PASSWORD JR

*English Dictionary for Speakers
of Portuguese at Beginner Level*

PASSWORD JR - English Dictionary
for Speakers of Portuguese at Beginner Level
K DICTIONARIES

© 2014 Martins Editora Livraria Ltda., São Paulo, para a presente edição.
© 2014 K Dictionaries Ltd.
kdl@kdictionaries.com

Tradução: Lina Maria Alvarenga
Edição: Erika Nogueira de Andrade Stupiello

Publisher	*Evandro Mendonça Martins Fontes*
Coordenação editorial	*Vanessa Faleck*
Design de capa	*Marcela Badolatto*
Produção editorial	*Heda Maria Lopes*
Preparação	*Rogério Bettoni*
	Lucas Torrisi
Revisão	*Juliana Amato Borges*
	Renata Sangeon
	Luciana Lima

Dados Internacionais de Catalogação na Publicação (CIP)
(Câmara Brasileira do Livro, SP, Brasil)

Password jr : English dictionary for speakers of
portuguese at beginner level / [translated by
Lina Maria Alvarenga and edited by Erika Nogueira
de Andrade Stupiello]. – São Paulo : Martins
Martins Fontes - selo Martins, 2014.

ISBN 978-85-8063-129-6

1. Inglês - Dicionários - Português.

14-02408   CDD-423.69

Índices para catálogo sistemático:

1. Inglês : Dicionários : Português   423.69

All rights reserved.
No part of this publication may be reproduced, stored in a retrieval system,
or transmitted, in any form or by any means, electronic, mechanical, photocopying,
recording or otherwise, without the written permission of the copyright holders.
We have made every effort to mark as such all words which we believe to be trademarks.
We should also like to make it clear that the presence of a word in the dictionary,
whether marked or unmarked, in no way affects its legal status as a trademark.

Todos os direitos desta edição reservados à
Martins Editora Livraria Ltda.
Av. Dr. Arnaldo, 2076
01255-000 São Paulo SP Brasil
Tel.: (11) 3116 0000
info@emartinsfontes.com.br
www.martinsfontes-selomartins.com.br

Aa

a [ə] *art.*
1 um, uma
They ate a banana, an apple and two oranges. ◆ It's a very good pen. ◆ a cup of tea.
■ Use **a** before a consonant sound: **a** house; **a** book.
■ Use **an** before a vowel sound (a, e, i, o, u): **an** apple; **an** orange; **an** umbrella. Use **a**: **a** university; **a** used car.
■ If **h** is not pronounced (as in hour, honour, honest), use **an**.
■ Compare:
an hour (h not pronounced).
a house (h pronounced).
2 a, ao, por
six dollars an hour. ◆ I go there twice a year.
■ Ver **a few; a lot (of); a little**.

abandon [ə'bandən] *v.* (**abandons, abandoning, abandoned**)
1 abandonar
The sailors abandoned the ship when it began to sink.
2 (= stop) □ **parar**
The police have to abandon the search because of the weather.

abandoned [ə'bandənd] *adj.* □ **abandonado**
an abandoned car.

abandonment [ə'bandənmənt] *n.* □ **abandono**

abbey ['abi] *n.* □ **abadia, mosteiro**
■ Ver **convent; monastery**.

abbreviation [ə,briːvi'eiʃn] *n.* □ **abreviação**
In this dictionary 'adj.' is the abbreviation for 'adjective'.

ABC [eibiː'siː] *n.* □ **alfabeto**
Do these children know their ABC from A to Z?
■ Ver **alphabet**.

abduct [əb'dʌkt] *v.* (**abducts, abducting, abducted**) □ **abduzir, sequestrar**
Terrorists abducted the Prime Minister.
■ The word we usually use is **kidnap**.
■ For planes and vehicles use **hijack**.

ability [ə'biləti] *n.* (*pl.* **abilities**) □ **habilidade, talento**
She has the ability to solve mathematical problems very quickly.

able¹ ['eibl] *adj.* □ **capaz**
be able to □ **conseguir, ser capaz de**
She is able to do it by herself. ◆ Will you be able to come tomorrow?
■ **was / were able** = managed to:
He was able to climb over the wall.
■ **can** means the same as **be able to**.

able² *adj.* □ **capaz, competente**
an able pupil / teacher.

aboard [ə'boːd] *adv., prep.* □ **a bordo**
All the passengers are aboard (the plane). ◆ We went aboard the ship.
All aboard! □ **Todos a bordo!**

abolish [ə'boliʃ] *v.* (**abolishes, abolishing, abolished**) □ **abolir**
The government abolished the tax.

abolition [,abə'liʃn] *n.* □ **abolição**
the abolition of slavery.

abortion [ə'boːʃn] *n.* □ **aborto**
The doctors told her to have an abortion because she was seriously ill.

about [ə'baut] *adv., prep.*
1 sobre
I'll think about it. ◆ What did they talk about? ◆ a book about animals.
2 por volta de
We arrived at about five o'clock. ◆ They are about the same age. ◆ about twenty people.
■ Ver **approximately, roughly**.
3 sobre
to wander about.
be about to □ **estar prestes a**
We were about to go out when it started to rain. ◆ The film is about to begin.
How about...?, What about...? □ **Que tal?**
How about going to a movie tonight? ◆ What about a cup of tea?

above [ə'bʌv] *adv., prep.*
1 acima de, por cima de
The plane flew above the clouds. ◆ The water rose above our knees.
2 acima de
The temperature is above 37º.
3 de cima, acima
Who lives on the floor above?
4 acima
The answer is in line 3 above.
■ antônimo: **below**
above all □ **acima de tudo, sobretudo**
Above all, don't lose hope!

abroad [ə'broːd] *adv.* □ **ao estrangeiro**
I'm going abroad next month.

absence ['absəns] *n.* □ **ausência**
I'll do his job in his absence.

absent ['absənt] *adj.* □ **ausente**
He was absent from school yesterday.

absolute ['absəluːt] *adj.* □ **absoluto, total**
the absolute truth.

absolutely ['absəluːtli] *adv.* □ **absolutamente**
You are absolutely right.

absorb [əb'soːb] *v.* (**absorbs, absorbing, absorbed**)
1 absorver
Cotton absorbs water, blood, etc. ◆ materials that absorb heat.
2 aprender
I can't absorb so much information.

absorption [əb'zoːpʃn] *n.* □ **absorção**
■ The verb is **absorb** (with a **b**).

abstract¹ ['abstrakt] *adj.* □ **abstrato**
an abstract idea.

abstract² *n.* □ **resumo**
The article begins with an abstract of the main points.

absurd [əb'soːd] *adj.* □ **ridículo, absurdo**
He looked absurd in those clothes. ◆ That's absurd! You're talking nonsense!

absurdity [əb'soːditi] *n.* □ **absurdo**

abuse¹ [ə'bjuːz] *v.* (**abuses, abusing, abused**)
1 abusar
He abused my trust. ◆ to abuse power.
2 maltratar

The police arrested the parents because they abused their children.
3 ofender
He abused me when I asked him to speak quietly.
abuse² [ə'bju:s] *n.*
1 abuso, excesso
drug abuse.
2 abuso
abuse of power.
3 molestamento
child abuse. ✦ sexual abuse.
4 insultos
They shouted abuse at us.
academic [akə'demik] *adj.* □ **acadêmico**
academic qualifications (a diploma, a degree, etc.). ✦ academic subjects in school, such as foreign languages. ✦ the academic year (= the university year).
accelerate [ək'seləreit] *v.* (**accelerates, accelerating, accelerated**) □ **acelerar**
The car began to accelerate.
accelerator [ək'seləreitə] *n.* □ **acelerador**
accent ['aksənt] *n.* □ **sotaque**
She speaks English with a foreign accent.
■ Ver **pronunciation**.
accept [ək'sept] *v.* (**accepts, accepting, accepted**)
1 aceitar
Please accept this small gift. ✦ She accepted his apology. ✦ to accept the invitation.
■ Compare with **receive**.
2 tolerar
She can't accept failure.
acceptable [ək'septəbl] *adj.*
1 aceitável
Is your idea acceptable to them?
2 tolerável
an acceptable level of noise.
acceptance [ək'septəns] *n.* □ **aceitação**
I got a letter of acceptance from the university.
access¹ ['akses] *n.* □ **acesso**
Access to the island is by boat or plane. ✦ I have access to their computer network.
access² *v.* (**accesses, accessing, accessed**) □ **acessar**
How do I access files for this program?
accident ['aksidənt] *n.* □ **acidente**
He had an accident. ✦ She was injured in a road accident.
■ Ver **crash; collision**.
by accident
1 por acaso, ao acaso
I met her by accident.
2 por engano
I took his bag by accident. I thought it was mine.
■ Ver **by chance; by mistake**.
accident and emergency ['aksidənt ənd i'mə:dʒənsi] *n. Brit.* [= **casualty (department)**] □ **pronto-socorro**
■ *Amer.* **emergency room**
accidental [,aksi'dentl] *adj.* □ **acidental**
It was an accidental meeting – it wasn't planned.
accidentally [,aksi'dentəli] *adv.* □ **acidentalmente**
He accidentally kicked me in the leg.
accommodate [ə'komədeit] *v.* (**accommodates, accommodating, accommodated**) □ **acomodar**
The hotel can accommodate six hundred guests.

accommodation [ə'komə'deiʃən] *n.* □ **acomodação**
to find cheap accommodation. ✦ The holiday costs $700 including accommodation.
■ *Amer.* **accommodations**
accompaniment [ə'kʌmpənimənt] *n.* □ **acompanhamento**
a song with piano accompaniment.
accompany [ə'kʌmpəni] *v.* (**accompanies, accompanying, accompanied**)
1 acompanhar
I'll accompany you to the door.
2 acompanhar
She accompanied me on the accordion.
be accompanied by □ **ser acompanhado de**
The Prime Minister was accompanied by his wife and daughter.
accomplish [ə'kʌmpliʃ] *v.* (**accomplishes, accomplishing, accomplished**) □ **concluir, realizar**
to accomplish the task. ✦ He accomplished nothing.
accomplishment [ə'kʌmpliʃmənt] *n.* □ **feito, realização**
Winning the prize was a great accomplishment for him.
■ Ver **achievement**.
accord [ə'ko:d] *n.* □ **acordo**
the peace accord.
of your own accord □ **por iniciativa própria**
She gave up her job of her own accord.
accordance [ə'ko:dəns] *n.*
in accordance with □ **de acordo com**
in accordance with the law
accordingly [ə'ko:diŋli] *adv.* □ **adequadamente, de modo apropriado**
This is a hospital, so please behave accordingly. ✦ She told him what to do, and he acted accordingly.
according (to) [ə'ko:diŋ] *prep.* □ **segundo, conforme**
It's 9:36 according to my watch. ✦ According to the teacher, the exam will be easier this time.
accordion [ə'ko:diən] *n.* □ **acordeão**
He plays the accordion very well.
account¹ [ə'kaunt] *n.*
1 conta
a bank account.
2 relato
He gave us an account of his trip to America.
on account of (= because of) □ **por causa de**
I couldn't come on account of my illness.
on no account □ **de jeito nenhum**
On no account must you leave them alone.
■ This expression always begins a sentence, and the auxiliary verb then comes before the subject (**must you**).
take something into account □ **considerar**
Did you take these facts into account?
accounts *n.* □ **contabilidade**
to keep (= prepare) the accounts of the business.
account² *v.* (**accounts, accounting, accounted**) □ **explicar**
account for
1 explicar
How do you account for your absence from school yesterday?
2 responder por
Heart attacks account for 60% of deaths from diseases.
accountancy [ə'kauntənsi] *n.* □ **contabilidade**
accountant [ə'kauntənt] *n.* □ **contador**

accumulate [əˈkjuːmjuleit] v. (**accumulates, accumulating, accumulated**) □ acumular
to accumulate a lot of money. ◆ Snow accumulated outside the door.

accumulation [əˌkjuːmjuˈleiʃən] n. □ acúmulo

accuracy [ˈakjurəsi] n. □ precisão, exatidão

accurate [ˈakjurət] adj. □ preciso, exato
an accurate description of the robber. ◆ Is your watch accurate?
- antônimo: **inaccurate**
- Ver **correct; exact; precise**.

accurately [ˈakjurətli] adv. □ precisamente, exatamente
He counted the figures accurately.

accusation [ˌakjuˈzeiʃən] n. □ acusação
Do you have proof for your accusation?

accuse [əˈkjuːz] v. (**accuses, accusing, accused**) □ acusar
They accused him of stealing the car. ◆ She was accused of murder.
the accused n. □ o acusado

accustomed [əˈkʌstəmd] adj. □ acostumado
be accustomed to □ estar acostumado a
I'm accustomed to this hot weather. ◆ We are not accustomed to studying eight hours a day.
become / get accustomed to (= be / get used to) □ acostumar-se a
I didn't like the way he behaved at first, but I got accustomed to it.
- Ver **be used to; get used to**.

ache[1] [eik] v. (**aches, aching, ached**) □ doer
My head aches.
- Compare:
hurt = because of a blow, an injury.
ache = because of stress, or a continual pain.

ache[2] n. □ dor
I've got a headache. ◆ If you have a toothache, go to the dentist.
- Compare:
pain = sharp, because of injury or a blow.
ache = dull and continual.

achieve [əˈtʃiːv] v. (**achieves, achieving, achieved**) □ alcançar
to achieve your aim ◆ With his last film he finally achieved success.

achievement [əˈtʃiːvmənt] n. □ realização
Winning a gold medal was her greatest achievement.
- Ver **accomplishment**.

acid [ˈasid] n., adj. □ ácido

acknowledge [əkˈnɒlidʒ] v. (**acknowledges, acknowledging, acknowledged**)
1 confirmar recebimento
I wish to acknowledge your letter of 10 May.
2 reconhecer
He acknowledged that it was a mistake.

acquaintance [əˈkweintəns] n.
1 conhecido
He isn't my friend, just an acquaintance.
2 conhecimento
I made his acquaintance at David's party.

acquainted [əˈkweintid] adj.
be acquainted with
1 ter conhecimento de
She is not acquainted with the facts.
2 conhecer
I'm acquainted with her.
become acquainted with □ tomar conhecimento de
She became acquainted with important politicians.

acquire [əˈkwaiə] v. (**acquires, acquiring, acquired**)
1 adquirir
to acquire a habit. ◆ He acquired the language in three months.
2 (= buy) □ adquirir
She acquired the dog in a pet shop.

acquisition [akwiˈziʃən] n. □ aquisição

acquit [əˈkwit] v. (**acquits, acquitting, acquitted**) □ absolver
He was acquitted of murder (at the trial).

acre [ˈeikə] n. □ acre

acrobat [ˈakrəbat] n. □ acrobata
- Ver **stuntman, juggler**.

acrobatic [ˌakrəˈbatik] adj. □ acrobático

across [əˈkrɒs] prep., adv.
1 para o outro lado
Dan swam across the pool.
2 do outro lado
We live across the street.
3 de largura
The road is 15 metres across.

act[1] [akt] n.
1 ato
I caught him in the act (of stealing). ◆ an act of courage.
2 ato
Act One (= the first act of a play).
3 número
a circus act
4 (= law) □ ato
an Act of Parliament.

act[2] v. (**acts, acting, acted**)
1 agir
It's time to act, not just to talk. ◆ They acted quickly to put out the fire.
2 (= behave) □ agir
You are acting like a child!
3 fazer o papel de
He acted (the part of) Othello in the play.

act as □ atuar
When the principal is ill, one of the teachers acts as head of the school.

acting[1] [ˈaktiŋ] n. □ interpretação, teatro
She studied acting at the school for drama.

acting[2] adj. □ interino
the acting manager

action [ˈakʃən] n. □ ação, ato
Now is the time for action. ◆ We watched the new player in action. ◆ You must take responsibility for your actions.
take action □ tomar providências, agir
We must take action at once to prevent the danger.

active[1] [ˈaktiv] adj. □ atuante, ativo
She is very active in the organization. ◆ He took an active part in the talks.

active[2] n. □ (voz) ativa
'I took the book' is in the active, but 'The book was taken by me' is in the passive
- You can also say **the active voice**.

activity [ˈaktiviti] n. (pl. **activities**) □ atividade

actor / adult

There's a lot of activity in the streets tonight. ◆ Fishing is one of my spare-time activities.
actor ['aktə] *n.* □ ator
actress ['aktris] *n.* (*pl.* **actresses**) □ atriz
actual ['aktʃuəl] *adj.* □ **real, verdadeiro**
What was the actual cost of the project? ◆ Those were his actual words.
actually ['aktʃuəli] *adv.*
1 na verdade
Actually, the film is better than the book.
2 realmente
I actually saw how it happened.
ad [ad] *n.* □ **anúncio**
Put an ad in the newspaper. ◆ an ad for a new drink
■ abbreviation for **advertisement**.
■ Compare **commercial**²:
a radio or TV broadcast advertising a product.
AD ['ei 'di:] *abbr.* □ **d.C.**
in 1310 AD.
■ Ver **BC**.
adapt [ə'dapt] *v.* (**adapts, adapting, adapted**)
1 adaptar-se
She adapted very quickly to her new home.
2 adaptar
His story was adapted for television.
adaptation [,adap'teiʃən] *n.* □ **adaptação**
add [ad] *v.* (**adds, adding, added**)
1 adicionar
Add a little more salt to the soup. ◆ I added my name to the list.
2 acrescentar
'And don't do that again', he added.
3 somar
If you add four and six you get ten.
■ The noun is **addition**.
addict ['adikt] *n.* □ **viciado**
drug addicts. ◆ a TV addict.
addicted [a'diktid] *adj.* □ **viciado**
He is addicted to drugs. ◆ She became addicted to alcohol.
addiction [a'dikʃən] *n.* □ **vício**
drug addiction.
addictive [a'diktiv] *adj.* □ **viciantes**
addictive drugs, such as heroin
addition [ə'diʃən] *n.*
1 adição
The room looked more cheerful with the addition of flowers.
2 soma
They learn addition and subtraction.
in addition (to) □ **além de**
In addition to Dan and David, there are two other players. ◆ In addition (to that), it is very dangerous.
additional [ə'diʃnl] *adj.* □ **adicional**
There are five additional exercises on page 60.
address¹ ['adres] *n.* □ **endereço**
Write your address on the envelope. ◆ Her address is 10 Flower St., London.
address² [ə'dres] *v.* (**addresses, addressing, addressed**) □ **endereçar**
You did not address the envelope correctly.
adequate ['adikwət] *adj.* □ **adequado**
an adequate answer. ◆ This equipment is not adequate for this job.
■ Ver **enough; good enough; satisfactory**.
■ antônimo: **inadequate**
adhesive plaster [əd'hi:siv 'pla:stə] *n.* □ **esparadrapo**
adhesive tape [əd'hi:siv 'teip] *n.* □ **fita adesiva**
adjective ['adʒiktiv] *n.* □ **adjetivo**
■ abreviação: **adj.**
adjust [ə'dʒʌst] *v.* (**adjusts, adjusting, adjusted**)
1 (= get used to) □ **adaptar-se**
to adjust to changes in the weather.
2 ajustar
Adjust the mirror and then start the car.
adjustment [ə'dʒʌstmənt] *n.*
1 adaptação
She has problems of adjustment.
2 ajuste
We have to make adjustments to the plan.
administer [əd'ministə] *v.* (**administers, administering, administered**) □ **administrar**
to administer a hospital / project
administration [əd,minis'treiʃən] *n.* □ **administração**
the administration of a business, a university, etc.
the Administration *n.* □ **Governo**
■ In Britain and other countries: **government**.
admirable ['admərəbl] *adj.* □ **admirável**
It was an admirable attempt, but it failed. ◆ an admirable achievement.
admiral ['admərəl] *n.* □ **almirante**
admiration [,admə'reiʃən] *n.* □ **admiração**
I have great admiration for their courage.
admire [əd'maiə] *v.* (**admires, admiring, admired**) □ **admirar**
They were admiring David's new car. ◆ I admire you for helping your friends so much.
admission [əd'miʃən] *n.*
1 entrada
free admission. ◆ The admission (fee) is 5 dollars.
2 (= confession) □ **reconhecimento**
an admission of guilt / failure.
admit [əd'mit] *v.* (**admits, admitting, admitted**)
1 admitir, assumir
She admitted her guilt. (= She admitted that she was guilty.) ◆ He admitted (to) stealing the money. ◆ I must admit (that) she was right.
■ antônimo: **deny**
2 admitir
This school admits only excellent pupils.
adolescence [,adə'lesns] *n.* □ **adolescência**
adolescent [,adə'lesnt] (= **teenager**) *adj., n.* □ **adolescente**
adopt [ə'dopt] *v.* (**adopts, adopting, adopted**) □ **adotar**
They adopted a child. ◆ We decided to adopt their ideas.
adopted [ə'doptid] *adj.* □ **adotado**
an adopted daughter.
adoption [ə'dopʃən] *n.* □ **adoção**
adorable [ə'do:rəbl] *adj.* □ **adorável**
What an adorable baby!
adore [ə'do:] *v.* (**adores, adoring, adored**) □ **adorar**
They adore their grandchildren.
adult¹ ['adʌlt] *n.* (= grown-up) □ **adulto**
a book for children and adults
adult² *adj.*
1 adulto
an adult giraffe

2 para adultos
an adult ticket
adulthood ['adʌlthud] *n.* □ **maturidade, maioridade**
advance[1] [əd'va:ns] *n.* □ **avanço**
advances in technology. ✦ They stopped the advance of the enemy.
in advance □ **adiantado**
He paid me in advance.
advance[2] *v.* (**advances, advancing, advanced**) □ **avançar**
Technology advances more and more every year. ✦ The soldiers advanced towards the border.
advanced [əd'va:nst] *adj.* □ **avançado**
advanced technology. ✦ an advanced course in English.
advantage [əd'va:ntidʒ] *n.* □ **vantagem**
I have an advantage over him because I speak English. ✦ the advantages and disadvantages of the system.
take advantage of □ **tirar proveito de, aproveitar-se de**
She took advantage of the opportunity. ✦ Don't take advantage of him.
adventure [əd'ventʃə] *n.* □ **aventura**
He wrote the story of his adventures in the African jungles.
adventurous [əd'ventʃərəs] *adj.* □ **aventureiro**
an adventurous trip. ✦ an adventurous person.
adverb ['advɜ:b] *n.* □ **advérbio**
Words such as 'quickly', 'well', 'very', and 'there' are adverbs.
■ abreviação: **adv.**
advertise ['advətaiz] *v.* (**advertises, advertising, advertised**) □ **anunciar**
to advertise a new product on TV. ✦ If you want to sell your car quickly, advertise it in the newspaper.
■ Compare:
advertise = for business purposes.
publicize = to make public, e.g. information, opinions.
publish = a book, an article, etc.
advertisement ['advɜ:tismənt] *n.* □ **anúncio**
I saw an advertisement for a new drink. ✦ She put an advertisement in the paper.
■ abreviação: **ad**
■ Compare **commercial**[2]:
commercial = a radio or TV broadcast advertising a product.
advertising ['advətaizɪŋ] *n.* □ **propaganda**
The company spends a lot of money on advertising.
advertising campaign ['advətaizɪŋ kam'pein] *n.* □ **campanha publicitária**
an advertising campaign for a new product.
advice [əd'vais] *n.* □ **conselho**
My advice to you is to try harder. ✦ Take my advice and apologize to them. ✦ I need your advice / some advice.
■ Do not say **an advice**, but **a piece of advice**:
Let me give you a piece of advice.
advise [əd'vaiz] *v.* (**advises, advising, advised**) □ **aconselhar**
She advised me not to go. ✦ I advise you to see a doctor.
adviser [əd'vaizə] *n.*, **advisor** □ **consultor**
an economic adviser.
aerial ['eəriəl] *n. Brit.* (= antenna) □ **antena**
aerobics [eə'rəubiks] *n.* □ **aeróbica**
She does aerobics regularly to lose weight.
aeroplane ['eərəplein] *n.* (Ver **airplane**).
aerosol ['eərəsɒl] *n., adj.* □ **aerossol**
an aerosol deodorant.

affair [ə'feə] *n.*
1 assunto
Don't interfere! It's not your affair.
2 caso, questão
Their quarrel was an ugly affair.
affect [ə'fekt] *v.* (**affects, affecting, affected**) □ **afetar**
Smoking may affect your health. ✦ Her bad manners did not affect my feelings for her.
■ The noun is **effect**, but do not confuse with the verb **to effect**.
affection [ə'fekʃən] *n.* □ **afeição, afeto**
She has great affection for her little brothers
affectionate [ə'fekʃənət] *adj.* □ **afetuoso**
She is very affectionate to her friends. ✦ He gave his daughter an affectionate kiss.
affectionately [ə'fekʃənətli] *adv.* □ **afetuosamente**
She smiled affectionately at him.
affluence ['afluəns] *n.* □ **riqueza**
She is very rich, but she does not make a show of her affluence.
affluent ['afluənt] *adj.* (= rich) □ **rico**
an affluent society
afford [ə'fɔ:d] *v.* (**affords, affording, afforded**)
can / can't afford □ **ter/não ter condição de**
I can't afford (to buy) a car. ✦ He must do what the boss tells him to do – he can't afford to lose his job.
afraid [ə'freid] *adj.* □ **com medo, assustado**
■ Ver **frightened; scared; fear**[2].
I'm afraid... □ **lamento que... / receio que...**
Are we late? – I'm afraid so. ✦ Can you come? – I'm afraid not. ✦ I'm afraid (that) the manager is at a meeting.
African American ['afrikən ə'merikən] *n., adj.* □ **afro-americano**
The Black citizens of the USA are called 'African Americans'.
after[1] ['a:ftə] *prep., conj.*
1 depois de, após
after breakfast. ✦ My name comes after yours on the list. ✦ What are you going to do after leaving school?
2 atrás
The dog is running after the cat.
3 depois de, após
After I leave school, I want to travel.
after all □ **afinal de contas**
He doesn't speak English very well. After all, he started to learn the language only last month. ✦ It wasn't so terrible after all.
after[2] *adv.* □ **depois, em seguida**
They arrived two days after. ✦ You go first and I'll come after.
afternoon [a:ftə'nu:n] *n.* □ **tarde**
It happened at four in the afternoon. ✦ We can meet this afternoon. ✦ on Saturday afternoon. ✦ tomorrow / yesterday afternoon.
afterward(s) ['a:ftəwəd(z)] *adv.* □ **depois**
Let's eat first and go to the cinema afterwards. ✦ two years afterwards.
again [ə'gen] *adv.* □ **de novo, novamente**
Don't do that again! ✦ I tried again but nobody answered.
again and again □ **repetidamente**
I've warned him again and again not to touch it.
against [ə'genst] *prep.*

1 contra
I'm against giving her the money. ◆ They voted against the plan. ◆ We are playing against a strong team tomorrow.
2 contra
Put the ladder against the tree. ◆ Put the bed against the wall.
age [eidʒ] *n.*
1 idade
What's his age? (= How old is he?) ◆ I left the army at the age of 21.
2 Idade, Era
the Stone Age.
for ages □ **há anos, por anos**
I waited there for ages.
with age □ **com a idade**
His hair was grey with age.
aged¹ [eidʒd] *adj.* □ **com a idade de**
a girl aged six.
aged² [ˈeidʒid] *adj., n.* □ **de idade, idoso**
her aged parents.
the aged □ **o idoso, os idosos**
agency [ˈeidʒənsi] *n.* (*pl.* **agencies**) □ **agência**
a travel agency. ◆ An employment agency helps people to find work.
agent [ˈeidʒənt] *n.* □ **agente, empresário**
a travel agent. ◆ This agent works for a famous actor.
aggression [əˈgreʃən] *n.* □ **agressão**
aggressive [əˈgresiv] *adj.* □ **agressivo**
his aggressive manner. ◆ She gets aggressive when she is hungry.
aggressively [əˈgresivli] *adv.* □ **agressivamente**
to behave aggressively.
ago [əˈgou] *adv.* □ **atrás (tempo)**
I bought it ten years ago. ◆ a few months ago ◆ a long time ago.
long ago □ **antigamente, no passado**
Long ago there was no electricity and people used candles.
■ Compare com **before**:
I bought my car a month ago.
I bought my car in July. He bought his car a month before (in June).
agonize [ˈagənaiz] *v.* (**agonizes, agonizing, agonized**) □ **agonizar**
She is agonizing whether to marry him or not.
agony [ˈagəni] *n.* (*pl.* **agonies**) □ **agonia**
The patient was in agony.
agree [əˈgri:] *v.* (**agrees, agreeing, agreed**)
1 concordar
I agree with you.
■ antônimo: **disagree**
2 concordar
She agreed to help me.
3 concordar
We agreed on a payment of $500 a month.
agreeable [əˈgri:əbl] *adj.* (= pleasant) □ **agradável**
an agreeable voice. ◆ agreeable weather.
agreement [əˈgri:mənt] *n.*
1 acordo
The Minister signed a trade agreement with Italy. ◆ We made an agreement; you can't break it now. ◆ to reach an agreement about...
2 estar de acordo
We are all in agreement about the plan.
■ antônimo: **disagreement**
agricultural [ˌagriˈkʌltʃərəl] *adj.* □ **agrícola**
agricultural land / products.
agriculture [ˈagrikʌltʃə] *n.* □ **agricultura**
Agriculture means raising animals and growing vegetables and fruit trees.
ahead [əˈhed] *adv., adj.*
1 à frente
Look straight ahead. ◆ There was a hill ahead of us.
2 à frente
We must think ahead if we want to succeed in this business.
3 à frente
Victor is ahead of the other runners. ◆ Her music is ahead of its time.
go ahead
1 Vá em frente!
Go ahead! Taste it.
2 ir em frente
He told us to go ahead with our plans.
aid¹ [eid] *n.*
1 (= help) □ **ajuda, socorro**
to send aid to a country, etc. ◆ They came to our aid. ◆ to walk with the aid of a stick.
■ Ver **first aid**.
2 aparelho que serve de auxílio
a hearing aid (for people who do not hear well).
aid² *v.* (**aids, aiding, aided**) □ **ajudar**
He aided the prisoner to escape.
aide [eid] *n.* □ **ajudante, assistente**
The Minister gives her aides a lot of work. ◆ a teacher's aide.
AIDS [eidz] *n.*, **Aids** □ **aids**
aim¹ [eim] *n.* □ **alvo, objetivo**
Her aim is to become a lawyer. ◆ He tried hard to achieve his aim.
■ Ver **purpose; goal**.
take aim at □ **mirar**
He took aim at the target and fired.
aim² *v.* (**aims, aiming, aimed**)
1 mirar
She aimed her gun at the target.
2 pretender
He aims to be a millionaire.
be aimed at □ **destinado**
products that are aimed at young people. ◆ These laws are aimed at protecting animals.
air¹ [eə] *n.* □ **ar**
There was not enough air to breathe in the cave. ◆ The air in this city is polluted (= dirty). ◆ I kicked the ball up in the air.
by air □ **de avião**
to travel by air.
air² *v.* (**airs, airing, aired**) □ **arejar**
I opened the windows to air the room.
airbag [ˈeəbag] *n.* □ **airbag**
An airbag in a car can save your life in a crash.
air-conditioned [ˈeəkənˌdiʃənd] *adj.* □ **com ar-condicionado**
an air-conditioned bus / office.
air-conditioner [ˈeəkənˌdiʃənə] *n.* □ **condicionador de ar**
air-conditioning [ˈeəkənˌdiʃəniŋ] *n.* □ **ar-condicionado**

aircraft ['eəkra:ft] *n.* (*pl.* **aircraft**) □ **aeronave**
The company bought two new aircraft. ♦ Helicopters and airplanes are aircraft.
aircraft-carrier ['eəkra:t,kariə] *n.* □ **porta-aviões**
air force ['eə fo:s] *n.* □ **Força Aérea**
air hostess ['eə ,houstis] *n. Brit.* □ **comissária de bordo**
■ *Amer.* **flight attendant**
airlift ['eəlift] *v.* (**airlifts, airlifting, airlifted**) □ **transportar, fazer ponte aérea**
Airplanes airlifted the wounded soldiers to a hospital.
airline ['eəlain] *n.* □ **companhia aérea**
an American airline.
airmail ['eəmeil] *n.* □ **correio aéreo**
to send a letter (by) airmail.
airplane ['eəplein] *n. Amer.* (= aeroplane, *Brit.*) □ **avião**
The airplane took off at exactly 5 o'clock. ♦ The airplane landed at the airport at 2 o'clock.
air pollution ['eə pə,lu:ʃən] *n.* □ **poluição do ar**
airport ['eəpo:t] *n.* □ **aeroporto**
air raid ['eə reid] *n.* □ **ataque aéreo, bombardeio**
aisle [ail] *n., adj.* □ **corredor**
I sat by the aisle on the plane, not by the window. ♦ an aisle seat.
alarm[1] [ə'la:m] *n.*
1 apreensão
The boy cried in alarm when he heard the thunder.
2 alarme
A burglar alarm may stop thieves from breaking into your house. ♦ a fire alarm. ♦ When the guard saw the robbers, he sounded the alarm.
3 (= alarm clock) □ **despertador**
to set the alarm for 5 o'clock.
alarm[2] *v.* (**alarms, alarming, alarmed**) □ **alarmar, assustar**
The noise alarmed the animal. ♦ They were alarmed to hear about her illness.
alarm clock [ə'la:m klok] *n.* □ **despertador**
to set the alarm clock for 5 o'clock.
■ Ver **alarm.**
album ['albəm] *n.*
1 álbum de imagens
a photograph album. ♦ a stamp album.
2 álbum musical
a great song from her latest album.
alcohol ['alkəhol] *n.* □ **álcool**
alcoholic [,alkə'holik] *adj.* □ **alcoólico**
Wines and beers are alcoholic drinks.
ale [eil] *n.* □ **um tipo de cerveja**
alert[1] [ə'lə:t] *adj.* □ **atento**
Don't drive if you are not feeling alert today. ♦ We are alert to the dangers.
alert[2] *n.* □ **alerta**
There was a bomb alert at the airport.
be on the alert □ **estar alerta**
The police were on the alert during the President's visit.
alert[3] *v.* (**alerts, alerting, alerted**) □ **alertar**
They alerted us to the dangers of such an adventure.
alias ['eiliəs] *n., adv.* □ **apelido, pseudônimo**
The criminal is using an alias, not his real name. ♦ William Smith, alias Bill Jones.
alibi ['alibai] *n.* □ **álibi**
He has an alibi for where he was on the night of the murder.
alien ['eiliən] *n., adj.* □ **alienígena; estrangeiro**

aliens from another planet ♦ alien countries (= foreign).
alight [ə'lait] *adj.* (= on fire) □ **em chamas**
The whole house was alight ten minutes after the fire started.
alike[1] [ə'laik] *adj.* □ **parecido, semelhante**
The two pictures are alike. ♦ The two brothers look alike.
alike[2] *adv.* □ **igualmente, da mesma maneira**
She treats all her pupils alike.
alive [ə'laiv] *adj.* □ **vivo**
The bird is still alive.
all[1] [o:l] *adj.* □ **todo**
It rained all day. ♦ That shop sells all kinds of paper. ♦ All her friends came to the wedding.
all[2] *pron., n.* □ **todos, tudo, só**
All of us work hard. ♦ We all know the answer. ♦ That's all for today.
all[3] *adv.* □ **só, sozinho**
He was sitting there all alone.
all along
1 o tempo todo
It was here all along. ♦ I knew all along that it was a lie.
2 ao longo de
all along the road.
all over
1 em todo
all over the world.
2 terminado, acabado
We had a problem, but that's all over now.
all right (= alright) □ **bom, bem, tudo certo, tudo bem**
The food is all right. ♦ The baby is all right now. ♦ All right, I'll come.
allege [ə'ledʒ] *v.* (**alleges, alleging, alleged**) □ **alegar**
He alleges that I cheated in the test, but it's not true.
alley ['ali] *n.* □ **beco, viela**
alliance [ə'laiəns] *n.* □ **aliança**
The two countries signed an alliance between them.
alligator ['aligeitə] *n.* □ **jacaré**
■ Ver **crocodile.**
allow [ə'lau] *v.* (**allows, allowing, allowed**) □ **permitir**
She allowed me to come in. ♦ They do not allow smoking in the cinema.
■ Ver **let**[2]; **permit.**
be not allowed (to) □ **não ter permissão**
You're not allowed to talk during the exam. ♦ Parking is not allowed here.
allowance [ə'lauəns] *n.* □ **mesada, semanada**
I give my son a weekly allowance of 15 dollars.
■ *Brit.* **pocket money**
all-terraine vehicle [,o:l tə'rein 'vi:əkl] *n.* □ **ATV, quadriciclo**
■ abreviação: **ATV**
ally [ə'lai] *n.* (*pl.* **allies**) □ **aliado**
During World War II, Britain and Russia were allies.
almond ['a:lmənd] *n.* □ **amêndoa**
I like nuts and almonds.
almost ['o:lmoust] *adv.* □ **quase**
It's almost ready. ♦ I'm almost 16. ♦ She almost dropped the vase.
■ Ver **nearly.**
alone [ə'loun] *adj., adv.*
1 sozinho
Are you alone? ♦ I don't like to eat alone.

2 (= only) □ **somente**
He alone knows the truth.
along¹ [ə'lɒŋ] *adv.*
1 para diante
Move along, please.
2 com, em companhia de
Come along with me.
along² *prep.* □ **ao longo de**
We walked along the road. ◆ They planted trees along the fence.
aloud [ə'laud] *adv.* □ **em voz alta**
She read the story aloud. ◆ They cried aloud for help.
alphabet ['alfəbit] *n.* □ **alfabeto**
■ Ver **ABC**.
alphabetical [,alfə'betikəl] *adj.* □ **alfabético**
alphabetically [,alfə'betikəli] *adv.* □ **em ordem alfabética**
already [ɔ:l'redi] *adv.* □ **já**
I've already seen it. ◆ It's ten o'clock already.
■ Both **yet** and **already** are used in interrogative sentences, but **already** shows surprise:
Is it 6 o'clock yet?
Is it 6 o'clock already?
alright [ɔ:l'rait] (Ver **all³**).
also ['ɔ:lsou] *adv.*
1 também
You'll also need money. ◆ I can sing and also play the guitar. ◆ It is not only ugly, but also expensive.
■ At the end of sentences **too** or **as well** are usually used:
Sara will come too.
He taught me English as well.
■ Use **not... either** instead of **also** in negative sentences:
I can't drive either.
2 além disso
Also, the air is cleaner there.
alter ['ɔ:ltə] *v.* (**alters, altering, altered**)
1 (= change) □ **alterar**
We'll have to alter the plan. ◆ She has altered a lot.
2 ajustar
My trousers are too long. Will you alter them for me?
alteration [,ɔ:ltə'reiʃən] *n.* □ **ajuste**
■ Ver **change¹**.
alternate [ɔ:l'tə:nət] *adj.* □ **alternado**
on alternate days □ **em dias alternados**
alternative¹ [ɔ:l'tə:nətiv] *adj.* □ **alternativo**
an alternative plan.
alternative² *n.*
1 alternativa
The road is blocked, the only alternative is to go by train.
2 (= choice) □ **opção, alternativa**
She has no alternative, she has to take the exam.
although [ɔ:l'ðou] *conj.*
1 embora
Although it was raining, we went out to play.
2 embora
He can drive, although not very well.
■ Ver **though**.
altogether [ɔ:ltə'geðə] *adv.*
1 no total
You owe me 100 dollars altogether.
■ Do not confuse with **all together.**
2 (= completely) □ **totalmente**
It's not altogether true.

aluminium [alju'miniəm] *n. Brit.*, **aluminum** *Amer.* □ **alumínio**
always ['ɔ:lweiz] *adv.*
1 sempre
I always go shopping on Tuesdays. ◆ I don't always eat breakfast. ◆ He is always late. ◆ She has always liked you.
2 (= forever) □ **sempre**
We'll always remember you.
am [am] *v.* (Ver **be**).
a.m. ['ei'em] *abbr.* □ **da manhã**
I usually get up at 6 a.m. ◆ It's still dark at 1 a.m.
■ Ver **p.m.**
amateur ['amətə] *n., adj.* □ **amador**
There are no amateurs in these teams, only professionals.
◆ an amateur footballer / photographer
■ antônimo: **professional**
amateurish [,amə'tə:riʃ] *adj.* □ **amador**
very amateurish acting
amaze [ə'meiz] *v.* (**amazes, amazing, amazed**) □ **espantar, pasmar**
He amazed me when he told me his real name.
be amazed □ **espantar-se**
I was amazed at her beauty. ◆ She was amazed to hear my story.
amazement [ə'meizmənt] *n.* □ **surpresa**
To my amazement, they started to sing. ◆ He looked at us in amazement.
amazing [ə'meiziŋ] *adj.* □ **surpreendente**
That was an amazing story.
amazingly [ə'meiziŋli] *adv.* □ **surpreendentemente**
It moved at an amazingly great speed.
ambassador [am'basədə] *n.* □ **embaixador**
the French ambassador to Spain.
■ Ver **embassy**.
ambition [am'biʃən] *n.*
1 ambição
Her ambition is to become a writer.
2 ambição
He will succeed because he has a lot of ambition.
ambitious [am'biʃəs] *adj.* □ **ambicioso**
an ambitious girl. ◆ Your plan is very ambitious.
ambulance ['ambjuləns] *n.* □ **ambulância**
Call an ambulance!
ambush¹ ['ambuʃ] *n.* □ **emboscada**
The soldiers lay in ambush. ◆ The robbers set an ambush.
ambush² *v.* (**ambushes, ambushing, ambushed**) □ **emboscar**
The robbers ambushed the travellers.
American [ə'meri:kən] *n., adj.* □ **americano, estadunidense**
an American citizen / TV show. ◆ Are you an American?
American Indian *n., adj.* (= Native American) □ **indígena americano**
ammunition [amju'niʃən] *n.* □ **munição**
They need more guns and ammunition.
among [ə'mʌŋ] *prep.* (mesmo que **amongst**) □ **entre**
They were hiding among the branches. ◆ Discuss it among yourselves.
■ For more than two persons or things use **among**; for two only use **between:**
Divide the money among you.
Divide the money between the two of you.
among other things □ **entre outras coisas**

We talked about this, among other things.

amount[1] [ə'maunt] *n.*
1 (= sum) □ **soma**
a large amount of money. ♦ to pay the full amount.
2 (= quantity) □ **quantidade**
small / large amounts of tea.
3 quantidade
a large amount of work. ♦ a certain amount of effort.

amount[2] *v.* (**amounts, amounting, amounted**)
amount to □ **totalizar**
The costs amount to 300 dollars. ♦ The cost of building a new house amounts to $100,000.

ample ['ampl] *adj.* □ **bastante**
You have ample time to catch the train.

amuse [ə'mju:z] *v.* (**amuses, amusing, amused**) □ **divertir**
His jokes amused us. ♦ She amused the audience with her tricks.

amusement [ə'mju:zmənt] *n.* □ **diversão**
To their amusement he fell into the water. ♦ I make these toys only for amusement.

amusements *n. pl.* □ **entretenimento, diversão**

amusement park [ə'mju:zmənt ,pa:k] *n.* □ **parque de diversões**

amusing [ə'mju:ziŋ] *adj.* □ **divertido**
an amusing person. ♦ The story wasn't very amusing.

an [an, ən] *art.* (Ver **a**).

anaesthetic [,anəs'θetik] *n.*, (= **anesthetic**) □ **anestésico**
Before an operation, the doctor gives the patient an anaesthetic.

analyse ['anəlaiz] *v. Brit.* (**analyses, analysing, analysed**), *Amer.* **analyze.**

analysis [ə'nalisis] *n.* (*pl.* **analyses**)
1 análise
an analysis of the situation / the text.
2 análise
a chemical analysis.

analyze ['anəlaiz] *v. Amer.* (**analyzes, analyzing, analyzed**)
1 analisar
to analyze the reasons for the failure.
2 analisar
to analyze blood, hair, etc. in a laboratory.

ancestor ['ansistə] *n.* □ **ancestral, antepassado**
My ancestors came to live here in 1886.

ancestry [ansestri] *n.* □ **ascendência**
She is of noble ancestry.

anchor ['aŋkə] *n.* □ **âncora**
The ship dropped anchor at the port.

anchovy ['antʃəvi] *n.* □ **anchova**

ancient ['einʃənt] *adj.* □ **antigo**
ancient civilizations. ♦ the ancient Greeks.

the ancients *n. pl.* □ **os antigos, os clássicos**

and [ənd, and] *conj.*
1 e
food and drink. ♦ They were laughing and shouting. ♦ six hundred and ten (= 610).
2 mais
Six and two are eight (6+2=8).

anesthetic [,anəs'θetik] *n.* (= **anaesthetic**) □ **anestésico**

angel ['eindʒəl] *n.* □ **anjo**

anger ['aŋgə] *n.* □ **raiva**
I was filled with anger when he pulled my hair. ♦ to feel anger towards him / her.

angle ['aŋgl] *n.* □ **ângulo**
Draw a line at an angle of 45°. ♦ An angle of 90° (= 90 degrees) is called a right angle.

angrily [aŋgrili] *adv.* □ **raivosamente**
'Don't touch it!', he shouted angrily.

angry [aŋgri] *adj.* (**angrier, angriest**) □ **zangado**
I was angry when he hit the child. ♦ She was angry with me. ♦ I was angry at / about the delay. ♦ an angry face.

get angry □ **zangar-se, enraivecer-se**
He got angry with me.

make someone angry □ **deixar alguém zangado**
His insults made me angry.

animal ['animəl] *n.* □ **animal**
wild animals such as lions, tigers and zebras. ♦ Horses, birds, snakes, fish, flies, and ants are all animals.

ankle ['aŋkl] *n.* □ **tornozelo**

anniversary [anə'və:səri] *n.* (*pl.* **anniversaries**) □ **aniversário**
Tomorrow is our 10th wedding anniversary.

announce [ə'nauns] *v.* (**announces, announcing, announced**) □ **anunciar, comunicar**
The teacher announces the date of the exam. ♦ to announce the winner of the competition.

announcement [ə'naunsmənt] *n.* □ **anúncio, comunicado**
The Prime Minister will make an important announcement today.

announcer [ə'naunsər] *n.* □ **apresentador, locutor**
An announcer tells the news on radio or television.

annoy [ə'noi] *v.* (**annoys, annoying, annoyed**) □ **irritar**
He annoyed me with his questions. ♦ This noise is annoying me.

annoyance [ə'noiəns] *n.* □ **irritação**
She gave me a look of annoyance.

annoyed [ə'noid] *adj.* □ **irritado**
He is annoyed with me.

annoying [ə'noiŋ] *adj.* □ **irritante**
an annoying delay.

annual ['anjuəl] *adj.* □ **anual**
Her annual income comes to 60,000 dollars. ♦ an annual meeting of the directors.

annually ['anjuəli] *adv.*
1 anualmente
They sell 80,000 cars annually.
2 (= once a year) □ **uma vez por ano**
A new telephone directory appears annually.

anonymous [ə'nonəməs] *adj.* □ **anônimo**
An anonymous caller warned the police about the robbery. ♦ an anonymous letter.

another [ə'nʌðə] *adj.* □ **outro, mais um**
Can I have another cup of coffee? ♦ I'll put on another shirt. ♦ I found another one in the kitchen.
■ Contrast with **other:**
Give me another book.
Give me the other book.
Give me the other books.

one another □ **um ao outro**
We must help one another. ♦ They respect one another.
■ **each other** is also possible.

answer[1] ['a:nsə] *n.* (= reply) **resposta**
1 resposta

Is that the right answer to your question? ✦ In answer to your letter I'd like to say that...
2 resposta, solução
This may be the answer to your problem.
answer² *v.* **(answers, answering, answered)** □ **responder**
Answer the question, please. ✦ Answer me! ✦ I answered her letter immediately.
■ Ver **reply**².
answer the door □ **atender a porta**
I'll answer the door. It must be the postman.
answer the (tele)phone □ **atender o telefone**
Who answered the phone?
answering machine *n.* □ **secretária eletrônica**
to leave a message on the answering machine.
ant [ænt] *n.* □ **formiga**
antenna [an'tenə] *n.* (= aerial) □ **antena**
anthem ['anθəm] *n.* **hino**
the national anthem.
anti- [anti-] *pref.* □ **anti-**
anticipate [an'tisəpeit] *v.* **(anticipates, anticipating, anticipated)** (= expect) □ **prever**
We don't anticipate any difficulties.
anticlockwise [anti'klokwaiz] *adj., adv.* □ **anti-horário**
■ *Amer.* **counterclockwise**
antique [an'ti:k] *adj.* □ **antigo, de antiguidade**
an antique piece of furniture. ✦ an antique shop (= a shop that sells antiques).
anti-Semitic [antisə'mitik] *adj.* □ **antissemita**
anti-Semitism [anti'semitizəm] *n.* □ **antissemitismo**
anxiety [aŋ'zaiəti] *n.* (*pl.* **anxieties**) □ **ansiedade**
His disappearance is causing them great anxiety.
anxious [aŋkʃəs] *adj.*
1 (= very worried) **preocupado**
I am anxious about her health.
2 (= eager) **ansioso**
He is anxious to meet you.
anxiously [aŋkʃəsli] *adv.* □ **ansiosamente**
The parents of the missing child waited anxiously by the phone.
any¹ ['eni] *adj.*
1 qualquer
Take any dress you want. ✦ Any child knows that.
2 algum
Is there any milk left? ✦ Do we have any oranges?
3 qualquer, nenhum
She did it without any help. ✦ I don't have any money.
■ Usually, **any** is used instead of some in negative and interrogative sentences.
■ Ver **some**.
any² *adv.* □ **um pouco**
Are you feeling any better?
any longer □ **mais tempo**
I can't wait any longer.
any more
1 mais
We don't go there any more.
2 nenhum
I can't give you any more (money).
■ American spelling **anymore** is possible only in meaning 1.
anybody ['eni,bodi] *pron.* (= **anyone**).
1 qualquer um, qualquer pessoa
Anybody can do that.
2 ninguém
I didn't see anybody.
3 alguém
Has anybody seen Dan?
■ Usually, **anybody** is used instead of **somebody** in negative and interrogative sentences.
anybody / anyone else □ **alguém, alguém mais**
Does anybody else know about this? ✦ I didn't tell anyone else about it.
anyhow ['enihau] *adv.* (= **anyway**).
anymore ['enimo:] *adv.* (**Ver any**²).
anyone ['eniwʌn] *pron.* (= **anybody**).
anything ['eniθiŋ] *pron.*
1 algo, alguma coisa
Has anything happened to him?
2 nada
I couldn't see anything in the dark.
■ Usually, **anything** is used instead of **something** in negative and interrogative sentences.
3 qualquer coisa
They will do anything for money.
anything else □ **algo mais, mais alguma coisa**
Would you like anything else to eat?
anyway ['eniwei] *adv.* (= **anyhow**)
1 de qualquer modo
Anyway, it's not relevant any more.
2 mesmo assim
There was no need to hurry, but I decided to run anyway.
3 mesmo
I don't want it anyway.
■ Don't confuse **anyway** with **any way:**
Is there any way to help him?
anywhere ['eniweə] *adv.*
1 algum lugar
Are you going anywhere this evening?
2 em lugar algum, em lugar nenhum
I didn't take her anywhere.
■ Usually, **anywhere** is used instead of **somewhere** in negative and interrogative sentences.
3 em qualquer lugar
Where shall I put it? – Anywhere. It doesn't matter.
anywhere else □ **mais algum lugar**
Is there anywhere else you'd like to go?
apart [ə'pa:t] *adv.*
1 de distância
The two buildings are 80 metres apart.
2 separado
They live apart.
apart from *prep.*
1 (= in addition to) □ **além de**
Ten people came to the party, apart from me.
2 (= except for) □ **menos, exceto**
Everybody came to the party, apart from me.
come / fall apart □ **ficar em pedaços**
The cup came apart in my hands.
take something apart □ **desmontar**
He is taking the engine apart.
apartment [ə'pa:tmənt] *n. Amer.* □ **apartamento**
How many rooms are there in your apartment?
■ *Brit.* **flat**
ape [eip] *n.* □ **símio**

Gorillas and chimpanzees are apes.
■ Ver **monkey**.
apologize [əˈpɒlədʒaiz] *v.* (**apologizes, apologizing, apologized**), **apologise** *v. Brit.* (**apologises, apologising, apologised**) □ **desculpar-se, pedir desculpas**
I apologize. ◆ She apologized to her friends for being late.
apology [əˈpɒlədʒi] *n.* (*pl.* **apologies**) □ **desculpa**
I owe you an apology. ◆ Please accept my apologies. ◆ I demand an apology.
appalling [əˈpɔːlɪŋ] *adj.* □ **horrível, horroroso**
The conditions in this prison are appalling.
apparatus [apəˈreitəs] *n.* □ **aparato, aparelhagem**
apparent [əˈparənt] *adj.* □ **aparente, óbvio**
It was apparent that they didn't like the idea.
apparently [əˈparəntli] *adv.* □ **aparentemente**
I didn't see the game, but it was very good, apparently. ◆ Apparently, she doesn't like your jokes.
appeal[1] [əˈpiːl] *n.*
1 apelo
They made an appeal for help.
2 apelo, atração
What has more appeal to you – big cities or small villages?
3 recurso
The court rejected (= did not accept) our appeal.
appeal[2] *v.* (**appeals, appealing, appealed**)
1 apelar, recorrer
The refugees appealed to our organization for help.
2 atrair
Swimming in winter does not appeal to me.
3 recorrer
to appeal to the High Court.
appealing [əˈpiːlɪŋ] *adj.* □ **atraente**
She has an appealing smile. ◆ an appealing idea.
appear [əˈpiə] *v.* (**appears, appearing, appeared**)
1 aparecer, surgir
The sun appeared behind the clouds.
■ antônimo: **disappear**
2 aparecer
The president appeared on television. ◆ Your name does not appear on the list.
3 parecer
She appears younger than she really is. ◆ It appears that he was right.
appearance [əˈpiərəns] *n.*
1 aparência
the sudden appearance of the police.
■ antônimo: **disappearance**
2 aparição
to make an appearance on television.
3 aparência
The building was like a hospital in appearance.
appendix [əˈpendiks] *n.* (*pl.* **appendixes, appendices**)
1 (= supplement) □ **apêndice**
an appendix at the end of the book
2 (= intestine tube) □ **apêndice**
The appendix sits in the lower right abdomen.
appetite [ˈapitait] *n.* □ **apetite**
He lost his appetite.
appetizing [ˈapitaizɪŋ] *adj.* □ **apetitoso**
The meal looks appetizing.
applaud [əˈplɔːd] *v.* (**applauds, applauding, applauded**) □ **aplaudir**

The audience applauded the dancers for 5 minutes.
applause [əˈplɔːz] *n.* □ **aplauso**
loud applause.
apple [ˈapl] *n.* □ **maçã**
appliance [əˈplaiəns] *n.* □ **aparelho**
electrical appliances such as washing machines and refrigerators.
applicant [ˈaplikənt] *n.* □ **candidato, interessado**
There were ten applicants for the job.
application [apliˈkeiʃən] *n.*
1 solicitação, inscrição
to make an application for a job. ◆ They turned down (= did not accept) my application.
2 aplicação
an invention with many applications in industry.
application form *n.* □ **formulário, ficha**
to fill in / out an application form (for a job, a passport, etc.).
apply [əˈplai] *v.* (**applies, applying, applied**)
1 candidatar-se, inscrever-se
She applied to the university. ◆ to apply for a job / a passport.
2 aplicar
Apply a little glue to the surface.
3 aplicar-se
The new rule applies in your case. ◆ What I have said does not apply to you.
4 aplicar
He applied his educational ideas in the classroom.
appoint [əˈpoint] *v.* (**appoints, appointing, appointed**) □ **nomear**
They appointed a new manager. ◆ They appointed him manager.
appointment [əˈpointmənt] *n.*
1 compromisso, hora marcada
I have an appointment with the manager at four o'clock. ◆ to make an appointment by telephone ◆ Cancel my appointment with the doctor.
2 nomeação
I congratulated her on her appointment as editor.
appreciate [əˈpriːʃieit] *v.* (**appreciates, appreciating, appreciated**) □ **reconhecer, ser grato por**
We appreciate your help. ◆ She does not appreciate my efforts.
appreciation [ə͵priːʃiˈeiʃən] *n.* □ **reconhecimento, gratidão**
He gave us a present to show his appreciation.
apprentice [əˈprentis] *n.* □ **aprendiz**
He worked as an apprentice to a carpenter.
approach[1] [əˈprəʊtʃ] *n.*
1 chegada, aproximação
With the approach of winter these birds fly to warmer countries.
2 abordagem
Each of them suggested a different approach to the problem.
approach[2] *v.* (**approaches, approaching, approached**) □ **aproximar-se**
The train is approaching platform 5.
appropriate [əˈprəʊpriət] *adj.* (= suitable) □ **adequado**
to wear appropriate clothes for a wedding. ◆ This is not an appropriate moment to talk about it.

■ antônimo: **inappropriate**

appropriately [ə'proupriətli] *adv.* □ **adequadamente**
Our guests did not behave appropriately so we will not invite them again.

approval [ə'pru:vəl] *n.* □ **aprovação**
She gave her approval to the project. ◆ I asked for her approval.

approve [ə'pru:v] *v.* (**approves, approving, approved**)
1 aprovar
I don't approve of the idea.
■ antônimo: **disapprove**
2 aprovar
The editor approved the article.

approximate [ə'proksimət] *adj.* □ **aproximado**
The train's approximate time of arrival is 9:30. ◆ The approximate cost is $2,000.

approximately [ə'proksimətli] *adv.* (= about) □ **aproximadamente**
There are approximately 30 pupils in our class.
■ Ver **roughly**.

apricot ['eiprikot] *n., adj.* □ **damasco**
apricot jam.

April ['eiprəl] *n.* □ **abril**
April the tenth (= 10th April). *Brit.* ◆ the tenth of April (= 10 April). *Brit.* ◆ April tenth (= April 10). *Amer.* ◆ in April 1993. ◆ on 4 April. ◆ on April 4. ◆ last April. ◆ next April.

apron ['eiprən] *n.* □ **avental**

aptitude ['aptitju:d] *n.* □ **aptidão**
an aptitude for languages / mathematics.
■ Ver **gift**.

Arab ['arəb] *n., adj.* □ **árabe**
The Arabs in Jordan. ◆ an Arab country.

Arabic ['arəbik] *adj.* □ **árabe**
Can you speak Arabic?

arch[1] [a:tʃ] *n.* □ **arco**
a bridge with three arches from ancient times.

arch[2] *v.* (**arches, arching, arched**) □ **arquear**
The cat arched its back.

archaeological [a:kio'lodʒikəl] *adj. Amer.,* **archeological** □ **arqueológico**

archaeologist [a:ki'olədʒist] *n. Amer.,* **archeologist** □ **arqueólogo**

archaeology [a:ki'olədʒi] *n. Amer.,* **archeology** □ **arqueologia**

archbishop [a:tʃ'biʃəp] *n.* □ **arcebispo**

architect ['a:kitəkt] *n.* □ **arquiteto**

architecture ['a:kitəktʃə] *n.* □ **arquitetura**
to study architecture. ◆ modern architecture.

are [a:] *v.* (Ver **be**).

area ['eəriə] *n.*
1 área, região
There aren't many discos in this area. ◆ in the London area. ◆ the desert areas of Egypt.
■ Ver **region**.
2 área
an area of 3 square kilometers. ◆ What's the area of this office?

area code ['eəriə ,koud] *n.* □ **código de área**

arena [ə'ri:nə] *n.* □ **arena**

aren't [a:nt] *v.* (mesmo que **are not**).

argue ['a:gju:] *v.* (**argues, arguing, argued**)
1 discutir

Don't argue with me! Do as you're told! ◆ I argued with him about the price.
2 discutir
to argue for / against the idea.

argument ['a:gju:mənt] *n.*
1 discussão
I had an argument with my neighbour about his dog. ◆ He did it without argument.
■ Ver **quarrel**.
2 argumento
arguments for and against the project.

arithmetic [ə'riθmətik] *n.* □ **aritmética**
He is not very good at arithmetic.

arm [a:m] *n.* □ **braço**
She carried a bag under her arm.
■ Don't confuse **arms** (= *plural of* **arm**) and **arms** (= weapons).

arm in arm □ **de braço(s) dado(s)**
They walked arm in arm.

with open arms □ **de braços abertos**
He welcomed me with open arms.

armchair ['a:mtʃeə] *n., adj.* □ **poltrona**
to sit in an armchair. ◆ an armchair detective.

armed [a:md] *adj.* □ **armado**
Don't shoot! He is not armed. ◆ an armed robber.

the armed forces *n.* □ **Forças Armadas**
The armed forces consist of the army, the navy and the air force.

armor ['a:mə] *n. Amer.,* **armour** *Brit.* □ **armadura**
In the past, knights wore armour to protect themselves.

arms [a:mz] *n.* (= weapons) □ **armas**
Arms are guns, tanks, missiles and other weapons.

army ['a:mi] *n.* (*pl.* **armies**) □ **exército**
He is a soldier in the British army.
■ Ver **military; air force; navy**.

aroma [ə'roumə] *n.* □ **aroma**
the aroma of fresh coffee.

around [ə'raund] *adv., prep.*
1 (= about) □ **por volta de**
I'll be back at around 5 o'clock. ◆ There were around 30 people there. ◆ It cost around 500 dollars.
2 (= round) □ **em volta de**
She put the collar around the dog's neck. ◆ Six people were sitting around the table.
3 por perto
We'll be around if you need us.
4 (= about) □ **por**
They left the toys lying around the room. ◆ They were running around the garden.
■ Ver **look around; turn around**.

arouse [ə'rauz] *v.* (**arouses, arousing, aroused**) □ **provocar**
His sudden appearance aroused suspicion.

arrange [ə'reindʒ] *v.* (**arranges, arranging, arranged**)
1 arrumar
She arranged the books on the shelf in alphabetical order. ◆ The clothes are arranged according to size.
2 combinar
We arranged to meet them at the hotel. ◆ The meeting was arranged for 12 April.
3 organizar
They are arranging a welcome party for her.

arrangement [ə'reindʒmənt] *n.*
1 arranjo
a flower arrangement.
2 acordo
We came to an arrangement over the price.
arrangements *n. pl.* □ **providências**
They are making arrangements to leave town. ◆ Who is in charge of the arrangements for the party?
arrest¹ [ə'rest] *v.* (**arrests, arresting, arrested**) □ **prender**
The police arrested the suspect. ◆ She was arrested for dangerous driving.
arrest² *n.* □ **prisão**
The police made several arrests.
under arrest □ **preso**
'You're under arrest!' said the policeman.
arrival [ə'raivəl] *n.* □ **chegada**
the arrival time of a train, a plane, etc. ◆ On your arrival (= When you arrive), please contact us.
arrive [ə'raiv] *v.* (**arrives, arriving, arrived**) □ **chegar**
What time did the plane arrive? ◆ We arrived at the hotel at 8. ◆ He will arrive in London late at night.
■ For small places use **arrive at**.
■ For big places (a country, a city, etc) use **arrive in**.
arrogance ['arəgəns] *n.* (= haughtiness) □ **arrogância**
arrogant ['arəgənt] *adj.* (= haughty) □ **arrogante**
an arrogant man. ◆ I don't like her because she is very arrogant.
arrogantly ['arəgəntli] *adv.* □ **arrogantemente**
to behave arrogantly.
arrow ['arou] *n.* □ **flecha**
to shoot an arrow (from a bow). ◆ Follow the arrows on the signs until you get to the place.
art [a:t] *n.* □ **arte**
to study art at school.
article ['a:tikl] *n.*
1 artigo (de texto)
There is an interesting article on drugs in the newspaper.
2 artigo
articles of clothing, such as shirts, skirts and trousers.
3 (grammar) □ **artigo**
The words 'a', 'an' and 'the' are articles.
artificial [a:ti'fiʃəl] *adj.* □ **artificial**
artificial flowers.
■ Ver **natural**.
artificial intelligence *n.* □ **inteligência artificial**
artillery [a:'tiləri] *n.* □ **artilharia**
artist ['a:tist] *n.* □ **artista**
an exhibition of the artist's works (paintings, sculptures, etc.).
artistic [a:'tistik] *adj.* □ **artístico**
an artistic flower arrangement.
as¹ [az] *conj.*
1 (= while; when) □ **enquanto, quando**
He fell as he was getting off the bus.
2 (= because) □ **como, uma vez que**
As she can't come, David will take her place.
3 como
Mary, as you know, is a professional player. ◆ As I said earlier, I don't like the idea.
as² *prep.* □ **como**
He works as a teacher. ◆ I always thought of her as a good driver, till the accident.

as... as *adv.* □ **tão... quanto**
She is as tall as me. ◆ He worked as fast as David. ◆ He is as good a driver as she is.
as far as □ **até**
We walked as far as the station. ◆ I read as far as page 90.
as far as I know □ **até onde eu sei**
As far as I know, she is not at home.
as good as □ **praticamente**
The car is as good as new.
as if (mesmo que **as though**) □ **como se**
He talks as if he knew the answers to everything.
as long as
1 enquanto
I don't want to see him as long as I live.
2 desde que
He may borrow your leather jacket as long as he returns it tomorrow.
■ Do not use the *future tense* after **as long as**; use the *present tense* as in the examples above.
as many as (Ver **many**).
as much as (Ver **much**).
as soon as □ **assim que, logo que**
Call me as soon as you get home. ◆ I'll start as soon as I'm ready.
■ Do not use the *future tense* after **as soon as**; use the *present tense* as in the examples above.
as soon as possible □ **o quanto antes, o mais cedo possível**
Please reply as soon as possible.
as usual □ **como sempre**
She is late, as usual.
as well □ **também**
Give me that bottle as well.
as well as
1 bem como
She can dance as well as sing. ◆ He speaks Spanish as well as English.
2 tão bem quanto
He cooks as well as my mother (does).
ash [aʃ] *n.* □ **cinza**
cigarette ash.
ashamed [ə'ʃeimd] *adj.* □ **envergonhado**
I'm ashamed that I was angry with you.
be ashamed of □ **ter vergonha de**
I'm ashamed of you! ◆ You should be ashamed of yourself for behaving like that.
be ashamed to □ **ter vergonha de**
I'm ashamed to admit that I lied.
ashore [ə'ʃo:] *adv.* □ **para a praia, em terra**
When their ship reached the port, the sailors went ashore.
ashtray ['aʃtrei] *n.* □ **cinzeiro**
aside [ə'said] *adv.* □ **de lado**
She moved aside to let me pass. ◆ He put the book aside and tried to sleep.
aside from *prep. Amer.* (= apart from) □ **com exceção de**
ask [a:sk] *v.* (**asks, asking, asked**)
1 perguntar
She didn't ask me that question. ◆ They asked him what to do. ◆ She asked me my name. ◆ Did you ask her about the money?
2 pedir

He asked me a favour. ◆ Let's ask the policeman to show us the way.
3 (= invite) □ **convidar**
I'll ask them to the party.
ask after someone □ **perguntar por**
He asked after you.
ask someone for □ **pedir**
I asked my parents for a motorbike. ◆ He asked for help.
ask for someone □ **perguntar por**
Phone them and ask for the manager.
asleep [ə'sli:p] *adj.* (= sleeping) □ **adormecido**
The baby is asleep.
■ antônimo: **awake**
fall asleep □ **cair no sono**
She fell asleep before supper.
aspect ['aspekt] *n.* □ **aspecto, detalhe**
They examined every aspect of the problem.
ass [as] *n.* (= donkey) □ **asno**
assassinate [ə'sasineit] *v.* (**assassinates, assassinating, assassinated**) □ **assassinar**
The terrorists assassinated the President.
■ Ver **kill; murder**².
assassination [əˌsasi'neiʃən] *n.* □ **assassinato**
The assassination attempt failed.
assault¹ [ə'sɔ:lt] *n.* □ **agressão**
assault² *v.* (**assaults, assaulting, assaulted**) □ **agredir**
The bank robber assaulted a policeman.
■ Ver **attack**².
assemble [ə'sembl] *v.* (**assembles, assembling, assembled**) □ **reunir-se**
The students assembled in the hall.
assembly [ə'sembli] *n.* (*pl.* **assemblies**) □ **reunião, assembleia**
assign [ə'sain] *v.* (**assigns, assigning, assigned**) □ **designar, incumbir**
The officer assigned different duties to the soldiers.
assignment [ə'sainmənt] *n.* □ **incumbência, tarefa**
homework assignments.
assist [ə'sist] *v.* (**assists, assisting, assisted**) □ **assistir, dar assistência**
The nurses assisted the doctor during the operation.
■ The usual word is **help**.
assistance [ə'sistəns] *n.* □ **assistência**
We offered them financial assistance. ◆ She was of great assistance to us.
assistant [ə'sistənt] *n.*, *adj.*
1 assistente
My assistant will take care of this problem. ◆ assistant manager.
2 *Brit.* □ **balconista**
a shop / sales assistant
■ *Amer.* (**sales**) **clerk**
associate [ə'sousieit] *v.* (**associates, associating, associated**)
1 relacionar-se com
He associates with criminals.
2 associar
We associate thunder with lightning.
association [əˌsousi'eiʃən] *n.* □ **associação**
the Football Association.
assume [ə'sju:m] *v.* (**assumes, assuming, assumed**) (= suppose) □ **supor**
I assume (that) you know what you're doing.

assumption [ə'sʌmpʃən] *n.* □ **suposição**
She made the wrong assumption.
assurance [ə'ʃuərəns] *n.* □ **garantia**
We want your assurance that you will finish the job today.
assure [ə'ʃuə] *v.* (**assures, assuring, assured**) □ **assegurar**
I assure you (that) there won't be any problems.
astonish [ə'stoniʃ] *v.* (**astonishes, astonishing, astonished**) □ **assombrar, espantar**
The news of their marriage astonished us. ◆ They were astonished at the beauty of the city.
astonishing [ə'stoniʃiŋ] *adj.* □ **assombroso, espantoso**
an astonishing success / achievement. ◆ the astonishing beauty of the city.
astonishment [ə'stoniʃmənt] *n.* □ **assombro, espanto**
To my astonishment, she agreed with me. ◆ They looked at us in astonishment.
astronaut ['astrənɔ:t] *n.* □ **astronauta**
Astronauts travel into space in a spaceship.
■ Ver **spaceman; specewoman**.
asylum [ə'sailəm] *n.* □ **asilo**
The refugees asked for asylum in Canada.
at [at] *prep.*
1 em
at the station / office. ◆ at home / work / school. ◆ at the party.
■ Use **in** when you mean 'inside' a room, building, etc.
2 em, a
I'm staying at a hotel. ◆ This bus does not stop at the village. ◆ I arrived at the airport at 5 o'clock.
■ Use **in** for big places (a country, a city, etc):
I arrived in London too late.
3 a
at 6 o'clock. ◆ at about 4:30. ◆ at noon / night / midnight. ◆ at (the age of) 20.
■ Use **on** for days:
on Sunday. ◆ on 4 May. ◆ on her birthday. ◆ on Tuesday evening.
■ Use **in** for months, years and seasons:
in July. ◆ in 1994. ◆ in (the) winter.
4 a
I drove at 80 km an hour. ◆ at the rate of 10 cars a day.
5 em, para, de
She threw the ball at me. ◆ He smiled at us. ◆ Look at me! ◆ They laughed at him.
6 de, com
We laughed at the joke. ◆ I'm surprised at you. ◆ I was shocked at the news. ◆ We were angry at the delay.
7 em
She is good at mathematics.
at all □ **de alguma forma**
Can he drive at all?
not at all
1 de forma nenhuma
She doesn't speak English at all.
2 De nada.
Thank you. – Not at all.
at first □ **no início, a princípio**
At first I didn't like English, but now I do.
at last □ **até que enfim, finalmente**
At last the train arrived. ◆ He came to a decision at last.
at least

1 no mínimo
It will cost you at least 5,000 pounds. ◆ There are at least 600 pupils in our school.
2 pelo menos
At least you have another chance.
at once (= immediately) □ **já, imediatamente**
Come here at once!
ate [et, eit] *v*. (Ver **eat**).
athlete ['æθliːt] *n*. □ **atleta**
athletic [əθ'letik] *adj*. □ **atlético**
an athletic figure / body.
athletics [əθ'letiks] *n*. □ **atletismo**
an athletics meeting (= a competition in running, jumping, etc.).
atlas ['ætləs] *n*. □ **atlas**
ATM [ˌei tiː 'em] *n*., *abbr*., *Amer*. (mesmo que **Automated Teller Machine**) □ **caixa eletrônico**
to draw money from an ATM.
■ *Brit.* **cash machine**
atmosphere ['ætməsfiə] *n*.
1 atmosfera
The temperature of the earth's atmosphere may rise because of air pollution.
2 ambiente
They discussed the problem in a friendly atmosphere.
atom ['ætəm] *n*., *adj*. □ **átomo**
to split the atom. ◆ an atom bomb.
atomic [ə'tomik] *adj*. □ **atômico**
an atomic bomb. ◆ atomic energy.
■ Ver **nuclear**.
attach [ə'tætʃ] *v*. (**attaches, attaching, attached**)
1 prender
to attach a label to a suitcase
2 (= enclose) □ **anexar**
He attached a letter to the package.
3 dar
I don't attach much importance to what he says.
be attached to □ **ser ligado a**
He is very attached to his uncle.
attachment [ə'tætʃmənt] *n*.
1 anexo
Send me the document as an attachment to your e-mail.
2 acessório
attachments on my new bicycle.
attack¹ [ə'tæk] *n*.
1 ataque
a surprise attack on the enemy. ◆ a strong attack on / against the government.
2 ataque
She died of a heart attack.
attack² *v*. (**attacks, attacking, attacked**) □ **atacar**
to attack the enemy. ◆ The dog attacked the burglar. ◆ She attacked the Prime Minister in a newspaper article.
attacker [ə'tækə] *n*. □ **atacante, agressor**
attempt¹ [ə'tempt] *n*.
1 tentativa
She made an attempt to fix it. ◆ He scored a goal at his first attempt.
2 atentado
The attempt on the President's life failed.
attempt² *v*. (**attempts, attempting, attempted**) (= try) □ **tentar**

They attempted to escape from prison.
attend [ə'tend] *v*. (**attends, attending, attended**)
1 comparecer
How many people attended the meeting? ◆ to attend a funeral / a lecture.
2 frequentar
They have to attend school until they are 16.
attendance [ə'tendəns] *n*.
1 frequência
The teacher checked attendance.
2 comparecimento
There was a large attendance at the funeral.
attendant [ə'tendənt] *n*. □ **atendente**
a museum attendant. ◆ an attendant at a petrol / gas station.
attention [ə'tenʃən] *n*. □ **atenção**
He is trying to attract attention with his funny hat. ◆ They listened with close attention.
draw someone's attention to □ **chamar a atenção de alguém para**
She drew my attention to my mistake.
pay attention (to) □ **prestar atenção (a)**
He never pays attention in class. ◆ She paid careful attention to what I was doing.
stand at / to attention □ **ficar em posição de sentido**
The soldiers stood to attention when the officer came in.
attic ['ætik] *n*. □ **sótão**
attitude ['ætitjuːd] *n*. □ **posicionamento, atitude**
What is your attitude to(wards) violence on television? ◆ Their attitude towards him changed completely. ◆ I don't like your negative attitude.
attorney [ə'tɜːni] *n*. □ **advogado, procurador**
You hire an attorney to speak for you in court.
■ Used mainly in American English. A more general word is **lawyer**.
attract [ə'trækt] *v*. (**attracts, attracting, attracted**)
1 atrair
Magnets attract needles, nails, etc. ◆ He was attracted to her.
2 atrair
to attract attention
attraction [ə'trækʃən] *n*.
1 atração
There are a lot of tourist attractions in London.
2 atração
He felt a strong attraction to her.
attractive [ə'træktiv] *adj*.
1 atraente
an attractive woman / man.
2 atraente
an attractive offer / idea.
■ antônimo: **unattractive**
ATV [ˌei tiː ˌviː] *n*., *abbr*. (mesmo que **all-terrain vehicle**) □ **ATV, quadriciclo**
aubergine ['əubəʒiːn] *n*. *Brit*. (= eggplant) □ **beringela**
auction ['ɔːkʃən] *n*. □ **leilão**
He bought the painting at an auction.
audience ['ɔːdiəns] *n*. □ **plateia, audiência**
There was a large audience at the rock concert. ◆ a TV audience.
audio, audio- ['ɔːdiəu] *adj*., *pref*. □ **áudio**
an audio book (= on tape). ◆ audio-visual aids.
August ['ɔːgəst] *n*. □ **agosto**

In August, 2002.
- See more examples at **April**.

aunt [a:nt] *n.* □ **tia**
My aunt and uncle are coming to visit us.

au pair [ˌəu 'peə] *n.* □ **au pair**
to work as an au pair abroad.

authentic [o:θentik] *adj.* □ **autêntico**
an authentic painting by the artist, not a copy. ◆ an authentic model of an ancient ship.

author ['o:θə] *n.* (= writer) □ **autor**
the author of this book / poem. ◆ She is the most successful author in Italy.

authorise ['o:θəraiz] *v. Brit.* (= **authorize**).

authority [o:'θorəti] *n.*
1 autoridade
He has the authority to arrest you.
2 (*pl.* **authorities**) □ **autoridades**
the health authorities. ◆ the Spanish authorities.

authorize ['o:θəraiz] *v.* (**authorizes, authorizing, authorized**) □ **autorizar**
I didn't authorize you to speak in my name.

autobiographical [ˌo:təbaio'grafikəl] *adj.* □ **autobiográfico**
an autobiographical novel.

autobiography [o:təbaio'grəfi] *n.* □ **autobiografia**

autograph ['o:təgra:f] *n.* □ **autógrafo**
to ask a pop star for his / her autograph.
- Ver **signature**.

automatic [o:tə'matik] *adj.* □ **automático**
an automatic machine / rifle.

automatically [o:tə'matikəli] *adv.* □ **automaticamente**
This television can be switched off automatically.

automobile ['o:təməbi:l] *n. Amer.* (= car) □ **automóvel, carro**

autumn ['o:təm] *n.* □ **outono**
In autumn the weather becomes cooler.
- The usual word in American English is **fall**.

available [ə'veiləbl] *adj.* □ **disponível**
Is the book available from the library? ◆ She is not available for interviews at the moment. ◆ Thanks to computers, more information is now available.
- antônimo: **unavailable**

avenue ['avinju:] *n.* □ **avenida**
- abreviação: **Ave.**
10 Liberty Ave.

average ['avərɪdʒ] *adj., n.*
1 média
The average age of the pupils in our class is 15. ◆ The average of 2, 4 and 6 is 4.
2 médio, regular
He is an average pupil.

on (the) average □ **em média**
I work 28 hours a week on average.

avoid [ə'void] *v.* (**avoids, avoiding, avoided**) □ **evitar**
We turned around to avoid (meeting) the teacher. ◆ She advised him to avoid (taking) drugs. ◆ He is avoiding me because he owes me money.

avoidance [ə'voidəns] *n.* □ **evitação, impedimento**
avoidance of danger.

awake [ə'weik] *adj.* □ **acordado**
Is he awake?
- antônimo: **asleep**

award[1] [ə'wo:d] *n.* □ **prêmio**
He won the award for Best Actor.
- Ver **prize; grant**.

award[2] *v.* (**awards, awarding, awarded**) □ **conceder**
They awarded her the first prize. ◆ to award a scholarship.

aware [ə'weə] *adj.* □ **ter ciência**
We are aware of the dangers. ◆ I'm aware that the plan is not perfect.
- antônimo: **unaware**

awareness [ə'weənis] *n.* □ **consciência**

away [ə'wei] *adv.*
1 de distância
The city is 5 kilometres away.
2 fora, ausente, longe
She is away on holiday.
3 para outra direção
I looked away because I couldn't watch it. ◆ Put the gun away!
- Ver **go away; keep away; right away; run away; throw away**.

awesome ['o:səm] *adj.* □ **incrível**
an awesome movie that thrilled me. ◆ an awesome sight.

awful ['o:ful] *adj.* (= terrible) □ **horrível**
The conditions in that prison are awful. ◆ an awful accident. ◆ The film was awful.

awfully ['o:fuli] *adv.* □ **muito, terrivelmente**
I'm awfully sorry! ◆ They played awfully.

awkward ['o:kwəd] *adj.*
1 esquisito
an awkward situation. ◆ The journalists asked him awkward questions. ◆ This is an awkward time to meet.
2 estranho
I felt awkward in their company. ◆ an awkward smile.
3 (= clumsy) □ **desengonçado**
He danced with awkward movements.

awkwardness ['o:kwədnis] *n.* □ **inconveniência, falta de jeito**
the awkwardness of my situation. ◆ I don't like the awkwardness of the dancers' movements.

axe[1] [aks] *n.*, **ax** *Amer.* □ **machado**
He chopped some wood with an axe.

axe[2] *Brit.*, **ax** *Amer.* □ **cortar, demitir**
The government axed the budget. ◆ The factory axed a lot of workers.

Bb

baby ['beibi] *n.* (*pl.* **babies**) ◻ **bebê**
She is going to have a baby. ◆ baby food / clothes.
baby carriage ['beibi ˌkaridʒ] *n. Amer.* ◻ **carrinho de bebê**
■ *Brit.* **pram**
babysit ['beibisit] *v.* (**babysits, babysitting, babysat**) ◻ **tomar conta de criança**
She babysits for her neighbours. ◆ I'm babysitting my little sister tonight.
babysitter ['beibiˌsitə] *n.* ◻ **babá**
bachelor ['batʃələ] *n., adj.* ◻ **solteiro, de solteiro**
a bachelor flat / apartment.
■ Ver **single**.
back[1] [bak] *adj.* ◻ **traseiro**
the back door.
back[2] *adv.*
1 para trás
He stepped back slowly when he saw the snake. ◆ to look back.
2 de volta
Put it back. ◆ Give it back to me. ◆ We ran to the park and back.
be back [bak] ◻ **estar de volta**
She'll be back in a minute.
■ Ver **call back; come back; get back; give back; go back; take back**.
back[3] *n.*
1 de costas
He lay on his back on the grass.
2 (= rear[2]) **fundo, verso**
We sat at the back of the bus. ◆ We sat in the back (of the car). ◆ Please sign on the back of the check.
3 final
The answers are at the back of the book.
behind someone's back ◻ **pelas costas (de alguém)**
They laugh at him behind his back.
get off someone's back ◻ **deixar em paz**
get off my back and stop nagging me
back[4] *v.* (**backs, backing, backed**)
1 dar ré
She backed (the car) into the parking space.
2 (= support) **apoiar**
We back Dan as our candidate for the Students' Council.
back away ◻ **afastar-se**
They backed away from the snake.
back someone / something up
1 apoiar
I told them what happened and Dina backed me up.
2 fazer cópia de segurança
We need to back up all this information (on the computer).
backache ['bakeik] *n.* ◻ **dor nas costas**
She suffers from backache. ◆ She has a backache.
backbone ['bakboun] *n.* (= spine) ◻ **coluna vertebral**
background ['bakgraund] *n.*
1 plano de fundo
You can see it in the background of the picture.
2 formação
people from different cultural backgrounds.
backpack ['bakpak] *n.* ◻ **mochila**
back seat ['bak 'siːt] *n.* ◻ **banco de trás**
I sat in the front seat and they sat in the back seat.
backstroke ['bakstrouk] *n.* ◻ **nado de costas**
backward[1] ['bakwəd] *adj.*
1 para trás
a backward step.
■ antônimo: **forward**
2 subdesenvolvido, atrasado
a backward country.
■ antônimo: **developed**.
3 atrasado
a backward child.
backward[2], **backwards** *adv.*
1 para trás
to walk backwards. ◆ to look backwards. ◆ to fall backwards.
■ antônimo: **forward(s)**
2 de trás para frente
Can you count backwards from ten to one?
backwards and forwards ◻ **para frente e para trás, de lá para cá**
We walked backwards and forwards along the street.
bacon ['beikən] *n.* ◻ **bacon, toucinho**
English people like eating bacon and eggs. ◆ Religious Jews and Muslims don't eat bacon.
bacteria [bak'tiəriə] *n. pl.* ◻ **bactérias**
bad [bad] *adj.* (**worse, worst**)
1 mau, ruim
a bad boy. ◆ a bad driver. ◆ bad eating habits.
2 ruim
bad news. ◆ a bad dream. ◆ a bad smell.
3 ruim
bad weather.
4 mau
bad luck.
5 prejudicial
Smoking is bad for you.
6 podre
bad eggs.
7 grave
She had a bad accident. ◆ a bad mistake.
bad language *n.* ◻ **linguagem chula, palavrão**
I won't listen to you if you use bad language.
be bad at ◻ **ser ruim em, ser péssimo em**
He is bad at mathematics.
go from bad to worse ◻ **de mal a pior**
After the new manager came, things went from bad to worse
too bad
1 uma pena
It's too bad you can't come.
2 Que pena!
I need more money. – Too bad! That's all you're going to get.
badge [badʒ] *n.*
1 distintivo
a policeman's badge.
2 emblema
a shirt with a school badge on the pocket.
badly ['badli] *adv.* (**worse, worst**)
1 mal
She sings badly. ◆ The building is badly built.

■ antônimo: **well**
2 desesperadamente
They need help badly.
3 gravemente
He was badly injured in the accident.
bad-tempered [,bad'tempəd] *adj.* □ **mal-humorado**
I become bad-tempered when I don't sleep well at night.
baffle ['bafl] *v.* (**baffles, baffling, baffled**) □ **intrigar**
This question still baffles scientists. ◆ The police are baffled by the mystery.
bag [bag] *n.* □ **sacola, saco**
a plastic shopping bag. ◆ a sandwich bag. ◆ a paper bag. ◆ a bag of crisps / potato chips. ◆ tea bags of 2 grams each. ◆ a bag of cement.
■ Ver **case**; **handbag**; **sack**.
baggage ['bagidʒ] *n.* (= luggage) □ **bagagem**
The bags and cases that you take with you when you travel are called 'baggage'. ◆ the baggage room at the bus station.
bagpipes ['bagpaips] *n.* □ **gaita de foles**
bait [beit] *n.* □ **isca**
bake [beik] *v.* (**bakes, baking, baked**) □ **assar**
to bake bread / a cake (in an oven).
baked [beikt] *adj.* □ **assado**
baked potatoes.
baked beans ['beikt ,bi:nz] *n. pl.* □ **feijão cozido com molho de tomate**
baker ['beikə] *n.* □ **padeiro, padaria**
I prefer to buy bread at the baker's (= the baker's shop).
bakery ['beikəri] *n. (pl.* **bakeries**) □ **padaria**
balance[1] ['baləns] *n.*
1 equilíbrio
She tried to keep her balance on the rope. ◆ He lost his balance and fell.
2 equilíbrio
a balance between work and play. ◆ a balance of power (between two countries).
3 saldo
There is a balance of 500 pounds in your bank account.
4 balança
a balance of trade.
balance[2] *v.* (**balances, balancing, balanced**) □ **equilibrar(-se), equilibrar**
He balanced on one leg. ◆ She balanced a ball on her head.
balanced ['balənst] *adj.* □ **balanceado, equilibrado**
a balanced diet
balcony ['balkəni] *n. (pl.* **balconies**) □ **sacada**
to sit on the balcony.
■ Ver **veranda(h)**.
bald [bo:ld] *adj.* □ **careca**
He is bald. ◆ He has a bald head.
go bald □ **ficar careca**
He is going bald.
ball [bo:l] *n.*
1 bola
a tennis ball. ◆ a football. ◆ to catch / kick / throw the ball.
2 novelo
a ball of wool.
3 baile
She bought a beautiful dress for the ball.
ballerina [balə'ri:nə] *n.* □ **bailarina**
ballet ['balei] *n.* □ **balé**
a ballet dancer.

balloon [bə'lu:n] *n.*
1 balão
to blow up a balloon (= to fill it with air). ◆ The balloon burst suddenly.
2 balão
to fly in a balloon.
ballot ['balət] *n.* □ **votação, cédula**
We held a ballot to choose a new leader. ◆ to vote by secret ballot.
ball-point (pen) ['bo:lpoint ('pen)] *n.* □ **(caneta) esferográfica**
ballroom ['bo:lrum] *n.* □ **salão de baile**
bamboo [bam'bu:] *n.* □ **bambu**
a bamboo chair.
ban[1] [ban] *n.* □ **proibição**
to put a ban on smoking.
ban[2] *v.* (**bans, banning, banned**) □ **proibir**
The school rules ban smoking in classrooms. ◆ The film was banned in many countries.
banana [bə'na:nə] *n.* □ **banana**
He peeled the banana and ate it.
band[1] [band] *n.*
1 banda
a rock / jazz band.
2 faixa
a barrel with metal bands round it.
3 fita
a hat with a red band.
4 filete
a cup with a gold band round the edge.
■ Ver **rubber band**; **elastic band**.
band[2] *v.* (**bands, banding, banded**)
band together □ **juntar-se**
The students banded together to protest (against) the new rules.
bandage[1] ['bandidʒ] *n.* □ **atadura**
The nurse put a bandage on his arm.
bandage[2] *v.* (**bandages, bandaging, bandaged**) □ **enfaixar**
The doctor bandaged my head / the wound.
Band-Aid™ ['band eid] *n. Amer.* □ **band-aid, curativo adesivo**
■ Ver **plaster**.
bandit ['bandit] *n.* □ **bandido**
Bandits robbed them.
bang[1] [baŋ] *n.*
1 pancada
He fell and got a bang on his head.
2 estrondo, explosão
She shut the door with a bang. ◆ The bomb exploded with a loud bang.
bang[2] *v.* (**bangs, banging, banged**)
1 bater com força
He banged on the door with his fist.
2 fechar com violência, disparar
Don't bang the door! ◆ We heard a gun bang twice.
bang your head on □ **bater a cabeça em**
He banged his head on the shelf.
banish ['baniʃ] *v.* (**banishes, banishing, banished**) □ **banir, expulsar**
In the past, the British government banished criminals to Australia.

banister(s) ['banistə] *n*. □ **corrimão**
The children were sliding down the banister.
bank □ [baŋk] *n*.
1 banco (instituição)
I have $500 in the bank. ♦ to borrow money from the bank. ♦ a bank account. ♦ a bank manager.
2 banco
a blood bank. ♦ a data bank.
3 margem, encosta
They walked along the river bank.
banker ['baŋkə] *n*. □ **banqueiro**
bank holiday ['baŋk 'holədi] *n*. □ **feriado bancário**
banknote ['baŋknout] *n*. □ **nota**
■ Ver **bill**.
bankrupt ['baŋkrʌpt] *adj*., *n*. □ **falido, quebrado**
go bankrupt □ **ir à falência**
The business went bankrupt.
bankruptcy ['baŋkrəptsi] *n*. □ **falência**
banner ['banə] *n*. □ **bandeira, faixa**
The demonstrators carried banners that said 'Give Peace a Chance'.
banquet ['bankwit] *n*. □ **banquete**
a wedding banquet.
baptism ['baptizəm] *n*. □ **batismo**
baptize [bap'taiz] *v*. (**baptizes, baptizing, baptized**), *Brit*. **baptise** □ **batizar**
He was baptized in this church. ♦ She was baptized Margaret.
bar¹ [ba:] *n*.
1 bar, lanchonete, café
to drink at the bar. ♦ a snack / coffee bar.
2 grade
We put bars on the windows. ♦ The criminal is now behind bars. (= He is in prison.)
3 barra
a bar of chocolate / soap.
bar² *v*. (**bars, barring, barred**) □ **bloquear**
The demonstrators barred the road.
barbed wire ['ba:bd 'waiə] *n*. □ **arame farpado**
a barbed wire fence.
barbecue ['ba:bikju:] *n*. □ **churrasco**
barber ['ba:bə] *n*. □ **barbeiro, barbearia**
to go to the barber's (= barbershop) to have a haircut.
■ Ver **hairdresser**.
bare [beə] *adj*.
1 nu, vazio
bare walls (with no pictures, etc.). ♦ The room was bare (of furniture).
2 descalço
to walk around in bare feet
barefoot ['beəfut] *adv*., *adj*. □ **descalço**
to walk barefoot
barely ['beəli] *adv*.
1 apenas
I was barely 6 when my mother died.
2 mal
I could barely breathe in the crowded room.
3 mal
She barely touched her food.
bargain¹ ['ba:gin] *n*.
1 (= deal) □ **trato**
Let's make a bargain – I'll cook and you'll wash the dishes.

2 pechincha
It's a real bargain at that price.
bargain² *v*. (**bargains, bargaining, bargained**) □ **negociar, pechinchar**
Try to bargain with him to cut the price.
bargaining ['ba:giniŋ] *n*. □ **barganha, pechincha**
After hours of bargaining they reached an agreement.
barge [ba:dʒ] *n*. □ **barcaça**
bark¹ [ba:k] *n*. □ **casca**
The bark of some trees is used for making medicines.
bark² *v*. (**barks, barking, barked**) □ **latir**
The dog barked at the postman.
barley ['ba:li] *n*. □ **cevada**
barmaid ['ba:meid] *n*. □ **garçonete**
barman ['ba:mən] *n*. (*pl*. **barmen**) □ **barman**
barn [ba:n] *n*. □ **celeiro**
barometer [bə'romitə] *n*. □ **barômetro**
baron ['barən] *n*. □ **barão**
baroness ['barənis] *n*. □ **baronesa**
barracks ['barəks] *n*. □ **quartel**
an army barracks.
barrel ['barəl] *n*.
1 barril
a barrel of beer. ♦ 20,000 barrels of oil.
2 cano
the barrel of a gun.
barricade¹ ['bari,keid] *n*. □ **barricada**
The crowd put up a barricade of furniture, carts, etc.
barricade² *v*. (**barricades, barricading, barricaded**) □ **bloquear, fazer barricada**
They barricaded the door to keep the attackers out.
barrier ['bariə] *n*. □ **barreira**
a police barrier. ♦ barriers at a football stadium.
barrow ['barou] *n*. □ **carrinho**
■ Ver **wheelbarrow**.
bartender ['ba:,tendə] *n*. *Amer*. □ **barman**
base¹ [beis] *n*.
1 base
the base of a triangle. ♦ the base of a statue.
2 base
an army base.
base² *v*. (**bases, basing, based**)
be based on □ **ser baseado em**
This movie is based on a bestseller. ♦ The story is based on facts.
baseball ['beisbɔ:l] *n*. □ **beisebol**
basement ['beismənt] *n*. □ **subsolo, porão**
He lives in a basement apartment. ♦ The clothing department is in the basement.
bases ['beisi:z] *n*. (*plural of* **basis** and **base**).
bash [baʃ] *v*. (**bashes, bashing, bashed**)
1 bater
She bashed her head on / against the wall.
2 golpear
The robber bashed her victim all over his body with a big stick.
basic ['beisik] *adj*. □ **básico**
basic principles. ♦ basic needs. ♦ a basic course in English.
basically ['beisikəli] *adv*. □ **basicamente**
Adults enjoy the book, but it's basically a children's book.
basin ['beisn] *n*.

basis / beat

1 (= washbasin) □ **pia**
A basin is a sink in a bathroom.
2 (= bowl) □ **tigela**
Put the flour and milk into a basin and mix well.
basis ['beisis] *n.* (*pl.* **bases** ['beisi:z]) □ **base**
a complaint without any basis. ◆ I wrote it on the basis of your ideas.
basket ['ba:skit] *n.*
1 cesto
a shopping basket. ◆ a bread basket. ◆ a basket of apples. ◆ a wastepaper basket.
2 cesta
to shoot / score a basket.
basketball ['ba:skitbo:l] *n.* □ **basquete**
bass [beis] *adj.* □ **grave, baixo, contrabaixo**
a bass voice / guitar.
bastard ['ba:stəd] *n.*
1 bastardo
A bastard is the son or daughter of an unmarried woman.
2 (= slang) □ **desgraçado**
You stupid / lucky bastard!
bat [bat] *n.*
1 morcego
Bats are active at night.
2 taco, raquete
a baseball bat. *Brit.* ◆ a pair of bats for table tennis.
batch [batʃ] *n.* □ **monte, fornada**
a batch of letters. ◆ a batch of cookies.
bath [ba:θ] *n.*
1 banho
to run a bath (= to fill it with water).
2 banho
I'll have a hot bath before supper. ◆ to give the baby a bath.
bathe [beið] *v.* (**bathes, bathing, bathed**)
1 banhar-se
They are bathing in the sea / river.
2 limpar, lavar
to bathe the wound and bandage it.
bather [beiðə] *n.* □ **banhista**
bathing [beiðiŋ] *n.* □ **banho**
bathrobe ['ba:θroub] *n.* □ **roupão de banho**
■ *Brit.* **bathing gown**
bathroom ['ba:θrum] *n.*
1 banheiro
You can have a shower or a bath in a bathroom.
2 (= toilet) *Amer.* □ **banheiro**
I need to go to the bathroom.
bathtub ['ba:θtʌb] *n.* □ **banheira**
battery ['batəri] *n.* (*pl.* **batteries**) □ **bateria**
Put three batteries in the flashlight. ◆ a car battery.
battle¹ ['batl] *n.*
1 batalha
Many soldiers were killed in (that) battle. ◆ to lose / win the battle
2 luta
the battle against crime and poverty
battle² *v.* (**battles, battling, battled**) □ **lutar**
They are battling for equal rights. ◆ to battle against crime.
battlefield ['batlfi:ld] *n.* □ **campo de batalha**
bay [bei] *n.* □ **baía**
The ship entered the bay.

bazaar [bə'za:] *n.* □ **bazar**
You can buy goods cheaply in a bazaar.
BC ['bi:'si:] *abbr.* □ **a.C.**
in (the year) 470 BC.
■ Ver **AD**.
be [bi:] *v.* (**am, is, are; was, were; been; being**)
1 estar
I'm (= I am) reading. ◆ He's (= He is) cooking. ◆ What are you doing? ◆ He was watching TV when the telephone rang.
■ Used as an auxiliary verb to form the *continuous* or *progressive tenses*.
2 ser
I was born in 1989. ◆ The car has been stolen. ◆ The money will be returned.
■ Used as an auxiliary verb to form the passive voice.
3 ser, estar
She is a lawyer. ◆ You're (= You are) wrong. ◆ It was expensive.
4 ser, estar
He is in the kitchen. ◆ My birthday is next Tuesday. ◆ The election was on Thursday.
5 estar
She has been to the doctor.
beach [bi:tʃ] *n.* □ **praia**
We go to the beach once a week. ◆ to play on the beach.
bead [bi:d] *n.* □ **conta**
She wore a string of beads.
beak [bi:k] *n.* □ **bico**
beam [bi:m] *n.*
1 viga
a wooden beam.
2 raio, feixe
a beam of light. ◆ a laser beam.
bean [bi:n] *n.* □ **grão, feijão**
green beans. ◆ baked beans. ◆ coffee beans.
bear¹ [beə] *n.* □ **urso**
The polar bear has white fur.
bear² *v.* (**bears, bearing, bore, borne**)
1 (= carry) □ **aguentar**
This chair cannot bear your weight.
2 arcar com
She bears a heavy responsibility. ◆ He bore all the costs.
3 parir, dar à luz
She bore three children.
■ Ver **born**.
can't bear (= can't stand) □ **não aguentar, não suportar**
I can't bear the pain. ◆ She can't bear him. ◆ I can't bear seeing him suffer so much.
bear in mind □ **ter em mente**
I'll bear your warning in mind. ◆ Bear in mind that we don't have enough money.
beard [biəd] *n.* □ **barba**
He has a white beard. ◆ He shaved off his beard.
bearded [biədid] *adj.* □ **barbado, barbudo**
beast [bi:st] *n.* (= animal) □ **besta, animal selvagem, fera**
a wild beast.
beat¹ [bi:t] *n.*
1 batimento, batida
the beat of the heart (= heartbeat). ◆ the beat of the drums.
2 batida
the beat of the music.

beat² *v.* (**beats, beating, beat, beaten**)
1 bater
to beat the drum. ◆ They beat him with a stick.
2 derrotar
She always beats me at chess. ◆ Brazil beat France 3-1.
■ Ver **defeat²**.
3 bater
My heart was beating fast.
4 bater
to beat an egg with a fork.
beating [bi:tiŋ] *n.* □ **surra**
He got a beating because he behaved so badly.
beautiful ['bju:təful] *adj.* □ **bonito, lindo**
a beautiful woman. ◆ a beautiful face / picture. ◆ The music was beautiful. ◆ What a beautiful day!
■ With men use **good-looking** or **handsome**.
beautifully ['bju:təfuli] *adv.* □ **lindamente**
He was beautifully dressed. ◆ They sing beautifully.
beauty ['bju:ti] *n.* □ **beleza**
the beauty of the sunset / the view. ◆ a woman of great beauty.
became [bi'keim] *v.* (Ver **become**).
because [bi'koz] *conj.* □ **porque**
I can't buy it, because I don't have enough money.
■ Ver **as; since²**.
because of *prep.* □ **devido a, por causa de**
She didn't go to school because of her illness. ◆ They came because of us.
become [bi'kʌm] *v.* (**becomes, becoming, became, become**) □ **tornar-se**
She became a lawyer in 1989. ◆ He is becoming famous.
become of □ **acontecer a**
What will become of you if you leave school? ◆ What became of his family after the war?
bed [bed] *n.*
1 cama
lie in bed. ◆ sit on the bed.
2 cama
Come on children! It's time for bed. ◆ I'm tired so I'm going to bed. ◆ Put the children to bed.
3 leito
the sea bed. ◆ the river bed.
4 canteiro
a flower bed.
make the bed □ **arrumar a cama**
bed and breakfast □ **hospedagem e café da manhã**
bedclothes ['bedkloυðz] *n.* □ **roupas de cama**
Sheets and blankets are bedclothes.
bedroom ['bedrum] *n.* □ **quarto**
bee [bi:] *n.* □ **abelha**
Bees make honey. ◆ A bee stung me on the arm.
beef [bi:f] *n.* □ **carne bovina**
beehive ['bi:haiv] *n.* □ **colmeia**
been [bi:n] *v.* (Ver **be**).
beer [biə] *n.* □ **cerveja**
a can of beer. ◆ Two beers, please.
beet [bi:t] *n.* □ **beterraba**
beetle ['bi:tl] *n.* □ **besouro**
beetroot ['bi:tru:t] *n.* □ **beterraba**
before¹ [bi'fo:] *adv.* □ **já, passado, antes, anteriormente**
I've seen that film before. ◆ He bought a car the month before. ◆ As I said before...
■ Ver **ago**.
before² *conj.* □ **antes que, antes de**
Tell him to do it now before he forgets. ◆ Before you say anything, listen to this. ◆ I read it before I signed.
■ Note that the *present tense* is used with **before** to refer to the future:
I will finish the book before I go to bed (*not* 'before I will go to bed').
before³ *prep.*
1 antes
She arrived before 11:30. ◆ He always drinks a glass of water before meals. ◆ My name comes before hers on the list.
2 (= in front of) □ **diante de**
They appeared before a large audience.
beforehand [be'fo:hand] *adv.* □ **de antemão**
I knew beforehand what to do.
beg [beg] *v.* (**begs, begging, begged**)
1 mendigar, pedir esmola
They beg (for money) in the subway.
2 implorar
He begged me to lend him some money.
I beg your pardon (Ver **pardon**).
began [bi'gan] *v.* (Ver **begin**).
beggar ['begə] *n.* □ **mendigo, pedinte**
begin [bi'gin] *v.* (**begins, beginning, began, begun**) □ **começar**
The lecture begins at 7 o'clock. ◆ It's beginning to rain. ◆ He began to cry. ◆ The first word begins with a capital letter.
■ Ver **start²**.
to begin with □ **para começar**
I won't buy it. To begin with, it's too expensive. Also, we don't need it.
beginner [bi'ginə] *n.* □ **iniciante**
a course of English for beginners.
beginning [bi'giniŋ] *n.* (= start¹) □ **começo, início**
Start at the beginning. ◆ at the beginning of the month / the book. ◆ In the beginning we didn't know what to do.
begun [bi'gʌn] *v.* (Ver **begin**).
behalf [bi'ha:f] *n.*
in behalf of *Amer.* (mesmo que **on behalf of** *Brit.*) □ **em nome de**
On behalf of all the workers here, I'd like to thank you. ◆ He is fighting on our behalf.
behave [bi'heiv] *v.* (**behaves, behaving, behaved**)
1 comportar-se
They behaved well / badly. ◆ How does she behave at school? ◆ You're behaving like a child.
2 (= behave yourself) □ **comportar-se**
The children behaved themselves at the party.
behavior [bi'heivjə] *n. Amer.*, **behaviour** *Brit.* □ **comportamento**
good behavior. ◆ Her behaviour towards us showed that she was angry.
behind¹ [bi'haind] *adv.* □ **para trás, atrás**
He did not look behind. ◆ The leader went in front and everybody walked behind.
behind with / in □ **atrasado**
They are behind with the payments. ◆ He is a month behind in the project.

behind² *prep.*
1 atrás de
I sit behind Victor in class. ♦ She hid behind a bush. ♦ Close the door behind you.
2 atrás de
We are years behind them in technology.
3 na retaguarda
They are behind us. (= They will support us.)
being¹ ['bi:iŋ] *v.* (Ver **be**).
He is being followed. (= Someone is following him.)
being² *n.* □ **ser**
a strange being from another planet. ♦ A human being is a man or a woman.
belief [bi'li:f] *n.* □ **crença**
belief in God. ♦ I lost my belief in them.
believe [bi'li:v] *v.* (**believes, believing, believed**)
1 acreditar
I believe her. ♦ I believe what she says.
2 acreditar, crer
Do you believe in God?
3 acreditar
He believes that you can do it.
I believe so / not □ **acredito que sim / não**
Is she coming today? – I believe not.
make believe (that) □ **fingir (que)**
They made believe (= pretended) that they were pilots.
bell [bel] *n.* □ **sino, campainha**
The church bells rang loudly. ♦ I rang the bell (= doorbell) but nobody answered the door. ♦ a bicycle bell
belly ['beli] *n.* (*pl.* **bellies**) □ **barriga**
belly-dance ['beli,da:nsə] *n.* □ **dança do ventre**
belong [bi'loŋ] *v.* (**belongs, belonged**) □ **pertencer a, ser o lugar de**
I belong here, with you. ♦ Put the book back where it belongs.
belong to □ **pertencer a**
It belongs to me. ♦ Who does this car belong to? ♦ These books belong to Dan.
■ **it belongs** (*not* "it's belong").
belongings [bi'loŋiŋz] *n.* □ **pertences**
personal belongings.
below¹ [bə'lou] *adv.*
1 abaixo
From the top of the hill we could see the valley below.
■ antônimo: **above**
2 abaixo
See line 5 below.
■ antônimo: **above**
below² *prep.*
1 abaixo de
The water is not deep here. It reaches below the knee. ♦ Sign above this line, not below it.
■ Compare with **under**:
under the table.
under the blanket.
2 abaixo de
The results of the exam were below average. ♦ The temperature is 6 degrees below zero. ♦ Young people below the age of 18 can't enter. ♦ The price should be below 50 dollars.
■ antônimo: **above**

■ With reference to age or price, **under** is also possible.
belt [belt] *n.* □ **cinto**
a leather belt. ♦ to put on a belt. ♦ He tightened his belt to stop his trousers from falling.
■ Ver **safety-belt; seat-belt**.
bench [bentʃ] *n.*
1 banco
They were sitting on a park bench.
2 bancada
a work bench.
bend¹ [bend] *n.* □ **curva**
a sharp bend in the road.
bend² *v.* (**bends, bending, bent**)
1 curvar-se, dobrar
She bent down and picked up her shoes. ♦ He bent his head. ♦ Try to bend your knees.
2 dobrar, entortar
Can you bend this piece of metal? ♦ The blade (of the knife) bent.
beneath [bi'ni:θ] *adv.*, *prep.*
1 (= below) □ **abaixo**
They looked down at the sea beneath.
2 (= under) □ **sob, embaixo de**
beneath his coat.
benefit¹ [benəfit] *n.*
1 benefício
I didn't get much benefit from the holiday. ♦ I did it for the benefit of the child.
2 (= advantage) □ **benefício**
What are the benefits of using a computer?
benefit² *v.* (**benefits, benefiting, benefited**), **benefitted** *Amer.* □ **beneficiar**
The new program will benefit both weak and good pupils.
benefit from □ **beneficiar-se de**
He benefited from my advice.
bent [bent] *v.* (Ver **bend²**).
beret ['berei] *n.* □ **boina**
berry ['beri] *n.* (*pl.* **berries**) □ **baga**
to pick berries.
■ Ver **blackberry; raspberry; strawberry**.
beside [bi'said] *prep.* (= by, next to) □ **ao lado de**
He sat beside me.
besides¹ [bi'saidz] *adv.* □ **além disso**
I'm too busy to go out. Besides, I have a cold.
besides² *prep.* (= in addition to) □ **além de**
Who else is coming besides Stella? ♦ Besides history, I like English and geography.
best¹ [best] *adj.* (**good, better, best**) □ **melhor**
This is the best film (that) I've ever seen. ♦ He is the best football player in the world.
best² *adv.*
1 melhor
She cooks well, I cook better, but he cooks best. ♦ Ruth did best in the exam.
2 mais
Of all my friends, I like Michael best.
best³ *n.* □ **o melhor**
We're all good at chess, but Ron is the best.
All (the) best! □ **Tudo de bom!**
do / try your best □ **fazer o seu melhor, fazer o melhor possível**

I'll do my best to help you. ♦ I tried my best to prevent it.
best man ['best 'man] *n*. ☐ **padrinho de casamento**
bestseller [,best'selə] *n*. ☐ **best-seller**
Her new book is a bestseller.
best-selling *adj*. ☐ **campeão de vendas, sucesso de vendas**
a best-selling novel.
bet[1] [bet] *v*. (**bets, betting, bet** or **betted**)
1 apostar
She bet me 10 dollars that she could fix it.
2 apostar, jogar
He bets on horses.
■ Ver **gamble**[2].
bet[2] *n*. ☐ **aposta**
He made a bet with me and I lost.
betray [bi'trei] *v*. (**betrays, betraying, betrayed**) ☐ **trair**
He is a traitor. He betrayed his country and his friends.
betrayal [bi'treiəl] *n*. ☐ **traição**
better[1] ['betə] *adj*. (**good, better, best**)
1 melhor
This computer is better than that one.
2 melhor
The patient is better today. ♦ I feel better now.
better[2] *adv*. (**well, better, best**)
1 melhor
I read English well, but she reads better. ♦ I speak English better than she does.
2 melhor
This dress suits you better.
better off ☐ **em melhor situação**
They used to be poor, but they are better off now. ♦ She is better off with her new boyfriend.
get better
1 (= improve) ☐ **ficar melhor, melhorar**
The situation got better. ♦ The weather is getting better.
2 (= recover) ☐ **melhorar**
The patient is still weak, but he'll soon get better.
had better (= 'd better) ☐ **é melhor (do que)**
You'd better hurry or you'll miss the train. ♦ She'd better tell her teacher about it.
between [bi'twi:n] *prep*.
1 entre
He sat between Dan and me. ♦ between the city and the sea
2 entre
You can come between 3 and 8.30.
3 entre
It costs between 20 and 25 dollars.
4 entre
He travels regularly between Paris and London.
5 entre
She divided the chocolate between the children.
■ In general, **between** is used for two people or things, but it can be used for more than two.
■ Ver **among**.
6 entre
There's no difference between these computers. ♦ There is a connection between the two events.
between you and me ☐ **cá entre nós**
Between you and me, the party was boring.
in between ☐ **entre uma coisa e outra**
I eat breakfast and supper, with a sandwich in between.
beware [bi'weə] *v*.

beware of ☐ **cuidado com**
Beware of the dog!
■ Used especially in the imperative on public notices.
bewildered [bi'wildəd] *adj*. ☐ **encantado**
The child was bewildered by what he saw at the circus.
bewitch [bi'witʃ] *v*. (**bewitches, bewitching, bewitched**) ☐ **enfeitiçar**
The wicked fairy bewitched the prince and turned him into a frog.
beyond [bi'jond] *prep*., *adv*. ☐ **além de, mais adiante**
The town is beyond those hills. ♦ The road continues beyond the village. ♦ We could see the river and the hills beyond.
bias ['baiəs] *n*. ☐ **parcialidade**
biased ['baiəst] *adj*. ☐ **tendencioso**
a biased opinion.
Bible ['baibl] *n*., **the Bible** ☐ **Bíblia, a Bíblia**
bicycle ['baisikl] *n*. ☐ **bicicleta**
He goes to school by bicycle. ♦ She is learning to ride a bicycle.
■ Ver **bike**.
big [big] *adj*. (**bigger, biggest**)
1 grande
a big house / umbrella. ♦ This is the biggest hotel in town. ♦ These trousers are too big for me. ♦ a big salary. ♦ a big family.
■ **large** is also possible.
■ antônimo: **small**
2 grande
a big success / problem.
■ Ver **great**.
3 (= elder) ☐ **mais velho**
my big sister.
■ antônimo: **little**
bigot ['bigət] *n*. ☐ **fanático, intolerante**
bigotry ['bigətri] *n*. ☐ **fanatismo, intolerância**
bike [baik] *n*.
1 (= bicycle) ☐ **bicicleta**
I ride my bike to school.
2 (= motorcycle) ☐ **moto**
She rides her bike to work.
bill [bil] *n*.
1 conta
a telephone bill. ♦ an electricity / electric bill.
2 *Brit*. ☐ **conta**
I asked the waiter for the bill.
■ *Amer*. **check**
3 *Amer*. ☐ **nota**
a ten-dollar bill.
■ *Brit*. **note**
billboard [bilbɔ:'d] *n*. ☐ **outdoor**
billboards by the roadside with their advertisements and notices.
billion ['biljən] *adj*., *n*. ☐ **bilhão**
six billion dollars. ♦ billions of dollars / people.
bin [bin] *n*.
1 lata de lixo
I peeled a banana and threw the skin into the bin.
■ Ver **litter bin; dustbin**.
2 lata, cesto
a bread-bin. ♦ a clothes bin (for dirty clothes).
bind [baind] *v*. (**binds, binding, bound**)

1 (= tie) □ **amarrar, prender**
They bound the burglar's hands behind his back.
2 cobrir com atadura
The nurse bound (up) my wound.
binoculars [bi'nokjuləz] *n. pl.* □ **binóculo**
biography [bai'ogrəfi] *n.* □ **biografia**
the biography of President Kennedy
biological [baiə'lodʒikəl] *adj.* □ **biológico**
biologist [bai'olədʒist] *n.* □ **biólogo**
biology [bai'olədʒi] *n.* □ **biologia**
bird [bə:d] *n.* □ **ave, pássaro**
All birds lay eggs. ✦ Birds usually build nests.
bird of prey *n.* □ **ave de rapina**
Eagles and hawks are birds of prey.
birth [bə:θ] *n.* □ **nascimento**
What's your date and place of birth? ✦ The baby weighed 3 kg at birth (= when it was born).
give birth to □ **dar à luz, parir**
She gave birth to twins.
birthday ['bə:θdei] *n.* □ **aniversário**
a birthday party / present. ✦ My birthday is next Tuesday on June 5.
birthplace ['bə:θpleis] *n.* □ **local de nascimento**
Where were you born – what is your birthplace?
biscuit ['biskit] *n. Brit.* □ **biscoito**
a packet of chocolate biscuits.
■ *Amer.* **cookie**
bishop ['biʃəp] *n.* □ **bispo**
A bishop is a priest of high rank in the Christian church.
bit [bit] *n.* □ **pedaço**
a bit of chocolate. ✦ bits of broken glass.
a bit (= a little)
1 um pouco
Wait a bit longer.
2 um pouco
I'm a bit worried. ✦ a bit more milk.
bit by bit □ **pouco a pouco**
Bit by bit he learnt how to do it.
come / fall to bits *n.* □ **ficar em pedaços, desmanchar**
The cake came / fell to bits in my hands.
bitch [bitʃ] *n.* □ **cadela**
My dog is a bitch.
bite¹ [bait] *n.*
1 mordida
I took a bite of the apple.
2 picada, mordida
a snake bite. ✦ a mosquito bite.
bite² *v.* (**bites, biting, bit, bitten**)
1 morder, roer
The dog bit me (in the leg). ✦ Stop biting your nails!
2 picar, morder
I was bitten by mosquitoes.
■ Ver **sting²**.
bitter ['bitə] *adj.*
1 amargo
a bitter taste. ✦ These almonds taste bitter.
2 amargo
a bitter disappointment. ✦ the bitter truth.
3 cortante
a bitter wind.
feel bitter (about) □ **decepcionar-se (com)**
They felt bitter about their examination marks.

bitterly ['bitəli] *adv.* □ **amargamente**
He was bitterly disappointed.
bitterness ['bitənis] *n.* □ **amargor, amargura**
black¹ [blak] *adj.* □ **preto**
black shoes. ✦ black coffee.
black² *n.*
1 preto
She was dressed in black. ✦ The door was painted black.
2 negro
The Blacks now have equal rights with The Whites in South Africa.
blackberry ['blakbəri] *n.* (*pl.* **blackberries**) □ **amora silvestre**
blackbird ['blakbə:d] *n.* □ **melro**
blackboard ['blakbɔ:d] *n.* □ **quadro-negro, lousa**
I need a piece of chalk to write on the blackboard.
blackcurrant ['blak'kʌrənt] *n.* □ **cassis, groselha preta**
blackmail¹ ['blakmeil] *n.* □ **chantagem**
They used blackmail to get money from him.
blackmail² *v.* (**blackmails, blackmailing, blackmailed**) □ **chantagear**
He tried to blackmail me.
blacksmith ['blaksmiθ] *n.* □ **ferreiro**
blade [bleid] *n.* □ **lâmina**
a sharp blade. ✦ the blade of the knife / the sword.
■ Ver **razor-blade**.
blame¹ [bleim] *n.* □ **culpa**
get the blame (for) □ **levar a culpa (por)**
He got the blame for the accident.
put / lay the blame on □ **pôr a culpa em**
She put / laid all the blame on me.
take the blame (for) □ **levar a culpa (por)**
You made the mistakes, but I took the blame for you.
blame² *v.* (**blames, blaming, blamed**) □ **culpar**
He blamed her for the failure of the plan. ✦ Don't blame me if we get there late.
blank¹ [blaŋk] *adj.*
1 em branco
a blank page. ✦ a blank cassette.
2 sem expressão
a blank look on his face.
blank² *n.* □ **espaço em branco**
Fill in the blanks in this form. ✦ Fill in the blanks with suitable words.
blanket ['blaŋkit] *n.* □ **cobertor**
If you feel cold, take another blanket.
blast¹ [bla:st] *n.*
1 rajada
a blast of hot air.
2 (= explosion) □ **explosão**
Six people were injured in the blast.
3 sopro
to blow a blast on a whistle / trumpet.
blast² *v.* (**blasts, blasting, blasted**) □ **explodir**
They blasted through the mountain to build a road.
blaze¹ [bleiz] *n.* □ **incêndio**
The blaze destroyed the whole building.
blaze² *v.* (**blazes, blazing, blazed**) □ **arder**
The fire blazed for hours. ✦ The sun blazed down.
blazer ['bleizə] *n.* □ **blazer**
bleak [bli:k] *adj.* □ **gelado, frio**
a bleak winter day.

bleed [bli:d] *v.* (**bleeds, bleeding, bled**) ▫ **sangrar**
Your nose is bleeding. ◆ He began to bleed.
blend¹ [blend] *v.* (**blends, blending, blend**)
1 (= mix) ▫ **misturar, misturar-se**
Blend the butter and flour (together). ◆ Oil and water do not blend.
2 combinar, ornar
The curtains blend well with the furniture.
blend² *n.* ▫ **mistura**
a blend of coffee / tobacco.
blender ['blendə] *n.* ▫ **liquidificador**
bless [bles] *v.* (**blesses, blessing, blessed**) ▫ **abençoar**
The old man blessed them.
be blessed with ▫ **ser abençoado com**
He is blessed with a wonderful voice.
Bless you! ▫ **Saúde!**
You say 'Bless you!' to someone when he / she sneezes.
blessing ['blesiŋ] *n.* ▫ **bênção**
He gave his blessing to their marriage.
blew [blu:] *v.* (Ver **blow²**).
blind¹ [blaind] *adj.* ▫ **cego**
She is blind. ◆ a blind man with a guide dog.
the blind ▫ **os cegos**
Louis Braille invented a special alphabet for the blind.
go blind ▫ **ficar cego**
The old dog is going blind.
blind² *v.* (**blinds, blinding, blinded**) ▫ **ficar cego, cegar**
He was blinded when he was 5. ◆ The car's lights blinded us.
blind³ *n.* (mesmo que **blinds**) ▫ **persiana, veneziana**
to pull down the blinds. ◆ to raise the blinds.
blindfold¹ ['blaindfould] *v.* (**blindfolds, blindfolding, blindfolded**) ▫ **vendar**
The guards blindfolded the prisoners.
blindfold² *n.* ▫ **venda**
blinding ['blaindiŋ] *adj.* ▫ **ofuscante**
a blinding light.
blindness ['blaindnis] *n.* ▫ **cegueira**
blink *v.* (**blinks, blinking, blinked**) ▫ **piscar**
He blinked in the bright light.
blister ['blistə] *n.* ▫ **bolha**
After the long walk, my feet were covered with blisters.
blizzard ['blizəd] *n.* ▫ **nevasca**
I'm afraid to go out in this blizzard.
block¹ [blɒk] *n.*
1 bloco
a concrete block.
2 bloco
wooden blocks for playing.
3 bloco
an office block. ◆ an apartment block.
4 quadra, quarteirão
The post office is two blocks away.
5 bloqueio
a road block.
block² *v.* (**blocks, blocking, blocked**) ▫ **bloquear**
The police blocked all the roads to the airport.
blockade¹ [blɒ'keid] *n.* ▫ **bloqueio**
a blockade of the town.
blockade² [blɒ'keid] *v.* (**blockades, blockading, blockaded**) ▫ **bloquear**
Ships blockaded the port.

blockage ['blɒkidʒ] *n.* ▫ **obstrução**
a blockage in the pipe.
blocked [blɒkt] *adj.* ▫ **bloqueado**
blockbuster ['blɒkbʌstə(r)] *n.* ▫ **sucesso de vendas**
The movie wasn't just successful – it was a blockbuster!
blond [blɒnd] *adj., n.* ▫ **loiro**
blond hair
blonde [blɒnd] *adj., n.* ▫ **loira**
a tall blonde (woman).
blood [blʌd] *n.* ▫ **sangue**
His hands were covered with blood. ◆ She lost a lot of blood.
blood pressure ['blʌd 'preʃə] *n.* ▫ **pressão sanguínea**
She suffers from high blood pressure.
blood test ['blʌd 'test] *n.* ▫ **exame de sangue**
to have a blood test.
bloody¹ ['blʌdi] *adj.* (**bloodier, bloodiest**)
1 ensanguentado, sangrento
a bloody nose.
2 sangrento
a bloody battle.
bloody² *adj., adv. Brit.* (= very) ▫ **muito**
He's a bloody fool. ◆ That was bloody good!
bloom [blu:m] *v.* (**blooms, blooming, bloomed**) ▫ **florescer**
The roses are blooming.
blossom¹ ['blɒsəm] *n.* ▫ **floração**
The orange trees are in blossom.
blossom² *v.* (**blossoms, blossoming, blossomed**) ▫ **florir**
The apple trees blossomed early in the season.
blouse [blauz] *n.* ▫ **blusa**
She was wearing a yellow blouse.
blow¹ [blou] *n.*
1 soco, golpe
He struck me a blow on the chin. ◆ She received a hard blow on the head.
2 baque, golpe
His father's death was a great blow to him.
blow² *v.* (**blows, blowing, blew, blown**)
1 soprar
The wind is blowing hard.
2 varrer
The wind blew the papers from her desk.
3 ser levado
The dry leaves were blowing in the wind.
4 soprar
to blow on hot food to cool it. ◆ to blow the dust off the book.
5 soprar
The referee blew the whistle for half-time.
6 assoar
She gave the child a handkerchief to blow his nose.
blow out ▫ **apagar com o sopro**
I blew out the candle.
blow over ▫ **passar**
The storm will soon blow over.
blow up
1 (= explode) **explodir**
Enemy soldiers blew up the bridge. ◆ The plane blew up.
2 estourar
to blow up balloons / tyres.
blue¹ [blu:] *adj.* ▫ **azul**

a blue shirt. ◆ The sky is blue.
blue² *n.* □ **azul**
She was dressed in blue. ◆ The walls were painted blue.
bluff¹ [blʌf] *n.* □ **blefe**
bluff² *v.* (**bluffs, bluffing, bluffed**) □ **blefar**
He is only bluffing. He is not going to do it.
blunt [blʌnt] *adj.*
1 cego, sem ponta
a blunt knife. ◆ The pencil is blunt.
■ antônimo: **sharp**
2 brusco
He was blunt with me and said that my work was terrible.
bluntly ['blʌntli] *adv.* (= frankly) □ **com franqueza**
I'll have to speak bluntly to him.
blurred [blə:rd] *adj.* □ **embaçado**
a blurred photograph. ◆ My vision is blurred without my glasses.
blush [blʌʃ] *v.* (**blushes, blushing, blushed**) □ **corar, enrubescer**
She blushes when I look at her.
boar [bɔ:] *n.* □ **javali**
board¹ [bɔ:d] *n.*
1 tábua
a floor board. ◆ an ironing board.
2 quadro
a notice / bulletin board.
■ Ver **blackboard**.
3 conselho
the board of directors (of a company).
4 refeições
room and board. ◆ full board (= all meals). ◆ half board (= breakfast and one other meal).
on board □ **a bordo**
There are 400 passengers on board (the plane). ◆ We went on board at 8 o'clock.
■ Ver **aboard**.
board² *v.* (**boards, boarding, boarded**) □ **embarcar**
to board the train / ship / plane.
boarder [bɔ:'də] *n.*
1 interno
These boys are boarders at the boarding school.
2 (= lodger) **hóspede**
How many boarders are there at this boarding house?
boarding card ['bɔ:diŋ 'ka:d] *n.* □ **cartão de embarque**
boarding house ['bɔ:diŋ 'haus] *n.* □ **pensão, pousada**
boardingschool ['bɔ:diŋ'sku:l] *n.* □ **internato**
boast¹ [boust] *v.* (**boasts, boasting, boasted**) □ **gabar-se**
He boasted about his high salary. ◆ She boasts that she is the best pupil in class.
boast² *n.* □ **fanfarronice**
boat [bout] *n.* □ **barco**
a motor boat. ◆ a fishing boat. ◆ We are going to America by boat.
body ['bodi] *n.* (*pl.* **bodies**) □ **corpo**
They covered themselves with blankets to keep their bodies warm. ◆ the human body.
bodyguard ['bodiga:d] *n.* □ **guarda-costas**
The President's bodyguards protected him from the attackers.
bogus ['bougəs] *adj.* □ **falso, fictício**
a bogus policeman.
boil [boil] *v.* (**boils, boiling, boiled**)

1 ferver
Water boils at 100° C. ◆ The kettle is boiling.
2 cozinhar
Boil the rice for 20 minutes.
boil over □ **ferver e transbordar**
Careful, the milk is boiling over!
boiled [boild] *adj.* □ **fervido**
boiled water.
boiler ['boilə] *n.* □ **caldeira**
boiling ['boiliŋ] *adj.* □ **fervente, muito quente**
boiling water. ◆ The weather is boiling hot today.
bold [bould] *adj.* □ **ousado**
a bold leader / plan.
boldly ['bouldli] *adv.* □ **ousadamente**
boldness ['bouldnis] *n.* □ **ousadia**
bolt¹ [boult] *n.*
1 trinco
Do you have a bolt on the door?
2 ferrolho
Four bolts hold the door in place. ◆ to tighten a bolt.
bolt² *v.* (**bolts, bolting, bolted**)
1 aferrolhar
I bolted the door.
2 disparar
The horse bolted when it heard the shot.
bomb¹ [bom] *n.* □ **bomba**
The bomb did not go off (= explode). ◆ a time bomb.
bomb² *v.* (**bombs, bombing, bombed**) □ **bombardear**
Two aircraft bombed the bridge.
bomber ['bomə] *n.*
1 bombardeiro
The bombers flew low and dropped their bombs on the city.
2 pessoa que coloca bombas
The bomber placed a bomb at the side of the road.
bone [boun] *n.* □ **osso**
She broke a bone in her hand. ◆ a fish with a lot of bones.
bonfire ['bonfaiə] *n.* □ **fogueira**
to build / make a bonfire. ◆ to sit around a bonfire.
■ Ver **campfire**.
bonnet ['bonit] *n.*
1 *Brit.* **capô**
■ *Amer.* **hood**
2 touca
In the past, women and girls wore bonnets.
bonus ['bounəs] *n.* □ **bônus**
She got a bonus for being such a good worker.
book¹ [buk] *n.*
1 livro
I like to read books about animals. ◆ cook books. ◆ to borrow a book from the library.
2 talão, caderno
a cheque / check book. ◆ Write your homework in your exercise book.
■ Ver **notebook**.
3 (= telephone directory) □ **lista telefônica, catálogo telefônico**
Look up the number in the book.
book² *v.* (**books, booking, booked**) □ **reservar**
They booked a room in a good hotel. ◆ We booked seats on the flight to Paris. ◆ to book a table at a restaurant.
■ Ver **(make a) reservation; reserve**.
be booked up; be fully booked □ **lotado**

We couldn't get a ticket / room. They were fully booked.
bookcase ['bukkeis] *n*. □ **estante**
booking ['bukiŋ] *n*. □ **reserva**
booking office ['bukiŋ ˌofis] *n*. □ **bilheteria**
book-keeping ['buk,ki:piŋ] *n*. □ **contabilidade**
booklet ['buklit] *n*. □ **livreto**
bookshelf ['bukʃelf] *n*. □ **estante**
bookshop ['bukʃop] *n*. *Brit*. □ **livraria**
The book is available in the bookshops.
bookstore ['buksto:] *n*. *Amer*. (= bookshop) □ **livraria**
boot [bu:t] *n*.
1 bota
rubber boots. ♦ to put on / take off your boots.
2 *Brit*. **porta-malas**
■ *Amer*. **trunk**
booth [bu:θ] *n*.
1 cabine
a telephone booth.
2 barraca, estande
a booth at a fair / an exhibition.
border ['bo:rdə] *n*.
1 fronteira
to cross the border. ♦ the Syrian border.
2 (= edge) **borda**
the border of a tablecloth. ♦ the border of a lake.
bore¹ [bo:] *v*. (Ver **bear**²).
bore² *v*. (**bores, boring, bored**)
1 entediar, aborrecer
The lecture bored me. ♦ Am I boring you? ♦ She bores us with her stories.
2 abrir buraco, perfurar
to bore a hole.
bored [bo:d] *adj*. □ **entediado**
He is bored. ♦ I was bored with the film and left in the middle.
get bored (with) □ **entediar-se (com)**
I'm getting bored with this game.
boredom ['bo:dəm] *n*. □ **tédio**
The boredom was unbearable. ♦ They did it out of boredom.
boring ['bo:riŋ] *adj*. □ **entediante, chato**
a boring film / book / job.
■ Ver **dull**.
born [bo:n] *adj*. □ **nato, nascido**
be born □ **nascer**
I was born in 1986. ♦ Where and when were you born?
borne [bo:n] *v*. (Ver **bear**²).
borrow ['borou] *v*. (**borrows, borrowing, borrowed**) □ **tomar emprestado**
He borrowed 100 dollars from me. ♦ to borrow a book from the library.
■ Ver **lend; loan**².
can I borrow...? □ **posso tomar emprestado...?**
Can I borrow your car for the weekend?
borrower ['borouə] *n*. □ **aquele que toma emprestado**
boss¹ [bos] *n*. □ **chefe, patrão**
The boss gave me a day off because I was ill.
boss² *v*. (**bosses, bossing, bossed**)
boss around / about □ **mandar em**
Stop bossing me around – I'm not your slave!
bossy ['bosi] *adj*. □ **mandão**
botanic(al) [bo'tanik(əl)] *adj*. □ **botânico**
the Botanical Gardens.

botany ['botəni] *n*. □ **botânica**
both [bouθ] *adj*., *pron*. □ **ambos, os dois**
Both players are good. ♦ I held it in both hands. ♦ on both sides of the road. ♦ They both saw it. ♦ Both of them saw it.
both... and □ **tanto... quanto, e... e**
I want both the book and the cassette. ♦ She is both clever and beautiful.
bother¹ ['boðə] *v*. (**bothers, bothering, bothered**)
1 incomodar
What's bothering you? ♦ Stop bothering me with your questions. ♦ Sorry to bother you, but... ♦ It doesn't bother me.
■ Ver **trouble**².
2 dar-se ao trabalho de
He didn't even bother to apologize. ♦ Please don't bother – I'll take a taxi.
bother² *n*. □ **incômodo**
I don't want to be a bother, but can you help me with this? ♦ Certainly, it's no bother at all.
bothered ['boðəd] *adj*. □ **incomodado**
I'm not bothered. I'm sure everything will be OK.
bottle ['botl] *n*. □ **garrafa**
I drank a bottle of water.
bottle opener ['botl 'oupənə] *n*. □ **abridor de garrafa**
bottom¹ ['botəm] *n*.
1 pé
at the bottom of the page. ♦ at the bottom of the stairs.
■ antônimo: **top**
2 fundo
the bottom of the sea.
3 nível mais baixo
He is at the bottom of the class in English.
■ antônimo: **top**
4 bunda
He fell on his bottom.
from the bottom of your heart □ **do fundo do seu coração**
He thanked her from the bottom of his heart.
get to the bottom of □ **chegar ao fundo de**
I intend to get to the bottom of this.
bottom² *adj*. □ **mais baixo**
the bottom shelf / drawer
■ antônimo: **top**
bought [bo:t] *v*. (Ver **buy**).
boulder ['bouldə] *n*. □ **pedra grande e redonda**
A large boulder fell from the mountain and blocked the road.
bounce [bauns] *v*. (**bounces, bouncing, bounced**)
1 quicar
He bounced on the bed. ♦ The ball bounced down the stairs.
2 fazer quicar
She bounced the ball several times and then shot at the basket.
bound¹ [baund] *v*. (Ver **bind**).
bound² *adj*.
be bound for □ **destinar-se a, ir para**
The ship is bound for Greece.
be bound to □ **estar fadado a**
Sooner or later, it was bound to happen. ♦ They win every game, so they are bound to take the championship.
bound³ *n*. □ **limite**
out of bounds □ **fora dos limites**
The military camp is out of bounds to civilians.

boundary ['baundəri] *n.* (*pl.* **boundaries**) □ **fronteira, divisa**
This river forms a boundary between the two countries.
♦ They put up a fence as a boundary between their lands.
■ Ver **border**.

bouquet [bu'kei] *n.* □ **buquê**
He gave her a bouquet of roses. ♦ a bride's bouquet.

bow[1] [bou] *n.*
1 arco
A bow is a weapon for shooting arrows.
2 arco
Can you play the violin without a bow?
3 laço
to tie a ribbon / shoelace in a bow.

bow[2] [bau] *n.* □ **reverência**
to make a deep bow

bow[3] [bau] *v.* (**bows, bowing, bowed**)
1 curvar-se
The actors bowed to the audience.
2 curvar
He bowed his head in shame.

bowel ['bauəl] *n., adj.* □ **intestino, intestinal**
to empty your bowels. ♦ a bowel movement.

bowl [boul] *n.* □ **tigela**
a salad bowl. ♦ a bowl of cereal with milk. ♦ a sugar bowl.
♦ a bowl of soup.
■ Ver **dish, plate**.

bowling ['bouliŋ] *n.* □ **boliche**
Bowling is my hobby.

box [boks] *n.*
1 caixa, estojo
a box of matches. ♦ a box of chocolates. ♦ a cardboard box, such as a shoebox. ♦ a jewel-box.
■ Ver **carton; case; packet**.
2 espaço
Fill in the boxes in the form.
3 cabine
a telephone box.
■ Ver **PO Box**.

boxer ['boksə] *n.* □ **boxeador, pugilista**

boxing ['boksiŋ] *n.* □ **boxe, pugilismo**
a boxing match. ♦ boxing gloves.

box office ['boks ˌofis] *n.* □ **bilheteria**
You buy tickets for a film or show at the box office.

boy [boi] *n.* □ **menino, garoto**
a good boy. ♦ There are 15 boys and 16 girls in our class.

boycott[1] ['boikot] *n.* □ **boicote**
an economic boycott.

boycott[2] *v.* (**boycotts, boycotting, boycotted**) □ **boicotar**
The students boycotted his lectures.

boyfriend ['boifrend] *n.* □ **namorado**
Her boyfriend is 18 years old.

boyhood ['boihud] *n.* □ **infância, meninice**

Boy Scout ['boi'skaut] *n.* □ **escoteiro**

bra [bra:] *n.* □ **sutiã**

bracelet ['breislit] *n.* □ **bracelete, pulseira**
a gold bracelet.

brackets ['brakits] *n. pl.*
round brackets (mesmo que **parentheses**) □ **parênteses**
square brackets □ **colchetes**

braid [breid] *n. Amer.* □ **trança**
She wears her hair in braids.
■ *Brit.* **plait**

brain [brein] *n.*
1 cérebro
The human brain weighs about 1.4 kg.
2 (= **brains**) **cabeça, cérebro**
He has a good brain. ♦ Use your brains!

brainwash ['breinwoʃ] *v.* (**brainwashes, brainwashing, brainwashed**) □ **fazer lavagem cerebral**
brainwashing by TV commercials

brake[1] [breik] *n.* □ **freio, breque**
She stepped on the brakes to stop the car.

brake[2] *v.* (**brakes, braking, braked**) □ **frear**
The driver braked suddenly in order not to hit the child.

branch[1] [bra:ntʃ] *n.*
1 galho
The child was hiding among the branches.
2 filial
a bank with branches all over the country ♦ The company has a branch in America.

branch[2] *v.* (**branches, branching, branched**) □ **bifurcar-se**
The road branches here.

brand [brand] *n.* □ **marca**
I don't like this brand of coffee.

brand-new [ˌbrand'nju:] *adj.* □ **novo em folha**
a brand-new car

brass [bra:s] *n.* □ **latão**
a jacket with brass buttons

brave [breiv] *adj.* (= **courageous**) □ **bravo, corajoso**
a brave woman. ♦ It was brave of him to save the drowning child.

bravely ['breivli] *adv.* □ **bravamente, corajosamente**
They fought bravely.

bravery ['breivəri] *n.* (= **courage**) □ **bravura, coragem**
They got a medal for bravery in battle. ♦ an act of bravery.

bread [bred] *n.* □ **pão**
brown bread. ♦ I bought two loaves of bread. ♦ I ate a slice of bread and some cheese.

breadth [bredθ] *n.* (= **width**) □ **largura**
the length and breadth of a swimming pool.
■ The adjective is **broad**.

break[1] [breik] *n.*
1 intervalo, pausa
to take a break. ♦ a coffee / lunch break. ♦ They worked for hours without a break. ♦ There is a break of 5 minutes between lessons.
■ Ver **recess**.
2 abertura
a break in the fence.

break[2] *v.* (**breaks, breaking, broke, broken**)
1 quebrar
Who broke the vase? ♦ Did you break the window? ♦ She fell and broke her leg.
2 quebrar
The cup broke into pieces. ♦ Glass breaks easily.
3 quebrar
My watch is broken (= not working).
■ Ver **break down; broken**.
4 romper
Be careful not to break the rope / chain.
■ Compare with **tear**:
Use **tear** for paper, cloth, etc.
5 arrebentar

The string broke.
6 infringir, quebrar
Criminals break the law. ♦ to break a promise.
break down
1 quebrar, parar de funcionar
The car broke down.
2 desatar a chorar
He broke down when he heard about the accident.
3 derrubar
The firemen broke down the door.
break in □ **arrombar**
The thieves broke in through the window.
break into
1 arrombar
Burglars broke into the bank yesterday.
2 desatar a
They broke into song. ♦ to break into tears / laughter.
break off □ **romper**
The two countries broke off relations.
break out
1 começar
When did World War II break out? ♦ No one knows how the fire broke out.
2 (= escape) **escapar, fugir**
The prisoner broke out of prison with someone's help.
break up
1 dispersar
The crowd began to break up. ♦ The police used tear gas to break up the demonstration.
2 separar
A policeman broke up the fight.
break up with (= split up with) □ **romper, terminar**
She broke up with her boyfriend.
breakdown ['breikdaun] *n*.
1 pane, falha
We had a breakdown (= Our car broke down) on the motorway.
2 colapso, esgotamento
She had a nervous breakdown.
breakfast [brekfəst] *n*. □ **café da manhã, desjejum**
I had breakfast at 8 o'clock. ♦ What would you like for breakfast?
breakthrough ['breikθru:] *n*. □ **grande avanço, progresso**
a breakthrough in the treatment of the disease
breast [brest] *n*.
1 peito, seio
A mother can give milk to her baby from her breasts.
2 peito
He held his child to his breast.
■ Ver **chest**.
breast-stroke ['breststrouk] *n*. □ **nado de peito**
breath [breθ] *n*. □ **respiração, fôlego**
Take a deep breath. ♦ He ran so fast that he was out of breath.
■ Ver **breathing**.
hold your breath □ **prender a respiração**
Hold your breath for 5 seconds and then breathe out. ♦ He held his breath when the teacher started to read out his grades.
breathe [bri:ð] *v*. (**breathes, breathing, breathed**) □ **respirar**

It's so hot here that I can't breathe. ♦ He was still breathing when they took him to hospital.
breathe in / out □ **inspirar / expirar**
The doctor told me to breathe in deeply and breathe out slowly.
breathing ['bri:ðiŋ] *n*. □ **respiração**
Deep breathing is good for you.
breathless ['breðlis] *adj*. □ **sem fôlego**
By the time I got to the 4th floor I was completely breathless.
breed[1] [bri:d] *v*. (**breeds, breeding, bred**)
1 criar
to breed cattle
2 reproduzir-se, procriar
Rabbits breed fast.
breed[2] *n*. □ **raça**
What breed is this dog?
breeding ['bri:diŋ] *n*. □ **acasalamento, reprodução**
the breeding season (for animals)
breeze [bri:z] *n*. □ **brisa**
bribe[1] [braib] *n*. □ **suborno**
He offered the guard a bribe to help him escape.
bribe[2] *v*. (**bribes, bribing, bribed**) □ **subornar**
to bribe a judge / policeman.
brick [brik] *n*. □ **tijolo**
a brick wall.
bride [braid] *n*. □ **noiva**
a bride on her wedding day.
bridegroom ['braidgrum] *n*. (= **groom**) □ **noivo**
They drank a toast to the bride and bridegroom.
bridesmaid ['braidsmeid] *n*. □ **padrinho**
■ Ver **best man**.
bridge[1] [bridʒ] *n*. □ **ponte**
to cross the bridge. ♦ to build a bridge over a river.
bridge[2] *v*. (**bridges, bridging, bridged**) □ **transpor**
He tried to bridge the gap between them.
brief[1] [bri:f] *adj*. (= short) □ **breve, rápido**
a brief reply / report. ♦ Her comments were brief and to the point. ♦ a brief visit.
in brief □ **em resumo**
These are the facts in brief.
brief[2] *v*. (**briefs, briefing, briefed**) □ **informar**
My job is to brief the new students about school rules.
briefcase ['bri:fkeis] *n*. □ **pasta**
briefly ['bri:fli] *adv*. □ **resumidamente**
I told her briefly what we were planning to do.
brigade [bri'geid] *n*. □ **brigada**
a brigade of soldiers. ♦ the Fire Brigade (= fire department, *Amer.*).
bright [brait] *adj*.
1 claro
a bright day.
2 brilhante
a bright light.
3 claro
the bright blue sky.
4 (= clever) **brilhante**
a bright child. ♦ the brightest pupil in class. ♦ a bright idea.
brighten ['braitn] *v*. (**brightens, brightening, brightened**)
1 clarear
The sky is brightening.

brightness / bubble

2 **alegrar-se**
His face brightened when he saw his presents.
3 **dar vida, animar**
These flowers will brighten up the place.
brightness ['braitnis] *n.* □ **brilho, claridade**
the brightness of the sun
brilliance ['briljəns] *n.* □ **brilho**
the brilliance of the light.
brilliant ['briliənt] *adj.*
1 **brilhante**
a brilliant light. ◆ brilliant sunshine.
2 **brilhante**
a brilliant idea. ◆ a brilliant career. ◆ a brilliant scientist.
brilliantly ['briliəntli] *adv.* □ **brilhantemente**
She planned everything brilliantly.
brim [brim] *n.* □ **borda**
to fill a glass to the brim.
bring [briŋ] *v.* (**brings, bringing, brought**)
1 **trazer**
She brought a friend with her. ◆ I asked him to bring me a glass.
2 **trazer**
Take this ring. It will bring you luck.
bring about □ **trazer**
The floods brought about destruction.
bring back
1 **devolver**
I'll bring it back tomorrow. ◆ Don't forget to bring back the book.
2 **trazer de volta**
It brought back memories of my childhood.
bring someone up □ **educar, criar**
to bring up children. ◆ My parents brought me up to respect other people.
■ *Amer.* also **raise**
bring something up
1 (= raise) **trazer à baila**
He brought up the subject of money. ◆ You should bring up the problem at the meeting.
2 (= vomit) **vomitar**
brisk [brisk] *adj.* □ **revigorante**
I go for a brisk walk every day.
bristle ['brisl] *n.* □ **cerda, pelo**
a brush with stiff bristles. ◆ the bristles on his face.
British ['britiʃ] *adj.* □ **britânico**
a British passport. ◆ the British Isles.
Britisher ['britiʃə] *n.* (mesmo que **Briton**) □ **bretão, britânico**
People who come from Great Britain call themselves 'Britishers'.
brittle ['britl] *adj.* □ **frágil**
Thin glass is brittle.
broad [bro:] *adj.* □ **largo, de largura**
a broad road. ◆ The river is ten metres broad.
■ antônimo: **narrow**
■ The usual word is **wide**.
■ The noun is **breadth**.
broadcast[1] ['bro:dka:t] *n.* □ **transmissão**
a TV broadcast.
broadcast[2] *v.* (**broadcasts, broadcasting, broadcast**)
□ **transmitir**

This channel broadcasts the news as well. ◆ The football game was broadcast live. ◆ The radio broadcast the play yesterday.
broadcaster ['bro:dka:tə] *n.* □ **transmissor**
broaden ['bro:dn] *v.* (**broadens, broadening, broadened**)
□ **alargar**
The road begins to broaden here. ◆ to broaden the road.
■ Ver **widen**.
brochure ['brouʃuə] *n.* □ **folheto**
a travel brochure. ◆ an advertising brochure.
broil [broil] *Amer. v.* (**broils, broiling, broiled**) (= grill)
□ **grelhar**
to broil meat / fish.
broke [bouk] *v.* (Ver **break**[2]).
broken[1] ['broukən] *v.* (Ver **break**[2]).
broken[2] *adj.*
1 **quebrado**
a broken arm. ◆ broken glass.
2 **quebrado**
The refrigerator is broken.
bronze [bronz] *n.* □ **bronze**
They had swords made of bronze. ◆ a bronze medal. ◆ a bronze statue.
brooch [broutʃ] *n.* □ **broche**
She was wearing a pearl brooch.
broom [bru:m] *n.* □ **vassoura**
to sweep the floor with a broom.
brother ['brʌðə] *n.* □ **irmão**
I have two brothers and one sister. ◆ My younger brother is 12 and my elder brother is 18.
brother-in-law ['brʌðərinlo:] *n.* (*pl.* **brothers-in-law**)
□ **cunhado**
brought [bro:t] *v.* (Ver **bring**).
brow [brau] *n.*
1 (= eyebrow) □ **sobrancelha**
2 (= forehead) □ **testa, fronte**
brown [braun] *adj., n.* □ **marrom, castanho, bronzeado**
I have brown eyes, but my sister's eyes are blue. ◆ He is very brown after a week at the beach.
browse [brauz] *v.* (**browses, browsing, browsed**) □ **dar uma olhada, navegar**
to browse through the books in the library / sites on the Internet. ◆ We spent the afternoon browsing in the shopping mall.
browser ['brauzə] *n.* □ **navegador de internet**
bruise [bru:z] *n.* □ **hematoma**
He was covered with bruises.
brush[1] [brʌʃ] *n.* □ **escova, brocha, pincel**
a hair-brush. ◆ to paint the door / wall with a brush. ◆ to paint a picture with a brush.
brush[2] *v.* (**brushes, brushing, brushed**) □ **escovar**
I need to brush my hair. ◆ Brush your jacket (with a clothes-brush). ◆ Did you brush your teeth?
brutal ['bru:tl] *adj.* □ **brutal**
a brutal murder. ◆ a brutal dictator.
■ Ver **cruel**.
brutally ['bru:təli] *adv.* □ **brutalmente**
He was brutally murdered.
bubble[1] ['bʌbl] *n.* □ **bolha**
soap bubbles. ◆ a bubble of air.
bubble[2] *v.* (**bubbles, bubbling, bubbled**) □ **borbulhar, ferver**
Boil the water until it bubbles.

buck [bʌk] *n.* □ **dólar**
You owe me five bucks.
bucket [ˈbʌkit] *n.* (= pail) □ **balde**
a bucket of water / sand.
buckle [ˈbʌkl] *n.* □ **fivela**
bud [bʌd] *n.* □ **botão**
The orange trees were covered in buds.
Buddhist [ˈbudist] *adj.*, *n.* □ **budista**
a Buddhist temple. ♦ He is a Buddhist.
buddy [ˈbʌdi] *n.* (*pl.* **buddies**) *Amer.* □ **parceiro, colega**
He and I were buddies.
■ *Brit.* **mate; pal**
budge [bʌdʒ] *v.* (**budges, budging, budged**) □ **mover**
The door is stuck and I can't budge it.
budget[1] [ˈbʌdʒit] *n.* □ **orçamento**
What is the budget for this project? ♦ to live on a low budget. ♦ a weekly budget.
budget[2] *v.* (**budgets, budgeting, budgeted**) □ **incluir no orçamento**
They budgeted five million dollars for the project.
budgie [ˈbʌdʒi] *n.* □ **periquito**
I keep budgies and other birds as pets.
■ Ver **parrot**.
bug [bʌg] *n.*
1 inseto
The sack of flour was full of bugs.
2 micróbio
a flu bug. ♦ I caught a bug last week.
3 vírus
The system / program is full of bugs.
build [bild] *v.* (**builds, building, built**)
1 construir
to build a house / bridge. ♦ The bird built the nest very quickly.
2 construir
to build a company / settlement.
3 construir
to build a road.
builder [ˈbildə] *n.* □ **construtor**
building [ˈbildiŋ] *n.* □ **prédio, edifício**
These buildings are 100 years old. ♦ a 16-storey / story building (= a building with 16 floors).
built [bilt] *v.* (Ver **build**).
bulb [bʌlb] *n.*
1 lâmpada
a light bulb
2 bulbo
Onions grow from bulbs.
bulge[1] [bʌldʒ] *n.* □ **saliência**
The gun made a bulge in his pocket.
bulge[2] *v.* (**bulges, bulging, bulged**) □ **fazer volume**
His pockets bulged with sweets.
bulky [ˈbʌlki] *adj.* (**bulkier, bulkiest**) □ **volumoso**
a bulky machine.
bull [bul] *n.* □ **touro**
■ Ver **ox**.
bulldozer [ˈbuldouzə] *n.* □ **escavadora**
bullet [ˈbulit] *n.* □ **bala, projétil**
He shot six bullets, but he missed the target.
bulletin-board [ˈbulətin ˌbɔːd] *n. Amer.* □ **quadro de avisos**
to put up a notice on the bulletin-board.
■ *Brit.* **notice-board**

bully[1] [ˈbuli] *n.* (*pl.* **bullies**) □ **valentão**
Two bullies in this class force other pupils to give them money.
bully[2] *v.* (**bullies, bullying, bullied**) □ **intimidar**
He bullies all the pupils in class. ♦ He bullied me into giving him the money.
bump[1] [bʌmp] *n.*
1 batida, galo
The car got a bump. ♦ I heard a bump when something fell to the ground. ♦ I got a bump on the head.
2 galo, calombo
He had a bump on his head.
3 lombada
I drove slowly because there were a lot of bumps in the road.
bump[2] *v.* (**bumps, bumping, bumped**)
1 bater, colidir
The car bumped against a tree.
2 bater
I bumped my head on the window.
bump into □ **topar com**
I bumped into an old friend on my way to the bank.
bumper [ˈbʌmpə] *n.* □ **para-choque**
bumpy [ˈbʌmpi] *adj.* (**bumpier, bumpiest**)
1 cheio de altos e baixos
a bumpy journey.
2 acidentada
a bumpy road.
bun [bʌn] *n.*
1 pão doce
I had a cup of tea and a bun for breakfast.
2 *Amer.* **pão de hambúrguer**
a hamburger bun.
■ Ver **roll**.
bunch [bʌntʃ] *n.*
1 cacho
a bunch of grapes / bananas.
2 molho, maço
a bunch of keys / flowers.
3 bando
a bunch of kids.
bundle [ˈbʌndl] *n.* □ **maço, trouxa**
a bundle of letters. ♦ He tied some clothes into a bundle.
bungalow [ˈbʌŋgəlou] *n.* □ **bangalô**
bunk [bʌŋk] *n.* □ **beliche**
bunk bed [ˈbʌŋk ˌbed] *n.* □ **cama-beliche**
bunny [ˈbʌni] *n.* (*pl.* **bunnies**) **coelhinho**
■ Ver **rabbit**.
buoy [boi] *n.* □ **boia**
burden [ˈbɜːdn] *n.* □ **fardo**
to carry a heavy burden.
burger [ˈbɜːgə] *n.* (= hamburger) □ **hambúrguer**
burglar [ˈbɜːglə] *n.* □ **ladrão**
A burglar broke into our house last night.
burglar alarm [ˈbɜːglə əˈlɑːm] *n.* □ **alarme contra ladrão**
burglary [ˈbɜːgləri] *n.* (*pl.* **burglaries**) □ **roubo**
There are a lot of burglaries in this part of town.
burgle [ˈbɜːgl] *v.* (**burgles, burgling, burgled**) □ **assaltar**
My apartment was burgled.
■ Ver **break into**.
burial [ˈberiəl] *n.* □ **enterro**

The burial took place on Tuesday.
■ The verb is **bury**.
buried ['berid] *v.* (Ver **bury**).
burn¹ [bəːn] *n.* ▫ **queimadura**
The doctor says that the burns on his arms are not serious.
burn² *v.* (**burns, burning, burned** or **burnt**)
1 queimar
The fire burned for hours. ✦ Paper burns easily.
2 queimar
to burn wood / coal. ✦ The house was burnt to the ground. ✦ He burnt the toast again.
■ Note:
I burnt my hand (accidentally).
burn down ▫ **incendiar**
They burned the house down. ✦ The building burned down.
burning ['bəːniŋ] *adj.* ▫ **em chamas**
They escaped from the burning house.
burrow ['bʌrou] *n.* ▫ **toca**
Rabbits live in burrows.
burst¹ [bəːst] *n.*
1 ruptura
a burst in the water pipe
2 explosão
a burst of laughter
burst² *v.* (**bursts, bursting, burst**)
1 estourar
The child burst the balloon. ✦ The pipe burst. ✦ The bag was so full that it burst.
2 sair correndo
He burst out of the room.
burst into
1 estourar, desatar a
to burst into tears / laughter. ✦ They burst into song.
2 irromper
The plane burst into flames.
burst out crying / laughing ▫ **desatar a chorar / rir, cair no choro / na risada**
She burst out laughing when she heard the joke.
bury ['beri] *v.* (**buries, burying, buried**)
1 enterrar
They buried the dead child.
2 enterrar
The pirates buried the treasure there.
bus [bʌs] *n.* ▫ **ônibus**
I go to school by bus. ✦ I get on the bus at 7:15 and get off at about 7:30.
bus station ['bʌs 'steiʃən] *n.* ▫ **estação rodoviária**
bus stop ['bʌs 'stɔp] *n.* ▫ **ponto/parada de ônibus**
There are five bus stops between the bus station and my house.
bush [buʃ] *n.* ▫ **tufo, arbusto, moita**
rose bushes.
busier, busiest ['biziə, 'biziist] (Ver **busy**).
busily ['bizili] *adv.* ▫ **ativamente**
The ants were busily collecting food.
business ['biznis] *n.*
1 comércio, negócios
Business is good, especially during the holiday seasons. ✦ We do business with them. ✦ to go into business.
2 negócio, empresa
He is the owner of two businesses in Paris.

It's none of your business! ▫ **Não é da sua conta!**
Who told you? – It's none of your business.
on business ▫ **a trabalho**
Are you here on business or for pleasure?
businessman ['bizinismən] *n.* (*pl.* **businessmen**) ▫ **empresário, homem de negócios**
business people ['bizinis 'piːpl] *n.* ▫ **executivos, empresários**
businesswoman ['biziniswumən] *n.* (*pl.* **business-women**) ▫ **empresária, mulher de negócios**
a successful businesswoman.
busy ['bizi] *adj.* (**busier, busiest**)
1 ocupado, atarefado
I can't come. I'm busy. ✦ He is busy with his homework.
2 cheio, atarefado
I had a busy day at work.
3 cheio, congestionado
The streets of the city centre are very busy at this hour. ✦ a busy market.
4 (= **engaged,** *Brit.*) *Amer.* **ocupado**
The line is busy. I'll dial the other number.
but¹ ['bʌt] *conj.*
1 mas
It's a simple plan, but a good one. ✦ I don't want it, but I'll take it anyway.
■ Ver **however; yet²**.
2 mas
My purpose is not to take your money, but to help you.
but² *prep.* (= except) ▫ **a não ser**
There's no one here but Ron.
butcher ['butʃə] *n.* ▫ **açougueiro, açougue**
I bought some meat at the butcher's (= butcher's shop).
butter¹ ['bʌtə] *n.* ▫ **manteiga**
I spread butter on a slice of bread. ✦ bread and butter.
butter² *v.* (**butters, buttering, buttered**) ▫ **passar manteiga, untar com manteiga**
I buttered a slice of toast.
butterfly ['bʌtəflai] *n.* (*pl.* **butterflies**) ▫ **borboleta**
button ['bʌtn] *n.*
1 botão
to undo / open the buttons. ✦ to do up the buttons.
2 botão
To start the machine, push / press the red button.
buy [bai] *v.* (**buys, buying, bought**) ▫ **comprar**
She bought it for 50 dollars. ✦ He bought me a present. ✦ He bought a present for me. ✦ Where did you buy it?
buzz¹ [bʌz] *n.* ▫ **zumbido**
the buzz of the bees / plane.
buzz² *v.* (**buzzes, buzzing, buzzed**) ▫ **zumbir**
The bees are buzzing over the flowers.
buzzword ['bʌzwəːd] *n.* ▫ **palavra da moda, modismo**
'Recycling' is a recent buzzword.
by¹ [bai] *adv.*
1 perto de
I live close by.
2 por perto
She passed by, but she didn't see me.
by² *prep.*
1 perto de, junto a
He sat by me / by my side. ✦ They live by the lake.
2 por
He walked by me without saying hello.

3 de
to go by car / bus.
4 por, com
It is done automatically by computer. ◆ It works by electricity. ◆ Did you pay in cash or by credit card?
5 de, por
a poem by Shakespeare. ◆ The palace was built by a famous architect.
6 antes de gerúndio indica modo e não se traduz
You can save time by using a computer.
7 por
He went out by the back door.
8 por volta de
Be here by six o'clock. ◆ They will finish the work by noon.
9 com
I was surprised by his reaction.
10 por
a room 4 metres by 6.
11 não se traduz
It's shorter by 30 centimetres. ◆ It's cheaper by 5 dollars.
12 por
I recognized him by his hat. ◆ It's 3:30 by my watch.
■ Ver **by accident; by chance; by far; by mistake**.
by himself / myself, etc.
1 sozinho
She built it by herself.
2 sozinho
He was all by himself.
by the way (= incidentally) □ **a propósito**
By the way, how is your friend David?
bye [bai] *excl.* **(mesmo que bye-bye)** □ **tchau**
I'll call you later. Bye.
by-product ['baiprodəkt] *n.* □ **subproduto**
bystander ['baistandə] *n.* □ **espectador, curioso**
Many bystanders were hurt when the cars crashed.
byte [bait] *n.* □ **byte**
How many bytes does your computer's memory have?

Cc

C [si:]
1 (= Celsius) □ **C**
The temperature is 25º C (= 25 degrees Celsius).
2 (= century) □ **século**
C21 (= twenty-first century)
3 (= 100) □ **C**
CC (= 200).

cab [kab] *n.*
1 (= taxi) **táxi**
I took a cab (= I went by cab) to the airport.
2 boleia
A cab is the place where the driver sits in a truck, train or bus.

cabbage ['kabidʒ] *n.* □ **repolho**

cabin ['kabin] *n.*
1 camarote
the captain's cabin (on a ship).
2 cabana
He lived in a cabin in the middle of the forest.
3 cabine
the first-class cabin (on a plane).

cabinet ['kabinit] *n.*
1 armário
a medicine cabinet (for keeping medicines). ♦ a filing cabinet (for keeping files in an office).
■ Ver **cupboard; closet**.
2 (= the Cabinet) **o Gabinete**
a cabinet meeting. ♦ a cabinet minister.

cable ['keibl] *n.*
1 cabo
a telephone cable.
2 cabo
This cable is strong enough to pull a truck.
3 (= telegram) **telegrama**
to send a cable.

cable-car ['keiblka:] *n.* □ **bonde, teleférico**

cable television ['keibl 'teliviʒən] *n.* (mesmo que **cable TV**) □ **televisão a cabo**

cactus ['kaktəs] *n.* □ **cacto**

café ['kafei] *n.* (= coffee shop) □ **cafeteria**

cafeteria [kafə'tiəriə] *n.* □ **refeitório, restaurante self-service**
I eat lunch at the cafeteria.

cage [keidʒ] *n.* □ **jaula, gaiola**
a lion in its cage at the zoo. ♦ The bird escaped from its cage.

cake ['keik] *n.* □ **bolo**
to bake / make a cake. ♦ a birthday cake. ♦ a chocolate cake.

calculate ['kalkjuleit] *v.* (**calculates, calculating, calculated**) □ **calcular**
to calculate the cost

calculated ['kalkjuleitid] *adj.* □ **calculado**
a calculated risk.

calculation [,kalkju'leiʃən] *n.* □ **cálculo**
Her calculations are correct / wrong.

calculator ['kalkjuleitər] *n.* □ **calculadora**
a pocket calculator.

calendar ['kaləndə] *n.*
1 calendário
the Chinese / Jewish / Muslim calendar. ♦ Look at the calendar and tell me the date.
2 *Amer.* **agenda**
The exam is next Tuesday. Please make a note in your calendars.
■ *Brit.* **diary**

calf [ka:f] *n.* (*pl.* **calves**) □ **bezerro, cria**

call¹ [ko:l] *n.*
1 chamado
a call for help.
2 chamado
The doctor received a call at midnight.
3 ligação, chamada, telefonema
I have to make a call (= to telephone). ♦ I'll give you a call. (= I'll telephone you.)
4 visita
I paid him a call. (= I visited him.)

call² *v.* (**calls, calling, called**)
1 chamar, gritar
They called for help. ♦ 'Who's there?', he called.
2 (= phone; ring) **telefonar, ligar**
I'll call you later. ♦ Thank you for calling.
3 chamar
Please call the doctor. ♦ Did you call me? ♦ They called the police. ♦ Please call (me) a taxi.
4 chamar
They called the baby Sharon. ♦ He called me a liar.
5 chamar
The postman calls around 10 every morning.
be called □ **chamar-se**
She is called Ruth. ♦ The song is called 'The Wall'.
call someone back ♦ **ligar de volta, retornar a ligação**
I'm busy now. Can I call you back?
call collect *Amer.* □ **ligar a cobrar**
■ *Brit.* **reverse the charges**
■ Ver **collect²**.
call for □ **ir buscar**
They will call for us at seven.
call off □ **cancelar, suspender**
to call off the match / search. ♦ The meeting was called off.
■ Ver **cancel**.
call on □ **visitar**
He'll call on you tonight.
call someone up
1 ligar para, telefonar
I'll call you up tomorrow.
2 convocar
The army calls up 18-year-olds. ♦ My brother was called up last week.
■ *Amer.* **draft**
■ Ver **conscript**.

call-box ['ko:lboks] *n.* (= telephone box) □ **cabine telefônica, orelhão**

calm¹ [ka:m] *adj.* □ **calmo**
Try to keep calm. ♦ a calm voice. ♦ The sea is calm.

calm² *v.* (**calms, calming, calmed**)
calm down □ **acalmar-se**
Calm down! I won't hurt you. ♦ The storm / sea calmed down. ♦ Try to calm the baby (down).

calmly ['kaːmli] *adv*. □ **calmamente, com calma**
calorie ['kaləri] *n*. □ **caloria**
How many calories are there in a slice of bread?
calves [kaːvz] *n*. (*plural of* **calf**).
came [keim] *v*. (Ver **come**).
camel ['kaməl] *n*. □ **camelo**
Camels can live in the desert without water for many days.
camera ['kamərə] *n*. □ **câmera**
to take photographs with a camera. ♦ a video camera.
cameraman, camerawoman ['kamərəˌman, 'kamərəˌwumən] *n*. □ **cinegrafista**
The TV cameraman filmed the riot.
■ Ver **photographer**.
camouflage[1] ['kaməflaːʒ] *n*. □ **camuflagem**
The tanks were covered with nets as camouflage.
camouflage[2] *v*. (**camouflages, camouflaging, camouflaged**) □ **camuflar**
The soldiers camouflaged themselves with mud and branches.
camp[1] [kamp] *n*. □ **acampamento**
to pitch a camp (= to put up tents). ♦ an army camp. ♦ a holiday camp.
camp[2] *v*. (**camps, camping, camped**) □ **acampar**
Let's camp here for the night.
go camping □ **ir acampar**
We went camping in the mountains.
camper ['kampə] *n*.
1 campista
The campers set up camp at the top of the hill.
2 trailer, reboque
My father drives the camper that the family eats and sleeps in when we go camping.
campaign[1] [kam'pein] *n*.
1 campanha
an advertising campaign. ♦ a campaign against smoking.
2 campanha
a military campaign.
campaign[2] *v*. (**campaigns, campaigning, campaigned**) □ **fazer campanha**
They are campaigning against smoking.
campfire ['kampfaiə] *n*. *Amer*. □ **fogueira**
to build / make a campfire. ♦ to sit around a campfire.
camping ['kampiŋ] *n*. □ **camping**
can[1] [kan] *n*. □ **lata**
a can of beer. ♦ a can of peas.
■ Ver **tin**.
can[2] *v*.
1 poder, ser capaz de, conseguir
I can do it now. ♦ You can write more clearly. ♦ She can't / cannot stay. ♦ This computer can talk.
■ **cannot** is one word. Short form: **can't**.
■ Ver **be able to; could**.
2 saber
Can you drive? ♦ I can't swim.
3 (= may) **poder, ter permissão de**
Can I come in? ♦ You can't (= are not allowed to) park here. ♦ You can go now.
4 poder
It can't be true.
5 poder
Can I help you? ♦ Can you help me, please?

canal [kə'nal] *n*. □ **canal**
the Suez Canal.
■ Ver **channel**.
canary [kə'neəri] *n*. (*pl*. **canaries**) □ **canário**
cancel ['kansəl] *v*. (*Amer*. **cancels, canceling, canceled**; *Brit*. **cancelling, cancelled**) □ **cancelar**
The meeting was cancelled. ♦ to cancel a match / flight.
cancellation [ˌkanse'leiʃən] *n*. □ **cancelamento**
cancer ['kansə] *n*. □ **câncer**
Smoking can cause lung cancer. ♦ Is there a cure for cancer?
candidacy ['kandidəsi] *n*., **candidature** *Brit*. □ **candidatura**
candidate ['kandidət] *n*.
1 candidato
Our candidate for Mayor is Michael Hanks. ♦ We're interviewing five candidates for the job.
2 (= examinee) **candidato**
All the candidates passed the exam.
candle ['kandl] *n*. □ **vela**
to light a candle.
candlestick ['kandlstik] *n*., *n*. □ **castiçal**
candy ['kandi] *n*. *Amer*. (*pl*. **candies**) □ **doce, guloseima**
Would you like a candy? ♦ You eat too much candy. ♦ a bag of candies.
■ *Brit*. **sweet**
cane [kein] *n*.
1 cana
bamboo canes. ♦ sugar cane.
2 bengala
The old man walks with a cane.
3 vara
Teachers used to punish pupils with a cane.
canned [kand] *adj*. □ **enlatado**
canned meat. ♦ canned beer.
■ Ver **tinned**.
cannibal ['kanibəl] *n*. □ **canibal**
cannon ['kanən] *n*. □ **canhão**
cannot ['kanot] *v*. (Ver **can**).
canoe [kə'nuː] *n*. □ **canoa**
can't [kaːnt] *v*. (Ver **can**).
canteen [kan'tiːn] *n*.
1 cantil
to drink from a water canteen.
2 cantina
I had lunch at the canteen.
canvas ['kanvəs] *n*.
1 lona
Tents and sails are made of canvas.
2 tela
Artists use canvas for their paintings.
cap [kap] *n*.
1 boné, gorro, touca
a nurse's cap. ♦ a bathing cap. ♦ a peaked cap. ♦ a flat cap. ♦ a soldier's cap.
■ Ver **hat**.
2 tampa
Put the cap back on the tube of toothpaste. ♦ To open the bottle, twist the cap.
■ Ver **top**[2].
capability [ˌkeipə'biliti] *n*. (*pl*. **capabilities**) □ **capacidade**
capable ['keipəbl] *adj*.
1 capaz
He is capable of solving the problem.

■ Ver **be able to**.
2 capaz
She is a very capable manager.
capacity [kə'pasəti] *n.* ☐ **capacidade**
The fuel tank in my car has a capacity of 40 litres.
capital ['kapitl] *n.*
1 capital
What is the capital of France?
2 (= **capital letter**) **caixa alta, letra maiúscula**
Write your name in capitals.
3 capital
He needs more capital for the business.
capsize [kap'saiz] *v.* (**capsizes, capsizing, capsized**) ☐ **virar, emborcar**
The boat capsized. ♦ A big wave capsized the boat.
captain ['kaptən] *n.*
1 capitão, capitã
the captain of the ship / plane. ♦ He is a captain in the army.
2 capitão, capitã
Who is the captain of the Brazilian team?
captive ['kaptiv] *n.* (= prisoner) ☐ **cativo**
captivity [kap'tiviti] *n.* ☐ **cativeiro**
animals in captivity (usually in a zoo).
capture¹ ['kaptʃə] *n.* ☐ **captura**
the capture of the thief.
capture² *v.* (**captures, capturing, captured**)
1 capturar
They captured six enemy soldiers. ♦ The spider captured a fly.
2 tomar
to capture a city.
car [ka:] *n.*
1 carro
He goes / drives to work by car. ♦ a racing car.
■ Ver **car park**.
2 *Amer.* **carro**
the restaurant car on a train.
■ *Brit.* (**railway**) **carriage**
caravan ['karəvan] *n.*
1 trailer
People on holiday sometimes live in caravans.
■ *Amer. trailer*
2 caravana
The caravan will travel across the desert for 10 days.
card [ka:d] *n.*
1 cartão
a birthday card. ♦ a New Year's card.
■ Ver **postcard**.
2 cartão
a membership card. ♦ a phone card. ♦ an identity card.
■ Ver **credit card**.
3 (= school report) *Brit.* **boletim**
a report card.
4 carta
a pack of cards. ♦ to play cards.
card index *n.* ☐ **fichário**
cardboard ['ka:dbo:d] *n.* ☐ **papelão**
a cardboard box.
cardigan ['ka:digən] *n.* ☐ **cardigã**
cardinal ['ka:dənl] *n.* ☐ **cardeal, cardinal**
care¹ [keə] *n.* ☐ **cuidado**
Move it with care. It breaks easily.

take care ☐ **tomar cuidado**
You should take more care when you're driving. ♦ Take care not to break it.
take care of ☐ **cuidar de**
Sara takes care of our children when we go on holiday. ♦ I'll take care of this problem. ♦ Take good care of these discs. They are very expensive.
■ Ver **look after**.
care² *v.* (**cares, caring, cared**) ☐ **importar-se**
I don't care what she says. ♦ Who cares? ♦ I couldn't care less. (= I don't care at all.)
care about ☐ **importar-se com**
I care about her future and I'm going to help.
care for
1 ligar
I don't care much for computer games.
2 cuidar
Who's caring for the children while you are away?
Would you care for...? (= Would you like...?) ☐ **Você gostaria de...?**
Would you care for a cup of tea?
career [kə'riə] *n.* ☐ **carreira**
a career in sport. ♦ to choose a career as a teacher.
careful ['keəful] *adj.* ☐ **cuidadoso**
a careful driver.
be careful ☐ **ter cuidado, ser cuidadoso, ter o cuidado de**
Be careful when you cross the road. ♦ Be careful with that vase! ♦ I was careful not to touch it.
carefully ['keəfuli] *adv.*
1 cuidadosamente, com cuidado
Drive carefully. The road is slippery.
2 atenciosamente, com cuidado
Listen carefully! ♦ The trip was carefully planned.
caregiver [keə'givə] *n.* (= carer) ☐ **cuidador**
careless ['keəlis] *adj.*
1 descuidado
a careless driver.
2 descuidado, displicente
He is careless about his clothes. ♦ careless work.
carelessly ['keəlisli] *adv.* ☐ **descuidadamente, displicentemente**
If you drive carelessly, you may cause an accident.
carelessness ['keəlisnis] *n.* ☐ **descuido, displicência**
carer ['keərə] *n.* ☐ **cuidador**
She works as a carer for sick old people.
caretaker ['keə,teikə] *n. Brit.* ☐ **zelador**
a school caretaker.
■ *Amer.* **janitor**
cargo ['ka:gou] *n.* ☐ **carga, carregamento**
a cargo of oranges / wheat.
carnival ['ka:nivəl] *n.* ☐ **parque de diversões, carnaval**
carousel [karə'sel] *n.* ☐ **carrossel**
car park [ka: pa:k] *n. Brit.* ☐ **estacionamento**
■ *Amer.* **parking lot; parking garage**
carpenter ['ka:pəntə] *n.* ☐ **carpinteiro**
carpentry ['ka:pəntri] *n.* ☐ **carpintaria**
carpet ['ka:pit] *n.* ☐ **carpete, tapete**
carriage ['karidʒ] *n.*
1 carruagem
to ride in a carriage.
2 *Brit.* **vagão**
a first-class carriage.
■ *Amer.* **car**

carried ['karid] *v.* (Ver **carry**).
carrier bag ['karɪə 'bag] *n.* □ **sacola, saco**
carrot ['karət] *n.* □ **cenoura**
  carrot juice.
carry ['kari] *v.* (**carries, carrying, carried**)
  1 carregar, levar, portar
  She carried her baby on her back. ◆ Carry this box to the car. ◆ That policeman is carrying a gun.
  2 transportar
  This pipeline carries oil to several countries. ◆ The ship is carrying a cargo of coal.
carry on □ **continuar**
  Carry on with your work. ◆ They carried on talking even when the teacher came in.
  ■ Ver **continue; go on; keep on**.
carry out □ **executar, realizar**
  He carried out my orders. ◆ to carry out a plan.
cart [ka:t] *n.*
  1 carroça
  horse and cart.
  2 *Amer.* **carrinho**
  a shopping cart (= supermarket trolley, *Brit.*). ◆ a baggage cart (= a luggage trolley, *Brit.*).
carton ['ka:tən] *n.* □ **embalagem, caixa**
  a carton of milk / eggs.
cartoon [ka:'tu:n] *n.*
  1 cartum, tirinha
  a newspaper cartoon.
  2 desenho animado
  a TV cartoon.
carve [ka:v] *v.* (**carves, carving, carved**)
  1 esculpir
  He carved a statue out of wood.
  2 entalhar
  She carved her name on the door.
  3 trinchar
  to carve the chicken.
case[1] [keis] *n.*
  1 caixa
  a case of wine / oranges. ◆ a glass case (in museums).
  ■ Ver **crate**.
  2 mala
  I helped her carry the cases to the car.
  ■ Ver **briefcase, suitcase**.
  3 estojo
  a pillowcase. ◆ a case for glasses / a camera.
case[2] *n.*
  1 caso
  In some cases I do it myself.
  2 caso
  If that's the case, there's still hope.
  3 caso
  His case will come before the court tomorrow. ◆ a divorce case. ◆ a murder case.
in any case (= anyway) □ **em todo caso, de qualquer forma**
  In any case, I don't care any more.
in case □ **caso**
  Take your coat with you in case it rains.
in case of □ **em caso de**
  In case of emergency call 100.
in that case □ **nesse caso**
  It's very expensive. – In that case, we'll buy only one.
just in case □ **por precaução, por via das dúvidas**
  The sky is clear, but take an umbrella just in case.
cash[1] [kaʃ] *n.* □ **em espécie, à vista, em dinheiro**
  Are you paying (in) cash or by credit card?
cash[2] *v.* (**cashes, cashing, cashed**) □ **descontar**
  She cashed a check / cheque for 100 dollars.
cash card ['kaʃ ,ka:d] *n.* □ **cartão de saque**
  You can use a cash card only to draw money out of an ATM.
  ■ Ver **credit card**.
cash desk ['kaʃ ,desk] *n. Brit.* □ **caixa**
cashier [ka'ʃɪə] *n.* □ **caixa**
cash machine ['kaʃ mə'ʃi:n] *n.* (mesmo que **cash dispenser; cashpoint**) □ **caixa eletrônico**
  to draw money out of a cash machine.
  ■ *Amer.* **ATM**
cassette [kə'set] *n.* □ **fita cassete**
  a video cassette. ◆ to play a cassette.
cassette player [kə'set ,pleɪə] *n.* □ **toca-fitas**
cassette recorder [kə'set rɪ'kɔ:də] *n.* **gravador**
cast [ka:st] *n. Amer.* □ **gesso**
  His leg was in a cast for four weeks.
  ■ *Brit.* **plaster**.
castle ['ka:sl] *n.* □ **castelo**
casual ['kaʒuəl] *adj.*
  1 casual, por acaso
  a casual meeting. ◆ a casual remark.
  2 casual, informal
  casual clothes.
  3 descontraído
  I tried to sound casual to hide my excitement.
casually ['kaʒuəli] *adv.*
  1 casualmente
  He glanced casually at the picture.
  2 informalmente
  She was casually dressed.
casualty ['kaʒuəlti] *n.* (*pl.* **casualties**) □ **baixa, vítima**
  The enemy suffered heavy casualties.
casualty (department) *n. Brit.* (mesmo que **casualty ward**) (= accident and emergency) □ **pronto-socorro, emergência**
  ■ *Amer.* **emergency room**
cat [kat] *n.* □ **gato**
  to feed the cat. ◆ A kitten is a young cat.
catalog ['katəlɒg] *n. Amer.*, **catalogue** *Brit.* □ **catálogo, lista telefônica**
catapult ['katəpʌlt] *n. Brit.* □ **catapulta, estilingue, atiradeira**
  ■ *Amer.* **slingshot**
catch [katʃ] *v.* (**catches, catching, caught**)
  1 pegar
  Catch the ball!
  2 capturar
  The police are trying to catch the criminal. ◆ The fisherman caught a big shark. ◆ The fox was caught in a trap.
  3 flagrar
  She caught him stealing her jewels.
  4 prender
  I caught my fingers in the door.
  5 pegar, tomar

I'll catch the next train.
- antônimo: **miss²**

6 contrair
to catch a disease. ♦ I caught a cold.

7 entender
Did you catch his meaning? ♦ Sorry, I didn't catch your name.

catch fire □ **pegar fogo**
The curtains caught fire.

catch up (with) □ **alcançar**
Walk faster if you want to catch up with the others. ♦ She was absent from school for a month, but she managed to catch up.

caterpillar ['katəpilə] *n.* □ **lagarta**
A caterpillar develops into a butterfly or moth.

cathedral [kə'θi:drəl] *n.* □ **catedral**

Catholic ['kaθəlik] *adj.* □ **católico**
a Catholic priest.

cattle ['katl] *n.* □ **gado**
a herd of cattle (cows and bulls).

caught [kɔ:t] *v.* (Ver **catch**).

cauliflower ['kɔliflauə] *n.* □ **couve-flor**

cause¹ [kɔ:z] *n.*
1 causa, motivo
What was the cause of the accident?
2 causa
He devoted his life to the cause of world peace. ♦ The money is for a good cause.

cause² *v.* (**causes, causing, caused**) □ **causar**
What caused the accident? ♦ She caused them a lot of trouble.

caution¹ ['kɔ:ʃən] *n.* □ **cautela, cuidado**
Drive with caution. The road is slippery. ♦ Caution! Narrow path.
- Ver **care; careful**.

caution² *v.* (**cautions, cautioning, cautioned**) □ **alertar**
She cautioned the child not to talk to strangers.
- The usual word is **warn**.

cautious ['kɔ:ʃəs] *adj.* (= careful) □ **cauteloso**
a cautious driver. ♦ She is cautious about taking medicines.

cautiously ['kɔ:ʃəsli] *adv.* □ **cautelosamente**

cave [keiv] *n.* □ **gruta, caverna**

CD ['si:'di:] *n.* (= compact disc) □ **CD**

cease [si:s] *v.* (**ceases, ceasing, ceased**) □ **deixar de, cessar**
The organization ceased to exist after five years. ♦ to cease fire in combat.

cease-fire ['si:s,faiə] *n.* □ **cessar-fogo**

ceiling ['si:liŋ] *n.* □ **teto**
a high / low ceiling.

celebrate ['seləbreit] *v.* (**celebrates, celebrating, celebrated**) □ **celebrar, comemorar**
How do you usually celebrate your birthday?

celebration [,selə'breiʃən] *n.* □ **celebração, comemoração**
There were celebrations everywhere when our team won.

celery ['seləri] *n.* □ **aipo, salsão**

cell [sel] *n.*
1 cela
The prisoner was alone in his cell.
2 célula
blood cells.

cellar ['selə] *n.* □ **adega**
a wine cellar.

cello ['tʃelou] *n.* □ **violoncelo**

cellphone ['selfoun] *n.* (= **cellular phone**) □ **celular**

cellular phone ['seluːlə foun] *n.* (= **cellphone, mobile phone**) □ **telefone celular**
What's your cellular phone number?

Celsius ['selsiəs] *n.* (= **centigrade**) □ **Celsius, centígrados**
The temperature is 30° C (= 30 degrees Celsius).

cement [sə'ment] *n.* □ **cimento**
a bag / sack of cement.
- Ver **concrete²**.

cemetery ['semətri] *n.* (*pl.* **cemeteries**) □ **cemitério**
The leaders of the nation are buried in this cemetery. ♦ a Jewish / Catholic cemetery.

cent [sent] *n.* □ **centavo**
It costs $5.99 (= 5 dollars and 99 cents).

center ['sentə] *n. Amer.*, **centre** *Brit.*
1 centro, meio
in the center of the circle.
2 centro
a shopping centre. ♦ a sports center.

centigrade ['sentigreid] *n.* (Ver **Celsius**).

centiliter ['sentiliːtə] *n. Amer.*, **centilitre** *Brit.* □ **centilitro**
This bottle contains 300 cl (= 300 centilitres) of juice.
- abreviação: **cl**

centimeter ['sentimiːtə] *n. Amer.*, **centimetre** *Brit.* □ **centímetro**
The size of the page is 20 cm by 13 cm (= 20 centimeters by 13 centimeters).
- abreviação: **cm**

central ['sentrəl] *adj.* □ **central**
to live in a central area.

central heating ['sentrəl 'hi:tiŋ] *n.* □ **aquecimento central**

centre ['sentə] *n. Brit.* (= **center**)
1 centro, meio
in the center of the circle.
2 centro
a shopping centre. ♦ a sports center.

century ['sentʃuri] *n.* (*pl.* **centuries**) □ **século**
in the 16th (= sixteenth) century. ♦ at the end of the 20th century.

cereal ['siəriəl] *n.*
1 cereal
Wheat and rice are cereals.
2 cereal
a bowl of cereal.

ceremonial [,serə'mouniəl] *adj.* □ **cerimonial**

ceremony ['serəməni] *n.* (*pl.* **ceremonies**) □ **cerimônia**
a wedding ceremony. ♦ the opening ceremony of the Olympic Games.

certain¹ ['sə:tn] *adj.* □ **certo**
It is certain (that) he will accept the offer. ♦ I'm certain (= I'm sure) she'll pass the test.

for certain □ **com certeza**
I don't know for certain when he will come.

make certain □ **certificar-se**
Make certain (that) the door is locked.

certain² *adj.* □ **certo**
Certain areas are colder than others.

certainly ['sə:tnli] *adv.*
1 certamente, com certeza

The plan will certainly fail without your help. ◆ He certainly didn't mean to hurt you.
2 (= of course) **claro, com certeza**
May I use the phone? – Certainly.
certainly not □ **claro não, certamente não**
May I take the car? – Certainly not.
certainty ['sə:tnti] *n.* □ **certeza**
There's no certainty that he will win.
certificate [sə'tifikət] *n.*
1 certidão
a birth certificate.
2 atestado
I was ill. Here's the doctor's certificate.
certify ['sə:tifai] *v.* (**certifies, certifying, certified**) □ **certificar, atestar**
I certify that this is a true photograph of J. Smith.
chain¹ [tʃein] *n.* □ **corrente**
a gold chain. ◆ The boat was pulled by a heavy chain.
chain² *v.* (**chains, chaining, chained**) □ **acorrentar**
The guards chained the prisoners to each other.
chair¹ [tʃeə] *n.* □ **cadeira**
to sit (down) on a chair.
chair² *v.* (**chairs, chairing, chaired**) □ **presidir**
She chaired the meeting.
chairman ['tʃeəmən] *n.* □ **diretor**
chairman of the board.
■ The word **chairman** also refers to a woman, but today **chairperson** is preferred for both men and women. The word **chairwoman** refers to a woman.
chalk [tʃo:k] *n.* □ **giz**
Take a piece of chalk and write the word on the blackboard. ◆ white chalk.
challenge¹ ['tʃalindʒ] *n.* □ **desafio**
Climbing the highest mountain in the world is a real challenge.
challenge² *v.* (**challenges, challenging, challenged**) □ **desafiar**
She challenged me to a game of tennis.
chameleon [kə'mi:liən] *n.* □ **camaleão**
champ [tʃamp] *n.* (= **champion**)
champagne [tʃam'pein] *n.* □ **champanhe**
champion¹ ['tʃampiən] *n.* □ **campeão**
the world boxing champion. ◆ a tennis champion.
champion² *v.* (**champions, championing, championed**) □ **defender**
to champion the rights of young people.
championship ['tʃampiənʃip] *n.* □ **campeonato**
Who won the tennis championship?
chance [tʃa:ns] *n.*
1 chance
He has no chance of winning. ◆ She has a good chance of success. ◆ What are their chances of surviving in the jungle?
2 chance
Give me a chance to prove myself. ◆ It's your last chance.
by chance □ **por acaso**
I found it by chance.
take a chance □ **correr risco, arriscar-se**
I don't trust him very much, but that's a chance I'll have to take.
change¹ [tʃeindʒ] *n.*

1 mudança
a change in the weather. ◆ a change for the better. ◆ to make some changes in the plan.
2 troco
Keep the change.
3 moedas, dinheiro trocado
Do you have any change? I want to make a phone call.
for a change □ **para variar**
Do it without my help for a change.
change² *v.* (**changes, changing, changed**)
1 mudar
They changed their address.
2 mudar
The town has changed a lot. ◆ When the traffic lights change to green you can cross the road.
3 trocar
Can you change 50 dollars? ◆ I changed 200 pounds into dollars.
4 trocar de roupa
Give me ten minutes to change.
change your mind □ **mudar de ideia**
I changed my mind and didn't go to the party.
channel ['tʃanl] *n.*
1 canal
channels that carry water to the fields.
2 canal
the English Channel. ◆ There's a good programme on Channel 2 tonight. ◆ I switched to another channel.
chapel ['tʃapəl] *n.* □ **capela**
chapter ['tʃaptə] *n.*
1 capítulo
The first chapter (of the book) is quite boring. ◆ Chapter 2 deals with the history of the Greeks. ◆ a new chapter in my life.
2 (= branch) *Amer.* □ **filial, sede regional**
The political party has a chapter in our town.
character ['karəktə] *n.*
1 caráter
She has a strong / weak character. ◆ The character of the town is changing.
2 personagem
The main character of the play is a prince called Hamlet.
characteristic¹ [,karəktə'ristik] *adj.* □ **característico**
It is characteristic of him to be so optimistic.
characteristic² *n.* □ **característica**
A characteristic of a good doctor is to be able to listen to patients.
charge¹ [tʃa:dʒ] *n.*
1 acusação
They arrested him on a charge of kidnapping.
2 cobrança, taxa
The books will be sent to you free of charge. ◆ 10% service charge (in a restaurant).
be in charge (of) □ **estar no comando (de)**
Who's in charge here? ◆ Ron is in charge of the office when the boss is away.
charge² *v.* (**charges, charging, charged**)
1 cobrar
How much did they charge you for it? ◆ They charged me ten dollars for the meal.
2 acusar
The police charged him with murder.

charity / cheerful

3 atacar
The police charged at the crowd.
charity ['tʃarəti] *n.*
1 caridade
to live on charity. ♦ to give (money) to charity.
2 (*pl.* **charities**) instituição de caridade
Charities give money to people who need it very much.
charm¹ [tʃa:m] *n.*
1 charme
She has a lot of charm.
2 amuleto
I always wear this ring. It's my lucky charm.
charm² *v.* (**charms, charming, charmed**) □ encantar
The child charmed us all with his sweet words.
charming ['tʃa:miŋ] *adj.* □ **charmoso, encantador**
a charming smile / person.
chart¹ [tʃa:t] *n.*
1 carta de navegação
to use a chart to navigate a ship.
■ Ver **map**.
2 gráfico
a weather chart. ♦ The sales chart for this year shows an increase in sales.
chart² *v.* (**charts, charting, charted**) □ traçar
He charted the course of the river.
chase¹ [tʃeis] *n.* □ **perseguição**
The police caught the robber after a short car chase.
chase² *v.* (**chases, chasing, chased**) □ **perseguir**
The cat is chasing a rat.
chase after □ **perseguir, ir atrás**
I chased after her to return her purse.
chase away □ **espantar**
to chase the flies away.
chat¹ [tʃat] *n.* □ **conversa, bate-papo**
I had a long chat with him about basketball.
chat² *v.* (**chats, chatting, chatted**) □ **conversar, bater papo**
We chatted about football.
chat show *n.* □ **programa de entrevista**
Politicians and actors appeared on the chat show on TV.
chatter¹ ['tʃatə] *n.* □ **tagarelice**
chatter² *v.* (**chatter, chattering, chattered**) □ **tagarelar**
The audience stopped chattering when the film began.
chauffeur ['ʃoufə] *n.* □ **chofer, motorista**
cheap [tʃi:p] *adj.*
1 barato
Is this watch cheaper than that one? ♦ a cheap hotel.
■ antônimo: **expensive**
2 *Amer.* mesquinho
Don't be so cheap! Give him some more money.
cheaply ['tʃi:pli] *adv.* □ **barato**
I bought it cheaply.
cheat¹ [tʃi:t] *v.* (**cheats, cheating, cheated**)
1 trapacear, roubar
He cheated me at cards.
2 colar
She was caught cheating on the exam.
cheat² *n.* □ **trapaceiro**
Don't let him play – he's a cheat!
check¹ [tʃek] *n.*
1 inspeção
a security check at the airport.

2 *Amer.* cheque
I'll write you a check for 500 dollars. ♦ I paid by check.
■ *Brit.* **cheque**
3 *Amer.* conta
I asked the waiter for the check.
■ *Brit.* **bill**
4 *Amer.* marca
Put a check by the correct answer.
■ *Brit.* **tick**
5 xeque
'You're in check!', said the chessplayer.
check² *v.* (**checks, checking, checked**)
1 conferir, verificar, conferir
Check your answer again. ♦ The mechanic checked the brakes and the tyres.
2 conferir, verificar
The teacher checks the names of the pupils who are present.
check in □ **dar entrada, fazer check in**
We checked in at the hotel at 2 pm.
check out
1 fechar a conta, fazer check out
They checked out of the hotel at 10 am.
2 checar, verificar, conferir
We checked out the suspect's story.
check up □ **checar, verificar, conferir**
I'm not sure I locked the door. – I'll go and check up.
♦ Please check up on the time of the train.
check³ *n.* □ **xadrez**
a skirt with a pattern of checks.
checked [tʃekt] *adj.* (mesmo que **check**) □ **xadrez**
a checked shirt.
checkers ['tʃekəz] *n. Amer.* □ **jogo de damas**
■ *Brit.* **draughts**
check-in ['tʃekin] *n.* □ **check-in**
the check-in desk at an airport.
checkout ['tʃekaut] *n.* □ **caixa**
to pay at the checkout.
■ Ver **cash desk**.
check-up ['tʃekʌp] *n.* □ **check-up**
I go to the doctor for a check-up every six months.
cheek [tʃi:k] *n.*
1 bochecha
She kissed the child on the cheek.
2 atrevimento, descaramento
You owe me money and you have the cheek to ask me for a loan.
cheeky ['tʃi:ki] *adj.* (**cheekier, cheekiest**) □ **atrevido, descarado**
Don't be so cheeky!
cheer¹ [tʃiə] *n.* □ **grito de entusiasmo**
the cheers of the football fans.
three cheers for □ **vivas**
Three cheers for the winner!
Cheers! □ **Saúde! (brinde)**
cheer² *v.* (**cheers, cheering, cheered**) □ **aplaudir, gritar com entusiasmo**
The fans cheered when he scored a goal.
cheer up □ **animar-se, alegrar-se**
Cheer up! You'll get another chance. ♦ I bought him a present to cheer him up.
cheerful ['tʃiəful] *adj.* □ **animado, alegre**
She is cheerful today. ♦ He is in a cheerful mood.

cheerfully ['tʃiəfuli] *adv.* ▫ **com ânimo, alegremente**
She smiled cheerfully.
cheerio [tʃiəri'ou] *excl. Brit.* (= bye) ▫ **tchau**
Cheerio, everybody! See you tomorrow!
■ Ver **See you later!; See you soon!**
cheerleader ['tʃiəli:də] *n.* ▫ **líder de torcida**
The group of cheerleaders sang and danced at the football game.
cheese [tʃi:z] *n.* ▫ **queijo**
a cheese sandwich.
chef [ʃef] *n.* ▫ ***chef* de cozinha**
chemical[1] ['kemikəl] *n.* ▫ **produto químico, substância química**
Some chemicals are used to give taste to foods.
chemical[2] *adj.* ▫ **químico**
a chemical process.
chemist ['kemist] *n.*
  1 químico
  Chemists can make perfumes, cosmetic creams, etc. in a lab.
  2 *Brit.* **farmácia**
  He bought vitamin pills at the chemist's (shop).
  ■ *Amer.* **druggist**
  ■ Ver **drugstore; pharmacy**.
chemistry ['kemistri] *n.* ▫ **química**
cheque [tʃek] *n. Brit.* ▫ **cheque**
I paid by cheque. ◆ I'll write you a cheque for 200 dollars.
■ *Amer.* **check**
cheque-book ['tʃekbuk] *n.* ▫ **talão de cheques**
cherry ['tʃeri] *n.* (*pl.* **cherries**) ▫ **cereja**
chess [tʃes] *n.* ▫ **xadrez**
to play chess
chest [tʃest] *n.*
  1 peito
  I have pains in my chest.
  ■ Ver **breast**.
  2 (= trunk) **baú, caixa**
  She packed her clothes in a chest.
chest of drawers *n.* ▫ **cômoda**
chew [tʃu:] *v.* (**chews, chewing, chewed**) ▫ **mastigar**
Chew your food well before you swallow it.
chewing-gum ['tʃu:iŋgʌm] *n.* (= **gum**) ▫ **goma de mascar, chiclete**
chick [tʃik] *n.* ▫ **pintinho**
a hen and its chicks. ◆ The mother bird is feeding her chicks.
chicken ['tʃikin] *n.* ▫ **galinha, frango**
to feed the chickens. ◆ I had chicken soup for lunch. ◆ roast chicken.
■ Ver **cock; rooster**.
chief[1] [tʃi:f] *adj.* (= main) ▫ **principal**
This is the chief reason for his decision to leave.
chief[2] *n.* ▫ **chefe**
the chief of the tribe. ◆ the Chief of Police.
chiefly ['tʃi:fli] *adv.* (= mainly) ▫ **principalmente**
The plan failed chiefly because there was a delay.
child [tʃaild] *n.* (*pl.* **children**)
  1 criança
  When I was a child I ate a lot of sweets. ◆ There are 25 children in my class.
  2 filho
  She is an only child. ◆ One of their children is a soldier.

childhood ['tʃaildhud] *n.* ▫ **infância**
They had a happy childhood.
childish ['tʃaildiʃ] *adj.* ▫ **infantil**
Don't be so childish! ◆ a childish joke. ◆ childish laughter.
children ['tʃildrən] *n.* (Ver **child**).
chilly ['tʃili] *adj.* (**chillier, chilliest**) ▫ **gelado**
a chilly morning.
chime[1] [tʃaim] *n.* ▫ **som**
the chimes of the bells / clock.
chime[2] *v.* (**chimes, chiming, chimed**) ▫ **soar**
The church bells chimed. ◆ The clock chimed 7.
chimney ['tʃimni] *n.* ▫ **chaminé**
Smoke from the factory chimney rose up into the sky.
chimpanzee [tʃimpən'zi:] *n.* (mesmo que **chimp**) ▫ **chimpanzé**
chin [tʃin] *n.* ▫ **queixo**
china ['tʃainə] *n.* ▫ **porcelana**
a china cup / doll. ◆ a set (= plates, cups) of china.
■ The country **China** is spelt with a capital C.
chip [tʃip] *n.*
  1 lasca
  chips of wood / stone / glass.
  2 (= microchip) **chip**
  3 *Brit.* **batata frita, fritas**
  fish and chips.
  ■ *Amer.* (**French**) **fries**
  4 *Amer.* **salgadinho**
  a bag of chips.
  ■ *Brit.* **crisps**
chirp[1] [tʃə:p] *n.* ▫ **pio**
chirp[2] *v.* (**chirps, chirping, chirped**) ▫ **piar**
The birds were chirping among the trees.
chocolate ['tʃokələt] *n.* ▫ **chocolate**
a bar of milk chocolate. ◆ a box of chocolates. ◆ I don't like chocolate. ◆ chocolate cake / cookies. ◆ a cup of hot chocolate.
choice [tʃois] *n.*
  1 opção, escolha
  Take your choice. (= You can choose any one you like.) ◆ You made the right choice. ◆ I have no choice. I have to do it. ◆ You have several choices.
  2 variedade
  There is a wide choice of cheeses here.
choir ['kwaiə] *n.* ▫ **coro**
the church choir.
choke [tʃouk] *v.* (**chokes, choking, choked**) ▫ **engasgar, sufocar**
He choked on a chicken bone. ◆ The smoke made her choke. ◆ Stop it! You are choking him.
choose [tʃu:z] *v.* (**chooses, choosing, chose, chosen**) ▫ **escolher, optar**
I chose this car because it's cheaper. ◆ You can choose whether to pay by credit card or in cash.
chop[1] [tʃop] *n.* ▫ **costeleta**
lamb chops.
chop[2] *v.* (**chops, chopping, chopped**)
  1 picar
  to chop vegetables / meat.
  2 cortar
  I chopped some wood for the fire.
chore [tʃo:] *n.* ▫ **tarefa de rotina, afazeres**
I have to do the chores before I can go out.

chorus ['kɔːrəs] *n.*
1 coral, coro
He sings in the chorus. He doesn't sing solo.
2 refrão, estribilho
Everybody in the hall sang the chorus.
chose [tʃouz] *v.* (Ver **choose**).
chosen [tʃouzn] *v.* (Ver **choose**).
christen ['krisn] *v.* (**christens, christening, christened**) □ **batizar**
They christened her Monica.
christening ['krisniŋ] *n.* □ **batismo**
Christian ['kristʃən] *adj.*, *n.* □ **cristão, cristã**
the Christian Church. ✦ She is a Christian.
Christianity [kristi'anəti] *n.* □ **cristianismo**
Christian name ['kristʃən 'neim] *n.* □ **nome de batismo**
His Christian name is Victor and his surname is Newman.
■ Many people, especially non-Christians, use **first name** instead.
Christmas ['krisməs] *n.* □ **Natal**
I wish you a merry Christmas. ✦ I sent her a Christmas card. ✦ At Christmas people buy a lot of presents.
chuckle[1] ['tʃʌkl] *n.* □ **risadinha**
chuckle[2] *v.* (**chuckles, chuckling, chuckled**) □ **rir com discrição**
He chuckled at the joke.
church [tʃɔːtʃ] *n.* □ **igreja**
They go to church every Sunday.
cigar [si'gaː] *n.* □ **charuto**
cigarette [sigə'ret] *n.* □ **cigarro**
He smokes a pack of cigarettes a day.
cinema ['sinəmə] *n.* □ **cinema**
to go to the cinema
■ Ver **movies; movie theatre**.
cinnamon ['sinəmən] *n.* □ **canela**
circle[1] ['sɔːkl] *n.* □ **círculo**
to draw a circle. ✦ the diameter of a circle. ✦ They sat in a circle.
circle[2] *v.* (**circles, circling, circled**)
1 fazer um círculo em volta de algo
Circle the correct answers.
2 rodear
The helicopter circled over the area.
circuit ['sɔːkit] *n.* □ **circuito**
an electricity circuit. ✦ The racing cars did five circuits of the track.
circular[1] ['sɔːkjulə] *adj.* □ **circular**
a circular table. ✦ a circular bus route.
circular[2] *n.* (mesmo que **circular letter**) □ **circular**
The manager sent a circular to all the workers.
circulate ['sɔːkjuleit] *v.* (**circulates, circulating, circulated**)
1 circular
Blood circulates through the body.
2 circular
He circulated among the guests.
3 circular
The report was circulated among all the members.
circulation [,sɔːkju'leiʃən] *n.*
1 circulação
Exercise improves your blood circulation.
2 circulação
This newspaper has a large circulation.

circumference [sə'kʌmfərəns] *n.* □ **circunferência**
the circumference of a circle. ✦ The circumference of the earth is about 42,000 km.
circumstances ['sɛːkəmstansiz] *n. pl.* □ **circunstâncias**
in / under the circumstances □ **nessas circunstâncias**
Under the circumstances, we were lucky not to lose the game.
under no circumstances □ **em hipótese alguma**
Under no circumstances should you go there alone.
■ Note that the auxiliary verb precedes the pronoun when this expression begins the sentence.
circus ['sɔːkəs] *n.* □ **circo**
circus acrobats / clowns.
citizen ['sitizn] *n.* □ **cidadão**
a French / British citizen. ✦ the citizens of Paris.
■ Ver **national**[2].
citizenship ['sitiznʃip] *n.* □ **cidadania**
Australian citizenship.
city ['siti] *n.* (*pl.* **cities**) □ **cidade**
What is the capital city of Spain?
civil ['sivl] *adj.*
1 civil
civil rights.
2 (= polite) **civilizado, educado**
I expect a civil answer from you.
the Civil Service *n.* □ **a administração pública**
civil war *n.* □ **guerra civil**
civilian[1] [si'viljen] *n.* □ **civil**
Five civilians were killed in the bombing.
civilian[2] *adj.* □ **civil**
civilian clothes
civilization [sivilai'zeiʃən] *n.*, **civilisation** *Brit.* □ **civilização**
ancient civilizations.
civilized ['sivilaizd] *adj.*, **civilised** *Brit.* □ **civilizado**
a civilized society. ✦ to behave in a civilized way.
cl *abbr.* (Ver **centiliter**) □ **cl**
claim[1] [kleim] *n.*
1 reivindicação
The workers' pay claims are high.
2 afirmação, alegação
I don't accept the claim that these drugs are harmless.
claim[2] *v.* (**claims, claiming, claimed**)
1 alegar
He claims (that) he has a black belt in karate.
2 reclamar, reivindicar
The workers claimed a 5% pay rise.
clap[1] [klap] *v.* (**claps, clapping, clapped**) □ **aplaudir, bater palmas**
The audience clapped wildly.
clap[2] *n.* □ **aplauso, palmas**
clarify ['klarəfai] *v.* (**clarifies, clarifying, clarified**) □ **esclarecer**
Please clarify what you mean.
clash [klaʃ] *v.* (**clashes, clashing, clashed**)
1 entrar em conflito
Demonstrators clashed with the police.
2 coincidir
The dates of the two concerts clash.
clasp[1] [klaːsp] *n.* □ **fecho, fivela**
the clasp on a necklace ✦ the clasp on a purse
clasp[2] *v.* (**clasps, clasping, clasped**) □ **apertar**
He clasped my hand warmly.

class [klɑːs] *n.*
1 classe, turma
small classes of 8 pupils each. ◆ The whole class came to my birthday.
2 (= lesson, *Brit.*) *Amer.* **aula**
I have a history class at 10.
3 turma
the class of 1976.
4 classe
the working class.
5 classe
to travel first class.
6 categoria
a first-class player.
classical [ˈklasikəl] *adj.* □ **clássico**
classical music.
classification [ˌklasifiˈkeiʃən] *n.* □ **classificação**
classify [ˈklasifai] *v.* (**classifies, classifying, classified**) □ **classificar**
The librarian classified the books in alphabetical order.
classmate [ˈklɑːsmeit] *n.* □ **colega de classe**
She's my classmate – she sits next to me in school.
classroom [ˈklɑːsrum] *n.* □ **sala de aula, classe**
clatter [ˈklatə] *n.* □ **barulho**
There was clatter of dishes from the kitchen.
clause [klɔːz] *n.* **oração**
  dependent clause *n.* (mesmo que **subordinate clause**) □ **oração subordinada**
  main clause *n.* □ **oração principal**
claw [klɔː] *n.* □ **garra**
Cats and eagles have claws.
claws *n. pl.* □ **pinças**
A crab has strong claws.
clay [klei] *n.* □ **argila**
clay pots.
clean¹ [kliːn] *adj.*
1 limpo
a clean shirt. ◆ My hands are clean.
■ antônimo: **dirty**
2 puro
clean air. ◆ clean drinking water.
■ antônimo: **polluted**
3 limpo
a clean piece of paper.
clean² *v.* (**cleans, cleaning, cleaned**) □ **limpar**
He cleaned the windows with a cloth. ◆ Clean (= Brush) your teeth.
clean³ *n.* (mesmo que **cleaning**) □ **limpeza**
I gave the car a good clean.
clear¹ [kliə] *adj.*
1 claro
Your answer is not clear. ◆ It's not clear why he did it. ◆ Is that clear? – Yes, sir.
2 (= obvious) **óbvio**
It was clear that he wasn't pleased to see us.
3 nítido
a clear photograph.
4 claro
a clear day.
5 transparente
clear glass.
6 puro
clear water. ◆ clear soup.
7 livre, sem movimento
The road is clear.
clear² *v.* (**clears, clearing, cleared**)
1 esvaziar, tirar
to clear the streets of snow. ◆ Police cleared the area. ◆ After lunch I cleared the table.
2 abrir
The sky cleared. ◆ The fog is clearing.
clear something away □ **retirar coisas de algo**
Clear away the food from the table.
clear off □ **Cai fora!**
Clear off! And don't come here again!
clear up □ **abrir**
The weather is clearing up.
clearly [ˈkliəli] *adv.*
1 com clareza
I couldn't see / hear him clearly. ◆ She explained the point clearly.
2 (= obviously) **obviamente, claramente**
Clearly, we have to decide now. ◆ She is clearly the best pupil in class.
clerical [ˈklerikəl] *adj.* □ **de escritório**
a clerical job.
clerk [klɑːk] *n.*
1 caixa
a bank clerk.
2 *Amer.* **balconista, vendedor**
a sales clerk.
■ *Brit.* **shop assistant**
clever [ˈklevə] *adj.*
1 inteligente
a clever child. ◆ a clever reply. ◆ a clever trick. ◆ He is the cleverest pupil in class.
■ **smart** is more usual in American English.
2 hábil
She is clever at arranging flowers.
cleverly [ˈklevəli] *adv.* □ **com inteligência**
Everything was cleverly planned. ◆ He dealt with the problem cleverly.
cleverness [ˈklevənis] *n.* □ **inteligência**
click¹ [klik] *n.* □ **clique**
Press the button until you hear a click.
click² [klik] *v.* (**clicks, clicking, clicked**) □ **estalar**
He clicked his fingers and the dog came running.
client [ˈklaiənt] *n.* □ **cliente**
This lawyer / accountant has many clients. ◆ The bank may lose many clients because of the scandal.
■ **customer** is used for shops or businesses.
cliff [klif] *n.* □ **penhasco**
climate [ˈklaimət] *n.* □ **clima**
In winter, birds fly from Europe to a warmer climate.
climb¹ [klaim] *n.* □ **escalada**
The climb to the top of the mountain was very hard.
climb² *v.* (**climbs, climbing, climbed**)
1 escalar
We climbed the mountain. ◆ to climb a tree / wall. ◆ to climb the stairs.
2 entrar, subir
She climbed into her car.

climb down / up □ **subir / descer**
He climbed down the ladder.
climber ['klaimə] *n.* □ **alpinista**
He is a mountain climber.
climbing ['klaimiŋ] *n.* □ **alpinismo**
We go climbing every summer.
cling [kliŋ] *v.* (**clings, clinging, clung**) □ **agarrar-se a**
The child clung to his mother with fear. ◆ His shirt clung to his wet body.
clinic ['klinik] *n.* □ **clínico**
clip¹ [klip] *n.* □ **clipe, grampo**
a paper clip. ◆ a hair clip.
clip² *v.* (**clips, clipping, clipped**)
 1 prender com clipe / grampo
to clip papers together (with a paper clip).
 2 aparar, cortar
She clipped her nails. ◆ to clip pictures from newspapers.
cloak [klouk] *n.* □ **manto, capa**
cloakroom ['kloukrum] *n.* □ **vestiário**
Leave your coat in the cloakroom.
 ■ Use **locker-room** for a swimming pool, etc.
clock [klok] *n.* □ **relógio de parede / mesa**
The clock is fast / slow. ◆ I set the alarm clock for 6 o'clock.
 ■ Compare with **watch**.
 (a)round the clock □ **24 horas por dia, sem parar**
They are working around the clock to finish the project on time.
clockwise ['klokwaiz] *adj.*, *adv.* □ **sentido horário**
Move your finger clockwise.
 ■ antônimo: *Brit.* **anticlockwise**; *Amer.* **counterclockwise**
clone [kloun] *v.* (**clones, cloning, cloned**) □ **clonar**
The scientists cloned a sheep.
close¹ [klous] *adj.*
 1 perto, próximo
My house is close to the beach. ◆ The two offices are close together.
 ■ Ver **near**.
 2 íntimo
a close friend.
 3 perto de
There were close to 200 people at the party.
 ■ Ver **nearly**.
 4 acirrado
The contest was very close. He almost lost.
 5 cuidadoso
Pay close attention to what he says. ◆ Keep a close watch on them.
close² *adv.* □ **perto de, próximo a**
I live close to the hospital. ◆ Don't get too close to the monkeys! ◆ Bring it closer.
 close by □ **bem perto**
We live close by.
 get / come closer □ **chegar mais perto de**
She got / came closer to the house.
close³ [klouz] *v.* (**closes, closing, closed**) □ **fechar**
Close your eyes for a moment. ◆ The door closed automatically. ◆ The banks close at 1 pm today.
 ■ **shut** can be used instead of **close**, but in the **-ing** form **close** is preferred:
Quick! The doors are closing.
 close down (= shut down) □ **fechar, encerrar atividade**
The business closed down because of financial difficulties.

closed [klouzd] *adj.*
 1 fechado
The banks are closed today. ◆ The door is closed. ◆ with closed eyes
 2 completo
The list is closed.
 3 encerrado
The matter is closed.
closely ['klousli] *adv.* (= carefully) □ **de perto, minuciosamente**
He examined the picture closely. ◆ I watched them closely.
closet ['klozit] *n.* □ **closet, armário**
a clothes / linen closet. ◆ a walk-in clothes closet.
 ■ The more usual word in British English is **cupboard**.
cloth [kloθ] *n.*
 1 tecido
cotton cloth. ◆ several metres of cloth.
 2 pano
to wipe the table with a cloth.
 ■ *pl.* **cloths** (not to be confused with **clothes**).
 3 toalha de mesa
a tablecloth.
clothe [klouð] *v.* (**clothes, clothing, clothed**) □ **vestir**
She clothed the baby all in white.
 ■ **dress** is more common.
clothes [klouðz] *n. pl.* □ **roupas**
He took off his clothes and had a shower. ◆ What clothes was she wearing? ◆ Wait until I change my clothes.
 ■ singular: an article (or item) of clothing.
 ■ Ver **outfit**.
clothes-peg ['klouðzpeg] *n. Brit.* □ **prendedor de roupa**
clothespin ['klouðzpin] *n. Amer.* □ **prendedor de roupa**
clothing ['klouðiŋ] *n.* □ **vestuário, roupa**
Prices of clothing rose by 5%.
cloud [klaud] *n.* □ **nuvem**
There isn't a cloud in the sky. ◆ dark clouds. ◆ a cloud of dust / smoke.
cloudy ['klaudi] *adj.* (**cloudier, cloudiest**) □ **nublado**
a cloudy sky.
clown [klaun] *n.* □ **palhaço**
The clown (at the circus) made me laugh.
club [klʌb] *n.*
 1 clube
a youth club. ◆ a tennis club. ◆ Are you a member of the club?
 ■ Ver **nightclub**.
 2 bastão, cacetete
Some policemen carry clubs.
 3 taco
a golf club
clubs *n.* **paus**
the eight of clubs.
clue [klu:] *n.*
 1 pista
The police looked for clues in the room where she was murdered.
 2 dica
the clues of a crossword puzzle.
 I haven't (got) a clue □ **Eu não faço ideia**
I haven't got a clue how it works. ◆ Where is he? – I haven't a clue.
clumsily ['klʌmzili] *adv.* □ **desajeitadamente**
to walk clumsily.

clumsiness ['klʌmzinis] *n.* □ **falta de jeito**
clumsy ['klʌmzi] *adj.* (**clumsier, clumsiest**) □ **desajeitado**
Don't let him wash the dishes. He is so clumsy he may break something.
clung [klʌŋ] *v.* (Ver **cling**).
clutch [klʌtʃ] *v.* (**clutches, clutching, clutched**) □ **agarrar**
The frightened child clutched his father's hand.
clutch at □ **agarrar**
The drowning man clutched at the boat.
cm *abbr.* (Ver **centimeter**) □ **cm**
The size of the page is 20 cm by 13 cm. ◆ a stick 30 cm long.
c/o *abbr.* (= care of) □ **a/c, aos cuidados de**
He addressed the letter 'Jack Smith c/o Jill Jones'.
Co. *abbr.* (= **company**)
coach[1] [koutʃ] *n.*
1 (= trainer) □ **treinador**
a football / swimming coach.
2 (= bus) □ **ônibus-leito**
He took the coach (from London) to Scotland.
3 carruagem
The Queen travels in a coach on special days.
4 instrutor
He took a coach to prepare for the exam.
coach[2] *v.* (**coaches, coaching, coached**) □ **treinar, dar aulas**
Who coached the Brazilian team last year? ◆ She coached me in English so I could catch up with the class.
coal [koul] *n.*
1 carvão
They use coal as fuel. ◆ a sack of coal.
2 brasa
burning / hot coals.
coalmine ['koulmain] *n.* □ **mina de carvão**
coarse [ko:s] *adj.* □ **áspero**
coarse skin. ◆ coarse sand.
coast [koust] *n.* □ **costa, litoral**
the north coast.
■ Compare:
shore = seaside; land along the edge of the sea, lake or broad river, especially used in expressions like **to**, **from**, **by the shore**.
They swam to the shore.
coast = land next to the sea, usually used with **east**, **west**, etc. and with names of seas.
beach = sand or stones along a seaside, where people go on holiday.
coastguard ['koustga:d] *n.* □ **guarda costeira**
coat[1] [kout] *n.*
1 casaco
It was hot, so I took off my coat. ◆ Put your coat on. It's cold outside. ◆ a raincoat.
2 pelagem
An animal's coat is the fur, wool or hair that covers its body.
3 demão, camada
a coat of paint
coat[2] *v.* (**coats, coating, coated**) □ **cobrir**
I coated the cake with chocolate. ◆ The table was coated with dust.
coat-hanger ['kout,haŋə] *n.* (= **hanger**) □ **cabide**
cobweb(s) ['kobweb(z)] *n. Brit.* □ **teia de aranha**
A spider spins cobwebs to catch insects.
■ *Amer.* **spiderweb**
cock [kok] *n. Brit.* □ **galo**
Cocks crow early in the morning.
■ *Amer.* **rooster**
cockpit ['kokpit] *n.* □ **cockpit, cabine**
Pilots sit in the cockpit when they fly a plane.
cockroach ['kokrout∫] *n.* □ **barata**
■ *Amer.* **roach**
cocktail ['kokteil] *n.* □ **coquetel**
cocoa ['koukou] *n.* □ **chocolate, cacau**
Would you like a (cup of) cocoa? ◆ Chocolates are made from cocoa.
coconut ['koukənʌt] *n.* □ **coco**
cod [kod] *n.* (*pl.* **cod**) □ **bacalhau**
code [koud] *n.*
1 código
The message was written in code.
2 (= dial[ling] code) **código de área**
What's the code for London?
■ *Amer.* **area code**
3 □ **regulamento**
the Highway Code (= traffic rules) ◆ a code of conduct (= how to behave)
coffee ['kofi] *n.* □ **café**
I had coffee and cake for breakfast. ◆ a cup of coffee. ◆ Two coffees, please. ◆ black coffee (without milk).
coffee break ['kofi 'breik] *n.* □ **coffee break, intervalo**
to take a coffee break.
coffee shop ['kofi ˌʃop] *n.* (= café) □ **cafeteria, cantina, lanchonete**
coffin ['kofin] *n.* □ **caixão**
coil[1] [koil] *n.* □ **rolo**
coils of smoke. ◆ a coil of rope.
coil[2] *v.* (**coils, coiling, coiled**) □ **enrolar**
The snake coiled itself round the branch. ◆ to coil a rope.
coin [koin] *n.* □ **moeda**
gold coins. ◆ a ten-cent coin.
coincidence [kou'insidəns] *n.* □ **coincidência**
What a coincidence! I'm going to India, too.
by coincidence □ **por coincidência**
By coincidence, they were there at the same time.
cold[1] [kould] *adj.*
1 frio
a cold wind. ◆ It's cold outside. ◆ hot and cold water.
2 frio
My hands are cold. ◆ Your tea is getting cold.
3 frio
a cold welcome. ◆ a cold person.
I'm cold, I feel cold □ **eu estou com frio, eu sinto frio**
I'm cold. May I have another blanket?
cold[2] *n.*
1 frio
I came back inside quickly because of the cold.
2 resfriado
I've got a cold.
catch (a) cold □ **pegar um resfriado**
I caught a bad cold.
coldly ['kouldli] *adv.* □ **friamente**
He looked at me coldly.
coldness ['kouldnis] *n.*
1 frieza
the coldness of the water.

2 frieza
His coldness made us feel unwelcome.
collapse[1] [kə'laps] *v.* (**collapses, collapsing, collapsed**) ◻ **desabar**
The bridge / building collapsed. ♦ He collapsed at the end of the marathon race.
collapse[2] *n.* ◻ **colapso**
collar ['kolə] *n.*
1 gola, colarinho
The collar of my shirt is too tight.
2 coleira
Is there a name on the dog's collar?
colleague ['koli:g] *n.* ◻ **colega**
collect[1] [kə'lekt] *v.* (**collects, collecting, collected**)
1 juntar
We collected wood for the fire.
2 colecionar
She collects stamps / coins.
3 pegar
I have to collect my child from school.
collect[2] *adj., adv. Amer.* (Ver **call collect**) ◻ **a cobrar**
a collect call. ♦ to call collect.
■ Compare:
a reverse charge call = ◻ **uma ligação a cobrar.**
reverse the charges = ◻ **fazer ligação a cobrar.**
collection [kə'lekʃən] *n.*
1 coleção
a collection of paintings. ♦ a stamp collection.
2 coleta
The rubbish collection begins early in the morning.
collective [kə'lektiv] *adj.* ◻ **coletivo**
It was a collective decision.
collector [kə'lektə] *n.* ◻ **colecionador**
a stamp collector.
college ['kolidʒ] *n.* ◻ **faculdade**
I graduated from college last year. ♦ a College of Education. ♦ I'm going to college next year.
collide [kə'laid] *v.* (**collides, colliding, collided**) ◻ **colidir**
The two cars collided. ♦ The car collided with a bus.
collision [kə'liʒən] *n.* ◻ **colisão**
The drivers were killed in the collision. ♦ There was a collision between two planes.
■ Ver **head-on**.
colon ['koulən] *n.* ◻ **cólon**
colonel ['kə:nl] *n.* ◻ **coronel**
colony ['koləni] *n.* (*pl.* **colonies**) ◻ **colônia**
Kenya was one of the British colonies in Africa.
color[1] ['kʌlə] *n. Amer.,* **colour** *Brit.* ◻ **cor**
What color is your car? ♦ Red, blue, green and yellow are colours.
■ Compare:
paint = for walls, and paintings, etc.
dye = for hair and clothing.
color[2] *v. Amer.* (**colors, coloring, colored**), **colour** *Brit.* (**colours, colouring, coloured**) ◻ **colorir**
The children coloured their drawings with crayons.
■ Compare:
paint = with a brush.
dye = hair, clothing.
color-blind ['kʌlə blaind] *adj. Amer.,* **colour blind** *Brit.* ◻ **daltônico**

colored ['kʌləd] *adj. Amer.,* **coloured** *Brit.* ◻ **colorido**
coloured chalks / pencils. ♦ coloured paper.
colorful ['kʌləful] *adj. Amer.,* **colourful** *Brit.* ◻ **colorido**
The garden was full of colourful flowers. ♦ colorful posters.
column ['koləm] *n.*
1 coluna
stone columns.
2 coluna
This page has two columns. ♦ You'll find the story (in the newspaper) on p. 6, column 5.
comb[1] [koum] *n.* ◻ **pente**
comb[2] *v.* (**combs, combing, combed**) ◻ **pentear**
Comb your hair.
combat ['kombat] *n.* ◻ **combate**
He was killed in combat. ♦ armed combat.
combat boots ['kombat 'bu:ts] *n. pl.* ◻ **coturno**
combination [kəmbi'neiʃən] *n.*
1 combinação
The city is a combination of old and new (buildings). ♦ His money, in combination with her influence, will help us very much.
2 segredo
I can't open the safe. I can't remember the combination.
combination lock [kəmbi'neiʃən ,lok] *n.* ◻ **cadeado com combinação**
combine [kəm'bain] *v.* (**combines, combining, combined**)
1 combinar
Is it possible to combine business with pleasure? ♦ They combined their money for the project.
2 unir-se
They combined against their competitor.
combined [kəm'baind] *adj.* ◻ **combinado, em conjunto**
Thanks to the combined efforts of all the workers, we finished the job on time.
come [kʌm] *v.* (**comes, coming, came, come**)
1 vir
Come here! ♦ Are you coming (with us)? ♦ Don't come near me!
2 vir, chegar
What time did she come? ♦ The train came late.
3 ocorrer
His success came as a surprise to us.
4 vir
The letter B comes after A.
come about ◻ **acontecer, ocorrer**
How did the accident come about?
■ Ver **happen; take place**.
come across ◻ **deparar com**
I came across this book in the storeroom. ♦ I came across an old friend at Dan's party.
come along
1 vir
Come along, it's getting late.
2 vir junto
We asked her to come along (with us).
come apart ◻ **desmontar**
When I picked up the chair, it came apart in my hands.
come back (= return) ◻ **voltar, retornar**
She'll never come back.
come back to ◻ **voltar**

I can't remember his name at the moment, but it will come back to me.
come by
1 conseguir
How did you come by this beautiful picture?
2 aparecer, chegar
I'll come by at 8 o'clock.
come down
1 descer
He came down the hill at full speed.
2 baixar
Prices did not come down last year.
3 (= collapse) **desabar**
The roof came down suddenly.
come from
1 ser de
My parents came from Turkey. ◆ Where do you come from?
2 vir de
Where is the noise coming from?
come in ▫ **entrar**
May I come in? ◆ He came into the office with his dog.
come off ▫ **soltar-se**
A button came off my shirt.
come on
1 vir
Come on, we'll be late.
2 acender
A warning light came on.
come out
1 sair
Come out with your hands up!
2 ser publicado
Her first novel came out in 1987.
3 aparecer, vir à tona
The truth will come out soon.
come out of ▫ **sair de**
When did he come out of prison? ◆ He will come out of hiding soon.
come true ▫ **virar realidade, realizar-se**
Her dream of becoming a doctor came true at last.
come up ▫ **surgir**
This question did not come up at the meeting.
come up to ▫ **chegar até**
The water came up to her neck.
to come ▫ **que está por vir, vindouro**
He will be a famous scientist in years to come.
comedian [kəˈmiːdiən] *n.* ▫ **comediante**
comedy [ˈkomədi] *n.* (*pl.* **comedies**) ▫ **comédia**
comfort[1] [ˈkʌmfət] *n.*
1 conforto
to live in comfort.
2 conforto
He finds comfort in his faith. ◆ It's a comfort to know that she is out of danger.
3 alívio
She is a comfort to her parents.
comforts *n. pl.* ▫ **comodidades**
a hotel with all the comforts.
comfort[2] *v.* (**comforts, comforting, comforted**) ▫ **confortar, consolar**
We came to comfort him in his hour of sorrow. ◆ to comfort a crying child.

comfortable [ˈkʌmfətəbl] *adj.*
1 confortável
This chair is not comfortable. ◆ comfortable clothes.
2 à vontade, confortável
Make yourself comfortable. ◆ I don't feel comfortable in this weather.
■ antônimo: **uncomfortable**
■ Compare with **convenient**:
convenient = suitable (time, place).
comfortably [ˈkʌmfətəbli] *adv.* ▫ **confortavelmente**
He was comfortably dressed. ◆ to sleep comfortably
comic[1] [ˈkomik] *adj.* ▫ **cômico, divertido**
a comic song. ◆ a comic actor.
comic[2] *n.*
1 humorista
He is a comic.
2 (= comic book) ▫ **revista em quadrinhos, gibi**
comical [ˈkomikəl] *adj.* ▫ **cômico, engraçado**
a comical hat
comics [ˈkomiks] *n.* ▫ **revista em quadrinhos, gibi**
I like reading comics.
comma [ˈkomə] *n.* ▫ **vírgula**
command[1] [kəˈmaːnd] *n.*
1 comando, ordem
They obeyed the officer's commands. ◆ He gave the command to attack.
2 comando
Who is in command of this force? ◆ He took command when the captain died.
command[2] *v.* (**commands, commanding, commanded**) ▫ **mandar, ordenar**
The officer commanded his men to attack.
■ The more usual word is **order**.
commander [kəˈmaːndə] *n.* ▫ **comandante**
comment[1] [ˈkoment] *n.*
1 (= remark) ▫ **comentário**
She made some nice comments about my new clothes.
2 Sem comentário!
'No comment!', he said to the reporters.
comment[2] *v.* (**comments, commenting, commented**) ▫ **comentar**
'This is not what I expected', she commented. ◆ The minister was asked to comment on the scandal.
commentary [ˈkoməntəri] *n.* (*pl.* **commentaries**) ▫ **comentário**
They listened to the radio commentary on the race.
commentator [ˈkoməntətə] *n.* ▫ **comentarista**
a sports commentator.
commerce [ˈkoməːs] *n.* ▫ **comércio**
commercial[1] [kəˈməːʃəl] *adj.* ▫ **comercial**
a commercial vehicle. ◆ a course in commercial English.
commercial[2] *n.* ▫ **comercial, vinheta publicitária**
TV commercials.
■ Ver **ad; advertisement**.
commit [kəˈmit] *v.* (**commits, committing, committed**) ▫ **cometer**
to commit murder / a crime. ◆ He committed suicide. (= He killed himself.)
committee [kəˈmiti] *n.* ▫ **comitê**
The committee came to the conclusion that...
common [ˈkomən] *adj.*
1 comum

Kangaroos are very common in Australia. ✦ a common Spanish custom. ✦ 'Big' is a very common word. ✦ These problems are common to all teenagers. ✦ All of us here have a common goal.
2 vulgar
an unpleasant, common person, with no culture.
have something in common □ **ter algo em comum**
They have a lot in common. ✦ We have nothing in common. ✦ What do these words have in common?
common sense ['komən sens] *n.* □ **bom senso**
Use your common sense. We can't leave him here alone.
communicate [kə'mju:nikeit] *v.* (**communicates, communicating, communicated**) □ **comunicar-se**
They communicated by radio. ✦ They communicate with me by fax.
communication [kə,mju:ni'keiʃən] *n.* □ **comunicação**
I don't speak French very well, so we had communication problems. ✦ Communication with the pilot was cut off. ✦ Television is an important means of communication.
communications *n.* □ **comunicações**
Communications were bad during the storm. ✦ a communications satellite.
community [kə'mju:nəti] *n.* (*pl.* **communities**) □ **comunidade**
the Irish and the Black communities in New York.
community center [kə'mju:nəti 'sentə] *n. Amer.*, **community centre** *Brit.* □ **centro comunitário**
commute [kə'mju:t] *v.* (**commutes, commuting, commuted**) □ **viajar diariamente para trabalhar**
I'm tired of commuting from my home village to the city every day.
commuter [kə'mju:tə] *n.* □ **pessoa que viaja diariamente para trabalhar**
compact disc [kəm'pakt 'disk] *n.* (= CD) □ **CD**
compact disc player *n.* □ **aparelho de CD, CD player**
companion [kəm'panjən] *n.* □ **companheiro**
my companions on the trip
company ['kʌmpəni] *n.* (*pl.* **companies**)
1 companhia, empresa
an insurance company. ✦ The company lost 5 million dollars.
2 companhia
I enjoy their company. ✦ We're expecting company (= visitors).
3 companhia militar
a company of soldiers
keep someone company □ **fazer companhia a alguém**
We kept him company until his parents came.
comparative [kəm'parətiv] *n., adj.* □ **comparativo**
'Stronger' is the comparative (form) of 'strong'.
■ Ver **superlative**.
compare [kəm'peə] *v.* (**compares, comparing, compared**) □ **comparar**
Compare the two meanings. ✦ He compared his answers with mine.
compared [kəm'peəd] *adj.* □ **comparado**
Compared to / with my computer, mine is very slow.
comparison [kəm'parisən] *n.* □ **comparação**
She made a comparison between the two styles. ✦ A bicycle is very slow in comparison to / with a car.
compartment [kəm'pa:tmənt] *n.*
1 cabine
a first-class compartment (on a train)
2 compartimento
a secret compartment in a suitcase. ✦ the glove compartment (in a car).
compass ['kʌmpəs] *n.*
1 bússola
You'll need a compass and a map to find your way in the desert.
2 (= compasses) **compasso**
to draw a circle with (a pair of) compasses
compel [kəm'pel] *v.* (**compels, compelling, compelled**) □ **obrigar**
He compelled them to work ten hours a day. ✦ He was compelled to do it.
■ The noun is **compulsion**.
compensate ['kompənseit] *v.* (**compensates, compensating, compensated**) □ **compensar**
The insurance company compensated him for the damage.
compensation [,kompen'seiʃən] *n.* □ **compensação**
compete [kəm'pi:t] *v.* (**competes, competing, competed**) □ **competir**
to compete in a race ✦ She is competing for the gold medal. ✦ Our company can't compete with the big companies.
competition [kompə'tiʃən] *n.* □ **competição**
a chess / sports competition. ✦ to take part in a competition. ✦ There's strong competition between the two companies.
■ Ver **contest**.
competitive [kəm'petətiv] *adj.* □ **competitivo**
a competitive sport.
competitor [kəm'petitə] *n.* □ **competidor**
complain [kəm'plein] *v.* (**complains, complaining, complained**) □ **reclamar, queixar-se**
Stop complaining! ✦ They complained to the teacher about Tony. ✦ She complained about the noise.
complaint [kəm'pleint] *n.* □ **reclamação**
a letter of complaint. ✦ Write to the manager if you have any complaints. ✦ to make a complaint (= to complain).
complement ['kompləmənt] *v.* (**complements, complementing, complemented**) □ **complementar**
Your shoes complement your dress – they go well together.
■ Do not confuse with **compliment**.
complete[1] [kəm'pli:t] *adj.*
1 completo
a complete list.
■ antônimo: **incomplete**
2 (= finished) **terminado**
The work on the project is complete.
3 total
a complete stranger. ✦ It was a complete surprise.
complete[2] *v.* (**completes, completing, completed**) □ **completar, terminar**
Complete the sentences (in this exercise). ✦ The project will be completed next month. ✦ I need one more stamp to complete the collection.
completely [kəm'pli:tli] *adv.* □ **totalmente, completamente**
I completely forgot to send it. ✦ He was completely bald.
complex[1] ['kompleks] *adj.* □ **complexo, complicado**
a complex problem / subject.
complex[2] *n.* □ **complexo**
A sports complex has a stadium, swimming pools, etc.

complicate ['komplikeit] *v.* (**complicates, complicating, complicated**) □ **complicar**
to complicate the situation

complicated ['komplikeitid] *adj.* □ **complicado**
It's too complicated to explain how it works. ◆ a complicated situation.

complication ['komplikeiʃən] *n.* □ **complicação**

compliment[1] ['kompləmənt] *n.* □ **elogio**
pay someone a compliment □ **fazer um elogio a alguém**
The teacher paid him a compliment on his good work.

compliment[2] *v.* (**compliments, complimenting, complimented**) □ **elogiar**
She complimented us for working as a team. ◆ I complimented her on her new hairstyle.
■ Do not confuse with **complement**.

complimentary ['komplə'mentəri] *adj.*
1 complementar
The speaker made some complimentary remarks before he began his lecture.
2 (= free) □ **gratuito**
a complimentary ticket to the concert.

component [kəm'pounənt] *n.* □ **componente**
the components of the machine.

compose [kəm'pouz] *v.* (**composes, composing, composed**) □ **compor**
to compose a poem. ◆ Who composed this opera?
be composed of □ **ser composto de**
Water is composed of oxygen and hydrogen. ◆ The committee is composed of a judge and two professors.

composer [kəm'pouzə] *n.* □ **compositor**
Mozart and Bach were famous composers.

composition [kompə'ziʃən] *n.* □ **redação**
Write a composition of 200 words.

compound noun ['kompaund 'naun] *n.* □ **substantivo composto**
The words 'blackboard' and 'mother-in-law' are compound nouns.

comprehension [,kompri'henʃən] *n.* □ **compreensão**
a test in reading and listening comprehension.

comprehensive ['kompri'hensiv] *adj.* □ **abrangente**
a comprehensive book on grammar.

comprehensive school [,kompri'hensiv sku:l] *n.* □ **escola inclusiva**

compromise[1] ['komprəmaiz] *n.* □ **meio-termo, acordo**
They reached a compromise after arguing for an hour.

compromise[2] *v.* (**compromises, compromising, compromised**) □ **chegar a um acordo**
They compromised on the price

compulsion [kəm'pʌlʃən] *n.* □ **compulsão**
He did it under compulsion.

compulsory [kəm'pʌlsəri] *adj.* □ **obrigatório, compulsório**
Is geography a compulsory subject? ◆ In some countries, military service is compulsory.
■ antônimo: **optional**

computer [kəm'pju:tə] *n.* □ **computador**
The whole process is done by computer. ◆ PC means 'personal computer'. ◆ a computer game. ◆ a computer program.

computer-literate [kəm'pju:tə 'litərət] *adj.* □ **alfabetizado digital**
Most young people today are computer-literate – they know a lot about computers and how to use them.

computerize [kəm'pju:təraiz] *v.* (**computerizes, computerizing, computerized**), **computarise** *Brit.* □ **informatizar**
to computerize the library / school records.

computerized [kəm'pju:təraizd] *adj.* □ **informatizado**
The factory is completely computerized.

conceal [kən'si:l] *v.* (**conceals, concealing, concealed**) (= hide) □ **esconder, ocultar**
He tried to conceal his disappointment. ◆ He concealed the gun under his coat.

conceited [kən'si:tid] *adj.* □ **convencido, vaidoso**

concentrate ['konsəntreit] *v.* (**concentrates, concentrating, concentrated**) □ **concentrar-se**
I can't concentrate with all this noise. ◆ Concentrate on your driving!

concentration ['konsəntreiʃən] *n.* □ **concentração**
He lost his concentration because of your jokes. ◆ a concentration camp.

concern[1] [kən'sə:n] *n.*
1 conta
It's not my concern. Let him solve his own problems.
2 preocupação
There's no cause for concern. The danger is over.

concern[2] *v.* (**concerns, concerning, concerned**)
1 dizer respeito a
It does not concern me and I will not interfere in this matter.
2 envolver
The letter concerns you.
3 preocupar-se
The report concerns the problems of air pollution. ◆ The book is concerned with teaching methods.
4 preocupar
What concerns me most is the rise in violence among youth.

concerned [kən'sə:nd] *adj.* □ **preocupado**
They are concerned about his future.
as far as I'm concerned □ **no que me diz respeito**
You can use it, as far as I'm concerned.

concerning [kən'sə:niŋ] *prep.* □ **referente a**
I'm writing to you concerning your complaint. ◆ There's new information concerning the accident.

concert ['konsət] *n.* □ **show, concerto, apresentação**
a rock concert.

concise [kən'sais] *adj.* □ **conciso**
a concise summary.

conclude [kən'klu:d] *v.* (**concludes, concluding, concluded**)
1 concluir
They concluded that it was my fault.
2 concluir, terminar
He concluded his show with a song.

conclusion [kən'klu:ʒən] *n.* □ **conclusão**
to come to the conclusion (= conclude) that...
in conclusion □ **para terminar**
And in conclusion, I wish to thank you all for coming to my party.

concrete[1] ['konkri:t] *adj.* □ **concreto**
concrete objects (e.g. a pen, a chair).

concrete[2] *n.* □ **concreto**
The roof was made of concrete.

condemn [kən'dem] *v.* (**condemns, condemning, condemned**)
1 condenar
We should all condemn acts of violence.

2 condenar
The judge condemned the robber to 10 years in prison. ◆ The murderer was condemned to death.
condemnation [kondem'neiʃən] *n.* □ **condenação**
condition¹ [kən'diʃən] *n.*
1 estado
The roads are in good condition. ◆ The patient's condition is better.
2 condição
He made a condition that we couldn't accept. ◆ We have to pay in advance. This is one of their conditions.
on condition that □ **com a condição de (que)**
You can take the car on condition that you drive carefully.
■ on condition that you **drive** (*not* 'that you will drive').
conditions *n. pl.* □ **condições**
I don't like driving in bad weather conditions. ◆ The conditions in prison were terrible.
condition² *v.* (**conditions, conditioning, conditioned**)
1 condicionar
These soldiers are conditioned to react quickly.
2 condicionar (produtos cosméticos)
a cream that conditions the skin.
conditional [kən'diʃənəl] *adj.* □ **condicional**
His agreement to help is conditional on your cooperation.
conditional clause [kən'diʃənəl 'klo:z] *n.* □ **oração condicional**
condolences [kən'doulənsiz] *n. pl.* □ **condolências, pêsames**
Please accept my condolences (on the death of your wife).
conduct¹ ['kondʌkt] *n.* (= behavior / behaviour) □ **conduta**
conduct² *v.* (**conducts, conducting, conducted**)
1 realizar
to conduct an investigation.
2 conduzir
She conducted the tourists around the museum.
3 reger
The orchestra was conducted by a famous conductor.
conductor [kən'dʌktə] *n.*
1 maestro
The conductor at tonight's concert is...
2 cobrador
The conductor asked to see my ticket.
cone [koun] *n.*
1 cone
A clown's hat is in the shape of a cone.
2 casquinha de sorvete
an ice-cream cone.
3 pinha
A cone is the fruit of a pine or fir tree.
confer [kən'fɜ:] *v.* (**confers, conferring, conferred**) □ **debater, discutir**
to confer with a lawyer.
conference ['konfərəns] *n.* □ **conferência, palestra**
a conference on computer technology.
confess [kən'fes] *v.* (**confesses, confessing, confessed**)
1 confessar, admitir
He confessed that he was a criminal. ◆ She confessed to the crime.
■ Ver **admit**.
2 confessar, admitir
I must confess (that) I was scared.

confession [kən'feʃən] *n.* □ **confissão**
He made a confession of his crimes to the police.
confidence ['konfidəns] *n.*
1 confiança
He doesn't have enough confidence to speak English. ◆ She was full of confidence.
2 (= trust) confiança
He lost his confidence in them. ◆ I have complete confidence in him.
in confidence □ **em confidência**
I'm telling you this in confidence.
confident ['konfidənt] *adj.* □ **confiante**
He is confident (that) they will win. ◆ She is a very self-confident teacher.
confidential ['konfidənʃəl] *n.* □ **confidencial**
This letter is confidential.
confidently ['konfidəntli] *adv.* □ **confiantemente, com confiança**
She smiled confidently.
confirm [kən'fɜ:m] *v.* (**confirms, confirming, confirmed**) □ **confirmar**
This letter confirms my suspicions. ◆ He refused to confirm or deny the rumours. ◆ I must telephone to confirm my flight. ◆ He wrote to confirm the date of his arrival.
confirmation [,konfə'meiʃən] *n.* □ **confirmação**
Did you get a confirmation of our flight?
conflict¹ ['konflikt] *n.* □ **conflito**
The peace treaty between the two countries ended a conflict of 100 years.
conflict² [kən'flikt] *v.* (**conflicts, conflicting, conflicted**) □ **conflitar, divergir**
His story conflicted with the police report.
confuse [kən'fju:z] *v.* (**confuses, confusing, confused**)
1 confundir
He confused me with all those questions.
2 confundir
I think you're confusing me with someone else. ◆ Don't confuse the words 'peace' and 'piece'.
confused [kən'fju:zd] *adj.* □ **confuso**
I'm confused. ◆ His story was a little confused.
get confused □ **ficar confuso**
She got confused and gave us the wrong key.
confusing [kən'fju:ziŋ] *adj.* □ **confuso**
The instructions are not clear enough. In fact, they are quite confusing.
confusion [kən'fju:ʒən] *n.*
1 confusão
There was some confusion about the dates.
2 confusão
In all the confusion, the robbers escaped.
congratulate [kən'gratjuleit] *v.* (**congratulates, congratulating, congratulated**) □ **parabenizar**
I congratulated them on their marriage. ◆ I congratulated her on winning the medal.
congratulations [kən,gratju'leiʃənz] *n. pl.* □ **parabéns**
Congratulations on your success. ◆ Please give them my congratulations.
conjunction [kən'dʒʌnkʃən] *n.* □ **conjunção**
The words 'and', 'but', 'because' and 'if' are conjunctions.
■ abreviação: **conj.**
conjurer ['kʌndʒərə] *n.*, **conjuror** □ **mágico**
The conjurer made the rabbit disappear.
■ Ver **magician**.

connect [kə'nekt] *v.* (**connects, connecting, connected**)
1 conectar, ligar
He connected the electric wires. ◆ The two towns are connected by a bridge.
2 passar a ligação
Hold on, please. I'll connect you with the manager.
connection [kə'nekʃən] *n.*
1 conexão
Is there a connection between the two events? ◆ There's no connection between his illness and his eating habits.
2 ligação
I couldn't hear him very well because of a bad connection.
3 baldeação
The bus / train was late so I missed my connection.
in connection with □ **com relação a**
I'm writing to you in connection with your complaint.
connections *n. pl.* **relações**
He has good connections with the Minister.
conquer ['kɔŋkə] *v.* (**conquers, conquering, conquered**)
□ **conquistar**
The Germans conquered most of Europe in the Second World War.
conquest ['kɔŋkwest] *n.* □ **conquista**
conscience ['kɔnʃəns] *n.* □ **consciência**
have a clear conscience □ **ter a consciência tranquila**
I did what I had to do. I have a clear conscience.
have a guilty conscience □ **ter a consciência pesada**
He has a guilty conscience because he didn't warn them.
conscientious [kɔnʃi'enʃəs] *adj.* □ **consciencioso**
a conscientious pupil.
conscious ['kɔnʃəs] *adj.*
1 consciente
The patient was conscious during the operation.
■ antônimo: **unconscious**
2 (= aware) **ciente**
She was conscious (of the fact) that she had to act.
consciousness ['kɔnʃəsnis] *n.* □ **consciência**
He lost consciousness.
conscript[1] ['kɔnskript] *n.* □ **conscrito, recruta**
conscript[2] *v.* (**conscripts, conscripting, conscripted**)
□ **recrutar**
The army conscripts all young men of 18.
■ Ver **call up, draft**[2]**, join up**
conscription [kən'skripʃən] *n.* □ **recrutamento**
consent [kən'sent] *n.* □ **consentimento**
The patient gave his consent to the operation.
consequence ['kɔnsikwəns] *n.* □ **consequência**
I got up late, and as a consequence I missed the bus.
■ Ver **result**.
consequences ['kɔnsikwənsiz] *n. pl.* □ **consequências**
The failure had terrible consequences.
consequently ['kɔnsikwəntli] *adv.* □ **consequentemente**
The teachers were on strike, and consequently the exams were postponed.
conservation [kɔnsə'veiʃən] *n.* □ **conservação**
Conservation means the protection of forests, animals, etc.
conservative [kən'sə:vətiv] *adj., n.* □ **conservador**
My father has conservative ideas about politics. He is a conservative.
consider [kən'sidə] *v.* (**considers, considering, considered**)
1 ponderar
We will consider your ideas. ◆ I'm considering selling the house.
2 levar em conta
We have to consider the children and not just ourselves.
3 (= reckon) **considerar**
They are considered (to be) good parents. ◆ I do not consider this book suitable for children.
considerable [kən'sidərəbl] *adj.* □ **considerável**
a considerable amount of money. ◆ I had considerable difficulty in finding the place.
considerably [kən'sidərəbli] *adv.* □ **consideravelmente**
Our team is considerably stronger than yours.
considerate [kən'sidərət] *adj.* □ **atencioso**
Please be considerate towards the other guests.
■ antônimo: **inconsiderate**
consideration [kən,sidə'reiʃən] *n.*
1 ponderação
After much consideration, he decided to sell the business.
2 respeito
Don't make so much noise. Show some consideration for the neighbours.
3 consideração
One of the considerations for accepting the job is the high salary.
take into consideration □ **levar em consideração**
We'll take all these facts into consideration.
considering [kən'sidəriŋ] *prep., conj.* □ **em vista de, considerando-se que**
Considering that she was ill, she did a good job.
consist (of) [kən'sist (ov)] *v.* (**consists, consisting, consisted**) □ **consistir em, compor-se de**
The class consists of 13 girls and 12 boys. ◆ The book consists of 12 units.
■ Ver **be composed of**.
■ Compare with **include, contain**:
consist of = altogether.
include, contain = part of the whole.
consistent [kən'sistənt] *adj.* □ **consistente**
Sometimes you write 'colour' and sometimes 'color'. Be consistent!
■ antônimo: **inconsistent**
consolation [,kɔnsə'leiʃən] *n.* □ **consolação**
It was a consolation to know that no one was hurt
console [kən'səul] *v.* (**consoles, consoling, consoled**)
□ **consolar**
They tried to console the parents of the dead child.
consonant ['kɔnsənənt] *n.* □ **consoante**
Letters that are not vowels (= a, e, i, o, u) are consonants.
◆ The sounds /b/ and /k/ are consonants.
conspicuous [kən'spikjuəs] *adj.* □ **conspícuo, evidente, visível**
His scar was very conspicuous.
conspiracy [kən'spirəsi] *n.* (= plot) □ **conspiração**
There was a conspiracy to kill the king.
conspirator [kən'spireitə] *n.* □ **conspirador**
constable ['kʌnstəbl] *n. Brit.* (= policeman) □ **guarda, policial**
constant ['kɔnstənt] *adj.*
1 constante
They live in constant fear. ◆ There were constant interruptions during his speech.

2 constante
a constant speed.
constantly ['kɒnstəntli] *adv.* ▫ **constantemente**
The weather is constantly changing.
constitution [,kɒnsti'tju:ʃən] *n.* ▫ **constituição**
the Constitution of the United States.
construct [kən'strʌkt] *v.* (**constructs, constructing, constructed**) (= build) ▫ **construir**
to construct a bridge.
construction [kən'strʌkʃən] *n.*
1 construção
The construction of the palace took 5 years.
2 construção
That tower is a beautiful construction.
construction worker [kən'strʌkʃən ,wɜːkə] *n.* ▫ **operário da construção**
constructive [kən'strʌktiv] *adj.* ▫ **construtivo**
constructive talks / suggestions.
consul ['kɒnsəl] *n.* ▫ **cônsul**
consult [kən'sʌlt] *v.* (**consults, consulting, consulted**)
1 consultar
You should consult a doctor before going on a diet. ◆ to consult a dictionary / map.
2 consultar
He consulted with his parents about the deal.
consultant [kən'sʌltənt] *n.* ▫ **consultor**
a computer / business consultant.
consultation [,kɒnsəl'teiʃən] *n.* ▫ **consulta**
consume [kən'sju:m] *v.* (**consumes, consuming, consumed**) ▫ **consumir**
It is not advisable to consume too much sugar. ◆ This car consumes very little fuel.
consumer [kən'sju:mə] *n.* ▫ **consumidor**
We advise consumers to compare prices before buying.
consumption [kən'sʌmpʃən] *n.* ▫ **consumo**
There is an increase in the consumption of milk. ◆ The fuel consumption of this car is very high.
contact[1] ['kɒntakt] *n.*
1 contato
There's no contact between the wires.
2 contato
We wrote to each other for a year and then I lost contact with her. ◆ I made contact with our agent in Paris.
contact[2] *v.* (**contacts, contacting, contacted**) ▫ **entrar em contato com, comunicar-se com**
I contacted him by telephone. ◆ If you have any information, please contact the police.
contact lens ['kɒntakt 'lenz] *n.* (*pl.* **contact lenses**) ▫ **lentes de contato**
I wear contact lenses.
contagious [kən'teidʒəs] *adj.* ▫ **contagioso**
a contagious disease.
contain [kən'tein] *v.* (**contains, containing, contained**)
1 conter
The wallet contained 100 dollars. ◆ This bottle contains 1 litre of oil. ◆ This drink does not contain sugar.
2 conter
The book contains a chapter on drugs. ◆ The book contains 12 chapters.
■ Ver **include, consist of**.
container [kən'teinə] *n.*
1 recipiente
Boxes, bags, and barrels are all containers.
2 contêiner
They are loading the containers onto the ship.
contempt [kən'tempt] *n.* (= scorn) ▫ **desprezo**
He felt contempt for us.
content[1] [kən'tent] *adj.* ▫ **contente, feliz**
He is content with his salary.
content[2] ['kɒntent] *n.* ▫ **conteúdo**
For the content (of the composition) you get 5 points.
contented [kən'tentid] *adj.* (= satisfied) ▫ **satisfeito**
contented workers. ◆ a contented smile.
■ antônimo: **discontented**
contents ['kɒntents] *n.*
1 conteúdo, teor
the contents of a bag / bottle / room.
2 sumário
You'll find the table of contents at the beginning of the book.
■ Ver **content**[2].
contest ['kɒntest] *n.* ▫ **concurso, campeonato**
a beauty contest. ◆ a boxing / dancing contest.
■ Ver **competition**.
contestant ['kɒntestənt] *n.* ▫ **competidor**
■ Ver **competitor**.
context ['kɒntekst] *n.* ▫ **contexto**
Guess the meaning of the word from the context.
continent ['kɒntinənt] *n.* ▫ **continente**
Asia and Africa are continents.
continual [kən'tinjuəl] *adj.*
1 contínuo
They are under continual pressure to finish the job on time. ◆ continual rain / pain.
2 intermitente
There were continual interruptions during the work.
■ Compare with **continuous**:
continuous = without a break.
continual = with breaks.
continually [kən'tinjuəli] *adv.* ▫ **continuamente**
He is continually complaining. ◆ I continually warned them about it.
continuation [kən,tinju'eiʃən] *n.* ▫ **continuação**
We'll hear the continuation of the story tomorrow.
continue [kən'tinju:] *v.* (**continues, continuing, continued**) ▫ **continuar**
They continued to play. ◆ They continued playing. ◆ Let's continue the interview tomorrow. ◆ The meeting continued for 2 hours. ◆ If the rain continues, there will be no games tomorrow. ◆ The path continued to the top of the hill. ◆ They continued along the path until they came to the cave.
continuous[1] [kən'tinjuəs] *adj.*
1 contínuo
a continuous line.
2 contínuo
continuous rain / noise.
■ Ver **continual**.
continuous[2] *n.* (= **progressive**) (**grammar**) ▫ **contínuo**
The present continuous, e.g. 'I am writing'. ◆ the past continuous.
continuously [kən'tinjuəsli] *adv.* ▫ **continuamente**
They worked continuously for 5 hours.

contract[1] ['kontrakt] *n.* □ **contrato**
to sign a contract.

contract[2] *v.* (**contracts, contracting, contracted**) □ **contrair**
In speech, we often contract 'do not' to 'don't'.

contradict [kontrə'dikt] *v.* (**contradicts, contradicting, contradicted**)
1 contradizer
The facts contradict your story. ◆ She contradicted herself.
2 opor-se
Don't contradict your father!

contradiction [,kontrə'dikʃən] *n.* □ **contradição**
There's no contradiction between the two reports. ◆ His actions are in contradiction to our principles.

contradictory [,kontrə'diktəri] *adj.* □ **contraditório**

contrary[1] ['kontrəri] *adj.* □ **contrário**
in contrary directions. ◆ contrary to the doctor's orders.

contrary[2] *n.* □ **contrário**
on the contrary □ **pelo contrário**
I don't hate rock music. On the contrary, I enjoy it very much.

contrast[1] ['kontra:st] *n.* □ **contraste**
This poor neighbourhood is in sharp contrast to the other parts of the city.
in contrast with / to □ **em contraste com/a**
In contrast to the hot days here, the nights are quite cold.
by / in contrast □ **ao contrário, em contraste**
Dan likes rock music, but his brother, in contrast, likes classical music.

contrast[2] [kən'tra:st] *v.* (**contrasts, contrasting, contrasted**) □ **comparar, contrastar**
The book contrasts the technology of the 19th century with modern technology.

contribute [kən'tribjut] *v.* (**contributes, contributing, contributed**) □ **contribuir**
to contribute (money) to charity. ◆ They contributed clothes and blankets for the refugees. ◆ Her help contributed a lot to our success.

contribution [,kontri'bju:ʃən] *n.* □ **contribuição**
He made a contribution of 50 dollars.

control[1] [kən'troul] *n.*
1 controle
The city is under the control of the enemy. ◆ He is in full control of the situation.
2 controle
passport control (at the airport).
lose control (of) □ **perder o controle (de)**
He lost control of the car, and it turned over.
bring something under control □ **conseguir controlar algo**
The firemen managed to bring the fire under control.
be under control □ **estar sob controle**
Don't worry! Everything is under control.

control[2] *v.* (**controls, controlling, controlled**) □ **controlar**
He couldn't control the horse. ◆ Who controls the company?

controls [kən'troulz] *n.* □ **controles**
control tower [kən'troul tauə] *n.* □ **torre de controle**
controversial [kontrə'vəʃəl] *adj.* □ **controverso, polêmico**
a controversial issue.

controversy ['kontrəvəsi] *n.* □ **controvérsia**
convenience [kən'vi:njəns] *n.* □ **conveniência**
For convenience, I pay by credit card.

convenient [kən'vi:njənt] *adj.* □ **conveniente**
I will come when it is convenient for me. ◆ Is this a convenient time for a meeting? ◆ It's very convenient to live near a supermarket.
■ antônimo: **inconvenient**
■ Ver **comfortable**.

convent ['konvənt] *n.* □ **convento**
conversation [konvə'seiʃən] *n.* □ **conversa**
I had an interesting conversation with Mary about computers. ◆ a telephone conversation.

converse [kən'və:s] *v.* (**converses, conversing, conversed**) □ **conversar**
They conversed in Japanese.

convert [kən'və:t] *v.* (**converts, converting, converted**)
1 converter
They converted the house into a restaurant.
2 converter
He converted to Islam.

convict[1] ['konvikt] *n.* □ **condenado, presidiário**
convict[2] *v.* (**convicts, convicting, convicted**) □ **condenar**
He was convicted of murder.

conviction [kən'vikʃən] *n.*
1 condenação
This is her second conviction for stealing.
2 convicção
She spoke with deep conviction. ◆ my political and religious convictions.
■ Ver **convince, convinced**.

convince [kən'vins] *v.* (**convinces, convincing, convinced**) (= persuade) □ **convencer**
She convinced me that it is a good job. ◆ What convinced you to buy it?

convinced [kən'vinst] *adj.* □ **convencido, convicto**
I'm convinced that he is innocent.

convincing [kən'vinsiŋ] *adj.* □ **convincente**
Your speech was very convincing.

convoy ['konvoi] *n.* □ **comboio**
The ships sailed in convoy.

cook[1] [kuk] *n.* □ **cozinheiro**
I work as a cook in a hotel.

cook[2] *v.* (**cooks, cooking, cooked**)
1 cozinhar
What did you cook for supper? ◆ He cooks his own meals.
2 cozinhar
Let the rice cook for 20 minutes.
■ Ver **bake; boil; broil; fry; grill**[2]; **roast**[2]; **toast**[2].

cooked [kukt] *adj.* □ **cozido**
The meat is not properly cooked.
■ antônimo: **raw**

cooker ['kukə] *n.* □ **fogão**
■ Ver **oven; stove**.

cookery ['kukəri] *n.* □ **culinária**
cookery lessons / classes. ◆ a cookery book (= cookbook).

cookie ['kuki] *n. Amer.* □ **biscoito, cookie**
■ *Brit.* **biscuit**

cooking ['kukiŋ] *n.*
1 culinária
I do all the cooking. ◆ cooking oil. ◆ cooking lessons / classes.
2 culinária
Chinese / French cooking.

cool / costume

cool¹ [ku:l] *adj.*
1 fresco
cool weather. ◆ It's cooler in the shade.
2 gelado
a cool drink.
3 (= attractive, great, fashionable) □ **legal, bacana**
I like your new boots – they're really cool!
Keep cool! (= Don't get angry / excited / frightened!) □ **Fica frio!**
cool² *v.* (**cools, cooling, cooled**) □ **resfriar, esfriar, refrescar**
I cooled his forehead with a wet cloth. ◆ Allow the pudding to cool and put it in the refrigerator.
cool down
1 esfriar
Don't drink your tea yet. Let it cool down.
2 acalmar, esfriar a cabeça
Cool down! He is only joking. ◆ It was difficult to cool him down.
cooperate [kou'opəreit] *v.* (**cooperates, cooperating, cooperated**), co-operate □ **cooperar**
The two companies are cooperating in the research. ◆ He refuses to cooperate with the police.
cooperation [kouopə'reiʃən] *n.* □ **cooperação**
Thank you for your cooperation. ◆ It was organized in co-operation with another school.
cooperative [kou'opərətiv] *adj.* □ **cooperativo**
He wasn't very cooperative when I asked him for information.
cop [kop] *n.* (= policeman; policewoman) □ **tira, policial**
The cops caught the robber.
cope [koup] *v.* (**copes, coping, coped**) □ **enfrentar, encarar**
He couldn't cope with his problems at work. ◆ Can you cope with the extra work?
copper ['kopə] *n.* □ **cobre**
copy¹ ['kopi] *n.* (*pl.* **copies**)
1 cópia
He made two copies of the letter. ◆ a copy of a painting.
2 exemplar
They sold ten thousand copies of the dictionary last year.
copy² *v.* (**copies, copying, copied**)
1 copiar, gravar
Copy the questions from the blackboard. ◆ I copied the file onto a floppy disc.
2 colar
How can we prevent copying in exams?
■ The more usual word is **cheat**.
3 (= imitate) **imitar**
This singer is trying to copy Elvis Presley.
cord [ko:d] *n.* □ **cordão**
to tie a parcel with cord
core [ko:] *n.* □ **miolo**
the core of the apple
cork [ko:k] *n.* □ **rolha**
to pull out a cork with a corkscrew
corkscrew ['ko:kskru:] *n.* □ **saca-rolhas**
corn [ko:n] *n.*
1 *Brit.* **grão**
a field of corn (= wheat, oats, etc.).
2 *Amer.* **milho**
■ *Brit.* **maize**

corn on the cob *n.* □ **espiga de milho, milho cozido**
corner ['ko:nə] *n.* □ **canto, esquina**
Put it in the corner. ◆ Meet me at / on the corner of A and B streets. ◆ They live around the corner (= not far from here).
cornflakes ['ko:nfleiks] *n. pl.* □ **flocos de milho**
to have cornflakes for breakfast.
corporal ['ko:pərəl] *n.* □ **cabo**
corporation [,ko:pə'reiʃən] *n.* □ **corporação**
He works for an American corporation.
■ Ver **company**.
corpse [ko:ps] *n.* □ **cadáver**
correct¹ [kə'rekt] *adj.* (= right) □ **correto, certo**
a correct answer. ◆ Is that the correct time?
■ antônimo: **incorrect**
correct² *v.* (**corrects, correcting, corrected**)
1 corrigir
Correct me if I'm wrong, but didn't I ask you to come early? ◆ She corrects us when we make mistakes.
2 corrigir
I corrected your homework / exams.
correction [kə'rekʃən] *n.* □ **correção**
The teacher marked the corrections in red ink.
correctly [kə'rektli] *adv.* □ **corretamente**
I hope I pronounced your name correctly.
correspond [korə'spond] *v.* (**corresponds, corresponding, corresponded**)
1 corresponder
The description you gave corresponds with hers. ◆ The dates on the letter and envelope do not correspond.
2 corresponder-se
I corresponded with her for a long time.
correspondence [,korə'spondəns] *n.* □ **correspondência**
Our correspondence went on for 5 months. ◆ My secretary reads my correspondence (= letters, faxes, etc.).
corridor ['korido:] *n.* □ **corredor**
corrupt¹ [kə'rʌpt] *adj.* □ **corrupto**
a corrupt judge.
corrupt² *v.* (**corrupts, corrupting, corrupted**) □ **corromper**
Some say that television corrupts young people.
corruption [kə'rʌpʃən] *n.* □ **corrupção**
cosmetic [koz'metik] *n.* □ **cosmético**
Lipstick, face cream, etc. are cosmetics.
cost¹ [kost] *n.*
1 custo
The cost of building the bridge came to 1 million dollars. ◆ I'll cover the costs of the trial. ◆ The company had to cut its costs by 20%.
2 custas
He saved the child from the burning house at the cost of his own life.
at all costs □ **custe o que custar, a todo custo**
We must find him at all costs.
cost² *v.* (**costs, costing, cost**) □ **custar**
The camera cost me 100 pounds. ◆ How much did the book cost? ◆ How much does it cost to use this machine? ◆ It costs a lot.
■ **it costs** (*not* 'it's cost').
costly ['kostli] *adj.* □ **custoso, caro**
The operation was very costly. ◆ a costly plan.
■ Ver **expensive**.
costume ['kostju:m] *n.* □ **traje**

the national costume of India. ◆ She makes costumes for the theatre.
■ Ver **swimming costume**.
cosy ['kouzi] *adj. Brit.* (**cosier, cosiest**) (= cozy, *Am.*) □ **aconchegante**
a cosy room / atmosphere.
cot [kot] *n.*
1 *Brit.* **berço**
■ *Amer.* **crib**
2 (= camp bed) *Amer.* **cama de lona**
cottage ['kotidʒ] *n.* □ **chalé**
cotton ['kotn] *n.* □ **algodão**
a cotton shirt. ◆ These socks are made of cotton.
cotton wool ['kotn 'wul] *n.* □ **algodão**
The nurse cleaned the wound with cotton wool.
■ *Amer.* **cotton**
couch [kautʃ] *n.* (= sofa) **sofá**
He was lying on the couch.
cough[1] [kof] *n.* □ **tosse**
Coughs and sneezes spread diseases.
cough[2] *v.* (**coughs, coughing, coughed**) □ **tossir**
The smoke made him cough.
could [kud] *v.*
1 conseguir
When I was young, I could swim fast. ◆ I looked for the ring, but I couldn't find it.
■ In this meaning **was / were able to** means the same as **could**.
2 poder
I could hear (= I heard) him shouting. ◆ We could smell something burning.
3 poder
She said (that) she couldn't come.
4 (= might) **poderia**
It could be true. ◆ It could rain tomorrow. ◆ Could you help me, please? ◆ Could I talk to you for a moment?
could have (done) □ **poderia ter**
Dan could have broken it. (= It is possible that Dan broke it.) ◆ He couldn't have done it. ◆ He could have killed you. ◆ I could have left early, but I didn't.
council ['kounsəl] *n.* □ **conselho, câmara**
the student council. ◆ the town council.
counselling ['kounsəliŋ] *n.*, **counseling** *Amer.* □ **aconselhamento**
Students who need counselling can see the counsellor today.
counsellor ['kounsələ] *n.*, **counselor** *Amer.* □ **conselheiro**
a student counsellor.
■ Do not confuse with **councillor** (= a member of a council).
count[1] [kaunt] *n.*, **Count** □ **conde**
count[2] *n.* □ **conta**
He got 212 votes by my count.
lose count (of) □ **perder a conta (de)**
I lost count of the number of points she scored.
count[3] *v.* (**counts, counting, counted**)
1 contar
count from one to ten ◆ He counted the money.
2 levar em consideração
You won because she helped you, so it doesn't count.
count on (= rely on) □ **contar com**
You can count on me. ◆ I'm counting on your help.

cosy / course

(not) counting □ **(sem) contar**
There are 150 guests, not counting the children.
countable ['kauntəbl] *adj.* □ **contável**
A countable noun is a noun that you can count, like 'chair', 'pen' and 'book'.
■ A countable noun is used with words that show numbers, such as **a**, **an** or **many**, and with numbers:
a book; an egg; many books; two pens.
■ antônimo: **uncountable**
counter ['kauntə] *n.* □ **balcão**
The barman put the beer on the counter. ◆ The clerk behind the counter was counting the money.
counterclockwise ['kauntə'klokwaiz] *adj., adv. Amer.* □ **sentido anti-horário**
Turn the wheel counterclockwise.
■ *Brit.* **anticlockwise**
■ antônimo: **clockwise**
countess ['kauntis] *n.* □ **condessa**
countless ['kauntlis] *adj.* □ **incontável**
There were countless mistakes in the report.
country ['kʌntri] *n.* (*pl.* **countries**) □ **país**
Germany, Spain and France are countries. ◆ What is the population of this country?
■ Ver **state; nation**.
the country □ **o campo**
They live in the country.
countryside ['kʌntrisaid] *n.* □ **área rural, interior, campo**
county ['kaunti] *n.* (*pl.* **counties**) □ **comarca, condado**
couple ['kʌpl] *n.* □ **casal, par**
married couples.
a couple of
1 alguns
I need a couple of men to help me.
2 (= a few) **alguns**
I asked him for a couple of dollars. ◆ We had to wait for a couple of minutes.
coupon ['ku:pon] *n.* □ **cupom**
Cut out the coupon in the newspaper ad.
courage ['kʌridʒ] *n.* (= bravery) □ **coragem, bravura**
She showed great courage when she saved the child. ◆ It takes courage (= You need courage) to do that.
courageous [kə'reidʒəs] *adj.* (= brave) □ **corajoso**
a courageous person / decision.
courageously [kə'reidʒəsli] *adv.* (= bravely) □ **corajosamente**
courgette [kuə'ʒet] *n.* □ **abobrinha**
■ *Amer.* **zucchini**
■ Ver **marrow**.
course [ko:] *n.*
1 curso
I'm taking a course in cooking. ◆ an English course.
2 decorrer, curso
He mentioned it three times in the course of the conversation.
3 prato
I had fish for the main course. ◆ a three-course dinner.
4 curso
The ship changed course.
5 pista, campo
a race-course. ◆ a golf-course.
of course □ **é claro, com certeza, certamente**

court / crazy

You're right, of course. ◆ Do you love me? – Of course (I do) (= Sure I do). ◆ Can I use the phone? – Of course (= Sure). ◆ Did you take it? – Of course not.
court [kɔːt] *n.*
1 (= court of law) **tribunal**
The prisoner was brought to court for trial. ◆ The court found him guilty.
2 quadra
a tennis court.
3 corte
the courts of the kings and queens of Europe.
courteous [ˈkɔːtiəs] *adj.* (= polite) □ **cortês, educado**
corteous behavior. ◆ a corteous letter of thanks.
courteously [ˈkɔːtiəsli] *adv.* □ **educadamente**
courtyard [ˈkɔːtˌjɑːd] *n.* □ **pátio**
cousin [ˈkʌzn] *n.* □ **primo**
cover¹ [ˈkʌvə] *n.*
1 capa
seat covers (in a car). ◆ I bought a plastic cover for the computer.
2 (= lid) **tampa**
He put the cover on the pot / box.
3 capa
a book with a hard cover. ◆ The cover story of a newspaper is the main story. ◆ Her picture appeared on the cover of several magazines.
4 abrigo
We took cover from the rain / gunfire.
cover² *v.* (**covers, covering, covered**)
1 cobrir
He covered his eyes with his hand. ◆ Don't cover the whole wall with posters. ◆ She covered the child (with a blanket).
2 cobrir
The reporter came to cover the President's visit.
be covered with □ **estar coberto de**
The box was covered with dust. ◆ The wall is covered with paintings.
covering [ˈkʌvərɪŋ] *n.* □ **cobertura, camada**
There was a covering of dead leaves on the ground.
cow [kau] *n.* □ **vaca**
to milk the cows
coward [ˈkauəd] *n.* □ **covarde**
You are a coward!
cowboy [ˈkauboi] *n.* □ **caubói**
cozy [ˈkouzi] *adj. Amer.* (**cozier, coziest**) (= cosy, *Brit.*) □ **aconchegante**
cozy room / atmosphere.
crab [krab] *n.* □ **caranguejo**
Crabs catch their food with their strong claws.
crack¹ [krak] *n.*
1 rachadura
There's a crack in the wall.
2 estalo
a crack of thunder. ◆ the crack of a whip.
crack² *v.* (**cracks, cracking, cracked**)
1 trincar
The mirror / wall cracked. ◆ The stone cracked the window-pane.
2 rachar
to crack nuts.
crackdown [ˈkrakdaun] *n.* □ **repressão**

a police crackdown on drugs. ◆ an official crackdown on drunk drivers.
cracker [ˈkrakə] *n.*
1 biscoitos
cheese and crackers.
2 (= firecracker) □ **bombinha**
crackle [ˈkrakl] *v.* (**crackles, crackling, crackled**) □ **crepitar**
The dry wood crackled in the fire.
cradle [ˈkreidl] *n.* □ **berço**
craft [krɑːft] *n.* □ **artesanato**
the craft of basket-weaving.
craftsman [ˈkrɑːftsmən] *n.* (*pl.* **craftsmen**) □ **artesão**
craftswoman [ˈkrɑːftswumən] *n.* (*pl.* **craftswomen**) □ **artesã**
crag [krag] *n.* □ **rochedo, penhasco**
cram [kram] *v.* (**crams, cramming, crammed**)
1 abarrotar, encher
She crammed her clothes into the suitcase. ◆ He crammed his mouth with cake.
2 (= swot) **estudar muito**
to cram for a history exam.
crane [krein] *n.* □ **guindaste**
The crane lifted the cars onto the ship.
crash¹ [kraʃ] *n.*
1 desastre
They were killed in a plane crash. ◆ a car crash.
2 barulho
I heard the crash of breaking glass. ◆ There was a loud crash when the tree fell.
crash² *v.* (**crashes, crashing, crashed**)
1 espatifar-se
The plane crashed (into a mountain). ◆ The car crashed into a tree.
2 bater
He crashed his car into a wall.
3 pifar
My computer crashed and I lost all the data.
crash barrier [kraʃ ˈbariə] *n.* □ **barreira contra acidentes**
crash-helmet [kraʃˌhelmit] *n.* □ **capacete**
Motorcyclists wear crash-helmets.
crate [kreit] *n.* □ **caixote, engradado**
a crate of oranges. ◆ a crate of beer.
crawl¹ [krɔːl] *n.* □ **nado crawl**
I usually swim the crawl.
crawl² *v.* (**crawls, crawling, crawled**)
1 engatinhar
Babies crawl before they learn to walk.
2 arrastar-se
The snake crawled up the tree. ◆ Ants crawled all over me.
■ Ver **creep**.
3 pulular
The place was crawling with insects.
crayon [ˈkreiən] *n.* □ **lápis de cera**
crazily [ˈkreizili] *adv.* □ **loucamente**
crazy [ˈkreizi] *adj.* (**crazier, craziest**) □ **louco, maluco, doido**
He is crazy (= mad). ◆ Are you crazy? It's too dangerous!
crazy about □ **louco por, doido por, maluco por**
I'm crazy about sports cars. ◆ He's crazy about her.
drive someone crazy □ **deixar alguém louco**
Your questions are driving him crazy.

go crazy ▫ **enlouquecer**
She will go crazy if he leaves her. ◆ They went crazy when their team won the championship.
creak¹ [kri:k] *n.* ▫ **rangido**
I heard a creak and then a door closing.
creak² *v.* (**creaks, creaking, creaked**) ▫ **ranger**
I heard the wooden stairs creaking.
cream [kr:m] *n.* ▫ **creme**
strawberries and cream. ◆ cream cake. ◆ I take cream in my coffee. ◆ shaving cream. ◆ a cream (-colored / coloured) dress.
creamy [ˈkri:mi] *adj.*
1 cremoso
creamy sauce. ◆ creamy chocolates. ◆ creamy soup.
2 creme
a creamy color / colour.
crease¹ [kri:s] *n.* ▫ **ruga, dobra, vinco**
The shirt is full of creases. Will you iron it for me?
crease² *v.* (**creases, creasing, creased**) ▫ **amarrotar, amassar**
I folded the trousers carefully so as not to crease them. ◆ This shirt does not crease.
create [kri'eit] *v.* (**creates, creating, created**)
1 criar
God created the world. ◆ to create a work of art.
2 criar
His announcement created a lot of excitement.
creation [kri'eiʃən] *n.*
1 criação
the creation of the world.
2 criação
This painting / play is one of her best creations.
creative [kri:'eitiv] *adj.* ▫ **criativo**
a creative game. ◆ He is a very creative teacher / artist.
creativity [ˌkri:ə'tiviti] *n.* ▫ **criatividade**
creator [kri'eitə] *n.* ▫ **criador**
She is the creator of one of the most famous characters in detective novels.
creature [ˈkri:tʃə] *n.* ▫ **criatura**
small creatures such as worms and ants. ◆ a creature from another planet.
credit [ˈkredit] *n.*
1 crédito
If you can't pay for it now, you can buy it on credit.
2 crédito
She deserves credit for her work. ◆ We caught the robber, but the police got all the credit.
credit card [ˈkredit 'ka:d] *n.* ▫ **cartão de crédito**
I paid by credit card.
creep [kri:p] *v.* (**creeps, creeping, crept**)
1 rastejar
The fox crept slowly towards the chicken.
■ Ver **crawl²**.
2 mover-se lentamente
I saw him creeping into the kitchen.
crescent [ˈkresent] *n.* ▫ **crescente, meia-lua**
crew [kru:] *n.* ▫ **tripulação, equipe**
The captain ordered his crew to help the passengers. ◆ a TV crew.
crib [krib] *n. Amer.* ▫ **berço**
■ *Amer.* **cot**
cricket [ˈkrikit] *n.*

1 grilo
I could hear the crickets chirping (= making sounds).
2 críquete
Cricket is a very popular game in India.
cried [kraid] *v.* (Ver **cry²**).
cries [kraiz] *v.* (Ver **cry²**).
crime [kraim] *n.* ▫ **crime**
He committed (= did) a crime. ◆ Murder and rape are serious crimes. ◆ Crime in this city is rising. ◆ a crime wave.
criminal¹ [ˈkriminl] *adj.* ▫ **criminoso, criminal, penal**
a criminal act / offence. ◆ to study criminal law.
criminal² *n.* ▫ **criminoso**
criminal record [ˈkriminl 'reko:d] *n.* ▫ **ficha criminal**
The suspect has a criminal record.
crimson [ˈkrimzn] *n., adj.* ▫ **carmesim, vermelho**
cripple [ˈkripl] *v.* (**cripples, crippling, crippled**) ▫ **aleijar, paralisar**
He was crippled in a road accident.
crisis [ˈkraisis] *n.* (*pl.* **crises**) ▫ **crise**
an economic / political crisis.
crisp [krisp] *adj.*
1 crocante
a crisp biscuit.
2 crocante
crisp lettuce.
crisps [krisps] *n. pl. Brit.* ▫ **salgadinho**
a bag of crisps.
■ *Amer.* **chips**
critic [ˈkritik] *n.*
1 crítico
a literary / film critic.
2 crítico
The Minister wrote an article in answer to his critics.
critical [ˈkritikəl] *adj.*
1 grave
The patient is in a critical condition.
2 crítico
a critical report. ◆ He was very critical of the plan.
critically [ˈkritikəli] *adv.* ▫ **gravemente**
He was critically wounded.
criticise [ˈkritisaiz] *v.* (Ver **criticize**). ▫ **criticar**
criticism [ˈkritisizəm] *n.*
1 crítica
Your criticism of my work is unfair.
2 crítica
literary criticism.
criticize [ˈkritisaiz] *v.* (**criticizes, criticizing, criticized**) (= **criticise**, *Brit*) ▫ **criticar**
The report criticizes the government. ◆ to criticize a painting / poem.
croak¹ [krouk] *n.* ▫ **coaxo**
the croaks of frogs.
croak² *v.* (**croaks, croaking, croaked**) ▫ **coaxar**
I could hear frogs croaking.
crockery [ˈkrokəri] *n.* ▫ **louça, utensílios de barro**
crocodile [ˈkrokədail] *n.* ▫ **crocodilo**
■ Ver **alligator**.
crook [kruk] *n.* ▫ **vigarista**
In the end, the crooks went to prison.
crooked [ˈkrukid] *adj.*
1 torto
crooked teeth

2 desonesto
a crooked businessman / deal.
■ antônimo: **straight¹**

crop [krop] *n.* □ **safra**
a good crop of tomatoes / wheat.

crops *n. pl.* □ **cultura**
The main crops they grow are wheat, rice and coffee.

cross¹ [kros] *adj.* (= angry) □ **bravo, zangado**
He was cross with me because I was late.

cross² *n.* □ **cruz**
The Pope wears a cross on his chest. ◆ He marked the wrong answers with a cross.

cross³ *v.* (**crosses, crossing, crossed**)
1 atravessar
to cross the road / bridge.
2 cruzar
He crossed his legs.

cross out □ **riscar**
I crossed out the whole paragraph.

cross someone's mind □ **passar pela cabeça de alguém**
Such thoughts never crossed my mind.

cross my heart! □ **eu juro!**
I won't tell anyone – cross my heart.

crossing ['krosiŋ] *n.* □ **travessia, faixa**
a pedestrian crossing (where cars must stop to let people cross the road).

crossroads ['krosroudz] *n.* □ **encruzilhada**
We came to a crossroads.
■ Ver **junction**.

crosswalk ['kroswo:k] *n. Amer.* □ **faixa de pedestres**
■ *Brit.* **pedestrian crossing**

crossword (puzzle) ['kroswəd ('pʌzl)] *n.* □ **palavras cruzadas**
I like to do crossword puzzles.

crouch [krautʃ] *v.* (**crouches, crouching, crouched**) □ **agachar-se**
The cat crouched, ready to jump on the bird.

crow¹ [krou] *n.* □ **corvo**

crow² *v.* (**crows, crowing, crowed**) □ **cocoricar**
The cock crows at dawn.

crowd¹ [kraud] *n.* □ **multidão**
There was a large crowd at the stadium.

crowd² *v.* (**crowds, crowding, crowded**) □ **aglomerar-se, lotar**
The fans crowded around the pop star. ◆ Demonstrators crowded the streets.

crowd into □ **apinhar-se**
Hundreds of people crowded into the hall.

crowded ['kraudid] *adj.* □ **lotado, superpopuloso**
The beach was crowded (with people). ◆ crowded cities (= cities with large populations).
■ Ver **overcrowded**.

crown¹ [kraun] *n.* □ **coroa**

crown² *v.* (**crowns, crowning, crowned**) □ **coroar**
When was Queen Elizabeth II crowned?

crucial ['kru:ʃəl] *adj.* □ **crucial**
This decision is crucial to their future. ◆ a crucial moment.

cruel ['kru:əl] *adj.* (**crueller, cruellest**) □ **cruel**
a cruel king. ◆ We teach them to love animals and not to be cruel to them.

cruelly ['kru:əli] *adv.* □ **cruelmente**
He treated them cruelly.

cruelty ['kru:əlti] *n.* □ **crueldade**
cruelty to children.

cruise¹ [kru:z] *n.* □ **cruzeiro**
They went on a cruise around the Mediterranean.

cruise² *v.* (**cruises, cruising, cruised**) □ **fazer um cruzeiro**
They are cruising around the world.

crumb [krʌm] *n.* □ **farelo, migalha**
You left biscuit crumbs all over the couch.

crumble ['krʌmbl] *v.* (**crumbles, crumbling, crumbled**) □ **esfarelar, desmoronar**
I crumbled a slice of bread for the birds. ◆ The walls are crumbling.

crumple ['krʌmpl] *v.* (**crumples, crumpling, crumpled**) □ **amassar**
He crumpled the letter and threw it into the waste-paper basket.

crunch [krʌntʃ] *v.* (**crunches, crunching, crunched**) □ **roer, mastigar**
The rabbit is crunching a carrot. ◆ a bone for the dog to crunch

crusade [kru:'seid] *n.*
1 Cruzada
The crusades took place in the Middle East during the Middle Ages.
2 cruzada
a crusade against organized crime.

crush [krʌʃ] *v.* (**crushes, crushing, crushed**) □ **esmagar**
I crushed the box when I sat on it. ◆ His arm was crushed in an accident.

crutch [krʌtʃ] *n.* □ **muleta**
He walks on crutches.

cry¹ [crai] *n.* (*pl.* **cries**) □ **grito, gritaria**
a cry for help. ◆ the cry of a wolf. ◆ the cries of children playing.

cry² *v.* (**cries, crying, cried**)
1 chorar
Stop crying! ◆ She cries when they tease her.
2 gritar
They cried for help. ◆ He cried (out) in pain.

crystal ['kristl] *n., adj.*
1 cristal
sugar / salt crystals
2 de cristal
a crystal necklace. ◆ a crystal vase.

cub [kʌb] *n.* □ **filhote de animal selvagem**
A cub is a young lion, tiger, fox or bear.
■ A young dog is a **puppy**.
■ A young cat is a **kitty**.

cube [kju:b] *n.* □ **cubo**
ice cubes. ◆ I cut the apple into cubes.

cubic ['kju:bik] *adj.* □ **cúbico**
one cubic meter / metre.

cuckoo ['kuku:] *n.* □ **cuco**

cuckoo clock ['kuku: 'klok] *n.* □ **relógio cuco**

cucumber ['kju:kʌmbə] *n.* □ **pepino**

cuddle¹ ['kʌdl] *n.* □ **abraço**
She gave me a cuddle.

cuddle² *v.* (**cuddles, cuddling, cuddled**) □ **abraçar**
She cuddled her doll.

cult [kʌlt] *n., adj.* □ **culto, cult**
He left home to join a religious cult. ◆ A cult movie is one that is very popular with a special group of people but not with everyone.

cultivate ['kʌltiveit] *v.* (**cultivates, cultivating, cultivated**)
1 cultivar
to cultivate the land.
2 cultivar
to cultivate vegetables and flowers.
cultivation [,kʌlti'veiʃən] *n.* □ **cultivo**
cultivation of the land.
cultural ['kʌltʃərəl] *adj.* □ **cultural**
the cultural differences between European and Asian countries. ◆ There's a rich cultural life here.
culture ['kʌltʃə] *n.* □ **cultura**
Greek culture; the culture of the Greeks. ◆ people from different cultures.
cunning¹ ['kʌniŋ] *adj.* (= sly) □ **astuto, sagaz**
a cunning trick ◆ He is as cunning as a fox.
cunning² *n.* □ **astúcia**
cup [kʌp] *n.*
1 xícara
He drank a cup of tea. ◆ a plastic / paper cup.
2 taça, copa
Who won the cup in the tennis championship?
cupboard ['kʌbəd] *n.* □ **armário**
a kitchen cupboard ◆ My clothes are in this cupboard.
■ Ver **closet; wardrobe**.
curb [kɜːb] *n. Amer.* □ **meio-fio**
■ *Brit.* **kerb**
cure¹ [kjuə] *n.* □ **cura**
Is there a cure for this disease?
cure² *v.* (**cures, curing, cured**) □ **curar**
to cure a patient / disease. ◆ He was cured of cancer.
curiosity [,kjuəri'ositi] *n.* □ **curiosidade**
He opened her letter out of curiosity.
curious ['kjuəriəs] *adj.*
1 curioso
I'm curious to know what was in the envelope.
2 (= inquisitive) **curioso**
curious neighbors / neighbours.
3 (= strange) **curioso**
She has curious habits.
curiously ['kjuəriəsli] *adv.* □ **curiosamente**
He looked at her curiously.
curl¹ [kɜːl] *n.* □ **cacho**
curl² *v.* (**curls, curling, curled**) □ **cachear, enrolar**
She curled her hair. ◆ Smoke curled from his pipe.
curly ['kɜːli] *adj.* (**curlier, curliest**) □ **cacheado, enrolado**
She has curly hair.
currant ['kʌrənt] *n.* □ **groselha**
currency ['kʌrənsi] *n.* (*pl.* **currencies**) □ **moeda**
The currency of the USA is the dollar. ◆ When you go abroad you need foreign currency.
current¹ ['kʌrənt] *adj.* □ **atual, corrente**
current events (= events that are in the news). ◆ the current year (= this year).
current² *n.* □ **corrente**
It is difficult to swim against the current. ◆ strong air currents. ◆ an electric current.
currently ['kʌrəntli] *adv.* □ **atualmente**
She is currently working on a new book.
curriculum [kə'rikjuləm] *n.* (*pl.* **curricula, curriculums**) □ **currículo**
the English curriculum. *Amer.* (= the English syllabus, *Brit.*) ◆ Our school curriculum includes English, art and computer studies.

■ *Brit.* **syllabus** = within a subject (e.g. 'the biology syllabus'); **curriculum** = all the subjects in a course.
curse¹ [kɜːs] *n.*
1 maldição, praga
The witch put a curse on the prince.
2 xingamento, palavrão
He shouted curses at the driver who almost hit him.
curse² *v.* (**curses, cursing, cursed**)
1 xingar
They cursed the player when he missed the goal.
2 amaldiçoar
The witch cursed them and turned them into sheep.
cursed [kɜːsid] *adj.* □ **amaldiçoado**
The place is cursed.
cursor [kɜːsə] *n.* □ **cursor**
You can move the cursor (on the computer screen) in all directions.
curtain [kɜːtn] *n.*
1 cortina
to draw (= open or close) the curtains.
■ *Amer.* also **drapes**
2 pano de boca
The curtain rises when the play begins.
curve¹ [kɜːv] *n.* (= bend) □ **curva**
a sharp curve in the road.
curve² *v.* (**curves, curving, curved**) □ **fazer curva**
The road curves sharply to the right.
curved [kɜːvd] *adj.* □ **curvo**
a sword with a curved blade.
cushion ['kuʃən] *n.* □ **almofada**
Put a cushion on the chair to make it more comfortable.
custard ['kʌstəd] *n.* □ **creme**
custom ['kʌstəm] *n.* □ **costume**
an old custom.
customs *n.*
1 imposto
How much customs did you pay on the camera?
2 alfândega
It didn't take me long to get through customs.
customary ['kʌstəməri] *adj.* □ **costumeiro**
It's customary for a bride to wear a white dress.
customer ['kʌstəmə] *n.* □ **cliente, freguês, consumidor, cliente**
to serve the customers (in a shop, restaurant, etc.
■ For lawyers, banks, etc. use **client**,
cut¹ [kʌt] *n.* □ **corte**
cuts on the face from shaving. ◆ I have a cut on my leg.
cut² *v.* (**cuts, cutting, cut**)
1 cortar
I cut the orange in half. ◆ Coconut doesn't cut easily. ◆ He cut his finger while cutting the bread.
■ Note: I cut myself (accidentally).
2 cortar
to cut cloth. ◆ He is cutting pictures out of the newspaper.
3 cortar, aparar
I have my hair cut at the barber's. ◆ She is cutting her nails. ◆ to cut the grass.
4 cortar, reduzir
to cut prices. ◆ to cut the budget by 10%.
cut back □ **cortar, reduzir**
We'll have to cut back on our expenses.
cut down □ **derrubar**
to cut down a tree.

cut down (on) □ **reduzir**
They need to cut down their expenses. ◆ I'm trying to cut down on smoking.
cut something off
1 cortar fora, arrancar
I cut off the branch. ◆ The animal's head was cut off.
2 cortar
They cut off the electricity.
be cut off
1 ficar isolado
The village was cut off by the snowstorm. ◆ They were cut off by the flood.
2 ser cortado
The electricity was cut off.
cut out (of) □ **cortar**
She is cutting pictures out of the newspaper.
cut up □ **cortar, picar**
to cut up vegetables.
cute [kju:t] *adj.* □ **gracioso**
a cute little girl. ◆ a cute hairstyle.
cutlery ['kʌtləri] *n.* □ **talheres, cutelaria**
silver cutlery (= silver knives, spoons and forks).

cybercafé ['saibəkafei] *n.* □ **cibercafé**
At a cybercafé you can send and get e-mails and also have a coffee or a meal.
cyberspace ['saibəspeis] *n.* □ **ciberespaço**
Cyberspace is the virtual 'world' of the Internet.
cycle^1 ['saikl] *n.*
1 (= bicycle) **bicicleta**
a cycle race.
2 (= motorcycle) **motocicleta**
cycle^2 *v.* (**cycles, cycling, cycled**) □ **andar de bicicleta**
He cycles to school every day. ◆ She cycled (= rode on her bicycle) down the street. ◆ We go cycling once a week.
cycling ['saikliŋ] *n.* □ **ciclismo**
cyclist ['saiklist] *n.* □ **ciclista**
cylinder ['silində] *n.*
1 cilindro
A beer can is in the shape of a cylinder.
2 tanque
divers with cylinders of oxygen on their backs.
cylindrical ['silindrikəl] *adj.* □ **cilíndrico**
cymbals ['simbəlz] *n. pl.* □ **pratos**

Dd

dad [dad] *n.* □ **papai**
My dad speaks English. ◆ Where's Mom, Dad?

daddy ['dadi] *n.* (*pl.* **daddies**) □ **paizinho, papaizinho**
Daddy! Dan is pulling my hair!

daffodil ['dafədil] *n.* □ **narciso**

daft [da:ft] *adj. Brit.* (= stupid) □ **tolo**
Don't be daft!

dagger ['dəgə] *n.* □ **adaga, punhal**

daily[1] ['deili] *adj.* □ **diário**
a daily newspaper. ◆ his daily visit to the hospital.

daily[2] *adv.* □ **diariamente**
We talk on the phone almost daily. ◆ Take one pill twice daily.

dainty ['deinti] *adj.* □ **delicado**
a dainty little girl.

dairy ['deəri] *n.* (*pl.* **dairies**) □ **leiteria, laticínios**
dairy products (= cheese, butter, yoghurt, etc.).

daisy ['deizi] *n.* (*pl.* **daisies**) □ **margarida**

dam [dam] *n.* □ **represa, barragem**

damage[1] ['damidʒ] *n.* □ **dano, prejuízo**
Alcohol may cause damage to the liver. ◆ Who will pay for the damage to the car?

damage[2] *v.* (**damages, damaging, damaged**) □ **danificar, prejudicar**
Many buildings were damaged by the fire. ◆ Loud music may damage your hearing.

damn [dam] *excl.* □ **Droga!**
Damn! I'll have to do it again.

damp [damp] *adj.* □ **úmido**
Wipe it with a damp cloth. ◆ damp walls.

dampen ['dampən] *v.* (**dampens, dampening, dampened**) □ **umedecer**
to dampen a cloth.

dampness ['dampnis] *n.* □ **umidade**

dance[1] [da:ns] *n.*
1 dança
a belly dance.
2 baile
Are you going to the dance tonight?

dance[2] *v.* (**dances, dancing, danced**) □ **dançar**
Would you like to dance? ◆ She dances very well. ◆ He is dancing with Sara.

dancer ['da:nsə] *n.* □ **dançarino**
a ballet dancer.

dancing ['da:nsɪŋ] *n.* □ **dança**
folk dancing. ◆ a dancing teacher (= a teacher for dancing).

danger ['deindʒə] *n.* □ **perigo**
Danger! Keep out! ◆ His life was in danger (= at risk). ◆ The patient is out of danger. ◆ the dangers of taking drugs. ◆ He is a danger to society.
■ The verb is **endanger**.

dangerous ['deindʒərəs] *adj.* □ **perigoso**
It's dangerous to play here. ◆ a dangerous man / adventure.
■ Ver **risky**.

dangerously ['deindʒərəsli] *adv.* □ **perigosamente**
You drive very dangerously. ◆ He is dangerously ill.

dare [deə] *v.* (**dares, daring, dared**) □ **atrever-se, ousar**
He doesn't dare (to) tell her. ◆ He dare not tell her. ◆ She wouldn't dare (to) fire me. ◆ I didn't dare (to) look at it.
■ Used especially in negative sentences and questions.

Dare you...? □ **Duvido que você...**
Dare you climb this hill?

don't you dare □ **não se atreva, não ouse**
Don't you dare touch it!

How dare you...? □ **Como você se atreve...?, Como você ousa...?**
How dare you speak to me like that?

I dare you □ **Eu desafio você a..., Eu duvido que você...**
I dare you to ask her to join us.

daring[1] ['deərɪŋ] *adj.* □ **atrevido, ousado**
a daring jump / plan.

daring[2] *n.* □ **atrevimento, ousadia**
He showed great daring in those dangerous times.

dark[1] [da:k] *adj.*
1 escuro
It's dark outside. ◆ It's getting dark. ◆ The room was dark.
2 escuro
a dark-green shirt
■ antônimo: **light**[2]
3 escuro
dark hair ◆ dark skin
■ antônimo: **fair**

dark[2] *n.* □ **escuro**
Why are you sitting in the dark? ◆ They don't dare go out after dark.

darken ['da:kən] *v.* (**darkens, darkening, darkened**)
1 escurecer
The sky darkened.
2 escurecer
to darken the room.

darkness ['da:knis] *n.* □ **escuridão**
The house was in complete darkness.

darling ['da:lɪŋ] *n.*
1 querido
Just a minute, darling.
2 queridinho
He is the darling of the teachers. ◆ The baby is a little darling.

dart[1] [da:t] *n.* □ **dardo**

darts *n.* □ **dardos**

dart[2] *v.* (**darts, darting, darted**) □ **disparar**
The rabbit darted away when it heard the noise.

dash[1] [daʃ] *n.*
1 (−) **travessão**
2 corrida curta, corridinha
He made a dash for shelter.

dash[2] *v.* (**dashes, dashing, dashed**) □ **correr, ir depressa**
It's getting late. I must dash. ◆ He dashed into a shop when it started to rain.

data ['deitə] *n.* □ **dados**
to store a lot of data in a computer. ◆ to collect data.

date[1] [deit] *n.*
1 data
What's the date (today)? ◆ What is your date of birth? ◆ to set a date for the exam.
2 encontro
I have a date with her tonight.
3 tâmara
Dates grow on palm trees.

date² v. (dates, dating, dated) ☐ **datar**
You forgot to date your letter.
out of date (= outdated) ☐ **desatualizado, antiquado**
The map is out of date. ◆ out-of-date ideas (= old-fashioned).
■ with hyphens when before a noun.
up to date (= updated) ☐ **atualizado, moderno**
Is this list up to date? ◆ an up-to-date dictionary. ◆ up-to-date techniques.
■ with hyphens when before a noun.
daughter ['dɔ:tə] *n.* ☐ **filha**
What's his daughter's name?
daughter-in-law ['dɔ:tərinlɔ:] *n.* (*pl.* **daughters-in-law**) ☐ **nora**
dawn [dɔ:n] *n.* ☐ **aurora, amanhecer**
The birds start singing at dawn.
day [dei] *n.*
1 dia
I bought it five days ago. ◆ What day is it today? – Friday. ◆ I visit them every day.
2 dia
Some animals sleep during the day.
3 época
in the days of the industrial revolution. ◆ In those days there were no computers.
a day ☐ **por dia, ao dia**
He prays three times a day. ◆ She earns 20 dollars a day.
day by day ☐ **dia a dia**
His condition is improving day by day.
day in, day out ☐ **dia sim, dia não**
She called us day in, day out.
some day ☐ **um dia**
Some day she will know the truth.
the day after tomorrow ☐ **depois de amanhã**
the day before yesterday ☐ **anteontem**
I called you the day before yesterday.
the other day ☐ **outro dia**
I met him the other day.
these days ☐ **hoje em dia**
It's difficult to be a teacher these days.
day-dream¹ ['deidri:m] *n.* ☐ **devaneio**
day-dream² v. (day-dreams, day-dreaming, day-dreamt / day-dreamed) ☐ **devanear, sonhar acordado**
Stop day-dreaming!
daylight ['deilait] *n.* ☐ **luz do dia**
It looks different in daylight.
daytime ['deitaim] *n.* ☐ **durante o dia**
Some animals sleep in the daytime.
daze¹ [deiz] *n.*
in a daze ☐ **atordoado**
He was in a daze for hours after the accident.
daze² v. (dazes, dazing, dazed) ☐ **atordoar**
She is still dazed by the blow on her head. ◆ He was dazed with drugs.
dazzle ['dazl] *v.* **(dazzles, dazzling, dazzled)** ☐ **ofuscar**
The strong light dazzled me. ◆ I was dazzled by the car's headlights.
dead¹ [ded] *adj.*
1 morto
dead fish / flowers. ◆ He is dead. He died 5 minutes ago.
2 sem carga, mudo
The battery is dead. ◆ The telephone is dead.

dead² adv. ☐ **totalmente, absolutamente**
I'm dead tired.
dead³ *n.*, **the dead** ☐ **os mortos**
to bury the dead
dead end ['ded end] *n.*
1 beco sem saída
Our search came to a dead end.
2 sem saída
a dead-end street.
deadline ['dedlain] *n.* ☐ **prazo final**
The deadline for (finishing) the project is May 26.
deadly ['dedli] *adj.* **(deadlier, deadliest)** ☐ **mortal**
a deadly weapon. ◆ one of the deadliest poisons.
deaf [def] *adj.* ☐ **surdo**
I'm deaf in one ear. ◆ How did she become deaf?
the deaf ☐ **os surdos**
The deaf use a special language called sign language.
deafen ['defən] *v.* **(deafens, deafening, deafened)** ☐ **ensurdecer**
We were deafened by the noise.
deafening ['defəniŋ] *adj.* ☐ **ensurdecedor**
The noise was deafening.
deafness ['defnis] *n.* ☐ **surdez**
deal¹ [di:l] *n.*, **a good great deal (of)** (= a lot [of]) ☐ **muito, bastante**
We spent a great deal of money. ◆ a great deal of time. ◆ They talked a good deal.
deal² *n.* ☐ **trato, acordo**
I made a lot of money on that deal. ◆ I'll make a deal with you.
deal³ v. (deals, dealing, dealt) ☐ **distribuir**
It's your turn to deal (the cards).
deal in ☐ **comercializar**
We deal in spare parts for cars.
deal with
1 lidar com
Don't worry, I'll deal with that problem. ◆ She dealt very well with the angry customers.
2 tratar de
The lecture dealt with the subject of dreams.
3 negociar
We deal with other companies also. ◆ They refused to deal with the kidnappers.
dealer ['di:lə] *n.*
1 comerciante
a car dealer. ◆ an art dealer.
2 traficante
a drug dealer.
■ Ver **merchant; trader**.
dealt [delt] *v.* (Ver **deal³**).
dear¹ [diə] *adj.*
1 caro, querido
His grandson is very dear to him. ◆ their dearest friends.
2 caro, prezado
Dear David, ◆ Dear Mrs. Segal, ◆ Dear Sir, ◆ Dear Madam,
3 (= expensive) **caro**
Fruit and vegetables are too dear at this time of year.
■ Not before a noun; do not say 'a dear hotel'.
■ antônimo: **cheap**
dear² *n.* ☐ **querido**
Would you like a biscuit, dear?
■ *Amer.* **honey**

■ Used to speak kindly to any loved person, a woman friend, a customer. Not used by a man to another man.
dear³ □ **ai, meu Deus!**
Oh dear! He fell off the bike. ♦ Dear me! It's four o'clock already.
dearly ['dɪəli] *adv.*
1 ternamente
They love their son dearly.
2 caro
I paid dearly for my mistakes.
death [deθ] *n.*
1 morte
They sold the house after their mother's death. ♦ He was shot to death by the police.
2 morte
The number of deaths from road accidents is increasing.
death sentence ['deθ 'sentəns] *n.* □ **sentença de morte**
debate¹ [di'beit] *n.* □ **debate**
a debate in parliament on taxes. ♦ a debate between the candidates (on TV, etc.).
debate² *v.* (**debates, debating, debated**)
1 debater
They debated the subject of school uniforms.
2 debater
I am debating whether to go or not.
debris ['debri:] *n.* □ **escombros**
the debris of the building that collapsed ♦ They searched among the debris from the crashed plane.
debt [det] *n.* □ **débito**
We borrowed a lot of money and we can't pay all our debts.
get into debt □ **contrair dívidas, endividar-se**
He got into debt when he started gambling.
decade ['dekeid] *n.* □ **década**
in the last two decades (= 20 years). ♦ the last decade of the 20th century (1991-2000).
decay¹ [di'kei] *n.* □ **cárie**
tooth decay.
decay² *v.* (**decays, decaying, decayed**) □ **apodrecer, cariar**
The dry leaves decayed after the rain. ♦ decaying teeth.
deceit [di'si:t] *n.* □ **engano**
They took his money by deceit.
deceitful [di'si:tfəl] *adj.*
1 dissimulado
a deceitful person.
2 enganador
a deceitful smile.
deceive [di'si:v] *v.* (**deceives, deceiving, deceived**) □ **enganar**
They deceived me. This diamond is not real. ♦ His smiles do not deceive me. He is not an honest man. ♦ Don't deceive yourself. They are not going to help you.
December [di'sembə] *n.* □ **dezembro**
It happened in December, 2010.
■ For more examples see **April**.
decency ['di:sənsi] *n.* □ **decência**
to behave with decency.
decent ['di:snt] *adj.*
1 decente
to wear decent clothes for a wedding.
2 decente
decent people.

decide [di'said] *v.* (**decides, deciding, decided**) □ **decidir**
They decided to stay for two more days. ♦ We decided not to buy it. ♦ I can't decide which one to take.
■ The noun is **decision**.
decimal [desiməl] *n.* □ **decimal**
The number 0.85 (= point eight five) is a decimal (number).
decision [di'siʒən] *n.* □ **decisão**
We made the decision (= We decided) to go ahead with the plan. ♦ When will you come to a decision? ♦ His decision to leave was wrong.
decisive [di'saisiv] *adj.*
1 decisivo
He scored the decisive goal at the last moment.
2 decidido, firme
a decisive person / answer.
deck [dek] *n.*
1 deque
We went up on deck to sit in the sun.
2 andar de cima
the top deck of the bus.
deck-chair ['dektʃeə] *n.* □ **espreguiçadeira, cadeira de lona**
declaration [deklə'reiʃən] *n.* □ **declaração**
a declaration of war. ♦ the declaration of independence.
declare [di'kleə] *v.* (**declares, declaring, declared**) □ **declarar**
They declared war on the terrorists. ♦ The chairman declared the meeting closed. ♦ He declared that he was innocent. ♦ Do you have anything to declare?
decline [di'klain] *v.* (**declines, declining, declined**)
1 declinar, recusar
to decline an invitation.
2 (= decrease) **diminuir, cair**
Sales of this product declined last year.
decorate ['dekəreit] *v.* (**decorates, decorating, decorated**)
1 decorar
They decorated the streets with flags. ♦ to decorate a cake. ♦ to decorate the office.
2 condecorar
Sergeant Lewis was decorated for bravery.
decoration [,dekə'reiʃən] *n.*
1 decoração
birthday party decorations.
2 condecoração
a decoration for bravery.
decrease¹ ['di:kri:s] *n.* □ **diminuição**
a 5% decrease in accidents.
■ antônimo: **increase**²
decrease² *v.* (**decreases, decreasing, decreased**) □ **diminuir**
The number of elephants in the area decreases from year to year. ♦ Interest in this game is decreasing. ♦ to decrease speed.
■ antônimo: **increase**
dedicate ['dedikeit] *v.* (**dedicates, dedicating, dedicated**)
1 dedicar
The author dedicated the book to his wife. ♦ I dedicate this song to you.
2 dedicar, devotar
She dedicated her life to helping poor families.
dedication [,dedi'keiʃən] *n.* □ **dedicação**

deed [di:d] *n.* □ **façanha, feito**
He did many good deeds in his life.
deep [di:p] *adj.*
1 fundo
a deep well / lake. ✦ The water is deep here.
2 de profundidade
The swimming pool is 3 metres deep.
■ The noun is **depth**.
3 fundo
a deep voice. ✦ Take a deep breath.
4 profundo
The baby was in a deep sleep. ✦ deep sorrow.
5 forte, carregado
The sky was deep blue.
How deep...? □ **Qual a profundidade...?**
How deep is that pool?
deepen ['di:pən] *v.* (**deepens, deepening, deepened**)
□ **aprofundar, ficar mais fundo**
to deepen the hole. ✦ The lake deepened after the rains.
deeply ['di:pli] *adv.* □ **profundamente**
He is deeply worried. ✦ She was deeply impressed.
deer [diə] *n.* (*pl.* **deer**) □ **cervo, veado**
default ['difo:lt] *adj.* □ **default, padrão**
to change the default password on your computer.
defeat[1] [di'fi:t] *n.* □ **derrota**
defeat in battle / the elections. ✦ The team has ten wins and two defeats.
defeat[2] *v.* (**defeats, defeating, defeated**) □ **derrotar**
We defeated them by two goals to one. ✦ The enemy was defeated.
defence [di'fens] *n. Brit.*, **defense** *Amer.* □ **defesa**
Attack is the best form of defence. ✦ the Defence Department.
defend [di'fend] *v.* (**defends, defending, defended**)
1 defender
He defended himself against the attacker. ✦ The army sent 2,000 soldiers to defend the city.
■ Compare with **protect**.
2 defender
We hired a good lawyer to defend you in court. ✦ She defended me when they blamed me for the failure.
defendant [di'fendənt] *n.* □ **acusado, réu**
The defendant is accused of murder.
defense [di'fens] *n. Amer.*, **defence** *Brit.* □ **defesa**
They fought bravely in defense of the country.
defensive [di'fensiv] *adj.* □ **defensivo, protetor**
defensive weapons. ✦ a defensive wall.
defiant [di'faiənt] *adj.* □ **insolente, provocador, desafiador**
defiant members (of the group) who refuse to obey their leader. ✦ a defiant look. ✦ a defiant speech.
defiantly [di'faiəntli] *adv.* **provocadoramente, desafiadoramente**
'I refuse!', he said defiantly.
deficient [di'fiʃənt] *adj.* □ **deficiente, pobre**
Her diet is deficient in vitamins.
define [di'fain] *v.* (**defines, defining, defined**) □ **definir**
How do you define 'love'?
definite ['definit] *adj.*
1 claro, categórico
I want a definite answer, Yes or No.
2 certo
Is it definite that they will come?

definite article ['definit 'a:tikl] *n.* □ **artigo definido**
'The' is the definite article.
■ Ver **indefinite article**.
definitely ['definitli] *adv.*
1 sem dúvida
This is definitely her best work.
2 com certeza
Are you going to help us? – Definitely.
definition [defi'niʃən] *n.* □ **definição**
Give me a definition of 'country'.
defy [di'fai] *v.* (**defies, defying, defied**) □ **desafiar**
They defied their parents and took the car without permission.
degenerate[1] [di'dʒenəreit] *v.* (**degenerates, degenerating, degenerated**) □ **degenerar**
Their freindly conversation degenerated into a fight. ✦ complaints that educational levels degenerated.
degenerate[2] [di'dʒenərət] *n.* □ **degenerado**
a moral degenerate.
degree [di'gri:] *n.*
1 grau
an angle of forty-five degrees (45°). ✦ Water boils at 100 degrees Celsius (100° C).
2 diploma
I have a degree in economics.
delay[1] [di'lei] *n.* □ **demora, atraso**
The ceremony began after a delay of one hour. ✦ I apologize for the delay in answering your letter.
without delay □ **sem demora**
We must send it without delay.
delay[2] *v.* (**delays, delaying, delayed**)
1 atrasar
The storm delayed all flights. ✦ We were delayed by a traffic jam. ✦ Don't delay!
2 (= postpone; put off) **adiar**
They delayed the interview for a few days.
delete [di'li:t] *v.* (**deletes, deleting, deleted**) □ **deletar, apagar, excluir**
The editor deleted all the insulting words in the article.
deletion [di'liʃən] *n.* □ **eliminação, supressão**
deli ['deli] *n.* (Ver **delicatessen**)
deliberate [di'libərət] *adj.* □ **deliberado, intencional**
It was a deliberate lie. ✦ It wasn't deliberate. I didn't mean to hurt her.
deliberately [di'libərətli] *adv.* □ **de propósito, deliberadamente**
You did it deliberately! ✦ You deliberately disobeyed my orders!
delicate ['delikət] *adj.* □ **delicado**
delicate skin. ✦ delicate glass. ✦ delicate fingers. ✦ a delicate perfume. ✦ a delicate situation.
delicatessen [delikə'tesn] *n.* □ **delicatéssen, mercearia**
■ *Amer.* also **deli**
delicious [di'liʃəs] *adj.* □ **delicioso**
a delicious cake. ✦ The pudding is delicious.
delight[1] [di'lait] *n.*
1 (= pleasure) **prazer**
To her great delight she got a 10 in English. ✦ He laughed with delight.
2 prazer
the delights of cooking.
take delight in (= enjoy) □ **ter prazer em**

He took great delight in teasing his sister.
delight² *v.* (**delights, delighting, delighted**) ▫ **deleitar, encantar**
It delighted us to see her play the piano.
be delighted ▫ **sentir prazer**
I'm delighted to hear that you won the first prize.
delightful [di'laitful] *adj.*
1 aprazível
We had a delightful time at the party.
2 agradável
a delightful house.
deliver [di'livə] *v.* (**delivers, delivering, delivered**)
1 entregar
The postman usually delivers the mail in the mornings.
2 entregar
They promised to deliver the bed tomorrow.
delivery [di'livəri] *n.* (*pl.* **deliveries**) ▫ **entrega**
The delivery of the refrigerator will be tomorrow.
delivery boy [di'livəri 'bɔi] *n.* ▫ **entregador**
I work as a delivery boy. I deliver pizzas.
demand¹ [di'ma:nd] *n.*
1 exigências
We cannot accept your demands.
2 demanda
There is a great demand for these computers.
to be in demand ▫ **haver procura por**
Good programmers are in great demand.
demand² *v.* (**demands, demanding, demanded**) ▫ **exigir**
We demand an apology from him. ◆ I demanded to see the manager.
democracy [di'mɔkrəsi] *n.* (*pl.* **democracies**) ▫ **democracia**
The USA is a democracy. ◆ There isn't enough democracy in this organization.
democrat ['deməkræt] *n.* ▫ **democrata**
democratic [demə'krætik] *adj.* ▫ **democrático**
democratic elections. ◆ democratic countries.
demolish [di'mɔliʃ] *v.* (**demolishes, demolishing, demolished**) ▫ **demolir**
to demolish an old building.
demonstrate ['deməstreit] *v.* (**demonstrates, demonstrating, demonstrated**)
1 demonstrar
He demonstrated (to us) how to build it.
2 manifestar-se
Thousands of people demonstrated against the government.
demonstration [,demən'streiʃən] *n.*
1 manifestação, passeata
demonstrations for peace. ◆ Many people took part in the demonstration against the hunting of whales.
2 demonstração
a demonstration of what the new machine can do.
demonstrator ['demənstreitə] *n.* ▫ **manifestantes**
Thousands of demonstrators protested against the new law.
den [den] *n.* ▫ **toca, covil**
Bears and lions live in dens.
denial [di'naiəl] *n.* ▫ **negativa**
He says that he did not cheat in the exam, and I believe his denial.
denied, denies [di'naid, di'niaz] *v.* (Ver **deny**).
denims ['denimz] *n.* (= jeans) ▫ **brim**

dense [dens] *adj.*
1 denso
dense fog.
2 fechado
a dense forest.
densely ['densli] *adv.* ▫ **densamente**
A densely populated city is a city with very many people.
density ['densiti] *n.* ▫ **densidade**
population density.
dent¹ [dent] *n.* ▫ **amassado**
There's a dent in the back of my car.
dent² *v.* (**dents, denting, dented**) ▫ **amassar**
The car behind me hit my car and dented it.
dental ['dentl] *adj.* ▫ **dental, dentário**
dentist ['dentist] *n.* ▫ **dentista**
I've got an appointment with the dentist on Tuesday. ◆ I have to go to the dentist's.
deny [di'nai] *v.* (**denies, denying, denied**) ▫ **negar**
She denies that she helped him. ◆ I deny these stories about me.
▪ antônimo: **admit**
deodorant [di:'oudərənt] *n.* ▫ **desodorante**
depart [di'pa:t] *v.* (**departs, departing, departed**) (= leave) ▫ **partir**
The train to London departs from platform 5 at 8:30 am.
department [di'pa:tmənt] *n.*
1 departamento
the English department (at a university). ◆ I work in the sales department. ◆ The toy department is on the third floor.
2 (= Ministry) *Amer.* **Ministério**
the Department of Defence.
department store [di'pa:t ,stɔ:] *n.* ▫ **loja de departamentos**
departure [di'pa:tʃə] *n.* ▫ **partida, embarque**
What is the departure time? (= When is the train, plane, etc. leaving?) ◆ His departure for Egypt was unexpected.
depend [di'pend] *v.* (**depends, depending, depended**)
1 depender
The success of the project depends on you. ◆ Young birds usually depend on their parents for food.
2 confiar
You can depend on that lawyer.
it depends ▫ **depende (de)**
I'm not sure I will come. It depends on the weather. ◆ It depends where we're going.
▪ **it depende** (*not* 'it's depend').
dependence [di'pendəns] *n.* ▫ **dependência**
dependent [di'pendənt] *adj.* ▫ **dependente**
He is dependent on his parents, because he doesn't have a job.
deposit¹ [di'pozit] *n.*
1 depósito
I make a deposit of 50 dollars in my savings account each month.
2 sinal
I paid a deposit on the new car.
deposit² *v.* (**deposits, depositing, deposited**) ▫ **depositar**
I deposited the money in your account.
depress [di'pres] *v.* (**depresses, depressing, depressed**) ▫ **deprimir**
Cold weather depresses me.
depressed [di'presd] *adj.* ▫ **deprimido**
He looked depressed.

depressing [di'presiŋ] *adj.* ▫ **deprimente**
a depressing book. ◆ The place was very depressing.
depression [di'preʃən] *n.* ▫ **depressão**
depth [depθ] *n.* ▫ **profundidade**
at a depth of six metres. ◆ What is the depth of the river here? ◆ The well is 10 metres in depth.
▪ Ver **deep**.
deputation [ˌdepju'teiʃən] *n.* ▫ **delegação**
The manager spoke to a deputation of the workers.
deputy ['depjuti] *n.* (*pl.* **deputies**) (= vice-)
1 substituto
a deputy school principal. ◆ a deputy minister.
2 substituto
You'll be my deputy when I'm on holiday.
derivative [di'rivətiv] *n.* ▫ **derivado**
'Deafness' is a derivative of 'deaf'.
descend [di'send] *v.* (**descends, descending, descended**) ▫ **descer**
The plane descended slowly. ◆ He descended the stairs.
▪ **come down** and **go down** are more usual.
descendant [di'sendənt] *n.* ▫ **descendente**
He is a descendant of Queen Victoria.
descent [di'sent] *n.* ▫ **descida**
The plane began its descent to the airport.
describe [di'skraib] *v.* (**describes, describing, described**) ▫ **descrever**
Can you describe the robber? ◆ He described the process in detail.
description [di'skripʃən] *n.* ▫ **descrição**
I gave the police a description of the man. ◆ a detailed description of the events.
desert[1] ['dezət] *n.* ▫ **deserto**
the Sahara Desert. ◆ It took them ten days to cross the desert on camels.
desert[2] [di'zeːt] *v.* (**deserts, deserting, deserted**)
1 largar, abandonar
He deserted his wife. ◆ to desert a place.
2 desertar
He deserted from the army.
deserted [di'zeːtid] *adj.* ▫ **deserto**
The streets were deserted. ◆ a deserted village.
desert island ['dezət 'ailənd] *n.* ▫ **ilha deserta**
deserve [di'zəːv] *v.* (**deserves, deserving, deserved**) ▫ **merecer**
He deserves a reward for his efforts. ◆ She did not deserve to win. ◆ You deserve a rest after working so hard.
▪ Ver **merit**[2].
design[1] [di'zain] *n.*
1 projeto
designs for a new shopping centre.
2 design
I like the design of this telephone.
3 desenho, padrão
wallpaper with a design of flowers.
4 projeto
The design of the car took two years.
design[2] *v.* (**designs, designing, designed**) ▫ **desenhar, projetar**
to design dresses / clothes. ◆ French engineers designed this plane.
designer [di'zainə] *n.* ▫ **designer**
a fashion designer.

desirable [di'zaiərəbl] *adj.* ▫ **desejável**
a desirable job.
desire[1] [di'zaiə] *n.* **desejo**
a desire to become famous. ◆ a desire for peace.
desire[2] *v.* (**desires, desiring, desired**) ▫ **desejar**
All he desires is to live in peace.
desk [desk] *n.*
1 mesa
Put your pens on the desk, please. ◆ a computer desk.
2 balcão
Let's ask at the information desk.
desktop computer ['desktop kəm'pjuːtə] *n.* ▫ **computador de mesa**
▪ Ver **laptop, palmtop**.
despair [di'speə] *n.* ▫ **desespero**
He was in despair after so many failures.
desperate ['despərət] *adj.*
1 desesperado
He is so desperate that he might do something stupid. ◆ She is desperate for work. ◆ He made a last desperate attempt to catch the rope before he drowned.
2 desesperador
The situation is desperate.
desperately ['despərətli] *adv.* ▫ **desesperadamente**
They tried desperately to save his life. ◆ They are desperately in need of money.
desperation [ˌdespə'reiʃən] *n.* ▫ **desespero**
In desperation, he started stealing food.
despise [di'spaiz] *v.* (**despises, despising, despised**) ▫ **desprezar**
How could you cheat him? I despise you.
▪ Ver **contempt**.
despite [di'spait] *prep.* ▫ **apesar de, a despeito de**
We continued to play despite the rain. ◆ Despite what you say, I think (that) we have a chance.
▪ **in spite of** can be used instead.
▪ Ver **although**.
dessert [di'zəːt] *n.* ▫ **sobremesa**
We had ice-cream for dessert. ◆ a pine-apple dessert.
destination [ˌdesti'neiʃən] *n.* ▫ **destino**
Rome was our final destination. ◆ He reached his destination at midnight.
destiny ['destəni] *n.* ▫ **destino**
destroy [di'stroi] *v.* (**destroys, destroying, destroyed**) ▫ **destruir**
The whole village was destroyed by the earthquake. ◆ The air force destroyed 200 enemy planes.
destroyer [di'stroiə] *n.* ▫ **destróier**
A destroyer is a small warship.
destruction [di'strʌkʃən] *n.* ▫ **destruição**
The storm caused destruction all over the country.
detach [di'tatʃ] *v.* (**detaches, detaching, detached**) ▫ **desprender, destacar**
You can detach this part of the machine. ◆ to detach a coupon from the newspaper.
detail ['diːteil] *n.* ▫ **detalhe**
He gave me all the details about the accident. ◆ We discussed every detail of the plan. ◆ For more details, please call 09-9232323.
go into detail(s) ▫ **entrar em detalhe(s)**
There's no need to go into detail. Just tell me who won.
in detail ▫ **em detalhes**

He explained everything in detail.
detailed ['di:teild] *adj.* ▫ detalhado
a detailed description.
detect [di'tekt] *v.* (**detects, detecting, detected**) ▫ detectar
The dog detected the drugs in his bag.
detection [di'tekʃən] *n.* ▫ detecção, descoberta
detective [di'tektiv] *n.* ▫ detetive
a private detective. ♦ The detective solved the murder case. ♦ a detective story.
deter [di'tə:] *v.* (**deters, deterring, deterred**) ▫ deter, impedir, intimidar
to deter criminals.
detergent [di'tə:dʒənt] *n.* ▫ detergente
laundry detergent (= washing-powder).
deteriorate [di'tiəriəreit] *v.* (**deteriorates, deteriorating, deteriorated**) ▫ deteriorar
The patient's condition is beginning to deteriorate. ♦ The situation is deteriorating.
determination [di,tə:mi'neiʃən] *n.* ▫ determinação
He has a great determination to succeed.
determine [di'tə:min] *v.* (**determines, determining, determined**) (= decide on, fix) ▫ determinar
They determined a date for their wedding.
determined [di'tə:mind] *adj.* ▫ determinado
She is determined to win the gold medal.
deterrent [di'terənt] *n.* ▫ meio de intimidação, impedimento
Is the death sentence a deterrent to murder?
detest [di'test] *v.* (**detests, detesting, detested**) ▫ detestar
I detest any kind of violence. ♦ They detest each other.
detour ['di:tuə] *n.* ▫ desvio
We made a detour to avoid the traffic jam.
develop [di'veləp] *v.* (**develops, developing, developed**)
1 desenvolver-se
The child / plant is developing well. ♦ The town developed beautifully. ♦ The disease developed quickly.
2 desenvolver
to develop the area.
3 desenvolver
I lift weights to develop my muscles.
4 revelar
to develop photographs.
5 desenvolver
They are developing a cure for the disease.
developed [di'veləpt] *adj.* ▫ desenvolvido
Developed countries have advanced industry.
developing country [di'veləpiŋ 'kʌntri] *n.* ▫ país em desenvolvimento
Many developing countries get help from the United Nations.
development [di'veləpmənt] *n.*
1 desenvolvimento
the development of a child. ♦ economic development.
2 desenvolvimento
The company spent 5 million dollars on research and development.
3 desenvolvimento
Are there any new developments in the trial?
device [di'vais] *n.* ▫ artifício, dispositivo
a device for closing plastic bags. ♦ a safety device which cuts off the electricity automatically.

devil ['devl] *n.* ▫ demônio
I don't believe in devils and ghosts.
the Devil *n.* o demônio, o diabo
devote [di'vout] *v.* (**devotes, devoting, devoted**) ▫ devotar, dedicar
He devotes his time and energy to helping weak pupils.
devoted [di'voutid] *adj.* ▫ devotado, dedicado
a devoted friend / mother.
devotion [di'vouʃən] *n.* ▫ devoção
devour [di'vauə] *v.* (**devours, devouring, devoured**) ▫ devorar
The tiger devoured the zebra. ♦ He devoured the cookies.
dew [dju:] *n.* ▫ orvalho
The flowers were wet with dew.
diabetes [daiə'bi:ti:z] *n.* ▫ diabetes
diagnose [daiəg'nouz] *v.* (**diagnoses, diagnosing, diagnosed**) ▫ diagnosticar
We must diagnose the disease before we treat it.
diagnosis [,daiəg,nousis] *n.* (*pl.* **diagnoses**) ▫ diagnóstico
What's the doctor's diagnosis?
diagonal [dai'agənl] *n.*, *adj.* ▫ diagonal
to draw a diagonal line.
diagram ['daiəgram] *n.* ▫ diagrama
The diagram shows how the system works.
dial¹ ['daiəl] *n.*
1 mostrador
the dial of a clock / watch.
2 indicador
The dial shows the number of kilometres.
3 dial
to move the dial to find a radio station.
4 discador
the dial of a telephone.
dial² *v.* (*Amer.* **dials, dialing, dialed**; *Brit.* **dialling, dialled**) ▫ discar
I dialled 08 232 615. ♦ Dial 144 for information.
dialect ['daiəlekt] *n.* ▫ dialeto
English has a lot of local dialects. ♦ I can't understand his dialect.
dialog ['daiəlog] *n. Amer.*, **dialogue** *Brit.* ▫ diálogo
diameter [dai'amitə] *n.* ▫ diâmetro
a circle 20 metres in diameter
diamond ['daiəmənd] *n.* ▫ diamante
a diamond ring.
diamonds *n.* ▫ ouros (cartas)
the seven of diamonds.
diaper ['daiəpə] *n. Amer.* ▫ fralda
to change the baby's diapers.
■ *Brit.* **nappy**
diary ['daiəri] *n.* (*pl.* **diaries**)
1 diário
She keeps a diary. (= She writes in her diary what happens to her each day.)
2 agenda
I'll check in my diary to see if I'm free tomorrow.
■ *Amer.* also **calendar**
dice [dais] *n.* (*pl.* **dice**) ▫ dado
to throw the dice.
dictate [dik'teit] *v.* (**dictates, dictating, dictated**)
1 ditar
The teacher dictated the new words to the class. ♦ She dictated a letter to her secretary.

2 dar ordem a alguém
You can't dictate to me. (= You can't tell me what to do.)
dictation [dik'teiʃən] *n*. □ **ditado**
We had a dictation in French.
dictator [dik'teitə] *n*. □ **ditador**
■ Ver **tyrant**.
dictionary ['dikʃənəri] *n*. (*pl*. **dictionaries**) □ **dicionário**
to look up a word in the dictionary.
did [did] *v*. (Ver **do**).
die [dai] *v*. (**dies, dying, died**) □ **morrer**
When did he die? ◆ She died of hunger / cancer. ◆ They died in an accident.
■ Ver **pass away**.
be dying
1 estar morrendo
She is dying (of cancer).
2 estar louco
I'm dying for an ice cream.
die down □ **apagar-se, abrandar, diminuir**
The fire / storm is dying down. ◆ The pain died down.
diet¹ ['daiət] *n*.
1 dieta
They live on a diet of rice and fish. ◆ a healthy diet.
2 regime
She wants to go on a diet because she is fat.
diet² *adj*. □ **dietético**
diet soft drinks.
diet³ *v*. (**diets, dieting, dieted**) □ **fazer regime, estar de regime**
No bread, please! I'm dieting.
differ ['difə] *v*. (**differs, differing, differed**) □ **diferir, diferenciar-se**
The boxes differed in size and colour. ◆ How do humans differ from animals?
difference ['difrəns] *n*.
1 diferença
What's the difference between these computers? ◆ There's a big difference between driving a car and driving a bus.
2 diferença
The difference in price between these two houses is only 3,000 dollars.
make any difference □ **fazer nenhuma diferença, fazer alguma diferença**
It doesn't make any difference (who will go). ◆ Does it make any difference (if I tell him now)?
make no difference □ **não fazer diferença, dar no mesmo**
It makes no difference to me: you can go or stay.
tell the difference □ **distinguir**
Can you tell the difference between them?
different ['difrənt] *adj*.
1 diferente
I did it in a different way. ◆ It looks different in daylight. ◆ This car is different from that one.
■ *Amer.* **different from**; **different than**.
2 diverso
These hats are made in different sizes and colours.
differentiate [ˌdifə'renʃieit] *v*. (**differentiates, differentiating, differentiated**) (= distinguish) □ **distinguir, diferenciar**
They are so similar – I can't differentiate between them.
differentiation [ˌdifərenʃi'eiʃən] *n*. □ **diferenciação**

differently ['difrəntli] *adv*. □ **diferentemente**
They behave differently in front of their parents.
difficult ['difikəlt] *adj*. □ **difícil**
a difficult question. ◆ The exam was not so difficult. ◆ It's difficult to pronounce your name.
■ antônimo: **easy**
■ Ver **hard**.
difficulty ['difikəlti] *n*. (*pl*. **difficulties**) □ **dificuldade**
Did you have any difficulty in finding the house? ◆ He moved his leg with difficulty.
dig [dig] *v*. (**digs, digging, dug**)
1 cavar, escavar
Who dug this hole? ◆ They are digging a tunnel.
2 cavoucar
to dig the garden.
dig up □ **desenterrar**
The archeologist dug up coins from ancient times.
digest [dai'dʒest] *v*. (**digests, digesting, digested**) □ **digerir**
It is not easy to digest this food. ◆ Baby food digests easily.
digestion [dai'dʒestʃən] *n*. □ **digestão**
dignified ['dignifaid] *adj*. □ **digno**
a dignified person.
dignity [digˈnəti] *n*. □ **dignidade**
to behave with dignity. ◆ He thinks it is beneath his dignity to help with the housework.
dilapidated [di'lapideited] *adj*. □ **em más condições, deteriorado**
a dilapidated building.
diligent ['dilidʒənt] *adj*. □ **diligente**
a diligent pupil / worker.
dilute [dai'lju:t] *v*. (**dilutes, diluting, diluted**) □ **diluir**
to dilute juice with water. ◆ to dilute paint.
dim¹ [dim] *adj*. (**dimmer, dimmest**) □ **fraco**
a dim light
dim² *v*. (**dims, dimming, dimmed**) □ **diminuir a intensidade**
He dimmed the lights.
dime [daim] *n*. □ **moeda de dez centavos de dólar**
diminish [di'miniʃ] *v*. (**diminishes, diminishing, diminished**) □ **diminuir**
The noise diminished. ◆ The number of elephants there is diminishing.
dimple ['dimpl] *n*. □ **covinha**
din [din] *n*. □ **estrépido, alarido**
The children made a terrible din when the bell rang.
dine [dain] *v*. (**dines, dining, dined**) □ **jantar**
We dined at an Indian restaurant.
dinghy ['diŋɡi] *n*. (*pl*. **dinghies**) □ **bote**
a rubber dinghy.
dining room ['dainiŋ ˌrum] *n*. □ **sala de jantar**
dinner ['dinə] *n*. □ **jantar**
What did you have for dinner last night? ◆ We had dinner at 1 o'clock.
■ Compare **lunch, supper**:
  lunch = a light midday meal.
  supper = a light evening meal.
dinosaur ['dainəso:] *n*. □ **dinossauro**
dip [dip] *v*. (**dips, dipping, dipped**)
1 mergulhar
He dipped his fingers in the water to see if it was hot enough. ◆ to dip a piece of bread in the sauce.

2 *Brit.* baixar
I dipped the headlights.
diploma [di'ploumə] *n.* □ **diploma**
a teaching diploma. ◆ a diploma in engineering.
diplomat ['dipləmæt] *n.* □ **diplomata**
diplomatic [diplə'mætik] *adj.* □ **diplomático**
diplomatic relations (with another country).
direct[1] [di'rekt] *adj.*
1 reto
in a direct line.
2 direto
direct flights to New York.
direct[2] *adv.* □ **direto**
He flew direct to London. ◆ The train goes direct to Rome.
direct object *n.* (grammar) □ **objeto direto**
■ Ver **indirect object**.
direct speech *n.* (grammar) □ **discurso direto**
■ Ver **indirect speech**.
direct[3] *v.* (**directs, directing, directed**)
1 ensinar o caminho, mostrar o caminho
Can you direct me to the airport, please?
2 dirigir
to direct a film / play.
3 encaminhar, direcionar
Please direct your complaints to the manager. ◆ He directed our attention to the fact that...
4 ordenar, comandar
A policeman directed the traffic.
5 dirigir
to direct a project / department.
direction [di'rekʃən] *n.* □ **direção**
Which direction did she go in? ◆ He went in the wrong direction.
directions [di'rekʃənz] *n. pl.*
1 instruções
Directions for use: 10 drops in a glass of water twice a day. ◆ His directions were not to leave the place.
2 orientação
I asked a policeman for directions how to get there.
directly [di'rektli] *adv.*
1 diretamente
He looked directly at them.
2 bem
My house is directly opposite the library.
3 imediatamente
We left directly after the speech.
director [di'rektə] *n.*
1 diretor
the board of directors (of a company, bank, etc.). ◆ the director of the project.
2 diretor
a television director.
directory [di'rektəri] *n.* □ **lista telefônica, catálogo telefônico**
to look up a number in the telephone directory
dirt [də:t] *n.*
1 sujeira
The wall was covered with dirt.
2 de terra
a dirt road.
dirty[1] ['də:ti] *adj.* (**dirtier, dirtiest**) □ **sujo**
dirty clothes / dishes. ◆ His hands were dirty.

dirty[2] *v.* (**dirties, dirtying, dirtied**) □ **sujar**
Try not to dirty your dress.
dis- [dis-] *pref.* □ **des-**
disobey (= not obey). ◆ dishonest (= not honest) . ◆ disconnect (= the opposite of connect).
disability [disə'biləti] *n.* □ **incapacidade, inaptidão**
disabled [dis'eibld] *adj.* □ **deficiente**
He is disabled. He sits in a wheelchair.
the disabled *n.* □ **deficientes**
disadvantage [disəd'va:ntidʒ] *n.* □ **desvantagem**
His lack of experience is a disadvantage. ◆ What are the advantages and disadvantages of the system?
disadvantaged [disəd'va:ntidʒd] *adj.* □ **menos favorecido**
disadvantaged sections of the population.
disagree [disə'gri:] *v.* (**disagrees, disagreeing, disagreed**) □ **discordar**
I disagree with you / your decision. ◆ We disagreed about the plan.
disagreement [,disə'gri:mənt] *n.*
1 desacordo, discordância
They are in disagreement over the plan.
2 (= argument) **desavença**
We had a disagreement about the money.
disappear [disə'piə] *v.* (**disappears, disappearing, disappeared**) □ **desaparecer, sumir**
The sun disappeared behind the clouds. ◆ When did he disappear?
make something disappear □ **fazer algo desaparecer**
The magician made the rabbit disappear.
disappearance [,disə'piərəns] *n.* □ **desaparecimento, sumiço**
His disappearance is a mystery.
disappoint [disə'point] *v.* (**disappoints, disappointing, disappointed**) □ **desapontar, decepcionar**
He disappointed us. He didn't try hard enough. ◆ Sorry to disappoint you, but it's just not possible.
disappointed [,disə'pointid] *adj.* □ **desapontado, decepcionado**
They were disappointed when the trip was cancelled. ◆ I was disappointed to hear that... ◆ They are disappointed in me. They expected me to win.
disappointing [,disə'pointiŋ] *adj.* □ **decepcionante**
a disappointing film / book. ◆ The results were disappointing.
disappointment [,disə'pointmənt] *n.* □ **desapontamento, decepção**
To their great disappointment, they were not invited. ◆ She couldn't hide her disappointment. ◆ His speech was a big disappointment.
disapproval [,disə'pru:vəl] *n.* □ **desaprovação**
disapprove [disə'pru:v] *v.* (**disapproves, disapproving, disapproved**) □ **desaprovar**
He wants to marry her but his family disapproves. ◆ They disapprove of him / his methods.
disaster [di'za:stə] *n.* □ **desastre**
Hundreds were killed in the disaster. ◆ natural disasters (= floods, earthquakes, etc.). ◆ an air disaster.
disastrous [di'za:strəs] *adj.* □ **desastroso**
disastrous floods. ◆ a disastrous mistake
disc [disk] *n., Amer.* **disk**
1 disco
We played some discs and danced.

■ Ver **record; compact disc**.
2 (= disk) **disco**
All the information can be stored on one disc.
■ Ver **floppy disk; hard disk**.
discharge¹ [dis'tʃɑːdʒ] *v*. (**discharges, discharging, discharged**) ▫ **dar alta, liberar**
They discharged him from hospital.
discharge² *n*. ▫ **descarga, despedida, alta**
disciple [di'saipl] *n*. ▫ **discípulo**
The religious leader has many disciples.
discipline¹ ['displin] *n*. ▫ **disciplina**
military discipline.
discipline² *v*. (**disciplines, disciplining, disciplined**) ▫ **disciplinar, disciplinar-se**
This pupil needs to be disciplined. ◆ You must discipline yourself to exercise every day.
disc-jockey ['disk'dʒɔki] *n*. (= **DJ**) ▫ **disc-jóquei, DJ**
disco ['diskou] *n*. ▫ **disco, discoteca**
disconnect [diskə'nekt] *v*. (**disconnects, disconnecting, disconnected**) ▫ **desconectar, desligar**
They may disconnect your telephone if you don't pay the bill. ◆ to disconnect (= unplug) the TV.
discontented [ˌdiskən'tentid] *adj*. (= dissatisfied) ▫ **descontente**
He is discontented with his salary.
discount ['diskaunt] *n*. ▫ **desconto**
You can get a 15% discount on these dresses. ◆ I bought it at a discount (of 20 dollars).
discourage [dis'kʌridʒ] *v*. (**discourages, discouraging, discouraged**) ▫ **desencorajar, desincentivar**
They did their best to discourage him from smoking.
■ antônimo: **encourage**
be discouraged ▫ **desanimar**
Don't be discouraged by his failure.
discover [dis'kʌvə] *v*. (**discovers, discovering, discovered**) ▫ **descobrir**
Who discovered America? ◆ They discovered a cure for the disease. ◆ I discovered that she was not a real doctor.
discovery [dis'kʌvəri] *n*. (*pl*. **discoveries**)
1 descobrimento
the discovery of America.
2 descoberta
a scientific discovery.
discriminate [dis'krimineit] *v*. (**discriminates, discriminating, discriminated**) ▫ **discriminar**
People should not be discriminated against because of their race or religion. ◆ This law discriminates in favour of men.
discrimination [disˌkrimi'neiʃən] *n*. ▫ **discriminação**
racial / religious discrimination.
discuss [dis'kʌs] *v*. (**discusses, discussing, discussed**) ▫ **discutir**
They discussed the problem. ◆ I'd like to discuss it with my partner.
discussion [dis'kʌʃən] *n*. ▫ **discussão**
Discussions on economic cooperation will start tomorrow. ◆ We had a long discussion about politics.
disease [di'ziːz] *n*. ▫ **doença**
Is there a cure for this disease?
■ Ver **illness**.
disgrace¹ [dis'greis] *n*. ▫ **desgraça**
He brought disgrace on his family.

■ Ver **shame**².
disgrace² *v*. (**disgraces, disgracing, disgraced**) ▫ **desgraçar**
She disgraced all of us by the way she behaved.
disguise¹ [dis'gaiz] *n*. ▫ **disfarce**
They went to the party in disguise.
disguise² *v*. (**disguises, disguising, disguised**)
1 disfarçar-se
They disguised themselves as policemen.
2 disfarçar
He tried to disguise his voice.
disgust¹ [dis'gʌst] *n*. ▫ **repugnância**
She looked at him in disgust when he killed the animal.
disgust² *v*. (**disgusts, disgusting, disgusted**) ▫ **enojar, repugnar**
The dirty tablecloth disgusted him. ◆ You disgust me!
be disgusted ▫ **ficar com nojo**
I was disgusted to see him eating with his fingers.
disgustedly [dis'gʌstidli] *adv*. ▫ **desgostosamente, repulsivamente**
disgusting [dis'gʌstiŋ] *adj*. (= revolting) ▫ **repugnante, nojento**
The taste / smell was disgusting.
dish [diʃ] *n*.
1 louça
He served the beans in a glass dish.
2 (= plate) **prato**
3 prato
a meat dish.
■ Ver **bowl; plate**.
the dishes *n*. ▫ **a louça**
It's your turn to wash the dishes.
dishonest [dis'ɔnist] *adj*. ▫ **desonesto**
a dishonest businessman
■ antônimo: **honest**
dishwasher ['diʃˌwɔʃə] *n*. ▫ **máquina de lavar louça**
disinfectant [ˌdisin'fektənt] *n*. ▫ **desinfetante**
disinterested [dis'intristid] *adj*. (= unbiased, fair, impartial) ▫ **desinteressado, imparcial**
I am not biased, so let me give you some disinterested advice.
■ Compare **uninterested**:
uninterested (= not interested).
disk [disk] *n*.
1 disco
All the information can be stored on one disk.
■ Ver **floppy disk; hard disk**.
2 (= disc) **disco**
We played some disks and danced.
disk drive ['disk 'draiv] *n*. ▫ **drive, unidade de disco**
diskette [dis'ket] *n*. (= floppy disk) ▫ **disquete**
dislike¹ [dis'laik] *n*. ▫ **aversão, desagrado**
She has a strong dislike of cats.
dislike² *v*. (**dislikes, disliking, disliked**) ▫ **ter aversão a, não gostar de**
I dislike driving at night. ◆ He dislikes them.
■ antônimo: **like; love**²
dismal ['dizməl] *adj*. ▫ **abatido, desolador**
a dismal look. ◆ dismal weather.
dismay¹ [dis'mei] *n*. ▫ **consternação, tristeza**
He looked at me in dismay when I told him the bad news.
dismay² *v*.

be dismayed ◻ **consternar-se**
He was dismayed to hear about the accident.
dismiss [dis'mis] *v.* (**dismisses, dismissing, dismissed**)
1 demitir
He was dismissed (from his job).
■ Ver **fire²**; **sack²**.
2 dispensar
The teacher dismissed the class early today.
dismissal [dis'misəl] *n.* **dispensa, demissão**
dismount [dis'maunt] *v.* ◻ (**dismounts, dismounting, dismounted**) ◻ **descer**
The police officer dismounted from his motorcycle.
■ The usual word is **get off** (his motorcycle / horse etc.).
disobedience [ˌdisə'biːdjəns] *n.* ◻ **desobediência**
They punished him for disobedience.
■ antônimo: **obedience**
disobedient [ˌdisə'biːdjənt] *adj.* ◻ **desobediente**
a disobedient child.
■ antônimo: **obedient**
disobey [disə'bei] *v.* (**disobeys, disobeying, disobeyed**) ◻ **desobedecer**
He disobeyed me / my order.
■ antônimo: **obey**
disorder [dis'ɔːdə] *n.*
1 desordem
She always leaves her room in disorder.
2 distúrbio
The police were ready to prevent any disorder.
disperse [dis'pəːs] *v.* (**disperses, dispersing, dispersed**) ◻ **dispersar, dispersar-se**
The police dispersed the demonstration. ◆ The animals dispersed in all directions.
display¹ [dis'plei] *n.* ◻ **mostra, exposição, expositor**
a fashion display. ◆ The treasure is on display at the museum.
display² *v.* (**displays, displaying, displayed**) ◻ **expor, exibir**
to display goods in shop windows.
displeased [dis'pliːzd] *adj.* ◻ **descontente, insatisfeito**
She is displeased with you.
■ antônimo: **pleased**
displeasure [dis'pleʒə] *n.* ◻ **desprazer, insatisfação**
disposable [dis'pouzəbl] *adj.* ◻ **descartável**
disposable diapers / cups.
disposal [dis'pouzəl] *n.* ◻ **descarte**
waste disposal.
dispose [dis'pouz] *v.* (**disposes, disposing, disposed**)
dispose of ◻ **descartar**
We must try to dispose of waste by recycling.
dispute ['dispjuːt] *n.*
1 contenda
a pay dispute between management and workers.
2 (= argument) **argumentação**
There's a lot of dispute over this issue. ◆ There was a dispute over who should go first.
disqualify [dis'kwɔlifai] *v.* (**disqualifies, disqualifying, disqualified**) ◻ **desclassificar**
Two athletes were disqualified because they took drugs.
disregard [disrə'gaːd] *v.* (**disregards, disregarding, disregarded**) ◻ **desconsiderar**
He disregarded my warnings.
disrespect ['disris'pekt] *n.* ◻ **desrespeito**

■ antônimo: **respect¹**
disrupt [dis'rʌpt] *v.* (**disrupts, disrupting, disrupted**) ◻ **desorganizar, interromper**
Snow disrupted traffic.
dissatisfied [di'satisfaid] *adj.* (= displeased) ◻ **insatisfeito**
Your teacher is dissatisfied with your work.
dissolve [di'zɔlv] *n.* (**dissolves, dissolving, dissolved**) ◻ **dissolver**
I dissolved the powder in water. ◆ Sugar dissolves in water.
■ Ver **melt**.
distance ['distəns] *n.* ◻ **distância**
What is the distance from the station to the airport? ◆ Keep a safe distance behind the car in front. ◆ He stood at a distance of 10 metres from the car.
in the distance ◻ **ao longe**
I could see a light in the distance.
distance learning ['distəns 'ləːniŋ] *n.* ◻ **ensino a distância**
Students study in distance learning courses by means of e-mail, TV, telephone and correspondence.
■ Ver **e-learning**.
distant ['distənt] *adj.* ◻ **distante**
distant villages. ◆ We heard a distant cry. ◆ It happened in the distant past.
distinct [dis'tiŋkt] *adj.*
1 distinto
The tracks in the snow were quite distinct. ◆ There's a distinct improvement in the patient's condition.
2 distinto
two distinct styles.
distinction [dis'tiŋkʃən] *n.*
1 distinção
Let's make a distinction between these suggestions.
2 menção honrosa
He got a distinction in the exam.
distinctly [dis'tiŋktli] *adv.* (= clearly) ◻ **distintamente**
I remember it distinctly. ◆ I distinctly remember what she said.
distinguish [dis'tiŋgwiʃ] *v.* (**distinguishes, distinguishing, distinguished**) (= differentiate) ◻ **distinguir**
I can't distinguish between the twins. ◆ Do you know what distinguishes people from animals?
distinguished [dis'tiŋgwiʃt] *adj.*
1 eminente
a distinguished scientist / actor. ◆ a distinguished athlete.
2 distinto
a distinguished lady.
3 notável
a distinguished career.
distract [dis'trakt] *v.* (**distracts, distracting, distracted**) ◻ **distrair**
Don't distract the driver's attention. ◆ The noise distracted me from my work.
distraction [dis'trakʃən] *n.* ◻ **distração**
distress [dis'tres] *n.* ◻ **angústia, pesar**
They spoke with distress about their son's illness. ◆ Her death caused him great distress.
in distress ◻ **em perigo**
a ship in distress.
distribute [dis'tribjut] *v.* (**distributes, distributing, distributed**)
1 distribuir
They distributed leaflets in the street.

2 distribuir
This company distributes our products in America.
■ Ver **give out, hand out**.
distribution [ˌditriˈbjuːʃən] *n.*
1 distribuição
the distribution of food and blankets to the refugees
2 distribuição
a distribution company.
district [ˈdistrikt] *n.* □ **região, distrito**
a mountainous district. ◆ He lives in a poor district.
■ Ver **area, region**.
distrust [disˈtrʌst] *v.* (**distrusts, distrusting, distrusted**)
□ **desconfiar**
They distrust him.
■ antônimo: **trust**^{2}
disturb [disˈtəːb] *v.* (**disturbs, disturbing, disturbed**)
□ **perturbar**
Do not disturb! ◆ He always disturbs me when I'm working.
■ Compare **interfere**^{2}.
disturbance [disˈtəːbəns] *n.*
1 desordem
He was punished for causing a disturbance in class.
2 tumulto
The police arrested him for creating a disturbance.
ditch [ditʃ] *n.* □ **fosso, vala**
They dug a ditch around their land.
dive [daiv] *v.* (**dives, diving, dived**)
1 submergir
The submarine dived to a depth of 150 metres.
2 mergulhar
He dived into the pool from the diving board.
■ The *past tense* in American English is **dived** or **dove**.
diver [ˈdaivə] *n.* □ **mergulhador**
divert [daiˈvəːt] *v.* (**diverts, diverting, diverted**)
1 desviar
to divert traffic (to a different road).
2 desviar
The noise diverted his attention.
divide [diˈvaid] *v.* (**divides, dividing, divided**)
1 dividir
We divided the money between ourselves. ◆ The policemen divided (up) into four groups.
2 dividir
If you divide 16 by 4 the answer is 4. ◆ 16 divided by 4 is 4.
■ The noun is **division**.
divine [diˈvain] *adj.* □ **divino**
divine justice.
diving [ˈdaiviŋ] *n.* □ **mergulho**
Let's go diving.
diving board [ˈdaiviŋboːd] *n.* □ **trampolim**
She dived into the pool from the diving board.
diving suit [ˈdaiviŋ sjuːt] *n.* □ **traje de mergulho**
The divers put on their diving suits.
division [diˈviʒən] *n.*
1 divisão
the division of the work between them.
2 divisão
Two divisions were sent to the border.
3 divisão
Our team is in the 1st division.
4 divisão, setor
The sales division.

5 divisão
multiplication and division.
divorce^1 [diˈvoːs] *n.* □ **divórcio**
She wants a divorce from her husband. ◆ Did you get a divorce?
divorce^2 *v.* (**divorces, divorcing, divorced**) □ **divorciar-se**
He divorced his wife. ◆ They got divorced.
divorced [diˈvoːst] *adj.* □ **divorciado**
I'm divorced.
DIY [ˌdiːaiˈwai] *abbr.* (= do it yourself) □ **faça você mesmo**
a DIY shop.
dizziness [ˈdizinis] *n.* □ **tontura**
dizzy [ˈdizi] *adj.* (**dizzier, dizziest**) □ **tonto**
I feel dizzy. ◆ The dance made me dizzy.
DJ [ˌdiːˈdʒei] *n.*, *abbr.* (= disc jockey) □ **DJ, disc-jóquei**
do [duː] *v.* (**does, doing, did, done**)
1 fazer
What are you doing? ◆ What do you usually do in the evenings? ◆ She didn't do a good job. ◆ Do me a favor / favour.
◆ Are you doing your homework?
■ Use **make** (*not* **do**) in these cases:
to make a mistake.
to make (a) noise.
to make peace with.
to make a cake.
2 ser bom, servir, bastar
Paper cups will do. (= Paper cups are good enough.) ◆ Five dollars will do. I don't need more.
3 ir, passar
She's doing very well at school. ◆ The patient is doing well.
4 usado como verbo auxiliar em orações negativas e, portanto, não é traduzido
I don't speak French. ◆ She doesn't come here often.
◆ Don't forget to send it.
5 usado como verbo auxiliar em orações interrogativas e, portanto, não é traduzido
Do you speak English?
6 usado como verbo auxiliar em orações interrogativas cujo sujeito seja um pronome interrogativo e, portanto, não é traduzido
What does she want? ◆ When did you see her?
7 usado para dar ênfase e pode ser traduzido como "realmente"
He did come to the party. ◆ I do want to come.
8 usado como verbo vicário para evitar a repetição do verbo principal
She promised to help, and she did. ◆ He speaks Spanish and so do I. ◆ Do you want it? – Yes, I do. ◆ Who took it? – I did.
9 usado em perguntas de confirmação
He came late, didn't he? ◆ We don't know her, do we?
10 usado para expressar polidez, boas maneiras, podendo ser traduzido como "por favor"
Do come here. ◆ Do please sit down.
could do with □ **gostar de**
I could do with a few hours' rest.
do away with □ **abolir, pôr fim a**
The school decided to do away with written exams.
do up
1 abotoar, amarrar
Help him to do up his coat / shoelaces.

■ antônimo: **undo**
2 pôr em ordem
to do the kitchen up
do without □ **passar sem**
I can't do without a car.
have to do with □ **ter a ver com**
His job has to do with films. ◆ I don't know who told her. I had nothing to do with it.
How are you doing? □ **Como você está?**
How is your brother doing these days?
How do you do? □ **Como vai?**
■ A formal greeting when meeting somebody for the first time. The reply is also: **How do you do?**
■ Informal greeting: **Pleased to meet you.**
What do you do? □ **O que você faz?**
What does he do (for a living)? (= What's his job?)
dock [dok] *n.* □ **cais, doca**
The ship is loading at the dock.
doctor [ˈdoktə] *n.*
1 médico
You'd better see a doctor. ◆ Call a doctor.
■ When you write 'Doctor' together with a person's name the short form is **Dr.**:
I have an appointment with Dr. Sol.
2 doutor
Dr. (= Doctor) Jones was a famous archaeologist.
document [ˈdokjumənt] *n.* □ **documento**
a top-secret document
documentary [ˌdokjuˈmentəri] *n.* (*pl.* **documentaries**) □ **documentário**
a documentary about life in China
dodge [dodʒ] *v.* (**dodges, dodging, dodged**) □ **esquivar--se de**
He dodged the blow. ◆ She entered the bus station to dodge the policeman.
does [dʌz] *v.* (Ver **do**).
dog [dog] *n.* □ **cachorro, cão**
a guide dog (for blind people) ◆ The dog barked and wagged its tail.
doing [ˈduːiŋ] *v.* (Ver **do**).
doll [dol] *n.* □ **boneca**
She hugged the doll.
dollar [ˈdolə] *n.* □ **dólar**
It costs fifty dollars ($50).
dolphin [ˈdolfin] *n.* □ **golfinho**
dome [doum] *n.* □ **cúpula**
The dome of the mosque is covered with gold.
domestic [dəˈmestik] *adj.*
1 doméstico
domestic life (= family life). ◆ domestic jobs such as cleaning and cooking.
2 doméstico
domestic animals.
3 doméstico
domestic flights (from one place to another in the same country).
domesticate [dəˈmestikeit] *v.* (**domesticates, domesticating, domesticated**) □ **domesticar**
People domesticated dogs and cats a very long time ago.
dominant [ˈdominənt] *adj.* □ **dominante**
the dominant person in the group. ◆ The dominant flower in the garden was the rose.

dominate [ˈdomineit] *v.* (**dominates, dominating, dominated**) □ **dominar**
Our team will dominate the football league this year.
donate [dəˈneit] *v.* (**donates, donating, donated**) □ **doar**
They donated money to the university. ◆ He donated the painting to the museum. ◆ to donate blood.
■ A person who donates is a **donor**.
donation [dəˈneiʃən] *n.* □ **doação**
She made large donations to hospitals and universities.
done [dʌn] *v.* (Ver **do**).
Have you done your homework? ◆ It can be done.
donkey [ˈdoŋki] *n.* □ **burro, jumento**
don't [dount] (mesmo que **do not**)
door [doː] *n.* □ **porta**
He knocked on the door. ◆ Close / Shut the door, please. ◆ The door is locked.
answer the door □ **atender a porta**
Will you answer the door?
next door □ **vizinho, da casa ao lado**
They live next door to us.
out of doors (also **outdoors**) □ **ao ar livre**
to exercise out of doors.
doorbell [ˈdoːbəl] *n.* □ **campainha**
to ring the doorbell.
doorway [ˈdoːwei] *n.* □ **entrada, à porta**
He stood in the doorway.
dormitory [ˈdoːmitəri] *n.* (*pl.* **dormitories**) □ **dormitório**
dose [dous] *n.* □ **dose**
Take one dose (of medicine) a day.
dot [dot] *n.* □ **ponto, pingo, bolinha**
There's a dot over the letter i. ◆ a red dress with white dots.
on the dot □ **em ponto**
The plane landed at six o'clock on the dot.
dot-com [ˈdotˈkom] *n.*, *adj.* □ **pontocom, online**
I bought it from a dot-com company on the Internet.
double[1] [ˈdʌbl] *adj.*
1 duplo, o dobro de
He had a double helping of pie. ◆ His income is double my income. ◆ My telephone number is two three seven, double three two (237332).
2 de casal
a double bed.
double[2] *adv.* □ **o dobro**
It costs double what it did a year ago.
double[3] *v.* (**doubles, doubling, doubled**) □ **dobrar**
The population of this city will double in 15 years. ◆ The company doubled its profits.
double agent [ˈdʌbl ˈeidʒənt] *n.* □ **agente duplo**
double-decker [ˌdʌblˈdekə] *n.* □ **ônibus de dois andares**
doubt[1] [daut] *n.* □ **dúvida**
I have no doubt that it will work. ◆ There's no doubt about it. ◆ There's some doubt about his honesty.
in doubt □ **em dúvida**
If you are in doubt, check it again.
no doubt □ **não tenha dúvida**
No doubt, he is the best.
without (a) doubt □ **sem (qualquer / nenhuma) dúvida**
It was without doubt their best game this year.
doubt[2] *v.* (**doubts, doubting, doubted**) □ **duvidar**
I doubt if they will come. ◆ I don't doubt that you're telling the truth.
doubtful [ˈdautful] *adj.* □ **incerto, duvidoso**
It is doubtful if he will stay.

doubtless / draw

to be doubtful □ duvidar de
He says he will pay me, but I'm doubtful.
doubtless ['dautlis] *adv.* □ **sem dúvida, indubitavelmente**
Doubtless she will win the game.
dough [dou] *n.* □ **massa**
doughnut ['dounʌt] *n.* □ **rosquinha**
dove [dʌv] *n.* □ **pombo**
The dove is a symbol of peace.
down[1] [daun] *adv.*
1 para baixo
He climbed down (from) the tree. ◆ Put it down on the floor.
 ▪ antônimo: **up**
 ▪ Ver **calm down; cut down; die down; fall down; go down; let down; lie down; put down; sit down; take down.**
2 em declínio
The temperature is down.
 ▪ antônimo: **up**
down[2] *prep.*
1 abaixo
They ran down the hill. ◆ to sail down the river.
2 (= along) **ao longo de**
to walk down the road
downhill [,daun'hil] *adv.* □ **ladeira abaixo**
They rode downhill on their bikes.
download ['daunloud] *v.* (**downloads, downloading, downloaded**) □ **baixar**
I download my e-mails every day.
downstairs[1] ['daun'steərz] *adv.* □ **em/para o andar de baixo**
He went downstairs to eat breakfast. ◆ Who lives downstairs?
 ▪ antônimo: **upstairs**
downstairs[2] *adj.* □ **no andar de baixo**
the downstairs apartment.
 ▪ antônimo: **upstairs**
downtown ['dauntaun] *adv., n.* □ **em / para / o centro da cidade, centro da cidade**
They went downtown.
downward(s) ['daunwəd(z)] *adv.* □ **para baixo**
He looked downwards at his shoes. ◆ He was lying face downwards.
 ▪ antônimo: **upward(s)**
doze[1] [douz] *n.* □ **soneca, cochilo**
doze[2] *v.* (**dozes, dozing, dozed**) □ **cochilar**
The old man is dozing in his chair.
dozen ['dʌzn] *n.* (*pl.* **dozen**) □ **dúzia**
a dozen eggs. ◆ two dozen (= 24) bottles. ◆ half a dozen (= 6).
dozens (of) □ **dúzias (de)**
I warned him dozens of times. ◆ How many people came? – Dozens.
Dr. *abbr.* (Ver **doctor**).
draft[1] [draːft] *n.*
1 *Amer.* **corrente de ar**
I'd better shut the window. There's a draft in here.
 ▪ *Brit.* **draught**
2 rascunho
a draft of an essay.
draft[2] *Amer.* (**drafts, drafting, drafted**) □ **convocar**
He was drafted after he left school.
 ▪ *Brit.* **conscript**[2]**; call up**

drafty ['draːfti] *adj. Amer.* □ **com corrente de ar**
It's a bit drafty in here.
 ▪ *Brit.* **draughty**
drag [drag] *v.* (**drags, dragging, dragged**)
1 arrastar
He dragged a heavy suitcase behind him. ◆ Don't drag your feet!
2 arrastar-se
The lecture started to drag.
dragon ['dragən] *n.* □ **dragão**
drain[1] [drein] *n.* □ **cano, bueiro**
The kitchen drain is blocked. ◆ He threw my keys down a drain in the road.
go down the drain □ **ir por água abaixo**
All the money we invested in this project went down the drain.
drain[2] *v.* (**drains, draining, drained**)
1 escorrer
Boil the vegetables for 5 minutes and drain them.
2 escorrer
Leave the plates / dishes to drain.
3 drenar; escoar
to drain a canal. ◆ The bath water quickly drained away.
drainpipe ['dreinpaip] *n.* □ **cano de esgoto**
drama ['draːmə] *n.*
1 (= play) **drama**
a TV drama.
2 teatro
She studies drama at university.
3 drama
There was a little drama when the pop star refused to go on stage.
dramatic [drə'matik] *adj.* □ **dramático**
a dramatic rescue operation. ◆ dramatic changes.
dramatically [drə'matikəli] *adv.* □ **dramaticamente**
drank [draŋk] *v.* (Ver **drink**[2]).
drapes [dreips] *n. pl. Amer.* □ **cortinas**
 ▪ Ver **curtain**.
drastic ['drastik] *adj.* □ **drástico**
drastic changes.
draught [draːft] *n. Brit.* □ **corrente de ar**
 ▪ *Amer.* **draft**
draughty ['draːfti] *adj. Brit.* □ **com corrente de ar**
 ▪ *Amer.* **drafty**
draughts [draːfts] *n. Brit.* □ **(jogo de) damas**
 ▪ *Amer.* **checkers**
draw[1] [droː] *n.*
1 (= tie[1]) **empate**
The game ended in a 2-2 draw.
2 sorteio
There is a draw to decide who will go.
draw[2] *v.* (**draws, drawing, drew, drawn**)
1 desenhar
She drew a beautiful picture. ◆ to draw a circle.
2 sacar
to draw a knife / gun.
3 (= pull) **puxar**
The carriage was drawn by 4 horses.
4 aproximar-se, entrar
Winter is drawing near. ◆ The train drew into the station.
5 retirar
to draw money from the bank.

6 (= attract) **atrair**
The circus is drawing big crowds. ◆ Sugar draws ants.
7 atrair
I'd like to draw your attention to the note on page 7.
8 retirar
They drew water from a well.
9 tirar, extrair
What conclusions did you draw from his explanations?
10 sortear
to draw the winning ticket.
11 empatar
The two teams drew two all (2-2).
12 puxar, abrir, fechar
to draw (= open or close) the curtains
draw lots ☐ **sortear, tirar à sorte**
They drew lots to decide who should go first.
draw (money) out ☐ **sacar dinheiro**
I drew out 200 dollars.
draw up ☐ **parar**
A blue car drew up outside the building.
draw something up ☐ **redigir**
She drew up a list of questions for the interview. ◆ to draw up a contract.
drawer [drɔ:] *n.* ☐ **gaveta**
She keeps the key in this drawer. ◆ the bottom / top drawer.
drawing ['drɔ:iŋ] *n.* ☐ **desenho, esboço**
a drawing of a ship. ◆ to do / make a drawing.
drawing-pin ['drɔ:iŋ'pin] *n. Brit.* ☐ **tachinha**
He put up her picture with a drawing-pin.
■ *Amer.* **thumbtack**
drawn [drɔ:n] *v.* (Ver **draw**²).
dreadful ['drɛdful] *adj.*
1 (= terrible) **horrível**
a dreadful accident.
2 (= awful) **horrível**
The film was dreadful.
dream¹ [dri:m] *n.*
1 sonho
I had a strange dream last night. ◆ A nightmare is a bad dream.
2 sonho
His dream was to become a film star.
dream² *v.* (**dreams, dreaming, dreamt** or **dreamed**)
1 sonhar
I dreamt that I saw her. ◆ She dreamt about lions again
2 sonhar
She dreams of becoming prime minister.
dreary ['drɪərɪ] *adj.*
1 sombrio
a dreary day.
2 monótono
dreary work.
drenched ['drɛntʃt] *adj.* ☐ **encharcado**
He was drenched with rain. ◆ She got drenched to the skin (= completely).
dress¹ [drɛs] *n.*
1 vestido
She wore a tight blue dress. ◆ She tried on several dresses and bought two of them.
2 traje
He wore formal dress at the ceremony.

dress² *v.* (**dresses, dressing, dressed**)
1 vestir, vestir-se
Help me dress the children. ◆ Just a minute! I'm dressing.
■ antônimo: **undress**
2 vestir-se
She dresses well / elegantly.
be dressed in ☐ **estar vestido de**
She was dressed in black.
dress up
1 arrumar-se, vestir-se elegantemente
They dressed up for the ceremony.
2 fantasiar-se
He dressed up as a cowboy.
get dressed ☐ **vestir-se**
I'm getting dressed. ◆ I got dressed quickly and went out.
dressing ['drɛsiŋ] *n.*
1 bandagem, curativo
to put a dressing on a cut
2 molho
A salad dressing is usually a mixture of oil and vinegar.
dressing gown ['drɛsiŋgaun] *n. Brit.* ☐ **roupão**
■ *Amer.* **robe**; **bathrobe**
dressing room ['drɛsiŋrum] *n.* ☐ **camarim**
dressing table ['drɛsiŋ ˌteibl] *n.* ☐ **penteadeira**
dressmaker ['drɛsˌmeikə] *n.* ☐ **costureira**
drew [dru:] *v.* (Ver **draw**²).
dried¹ ['draid] *v.* (Ver **dry**²).
dried² *adj.* ☐ **seco**
dried fruit.
drier¹ ['draiə] *n.* (= **dryer**)
1 secadora
He put the wet clothes in the drier.
2 (= hair-drier) **secador de cabelo**
drier² *adj.* (Ver **draw**²).
dries [draiz] *v.* (Ver **draw**²).
driest ['draiəst] *adj.* (Ver **draw**²).
drift [drift] *v.* (**drifts, drifting, drifted**)
1 ir à deriva
The boat drifted with the current.
2 ser levado
The clouds drifted away.
drill¹ [dril] *n.* ☐ **broca**
a dentist's drill. ◆ an electric drill.
drill² *v.* (**drills, drilling, drilled**)
1 brocar, perfurar
to drill a hole.
2 treinar
The teacher drilled the pupils in English spelling.
drink¹ [drɪŋk] *n.*
1 bebida
soft drinks (= drinks without alcohol). ◆ Can I have a cold drink? ◆ There's plenty of food and drink in the kitchen.
2 bebida, drinque
Would you like a drink? A cold beer perhaps?
drink² *v.* (**drinks, drinking, drank, drunk**)
1 beber
He drank his tea slowly. ◆ What would you like to drink?
2 beber
Policemen do not drink when they are on duty.
drip [drip] *v.* (**drips, dripping, dripped**) ☐ **pingar**
The tap is dripping. ◆ Water dripped from the roof.
drive¹ [draiv] *n.*

drive / duchess

1 percurso de carro
It's not a long drive to the airport.
- Note: a **ride** by bus / train.
2 (= driveway) **entrada para veículos**
3 (= disk drive) **drive, unidade de disco**
drive[2] *v.* (**drives, driving, drove, driven**)
1 dirigir
Can you drive? ◆ She usually drives to work.
2 levar de carro
Who drove you home? ◆ Victor drove me to the station.
driver ['draɪvə] *n.* □ **motorista**
a taxi driver. ◆ Do women drivers drive more carefully than men?
driver's license ['draɪvəz 'laɪsəns] *n. Amer.* □ **carteira de motorista**
- *Brit.* **driving licence**
driveway ['draɪvweɪ] *n.* □ **entrada para veículos**
Park the car in the driveway.
driving ['draɪvɪŋ] *n.* □ **ato de dirigir, direção**
I enjoy driving. ◆ Driving on wet roads is dangerous. ◆ to take driving lessons.
driving licence ['draɪvɪŋ 'laɪsəns] *n. Brit.* □ **carteira de motorista**
When did you get your driving licence?
- *Amer.* **driver's license**
driving test ['draɪvɪŋ 'test] *n.* □ **exame de direção**
I passed my driving test.
drizzle[1] ['drɪzl] *n.* □ **chuva fina, chuvisco**
drizzle[2] *v.* (**drizzles, drizzling, drizzled**) □ **chuviscar**
It's drizzling.
drop[1] [drɒp] *n.*
1 gota
drops of rain / sweat. ◆ a drop of blood.
2 (= fall) **queda**
a drop in the price of oil. ◆ a sharp drop in temperature.
- antônimo: **rise**
drop[2] *v.* (**drops, dropping, dropped**)
1 cair, deixar cair, derrubar
The vase dropped (from his hand) and broke. ◆ Be careful not to drop the tray.
2 deixar cair, derrubar
He dropped his hat on the bed.
3 cair
Prices dropped last month. ◆ The temperature is dropping.
4 deixar
I asked him to drop me (off) at the bank.
5 largar, parar
Drop everything and start working on this. ◆ Let's drop the subject.
drop by / in / around □ **visitar casualmente, dar uma passada**
Next time you are in town drop in and see us.
drop me a line □ **escrever**
Drop me a line when you get home.
drop out □ **deixar de frequentar, largar**
He dropped out (of school). ◆ When did she drop out of the race?
drop-out ['drɒpaʊt] *n.* □ **desistente**
drop-outs from school.
drought [draʊt] *n.* □ **seca, estiagem**
drove [drəʊv] *v.* (Ver **drive**[2]).

drown [draʊn] *v.* (**drowns, drowning, drowned**) □ **afogar-se, afogar**
He's drowning! ◆ She drowned in the lake. ◆ You almost drowned him.
- Compare **sink**:
The ship is sinking.
drug[1] [drʌg] *n.*
1 remédio, medicamento
A pain-killing drug makes a headache or pain go away.
2 droga
Does he take drugs? ◆ Hard drugs (heroin, etc.) are very dangerous.
drug abuse *n.* □ **abuso de drogas**
drug addict *n.* □ **adicto, dependente químico**
drug addiction *n.* □ **toxicomania, dependência química**
drug dealer *n.* □ **traficante**
drug[2] *v.* (**drugs, drugging, drugged**)
1 drogar, dopar
The robbers drugged the guard dog.
2 colocar droga
She drugged his drink.
druggist ['drʌgɪst] *n. Amer.* (= pharmacist) □ **farmacêutico**
- *Brit.* **chemist**
drugstore ['drʌgstɔː] *n. Amer.* □ **farmácia, drogaria**
A drugstore sells medicines as well as soft drinks, chocolates, cigarettes, newspapers, etc.
drum [drʌm] *n.*
1 tambor, bateria
to beat the drum. ◆ I play the drums (in the band).
2 tambor, barril
an oil drum.
drummer ['drʌmə] *n.* □ **baterista**
drunk[1] [drʌŋk] *v.* (Ver **drink**[2]).
drunk[2] *adj., n.* **bêbado**
I think he is drunk. ◆ two drunks outside the pub.
get drunk □ **ficar bêbado**
She got drunk after drinking two beers.
drunkenness ['drʌŋkənɪs] *n.* □ **embriaguez, bebedeira**
dry[1] [draɪ] *adj.* (**drier, driest**)
1 seco
Is the washing dry yet? ◆ The paint isn't dry yet.
2 seco
There is no water in this well. It's dry.
3 seco
a dry climate. ◆ It's drier in the south of the country.
4 seco
a dry wine.
dry[2] *v.* (**dries, drying, dried**)
1 secar
She dried her hair (with a dryer). ◆ This glue dries quickly.
2 secar, enxugar
Dry your hands on this towel.
dry up □ **secar totalmente**
The river dried up.
dry-clean [ˌdraɪˈkliːn] *v.* (**dry-cleans, dry-cleaning, dry-cleaned**) □ **lavar a seco**
to dry-clean a jacket, etc.
dry-cleaner's [ˌdraɪˈkliːnəz] *n.* □ **lavanderia que lava a seco**
dryer ['draɪə] *n.* (Ver **drier**)
dryness ['draɪnɪs] *n.* □ **secura, aridez**
duchess ['dʌtʃɪs] *n.* □ **duquesa**

The duchess and the duke did not come to the ball.
- Ver **duke**.

duck¹ [dʌk] *n.* ☐ **pato**

duck² *v.* (**ducks, ducking, ducked**) ☐ **abaixar-se de repente**
He ducked (his head) when the shooting began.

duckling [ˈdʌklıŋ] *n.* ☐ **patinho**

due [djuː] *adj.*
1 vencido
When is the telephone bill due? ◆ My rent is due on the first (day) of each month.
2 aguardado
The train is due (to arrive) at 9:30.
3 esperado
They are due to meet on May 10.
4 devido
When will they pay you what is due to you?

due to ☐ **devido a**
The failure was due to carelessness. ◆ His success is due to hard work.
- Ver **owing to**.

duel [ˈdjuəl] *n.* ☐ **duelo**

dug [dʌg] *v.* (Ver **dig**).

duke [djuːk] *n.* ☐ **duque**
- Ver **duchess**.

dull [dʌl] *adj.*
1 (= boring) **entediante, chato**
a dull book / person.
2 (= not bright) **opaco**
a dull color / colour.
3 (= not bright and sunny) **nublado**
It was a dull, cold day.
4 chato
a dull pain.
- antônimo: **sharp**

dumb [dʌm] *adj.*
1 mudo
He is deaf and dumb.
2 (= stupid) **idiota**
What a dumb question to ask!

dumbness [ˈdʌmnıs] *n.* ☐ **idiotice**

dump¹ [dʌmp] *n.* ☐ **depósito de lixo, lixão**
a rubbish / garbage dump.

dump² *v.* (**dumps, dumping, dumped**) ☐ **jogar, descarregar**
Where did you dump the junk?

dune [djuːn] *n.* ☐ **duna**
A dune is a small hill of sand near a beach or in a desert.

dungarees [ˌdʌŋgəˈriːz] *n.* ☐ **macacão**

dungeon [ˈdʌndʒən] *n.* ☐ **calabouço**

during [ˈdjuərıŋ] *prep.*
1 durante
Bears sleep during the winter.
2 durante
He broke his leg during the game.

dusk [dʌsk] *n.* (= twilight) ☐ **anoitecer, crepúsculo**
At dusk they come out of their hiding place.

dust¹ [dʌst] *n.* ☐ **pó, poeira**
The furniture was covered with dust.

dust² *v.* (**dusts, dusting, dusted**) ☐ **tirar o pó, espanar**
to dust the furniture.

dustbin [ˈdʌstbın] *n. Brit.* (= litter bin) ☐ **lata de lixo, lixeira**
- *Amer.* **garbage can; trash can**

duster [ˈdʌstə] *n.* ☐ **espanador**

dustman [ˈdʌstmən] *n. Brit.* (*pl.* **dustmen**) ☐ **lixeiro**
- *Amer.* **garbage man**

dustpan [ˈdʌstpan] *n.* ☐ **pá de lixo**

dusty [ˈdʌsti] *adj.* (**dustier, dustiest**) ☐ **empoeirado**
The furniture was dusty.

duty [ˈdjuːti] *n.* (*pl.* **duties**)
1 dever
It's your right and your duty to vote. ◆ What are your duties in the office?
2 imposto
You pay duty on certain goods that you bring from abroad.

off duty ☐ **de folga**
I'll be off duty at 7 pm.

on duty ☐ **de serviço, de plantão**
Policemen don't drink (alcohol) when they are on duty. ◆ The nurse was on duty from 7 am to 4 pm.

duty-free [ˈdjuːtiˈfriː] *adj.* ☐ **livre de impostos**
duty-free goods. ◆ a duty-free shop.

DVD [ˌdiːviːdiː] *n., abbr.* (= digital video / versatile disk) ☐ **DVD**
I can play DVDs on my computer.

dwarf [dwoːf] *n.* (*pl.* **dwarves, dwarfs**) ☐ **anão**
- Ver **midget**.

dwelling [ˈdwelıŋ] *n.* (= house, hut, etc.) ☐ **habitação, moradia**
human dwellings.

dye¹ [daı] *n.* ☐ **tintura, corante**
- Ver **color, colour**.

dye² *v.* (**dyes, dyeing, dyed**) ☐ **tingir**
She's dyeing her hair black. ◆ He dyes his hair. ◆ I dyed the blouse yellow.

dying [ˈdaııŋ] *v.* (Ver **die**) ☐ **morrendo**
He is dying.

dynamic [daıˈnamık] *adj.* ☐ **dinâmico**
We need a dynamic manager for this business.

dynamite [ˈdaınəmaıt] *n.* ☐ **dinamite**

Ee

E *abbr.* (= **East**) ▫ **Leste**

e- [iː-] *pref.* (= electronic communications) ▫ **e-**
e-mail / email. ◆ e-commerce. ◆ e-trade.

each[1] [iːtʃ] *adj.* ▫ **cada**
There was a small red book on each desk. ◆ She gave each one of them a piece.

each[2] *adv.* ▫ **cada**
The tickets cost 10 dollars each.

each[3] *pron.* ▫ **cada um**
I spoke to each of them. ◆ Each of them has a car.

each other ▫ **um ao outro**
They hate each other.
■ Ver **one another**.

eager [ˈiːgə] *adj.* ▫ **ávido**
He is eager to meet the pop singer.

eagerly [ˈiːgəli] *adv.* ▫ **avidamente**
The dog looked eagerly at the chocolate in my hand.

eagerness [ˈiːgənis] *n.* ▫ **avidez, impaciência**

eagle [ˈiːgl] *n.* ▫ **águia**

ear [iə] *n.* ▫ **ouvido, orelha**
He whispered something in her ear.

earache [ˈiəreik] *n.* ▫ **dor de ouvido**

earl [ɜːl] *n.* ▫ **conde**

early [ˈɜːli] *adj., adv.* (**earlier, earliest**) ▫ **cedo, adiantado, início**
early in the morning. ◆ You're too early. You'll have to wait an hour. ◆ The train was 5 minutes early. ◆ a woman in her early thirties (= a woman between the ages of 30-34).

earn [ɜːn] *v.* (**earns, earning, earned**) ▫ **ganhar**
She earns $10,000 a month.

earnings [ˈɜːniŋz] *n. pl.* (=) ▫ **renda**
What are your annual earnings? (= How much do you earn a year?)

earphones [ˈiəfounz] *n.* (*pl.*) (= **headphones**) ▫ **fones de ouvido**
a cassette player with a pair of earphones.

earring [ˈiəriŋ] *n.* ▫ **brinco**
She decided to wear her gold earrings.

earth [ɜːθ] *n.*
1 ▫ **Terra**
Our planet is called Earth. ◆ The Earth goes round the sun. ◆ It's the fastest animal on earth.
■ In this meaning, **Earth** is usually written with a capital E.
2 (= land; ground) **terra, chão**
The earth shook for five minutes.
3 (= soil) **terra**
I filled the flower-pots with earth.

What, Who, etc. on earth...? ▫ **Que, Quem etc. diabos ...?**
What on earth is she doing? ◆ How on earth did it happen?

earthquake [ˈɜːθkweik] *n.* ▫ **terremoto**
The earthquake destroyed whole villages.

ease [iːz] *n.* ▫ **facilidade**

with ease (= easily) ▫ **com facilidade**
She passed the test with ease.

easier [ˈiːziə] *adj.* (Ver **easy**).

easiest [ˈiːziist] *adj.* (Ver **easy**).

easily [ˈiːzili] *adv.* ▫ **facilmente**

east[1] [iːst] *adj.* ▫ **leste, oriental**
an east wind. ◆ the east bank of the river. ◆ East Africa.

east[2] *adv.* ▫ **para o leste**
to travel / sail east.

east of ▫ **a leste de**
two km east of the city.

east[3] *n.* ▫ **leste, oriente**
from the east.

the East *n.* ▫ **o Oriente**
He learned karate in the East (in Japan, China, etc).

the Middle East *n.* ▫ **o Oriente Médio**

the Far East *n.* ▫ **o Extremo Oriente**

Easter [ˈiːstə] *n.* ▫ **Páscoa**

eastern [ˈiːstən] *adj.* ▫ **oriental, do leste**
eastern England / Europe.

eastward(s) [ˈiːstwəd(z)] *adv.* ▫ **para o leste**
They sailed eastwards.

easy [ˈiːzi] *adj.* (**easier, easiest**) ▫ **fácil**
The exam was (too) easy. ◆ Italian is an easy language to learn. ◆ The second question was easier (than the first one). ◆ It's not easy for him to apologize. ◆ The easiest way to do it is by computer.
■ antônimos: **difficult; hard**

take it easy; take things easy ▫ **ter calma, não se afobar**
Take it easy! You lost only one game! ◆ He works too hard. The doctor advised him to take it easy.

easy chair [ˈiːzi ˈtʃeə] *n.* ▫ **poltrona**

eat [iːt] *v.* (**eats, eating, ate, eaten**) ▫ **comer**
He eats a lot. ◆ The bird was eaten by the cat. ◆ I don't eat meat.

echo[1] [ˈekou] *n.* ▫ **eco**

echo[2] *v.* (**echoes, echoing, echoed**) ▫ **ecoar**
His shouts echoed in the cave.

eclipse [iˈklips] *n.* ▫ **eclipse**
a total eclipse of the sun / moon.

eco-friendly [ˈiːkouˌfrendli] *adj.* ▫ **ecológico**
eco-friendly fuel.

ecological [ˌiːkəˈlɒdʒikəl] *adj.* ▫ **ecológico**
Chemicals from factories cause ecological problems.

ecology [iˈkɒlədʒi] *n.* ▫ **ecologia**

e-commerce [ˌiːˈkɒmɜːs] *n.* ▫ **e-commerce, comércio eletrônico**
E-commerce means buying and selling via the Internet.

economic [iːkəˈnɒmik] *adj.* ▫ **econômico**
economic problems. ◆ economic cooperation between the two countries.

economical [iːkəˈnɒmikəl] *adj.* ▫ **econômico**
an economical car. ◆ It's more economical to do it by computer.
■ antônimo: **uneconomical**

economics [iːkəˈnɒmiks] *n.* ▫ **economia**
I'm studying economics at university.

economise [iˈkɒnəmaiz] *v.* (Ver **economize**).

economist [iˈkɒnəmist] *n.* ▫ **economista**

economize [iˈkɒnəmaiz] *v.* (**economizes, economizing, economized**) ▫ **economizar, fazer economias**
Prices are rising. We must economize.

economy [iˈkɒnəmi] *n.* (*pl.* **economies**)
1 economia
An increase in tourism will improve the economy. ◆ The economies of these countries are in a bad state.
2 economia

They shut down one of their factories for reasons of economy.

edge [edʒ] *n*. □ **beirada, borda**
There was a glass on the edge of the table. ◆ The edges of the letter were a little burned.

edit ['edit] *v*. (**edits, editing, edited**) □ **editar**
She edits this newspaper.

edition [i'diʃn] *n*. □ **edição**
the morning edition of the news / newspaper. ◆ a new edition of the dictionary.

editor ['editə] *n*. □ **editor**
The editor changed two sentences in my article.

educate ['edjukeit] *v*. (**educates, educating, educated**) □ **educar, instruir**
She was educated at a private school. ◆ We must educate the public to protect the environment.

educated ['edjukeitid] *adj*. □ **instruído**
an educated person.

education [,edjukeiʃən] *n*. □ **educação, instrução**
the Ministry of Education. ◆ She got her university education abroad.

higher education *n*. □ **ensino superior**

educational [,edju'keiʃənəl] *adj*. □ **educativo, educacional**
an educational film. ◆ Educational Television.

eel [i:l] *n*. □ **enguia**

effect¹ [i'fekt] *n*. □ **efeito**
Noise has many harmful effects on our health. ◆ The book had a great effect (= influence) on her.
■ The verb is **affect** (*not* effect).

effect² *v*. (**effects, effecting, effected**) □ **efetuar, realizar**
The new government will effect many reforms.
■ Ver **carry out**.

effective [i'fektiv] *adj*. □ **efetivo, eficaz**
an effective way to stop smoking. ◆ This medicine is very effective.
■ antônimo: **ineffective**
■ Compare with **efficient**.

efficiency [i'fiʃənsi] *n*. □ **eficiência**
the efficiency of the machine / system.

efficient [i'fiʃənt] *adj*. □ **competente, eficiente**
an efficient worker. ◆ It's more efficient to do it by computer.
■ antônimo: **inefficient**
■ Ver **effective**.

efficiently [i'fiʃəntli] *adv*. □ **eficientemente, eficazmente**
The system now works more efficiently.

effort ['efət] *n*. □ **esforço**
It was a waste of time and effort. ◆ Please make an effort to come on time.

e.g., eg ['i:'dʒi:] *abbr*. (= for example) □ **p. ex.**
green vegetables, e.g. lettuce and cucumbers.

egg [eg] *n*. □ **ovo**
I had fried eggs for breakfast. ◆ The hen laid an egg.

eggplant ['egpla:nt] *n*. □ **beringela**

eight [eit] *adj., n*. □ **oito**
Four and four are eight. ◆ She is eight years old. ◆ It's eight o'clock.

eighteen [ei'ti:n] *adj., n*. □ **dezoito**
The story is on page eighteen.

eighteenth¹ [ei'ti:nθ] *adj*. □ **dezoito**
the eighteenth century (= 1701-1800).

eighteenth² *n*. □ **décimo oitavo, dezoito**

the eighteenth of May (= 18th May). *Brit*. ◆ May eighteenth (= May 18). *Amer*.

eighth¹ [eitθ] *adj., adv*. □ **oitavo, oito**
the eighth of June (= 8th June). *Brit*. ◆ June eighth (= June 8). *Amer*. ◆ the eighth floor. ◆ She came eighth in the race.

eighth² *n*. □ **oitavo**
one eighth (= 1/8) of the cake.

eightieth¹ ['eitiiθ] *adj*. (= 80th) □ **octogésimo**
her eightieth name on the list.

eightieth² *n*. (= 1/80) □ **um oitenta avos**
She only got an eightieth of the money.

eighty ['eiti] *adj., n*. □ **oitenta**
Fifty and thirty are eighty (50+30=80). ◆ He is eighty years old.

in the eighties □ **nos anos oitenta, na década de 1980**
music that was popular in the eighties.

either¹ ['aiðə, 'i:ðə] *adj., pron*. □ **qualquer dos dois, um ou outro, ambos**
You can sit in either armchair. ◆ Either one is comfortable. ◆ I don't like either of them.
■ Ver **neither²**.

either² *adv*. □ **também, tampouco**
If he doesn't come, I won't either. ◆ I don't smoke. – I don't either. ◆ She can't drive and I can't either.
■ Ver **neither**.

either... or □ **ou... ou**
We can do it either now or tomorrow. ◆ You can either pay by cash or by credit card.

elastic¹ [i'lastik] *adj*. □ **elástico**
elastic material.

elastic² *n*. □ **elástico**
a piece of elastic (for a dress, trousers, etc.).

elastic band [i] *n*. *Brit*. (= rubber band) □ **elástico**
Tie the papers together with an elastic band.

elbow ['elbou] *n*. □ **cotovelo**

elder ['eldə] *adj*. □ **mais velho**
My elder brother is a pilot. ◆ His elder daughter works with him.
■ **older** is also possible.
■ Ver **eldest**.

the elders *n. pl*. □ **os idosos, as pessoas de idade**
the elders of the village.

elderly ['eldəli] *adj*. □ **idoso**
a hospital for the elderly. ◆ an elderly man / woman.

eldest ['eldist] *adj., n*. □ **o mais velho**
her eldest son. ◆ She is the eldest of the three children.
■ **oldest** is also possible.
■ Ver **older**.

e-learning ['i:lə:niŋ] *n*. □ **ensino a distância**
an e-learning course for students who study at home.
■ Ver **distance learning**.

elect [i'lekt] *v*. (**elects, electing, elected**) □ **eleger**
They elected him president for 4 more years.
■ Ver **vote²**.

election [i'lekʃən] *n*. (also **elections**) □ **eleição**
The election will take place in June.

electric [i'lektrik] *adj*. □ **elétrico**
an electric guitar / kettle / car.
■ Compare with **electrical**.

electrical [i'lektrikəl] *adj*. □ **elétrico**
electrical engineer. ◆ electrical appliances (= refrigerators, washing-machines, etc.).

■ Ver **electric**.
electrician [,elek'triʃən] *n.* □ **eletricista**
electricity [,elek'trisəti] *n.* □ **eletricidade**
Turn the light off and save electricity. ◆ an electricity (= electric bill).
electronic [elek'tronik] *adj.* □ **eletrônico**
an electronic calculator.
electronic mail [elek'tronik 'meil] *n.* □ **correio eletrônico**
■ Ver **e-mail**.
electronics [elek'troniks] *n.* □ **eletrônica**
elegant ['eligənt] *adj.* □ **elegante**
You look elegant in this dress.
elegantly ['eligəntli] *adv.* □ **elegantemente**
element ['eləmənt] *n.* □ **elemento**
chemical elements.
elementary [,eli'mentəri] *adj.* □ **básico**
an elementary course / dictionary.
elementary school [,eli'mentəri ,skul] *n.* □ **ensino fundamental**
■ Ver **primary school**.
elephant ['elifənt] *n.* □ **elefante**
elevator ['eliveitə] *n. Amer.* □ **elevador**
I took the elevator to the sixth floor.
■ *Brit.* **lift**
eleven [i'levn] *adj., n.* □ **onze**
Five and six are eleven. (5+6=11). ◆ He is eleven years old. ◆ It's eleven o'clock.
eleventh [i'levnθ] *adj., n., adv.* □ **décimo primeiro, onze**
the eleventh of July (= 11th July). *Brit.* ◆ July eleventh (= July 11). *Amer.* ◆ the eleventh floor. ◆ He came eleventh.
eloquence ['eləkwəns] *n.* □ **eloquência**
eloquent ['eləkwənt] *adj.* □ **eloquente**
an eloquent speaker.
else [els] *adv.*
1 mais
What else can I say? ◆ Did anyone else go with you? ◆ Who else saw you?
2 outro
We went somewhere else. ◆ I took someone else's umbrella by mistake.
or else □ **senão, do contrário**
You'd better hurry, or else you'll be late.
elsewhere [,els'weə] *adv.* □ **outro lugar**
We had to go elsewhere. ◆ in France, Britain and elsewhere.
e-mail, email¹ ['i:meil] *n.* (= electronic mail) □ **e-mail, email**
What is her e-mail (address)? ◆ send an email.
e-mail, email² *v.* (**emails, emailing, emailed**) □ **mandar e-mail**
He promised to email us his answer.
embarrass [im'barəs] *v.* (**embarrasses, embarrassing, embarrassed**) □ **constranger**
His jokes embarrassed his wife. ◆ You are embarrassing them.
embarrassed [im'barəst] *adj.* □ **constrangido**
We were embarrassed by his behavior.
embarrassing [im'barəsiŋ] *adj.* □ **constrangedor**
an embarrassing situation / question.
embarrassment [im'barəsmənt] *n.*
1 constrangimento
She blushed with embarrassment.
2 constrangimento
The scandal caused them great embarrassment.
3 constrangimento
He is an embarrassment to his family.
embassy ['embəsi] *n.* (*pl.* **embassies**) □ **embaixada**
the American embassy in Tokyo.
■ Ver **ambassador**.
embrace¹ [im'breis] *n.* (= hug) □ **abraço**
a warm embrace.
embrace² *v.* (**embraces, embracing, embraced**) □ **abraçar**
They embraced when they finally met.
embroider [im'broidə] *v.* (**embroiders, embroidering, embroidered**) □ **bordar**
She embroidered the handkerchief with her name.
embroidered [im'broidəd] *adj.* □ **bordado**
an embroidered shirt.
embroidery [im'broidəri] *n.* □ **bordado**
emerald ['emərəld] *n.* □ **esmeralda**
an emerald ring.
emerald (green) *adj., n.* □ **verde-esmeralda**
emerge [i'mɜːdʒ] *v.* (**emerges, emerging, emerged**) □ **emergir**
His head emerged out of the water.
emergence [i'mɜːdʒəns] *n.* □ **emergência**
the emergence of new states and nations after the war.
emergency [i'mɜːdʒənsi] *n.* (*pl.* **emergencies**) □ **emergência**
Call the police in an emergency.
emergency room [i'mɜːdʒənsi ,rum] *n. Amer.* □ **setor de emergência, pronto-socorro**
■ *Brit.* **casualty (department); accident and emergency**
emigrate ['emigreit] *v.* (**emigrates, emigrating, emigrated**) □ **emigrar**
They emigrated (from Portugal) to Canada.
■ Ver **immigrate**.
emigration ['emigreiʃən] *n.* □ **emigração**
emotion [i'məuʃən] *n.* □ **emoção**
Love, hatred, fear and jealousy are all emotions. ◆ to speak with deep emotion.
emotional [i'məuʃənl] *adj.*
1 comovente
an emotional speech.
2 emocional
children with emotional problems.
3 comovido, emocionado
He gets very emotional when he talks about the baby.
emperor ['empərə] *n.* □ **imperador**
The emperor ruled his empire for fifty years.
■ Ver **empress**.
emphasis ['emfəsis] *n.* □ **ênfase**
The emphasis in this course is on individual work.
emphasise ['emfəsaiz] *v.* (Ver **emphasize**).
emphasize ['emfəsaiz] *v.* (**emphasizes, emphasizing, emphasized**) (= stress) □ **enfatizar**
She emphasized the importance of working together.
empire ['empaiə] *n.* □ **império**
the British Empire.
employ [im'ploi] *v.* (**employs, employing, employed**) □ **empregar**
She employed 80 workers for this job. ◆ The company employs 120 engineers.
be employed □ **ser/estar empregado**
He is employed as a technician.
■ Ver **unemployed**.

employee [ˌemploiˈiː] *n.* □ **empregado, funcionário**
The company will fire 200 employees.

employer [imˈploiə] *n.* □ **empregador**
This company is the biggest employer in the country.

employment [imˈploimənt] *n.* □ **emprego**
He found employment as a shop assistant.
■ Ver **unemployment**.

employment agency [imˈploimənt ˌeidʒənsi] *n.* □ **agência de empregos**
I got work through an employment agency.

empress [ˈempris] *n.* □ **imperatriz**
■ Ver **emperor**.

emptiness [ˈemptinis] *n.* □ **vazio, vácuo**

empty¹ [ˈempti] *adj.* (**emptier, emptiest**) □ **vazio**
The box was empty. ◆ empty bottles. ◆ The streets were empty.

empty² *v.* (**empties, emptying, emptied**) □ **esvaziar**
He emptied his glass into the sink. ◆ The streets began to empty.
■ antônimo: **fill**

enable [iˈneibl] *v.* (**enables, enabling, enabled**) □ **possibilitar**
The loan enabled us to finish the project.
■ Ver **make it possible (for)**

enchanted [inˈtʃɑːntid] *adj.* □ **encantado**
an enchanted forest.

be enchanted by □ **encantar-se com**
I was enchanted by her beauty.

encircle [inˈsɜːkl] *v.* (**encircles, encircling, encircled**) (= surround) □ **rodear, circundar**
Enemy forces encircled the town.

enclose [inˈklouz] *v.* (**encloses, enclosing, enclosed**)
1 anexar
I enclose a cheque for 100 dollars.
2 rodear, circundar
The garden is enclosed by a fence.

encounter¹ [inˈkauntə] *n.* □ **encontro**
It was an encounter, not a meeting.

encounter² *v.* (**encounters, encountering, encountered**) (= meet by chance) □ **encontrar**
I encountered him at the bus stop.

encourage [inˈkʌridʒ] *v.* (**encourages, encouraging, encouraged**) □ **encorajar, incentivar**
He encouraged me to try again.

encouraged [inˈkʌridʒd] *adj.* □ **encorajado, incentivado**
She felt encouraged by his words.

encouragement [inˈkʌridʒmənt] *n.* □ **encorajamento, incentivo**
He needs some encouragement.

encouraging [inˈkʌridʒiŋ] *adj.* □ **encorajador, incentivador**
The news was encouraging. ◆ The results are very encouraging.

encyclopedia [inˌsaiklə'piːdiə] *n.* (also **encyclopaedia**) □ **enciclopédia**

end¹ [end] *n.*
1 fim
the end of the story. ◆ at the end of the week / month.
2 fim, final
at the end of the line. ◆ at the end of the street.
3 extremidade, ponta
He tied together both ends of the rope.

come to an end □ **chegar ao fim**
Winter is coming to an end.

from beginning to end □ **do início ao fim**
I read it from beginning to end.

in the end (= at last; finally) □ **no final, finalmente**
She tried many times to stop smoking, and in the end she succeeded.

make ends meet □ **viver dentro do orçamento**
They find it difficult to make ends meet.

on end □ **a fio**
It rained for days on end.

put an end to □ **pôr / dar um fim em**
We must put an end to the quarrel.

end² *v.* (**ends, ending, ended**)
1 terminar, acabar
They ended the meeting at 5.
2 terminar, acabar
How does the story end? ◆ The match ended in a 1-1 draw. ◆ The road ends here.

end up □ **acabar, ir parar**
The careless driver ended up in hospital.

endanger [inˈdeindʒə] *v.* (**endangers, endangering, endangered**) □ **ameaçar, pôr em risco**
Too much alcohol endangers your health.

ending [ˈendiŋ] *n.*
1 final
a film with a happy ending.
2 terminação
Many adverbs have the ending '-ly'.

endless [ˈendlis] *adj.* □ **sem fim**
The delay seemed endless. ◆ endless discussions.

endlessly [ˈendlisli] *adv.* □ **infinitamente, incessantemente**
He complains endlessly about it.

endurance [inˈdjuərəns] *n.* □ **resistência**
I admire his endurance.

endure [inˈdjuə] *v.* (**endures, enduring, endured**) □ **resistir, aguentar**
She endured a lot of pain.

enemy [ˈenəmi] *n.* (*pl.* **enemies**) □ **inimigo**
The enemy attacked our forces. ◆ He has many enemies.

energetic [ˌenəˈdʒetik] *adj.* □ **vigoroso, forte**
an energetic person.

energy [ˈenədʒi] *n.*
1 energia
He is full of energy.
2 energia
to save energy. ◆ solar energy (= energy from the sun).

enforce [inˈfɔːs] *v.* (**enforces, enforcing, enforced**) □ **aplicar, fazer cumprir**
to enforce the law.

engage [inˈgeidʒ] *v.* (**engages, engaging, engaged**) □ **envolver-se, engajar-se**
to engage in a struggle.

engaged [inˈgeidʒd] *adj.*
1 *Brit.* □ **ocupado**
The line is engaged.
■ *Amer.* **busy**
2 noivo, comprometido
She is engaged to Dan. ◆ They are engaged.

engagement [inˈgeidʒmənt] *n.* □ **noivado**
an engagement ring.

engine ['endʒin] *n.*
1 motor
Start the engine.
2 (= locomotive) **locomotiva**
engine-driver ['endʒindraivə] *n. Brit.* ◻ **maquinista**
■ *Amer.* **engineer**
engineer [,endʒi'niə] *n.*
1 engenheiro
an electrical engineer.
2 (= engine-driver) *Amer.* **maquinista**
engineering [,endʒi'niəriŋ] *n.* **engenharia**
He is studying engineering at college.
enjoy [in'dʒoi] *v.* (**enjoys, enjoying, enjoyed**) ◻ **gostar de**
I enjoyed the book very much. ◆ She enjoys playing computer games.
enjoy oneself ◻ **divertir-se**
Did she enjoy herself (at the party)? ◆ Enjoy yourselves! (= Enjoy!, *Amer.*)
■ Ver **have a good time; have fun**.
enjoyable [in'dʒoiəbl] *adj.* ◻ **prazeroso, agradável**
an enjoyable film.
enjoyment [in'dʒoimənt] *n.* ◻ **prazer**
He gets great enjoyment from riding horses.
enlarge [in'la:dʒ] *v.* (**enlarges, enlarging, enlarged**) ◻ **aumentar, ampliar**
to enlarge a photograph.
enlargement [in'la:dʒmənt] *n.* **aumento, ampliação**
enlighten [in'laitn] *v.* (**enlightens, enlightening, enlightened**) ◻ **informar, esclarecer**
Please enlighten us about your plans.
enlightened [in'laitnd] *adj.* ◻ **informado, esclarecido**
They are very enlightened people.
enlightenment [in'laitnmənt]
the Enlightenment *n.* ◻ **o Iluminismo**
enormous [i'no:məs] *adj.* (= huge)
1 enorme
an enormous amount of money. ◆ an enormous dog / building.
2 enorme
an enormous success. ◆ enormous pleasure.
enormously [i'no:məsli] *adv.* ◻ **enormemente**
I enjoyed it enormously.
enough¹ [i'nʌf] *adv.* ◻ **suficiente, o bastante**
She is old enough to decide by herself. ◆ He is not tall enough to reach that shelf. ◆ That's not good enough.
enough² *adj., pron.* ◻ **suficiente, o bastante**
Do we have enough chairs? ◆ There is enough time for another game. ◆ You don't eat enough. ◆ That's enough!
have had enough (of) ◻ **estar satisfeito, estar farto (de)**
I've had enough. ◆ He has had enough of your nonsense.
enquire [in'kwaiə] *v. Brit.* (**enquires, enquiring, enquired**) (= inquire, *Amer.*) ◻ **perguntar, indagar**
I have to enquire about the times of the train. ◆ 'Where are you going?', he enquired.
enquire into *Amer.* (= inquire into) ◻ **investigar**
The police are enquiring into the case.
enquiry [in'kwaiəri] *n. Brit.* (*pl.* **enquiries**) (= inquiry, *Amer.*) ◻ **pergunta**
I made enquiries about the man.
enrol [in'roul] *v.* (**enrols, enrolling, enrolled**), **enroll** *Amer.* ◻ **matricular-se, inscrever-se**
She enrolled at Harvard University.

enrolment [in'roulmənt] *n. Amer.*, **enrollment** ◻ **matrícula, inscrição**
en route [an'ru:t] *adv.* ◻ **a caminho**
We are en route for London.
ensure [in'ʃuə] *v.* (**ensures, ensuring, ensured**), **insure** *Amer.* ◻ **garantir, assegurar**
We have to ensure their safety.
enter ['entə] *v.* (**enters, entering, entered**)
1 entrar
He entered the house by the back door.
■ to enter (*not* 'enter into') the house.
■ Ver **come in(to); get in(to); go into**.
2 enter
Press the 'Enter' key to enter the data on your computer.
enterprise ['entəpraiz] *n.* ◻ **empreendimento**
an industrial enterprise.
entertain [entə'tein] *v.* (**entertains, entertaining, entertained**)
1 entreter, divertir
He entertained us with his funny stories.
2 receber, recepcionar
He's entertaining some businessmen tonight.
entertaining [,entə'teiniŋ] *adj.* ◻ **divertido**
an entertaining story.
entertainment [,entə'teinmənt] *n.* ◻ **entretenimento, diversão**
enthusiasm [in'θju:ziazəm] *n.* ◻ **entusiasmo**
She didn't show much enthusiasm about the plan.
enthusiast [in'θju:ziast] *n.* ◻ **entusiasta**
chess / opera enthusiasts.
enthusiastic [in,θju:zi'astik] *adj.* **entusiasmado**
He was enthusiastic about my song. ◆ an enthusiastic manager.
enthusiastically [in,θju:zi'astikəli] *adv.* ◻ **com entusiasmo**
entire [in'taiə] *adj.* ◻ **inteiro**
We spent an entire day in the market. ◆ The entire village was destroyed.
■ Ver **whole; complete**.
entirely [in'taiəli] *adv.* (= completely) ◻ **inteiramente**
These are entirely new plans. ◆ I entirely agree with you.
entirety [in'tairəti] *n.* ◻ **totalidade**
to read it in its entirety.
entitle [in'taitl] *v.* (**entitles, entitling, entitled**)
be entitled to ◻ **ter direito a, ter direito de**
You are entitled to a vacation. ◆ I'm entitled to know why you did it.
entitled [in'taitld] *adj.* ◻ **intitulado**
She wrote an essay entitled 'My Plans for the Holidays'.
entrance ['entrəns] *n.*
1 entrada
The entrance to the cave is very narrow.
2 entrada
No entrance!
3 admissão
entrance examinations.
entry ['entri] *n.* (*pl.* **entries**) ◻ **entrada**
a No entry sign (on the road).
envelope ['envəloup] *n.* ◻ **envelope**
Write the address on the envelope.
envious ['enviəs] *adj.* ◻ **invejoso**
He is envious of my success.

- Compare with **jealous**.
- Ver **envy**.

enviously ['enviəsli] *adv*. □ **com inveja**
She watched them enviously.

environment [in'vaiərənmənt] *n*. □ **ambiente**
a good home environment for the child.
the environment □ **o meio ambiente**
to educate children to protect the environment.

environmental [in,vaiərən'mentəl] *adj*. □ **ambiental**
Smoke from factories causes environmental pollution.

envy[1] ['envi] *n*. □ **inveja**
He couldn't hide his envy of her success. ◆ She watched them with envy.
- Compare with **jealousy**.
- Ver also **envious**.

envy[2] *v*. (**envies, envying, envied**) □ **invejar**
I envy you. ◆ I envy him his beautiful voice.

epidemic [epi'demik] *n*. □ **epidemia**
a flu epidemic.

episode ['episoud] *n*. □ **episódio**
the final episode of a TV serial.

equal[1] ['i:kwəl] *adj*. □ **igual**
I divided the chocolate into 4 equal parts. ◆ equal rights. ◆ They are equal in size.

equal[2] *v*. (*Amer*. **equals, equaling, equaled**; *Brit*. **equalling, equalled**)
1 ser igual a
Six plus four equals ten (6+4=10).
2 empatar
She equalled the world record in 200 metres.
3 igualar
Only one man equalled him in strength.

equal[3] *n*. □ **igual**
We should treat all human beings as equals.

equality [i'kwoləti] *n*. □ **igualdade**
equality between the sexes (= between women and men).

equally ['i:kwəli] *adv*.
1 igualmente
They are all equally good. ◆ They both swim equally fast.
2 igualmente
I divided the chocolate equally between them.

equation [i'kweiʒən] *n*. □ **equação**

equator [i'kweitə] *n*. □ **equador**

equip [i'kwip] *v*. (**equips, equipping, equipped**) □ **equipar, aparelhar**
They equipped the boat with modern equipment.
equip oneself □ **equipar-se, aparelhar-se**
They equipped themselves with ropes.

equipment [i'kwipmənt] *n*. □ **equipamento**
sports equipment.

erase [i'reiz] *v*. (**erases, erasing, erased**)
1 *Amer*. **apagar**
He erased the drawing from the blackboard. ◆ Erase the blackboard.
- *Brit*. **rub out**
2 apagar
to erase the recording. ◆ to erase a file (from the computer).

eraser [i'reizə] *n*. *Amer*. □ **borracha, apagador**
- *Brit*. **rubber**

erect[1] [i'rekt] *v*. (**erects, erecting, erected**) □ **erguer, erigir, levantar**
to erect a building.

erect[2] *adj*. □ **ereto**
Very few homes stood erect after the storm.

errand ['erənd] *n*. □ **serviço; recado**

errand boy ['erənd ,boi] *n*. □ **mensageiro, garoto de recados**

error ['erə] *n*. □ **erro**
spelling errors (= spelling mistakes). ◆ I made an error. ◆ a computer error.
- Ver **mistake**.

erupt [i'rʌpt] *v*. (**erupts, erupting, erupted**) □ **entrar em erupção**
This volcano erupted last in 1965.

eruption [i'rʌpʃən] *n*. □ **erupção**

escalator ['eskəleitə] *n*. □ **escada rolante**
to go up / down the escalator.

escape[1] [i'skeip] *v*. (**escapes, escaping, escaped**)
1 fugir, escapar
The prisoner tried to escape. ◆ The bird escaped from the cage.
- Ver **flee; run away**.
2 vazar
Gas is escaping from the pipe.

escape[2] *n*. □ **fuga**
an escape attempt from prison.
make your escape □ **conseguir fugir**
He made his escape with the help of one of the guards.

escort [i'sko:t] *v*. (**escorts, escorting, escorted**)
1 escoltar
Two policemen escorted him into the court.
2 acompanhar
Dan will escort her home.

especially [i'speʃəli] *adv*. □ **especialmente**
I like watching games, especially basketball. ◆ He built the house especially for her. ◆ Do you like football? – Not especially.
- abreviação: **esp.**

essay ['esei] *n*. □ **ensaio**
Write an essay of 250 words about violence in sports.

essence ['esns] *n*. □ **essência**
the essence of his remarks.

essential [i'senʃəl] *adj*. □ **essencial**
It is essential that we (should) work together as a team.

establish [i'stabliʃ] *v*. (**establishes, establishing, established**) □ **fundar, estabelecer**
My family established this company.

establishment [i'stabliʃmənt] *n*. □ **estabelecimento, fundação**
the establishment of the company.
the Establishment *n*. □ **a Fundação**

estate [i'steit] *n*.
1 propriedade
He owns a large estate in England.
2 (= housing development, *Amer*.) *Brit*. **conjunto habitacional**
We live on a housing estate.

estate agent [i'steit ,eidʒənt] *n*. *Brit*. □ **corretor de imóveis**
- *Amer*. **real estate agent; realtor**

estimate[1] ['estməit] *n*. □ **estimativa**
The estimate for building the pool is $10,000.

estimate[2] *v*. (**estimates, estimating, estimated**) □ **estimar, avaliar, calcular**
She estimated the cost at $2,000. ◆ I estimate that the project will take six months.

etc. [it'setrə] *abbr.* (= etcetera) ▫ **etc.**
We need pencils, pens, notebooks, etc.
eternal [i'tɔ:nl] *adj.* ▫ **eterno**
eternal life / youth.
eternally [i'tɔ:nli] *adv.* ▫ **eternamente**
▪ Ver **for ever**.
ethnic ['eθnik] *adj.* ▫ **étnico**
ethnic minorities / groups.
EU ['i:'ju:] *abbr.* (= European Union) ▫ **UE, União Europeia**
Switzerland is not a member of the EU.
eucalyptus [,ju:kə'liptəs] *n.* ▫ **eucalipto**
euro ['juərou] *n.* ▫ **Euro**
Many European countries use the euro as their currency.
evacuate [i'vækjueit] *v.* (**evacuates, evacuating, evacuated**) ▫ **evacuar**
They evacuated the village because of the danger of floods.
evacuation [i,vækju'eiʃən] *n.* ▫ **evacuação**
The evacuation of all the people took 20 minutes.
evacuee [i,vækju'i:] *n.*
evacuees from the war zone / flood areas.
eve [i:v] *n.* ▫ **véspera, vésperas**
Christmas eve. ◆ on the eve of their wedding.
even[1] ['i:vən] *adj.*
1 plano, liso
an even surface.
▪ antônimo: **uneven**
2 par
even numbers (2, 4, 6, etc)
▪ Ver **odd**.
3 equilibrado, quite
The contest was very even (each of them could win). ◆ Here's the money I owe you. Now we are even.
get even with ▫ **ajustar as contas com**
I'll get even with you for telling them.
even[2] *adv.* ▫ **nem, até, até mesmo**
I don't even remember his name. ◆ I even talked to him. ◆ Even you can do it. ◆ It's hot here even in January.
even if ▫ **mesmo que**
I won't go even if he begs.
even so ▫ **mesmo assim**
It's very expensive, but even so it's worth buying.
even though (= although) ▫ **embora, mesmo que**
I'd like to go there even though it's late.
evening ['i:vniŋ] *n.* ▫ **noite**
It happened in the evening. ◆ What are you doing this evening? ◆ He called on Tuesday evening.
event ['ivent] *n.* ▫ **evento, acontecimento**
Climbing that mountain for the first time was a historic event.
eventually ['ivenʃuəli] *adv.* ▫ **finalmente, por fim**
He eventually agreed to talk.
ever ['evə] *adv.* ▫ **alguma vez, já**
Have you ever been to Paris? ◆ Did you ever touch a jellyfish? ◆ This is the best film I've ever seen.
ever since ▫ **desde (que), desde então**
Ever since I was a child, I've wanted to be a singer. ◆ No one has visited the village ever since (the earthquake).
for ever (= forever) ▫ **para sempre**
I'll keep it for ever.
if ever ▫ **se alguma vez**
I seldom, if ever, wear a hat.

than ever ▫ **do que nunca**
You play better than ever.
every ['evri] *adv.*
1 cada um, todos
Every pupil answered one question.
▪ Ver **each**.
2 todo, a cada
It happens every day. ◆ every three hours. ◆ every few days. ◆ every ten metres.
(every) now and then, (every) now and again ▫ **de vez em quando**
Every now and then he comes for a visit.
every other day ▫ **dia sim, dia não**
She calls every other day.
every time ▫ **toda vez, sempre que**
Every time he breaks something, he blames me.
everybody ['evribodi] *pron.* (= **everyone**) ▫ **todos, todo mundo**
Everybody knows him. ◆ Everybody is coming except David.
▪ **everybody** is used with a singular verb.
everyday ['evridei] *adj.* ▫ **de todo dia, diário**
everyday clothes. ◆ an everyday event.
▪ Compare with **every day**:
She visits me every day.
everyone ['evriwʌn] *pron.* (= **everybody**).
everything ['evriθiŋ] *pron.* ▫ **tudo, todas as coisas**
He told me everything. ◆ Everything here is mine.
everywhere ['evriweə] *adv.* ▫ **em todo lugar**
There are houses like that everywhere. ◆ He followed me everywhere I went.
evidence ['evidəns] *n.* ▫ **prova**
There's enough evidence to put him in jail. ◆ There's no evidence that she stole it.
▪ **a piece of evidence** (*not* 'an evidence').
give evidence ▫ **apresentar provas**
The witness gave evidence in court.
evident ['evidənt] *adj.* (= obvious) ▫ **evidente**
It is evident that she doesn't want to help.
evil[1] ['i:vl] *adj.* ▫ **mau**
an evil man.
evil[2] *n.* ▫ **mal, males**
Do no evil! ◆ the evils of war.
▪ Compare **good**[2].
ex- ['eks-] *pref.* (= former) ▫ **ex-**
an ex-soldier. ◆ her ex-husband. ◆ the ex-president.
exact [ig'zækt] *adj.* ▫ **exato**
an exact copy. ◆ the exact amount. ◆ What was the exact time of arrival? ◆ I don't remember his exact words.
▪ Ver **accurate; precise**.
to be exact ▫ **para ser exato**
He wants to stay a few more days – till Monday, to be exact.
exactly [ig'zæktli] *adv.* ▫ **exatamente**
Please tell us exactly what you saw. ◆ Where exactly did you see her? ◆ The plane landed at exactly 10 o'clock.
Exactly ▫ **exatamente**
So you think that it's a bad deal. – Exactly!
exaggerate [ig'zædʒəreit] *v.* (**exaggerates, exaggerating, exaggerated**) ▫ **exagerar**
You are exaggerating. No one can do it in 5 seconds. ◆ Don't exaggerate!
exaggeration [ig,zædʒə'reiʃən] *n.* ▫ **exagero**

It's not an exaggeration to say that she speaks English perfectly.
exam [ig'zam] *n.* (= examination) □ **exame**
I have an exam tomorrow.
examination [ig,zami'neiʃən] *n.*
1 (= exam) **exame**
Everybody has to take an entrance examination. ◆ She passed / failed her examination in history. ◆ a written examination. ◆ an oral examination.
2 exame
a careful examination of the facts. ◆ a medical examination.
examine [ig'zamin] *v.* (**examines, examining, examined**)
1 examinar
The doctor examined the patient. ◆ to examine the evidence.
2 (= test) **examinar**
The teacher examined us orally, not in writing.
example [ig'za:mpl] *n.* □ **exemplo**
Can you give me an example? ◆ Read the example first and then do the exercise.
for example □ **por exemplo**
She has many hobbies, for example, painting and crossword puzzles.
■ abreviação: **e.g.; eg**
■ Ver **for instance**.
excavation [,ekskə'veiʃən] *n.* □ **escavação**
exceed [ik'si:d] *v.* (**exceeds, exceeding, exceeded**)
1 exceder
The cost must not exceed $20,000.
2 exceder
to exceed the speed limit.
excellent ['eksələnt] *adj.* □ **excelente**
an excellent film / idea. ◆ He is in excellent physical condition. ◆ an excellent student.
except [ik'sept] *prep., conj.* □ **exceto, menos, a não ser**
Everyone came to the party except (for) Sara. ◆ The shop is open every day except (for) Saturday and Sunday. ◆ We couldn't do anything except wait. ◆ He calls every night except when he is busy.
■ **except** or **except for** takes a noun or pronoun (see the first two sentences above).
■ **except for** comes before 'a' or 'the'.
■ **except** comes before a verb or words like 'when', 'what', etc. (see the last two sentences above).
■ Ver **apart from**.
except that □ **só que**
My bag is the same as yours, except that it is black. ◆ I don't know anything about him, except that he is Indian.
exception [ik'sepʃən] *n.* □ **exceção**
He always comes early, but today is an exception.
with the exception of □ **exceto**
Everyone voted for me, with the exception of Elisa.
without exception □ **sem exceção**
You must all be here at 10 without exception.
exceptional [ik'sepʃənl] *adj.*
1 excepcional
The weather is exceptional for this time of year.
2 excepcional
exceptional talent.
exceptionally [ik'sepʃənli] *adv.* □ **excepcionalmente**
She is an exceptionally good swimmer.

exchange¹ [iks'tʃeindʒ] *n.* □ **troca, intercâmbio**
an exchange of ideas.
in exchange (for) (= in return for) □ **em troca (de)**
What will you give me in exchange (for this watch)?
exchange² *v.* (**exchanges, exchanging, exchanged**) □ **trocar**
They exchanged glances. ◆ We exchanged telephone numbers. ◆ I'd like to exchange these shoes. They are too tight. ◆ to exchange dollars for euros.
exchange rate [iks'tʃeindʒ 'reit] *n.* □ **taxa de câmbio**
What is the exchange rate for the dollar?
excite [ik'sait] *v.* (**excites, exciting, excited**) □ **excitar, empolgar**
Don't excite the baby before bedtime.
excited [ik'saitid] *adj.* □ **excitado, empolgado**
The fans got excited when he scored a goal. ◆ They are excited about going on holiday.
excitement [ik'saitmənt] *n.* □ **excitação, empolgação, euforia**
The Queen's visit caused great excitement.
exciting [ik'saitiŋ] *adj.* □ **excitante, empolgante**
The circus performance was very exciting. ◆ an exciting job.
exclaim [iks'kleim] *v.* (**exclaims, exclaiming, exclaimed**) □ **exclamar**
'What a beautiful flower!', she exclaimed ◆ 'Don't touch me!', he exclaimed angrily
exclamation [,eksklə'meiʃən] *n.* □ **exclamação**
'Careful!', 'Help!' and 'What a surprise!' are exclamations.
■ Ver **interjection**.
exclamation mark [,eksklə'meiʃən ,ma:k] *n. Brit.* □ **ponto de exclamação**
exclamation point [,eksklə'meiʃən ,point] *n. Amer.* □ **ponto de exclamação**
exclude [iks'klu:d] *v.* (**excludes, excluding, excluded**)
1 excluir
We must not exclude the possibility that it happened here.
2 excluir
We cannot exclude him from the discussions.
■ Ver **include**.
excluding [iks'klu:diŋ] *prep.* □ **fora**
There are 50 people in the orchestra, excluding the conductor.
■ antônimo: **including**
exclusion [iks'klu:ʒən] *n.* □ **exclusão**
exclusive [iks'klu:siv] *adj.*
1 exclusivo
an exclusive club.
2 exclusiva
an exclusive interview.
excursion [iks'kɔ:ʃən] *n.* (= trip) □ **excursão**
We went on a day excursion to the lake.
■ Ver **trip**.
excuse¹ [iks'kju:z] *n.*
1 desculpa, escusa
There's no excuse for such behaviour.
2 desculpa, justificativa, pretexto
You're late again! What's your excuse this time? ◆ It was just an excuse to make me stay. ◆ He was absent without a good excuse.
excuse² *v.* (**excuses, excusing, excused**)
1 (= forgive) **desculpar, perdoar**

Excuse me for asking, but are you invited?
2 desculpar
Nothing can excuse such behaviour.
3 dispensar
He was excused from training.
Excuse me
1 com licença
Excuse me, is this the way to the station?
2 (= Sorry, *Brit.*) *Amer.* **desculpe-me**
Excuse me.
3 (= Pardon?, *Brit.*) *Amer.* **como disse?**
Excuse me? (= I didn't hear what you said.)
execute ['eksikju:t] *v.* (**executes, executing, executed**) □ **executar**
The murderer was executed.
execution [,eksi'kju:ʃən] *n.* □ **execução**
executioner [,eksi'kju:ʃənə] *n.* □ **executor**
executive [ig'zekjutiv] *n.* □ **executivo**
a sales executive (= a sales manager).
exercise¹ ['eksəsaiz] *n.*
1 exercício físico
Walking is very good exercise. ◆ You should take more exercise. ◆ This exercise is good for your heart.
2 exercício
We have to do all the exercises on page 60.
exercise² *v.* (**exercises, exercising, exercised**) □ **exercitar**
You should exercise every day.
exercise book ['eksəsaiz ,buk] *n. Brit.* □ **caderno**
■ *Amer.* **notebook**
exhaust¹ [ig'zo:st] *v.* (**exhausts, exhausting, exhausted**) (= be tired out) □ **esgotar**
The long walk exhausted them.
exhaust² *n.* □ **exaustor, escapamento**
exhausted [ig'zo:stid] *adj.* (= be tired out) □ **exausto**
He was exhausted after climbing the mountain.
exhausting [ig'zo:stiŋ] *adj.* (= very tiring) □ **exaustivo**
an exhausting day.
exhaustion [ig'zo:stʃən] *n.* □ **exaustão**
She suffers from exhaustion.
exhibit¹ [ig'zibit] *n.*
1 obra exposta, objeto exposto
All the exhibits (in the museum) are from the 16th century.
2 (= exhibition) **exposição, mostra**
exhibit² *v.* (**exhibits, exhibiting, exhibited**) □ **exibir, expor**
The gallery is exhibiting his paintings. ◆ to exhibit evidence in court.
exhibition [eksi'biʃən] *n.* □ **exposição, mostra**
an art exhibition. ◆ an exhibition of photographs.
exile¹ ['eksail] *n.*
1 exílio
He went into exile. ◆ a political exile.
exile² *v.* (**exiles, exiling, exiled**) □ **exilar**
Napoleon was exiled from France.
exist [ig'zist] *v.* (**exists, existing, existed**) □ **existir**
We can't exist without food. ◆ Life may exist on other planets. ◆ That animal exists only in Africa.
existence [ig'zistəns] *n.* □ **existência**
I don't believe in the existence of ghosts.
exit ['egzit] *n.* (= way out) □ **saída**
an emergency exit.
expand [iks'pand] *v.* (**expands, expanding, expanded**)
1 expandir

Metals expand at high temperatures.
2 expandir
The company is expanding (its business).
expansion [iks'panʃən] *n.* □ **expansão**
The expansion of the business will cost a lot of money.
expect [iks'pekt] *v.* (**expects, expecting, expected**)
1 esperar, estar grávida
We're expecting visitors. ◆ What do you expect me to do?
◆ She is expecting. (= She is going to have a baby.)
2 (= suppose; guess) *Amer.* **supor**
I expect (that) you know him. ◆ Is she coming? – I expect so.
be expected to □ **espera-se que, supõe-se que**
The rain is expected to continue.
expectation [,ekspek'teiʃən] *n.* □ **expectativa**
There's no expectation of rain tomorrow.
beyond all expectations □ **além de todas as expectativas**
The plan succeeded beyond all expectations.
expedition [ekspi'diʃən] *n.* □ **expedição**
They went on an expedition to the jungle.
expel [iks'pel] *v.* (**expels, expelling, expelled**) □ **expulsar**
They expelled him from school. ◆ She was expelled from the club.
expense [iks'pens] *n.* □ **despesa**
Keeping a pet is not a big expense.
at someone's expense
1 à custa de alguém
He went abroad at the company's expense.
2 à custa de alguém
They laughed at her expense.
expenses *n. pl.* □ **despesas**
travelling / medical expenses. ◆ The insurance will cover the expenses.
expensive [iks'pensiv] *adj.* □ **caro**
expensive clothes. ◆ an expensive car. ◆ It's too expensive (for me).
■ antônimo: **cheap; inexpensive**
■ Ver **dear¹**.
experience¹ [iks'piəriəns] *n.*
1 experiência
You need a lot of experience in this job. ◆ She has 5 years' experience of working with children.
2 experiência
an unpleasant experience.
experience² *v.* (**experiences, experiencing, experienced**)
□ **vivenciar, passar por, enfrentar**
I experienced a lot of difficulty.
experienced [iks'piəriənst] *adj.* □ **experiente**
an experienced teacher / driver.
■ antônimo: **inexperienced**
experiment¹ [iks'perimənt] *n.* □ **experimento**
to carry out experiments on mice. ◆ a scientific / chemical experiment.
experiment² *v.* (**experiments, experimenting, experimented**) □ **fazer experiências**
Is it right to experiment on animals?
experimental [iks,peri'mentl] *adj.* □ **experimental**
experimental methods.
expert ['ekspərt] *n.* □ **expert, especialista**
an expert on stamps. ◆ an expert at arranging flowers.
◆ a computer expert.
expertise [,ekspə'ti:z] *n.*
1 perícia, competência, habilidade

their expertise in mountain-climbing.
2 competência, maestria
her expertise in American history.
3 competência, técnica
a legal expertise.
explain [iks'plein] *v.* (**explains, explaining, explained**) □ **explicar**
She explained the meaning of the word. ◆ I'm trying to explain to you why I did it. ◆ to explain the problem to him.
explanation [,eksplə'neiʃən] *n.* □ **explicação**
What is the explanation for his disappearance? ◆ He gave me a clear explanation of the grammar rule.
explode [iks'ploud] *v.* (**explodes, exploding, exploded**) □ **explodir**
The bomb exploded.
■ The noun is **explosion**.
exploit [iks'ploit] *v.* (**exploits, exploiting, exploited**) □ **explorar**
They exploit the workers terribly.
exploitation [,eksploi'teiʃən] *n.* □ **exploração**
exploration [,eksplə'reiʃən] *n.* □ **exploração**
the exploration of the North Pole.
explore [iks'plo:] *v.* (**explores, exploring, explored**) □ **explorar**
They explored the jungles of Africa.
explorer [iks'plo:rə] *n.* □ **explorador**
Marco Polo was a famous explorer.
explosion [iks'plouʒən] *n.* □ **explosão**
No one was killed in the explosion.
explosive[1] [iks'plousiv] *adj.* □ **explosivo**
an explosive gas.
explosive[2] *n.* □ **explosivo**
Dynamite is an explosive.
export[1] ['ekspo:t] *n.* □ **exportação**
All our production is for export.
exports □ **exportações**
Exports to the USA rose by 10% last year.
■ antônimo: **import(s)**
export[2] [eks'po:t] *v.* (**exports, exporting, exported**) □ **exportar**
What goods do you export to Europe?
■ Ver **import**[2].
exporter [eks'po:tə] *n.* □ **exportador**
■ Ver **importer**.
expose [iks'pouz] *v.* (**exposes, exposing, exposed**)
1 expor
Don't expose your skin to the sun for too long.
2 expor, mostrar
The reporter exposed the manager's lies.
express[1] [iks'pres] *v.* (**expresses, expressing, expressed**) □ **expressar**
They expressed their fears about the situation. ◆ Her face expressed sorrow.
to express oneself □ **expressar-se**
She expresses herself very well.
express[2] *adj.* □ **expresso**
an express bus. ◆ an express letter.
express[3] *adv.* □ **expresso**
to send a letter express.
express[4] *n.* □ **expresso**
the 10 a.m. express to the airport.
expression [iks'preʃən] *n.*

1 expressão
an expression of surprise on his face.
2 expressão
Explain the expression 'good for you'.
3 expressão
'Freedom of expression' means that you can say what you think.
expressway [iks'preswei] *n. Amer.* □ **via expressa**
■ *Brit.* **motorway**
expulsion [iks'pʌlʃən] *n.* □ **expulsão**
What was the reason for his expulsion from school?
■ The verb is **expel**.
exquisite ['ekskwizit] *adj.* □ **requintado, primoroso**
an exquisite view / painting.
extend [iks'tend] *v.* (**extends, extending, extended**)
1 estender
to extend the road / fence.
2 estender
He extended the visit for another week.
3 (= stretch) **ampliar**
The lake extends over a large area. ◆ The road extends for many kilometres.
4 estender
He extended his hand to me.
extension [iks'tenʃən] *n.*
1 ramal
His phone number is 5558351, extension 33.
2 anexo
an extension to a house.
extensive [iks'tensiv] *adj.* □ **abrangente**
extensive reading.
extent [iks'tent] *n.*
1 extensão
What is the extent of the damage?
2 extensão
The extent of her knowledge is amazing.
to a certain extent, to some extent □ **até certo ponto**
She is right, to some extent.
exterior[1] [iks'tiəriə] *adj.* □ **externo**
the exterior walls of a building.
■ antônimo: **interior**
exterior[2] *n.* □ **exterior**
the exterior of a building.
exterminate [iks'tə:mineit] *v.* (**exterminates, exterminating, exterminated**) □ **exterminar**
to exterminate the rats / mosquitoes.
external [iks'tə:nl] *adj.* □ **externo**
This oil is for external use only.
■ antônimo: **internal**
■ Ver **outside**.
extinct [iks'tiŋkt] *adj.*
1 extinto
These animals became extinct many years ago.
2 extinto
This volcano is now extinct.
extinction [iks'tiŋkʃən] *n.* □ **extinção**
These plants are in danger of extinction.
extinguish [iks'tiŋguiʃ] *v.* (**extinguishes, extinguishing, extinguished**) (= put out) □ **extinguir**
Please extinguish your cigarettes. ◆ They extinguished the fire very quickly.
extinguisher [iks'tiŋguiʃə] *n.* □ **extintor**

extra[1] ['ekstrə] *adj.* □ **extra, adicional**
Put an extra chair there.
extra[2] *adv.* □ **a mais**
You have to pay extra for meals.
extraordinarily [iks'tro:dənərəli] *adv.* □ **extraordinariamente**
an extraordinarily strong man.
extraordinary [iks'tro:dənəri] *adj.*
1 extraordinário
a person of extraordinary talents.
2 incrível, excepcional
How extraordinary!
extraterrestrial [ekstrətə'restriəl] *n., adj.* □ **extraterrestre**
In science fiction stories extraterrestrial beings from outer space are called 'aliens'.
extravagance [iks'travəgəns] *n.* □ **extravagância**
extravagant [iks'travəgənt] *adj.* □ **extravagante**
an extravagant man.
extravagantly [iks'travəgəntli] *adv.* □ **com extravagância, extravagantemente**
They lived extravagantly.
extreme [iks'tri:m] *adj.*
1 extremado
He has extreme opinions on education.
2 extremo
extreme pain / cold. ◆ You must take extreme care. It's dangerous.

3 extremo
in the extreme north of the country
extremely [iks'tri:mli] *adv.* □ **extremamente**
The exam was extremely difficult.
extremism [iks'tri:mizəm] *n.* □ **extremismo**
political extremism.
extremist [iks'tri:mist] *n., adj.* □ **extremista**
a political extremist. ◆ extremist politics.
eye [ai] *n.* □ **olho**
What colour are your eyes? ◆ Close your eyes.
catch someone's eye □ **chamar a atenção de alguém**
The vase in the shop-window caught my eye.
cry your eyes out □ **morrer de chorar**
He cried his eyes out when his toy broke.
keep an eye on □ **ficar de olho em**
Can you keep an eye on the baby for a moment?
not take your eyes off □ **não tirar os olhos de**
He couldn't take his eyes off the picture.
see eye to eye (with) □ **estar de acordo (com)**
We don't see eye to eye on this matter.
eyebrow ['aibrau] *n.* □ **sobrancelha**
eyelashes ['ailaʃiz] *n. pl.* □ **cílios**
eyelid ['ailid] *n.* □ **pálpebra**
eyesight ['aisait] *n.* □ **visão, vista**
She has good eyesight.
eye-witness ['ai'witnis] *n.* □ **testemunha ocular**
There were no eye-witnesses to the accident.

Ff

F *abbr.* (= Fahrenheit) ▫ **F**
Water freezes at 32° F.
fable ['feibl] *n.* ▫ **fábula**
the fable about the lion and the mouse.
face[1] [feis] *n.* ▫ **rosto**
a beautiful face. ◆ Your face is dirty.
face to face ▫ **cara a cara**
I met him face to face.
keep a straight face ▫ **ficar sério**
I couldn't keep a straight face when she put on her new hat.
to someone's face ▫ **na cara de alguém**
I told him to his face what I thought of him.
face[2] *v.* (**faces, facing, faced**)
1 encarar, olhar para
They faced each other. ◆ Face the camera and smile!
2 enfrentar, encarar
They are facing a serious problem. ◆ You'll have to face the truth.
be faced with ▫ **estar diante de**
We are faced with some difficult problems.
let's face it ▫ **convenhamos**
Let's face it – it was a mistake to sell it.
facilities [fə'silitiz] *n. pl.* ▫ **instalações**
sports facilities (= a gymnasium, a swimming-pool, etc.)
fact [fakt] *n.* ▫ **fato**
Tell me all the facts. ◆ I want facts, not opinions.
as a matter of fact ▫ **na verdade**
As a matter of fact, I don't know him very well.
in fact ▫ **na verdade**
I don't think he cheated; in fact, I know he didn't.
the fact is ▫ **o fato é (que)**
The fact is, I don't like him at all.
factor ['faktə] *n.* ▫ **fator**
There are many factors to think of, before we decide.
factory ['faktəri] *n.* (*pl.* **factories**) ▫ **fábrica**
I work in a shoe factory.
fade [feid] *v.* (**fades, fading, faded**) ▫ **desbotar**
The colour of the curtains is beginning to fade.
Fahrenheit ['farənhait] *n.* ▫ **Fahrenheit**
The temperature is 88° F (= 88 degrees Fahrenheit).
fail[1] [feil] *v.* (**fails, failing, failed**)
1 falhar, não conseguir
I failed my driving test. ◆ She tried to move it, but she failed.
2 reprovar
The teacher failed six pupils.
fail to do something
1 falhar em, não conseguir
He failed to reach the top shelf.
2 deixar de fazer algo
She failed to appear in court.
fail[2] *n.*, **without fail**
1 sem falta
I'll be there at 8 o'clock without fail.
2 sem falta
She visits her mother every day without fail.
failure ['feiljə] *n.* ▫ **fracasso**

The party was a failure. ◆ All our attempts ended in failure.
faint[1] [feint] *adj.*
1 fraco, leve
to speak in a faint voice. ◆ a faint smell of roses. ◆ a faint light.
2 sentir tonteira
I feel faint.
faint[2] *v.* (**faints, fainting, fainted**) ▫ **desmaiar**
He fainted from hunger.
fair[1] [feə] *adj.*
1 justo
a fair judge. ◆ They deserve a fair trial. ◆ It's not fair.
■ antônimo: **unfair**
2 razoável
The patient's condition is fair.
3 agradável
fair weather.
4 loiro
He is fair-haired. (= He has fair hair.)
fair[2] *n.* ▫ **parque de diversões, feira**
I won a teddy bear at the fair. ◆ a trade fair. ◆ a book fair.
fairly ['feəli] *adv.*
1 com justiça
They treated us fairly.
■ antônimo: **unfairly**
2 (= quite; rather) **bem**
I read the book fairly quickly. ◆ The questions are fairly difficult.
fairy ['feəri] *n.* (*pl.* **fairies**) ▫ **fada**
The good fairies saved the princess from the wicked fairy.
fairy tale ['feəri 'teil] *n.* ▫ **conto de fadas**
faith [feiθ] *n.*
1 fé
I have great faith in her ability. ◆ He has no faith in that doctor. ◆ their faith in God.
2 (= religion) ▫ **fé, crença**
the Christian / Muslim faith.
faithful ['feiθful] *adj.* ▫ **fiel**
a faithful friend / husband / wife.
■ antônimo: **unfaithful**
■ Ver **loyal**.
faithfully ['feiθfuli] *adv.* ▫ **fielmente**
They served the king faithfully.
Yours faithfully *Brit.* ▫ **atenciosamente**
■ You write **Yours faithfully** at the end of a formal and business letter when you begin with 'Dear Sir' or 'Dear Madam'.
■ *Amer.* **Yours truly**; **Sincerely yours**
fake[1] [feik] *adj.* ▫ **falso, de mentira**
a fake painting. ◆ fake jewellery.
■ antônimo: **genuine**
■ Ver **false; forged; phoney**.
fake[2] *n.* ▫ **falsificação**
That's not the original painting – it's a fake.
fake[3] *v.* (**fakes, faking, faked**) ▫ **falsificar**
He faked many works of art.
■ Ver **forge**.
fall[1] [fɔ:l] *n.*
1 tombo
I had a fall from the horse.
2 queda
a fall in the price of fruit.

fall / far

- antônimo: **rise**[1]
3 (= autumn) *Amer.* **outono**
in the fall of 1968.
fall[2] *v.* (**falls, falling, fell, fallen**)
1 cair
I fell (down the stairs) and broke my arm. ◆ She fell off the horse / ladder. ◆ He fell into the river.
2 cair
Rain / Snow is falling.
3 cair, decrescer
The temperature is falling. ◆ The prices of cars may fall again.
- antônimo: **rise**
4 cair
The leaves are beginning to fall.
fall apart ▫ **desmontar**
The toy fell apart in his hands.
fall asleep (= go to sleep) ▫ **cair no sono, dormir**
He fell asleep in front of the TV.
fall behind ▫ **atrasar-se**
She is falling behind in her schoolwork. ◆ They fell behind with their payments.
fall down ▫ **cair**
The tree may fall down in this storm.
fall ill ▫ **adoecer**
He fell ill suddenly.
fall in love ▫ **apaixonar-se**
They fell in love.
fall out (with) ▫ **discutir (com), brigar (com)**
She fell out with her friend.
fall through ▫ **falhar**
The plan fell through at the last minute.
fall to pieces ▫ **ficar em pedaços**
The book fell to pieces in my hands.
falls [fo:lz] *n. pl.* ▫ **catarata, queda d'água**
Niagara Falls.
false [fo:ls] *adj.*
1 falso
false information. ◆ Kittens are young cats. True or false?
2 falso, postiço
a false passport. ◆ a false beard. ◆ a false name.
- Ver **fake; forged; phoney**.
false alarm ['fo:ls ə,la:m] *n.* ▫ **alarme falso**
There was no fire. It was a false alarm.
fame [feim] *n.* ▫ **fama**
She achieved fame when she won the gold medal.
familiar [fə'miljə] *adj.* ▫ **familiar, conhecido**
This place looks familiar. ◆ a familiar voice. ◆ a familiar face.
be familiar with ▫ **estar familiarizado com**
I'm not familiar with this place. ◆ Are you familiar with this game?
- antônimo: **unfamiliar**
family ['faməli] *n.* (*pl.* **families**) ▫ **família**
a large family. ◆ Almost every family here has a dog. ◆ All my family enjoy swimming.
- *Brit.* A family has / have... (*singular* or *plural verb*); *Amer.* A family has... (*singular verb* only).
family name ['faməli 'neim] *n.* (= surname; last name) ▫ **nome de família, sobrenome**
family tree ['faməli 'tri:] *n.* ▫ **árvore genealógica**
famine ['famin] *n.* ▫ **fome, carestia**
There is (a) famine in that country because of the drought.

- Ver **hunger; starvation**.
famous ['feiməs] *adj.* ▫ **famoso**
She is a famous writer. ◆ Paris is famous for its beauty.
- The noun is **fame**.
fan [fan] *n.*
1 ventilador
He turned on / off the fan.
2 leque
She lost her fan.
3 torcedor, fã
football fans. ◆ She is a fan of this pop star.
fancy[1] ['fansi] *adj.* ▫ **luxuoso, extravagante**
a fancy hat / car. ◆ fancy food.
fancy[2] *v.* (**fancies, fancying, fancied**)
1 querer, estar a fim
What do you fancy for supper? ◆ Do you fancy a swim?
2 imaginar-se
He fancies himself as a film star.
Fancy...! ▫ **Imagine...!**
Fancy meeting you here!
fancy dress ['fansi 'dres] *n.* ▫ **fantasia**
They are going to a fancy dress party.
fantastic [fan'tastik] *adj.* ▫ **fantástico**
a fantastic book / holiday. ◆ a fantastic story.
fantasy ['fantəsi] *n.* (*pl.* **fantasies**) ▫ **fantasia**
to live in a world of fantasy.
FAQ [fak] *n., abbr.* (= Frequently Asked Questions) ▫ **FAQ, perguntas mais frequentes**
Many computer programs contain FAQs. ◆ The FAQ section in the machine's manual tells you what to do if something does not work.
far[1] [fa:] *adj.* ▫ **longe**
You can go on foot. It's not far.
- antônimo: **near**
- Ver **farther; farthest; further; furthest**.
far[2] *adv.*
1 longe
The station is not far from here. ◆ It's too far for me to see. ◆ far beyond the bridge.
- **far** is usually used in questions and negative sentences, and after **too** and **so**. In other sentences we use **a long way**:
The station is a long way from here.
2 bem, muito
This car is far better / bigger than yours.
How far...? ▫ **Qual a distância...?, Até onde...?, Até que ponto...?**
How far is it to the airport? ◆ How far did you get?
as far as
1 até
We walked as far as the station. ◆ I read as far as page 90.
2 pelo que eu sei
As far as I know, everybody wants to come.
by far ▫ **de longe**
He is by far the best student in class.
far away ▫ **muito longe**
The bank is not far away from here.
far from ▫ **longe de**
The problem is far from easy.
so far ▫ **até agora, até então**
So far he hasn't said a word. ◆ Everything is OK, so far.

■ Ver **till now; until now; up to now**.

so far, so good □ **até aqui, tudo bem / certo**

fare [feə] *n.* □ **tarifa**

How much is the bus fare to the market?

farewell [feə'wel] *n.* □ **despedida**

a farewell party / visit. ◆ He made his farewell and left.

■ Ver **goodbye**.

farm [fa:m] *n.* □ **fazenda**

to work on a farm.

farmer ['fa:mə] *n.* □ **fazendeiro, agricultor, lavrador**

farming ['fa:miŋ] *n.* □ **agricultura, lavoura**

farmyard ['fa:mja:d] *n.* □ **curral, cercado para animais**

farther ['fa:ðə] (= further) *adj., adv.* □ **mais distante, mais longe**

He can run farther than you.

farthest ['fa:ðist] (= furthest) *adj., adv.* □ **o mais longe, o mais distante**

He can throw the ball (the) farthest.

fascinate ['fasineit] *v.* (**fascinates, fascinating, fascinated**) □ **fascinar**

I love that girl. She fascinates me.

fascinating ['fasineitiŋ] *adj.* □ **fascinante**

a fascinating girl / story.

fascination [,fasi'neiʃən] *n.* □ **fascinação**

fashion ['faʃən] *n.* □ **moda**

She always dresses in the latest fashion. ◆ a fashion show. ◆ Is this hairstyle still in fashion?

come into fashion □ **vir a ser moda**

Leather clothes may come into fashion next year.

go out of fashion □ **sair de moda**

Jeans will never go out of fashion.

fashionable ['faʃnəbl] *adj.* □ **da moda**

fashionable clothes.

■ antônimo: **unfashionable; old-fashioned**

fashionably ['faʃnəbli] *adv.* □ **na moda**

They were fashionably dressed.

fashion designer ['faʃən di'zainə] *n.* □ **designer de moda**

fashion show ['faʃən ʃou] *n.* □ **desfile de moda**

fast¹ [fa:st] *adj.*

1 rápido

a fast car / train. ◆ Who is the fastest runner in the world?

■ antônimo: **slow**

■ Ver **quick**.

2 adiantado (relógio)

My watch is two minutes fast.

■ antônimo: **slow**

fast² *adv.*

1 rápido

Don't drive so fast. ◆ He runs faster than me. ◆ Take her to hospital as fast as possible.

■ antônimo: **slowly**

■ Ver **quickly**.

2 apertado

The rope is tied fast to the tree.

be fast asleep □ **estar em sono profundo**

He is fast asleep.

fast³ *n.* □ **jejum**

a fast of five days.

fast⁴ *v.* (**fasts, fasting, fasted**) □ **jejuar**

He fasts one day a week.

fasten ['fa:sn] *v.* (**fastens, fastening, fastened**)

1 apertar, fechar

Please fasten your seat-belts. ◆ He fastened his coat. ◆ to fasten the suitcase.

2 fixar

He fastened a sticker to his car.

fast food ['fa:st fu:d] *n.* □ **fast-food**

fast forward ['fɪst 'fɔ:wəd] *n., v.* (**fast forwards, fast forwarding, fast forwarded**) □ **função avançar, avançar**

to fast forward the videotape. ◆ Press the fast forward (button) on the tape recorder.

fat¹ [fat] *adj.* (**fatter, fattest**) □ **gordo**

a fat man. ◆ She is not so fat.

■ antônimo: **thin**

get fat □ **engordar**

He got fat from too many cakes.

fat² *n.* □ **gordura**

I like meat without fat on it.

fatal ['feitl] *adj.*

1 fatal

a fatal accident / disease.

2 fatal

a fatal mistake.

fatally ['feitli] *adv.* □ **fatalmente**

He was fatally wounded.

fate [feit] *n.*

1 destino

It was fate that brought them together.

2 destino

What will be the fate of these people?

fateful ['feitful] *adj.* □ **fatídico**

a fateful day for her.

father ['fa:ðə] *n.* □ **pai**

My father is a photographer.

■ Ver **dad; daddy**.

Father Christmas ['fa:ðə 'krisməs] *n.* □ **Papai Noel**

father-in-law ['fa:ðərinlɔ:] *n.* □ **sogro**

faucet ['fɔ:sit] *n. Amer.* □ **torneira**

to turn on / off the faucet. ◆ The faucet is dripping.

■ *Brit.* **tap**

fault¹ [fɔ:lt] *n.*

1 culpa

It's not my fault that she came late.

2 falha

There is a fault in one of the engines.

3 defeito

She is a good friend, but she has her faults.

find fault with □ **achar defeito em**

They are always finding fault with my cooking.

fault² *v.* (**faults, faulting, faulted**) □ **criticar**

It's hard to fault his singing.

faultless ['fɔ:ltlis] *adj.* □ **impecável**

His work was faultless.

faulty ['fɔ:lti] *adj.* □ **defeituoso, com defeito**

a faulty switch

favor¹ ['feivə] *n. Amer.*, **favour** *Brit.* □ **favor**

Will you do me a favour? ◆ Do me a favour and check it again.

to be in favour (of) □ **ser a favor de**

Are you in favour (of the new rules)?

favor² ['feivə] *v. Amer.* (**favors, favoring, favored**), **favour** *Brit.* (**favours, favouring, favoured**)

1 apoiar

I favour your plan.

2 favorecer, auxiliar
He favors his eldest son.
favorable ['feivərəbl] *adj. Amer.*, **favourable** *Brit.* □ **favorável**
a favourable impression / report.
favorite¹ ['feivərit] *adj. Amer.*, **favourite** *Brit.* □ **favorito, preferido**
Spaghetti is my favourite food.
favorite² *n. Amer.*, **favourite** *Brit.*
1 favorito, preferido
He is a great writer. He is one of my favorites.
2 favorito
Our team is the favourite.
favoritism ['feivəritizəm] *n. Amer.*, **favouritism** *Brit.* □ **favoritismo**
The teacher shows favoritism to students whose parents went to school with him.
fax¹ [faks] *n.* □ **fax**
Send him a fax.
fax² *v.* (**faxes, faxing, faxed**) □ **enviar por fax**
I faxed the documents to Paris.
fear¹ [fiə] *n.*
1 medo
I have a fear of heights. ◆ He was shaking with fear.
2 medo
There's no fear that the plan will fail.
fear² *v.* (**fears, fearing, feared**)
1 temer, ter medo de
They feared the witch.
2 temer
We fear for his life. ◆ I fear it will be too late.
■ Ver **afraid**.
fearless ['fiəlis] *adj.* □ **destemido**
a fearless soldier.
fearlessly ['fiəlisli] *adv.* □ **destemidamente**
They fought fearlessly.
feast [fi:st] *n.* □ **festim, banquete**
a wedding feast.
feat [fi:t] *n.* □ **feito, proeza**
Building the pyramids was an amazing feat.
feather ['feðə] *n.* □ **pena**
Feathers keep the bird warm.
feature ['fi:tʃə] *n.*
1 característica
What are the most important features of the new system?
2 reportagem
a special feature on life in China.
3 feição, traço
She has delicate features.
February ['februəri] *n.* □ **fevereiro**
in February, 2002
■ For examples of the use of the months see **April**.
fed [fed] *v.* (Ver **feed**).
 be fed up (with) □ **estar farto (de), estar cheio (de)**
He is fed up with his job.
fee [fi:] *n.*
1 honorários
The lawyer's fee was $800.
2 taxa
How much is the membership fee? ◆ entrance / registration fee.
3 (= fees) **taxa escolar**
college / tuition fees.
feeble ['fi:bl] *adj.* □ **fraco, débil**
a feeble old man ◆ a feeble cry for help.
feed [fi:d] *v.* (**feeds, feeding, fed**) □ **alimentar**
Did you feed the baby this morning? ◆ Who fed the chickens yesterday?
feed on □ **alimentar-se de**
Sharks feed on fish.
feedback ['fi:dbak] *n.* □ **feedback, retroalimentação, retorno**
The company got some positive feedback from the public.
◆ negative feedback about the government's new policy.
feel [fi:l] *v.* (**feels, feeling, felt**)
1 sentir-se
How do you feel? ◆ I feel fine. ◆ I don't feel very well.
2 sentir
He felt that something was wrong.
3 sentir
She felt a sting in her arm. ◆ Feel how soft this fur is.
4 tatear
He felt in his pockets for the key. ◆ She felt her way in the dark.
5 passar a sensação de
The coat felt soft.
6 sentir, achar
I feel that we should tell him.
feel like □ **estar a fim de**
I feel like going for a swim. ◆ Do you feel like (having) a drink?
feeling ['fi:liŋ] *n.*
1 sentimento
a feeling of disappointment.
2 sensibilidade
He lost all feeling in his right hand.
3 sensação
I have a feeling that he is hiding something.
hurt someone's feelings □ **magoar alguém**
How can I tell him without hurting his feelings?
feet [fi:t] *n. plural* (Ver **foot**).
fell [fel] *v.* (Ver **fall**²).
fellow¹ ['felou] *n. Brit.* □ **cara, sujeito**
He is a good fellow.
■ *Amer.* **guy**
fellow² *adj.* □ **colega**
my fellow workers / students.
felt [felt] *v.* (Ver **feel**).
felt-pen ['feltpen] *n.* (mesmo que **felt-tip pen**) □ **caneta hidrográfica**
female¹ ['fi:meil] *n.* □ **fêmea**
Is this cat a male or a female?
female² *adj.* □ **fêmea**
a female bird / child.
■ Compare **feminine**¹.
feminine¹ ['feminin] *adj.*
1 (grammar) □ **feminino**
'Lioness' is a feminine noun and 'lion' is a masculine noun.
2 feminino
a feminine voice.
feminine² *n.* (grammar) □ **feminino**
The feminine of 'prince' is 'princess'.

fence [fens] *n.* □ **cerca**
He built a fence around the garden.
fender ['fendə] *n. Amer.* □ **para-lama**
■ *Brit.* **wing**
ferocious [fə'rouʃəs] *adj.* □ **feroz**
a ferocious dog.
■ Ver **fierce**.
ferry ['feri] *n. (pl.* **ferries)** □ **balsa**
We crossed the river by ferry.
fertile ['fətail] *adj.* □ **fértil**
fertile soil / land
■ antônimo: **infertile**
fertilizer ['fətilaizə] *n.* □ **fertilizante**
chemical / organic fertilizer
festival ['festivəl] *n.*
1 festival
a film festival.
2 festa
a religious festival.
festivities ['festiviti:z] *n. pl.* □ **festividades**
The festivities ended with fireworks.
fetch [fetʃ] *v.* (**fetches, fetching, fetched**) □ **ir buscar**
Please fetch me some apples from the garden.
fête [feit] *n.* □ **festa**
the school / church fête.
feud [fju:d] *n.* □ **rixa, disputa**
a family feud (between two families).
fever ['fi:və] *n.* □ **febre**
He has a high fever. (= He has a temperature.)
feverish ['fi:vəriʃ] *adj.* □ **febril**
She is feverish. Let's call the doctor.
feverishly ['fi:vəriʃli] *adv.* □ **febrilmente, agitadamente**
He worked feverishly to finish early.
few [fju:] *adj., pron.* □ **poucos**
Few people knew the secret.
■ Use **few** with countable nouns; use **little** with uncountable nouns:
We have very little time left.
a few (= several) □ **alguns**
He decided to wait a few days. ◆ A few people waited outside.
■ Be careful:
a few = some.
few = not many.
quite a few □ **vários, um grande número**
There are quite a few mistakes in the book.
fewer ['fju:ə] *adj., pron.* □ **menos**
There were fewer questions than the last time. ◆ Fewer than 20 people came.
■ **fewer** is used with countable nouns ('fewer books'); **less** with uncountable nouns ('less time').
fewest ['fju:ist] *adj., pron.* □ **pouquíssimos**
The company sold the fewest cars last year.
■ **fewest** is used with countable nouns; **least** with uncountable nouns:
She ate the least. (food).
fiancé [fi'a:nsei] *n.* □ **noivo**
Her fiancé is 24 years old.
fiancée [fi'a:nsə] *n.* □ **noiva**
When did he and his fiancée get engaged?
fib[1] [fib] *n.* □ **lorota**
Don't tell fibs!

fib[2] *v.* (**fibs, fibbing, fibbed**) □ **contar lorotas**
I know you're fibbing.
fibber ['fibə] *n.* □ **mentiroso, loroteiro**
fiber ['faibə] *n. Amer.,* **fibre** *Brit.* □ **fibra**
cotton fibers.
fiction ['fikʃən] *n.* □ **ficção**
I enjoy reading fiction, especially novels.
■ Ver **non-fiction; science fiction**.
fictional ['fikʃənl] *adj.* □ **fictício, ficcional**
'Superman' is a fictional character.
fictitious [fik'tiʃəs] *adj.* □ **fictício**
a fictitious (= false) name. ◆ All the events in the story are fictitious.
fiddle[1] ['fidl] *v.* (**fiddles, fiddling, fiddled**) □ **brincar**
Stop fiddling with the fork and eat your food!
fiddle[2] *n.* (= violin) □ **rabeca**
fidget ['fidʒit] *v.* (**fidgets, fidgeting, fidgeted**) □ **manusear algo com inquietação**
He fidgeted with his sunglasses.
field [fi:ld] *n.*
1 campo, lavoura
a field of corn.
2 campo, área, esfera
He is an expert in the field of computers.
3 campo
an oil field.
4 campo
a football field.
fierce [fiəs] *adj.*
1 bravo, feroz
a fierce dog.
■ Ver **ferocious**.
2 forte
fierce winds.
fifteen [fif'ti:n] *adj., n.* □ **quinze**
She is fifteen years old. ◆ The story is on page fifteen. ◆ Three times five is fifteen (3x5=15).
fifteenth[1] [fif'ti:nθ] *adj.* □ **décimo quinto, quinze**
the fifteenth century (1401-1500). ◆ the fifteenth floor.
fifteenth[2] *adv.* □ **décimo quinto**
She finished fifteenth in the race.
fifteenth[3] *n.* □ **décimo quinto, quinze**
the fifteenth of June (= 15th June). *Brit.* ◆ June fifteenth (= June 15). *Amer.*
fifth[1] [fifθ] *adj., adv.* □ **quinto, cinco**
the fifth floor. ◆ I'm the fifth on the list. ◆ the fifth of July (= 5th July). *Brit.* ◆ July fifth (= July 5). *Amer.* ◆ He came fifth in the race.
fifth[2] *n.* □ **quinto**
one-fifth (= 1/5) of the money
fifties ['fiftiz] *n.* (Ver **fifty**).
fiftieth[1] ['fiftiθ] *adj.* □ **quinquagésimo**
their fiftieth wedding anniversary.
fiftieth[2] *adv.* □ **quinquagésimo**
Our came came in fiftieth in the race.
fiftieth[3] *n.* □ **quinquagésimo**
A 'fiftieth' is one of 50 parts.
fifty ['fifti] *adj., n.* □ **cinquenta**
He is fifty years old. ◆ It will start at eight fifty (8:50). ◆ The wall is fifty metres long.
in the fifties □ **nos anos cinquenta, na década de 1950**
This dance was popular in the fifties.

fig / finance

in your fifties □ **nos seus cinquenta anos, com cinquenta e poucos anos**
She is in her fifties.
fig [fig] *n.* □ **figo**
dried figs.
fight¹ [fait] *n.* □ **briga**
The two gangs had a fight.
fight² *v.* (**fights, fighting, fought**)
1 lutar
They fought bravely against the enemy.
2 brigar
The digs are fighting again.
3 brigar, lutar
Fight for your rights! ◆ to fight against crime.
fighter ['faitə] *n.*
1 guerreiro, lutador, combatente
Several fighters were wounded.
2 (= boxer) **lutador**
3 caça
fighter planes.
fighting ['faitiŋ] *n.* □ **briga**
street fighting between gangs.
figure¹ ['figə] *n.*
1 dígito
a telephone number of seven figures.
2 soma
He offered us a high figure for the house.
3 figura
She has a good figure.
4 vulto
I could see a figure in the dark.
5 figura, imagem
The figure on page VI shows the parts of the machine.
figures *n. pl.*
1 números
The sales figures of the company are higher this year.
2 números
I'm not very good at figures.
figure of speech *n.* □ **figura de linguagem**
If you say that someone is an angel, it's a figure of speech.
figure² *v.* (**figures, figuring, figured**) □ **imaginar**
I figure that he will finish the job next Monday.
figure out
1 entender, sacar
I can't figure out how he did it.
2 descobrir, achar
He figured out a way to do it more quickly.
file¹ [fail] *n.*
1 ficha, pasta
We have files on all our workers. ◆ Put this document in the file.
2 arquivo
Copy all these files onto a floppy disk.
3 lixa
a nail-file.
4 fila, coluna
They walked in (single) file.
file² *v.* (**files, filing, filed**)
1 lixar
She is filing her nails.
2 arquivar
File these letters under 'Complaints'.

fill [fil] *v.* (**fills, filling, filled**)
1 encher
He filled the glass (with water). ◆ She filled the boxes with books.
2 encher-se
Their eyes filled with tears.
3 obturar
The dentist filled one of my teeth. *Brit.*
fill in □ **preencher**
Please fill in this form. ◆ I filled in my name and address.
■ *Amer.* **fill out**
fill up □ **encher**
I filled up the fuel tank. ◆ He filled the jar up with sweets.
filling ['filiŋ] *n.*
1 obturação
I have two fillings in my teeth.
2 recheio
cake with chocolate filling.
film¹ [film] *n.*
1 filme
a television film. ◆ We went to see a film (at the cinema).
■ *Amer.* **movie**
2 filme
I need a new film for my camera.
film² *v.* (**films, filming, filmed**) □ **filmar**
They filmed the scene several times.
■ Ver **shoot**.
film star ['film 'sta:] *n. Brit.* □ **astro de cinema**
■ *Amer.* **movie star**
filter¹ ['filtə] *n.* □ **filtro**
an air filter. ◆ a coffee filter.
filter² *v.* (**filters, filtering, filtered**) □ **filtrar**
We filtered the water before we drank it.
filth [filθ] *n.* □ **sujeira, imundície**
The floor was covered in filth.
filthy ['filθi] *adj.* (**filthier, filthiest**) □ **imundo**
filthy clothes / hands.
fin [fin] *n.* □ **nadadeira, barbatana**
The fins help the fish to swim.
final¹ ['fainl] *adj.*
1 (= last) **final, último**
The final chapter of the book is disappointing. ◆ That's my final offer.
final² *n.* □ **final**
the Cup Final (= a game to decide which team will win the cup).
finals *n.* □ **exames finais**
He took his finals a few weeks ago.
finalize ['fainəlaiz] *v.* (**finalizes, finalizing, finalized**) □ **finalizar**
to finalize our plans.
finally ['fainəli] *adv.*
1 finalmente
They finally agreed to take it back.
2 por fim, finalmente
Finally, I would like to say that...
■ Meaning 1: **finally** comes before the verb. Meaning 2: **finally** usually begins the sentence.
finance¹ [fai'nans] *n.*
1 Fazenda
the Minister of Finance (= the Finance Minister).
■ In Britain: **the Chancellor of the Exchequer**. In the USA: **the Secretary of the Treasury**.

2 finanças
an expert in finance.
3 financiamento, verba
We can't get any finance for the project.
finances *n. pl.* □ **finanças**
The company's finances are not very good.
finance² *v.* (**finances, financing, financed**) □ **financiar**
The government will finance 45% of the research.
financial [fai'nanʃəl] *adj.* □ **financeiro**
They are in financial difficulties.
find [faind] *v.* (**finds, finding, found**)
1 achar, encontrar
Where did you find the ring? ◆ I can't find my watch. ◆ They found a solution to the problem.
2 achar
I find this game very amusing.
I find it difficult / hard to… □ **eu acho difícil…**
I find it hard to believe that he is guilty.
find out □ **descobrir**
I found out that he knew nothing about it.
■ Ver **discover**.
findings ['faindiŋz] *n. pl.* □ **descobertas**
What were the findings of the committee?
fine¹ [fain] *adj.*
1 bom
fine weather.
2 bem
I feel fine. ◆ How are you? – Fine, thank you.
3 de boa qualidade
fine food / clothes.
4 belo
a fine view.
5 (= OK) **tudo bem, certo, OK**
The meeting is tomorrow. – Fine, I'll be there.
6 (= delicate) **fino**
fine silk / lace
7 fino
fine powder / sand.
■ antônimo: **coarse**
8 fino
fine thread / hair. ◆ a pencil with a fine point.
■ antônimo: **thick**
fine² *n.* □ **multa**
He paid a fine of $150.
fine³ *v.* (**fines, fining, fined**) □ **multar**
The judge fined him $120 for speeding (= driving too fast)
finger ['fiŋgə] *n.* □ **dedo**
He dug a hole with his fingers.
keep your fingers crossed □ **torcer, cruzar os dedos**
I'm keeping my fingers crossed that you'll pass the test.
not lift a finger □ **não levantar um dedo**
They didn't lift a finger to help.
fingernail ['fiŋgəneil] *n.* (Ver **nail**) □ **unha**
I cut my fingernails regularly.
fingerprint ['fiŋgəprint] *n.* □ **(impressão) digital**
The police took the suspect's fingerprints.
finish¹ ['finiʃ] *n.* □ **fim**
The finish of the race was very exciting.
■ antônimo: **start**
finish² *v.* (**finishes, finishing, finished**) □ **terminar, acabar**
They will finish the job on time. ◆ She finished talking and sat down. ◆ What time does the game finish? ◆ School finishes at 2 pm today.
fir [fə:] *n.* (mesmo que **fir-tree**) □ **abeto**
fire¹ ['faiə] *n.*
1 incêndio
The firemen put out the fire very quickly. ◆ The fire broke out on the fifth floor.
2 fogo
to light a fire.
3 aquecedor
Switch on the electric fire.
4 fogo
The soldiers opened fire when they saw the enemy.
catch fire □ **pegar fogo**
The house caught fire very quickly.
on fire □ **em chamas**
The building is on fire.
set something on fire □ **pôr fogo em algo**
They set the car on fire. (= They set fire to the car.)
fire² *v.* (**fires, firing, fired**)
1 disparar, atirar
He fired one shot in the air.
■ Ver **shoot**.
2 despedir, demitir
The boss fired him because he was lazy. ◆ You're fired!
■ Ver **dismiss; sack²**.
fire-alarm ['faiərə,la:m] *n.* □ **alarme de incêndio**
fire brigade ['faiə bri'geid] *n. Brit.* □ **brigada de incêndio, corpo de bombeiros**
Call the fire brigade!
■ *Amer.* **fire department**
firecracker ['faiəkrakə] *n.* □ **bombinha**
fire-engine ['faiər,endʒin] *n.* □ **carro de bombeiro**
fire-escape ['faiəris,keip] *n.* □ **saída de incêndio**
In case of fire, use the fire-escape.
fire extinguisher ['faiər iks,tiŋgwiʃə] *n.* □ **extintor de incêndio**
firefighter ['faiə,faitə] *n.* □ **bombeiro**
The fire-fighters put out the fire very quickly.
fireman ['faiəmən] *n.* (*pl.* **firemen**) □ **bombeiro**
fireplace ['faiəpleis] *n.* □ **lareira**
■ Ver **hearth**.
fireproof ['faiəpru:f] *adj.* □ **à prova de fogo**
fireproof material.
fireside ['faiəsaid] *n.* □ **próximo à lareira**
to sit by the fireside.
firework ['faiəwə:k] *n.* □ **fogos de artifício**
We went to see the fireworks.
firm¹ [fə:m] *adj.*
1 firme
That shelf is not firm enough for the books. ◆ a firm handshake.
2 firme
He has firm muscles.
3 firme
She is firm with the pupils.
4 firme
a firm decision. ◆ a firm promise.
firm² *n.* □ **firma, empresa, escritório de advocacia**
a building firm.
■ Ver **company**.

firmly ['fɜːmli] *adv.*
1 firmemente, com firmeza
'Don't interfere!', he said firmly.
2 firme
Hold it firmly. ◆ Tighten the rope firmly.
first¹ [fɜːst] *adj., pron.* □ **primeiro**
This is my first visit to your country. ◆ She won the first prize. ◆ He was the first to arrive. ◆ the first of June (= 1st June). *Brit.* ◆ June first (= June 1). *Amer.*
first² *adv.*
1 primeiro
She came first in the race.
2 primeiro, primeiramente
First, I'd like to thank you all for your support.
3 pela primeira vez
When did you first meet them?
at first □ **a princípio, no início**
At first he hated the new house.
first of all □ **em primeiro lugar**
First of all, it's a very useful tool. Secondly, it's not expensive.
first aid ['fɜːst eid] *n.* □ **primeiros-socorros**
I gave the injured man first aid.
first class¹ [,fɜːst 'klɑːs] *n.* □ **primeira classe**
The seats are more comfortable in first class.
first class² *adj.* □ **de primeira classe**
a first-class ticket / seat ◆ The service here is first class.
first class³ *adv.*, **first-class** □ **de primeira classe**
to travel / fly first class.
first floor [,fɜːst 'flɔː] *n.*
1 *Brit.* **primeiro andar**
I live on the first floor.
■ *Amer.* **second floor**
2 *Amer.* **andar térreo**
■ *Brit.* **ground floor**
firstly ['fɜːstli] *adv.* □ **primeiramente, em primeiro lugar**
The book will be a success, firstly because it's funny and secondly because it's not expensive.
first name ['fɜːst 'neim] *n.* (= Christian name) □ **primeiro nome, nome de batismo**
Write down your first and last name.
■ Ver também **family name; surname**.
first-rate [,fɜːst'reit] *adj.* □ **de primeira (qualidade)**
a first-rate player. ◆ The service here is first-rate.
fish¹ [fiʃ] *n.* (*pl.* **fish** or **fishes**) □ **peixe**
I caught a lot of fish yesterday. ◆ We had fried fish for dinner.
■ The plural is usually **fish**. The plural **fishes** is used especially when we talk about different kinds of fish.
fish² *v.* (**fishes, fishing, fished**) □ **pescar**
We fish (= go fishing) every Sunday.
fisherman ['fiʃəmən] *n.* (*pl.* **fishermen**) □ **pescador**
fishing ['fiʃiŋ] *n.* □ **pescaria, ato de pescar**
Let's go fishing. ◆ My hobbies are fishing and tennis.
fist [fist] *n.* □ **punho**
He banged on the table with his fist.
fit¹ [fit] *adj.* (**fitter, fittest**)
1 adequado
This house is not fit to live in. ◆ I don't think he is fit for the job.
■ antônimo: **unfit**
2 em forma

She does exercises to keep fit. ◆ He is still ill and is not fit for work.
■ antônimo: **unfit**
fit² *n.* □ **ataque, acesso, crise**
a fit of coughing / anger.
fit³ *v.* (**fits, fitting, fitted**)
1 servir, assentar, encaixar-se
These shoes don't fit (me). ◆ The suit fits you exactly. ◆ The key doesn't fit the lock.
2 condizer
Your report does not fit the facts.
3 encaixar
to fit a lock on the door. ◆ Can you fit these pieces together?
4 caber
The clothes won't fit into one suitcase. ◆ Only four people can fit into the car.
fit in
1 encaixar
I can't fit any more books in. ◆ The car is so small that only two people can fit in.
2 encaixar
The doctor can fit you in tomorrow at 10.
fitness ['fitnis] *n.* □ **boa forma, aptidão física**
They trained hard to improve their physical fitness.
five [faiv] *adj., n.* □ **cinco**
Two and three are five (2+3=5). ◆ Come at five o'clock. ◆ She is five years old.
■ Ver **fifth**.
fix [fiks] *v.* (**fixes, fixing, fixed**)
1 consertar
to fix the car / a broken window.
■ Ver **mend; repair²**.
2 fixar
We fixed the blackboard to the wall.
3 combinar
They fixed a date for the meeting.
■ Ver **determine**.
fixed [fikst] *adj.*
1 fixo
fixed cupboards.
2 fixo
a fixed price.
fizzy ['fizi] *adj. Brit.* (= sparkling) □ **com gás, gasoso**
fizzy drinks (= sodas, *Amer.*).
■ antônimo: **still²**
flag [flag] *n.* □ **bandeira**
They waved their flags. ◆ the national flag of our country.
flagpole ['flagpoul] *n.* □ **mastro de bandeira**
flake [fleik] *v.* (**flakes, flaking, flaked**) □ **escamar, descascar**
My skin is beginning to flake (off).
flakes [fleiks] *n. pl.* □ **floco**
flakes of snow.
■ Ver **cornflakes; snowflakes**.
flame [fleim] *n.* □ **chama**
the flame of a candle.
(go up) in flames □ **(ficar) em chamas**
The building went up in flames. ◆ The car was in flames.
flap¹ [flap] *n.*
1 batida
the flap (= flapping) of wings.

flap / floppy disk

2 aba
The flap of the envelope was open.

flap² *v.* (**flaps, flapping, flapped**) □ bater, esvoaçar
The bird flapped its wings. ◆ The sails flapped in the wind.

flare [fleə] *v.* (**flares, flaring, flared**) □ chamejar
The match flared (up) in the darkness.

flash¹ [flaʃ] *n.*
1 clarão
a flash of lightning.
2 flash
Use a flash when there isn't enough light.
in a flash □ num instante
It disappeared in a flash.

flash² *v.* (**flashes, flashing, flashed**)
1 brilhar
Lightning flashed across the sky.
2 piscar
He flashed the lights of the car three times.
3 passar rápido
An aircraft flashed across the sky.

flashlight ['flaʃlait] *n. Amer.* □ lanterna
He shone the flashlight on me.
■ *Brit.* **torch**

flat¹ [flat] *adj.* (**flatter, flattest**)
1 plana
a flat surface.
2 murcho
a flat tyre / tire.

flat² *n.*
1 *Brit.* **flat, apartamento**
I rented a flat. ◆ a block of flats (= a building with a lot of flats).
■ *Amer.* **apartment**
2 pneu furado, pneu murcho
I have a flat. I'll have to change the tyre.
■ Ver **puncture**.

flatten ['flatn] *v.* (**flattens, flattening, flattened**)
1 aplainar, nivelar, abrir
They flattened the area with bulldozers. ◆ Use a rolling-pin to flatten the dough.
2 achatar
He flattened the flower when he stepped on it.

flatter ['flatə] *v.* (**flatters, flattering, flattered**)
1 bajular
He flatters the boss in order to get the good jobs.
2 favorecer
This dress / photograph flatters you.

feel / be flattered □ sentir-se lisonjeado
I felt flattered when they asked for my help.

flatter yourself □ vangloriar-se
You flatter yourself if you think that we need you.

flattery ['flatəri] *n.* □ bajulação
With a little flattery he got the car from his sister.

flavor¹ ['fleivə] *n. Amer.*, **flavour** *Brit.* □ sabor
What flavour of ice-cream do you like?

flavor² *v. Amer.* (**flavors, flavoring, flavored**), **flavour** *Brit.* (**flavours, flavouring, flavoured**) □ temperar
The sauce is flavoured with pepper.

-flavored *Amer.*, **-flavoured** *Brit.* □ com sabor de
chocolate-flavoured ice-cream.

flea [fli:] *n.* □ pulga

flee [fli:] *v.* (**flees, fleeing, fled**) □ fugir (de)
He fled the country.

■ Ver **escape; run away**.

fleet [fli:t] *n.* □ esquadra, frota
a fleet of ships.

flesh [fleʃ] *n.* □ carne
There was a deep cut in his flesh. ◆ The flesh of animals that we eat is called meat.

flew [flu:] *v.* (Ver **fly²**).

flex [fleks] *n. Brit.* □ fio
■ *Amer.* **cord**

flexible ['fleksibl] *adj.* □ flexível
flexible material. ◆ The plan is flexible.

flicker ['flikə] *v.* (**flickers, flickering, flickered**) □ tremular
The candle flickered and went out.

flies [flaiz] *n., v.* (Ver **fly¹; fly²**).

flight [flait] *n.*
1 voo
Flight No. 309 from London arrives at 9:30. ◆ I cancelled my flight.
2 voo
From here you can clearly see the eagles in flight.
3 lance
a flight of stairs.

flight attendant ['flait ə,tendənt] *n. Amer.* □ comissária de bordo
■ *Brit.* **air hostess; steward; stewardess**

fling [fliŋ] *v.* (**flings, flinging, flung**) □ lançar, jogar
He flung his attacker to the ground. ◆ She flung the ring at him.

flirt [flə:t] *v.* (**flirts, flirting, flirted**) □ flertar
He tried to flirt with her.

float [flout] *v.* (**floats, floating, floated**)
1 boiar, flutuar
Can you float on your back? ◆ Oil floats on water.
2 flutuar
The balloons floated in the sky.

flock [flok] *n.*
1 rebanho
a flock of sheep / goats.
■ Ver **herd**.
2 bando, rebanho
a flock of seagulls.

flood¹ [flʌd] *n.*
1 enchente
Many villages were destroyed in the floods.
2 enxurrada
We received a flood of letters.

flood² *v.* (**floods, flooding, flooded**)
1 inundar
The river flooded the fields.
2 encher, inundar
The customers flooded us with complaints.

floor [flo:] *n.*
1 chão
They sat on the floor.
2 andar
I live on the second floor. ◆ The office is on the tenth floor.
■ Also **storey** (*Brit.*) or **story** (*Amer*), but usually when stating the number of floors, e.g.:
a seven-storey building.
■ Ver **first floor; ground floor**.

floppy disk ['flopi 'disk] *n.* □ disquete

florist / follow

Copy this file onto a floppy disk.
■ Ver **hard disk**.
florist ['florist] *n*. □ **florista**
flour [flauə] *n*. □ **farinha de trigo**
a packet of white flour. ♦ to mix flour with water to make dough.
flourish ['flʌriʃ] *v*. (**flourishes, flourishing, flourished**) □ **florescer, prosperar**
His business is flourishing.
flow¹ [flou] *n*. □ **fluxo**
He stopped the flow of blood from the cut.
flow² *v*. (**flows, flowing, flowed**) □ **correr, fluir**
The river flows into the Mediterranean Sea. ♦ Tears flowed down her cheeks. ♦ The traffic is flowing smoothly.
flower ['flauə] *n*. □ **flor**
He picked some flowers. ♦ a bunch of flowers.
flowerbed ['flauəbed] *n*. □ **canteiro**
flowerpot ['flauəpot] *n*. □ **vaso**
flowery ['flauəri] *adj*. □ **florido**
a flowery dress.
flown [floun] *v*. (Ver **fly**²).
flu [flu:] *n*. □ **gripe**
He is in bed with the flu.
fluency ['flu:ənsi] *n*. □ **fluência**
She got the job because of her fluency in three languages.
fluent ['flu:ənt] *adj*. □ **fluente**
He speaks fluent French.
fluently ['flu:əntli] *adv*. □ **fluentemente**
They speak Spanish fluently.
fluid¹ ['flu:id] *n*. □ **líquido**
Drink plenty of fluids.
■ Ver **liquid**.
fluid² *adj*. □ **indefinido**
The situation is still fluid – we don't know how it will end.
flung [flʌŋ] *v*. (Ver **fling**).
flush [flʌʃ] *v*. (**flushes, flushing, flushed**)
1 dar descarga
to flush the toilet.
2 enrubescer, corar
He flushed with anger.
■ Compare with **blush**.
flute [flu:t] *n*. □ **flauta**
He plays the flute.
fly¹ [flai] *n*. (*pl*. **flies**) □ **mosca**
insects such as flies and mosquitoes.
fly² *v*. (**flies, flying, flew, flown**)
1 voar
Some birds fly together in a group (flock).
2 voar, ir de avião
The plane flew above the clouds. ♦ I'm flying to Brazil tomorrow.
3 pilotar
This pilot can fly planes and helicopters.
4 empinar
to fly a kite.
flyer ['flaiə] *n*.
1 aviador, voador
A flyer is a pilot or a passenger on an airplane.
2 flyer, folheto
fliers advertising the new restaurant.
flying¹ ['flaiŋ] *adj*. □ **voador**
flying insects.

flying² *n*. □ **de avião**
The only way to get there is by flying.
flying saucer ['flaiiŋ ˌsɔːsə] *n*. □ **disco voador**
foal [foul] *n*. □ **potro**
foam [foum] *n*. □ **espuma**
the foam of the waves. ♦ shaving foam.
focus¹ ['foukəs] *n*. □ **foco**
The photo is out of focus.
focus² *v*. (**focuses, focusing, focused**)
1 focar
to focus a camera / microscope.
2 concentrar
Try to focus your attention on this problem.
fog [fog] *n*. □ **neblina**
The fog is beginning to clear.
■ Compare with **mist**.
foggy ['fogi] *adj*. (**foggier, foggiest**) □ **nevoento, com névoa, com neblina**
It will be foggy tomorrow. ♦ a foggy day.
fold¹ [fould] *n*. □ **dobra**
to make folds in a piece of paper. ♦ the folds of a dress.
fold² *v*. (**folds, folding, folded**)
1 dobrar
I folded the letter (in half). ♦ Fold up your trousers.
■ antônimo: **unfold**
2 dobrar
The chair folds (up) easily.
fold your arms □ **cruzar os braços**
He folded his arms and waited.
folder ['fouldə] *n*. □ **fôlder, pasta**
folding ['fouldiŋ] *adj*. □ **dobrável**
a folding chair / bed.
folk [fouk] *n*. (= people) □ **pessoas**
Some folk still remember him.
■ *Amer*. **folks**
one's folks *n*. □ **a família de alguém**
How are your folks?
folk dance ['foukdɑːns] *n*. □ **dança folclórica**
folk song ['fouksoŋ] *n*. □ **música folclórica**
follow ['folou] *v*. (**follows, following, followed**)
1 seguir, vir depois de
Follow him. ♦ Follow me, please. ♦ The black car is following us. ♦ Tuesday follows Monday.
2 seguir
Follow the road until you see a tall building.
3 seguir
Follow the instructions on the package. ♦ I followed your advice.
4 entender, acompanhar
I don't follow. (= I don't understand.) ♦ I couldn't follow the lecturer / explanation.
as follows □ **como segue**
The results are as follows: Greece 8 points, Italy 10 points and Ireland 12 points.
it follows from □ **a partir de, segundo**
It follows from what you say that it is possible.
following ['folouiŋ] *adj*.
1 seguinte
She called the following (= next) day.
2 a seguir
Answer the following questions.

follow-up ['folouʌp] *n.* □ **continuação**
The movie is a follow-up of the successful book.

fond [fond] *adj.*
be fond of □ **gostar de**
I'm fond of him. ◆ She is fond of her cats.

food [fu:d] *n.* □ **comida, alimento**
There's plenty of food and drink. ◆ baby food.
food processor ['fu:d pro'sesə] *n.* □ **processador de alimentos**

fool¹ [fu:l] *n.* □ **tolo**
He is not a fool, although he sometimes behaves like one.
make a fool of □ **fazer alguém de bobo**
He made a fool of you. It's not a real diamond. ◆ Stop making a fool of yourself!

fool² *v.* (**fools, fooling, fooled**) □ **enganar**
You can't fool me!
fool about / around
1 perder tempo
Stop fooling around! We have a lot of work to do.
2 brincar
Don't fool about with that knife!

foolish ['fu:liʃ] *adj.* (= silly, stupid) □ **tolo, insensato**
It was foolish of you to ask. ◆ a foolish question / mistake.

foolishly ['fu:liʃli] *adv.* □ **tolamente, insensatamente**
I foolishly agreed to sign.

foolishness ['fu:liʃnis] *n.* (= stupidity) □ **tolice, insensatez**

foot [fut] *n.* (*pl.* **feet**)
1 pé
She has small feet. ◆ He stood on one foot.
2 sopé
the foot of the mountain.
3 pé (unidade de medida)
She is six foot / feet tall.
■ abreviação: **ft**.
on foot □ **a pé**
Shall we go by car or on foot?

football ['futbo:l] *n.*
1 (= soccer) **futebol**
to play football. ◆ a football player (= footballer). ◆ a football match / game. ◆ a football field / pitch.
2 (= ball) **bola de futebol**
3 (= American football) **futebol americano**
In American football the players pass the ball with their hands.

footballer ['futbo:lə] *n.* □ **jogador de futebol**
football pitch ['futbo:l ˌpitʃ] *n.* □ **campo de futebol**
footpath ['futpa:θ] *n.* □ **trilha, atalho**
footprint ['futprint] *n.* □ **pegada**
The bear left its footprints in the snow.
footstep ['futstep] *n.* □ **passo**
I heard her footsteps in the corridor.

for¹ [fo:] *conj.* (= because) □ **pois, porque, já que**
They stayed there, for they had nowhere else to go.
■ **because, since** and **as** are more common.

for² *prep.*
1 para
This present is for you.
2 para
What did you have for breakfast? ◆ to prepare for an exam ◆ Fruit juice is good for you.
3 por
He worked here for five years. (He is not working here now.) ◆ He has worked here for five years. (He is still working here.) ◆ I'm going away for a few days.
4 por
We walked for 10 kilometers.
5 para
The train for Berlin leaves in five minutes.
6 por
I bought it for 20 dollars.
7 para
He went to prison for robbery.
8 a favor
Are you for or against the plan?
9 por
I did it for my family. ◆ What can I do for you?
10 por
Wait for them.
11 por
I'm speaking for all the class.
12 para
He is tall for his age. ◆ It's cold for this time of year.
13 para
They invited me for 8:30.
14 para, por
For every correct answer you get 5 points.
for the first time □ **pela primeira vez**
I saw her yesterday for the first time.

forbid [fə'bid] *v.* (**forbids, forbidding, forbade, forbidden**) □ **proibir**
I forbid you to talk to him. ◆ Smoking is forbidden here.

force¹ [fo:s] *n.*
1 força
They used force to open the door.
2 força
the force of the earthquake / explosion.
■ Ver **power; strength**.
by force □ **à força**
He took it by force.

force² *v.* (**forces, forcing, forced**)
1 forçar, obrigar
I can't force you to stay. ◆ Nobody is forcing you to come.
2 forçar
The thief forced the lock.

forecast¹ ['fo:ka:st] *n.* □ **previsão**
What is the weather forecast for tomorrow? ◆ the company's sales forecast.
■ Ver **outlook**.

forecast² *v.* (**forecasts, forecasting, forecast, forecasted**) □ **prever**
The company forecasts a 5% increase in exports.

forehead ['fo:rid] *n.* (= brow) □ **testa, fronte**
He wiped the sweat from his forehead.

foreign ['forən] *adj.*
1 estrangeiro
a foreign language. ◆ a foreign country.
2 Relações Exteriores
the Foreign Minister.
■ Compare **strange**:
foreign = from / of a different country
strange = not known to you

foreigner ['forinə] *n.* □ **estrangeiro**
■ Ver **stranger**.

foreman ['fɔ:mən] *n.* (*pl.* **foremen**) ☐ **capataz**
foresee [fɔ:'si:] *v.* (**foresees, foreseeing, foresaw, foreseen**) ☐ **prever**
They did not foresee the difficulties.
foresight ['fɔ:sait] *n.* ☐ **presciência**
She had the foresight to insure her house.
forest ['fɔrist] *n.* ☐ **floresta**
They lost their way in the forest.
foretell [fɔ:'tel] *v.* (**foretells, foretelling, foretold**) (= predict) ☐ **predizer**
I can't foretell what will happen.
forever [fə'revə] *adv.* ☐ **para sempre**
I'll remember you forever.
foreword ['fɔ:wəd] *n.* (= preface) ☐ **prefácio**
You should read the foreword before you read the book itself.
forgave [fə'geiv] *v.* (Ver **forgive**).
forge [fɔ:dʒ] *v.* (**forges, forging, forged**) ☐ **forjar, falsificar**
He forged my signature.
■ Ver **fake³**.
forged [fɔ:dʒd] *adj.* ☐ **forjado, falsificado, falso**
The money / passport is forged.
■ Ver **fake**.
forger ['fɔ:dʒə] *n.* ☐ **falsificador**
forgery ['fɔ:dʒəri] *n.* (*pl.* **forgeries**) ☐ **falsificação**
She was sent to prison for forgery. ♦ The banknotes were forgeries.
■ Ver **fake²**.
forget [fə'get] *v.* (**forgets, forgetting, forgot, forgotten**) ☐ **esquecer**
Don't forget to lock the door! ♦ He forgot her address.
forgetful [fə'getful] *adj.* ☐ **esquecido**
He is getting very forgetful.
forgive [fə'giv] *v.* (**forgives, forgiving, forgave, forgiven**) ☐ **perdoar**
She will never forgive you for that mistake. ♦ He forgave me a long time ago. ♦ Forgive me for interrupting, but...
forgiveness [fə'givnis] *n.* ☐ **perdão**
to ask for forgiveness.
forgot [fə'gɔt] *v.* (Ver **forget**).
forgotten [fə'gɔtn] *v.* (Ver **forget**).
fork [fɔ:k] *n.*
1 garfo
knives, forks and spoons.
2 forquilha
a garden fork.
3 bifurcação
a fork in the road.
form¹ [fɔ:m] *n.*
1 meios
different forms of communication (e.g. telephone, radio).
2 formulário
Fill in this form. *Brit.* ♦ Fill out this form. *Amer.*
3 (= shape) **formato**
chocolate in the form of an egg.
4 (grammar) **forma**
The plural form of 'foot' is 'feet'.
5 *Brit.* **série**
She is in the fifth form.
■ *Amer.* **grade**
form² *v.* (**forms, forming, formed**)
1 formar, modelar
They formed a circle and began to dance. ♦ He formed a star out of chocolate.
2 formar-se
A cloud of smoke formed over the place.
3 formar, montar
to form a team / government / club.
4 (grammar) **formar**
Usually we form the plural of nouns by adding 's' or 'es'.
formal ['fɔ:məl] *adj.* ☐ **formal**
a formal dinner. ♦ This letter is in very formal English.
■ antônimo: **informal**
formally ['fɔ:məli] *adv.* ☐ **formalmente**
He was formally dressed. ♦ She spoke to me very formally.
■ antônimo: **informally**
former¹ ['fɔ:mə] *adj.*
1 anterior
the former Prime Minister. ♦ her former husband.
2 ex-
He is a former diplomat.
in former times ☐ **nos tempos antigos**
In former times, the Greeks believed in gods.
former² *adj., n.* ☐ **primeiro**
Both Venice and Rome are beautiful, but I liked the former (city) much more.
■ Ver **latter²**.
formerly ['fɔ:məli] *adv.* ☐ **anteriormente**
This building was formerly a prison.
formula ['fɔ:mjulə] *n.* (*pl.* **formulae** or **formulas**) ☐ **fórmula**
a mathematical / chemical formula.
fort [fɔ:t] *n.* ☐ **forte**
forth [fɔ:θ] *adv.*
and so forth ☐ **e assim por diante**
The plan tells you exactly where to wait, how long, and so forth.
forties ['fɔ:tiz] *n.* (Ver **forty**).
fortieth ['fɔ:tiiθ] *adj., n.* ☐ **quadragésimo**
her fortieth (40th) birthday.
fortnight ['fɔ:tnait] *n. Brit.* ☐ **quinzena**
They went away for a fortnight (= for two weeks). ♦ a fortnight ago.
fortress ['fɔ:tris] *n.* ☐ **fortaleza**
fortunate ['fɔ:tʃənət] *adj.* ☐ **afortunado**
I was fortunate (= lucky) to get that job.
■ antônimo: **unfortunate**
fortunately ['fɔ:tʃənətli] *adv.* (= luckily) ☐ **felizmente**
Fortunately, no one was killed.
■ antônimo: **unfortunately**
fortune ['fɔ:tʃən] *n.*
1 sorte
He had the good fortune to work with a good team.
2 fortuna
He made a fortune selling junk. ♦ The painting is worth a fortune.
3 sorte
She told him his fortune.
fortune teller ['fɔ:tʃən 'telə] *n.* ☐ **vidente, adivinho**
forty ['fɔ:ti] *adj., n.* ☐ **quarenta**
She is forty years old. ♦ The fence is forty metres long.
■ Ver **fortieth**.
in the forties ☐ **nos anos quarenta, na década de 1940**
This dance was popular in the forties.

in your forties □ nos seus quarenta anos, com quarenta e poucos anos
He is in his forties.
forum ['fɔːrəm] *n.* □ **fórum**
a forum on the Internet to discuss our problems.
forward ['fɔːwəd] *v.* (**forwards, forwarding, forwarded**) □ **encaminhar**
Please forward my letters to my new address.
forward(s) ['fɔːwəd(z)] *adv.*
1 para a frente
She moved forward slowly. ◆ It goes forwards and backwards.
2 adiantado
I put my watch two hours forward.
to look forward to □ **aguardar, esperar**
I'm looking forward to meeting you. ◆ I'm looking forward to our meeting.
fossil ['fɒsl] *n.* □ **fóssil**
fought [fɔːt] *v.* (Ver **fight²**).
foul¹ [faul] *adj.*
1 fétido
a foul taste / smell.
2 ruim, horrível
foul weather.
foul² *n.* □ **falta, infração**
That's the seventh foul of the team.
foul³ *v.* (**fouls, fouling, fouled**)
1 poluir
These factories foul the air.
2 cometer falta
That player was fouled again.
found¹ [faund] *v.* (Ver **find**).
found² *v.* (**founds, founding, founded**) □ **fundar**
They founded the organization in 1968.
foundation [faun'deɪʃən] *n.* □ **fundação**
the foundation of a youth movement.
foundations *n. pl.* □ **alicerces**
the foundations of the building.
founder ['faundə] *n.* □ **fundador**
Who was the founder of the company?
fountain ['fauntɪn] *n.* □ **fonte**
a fountain with a statue of an angel.
fountain-pen ['fauntɪnpen] *n.* □ **caneta-tinteiro**
four [fɔː] *adj., n.* □ **quatro**
It's four o'clock. ◆ He is four years old.
on all fours □ **de quatro**
We crawled on all fours.
four-legged ['fɔːlegd] *adj.* □ **de quatro patas**
a four-legged animal.
fourteen [fɔː'tiːn] *adj., n.* □ **catorze**
She is fourteen years old. ◆ It weighs fourteen kilos. ◆ It's fourteen minutes to six.
fourteenth [fɔː'tiːnθ] *adj., adv., n.* □ **décimo quarto, catorze**
the fourteenth floor. ◆ her fourteenth birthday. ◆ June fourteenth (= June 14). *Amer.* ◆ the fourteenth of June (= 14th June). *Brit.*
fourth¹ [fɔːθ] *adj., pron., adv.* □ **quarto, quatro**
the fourth floor. ◆ July fourth (= July 4). *Amer.* ◆ the fourth of July (= 4th July). *Brit.* ◆ She came fourth in the race.
fourth² *n.* □ **quarto**
One fourth of the pupils failed.
fox [fɒks] *n.* □ **raposa**

fraction ['frakʃən] *n.* □ **fração**
1/4 (= a quarter) and 1/2 (= a half) are fractions.
fracture¹ ['fraktʃə] *n.* □ **fratura**
He has a fracture in his left arm.
fracture² *v.* (**fractures, fracturing, fractured**) □ **fraturar**
He fractured his leg in the accident.
fragile ['fradʒaɪl] *adj.* □ **frágil**
These glasses are very fragile.
fragment ['fragmənt] *n.* □ **fragmento**
fragments of a (broken) vase. ◆ tiny fragments of glass.
fragrance ['freɪgrəns] *n.* □ **fragrância**
■ Ver **perfume; scent**.
frail [freɪl] *adj.* □ **fraco, debilitado**
The child is still frail after his illness.
frame¹ [freɪm] *n.* □ **batente, moldura, armação**
a window frame. ◆ He bought round frames (for his glasses).
frame² *v.* (**frames, framing, framed**) □ **emoldurar**
to frame a photograph / painting
framework ['freɪmwəːk] *n.* □ **chassi, estrutura**
the framework of a car.
frank [fraŋk] *adj.* □ **franco**
To be frank, you sing very badly. ◆ Can I be frank with you?
frankly [fraŋklɪ] *adv.* □ **francamente**
He spoke frankly about his problems.
fraud [frɔːd] *n.*
1 fraude
She was guilty of fraud.
2 impostor
He calls himself Dr. Jones but he is not a doctor. He is a fraud.
freckles ['freklz] *n. pl.* □ **sardas**
free¹ [friː] *adj.*
1 livre
After many years in prison, he is a free man again. ◆ This is a free country. ◆ I opened the cage and the bird went free.
2 livre
You are free to do as you wish.
3 grátis, de graça
a free ticket / gift. ◆ You can have it for free.
4 livre
Are you free tomorrow? ◆ I don't have much free time.
5 livre
Is this seat free?
free from / of □ **livre de**
free from worries. ◆ The area is free of pollution.
free of charge □ **grátis, de graça**
The service is free of charge.
set someone free □ **libertar alguém**
They set the bird / prisoner free.
free² *adv.* □ **de graça**
He travels free on buses.
free³ *v.* (**frees, freeing, freed**) □ **libertar**
They freed the hostages. ◆ He freed the animal from the trap.
■ Ver **release²**.
freedom ['friːdəm] *n.* □ **liberdade**
She had freedom of action to make the deal. ◆ freedom of speech (= freedom to say what you think). ◆ freedom fighters.
■ Ver **liberty**.

freely ['fri:li] *adv*. □ livremente
to speak freely.
freeway ['fri:wei] *n. Amer.* (= **expressway**) □ autoestrada, via expressa
■ *Brit.* **motorway**
free will [,fri: 'wil] *n*. □ livre-arbítrio
of your own free will □ por livre e espontânea vontade
He came of his own free will.
freeze [fri:z] *v*. (**freezes, freezing, froze, frozen**)
1 congelar
Water freezes at 0º C. ◆ to freeze vegetables / meat.
■ Ver **frozen²**.
2 congelar
I'm freezing!
3 congelar
It's freezing outside.
4 gelar
He froze when he saw the snake.
freeze to death □ morrer congelado
They froze to death on the mountain.
freezer ['fri:zə] *n*. □ **freezer, congelador**
freight [freit] *n*. □ **carga**
a freight train.
French fries ['frent∫ ,fraiz] *n. Amer.* (= **fries**) □ batata frita
■ *Brit.* **chips**
frequency ['fri:kwənsi] *n*. frequência
The police noted the frequency of his visits.
frequent ['fri:kwənt] *adj*. frequente
Her visits became more frequent.
frequently ['fri:kwəntli] *adv*. (= **often**) frequentemente
It happens frequently.
■ antônimo: **seldom**
fresh [fre∫] *adj*.
1 fresco
fresh bread / milk. ◆ fresh vegetables (not frozen, not canned).
2 fresco, doce, não salgada
fresh air. ◆ fresh water.
3 novo
to make a fresh start. ◆ fresh ideas.
4 novo, limpo
Write it on a fresh piece of paper. ◆ fresh sheets / towels.
freshman ['fre∫mən] *n*. □ **calouro**
A freshman at a university is a first-year student.
friction ['frik∫ən] *n*. □ fricção
Friday ['fraidei] *n*. □ sexta-feira
last / next Friday. ◆ on Friday.
fridge [fridʒ] *n*. (= **refrigerator**) □ **geladeira, refrigerador**
Keep the fish in the fridge.
fried¹ [fraid] *v*. (Ver **fry**).
fried² *adj*. □ **frito**
fried eggs.
friend [frend] *n*. □ **amigo**
Sara is my best friend. ◆ They are good friends.
make friends (with) □ fazer amigos, fazer amizade com
We made friends with him.
friendliness ['frendlines] *n*. □ **amizade, afabilidade**
friendly ['frendli] *adj*. (**friendlier, friendliest**) □ **simpático, amistoso**
They were friendly towards us.
■ antônimo: **unfriendly**
friendship ['frend∫ip] *n*. □ **amizade**

fries¹ [fraiz] *n*. (= **French fries**).
fries² *v*. (Ver **fry**).
fright [frait] *n*. □ susto
The sudden thunder gave me a fright.
frighten ['fraitn] *v*. (**frightens, frightening, frightened**) □ assustar, amedrontar
The noise frightened the baby. ◆ Horror films frighten me.
■ Ver **scare²**; **terrify**.
frightened ['fraitnd] *adj*. □ **com medo, amedrontado**
I'm frightened of him. ◆ Don't be frightened! ◆ a frightened animal / child.
■ Ver **afraid; scared; terrified**.
frightening ['fraitniŋ] *adj*. □ **assustador**
It's frightening to go there alone at night.
frightful ['fraitful] *adj*. □ **horrível, terrível**
a frightful experience.
fringe [frindʒ] *n*.
1 franja
You look nice with a fringe.
2 margem
on the fringe of the forest.
fro [frou] *adv*.
to and fro □ para lá e para cá, de um lado para o outro
He is walking impatiently to and fro.
frock [frok] *n*. □ **vestido**
■ **dress** is the usual word today.
frog [frog] *n*. □ sapo
The sounds that frogs make are called croaking.
from [from] *prep*.
1 de
from Paris to Madrid. ◆ It fell from the sky.
2 de
The office is open from 7 am to / until 4 pm. ◆ from 1972 to 1983.
3 de
I received a letter from her. ◆ I borrowed some money from the bank.
4 de
two kilometers from here
5 de
to protect them from danger. ◆ He saved me from drowning.
6 de
Butter is made from milk.
■ When you can see the material from which is made, use **made of:**
These shoes are made of leather.
7 de
They make from 5 to 8 machines a month.
8 de
The lights change from red to green.
9 de
They are different from the others.
10 de
They are suffering from hunger. ◆ Many are dying from the disease.
from the beginning □ desde o início
Read it from the beginning.
from now on □ de agora em diante
From now on, I'll check it myself.
from time to time □ de tempos em tempos
I visit them from time to time.

front¹ [frʌnt] *adj.*
1 dianteiro
the front seat of the car.
2 primeira
the front page (of a newspaper).
3 da frente
the front door.

front² *n.*
1 frente
the front of the building. ◆ You can sit in the front (of the car).
2 fronte
He was sent to the front.
in front ☐ **em frente**
a house with a garden in front ◆ He walked in front.
in front of
1 em frente (de)
He sits in front of me in class.
2 em frente de, diante de
She looked at the picture in front of her.
3 na frente de
He shouted at me in front of other people.

frontier ['frʌntiə] *n.* ☐ **fronteira**
to cross the frontier. ◆ a frontier town.
■ Ver **border**.

frost [frost] *n.* ☐ **geada**
There was a frost last night. ◆ Frost covered the ground.

frosty ['frosti] *adj.* ☐ **gelado**
a frosty morning / evening.

froth [froθ] *n.* ☐ **espuma**
the froth on a glass of beer.

frown¹ [fraun] *n.* ☐ **carranca, cenho**
He looked at me with a frown.

frown² *v.* (**frowns, frowning, frowned**) ☐ **franzir as sobrancelhas, fechar a cara**
My father frowned when he saw my grades.

froze [frouz] *v.* (Ver **freeze**).

frozen¹ ['frouzn] *v.* (Ver **freeze**).

frozen² *adj.* ☐ **congelado**
frozen vegetables / meat.

fruit [fru:t] *n.* ☐ **fruta**
You should eat more fruit and vegetables. ◆ fruit trees / juice. ◆ Would you like some fruit?
■ The plural is usually **fruit**. The plural **fruits** is used especially when we talk about different types of fruit:
bananas, oranges and other fruits.

frustrated [frʌs'treitid] *adj.* ☐ **frustrado**
to feel frustrated.

frustrating [frʌs'treitiŋ] *adj.* ☐ **frustrante**
It's frustrating when you don't get a chance to do something you want.

frustration [frʌs'treiʃən] *n.* ☐ **frustração**

fry [frai] *v.* (**fries, frying, fried**) ☐ **fritar**
I'm frying fish. ◆ Fry it in oil for five minutes.
■ Ver **fried²**.

frying ['fraiŋ] *n.* ☐ **fritura, ato de fritar**

frying-pan ['fraiŋpan] *n. Amer.* (mesmo que **fry-pan**) ☐ **frigideira**

ft. *abbr.* (= foot; feet) ☐ **pé (unidade de medida)**

fuel¹ ['fjuəl] *n.* ☐ **combustível**
Oil, coal and gas are kinds of fuel.

fuel² *v.* (*Amer.* **fuels, fueling, fueled**; *Brit.* **fuelling, fuelled**) ☐ **abastecer**
The plane fueled (up) and took off again.

fuel tank ['fjuəl ˌtank] *n.* ☐ **tanque de combustível**

fulfil [ful'fil] *v.* (**fulfils, fulfilling, fulfilled**), **fulfill** *Amer.*
1 cumprir
He fulfilled his promise. ◆ to fulfil your duties.
2 realizar
She fulfilled her dream of becoming a pilot.

fulfilment [ful'filmənt] *n. Amer.* (also **fulfillment**) ☐ **realização, satisfação**
the fulfillment of our hopes.

full [ful] *adj.*
1 cheio
The fuel tank is almost full. ◆ The hall was full.
2 completo
Write your full name. ◆ full details.
3 total
at full speed.
full of ☐ **cheio de**
The room was full of people. ◆ Your exam is full of spelling mistakes.
full up
1 lotado, cheio
The bus was full up.
2 satisfeito
I can't eat any more. I'm full (up).
in full ☐ **por extenso, na íntegra**
Write your name in full. ◆ The report was published in full.

full board ['fulbɔ:d] *n.* ☐ **pensão completa**
■ Ver **board¹**.

full stop ['ful 'stop] *n. Brit.* ☐ **ponto final**
■ *Brit.* **period**
■ Ver **dot; point**.

full-time [ful'taim] *adj., adv.* ☐ **de tempo integral, em tempo integral**
a full-time job. ◆ to work full-time.
■ Ver **part-time**.

fully ['fuli] *adv.* ☐ **totalmente**
I fully agree with you. ◆ fully automatic.

fully booked [ˌfuli 'bukt] *adj.* ☐ **lotado**
The hotel is fully booked.

fun [fʌn] *n.* ☐ **diversão, divertimento**
Have fun! (= Enjoy yourself / yourselves!) ◆ We had a lot of fun at the disco.
for fun ☐ **de brincadeira**
They do it for fun.
to make fun of ☐ **tirar sarro de, zombar**
It isn't nice to make fun of him / of his clothes.

function¹ ['fʌŋkʃən] *n.* ☐ **função**
the functions of a computer. ◆ What are the functions of the manager here?

function² *v.* (**functions, functioning, functioned**) (= operate) ☐ **funcionar**
My computer is not functioning properly.

fund [fʌnd] *n.* ☐ **fundo, verba**
a special fund for helping the refugees.

funds *n. pl.* ☐ **fundos, verbas**
to raise funds for the project.

fundamental [ˌfʌndə'mentl] *adj.*
1 fundamental
There's a fundamental difference between them.

funeral / fuzzy

2 fundamental
Water is fundamental for life.
funeral ['fju:nərəl] *n*. ☐ **funeral**
Many people attended his funeral.
funnel ['fʌnl] *n*.
1 funil
Use a funnel to pour the oil into the bottle.
2 chaminé
Black smoke was coming out of the ship's funnel.
funny ['fʌni] *adj*. (**funnier, funniest**)
1 engraçado
a funny joke. ✦ That's not funny!
2 estranho, esquisito
a funny smell / noise. ✦ There's something funny going on here.
■ Ver **odd; strange**.
fur [fɜ:] *n*. ☐ **pelo**
Foxes and bears have thick fur.
furious ['fjuəriəs] *adj*. ☐ **furioso**
She was furious with us.
furiously ['fjuəriəsli] *adv*. ☐ **furiosamente**
He shouted furiously at me.
furlough ['fɜ:lou] *n*. *Amer*. ☐ **licença**
The soldiers are now on furlough.
■ *Brit*. **leave**¹
furnace ['fɜ:nis] *n*. ☐ **fornalha**
You can heat metals to very high temperatures in a furnace.
furnish ['fɜ:niʃ] *v*. (**furnishes, furnishing, furnished**)
☐ **mobiliar**
to furnish the office.
furnished ['fɜ:niʃt] *adj*. ☐ **mobiliado**
a furnished flat / apartment.
furniture ['fɜ:nitʃə] *n*. ☐ **mobília, mobiliário**
The furniture was new. ✦ a piece of furniture (= a chair, a bed, etc.).
furry ['fɜ:ri] *adj*. (**furrier, furriest**) ☐ **peludo**
a furry animal / toy.
further ['fɜ:ðə] *adj*., *adv*.
1 adicional
For further details please call... ✦ I have nothing further to say.

2 (= farther) **mais além**
I can't go any further.
until further notice ☐ **até segunda ordem**
You will wait here until further notice.
furthermore ['fɜ:ðə'mɔ:] *adv*. (= in addition; moreover) **além disso**
Vegetables are good for you. Furthermore, they are low in calories.
furthest ['fɜ:ðist] (= farthest) *adj*., *adv*. ☐ **o mais distante, mais longe**
the furthest end of the street ✦ Who swam the furthest?
fury ['fjuəri] *n*. (= rage) ☐ **fúria**
fuse [fju:z] *n*. ☐ **fusível**
I'll check the fuses to see why there is no light.
fuss¹ [fʌs] *n*. ☐ **estardalhaço**
Don't make such a fuss. I'm only five minutes late.
get into a fuss ☐ **fazer um escândalo**
Don't get into a fuss. There is plenty of time.
fuss² *v*. (**fusses, fussing, fussed**) ☐ **alvoroçar-se**
Don't fuss! There's still plenty of time.
fuss over ☐ **paparicar, mimar**
They are always fussing over their children.
fussy ['fʌsi] *adj*.
1 ☐ **meticuloso**
She is fussy about her food.
2 ☐ **exigente**
fussy parents.
future¹ ['fju:tʃə] *n*. ☐ **futuro**
Who knows what will happen in the future? ✦ The future of this project is uncertain. ✦ the computer / car of the future.
in future ☐ **no futuro**
Try to be more careful in future.
future² *adj*. ☐ **futuro**
my future wife. ✦ the future tense. ✦ future events / plans.
fuzzy ['fʌzi] *adj*.
1 (= unclear) ☐ **indistinto, não nítido**
a fuzzy photo. ✦ I can't hear you well. – your voice sounds fuzzy.
2 (= confused) ☐ **confuso**
fuzzy thinking / ideas.

Gg

g *abbr.* (= gram[s]) □ **g**
It weighs 100g.
gadget ['gadʒit] *n.* □ **engenhoca**
an electrical gadget for opening tins.
gag [gag] *v.* (**gags, gagging, gagged**) □ **amordaçar**
The robbers tied him up and gagged him.
gain [gein] *v.* (**gains, gaining, gained**)
 1 ganhar
 to gain experience.
 2 ganhar, conseguir
 They gained an advantage over us. ◆ How can we gain their support?
 3 ganhar
 They did it just to gain time.
 4 engordar
 The baby gained 600 grams.
gain on □ **aproximar-se, chegar perto**
Run faster – they are gaining on us.
galaxy ['galəksi] *n.* (*pl.* **galaxies**) □ **galáxia**
gale [geil] *n.* □ **vendaval**
The ship almost sank in the gale.
 ■ Ver **storm**.
gallery ['galəri] *n.* (*pl.* **galleries**) □ **galeria**
an art gallery.
gallon ['galən] *n.* □ **galão**
gallop¹ ['galəp] *n.* □ **galope**
to go for a gallop (on a horse).
gallop² *v.* (**gallops, galloping, galloped**) □ **galopar**
The horses galloped through the field.
gallows [galouz] *n.* □ **forca**
He was sent to the gallows.
gamble¹ [gambl] *n.* □ **risco**
It's a gamble to put all our money in that business.
gamble² *v.* (**gambles, gambling, gambled**) □ **jogar**
He gambles at cards / on horses. ◆ I don't gamble.
 ■ Ver **bet**.
gambler [gamblə] *n.* □ **jogador**
gambling ['gamblin] *n.* □ **jogo, jogatina**
Gambling is illegal there.
game [geim] *n.*
 1 partida, jogo
 We played a game of tennis / chess. ◆ video games.
 ■ Ver **match**.
 2 carne de caça
 big game (e.g. deer, tigers).
games [geimz] *n. pl.* □ **jogos**
the Olympic Games.
gang¹ [gaŋ] *n.*
 1 gangue
 a gang of thieves. ◆ street gangs.
 2 turma, galera
 I'm going on a trip with the gang.
gang² *v.* (**gangs, ganging, ganged**)
gang together / up □ **conspirar, atacar em bando**
They ganged up against him.
gangster ['gaŋstə] *n.* □ **gângster, bandido**
gangway ['gaŋwei] *n.* □ **prancha de embarque e desembarque**
The passengers climbed down the gangway one by one.
gaol [dʒeil] *n. Brit.* (= **jail**¹).
gap [gap] *n.*
 1 fenda
 a gap in the fence.
 2 brecha
 a gap between two teeth.
 3 lacuna
 The gap between the rich and the poor is widening in some countries.
 ■ Ver **generation gap**.
 4 intervalo
 After a gap of seven years, she wrote another book.
gape [geip] *v.* (**gapes, gaping, gaped**) □ **embasbacar-se**
They stood there and gaped at the treasure.
gaping ['geipiŋ] *adj.* □ **muito aberto e profundo**
a gaping wound / hole.
garage ['gara:dʒ] *n.*
 1 garagem
 He opened the garage door by remote control.
 2 *Brit.* **posto de combustível**
 I bought oil for my car at the garage.
 ■ The usual word is **petrol station**.
 ■ *Amer.* **gas station**
 3 oficina
 a garage mechanic.
garbage ['ga:bidʒ] *n. Amer.* (= **trash**) □ **lixo**
Throw it in the garbage.
 ■ *Brit.* **rubbish**
garbage can ['ga:bidʒ 'kan] *n. Amer.* (= **trash can**) □ **lata de lixo**
 ■ *Brit.* **dustbin**
garden ['ga:dn] *n.* □ **jardim**
a rose garden (= a garden of roses). ◆ He is working in the garden.
gardens *n. pl.* □ **jardins**
gardener ['ga:dnə] *n.* □ **jardineiro**
gardening ['ga:dniŋ] *n.* □ **jardinagem**
gardening tools (e.g. a fork, a rake, a hoe).
garlic ['ga:lik] *n.* □ **alho**
gas [gas] *n.*
 1 gás
 Oxygen is a gas. ◆ He turned on / off the gas.
 2 (= **gasoline**) *Amer.* **gasolina**
 We need some gas. The fuel tank is almost empty.
 ■ *Brit.* **petrol**
gas station *n.* □ **posto de combustível**
 ■ *Brit.* **petrol station**
gasoline ['gasəli:n] *n. Amer.* (= **gas**) □ **gasolina**
 ■ *Brit.* **petrol**
gasp¹ [ga:sp] *n.* □ **arfada**
gasp² *v.* (**gasps, gasping, gasped**)
 1 ofegar
 He was gasping for air when he got to the sixth floor.
 2 falar ofegantemente
 She gasped with astonishment.
gate [geit] *n.* □ **portão**
He left the gate open and the horses got away. ◆ the gates of the stadium.
gateway ['geitwei] *n.* □ **portão, passagem**
gather ['gaðə] *v.* (**gathers, gathering, gathered**)
 1 reunir-se
 They gathered round the pop star.

2 juntar, reunir
He gathered (up) his toys and put them in the box. ◆ to gather information.
3 deduzir
I gather that you know already what happened.
gathering ['gaðəriŋ] *n.* □ **reunião**
a gathering of the workers. ◆ a family gathering.
gauge¹ [geidʒ] *n.* □ **medidor**
the fuel gauge (in a car).
gauge² *v.* (**gauges, gauging, gauged**) □ **medir**
This instrument gauges the pressure.
gave [geiv] *v.* (Ver **give**).
gay [gei] *adj.*
1 (= cheerful) **alegre**
gay music.
2 (= homosexual) **gay**
He is gay.
gaze¹ [geiz] *v.* (**gazes, gazing, gazed**) □ **olhar fixamente**
He gazed curiously at the picture.
■ Ver **stare**.
gaze² *n.* □ **olhar fixo**
GB, G.B. ['dʒi:'bi:] *abbr.* (= Great Britain) □ **Grã-Bretanha**
gear [giə] *n.*
1 equipamento
camping / diving gear.
■ Ver **equipment**.
2 marcha
to change gears.
geese [gi:s] *n.* (*plural of* **goose**) □ **gansos**
gem [dʒem] *n.* □ **gema**
A gem is a precious stone.
gender ['dʒendə] *n.*
1 (grammar) **gênero**
masculine or feminine gender in English pronouns.
2 (= sex) **gênero**
discrimination based on class, gender, race or religion.
■ Compare:
In grammar, **masculine** or **feminine gender**; for differences between the sexes, **male** or **female gender**.
general¹ ['dʒenərəl] *n.* □ **general**
He is a general in the American army.
general² *adj.*
1 vago, genérico
Your description is too general.
2 geral, comum
a matter of general interest. ◆ Telephones are in general use today.
in general □ **em geral**
In general, it's not very cold here in winter.
general election ['dʒenərəl i'lekʃən] *n.* □ **eleição**
In my country, you can vote in the general election when you are 18.
general knowledge ['dʒenərəl 'nolidʒ] *n.* □ **conhecimentos gerais**
The exam also tests your general knowledge.
generalise ['dʒenərəlaiz] *v. Brit.* (= **generalize**).
generalize ['dʒenərəlaiz] *v.* (**generalizes, generalizing, generalized**) □ **generalizar**
Don't generalize – they're not all bad.
generally ['dʒenərəli] *adv.* □ **geralmente**
We generally have breakfast at 8:30.

generally speaking □ **em termos gerais**
Generally speaking, it's a good book.
generate ['dʒenəreit] *v.* (**generates, generating, generated**) □ **gerar**
to generate heat / electricity.
generation [,dʒenə'reiʃən] *n.* □ **geração**
the younger generation. ◆ All three generations – children, parents and grandparents – were there. ◆ the next generation of computers.
generation gap [,dʒenə'reiʃən 'gap] *n.* □ **conflito de gerações**
We have a generation gap when the younger and the older generations don't understand each other.
generator ['dʒenəreitə] *n.* □ **gerador**
generosity [,dʒenə'rositi] *n.* □ **generosidade**
generous ['dʒenərəs] *adj.*
1 generoso
It was generous of you to help them. ◆ She is generous with her money.
2 generoso
He gives generous donations to the hospital.
generously ['dʒenərəsli] *adv.* □ **generosamente**
genius ['dʒi:njəs] *n.* □ **gênio**
Einstein was a genius.
gentle ['dʒentl] *adj.*
1 leve, gentil, delicado
a gentle touch / voice / breeze.
2 cuidadoso
Be gentle (= careful) with the vase.
gentleman ['dʒentlmən] *n.* (*pl.* **gentlemen**)
1 cavalheiro
He is a real gentleman.
2 cavalheiro, senhor
The gentleman with the blue suit asked me to give you this.
Ladies and gentlemen! □ **Senhoras e senhores!**
gently ['dʒentli] *adv.* □ **delicadamente**
Put it gently on the table. ◆ 'Don't worry', he said gently.
Gents ['dʒents] *n. Brit.* □ **banheiro masculino**
Where is the Gents, please?
■ *Amer.* **men's room**
genuine ['dʒenjuin] *adj.*
1 genuíno
genuine diamonds / leather. ◆ a genuine painting by Van Gogh.
2 genuíno
His sorrow is genuine.
genuinely ['dʒenjuinli] *adv.* □ **genuinamente**
She was genuinely sorry.
geographic(al) [dʒiə'grafik(əl)] *adj.* □ **geográfico**
geography [dʒi'ogrəfi] *n.* □ **geografia**
geometric(al) [dʒiə'metrik(əl)] *adj.* □ **geométrico**
geometric figures (e.g. triangles, squares).
geometry [dʒi'omətri] *n.* □ **geometria**
germ [dʒə:m] *n.* □ **germe**
Germs can cause diseases.
gesture ['dʒestʃə] *n.*
1 gesto
He made a gesture of impatience.
2 gesto
I invited him as a friendly gesture.
get [get] *v.* (**gets, getting, got;** *Amer.* **gotten**)
1 conseguir, arrumar
He got a good job. ◆ Where did you get this book?

■ Ver **buy; obtain**.
2 tirar; ganhar
I got a good mark in the exam. ◆ She got nice presents from her friends.
■ Ver **receive**.
3 pegar
Please get me my umbrella. ◆ Can you get Dan from school? ◆ Can I get you anything (to eat)?
■ Ver **bring; fetch**.
4 chegar
The train got to Berlin at 10:30. ◆ He got home early.
■ Ver **arrive; reach²**.
5 entender
He didn't get the joke.
■ Ver **understand; catch**.
6 ficar
She got angry. ◆ He is getting fat. ◆ The soup is getting cold.
■ Ver **become; grow**.
7 ser (quando seguido de verbo no particípio passado não é traduzido)
He got caught (= was caught) by the police. ◆ Get dressed! ◆ They got married (= were married).
have got (= have) ▫ **ter**
I've got a good chance to win. ◆ She has got a lot of friends.
have got to (= have to) ▫ **ter de**
You've got to tell her. ◆ She's got to stay.
get along (with) (= get on)
1 dar-se com
They get along well with each other.
2 dar-se
He is getting along well at work.
get around ▫ **espalhar-se**
The news got around very quickly.
get away ▫ **sair, fugir**
Try to get away early from the party. ◆ The prisoner got away (= escaped).
get away with ▫ **dar-se bem, safar-se**
He won't get away with murder.
get back (= return) ▫ **voltar, retornar**
What time did he get back? ◆ She got back yesterday.
get by (= manage) ▫ **virar-se, sobreviver**
He gets by on a small pension.
get down ▫ **descer**
Get down from that tree!
get down to ▫ **começar a**
Let's get down to business.
get in (= enter) ▫ **entrar**
The door was locked. How did he get in?
get in / into ▫ **entrar**
He got into the car. ◆ Something got into my eye.
get off
1 descer
I'm getting off at the next stop. ◆ He got off the bus / bike.
2 (= leave) **sair**
I will get off work early to meet you.
get on
1 subir, entrar
The passengers got on the train.
2 (= get along) **progredir**
She is getting on well at school.
get on with
1 (= get along) **dar-se (com)**
They get on well with each other.
2 continuar
Stop talking and get on with your work.
get out (of)
1 sair
Get out! ◆ The door was locked. I couldn't get out. ◆ When did he get out of hospital?
2 sair, descer
to get out of a car / boat.
get... out (of) ▫ **tirar**
The key was stuck and I couldn't get it out. ◆ They got the child out of the burning house.
get over ▫ **superar**
It was a great disappointment for him, but he'll get over it.
get through
1 fazer contato
I rang several times, but I couldn't get through.
2 chegar ao fim, terminar
I got through the book in four hours.
3 passar por, atravessar
They helped us get through that difficult time.
4 (= pass) **passar**
She got through her exam easily.
get together ▫ **reunir-se**
We should get together to discuss the matter.
get up ▫ **levantar-se**
I usually get up at 7 o'clock. ◆ She got up from the armchair.
get up to
1 (= reach) ▫ **chegar até, alcançar**
I got up to page 122. ◆ The water got up to his neck.
2 aprontar, fazer
What's she getting up to now?
get used to ▫ **acostumar-se**
I got used to the heat after a few days. ◆ You'll soon get used to living in this village.
■ Ver **accustomed**.
ghastly ['gɑːstli] *adj.* ▫ **feio, medonho**
a ghastly accident / crime.
ghost [goust] *n.* (= phantom) ▫ **fantasma**
They say that ghosts haunt this house.
ghostly ['goustli] *adj.* ▫ **fantasmagórico**
giant ['dʒaɪənt] *n., adj.* ▫ **gigante**
giant creatures.
giddy ['gɪdi] *adj.* (= dizzy) ▫ **tonto, com vertigem**
I feel giddy.
gift [gɪft] *n.*
1 (= present) **presente**
a birthday / wedding gift. ◆ a gift shop.
2 (= talent) **talento, dom**
He has a gift for languages.
gifted ['gɪftɪd] *adj.* (= talented) ▫ **talentoso**
a gifted athlete / artist. ◆ gifted children.
gigantic [dʒaɪ'gæntɪk] *adj.* ▫ **gigantesco**
a gigantic statue.
giggle¹ ['gɪgl] *n.* ▫ **risadinha**
giggle² *v.* (**giggles, giggling, giggled**) ▫ **dar risadinhas**
They stopped giggling when the teacher looked at them.
ginger¹ ['dʒɪndʒə] *n.* ▫ **gengibre**
a ginger biscuit.

ginger² *adj.* ▫ **ruivo**
a ginger cat. ♦ ginger hair.
gipsy ['dʒipsi] *n.* (*pl.* **gipsies**) (= **gypsy**).
giraffe [dʒi'ra:f] *n.* ▫ **girafa**
girl [gə:l] *n.*
1 garota, menina
When I was a little girl, I played with dolls.
2 garota, menina
There are 12 girls and 10 boys in our class.
3 (= daughter) **filha, menina**
I have two boys and a girl.
girlfriend ['gə:lfrend] *n.* ▫ **namorada**
His girlfriend is 19 years old.
girlhood ['gə:lhud] *n.* ▫ **mocidade**
She spent her girlhood with her grandparents.
Girl Guide ['gə:l 'gaid] *n.* ▫ **escoteira**
■ *Amer.* **Girl scout**
give [giv] *v.* (**gives, giving, gave, given**)
1 dar
Who gave it to you? ♦ Give me that letter! ♦ What did you give her for her birthday?
2 dar
Who gave you permission? ♦ Let me give you a piece of advice.
3 dar
Can you give me an example?
4 dar
Please give him my regards.
5 pensar com carinho
I will give a lot of thought to your suggestion.
6 pagar
I gave (= paid) 130 dollars for this watch.
7 dar
to give a party.
8 dar, causar
The noise is giving me a headache.
9 dar
He gave a shout / laugh / sigh.
give away
1 doar
They gave their old furniture away.
2 contar, revelar
Don't give away the secret.
give back ▫ **devolver**
Give it back (to me)! ♦ Give me back the cassette I lent you.
■ Ver **return²**.
give in (to) ▫ **ceder (a)**
At first, my parents did not allow me to go, but finally they gave in. ♦ The soldiers did not give in.
■ Ver **surrender**.
give off ▫ **exalar**
The fish gave off a terrible smell.
give out ▫ **distribuir**
The teacher gave out the exam papers.
■ Ver **distribute**.
give up ▫ **desistir**
I give up – what's the answer? ♦ She won't give up. She'll try again and again.
give (something) up
1 parar de fazer algo
He is trying to give up smoking.

2 largar
She had to give up a good job when she moved to another city.
give oneself up ▫ **entregar-se**
He gave himself up (to the police).
■ Ver **surrender**.
given ['givn] *v.* (Ver **give**).
glad [glad] *adj.* (= happy) ▫ **feliz**
I'm glad to see you. ♦ I was glad to receive your letter.
gladly ['gladli] *adv.* ▫ **com muito prazer**
He gladly agreed to lend us the money.
gladness ['gladnis] *n.* (= happiness) ▫ **felicidade**
glance¹ [gla:ns] *n.* ▫ **olhar**
They exchanged glances.
glance² *v.* (**glances, glancing, glanced**) ▫ **olhar de relance**
He glanced at his watch.
glare¹ [gleə] *n.*
1 luminosidade
the glare of the (car's) headlights.
2 olhar furioso
She gave me an angry glare.
glare² *v.* (**glares, glaring, glared**)
1 brilhar
The sun is glaring (in my eyes).
2 olhar furiosamente
They glared (angrily) at each other.
glaring ['gleəriŋ] *adj.* ▫ **forte, brilhante, notório**
glaring lights. ♦ glaring colors / colours. ♦ a glaring mistake.
glass [gla:s] *n.*
1 vidro
broken glass. ♦ Mirrors are made of glass. ♦ a glass door.
2 copo, taça
He drank two glasses of milk. ♦ A wineglass is a special glass for wine.
glasses ['glasiz] *n. pl.* ▫ **óculos**
He wears glasses. ♦ She put on her glasses and started to read. ♦ a pair of glasses.
■ Ver **sunglasses**.
gleam¹ [gli:m] *n.*
1 brilho
a gleam of light / fire.
2 centelha
a gleam of hope.
gleam² *v.* (**gleams, gleaming, gleamed**) ▫ **brilhar, cintilar**
His eyes gleamed with pleasure.
glide [glaid] *v.* (**glides, gliding, glided**) ▫ **deslizar**
The boat glided across the water. ♦ The eagle glided over the valley.
glider ['glaidə] *n.* ▫ **planador**
■ Ver **hang-glider**.
gliding ['glaidiŋ] *n.* ▫ **planador, asa-delta**
glimmer¹ ['glimə] *n.*
1 luz trêmula
the glimmer of a candle.
2 fio
a glimmer of hope.
glimmer² *v.* (**glimmers, glimmering, glimmered**) ▫ **cintilar**
The lights of the village glimmered in the distance.
glimpse¹ [glimps] *n.* ▫ **relance**
catch a glimpse of ▫ **ver de relance**
I only caught a glimpse of the robber.

glimpse² *v.* (**glimpses, glimpsing, glimpsed**) ▫ **ver de relance**
I glimpsed someone behind the bushes.

glisten ['glisn] *v.* (**glisten, glistening, glistened**) ▫ **faiscar, cintilar**
Their eyes glistened with tears.

glitter¹ ['glitə] *n.* ▫ **esplendor, brilho**
the glitter of the gold coins.

glitter² *v.* (**glitters, glittering, glittered**) **resplandecer**
The diamond glittered in the light.

gloat [glout] *v.* (**gloats, gloating, gloated**) ▫ **vangloriar-se**
He is gloating over the defeat of our team.

global ['gloubəl] *adj.* ▫ **global**
a global problem. • The world is one global village today. • global warming (= the Earth's temperature is rising).

globe [gloub] *n.*
1 globo
Show me where Egypt is on the globe.
2 (= the Earth) **mundo**
people from all over the globe (= world).

gloomily ['glu:mili] *adv.* ▫ **melancolicamente, com tristeza**
He looked gloomily at his sick dog.

gloomy ['glu:mi] *adj.* (**gloomier, gloomiest**)
1 sombrio, escuro
gloomy sky / weather.
2 sombrio, triste
a gloomy face.

glorious ['glo:riəs] *adj.*
1 glorioso
a glorious victory.

glory ['glo:ri] *n.*
1 glória
the glory of the war heroes.
2 glória
They saw the palace in all its glory.

glossy ['glosi] *adj.* ▫ **brilhoso**
glossy hair.

glove [glʌv] *n.* ▫ **luva**
leather / rubber gloves. • He put on his gloves and went out. • I never wear gloves.

glow¹ [glou] *n.* ▫ **incandescência, fulgor**
the glow of burning coals. • the glow of the sunset.

glow² *v.* (**glows, glowing, glowed**) ▫ **reluzir, fulgir**
A cigarette glowed in the dark.

glue¹ [glu:] *n.* ▫ **cola**
to mend a broken chair with glue
■ Ver **gum**.

glue² *v.* (**glues, gluing, glued**) ▫ **colar**
He glued the pieces together.
■ Ver **stick²**.

gm *abbr.* (= **gram(s)**) ▫ **g**
It weighs 50 gm.

gnaw [no:] *v.* (**gnaws, gnawing, gnawed**) ▫ **roer**
The dog was gnawing at a bone. • The mice gnawed through the sack.

go¹ [go:] *n.* ▫ **vez**
It's my go. (= It's my turn.)
at one go ▫ **de uma vez só**
He swallowed them at one go.
have a go (at) ▫ **tentar**
If you can't fix it, let me have a go (at it).

go² *v.* (**goes, going, went, gone**)
1 ir
Where are you going? • I'm going home. • She goes to the beach once a week.
2 ir de
to go by bus / ship / plane. • I went to Paris by train.
3 ir
Does this train go to Amsterdam? • This path goes to the top of the mountain.
4 ficar
He went blind when he was 12. • to go mad.
5 ir embora, passar
My headache will go after a short rest.
6 ir
The party went well. • Everything is going according to plan.
be going to (Ver **going**).
go after (= chase) ▫ **ir atrás, perseguir**
The police went after the robbers.
go ahead ▫ **ir em frente, prosseguir**
They are going ahead with their plans. • Go ahead, take it! *Amer.*
go around
1 girar
The earth goes around the sun.
2 atender à demanda
There isn't enough food to go around.
■ *Brit.* **go round**
go away
1 ir embora, sair, ficar fora, viajar
Don't go away! • I'm going away for a few days.
2 ir embora, sair
Go away! I'm trying to work.
3 ir embora, sumir
The problem won't go away just by talking.
go back
1 (= return) **voltar, retornar**
When are you going back to school?
2 remontar
These customs go back to the 11th century.
go by
1 (= pass) **passar-se, passar**
Six months went by • As time went by, he became more and more afraid.
2 ir de
I go to school by bus.
3 seguir, obedecer
We have to go by the rules.
go down
1 baixar
The price of vegetables is going down.
2 descer
She went down the stairs.
■ Ver **descend**.
go for a walk ▫ **sair para caminhar**
Let's go for a walk.
go into
1 (= enter) **entrar**
He went into the kitchen.
2 entrar
I don't want to go into details.

go off
1 (= explode) **explodir, disparar**
The bomb went off. ✦ The gun went off.
2 disparar, tocar
The alarm went off at exactly 7 o'clock.
3 (= go bad) *Brit.* **estragar**
The fish / milk has gone off.
go on
1 (= happen) **acontecer**
Find out what's going on there.
2 (= continue) **continuar**
Go on, I'm listening. ✦ He went on eating.
3 (= go by) **passar-se**
As the days went on, she became more and more impatient.
4 sair de
to go on holiday / business. ✦ They went on a trip.
5 acender
Suddenly all the lights went on.
go out
1 sair
He went out a few minutes ago.
2 sair
We don't go out much.
3 apagar-se
The fire is going out. ✦ Suddenly the lights went out.
go out with □ **sair com**
He is going out with Sharon.
go over
1 examinar
He went over his answers again.
2 ir para
Go over to the other side, please.
go round
1 girar sem parar
The wheel was going round and round.
2 atender à demanda
There aren't enough chairs to go round.
▪ Ver **go around**.
3 visitar, passar em
I'm going round to my aunt.
go through
1 passar por
to go through town.
2 (= go over) **examinar**
My lawyer will go through the contract.
3 atravessar, passar por
She went through a difficult time.
4 revistar
The policeman went through my things.
go up
1 subir
House prices are going up.
2 subir
She went up the stairs. ✦ to go up in an elevator.
3 arder, queimar
The house went up in flames.
go without □ **ficar sem**
You'll have to go without a car today. ✦ They went without food (= They didn't eat anything) for two days.
go-ahead ['gouəhed] *n.* □ **sinal verde**
They got the go-ahead for the project.
goal [goul] *n.*

1 gol
He scored two goals. ✦ Our team won by two goals to one. (= We beat them 2-1.)
2 objetivo
What's your goal in life?
▪ Ver **aim; purpose**.
goalkeeper ['goulki:pə] *n.* □ **goleiro**
goat [gout] *n.* □ **cabra**
goat's milk
god [god] *n.* □ **deus**
Apollo was the Greek god of war.
▪ Ver **goddess**.
God [god] *n.* □ **Deus**
Thank God, he is alive.
Oh (my) God! □ **Meu Deus!**
Good God! □ **Santo Deus!**
▪ Ver **goodness; gosh**.
goddess ['godis] *n.* □ **deusa**
the Greek goddess of love.
godfather ['godf:ðə] *n.* □ **padrinho**
godmother ['godmʌðə] *n.* □ **madrinha**
goggles ['goglz] *n. pl.* □ **óculos de proteção**
Goggles protect your eyes from dust, wind, water, etc.
going ['gouiŋ]
be going to □ **ir, tornar-se**
I'm going to (= I intend to) do it myself. ✦ She's going to be (= She'll be) 18 next month. ✦ It's going to rain.
gold [gould] *n., adj.* □ **ouro, de ouro**
This ring is made of gold. ✦ a gold medal. ✦ a gold chain.
golden ['gouldən] *adj.*
1 de ouro, dourado
a golden crown / necklace.
2 dourado
golden hair / skin.
golden wedding ['gouldən 'wediŋ] *n.* □ **bodas de ouro**
goldfish ['gouldfiʃ] *n.* □ **peixinho dourado**
goldmine ['gouldmain] *n.* □ **mina de ouro**
goldsmith ['gouldsmiθ] *n.* □ **ourives**
golf [golf] *n.* □ **golfe**
I play golf once a week.
golf course ['golf 'ko:s] *n.* □ **campo de golfe**
gone [gon] *v.* (Ver **go**²).
good¹ [gud] *adj.* (**better, best**)
1 bom
This pen is good, but that one is better. ✦ He is a good cook. ✦ All her books are good, but this one is the best. ✦ This exercise isn't much good. ✦ She is good at mathematics.
2 bom
This is good news.
3 bom
You have a good chance of winning.
4 bom
Fruit juice is good for you.
5 bom, bem
She has a good figure. ✦ You look good in that suit.
6 bondade
It was good of you to help him.
7 bom
Good morning / evening! ✦ Good night!
8 válido
The ticket is good for another week.
9 ótimo
Are you ready? Good. Let's go.

a good deal of (= a great deal of; a lot of) ▫ **muito**
He spent a good deal of money.
all in good time ▫ **tudo a seu tempo, na hora certa**
I'll take care of it, all in good time.
Good for you! ▫ **Que bom!**
I passed the test. – Good for you!
have a good time ▫ **divirta-se**
We had a good time at the party.
■ Ver **enjoy**.
in good time ▫ **a tempo, rapidamente**
We have to be ready in good time.
good² *n.*
1 bem
He knows the difference between good and evil.
2 bem
What good is it talking about it?
do you good ▫ **vai fazer-lhe bem**
Take a few days off. It will do you good.
for good ▫ **para sempre**
They came here for good.
for your own good ▫ **para o seu próprio bem**
She did it for your own good.
it's no good (= it's no use) ▫ **não adianta**
It's no good shouting; they won't hear you.
not be any good, be no good ▫ **não servir para nada**
This camera isn't any good.
good afternoon [ˌgud ɑːftˈnuːn] ▫ **boa tarde**
Good afternoon, everybody!
goodbye [gudˈbaɪ] ▫ **tchau, até logo, adeus**
Goodbye! See you tomorrow. ◆ He kissed them goodbye.
■ Ver **farewell**.
good-looking [gudˈlukɪŋ] *adj.* ▫ **bonito, de boa aparência**
a good-looking man / woman.
■ **handsome** usually describes men.
■ **beautiful** and **pretty** usually describe women and objects.
good-natured [ˌgudˈneɪtʃəd] *adj.* ▫ **de gênio bom**
a good-natured child.
goodness [ˈgudnɪs] *n.* ▫ **bondade, virtude**
for goodness' sake ▫ **por Deus!**
For goodness' sake, keep quiet!
goodness (me) ▫ **Santo Deus!, Minha nossa!**
Goodness! What a beautiful palace!
thank goodness ▫ **graças a Deus**
Thank goodness, he is alive!
goods [gudz] *n. pl.* ▫ **aparelhos, produtos, bens**
electrical goods.
good-tempered [gudˈtempəd] *adj.* ▫ **de bom gênio**
He is very good-tempered.
goose [guːs] *n.* (*pl.* **geese**) ▫ **ganso**
gooseberry [ˈguzberi] *n.* (*pl.* **gooseberries**) ▫ **groselha**
She made jam from gooseberries.
gorgeous [ˈgɔːdʒəs] *adj.* ▫ **lindo, ótimo**
a gorgeous dress / party. ◆ The weather was gorgeous.
gorilla [gəˈrɪlə] *n.* ▫ **gorila**
gosh [gɒʃ] ▫ **Nossa!**
Gosh! What a big melon!
gossip¹ [ˈgɒsɪp] *n.*
1 fofoca
Don't believe it. It's just gossip.
2 fofoqueiro
You are such a gossip!

gossip² *v.* (**gossips, gossiping, gossiped**) ▫ **fofocar**
They are gossiping about politicians.
got [gɒt] *v.* (Ver **get**).
have got *v.* (Ver **get**).
gotten [ˈgɒtn] *v.* (Ver **get**).
govern [ˈgʌvən] *v.* (**governs, governing, governed**) ▫ **governar**
In Britain, the Prime Minister, the Cabinet and Parliament govern the country.
governess [ˈgʌvənɪs] *n.* ▫ **governadora**
government [ˈgʌvən,mənt] *n.* ▫ **governo**
The government will discuss the problem of unemployment.
governor [ˈgʌvənə] *n.*
1 governador
the Governor of the State of California.
2 diretor
the Governor of the State Bank.
3 diretor
the prison governor.
gown [gaun] *n.*
1 vestido de noiva
a wedding gown (= a wedding dress).
■ Ver **dressing gown**; **nightgown**.
2 toga, beca
Lawyers wear black gowns.
grab [græb] *v.* (**grabs, grabbing, grabbed**) ▫ **arrancar**
He grabbed the letter from my hand.
■ Ver **snatch**.
grace [greɪs] *n.*
1 graça
They dance with grace.
2 dar graças
to say grace (before or after a meal).
graceful [ˈgreɪsful] *adj.* ▫ **gracioso**
a graceful dancer.
gracefully [ˈgreɪsfuli] *adv.* ▫ **graciosamente**
to dance gracefully.
graciously [ˈgreɪʃəsli] *adv.* ▫ **delicadamente**
She asked us graciously to sit down.
grade¹ [greɪd] *n.*
1 *Amer.* **nota**
They got good grades on their exams.
■ *Brit.* **mark**
2 *Amer.* **série**
He is in the eighth grade.
■ In British English **form** is used for ages 11-18, and **year** is used for all ages.
3 tipo, qualidade
There are several grades of petrol. ◆ low-grade apples.
grade² *v.* (**grades, grading, graded**)
1 classificar
They grade the eggs according to size.
2 *Amer.* **dar nota, corrigir**
I have to grade all these exam papers.
■ *Brit.* **mark**²
grade crossing [ˌgreɪd ˈkrɒsɪŋ] *n. Amer.* ▫ **passagem de nível**
■ *Brit.* **level crossing**
graded [ˈgreɪdɪd] *adj.* ▫ **graduado**
graded tests / courses.

gradual ['gradjuəl] *adj.* ▫ **gradual, gradativo**
a gradual increase in the number of students.
gradually ['gradjuəli] *adv.* ▫ **gradualmente, gradativamente**
The patient's condition is gradually improving.
graduate¹ ['gradjuət] *n.*
1 formado
a graduate of Oxford / in law.
2 formado
a high-school graduate.
graduate² ['gradjueit] *v.* (**graduates, graduating, graduated**)
1 formar-se
She graduated in Economics. ♦ He graduated from Cambridge University in 2001.
2 *Amer.* **formar-se**
I graduated from high school in 1999.
graduation [,gradju'eiʃən] *n.* ▫ **formatura**
After graduation, I will go abroad for 3 months.
grain [grein] *n.*
1 grão
to grow grain.
2 grão
grains of wheat / rice. ♦ grains of sand.
gram [gram] *n.* (= **gramme**) ▫ **grama**
fifty grams (= 50g) of sugar.
grammar ['gramə] *n.* ▫ **gramática**
a grammar book.
grammar school ['gramə 'skuːl] *n. Brit.* ▫ **escola de ensino médio**
grammatical [grə'matikəl] *adj.* ▫ **gramatical**
a grammatical mistake. ♦ That sentence is not grammatical.
grammatically [grə'matikəli] *adv.* ▫ **gramaticalmente**
a grammatically correct sentence.
gramme [gram] *n.* (= **gram**).
grand [grand] *adj.* ▫ **grandioso, formidável**
a grand palace / wedding
grandchild ['grantʃaild] *n.* (*pl.* **grandchildren**) ▫ **neto, neta**
grandad ['grandad] *n.* (mesmo que **grand-dad; grandpa**) ▫ **vovô, vô**
Did you bring me a present, Grandad?
■ *Amer.* also **granddaddy**
granddaughter ['gran,doːtə] *n.* ▫ **neta**
grandfather ['grandfaːðə] *n.* ▫ **avô**
■ Ver **grandpa; grandad.**
grandma ['granmaː] *n.* ▫ **vovó, vó**
My grandma is 85 years old.
grandmother ['granmʌðə] *n.* ▫ **avó**
■ Ver **grandma; granny.**
grandpa ['granpaː] *n.* (= **grandad**) ▫ **vovô, vô**
■ Ver **grandfather.**
grandparents ['granpeərənts] *n. pl.* ▫ **avós**
grandson [gransʌn] *n.* ▫ **neto**
My grandson visits me every week.
grandstand ['grandstand] *n.* ▫ **tribuna de honra; arquibancada**
granny ['grani] *n.*, **grannie** ▫ **vovó, vó**
Will you tell me a story, Granny?
■ Ver **grandmother.**
grant¹ [graːnt] *n.* ▫ **bolsa de estudo**
They gave him a student grant (so now he can study at university).
grant² *v.* (**grants, granting, granted**) ▫ **conceder**
They granted him a visa. ♦ The company granted us $100,000 for reseach.
take something for granted ▫ **dar algo por certo**
I take it for granted that you know the job.
grape [greip] *n.* ▫ **uva**
a bunch of grapes. ♦ grape juice.
grapefruit ['greipfruːt] *n.* ▫ **grapefruit, toranja**
graph [graf] *n.* **gráfico**
The graph shows a rise in sales in 2001.
grasp¹ [graːsp] *n.* **domínio, controle, pegada**
I lost my grasp on the box and it fell.
grasp² *v.* (**grasps, grasping, grasped**)
1 agarrar, estender a mão
The child grasped his mother's hand firmly. ♦ He grasped at the rope. (= He tried to hold it.)
2 (= understand) **entender, sacar**
He couldn't grasp the importance of the project.
grass [graːs] *n.* ▫ **capim, grama**
Cows eat grass. ♦ Keep off the grass! (= Don't walk on the grass!)
grasshopper ['graːshopə] *n.* ▫ **gafanhoto**
grassy ['graːsi] *adj.* ▫ **herboso**
grassy land.
grate [greit] *v.* (**grates, grating, grated**) ▫ **ralar**
to grate some cheese.
grated ['greitid] *adj.* ▫ **ralado**
grated carrots.
grateful ['greitful] *adj.* ▫ **grato**
I am grateful to you for your help. ♦ We are grateful that you didn't tell anybody.
■ antônimo: **ungrateful**
gratefully ['greitfuli] *adv.* ▫ **com gratidão, reconhecidamente**
I accepted their offer gratefully.
grater ['greitə] *n.* ▫ **ralador**
gratitude ['gratitjuːd] *n.* ▫ **gratidão**
He showed his gratitude by inviting us to dinner.
grave¹ [greiv] *adj.* ▫ **grave**
a grave mistake. ♦ The situation is grave.
grave² *n.* ▫ **túmulo**
He put flowers on his mother's grave.
gravel ['gravəl] *n.* ▫ **cascalho**
a gravel path.
gravely ['greivli] *adv.* ▫ **gravemente**
She is gravely ill.
gravestone ['greivstoun] *n.* ▫ **lápide**
One gravestone had no name on it.
graveyard ['greivjaːd] *n.* ▫ **cemitério**
■ Ver **cemetery.**
gravity ['gravəti] *n.* ▫ **gravidade**
When you drop something, it falls to the ground because of the force of gravity.
gray [grei] *adj.*, *n. Amer.*, **grey** *Brit.* ▫ **cinza**
gray hair. ♦ She was dressed in gray.
graze [greiz] *v.* (**grazes, grazing, grazed**)
1 esfolar
He fell and grazed his knee.
2 arranhar
The car grazed the wall.

3 pastar
The cattle are grazing in the fields.
grease¹ [gri:s] *n.*
1 gordura
You can use grease instead of margarine.
2 gordura, graxa
The dishes were covered with grease. ◆ Put some grease on to make the wheels turn smoothly.
grease² *v.* (**greases, greasing, greased**) ▫ **untar**
to grease the frying-pan.
greasy ['gri:zi] *adj.* (**greasier, greasiest**) ▫ **gorduroso**
greasy fingers. ◆ greasy food.
great [greit] *adj.*
1 grande
a great amount of work. ◆ a great distance.
2 grande
a great success.
3 grande
a great event.
4 grande
a great leader / musician.
5 ótimo
We had a great time. ◆ It's a great idea. ◆ I feel great.
■ Ver **big, large**.
a great deal (of) (= a lot (of)) ▫ **muito**
a great deal of money / time / effort. ◆ They talked a great deal.
a great many ▫ **muitos**
a great many people.
great-grandfather ['greit'granfa:ðə] *n.* ▫ **bisavô**
great-grandmother ['greit'granmʌðə] *n.* ▫ **bisavó**
greatly ['greitli] *adv.* ▫ **muito, extremamente**
We were greatly surprised to hear that.
greatness ['greitnis] *n.* ▫ **grandeza**
greed [gri:d] *n.*
1 ganância
He takes money even from his poor mother. It's just greed.
2 voracidade
Her greed is amazing. She ate the whole cake.
greedily ['gri:dili] *adv.* ▫ **gananciosamente; avidamente**
greedy ['gri:di] *adj.* ▫ **guloso, ganancioso**
Don't be so greedy! Leave some ice-cream for your sister.
green¹ [gri:n] *adj.* ▫ **verde**
green eyes. ◆ I painted the fence green.
green² *n.*
1 verde
She was dressed in green.
2 área verde
the village green.
greens *n. pl.* **folhas**
You should eat more greens.
greengrocer ['gri:n,grousə] *n. Brit.* ▫ **verdureiro**
to buy vegetables and fruit at the greengrocer's.
greengrocery ['gri:n,grousəri] *n. Brit.* (*pl.* **greengroceries**) ▫ **quitanda, mercadinho, sacolão**
■ *Amer.* **produce store**
greenhouse ['gri:nhaus] *n.* ▫ **estufa**
You can grow flowers, vegetables and plants in a greenhouse. ◆ the greenhouse effect (= global warming).
greet [gri:t] *v.* (**greets, greeting, greeted**) ▫ **cumprimentar, receber**
She greeted us with a smile.

greeting ['gri:tiŋ] *n.* ▫ **cumprimento**
'Hello' and 'Dear Sir' are greetings.
greetings *n. pl.* ▫ **saudação**
Give my greetings to your mother. ◆ a greetings card (e.g. a birthday card).
grenade [grə'neid] *n.* ▫ **granada**
The grenade did not explode.
grew [gru:] *v.* (Ver **grow**)
grey [grei] *adj.*, *n. Brit.*, **gray** *Amer.* ▫ **grisalho, cinza**
grey hair. ◆ He was dressed in grey.
grief [gri:f] *n.* ▫ **dor, pesar, desgosto**
She died of grief.
grievance ['gri:vəns] *n.* ▫ **queixa**
The boss promised to deal with the workers' grievances.
grieve [gri:v] *v.* (**grieves, grieving, grieved**) ▫ **lamentar, sofrer**
They are still grieving over their son's death.
■ Ver **mourn**.
grill¹ [gril] *n.* ▫ **grelha, grill**
Put the chicken under / on the grill for 40 minutes.
grill² *v.* (**grills, grilling, grilled**)
1 grelhar
to grill fish / steaks.
■ *Amer.* also **broil**
2 (= question; interrogate) **interrogar**
The police grilled the prisoner.
grin¹ [grin] *n.* ▫ **sorriso largo**
He looked at us with a grin on his face.
grin² *v.* (**grins, grinning, grinned**) ▫ **dar um sorriso largo**
He grinned from ear to ear.
grind [graind] *v.* (**grinds, grinding, ground**) ▫ **moer**
to grind wheat / coffee. ◆ to grind meat (= to mince meat, *Brit.*).
■ Ver **ground**.
grinder ['graində] *n.* ▫ **moedor**
a coffee grinder.
grip¹ [grip] *n.* ▫ **pegada**
He lost his grip on the rope and fell.
grip² *v.* (**grips, gripping, gripped**) ▫ **agarrar**
She gripped my hand.
grit [grit] *n.* ▫ **grão de areia**
groan¹ [grəun] *n.* ▫ **gemido**
groans of pain.
groan² *v.* (**groans, groaning, groaned**) ▫ **gemer**
He groaned with pain.
grocer ['grousə] *n.* ▫ **dono de quitanda, mercadinho, sacolão**
She bought bread and tea at the grocer's.
groceries ['grousəri:z] *n. pl.* ▫ **mantimentos, gêneros alimentícios**
grocery ['grousəri] *n.* (mesmo que **grocery shop**; **the grocer's**) ▫ **quitanda, mercadinho, sacolão**
groom [gru:m] *n.*
1 cavalariço
The groom brushed and cleaned the horse.
2 (= bridegroom) **noivo**
Let's drink to the bride and groom.
groove [gru:v] *n.*
1 sulco, canaleta
This door slides along a groove.
2 ranhura
grooves in a record

grope [group] *v.* (**gropes, groping, groped**) ◻ **tatear**
He groped in the dark for the light switch.

gross [grous] *adj.* ◻ **nojento**
That's gross (= disgusting)!

ground¹ [graund] *adj.* ◻ **moído**
ground coffee. ✦ ground meat (= minced meat, *Brit.*).

ground² *v.* (Ver **grind**).

ground³ *n.*
1 chão
They sat on the ground. ✦ The tree fell to the ground.
■ Ver **earth; soil**.
2 pátio, campo
a playground (for children). ✦ a sports ground.

grounds *n. pl.* ◻ **terreno**
the school grounds.

ground floor ['graund 'flo:] *n. Brit.* ◻ **térreo**
■ *Amer.* **first floor**

group [gru:p] *n.*
1 grupo
a group of tourists / houses.
2 banda, grupo
a pop group.

grove [grouv] *n.* ◻ **pequeno bosque, pomar**
an orange grove. ✦ an olive grove.

grow [grou] *v.* (**grows, growing, grew, grown**)
1 desenvolver-se
Oranges grow well in Spain.
2 crescer, aumentar
The world population is growing rapidly.
3 cultivar, deixar crescer
She grows vegetables in her garden. ✦ I'm growing a beard.
4 aumentar
My suspicions grew when he did not come back.
5 (= become; get) **ficar**
to grow old. ✦ It began to grow dark.
grow up ◻ **crescer**
They grew up together in the same village. ✦ What do you want to be when you grow up?

growing ['grouwiŋ] *adj.* ◻ **crescente**
a growing number of students.

growl¹ [graul] *v.* (**growls, growling, growled**) ◻ **rosnar**
The dog growled at him.

growl² *n.* ◻ **rosnado, urro**
The bear gave a growl.

grown¹ [groun] *v.* (Ver **grow**).

grown² *adj.* ◻ **crescido, adulto**
a grown man.

grown-up¹ ['grounʌp] *n.* (= adult) ◻ **adulto**
books for grown-ups.

grown-up² *adj.* ◻ **adulto**
They have a grown-up daughter.

growth [grouθ] *n.* ◻ **crescimento**
the growth of a baby / plant.

grub [grʌb] *n.*
1 (= food) **rango**
Is there any grub in the house? I'm hungry.
2 larva
A grub is a young insect that looks like a worm.

grubby ['grʌbi] *adj.* (**grubbier, grubbiest**) ◻ **encardido**
grubby hands.

grudge¹ [grʌdʒ] *n.* ◻ **rancor, ressentimento**

have a grudge against ◻ **guardar rancor de, ter ressentimento contra**
He has a grudge against me.

grudge² *v.* (**grudges, grudging, grudged**) ◻ **invejar**
not grudge ◻ **não invejar**
I don't grudge him his success.

grumble ['grʌmbl] *v.* (**grumbles, grumbling, grumbled**)
◻ **resmungar, manifestar desgosto**
He often grumbles about his job.

grumpy ['grʌmpi] *adj.* (**grumpier, grumpiest**) ◻ **rabujento**
He is grumpy because he is tired.

guarantee¹ [garən'ti] *n.*
1 garantia
This camera has a year's guarantee.
2 garantia
There's no guarantee that it will succeed.

guarantee² *v.* (**guarantees, guaranteeing, guaranteed**)
◻ **garantir**
I can't guarantee that he will agree.
be guaranteed
1 ter garantia
The watch is guaranteed for one year.
2 ser garantido
Success is guaranteed.

guard¹ [ga:d] *n.*
1 guarda
a security guard. ✦ The guard was armed.
2 guarda
The president inspected the guard of honour. *Brit.* ✦ The president inspected the honor guard. *Amer.*
3 guarda
a prison guard.
be on guard ◻ **de guarda**
The policemen are on guard outside the building.

guard² *v.* (**guards, guarding, guarded**) ◻ **guardar, vigiar**
The dog guarded the place. ✦ to guard the prisoners.

guardian ['ga:diən] *n.* ◻ **guardião**

guerrilla [gə'rilə] *n.*, **guerilla** ◻ **guerrilha**
guerrilla fighters.

guess¹ [ges] *n.* ◻ **palpite**
Have a guess. (= Try to guess.) ✦ My guess is that they will be back.

guess² *v.* (**guesses, guessing, guessed**)
1 adivinhar
Can you guess my age? ✦ Guess how much it cost me.
2 (= suppose) *Amer.* **achar, supor**
I guess you know what to do.
I guess so / not ◻ **achar, supor**
Will he come too? – I guess so.

guest [gest] *n.*
1 convidado
He invited 250 guests to the wedding.
2 hóspede
hotel guests.

guidance ['gaidəns] *n.*
1 orientação
The new workers will need a lot of guidance.
2 orientação
educational guidance (for students who need advice).

guide¹ [gaid] *n.*
1 guia
The tour guide took us to the palace.

2 (= guidebook) **guia, manual**
a guide to Europe. ◆ a guide to gardening.

guide² *v.* (**guides, guiding, guided**)
1 guiar
She guided us round the museum. ◆ Guide-dogs guide the blind when they go out.
2 orientar
If you are not sure what to do, your teachers will guide you.

guidebook ['gaidbuk] *n.* (= **guide**) □ **guia**
a guidebook to France.

guilt [gilt] *n.*
1 culpa
It will be difficult to prove his guilt.
■ antônimo: **innocence**
2 culpa
Don't you feel any guilt after lying to them?

guilty ['gilti] *adj.* (**guiltier, guiltiest**)
1 culpado
The judge found him guilty of stealing. ◆ I'm not guilty. I'm innocent.
2 culpado
I feel guilty about leaving them.

guinea pig ['ginipig] *n.*
1 porquinho-da-índia
I keep a guinea pig as a pet.
2 cobaia
They asked patients to be guinea pigs to test a new medicine.

guitar [gi'ta:] *n.* □ **violão**
He plays the guitar very well.

guitarist [gi'ta:rist] *n.* □ **violonista**

gulf [gʌlf] *n.* □ **golfo**
the Persian Gulf ◆ the Gulf of Mexico

gulp¹ [gʌlp] *n.* □ **gole**
He emptied the glass in one gulp.

gulp² *v.* (**gulps, gulping, gulped**) □ **engolir apressadamente**
He gulped down a cup of tea.

gum [gʌm] *n.*
1 (= chewing gum) **chiclete**
Don't chew gum in class.
2 goma, cola
Use gum to stick these pieces of paper together.

■ Ver **glue¹**.

gums [gʌmz] *n. pl.* □ **gengivas**
The dentist examined my teeth and gums.

gun [gʌn] *n.*
1 arma
He aimed the gun at the target and fired.
■ Ver **pistol; rifle**.
2 arma, armamento
heavy guns.

gunman ['gʌnmən] *n.* (*pl.* **gunmen**) □ **homem armado**
Two gunmen robbed the bank.

gunpowder ['gʌnpaudə] *n.* □ **pólvora**

gush [gʌʃ] *v.* (**gushes, gushing, gushed**) □ **esguichar, jorrar**
Blood gushed from the wound.

gust [gʌst] *n.* □ **rajada**
a gust of wind.

guts [gʌts] *n. pl.* □ **coragem**
You don't have the guts to do it.
■ Ver **courage**.

gutter ['gʌtə] *n.*
1 calha
A gutter is a pipe that carries rainwater down from the roof.
2 sarjeta
My keys fell into the gutter.

guy [gai] *n. Amer.* □ **cara**
He is a nice guy.
■ Ver **fellow¹**.

guys *n. pl.* □ **turma, pessoal**
She is one of the guys now.

gym [dʒim] *n.*
1 (= gymnasium) **ginásio, quadra**
The pupils do gymnastics in the gym.
2 academia
He goes to the gym every day to lift weights.
3 (= gymnastics) **ginástica**
gym shoes.

gymnasium [dʒim'neizjəm] *n.* (= **gym**) □ **ginásio**

gymnastics [dʒim'nastiks] *n.* (= **gym**) □ **ginástica**
They do gymnastics in the gym. ◆ our gymnastics teacher.

gypsy ['dʒipsi] *n.* (*pl.* **gypsies**) (= **gipsy**) □ **cigano**
a gypsy woman.

Hh

habit ['habit] *n.* □ **hábito**
She has a bad habit of biting her nails. ◆ That's the second time you're late. Don't make a habit of it!
habitual [ə'bitjuəl] *adj.*
1 habitual
a habitual act.
2 inveterado
a habitual liar.
had [had] *v.* (Ver **have**).
had better (Ver **better**).
hacker ['hakə] *n.* □ **hacker**
Hackers broke into the computers.
■ The verb is **hack**.
hail[1] [heil] *n.* □ **granizo**
hail[2] *v.* (**hails, hailing, hailed**) □ **chover granizo**
It's hailing.
hailstone ['heilstoun] *n.* □ **granizo**
hair [heə] *n.*
1 cabelo
She has long hair. ◆ Comb / Brush your hair!
2 cabelo
There's a hair in the soup.
■ Compare:
long hair.
a long hair.
have / get your hair cut □ **ter seu cabelo cortado**
I had my hair cut yesterday.
hairbrush ['heəbrʌʃ] *n.* □ **escova de cabelo**
haircut ['heəkʌt] *n.* □ **corte de cabelo**
I need a haircut. ◆ a short haircut.
have a haircut □ **fazer um corte de cabelo**
He had a haircut.
hairdresser ['heə‚dresə] *n.* □ **cabeleireiro**
men's hairdresser. ◆ She went to the hairdresser's.
hair-drier ['heədraiə] *n.*, **hair-dryer** □ **secador de cabelo**
hairpin ['heəpin] *n.* □ **grampo, prendedor de cabelo**
hairstyle ['heəstail] *n.* □ **penteado, corte de cabelo, estilo de cabelo**
I like your new hairstyle.
hairy ['heəri] *adj.* (**hairier, hairiest**) □ **cabeludo, peludo**
half[1] [ha:f] *adj.* □ **meio**
half a kilo of sugar. ◆ We waited for half an hour.
half[2] *n.* (*pl.* **halves**)
1 meio, metade
Cut the apple in half. ◆ Half of them came. ◆ Two halves make a whole.
2 tempo (esporte)
They played better in the second half.
half[3] *adv.* □ **meio, half pela metade**
The bottle is half empty. ◆ half-cooked.
half past □ **... e meia; ... e trinta**
It's half past six. (= It's 6:30.)
half-term [‚ha:f'tə:m] *n. Brit.* □ **recesso escolar no meio do ano**
We are going on holiday at half-term.
■ *Amer.* **midterm**
half-time [‚ha:f'taim] *n.* □ **intervalo (esporte)**
At half-time, the score was 1-1.

halfway [‚ha:f'wei] (= midway) *adj., adv.* □ **meio caminho, metade do caminho**
I'll meet you halfway.
hall [ho:l] *n.*
1 saguão
The hall of a hotel.
2 sala
a concert hall.
3 prefeitura, câmara
the town / city hall.
hallo [ha'lou] □ **olá**
Halloween [‚halou'i:n] *n.* □ **halloween, dia das bruxas**
Some people believe that ghosts and witches appear at Halloween.
halt[1] [ho:lt] *n.* □ **parada**
The bus came to a halt.
halt[2] *v.* (**halts, halting, halted**) □ **parar**
'Halt!', the policeman called.
halve [ha:v] *v.* (**halves, halving, halved**)
1 dividir ao meio
I halved the apple.
2 reduzir à metade
to halve the number of accidents.
halves [ha:vz] *n. plural of* **half**[2] □ **metades**
ham [ham] *n.* □ **presunto**
a ham sandwich.
hamburger ['hambə:gə] *n.* (also **burger**) □ **hambúrguer**
Two hamburgers and chips, please.
hammer[1] ['hamə] *n.* □ **martelo**
to knock nails into wood with a hammer.
hammer[2] *v.* (**hammers, hammering, hammered**)
1 martelar
He hammered the nail into the wall.
2 golpear insistentemente
to hammer on the door.
hammock ['hamək] *n.* □ **rede**
to sleep in a hammock.
hamster ['hamstə] *n.* □ **hamster**
I keep a hamster as my pet.
hand[1] [hand] *n.*
1 mão
We shook hands. ◆ He held the book in his hand. ◆ She raised her hand.
2 ponteiro
the minute / hour hand.
3 mão, ajuda
Give me a hand with these boxes.
4 aplauso
Let's give her a big hand.
(close / near) at hand □ **à mão**
At night I put the alarm clock close at hand.
by hand □ **à mão**
These shoes were made by hand.
to get out of hand □ **sair do controle**
The situation got out of hand.
hand in hand □ **de mãos dadas**
They walked hand in hand.
hands up
1 mãos ao alto
Hands up! Now drop your gun!
2 levante a mão
Hands up, who would like to answer?

in good hands ▫ em boas mãos
Don't worry – your children are in good hands.
lay your hands on ▫ pôr as mãos em
The police are trying hard to lay their hands on the murderer.
on the one hand... on the other (hand) ▫ por um lado... por outro (lado)
On the one hand, I like to eat. On the other hand, I don't want to get fat.
hand² *v.* (**hands, handing, handed**) ▫ **passar, dar**
Please hand me that book!
hand down ▫ **passar**
These customs are handed down from generation to generation.
hand in ▫ **entregar**
I have to hand in the report tomorrow.
hand out ▫ **distribuir**
The teacher handed out the exam papers.
■ Ver **distribute**.
hand over (to) ▫ **entregar (para)**
They handed him over to the police. ♦ The prisoners handed over their guns.
handbag ['handbag] *n*. ▫ **bolsa**
■ *Amer.* also **purse**
handbook ['handbuk] *n*. (= manual) ▫ **manual**
a handbook of instructions.
handcuffs ['handkʌfs] *n. pl.* ▫ **algemas**
They took him to prison in handcuffs.
handful ['handful] *n.*
1 punhado
a handful of nuts / sand.
2 pequena quantidade
Only a handful of people came to the lecture.
hand grenade ['hand grə,neid] *n*. (also **grenade**) ▫ **granada de mão**
handicap ['handikap] *n.*
1 desvantagem
In this job, it is a handicap if you don't speak a foreign language.
2 deficiência
children with physical or mental handicaps.
handicapped ['handikapt] *adj.* ▫ **deficiente**
He is physically handicapped ♦ the handicapped (= people with a physical or mental handicap).
■ Ver **disabled**.
handkerchief [,haŋkətʃif] *n.* ▫ **lenço**
a paper handkerchief (= a tissue).
handle¹ ['handl] *n.* ▫ **cabo, asa, maçaneta**
the handle of the knife / bucket. ♦ Hold the cup by the handle. ♦ He turned the handle, but the door did not open.
handle² *v.* (**handles, handling, handled**)
1 manusear
You must wash your hands before you handle food.
2 (= deal with) **lidar com**
She can handle the problem. ♦ He doesn't know how to handle children.
handlebars ['handlbɑːz] *n. pl.* ▫ **guidão**
hand luggage ['hand 'lʌgidʒ] *n. Brit.* ▫ **bagagem de mão**
■ *Amer.* **carry-on bag(s)**
handmade [,hand'meid] *adj.* ▫ **feito à mão, artesanal**
handmade shoes.
handshake ['handʃeik] *n.* ▫ **aperto de mão**

■ Ver **shake hands (with)**.
handsome ['hansəm] *adj.* ▫ **bonito**
a handsome man.
■ **handsome** usually describes men.
■ Ver **good-looking**.
handwriting ['hand,raitiŋ] *n.* ▫ **letra, caligrafia**
I can't read his handwriting.
handy ['handi] *adj.* (**handier, handiest**)
1 útil
A computer is very handy for keeping accounts.
2 à mão
She keeps her medicine handy.
come in handy ▫ **vir a calhar, ser útil**
Don't throw the string away. It may come in handy.
handyman ['handimən] *n.* (*pl.* **handymen**) ▫ **faz-tudo**
hang¹ [haŋ] *v.* (**hangs, hanging, hung**)
1 pendurar
He is hanging (up) the washing. ♦ I hung the shirt on a hanger.
2 pender
One lamp hung from the ceiling.
hang² *v.* (**hangs, hanging, hanged**) ▫ **enforcar**
He was hanged for murder.
hang about / around ▫ **passar o tempo, ficar**
A few boys were hanging about in the street.
■ Ver **loiter**.
hang on
1 esperar
Hang on! We're going to get you out of there.
2 esperar
Hang on a minute!
■ Ver **hold on**.
hang on to ▫ **segurar-se**
He hung on to the rope.
hang up ▫ **desligar (telefone)**
Don't hang up! Let me speak to her.
■ Ver **ring off**.
hanger ['haŋə] *n*. (= **coat-hanger**) ▫ **cabide**
to hang a shirt, coat, etc. on a hanger.
hang-glider ['haŋ'glaidə] *n.* ▫ **asa-delta**
hang-gliding ['haŋ'glaidiŋ] *n.* ▫ **voo livre, asa-delta**
hangman ['haŋmən] *n.* (*pl.* **hangmen**) ▫ **carrasco**
hanky ['haŋki] *n.*, **hankie** ▫ **lenço**
A hanky is a handkerchief.
happen ['hapn] *v.* (**happens, happening, happened**) ▫ **acontecer**
What happened there? ♦ How did the accident happen? ♦ Do you know what happened to her?
■ **What happened?** (*not* 'What was happened?').
happen to ▫ **acontecer**
I happened to meet her yesterday. ♦ He happened to be there when it started.
happening ['hapəniŋ] *n.* ▫ **acontecimento, evento**
happily ['hapili] *adv.*
1 feliz, com felicidade
They lived happily together.
2 felizmente
Happily, nothing happened to him.
happiness ['hapinis] *n.* (= joy) ▫ **felicidade**
happy ['hapi] *adj.* (**happier, happiest**)
1 feliz

harassment / hasten

The presents made the children happy. ◆ This is one of the happiest days of my life.
- antônimo: **unhappy; sad**

2 feliz
I'm not happy with the results.
- Ver **glad**.

be happy to ▫ **ficar feliz em**
I'll be happy to help you. ◆ I was happy to hear that you passed the exam.

Happy Birthday! ▫ **Feliz aniversário!**
Happy New Year! ▫ **Feliz Ano-Novo!**
Many Happy Returns! ▫ **Muitas felicidades!**

harassment ['harəsmənt] *n.*
sexual harassment *n.* ▫ **assédio**
She accused her boss of sexual harassment.

harbor ['ha:bə] *n. Amer.*, **harbour** *Brit.* ▫ **porto**
The ship reached harbour at last.
- Ver **port**.

hard[1] [ha:d] *adj.*

1 duro
The ground here is too hard. ◆ Nuts have a hard shell.
- antônimo: **soft**

2 (= difficult) **difícil, duro**
It's a hard question. ◆ It's hard for him to admit it. ◆ I find it hard to believe that...
- antônimo: **easy**

3 árduo, duro, pesado
hard work.
- antônimo: **light**

4 duro, difícil
He had a hard life.
- antônimo: **easy**

5 pesado
hard drugs.

6 duro
Don't be too hard on him.

hard[2] *adv.*

1 arduamente
She works hard.

2 com força
He hit me hard.

3 muito, forte
It's raining hard.

4 muito
to think hard.
- **hard** is both an adjective and an adverb.
- **hardly** has a different meaning entirely.
- Ver **hardly**.

hardback ['ha:dbak] *n.* ▫ **capa dura**
I bought the book in hardback.
- Ver **paperback**.

hard-boiled ['ha:dboild] *adj.* ▫ **duro, bem cozido**
I wanted my egg hard-boiled, not soft-boiled.

hard disk [ha:d 'disk] *n.* ▫ **HD, disco rígido**
- Ver **floppy disk**.

harden ['ha:dn] *v.* (**hardens, hardening, hardened**) ▫ **endurecer**
This glue hardens very fast.

hard feelings ['ha:d 'fi:liŋs] *n.* ▫ **ressentimento**
no hard feelings ▫ **sem ressentimentos**
There are no hard feelings between them.

hard labor ['ha:d 'leibə] *n. Amer.*, **hard labour** *Brit.* ▫ **trabalhos forçados**

hardly ['ha:dli] *adv.*

1 mal
I could hardly see it. ◆ We hardly know them.

2 quase não
This is hardly the time for silly games.

3 quase nunca
I have hardly any money. ◆ She hardly ever comes alone.

hardware ['ha:dweə] *n.*

1 hardware
I bought the hardware at the new computer supermarket, but I got the software at a different place.

2 ferragens
I bought this hammer in the hardware department.

hare [heə] *n.* ▫ **lebre**
- Ver **rabbit**.

harm[1] [ha:m] *n.* ▫ **mal**
The scandal did them a lot of harm. ◆ It won't do you any harm.

come to harm ▫ **ferir**
He had an accident, but he came to no harm.

there's no harm in ▫ **não haver mal em**
The chances are not good, but there's no harm in trying.

harm[2] *v.* (**harms, harming, harmed**) ▫ **prejudicar, fazer mal**
Smoking harms the lungs. ◆ It wouldn't harm you to help a little.
- Ver **damage**[2].

harmful ['ha:mful] *adj.* ▫ **prejudicial**
Too much alcohol can be harmful.

harmless ['ha:mlis] *adj.* ▫ **inofensivo**
Don't be frightened! This snake is harmless.

harmony ['ha:məni] *n.* ▫ **harmonia**
They live in harmony. ◆ They sang in harmony.

harness ['ha:nis] *n.* ▫ **arreios**

harp [ha:p] *n.* ▫ **harpa**
I can play the harp.

harsh [ha:ʃ] *adj.*

1 duro, severo
a harsh punishment. ◆ harsh laws.

2 áspero
a harsh voice.

harshly ['ha:ʃli] *adv.* ▫ **asperamente, grosseiramente**
They treated us harshly.

harvest[1] ['ha:vist] *n.*

1 colheita
The grape harvest is next month.

2 colheita
We had a good harvest of tomatoes this year.

harvest[2] *v.* (**harvests, harvesting, harvested**) ▫ **colher**
We are going to harvest (the wheat) next week.

has, hasn't [haz, 'haznt] *v.* (Ver **have**).

hash [haʃ] *n.* (#) ▫ **cerquilha**
Press the phone number and then the hash (sign).
- *Amer.* also **pound sign**

haste [heist] *n.* ▫ **pressa**
In my haste, I forgot to take the key.

hasten ['heisn] *v.* (**hastens, hastening, hastened**) (= hurry) ▫ **acelerar, apressar-se**
They hastened to catch the train.

hastily ['heistili] *adv.* □ **apressadamente, com pressa**
He prepared the meal hastily.

hasty ['heisti] *adj.*
1 apressado, rápido
a hasty meal.
2 precipitado
a hasty decision. ◆ Let's not be too hasty. We have enough time to decide.

hat [hat] *n.* □ **chapéu**
He put on his hat and left. ◆ She took off her hat. ◆ She is wearing a hat.

hatch [hatʃ] *v.* (**hatches, hatching, hatched**) □ **sair do ovo, chocar**
Look! The chicks are hatching.

hatchet ['hatʃit] *n.* □ **machadinha**
■ Ver **axe¹**.

hate¹ [heit] *n.* (= hatred) □ **ódio**

hate² *v.* (**hates, hating, hated**)
1 odiar, detestar
I hate him. ◆ She hates tea. ◆ I hate washing the dishes.
2 odiar, detestar
I hate to say this, but...

hated ['heitid] *adj.* □ **odiado**
He is the most hated politician in the country.

hateful ['heitful] *adj.* □ **odioso**
Don't be so hateful! ◆ hateful weather.

hatred ['heitrid] *n.* (= hate) □ **ódio**
He looked at us with hatred.

haughtiness ['hɔ:tinis] *n.* (= arrogance) □ **soberba, arrogância**

haughty ['hɔ:ti] *adj.* (**haughtier, haughtiest**) (= arrogant) □ **arrogante**
a haughty attitude

haul [hɔ:l] *v.* (**hauls, hauling, hauled**) □ **puxar**
The horse was hauling a cart.

haunt [hɔ:nt] *v.* (**haunts, haunting, haunted**)
1 assombrar
Ghosts haunt this house.
2 assombrar
His accusing look still haunts me.

haunted ['hɔ:ntid] *adj.* □ **assombrado**
a haunted house.

have¹ [hav] *v.* (**has, had**) □ **ter (como verbo auxiliar, às vezes não é traduzido)**
I have (= I've) seen that film. ◆ She has written three letters since June. ◆ I haven't seen him for three days. ◆ They haven't come yet. ◆ When I arrived, the bus had already left. ◆ I've been waiting here since 8 o'clock.

have² *v.* (**has, having, had**)
1 ter, possuir
She has black hair. ◆ How many children do you have? ◆ We had enough food for a week.
■ Negative: **have not** or **do not have**.
■ Questions: **have you?** or **do you have?**
■ **have got** is also possible:
We have (= We've) got a large house. ◆ Have you got enough money? ◆ They haven't got any children.
2 tomar, ter
We have breakfast at 8 am. ◆ I didn't have anything to eat for dinner.
3 sofrer, fazer
We had an accident. ◆ She had an operation.
4 ter
I have a headache. ◆ He has cancer.
■ **have got** is also possible:
She's got (= She has got) a headache.
■ Meanings 1, 4 [no be+ -ing]: Do *not* say '**is / are**' etc. '**having**'.

had better (Ver **better**).

have to □ **ter de**
I have to send it now. ◆ You don't have to go. ◆ She doesn't have to say anything. ◆ I had to go and visit her.
■ Ver **must**.
■ **will have to** is the *future tense* of **have to** and of **must**.
■ **had to** is the *past tense* of **have to** and of **must**.

have got to □ **ter de**
I have (= I've) got to send it now. ◆ She's got (= She has got) to come.

have nothing to do with □ **não ter nada a ver com**
It was his decision. I had nothing to do with it.

have something (done) □ **ter algo (feito)**
He has his hair cut every two months. ◆ I had my eyes tested yesterday.

haven't ['havnt] (mesmo que **have not**).

hawk [hɔ:k] *n.* □ **falcão**

hay [hei] *n.* □ **feno**

hay fever ['hei 'fi:və] *n.* □ **rinite alérgica**

hazard ['hazəd] *n.* □ **perigo**
a health hazard. ◆ Bad roads are a hazard to drivers.
■ Ver **risk¹**.

hazardous ['hazədəs] *adj.* (= dangerous) □ **perigoso**
hazardous chemicals. ◆ Smoking is hazardous to your health.

haze [heiz] *n.* □ **neblina, cerração**

hazelnut ['heizlnʌt] *n.* □ **avelã**

hazy ['heizi] *adj.* □ **enevoado**
a hazy day.

he [hi:] *pron.* □ **ele**
He works hard. ◆ He doesn't know me. ◆ He came with his wife.

head¹ [hed] *n., adj.*
1 cabeça
She shook her head (to say 'no'). ◆ The stone hit me on the head.
2 cabeça
Who put that idea into your head? ◆ Use your head! (= Think!)
3 cabeça
the head of the nail / pin.
4 diretor, chefe
Dr. Brown is the head of the department.
5 matriz
the head office.

a head, per head □ **por pessoa**
The meal cost $12 a head.

at the head of the table □ **à cabeceira da mesa**
He sat at the head of the table.

go to your head □ **subir à sua cabeça**
Success went to his head.

hang your head □ **baixar a cabeça**
She hung her head in shame.

head first □ **de cabeça**
He jumped head first into the pool.

heads or tails □ **cara ou coroa**
We tossed heads or tails to decide who goes first.

can't make head or tail of □ não entender, não decifrar
I can't make head or tail of these signs.
put our / your / their heads together □ pôr nossas / suas cabeças para pensar
Let's put our heads together and find a solution to the problem.
head² *v.* (**heads, heading, headed**)
1 encabeçar
His name heads the list. ♦ She headed the team of scientists.
2 dirigir-se
The boat headed towards the beach.
3 cabecear
He headed the ball into the net.
head for □ ir em direção a, tomar o rumo de
They headed (for) home.
headache ['hedeik] *n.* □ dor de cabeça
I have a headache.
heading ['hediŋ] *n.* □ título
What is the heading of the article?
■ Ver **headline**; **title**.
headlight ['hedlait] *n.* (also **headlamp**) □ farol
to switch on / off the headlights.
headline ['hedlain] *n.* □ manchete
The scandal is still in the headlines of all the newspapers.
headlines *n. pl.* □ manchetes
the news headlines (on TV).
headmaster ['hed'ma:stə] *n.* (= principal) □ diretor
headmistress ['hed'mistris] *n.* (= principal) □ diretora
head-on [,hed'on] *adj.* □ de frente
a head-on collision (between a car and a bus).
headphones ['hed'founz] *n. pl.* □ fones de ouvido
He put on the headphones and listened to the cassette.
headquarters ['hed'kwo:təz] *n.* □ sede, quartel-general
The company's headquarters is / are in New York. ♦ the army headquarters.
■ abreviação: **HQ**
headway ['hedwei] *n.*
make headway □ avançar, progredir
We are not making much headway in our negotiations.
heal [hi:l] *v.* (**heals, healing, healed**) □ sarar, cicatrizar
The wound healed completely. ♦ This will help to heal the cut.
health [helθ] *n.* □ saúde
He is in good health. ♦ Is it good or bad for her health? ♦ the Ministry of Health.
healthy ['helθi] *adj.* (**healthier, healthiest, healthful**)
1 saudável
a healthy child.
■ antônimo: **unhealthy; sick**
2 *Amer.* **saudável**
healthy food.
■ antônimo: **unhealthy**
heap¹ [hi:p] *n.* □ monte, pilha
a heap of toys / sand.
■ Ver **pile**.
heap² *v.* (**heaps, heaping, heaped**) □ amontoar, encher
The gardener heaped (up) the dead leaves. ♦ He heaped the plate with food.
hear [hiə] *v.* (**hears, heard**) □ ouvir, escutar
He doesn't hear very well. ♦ I listened but I heard nothing. ♦ I didn't hear you come in.

hear about □ saber sobre
I heard about the accident on the news.
hear from □ ter notícias
Have you heard from your family?
hear of □ ouvir falar de
I've never heard of him. Who is he? ♦ Have you ever heard of UFOs?
will / would not hear of □ não dar ouvidos, não querer saber
I can do it, but they won't hear of it. ♦ She wanted to marry him, but her parents wouldn't hear of it.
hearing ['hi:riŋ] *n.* □ audição
His hearing isn't very good.
heart [ha:t] *n.*
1 coração
My heart was beating fast.
2 coração
She has a kind heart.
3 meio, centro
in the heart of the forest.
4 coração
a cake in the shape of a heart.
hearts *n.* □ copas
the eight of hearts.
after your own heart □ que agrada profundamente
He is a man after my own heart.
break someone's heart □ partir o coração de alguém
She broke his heart.
by heart □ de cor
to learn the poem by heart. ♦ I know the rules by heart.
from the bottom of my heart □ do fundo do meu coração
I thank you from the bottom of my heart.
lose heart □ desanimar
Don't lose heart – you still have a chance to win.
not have the heart to... □ não ter coragem de
I didn't have the heart to take it from him.
take something to heart □ levar a sério
He took my refusal to heart.
heart attack ['ha:t ə'tak] *n.* □ ataque cardíaco
He died of a heart attack.
heartbeat ['ha:tbi:t] *n.* □ batimento cardíaco
I listened to his heartbeat.
hearth [ha:θ] *n.* (= fireplace) □ lareira
to sit by the warm hearth.
heartless ['ha:tlis] *adj.* □ sem coração, impiedoso
a heartless man.
heartlessly ['ha:tlisli] *adv.* □ impiedosamente
heat¹ [hi:t] *n.* □ calor
the heat of the sun. ♦ I can't work in this heat.
heat² *v.* (**heats, heating, heated**) □ aquecer, esquentar
to heat (up) the meal. ♦ to heat the room. ♦ Let the oven heat up before you put the bread in.
heater ['hi:tə] *n.* □ aquecedor
Switch on the (electric / gas) heater.
heating ['hi:tiŋ] *n.* □ aquecedor
The heating isn't working. ♦ central heating (for the whole building).
heaven ['hevn] *n.* □ céu
We believe that good people go to heaven when they die.
Good Heavens! □ (Minha) nossa!
Good Heavens! What a big egg!

heavily ['hevili] *adv.*
1 pesadamente
He sat heavily in the armchair.
2 excessivamente
It rained heavily.
heaviness ['hevinis] *n.* □ **peso**
the heaviness of his burden.
heavy ['hevi] *adj.* (**heavier, heaviest**)
1 pesado
I can't lift it. It's too heavy. ♦ I'll take the heavier suitcase.
2 forte
heavy rain.
3 pesado
a heavy fine.
4 pesado
heavy traffic.
■ antônimo: **light**
How heavy...? □ **Quão pesado...?**
How heavy is the car?
hectare ['hekta:] *n.* □ **hectare**
hectic ['hektik] *adj.* □ **agitado**
I had a hectic day at work.
he'd [hi:d] (mesmo que **he had**; **he would**).
hedge [hedʒ] *n.* □ **cerca viva**
hedgehog ['hedʒhog] *n.* □ **ouriço**
heel [hi:l] *n.* □ **salto**
I don't wear (shoes with) high heels.
height [hait] *n.*
1 altitude
What's the height of the mountain? ♦ It's 800 metres (= metres) in height.
■ Ver **high**.
2 auge
the height of passion.
heights *n. pl.*
1 altura
I'm afraid of heights.
2 alturas
From the heights we could see all the villages below.
heir [eə] *n.* □ **herdeiro**
The prince is heir to the throne (= will become king).
heiress ['eəris] *n.* □ **herdeira**
She is an heiress to a rich family.
held [held] *v.* (Ver **hold**²).
helicopter ['helikoptə] *n.* □ **helicóptero**
a helicopter pilot.
hell [hel] *n.* □ **inferno**
he'll [hi:l] (mesmo que **he will**).
hello [he'lou]
1 alô
Hello! This is David speaking.
2 (= **hi**) **olá**
Hello, Mary! What are you doing here?
■ **hi** is more common in American English.
helmet ['helmit] *n.* □ **capacete**
Soldiers and firemen wear helmets. ♦ a crash-helmet (for motorcyclists, etc.).
help¹ [help] *n.*
1 ajuda, auxílio, socorro
Thank you for your help. ♦ to call for help. ♦ Do you need any help?
■ Ver **aid; assistance**.

2 ajuda
They were a great help (to us).
help² *v.* (**helps, helping, helped**) □ **ajudar, auxiliar, socorrer**
Could you help me to move the table? ♦ She helped me with my homework. ♦ Can I help you?
Help! □ **Socorro!**
Help! Someone is drowning!
can't / couldn't help □ **não poder deixar de**
I couldn't help laughing.
help yourself
1 servir-se
She helped herself to a drink.
2 ficar à vontade
Can I borrow a pen? – Sure, help yourself.
a helping hand □ **ajuda, força**
He is always ready to give us a helping hand.
helpful ['helpful] *adj.* □ **útil, prestativo**
a helpful suggestion. ♦ He was very helpful (to us).
■ antônimo: **unhelpful**
helping ['helpiŋ] *n.* □ **porção**
a big helping of rice. ♦ He asked for another helping of ice-cream.
helpless ['helplis] *adj.* □ **incapaz, desamparado, sem remédio**
a helpless old man.
helplessly ['helplisli] *adv.* □ **impotentemente**
He looked helplessly at his burning house.
helplessness ['helplisnis] *n.* □ **impotência, desamparo**
hem [hem] *n.* □ **bainha**
hemisphere ['hemisfiə] *n.* □ **hemisfério**
the northern / southern hemisphere.
hen [hen] *n.*
1 galinha
Hens lay eggs. ♦ They keep hens on their farm.
2 fêmea de qualquer ave doméstica
A hen is the female of any kind of bird.
■ Ver **cock**.
her¹ [hɔ:] *adj.* □ **dela, seu**
Her hair is black. ♦ Is that her umbrella?
■ Ver **hers**.
her² *pron.* □ **a, lhe, ela** (precedido de preposição)
I saw her yesterday. ♦ He bought her a present. ♦ Dr. Clark treated her. ♦ We think about her every day.
herb [hə;b] *n.* □ **erva**
We use herbs in cooking and in medicine.
herd [hə:d] *n.* □ **rebanho, manada**
a herd of cattle / elephants.
■ Ver **flock**.
here [hiə] *adv.*
1 aqui
I found it here. ♦ Come here! ♦ Let's get out of here!
2 aqui, aí
Here is the book you wanted. ♦ Here they come!
here you are □ **aqui está**
Can I have an apple? – Yes, here you are.
here we are □ **cá estamos**
Here we are! This is the place.
hero ['hiərou] *n.* (*pl.* **heroes**)
1 herói
war heroes. ♦ She is a hero. She saved my son from drowning.

2 protagonista, herói
the hero of the play.
- Ver **heroine**.

heroic [hi'rouik] *adj*. □ **heroico**

heroin ['herouin] *n*. □ **heroína**
He is addicted to heroin.

heroine ['herouin] *n*.
1 protagonista, mocinha
Who plays the heroine in the film?
2 (= hero) **heroína**

heroism ['herouizm] *n*. □ **heroísmo**
an act of heroism.

hers [hɔ:z] *pron*. □ **dela**
Whose is this coat? – It's hers. ◆ She is a friend of hers.

herself [hɔ:'self] *pron*.
1 se, si mesma, si própria
She looked at herself in the mirror. ◆ She was proud of herself.
- Note the meaning of:
She cut herself. □ **Ela se cortou.**
She hurt herself. □ **Ela se machucou.**
She enjoyed herself. □ **Ela se divertiu.**
2 ela mesma
She bought it herself. ◆ Edna herself gave it to me.

by herself
1 sozinha
She is all by herself.
2 por conta própria
She solved the problem by herself.

he's [hi:z] (mesmo que **he is**; **he has**).

hesitant ['hezitənt] *adj*. □ **hesitante, indeciso**

hesitate ['heziteit] *v*. (**hesitates, hesitating, hesitated**) □ **hesitar**
She hesitated before answering. ◆ If you need help, don't hesitate to come to us.

hesitation [ˌhezi'teiʃən] *n*. □ **hesitação**
I answered without hesitation.

hey [hei] □ **ei**
Hey! What are you doing?

hi [hai] □ **oi**
Hi, Dina. How are you?
- Ver **hello**.

hiccup ['hikʌp] *n*. (mesmo que **hiccough**) □ **soluço**

hid *v*. (Ver **hide**).

hidden¹ ['hidn] *v*. (Ver **hide**).

hidden² *adj*. □ **escondido**
a hidden microphone. ◆ The letter was hidden in a shoe box.

hide [haid] *v*. (**hides, hiding, hid, hidden**)
1 esconder
He hid the money here.
2 esconder
She is hiding behind the bushes.
3 esconder
She couldn't hide her disappointment. ◆ I have nothing to hide.

hide-and-seek ['haidənd'si:k] *n*. □ **esconde-esconde**
to play hide-and-seek.

hideous ['hidiəs] *adj*.
1 hediondo
a hideous crime.

2 horroroso
a hideous hat.

hide-out ['haidaut] *n*. □ **esconderijo**
The robbers used a cave as a hide-out.

hiding ['haidiŋ] *n*. □ **esconderijo**
The prisoner escaped and went into hiding.

get a good hiding □ **levar uma boa surra**
The boy got a good hiding from his father for staying out late.

high¹ [hai] *adj*.
1 alto
a high wall. ◆ What's the highest mountain in the world? ◆ The shelf is too high.
- antônimo: **low**
- We use **tall** to talk about people, animals and trees.
2 de altura
The ceiling is 2.50 meters / metres high.
- We use **tall** to talk about people:
She is 1.70 meters / metres tall.
3 alto
a high salary. ◆ high temperatures / prices.
- antônimo: **low**

How high...? □ **Qual é a altura...?, Qual é a altitude...?**
How high is the mountain?
- for a person: **How tall...?**

high² *adv*. □ **alto**
Can you throw the ball higher?

high-class [ˌhai'kla:s] *adj*. □ **alta classe, de primeira classe**
a high-class restaurant.

high jump ['hai,dʒʌmp] *n*. □ **salto em altura**
She broke the record in the high-jump.

highlight ['hailait] *n*. □ **ponto alto**
Visiting the pyramids was the highlight of our trip.

highly ['haili] *adv*.
1 altamente
highly intelligent.
2 muito bem
He speaks highly of you.

Highness ['hainis] *n*. □ **Alteza**
His Highness the Prince of Wales.

high school ['hai ˌsku:l] *n*. *Amer*. □ **ensino médio, colégio**
I graduated from high school in 1994.
- *Brit*. **secondary school; grammar school**

highway ['haiwei] *n*. □ **rodovia**

highwayman ['haiweimən] *n*. □ **ladrão de estrada, salteador**
In the past, highwaymen robbed travellers.

hijack ['haidʒak] *v*. (**hijacks, hijacking, hijacked**) □ **sequestrar**
to hijack a plane / van.
- Ver **kidnap**.

hijacker ['haidʒakə] *n*. □ **sequestrador**

hike¹ [haik] *n*. □ **caminhada**
They went on a long hike.

hike² *v*. (**hikes, hiking, hiked**) □ **caminhar**
We hiked everywhere and never took a bus or train on our holiday.

hiker ['haikə] *n*. □ **caminhante, que faz caminhada**
Hikers often sleep outdoors.

hill [hil] *n*. □ **colina, morro, ladeira**
We could see the village from the top of the hill. ◆ to walk up the hill.

hilly ['hili] *adj.* ▫ **montanhoso**
a hilly area.

him [him] *pron.* ▫ **o, lhe, ele (precedido de preposição)**
I know him. ♦ She bought him a present. ♦ Dr. Segal treated him. ♦ I'll talk to him.

himself [him'self] *pron.*
1 se, si mesmo, si próprio
He looked at himself in the mirror. ♦ He was proud of himself.
■ Note the meaning of:
He cut himself. ▫ **Ele se cortou.**
He hurt himself. ▫ **Ele se machucou.**
He enjoyed himself. ▫ **Ele se divertiu.**
2 ele mesmo
He bought it himself. ♦ David himself gave it to me.
by himself
1 sozinho
He lives by himself.
2 por conta própria
He solved the problem by himself.

hinge [hindʒ] *n.* ▫ **dobradiça**
I must oil the hinges of the door.

hint¹ [hint] *n.* ▫ **dica**
Can you give me a hint – maybe the first letter of the missing word?

hint² *v.* (**hints, hinting, hinted**) ▫ **insinuar, dar a entender**
He looked at his watch to hint that he was in a hurry.

hip¹ [hip] *n.* ▫ **quadril**
He stood there with his hands on his hips.

hip²
Hip, hip, hurray (Ver **hurrah**).

hippie ['hipi] *n.* ▫ **hippie**
My dad was a hippie when he was young.

hippo ['hipou] *n.* (= **hippopotamus**).

hippopotamus [hipə'potəməs] *n.* (*pl.* **hippopotami** or **hippopotamuses**) ▫ **hipopótamo**

hire¹ ['haiə] *n.* ▫ **aluguel**
bicycles for hire.

hire² *v.* (**hires, hiring, hired**)
1 alugar
He hires a car when he goes on holiday. ♦ to hire a suit.
■ Ver **rent**.
2 contratar
to hire a lawyer / guide.

hire out *Brit.* ▫ **alugar**
She hires out motor-boats.
■ *Amer.* **rent**
■ Ver **rent²**; **let**.

his¹ [hiz] *adj.* ▫ **dele, seu**
I read one of his books. ♦ His hair is black.

his² *pron.* ▫ **dele**
That coat is his, not mine.

hiss¹ [his] *n.* ▫ **chiado**
When you iron wet clothes you hear a hiss.

hiss² *v.* (**hisses, hissing, hissed**)
1 sibilar
The snake hissed.
2 vaiar
The crowd hissed the speaker.

historian [his'to:riən] *n.* ▫ **historiador**

historic [his'to:rik] *adj.* ▫ **histórico**
This is a historic moment for our people.

historical [his'to:rikəl] *adj.* ▫ **histórico**
historical documents.

history ['histəri] *n.* ▫ **história**
I got a good grade in history. ♦ the history of America.

hit¹ [hit] *n.*
1 golpe
a direct hit on the target.
2 sucesso
The film became a hit in Europe.

hit² *v.* (**hits, hitting, hit**) (= strike)
1 bater, acertar
He hit me with his umbrella. ♦ to hit a ball (with a racket, etc.).
2 atropelar
A car hit him.
3 bater
He hit his head against the branch.

hit-and-run *adj., n.* ▫ **relativo ao motorista que atropela alguém e foge**
a hit-and-run accident.

hitch [hitʃ] *v.* (**hitches, hitching, hitched**)
1 pegar carona
to hitch a lift / ride.
2 (= hitchhike) **viajar de carona**

hitchhike ['hitʃhaik] *v.* (**hitchhikes, hitchhiking, hitchhiked**) ▫ **viajar de carona**
We hitchhiked across Italy.

hitchhiker ['hitʃhaikə] *n.* ▫ **caronista**

hi-tech [,hai'tek] (mesmo que **high tech**) *n., adj.* ▫ **alta tecnologia, altamente tecnológico**
Hi-tech is used a lot in industry today. ♦ a hi-tech industry.

hive [haiv] *n.* (= **beehive**) ▫ **colmeia, enxame**

hoard¹ [hoːd] *n.* ▫ **estoque**
I found a hoard of sweets in his room.

hoard² *v.* (**hoards, hoarding, hoarded**) ▫ **acumular, estocar**
Ants hoard grain for the winter.

hoarse [hoːs] *adj.* ▫ **rouco**
He had a hoarse voice. ♦ She got hoarse from shouting.

hoarsly ['hoːsli] *adj.* ▫ **roucamente**

hoax [houks] *n.* ▫ **trote, brincadeira, alarme falso**
Someone called to warn us of a bomb, but it was a hoax.

hobby ['hobi] *n.* (*pl.* **hobbies**) (= pastime) ▫ **hobby**
My hobbies are tennis and collecting stamps.

hockey ['hoki] *n.* ▫ **hoquei**
ice hockey.

hoe [hou] *n.* ▫ **enxada**
hoes, forks and other garden tools.

hoist [hoist] *v.* (**hoists, hoisting, hoisted**) ▫ **içar**
to hoist a flag.

hold¹ [hould] *n.* ▫ **segurada, pegada**
He kept a firm hold of the rope. (= He held it firmly.)
get hold of
1 conseguir
He got hold of the information.
2 encontrar
I'll have to call later. I can't get hold of him.
3 segurar, agarrar
He got hold of the rope.

hold² *v.* (**holds, holding, held**)
1 segurar
She held an umbrella in her hand. ♦ Hold my hand!

2 comportar, ter capacidade para
The fuel tank holds 47 liters / litres. ◆ The car holds five people.
3 ter
She holds an American passport. ◆ Who holds the world record in the high jump?
4 realizar
We held the meeting in my office.
5 não desligar
Hold the line, please!
hold back
1 reter
The police held the crowd back.
2 segurar
She couldn't hold back her tears.
3 esconder
I'm sure he is holding something back.
Hold it! □ **Pare!**
Hold it! Don't touch that button! ◆ Hold it! We can't start without him.
hold on □ **esperar**
Hold on a moment!
■ Ver **hang on**.
hold out □ **esticar**
I held out my hand to take the rope.
hold up
1 segurar
What is holding up the traffic? ◆ Sorry to hold you up.
2 (= rob) roubar, assaltar
They held up a bank.
be held up □ **ficar detido**
The plane was held up for 2 hours. ◆ We were held up by a traffic jam.
hold-up ['hould∧p] *n*.
1 assalto
There was a hold-up at the bank.
2 (= delay) atraso, demora
There is a hold-up on the freeway / motorway.
hole [houl] *n*. **furo; buraco**
There's a hole in my pocket. ◆ to dig a hole in the ground ◆ The dentist fill a hole in my tooth.
holiday ['holidei] *n*.
1 férias
Take two weeks' holiday. ◆ They are on holiday. ◆ the school holidays. ◆ We are going to Turkey for our summer holidays.
■ *Amer.* **vacation**
2 feriado
a bank holiday. ◆ a public holiday.
3 feriado
Easter is a Christian holiday. ◆ the Jewish holidays.
holidaymaker ['holideimeikə] *n. Brit.* □ **veranista, pessoa que está de férias**
holidaymakers at summer camps or by the sea.
■ *Amer.* **vacationer**
hollow ['holou] *adj*. □ **oco, vazio**
a hollow tree.
Holocaust ['holəko:st] *n*.
the Holocaust □ **o Holocausto**
holy ['houli] *adj*. **(holier, holiest)** □ **sagrado**
the Holy Bible. ◆ Jerusalem is a holy city for Jews, Christians and Muslims.

home¹ [houm] *adj*. □ **residencial**
What is your home address?
home² *adv*. □ **para casa**
Let's go home. ◆ She went home. ◆ I got home at 5:30.
home³ *n*.
1 casa, lar
He stayed at home. ◆ The teacher visited her in her home.
■ A **home** can be a *flat*, an apartment, a house or even a tent.
2 asilo
an old people's home.
at home □ **em casa**
Is he at home? (= Is he home?). *Amer.* ◆ I work at home.
Make yourself at home! □ **Sinta-se em casa!; Fique à vontade!**
homeland ['houmlənd] *n*. □ **terra natal**
She is now living in Europe, but Mexico is her homeland.
homeless ['houmlis] *adj*. □ **sem-teto**
the homeless (= people who have no home).
homemade [,houm'meid] *adj*. □ **caseiro, feito em casa**
homemade jam.
homesick ['houmsik] *adj*. □ **com saudades de casa**
He felt homesick.
homework ['houmwə:k] *n*. □ **tarefa, dever de casa**
Do your homework now and play later.
homosexual [,homə'sek∫uəl] *adj*., *n*. □ **homossexual**
honest ['onist] *adj*. □ **honesto, sincero**
an honest person. ◆ I want an honest answer. ◆ To be honest (= To tell you the truth), I don't know what to do.
■ antônimo: **dishonest**
honestly ['onistli] *adv*. □ **honestamente, sinceramente**
I honestly don't know where they are.
honesty ['onisti] *n*. □ **honestidade**
honey ['h∧ni] *n*. □ **mel**
Bees make honey.
honeymoon ['h∧nimu:n] *n*. □ **lua de mel**
They went to Paris for their honeymoon.
honk [hoŋk] *v. Amer.* **(honks, honking, honked)** □ **buzinar**
The drivers were honking – the noise was terrible.
■ *Brit.* **hoot**
honor¹ ['onə] *n. Amer.*, **honour** *Brit.* □ **honra**
It's a great honor to have the Prime Minister here today. ◆ to protect the honour of the family.
be an honor / honour to □ **ser motivo de honra para**
She is an honour to her school.
in honor / honour of □ **em homenagem a**
They gave a party in honor of the guest.
Your Honor / Honour □ **Meritíssimo**
I'm not guilty, your Honour.
honor² ['onə] *v. Amer.* **(honors, honoring, honored), honour** *Brit.* **(honours, honouring, honoured)** □ **honrar**
to honor your parents.
honorable ['onərəbl] *adj. Amer.*, **honourable** *Brit.* □ **honrado**
an honorable person / solution.
hood [hud] *n*.
1 capuz
He covered his head with the hood.
2 *Amer.* **capô**
■ *Brit.* **bonnet**
hoof [hu:f] *n*. (*pl*. **hoofs** or **hooves**) □ **casco**
Horses, cows and giraffes have hoofs.

hook [huk] *n.* □ **gancho, anzol**
to hang a towel on a hook. ◆ a fish-hook.
hooky ['huki] *n. Amer.*
  play hooky □ **matar aula**
  ■ *Brit.* **play truant**
hooligan ['hu:ligən] *n.* □ **hooligan, desordeiro, vândalo**
hooray [hu'rei] (Ver **hurrah**).
hoot¹ [hu:t] *n.*
  1 toque, buzinada
  He gave two hoots on the car horn.
  2 pio
  the hoot of the owl.
hoot² *v.* (**hoots, hooting, hooted**) □ **buzinar**
  The driver hooted impatiently.
  ■ *Amer.* **honk**
hooves [hu:vz] *v. pl.* (Ver **hoof**).
hop¹ [hop] *v.* (**hops, hopping, hopped**) □ **pular, saltar**
  He hopped on his left foot. ◆ The frog hopped out of the water.
hop² *n.* □ **pulo, salto**
hope¹ [houp] *n.*
  1 esperança
  There's no hope of finding them. ◆ We are full of hope.
  2 esperança
  Nobody wants to help me. You are my last hope.
  give up hope □ **perder as esperanças**
  Don't give up hope! I'm sure they will find him.
  in the hope of □ **na esperança de**
  I talked to him in the hope of solving the problem.
hope² *v.* (**hopes, hoping, hoped**) □ **esperar, ter esperança**
  I hope to meet her again. ◆ I hope (that) he will win.
  I hope so □ **Espero que sim.**
  Will he come too? – I hope so.
  I hope not □ **Espero que não.**
  Do we have to do it now? – I hope not.
hopeful ['houpful] *adj.* □ **esperançoso**
  I'm hopeful about her future.
hopefully ['houpfuli] *adv.*
  1 esperançosamente
  'Can you lend us the money?', he asked hopefully.
  2 tomara que
  Hopefully, we'll finish the job on time.
hopeless ['houplis] *adj.*
  1 irremediável
  a hopeless situation.
  2 péssimo
  I'm hopeless at mathematics.
hopelessly ['houplisli] *adv.* □ **desesperadamente**
  He was hopelessly confused.
horizon [hə'raizn] *n.* □ **horizonte**
  We could see a ship on the horizon.
horizontal [hori'zontl] *adj.* □ **horizontal**
  horizontal and vertical lines.
horn [ho:n] *n.*
  1 chifre
  Goats, bulls and deer have horns.
  2 trompa
  She plays the horn.
  3 buzina
  The driver sounded the horn.
horrible ['horibl] *adj.*
  1 horrível
  a horrible crime.
  2 horrível
  a horrible smell.
horrid ['horid] *adj.* □ **horroroso**
  horrid weather. ◆ Don't be so horrid!
horrified ['horifaid] *adj.* □ **horrorizado**
  They were horrified to hear of her death.
horrify ['horifai] *v.* (**horrifies, horrifying, horrified**) □ **horrorizar**
  What they saw horrified them.
horror ['horə] *n.* □ **horror**
  The children ran away in horror.
horror film ['horə ‚film] *n.* □ **filme de terror**
horse [ho:s] *n.* □ **cavalo**
  Can you ride a horse? ◆ He fell off the horse.
  on horseback □ **a cavalo**
  Policemen on horseback stopped the crowd.
horseshoe ['ho:s‚ʃu:] *n.* □ **ferradura**
hose [houz] *n.* (mesmo que **hose-pipe**) **mangueira**
  a garden hose.
hospitable ['hospitəbl] *adj.* □ **hospitaleiro**
  They are very hospitable to visitors.
  ■ *Amer.* **inhospitable**
hospital ['hospitl] *n.* □ **hospital**
  She is in hospital. (= She is in **the** hospital, *Amer.*) – she had an accident. ◆ He visited a patient at the hospital.
hospitality [‚hospi'taliti] *n.* □ **hospitalidade**
  He thanked them for their hospitality.
host [houst] *n.* □ **anfitrião**
  The guests thanked their host and went home.
  ■ Ver **hostess**.
hostage ['hostidʒ] *n.* □ **refém**
  The hijackers refused to release the hostages.
hostel ['hostəl] *n.* □ **albergue**
  a youth hostel.
hostess ['houstis] *n.*
  1 anfitriã
  The hostess introduced me to the other guests.
  2 (= **air-hostess**) **comissária de bordo**
  ■ Ver **host**.
hostile ['hostail] *adj.*
  1 hostil
  They were hostile to us.
  2 inimigo, hostil
  hostile aircraft.
  ■ The noun is **hostility**.
hostility [ho'ʊtiliti] *n.* □ **hostilidade**
hot [hot] *adj.* (**hotter, hottest**)
  1 quente, com calor
  hot water (for a bath, etc.). ◆ It's hot today. Turn on the air-conditioner! ◆ I'm hot. Is there a cold drink for me?
  ■ Ver **warm**.
  2 apimentado, picante
  The sauce is very hot.
hot-air balloon ['hot‚eə bə'lu:n] *n.* □ **balão**
  to fly in a hot-air balloon.
hot dog ['hot ‚dog] *n.* □ **cachorro-quente**
hotel [hou'təl] *n.* □ **hotel**
  I booked a room at the hotel. ◆ I'm staying at that hotel.
  ■ Ver **check in; check out**.
hour ['auə] *n.* □ **hora**

I work eight hours a day. ♦ I'll be back in half an hour.
■ **an** hour (*not* 'a hour').
at an early hour □ **cedo**
hours *n. pl.* □ **horário**
Our office hours are from 9 to 5. ♦ visiting hours.
hourly ['auəli] *adv.* □ **de hora em hora**
You must check it hourly.
house¹ [haus] *n.*
1 casa
We went to his house. ♦ He has a large house by the sea.
■ Ver **home²**.
2 casa (de ópera, de espetáculos)
the opera-house.
house² *v.* (**housed, housing, housed**) □ **abrigar**
to house the homeless. ♦ The refugees were housed in an army camp.
housekeeper ['hauski:pə] *n.* **governanta, empregada**
They employ a housekeeper.
housewife ['hauswaif] *n.* (*pl.* **housewives**) □ **dona de casa**
housework ['hauswə:k] *n.* □ **serviço doméstico**
to do the housework (= cleaning, cooking, etc.).
housing ['hauziŋ] *n.* □ **habitação**
There's a need for more housing.
housing estate ['hauziŋ i'steit] *n. Brit.*, **housing development** *Amer.* □ **conjunto habitacional**
She lives on a housing estate.
hover ['hovə] *v.* (**hovers, hovering, hovered**) □ **pairar**
The helicopter hovered over the boat.
hovercraft ['hovəkra:ft] *n.* □ **aerodeslizador, hovercraft**
There were 100 passengers on board the hovercraft. ♦ to go by hovercraft.
how [hau] *adv.*
1 como
How did you do it? ♦ I don't know how to get there. ♦ Do you know how to use it?
2 como
How are you? – Fine, thanks. ♦ How is your sister?
■ Compare with **What ... like?**:
What's his sister like? (Tell me about her appearance, her character.)
3 como
How was the party?
How about...? (= What about...?) □ **Que tal...?**
How about a cup of tea? ♦ How about going to the cinema?
How come...? □ **Como é que...?, Por que...?**
How come you failed the exam?
How do you do? □ **Como vai?**
■ Used when meeting somebody for the first time. The answer is also **How do you do?**
■ **Pleased to meet you** is more usual.
How many...? □ **Quantos...?**
How many chairs do you need?
How much...?
1 Quanto...?
How much money do you have? ♦ How much sugar is there?
2 Quanto é?, Quanto custa?
How much is that bag? (= How much does that bag cost?).
■ Compare:
how many books / people

How long...?
1 Qual o comprimento...?
How long is this road?
2 Quanto tempo...?
How long did you wait?
How often...? □ **Com que frequência...?**
How often do you visit her?
How old...? □ **Qual a idade...? Quantos anos...?**
How old is she? ♦ How old are you?
■ Ver **how deep; how far; how high; how tall; how wide**.
however [hau'evə] *adv.*
1 no entanto, contudo
The plan is perfect. However, it may cost a lot. ♦ We all agree. There is, however, one small problem.
■ Compare:
The plan is perfect. But it may cost a lot. (No comma after 'But'.)
2 por mais que
However hard I tried, I couldn't remember the name.
3 (= how) **como**
However did he get in?
howl¹ [haul] *n.* □ **uivo**
the howls of the wolves. ♦ the howl of the wind.
howl² *v.* (**howls, howling, howled**) □ **uivar**
We could hear the wind howling. ♦ The dog howled with pain.
HQ [eitʃ'kju:] *abbr.* (Ver **headquarters**).
hug¹ [hʌg] *n.* □ **abraço**
Come on, give your father a hug.
hug² *v.* (**hugs, hugging, hugged**) □ **abraçar**
She hugged her mother.
huge [hju:dʒ] *adj.* (= enormous) □ **enorme, grandioso**
a huge building. ♦ a huge success.
hullo ['hʌ'lou] (= **hello**).
hum [hʌm] *v.* (**hums, humming, hummed**)
1 zumbir
Bees and flies hum.
2 cantarolar
She was humming a beautiful tune.
human¹ ['hju:mən] *adj.* □ **humano**
the human body / race.
human² *n.* (mesmo que **human being**) □ **humano**
Only humans (= human beings) have the ability to speak.
human rights *n.* □ **direitos humanos**
the human race *n.* □ **a espécie humana**
humane ['hju:mein] *adj.* □ **humano, humanitário**
He showed a humane attitude to the prisoners.
humanity [hju'manəti] *n.* □ **humanidade**
crimes against humanity.
humble ['hʌmbl] *adj.*
1 humilde
a humble person.
2 humilde
his humble home.
humbly ['hʌmbli] *adv.* □ **humildemente**
'I apologize', he said humbly.
humiliate [hju'milieit] *v.* (**humiliates, humiliating, humiliated**) □ **humilhar**
She humiliated him in front of his friends.
humiliated [hju'milieitid] *adj.* □ **humilhado**
She felt humiliated.

humiliating [hju'mileitiŋ] *adj.* ▫ **humilhante**
a humiliating defeat.

humiliation [ˌhjumili'eiʃən] *n.* ▫ **humilhação**

humor ['hju:mə] *n. Amer.*, **humour** *Brit.* ▫ **humor**

have a sense of humor ▫ **ter senso de humor**
She has a great sense of humor.

humorous ['hju:mərəs] *adj. Amer.*, **humourous** *Brit.*
▫ **engraçado**
a humorous story / writer.

humorously ['hju:mərəsli] *adv. Amer.*, **humourously** *Brit.*
▫ **de modo engraçado, jocosamente**

humour ['hju:mə] *n. Brit.*, **humor** *Amer.* ▫ **humor**

hump [hʌmp] *n.* ▫ **corcova**
A camel has a hump.

hundred ['hʌndrəd] *adj., n.* ▫ **cem, centena**
I need one hundred blankets. ◆ She's a hundred years old.
◆ two hundred and twenty (= 220).

hundreds of ▫ **centenas de**
Hundreds of people saw it.

hundredth[1] ['hʌndrədθ] *adj.* (= 100th) ▫ **centésimo**
the hundredth anniversary of the victory.

hundredth[2] *n.* (= 1/100) ▫ **centésimo**
one hundredth of the money.

hung [hʌŋ] *v.* (Ver **hang**).

hunger ['hʌŋgə] *n.* ▫ **fome, inanição**
They died of hunger.

hungry ['hʌŋgri] *adj.* (**hungrier**, **hungriest**) ▫ **faminto, com fome**
I'm not hungry. I'll eat later.

hunt[1] [hʌnt] *v.* (**hunts, hunting, hunted**) ▫ **caçar**
Some animals hunt at night. ◆ They hunt foxes for sport.

hunt[2] *n.* ▫ **caça; caçada**
a fox-hunt. ◆ After a long hunt they caught the murderer.

hunter ['hʌntə] *n.* ▫ **caçador**

hunting ['hʌntiŋ] *n.* ▫ **caça**
They live by hunting. ◆ hunting dogs

hurl [hɜ:l] *v.* (**hurls, hurling, hurled**) ▫ **lançar**
They hurled stones at the soldiers.

hurrah [hu'rei] *n., abbr.*, **hooray, hurray** ▫ **viva**
Hurrah for the winner!
Hip, hip, hurray ▫ **Viva!**

hurricane ['hʌrikən] *n.* ▫ **furacão**

hurriedly ['hʌridli] *adv.* ▫ **apressadamente**
They left town hurriedly.

hurry[1] ['hʌri] *n.* ▫ **pressa**
There's no hurry. ◆ What's the hurry?
in a hurry ▫ **com pressa**
He drank his tea in a hurry.
to be in a hurry ▫ **estar com pressa**
I'm not in a hurry.

hurry[2] *v.* (**hurries, hurrying, hurried**)
1 correr
Let's hurry. We're late. ◆ She hurried home.
2 apressar
Stop hurrying me!
hurry up ▫ **depressa!, anda logo!**
Hurry up, you'll be late!

hurt[1] [hɜ:t] *v.* (**hurts, hurting, hurt**)
1 machucar
He hurt his knee when he fell.
2 machucar, doer
Stop it – you're hurting me! ◆ My leg hurts.
3 magoar, ferir
He hurt her feelings.
get hurt ▫ **machucar-se, ferir-se**
She got hurt when she climbed the tree.
it won't / wouldn't hurt ▫ **não vai / não iria tirar pedaço**
It won't hurt you to help a little.

hurt[2] *adj.* ▫ **magoado**
She was very hurt when you did not invite her.
■ Ver **insulted**.

husband ['hʌzbənd] *n.* ▫ **marido**
What's her husband's name?
■ Ver **wife**.

hush! [hʌʃ] ▫ **psiu!, silêncio!**
Hush, you'll wake the baby.

hut [hʌt] *n.* ▫ **cabana**
They built wooden huts.

hydrogen ['haidrədʒən] *n.* ▫ **hidrogênio**

hygiene ['haidʒi:n] *n.* ▫ **higiene**
Good hygiene can prevent diseases.

hygienic [hai'dʒi:nik] *adj.* ▫ **higiênico**
The hygienic conditions here are good.
■ antônimo: **unhygienic**

hymn [him] *n.* ▫ **hino**

hypermarket ['haipəma:kit] *n.* ▫ **hipermercado**
A hypermarket is a very big supermarket.

hyphen ['haifən] *n.* ▫ **hífen**
I write 'notice-board' with a hyphen.

hypocrisy [hi'pokrəsi] *n.* ▫ **hipocrisia**

hypocrite ['hipəkrit] *n.* ▫ **hipócrita**
Hypocrites say one thing and do the opposite.

hypocritical [hipə'kritikəl] *adj.* ▫ **hipócrita**
a hypocritical liar.

Ii

I[1] [ai] *pron.* □ **eu**
I don't know. ✦ I'm hungry. ✦ I was there.
I[2] (= 1) □ **I**
King Richard III.
ice [ais] *n.* □ **gelo**
Would you like ice in your drink?
iceberg ['aisbə:g] *n.* □ **iceberg**
ice-cream [,ais'kri:m] *n.* (mesmo que **ice cream**) □ **sorvete**
Two ice-creams, please. ✦ We had ice-cream for dessert.
ice cube ['aiskju:b] *n.* □ **cubo de gelo**
He put two ice cubes in his drink.
ice hockey ['ais ,hoki] *n.* □ **hóquei no gelo**
ice lolly [,ais 'loli] *n.* (*pl.* **ice lollies**) □ **picolé**
■ *Amer.* **Popsicle™**
ice rink ['aisriŋk] *n.* □ **pista de patinação no gelo**
ice skating ['ais ,skeitiŋ] *n.* □ **patinação no gelo**
icicle ['aisikl] *n.* □ **sincelo**
icing ['aisiŋ] *n.* □ **cobertura, glacê**
a cake with chocolate icing.
icy ['aisi] *adj.* (**icier, iciest**)
1 gelado
icy roads.
2 gélido
icy winds.
I'd [aid] (mesmo que **I had** ou **I would**).
ID [,ai'di:] *n.* □ **carteira de identidade**
Can I see your ID? ✦ an ID card.
■ Ver **identity card; identification**.
idea [ai'diə] *n.* □ **ideia**
It's a good idea. ✦ I have an idea. Let's go swimming.
✦ I have no idea who did it. ✦ They have their own ideas about education.
ideal [ai'diəl] *adj.* □ **ideal**
ideal weather for a trip.
identical [ai'dentikəl] *adj.* □ **idêntico**
These keys are identical (in size). ✦ identical twins.
identification [ai,dentifi'keiʃən] *n.*
1 identificação
The identification of the bodies was very difficult.
2 (= ID) **identificação**
Do you have any identification?
identify [ai'dentifai] *v.* (**identifies, identifying, identified**) □ **identificar**
The wife identified the body. ✦ The witness can identify the robber. ✦ to identify the problem.
identify yourself □ **identifique-se**
Did she identify herself?
identity [ai'dentiti] *n.* (*pl.* **identities**) □ **identidade**
The police have proof of his identity.
identity card [ai'dentiti 'ka:d] *n.* □ **carteira de identidade**
Can I see your identity card?
■ Ver **ID**.
idiom ['idiəm] *n.* □ **expressão idiomática**
■ Different kinds of **idioms**:
1 (phrasal verbs [verb + preposition or verb + adverb])
bring up □ **criar, educar**
put up with □ **aguentar, suportar**
2 (expressions or phrases)

off the peg □ **padrão, que não foi feita sob medida (roupa)**
It's out of the question. □ **Isto está fora de cogitação.**
■ Idioms normally cannot be translated word for word, since the meaning of the whole phrase is different from the meanings of the separate words.
idiot ['idiət] *n.* □ **idiota**
Don't touch it, you idiot!
idiotic [,idi'otik] *adj.* □ **idiota**
an idiotic idea.
idle ['aidl] *adj.*
1 à toa
She doesn't like to be idle.
2 (= lazy) **preguiçoso**
an idle student.
idleness ['aidlnis] *n.* □ **ociosidade**
He doesn't get anything done because of his idleness.
idol ['aidl] *n.*
1 ídolo
The film star was the idol of millions of fans.
2 ídolo
They worship a stone idol in the shape of a snake.
i.e. ['ai'i:] *abbr.*, **ie** (= that is) □ **i.e., isto é**
the media, i.e. television, radio and newspapers.
if [if] *conj.*
1 se
You can stay here if you like. ✦ If it rains, I'll stay at home.
✦ I won't go, if she does not apologize.
■ Note the use of the *present tense* in the 'if' clause, despite the future reference.
2 se
If I had enough money, I would buy a computer. ✦ What would you do, if you won two million dollars?
■ This is an 'unreal' condition relating to the present or future. Note the use of the *past tense* in the 'if' clause, and 'would' in the main clause.
3 se
If you had studied for the exam, you would have passed.
■ This is the unreal condition relating to the past. Note the use of the *past perfect tense* in the 'if' clause, and 'would have' in the main clause. The example sentence means that you did not study and so you did not pass.
4 (= whether) **se**
She asked if we could do it. ✦ I don't know if she can come.
if I were you □ **se eu fosse você**
If I were you, I wouldn't buy this car.
if necessary □ **se necessário**
We'll start from the beginning if necessary.
if only □ **se ao menos**
If only I could find it.
ignorance ['ignərəns] *n.* □ **ignorância**
ignorant ['ignərənt] *adj.* □ **ignorante**
She is ignorant of our plans. ✦ He is ignorant about business. ✦ an ignorant fool.
ignore [ig'no:] *v.* (**ignores, ignoring, ignored**) □ **ignorar**
I smiled at her, but she ignored me. ✦ He ignored our warnings.
I'll [ail] (mesmo que **I will** ou **shall**).
ill [il] *adj.* □ **doente**
She is very ill. ✦ I feel ill.
■ **sick** is the usual word in American English.
be taken ill □ **ficar doente**
She was taken ill suddenly.

fall ill □ **passar mal**
He fell ill when he heard the bad news.
illegal [i'li:gəl] *adj.* □ **ilegal**
In most countries, it is illegal to sell drugs. ◆ an illegal immigrant.
■ antônimo: **legal**
illegally [i'li:gəli] *adv.* □ **ilegalmente**
They entered the country illegally.
illegible [i'ledʒəbl] *adj.* □ **ilegível**
Your handwriting is illegible – write your composition again. ◆ an illegible signature.
■ antônimo: **legible**
illiterate [i'litərət] *adj., n.* □ **analfabeto, sem instrução**
illiterate people. ◆ Illiterates cannot read.
■ antônimo: **literate**
illness ['ilnis] *n.* □ **doença**
a serious illness. ◆ She'll get over her illness.
■ Ver **disease; sickness**.
■ Compare:
  illness = when you feel unwell / ill.
  disease = an illness with a nameor that affects a certain part of your body (e.g. cancer).
ill-treat [,il'tri:t] *v.* (**ill-treats, ill-treating, ill-treated**) □ **maltratar**
The parents ill-treated their child.
ill-treatment [,il'tri:tmənt] *n.* □ **maus-tratos**
illuminate [i'lu:mineit] *v.* (**illuminates, illuminating, illuminated**) □ **iluminar**
The sunlight illuminated the room.
illustrate ['iləstreit] *v.* (**illustrates, illustrating, illustrated**)
 1 **ilustrar**
to illustrate a book.
 2 **ilustrar**
He gave an example to illustrate what he meant.
illustration [,iləs'treiʃən] *n.* □ **ilustração**
book illustrations
I'm [aim] = **I am**
image ['imidʒ] *n.*
 1 **imagem**
The dog watched the images on the TV screen. ◆ He suddenly saw his image in the mirror.
 2 **imagem**
That's exactly the image I had of the city – clean and beautiful.
 3 **imagem**
He wants to improve his public image.
imaginary [i'mædʒinəri] *adj.* □ **imaginário**
All the characters in the book are imaginary.
imagination [i,mædʒi'neiʃən] *n.*
 1 **imaginação**
There's not enough imagination in his stories.
 2 **imaginação**
Nobody is following us – it's all in your imagination.
imaginative [i'mædʒinətiv] *adj.* □ **imaginativo**
an imaginative child / writer
■ antônimo: **unimaginative**
imagine [i'mædʒin] *v.* (**imagines, imagining, imagined**)
 1 **imaginar**
Can you imagine life without money? ◆ Imagine that you are the Emperor of Rome!
 2 (= suppose, guess) **imaginar**
I imagine (that) she knows what she is doing.

imitate ['imiteit] *v.* (**imitates, imitating, imitated**) □ **imitar**
Don't imitate their bad habits. ◆ She imitated her teacher.
imitation [,imi'teiʃən] *n.*
 1 **imitação**
He did a funny imitation of the boss.
 2 **imitação**
It's not a real diamond. It's an imitation. ◆ imitation leather.
immediate [i'mi:diət] *adj.* □ **imediata**
I demand an immediate answer.
immediately [i'mi:diətli] *adv.* □ **imediatamente**
Come here immediately!
■ Ver **at once; right away**.
immense [i'mens] *adj.* □ **imenso**
immense difficulties. ◆ an immense statue.
immensely [i'mensli] *adv.* □ **imensamente**
I enjoyed the film immensely.
immigrant ['imigrənt] *n.* □ **imigrante**
Immigrants from many countries come to America every year.
immigrate ['imigreit] *v.* (**immigrates, immigrating, immigrated**) □ **imigrar**
They immigrated from France.
■ Ver **emigrate**.
immigration [,imi'greiʃən] *n.* □ **imigração**
immoral [i'morəl] *adj.* □ **imoral**
It's immoral to steal.
■ antônimo: **moral**
immortal [i'mo:tl] *adj.* □ **imortal**
The Greeks believed that their gods were immortal.
■ antônimo: **mortal**
immune [i'mju:n] *adj.* □ **imune**
They were immune to the disease.
immunize ['imjunaiz] *v.* (**immunizes, immunizing, immunized**), **immunise** *Brit.* □ **imunizar**
Babies are immunized against many diseases.
impartial [im'pa:ʃəl] *adj.* (= fair) □ **imparcial**
an impartial judge.
impatience [im'peiʃəns] *n.* □ **impaciência**
impatient [im'peiʃənt] *adj.* □ **impaciente**
Why are you so impatient with them? ◆ Don't be so impatient – it will start soon.
■ antônimo: **patient**
impatiently [im'peiʃəntli] *adv.* □ **impacientemente**
'I know, I know', he said impatiently.
imperative [im'perətiv] *n.* (grammar) □ **imperativo**
'Look!' and 'Sit down!' are in the imperative.
impertinent [im'pə:tinənt] *adj.* (= impudent) □ **impertinente**
impertinent questions. ◆ an impertinent child.
■ antônimo: **polite**
implication [,impli'keiʃən] *n.* □ **implicação**
The implication from what you say is that we can't continue with the project. ◆ What are the implications of this action?
■ The verb is **imply**.
implore [im'plo:] *v.* (**implores, imploring, implored**) □ **implorar**
We implore you not to punish him.
■ **beg** means the same.
imply [im'plai] *v.* (**implies, implying, implied**) □ **implicar**
Are you implying that it's my fault? ◆ His answer implied that he was not happy.
■ The noun is **implication**.

impolite [ˌimpəˈlait] *adj.* (= rude) ☐ **indelicado, grosso, mal-educado**
It was impolite to refuse them.
■ antônimo: **polite**
impolitely [ˌimpəˈlaitli] *adv.* ☐ **indelicadamente**
import[1] [ˈimpɔ:t] *n.* (mesmo que **imports**) ☐ **importação**
Food imports increased by 5 percent.
■ Ver **export**[1].
import[2] *v.* (**imports, importing, imported**) ☐ **importar**
We import cars from America and Japan.
■ Ver **export**[2].
importance [imˈpɔ:təns] *n.* ☐ **importância**
This discovery is of great importance.
important [imˈpɔ:tənt] *adj.* ☐ **importante**
an important decision. ◆ an important person. ◆ It's important to read the questions carefully.
■ antônimo: **unimportant**
imported [imˈpɔ:tid] *adj.* ☐ **importado**
imported cars.
importer [imˈpɔ:tə] *n.* ☐ **importador**
■ Ver **exporter**.
impose [imˈpouz] *v.* (**imposes, imposing, imposed**)
1 impor
to impose high taxes on cigarettes.
2 impor
Teachers should not impose their opinions on pupils.
impossible [imˈpɔsibl] *adj.*
1 impossível
It's impossible to finish the job by Thursday.
■ antônimo: **possible**
2 impossível
an impossible situation.
impress [imˈpres] *v.* (**impresses, impressing, impressed**) ☐ **impressionar**
She impressed all of us.
be impressed by ☐ **ficar impressionado com**
We were impressed by his talent.
impression [imˈpreʃən] *n.* ☐ **impressão**
What's your impression of the play? ◆ He made a good impression on them.
impressive [imˈpresiv] *adj.* ☐ **impressionante**
Her speech was very impressive. ◆ an impressive building.
imprison [imˈprizn] *v.* (**imprisons, imprisoning, imprisoned**) (= jail) ☐ **prender, encarcerar**
He was imprisoned for robbing a bank.
imprisonment [imˈpriznmənt] *n.* ☐ **de prisão**
The judge sentenced her to five years' imprisonment.
improbable [imˈprɔbəbl] *adj.* ☐ **improvável**
It is improbable that they will win. ◆ an improbable reason.
■ antônimo: **probable**
improve [imˈpru:v] *v.* (**improves, improving, improved**) ☐ **melhorar**
You will have to improve your English. ◆ Her health is improving.
improvement [imˈpru:vmənt] *n.* ☐ **melhora**
We want to see a big improvement in your work. ◆ an improvement in the weather.
impudent [ˈimpjudənt] *adj.* (= impertinent) ☐ **insolente, malcriado**
an impudent question. ◆ an impudent child.

impulse [ˈimpʌls] *n.* ☐ **impulso**
I felt an impulse to slap him in the face.
impulsive [imˈpʌlsiv] *adj.* ☐ **impulsivo**
an impulsive decision. ◆ He is very impulsive.
in [in] *prep.*
1 em
in the north. ◆ in Italy. ◆ We arrived in New York at midnight.
■ Ver **at**.
2 em
in the room / box. ◆ in the water. ◆ in the garden. ◆ She is still in bed. ◆ I read about it in the newspaper.
■ **in** the street. *Brit.* ◆ **on** the street. *Amer.*
■ Ver **at**.
3 em
in 1994. ◆ in June. ◆ in winter. ◆ in the morning.
■ Ver **at**.
4 em
I'll be back in an hour. ◆ in a few days.
5 em
He is in good health. ◆ The place was in a mess.
6 em
to walk in the rain. ◆ to sit in the shade.
7 em
They sat in a circle.
8 de
She was dressed in red.
9 em
They spoke in English.
10 em
They buy coffee in large quantities.
in all ☐ **ao todo**
There are twenty questions in all.
inability [ˌinəˈbiliti] *n.* ☐ **incapacidade**
His inability to pay attention worries me.
■ The adjective is **unable**.
inaccurate [inˈakjurət] *adj.* (= incorrect) ☐ **impreciso, inexato**
an inaccurate description. ◆ The information was inaccurate.
■ antônimo: **accurate**
inaccurately [inˈakjurətli] *adv.* ☐ **imprecisamente, incorretamente**
inadequate [inˈadekwət] *adj.*
1 insuficiente
inadequate income.
2 inadequado
The equipment is inadequate for this purpose.
■ antônimo: **adequate**
incapable [inˈkeipəbl] *adj.* ☐ **incapaz**
He is incapable of cooking an omelette.
■ antônimo: **capable**
inch [intʃ] *n.* ☐ **polegada**
incident [ˈinsidənt] *n.* ☐ **incidente**
There was an unpleasant incident at the office today.
incidental [ˌinsiˈdentl] *adj.* ☐ **episódico, eventual**
incidental details.
incidentally [ˌinsiˈdentli] *adv.* (= by the way) ☐ **a propósito, aliás**
It was a good party. Incidentally, your friend David was there.
inclined [inˈklaind] *adj.*

be inclined to □ **estar inclinado a**
I'm inclined to accept his offer.

include [in'klu:d] *v.* (**includes, including, included**)
1 incluir
The price includes drinks. ◆ The team included two scientists.

■ Ver **consist of; contain**.

2 incluir
They included a chapter on air pollution.

be included □ **estar incluído**
Two batteries are included.

including [in'klu:diŋ] *prep.* □ **inclusive**
Everyone refused, including me. ◆ It costs 25 dollars, including postage and packing.

■ antônimo: **excluding**

inclusion [in'klu:ʒən] *n.* □ **inclusão**
■ The verb is **include**.

inclusive [in'klu:siv] *adj.* □ **inclusive**
from Monday the 18th to Tuesday the 26th inclusive.

income ['iŋkʌm] *n.* □ **renda, rendimento**
His income comes to $40,000 a year.

income tax ['iŋkʌm'taks] *n.* □ **imposto de renda**

incomplete [,inkəm'pli:t] *adj.* □ **incompleto**
The information is incomplete. ◆ an incomplete report.

■ antônimo: **complete**

inconsiderate [,inkən'sidərət] *adj.* □ **desatencioso**
inconsiderate drivers. ◆ It was inconsiderate of you to make so much noise.

■ antônimo: **considerate**

inconsistent [,inkən'sistənt] *adj.*
1 inconsistente
Your work is very inconsistent. Sometimes it's good and sometimes it's bad.
2 inconsistente
Your story is inconsistent with the facts.

■ antônimo: **consistent**

inconvenience [,inkən'vi:niəns] *n.* □ **inconveniência**
We apologize for the inconvenience.

inconvenient [,inkən'vi:niənt] *adj.* □ **inconveniente**
He phoned at an inconvenient time. ◆ It's inconvenient for me to meet you at the office.

■ antônimo: **convenient**

■ Compare **uncomfortable**:
uncomfortable = physical, feelings.

incorrect [inkə'rekt] *adj.* (= wrong) □ **incorreto**
an incorrect answer.

■ antônimos: **accurate; correct; right**

incorrectly [inkə'rektli] *adv.* □ **incorretamente**
You answered all the questions incorrectly.

increase[1] [in'kri:s] *v.* (**increases, increasing, increased**)
1 (= go up) **subir, aumentar**
Our exports will increase by 5% next year. ◆ Housing prices are increasing.
2 aumentar
He increased the speed.

■ antônimo: **decrease**[2]

increase ['inkri:s] *n.* □ **aumento**
an increase of 10% in sales. ◆ a wage increase.

■ antônimo: **decrease**

■ Ver **rise**[1]; **raise**[1].

incredible [in'kredəbl] *adj.* (= unbelievable) □ **incrível**
an incredible story. ◆ It can fly at an incredible speed.

incredibly [in'kredəbli] *adv.* □ **incrivelmente**
He is incredibly lazy.

incurable [in'kju:rəbl] *adj.* □ **incurável**
an incurable disease.

■ antônimo: **curable**

indeed [in'di:d] *adv.*
1 (= certainly) □ **com certeza**
Yes indeed!
2 (= really) □ **realmente**
I'm very glad indeed to see you.

indefinite article [in'definit 'a:tikl] *n.* (grammar) □ **artigo indefinido**
The indefinite articles in English are 'a' and 'an'.

indefinitely [in'definitli] *adv.* □ **indefinidamente**
They postponed the meeting indefinitely.

independence [indi'pendəns] *n.* □ **independência**
The country achieved independence in 1947. ◆ economic independence. ◆ He doesn't want to lose his independence.

independent [indi'pendənt] *adj.* □ **independente**
an independent country. ◆ Although she is very old, she is still independent.

■ antônimo: **dependent**

index ['indeks] *n.* □ **índice**
There is an index at the end of the book.

Indian ['indiən] *n., adj.*
1 indiano
My Indian friend lives in the capital, Delhi.
2 índio
cowboys and Indians.

indicate ['indikeit] *v.* (**indicates, indicating, indicated**)
1 indicar
He indicated where I should sign.
2 indicar
Their answers indicate that they don't know anything about it.
3 (= signal) *Brit.* **sinalizar**
Indicate when you turn right or left.

indication [,indi'keiʃən] *n.* □ **indicação**
There's no indication that she will change her decision.

indicator ['indikeitə] *n.* □ **seta**
■ *Amer.* **turn signal**

indifferent [in'difrənt] *adj.* (= uninterested) □ **indiferente**
She was indifferent to our troubles.

indignant [in'dignənt] *adj.* □ **indignado**
He became very indignant when they blamed him.

indignantly [in'dignəntli] *adv.* □ **indignadamente**
'That's not your business', he said indignantly.

indignation [,indig'neiʃən] *n.* □ **indignação**

indirect [indi'rekt] *adj.* □ **indireto**
an indirect answer. ◆ an indirect flight to New York.

■ antônimo: **direct**

indirect object [indi'rekt 'obdʒikt] *n.* (grammar) □ **objeto indireto**
The word 'him' in the sentence 'I gave him the book' is the indirect object of the verb.

■ Ver **direct object**.

indirectly [indi'rektli] *adv.* □ **indiretamente**
He is indirectly responsible for the failure.

indirect speech [indi'rekt spi:tʃ] *n.* (grammar) (mesmo que **reported speech**) □ **discurso indireto**

■ Compare:
I said that I would go. (indirect speech)
I will go. (direct speech)

individual[1] [indi'vidjuəl] *n.* □ **indivíduo**
Every individual has the right to speak freely.
individual[2] *adj.*
1 individual
the individual needs of the pupils.
2 individual
They checked each individual case.
3 particular
The pupils here have individual lessons in mathematics.
individually [,indi'vidjuəli] *adv.* □ **separadamente, individualmente**
He spoke to each of them individually.
indoor ['indo:] *adj.* □ **interno**
an indoor swimming-pool.
■ antônimo: **outdoor**
indoors [,in'do:z] *adv.* □ **em lugar fechado**
It's cold. Let's go indoors. ◆ to do sports indoors.
■ antônimo: **outdoors**
indulge [in'dʌldʒ] *v.* (**indulges, indulging, indulged**) □ **satisfazer, deliciar-se**
to indulge a child. ◆ He is indulging himself with a good meal.
industrial [in'dʌstriəl] *adj.* □ **industrial**
an industrial country / area.
industrious [in'dʌstriəs] *adj.* □ **diligente, esforçado**
an industrious worker.
industry ['indəstri] *n.* (*pl.* **industries**) □ **indústria**
the car industry.
inefficient [inə'fiʃənt] *adj.* □ **ineficiente**
an inefficient system. ◆ an inefficient manager.
■ antônimo: **efficient**
inefficiently [inə'fiʃəntli] *adv.* □ **ineficientemente**
inevitable [in'evitəbl] *adj.* □ **inevitável**
The delay was inevitable because of the storm.
inevitably [in'evitəbli] *adv.* □ **inevitavelmente**
More cars on the roads will inevitably mean more accidents.
inexpensive [iniks'pensiv] *adj.* (= cheap) □ **barato**
an inexpensive watch.
■ antônimo: **expensive**
inexperienced [,iniks'piəriənst] *adj.* □ **inexperiente**
an inexperienced teacher.
■ antônimo: **experienced**
infamous ['infəməs] *adj.* (= notorious) □ **infame, abominável**
an infamous criminal.
■ 'infamous' does *not* mean 'not famous'.
infancy ['infənsi] *n.* □ **infância**
infant ['infənt] *n.* □ **criança**
infantry ['infəntri] *n.* □ **infantaria**
infect [in'fekt] *v.* (**infects, infecting, infected**) □ **contaminar, infectar**
to infect people with a virus. ◆ to infect a computer program.
infected [in'fektid] *adj.* □ **infectado, infeccionado**
The wound is infected.
infection [in'fekʃən] *n.* □ **infecção**
an ear infection.
infectious [in'fekʃəs] *adj.* □ **infeccioso**
an infectious disease.
■ Compare **contagious**:
contagious = passed on by touch.
infectious = passed on in the air.

inferior [in'fiəriə] *adj.* □ **inferior**
He feels inferior to them. ◆ goods of inferior quality.
■ antônimo: **superior**
infinite ['infinit] *adj.* □ **infinito**
There is an infinite number of fish in the sea.
infinitely ['infinitli] *adv.* □ **infinitamente**
This computer is infinitely better than the others.
infinitive [in'finətiv] *n.* (grammar) □ **infinitivo**
■ The infinitive in English is sometimes used with **to** and sometimes without **to**:
He wants to go.
He must go.
inflatable [in'fleitəbl] *adj.* □ **inflável**
an inflatable boat.
inflate [in'fleit] *v.* (**inflates, inflating, inflated**) □ **inflar, encher**
to inflate the tyres.
■ **blow up** is the usual word.
inflation [in'fleiʃən] *n.* □ **inflação**
influence[1] ['influəns] *n.*
1 influência
The book had a strong influence on her. ◆ She is a good influence on him.
2 influência
He used his influence to get a job for his son.
influence[2] *v.* (**influences, influencing, influenced**) □ **influenciar**
What influenced you to change your decision?
be influenced □ **ser influenciado**
He is easily influenced. ◆ Her music is influenced by Indian music.
influential [,influ'enʃəl] *adj.* □ **influente**
an influential man / newspaper.
inform [in'fo:m] *v.* (**informs, informing, informed**) □ **informar**
We informed him about our decision.
■ Ver **notify**.
inform on □ **delatar, entregar**
He did not want to inform on his friends.
informal [in'fo:ml] *adj.* □ **informal**
informal clothes (= jeans, T-shirt, etc.). ◆ an informal discussion. ◆ 'Cop' is an informal word for 'policeman'.
■ antônimo: **formal**
informally [in'fo:mli] *adv.*
1 informalmente
They discussed it informally.
2 informalmente
They dressed informally.
■ antônimo: **formally**
information [,info:'meiʃən] *n.* □ **informação**
I need more information about the plan. ◆ I'd like some information about hotels in Morocco.
■ a piece of information (not 'an information').
information technology [,info:'meiʃən tek'nolədʒi] *n.* (mesmo que **IT**) □ **TI, tecnologia da informação**
He teaches information technology to students of electronics and computer sciences.
infrequent [in'fri:kwənt] *adj.* □ **raro, esporádico**
His visits became infrequent.
■ antônimo: **frequent**
infrequently [in'fri:kwəntli] *adv.* □ **raramente, esporadicamente**
■ antônimo: **frequently**

ingredient [in'gri:diənt] *n*. □ **ingrediente**
Ingredients: potatoes, vegetable oil, salt.
inhabitant [in'habitənt] *n*. □ **habitante**
a city of two million inhabitants.
inhabited [in'habitid] *adj*. □ **habitado**
Is the island inhabited?
inherit [in'herit] *v*. (**inherits, inheriting, inherited**) □ **herdar**
She inherited the house from her uncle.
inheritance [in'heritəns] *n*. □ **herança**
initial [i'niʃəl] *adj*. □ **inicial**
My initial reaction was to laugh. ♦ The project is still in its initial stages.
initially [i'niʃəli] *adv*. (= at first) □ **inicialmente, a princípio**
Initially, we all agreed.
initials [i'niʃəlz] *n. pl*. □ **iniciais**
My initials are DJ (David Jones).
initiate [i'niʃieit] *v*. (**initiates, initiating, initiated**) □ **iniciar**
He initiated the talks.
inject [in'dʒekt] *v*. (**injects, injecting, injected**) □ **injetar, aplicar injeção**
The doctor injected him against the disease.
injection [in'dʒekʃən] *n*. (= shot) □ **injeção**
The doctor gave her an injection.
injure ['indʒə] *v*. (**injures, injuring, injured**) □ **ferir**
The bomb injured several people.
■ Ver **wound³**.
be injured □ **ser ferido**
He was seriously injured in the accident.
injured ['indʒəd] *adj*. □ **ferido**
her injured leg.
the injured *n*. □ **os feridos**
The injured were taken to hospital.
injury ['indʒəri] *n*. (*pl*. **injuries**) □ **ferimento**
He cannot play because of his injury. ♦ She has head injuries.
injustice [in'dʒʌstis] *n*. □ **injustiça**
I'm angry at the injustice that she suffered.
■ antônimo: **justice**
■ Ver **wrong³**.
ink [iŋk] *n*. □ **tinta**
to write in ink.
inn [in] *n*. □ **pousada, hospedaria**
inner ['inə] *adj*. □ **interior, íntimo**
an inner room. ♦ his inner emotions.
innocence ['inəsens] *n*. □ **inocência**
He proved his innocence.
■ antônimo: **guilt**
innocent ['inəsent] *adj*.
1 inocente
I can prove that she is innocent (of the crime).
■ antônimo: **guilty**
2 inocente, ingênuo
an innocent question. ♦ He is so innocent that he believes everything.
innocently ['inəsentli] *adv*. □ **inocentemente**
input ['input] *n*. □ **dado, informação**
Input is the information that is put into a computer.
inquire [in'kwaiə] *v*. (**inquires, inquiring, inquired**) (= **enquire**, *Brit*.) □ **perguntar, pedir informações**
to inquire about the times of the trains. ♦ 'Where are you going?', she inquired.

inquire into □ **investigar**
The police are inquiring into the case.
inquiry [in'kwaiəri] *n*. (*pl*. **inquiries**) (= **enquiry**, *Brit*.)
1 pergunta, indagação
I made inquiries about the company. ♦ We had many inquiries about our ad.
2 investigação, inquérito
The police decided to continue their inquiries into the case.
inquisitive [in'kwizitiv] *adj*. □ **curioso**
inquisitive neighbours.
■ Ver **curious**.
insane [in'sein] *adj*. (= mad) □ **insano, louco**
She is insane.
■ antônimo: **sane**
insect ['insekt] *n*. □ **inseto**
Ants, beetles, and flies are all insects.
insecure [,insi'kjuə] *adj*.
1 inseguro
This ladder looks insecure.
2 incerto
an insecure future / situation.
3 inseguro
to feel insecure.
■ antônimo: **secure**
insecurity [,insi'kjuəriti] *n*. □ **insegurança**
Her insecurity is the reason for her failure. ♦ a feeling of insecurity.
insert [in'sət] *v*. (**inserts, inserting, inserted**) □ **inserir**
Insert the coins and press the button. ♦ to insert words in a sentence.
inside¹ ['insaid] *adj*. □ **interno**
the inside pages of the newspaper.
inside² [in'said] *adv*. □ **para dentro, dentro de**
Let's go inside. ♦ There was nothing inside.
■ antônimo: **outside**
inside³ *prep*. □ **dentro**
There was nothing inside the box. ♦ She put it inside the safe.
■ antônimo: **outside**
inside⁴ *n*. □ **interior, do lado de dentro**
the inside of the car. ♦ He locked the door from the inside.
■ antônimo: **outside**
inside out □ **às avessas**
He put on his socks inside out.
insignificant [,insig'nifikənt] *adj*. (= unimportant) □ **insignificante**
an insignificant difference / number.
■ antônimo: **significant**
insist [in'sist] *v*. (**insists, insisting, insisted**)
1 insistir
He insisted that we stay one more week. ♦ She insisted on going alone.
2 insistir
He insists that he is innocent.
insistence [in'sistəns] *n*. □ **insistência**
insistent [in'sistənt] *adj*. □ **insistente**
I didn't want to take the money, but she was very insistent.
insolence ['insələns] *n*. □ **insolência**
insolent ['insələnt] *adj*. □ **insolente**
insolent behaviour / remarks. ♦ insolent children.
■ Ver **rude; impolite; impertinent**.
■ antônimo: **polite**

inspect [in'spekt] *v.* (**inspects, inspecting, inspected**)
 1 inspecionar, examinar
 He inspected my passport carefully.
 2 inspecionar
 to inspect a restaurant.
inspection [in'spekʃən] *n.* □ **inspeção**
inspector [in'spektə] *n.*
 1 inspetor
 Inspector Jones will investigate the murder case.
 2 inspetor
 An inspector will visit our school today.
inspiration [,inspə'reiʃən] *n.* □ **inspiração**
 Many artists find inspiration in the stories of the Bible.
inspire [in'spaiə] *v.* (**inspires, inspiring, inspired**)
 1 inspirar
 Her beauty inspired him to write this poem.
 2 inspirar
 His promises inspired us with hope.
install [in'stɔ:l] *v. Amer.* (**installs / instals, installing, installed**) (= put in) □ **instalar**
 to install an alarm system.
installation [,instə'leiʃən] *n.*
 1 instalação
 the installation of the washing machine.
 2 instalação
 a military installation.
installment [in'stɔ:lmənt] *n. Amer.*, **instalment** *Brit.*
 1 parcela
 I paid for the TV in five monthly instalments.
 2 parte, capítulo
 Today we will listen to the last installment of the story (on the radio).
instance ['instəns] *n.* □ **ocasião, instância**
 He showed his courage in many instances.
 for instance (= for example) □ **por exemplo**
 Some animals, monkeys for instance, have two legs.
instant[1] ['instənt] *adj.*
 1 instantâneo
 The book was an instant success.
 2 instantâneo
 instant coffee / soup.
instant[2] *n.* (= moment) □ **instante**
 He thought for an instant and then answered.
 this instant □ **já, agora mesmo**
 Come here this instant! (= at once!)
instantly ['instəntli] *adv.* □ **imediatamente**
 He replied instantly.
instead [in'sted] *adv.* □ **em vez de, como substituto**
 There was no butter, so he bought margarine instead.
 instead of □ **em vez de, ao invés de**
 They sent me instead of David. ◆ Read the instructions instead of asking me.
instinct ['instiŋkt] *n.* □ **instinto**
 Birds learn to fly by instinct.
instinctive [in'stiŋktiv] *adj.* □ **instintivo**
 We have an instinctive fear of snakes.
instinctively ['instiŋktivli] *adv.* □ **instintivamente**
 Instinctively, I covered my head with my hands.
institute ['institju:t] *n.* □ **instituto**
 a research institute. ◆ the Institute of Technology.
institution [,insti'tju:ʃən] *n.* □ **instituição**
 an educational institution. ◆ financial institutions.

instruct [in'strʌkt] *v.* (**instructs, instructing, instructed**)
 □ informar, instruir, dar instruções
 The boss instructed me to wait for you. ◆ He instructed us in how to use the equipment. ◆ to instruct pupils in road safety.
instruction [in'strʌkʃən] *n.*
 1 instrução
 driving / swimming instruction.
 2 instruções
 Read the instructions first.
 3 instruções
 My instructions are to wait here.
instructional [in'strʌkʃənl] *adj.* □ **instrutivo**
 instructional television.
instructor [in'strʌktə] *n.* □ **instrutor**
 a driving instructor. ◆ a ski instructor.
instrument ['instrəmənt] *n.*
 1 aparelho, instrumento
 optical instruments (e.g. a telescope, microscope).
 ■ Ver **tool**.
 2 (= musical instrument) **instrumento**
insufficient [,insə'fiʃənt] *adj.* (= not enough) □ **insuficiente**
 One hour is insufficient to finish the exam.
 ■ antônimo: **sufficient**
insult[1] ['insʌlt] *n.* □ **insulto**
 They shouted insults at each other.
insult[2] *v.* (**insults, insulting, insulted**) □ **insultar**
 He didn't mean to insult you. ◆ I felt insulted.
insulted ['insʌltid] *adj.* □ **insultado**
 I felt insulted when she turned her back on me.
 ■ Ver **hurt**[2].
insulting ['insʌltiŋ] *adj.* □ **insultante**
 an insulting remark.
insurance [in'ʃuərəns] *n.* □ **seguro**
 The insurance company will pay for the damage. ◆ life insurance.
insure [in'ʃuə] *v.* (**insures, insuring, insured**)
 1 segurar, ter seguro
 I insured the house against fire. ◆ Are you insured?
 2 (= ensure, *Brit.*) *Amer.* **assegurar**
 We have to insure their safety.
intellect ['intilekt] *n.* □ **intelecto**
intelligence [in'telidʒəns] *n.*
 1 inteligência
 a pupil of high intelligence. ◆ an intelligence test.
 2 inteligência
 military intelligence.
intelligent [in'telidʒənt] *adj.* □ **inteligente**
 She is very intelligent. ◆ an intelligent answer.
 ■ Ver **clever**.
intelligently [in'telidʒəntli] *adv.* □ **inteligentemente**
intend [in'tend] *v.* (**intends, intending, intended**) □ **pretender, intencionar**
 He intends to stay there another week. ◆ What do you intend to do?
 ■ The noun is **intention**.
 ■ Ver **propose**[2].
 be intended for □ **ser destinado a, ser voltado para**
 The book is intended for children and adults.
intense [in'tens] *adj.* □ **intenso**
 intense heat. ◆ intense hatred.

intensely [in'tensli] *adv.* □ **intensamente**
He dislikes her intensely.
intention [in'tenʃən] *n.* □ **intenção**
She has no intention of selling the house.
intentional [in'tenʃənl] *adj.* □ **intencional, proposital**
It was not intentional. I forgot to invite him.
■ antônimo: **unintentional**
intentionally [in'tenʃənli] *adv.* □ **intencionalmente**
She didn't say that intentionally.
interactive [intər'aktiv] *adj.* □ **interativo**
an interactive computer program. ◆ interactive video games.
intercom ['intəkom] *n.* □ **interfone, rádio comunicador**
to speak on the intercom.
interest[1] ['intrəst] *n.*
1 interesse
He looked at the picture with some interest. ◆ to show interest in music.
2 interesse
They asked me about my hobbies and interests.
3 interesse
They want to protect their interests.
4 juros
I got a loan at 8% interest.
take an interest in □ **ter interesse em**
She takes an interest in politics.
interest[2] *v.* (**interests, interesting, interested**) □ **interessar**
His stories interested the children. ◆ Football does not interest me.
be interested (in) □ **estar interessado em**
I'm interested in this subject. ◆ Are you interested (in joining the club)?
■ antônimo: **uninterested**
■ Ver **disinterested; unbiased; impartial**.
interesting ['intrəstiŋ] *adj.* □ **interessante**
The lecture wasn't very interesting. ◆ I met some interesting people.
■ antônimo: **uninteresting; boring**
interfere [intə'fiə] *v.* (**interferes, interfering, interfered**)
1 interferir
Don't interfere in their quarrel.
2 interferir
The noise here interferes with my work.
■ Compare with **disturb**:
  Don't disturb me.
  Don't interfere with my plans.
interference [,intə'fiərəns] *n.*
1 interferência
interference in their affairs.
2 (= disturbance) **interferência**
I can't hear the radio programme. There's too much interference from other stations.
interior [in'tiəriə] *n., adj.* □ **interior, íntimo**
The interior of the palace is very impressive. ◆ an interior room. ◆ the Interior Minister.
■ antônimo: **exterior**
interjection [intə'dʒekʃən] *n.* (grammar) □ **interjeição**
The words 'Wow!' and 'Oh!' are interjections.
intermediate [intə'mi:diət] *adj.*
1 intermediário
intermediate learners of English.

2 intermediário
an intermediate level. ◆ at an intermediate stage.
intermission [intə'miʃən] *n.* □ **intervalo**
■ Ver **interval**.
internal [in'tə:nl] *adj.* □ **interno, doméstico**
the internal affairs of the country.
■ antônimo: **external**
international [intə'naʃnəl] *adj.* □ **internacional**
an international telephone call. ◆ international trade.
internet ['intənət] *n.* (= **the** net, the web) □ **internet**
to look up information on the Internet. ◆ an Internet site.
interpret [in'tə:prit] *v.* (**interprets, interpreting, interpreted**)
1 servir de intérprete, interpretar
to interpret his meaning. ◆ to interpret a dream.
2 (= translate) **traduzir**
I don't speak Chinese. Can you interpret for me?
■ Compare **interpret**:
  interpret = translate speech as it is being spoken.
  translate = translate speech or especially writing.
interpretation [in,tə:pri'teiʃən] *n.* □ **interpretação**
the interpretation of the dream.
interpreter [in'tə:pritə] *n.* □ **intérprete**
■ The interperters worked hard at the international conference.
■ Ver **translator**.
interrogate [in'terəgeit] *v.* (**interrogates, interrogating, interrogated**) □ **interrogar**
to interrogate the suspect / witness.
■ Ver **grill**[2].
interrogation [in,terə'geiʃən] *n.* □ **interrogação**
interrogative [intə'rogətiv] *adj.* (grammar) □ **interrogativo**
An interrogative sentence asks a question.
interrupt [intə'rʌpt] *v.* (**interrupts, interrupting, interrupted**) □ **interromper**
Stop interrupting me when I'm talking! ◆ Sorry to interrupt, but you have a visitor.
interruption [,intə'rʌpʃən] *n.* □ **interrupção**
I don't want any interruptions until we finish the meeting.
interval ['intəvəl] *n.*
1 intervalo
There is an interval in the middle of the show.
■ *Amer.*: **intermission**
2 intervalo
After an interval of 2 hours, it started raining again.
at intervals
1 em intervalos
We dug holes at intervals of 5 metres / meters.
2 a cada
Buses leave here at 15-minute intervals.
interview[1] ['intəvju:] *n.*
1 entrevista
He said that in a TV interview.
2 entrevista
I have an interview for the job today.
interview[2] *v.* (**interviews, interviewing, interviewed**) □ **entrevistar**
They interviewed me for the job. ◆ The Prime Minister was interviewed on television.
interviewer ['intəvju:ə] *n.* □ **entrevistador**
into ['intu] *prep.*
1 em

He went into the kitchen. ✦ I threw it into the water. ✦ She got into the car.
2 em, para
The water turned into ice. ✦ Translate the passage into English.
3 em
He divided the class into two groups.
4 em
The car crashed into a tree.
intonation [intə'neiʃən] *n*. □ **entonação**
introduce [intrə'dju:s] *v*. (**introduces, introducing, introduced**)
1 apresentar
He introduced me to his parents. ✦ I introduced myself.
2 introduzir
to introduce a subject ✦ to introduce new methods.
introduction [,intrə'dʌkʃən] *n*.
1 introdução
the introduction of the new system.
2 apresentação
Our next guest needs no introduction.
3 introdução
He wrote an introduction to his new book.
4 (= a book for beginners) **introdução**
'An Introduction to Grammar'.
invade [in'veid] *v*. (**invades, invading, invaded**) □ **invadir**
They invaded the country with a large army.
■ The noun is **invasion**.
invader [in'veidə] *n*. □ **invasor**
invalid ['invəlid] *n*. □ **inválido**
He became an invalid after the accident.
invaluable [in'valjuəbl] *adj*. □ **inestimável**
His help is invaluable (to us).
■ Be careful: 'valuable' is **not** the opposite of 'invaluable'
invasion [in'veiʒən] *n*. □ **invasão**
The German invasion of Poland was in 1939.
■ The verb is **invade**.
invent [in'vent] *v*. (**invents, inventing, invented**)
1 inventar
Edison invented the microphone.
2 (= make up) **inventar**
to invent an excuse.
invention [in'venʃən] *n*. □ **invenção**
the invention of printing. ✦ the greatest inventions of the 20th century.
inventor [in'ventə] *n*. □ **inventor**
inverted commas [in'və:tid 'koməz] *n. Brit*. □ **aspas**
■ Ver **quotation marks**.
invest [in'vest] *v*. (**invests, investing, invested**) □ **investir**
He invested a lot of money in the business.
investigate [in'vestigeit] *v*. (**investigates, investigating, investigated**) □ **investigar**
The police are investigating the case.
investigation [in'vestigeiʃən] *n*. □ **investigação**
There will be a full investigation of the crime.
investment [in'vestmənt] *n*. □ **investimento**
an investment of $5 million.
investor [in'vestə] *n*. □ **investidor**
invisible [in'vizəbl] *adj*. □ **invisível**
Viruses are invisible to the eye.
■ antônimo: **visible**
invitation [invi'teiʃən] *n*. □ **convite**
I sent them an invitation to our wedding.

invite [in'vait] *v*. (**invites, inviting, invited**) □ **convidar**
We invited him for dinner. ✦ They did not invite me to the party.
invoice ['invois] *n*. □ **fatura**
involve [in'volv] *v*. (**involves, involving, involved**)
1 implicar, exigir
The project involves large investments.
2 envolver
Don't involve me in this quarrel!
be involved (in) □ **estar envolvido (em)**
I'm not involved in this business. ✦ Two buses were involved in the accident.
involvement [in'volvmənt] *n*. □ **envolvimento**
The police can't prove his involvement in the robbery.
inward(s) ['inwəd(z)] *adv*. □ **para dentro**
The door opens inwards.
■ antônimo: **outward(s)**
iron¹ ['aiən] *n*.
1 ferro
Steel is made from iron.
2 ferro de passar
Be careful not to burn the shirt with the iron.
iron² *v*. (**irons, ironing, ironed**) □ **passar roupa**
I finished ironing the clothes.
ironing ['aiəniŋ] *n*.
1 roupa para passar
a pile of ironing.
2 passar a roupa
to do the ironing.
ironing board [ronəniŋ bo:d] *n*. □ **tábua de passar**
irregular [i'regjulə] *adj*.
1 (= grammar) **irregular**
irregular verbs.
2 irregular
irregular conduct.
3 irregular
His pulse was irregular. ✦ Her visits became irregular.
■ antônimo: **regular**
irrelevant [i'relivənt] *adj*. □ **irrelevante**
The fact that he is rich is irrelevant.
■ antônimo: **relevant**
irresponsibility ['iri,sponsə'biliti] *n*. □ **irresponsabilidade**
irresponsible [iri'sponsəbl] *adj*. □ **irresponsável**
irresponsible behavior / behaviour. ✦ It was irresponsible to put it near the fire. ✦ He is irresponsible about money.
■ antônimo: **responsible**
irritable ['iritəbl] *adj*. □ **irritadiço, sensível**
He is very irritable today.
irritate ['iriteit] *v*. (**irritates, irritating, irritated**)
1 irritar
His remarks irritated me.
2 irritar
The smoke irritates my eyes.
irritating ['iriteitiŋ] *adj*. □ **irritante**
irritation [,iri'teiʃən] *n*.
1 irritação
The delays caused a lot of irritation among the passengers.
2 irritação
This glue may cause irritation to your skin.
is [iz] *v*. (Ver **be**).
Islam ['izla:m] *n*. □ **Islã**
Islamic [iz'lamik] *adj*. □ **islâmico**
Islamic law / culture.
■ Ver **Muslim**.

island ['ailənd] *n.* □ **ilha**
a desert island (= an island where nobody lives).
isn't ['iznt] (mesmo que **is not**).
isolate ['aisəleit] *v.* (**isolates, isolating, isolated**) □ **isolar**
to isolate people with an infectious disease.
be isolated □ **ser / estar / ficar isolado**
The villages were isolated by the floods.
isolated ['aisəleitid] *adj.* □ **isolado, remoto**
an isolated farm.
isolation [,aisə'leiʃən] *n.* □ **isolamento**
to keep dangerous prisoners in isolation.
issue¹ ['iʃu:] *n.*
1 questão
The government will discuss the issue of unemployment.
2 edição, exemplar, número
the latest issue of the magazine.
3 emissão
a special issue of stamps.
issue² *v.* (**issues, issuing, issued**)
1 emitir
to issue a passport / visa. ◆ to issue stamps.
2 distribuir, entregar
We issued them with the most modern equipment.
it [it] *pron.*
1 não é traduzido quando ocorre como sujeito de verbos impessoais ou auxiliares
It's hot today. ◆ What time is it? – It's five o'clock.
2 não é traduzido quando ocorre como sujeito de verbos impessoais ou auxiliares
It's impossible. ◆ Does it matter?
3 ele, ela
The pen is very expensive. It costs 50 dollars. ◆ The dog barked because it heard a noise.
■ Pet animals are often referred to as **he / she** instead of **it**.
■ **it** is used for a baby when the sex is unknown:
Is it a boy or a girl?
4 o, a, lhe, ele, ela
I took the box and opened it. ◆ I opened the safe, but there was nothing in it. ◆ The dog was hungry, so I gave it something to eat.
itch¹ [itʃ] *n.* □ **coceira**
I have an itch.

itch² *v.* (**itches, itching, itched**) □ **coçar**
My nose is itching.
■ Ver **scratch**.
itchy ['itʃi] *adj.* □ **que coça, comichoso**
an itchy nose.
it'd [itəd] (mesmo que **it had** ou **would**).
item ['aitəm] *n.*
1 peça
One of the items was sold for $120,000. ◆ an item of clothing.
2 artigo
an item of news (in the paper).
it'll [itl] (mesmo que **it will**).
it's [its] (mesmo que **it is, it has**) □ **não é traduzido quando ocorre como sujeito de verbos impessoais ou auxiliares**
It's (= It is) raining. ◆ It's (= It is) a difficult question. ◆ It's (= It has) succeeded.
■ Do not confuse with **its**.
■ Ver **'s**.
its [its] *pron., adj.* □ **seu, sua**
The dog wagged its tail. ◆ The company doubled its exports.
■ Compare **his¹, her¹**.
itself [it'self] *pron.*
1 se, si mesmo, ele mesmo
The bird cleaned itself.
■ Compare:
The dog hurt itself (accidentally).
2 próprio
The system itself is wrong.
by itself
1 sozinho, por si só
A young bird can't eat by itself. ◆ The door will open by itself.
2 (= alone) sozinho
The cat stayed in the house by itself for two days.
in itself □ **em si**
A car is not dangerous in itself. It all depends on the driver.
I've [aiv] (mesmo que **I have**)
I've seen it before.
ivory ['aivəri] *n.* □ **marfim**
ivy ['aivi] *n.* □ **hera**

Jj

jack [dʒak] *n.*
1 valete
the jack of hearts.
2 macaco (peça mecânica)
You need a jack to change a tire / tyre.
jackal ['dʒakl] *n.* □ **chacal**
Jackals were howling and dogs were barking – what a noise!
jacket ['dʒakit] *n.* □ **jaqueta, paletó**
a sports jacket. ♦ a leather jacket. ♦ a dinner jacket.
jackpot ['dʒakpɒt] *n.* □ **sorte grande**
to win the jackpot.
jagged ['dʒagid] *adj.* □ **pontudo**
jagged rocks.
jaguar ['dʒagjuə] *n.* □ **jaguar**
jail¹ ['dʒeil] *n.* (= prison) □ **cadeia**
He was sent to jail.
jail² *v.* (**jails, jailing, jailed**) (= imprison) □ **prender**
be jailed □ **ser preso**
She was jailed for five years.
jam¹ [dʒam] *n.* □ **geleia**
a jar of strawberry jam.
  ■ *Amer.* **jelly**
jam² *n.* (Ver **traffic jam**).
jam³ *v.* (**jams, jamming, jammed**)
1 emperrar
The door jammed and we couln't open it.
2 bloquear
A bus is jamming the road.
jammed ['dʒamd] *adj.* □ **emperrado**
The lock is jammed and won't open.
janitor ['dʒanitə] *n. Amer.* □ **zelador**
  ■ *Brit.* **caretaker**
January ['dʒanjuəri] *n.* **janeiro**
It happened in January, 2002.
  ■ For examples of the use of the months, see **April**.
jar [dʒa:] *n.* □ **vidro**
a jar of honey / coffee. ♦ a jam jar.
javelin ['dʒavəlin] *n.* □ **dardo de arremesso**
jaw [dʒɔ:] *n.* □ **mandíbula**
the upper / lower jaw.
jaws [dʒɔ:z] *n. pl.* □ **mandíbula**
the jaws of the shark.
jazz [dʒaz] *n.* □ **jazz**
a jazz band.
jealous ['dʒeləs] *adj.*
1 ciumento
a jealous husband.
2 com ciúmes
They are jealous of my success.
  ■ Ver **envious**.
jealously ['dʒeləsli] *adv.* □ **com ciúmes**
He looked jealously at my car.
jealousy ['dʒeləsi] *n.* □ **ciúmes**
jeans [dʒi:ns] *n.* □ **calças jeans**
a pair of jeans ♦ He wore tight jeans.
jeep [dʒi:p] *n.* □ **jipe**
jeer¹ [dʒi:r] *v.* (**jeers, jeering, jeered**) □ **zombar**
The audience jeered at the speaker.
jeer² *n.* □ **zombaria, chacota**
jelly ['dʒeli] *n.*
1 gelatina
to have jelly for dessert.
2 (= jam) *Amer.* **geleia**
jellyfish ['dʒelifiʃ] *n.* □ **água-viva**
There were a lot of jellyfish on the beach. ♦ He was stung by a jellyfish.
jerk¹ [dʒɜ:k] *n.*
1 tranco, solavanco
The train stopped with a jerk.
2 cretino
What a jerk! He does the stupidest things.
jerk² *v.* (**jerks, jerking, jerked**)
1 dar um tranco
The bus jerked to a halt. (= It stopped suddenly.)
2 fazer um movimento brusco
He jerked his hand into the water and pulled out a fish.
jersey [dʒɜ:zi] *n.* □ **jérsei, camisa de malha**
Jesus (Christ) ['dʒi:zəs (kraist)] *n.* □ **Jesus (Cristo)**
jet [dʒet] *n.*
1 jato
to fly to London by jet.
2 jato
a jet of gas / water.
jet lag ['dʒet lag] *n.* □ **indisposição devido à mudança de fuso horário**
She suffered from jet lag after the long flight.
Jew [dʒu:] *n.* □ **judeu, judia**
How many Jews live in America?
  ■ The adjective is **Jewish**.
jewel ['dʒu:əl] *n.*
1 joia
She doesn't wear any jewels.
2 joia
A diamond is a jewel.
jeweler ['dʒu:ələ] *n. Amer.*, **jeweller** *Brit.* □ **joalheiro**
jewellery ['dʒu:əlri] *n. Brit.*, **jewelry** *Amer.* □ **joias**
gold jewellery
Jewish ['dʒu:wiʃ] *adj.* □ **judaico, judeu, judia**
the Jewish religion (= Judaism). ♦ She is Jewish.
jigsaw (puzzle) ['dʒigsɔː(pʌzl)] *n.* □ **quebra-cabeça**
jingle¹ ['dʒiŋgl] *n.* □ **tilintar, música para propaganda**
the jingle of bells.
jingle² *v.* (**jingles, jingling, jingled**) □ **tilintar**
He jingled the coins in his pocket.
job [dʒɒb] *n.*
1 trabalho, emprego
You did a good job. ♦ She has a good job. ♦ He is looking for a job.
2 trabalho, tarefa
It's not my job to clean the office.
it's a good job... *Brit.* □ **bom trabalho**
It's a good job you were there to help us.
out of a job (= unemployed) □ **sem emprego**
She is out of a job.
jockey ['dʒɒki] *n.* □ **jóquei**
A jockey rides horses in races.
  ■ Ver **disc-jockey**.
jog¹ ['dʒɒg] *v.* (**jogs, jogging, jogged**)
1 correr
She jogs around the park every morning.

2 empurrar
He jogged me and I spilled my coffee.
jog² *n.* □ **corrida**
Let's go for a jog – it's good exercise.
jogging ['dʒɒgɪŋ] *n.* □ **corrida**
I like jogging and swimming. ◆ I go jogging every evening, but she goes running.
join [dʒɔɪn] *v.* (**joins, joining, joined**)
1 associar-se
He joined the organization in 2001.
2 juntar-se a
Would you like to join me for a swim?
3 unir
The bridge joins the two cities. ◆ He joined two ropes together.
4 encontrar-se
The two roads join here.
join in □ **participar**
Would you like to join in (the game)?
join the army □ **entrar para o exército**
He joined the army in 1999.
join up □ **alistar-se**
He joined up when he was 18.
■ Ver **draft²; conscript.**
joint¹ [dʒɔɪnt] *adj.* □ **conjunto**
They have a joint bank account.
joint² *n.*
1 junta, articulação
the finger joints.
2 junta, encaixe
the joints in a water pipe.
3 quarto
a joint of beef.
jointly ['dʒɔɪntli] *adv.* □ **juntamente, conjuntamente**
joke¹ [dʒəʊk] *n.* □ **piada**
He told me a funny joke.
play a joke on □ **pregar uma peça em**
He played a joke on me by hiding my car keys.
joke² *v.* (**jokes, joking, joked**) □ **brincar**
I was only joking. It isn't really true.
■ Ver **practical joke.**
jolly¹ ['dʒɒli] *adj.* □ **alegre**
a jolly person.
jolly² *adv. Brit.* (= very) □ **muito, extremamente**
It was a jolly good game.
jolt¹ [dʒəʊlt] *n.* □ **sacudida, tranco**
The bus stopped with a jolt.
jolt² *v.* (**jolts, jolting, jolted**)
1 sacolejar
The jeep jolted along the track.
2 abalar
The explosion jolted the buildings around.
jot [dʒɒt] *v.* (**jots, jotted, jotting**)
jot down □ **anotar**
He jotted down a few ideas in his notebook.
journal ['dʒɜːnl] *n.*
1 periódico
a medical / scientific journal.
■ Ver **magazine; monthly³; weekly².**
2 (= diary) **diário**
The children kept a journal of their trip abroad.
journalism ['dʒɜːnəlɪzəm] *n.* □ **jornalismo**

journalist ['dʒɜːnəlɪst] *n.* □ **jornalista**
She works as a journalist on a local newspaper.
■ Ver **reporter.**
journey ['dʒɜːni] *n.*
1 viagem
a half-hour journey to work. ◆ Did you have a good journey?
2 jornada
a journey around the world. ◆ a journey through the jungle.
■ Ver **travel².**
joy [dʒɔɪ] *n.* (= happiness) □ **felicidade**
They jumped for joy when they got their presents.
joyful ['dʒɔɪful] *adj.* (= very happy) □ **alegre**
They were joyful over the team's victory.
joyfully ['dʒɔɪfuli] *adv.* □ **alegremente**
joyriding ['dʒɔɪraɪdɪŋ] *n.* □ **passear em alta velocidade sem a autorização do dono do veículo**
They stole some motorbikes and went joyriding at 120 kph until the police arrested them.
joystick ['dʒɔɪstɪk] *n.* □ **controle de video game**
You need a joystick to play this video game.
jubilee ['dʒuːbɪliː] *n.* □ **jubileu**
a silver jubilee (= 25 years) of a reign / the foundation of an organization, etc. ◆ a golden jubilee (= 50 years). ◆ a diamond jubilee (= 60 years).
Judaism [dʒuːdeɪˈɪzm] *n.* □ **judaísmo**
judge¹ [dʒʌdʒ] *n.*
1 juiz
The judge sent the criminal to prison.
2 jurados
the judges at a beauty contest.
judge² *v.* (**judges, judging, judged**)
1 ponderar
It's difficult to judge which plan is better.
2 julgar
They asked me to judge the dancing competition.
judgement ['dʒʌdʒmənt] *n.*, **judgment**
1 julgamento
In my judgement, our chances are good.
2 discernimento
He showed good judgement in choosing her for the job.
3 julgamento
The judgment surprised everyone in court.
judo ['dʒuːdəʊ] *n.* □ **judô**
to learn judo.
jug [dʒʌg] *n.* □ **jarra**
a water jug. ◆ a jug of wine.
■ *Amer.* **pitcher**
juggle ['dʒʌgl] *v.* (**juggles, juggling, juggled**) □ **fazer malabarismo**
Now I'll try to juggle (with) five apples.
juggler ['dʒʌglə] *n.* □ **malabarista**
juice [dʒuːs] *n.* □ **suco**
a glass of orange juice. ◆ Add lemon juice to the salad.
juicy ['dʒuːsi] *adj.* (**juicier, juiciest**) □ **suculento**
a juicy fruit.
July [dʒuˈlaɪ] *n.* □ **julho**
■ For examples of the use of the months, see **April.**
jumble ['dʒʌmbl] *n.* □ **miscelânia**
a jumble of clothes / papers.
jumbo jet ['dʒʌmbəʊ dʒet] *n.* □ **avião jumbo**
This airplane is a jumbo jet, and can take over 400 passengers.

jump¹ [dʒʌmp] *n.* □ **pulo, salto**
She won a medal in the high jump. ◆ a jump of 7 metres.
jump² *v.* (**jumps, jumping, jumped**)
1 pular
He jumped over the fence. ◆ The cat jumped off the roof.
2 pular
She jumped out of bed.
3 pular
You made me jump!
jump at □ **ter o prazer de aceitar**
She jumped at the chance.
jump to conclusions □ **tirar conclusões apressadas**
Don't jump to conclusions!
jumper ['dʒʌmpə] *n. Brit.* (= sweater) □ **suéter, pulôver**
jump rope ['dʒʌmp roup] *n. Amer.* □ **corda de pular**
■ *Brit.* **skipping-rope**
junction ['dʒʌŋkʃən] *n.* □ **cruzamento, entroncamento**
Turn left at the next junction.
■ *Amer.* **intersection**
June [dʒu:n] *n.* □ **junho**
■ For examples of the use of the months, see **April**.
jungle ['dʒʌngl] *n.* □ **selva**
a journey in the jungles of South America.
junior ['dʒu:niə] *adj., n.*
1 mais novo, mais jovem
He is my junior by two years.
2 Júnior
David Topaz, Junior.
3 subalterno, júnior
a junior officer.
■ antônimo: **senior**
junior high (school) ['dʒu:niə 'hai (sku:l)] *n. Amer.* □ **escola de ensino fundamental**
junior school ['dʒu:niə 'sku:l] *n. Brit.* (= primary school) □ **escola de ensino fundamental**
junk [dʒʌŋk] *n.* □ **coisas velhas**
Throw away all the junk in the cupboard.
junk food [dʒʌŋk fu:d] *n.* □ **junk food, comida pronta de baixo valor nutricional**
junk food like hamburgers, chips and sweets.
jury ['dʒuəri] *n.* (*pl.* **juries**) □ **júri, corpo de jurados**
The jury found her not guilty. (= innocent).
just¹ [dʒʌst] *adj.* □ **justo**
a just decision / punishment.
■ antônimo: **unjust**
just² *adv.*

1 acabar de
She just went out. *Amer.*
She has just gone out.
2 (= exactly) **exatamente**
That's just what I need.
3 (= only) **só**
I just want to see him. ◆ It's just a joke.
4 simplesmente
I just don't know what to do!
5 só
I only just passed the test.
just a minute / moment □ **só um minuto/momento**
Just a minute – I forgot to lock the door.
just as
1 exatamente
My computer is just as good as yours.
2 assim que, quando
She telephoned just I came in.
just now
1 no momento
She isn't here just now.
2 agora há pouco
I saw him just now.
justice ['dʒʌstis] *n.*
1 justiça
We demand justice!
■ antônimo: **injustice**
2 Justiça
to bring criminals to justice. ◆ a court of justice.
3 juiz, juíza
Justice Jones.
justification [ˌdʒʌstifi'keiʃən] *n.* □ **justificativa**
There is no justification for raising prices.
justified ['dʒʌstifaid] *adj.* □ **justificado**
His criticism is justified.
■ antônimo: **unjustified**
justify ['dʒʌstifai] *v.* (**justifies, justifying, justified**) □ **justificar**
I'm not trying to justify his actions.
justify yourself □ **justificar-se**
He tried to justify himself.
justly ['dʒʌstli] *adv.* □ **justamente, com justiça**
to act justly. ◆ to deal justly with those who break the law.
juvenile delinquent ['dʒu:vənail di'linkwənt] *n.* (= young criminal) □ **delinquente juvenil**
special lawcourts for juvenile delinquents

Kk

K [kei] (= 1,000) □ **mil**
  The house cost us $90K.
kangaroo [kaŋgəˈruː] *n.* □ **canguru**
karate [kəˈrɑːtə] *n.* □ **caratê**
  In karate you fight with your hands and feet.
keen [kiːn] *adj.*
  1 (= eager) **ávido**
  He is a keen tennis player. ◆ She is keen to succeed.
  2 penetrante
  keen eyesight.
  be keen on
  1 gostar muito de
  She is keen on pop music. ◆ He is keen on her.
  2 sentir muita vontade de
  She is keen on travelling abroad.
keep [kiːp] *v.* (**keeps, keeping, kept**)
  1 guardar
  Where do you keep your medicines? ◆ 'Keep the change!', he said to the taxi driver
  2 continuar
  Keep walking! ◆ She kept asking questions about you. ◆ He keeps forgetting my name.
  3 manter
  Keep the room locked. ◆ This will keep you warm.
  4 ficar
  Keep calm! ◆ Keep still! (= Don't move!)
  5 deixar
  Don't keep her waiting.
  6 guardar, manter
  to keep a secret. ◆ He kept his promise.
  7 guardar
  I'll keep a place for you.
  8 deter
  What kept you?
  9 criar
  They keep hens.
  keep away from □ **manter-se longe de**
  Keep away from the fire!
  keep someone from □ **impedir**
  His illness kept him from going abroad.
  keep something down □ **manter**
  Keep your head down! ◆ Keep your voice down! (= Speak more quietly!)
  keep something from someone □ **esconder, reter**
  We can't keep this information from him.
  keep off □ **manter-se longe de**
  Keep off the grass!
  keep on [doing] □ **continuar**
  I told him to stop but he kept on running.
  keep out □ **manter distância**
  The sign said, 'Danger. Keep out!'.
  keep... out □ **manter... distante**
  They built a fence to keep the wolves out.
  keep up with you □ **acompanhar-lhe**
  Don't walk so fast! The children can't keep up with you.
keeper [ˈkiːpə] *n.*
  1 mantenedor, guardião, guarda
  a zoo keeper.
  2 (= goalkeeper) **goleiro**
kennel [kenl] *n.* □ **canil, casa de cachorro**
kept [kept] *v.* (Ver **keep**).
kerb [kɜːb] *n. Brit.,* **curb** *Amer.* □ **guia, meio-fio, sarjeta**
kerosene [ˈkerəsiːn] *n. Amer.* □ **querosene**
  We use kerosene to heat the house.
  ■ *Brit.* **paraffin**
ketchup [ˈketʃəp] *n.* □ **ketchup**
kettle [ˈketl] *n.* □ **chaleira**
  Put the kettle on! (= Boil water in the kettle.)
key[1] [kiː] *n.*
  1 chave
  Where are my car keys? ◆ This is the key to the safe.
  2 tecla
  to press a key on a computer keyboard. ◆ piano keys.
  3 legenda (de gráficos, mapas, tabelas etc.)
  There is a key at the back of the book.
key[2] *v.* (**keys, keying, keyed**)
  key in □ **teclar**
  Key in the name of the file.
keyboard[1] [ˈkiːbɔːd] *n.* □ **teclado**
  He typed the letters GCE on the keyboard.
keyboard[2] *v.* (= **key in**)
keyhole [ˈkiːhoul] *n.* □ **fechadura**
  to look through the keyhole.
kg *abbr.* = **kilogram / kilogramme(s)** □ **kg**
  The box weighs 25 kg.
khaki [ˈkɑːki] *adj., n.* □ **cáqui**
  Soldiers wear khaki uniforms.
kick[1] [kik] *n.*
  1 chute
  He gave the ball a kick. ◆ a karate kick.
  2 curtir, divertir-se
  She gets a kick out of surfing.
kick[2] *v.* (**kicks, kicking, kicked**) □ **chutar**
  to kick the ball. ◆ He kicked me in the leg.
kick someone out □ **expulsar**
  They kicked him out of the disco.
kick-off [ˈkikˈɔːf] *n.* □ **pontapé inicial**
  The kick-off is at 4:30.
kid[1] [kid] *n.*
  1 criança
  He is coming with his wife and kids. ◆ The kids are playing in the street. ◆ my kid sister / brother (= my younger sister / brother).
  2 cabrito
  A kid is a young goat.
kid[2] *v.* (**kids, kidding, kidded**)
  1 (= joke) **brincar**
  I was only kidding. I didn't really mean it. ◆ I'm not kidding. (= I'm serious.)
  2 pregar peças
  You're kidding (me)!
kidnap [ˈkidnap] *v.* (**kidnaps, kidnapping, kidnapped**) □ **sequestrar**
  The child was kidnapped by two men.
  ■ Compare with **hijack**.
kidnapper [ˈkidnapə] *n.* □ **sequestrador**
  The kidnappers wanted a ransom of a million dollars.
kidnapping [ˈkidnapiŋ] *n.* □ **sequestro**
kidney [ˈkidni] *n.* □ **rim**
kill [kil] *v.* (**kills, killing, killed**) □ **matar**

He killed his victims with a knife. ♦ They were killed in an accident.
kill yourself □ **matar-se**
She killed herself.
killer ['kɪlə] *n.* □ **matador, assassino**
The police found the killer.
killing ['kɪlɪŋ] *n.* □ **assassinato**
a series of killings.
kilo ['ki:lou] *n.* (= kilogram[me]) □ **quilo**
two kilos of rice.
■ abreviação: **kg**
kilometer ['kɪləmitə] *n. Amer.*, **kilometre** *Brit.* □ **quilômetro**
The airport is 5 km (= kilometers) from here.
■ abreviação: **km**
kilowatt ['kɪləwot] *n.* (= 1000 watt) □ **quilowatt**
A kilowatt is a measure of electric power.
■ abreviação **kw**
kilt [kɪlt] *n.* □ **saia escocesa**
kind¹ [kaind] *adj.* □ **gentil**
a kind man. ♦ She was kind to them. ♦ It was kind of you to help them.
■ antônimo: **unkind**
kind² *n.* (= sort, type) □ **tipo**
different kinds of pens. ♦ all kinds of people. ♦ What kind of computer is this?
a kind of □ **uma espécie de/um tipo de**
A hut is a kind of house.
kind of (= sort of) □ **meio, mais ou menos**
He was kind of worried. ♦ Did he give you permission? – Kind of.
kindergarten [ɪndəga:tn] *n.* □ **jardim de infância**
kind-hearted [,kaind'ha:tid] *adj.* □ **generoso, de bom coração**
a kind-hearted person.
kindly¹ ['kaindli] *adv.*
1 gentilmente
He treated them kindly.
■ antônimo: **unkindly**
2 por gentileza, fazer o favor de
Would you kindly wait outside?
kindly² *adj.* □ **gentil**
a kindly old woman.
kindness ['kaindnis] *n.* □ **gentileza**
to thank them for their kindness.
king [kɪŋ] *n.* □ **rei**
He became king when he was 17.
kingdom ['kɪŋdəm] *n.* □ **reino**
The Queen ruled over a small kingdom. ♦ the United Kingdom (= England, Wales, Scotland and Northern Ireland).
kiosk ['ki:osk] *n.*
1 quiosque
He bought a cold drink at the kiosk.
2 (= telephone kiosk) **orelhão, cabine telefônica**
kiss¹ [kɪs] *n.* □ **beijo**
Give me a kiss!
kiss² *v.* (**kisses, kissing, kissed**) □ **beijar**
He kissed me on the cheek. ♦ They kissed and then said 'Good night'.
kit [kɪt] *n.*
1 kit
a first-aid kit (bandages, plasters, etc.). ♦ tennis kit (tennis clothes and racket)

2 kit
a model airplane kit.
kitchen ['kɪtʃin] *n.* □ **cozinha**
He went into the kitchen to cook dinner. ♦ a kitchen cupboard.
kite [kait] *n.* □ **pipa**
They enjoy flying kites.
kitten ['kɪtn] *n.* □ **gatinho, filhote de gato**
My cat had four kittens yesterday.
km *abbr.* (= **kilometer**) □ **km**
I live 5 km from the airport.
knead [ni:d] *v.* (**kneads, kneading, kneaded**) □ **amassar**
to knead dough.
knee [ni:] *n.* □ **joelho**
I fell and hurt my knee.
kneel [ni:l] *v.* (**kneels, kneeling, kneeled or knelt**) □ **ajoelhar-se**
He knelt (down) to look for the needle.
knew [nju:] *v.* (Ver **know¹**).
knickers ['nɪkəz] *n. Brit.* □ **calcinha**
a pair of knickers.
■ *Amer.* **panties**
knife [naif] *n.* (*pl.* **knives**) □ **faca**
Cut it with a sharp knife.
knight [nait] *n.*
1 cavaleiro
The knight killed the dragon.
2 cavaleiro
Knights add the title 'Sir' to their names.
knit [nɪt] *v.* (**knits, knitting, knitted**) □ **tricotar**
to knit a sweater (from wool).
knitting ['nɪtɪŋ] *n.* □ **tricô**
knitting-needle ['nɪtɪŋni:dl] *n.* □ **agulha de tricô**
knives [naivz] *n.* (*pl.* **knife**) □ **facas**
knob [nob] *n.*
1 maçaneta
He turned the knob, but the door was locked.
2 botão
Turn down the volume with the knob on the left.
knock¹ [nok] *n.* □ **golpe, batida**
He got a knock on the head. ♦ There was a knock on the door.
knock² *v.* (**knocks, knocking, knocked**)
1 bater
He knocked on / at the door.
2 derrubar
She knocked the book off the shelf.
3 bater
I knocked my head on the car door.
knock someone down □ **derrubar a golpes**
He knocked me down with one punch. ♦ She was knocked down by a bus.
knock something down □ **demolir, derrubar**
They knocked down the old houses here.
knock someone out □ **nocautear**
He knocked the other boxer out after 2 minutes.
knock something over □ **derrubar**
Be careful not to knock over the vase.
knot¹ [not] *n.* □ **nó**
to tie a knot in a rope. ♦ Try to undo / untie this knot.
knot² *v.* (**knots, knotting, knotted**) □ **dar nó, amarrar**
He knotted two ropes together.

know¹ [nou] *v.* (**knows, knew, known**)
1 saber
Who knows the answer? ♦ You don't know all the facts. ♦ Does she know where he is?
2 conhecer
Do you know him? ♦ I know the place.
[no be + ing]. Do *not* say 'I am knowing this', only 'I know this'.
know how to do something ◻ **saber como fazer algo**
Do you know how to drive? (= Can you drive?)
get to know someone ◻ **conhecer alguém**
I'd like to get to know them better.
let someone know ◻ **informar alguém**
Let me know if you decide to go.
know² *n.*
in the know ◻ **informado**
People in the know say that will be a war soon.

know-how ['nouhau] *n.* ◻ **know-how, conhecimento**
Does that company have the know-how to make airplanes? ♦ I have the know-how to do the job.
knowledge ['nolidʒ] *n.*
1 conhecimento
She has a good knowledge of mathematics.
2 conhecimento
They did it without my knowledge.
known [noun] *v.* (Ver **know**).
knuckle [nʌkl] *n.* ◻ **junta, articulação dos dedos**
Koran [koˈrɑːn] *n.* ◻ **o Alcorão**
The Koran is the holy book of the Muslims.
kosher [ˈkouʃə] *adj.* ◻ **kosher**
kph *abbr.* (mesmo que **kilometers per hour**) ◻ **km/h**
The speed limit here is 90 kph. ♦ I was driving at 50 kilometers per hour.

LI

l. *abbr.*
 1 (= line) (*pl.* **ll.**) **l.**
 page 50, ll. 25-32
 2 (= liter / litre(s)) **l**
 3 (L = 50) **L**
 CL (= 150).
 4 (L = large size clothes) **G**

lab [lab] *n.* (= laboratory) □ **laboratório**
 a science lab.

label¹ ['leibl] *n.* □ **etiqueta, rótulo**
 The label on the shirt says 'Made in Hong Kong'. ◆ The label on the bottle says 'Poison'. ◆ to put labels (with your name and address) on the suitcases.

label² *v.* (*Brit.* **labels, labelling, labelled**; *Amer.* **labeling, labeled**) □ **etiquetar, rotular**
 to label the luggage with your name and address.

labor ['leibə] *n. Amer.*, **labour** *Brit.*
 1 trabalho
 manual labor (= work that you do with your hands).
 2 mão de obra
 skilled labor.

laboratory [lə'borətəri] *n.* (*pl.* **laboratories**) □ **laboratório**
 a physics / language laboratory. ◆ to do experiments in the laboratory.
 ■ abreviação: **lab**

laborer ['leibərə] *n. Amer.*, **labourer** *Brit.* □ **trabalhador, operário**
 a farm laborer.

lace [leis] *n.*
 1 renda
 lace curtains.
 2 cadarço
 shoe-laces.

lack¹ [lak] *n.* □ **escassez, falta**
 There is a lack of good secretaries. ◆ His lack of confidence is a big problem.

lack² *v.* (**lacks, lacking, lacked**) □ **carecer**
 She lacks experience.

lacking ['lakiŋ] *adj.* □ **carente de**
 Money is lacking for research. ◆ He is not lacking in courage.

lad [lad] *n. Brit.* □ **cara**
 He's a nice lad.
 ■ *Amer.* **guy**

ladder ['ladə] *n.* □ **escada**
 She climbed the ladder to pick some apples. ◆ Put the ladder against the wall.
 ■ Ver **stepladder**.

Ladies ['leidi:z] *n. Brit.* □ **banheiro feminino**
 Is there a Ladies on this floor?
 ■ *Amer.* **ladies' room**

lady ['leidi] *n.* (*pl.* **ladies**) □ **senhora, relativo a mulher, feminino**
 an old lady. ◆ ladies' fashions.

lag [lag] *v.* (**lags, lagging, lagged**) □ **ficar para trás, ir vagarosamente**
 He lagged behind (the others).

laid [leid] *v.* (Ver **lay²**).

lain [lein] *v.* (Ver **lie³**).

lake [leik] *n.* □ **lago**
 They went for a swim in the lake.

lamb [lam] *n.* □ **carneiro**
 lamb's wool.

lame [leim] *adj.* □ **manco**
 a lame horse.
 ■ Ver **limp¹,²**.

lamp [lamp] *n.*
 1 abajur
 a table lamp.
 ■ **light bulb** □ **lâmpada**
 2 farol, lâmpada, lanterna
 a bicycle lamp. ◆ a street lamp.
 ■ *Amer.* **flashlight**
 ■ *Brit.* **torch**

lamp-post ['lampəust] *n.* □ **poste de luz**

lampshade ['lampʃeid] *n.* □ **abajur, quebra-luz**

land¹ [land] *n.*
 1 terra
 to travel by land. ◆ After ten days at sea, we reached land.
 2 terras
 He doesn't want to sell his land.
 3 (= soil) **solo**
 fertile land.
 4 (= country) **terra**
 They live in a foreign land.

land² *v.* (**lands, landing, landed**)
 1 pousar, aterrissar
 The plane landed safely (at the airport). ◆ We landed in New York at 5:30.
 ■ Ver **take off**.
 2 pousar, aterrissar
 The pilot landed the helicopter safely.

landing ['landiŋ] *n.*
 1 pouso, aterrissagem
 The plane made an emergency landing.
 ■ antônimo: **take-off**
 2 patamar
 He climbed the stairs and stopped on the landing.

landlady ['landleidi] *n.* (*pl.* **landladies**)
 1 senhoria, proprietária
 The landlady wants me to pay the rent tomorrow.
 2 dona
 The landlady brought food and drink to their table.

landlord ['landlo:d] *n.*
 1 senhorio, proprietário
 The landlord raised the rent.
 2 dono
 The landlord said we could stay for one night only.

landscape ['landskeip] *n.* □ **paisagem**
 a beautiful mountainous landscape.
 ■ Ver **view**.

lane [lein] *n.*
 1 pista
 a motorway with four lanes
 2 estrada
 narrow country lanes
 3 caminho
 A lane is a narrow street between buildings.
 4 raia
 The American swimmer is in lane 3.

language ['laŋgwidʒ] *n.* □ **língua, idioma**
to learn a foreign language.
- Ver **mother tongue**.

lap [lap] *n.*
1 colo
The child sat on his mother's lap.
2 volta
The British runner was leading in the last lap.

laptop ['laptop] *n.* □ **laptop**
Business people often take them their laptops with them on their travels.
- Ver **desktop computer; palmtop**.

large [la:dʒ] *adj.* □ **grande**
a large (= big) house • a large (= big) family. • a dress in a large size. • a large amount of money. • a large number of people.
- antônimo: **small**
- Ver **big; great**.

largely ['la:dʒli] *adv.* □ **em grande medida**
He is largely responsible for the failure.

laser ['leizə] *n.* □ **laser, a laser**
Doctors use lasers in some operations. • a laser printer.

last¹ [last] *adj.*
1 último
the last name on the list. • This is your last chance. • The last bus leaves at midnight.
2 (= latest) **último, mais recente**
Your last book is very good.
3 passado, anterior
I saw her last week / month. • It rained last night.
the last time □ **a última vez**
The last time I saw him, he was ill. • That was the last time I went there.

last² *adv.*
1 último
I finished last in the race.
2 última vez
I last saw her two months ago. • When did you last see him?
last but not least □ **por último, mas não menos importante**
I would like to thank my uncle Dan, my sister Sharon and, last but not least, Mrs. Brown.

last³ *n., pron.* □ **último**
I was the last to arrive.
at last □ **finalmente**
He scored a goal at last.

last⁴ *v.* (**lasts, lasting, lasted**)
1 durar
The meeting lasted two hours. • The exam lasts three hours.
2 durar
These flowers won't last long.
3 durar
The water lasted us two days.

lastly ['la:stli] *adv.* □ **por último, finalmente**
Lastly, I would like to thank you all for your help.

last name *n.* □ **sobrenome**
Write down your first and last name.
- Also possible to say **family name** or **surname**.

late¹ [leit] *adj.*
1 tarde
It's late. Let's close the shop. • It's too late to do anything about it.
2 atrasado, tarde
You're late! You can't go in. • The train was 10 minutes late. • Hurry, it's getting late.
3 passado
in late summer. • in the late sixties.
- antônimo: **early**
4 falecido
her late husband.
- Ver **later; latest**.

late² *adv.* □ **até tarde, tarde**
I am working late tonight. • The airplane arrived late at night.

latecomer ['leitkʌmə] *n.* □ **retardatário**
We'll have to wait for the latecomers.

lately ['leitli] *adv.* (= recently) □ **ultimamente**
Have you been here lately? • She hasn't visited us lately.

later ['leitə] *adv.* □ **posteriormente, mais tarde, depois**
Later, we met at my office. • She sent it back two days later.
later (on) □ **mais tarde**
We'll talk later (on).
no later than □ **até**
The telephone bill must be paid no later than 22 June.
see you (later) □ **até mais (tarde)**
See you later at school!

latest ['leitist] *adj.* □ **último, mais recente**
the latest fashion. • His latest book is a bestseller.
at the latest □ **no mais tardar**
We'll be there at 8 at the latest.

latter¹ ['latə] *adj.* □ **segundo**
in the latter half of the century.

latter² *n., pron.* □ **segundo, último (de dois)**
Both plan A and plan B are good, but the latter will cost more (than the former).

laugh¹ [la:f] *v.* (**laughs, laughing, laughed**) □ **rir**
They laughed at the joke. • They laughed at him. • I couldn't stop laughing.
make someone laugh □ **fazer alguém rir**
He makes me laugh. • The joke made me laugh.

laugh² *n.* □ **risada**
'Stop it!', he said with a laugh.
for a laugh □ **só pra se divertir**
They did it for a laugh.

laughter ['la:ftə] *n.* □ **risadas**
They heard laughter in the other room.

launch [lo:ntʃ] *v.* (**launches, launching, launched**)
1 lançar
to launch a missile / satellite.
2 lançar
The ship was launched only last month.

launderette [lo:n'dret] *n.*, **laundrette** □ **lavanderia automática**

laundromat ['lo:ndrə'mat] *n. Amer.* □ **lavanderia automática**

laundry ['lo:ndri] *n.* (*pl.* **laundries**)
1 lavanderia
to take the dirty clothes to the laundry.
2 lavar roupa
to do (= wash) the laundry.

lava ['la:və] *n.* **lava**
Lava came out of the volcano.

lavatory ['la:vətəri] *n.* (*pl.* **lavatories**) (= toilet) □ **banheiro, toalete**
Where's the lavatory?
- *Amer.* **bathroom; washroom**

law [lo:] *n.*
1 lei
There's a law against it. ◆ Stealing is against the law.
2 direito
I'm studying law (at university).
break the law □ **infringir a lei**
They sent him to prison because he broke the law.

lawcourt ['lo:ko:t] *n.* (mesmo que **court of law**) □ **tribunal**

lawful ['lo:ful] *adj.* □ **por direito, legal, lícito**
the lawful owner of the house. ◆ her lawful husband.
- antônimo: **unlawful**
- Ver **legal**.

lawn [lo:n] *n.* □ **grama; gramado**
to mow the lawn (= to cut the grass). ◆ to sit on the lawn.

lawnmower ['lo:nməuə] *n.* □ **cortador de grama**

lawyer ['lo:jə] *n.* □ **advogado**
to consult a lawyer. ◆ The accused hired a good lawyer.
- *Amer.* **attorney**

lay¹ [lei] *v.* (Ver **lie³**).
He lay on the bed.

lay² *v.* (**lays, laying, laid**)
1 colocar, pôr
He laid the parcel on the desk. ◆ She laid her hand on my shoulder.
2 pôr, botar
Birds, fish and insects lay eggs.
3 pôr, arrumar
to lay the table (= to set the table).

layer ['leiə] *n.* □ **camada, demão**
a thin layer of dust. ◆ another layer of paint.

lazily ['leizili] *adv.* □ **preguiçosamente, vagarosamente**
He got up lazily.

laziness ['leizinis] *n.* □ **preguiça**

lazy ['leizi] *adj.* (**lazier, laziest**) □ **preguiçoso**
He is the laziest pupil in the class. ◆ She is too lazy to write us a letter.

lb *abbr.* (= pound(s)), **lb.** □ **libra**
It weighs 7 lb (= pounds).

lead¹ [led] *n.*
1 chumbo
Lead is a heavy metal.
2 ponta, grafite
The lead may break if you press on the pencil.

lead² [li:d] *n.* □ **vantagem, dianteira**
We have a lead over all our competitors.
be in the lead □ **estar na liderança**
The Australian runner was in the lead from the beginning.

lead³ [li:d] *n.*
1 pista
The police have a lead on the murder.
2 (= leash) **coleira**
to keep the dog on a lead.

lead⁴ [li:d] *v.* (**leads, leading, led**)
1 levar, conduzir
He led us into the cave.
2 levar
Where does this path lead to?
3 liderar
Our team is leading 2-1.
4 levar
Even one mistake may lead to failure.
5 liderar
He is the right man to lead the party.
6 liderar
to lead a discussion.

leader ['li:də] *n.*
1 líder
The party needs a strong leader.
2 líder
Our company is a leader in the field of computers.

leadership ['li:dəʃip] *n.*
1 liderança
The new leadership will make changes.
2 liderança
We need someone with the necessary skills of leadership.

leading ['li:diŋ] *adj.*
1 primeiro, líder
the leading company in laser technology.
2 principal
a leading scientist / writer.

leaf [li:f] *n.* (*pl.* **leaves**) □ **folha**
In autumn, a lot of leaves fall from the trees.

leaflet ['li:flit] *n.* □ **folheto**
advertising leaflets. ◆ a leaflet about the new bus lines.

league [li:g] *n.* □ **liga**
the football league.

leak¹ [li:k] *n.* □ **vazamento**
There's a leak in the roof. ◆ a gas leak.

leak² *v.* (**leaks, leaking, leaked**)
1 vazar
Oil is leaking from the engine.
2 vazar
The boat is leaking. ◆ The roof is leaking.
- Compare with **drip**:
The tap is dripping.
3 vazar
to leak secret information.

lean¹ [li:n] *adj.*
1 esguio
a tall, lean man.
- Ver **thin**.
2 magro
lean meat.

lean² *v.* (**leans, leaning, leaned or leant**)
1 apoiar-se, debruçar-se
Lean on me. ◆ She was leaning against the tree. ◆ Don't lean out of the window!
2 apoiar
I leaned the ladder against the wall.

leap¹ [li:p] *n.* □ **salto**

leap² *v.* (**leaps, leaping, leaped or leapt**) □ **saltar**
The cat leapt over the fence.

leap year ['li:p ˌjiə] *n.* □ **ano bissexto**

learn [lə:n] *v.* (**learns, learning, learned or learnt**)
1 aprender, decorar
I'm learning to drive. ◆ She learnt the poem by heart. ◆ He learnt how to open it.
- Compare **study**:
(at a certain school) study music / law (etc.). at university.
study for an exam.

2 saber
I learnt about it from the newspaper.
learn your lesson □ **aprender a lição**
He won't do it again. He learnt his lesson.
learned ['lə:nid] *adj.* □ **culto**
a learned professor.
learner ['lə:nə] *n.* □ **iniciante, aprendiz**
a grammar book for learners of English. ◆ a learner driver.
learning ['lə:niŋ] *n.*
1 erudição, saber
a man of great learning.
2 aprendizado
The book makes learning easier.
leash [li:ʃ] *n. Amer.* □ **coleira**
Keep the dog on a leash.
■ *Brit.* **lead**
least[1] [li:st] *pron., adj.*
1 a menor quantidade
I have a little money, he has less, and she has the least.
2 menor
That's the least of my problems.
least[2] *adv.* □ **menos**
I bought the least expensive computer.
at least
1 pelo menos, no mínimo
There were at least 100 people outside.
2 pelo menos
At least you learned something from your mistake.
3 pelo menos
I hit the target. At least, I think I did.
not in the least (= not at all) □ **nem de longe, de maneira nenhuma**
Are you tired? – Not in the least.
leather ['leðə] *n.* □ **couro**
The bag is made of leather. ◆ a leather jacket.
■ Ver **skin**.
leave[1] [li:v] *n.* □ **licença**
When you are ill you can take sick leave. ◆ The soldiers are on leave.
■ Ver **holiday**.
leave[2] *v.* (**leaves, leaving, left**)
1 sair, partir
He asked to leave the room. ◆ We are leaving at 10 o'clock. ◆ The plane leaves in an hour.
2 (= quit) **largar, deixar**
She left school at the age of 15. ◆ He left his job a month ago.
3 deixar
Who left the window open? ◆ Don't leave the baby alone.
4 deixar
Leave some cake for your brother! ◆ She left me a note.
5 deixar
He left the keys at the office.
6 deixar
Leave it to me! I'll deal with it.
7 deixar
She left them a fortune.
leave someone alone □ **deixar alguém em paz**
Leave me alone!
leave something alone □ **não mexer em algo**
Leave the camera alone!
leave... behind □ **esquecer / deixar... em algum lugar**

I left my umbrella behind.
leave for □ **ir para**
We have to leave for the airport early.
leave out
1 omitir
You left out a word here. ◆ He left some details out (on purpose).
2 deixar de fora, excluir
They left him out of the game.
leaves [li:vz] *n.* (*plural of* **leaf**) □ **folhas**
lecture[1] ['lektʃə] *n.* (= talk[1]) □ **conferência, palestra, aula**
She gave an interesting lecture on dreams.
lecture[2] *v.* (**lectures, lecturing, lectured**) □ **falar sobre, dar aula de**
He lectures on modern literature.
lecturer [ecturʃərə] *n.* □ **conferencista, palestrante, professor**
led [led] *v.* (Ver **lead**[4]).
ledge [ledʒ] *n.* □ **peitoril**
a window-ledge.
leek [li:k] *n.* □ **alho-poró**
left[1] [left] *v.* (Ver **leave**[2]).
■ **be left over** (Ver **over**[2]).
left[2] *adj., adv., n.* □ **esquerda, esquerdo, à esquerda**
Raise your left hand! ◆ Turn left at the next traffic-lights! ◆ on the left. ◆ Do you support the Left or the Right in politics?
■ antônimo: **right**
left-hand [left'hand] *adj.* □ **esquerdo**
the left-hand side of the road.
left-handed [left'handid] *adj.* □ **canhoto, para canhotos**
He is left-handed. ◆ left-handed scissors.
left luggage office ['left 'lʌgidʒ 'ofis] *n. Brit.* □ **depósito de bagagem**
I put my suitcases in the Left Luggage Office at the station for a few hours.
■ *Amer.* **baggage room**
leg [leg] *n.*
1 perna
He stood on his left leg. ◆ She has long legs.
■ Compare **foot**.
2 perna
A horse has four legs.
3 perna
a chair with three legs (= a 3-legged chair).
legal ['li:gəl] *adj.*
1 legal, lícito
The deal is legal. ◆ Is it legal to drive without insurance?
■ antônimo: **illegal**
2 jurídico
to get legal advice (from a lawyer).
legally ['li:gəli] *adv.* □ **legalmente**
They imported these goods legally. ◆ They are legally married.
legend ['ledʒənd] *n.* □ **lenda**
the legend of King Arthur.
legendary ['ledʒendəri] *adj.* □ **lendário**
legendary heroes.
legible ['ledʒəbl] *adj.* □ **legível**
Your handwriting is very bad – it's hardly legible.
■ antônimo: **illegible**
legitimate [li'dʒitimət] *adj.*

1 legítimo
their legitimate rights.
2 legítimo
his legitimate child.
leisure ['leʒə] *n., adj.* □ **lazer**
They now have more leisure (time). ♦ leisure activities.
leisurely ['leʒəli] *adv., adj.* □ **sem pressa, despreocupadamente**
to work leisurely. ♦ They had a leisurely breakfast.
lemon ['lemən] *n.* □ **limão**
lemon juice. ♦ to put a slice of lemon in your tea.
lemonade [,lemə'neid] *n.* □ **limonada**
lend [lend] *v.* (**lends, lending, lent**) □ **emprestar**
Could you lend me 100 dollars? ♦ She lent him a book for the weekend.
■ Ver **borrow**.
length [leŋθ] *n.*
1 comprimento
The room is five metres in length. ♦ to measure the length, height and width of the table.
■ Ver **long; how long**.
2 tamanho, extensão
the length of a book
3 período
for a short length of time.
lengthen ['leŋθən] *v.* (**lengthens, lengthening, lengthened**) □ **encompridar, alongar**
to lengthen the skirt (= make it longer) ♦ The days lengthened as summer came nearer.
■ antônimo: **shorten**
lengthy ['leŋθi] *adj.* (**lengthier, lengthiest**) □ **comprido, longo**
lengthy discussions. ♦ a lengthy speech.
lens [lenz] *n.* (*pl.* **lenses**) □ **lente**
Lenses are used in glasses, telescopes, etc.
■ Ver **contact lens**.
lent [lent] *v.* (Ver **lend**).
lentil ['lentil] *n.* □ **lentilha**
lentil soup.
leopard ['lepəd] *n.* □ **leopardo**
A leopard has yellow fur with black spots.
less[1] [les] *adj.* (**little, less, least**) □ **menos**
He paid less money for his car. ♦ Next time put in less sugar.
■ Ver **fewer**.
less[2] *adv., pron.* □ **menos, cada vez menos**
This TV is less expensive than that one. ♦ She eats less now. ♦ It's becoming less and less difficult.
less[3] *prep.* □ **menos**
2,000 pounds, less 10% tax
lessen ['lesn] *v.* (**lessens, lessening, lessened**) □ **diminuir**
to lessen the risk. ♦ The pain is lessening.
lesson ['lesn] *n.*
1 aula
The English lesson starts at 10 o'clock. ♦ to take driving lessons.
2 lição
He won't do it again. He learnt his lesson.
■ Ver **moral**[2].
let[1] [let] *v.* (**lets, letting, let**) □ **alugar**
We let our house for a year. ♦ She let the room to her friend.
■ Ver **rent**[2].

let[2] *v.* (**lets, letting, let**) □ **deixar, permitir**
He lets me use his computer. ♦ She didn't let us come in. ♦ Don't let them touch anything!
■ Compare with **allow**:
 He **let** me park there.
 He **allowed** me to park there.
let me... □ **deixe que eu... deixe-me...**
Let me help you with these bags.
let's... (mesmo que **let us**) □ **vamos**
Let's try again! ♦ Let's not fight about it!
let someone down □ **decepcionar**
I relied on him, but he let me down.
let someone go □ **soltar alguém**
Let him go!
let go (of) □ **largar (de)**
Let go of my hand!
let someone in □ **deixar alguém entrar**
Let me in! ♦ Let the dog in.
let someone in on □ **incluir alguém em**
We'll have to let her in on the plans.
let someone know □ **avisar alguém**
Let me know if you change your mind.
let someone off □ **liberar alguém**
The police let him off with a warning.
let someone out □ **deixar alguém sair**
to let the cat out. ♦ Let me out!
letter ['letə] *n.*
1 letra
capital letters (A, B, C, etc.) and small letters (a, b, c, etc.). ♦ the letters of the alphabet.
2 carta
He sent a letter to his uncle. ♦ I got a letter from the company.
letter-box ['letəboks] *n.*
1 caixa de correspondência
There were two letters in the letter-box.
■ *Amer.* **mailbox**
2 caixa de correspondência
The postman collected the post from the letter-box.
lettuce ['letis] *n.* □ **alface**
a lettuce and tomato salad.
level[1] ['levl] *adj.*
1 plano
level ground.
2 uniforme
The painting is not level.
3 raso
a level teaspoon of sugar.
level[2] *n.*
1 nível
an elementary / intermediate level. ♦ an advanced-level student.
2 nível
a high level of unemployment.
3 nível
0 meters above sea level.
level crossing ['levl 'krosiŋ] *n. Brit.* □ **passagem de nível (cruzamento entre uma ferrovia e uma rodovia)**
■ *Amer.* **grade crossing**
lever ['li:və] *n.*
1 alavanca
They used a lever to lift the heavy rock.

2 alavanca
Pull this lever to switch on the electricity.
liable ['laiəbl] *adj.*
  be liable to ☐ **estar sujeito a**
  Everyone is liable to make mistakes.
liar ['laiə] *n.* ☐ **mentiroso**
  He called her a liar.
  ■ Ver **lie¹**; **lie²**.
liberal ['libərəl] *adj.* ☐ **liberal**
  Our school has a liberal policy about discipline.
liberate ['libəreit] *v.* (**liberates, liberating, liberated**) ☐ **libertar**
  The army liberated the city in May 1945. ◆ to liberate them from slavery.
liberation [,libə'reiʃən] *n.* ☐ **libertação**
liberty ['libəti] *n.* ☐ **liberdade**
  They enjoy a great deal of liberty.
  ■ Ver **freedom**.
librarian [lai'breəriən] *n.* ☐ **bibliotecário**
library ['laibrəri] *n.* (*pl.* **libraries**) ☐ **biblioteca**
  I borrowed this book from the library. ◆ a public library.
licence ['laisəns] *n. Brit.*, **license** *Amer.* ☐ **licença, carteira de motorista**
  a driving licence. *Brit.* ◆ a driver's license. *Amer.*
license ['laisəns] *v.* (**licenses, licensing, licensed**) ☐ **dar licença a, autorizar**
  be licensed ☐ **ter licença**
  This shop is not licensed to sell alcohol.
licensed ['laisənst] *adj.* ☐ **credenciado; autorizado**
  a licensed doctor / pilot. ◆ a licensed restaurant.
license plate ['laisəns pleit] *n. Amer.* ☐ **placa de identificação do veículo**
  ■ *Brit.* **number-plate**
lick¹ [lik] *n.* ☐ **lambida**
  Can I have a lick of your ice-cream?
lick² *v.* (**licks, licking, licked**) ☐ **lamber**
  He licked his ice-cream. ◆ She licked the stamp and stuck it on the envelope.
lid [lid] *n.*
  1 tampa
  to take off the lid (from the pot) ◆ Screw the lid on the jar.
  2 (= eyelid) **pálpebra**
lie¹ [lai] *n.* **mentira**
  to tell lies. ◆ That's a lie!
lie² *v.* (**lies, lying, lied**) ☐ **mentir**
  Don't lie to me! ◆ You're lying! ◆ He lied about his age.
lie³ *v.* (**lies, lying, lay, lain**)
  1 deitar-se
  He was lying in bed. ◆ She lay on her back on the grass.
  2 estar situado
  There were dirty clothes lying on the floor.
  lie down ☐ **deitar-se**
  I'm going to lie down for a while.
lieutenant [ləf'tenənt] *n.* ☐ **tenente**
  He is a lieutenant in the British army.
life [laif] *n.*
  1 vida
  There's no life on the moon.
  2 vida
  Life was hard during the war. ◆ She had a happy life.
  3 (*pl.* **lives**) **vida**
  He risked his life to save me. ◆ They risked their lives to save us. ◆ They lost their lives (= They were killed) in the fire. ◆ She saved my life.
  4 (*pl.* **lives**) **vida**
  They lived there all their lives.
  5 (*pl.* **lives**) **vida**
  Six lives were lost in the fire.
  come to life ☐ **ganhar vida, animar-se**
  At night the streets come to life.
  lead a life ☐ **levar uma vida**
  She leads a busy life.
lifebelt ['laifbelt] *n.* (= life preserver) ☐ **cinto salva-vidas**
  The lifebelts saved them from drowning.
lifeboat ['laifbout] *n.* ☐ **bote salva-vidas**
  They escaped from the sinking ship by lifeboat.
lifebuoy ['laifboi] *n.* ☐ **boia de salvamento**
lifeguard ['laifgɑ:d] *n.* ☐ **salva-vidas, guarda-vidas**
  The lifeguard saved me from drowning.
life jacket ['laif,dʒakit] *n.* ☐ **colete salva-vidas**
  Put on your life-jackets.
life preserver ['laif pri,zə:və] *n. Amer.* (= lifebelt) ☐ **cinto salva-vidas**
life sentence ['laif 'sentəns] *n.* ☐ **prisão perpétua**
  He got a life sentence.
lifestyle ['laifstail] *n.* ☐ **estilo de vida**
  He has a healthy lifestyle. ◆ You need to change your lifestyle.
lifetime ['laiftaim] *n.* ☐ **tempo de vida**
  once in a lifetime. ◆ He saw many changes in his lifetime.
lift¹ [lift] *n.*
  1 *Brit.* **elevador**
  You take the lift and I'll use the stairs.
  ■ *Amer.* **elevator**
  2 carona
  Would you like a lift? – Yes, thank you. ◆ David gave me a lift (to the station).
  ■ *Amer.* **ride**
lift² *v.* (**lifts, lifting, lifted**) ☐ **erguer, levantar**
  The box is too heavy. I can't lift it. ◆ to lift weights.
light¹ [lait] *n.*
  1 luz
  the light of the sun / a candle.
  2 (*pl.* **lights**) **luz, luzes**
  Turn / Switch the lights on! ◆ Turn / Switch the lights off! ◆ Suddenly the lights went out.
  3 fogo
  Have you got a light? – No, sorry, I don't smoke.
  4 semáforo, sinal
  Turn left at the next (traffic) lights. ◆ to go through a red light.
  ■ Ver **traffic lights**.
  set light to ☐ **pôr fogo em**
  He set light to the papers.
light² *adj.*
  1 claro
  a light room. ◆ It's still light outside.
  2 claro
  a light-green sweater.
  3 leve
  This box is very heavy, but this one is lighter.
  4 leve
  light rain. ◆ a light meal. ◆ light clothes.
light³ *v.* (**lights, lighting, lit** or **lighted**)

light-bulb / listener

1 acender
to light a match / cigarette. ◆ They lit a fire.
2 acender
The streets were lit with neon lights.
light-bulb ['laitbʌlb] *n*. (= **bulb**) □ **lâmpada**
a 60 watt light-bulb.
lighter ['laitə] *n*. □ **isqueiro**
a cigarette lighter.
lighthouse ['laithaus] *n*. □ **farol**
lighting ['laitiŋ] *n*. □ **iluminação**
street lighting.
lightly ['laitli] *adv*. □ **levemente**
He touched me lightly on the shoulder.
lightning ['laitniŋ] *n*. □ **raio, relâmpago**
thunder and lightning ◆ He was struck by lightning.
like¹ [laik] *v*. (**likes, liked**)
1 gostar
I like him. ◆ I don't like ice-cream. ◆ She didn't like the film. ◆ I like working here.
■ antônimo: **dislike²**
2 querer
Do what you like! ◆ Take as many as you like!
■ [no be + ing]. Do *not* say **am / are** etc. **liking**.
would like □ **gostaria, gostaríamos, gostariam**
Would you like some more tea? ◆ I'd (= I would) like to see it.
like² *prep., conj*.
1 como, feito
She has a watch like mine. ◆ He cried like a baby. ◆ I can't do it like you can.
2 tal como
We saw animals there, like lions, elephants and giraffes.
■ Ver **such as**.
3 como
How can you live in a place like that?
what is... like? □ **Como é...?**
What's the weather like in Italy? ◆ What's she like?
likely ['laikli] *adj*. □ **provável, propenso**
It's very likely that they will agree. ◆ He is likely to change his mind.
■ antônimo: **unlikely**
■ Ver **probable**.
likeness ['laiknis] *n*. □ **semelhança**
There's a strong likeness between the two brothers.
likewise ['laikwaiz] *adv*. (= the same) □ **da mesma forma**
Watch how I do it and then do likewise.
lily ['lili] *n*. (*pl*. **lilies**) □ **lírio**
limb [lim] *n*. □ **membro**
lime [laim] *n*. □ **limão, lima**
limit¹ ['limit] *n*. □ **limite**
There's a limit to what we can do. ◆ There's an age limit for voting.
■ Ver **speed limit**.
limit² *v*. (**limits, limiting, limited**) □ **limitar**
They limited the number of guests to 200. ◆ Please limit your speech to ten minutes.
limited ['limitid] *adj*. □ **limitado**
There's a limited number of tickets.
limp¹ [limp] *n*. □ **coxeadura, manqueira**
He walks with a limp.
limp² *v*. (**limps, limping, limped**) □ **mancar**
He is limping but will continue to play.

line¹ [lain] *n*.
1 linha
to draw a line with a ruler. ◆ a straight line.
2 linha
page 36 line 15. ◆ Please start each paragraph on a new line.
3 (= **row**) **fileira, fila**
a long line of cars. ◆ lines of trees. ◆ to stand in line. *Amer*.
4 linha
The line is busy. ◆ The telephone lines are down because of the storm.
5 varal, linha
to hang the washing on the line. ◆ a fishing-line.
6 linha
the last stop on line No. 4.
7 linha
The train stopped because the line was blocked.
8 ruga
the lines on his forehead.
line² *v*. (**lines, lining, lined**) □ **ladear, enfileirar-se**
They lined the street to welcome the President.
be lined with
1 alinhar
The road was lined with trees.
2 forrar
The jacket is lined with fur.
line up □ **fazer fila**
People lined up to buy tickets.
linen ['linin] *n*. □ **roupa de cama e mesa**
liner ['lainə] *n*. □ **navio**
There were 500 passengers on board the liner. ◆ an airliner.
linger ['liŋgə] *v*. (**lingers, lingering, lingered**) □ **demorar-se**
They lingered in the museum after the tour ended.
lining ['lainiŋ] *n*. □ **forro**
a coat with a fur lining.
link¹ [liŋk] *n*.
1 elo
Add a few more links to this gold chain.
2 elo
There's a strong link between smoking and heart disease.
link² *v*. (**links, linking, linked**) □ **ligar, conectar**
The tunnel links the two countries.
lion ['laiən] *n*. □ **leão**
The lion roared angrily.
lioness ['laiənis] *n*. □ **leoa**
lip [lip] *n*. □ **lábio**
the upper / lower lip.
lipstick ['lipstik] *n*. □ **batom**
She doesn't wear lipstick. ◆ to put on some lipstick.
liquid¹ ['likwid] *n*. □ **líquido**
Boil the liquid and add in the vegetables.
liquid² *adj*. □ **líquido**
liquid food / soap.
list¹ [list] *n*. □ **lista**
a shopping list. ◆ Your name is not on the list.
list² *v*. (**lists, listing, listed**) □ **listar**
List the names in alphabetical order.
listen ['lisn] *v*. (**listens, listening, listened**) □ **ouvir, escutar**
Listen! Can you hear the noise? ◆ Listen carefully to what I have to tell you. ◆ He was listening to the radio.
listener ['lisnə] *n*. □ **ouvinte**

lit [lit] *v.* (Ver **light³**).

liter ['li:tə] *n. Amer.*, **litre** *Brit.* □ **litro**
a liter of milk. ♦ 5 liters (= l.) of gasoline.

literature ['litrətʃə] *n.* □ **literatura**
I'm studying Chinese literature.

litter¹ ['litə] *n.*

1 lixo
After the picnic they collected the litter. ♦ Please don't throw your litter on the grass.
■ **refuse²**, **rubbish**, **garbage**, **trash** mean the same.

2 ninhada
My cat had a litter of six kittens.

litter² *v.* (**litters, littering, littered**) □ **sujar, jogar lixo**
be littered with □ **estar sujo**
The streets were littered with paper.

litter bin ['litəbin] *n. Brit.* □ **lata de lixo**
Throw the litter in the litter bin.
■ *Amer.* **trash basket; trash can**

little¹ ['litl] *adj.*

1 pequeno
little eyes. ♦ a little garden.
■ Ver **small**.

2 pequenino
a little girl. ♦ my little brother.

3 pouco
We have very little money.
■ Ver **less; least**.
a little □ **um pouco**
He needs a little more time. ♦ I speak a little Spanish.
■ Compare:
 He has little money.
 He has a little money.

little² *adv.* □ **pouco**
I ate very little at lunch.
little by little □ **pouco a pouco**
Little by little he learnt how to do it.

little³ *pron.* □ **pouco, um pouco**
I remember very little of what he said. ♦ Give me a little.

live¹ [laiv] *adj.*

1 vivo
There was a live spider in the jar.
■ Ver **alive**.

2 ao vivo
a live broadcast. ♦ a live concert

3 eletrizado
a live wire.

live² [laiv] *adv.* □ **ao vivo**
They will broadcast the game live.

live³ [liv] *v.* (**lives, living, lived**)

1 viver
I don't know how long he will live. ♦ She lived to the age of 89. ♦ You can't live without air.

2 morar
I live in Paris. ♦ She lives at 10 Johnson St. ♦ Where do you live?
live on something

1 viver de
Some animals live on fruit.

2 viver com
He lives on a small salary.
live through □ **passar por**
They lived through a difficult time.

livelihood ['laivlihud] *n.* □ **subsistência, vida**
He earns his livelihood from teaching.

lively ['laivli] *adj.* (**livelier, liveliest**) □ **alegre, animado**
The children are very lively. ♦ a lively conversation.

liver ['livə] *n.* □ **fígado**
Too much alcohol may cause damage to the liver.

lives [laivz] *n. pl. of* **life**

livestock ['laivstok] *n.* □ **rebanho**
They sold their livestock (= sheep, cows, etc.).

living¹ ['liviŋ] *adj.* □ **vivo**
He is the greatest living football player.

living² *n.* □ **viver**
What do you do for a living?
■ Ver **standard of living**.
make a living □ **ganhar a vida**
He makes a living by writing.

living room ['liviŋ rum] *n.* □ **sala de estar**
They are watching TV in the living-room.
■ *Brit.* **sitting room**.

lizard ['lizəd] *n.* □ **lagarto**

load¹ [loud] *n.* □ **carga**
a heavy load.

load² *v.* (**loads, loading, loaded**)

1 colocar, carregar
They loaded the boxes onto the truck. ♦ They finished loading the ship.
■ antônimo: **unload**

2 carregar
to load a gun.

3 carregar
to load a file (onto a computer).

4 carregar
The plane to Istanbul is now loading.

loaded ['loudid] *adj.*

1 cheio
loaded baskets.

2 carregado
The gun is loaded. ♦ a loaded gun.

loaf [louf] *n.* (*pl.* **loaves**) □ **filão**
I bought a loaf of white bread.

loan¹ [loun] *n.* □ **empréstimo**
I asked for a loan of 10,000 dollars.
on loan □ **emprestado**
I got the book on loan from the library.

loan² *v.* (**loans, loaning, loaned**) (= lend) □ **emprestar**
I'll loan you the money. ♦ She loaned me her car for the weekend.

loaves [louvz] *n. pl. of* **loaf**

lobby ['lobi] *n.* (*pl.* **lobbies**) □ **saguão, lobby**
We met in the hotel lobby.

lobster ['lobstə] *n.* □ **lagosta**

local ['loukəl] *adj.* □ **local**
a local newspaper. ♦ a local (telephone) call.

locality [lə'kaləti] *n.* □ **localidade**

locate [lou'keit] *v.* (**locates, locating, located**) □ **localizar**
The police located the missing child. ♦ to locate the place on the map.

be located (= be situated) □ **estar localizado, estar situado**
The factory is located outside the town.

location [lou'keiʃən] *n.* □ **localização**
This is a suitable location for a school. ♦ Find the exact location of the ship.

lock¹ [lok] *n.* □ **fechadura**
I must oil the lock.
■ Ver **padlock**.

lock² *v.* (**locks, locking, locked**)
1 trancar
I forgot to lock the door. ◆ Lock the safe / drawer.
2 trancar, travar
The door locks automatically.
be locked □ **estar trancado**
The door was locked.
lock something away □ **trancar algo em algum lugar**
I must lock away the jewels.
be locked in □ **ficar trancado do lado de dentro**
I'm locked in!
lock someone out □ **trancar alguém do lado de fora**
He locked himself out.
lock up □ **trancar tudo**
Don't forget to lock up when you leave.

locker ['lokə] *n.* □ **armário**
I lost the key to my locker.

locomotive [loukə'moutiv] *n.* □ **locomotiva**

locust ['loukəst] *n.* □ **gafanhoto**

lodge [lodʒ] *v.* (**lodges, lodging, lodged**) □ **hospedar-se**
I'm lodging with a nice family. ◆ I lodged at their house in Washington.
■ Compare **stay**:
to stay at a hotel.
to stay at your friend's house.

lodger ['lodʒə] *n.* □ **hóspede, inquilino**

lodgings ['lodʒiŋs] *n. pl.* □ **cômodo de aluguel**
to stay / live in lodgings.

log [log] *n.* □ **lenha, tora, tronco**
to cut logs for a fire.

loiter (about) ['loitə (ə'baut)] *v.* (**loiters, loitering, loitered**) □ **vadiar**
Some strangers were loitering about outside my house.
■ Ver **hang about / around**.

loitering ['loitəriŋ] *n.* □ **vadiagem**
He was arrested for loitering.

lollipop ['lolipop] *n.* □ **pirulito**
He licked his lollipop.

lolly ['loli] *n. Brit.* (*pl.* **lollies**)
1 (= lollipop) **pirulito**
2 (= ice lolly) **picolé**

loneliness ['lounlinis] *n.* □ **solidão**

lonely ['lounli] *adj.* (**lonelier, loneliest**)
1 sozinho, solitário
to feel lonely.
2 isolado
a lonely village.

lonesome ['lounsəm] *adj. Amer.* □ **solitário**
I'm lonesome in this place.

long¹ [loŋ] *adj.*
1 longo, comprido
a long dress. ◆ Her hair is longer than mine. ◆ This is the longest road in Canada.
■ antônimo: **short**
2 longo
a long film / holiday.
■ antônimo: **short**
3 de comprimento
The fence is 2 km long.
a long time □ **muito tempo**
We waited for a long time.
how long...?
1 Qual o comprimento...?
How long is this road?
2 Qual a duração...?, Quanto tempo tem...?
How long is the film?
3 Por quanto tempo...?
How long will you stay there?
get longer □ **ficar mais longo**
His hair got longer and longer.

long² *adv.* □ **muito tempo, muito mais tempo, pouco tempo**
We couldn't stay (for) long. ◆ You won't have to wait much longer. ◆ It didn't take me long to find it. ◆ Will you be out for long? ◆ How long will it take? – Not long.
as long as
1 enquanto
As long as I'm the boss, I give the orders.
2 desde que
You can take the car as long as you bring it back before eight.
■ Do not confuse with:
My hair is as long as yours.
before long (= soon) □ **em breve**
He will forget this before long.
long after / before □ **muito tempo depois / antes**
She started working here long before her marriage.
long ago □ **há muito tempo**
It happened long ago.
no longer, not any longer □ **não mais**
He doesn't go there any longer. ◆ She no longer lives here

long³ *v.* (**longs, longing, longed**)
1 ansiar
We are longing to see you again.
2 ansiar
How she longed for those days!

long-distance ['loŋ,distəns] *adj., adv.* □ **interurbano**
a long-distance phone call. ◆ to phone long distance.

longing ['loŋiŋ] *n.* □ **desejo, anseio**
a longing for home.

long jump ['loŋ ,dʒʌmp] *n.* □ **salto em distância**
She won a medal in the long-jump.

loo [lu:] *n. Brit.* □ **banheiro**
The bus stopped so that passengers could go to the loo.

look¹ [luk] *n.*
1 olhar, olhada
He gave me an angry look.
2 aparência, visual
The place had a cheerful look.
have a look □ **dar uma olhada**
Can I have a look at the letter?
take a look □ **dar uma olhada**
Take a look at this photograph.
I don't like the look of □ **não gosto da aparência**
I don't like the look of this wound.
looks *n.* □ **aparência, visual**
He's got good looks. (= He's good-looking.)

look² *v.* (**looks, looking, looked**)
1 olhar
Look over there. Can you see the tree? ◆ He looked at m and smiled. ◆ She looked into the mirror. ◆ to look out (o the window.

2 parecer, aparentar
He looks bored / tired.
3 olhar
Did you look under the bed? ◆ Keep looking!
look after □ **cuidar, tomar conta**
Who's looking after the baby? ◆ Dani looks after the shop when I'm not there.
look around □ **olhar ao redor**
Look around you. Can you see anything different in the room?
it looks as if □ **parece que**
It looks as if it's going to rain.
look at
1 olhar
What are you looking at? ◆ She looked at me and smiled.
2 (= examine) **olhar**
Let the doctor look at your eye.
look down on □ **desprezar**
They look down on people from our neighbourhood.
look for □ **procurar**
What are you looking for? ◆ I'm looking for my keys. ◆ We looked for him everywhere.
look forward to □ **aguardar ansiosamente**
I'm looking forward to meeting you next month. ◆ They are looking forward to the trip to India.
look into □ **examinar, investigar**
I looked into your complaint.
look like □ **parecer-se com, ser como**
She looks like (= resembles) her mother. ◆ It looks like a ball. ◆ What does he look like? – He's tall and good-looking.
look out! (= be careful) □ **cuidado!**
Look out! There's a hole in the road!
look over □ **dar uma olhada**
Look over the report and tell me what you think.
look round
1 olhar ao redor
He looked round and saw someone following him.
2 (= look around) **olhar em volta**
She looked round to find a place to sit.
look through □ **olhar através**
to look through the telescope.
look up □ **levantar os olhos**
The child looked up at me.
look something up □ **procurar**
to look up a word in a dictionary.
lookout ['lukaut] *n.*
1 vigia
One boy acted as a lookout to warn us if the teacher was coming. ◆ to be on the lookout.
2 (mesmo que **look-out point**) □ **mirante**
a lovely view from the look-out point at the top of the mountain.
loop [lu:p] *n.* □ **laço**
to make a loop in the rope.
loose [lu:s] *adj.*
1 solto
The dog is loose.
2 solto
One of the screws is loose. ◆ The rope was loose. ◆ a loose button.
3 largo, folgado
She wore a loose dress.

get loose □ **soltar-se**
The animal got loose and ran away.
loosely ['lu:sli] *adv.* □ **frouxamente**
to tie the rope loosely.
loosen ['lu:sn] *v.* (**loosens, loosening, loosened**) □ **afrouxar**
He loosened his tie. ◆ to loosen the screws.
■ antônimo: **tighten**
lord [lo:d] *n.* □ **lorde**
the Lord (= God) □ **o Senhor**
lorry ['lori] *n. Brit.* (*pl.* **lorries**) □ **caminhão**
They loaded the lorry with furniture. ◆ a lorry driver.
■ *Amer.* **truck**
lose [lu:z] *v.* (**loses, losing, lost**)
1 perder
I lost my wallet.
2 perder
They lost the game.
■ antônimo: **win**
3 perder
We lost a lot of money last year.
4 perder
I'm losing my patience! ◆ They lost interest in the game.
5 perder
She lost consciousness. ◆ I lost my appetite. ◆ He lost his balance and fell ◆ She lost 5 kilos.
lose your life □ **morrer**
Hundreds lost their lives in the floods.
lose your way □ **perder-se**
They lost their way in the forest.
loser [ose:zə] *n.* □ **perdedor, fracassado**
■ antônimo: **winner**
loss [los] *n.*
1 perda
I reported the loss of my ID card.
2 baixa
The enemy suffered heavy losses.
3 prejuízo
The company had a loss of $30 million. ◆ Their losses came to 5 million.
at a loss □ **abaixo do preço**
He sold the car at a loss.
be at a loss □ **ficar sem palavras, estar perplexo**
I'm at a loss what to say.
lost¹ [lost] *v.* (Ver **lose**).
lost² *adj.* □ **perdido**
the lost treasure.
be lost
1 estar perdido
The suitcase is lost.
2 estar perdido
I think we're lost. This is not the way back.
3 estar perdido
I'm lost without your support.
get lost
1 perder-se
The documents got lost.
2 perder-se, ficar perdido
He got lost in the forest.
3 (= Get lost!; Go away!; Leave me alone!) **Cai fora!**
lost and found ['lost and 'faund] *Amer.* □ **achados e perdidos**

lot / lump

Let's look for the bags at the lost property (office).
■ *Brit.* **lost property**
lot [lɒt] *n., adv.*
a lot □ **muito**
We talked a lot. ✦ Your computer is a lot better than mine. ✦ I like him a lot.
a lot of; lots of (= much; many) □ **muito, muitos**
He lost a lot of money. ✦ She invited a lot of people. ✦ He bought me lots of presents.
lotion [ˈlouʃən] *n.* □ **loção**
suntan lotion. ✦ body lotion.
lottery [ˈlɒtəri] *n.* □ **loteria**
loud [laud] *adj., adv.* □ **alto**
Turn down the music. It's too loud. ✦ loud voices. ✦ a loud noise. ✦ Could you speak a bit louder?
out loud □ **em voz alta**
Read the letter out loud.
■ antônimo: **silently**
loudly [ˈlaudli] *adv.* □ **alto**
They laughed loudly.
loudspeaker [ˌlaudˈspiːkə] *n.* □ **alto-falante**
lounge [laundʒ] *n.* □ **saguão**
They met in the lounge of the hotel. ✦ The passengers waited in the lounge.
lovable [ˈlʌvəbl] *adj.* □ **adorável**
a lovable child / kitten.
love[1] [lʌv] *n.*
1 amor
their love for their children. ✦ Her love for him was very strong.
■ antônimo: **hate; hatred**
2 amor
Yes, my love.
3 com (muito) amor
Love, Sara. ✦ Lots of love from us all, David.
4 zero (tênis)
The score is 30 – love.
be in love (with) □ **estar apaixonado (por)**
He is in love with her.
fall in love (with) □ **apaixonar-se (por)**
She fell in love with him.
give / send my, her, etc. love (to) □ **mandar lembranças**
Give my love to Edna. ✦ They send their love.
love[2] *v.* (**loves, loved**) □ **amar, adorar**
She loves her husband. ✦ They love their children very much. ✦ I love to play basketball.
■ [no be + ing]. Do *not* say **am / are** etc. **loving**
would love □ **adoraria, adoraríamos, adorariam**
Would you like to join us? – We'd (= We would) love to. ✦ I'd love to go, but I'm busy.
lovely [ˈlʌvli] *adj.* (**lovelier, loveliest**)
1 lindo, adorável
What a lovely dress! ✦ You look lovely!
2 ótimo, adorável
We had a lovely holiday. ✦ a lovely day.
lover [ˈlʌvə] *n.*
1 amante
Her lover is 35 years old.
2 amantes, enamorados
young lovers.
loving [ˈlʌviŋ] *adj.* □ **amoroso**
loving parents.

lovingly [ˈlʌviŋli] *adv.* □ **carinhosamente**
low[1] [lou] *adj.*
1 baixo
a low fence. ✦ a low ceiling.
■ Compare:
a **short** person.
2 baixo
low temperatures. ✦ The lowest price was $2,500.
3 baixo
to speak in a low voice.
■ antônimo: **high**
■ Ver **lower**[1].
low[2] *adv.* □ **baixo**
The plane flew low over the village.
lower[1] [ˈlouə] *adj.*
1 inferior
the lower lip.
■ antônimo: **upper**
■ Ver **bottom**[2].
2 mais baixo
This table is lower than that one. ✦ to buy it at a lower price.
■ antônimo: **higher**
lower[2] *v.* (**lowers, lowering, lowered**)
1 abaixar
Lower your voice.
2 baixar
to lower the flag.
3 baixar, diminuir
He lowered the price. ✦ to lower the temperature.
■ antônimo: **raise**
loyal [ˈlɔiəl] *adj.* □ **leal**
a loyal friend. ✦ She is loyal to her country.
■ Ver **faithful**.
loyalty [ˈlɔiəlti] *n.* □ **lealdade**
She proved her loyalty to us.
luck [lʌk] *n.*
1 sorte
We can do it with a little luck. ✦ It brings good luck.
2 boa sorte
Wish me luck! ✦ I wish you lots of luck with your new job.
good luck! □ **boa sorte!**
be in luck □ **estar com sorte**
You're in luck – this is the last ticket.
luckily [ˈlʌkili] *adv.* □ **felizmente**
Luckily, I had a spare key.
lucky [ˈlʌki] *adj.* (**luckier, luckiest**)
1 afortunado, sortudo
We were lucky (to find you there).
2 de sorte
My lucky number is 5.
■ antônimo: **unlucky**
luggage [ˈlʌgidʒ] *n.* □ **bagagem**
I put a name label on my luggage.
■ *Amer.* **baggage**
■ Ver **left luggage office**.
lukewarm [ˈluːkwɔːm] *adj.* □ **morno, tépido**
lukewarm water.
lullaby [ˈlʌləbai] *n.* (*pl.* **lullabies**) □ **cantiga de ninar**
She sang her child a lullaby.
lump [lʌmp] *n.*
1 torrão
Two lumps (of sugar), please.

2 pelota
There are lumps in the sauce.
3 calombo, galo
The lump on my head hurts.
lunch¹ [lʌntʃ] *n.* □ **almoço**
What did you have for lunch? ♦ We had lunch at a restaurant.
■ Compare:
  lunch = only at midday.
  dinner = the main meal, at midday or in the evening.
lunch² *v.* (**lunches, lunching, lunched**) □ **almoçar**
We lunched at the cafeteria.
lunch-time ['lʌntʃtaim] *n.* □ **hora do almoço**
He's at lunch-time.
lung [lʌŋ] *n.* □ **pulmão**
Smoking can cause damage to the lungs.
luxurious [lʌk'ʃuəriəs] *adj.* □ **luxuoso**
a luxurious hotel.
luxury ['lʌkʃəri] *n.*
1 luxo
a life of luxury.
2 luxo
a luxury car / hotel.
3 luxo
Going abroad every year is a luxury that I cannot afford.
lying ['laiŋ] *v.* (Ver **lie²**; **lie³**).
lyrics ['liriks] *n. pl.* □ **letra (de música)**
I like the tune of that song, but not the lyrics.

Mm

m. *abbr.*, **m**
 1 (= meter / metre) **m**
  the 800m race.
 2 (= million) **milhão**
  $50m.
 3 (= M (1000)) **mil**
  MMM (= 3000)
 4 (= M [medium size clothes]) **M**
ma [ma:] *n.*, *abbr.* (= mother) □ **mãe**
 It's time to go, Ma.
machine [məˈʃiːn] *n.* □ **máquina**
 How do you operate this machine? ◆ a machine for cutting meat ◆ The machine doesn't work.
machine-gun [məˈʃiːngʌn] *n.* □ **metralhadora**
 A machine-gun is an automatic weapon.
machinery [məˈʃiːnəri] *n.*
 1 máquina
  the machinery of a clock.
 2 maquinário
  The machinery in this factory is very old.
mad [mad] *adj.* (**madder, maddest**)
 1 (= mentally ill) **demente, louco**
  The doctor says that she is not mad.
 2 (= crazy) **louco**
  You're mad to go there alone!
 3 (= angry) **bravo**
  She is mad at you.
 be mad about □ **ser louco por**
  He is mad about her. ◆ She is mad about pop music.
 drive someone mad □ **deixar alguém louco**
  The noise is driving me mad.
 go mad □ **ficar louco, enlouquecer**
  He went mad when his daughter died.
madam [ˈmadəm] *n.* □ **senhora, madame**
 Can I help you, madam?
 Dear Madam □ **Prezada senhora**
  When you write a formal letter to a woman you begin with Dear Madam.
 ■ Ver **sir**.
made [meid] *v.* (Ver **make**).
 be made of □ **ser feito de**
  These shoes are made of leather.
 be made from □ **ser feito de**
  Butter is made from milk.
 be made up of □ **ser constituído de**
  The committee is made up of six people. ◆ Water is made up of oxygen and hydrogen.
madly [ˈmadli] *adv.* □ **loucamente**
 He is madly in love with her.
madman [ˈmadmən] *n.* (*pl.* **madmen**) □ **louco, doido**
madness [ˈmadnis] *n.* □ **loucura**
madwoman [ˈmadwumən] *n.* (*pl.* **madwomen**) □ **louca, doida**
magazine [magəˈziːn] *n.* □ **revista**
 a computer magazine. ◆ a woman's magazine.
maggot [ˈmagət] *n.* □ **larva de inseto**
magic¹ [ˈmadʒik] *n.*
 1 magia
  The witch used magic against the princess.
 2 mágica
  Magicians do magic to entertain people.
 3 magia
  The place lost its magic.
 as if by magic, like magic □ **como num passe de mágica, feito mágica**
  As if by magic, the rain suddenly stopped.
magic² *adj.* □ **mágico**
 magic words.
magic wand *n.* □ **varinha mágica**
magical [ˈmadʒikəl] *adj.*
 1 mágica
  magical beauty.
 2 (= magic²) **mágico**
  The witch used her magical powers.
magically [ˈmadʒikəli] *adv.* □ **magicamente**
 He made the rabbit disappear magically.
magician [məˈdʒiʃən] *n.*
 1 mágico
  There was a magician at the party.
 2 mago
  The magician helped the prince to kill the dragon.
magistrate [ˈmadʒistreit] *n.* □ **magistrado**
magnet [ˈmagnit] *n.* □ **ímã**
magnetic [magˈnetik] *adj.* □ **magnético**
magnificent [magˈnifisnt] *adj.* □ **magnífico**
 a magnificent palace. ◆ a magnificent ceremony.
magnify [ˈmagnifai] *v.* (**magnifies, magnifying, magnified**) □ **aumentar, ampliar**
 to magnify an insect under a microscope. ◆ to magnify a picture.
magnifying glass [ˈmagnifaiiŋ glaːs] *n.* □ **lente de aumento**
maid [meid] *n.* □ **empregada doméstica**
 We hired a maid to do the housework.
mail¹ [meil] *n.* □ **correio, correspondência**
 Send the book by mail. ◆ electronic mail. ◆ Is there any mail for me?
 ■ *Brit.* usually **post** (but **electronic mail** and **e-mail** also in British English).
mail² *v.* (**mails, mailing, mailed**) □ **enviar por correio**
 Please mail the check to our new address.
 ■ *Brit.* usually **post**
mailbox [ˈmeilbɔks] *n.* *Amer.*
 1 caixa de correspondência
  There's a letter in the mailbox.
 2 (= postbox) **caixa do correio**
  The mailman collected the letters from the mailbox.
 ■ Ver **letter-box**.
mailman [ˈmeilmən] *n.* (*pl.* **mailmen**) *Amer.* □ **carteiro**
 ■ *Brit.* **postman**
main [mein] *adj.* (= principal)
 1 principal
  What are the main points of the lecture? ◆ That's the main reason for not going.
 2 principal
  the main entrance. ◆ the main street.
main course *n.* □ **prato principal**
 We had fish as the main course.
main road *n.* □ **estrada principal**
mainly [ˈmeinli] *adv.* □ **principalmente**

He refused, mainly because it was late. ✦ The tourists were mainly from France.

maintain [mein'tein] *v.* (**maintains, maintaining, maintained**)
1 manter
to maintain law and order. ✦ He maintained a speed of 50 kph.
2 manter
to maintain a car / building.

maintenance ['meintənəns] *n.* ▫ **manutenção**
The maintenance costs of the car are very high.

maize [meiz] *n. Brit.* ▫ **milho**
■ *Amer.* **corn**
■ Ver **corn on the cob**.

Majesty ['madʒəsti] *n.* (*pl.* **Majesties**) ▫ **majestade**
Her Majesty (the Queen). ✦ Your Majesty.

major[1] ['meidʒə] *adj.* ▫ **principal, importante**
major cities. ✦ a major problem. ✦ the major cause of the disease.
■ antônimo: **minor**

major[2] *n.* ▫ **major**
He is a major in the army.

majority [mə'dʒɔriti] *n.* ▫ **maioria**
The majority of the pupils agreed.
■ antônimo: **minority**

make[1] [meik] *n.* ▫ **marca**
What make is your car? ✦ a TV of Japanese make.

make[2] *v.* (**makes, making, made**)
1 fazer
He is making a cake. ✦ He made her a cup of tea. ✦ They make six cars a day in this factory.
■ Ver **do**.
■ Ver **made**.
2 cometer, fazer
She made a mistake. ✦ They tried not to make a noise. ✦ to make an effort. ✦ to make peace. ✦ We made an agreement.
3 preparar
to make breakfast / tea.
4 fazer
He made me laugh. ✦ They made us wait for two hours.
■ made me laugh (*not* 'made me to laugh').
■ made us wait (*not* 'made us to wait').
5 tornar
to make it more interesting.
6 (= earn) **ganhar**
She makes $2,000 a month.
7 (= estimate) **calcular, estimar**
I make the distance about 8 km. ✦ What do you make the time?
8 ser, dar
Four and six make ten (4+6=10).
9 ser
He'll make a good doctor.
10 fazer
They made him chairman.
11 tomar, dar, fazer
to make a decision (= to decide). ✦ to make a guess (= to guess). ✦ to make a call (= to telephone).

make do with ▫ **virar-se, contentar-se**
You'll have to make do with a small TV set.

make something into ▫ **transformar algo em**
They made the prison into a school.

make it ▫ **ir, chegar**
I'm afraid I can't make it to the meeting.

make of ▫ **achar**
What do you make of this letter? ✦ I couldn't make much of his speech.

be made of (Ver **made**).

make out
1 decifrar
I couldn't make out the address on the envelope.
2 entender
I can't make out why they left it here.

make up
1 maquiar-se
How long does it take you to make up?
2 inventar, bolar
to make up an excuse.
3 fazer as pazes com, reconciliar-se
I want you to make up with him.

be made up of (Ver **made**).

make up for ▫ **compensar**
Her talent does not make up for her laziness.

make it up to ▫ **compensar**
I'm sorry I can't keep my promise, but I'll make it up to you.

maker ['meikə] *n.* ▫ **fabricante**
a car maker. ✦ a wine maker. ✦ a shoemaker.

make-up ['meikʌp] *n.* ▫ **maquiagem**
She doesn't wear make-up. ✦ I put on my make-up.

male [meil] *adj., n.* ▫ **masculino, macho**
a male choir. ✦ a male bird. ✦ males and females.
■ Ver **masculine**.

mall [mɔ:l] *n.* (= **shopping mall**) ▫ **shopping center**
I'm going to the mall to do some shopping.

mammal ['maməl] *n.* ▫ **mamífero**
Whales are mammals, not fish.

man[1] [man] *n.* (*pl.* **men**)
1 homem
men, women and children. ✦ an old man.
2 homem, ser humano
Only man (= human beings) can speak a language. ✦ modern man.

man[2] *v.* (**mans, manning, manned**) ▫ **tripular, manejar, operar**
Two astronauts manned the spaceship.

manage ['manidʒ] *v.* (**manages, managing, managed**)
1 conseguir
He managed to open it.
2 virar-se, arranjar-se
I can't manage without a car.
3 gerenciar
Who manages this department? ✦ to manage a project.

management ['manidʒmənt] *n.*
1 gerenciamento
The company is losing money because of bad management.
2 gerência
The management agreed to raise the workers' pay.

manager ['manidʒə] *n.* ▫ **gerente**
She's the bank manager. ✦ He is a hotel manager. ✦ to complain to the manager.
■ A **manager** can also be a woman.

manageress ['manidʒəris] *n.* ▫ **gerente**
the manageress of the shop / restaurant.

managing director ['manidʒiŋ di'rektə] *n*. □ **diretor executivo, diretor administrativo**

mane [mein] *n*. □ **juba, crina**
Lions and horses have manes.

maneuver [mə'nu:və] *n*. *Amer*. (= **manoeuvre**) □ **manobra**
army maneuvers.

mango ['maŋgou] *n*. □ **manga**

manhood ['manhud] *n*. □ **maturidade (masculina), idade adulta, virilidade**
to reach manhood.
■ Ver **womanhood**.

mankind [man'kaind] *n*. □ **humanidade**
the history of mankind.

man-made [,man'meid] *adj*. □ **fabricado, artificial**
a man-made lake.
■ antônimo: **natural**

manner ['manə] *n*.
1 jeito
to speak in a very polite manner.
2 jeito
Her informal manner surprised us.

manners ['manəz] *n*. *pl*. □ **maneiras, modos**
It's bad manners to point at people. ◆ He has good manners.
Mind your manners! □ **Tenha modos!**

manoeuvre [mə'nu:və] *n*. *Brit*. (= **maneuver**).

manpower ['manpauə] *n*. □ **força de trabalho, mão de obra**
a shortage of manpower in the construction industry.

mansion ['manʃən] *n*. □ **mansão**
A film star lives in that beautiful mansion.

mantelpiece [mantl'pi:s] *n*. □ **consolo de lareira**

manual¹ ['manjuəl] *adj*. □ **manual**
manual work. ◆ a car with manual gears.

manual² *n*. (= handbook) □ **manual**
a car manual. ◆ an instruction manual for a washing-machine.

manually ['manjuəli] *adv*. □ **manualmente**
You can operate the machine automatically or manually.

manufacture¹ [,manju'faktʃə] *n*. □ **fabricação**
They stopped the manufacture of these toys.
■ Ver **production**.

manufacture² *v*. (**manufactures, manufacturing, manufactured**) □ **fabricar, manufaturar**
The company manufactures computers.
■ Ver **produce**.

manufacturer [,manju'faktʃərə] *n*. □ **fabricante**
a car manufacturer. ◆ a chocolate manufacturer.

many ['meni] *adj*. (**more, most**) □ **muitos**
We received many (= a lot of) complaints. ◆ Many people saw it. ◆ Many of them continue to work here.
■ Use **much** with uncountable nouns (e.g. much water) and **many** with countable nouns (e.g. many books).
as many as
1 tantos quantos
Take as many as you want.
2 exatamente, nem mais nem menos do que
There were as many as 200 birds there.
How many...? □ **Quantos...?**
How many students are there in your class? ◆ How many (pencils) do you need?
■ Compare **how much**:
how much money / water.
many a time □ **muitas vezes**
too many □ **muitos, demais**
There are too many problems in this plan.
■ Compare **too much**:
too much money / water.

map [map] *n*. □ **mapa**
Can you find Alaska on the map? ◆ a street map of London.

marathon ['marəθən] *n*. □ **maratona**

marble ['ma:bl] *n*.
1 mármore
a marble floor.
2 bolinha de gude
to play marbles.

March [ma:tʃ] *n*. □ **março**
It happened in March, 1993.
■ For examples of the use of the months, see **April**.

march¹ ['ma:tʃ] *n*.
1 marcha
a long march.
2 marcha, passeata
to take part in a peace march.

march² *v*. (**marches, marching, marched**) □ **marchar**
The soldiers marched through the streets. ◆ They marched through the town to protest against the war.

margarine ['ma:dʒəri:n] *n*. □ **margarina**

margin ['ma:dʒin] *n*. □ **margem**
Write a note in the margin.

mark¹ [ma:k] *n*.
1 marca
There are dirty marks on the shirt. ◆ What are these marks on the ground?
2 nota
He got good marks in French.
■ *Amer*. **grade**
3 sinal
punctuation marks
■ Ver **exclamation mark; question mark; quotation marks**.

mark² *v*. (**marks, marking, marked**)
1 marcar
Mark a wrong answer with an x. ◆ He marked the place on the map.
2 corrigir, dar nota
I have to mark all these exam papers.
■ *Amer*. **grade**

market¹ ['ma:kit] *n*.
1 mercado
They went to the market to buy fruit and vegetables.
2 mercado
This is the best computer on the market. ◆ There is a big market for this product.

market² *v*. (**markets, marketing, marketed**) □ **comercializar**
Our company markets this product in Europe.

marketing ['ma:kitiŋ] *n*. □ **marketing**

marmalade ['ma:məleid] *n*. □ **geleia de fruta cítrica**
I had toast and marmalade for breakfast.

marriage ['maridʒ] *n*.
1 casamento
They had a happy marriage.

2 (= wedding) **cerimônia de casamento**
The marriage took place in church.
married ['marid] *adj.* □ **casado**
a married woman. ✦ He is married to Dana. ✦ I'm not married. I'm single.
get married □ **casar-se**
When are you getting married? ✦ They got married last month.
marrow ['marou] *n. Brit.* □ **abóbora**
■ *Amer.* **squash**
marry ['mari] *v.* (**marries, marrying, married**)
1 casar-se
He asked me to marry him. ✦ They married and had three children.
2 casar
They married two of their children.
■ The noun is **marriage**.
marsh ['ma:ʃ] *n.* □ **pântano**
marvel[1] ['ma:vəl] *n.* □ **maravilha**
the marvels of technology.
marvel[2] *v.* (*Amer.* **marvels, marveling, marveled** *Brit.* **marvelling, marvelled**) □ **maravilhar-se**
They marveled at the size of the statue.
marvellous ['ma:vələs] *adj. Brit.*, **marvelous** *Amer.* (= wonderful) □ **maravilhoso**
The weather was marvellous.
masculine ['maskjulin] *adj.*
1 masculino
a masculine voice.
2 masculino
The word 'lion' is masculine, and 'lioness' is feminine.
■ Ver **male**.
mash [maʃ] *v.* (**mashes, mashing, mashed**) □ **amassar**
to mash the potatoes.
mashed potatoes [maʃt pə'teitouz] *n.* □ **purê de batata**
mask [ma:sk] *n.* □ **máscara**
The robbers wore masks. ✦ a gas mask.
masked ['ma:skt] *adj.* □ **mascarado**
masked robbers.
Mass [mas] *n.* □ **missa**
mass[1] [mas] *n.*
1 conjunto
a mass of rock. ✦ masses of clouds.
2 massa
masses of people.
mass[2] *adj.* □ **de massa**
the mass media (= radio, television and newspapers).
massacre[1] ['masəkə] *n.* □ **massacre**
■ Ver **slaughter**[1].
massacre[2] *v.* (**massacres, massacring, massacred**) □ **massacrar**
The soldiers massacred the whole population of the village.
■ Ver **slaughter**[2].
massage[1] ['masa:ʒ] *n.* □ **massagem**
massage[2] *v.* (**massages, massaging, massaged**) □ **massagear**
to massage the body.
massive ['masiv] *adj.* □ **enorme, vultuoso**
a massive building. ✦ massive sums of money.
mast [ma:st] *n.* □ **mastro**
master[1] ['ma:stə] *n.* □ **mestre, dono**
The dog soon learnt to obey its master. ✦ The slave served his master for 30 years.

■ Ver **owner**.
master[2] *v.* (**masters, mastering, mastered**) □ **dominar**
to master a foreign language.
masterpiece ['ma:stəpi:s] *n.* □ **obra-prima**
This painting is a masterpiece.
mat [mat] *n.*
1 capacho, tapete
a bathmat. ✦ a doormat.
2 tatame
a judo mat.
3 descanso, suporte
Put the glasses on mats.
match[1] [matʃ] *n.*
1 fósforo
a box of matches. ✦ to strike a match (= to light it).
2 jogo, partida
a football match (= game). ✦ a boxing match.
■ a tennis match (*not* 'game').
3 combinação
This tie is a good match for your shirt.
4 páreo
She is a very good swimmer. You're no match for her.
5 partido
He is a good match.
match[2] *v.* (**matches, matching, matched**)
1 combinar
That shirt doesn't match your suit.
2 combinar
Match the words in column A with the words in column B.
matchbox ['matʃboks] *n.* □ **caixa de fósforos**
matchmaker ['matʃmeikə] *n.* □ **casamenteiro**
mate[1] [meit] *n.*
1 colega, parceiro, amigo
He's going to the beach with his mates.
■ *Amer.* **buddy; pal**
■ **friend** is the usual word.
2 colega
my classmates. ✦ my roommate.
3 parceiro
These birds never change their mates.
mate[2] *v.* (**mates, mating, mated**) □ **acasalar-se**
Animals mate during the mating season.
material[1] [mə'tiəriəl] *n.*
1 material
building materials.
2 matéria
reading material (for an exam, etc.).
3 material
writing materials (= pens, pencils, etc.).
4 tecido
material for dresses, curtains, etc.
material[2] *adj.* □ **material**
material needs (food, clothing, etc.).
math [maθ] *n. Amer.*, **maths** *Brit.* □ **matemática**
my math teacher. ✦ She is good at maths.
■ Ver **mathematics**.
mathematical [,maθə'matikəl] *adj.* □ **matemático**
a mathematical problem.
mathematically [,maθə'matikəli] *adv.* □ **matematicamente**
mathematician [,maθəma'tiʃən] *n.* □ **matemático (pessoa que estuda matemática)**
mathematics [maθə'matiks] *n.* □ **matemática**

I have an exam in mathematics.
- abreviação: **math, maths**.

matter¹ ['matə] *n.*

1 material
reading matter (= books, newspapers, etc.). ◆ The label on the envelope says 'Printed matter'.

2 assunto
It's a personal matter. ◆ He discussed the matter with the manager.

as a matter of fact □ **na verdade**
As a matter of fact, I talked to him about it.

be the matter (with) □ **ter um problema (com)**
There's something the matter with the car.

no matter what, who, etc. □ **não importa o quê, quem, etc.**
I will not change my mind, no matter what he says.

What's the matter? □ **O que foi?, Qual o problema?**
What's the matter? Are you ill? ◆ What's the matter with the TV?

matter² *v.* (**matters, mattered**) □ **importar**
What does it matter (who did it)? ◆ Does it matter when we come? ◆ It doesn't matter.
- [no be + -ing]. Do *not* say 'It isn't mattering', only 'It doesn't matter'.

mattress ['matris] *n.* □ **colchão**
He sleeps on a mattress on the floor.

mature¹ [mə'tjuəʳ] *adj.*

1 maduro
mature trees / animals.

2 maduro
He is young but very mature.

mature² *v.* (**matures, maturing, matured**) □ **amadurecer**
Some animals mature faster than others. ◆ He matured a lot after he joined the army.

maturity [mə'tjuəriti] *n.* □ **maturidade**
Some animals reach maturity very quickly.

mauve [mouv] *adj., n.* □ **malva**
- Ver **purple; violet**.

maximum ['maksiməm] *adj., n.* □ **máximo**
the maximum temperatures. ◆ This truck can carry a maximum of 5 tons.
- antônimo: **minimum**.

May [mei] *n.* □ **maio**
It happened in May, 2000.
- See **April** for examples of the use of the months.

may [mei] *v.*

1 poder, ser possível, ser provável
He may be in his room.
- Compare:
Maybe he is in his room.

2 talvez
Talk to David – he may help you. ◆ She may arrive late.
- **might** is also possible.

3 (= can) **poder, ter permissão**
You may use a dictionary in the exam. ◆ May I come in?

4 desejar
May you be happy!

may have □ **poder ter**
You may have seen him at the party.

maybe ['meibi:] *adv.* (= perhaps) □ **pode ser, talvez**
Maybe you are right. ◆ Are you going to tell him? – Maybe.

mayor ['meəʳ] *n.* □ **prefeito**
the mayor of New York.

mayoress ['meəris] *n.* □ **prefeita**

me [mi:] *pron.*

1 me
He bought me a present. ◆ She saw me. ◆ They looked at me. ◆ He telephoned me.

2 eu
Who is it? – It's me! ◆ Who wants to go? – Not me!

meadow ['medou] *n.* □ **campina, prado**
The cows are in the meadow.

meal [mi:l] *n.* □ **refeição, prato**
to prepare a meal. ◆ I eat a hot meal for lunch.

mean¹ [mi:n] *v.* (**means, meaning, meant**)

1 significar, querer dizer
What does this word mean? ◆ This road sign means 'stop'.

2 querer dizer
What do you mean? ◆ You know what I mean.
- [no be + -ing]. Do *not* say 'is / are, etc., meaning' in meanings **1** and **2**, only 'mean, means, meant'.

3 ter a intenção de, pretender
I didn't mean to hurt you. ◆ I meant to send it today, but I forgot.

it means (that) □ **significa (que), quer dizer (que)**
It means that we are in trouble.
- *it means* (*not* 'it's mean').

mean something to □ **significa muito para**
Your friendship means a lot to me.

mean well □ **ser bem-intencionado, ter boa vontade**
She means well, but don't listen to her advice.

be meant to □ **dever (fazer algo), ser para (fazer algo)**
You're meant to pay it today. ◆ It's not meant to be easy.

mean² *adj.*

1 sovina
Don't be so mean! Give him some more money!

2 mesquinho
It was mean of you to hurt his feelings.

meaning ['mi:niŋ] *n.*

1 significado
Explain the meaning of this word. ◆ What is the meaning of these codes?

2 sentido
to find meaning in life.

meaningful ['mi:niŋful] *adj.*

1 significativo, importante
a meaningful relationship.

2 significativo
a meaningful look.

meaningless ['mi:niŋlis] *adj.* □ **sem sentido, inexpressivo**
His advice is meaningless.

meanness ['mi:nis] *n.* □ **maldade; mesquinhez**
- Ver **mean²**.

means [mi:nz] *n.* □ **meios**
Find the means to do it. ◆ means of transport (= trains, buses, etc.).

a man of means □ **um homem de posses**

by means of □ **por meio de**
They communicated by means of radio.

by all means (= certainly) □ **com certeza**
Can I wait here? – By all means.

by no means (= not at all) □ **de jeito nenhum, absolutamente**
I am by no means certain that we are ready.

meant [ment] *v.* (Ver **mean¹**).

meantime ['mi:ntaim] *n.*
in the meantime □ **nesse ínterim**
In the meantime you can do something else.
meanwhile ['mi:nwail] *adv.* □ **enquanto isso**
Meanwhile you can use my computer. ◆ He went to look for his brother. Meanwhile, his parents waited at home.
measles ['mi:zlz] *n.* □ **sarampo**
measure[1] ['meʒə] *n.* □ **medida**
A metre is a measure of length.
■ Compare with **measurement**.
measures *n. pl.* □ **medidas**
The government will take measures to reduce unemployment. ◆ safety measures to prevent accidents. ◆ security measures (against attacks, robbery, etc.).
measure[2] *v.* (**measures, measuring, measured**)
1 medir
I measured the length of the bed. ◆ to measure the room.
2 medir, ter determinada medida
The room measures 4 meters by 6.
measurement ['meʒəmənt] *n.* □ **medida**
What are the measurements of the box?
meat [mi:t] *n.* □ **carne**
mechanic [mi'kanik] *n.* □ **mecânico**
a car mechanic.
mechanical [mi'kanikəl] *adj.* □ **mecânico**
a mechanical toy. ◆ The car didn't start because of a mechanical problem.
mechanics [mi'kaniks] *n.* □ **mecânica**
mechanism ['mekənizəm] *n.* □ **mecanismo**
the mechanism of a toy.
medal ['medl] *n.* □ **medalha**
She won two gold medals in the Olympic Games. ◆ They gave him a medal for bravery.
meddle ['medl] *v.* (**meddles, meddling, meddled**) (= interfere) □ **meter-se, intrometer-se**
Don't meddle in their affairs!
media ['mi:diə] *n. pl.* □ **mídia**
medical[1] ['medikəl] *adj.*
1 médico
to get medical treatment.
2 de medicina
a medical student.
medical[2] *n.* (mesmo que **a medical examination**) □ **exame médico**
to have a medical.
medicine ['medsin] *n.*
1 medicina
modern medicine.
2 remédio, medicamento
Take this medicine twice a day.
medieval [ˌmedi'i:vəl] *adj.*, **mediaeval** □ **medieval**
a medieval building.
■ Ver **Middle Ages**.
mediocre [mi:di'oukə] *adj.* □ **medíocre**
a mediocre football player.
Mediterranean [ˌmeditə'reiniən] *adj.* □ **mediterrâneo**
Mediterranean food
the Mediterranean *n.* □ **o Mediterrâneo**
the Mediterranean Sea. ◆ to cruise around the Mediterranean.
medium ['mi:diəm] *adj.* □ **médio**
He is of medium height. ◆ a medium-sized pizza (= a pizza of medium size).

meet [mi:t] *v.* (**meets, meeting, met**)
1 encontrar
I'll meet you at 8 o'clock. ◆ Where did you meet the first time? ◆ I met Dan yesterday at the bank.
2 conhecer
Meet my son David. ◆ Pleased to meet you!
3 atender
to meet the needs of the children. ◆ to meet the demands of the workers.
meeting ['mi:tiŋ] *n.*
1 reunião
The teachers had a meeting to discuss the problem.
2 encontro
I remember our first meeting.
melody ['melədi] *n.* (*pl.* **melodies**) □ **melodia**
melon ['melən] *n.* □ **melão**
melt [melt] *v.* (**melts, melting, melted**) □ **derreter**
The snow is beginning to melt. ◆ Sugar melts in water. ◆ to melt some butter.
■ Ver **dissolve**.
member ['membə] *n.*
1 membro
a member of the club. ◆ The committee has six members.
2 membro
a member of the family.
membership ['membəʃip] *n.*
1 participação como sócio ou membro, afiliação
He started his membership in the club in 2000.
2 (= membership fee) **taxa de adesão**
Membership is $50 a year.
memo ['memou] *n.* (mesmo que **memorandum**) □ **memo, memorando**
I sent them a memo about the sale.
memorable ['memərəbl] *adj.* □ **memorável**
a memorable adventure.
memorial [mi'mo:riəl] *n.* □ **memorial**
This statue is a memorial to the dead soldiers.
memorise ['meməraiz] *v. Brit.* (Ver **memorize**).
memorize ['meməraiz] *v.* (**memorizes, memorizing, memorized**) □ **memorizar**
I memorized their telephone numbers.
memory ['meməri] *n.* (*pl.* **memories**)
1 memória
You have a good memory
2 lembrança
I have very pleasant memories of that day.
3 memória
a computer memory.
in memory of □ **em memória de**
They built a statue in memory of the soldiers who died there.
men [men] *n. pl. of* **man**
menace ['menəs] *n.* (= danger; threat) □ **ameaça**
Drugs are a menace to society.
mend [mend] *v.* (**mends, mending, mended**) □ **emendar, consertar**
to mend a broken vase.
■ Ver **fix**; **repair**[2].
mental ['mentl] *adj.* □ **mental**
his mental development. ◆ a mental effort. ◆ a mental illness.
mentality [men'taliti] *n.* □ **mentalidade**

mentally ['mentəli] *adv.* □ **mentalmente**
He is mentally ill.
mention[1] ['menʃən] *v.* (**mentions, mentioning, mentioned**) □ **mencionar**
Don't mention his name in front of them. ◆ They didn't mention these facts in the report.
Don't mention it. (= **You're welcome.**) □ **De nada.**
Thank you. – Don't mention it.
not to mention □ **sem falar**
We enjoyed the meal very much, not to mention the dessert.
mention[2] *n.* □ **menção**
There's no mention of the incident in the newspaper.
menu ['menju:] *n.*
1 cardápio
What's on the menu today?
2 menu
Press this key and the menu will appear on the screen.
meow [mi'au] *n., v.* (= **miaow**[1]; **miaow**[2]).
MEP ['em i: 'pi:] *abbr.* (mesmo que **Member of the European Parliament**) □ **Membro do Parlamento Europeu**
merchandise ['mɔːtʃəndaiz] *n.* □ **mercadoria**
They sell merchandise of good quality.
merchant ['mɔːtʃənt] *n.* □ **comerciante**
a wine merchant.
■ Ver **trader**.
merciful ['mɔːsiful] *adj.* □ **misericordioso**
The king was merciful to them.
merciless ['mɔːsilis] *adj.* □ **impiedoso**
mercilessly ['mɔːsilisli] *adv.* □ **impiedosamente**
They beat him mercilessly.
mercy ['mɔːsi] *n.* □ **misericórdia**
The thief asked the judge for mercy. ◆ He had mercy on the child (and didn't punish him).
■ Ver **pity**.
be at the mercy of □ **à mercê de**
The ship was at the mercy of the sea.
mere [miə] *adj.* □ **mero**
He is a mere child.
merely ['miəli] *adv.* □ **meramente**
They did it merely because they were bored.
merge [mɔːdʒ] *v.* (**merges, merging, merged**) □ **fundir-se**
This company will merge with a bigger company.
merit[1] ['merit] *n.* □ **mérito**
We discussed the merits of the plan.
merit[2] *v.* (**merits, meriting, merited**) (= deserve) □ **merecer**
This problem merits careful attention.
mermaid ['mɔːmeid] *n.* □ **sereia**
merry ['meri] *adj.* (**merrier, merriest**) □ **feliz**
a merry party. ◆ Merry Christmas!
merry-go-round ['merigou,raund] *n.* (= **carousel; roundabout**) □ **carrossel**
mess[1] [mes] *n.* □ **bagunça**
Your room is always in a mess!
look a mess □ **estar horrível**
You look a mess!
to be in a mess □ **estar em maus lençóis**
She is in a mess. She needs our help.
mess[2] *v.* (**messes, messing, messed**) □ **sujar**
Don't mess the floor with your dirty shoes!
mess about / around □ **brincar**
Don't mess about with the knife! ◆ Stop messing around! We have a lot of work to do.

mess up
1 atrapalhar
The weather messed up our plans to go on a trip.
2 bagunçar
Who messed up my desk?
message ['mesidʒ] *n.*
1 recado
Would you like to leave a message? ◆ Could you give a message to George, please?
2 mensagem
The book has no message.
messenger ['mesindʒə] *n.* □ **mensageiro**
Messiah [mə'saiə] *n.* □ **Messias**
to pray for the coming of the Messiah.
messy ['mesi] *adj.* (**messier, messiest**)
1 bagunçado
a messy room.
2 malfeito
a messy job.
met [met] *v.* (Ver **meet**).
metal ['metl] *n.* □ **metal**
Silver and gold are precious metals. ◆ a metal box.
metallic [mə'talik] *adj.* □ **metálico**
meter ['miːtə] *n.*
1 medidor
an electricity meter. ◆ The taxi-driver switched on the meter.
■ Ver **parking meter**.
2 *Amer.* **metro**
The pool is two meters deep. ◆ The room is 4m (= meters) by 6.
■ *Brit.* **metre**
method ['meθəd] *n.* □ **método**
teaching methods. ◆ a new method for recycling paper.
metre ['miːtə] *n. Brit.* □ **metro**
The fence is two metres high. ◆ The room is 4m (= metres) by 6.
■ *Amer.* **meter**
metric ['metrik] *adj.* □ **métrico**
the metric system.
mg *abbr.*, **mg.** (= milligram) □ **mg**
The pill contains 50 mg of vitamin C.
miaow[1] [mi'au] *n. Brit.*, meow *Amer.* □ **miau**
miaow[2] *v. Brit.* (**miaows, miaowing, miaowed**) (= meow) □ **miar**
The cat is miaowing outside.
mice [mais] *n. pl. of* **mouse**
microbe ['maikroub] *n.* □ **micróbio**
microphone ['maikrəfoun] *n.* (= **mike**) □ **microfone**
Speak into the microphone.
microscope ['maikrəskoup] *n.* □ **microscópio**
He examined the blood under the microscope.
microscopic [maikrəs'kopik] *adj.* □ **microscópico**
microwave (oven) ['maikrəweiv ('ʌvn)] *n.* □ **(forno de) micro-ondas**
mid [mid] *adj., pref.*, **mid-** □ **em meados de; no meio de**
in mid winter. ◆ mid-morning coffee (around 10 o'clock).
midday [mid'dei] *n.* (= noon) □ **meio-dia**
at midday (= at 12 o'clock).
middle[1] ['midl] *n.* □ **meio**
in the middle of the room. ◆ in the middle of the night.

be in the middle of □ **estar no meio de**
I'm in the middle of doing my homework.
middle² *adj.* □ **do meio**
the middle drawer.
middle-aged [,midl'eidʒd] *adj.* □ **meia-idade**
a middle-aged man, about 50 years old.
Middle Ages ['midl ,eidʒiz] *n.*
the Middle Ages □ **a Idade Média**
■ Ver **medieval**.
middle class ['midl ,kla:s] *n., adj.* □ **classe média, de classe média**
middle-class families.
■ Ver **upper class; working class**.
Middle East ['midl 'i:st] *n.* (mesmo que **the Middle East**) □ **Oriente Médio**
the Middle East conflict. ◆ the countries of the Middle East.
middleman ['midlman] *n.* (*pl.* **middlemen**) □ **intermediário**
midget ['midʒit] *n., adj.* □ **anão, pequenino**
a midget camera.
■ Ver **dwarf**.
midnight ['midnait] *n.* □ **meia-noite**
at midnight.
midterm [mid'tə:m] *n. Amer.* □ **recesso escolar no meio do ano**
We're going on vacation at midterm.
■ *Brit.* **half-term**
midway [mid'wei] *adv., adj.* (= halfway) □ **a meio caminho, na metade do caminho**
midway between London and Liverpool. ◆ I'll meet you midway.
midweek [mid'wi:k] *n., adv., adj.* □ **meio da semana**
to travel midweek, not at the weekend. ◆ Midweek prices at hotels are cheaper. ◆ to go in / at midweek.
midwife ['midwaif] *n.* (*pl.* **midwives**) □ **parteira**
might [mait] *v.*

1 poderia, seria possível, seria provável
He said that he might stay there another day.
■ The example sentence above is the indirect speech of:
He said: 'I may stay there another day'.
2 talvez
It might rain tomorrow. ◆ He might help you.
■ **may** is also possible, but **might** suggests less probability.
3 (= may) **talvez**
She might be in her room.
4 (= may) **poder, poderia**
Might I suggest something?
might have (done) □ **poderia ter (feito)**
You might have broken your leg. ◆ He might have succeeded.
mighty ['maiti] *adj.* (**mightier, mightiest**) □ **poderoso**
a mighty army.
migrant ['maigrənt] *n.* □ **migrante**
Migrant workers go from place to place looking for work.
migrate [mai'greit] *v.* (**migrates, migrating, migrated**) □ **migrar**
These birds migrate every winter.
mike [maik] *n.* (= microphone) □ **microfone**
mild [maild] *adj.*

1 suave

Mild cheese doesn't have a sharp taste. ◆ a mild soap.
2 leve
a mild punishment. ◆ mild criticism.
3 ameno
mild weather.
mile [mail] *n.* □ **milha**
The airport is 3 miles from here.
military ['militəri] *adj.* □ **militar**
a military camp. ◆ He wore a military uniform.
■ In the following phrases, **army** is used:
an army officer.
an army base.
the military *n.* □ **as forças armadas**
milk¹ [milk] *n.* □ **leite**
Do you take milk in your coffee? ◆ a glass of milk.
milk chocolate *n.* □ **chocolate ao leite**
milk² *v.* (**milks, milking, milked**) □ **ordenhar**
to milk cows / goats.
milkman ['milkman] *n.* (*pl.* **milkmen**) □ **leiteiro**
milky ['milki] *adj.*
1 com leite
milky coffee (= with a lot of milk).
2 leitoso
milky liquid.
mill [mil] *n.*
1 fábrica, usina
a paper mill. ◆ a steel mill.
2 moinho
They grind flour at that old mill.
3 moedor
a coffee mill (= a coffee grinder).
millennium [mi'leniəm] *n.* (*pl.* **millenniums, millennia**) (mesmo que **1,000 years**) □ **milênio**
the beginning of a new millennium.
miller ['milə] *n.* □ **moleiro**
milligram ['miligram] *n.* □ **miligrama**
50 mg (= milligrams) of vitamin C.
millimeter ['milimi:tə] *n. Amer.*, **millimetre** *Brit.* □ **milímetro**
a 16 mm (= millimeter) film. ◆ There are ten millimetres in a centimetre.
million ['miljən] *n., adj.* □ **milhão**
ten million dollars (= $10m). ◆ millions of people. ◆ half a million.
millionaire [,milljə'neə] *n.* □ **milionário**
millionth¹ ['miljənθ] *adj.* □ **milionésimo**
the millionth tourist to arrive this year.
millionth² *n.* □ **milionésimo**
a millionth of a second.
mime¹ [maim] *v.* (**mimes, miming, mimed**) □ **imitar, fazer mímica**
He mimed the act of milking a cow.
mime² *n.* □ **mímica**
■ Ver **pantomime**.
mimic¹ ['mimik] *v.* (**mimics, mimicking, mimicked**) □ **imitar**
He mimicked his boss.
mimic² *n.* □ **mímico**
mince [mins] *v.* (**minced, mincing, minced**) □ **moer**
Mince a kilo of beef.
■ *Amer.* also **grind**
minced [minst] *adj.* □ **moído**

minced beef.
■ *Amer.* **ground**[1]
mind[1] [maind] *n.*
1 mente, cabeça
She has a sharp mind. ◆ He is one of the brightest minds in America.
2 mente, cabeça
There's no one there. It's just in your mind. ◆ I can't get it out of my mind. (= I can't stop thinking about it.)
3 mente
He has a sick mind. (= He is crazy.)
4 a meu ver
to my mind (= in my opinion).
be out of your mind □ **não estar no seu juízo perfeito**
Are you out of your mind?
bear / keep in mind □ **ter em mente**
Bear in mind that the meeting is tomorrow.
change your mind □ **mudar de ideia**
I changed my mind. I'm not going.
come to mind □ **vir à mente**
The first thought that came to mind was to run away.
cross your mind □ **passar pela sua cabeça**
It never crossed my mind that she was unhappy.
have something on your mind □ **ter algo na cabeça**
I have a lot on my mind right now.
make up your mind (= decide) □ **tomar uma decisão**
I can't make up my mind what to wear.
mind[2] *v.* (**minds, minding, minded**)
1 importar-se
Do you mind if I close the window? ◆ You can take it. He won't mind. ◆ I'll wait here, if you don't mind.
■ [no be + -ing] in this meaning. Do *not* say 'am / is, etc., minding'.
2 ter cuidado com
Mind the step!
3 (= look after; take care of) **olhar, cuidar**
I can't come now – I'm minding the baby.
Do you mind...?
1 Você se importa de ...?
Do you mind waiting outside?
2 Você se importa se ...?
Do you mind if I sit here?
Would you mind...? □ **Você poderia ...?**
Would you mind closing the window?
I don't mind □ **Eu não ligo**
Would you like tea or coffee? – I don't mind. ◆ I don't mind waiting here.
mind your own business □ **cuidar da sua própria vida**
never mind □ **esqueça, deixe para lá**
Never mind, you can try again tomorrow.
mine[1] [main] *pron.* □ **meu, minha**
a friend of mine. ◆ Whose pen is this? – It's mine. ◆ That car is mine. (= That is my car.)
mine[2] *n.*
1 mina
a coal mine. ◆ a gold mine.
2 mina
He was wounded by a mine.
mine[3] *v.* (**mines, mining, mined**) □ **explorar, extrair, minerar**
They are mining for gold.
minefield ['mainfi:ld] *n.* □ **campo minado**

miner ['mainə] *n.* □ **mineiro**
a coal miner.
mineral ['minərəl] *n.* □ **mineral**
vitamins and minerals. ◆ This area is rich in minerals.
mineral water ['minərəl 'wotə] *n.* □ **água mineral**
miniature ['miniatʃə] *adj.* □ **miniatura**
a miniature camera.
minimal ['minimal] *adj.* □ **mínimo**
minimal damage.
minimum[1] ['minimam] *n.* □ **mínimo**
We need a minimum of 20,000 dollars. ◆ It will take 3 years (at the) minimum.
■ antônimo: **maximum**
minimum[2] *adj.* □ **mínimo**
with minimum effort. ◆ the minimum wage.
■ antônimo: **maximum**
minister ['ministə] *n.*
1 ministro
the Minister of Education.
■ *Amer.* **Secretary**
2 pastor protestante
A minister is a priest (in some Christian churches).
ministry ['ministri] *n.* (*pl.* **ministries**) □ **Ministério**
the Ministry of Defence. ◆ the Ministry of Agriculture. ◆ the Health Ministry.
■ *Amer.* **department**
minor[1] ['mainə] *n.* □ **menor**
minor[2] *adj.* □ **pequeno, de pouca importância**
a minor problem. ◆ She had a minor part in the film. ◆ He suffered minor injuries in the accident.
■ antônimo: **major**
minority [mai'noriti] *n.* (*pl.* **minorities**) □ **minoria**
Only a small minority voted for him. The majority voted for Dina. ◆ A small minority of the students failed the exam.
■ Ver **majority**.
mint [mint] *n.*
1 hortelã, menta
mint tea. ◆ mint chewing-gum.
2 bala de hortelã, bala de menta
a packet of mints.
minus ['mainəs] *prep.*
1 menos
Ten minus four is six (10-4=6).
2 (= below zero) **menos**
a temperature of minus 7 degrees (-7° C).
minute[1] [mai'nju:t] *adj.* (= tiny) □ **minúsculo**
minute specks of dust.
minute[2] ['minit] *n.*
1 minuto
The train was five minutes late. ◆ They came a few minutes ago. ◆ It's six minutes past ten. (= 10:06)
2 (= moment) **minuto**
Wait a minute! ◆ Just a minute! ◆ at the last minute.
in a minute □ **em um minuto, logo**
I'll be back in a minute.
miracle ['mirəkl] *n.* □ **milagre**
It's a miracle that he recovered from his illness.
miraculous [mi'rakjuləs] *adj.* □ **milagroso**
a miraculous escape.
miraculously [mi'rakjuləsli] *adv.* □ **milagrosamente**
Miraculously, no one died.
mirror ['mirə] *n.* □ **espelho**
to look in the mirror.

misbehave [ˌmisbi'heiv] *v.* (**misbehaves, misbehaving, misbehaved**) □ **comportar-se mal**
Some of the class misbehaved during the lecture.
misbehavior [ˌmisbi'heivjə] *n. Amer.*, **misbehaviour** *Brit.* □ **comportamento indevido**
mischief ['mistʃif] *n.* □ **travessura**
The children got into mischief again.
mischievous ['mistʃi:vəs] *adj.* □ **arteiro, danado**
a mischievous child.
miser ['maizə] *n.* □ **sovina, avarento**
miserable ['mizərəbl] *adj.*
1 muito triste
to feel miserable.
2 miserável
They lived in miserable conditions.
3 horrível
miserable weather.
miserly ['maizəli] *adj.* □ **avaramente**
misery ['mizəri] *n.* □ **miséria**
to live in misery.
misfortune [mis'fɔ:tʃən] *n.* □ **azar**
I had the misfortune to break my arm.
mislay [mis'lei] *v.* (**mislays, mislaying, mislaid**) □ **perder, guardar em lugar não lembrado**
I always mislay things and can't find them later. ♦ It's not lost, just mislaid.
mislead [mis'li:d] *v.* (**misleads, misleading, misled**) □ **enganar, induzir a erro**
They misled me when they promised me the job.
misleading [mis'li:diŋ] [misprə'nauns] *adj.* □ **enganoso**
The information was misleading.
mispronounce [misprə'nauns] *v.* (**mispronounced, mispronouncing, mispronounced**) □ **pronunciar incorretamente**
He mispronounced 's' as 'z'.
Miss [mis] □ **senhorita**
You can go in, Miss. ♦ Dear Miss Jones,
■ Ver **Mrs**; **Ms**.
miss¹ [mis] *n.* □ **errar, não acertar em**
three hits and one miss.
miss² *v.* (**misses, missing, missed**)
1 errar
The bomb missed the target. ♦ He threw the ball at me, but he missed.
2 perder
Hurry up or we'll miss the train!
3 perder
You missed a good party last night.
4 perder
She missed the opportunity to see them.
5 sentir falta de, ter saudade de
Did you miss me?
missile ['misail] *n.*
1 míssil
ground-to-air missiles
■ Ver **rocket**.
2 projétil
They began to throw bottles, stones and other missiles.
missing ['misiŋ] *adj.* □ **desaparecido, ausente**
The police found the missing child. ♦ They are looking for the missing jewels. ♦ One page is missing from her diary.

mission ['miʃən] *n.* □ **missão**
Their mission was to bomb the bridge.
missionary ['miʃənəri] *n.* (*pl.* **missionaries**) □ **missionário**
misspell [mis'spel] *v.* (**misspells, misspelling, misspeled / misspelt**) □ **pronunciar incorretamente**
You've misspelt my name – it's written with a 'c' not a 'k'.
mist [mist] *n.*
1 neblina
Drive more slowly when there is mist in the air.
■ Ver **fog**.
2 garoa
Wipe the mist from the mirror.
mistake¹ [mis'teik] *n.* □ **erro**
to make a mistake. ♦ Please correct your spelling mistakes. ♦ It was a mistake to tell him.
■ Ver **error**.
by mistake □ **por engano**
I took his umbrella by mistake.
mistake² *v.* (**mistakes, mistaking, mistook, mistaken**)
1 compreender mal, confundir
He missed the test because he mistook the date.
2 confundir-se, tomar uma coisa por outra
Sorry. I mistook you for your sister.
mistaken [mis'teikən] *adj.*
1 errado, enganado
It was in 1989, if I'm not mistaken.
2 errado, equivocado
mistaken ideas.
Mister ['mistə] *n.* (= Mr.) □ **senhor**
mistook [mis'tuk] *v.* (Ver **mistake**²).
misty ['misti] *adj.* □ **nublado**
misty weather.
misunderstand [ˌmisʌndə'stænd] *v.* (**misunderstands, misunderstanding, misunderstood**) □ **entender mal**
They misunderstood the instructions. ♦ Don't misunderstand me.
misunderstanding [ˌmisʌndə'stændiŋ] *n.* □ **engano, mal-entendido**
There's some misunderstanding about the new tax. ♦ They were angry with me, but it was all a misunderstanding.
mitten ['mitn] *n.* □ **mitene**
mix [miks] *v.* (**mixes, mixing, mixed**)
1 misturar
Mix the milk with the flour.
2 misturar-se
Oil and water don't mix.
3 misturar
to mix business with pleasure.
mix up
1 confundir
I mixed him up with someone else.
2 misturar
Don't mix up the files! I arranged them alphabetically.
mix-up *n.* □ **confusão**
Sorry about the mix-up with the money.
mixed [mikst] *adj.* □ **misto**
a mixed school (for boys and girls). ♦ I have mixed feelings about this.
be / get mixed up □ **estar / ficar confuso**
He got mixed up and forgot what to say.
mixer ['miksə] *n.* □ **mixer, batedeira**
a food-mixer.

mixture ['mikstʃə] *n.* □ **mistura; mescla**
a mixture of flour, milk and eggs. ◆ a mixture of old and new buildings.
mm *abbr.* (= millimeter / millimetre) □ **mm**
a 16mm film.
moan[1] [moun] *n.* □ **gemido**
moan[2] *v.* (**moans, moaning, moaned**)
1 gemer
to moan with pain.
2 queixar-se
He is always moaning about his salary.
mob [mob] *n.* □ **multidão**
The police could not stop the angry mob.
mobile ['moubail] *adj.* □ **móvel**
a mobile phone. ◆ Old people are usually not as mobile as younger people.
mock [mok] *v.* (**mocks, mocking, mocked**) □ **zombar**
They mocked him. (= They laughed at him.)
■ The noun is **mockery**.
modal ['moudl] *n.* (mesmo que **modal verb**) □ **verbo modal**
■ Modal verbs:
can; could; may; might; shall; should; must; will; would; ought to.
■ Modal verbs are followed by the infinitive without 'to' (except **ought to**):
He must go (*not* 'must to go').
■ Modal verbs have the same form for all persons (e.g. I can, she can).
■ You make questions and negative sentences without 'do' or 'did':
Must he go?
You should not come.
model[1] ['modl] *n.*
1 modelo
a model of the building. ◆ a model airplane. ◆ the latest models of motorcycles.
2 modelo
a fashion model. ◆ an artist's model.
3 modelo, exemplar
a model pupil.
model[2] *v.* (**models, modelling, modelled**)
1 trabalhar como modelo (em moda)
She models swimsuits at fashion shows.
2 apresentar, exibir
to model a car on a computer screen.
3 modelar
He modelled a small animal out of wax.
modelling ['modliŋ] *n.* □ **modelagem**
modem ['moudem] *n.* □ **modem**
You need a modem to send emails.
moderate[1] ['modərət] *adj.*
1 moderado
moderate political opinions.
■ antônimo: **extremist**
2 moderado
a moderate increase in prices.
3 moderado
moderate weather.
moderate[2] *n.* □ **moderado**
■ antônimo: **extremist**
moderate[3] ['modəreit] *v.* (**moderates, moderating, moderated**)
1 moderar
He must learn to moderate his language.
2 mediar
to moderate a discussion.
moderately ['modəreitli] *adv.*
1 moderadamente
He was moderately wounded.
2 moderadamente
moderately successful.
3 moderadamente
Prices increased moderately.
4 moderadamente
moderately long.
modern ['modən] *adj.* □ **moderno**
modern equipment. ◆ modern furniture. ◆ modern art.
modest ['modist] *adj.*
1 modesto
She is very modest about her great achievements.
2 modesto
They live in a modest little house.
3 modesto
a modest dress.
■ antônimo: **immodest**
modestly ['modistli] *adv.* □ **modestamente**
modesty ['modisti] *n.* □ **modéstia**
moist [moist] *adj.* □ **úmido**
Plants grow well in moist soil.
moisten ['moisn] *v.* (**moistens, moistening, moistened**) □ **umedecer**
Moisten the cloth and clean the window.
moisture ['moistʃə] *n.* □ **umidade**
mold[1] [mould] *n. Amer.* (= **mould**[1])
1 bolor, mofo
The bread is not fresh. There's mold on it.
2 molde
Pour the hot jelly into molds.
mold[2] *v. Amer.* (**molds, molding, molded**) (= **mould**[2]) □ **moldar**
He molds little animals out of clay.
moldy ['mouldi] *adj. Amer.* (= **mouldy**) □ **bolorento, de mofo**
moldy bread. ◆ a moldy smell.
mole [moul] *n.*
1 toupeira
The gardener killed the mole.
2 verruga
He had a mole on his face.
mom [mʌm] *n. Amer.* (= **mum**) □ **mãe, mamãe**
Can I do it later, Mom?
moment ['moumənt] *n.* □ **momento**
Just a moment! (= Wait a moment!). ◆ He stopped for a moment. ◆ at the last moment.
at the moment □ **no momento**
She is working with us at the moment.
for the moment □ **no momento**
We need only two people for the moment.
in a moment □ **em um minuto, já, já**
I'll be back in a moment.
the moment □ **na hora (em que), no momento (em que)**
The moment (that) he saw me he ran away.
momma ['mʌmə] *n. Amer.* (= mother) □ **mamãe**
Let me help you, Momma.

mommy ['mʌmi] *n. Amer.* (*pl.* **mommies**) □ **mãezinha, mamãezinha**
Can I come too, Mommy?
■ *Brit.* **mummy**

monarch ['monək] *n.* □ **monarca**

monarchy ['monəki] *n.* (*pl.* **monarchies**) □ **monarquia**

monastery ['monəstəri] *n.* (*pl.* **monasteries**) □ **mosteiro**

Monday ['mʌndei] *n.* □ **segunda-feira**
They will come on Monday. ◆ I saw her last Monday. ◆ It's my birthday next Monday.

money ['mʌni] *n.* □ **dinheiro**
How much money did you lose? ◆ He spends a lot of money on books. ◆ It costs a lot of money. ◆ a large sum of money

monk [mʌŋk] *n.* □ **monge**
■ Ver **nun**.

monkey ['mʌŋki] *n.* □ **macaco**

monotonous [mə'notənəs] *adj.* □ **monótono**
monotonous work. ◆ a monotonous voice.

monster ['monstə] *n.* □ **monstro**
an ugly monster with three heads.

monstrous ['monstrəs] *adj.* □ **monstruoso**
a monstrous creature. ◆ a monstrous crime.

month [mʌnθ] *n.* □ **mês**
two months ago. ◆ It happened last month. ◆ Come again next month. ◆ He came here for a month.
a month □ **por mês**
She earns $1,000 a month. ◆ He visits us once a month.

monthly¹ ['mʌnθli] *adj.* □ **mensal**
a monthly visit. ◆ a monthly income of $2000.

monthly² *adv.* □ **mensalmente**
I am paid monthly.

monthly³ *n.* □ **publicação mensal**
This magazine is a monthly.

monument ['momjumənt] *n.* □ **monumento**
a monument in memory of the hero.

moo¹ [mu:] *n.* □ **mugido**

moo² *v.* (**moos, mooing, mooed**) □ **mugir**
The cow mooed.

mood [mu:d] *n.* □ **humor**
She is in a good mood. ◆ I'm not in the mood for playing games.

moody ['mu:di] *adj.* □ **de lua, melancólico**
He looks moody.

moon [mu:n] *n.* □ **lua**
The landing on the moon was successful. ◆ There's a full moon tonight.

moonlight ['mu:nlait] *n.* □ **luar**

moonlit ['mu:nlit] *adj.* □ **enluarado**
a moonlit night.

mop¹ [mop] *n.* □ **esfregão**
a floor mop.

mop² *v.* (**mops, mopping, mopped**) □ **esfregar**
to mop the floor.

mop up □ **limpar**
Mop up the milk from the table.

moped ['mouped] *n.* □ **bicicleta motorizada**
to ride on a moped.

moral¹ ['morəl] *adj.* □ **moral**
a moral problem / question. ◆ a moral person. ◆ He refused to do it for moral reasons.
■ antônimo: **immoral**

moral² *n.* (= lesson²) □ **moral**
What is the moral of the story?

morale [mə'ra:l] *n.* □ **o moral, estado de espírito**
Their morale is high.

morality [mə'roliti] *n.* □ **moralidade**
■ antônimo: **immorality**

morally ['morəli] *adv.* □ **moralmente**
It's morally wrong to do this.

more¹ [mo:] *adj.* □ **mais**
I need more money. ◆ Give me one more apple. ◆ Put some more sugar in it.

more² *pron.* □ **mais**
Show me more of your tricks. ◆ That's not enough – I want more. ◆ I can't eat any more. ◆ Give him a little more.
the more... the more... □ **quanto mais... mais...**
The more you hope, the more you will be disappointed.

more³ *adv.* □ **mais**
He is more intelligent than I thought. ◆ Drive more slowly! ◆ This question is much more difficult.
■ With short words we use **-er** instead of **more:**
fast – faster.
hard – harder.
more or less □ **mais ou menos**
We are more or less the same height.
not any more □ **não mais**
I don't go there any more.
once more □ **mais uma vez, de novo**
You can try once more.

moreover [mo:'rouvə] *adv.* □ **além disso, além do mais**
This computer is better than the others. Moreover, it is cheaper.

morning ['mo:niŋ] *n.* □ **manhã**
early in the morning. ◆ on Monday morning. ◆ I'll send it tomorrow morning.

mortgage¹ ['mo:gidʒ] *n.* □ **hipoteca**

mortgage² *v.* (**mortgages, mortgaging, mortgaged**) □ **hipotecar**
They mortgaged their house.

Moslem *n.* (Ver **Muslim**).

mosque [mosk] *n.* □ **mesquita**

mosquito [mə'ski:tou] *n.* □ **pernilongo**
Mosquitoes bit me on the face.

moss [mos] *n.* □ **musgo, limo**

most¹ [moust] *adj., pron.*
1 maioria de, maior parte de
He made the most mistakes. ◆ They ate the most food. ◆ She reads the most.
2 a maioria de
In most cases. ◆ Most of them knew the answer. ◆ They are here most of the time.
at (the) most □ **no máximo**
The journey will take 2 hours at the most.
make the most of □ **aproveitar o máximo**
We don't have much time, so let's make the most of it.

most² *adv.* □ **o mais, mais**
It's the most expensive computer there is. ◆ Who helped you most?
■ With short words you use **-est** instead of **most:**
fast - fastest.
easy - easiest.

mostly ['moustli] *adv.* □ **principalmente**
It snows mostly in the north of the country. ◆ The tourists in this group are mostly Americans.

motel [mou'tel] *n.* □ motel
moth [mɔθ] *n.* □ mariposa, traça
mother ['mʌðə] *n.* □ mãe
My mother is a dentist. ◆ It's not here, Mother.
mother-in-law ['mʌðərinlɔː] *n.* (*pl.* **mothers-in-law**) □ sogra
My mother-in-law is coming for a visit.
mother tongue ['mʌðə tʌŋ] *n.* □ língua materna
My mother tongue is Italian.
motion ['mouʃən] *n.* □ movimento
Don't get up when the bus is in motion.
motive ['moutiv] *n.* □ motivo
What was the motive for the murder?
motor ['moutə] *n.* □ motor
an electric motor.
■ **engine** is the usual word for cars.
motorbike ['moutəbaik] *n.* (= motorcycle) □ motocicleta, moto
Can you ride a motorbike?
motorboat ['moutəbout] *n.* □ barco a motor
motor car ['moutə kaː] *n. Brit.* (= car) □ carro
motorcycle ['moutəsaikl] *n.* □ motocicleta
motorcyclist ['moutə,saiklist] *n.* □ motociclista
The motorcyclist rode on a red motorbike.
motorist ['moutərist] *n.* □ motorista
■ **driver** is the usual word.
motor racing ['moutə 'reisiŋ] *n.* □ corrida de carro, automobilismo
motorway ['moutəwei] *n. Brit.* □ autoestrada, via expressa
■ *Amer.* **expressway; freeway**
mould[1] [mould] *n. Brit.*, **mold** *Amer.*
1 bolor
The bread is not fresh. There is mould on it.
2 forma, molde
Pour the hot jelly into moulds.
mould[2] *v. Brit.* (**moulds, moulding, moulded**) (= **mold**[2], *Amer.*) □ moldar
She moulds little animals out of clay.
mouldy ['mouldi] *adj. Brit.*, **moldy** *Amer.* □ embolorado, bolorento
mouldy bread.
Mount [maunt] *n.* □ monte
Mount Everest (= Mt Everest).
mount [maunt] *v.* (**mounts, mounting, mounted**) (= get on) □ montar
They mounted their horses.
■ antônimo: **dismount (from)**
mountain ['mauntən] *n.* □ montanha
They climbed the mountain. ◆ Which is the highest mountain in the world?
mountaineer [,maunti'niə] *n.* □ montanhista, alpinista
mountaineering [,maunti'niəriŋ] *n.* □ montanhismo, alpinismo
mountainous ['mauntənəs] *adj.* □ montanhoso
a mountainous area.
mourn [mɔːn] *v.* (**mourns, mourning, mourned**) □ lamentar a morte de
They are mourning for their child.
mourner ['mɔːnə] *n.* □ lamentador
mourning ['mɔːniŋ] *n.* □ luto
They are in mourning.
mouse [maus] *n.* (*pl.* **mice**)
1 rato
The cat almost caught the mouse.
2 mouse
I use the mouse for computer games.
moustache [mə'staːʃ] *n.* (= **mustache**) □ bigode
He is growing a moustache.
mouth [mauθ] *n.* □ boca
Open your mouth, please.
move[1] [muːv] *n.*
1 passo
What's the next move?
2 jogada
Do you know all the moves in chess?
3 movimento, passo
The police are watching his moves.
4 mudança
The move (to the new house) will be tomorrow.
get a move on (= hurry[2]) □ apressar-se, andar logo
move[2] *v.* (**moves, moving, moved**)
1 mover-se, mexer-se, mexer
Don't move! ◆ The train started moving. ◆ He can't move his legs.
2 mudar
I moved to the front seat. ◆ They are moving the factory to another area.
3 mudar-se
We are moving house next month. ◆ They don't live here any more – they moved last year.
4 mexer-se
You have to move quickly if you want to save the company.
5 comover, emocionar
His story moved them.
move in □ mudar-se
When are you moving in?
move on □ passar para
Let's move on to the next question.
move over □ afastar-se
I moved over to let her sit by the window.
movement ['muːvmənt] *n.*
1 movimento
The boxer's movements were very quick. ◆ the movement of the trees in the wind.
2 movimento
a youth movement.
movie ['muːvi] *n. Amer.* □ filme, cinema
Would you like to go to a movie? ◆ movie stars
■ *Brit.* **film**
the movies (= the cinema) □ o cinema
to go to the movies.
movie theater ['muːvi 'θiətə] *n. Amer.* □ cinema
■ *Brit.* **cinema**
mow [mou] *v.* (**mows, mowing, mowed, mown**) □ aparar
to mow the grass.
mower ['mouə] *n.* □ cortador de grama
MP [em piː] *abbr.* □ Membro do Parlamento
Mr. *abbr.*, **Mr** (= Mister) Sr.
Mr. (David) Jones. ◆ Dear Mr Jones, (beginning a letter)
Mrs. *abbr.*, **Mrs** (mesmo que **Mistress**) (*pl.* **Mmes**) □ Sra.
Mrs (Edna) Frost. ◆ Dear Mrs Frost, (beginning a letter)
Ms. *abbr.*, **Ms** (mesmo que **Miss**) (*pl.* **Mses**) □ Srta.
Ms (Esther) Williams.
Mt. *abbr.*, **Mt** (= Mount) □ Mt.
Mt Everest.

much [mʌtʃ] *adj.*, *pron.*, *adv.*
1 muito
I don't have much money. ♦ She didn't say much. ♦ He doesn't know much about computers.
■ **much** is usually used in questions and negative sentences, and after 'as', 'how', 'so', 'too' and 'very'. In other sentences we use **a lot of**.
■ Ver **many**.
2 muito
I feel much better now. ♦ This box is much heavier than that box.
■ Ver **much more**.
as much as □ **tanto... quanto**
Take as much (food) as you want.
How much...? □ **Quanto...?**
How much will it cost? ♦ How much time do you need?
■ Ver **How many...?**
much more □ **muito mais**
This question is much more difficult than the first one.
not (very) much □ **não muito**
Did you enjoy the book? – No, not very much. ♦ It doesn't matter much to me.
so much □ **tanto**
There is so much food that we can't eat it all. ♦ They suffered so much.
too much □ **demais, muito**
There's too much salt in the soup. ♦ It cost too much.
very much □ **muito**
I enjoyed the film very much.
mud [mʌd] *n.* □ **lama, barro**
Your shoes are covered with mud.
muddle[1] ['mʌdl] *n.*
1 bagunça
Your room is in a terrible muddle (= in a mess). ♦ How can we get out of this muddle (= mess)?
2 confusão
to get in a muddle (= to become confused)
muddle[2] *v.* (**muddles, muddling, muddled**) □ **atrapalhar**
muddle something (up) □ **bagunçar**
Don't muddle up the papers on my desk.
muddle someone (up) (= confuse) □ **confundir**
You're muddling me up with these questions.
muddy ['mʌdi] *adj.* (**muddier, muddiest**)
1 barrento
the muddy water of the river.
2 barrento, enlameado
The roads are muddy after the rain.
mug[1] [mʌg] *n.* □ **caneca**
She drank a mug of beer.
mug[2] *v.* (**mugs, mugging, mugged**) □ **assaltar**
Two people mugged me and took my money.
mugger ['mʌgə] *n.* □ **assaltante**
mule [mju:l] *n.* □ **mula**
The mules carried our food and equipment.
multicolored [,mʌlti'kʌləd] *adj. Amer.*, **multicoloured** *Brit.* □ **multicolorido**
multicolored flags.
multiple-choice test ['mʌltiplt∫ois ,test] *n.* □ **teste de múltipla-escolha**
multiplication [,mʌltipli'kei∫ən] *n.* □ **multiplicação**
to learn multiplication, division, addition and subtraction.

multiplication table [,mʌltipli'kei∫ən 'teibl] *n.* □ **tabuada**
multiply ['mʌltiplai] *v.* (**multiplies, multiplying, multiplied**)
1 □ **multiplicar, vezes**
If you multiply 5 by 2 you get 10 (5x2=10). ♦ Six multiplied by ten is sixty (6x10=60).
2 □ **multiplicar-se**
Rabbits multiply quickly.
mum [mʌm] *n. Brit.*, **mom** *Amer.* □ **mãe**
Can I go now, Mum?
mumble ['mʌmbl] *v.* (**mumbles, mumbling, mumbled**) □ **resmungar**
She mumbled something, but I couldn't hear what she said.
mummy ['mʌmi] *n. Brit.* (*pl.* **mummies**) □ **mamãezinha, mãezinha**
Tell me a story, Mummy.
■ *Amer.* **mommy**
mumps [mʌmps] *n.* □ **caxumba**
murder[1] ['mɔ:də] *n.* □ **assassinato, crime**
She is accused of murder. ♦ The police found the murder weapon.
murder[2] *v.* (**murders, murdering, murdered**) □ **assassinar**
He murdered her with a knife.
murderer ['mɔ:dərə] *n.* □ **assassino**
She is not the murderer.
murderess ['mɔ:dəris] *n.* □ **assassina**
murderous ['mɔ:dərəs] *adj.* □ **assassino**
a murderous attack.
murmur[1] ['mɔ:mə] *n.* □ **murmúrio, barulhinho**
the murmur of the waves. ♦ the murmur of the wind in the trees.
murmur[2] *v.* (**murmurs, murmuring, murmured**) □ **murmurar**
He murmured something in his sleep.
muscle ['mʌsl] *n.* □ **músculo**
He has strong muscles.
muscular ['mʌskjulə] *adj.* □ **musculoso, muscular**
muscular arms.
museum [mju'ziəm] *n.* □ **museu**
There's a new exhibition at the Science Museum.
mushroom ['mʌ∫rum] *n.* □ **cogumelo**
mushroom soup.
music ['mju:zik] *n.*
1 música
pop / rock music. ♦ What kind of music do you like?
2 partitura, notação musical
They can't read music. ♦ Who wrote the music?
musical[1] ['mju:zikəl] *adj.* □ **musical**
He plays the piano, the guitar and other musical instruments.
musical[2] *n.* □ **musical**
musician [mju'zi∫ən] *n.* □ **músico, musicista**
There are five musicians in the band.
Muslim ['muzlim] (= **Moslem**) *n.*, *adj.* □ **muçulmano**
He is a Muslim. ♦ Muslim holidays.
must [mʌst] *v.*
1 dever
You must pay him today. ♦ He must tell them the truth. ♦ Must I send it now? – No, you don't have to.
■ Be careful not to use 'to' after 'must'.
■ In negative sentences use **do not have to**, because **must not** has a different meaning.
■ For the *past tense* use **had to**.
■ Ver **have to**.

2 dever
You must be hungry. ◆ She must be disappointed.
must not □ **estar proibido de**
You mustn't smoke here. ◆ You mustn't tell anyone.
must have (done) □ **dever ter (feito)**
He is not here. He must have gone to the dentist.
mustache [məs'ta:ʃ] *n. Amer.* (= **moustache**) □ **bigode**
mustard ['mʌstəd] *n.* □ **mostarda**
mustn't ['mʌsnt] (mesmo que **must not**)
mutiny[1] ['mju:tini] *n.* (*pl.* **mutinies**) □ **motim**
mutiny[2] *v.* (**mutinies, mutinying, mutinied**) □ **amotinar-se**
The sailors mutinied against their captain.
mutter ['mʌtə] *v.* (**mutters, muttering, muttered**) □ **resmungar, murmurar**
He muttered something about the waste of money and time.
mutton ['mʌtn] *n.* □ **carne de carneiro**
mutual ['mju:tʃuəl] *adj.*
1 mútuo
mutual respect.
2 em comum
They have mutual interests. ◆ a mutual friend.
muzzle [mʌzl] *n.* □ **focinheira**
This dog bites, so it has a muzzle on.
my [mai] *adj.* □ **meu, minha**
My hair is black. ◆ My friends are coming tonight. ◆ Where are my keys?
■ Ver **mine**.

myself [mai'self] *pron.*
1 me, eu mesmo
I looked at myself in the mirror. ◆ I bought myself a pair of jeans. ◆ I'm proud of myself.
■ Note:
I cut myself (by accident).
I hurt myself (when I fell, etc.).
2 eu mesmo
I sent it myself. ◆ I myself gave it to him.
by myself
1 sozinho
I live by myself.
2 por conta própria
I fixed it by myself.
mysterious [mi'stiəriəs] *adj.* □ **misterioso**
the mysterious disappearance of the woman.
mysteriously [mi'stiəriəsli] *adv.* □ **misteriosamente**
Many people got ill mysteriously.
mystery ['mistəri] *n.* (*pl.* **mysteries**) □ **mistério**
The detective solved the mystery.
mystery novel ['mistəri ˌnovl] *n.* □ **romance de mistério**
myth [miθ] *n.*
1 mito
Everybody thinks that he was a hero, but it's a myth.
2 mito
ancient Greek myths (= old stories about the Greek gods and heroes).

Nn

n. *abbr.* (= noun) □ **n.**
N *abbr.* (= North) □ **N**
nag [nag] *v.* (**nags, nagging, nagged**) □ **resmungar, amolar, atazanar**
Stop nagging! ◆ He is nagging me to buy him a computer.
nail¹ [neil] *n.*
  1 prego
  to hammer a nail into the wall. ◆ I need a hammer and nails to mend the chair.
  2 unha
  Cut your nails. Don't bite them!
  ■ Ver **fingernail; toenail.**
nail² *v.* (**nails, nailing, nailed**) □ **pregar**
He nailed the sign to the wall.
naive [nai'i:v] *adj.* □ **ingênuo**
I don't believe them. I'm not so naive.
naked ['neikid] *adj.* □ **nu**
She was naked. ◆ his naked body.
  with the naked eye □ **a olho nu**
  You can't see a virus with the naked eye.
name¹ [neim] *n.*
  1 nome
  What's your name? ◆ Her name is not on the list. ◆ What is the name of this tree?
  ■ Ver **family name; first name.**
  2 fama
  This neighborhood has a bad name.
  call someone names □ **xingar alguém**
  They called him names. (= They called him a liar, a coward, etc.)
name² *v.* (**names, naming, named**)
  1 nomear, dar nome
  They named her Diana.
  2 enumerar, citar
  Can you name the months of the year? ◆ Name two reasons for this decision.
namely ['neimli] *adv.* □ **a saber, isto é**
He will achieve his goal, namely to win three gold medals.
nanny ['nani] *n.* (*pl.* **nannies**) □ **babá**
nap¹ [nap] *n.* □ **soneca, cochilo**
He had a nap on the sofa.
nap² *v.* (**naps, napping, napped**) □ **cochilar**
She usually naps for an hour after lunch.
napkin ['napkin] *n.* □ **guardanapo**
He wiped his mouth with a paper napkin.
  ■ *Brit.* also **serviette**
nappy ['napi] *n. Brit.* (*pl.* **nappies**) □ **fralda**
I changed the baby's nappy.
  ■ *Amer.* **diaper**
narrow¹ ['narou] *adj.* □ **estreito**
a narrow bridge. ◆ The road gets narrower here.
  ■ antônimo: **broad; wide**
  a narrow escape □ **por um triz**
  The plane almost crashed into the mountain. It was a narrow escape.
narrow² *v.* (**narrows, narrowing, narrowed**)
  1 estreitar
  The road narrows here.
  2 diminuir
  to narrow the gap between the rich and the poor.
narrowly ['narouli] *adv.* □ **quase, por pouco**
The plane narrowly missed hitting the tower.
nasty ['na:sti] *adj.* (**nastier, nastiest**)
  1 nojento
  a nasty smell.
  2 grosseiro, mau
  Don't be so nasty to your brother!
  3 feio
  a nasty (= bad) accident.
nation ['neiʃən] *n.* □ **nação**
all the nations of the world. ◆ industrial nations (= industrial countries).
national¹ ['naʃənəl] *adj.* □ **nacional**
What's the national food of Hungary?
national anthem *n.* □ **hino nacional**
national² *n.* □ **cidadão**
American nationals in France.
nationality [,naʃə'naləti] *n.* (*pl.* **nationalities**) □ **nacionalidade**
British nationality.
native¹ ['neitiv] *adj.* □ **nativo**
  native country *n.* □ **país de origem, pátria**
  native speaker *n.* □ **falante nativo**
  native speakers of English.
native² *n.* □ **natural, nativo**
a native of Paris / France.
Native American ['neitiv ə'meri:kən] (= American Indian) *n., adj.* □ **nativo americano, indígena americano**
Native American tribes.
natural ['natʃərəl] *adj.* □ **natural**
natural resources (e.g. coal, oil, gold). ◆ natural foods. ◆ It's natural to feel angry when people cheat you.
  ■ Ver **unnatural; man-made; artificial.**
naturally ['natʃərəli] *adv.*
  1 naturalmente
  Naturally, you'll need some time to think about it.
  2 naturalmente
  Try to behave naturally.
  3 naturalmente
  She is naturally blond.
nature ['neitʃə] *n.*
  1 natureza
  the beauty of nature. ◆ the laws of nature.
  2 natureza
  It's not in his nature to lie. ◆ his real nature.
  3 natureza
  What's the nature of her illness?
naughtiness ['no:tinis] *n.* □ **traquinagem, travessura**
naughty ['no:ti] *adj.* (**naughtier, naughtiest**) □ **levado, traquina**
a naughty child
naval ['neivəl] *adj.* □ **naval**
a naval officer.
navigate ['navigeit] *v.* (**navigates, navigating, navigated**) □ **navegar, pilotar**
to navigate with a map and compass. ◆ to navigate a boat / an airplane.
navigation [navi'geiʃən] *n.* □ **navegação**
navigator ['navigeitə] *n.* □ **navegador**
navy ['neivi] *n.* (*pl.* **navies**) □ **marinha**
He is in the navy.

near¹ [niə] *adj.* □ **perto, próximo**
The school is very near. ◆ The nearest bank is 2 km from here. ◆ the near future (= very soon).
■ Ver **close¹**.
get nearer (= get closer) □ **aproximar-se**
Her wedding day is getting nearer.
near² *adv., prep.* □ **perto (de), próximo (a)**
He wants to sit near me. ◆ We live near (to) the school.
bring something nearer (= bring closer) □ **trazer algo para mais perto**
Bring the chair nearer.
come near / nearer □ **chegar perto / mais perto**
Don't come too near me! ◆ Come nearer. I want to look at you.
nearby [niə'bai] *adj., adv.* □ **próximo**
He lives in a nearby street. ◆ He lives nearby. (= He lives near here.)
nearly ['niəli] *adv.* □ **quase**
It's nearly four o'clock. ◆ I'm nearly 17. ◆ We're nearly there.
■ **nearly** cannot be used for colours, shapes or features, or in phrases with 'nothing', 'no-one', 'never', etc.; **almost** is used in all cases:
She said almost nothing.
almost green; almost round; almost human.
not nearly □ **nem perto**
One million dollars is not nearly enough for this project.
near-sighted [,niə'saitid]
neat [ni:t] *adj.*
1 asseado, em ordem
He always keeps his room neat and tidy.
2 caprichado, elegante
She has neat handwriting.
neatly ['ni:tli] *adv.* □ **em ordem, bem arrumado**
I arranged the books neatly.
necessarily [,nesi'serili] *adv.* □ **necessariamente**
This is not necessarily true.
necessary ['nesisəri] *adj.* □ **necessário**
We'll do whatever is necessary. ◆ Is it necessary to do it here?
necessity [ni'sesəti] *n. (pl.* **necessities**)
1 necessidade
There's no necessity to check it again.
2 necessidade
For disabled people, a car is a necessity.
neck [nek] *n.*
1 pescoço
I put the necklace around her neck.
2 gola
a sweater with a round neck
■ For shirts, jackets, etc. use **collar**.
necklace ['nekləs] *n.* □ **colar, gargantilha**
She wore a pearl necklace.
need¹ [ni:d] *n.* □ **necessidade**
There's no need to apologize. ◆ He felt the need to visit them.
be in need of □ **estar precisando de**
I'm in need of a hot bath.
need² *v.* (**needs, needing, needed**) □ **precisar de, necessitar de**
We need more volunteers. ◆ Do you need any help?

need to (= have to) □ **ter de**
He needs to try harder. ◆ You don't need to pay now.
■ In negative sentences, **needn't** can be used instead of **don't / doesn't need to**: He **needn't** wait for them. Or: He **doesn't** need to wait for them.
■ Questions can be formed in two ways: **Need** you come? or: **Do** you **need** to come?
needle ['ni:dl] *n.*
1 agulha
I need a needle and thread to sew on this button. ◆ a knitting needle.
2 ponteiro
the needle of a compass.
needless ['ni:dlis] *adj.* □ **desnecessário**
You caused us needless worry.
needlessly ['ni:dlisli] *adv.* □ **desnecessariamente**
needn't (Ver **need²**).
negative¹ ['negətiv] *adj.* □ **negativo**
a negative sentence.
■ Ver **positive**.
negative² *n.*
1 negativo
He answered in the negative.
2 negativo
to develop photographs from the negative.
neglect¹ [ni'glekt] *v.* (**neglects, neglecting, neglected**) □ **negligenciar**
Don't neglect your health. ◆ He started to neglect his studies.
neglect² *n.* □ **negligência, abandono**
The house was in a state of neglect.
neglected [ni'glektid] *adj.* □ **negligenciado**
a neglected house. ◆ neglected children.
negligence ['neglidʒəns] *n.* □ **negligência**
Medical negligence led to her death.
negligent ['neglidʒənt] *adj.* □ **negligente**
He was negligent in his work.
negotiate [ni'gouʃieit] *v.* (**negotiates, negotiating, negotiated**) □ **negociar**
The workers are negotiating with the manager about their pay.
negotiation [ni,gouʃi'eiʃən] *n.* □ **negociação**
The negotiations for peace are continuing.
neigh¹ [nei] *n.* □ **relincho**
neigh² *v.* (**neighs, neighing, neighed**) □ **relinchar**
The horse neighed when I touched it.
neighbor ['neibə] *n. Amer.,* **neighbour** *Brit.* □ **vizinho**
I invited our next-door neighbor to the party.
neighborhood ['neibəhud] *n. Amer.,* **neighbourhood** *Brit.* □ **vizinhança, bairro**
He lives in a rich neighborhood.
neighboring ['neibəriŋ] *adj. Amer.,* **neighbouring** *Brit.* □ **vizinho**
neighboring countries.
neighborly ['neibəli] *adj. Amer.,* **neighbourly** *Brit.* □ **amistoso, prestativo**
neighborly relations.
neither¹ ['naiðə, 'ni:ðə(r)] *adj., pron.* □ **nenhum dos dois, nem um, nem outro**
Neither answer was correct. ◆ Neither of the answers was correct. ◆ Would you like tea or coffee? – Neither, thank you.
■ **neither** is in itself negative and so does not require another negative word (e.g. not) in the same sentence.

■ **neither** is followed by a singular noun and verb; **neither of** is followed by a plural noun and singular verb (see the first two sentences).

neither² *adv.* (= nor) □ **também não, nem**
I can't drive and neither can Dan. ◆ I don't speak French. – Neither do I.

■ Note the inverted word order after **neither** – first the auxiliary verb and then the subject.

neither... nor □ **nem..., nem**
Neither you nor I was / were there. ◆ Neither Guy nor Naomi likes / like fish. ◆ I speak neither German nor French.

■ Note that the verb after **neither... nor** can be singular or plural.

neon ['ni:on] *n.*, *adj.* □ **neon**

nephew ['nefju:] *n.* □ **sobrinho**
My nephew and niece came to visit me.

nerd [nə:d] *n.* □ **nerd**
That nerd wears weird clothes and isn't interested in anything except computers.

nerve [nə:v] *n.*
1 nervo
He cannot walk because of the damage to his nerves.
2 coragem
They didn't have the nerve to tell him the truth.
3 coragem
She had the nerve to ask me for money.

nerves *n. pl.*
1 nervos
strong nerves.
2 nervos
Take this medicine to calm your nerves.
get on your nerves □ **dar nos nervos, irritar**
He got on my nerves with his silly jokes. ◆ You're getting on my nerves!

nervous ['nə:vəs] *adj.*
1 nervoso
the nervous system.
2 nervoso
I'm nervous because this is my first time on TV. ◆ a nervous laugh.
get nervous □ **ficar nervoso**
I always get nervous before an exam.

nervously ['nə:vəsli] *adv.* □ **nervosamente**
She laughed nervously.

nervousness ['nə:vəsnis] *n.* □ **nervosismo**

nest¹ [nest] *n.* □ **ninho**
a bird's nest. ◆ an ants' nest.

nest² *v.* (**nests, nesting, nested**) □ **fazer ninho, aninhar-se**
The birds nested on top of the tree.

net [net] *n.* □ **rede**
a fishing net.
the net (= internet) □ **a rede, net, internet**
to surf the net.

network ['netwə:k] *n.* □ **network, rede**
a computer network. ◆ a network of roads. ◆ television networks.

neutral ['nju:trəl] *adj.*, *n.* □ **neutro**
Switzerland was a neutral country in the war. ◆ to remain neutral. ◆ put the car in neutral (= neutral gear).

never ['nevə] *adv.* □ **nunca, jamais**
I'll never forget you. ◆ She never saw him again after that day.

never mind □ **tudo bem, deixe para lá**
Never mind, you can try again tomorrow.

nevertheless [,nevəðə'les] *adv.* (= in spite of this) □ **apesar disso, todavia, contudo**
They knew that there was no chance. Nevertheless, they decided to try.

new [nju:] *adj.* □ **novo**
I bought a new car. ◆ new ideas.

new to
1 novo em
I'm new to this town.
2 novo para
This area is new to me.

New Year's Eve □ **véspera de ano-novo**

newcomer [nju:'kʌmə] *n.* □ **recém-chegado**

newly ['nju:li] *adv.* □ **recém, recentemente**
They are newly married.

news [nju:z] *n.*
1 noticiário
the nine o'clock news. ◆ I heard about it on the news.
2 notícia
That's good news. When is the wedding?

■ **news** takes a singular verb:
The news is good.

■ **a piece of news** or **a news item** (*not* 'a news')

newsagent ['nju:z,eidʒənt] *n. Brit.* □ **jornaleiro**
■ *Amer.* **newsdealer**

newscaster ['nju:zka:stə] *n.* (mesmo que **newsreader**) □ **âncora**

news conference ['nju:z 'konfərəns] *n.* □ **coletiva de imprensa**

newsflash ['nju:zflaʃ] *n.* □ **notícia de última hora**

newspaper ['nju:zpeipə] *n.* (Ver **paper**) □ **jornal**
I read it in the newspaper. ◆ a newspaper article.

next¹ [nekst] *adj.*
1 próximo
next week. ◆ They are coming next Monday. ◆ Turn right at the next traffic light. ◆ The next train leaves at 11.
2 próximo, outro
in the next room.
(the) next day □ **(o) dia seguinte**
The next day, he came alone.
next time □ **próxima vez**
Next time try to come early!
next to (= beside) □ **ao lado de**
He sat next to me.
next to nothing (= hardly anything) □ **quase nada**
He earns next to nothing – he is very badly paid.
the next □ **o seguinte, o próximo**
The bus was full, so we took the next.

next² *adv.*
1 depois, em seguida
What did you do next?
2 o próximo
You're next.

next door [,nekst 'do:] *adj.*, *adv.* □ **vizinho, ao lado**
the next-door apartment. ◆ my next-door neighbor. ◆ They live next door.

nibble¹ ['nibl] *n.* □ **bocado, pedaço**
Can I have a nibble of your chocolate?

nibble² *v.* (**nibbles, nibbling, nibbled**) □ **mordiscar**
The mouse nibbled (on) the cheese.

nice [nais] *adj.*
1 (= pleasant) **bom, agradável**
nice weather. ♦ It's a nice day.
2 legal
a nice girl.
3 legal, de bom gosto
It's not nice to point at people.
nice to see you □ **prazer em vê-lo**
nice to meet you (= pleased to meet you) □ **prazer em conhecê-lo**
nicely ['naisli] *adv.*
1 bem, primorosamente
You arranged the flowers nicely.
2 com modos, direito
You can have ice cream if you ask nicely.
nickname¹ ['nikneim] *n.* □ **apelido**
Her nickname is 'Ginger'.
nickname² *v.* (**nicknames, nicknaming, nicknamed**) □ **apelidar**
be nicknamed □ **ser apelidado de**
She is nicknamed 'Angel'.
niece [ni:s] *n.* □ **sobrinha**
■ Ver **nephew**.
night [nait] *n.*
1 noite
I was awake all night. ♦ Discos are open till late at night.
2 à noite
on Saturday night.
■ Ver **tonight**.
last night □ **ontem à noite**
She slept very well last night. ♦ I called you last night at 8.
nightclub ['naitklʌb] *n.* □ **casa noturna, boate**
nightdress ['naitdres] *n.* (mesmo que **nightie**) □ **camisola**
■ *Amer.* also **nightgown**
nightingale ['naitiŋgeil] *n.* □ **rouxinol**
nightly ['naitli] *adj., adv.* □ **noturno, à noite**
a nightly TV show.
nightmare ['naitmeə] *n.* □ **pesadelo**
She had a nightmare last night. ♦ It's a nightmare to drive in this city.
night school [nait sku:l] *n.* □ **escola noturna, curso noturno**
■ *Brit.* **evening classes**
night shift ['nait ʃift] *n.* □ **turno da noite**
to work (on) the night shift.
night-time ['naitaim] *n.* □ **noite**
at night-time.
nil [nil] *n.* □ **zero**
Our team won the game two-nil (2-0).
■ Ver **zero**.
nine [nain] *adj., n.* □ **nove**
It's nine o'clock. ♦ The show starts at nine. ♦ She is nine years old. ♦ Four and five are nine (4+5=9).
■ Ver **ninth**.
nineteen [nain'ti:n] *adj., n.* □ **dezenove**
nineteenth [,nain'ti:nθ] *adj., adv., n.* □ **décimo nono, dezenove**
the nineteenth floor. ♦ the nineteenth century. ♦ the nineteenth of July (= 19th July). *Brit.* ♦ July nineteenth (= July 19). *Amer.*
nineties ['naintiz] *n.* (Ver **ninety**).
ninetieth ['naintiəθ] *adj., adv., n.* □ **nonagésimo**
the ninetieth name on the list.
ninety ['nainti] *adj., n.* □ **noventa**
He is ninety years old. ♦ ninety thousand (= 90,000).
the nineties (= 90's) □ **os anos noventa, a década de 1990**
in the early nineties (= in the first years of the 90's).
ninth¹ ['nainθ] *adj., adv., pron.* □ **nono, nove**
the ninth floor. ♦ the ninth of April (= 9th April). *Brit.* ♦ April ninth (= April 9). *Amer.* ♦ She came ninth in the race.
ninth² *n.* □ **nono**
a ninth (= 1/9) of the budget.
nipple ['nipl] *n.* □ **mamilo**
nitrogen ['naitrədʒən] *n.* □ **nitrogênio**
No. *abbr.*, **no.** (= number) □ **N°, n°**
room no. 137.
no [nou]
1 não
Do you know him? – No, I don't. ♦ Would you like to come? – No, thank you.
2 nenhum
There's no one here. (= There isn't anyone here.) ♦ There are no towels. (= There aren't any towels.) ♦ I have no money. (= I don't have any money.)
3 nenhum
No other pupil got a 10.
4 nada
no less than 100 dollars. ♦ no fewer than 150 people. ♦ no later than Tuesday.
5 é proibido
No parking! ♦ No smoking!
no one (Ver **nobody**).
noble ['noubl] *adj.*
1 nobre
a noble family.
2 nobre
It was noble of you to forgive him.
nobody ['noubədi] *pron.* (mesmo que **no one**) □ **ninguém**
Nobody knows what happened. ♦ There was nobody there. (= There wasn't anybody there.) ♦ I told nobody. (= I didn't tell anybody.)
nod¹ [nod] *n.* □ **sinal afirmativo com a cabeça**
He gave me a nod.
nod² *v.* (**nods, nodding, nodded**) □ **assentir com a cabeça**
They nodded in agreement. ♦ She nodded to me to take a seat.
noise [noiz] *n.*
1 barulho, ruído
I heard a noise in the kitchen. ♦ Who is making these noises?
2 barulho
Stop making so much noise!
noisily ['noizli] *adv.* □ **ruidosamente, barulhentamente**
noisy ['noizi] *adj.* (**noisier, noisiest**) □ **barulhento**
It's too noisy in here. ♦ a noisy class.
■ antônimo: **quiet**
non- [non] *pref.* □ **não, sem**
a non-smoker (= a person who does not smoke). ♦ non-violence (= without violence). ♦ non-stop (train, flight, etc).
none [nʌn] *pron.* □ **nenhum, nada, ninguém**
None of them waited. ♦ None of the questions is easy. ♦ She wanted some milk, but there was none left.
nonetheless [,nʌnðə'les] *adv.* (= anyway; nevertheless) □ **todavia, contudo, entretanto**

non-fiction [nonˈfikʃən] *n.* □ **não ficção**
I like to read non-fiction, such as biographies and travel books.
■ Ver **fiction**.

nonsense [ˈnonsəns] *n.* □ **besteira, bobagem**
Don't talk nonsense! ◆ It's nonsense to say that he is rich.

non-smoker [nonˈsmoukə] *n.* □ **não fumante**

non-stop [nonˈstop] *adj.*, *adv.*
1 sem escala, direto
a non-stop flight to New York.
2 sem parar
to talk non-stop.

noodles [ˈnu:dlz] *n. pl.* □ **macarrão**

noon [nu:n] *n.* (= midday) □ **meio-dia**
We met at noon.

no one (Ver **nobody**).

nor [no:] *conj.*, *adv.* □ **nem**
I don't speak Chinese. – Nor do I. ◆ If you don't go, nor will I. ◆ Neither she nor I will come.
■ Ver **neither**[2].

normal [ˈno:məl] *adj.* □ **normal**
Arriving late is normal. ◆ at the normal (= usual) time.

normally [ˈno:məli] *adv.*
1 normalmente
They aren't behaving normally.
2 (= usually) **normalmente**
I normally go to school by bus.

north[1] [no:θ] *n.* □ **norte**
I live in the north (of the country).
to the north of □ **ao norte de**
They live 25 km to the north of the city.

north[2] *adj.* □ **norte**
a north wind. ◆ North America. ◆ the North Pole.

north[3] *adv.* □ **sentido norte**
We travelled north.
north of □ **ao norte de**
10 km north of the airport.

northerly [ˈno:ðəli] *adj.* □ **do norte, norte**
northerly winds.

northern [ˈno:ðən] *adj.* □ **setentrional**
northern Europe.

nose [nouz] *n.*
1 nariz
Breathe in through your nose.
2 parte dianteira
the nose of the plane.
blow your nose □ **assoar seu nariz**
He blew his nose.

nostril [ˈnostril] *n.* □ **narina**

nosy [ˈnouzi] *adj.* (**nosier, nosiest**) □ **curioso, intrometido**
nosy people next door.

not [not] *adv.*
1 não
He does not (= doesn't) know. ◆ I'm not staying. ◆ It's not (= It isn't) heavy. ◆ I asked him not to come.
2 não
Don't (= Do not) wait for us.

not at all
1 de jeito nenhum
Am I boring you? – Not at all.
2 de nada
Thanks for your advice. – Not at all.

not only... but also □ **não só... como também**
They came not only with their children, but also with their dog. ◆ She not only sings, but also plays the piano. (= Not only does she sing, but she also plays the piano.)

note[1] [nout] *n.*
1 bilhete
He wrote me a note in the middle of the meeting. ◆ a note (= a short letter) of explanation.
2 nota
See the note on page 830.
3 *Brit.* **nota**
a fifty-pound note (= a £50 note)
■ *Amer.* **bill**
4 nota musical
He played a few notes on the piano.
make a note of (= write down) □ **tomar nota de, anotar**
She made a note of the time and place of the accident.
notes *n. pl.* □ **anotações**
The speaker looked at his notes.
take notes □ **tomar nota, fazer anotações**
Some of the students took notes at the lecture.

note[2] *v.* (**notes, noting, noted**) □ **notar**
Note that there are two possible answers here.
note down □ **tomar nota, anotar**
Please note down what I say.

notebook [ˈnoutbuk] *n.* □ **caderno**
I wrote down the main points in my notebook.
■ Ver **exercise book**.

notepad [ˈnoutpad] *n.* □ **bloco de anotações**

notepaper [ˈnoutpeipə] *n.* □ **papel para anotações**

nothing [ˈnʌθiŋ] *pron.* □ **nada**
There's nothing in the box. ◆ I saw nothing. (= I didn't see anything.) ◆ I have nothing to say.
come to nothing □ **não dar em nada**
Their plans came to nothing in the end.
for nothing
1 para nada
Our efforts were all for nothing.
2 de graça, sem razão, por nada
I got the radio for nothing.
have nothing to do with □ **não ter nada a ver com**
I don't know who did it. I had nothing to do with it.
nothing but
1 nada além de, só, apenas
He took nothing but a few books.
2 não passar de
She is nothing but a liar.

notice[1] [ˈnoutis] *n.*
1 cartaz, anúncio
to put up a notice. ◆ The notice on the wall says 'No Parking'
◆ notices of births, marriages and deaths in the newspaper
■ Ver **advertisement; announcement**.
2 aviso
He gave us two weeks' notice to prepare.
at short notice □ **em cima da hora**
We had to prepare everything at very short notice.
give in / hand in your notice □ **pedir demissão**
She handed in her notice yesterday.
■ Ver **resignation**.
take no notice of □ **não ligar para**
Take no notice of him. ◆ He didn't take any notice of what I said.
until further notice □ **até segunda ordem**
Be here at 8 every day until further notice.

notice² *v.* (**notices, noticing, noticed**) □ **notar**
I noticed that he was sad. ◆ Did you notice anything strange in his speech?
noticeable ['noutisəbl] *adj.* □ **notável, perceptível**
a noticeable improvement in the patient's health.
noticeboard ['noutisbɔːd] *n.* Brit. □ **quadro de avisos**
I put the list of names on the notice-board.
■ *Amer.* **bulletin board**
notify ['noutifai] *v.* (**notifies, notifying, notified**) □ **notificar**
Why didn't you notify the police (of the theft)?
■ Ver **inform; let someone know**.
notion ['nouʃən] *n.* □ **noção, ideia, opinião**
She has strange notions about education.
■ Ver **idea**.
notorious [nə'tɔːriəs] *adj.* (= infamous) □ **notório**
a notorious criminal.
nought ['nɔːt] *n.* (mesmo que **naught**) □ **zero**
nought point four (= 0.4).
■ Ver **zero**.
noun [naun] *n.* □ **substantivo**
countable nouns (= nouns that you can count, e.g. 'a chair', 'a bed'). ◆ uncountable nouns (= nouns that you cannot count, e.g. 'sugar', 'money').
nourishing ['nʌriʃiŋ] *adj.* (= nutritious) □ **nutritivo**
nourishing food.
novel ['nɔvəl] *n.* □ **romance**
a detective novel
novelist ['nɔvəlist] *n.* □ **romancista**
She is a famous novelist.
November [nə'vembə] *n.* □ **novembro**
Is it cold here in November?
■ See **April** for more examples.
now [nau] *adv.*
1 agora
I'm busy now. ◆ What are you doing now? ◆ until now.
2 agora
Now turn to page 65 in your books.
(every) now and then, (every) now and again □ **de vez em quando**
I visit them every now and then.
for now □ **por enquanto**
That's all for now.
from now on □ **de agora em diante**
From now on, you'll come at 8 every day.
nowadays ['nauədeiz] *adv.* □ **hoje em dia, atualmente**
Nowadays, computers are cheaper than in the past. ◆ I don't go there often nowadays.
nowhere ['nouweə] *adv.* □ **nenhum lugar**
There's nowhere to hide it. ◆ Where are you going? – Nowhere.
nowhere near □ **nem perto**
Your plan is nowhere near what we need.
nuclear ['njuːkliə] *adj.* □ **nuclear**
nuclear energy / weapons.
nudge¹ [nʌdʒ] *n.* □ **cutucada, cotovelada**
He gave me a nudge.
nudge² *v.* (**nudges, nudging, nudged**) □ **cutucar com o cotovelo**
He nudged me when the teacher looked at me.
nuisance ['njuːsns] *n.* □ **incômodo**
The smoke from the factory is a nuisance. ◆ There's a traffic jam again. What a nuisance!
numb [nʌm] *adj.*

1 dormente
My fingers were numb with cold.
2 entorpecido
He was numb with shock.
number¹ ['nʌmbə] *n.*
1 número
What's your telephone number? ◆ even numbers (2, 4, 6, etc). ◆ odd numbers (1, 3, 5, etc.).
■ Ver **no**.
2 número
The number of students increased by 10% last year.
a number of (= several) □ **uma série de, vários**
There were a number of problems.
a large number of □ **um grande número de**
a large number of people / cars. ◆ Large numbers of birds died there.
a small number of (= a few) □ **um pequeno número de**
in large numbers □ **em grande quantidade**
They attacked in large numbers.
number² *v.* (**numbers, numbering, numbered**)
1 enumerar
Number the pages.
2 totalizar
The police force numbered 2,000.
numbered ['nʌmbəd] *adj.* □ **numerado**
The seats are not numbered.
number plate ['nʌmbə 'pleit] *n.* Brit. □ **placa**
■ *Amer.* **license plate**
numerous ['njuːmərəs] *adj.* (= very many) □ **inúmeros**
We received numerous complaints.
nun [nʌn] *n.* □ **freira**
Nuns live in convents.
■ Ver **monk**.
nurse¹ [nɜːs] *n.*
1 enfermeira
She works as a nurse in a hospital.
2 (= nursemaid) **cuidador, enfermeira**
nurse² *v.* (**nurses, nursing, nursed**) □ **cuidar**
I nursed my brother when he was ill.
nursery ['nɜːsri] *n.* (*pl.* **nurseries**)
1 creche
a day nursery.
2 quarto de brinquedo
The children are playing in the nursery.
3 viveiro
I bought some plants at the nursery.
nursery rhyme ['nɜːsri 'raim] *n.* □ **cantiga de ninar**
nursery school ['nɜːsri 'skuːl] *n.* □ **creche, escola maternal**
nursing ['nɜːsiŋ] *n.* □ **enfermagem**
She studied nursing.
nursing home ['nɜːsiŋ ˌhoum] *n.* □ **casa de repouso**
nut [nʌt] *n.*
1 noz, castanha
roasted nuts.
2 porca
Tighten the nut.
be nuts (about) (= be crazy (about)) □ **ser doido (por)**
He is nuts about sports cars.
nutritional [njuːˈtriʃənl] *adj.* □ **nutricional**
The nutritional value of the food is printed on the label.
nutritious [njuːˈtriʃəs] *adj.* (= nourishing) □ **nutritivo**
Bananas are nutritious.
nylon ['nailən] *n.* □ **náilon**
Put the shirt in a nylon bag. ◆ nylon bags for sandwiches.

Oo

O, o [ou] *n.* □ **zero**
room three-o-nine (309) ◆ My number is o eight two three o seven (082307).
■ Ver **zero**.

O [ou] = **Oh**

oak [ouk] *n.* □ **carvalho**
an oak table

oar [ɔ:] *n.* □ **remo**
You use oars to row a boat.

oasis [ou'eisis] *n.* (*pl.* **oases**) □ **oásis**

oath [ouθ] *n.*
1 juramento
A witness takes an oath (= swears to tell the truth) in court.
2 (= swear-word) **palavrão**

oats [outs] *n. pl.* □ **aveia**

obedience [ə'bi:djəns] *n.* □ **obediência**

obedient [ə'bi:djənt] *adj.* □ **obediente**
An obedient boy does what his parents tell him.
■ antônimo: **disobedient**

obediently [ə'bi:djəntli] *adv.* □ **obedientemente**

obey [ə'bei] *v.* (**obeys, obeying, obeyed**) □ **obedecer**
to obey the law. ◆ The soldier refused to obey his officer.
■ antônimo: **disobey**

object[1] ['ɔbdʒikt] *n.*
1 objeto
a red plastic object.
2 (= purpose) **objetivo**
What is your object in life?
3 objeto
the direct object. ◆ an indirect object.

object[2] [əb'dʒekt] *v.* (**objects, objecting, objected**) □ **opor-se, protestar**
No one objected to the plan. ◆ I object!

objection [əb'dʒekʃən] *n.* □ **objeção**
I have no objection (to the plan). ◆ I have one objection – it's too expensive.

objective[1] [əb'dʒektiv] *adj.* □ **objetivo**
An objective report is based on facts only, not ideas or opinions.

objective[2] *n.* (= purpose) □ **objetivo**
The objective is to finish the project by April

objectively [əb'dʒektivli] *adv.* □ **objetivamente**

obligation [ɔbli'geiʃən] *n.* □ **obrigação**
I have an obligation to tell them.
to be under an obligation to □ **ter a obrigação de**
You are under no obligation to buy.

oblige [ə'blaidʒ] *v.* (**obliges, obliging, obliged**) □ **fazer um favor a, obrigar**
be obliged to □ **ser obrigado a**
You are not obliged to tell them anything. ◆ We were obliged to move to another town.
I'm much obliged (to you) □ **Sou muito agradecido (a você)**

oblong ['ɔblɔŋ] *n., adj.* (= rectangle, rectangular) □ **retângulo, retangular**
an oblong table

obscure [əb'skjuə] *adj.*
1 obscuro
an obscure politician, unknown to the voters.
2 pouco claro
His statement was too obscure to understand immediately.

observance [əb'zɔ:vəns] *n.* □ **observância**
observance of the rules.

observant [əb'zɔ:vənt] *adj.*
1 praticante
an observant Christian / Muslim / Jew.
2 observador
He notices everything – he is very observant.

observation [ˌɔbzə:'veiʃən] *n.* □ **observação**
You can learn a lot about people by observation.
■ The verb is **observe**.
under observation □ **sob observação**
The suspect is under observation. ◆ to keep the patient under observation

observatory [əb'zɔ:vətri] *n.* □ **observatório**

observe [əb'zɔ:v] *v.* (**observes, observing, observed**)
1 observar
Observe carefully how they do it. ◆ He observed someone watching him.
2 (= remark) **observar**
'It's possible', she observed.
3 cumprir, obedecer
to observe the law.

obsess [əb'ses] *v.* □ **obsedar, molestar**
be obsessed with □ **ser obcecado por**
She is obsessed about cleanliness.

obsession [əb'seʃən] *n.* □ **obsessão**
Computer games are an obsession with him.

obstacle ['ɔbstəkl] *n.* □ **obstáculo**
The horses have to jump over fences and other obstacles. ◆ an obstacle to peace.

obstinacy ['ɔbstinəsi] *n.* □ **obstinação**

obstinate ['ɔbstinət] *adj.* (= stubborn) □ **obstinado**
She is so obstinate – it's impossible to convince her.

obstinately ['ɔbstinətli] *adv.* □ **obstinadamente**

obstruct [əb'strʌkt] *v.* (**obstructs, obstructing, obstructed**)
1 obstruir
A fallen tree obstructed the road.
2 atrapalhar
Sit down! You're obstructing my view.

obstruction [əb'strʌkʃən] *n.* □ **obstrução**
The accident is causing an obstruction on the road.

obtain [əb'tein] *v.* (**obtains, obtaining, obtained**) (= get) □ **obter**
Where can I obtain the medicine? ◆ to obtain information.

obvious ['ɔbviəs] *adj.* □ **óbvio**
It was obvious that he was tired. ◆ The reasons are obvious – he wants to be rich and famous.

obviously ['ɔbviəsli] *adv.* □ **obviamente**
Obviously, this is not the right time to talk about it. ◆ I need more time. – Obviously!

occasion [ə'keiʒən] *n.*
1 ocasião
I saw him on two occasions last month. ◆ On that occasion the police arrived quickly.
2 ocasião
The party was a big occasion in their life.

occasional [ə'keiʒənl] *adj.* □ **ocasional**
an occasional visit from time to time.

occasionally [ə'keiʒənli] *adv.* (= once in a while) □ **ocasionalmente**
I see them occasionally.
occupation [ˌɔkju'peiʃən] *n.*
1 (= job) **profissão**
Please write your name, address and occupation.
2 ocupação
Playing video games is her occupation in the evenings.
3 ocupação
The army left the conquered country after 10 years of occupation.
occupied ['ɔkjupaid] *adj.*
1 (= taken) **ocupado**
These seats are occupied. ◆ occupied territories.
2 (= busy) **ocupado**
My hobby keeps me occupied after work.
occupy ['ɔkjupai] *v.* (**occupies, occupying, occupied**)
1 ocupar
She occupies the house next door.
2 ocupar
They occupied the enemy country. ◆ The rebels occupied the TV station.
3 ocupar
My hobby occupies most of my time.
4 ocupar
The bed occupies most of the bedroom.
occur [ə'kɔː] *v.* (**occurs, occurring, occurred**)
1 (= happen) **ocorrer**
The accident occurred early this morning.
2 ocorre
This problem occurs everywhere.
occur to □ **ocorrer a alguém**
It never occurred to me that they needed help.
occurrence [ə'kʌrəns] *n.* (= happening) □ **ocorrência**
ocean ['ouʃən] *n.* □ **oceano**
o'clock [ə'klɔk] *adv.* □ **hora**
at two o'clock ◆ It's six o'clock.
■ Use **o'clock** only with full hours.
■ Compare:
  It's six twenty (6:20).
October [ɔk'toubə] *n.* □ **outubro**
It happened in October, 2001.
■ For more examples of the use of the months, see **April**.
octopus ['ɔktəpəs] *n.* □ **polvo**
odd [ɔd] *adj.*
1 (= strange) **estranho, esquisito**
odd clothes. ◆ It's odd that she didn't telephone.
2 ímpar
an odd number (1, 3, 5, etc.).
■ antônimo: **even**
3 avulso
odd socks (from different pairs).
4 e tantos, e poucos
twenty-odd years.
the odd one out, the odd man out □ **o que sobra, o que não faz parte**
Which is the odd one out?
odd jobs *n. pl.* □ **trabalhos esporádicos, bicos**
to do odd jobs around the house
oddly ['ɔdli] *adv.* (= strangely) □ **estranhamente**
They behaved very oddly.
odds ['ɔdz] *n. pl.* □ **chances**
The odds are against us.
odds and ends [ˌɔdz ənd 'endz] *n.* □ **bugigangas, quinquilharias**
Her room was full of odds and ends.
odor ['oudə] *Amer.*, **odour** *Brit.* □ **odor**
The odor was very unpleasant – it was a nasty smell.
■ Ver **smell**[1]; **stink**[1].
of [ɔv] *prep.*
1 de
the end of the film. ◆ a friend of mine. ◆ a kilo of sugar. ◆ the house of my parents (= my parents' house). ◆ the keys of the car (= the car keys).
■ Compare:
  a bottle of wine.
  a wine bottle.
2 de
the tenth of May. ◆ We are proud of you. ◆ They accused him of stealing.
3 de
some of the teachers. ◆ He is afraid of the dark. ◆ This shirt is made of cotton.
4 de
10 km south of the airport. ◆ a quarter of nine (8:45). *Amer.* ◆ a teacher of English.
5 de
It reminds me of my childhood.
of all... □ **só, somente**
Why me of all people? ◆ She is late today of all days.
of course (Ver **course**).
off[1] [ɔːf] *prep.*
1 de
I fell off the horse. ◆ 200 meters off the target.
2 de
off the shore.
off duty (Ver **duty**).
off[2] *adv.*, *adj.*
1 distante, de distância
Their wedding day is not far off. ◆ The airport is 5 km off.
2 cancelado
The wedding is off.
■ antônimo: **on**
3 desligado
The light is off. ◆ The radio is off.
■ antônimo: **on**
4 de folga
Take a day off.
5 de desconto
They sell them at 20% off.
must be off □ **precisar partir**
I must be off. It's getting late.
off and on, on and off □ **intermitentemente**
It rained on and off yesterday.
■ Ver **come off; cut off; get off; go off; keep off; put off; switch off; take off; turn off**.
offence [ə'fens] *n. Brit.*, **offense** *Amer.* □ **delito**
to commit (= do) a serious offence. ◆ traffic offences.
No offence □ **Não se ofenda**
No offence, but I don't need any help.
take offence (= feel insulted) □ **ofender-se**
He took offence because I asked him to wait outside.
offend [ə'fend] *v.* (**offends, offending, offended**) □ **ofender**

I didn't mean to offend you.
- Compare with **insult**[2].

offender [ə'fendə] *n.* □ **delinquente**
juvenile offenders (= young criminals).
- Ver **juvenile delinquent**.

offer[1] ['ofə] *v.* (**offers, offering, offered**) □ **oferecer**
She offered me a job. ◆ He offered us his help. ◆ I offered them some tea and cake. ◆ How much are you offering for his car?
- she offered me (*not* 'to me').
- Compare with **propose; suggest**.

offer[2] *n.* □ **oferta, proposta**
I accepted his offer of help. ◆ a job offer. ◆ an offer of marriage.
- Compare with **proposal; suggestion**.

office ['ofis] *n.*
1 escritório, sala
The manager's office is on the second floor. ◆ office equipment.
2 *Brit.* **Ministério**
the Foreign Office. ◆ the Home Office.
- **Office** is used only for the above; otherwise **Ministry** is used.
- *Amer.* **Department**
3 cargo
She held the office of President for 5 years.

office block ['ofis blok] *n.* □ **prédio comercial, conjunto de escritórios**

office hours ['ofis 'auə] *n. pl.* □ **horário de expediente**

officer ['ofisə] *n.*
1 oficial
an air force officer.
2 inspetor
a customs officer.
3 policial
Excuse me, officer, where is the police station? ◆ a police officer (= a policeman or policewoman).

official[1] [ə'fiʃəl] *adj.* □ **oficial**
an official visit. ◆ an official announcement.
- antônimo: **unofficial**

official[2] *n.* □ **autoridade**
government officials.

officially [ə'fiʃəli] *adv.* □ **oficialmente**

offspring ['ofspriŋ] *n.* □ **filhote, prole**
How many offspring does a tiger usually have?

often ['ofn] *adv.* □ **frequentemente**
We often talk about it. ◆ I don't visit them very often.
- antônimo: **seldom**

How often...? □ **Com que frequência...?**
How often do you write them a letter?

every so often □ **de tempos em tempos**
Every so often she comes for a visit.

oh [ou] *excl.*
1 oh!, ah!
Oh yes, of course.
2 Ah, é?, É?
He passed the test. – Oh? When?

oh dear □ **minha nossa!**
Oh dear! What happened to you?

oh well □ **bem / bom**
Oh well, we'll do it some other time.

oil[1] [oil] *n.*
1 petróleo
We use oil as fuel.
2 óleo
engine oil.
3 óleo, azeite
Fry the fish in oil. ◆ olive oil.
4 óleo
suntan oil.

oil[2] *v.* (**oils, oiling, oiled**) □ **lubrificar**
to oil the hinges (of the door).

oilfield ['oilfi:ld] *n.* □ **campo de petróleo**
oil painting [oil 'peintiŋ] *n.* □ **pintura a óleo**
oil rig [oil rig] *n.* □ **plataforma de petróleo**
oil slick [oil slik] *n.* □ **mancha de óleo**
oil tanker [oil 'taŋkə] *n.* □ **petroleiro**
oil well [oil wel] *n.* □ **poço de petróleo**
oily ['oili] *de adj.* (**oilier, oiliest**) □ **oleoso**
an oily liquid. ◆ oily food.

OK [ou'kei] *excl.* □ **tudo bem, OK**
Try to come early. – OK.

okay[1] [ou'kei] *adj., adv.*, **OK** □ **ok, bom, certo, tudo bem**
Everything is okay. ◆ It's okay with me. (= I agree.) ◆ He did OK in the test. ◆ Are you okay?

okay[2] *n.*, **OK** □ **OK, permissão**
I gave them the okay to start.

okay[3] *v.* (**okays, okaying, okayed**) □ **autorizar**
They okayed the project.

old [ould] *adj.*
1 idoso
an old man. ◆ the oldest woman in the village.
- antônimo: **young**
- Ver **older**.
2 velho
old books / clothes. ◆ old customs.
- antônimo: **new**
3 velho
an old friend of mine.
4 de idade
She is 12 years old.

How old...? □ **Que idade...?, Quantos anos...?**
How old is she? ◆ How old are you?

get old □ **envelhecer**
He is getting old.

the old *n.* □ **os idosos**
a special club for the old.

older *adj.* □ **mais velho**
Dan is older than me.

old age [ould 'eidʒ] *n.* □ **velhice, terceira idade**
He has more time for his hobbies in his old age.

old-age pension [ould 'eidʒ 'penʃən] *n.* □ **aposentadoria por velhice**

old-fashioned [,ould'faʃənd] *adj.* □ **fora de moda, antigo**
old-fashioned clothes. ◆ Her views are very old-fashioned.

olive ['oliv] *n.* □ **azeitona, oliva**
black / green olives. ◆ olive oil.

Olympic [ə'limpik] *adj.* □ **olímpico**
the Olympic Games *n.* □ **os Jogos Olímpicos**

omelette ['omlit] *n. Amer.*, **omelet** □ **omelete**
I had an omelette for breakfast.

omission [ə'miʃən] *n.* □ **omissão**
errors and omissions (in a book).

omit [ə'mit] *v.* (**omits, omitting, omitted**) (= leave out) □ **omitir**
They omitted my name from the list.
on [on] *adv., prep.*
1 sobre, em
There is a book on the table. ◆ Sit on the floor. ◆ on the wall.
2 em
on Friday. ◆ on 5th June. *Brit.* ◆ on June 5. *Amer.*
▪ Ver **in**.
3 em, ao, por
There's nothing worth seeing on TV tonight. ◆ There's a tree on the right (side). ◆ I spoke to her on the phone. ◆ Look at the picture on page 50.
4 sobre
a book on wild animals. ◆ a lecture on poetry.
5 ligado
The TV was on. ◆ Switch the lights on.
▪ antônimo: **off**
6 no momento em que, quando
On his arrival, he telephoned them. ◆ On hearing the shouts, the dog barked.
7 indica ação continuada
to read on. ◆ to walk on.
▪ Ver **come on; depend on; get on; go on; hang on; keep on; put on; rely on; switch on; try on; turn on**.
▪ Ver **on (the) average; on business; on fire; on holiday; on purpose; on sale; on time**.
on and off, off and on □ **intermitentemente**
It rained on and off yesterday.
on and on □ **sem parar**
once¹ [wʌns] *adv.*
1 uma vez
She visits them once a week. ◆ I saw her only once.
2 no passado
This building was once a prison.
all at once (= suddenly) □ **de repente**
All at once he got up and left the room.
at once
1 (= immediately) **já, imediatamente**
Tell him to come here at once!
2 ao mesmo tempo
Don't all talk at once.
for once □ **pelo menos uma vez**
For once she wasn't late.
once again, once more □ **mais uma vez**
I want to see it once more.
once and for all □ **(de) uma vez por todas**
We have to take care of this problem once and for all.
once in a while (= occasionally) □ **de vez em quando**
Once in a while we play tennis together.
once or twice □ **uma vez ou outra, poucas vezes**
They met once or twice.
once upon a time □ **era uma vez**
Once upon a time there was a king…
once² *conj.* (= as soon as) □ **quando, assim que**
Once you decide, that's it.
▪ once you decide (*not* 'will decide').
one¹ [wʌn] *n., adj.* □ **um**
It's one o'clock. ◆ She is one year old. ◆ One and two are three (1+2=3).
one by one □ **um por um, um a um**
One by one they left the room. ◆ She counted them one by one.

one² *pron., n.* (*pl.* **ones**)
1 um; em certas expressões não é traduzido
I sold my old computer. This is a new one. ◆ There were two buses. The first one was full.
2 um
Which skirt do you want? – That one. ◆ These are the pictures – leave the ones you don't need.
3 só uma pessoa
One cannot do this alone.
▪ **you** is usually used instead of **one** in this last meaning.
one another (Ver **another**).
one of □ **um de**
One of the pupils was late. ◆ One of them agreed.
one-on-one, one-to-one □ **personalizado, individual, pessoal**
one-on-one teaching (= one teacher to one student).
Which one…? □ **Qual…?**
Which one do you prefer? ◆ Give me those books, please. – Which ones?
oneself [wʌn'self] *pron.*
1 se, si mesmo, si próprio
to wash oneself
2 sozinho, por si mesmo
One must do it oneself.
▪ **you… yourself** is usually used instead of **one… oneself**.
(all) by oneself
1 sozinho
It's difficult to live by oneself.
2 sozinho
One must learn to do it by oneself.
one-way ['wʌn'wei] *adj.*
1 (de) mão única
a one-way street.
2 só de ida
a one-way ticket.
onion ['ʌnjən] *n.* □ **cebola**
on-line ['onlain] *adj., adv.,* **online** □ **online, na internet**
on-line banking. ◆ online ads. ◆ You can get the results online. ◆ to go online.
only¹ ['ounli] *adj.* □ **único**
I was the only American in the group. ◆ That's the only solution.
an only child □ **filho único**
She was an only child.
only² *adv.* □ **só, somente, apenas**
It's only a game. ◆ I have only one brother.
▪ The position of **only** in a sentence can change the meaning:
Only David closed the door.
David only closed the door.
David closed only the door.
David closed the only door.
not only… but also (Ver **not**).
only³ *conj.* (= but) □ **só que, mas**
He wants to do it, only he doesn't know how.
onto ['ontu] *prep.* (mesmo que **on to**) □ **em, sobre**
The book fell onto the floor. ◆ Throw it onto the bed.
▪ Use **onto** only with verbs of motion.
onward(s) ['onwəd(z)] *adv.*
1 em frente
to move onwards.

2 em diante
from April onwards.
open¹ ['oupən] *adj.*
1 aberto
Leave the door open. ◆ Is the bank still open?
- antônimo: **closed**
2 aberto
The competition is open to everyone.
3 aberto
an open person.
- antônimo: **closed, shut**
in the open air □ **ao ar livre**
They slept in the open air.
with open arms □ **de braços abertos**
He welcomed me with open arms.
open² *v.* (**opens, opening, opened**)
1 abrir
Will you open the window, please? ◆ Open your books to page 65. ◆ I opened my eyes / mouth.
- **turn on** the tap / faucet / gas (*not* 'open').
2 abrir
When does the bank open? ◆ The door opens from the inside. ◆ The door opened and the boss came in.
- Compare:
    The door opened. (*Not* was opened.)
    The door was opened by a servant.
3 (= begin) **começar**
Every sentence opens with a capital letter. ◆ The meeting will open in half an hour.
4 abrir
I opened a bank account.
5 abrir
They opened fire on the enemy.
- antônimo: **close³**
open-air ['oupəneə] *adj.* □ **ao ar livre**
an open-air concert.
opener ['oupənə] *n.* □ **abridor**
a can opener. *Amer.* ◆ a tin opener. *Brit.*
opening ['oupəniŋ] *n., adj.*
1 abertura
an opening in the fence.
2 (= beginning) **abertura**
the opening of the letter.
3 abertura
the opening of the games. ◆ the opening ceremony.
- antônimo: **closing**
4 vaga
an opening for a secretary.
openly ['oupənli] *adv.* □ **abertamente**
They talk openly about their problems.
opera ['opərə] *n.* □ **ópera**
operate ['opəreit] *v.* (**operates, operating, operated**)
1 operar
Learn how to operate this machine. ◆ How does the system operate? (= function)
2 operar
The new surgeon will operate on these patients.
operation [,opə'reiʃən] *n.*
1 operação, cirurgia
She had an operation on her arm.
2 operação
a rescue operation. ◆ a military operation.

3 operação, funcionamento
The machine is now in operation.
operator [opə'reitə] *n.*
1 operador
a computer operator.
2 telefonista
Hello? Operator? I'd like to call New York.
opinion [ə'pinjən] *n.*
1 opinião
What's your opinion of the plan?
2 opinião, parecer
the doctor's opinion.
in my opinion (= I think) □ **na minha opinião**
In my opinion, it is possible.
opponent [ə'pounənt] *n.*
1 oponente, adversário
The boxer beat his opponent easily. ◆ a political opponent.
2 opositor
the opponents of the project.
- antônimo: **supporter**
opportunity [opə'tju:nəti] *n.* (*pl.* **opportunities**) □ **oportunidade**
I didn't have the opportunity to tell her.
take the opportunity □ **aproveitar a oportunidade**
I'd like to take this opportunity to thank you all.
oppose [ə'pouz] *v.* (**opposes, opposing, opposed**) □ **opor-se**
Only two people opposed the plan. ◆ to oppose the government.
- antônimo: **support²**
be opposed to □ **ao contrário de, em contraste a**
They are opposed to the project.
as opposed to □ **ao contrário de, em contraste a**
military men as opposed to civilians.
opposite¹ ['opəzit] *adj., adv.*
1 oposto, em frente
on the opposite page. ◆ on the opposite side of the river. ◆ He sat opposite (me).
2 oposto
in the opposite direction.
- antônimo: **same**
opposite² *prep.* □ **do lado oposto, em frente**
at the building opposite the bank.
opposite³ *n.* □ **oposto, contrário**
The opposite of 'tall' is 'short'.
opposition [opə'ziʃən] *n.* □ **oposição**
There's strong opposition to the plan.
- antônimo: **support¹**
optical ['optikəl] *adj.* □ **óptico**
optician [op'tiʃən] *n.* □ **oculista, que trabalha na ótica**
optimism ['optimizəm] *n.* □ **otimismo**
- antônimo: **pessimism**
optimist ['optimist] *n.* □ **otimista**
- antônimo: **pessimist**
optimistic [,opti'mistik] *adj.* □ **otimista**
I am optimistic about his chances of winning.
- antônimo: **pessimistic**
option ['opʃən] *n.* □ **opção**
I have no option (= choice). I have to pay. ◆ You have two options: go with me or not go at all.
optional ['opʃnl] *adj.* □ **opcional**
Art is an optional subject in our school.

■ antônimo: **compulsory**
or [ɔ:] *conj.*
1 ou
Do you want to play or not? ◆ Is it in English or in French?
■ Ver **either... or**.
2 (= otherwise) **senão**
Do it carefully or you'll break something.
■ Ver **neither... nor**.
oral ['ɔ:rəl] *adj.* □ **oral**
an oral test in English.
orange[1] ['ɔrindʒ] *n., adj.* □ **laranja**
He peeled an orange and gave me half. ◆ orange juice (= the juice of an orange).
orange[2] *adj., n.* □ **(cor de) laranja**
an orange balloon.
orbit[1] ['ɔ:bit] *n.* □ **órbita**
orbit[2] *v.* (**orbits, orbiting, orbited**) □ **orbitar**
The satellite is orbiting the Earth.
orchard ['ɔ:tʃəd] *n.* □ **pomar**
orchestra ['ɔ:kəstrə] *n.* □ **orquestra**
orchid ['ɔ:kid] *n.* □ **orquídea**
ordeal [ɔ:'di:l] *n.* □ **suplício, provação**
It was a terrible ordeal to walk for two days in the desert without water.
order[1] ['ɔ:də] *n.*
1 ordem, organização
in alphabetical order. ◆ The books are in the wrong order.
2 ordem
to put the room in order.
3 ordem
It was difficult for the teacher to keep order in class. ◆ law and order.
4 ordem, injunção
The soldier obeyed the officer's orders (= commands). ◆ I have orders to send it at once.
5 pedido
The waiter took our order. ◆ an order for sixty books.
6 ordem
a court order.
in order
1 em ordem
His passport is in order.
2 em ordem
Everything in the room was in order.
3 em ordem
to discuss the questions in order.
in order to □ **a fim de, para**
I run 8 km every day in order to keep fit.
in order that □ **a fim de, para**
I came early in order that we might talk in private.
out of order
1 quebrado, com defeito
The telephone is out of order. (= It is not working.)
2 fora de ordem
The books are out of order.
order[2] *v.* (**orders, ordering, ordered**)
1 (= command) **ordenar, mandar**
The doctor ordered me to stay in bed. ◆ The robber ordered us not to move.
2 pedir, solicitar
I ordered a pizza and apple juice. ◆ We have to order two tons of rice.

ordinarily ['ɔ:dənərili] *adv.* (= usually) □ **geralmente**
ordinary ['ɔ:dinri] *adj.* □ **comum**
ordinary people. ◆ an ordinary house.
■ antônimo: **extraordinary**
out of the ordinary (= unusual) □ **fora do comum, extraordinário**
We didn't notice anything out of the ordinary.
organ ['ɔ:gən] *n.*
1 órgão
Smoking is harmful to the heart and lungs and to other organs as well.
2 órgão
I can play the organ.
organic [ɔ:'ganik] *adj.* □ **orgânico**
organic farming.
organise ['ɔ:gənaiz] *v. Brit.* (Ver **organize**).
organization [ˌɔ:gənai'zeiʃən] *n.*, **organisation** *Brit.*
1 organização
to join the organization. ◆ a student organization.
2 organização
The office needs more organization.
3 organização
They are busy with the organization of the party.
organize ['ɔ:gənaiz] *v.* (**organizes, organizing, organized**), **organise** *Brit.* □ **organizar**
to organize a team. ◆ She organizes all our parties.
organized ['ɔ:gənaizd] *adj.*, **organised** *Brit.*
1 organizado
an organized group.
2 organizado
an organized person.
get organized □ **organizar-se**
They got organized very quickly.
organizer ['ɔ:gənaizə] *n. Brit.*, **organiser** □ **organizador**
oriental [ˌɔ:ri'entl] *adj.* □ **oriental**
oriental art.
origin ['ɔridʒin] *n.*
1 origem
words of Arabic / Latin origin. ◆ the origins of life on earth.
2 origem
African-Americans are black Americans of African origin.
original[1] [ə'ridʒinəl] *adj.* □ **original**
Her ideas are very original. ◆ original paintings.
original[2] *n.* □ **original**
The translation of the poem is not as good as the original. ◆ I have a copy of the document and also the original.
originally [ə'ridʒinəli] *adv.* □ **originalmente**
The organization was originally very small. ◆ I am originally from Italy.
ornament ['ɔ:nəmənt] *n.*
1 ornamento, enfeite
glass / gold ornaments.
2 enfeite
a dress with gold threads for ornament.
ornamental [ɔ:nə'mentl] *adj.* □ **ornamental**
ornamental trees.
orphan[1] ['ɔ:fən] *n.* □ **órfão**
orphan[2] *v.*
be orphaned □ **ficar órfão**
She was orphaned when she was five.
orphanage ['ɔ:fənidʒ] *n.* □ **orfanato**
ostrich ['ɔ:stritʃ] *n.* □ **avestruz**

other ['ʌðə] *adj.*, *pron.*
 1 outro
 Where is the other shoe? ◆ One bag is here. Where is the other (one)?
 2 outro
 The other players will come later. ◆ There were no other questions. ◆ I have other plans.
 ■ Ver **another**.
others *pl.* □ **outros**
 Some people agreed, others didn't. ◆ Don't tell the others.
other than (= except) □ **a não ser, exceto**
 Nobody knows other than Iris.
some other time □ **uma outra vez**
 I'll come some other time.
the other day □ **outro dia**
 I spoke to him on the phone the other day.
otherwise[1] ['ʌðəwaiz] *conj.* □ **senão, do contrário**
 Come early, otherwise we'll go without you.
otherwise[2] *adv.*
 1 fora isso
 He talks a lot, but otherwise he is very nice.
 2 diferentemente
 They wanted her to join them, but she decided otherwise.
ought [o:t] *v.* (= should)
 1 dever
 You ought to tell him the truth. ◆ She ought to visit them.
 2 dever
 It's a beautiful film. You ought to see it. ◆ You ought to see a doctor.
 3 dever
 They ought to be there by now. ◆ She ought to win the game.
ounce [auns] *n.* □ **onça**
 There are sixteen ounces in a pound.
 ■ abreviação: **oz**
our [auə] *adj.* □ **nosso, nossa**
 Our car is red. ◆ This is our plan.
ours [auəz] *pron.* □ **nosso, nossa**
 He is a friend of ours. ◆ Whose car is that? – It's ours.
ourselves [,auə'selvz] *pron.*
 1 nos, nós mesmos
 We built ourselves a shelter. ◆ We are proud of ourselves. ◆ We want it for ourselves.
 2 nós mesmos
 We checked it ourselves.
 (all) by ourselves
 1 sozinhos
 We sat there by ourselves.
 2 por conta própria
 We built it all by ourselves.
out [aut] *adv.*, *adj.*
 1 fora
 Throw it out. ◆ to hang the wash out.
 2 fora
 He is out. ◆ We're eating out tonight.
 ■ antônimo: **in**
 3 desligado, apagado
 The lights are out (= not on). ◆ The fire is out.
 ■ Ver **come out; get out; go out; keep out; put out; run out; turn out**.
out of *prep.* [aut ov]
 1 fora de
 Can frogs live out of water?
 2 para fora de
 The bird flew out of the cage. ◆ He took something out of his pocket.
 3 por
 She helped him out of pity.
 4 dentre
 Two out of three people think so.
 5 sem
 We are out of coffee.
 6 com
 She made a box out of cardboard.
 out of danger □ **fora de perigo**
 The patient is now out of danger.
 out of date (Ver **date**).
 out of order (Ver **order**).
 out of reach □ **fora do alcance**
 Keep the medicine out of reach of little children.
 out of work (= unemployed) □ **desempregado**
 Many people are out of work in this town.
outbreak ['autbreik] *n.* □ **deflagração**
 an outbreak of war.
outburst ['autbə:st] *n.* □ **explosão**
 an outburst of anger.
outcome ['autkʌm] *n.* (= result)
 1 resultado
 the outcome of the elections.
 2 resultado
 The outcome of the war.
outcry ['autkrai] *n.* (*pl.* **outcries**) □ **clamor, protesto**
 a public outcry against the new taxes.
outdated [aut'deitid] *adj.* (= out of date) □ **ultrapassado**
 outdated opinions / methods.
outdoor ['autdo:] *adj.* □ **ao ar livre**
 outdoor sports / activities.
 ■ antônimo: **indoor**
outdoors [aut'do:z] *adv.* □ **ao ar livre**
 to eat and sleep outdoors.
 ■ antônimo: **indoors**
outer ['autə] *adj.* □ **externo**
 the outer walls.
 ■ antônimo: **inner**
 ■ Ver **exterior; external**.
outer space ['autə ,speis] *n.* □ **espaço sideral**
outfit ['autfit] *n.* □ **roupa, traje**
 I have to buy a new outfit for their wedding. ◆ a tennis outfit.
 ■ Ver **clothes**.
outing ['autiŋ] *n.* (= excursion) □ **passeio, excursão**
 to go on an outing. ◆ a school outing to a museum.
outline ['autlain] *n.*
 1 esboço, contorno
 to draw the outline of the building.
 2 esboço, linhas gerais
 an outline for an essay. ◆ He told us the plan in outline.
outlook ['autluk] *n.*
 1 ponto de vista
 an optimistic outlook on life.
 2 previsão
 What's the weather outlook for tomorrow?
 3 perspectiva
 The economic outlook is not good.
 ■ Ver **forecast**[1].

out of (Ver **out**).
output ['autput] *n.* □ **produção**
The factory's output will increase this year.
outrageous [aut'reidʒəs] *adj.* □ **absurdo, escandaloso**
outrageous prices / conduct. ◆ What they are doing is outrageous.
■ Ver **shocking**.
outset ['autset] *n.*
from the outset □ **início, princípio**
There were problems from the outset.
outside[1] ['autsaid] *adj.* (= external) □ **externo**
the outside walls.
outside[2] *n.* □ **exterior, parte externa, lado de fora**
Paint the inside and the outside of the house. ◆ Open the door from the outside.
outside[3] [aut'said] *adv.* □ **lá fora, na parte externa**
It's cold outside. ◆ She is waiting outside. ◆ Let's go outside. ◆ We heard a noise from outside.
■ antônimo: **inside**
outside[4] *prep.* □ **do lado de fora**
Leave it outside the door.
outsider ['autsaidə] *n.* □ **excluído**
The new pupil feels like an outsider, because nobody plays with him.
outskirts ['autskə:ts] *n.* □ **periferia, arredores**
on the outskirts of the city
outstanding [aut'standiŋ] *adj.* (= excellent) □ **notável**
an outstanding achievement. ◆ an outstanding teacher. ◆ Their work is outstanding.
outward[1] ['autwəd] *adj.* □ **externa**
outward appearance. ◆ an outward show of sympathy.
outward[2] ['autwəd] *adv.*, **outward(s)** □ **para o lado de fora**
The door opens outwards.
■ antônimo: **inward(s)**
outwards (Ver **outward**[2]).
oval ['ouvəl] *adj.*, *n.* □ **oval**
an oval mirror.
oven ['ʌvn] *n.* □ **forno**
to bake a cake in the oven. ◆ Turn on the oven. ◆ Turn off the oven.
■ Ver **cooker; stove**.
over[1] ['ouvə] *adj.* □ **acabado, terminado**
The meeting is over. ◆ The storm is over.
over[2] *adv.*, *prep.*
1 por cima
The plane flew over the village.
■ **above** is used when meaning higher than a certain point, e.g. above the knees.
2 sobre
He put a coat over her shoulders.
3 sobre
We have an advantage over them.
4 mais de
She worked there for over 15 years. ◆ toys for children of six and over.
5 para o lado
Move over a bit.
6 não é traduzido em certas expressões, e a ação passa a ser expressa apenas pelo verbo
to bend over. ◆ I fell over and quickly got up.
■ Ver **boil over; get over; go over; look over; pull over; run over; turn over**.

over! □ **Câmbio!**
Get ready to land (the plane). Over!
all over □ **por toda parte**
all over the world ◆ I looked all over for the child.
all over again □ **tudo de novo, tudo outra vez**
I have to write it all over again.
be left over □ **estar sobrando**
There's a lot of food left over.
over and over (again) □ **repetidamente**
He played the disc over and over again.
over here / there □ **aqui / lá**
Come over here. (= Come here.) ◆ I found it over there.
over- ['ouvə] *pref.* □ **demais, além da conta**
to overeat (= eat too much). ◆ to be over-confident (= to be too confident).
overall[1] ['ouvərɔ:l] *adj.*, *adv.* □ **total, no total**
the overall cost of the project. ◆ It will cost $2 million overall.
overall[2] *n. Brit.* □ **jaleco, avental**
■ *Amer.* **smock**
overalls ['ouvərɔ:lz] *n.*
1 *Brit.* **macacão**
The mechanic put on his overalls.
■ *Amer.* **coveralls; overall**
2 *Amer.* **macacão**
The farmer was wearing overalls.
■ *Brit.* **dungarees**
overboard ['ouvəbɔ:d] *adv.* □ **ao mar**
to fall / jump overboard
overcharge [,ouvə'tʃɑ:dʒ] *v.* (**overcharges, overcharging, overcharged**) □ **cobrar a mais**
The store overcharged me. ◆ I was overcharged by the taxi driver.
overcoat ['ouvəkout] *n.* □ **sobretudo**
overcome [,ouvə'kʌm] *v.* (**overcomes, overcoming, overcame, overcome**)
1 superar
He overcame his fear and jumped into the water. ◆ to overcome a problem.
2 vencer, superar
to overcome the enemy.
overcrowded [,ouvə'kraudid] *adj.* □ **superpopulado, lotado**
overcrowded cities. ◆ The beach was overcrowded.
overdue [,ouvə'dju:] *adj.* □ **atrasado**
The train is overdue. ◆ The telephone bill / library book is overdue.
overestimate [,ouvər'estimeit] *v.* (**overestimates, overestimating, overestimated**) □ **superestimar**
to overestimate the cost / distance. ◆ I overestimated the importance of this.
overflow [,ouvə'flou] *v.* (**overflows, overflowing, overflowed**) □ **transbordar**
The river overflowed its banks. ◆ The bath is overflowing.
overhaul [ouvə'hɔ:l] *n.*, *v.* (**overhauls, overhauling, overhauled**) □ **revisão, revisar**
to take in the car for an overhaul ◆ The garage is overhauling my car.
overhead[1] ['ouvə'hed] *adj.* □ **suspenso**
overhead wires.
overhead[2] *adv.* □ **acima, por cima, acima da cabeça**
A plane flew overhead.
overhear [,ouvə'hiə] *v.* (**overhears, overhearing, overheard**) □ **ouvir por acaso**
I overheard their conversation.

overlap [,ouvə'lap] *v.* (**overlaps, overlapping, overlapped**) □ **coincidir, sobrepor-se**
The meanings of these two words overlap.

overlook [,ouvə'luk] *v.* (**overlooks, overlooking, overlooked**)
1 (= ignore) **ignorar**
I can't overlook the risks. ◆ He overlooked their lies.
2 (= miss) **deixar passar**
Check it again. Maybe you overlooked something.
3 ter vista para
My room overlooks the sea.

overnight [ouvə'nait] *adj., adv.*
1 noturno, durante a noite
an overnight journey. ◆ to stay overnight.
2 repentino, da noite para o dia
an overnight success.

overseas ['ouvəsi:z] *adj., adv.* □ **estrangeiro, no exterior**
overseas students / markets. ◆ to live overseas.

oversee [ouvə'si:] *v.* (**oversees, overseeing, oversaw, overseen**) □ **supervisionar**
The manager oversees the workers to make sure they are doing the job well.

oversleep [ouvə'sli:p] *v.* (**oversleeps, oversleeping, overslept**) □ **dormir demais**
I overslept and was late for the meeting.

overtake [ouvə'teik] *v.* (**overtakes, overtaking, overtook, overtaken**) □ **ultrapassar**
An ambulance overtook us.

overtime ['ouvətaim] *n., adv.* □ **hora extra, além do período estabelecido**
to work overtime.

overtook [ouvə'tuk] *v.* (Ver **overtake**).

overturn [ouvə'tə:n] *v.* (**overturns, overturning, overturned**) □ **capotar**
The car / boat overturned.

overweight [ouvə'weit] *adj.* □ **muito pesado**
I am overweight. I must go on a diet.

overwhelm [ouvə'welm] *v.* □ **subjugar**
be overwhelmed □ **ser dominado, ser derrotado, ser subjugado**
They were overwhelmed with sorrow.

overwhelming [,ouvə'welmiŋ] *adj.* □ **arrasador**
an overwhelming victory.

owe [ou] *v.* (**owes, owing, owed**) □ **dever**
He owes me 100 dollars. ◆ How much does she owe you?
◆ You owe me an explanation. ◆ I owe him my life.

owing to *prep.* (= because of) □ **devido a, graças a**
There will be delays owing to the weather.
■ Ver **due to**.

owl [aul] *n.* □ **coruja**

own[1] [oun] *v.* (**owns, owning, owned**) □ **ser dono, possuir**
Who owns the house? ◆ I don't own this car. It belongs to my brother.

own up (= admit) □ **confessar, admitir**
He owned up to stealing the car.

own[2] *adj., pron.*
1 próprio
I prefer to use my own tools. ◆ I have my own car. (= I have a car of my own.)
2 próprio
They cook their own meals.

get your own back □ **dar o troco**
He cheated me, but I'll get my own back one day.

in your own time
1 (= on your own time) **em seu horário livre**
Do this on your own time, not at work!
2 com calma
It's not urgent. You can do it in your own time.

of your own □ **próprio**
She has problems of her own. ◆ I have a car of my own.

on your own
1 (= alone) **sozinho**
He lives on his own.
2 sozinho, por conta própria
I wrote it on my own (= by myself).

with my own eyes □ **com meus próprios olhos**
I saw it with my own eyes.

owner ['ounə] *n.* □ **dono, proprietário**
Who is the owner of the car? ◆ a dog owner.

ownership ['ounəʃip] *n.* □ **propriedade**

ox [oks] *n.* (*pl.* **oxen**) □ **boi**

oxygen ['oksidʒən] *n.* □ **oxigênio**

oyster ['oistə] *n.* □ **ostra**

oz *abbr.* (= ounce) □ **onça**

ozone ['ouzoun] *n.* □ **ozônio**
the ozone layer in the atmosphere.

Pp

p *abbr.*, **p.**
1 (= pence; penny) *Brit*. **cent.**
The price is 80 p.
2 (= page) (*pl.* **pp.**) **pág., p.**
See p 28 and pp 35-43.
3 (= P, Parking) **E**
pace [peis] *n*.
1 ritmo, velocidade
at a slow / fast pace.
2 (= step) **passo**
Come forward a few paces.
keep pace with □ **acompanhar o passo de**
Let's walk more slowly. They can't keep pace with us. ◆ to keep pace with the new technological developments.
pack¹ [pak] *n*.
1 (= backpack) **mochila**
They put their packs on their backs and went their way.
2 *Amer*. **pacote, maço**
a pack of cigarettes / gum.
■ *Brit*. **packet**
3 pacote, fardo
a pack of envelopes. ◆ a six-pack of beer (a pack of six cans of beer).
4 *Brit*. **baralho**
a pack of cards.
■ *Amer*. **deck**
5 bando
a pack of wolves. ◆ a pack of thieves.
6 monte
a pack of lies.
pack² *v*. (**packs, packing, packed**) □ **fazer as malas, empacotar**
It's time to start packing. ◆ Pack the suitcase. ◆ He packed the books in boxes.
■ antônimo: **unpack**
package ['pakidʒ] *n*. □ **pacote**
I wrapped the package in brown paper. ◆ a package of cookies. *Amer*.
■ Ver **packet; parcel.**
package tour ['pakidʒ tuə] *n*. □ **pacote turístico**
In a package tour, your guide arranges the travel, the meals and the visits.
packaging ['pakidʒiŋ] *n*. □ **empacotamento**
packet ['pakit] *n*. □ **pacote, embalagem**
a packet of cornflakes. ◆ a packet of biscuits. ◆ a packet of cigarettes.
■ *Amer*. a **box** of cornflakes; a **package** of cookies; a **pack** of cigarettes.
packing ['pakiŋ] *n*. □ **embalagem, empacotamento**
I'll do the packing. ◆ packing and postage.
pact [pakt] *n*. □ **pacto, tratado**
The two countries signed a peace pact.
pad [pad] *n*.
1 bloco
a writing pad.
■ Ver **notebook; notepad.**
2 joelheira, enchimento
Football players wear knee pads. ◆ She wears dresses with shoulder pads. ◆ a pad of cotton.

paddle¹ ['padl] *n*. □ **remo curto**
paddle² *v*. (**paddles, paddling, paddled**)
1 remar
The diver paddled and rose above the water.
2 remar
He paddled across the river.
■ Ver **row³.**
3 (= wade) **passar com dificuldade por local que dificulte os movimentos**
to paddle along the shore.
padlock ['padlok] *n*. □ **cadeado**
page [peidʒ] *n*.
1 página
There is a picture on p. (= page) 28. ◆ the front (= first) page (of a newspaper).
2 página, folha
to tear a page out of the notebook.
paid [peid] *v*. (Ver **pay**).
pail [peil] *n*. (= bucket) □ **balde**
pain [pein] *n*. □ **dor**
I felt a sharp pain in my back. ◆ She's in pain.
■ Ver **ache.**
take great pains □ **se dar o trabalho de fazer algo**
She took great pains to correct every mistake.
painful ['peinful] *adj*. □ **doloroso**
a painful injury. ◆ a painful memory.
painfully ['peinfuli] *adv*. □ **dolorosamente**
painless ['peinlis] *adj*. □ **indolor**
The treatment is painless.
painlessly ['peinlisli] *adv*. □ **de modo indolor**
painstaking ['peinzteikiŋ] *adj*. □ **meticuloso, esmerado**
painstaking research.
paint¹ [peint] *n*. □ **tinta**
The paint is still wet. ◆ The artist uses a lot of blue paint in his pictures.
■ Ver **color¹.**
paint² *v*. (**paints, painting, painted**)
1 pintar
I painted the walls white.
2 pintar
A famous artist painted this picture.
■ Compare with **draw**:
to paint with a brush, pencil or pen.
paintbrush ['peintbrʌʃ] *n*. □ **pincel**
painter ['peintə] *n*.
1 pintor
The painter finished painting the house.
2 pintor
The painter sold all his paintings.
painting ['peintiŋ] *n*. □ **pintura**
an oil painting.
pair [peə] *n*. □ **par**
a pair of socks. ◆ a pair of scissors. ◆ The pupils worked in pairs.
■ Ver **couple.**
pajamas [pə'dʒɑ:məz] *Amer*., **pyjamas** *Brit*. □ **pijama**
pal [pal] *n*. (= buddy, friend) □ **camarada, amigo**
palace ['paləs] *n*. □ **palácio**
The Queen invited them to the palace.
pale [peil] *adj*. □ **pálido**
You look pale.
palm¹ [pa:m] *n*. □ **palma**
in the palm of my hand.

palm² *n.* (mesmo que **palm-tree**) □ palmeira
palmtop ['pa:mtɔp] *n., adj.* □ palmtop
You can hold a palmtop computer in the palm of your hand.
▪ Ver **laptop; desktop computer**.
pan [pæn] *n.*
1 panela
pots and pans.
▪ Ver **frying pan; saucepan**.
2 forma
a cake pan. *Amer.* (= a cake tin, *Brit.*)
pancake ['pænkeik] *n.* □ panqueca
pane [pein] *n.* □ vidraça
panel ['pænl] *n.*
1 painel
a door with panels.
2 painel
a control panel of a TV.
3 painel
a panel of experts.
panic¹ ['pænik] *n.* □ pânico
They were in a panic.
panic² *v.* (**panics, panicking, panicked**) □ entrar em pânico
Don't panic!
pant [pænt] *v.* (**pants, panting, panted**) □ ofegar
She was panting after the run.
panther ['pænθə] *n.* □ pantera
panties ['pæntiz] *n. pl.* □ calcinha
▪ Ver **knickers**.
pantomime ['pæntəmaim] *n.*
1 (= mime) **mímica**
He did a pantomime of riding a horse.
2 *Brit.* **pantomima**
A pantomime is a musical play of children's stories.
pants [pænts] *n. pl.*
1 *Amer.* **calças**
I put on my pants. ◆ I took off my pants.
▪ *Brit.* **trousers**
2 *Brit.* **cuecas**
▪ *Amer.* **underpants**
pantyhose ['pæntihouz] *n. Amer.* □ meia-calça
▪ *Brit.* **tights**
paper ['peipə] *n.*
1 papel
Wrap the package in brown paper. ◆ a paper bag. ◆ a paper towel.
▪ Ver **toilet paper; tissue paper**.
2 (= newspaper) **jornal**
a daily paper. ◆ I read about it in the paper.
3 prova, exame
The teacher checked the exam papers.
4 *Amer.* **trabalho**
We have to hand in the history papers tomorrow.
▪ *Brit.* **essay**
5 dissertação, artigo
Dr. Jones wrote a paper on the new medicine.
a piece of paper / a sheet of paper □ um pedaço de papel / uma folha de papel
papers *n. pl.*
1 documentos
The policeman asked to see my papers.

2 papelada
The letter is among the papers on my desk.
paperback ['peipəbæk] *n.* □ brochura
▪ Compare **paperback, hardback**:
paperback = a book with a paper cover.
hardback = a book with a hard cover.
paper-clip ['peipəklip] *n.* □ clipe de papel
paprika ['pæprikə] *n.* □ páprica
parachute¹ ['pærəʃu:t] *n.* □ paraquedas
parachute² *v.* (**parachutes, parachuting, parachuted**) □ saltar de paraquedas
to parachute behind enemy lines.
parade¹ [pə'reid] *n.* □ parada, desfile
a military parade.
parade² *v.* (**parades, parading, paraded**) □ desfilar
They paraded along the main road.
paradise ['pærədais] *n.* (= heaven) □ paraíso
paraffin ['pærəfin] *n. Brit.* □ parafina
▪ *Amer.* kerosene.
paragraph ['pærəgra:f] *n.* □ parágrafo
A paragraph always starts on a new line. ◆ Read the first paragraph.
parallel ['pærəlel] *adj.* □ paralelo
Parallel lines never meet.
paralyse ['pærəlaiz] *v. Brit.* (**paralyses, paralysing, paralysed**), **paralyze** *Amer.* (**paralyzes, paralyzing, paralyzed**) paralisar
The snake's poison paralyzed him. ◆ Fear paralysed him.
paralysed ['pærəlaizd] *adj. Brit.*, **paralyzed** *Amer.* □ paralisado
His legs are paralysed.
paralysis [pə'rælɔsis] *n.* □ paralisia
parcel ['pa:sl] *n.* □ pacote
We sent her a parcel of books. ◆ a food parcel.
▪ *Amer.* also **package**
pardon¹ ['pa:dn] *n.* □ perdão
I beg your pardon
1 (= Sorry!) **Me desculpe!, Sinto muito!**
2 (= Pardon?) **Como?**
I beg your pardon, what was the question?
▪ *Amer.* usually **excuse me?**
pardon² *v.* (**pardons, pardoning, pardoned**)
1 (= forgive) **perdoar**
Pardon my curiosity, but where are you going?
2 indultar
The President pardoned two prisoners.
Pardon? □ Perdão?, Como?
Pardon, what did you say?
pardon me
1 (= Pardon?) **Como?**
2 (= Sorry!) **Me desculpe!; Perdão!**
Pardon me, I didn't mean to interrupt.
▪ Ver **excuse me**.
parent ['peərənt] *n.* □ genitor, pais
My parents want to see you.
parentheses [pə'renθəsi:z] *n. pl. Amer.* □ parênteses
Put the word in parentheses.
▪ *Brit.* **(round) brackets**
park¹ [pa:k] *n.* □ parque
park² *v.* (**parks, parking, parked**) □ estacionar
I parked the car in a parking lot. ◆ You can't park here.

parking ['pɑːkiŋ] *n.* □ **estacionamento**
No parking!
parking garage ['pɑːkiŋ 'gɑrɑːdʒ] *n. Amer.* □ **estacionamento**
▪ *Brit.* **car park**
parking lot ['pɑːkiŋ 'lot] *n. Amer.* □ **estacionamento**
▪ *Brit.* **car park**
parking meter ['pɑːkiŋ 'miːtə] *n.* □ **parquímetro**
parking space ['pɑːkiŋ speis] *n.* (mesmo que **parking place**) □ **local para estacionar, vaga**
It was difficult to find a parking space.
parking ticket ['pɑːkiŋ 'tikit] *n.* □ **multa por estacionamento proibido**
He got a parking ticket for parking on the sidewalk.
parliament ['pɑːləmənt] *n.* □ **parlamento**
a member of parliament (= MP).
parlor ['pɑːlə] *n. Amer.*, **parlour** *Brit.*
1 quiosque
an ice-cream parlor. ◆ a pizza parlour.
2 salão
a beauty parlour.
parrot ['pɑrət] *n.* □ **papagaio**
parsley ['pɑːsli] *n.* □ **salsinha**
part¹ [pɑːt] *n.*
1 parte
I read only part of the story. ◆ Divide the money into four parts.
2 peças
We sell (spare) parts for cars.
3 bandas, arredores
We don't see many foreigners in these parts.
4 papel
He played the part of Romeo.
5 parte, capítulo
a TV series in six parts.
in part □ **em parte**
They decided to stay, in part because of the weather.
on the part of, on your part □ **da parte de, de sua parte**
It was a good decision on their part.
play a part (in) □ **ter um papel (em)**
She played an important part in building the organization.
take part (in) (= participate) □ **tomar parte (em), fazer parte (de), participar**
We all took part in the race.
part² *v.* (**parts, parting, parted**) □ **separar-se**
We parted with a handshake.
partial ['pɑːʃəl] *adj.* □ **parcial**
a partial success.
participant [pɑːˈtisipənt] *n.* □ **participante**
The participants enjoyed the discussion.
participate [pɑːˈtisipeit] *v.* (**participates, participating, participated**) (= take part) □ **participar**
Did you participate in the race? ◆ She participated in the discussion.
participation [pɑːˌtisiˈpeiʃən] *n.* □ **participação**
participle ['pɑːtisipl] *n.* □ **particípio**
In 'I am standing', the word 'standing' is the present participle. In 'I have written', 'written' is the past participle.
particular [pəˈtikjulə] *adj.*
1 específico
a particular kind of paper.
2 especial
Do it with particular care.
3 exigente
He is very particular about what he eats.
in particular □ **em particular**
She likes juice, orange juice in particular. ◆ Is there anything in particular you want?
particularly [pəˈtikjuləli] *adv.* (= specially) □ **particularmente**
I'm particularly worried about Ruth. ◆ Did you enjoy the film? – Not particularly.
partly ['pɑːtli] *adv.* □ **parcialmente**
It was partly your fault. ◆ The door was partly open.
partner ['pɑːtnə] *n.*
1 parceiro, sócio
business partners.
2 parceiro
my dancing partner.
partnership ['pɑːtnəʃip] *n.* □ **parceria, sociedade**
I want to go into partnership with him.
part of speech ['pɑːt əv spiːtʃ] *n.* □ **categoria gramatical**
'Adjective', 'noun' and 'verb' are parts of speech.
part-time [ˌpɑːˈtaim] *adj., adv.* □ **meio período, meio expediente**
a part-time job. ◆ to work part-time.
party ['pɑːti] *n.* (*pl.* **parties**)
1 festa
to have a party. ◆ I invited them to my birthday party.
2 partido
a political party.
3 (= group) **grupo**
a party of tourists.
4 partes
the parties to the agreement.
pass¹ [pɑːs] *n.*
1 passe
He gave me a pass and I scored a goal.
2 aprovação
I got a pass in biology and a fail in maths. ◆ I got a pass in my philosophy course.
3 passe, credencial
You need a pass to get in.
4 passe
a monthly bus pass.
5 desfiladeiro
a mountain pass.
pass² *v.* (**passes, passing, passed**)
1 passar
The street was so narrow that the bus couldn't pass. ◆ We passed a park on the way to the station.
2 passar
Could you pass me the salt, please? ◆ I passed him the ball.
3 passar, ser aprovado
Did you pass the test?
▪ antônimo: **fail**
4 (= go by) **passar-se**
Eight hours passed before he called.
5 passar
How did you pass the time?
6 passar, ser aprovado
to pass new laws.
pass something around / round □ **passar / fazer circular algo para as pessoas**
Pass the photograph around, please.

pass away (= die) □ **falecer**
He passed away at midnight.
pass by □ **passar**
They waved at us as we passed by.
pass on (to)
1 passar (para)
Pass on this information to the manager.
2 passar para, seguir
Let's pass on to the next paragraph.
pass out (= faint) □ **desmaiar**
He passed out when he saw the blood.
pass through □ **atravessar**
We passed through the city on our way to the airport.
passage ['pasidʒ] *n.*
1 trecho, passagem
Read the passage and answer the questions.
2 (= corridor) **corredor**
The office is at the end of the passage.
passenger ['pasindʒə] *n.* □ **passageiro**
There were 400 passengers on the plane. ♦ All the passengers got off the bus.
passer-by [ˌpaːsə'bai] *n.* (*pl.* **passers-by**) □ **pedestre, transeunte**
Two passers-by caught the thief.
passion ['paʃən] *n.* □ **paixão**
He had a great passion for her. ♦ to speak with passion.
passionate ['paʃənət] *adj.* □ **apaixonado**
a passionate kiss. ♦ a passionate speech.
passionately ['paʃənətli] *adv.* □ **apaixonadamente**
She hated them passionately.
passive ['pasiv] *n.* □ **passivo**
'The letter was written by me' is a sentence in the passive.
■ antônimo: **active**
passport ['paːspɔːt] *n.* □ **passaporte**
I have to renew my passport. ♦ a German passport.
password ['paːswəd] *n.* □ **senha**
The guard ordered me to say the password. ♦ You can enter this (computer) file only if you know the password.
past[1] [paːst] *adj.*
1 (= last) **último, passado**
the past two weeks.
2 passado
your past mistakes.
■ Do not confuse with **passed** (the *past tense* of the verb *pass*).
past[2] *n.* □ **passado**
In the past, people lived in caves. ♦ We don't know anything about his past.
the past (tense) □ **o (tempo) pretérito**
The past tense of 'eat' is 'ate'.
past[3] *prep., adv.*
1 depois de
It's half past eight (= 8:30). ♦ It's six minutes past ten (= 10:06).
■ American English also:
It's six minutes after ten (= 10:06).
2 mais de
She is past 40.
3 além de
I live just past the traffic-lights. ♦ The bus went past without stopping.

paste[1] [peist] *n.*
1 cola
wallpaper paste (= paste for sticking wallpaper)
■ Ver **glue**.
2 pasta, patê
Spread olive paste on bread.
■ Ver **spread**[1].
paste[2] *v.* (**pastes, pasting, pasted**) □ **colar**
to paste pieces of paper together.
pastime ['paːstaim] *n.* (= hobby) □ **passatempo**
Their favourite pastime is riding horses.
pastry ['peistri] *n.*
1 massa
You mix flour, water and fat to make pastry.
■ Compare **pastry, dough**:
pastry = for making a pie.
dough = for making bread.
2 (*pl.* **pastries**) **doces de confeitaria**
We had pastries and milk for breakfast.
pat[1] [pat] *v.* (**pats, patting, patted**) □ **dar tapinhas em**
She patted the dog. ♦ He patted me on the back.
■ Ver **stroke**.
pat[2] *n.* □ **tapinha**
He gave me a pat on my shoulder.
patch [patʃ] *n.*
1 remendo
He wore jeans with patches on the knees.
2 sinal, mancha
My cat has a white patch on its head.
3 tapa-olho
an eye-patch.
path [paːθ] *n.* □ **caminho, trilha**
This path leads to the cave.
patience ['peiʃəns] *n.* □ **paciência**
I'm losing my patience. ♦ She has a lot of patience with children.
■ antônimo: **impatience**
patient[1] ['peiʃənt] *adj.* □ **paciente**
Be patient. They will be here soon. ♦ He was patient with us.
■ antônimo: **impatient**
patient[2] *n.* □ **paciente**
The condition of the patient is improving. ♦ This dentist has a lot of patients.
patiently ['peiʃəntli] *adv.* □ **pacientemente, com paciência**
Wait patiently for your turn!
patrol[1] [pə'troul] *n.* □ **patrulha**
to make patrols along the border. ♦ an army patrol.
patrol[2] *v.* (**patrols, patrolling, patrolled**) □ **patrulhar**
A security guard patrols the building.
patter[1] ['patə] *n.* □ **tamborilada, passinho**
the patter of rain on the roof. ♦ the patter of children's feet in the corridor.
patter[2] *v.* (**patters, pattering, pattered**) □ **tamborilar**
Rain pattered against / on the window.
pattern ['patən] *n.*
1 estampa
a carpet with a pattern of flowers.
2 molde
I saw a pattern in the magazine for knitting a sweater.
pause[1] [pɔːz] *n.* □ **pausa**
There was a pause in the conversation.

pause² v. (pauses, pausing, paused) □ **fazer uma pausa**
He paused to drink some water and then said...

pavement ['peivmənt] *n. Brit.* □ **calçada**
Keep to the pavement! ◆ Don't ride your bike on the pavement.
■ *Amer.* **sidewalk**

paw [pɔ:] *n.* □ **pata**

pay¹ [pei] *n.* □ **pagamento**
When do you get your pay?
■ Ver **salary; wages**.

pay² v. (pays, paying, paid)
1 pagar
How much did you pay (him) for the car? ◆ I paid her $300 for her work. ◆ to pay the telephone bill.
2 compensar
Crime doesn't pay. ◆ It pays to be patient.

pay attention (to) □ **prestar atenção (a)**
You're not paying attention. ◆ Don't pay attention to her.

pay someone a compliment □ **fazer um elogio a alguém**
He paid me a big compliment.

pay someone a visit □ **fazer uma visita a alguém**
I'll pay them a visit.

payment ['peimənt] *n.* □ **pagamento**
a cash payment. ◆ ten monthly payments of 50 dollars each.

pay phone [pei foun] *n.* □ **telefone público, orelhão**

PC ['pi:'si:] *n., abbr.*
1 (= personal computer) **PC**
2 (= police constable) *Brit.* **policial**

pea [pi:] *n.* □ **ervilha**
a bag of frozen peas. ◆ pea soup.

peace [pi:s] *n.*
1 paz
peace talks. ◆ to make peace (with...).
2 paz
Go away and leave me to work in peace!

peace of mind □ **paz de espírito**

peaceful ['pi:sful] *adj.*
1 pacífico
a peaceful solution. ◆ a peaceful demonstration.
2 tranquilo, sossegado
a peaceful evening.

peacefully ['pi:sful] *adv.* □ **pacificamente**
to live peacefully together. ◆ to sleep peacefully.

peacefulness ['pi:sfulnis] *n.* □ **tranquilidade, sossego**

peach [pi:tʃ] *n.* □ **pêssego**

peacock ['pi:kok] *n.* □ **pavão**

peak [pi:k] *n.*
1 pico
The mountain peaks were covered with snow.
2 auge
at the peak of her career.
3 pala
A hat with a peak is called 'a peaked cap'.

peanut ['pi:nʌt] *n.* □ **amendoim**
a bag of roasted peanuts. ◆ peanut butter.

pear [peə] *n.* □ **pera**

pearl [pe:l] *n.* □ **pérola**
a pearl necklace

peasant ['peznt] *n.* □ **camponês**

pebble ['pebl] *n.* □ **pedregulho**

peck [pek] *v.* **(pecks, pecking, pecked)** □ **bicar**
The birds pecked at the pieces of bread.

peculiar [pi'kju:ljə] *adj.* (= strange) □ **peculiar**
Their behaviour seemed very peculiar to us. ◆ a peculiar smell.

peculiarity [,pikju:li'ariti] *n.* □ **peculiaridade**

pedal¹ ['pedl] *n.* □ **pedal**
the brake pedal. ◆ to step on the pedal.

pedal² v. (pedals, pedalling, pedalled) □ **pedalar**
He pedalled (the bicycle) up the hill.

pedestrian [pi'destriən] *n.* □ **pedestre**
Careful pedestrians always walk on the sidewalk.

pedestrian crossing [pi'destriən 'krosiŋ] *n.* □ **faixa de pedestre**
to cross the road at a pedestrian crossing.
■ *Amer.* **crosswalk**

pedestrian mall [pi'destriən mo:l] *n. Amer.* □ **calçadão**

pedestrian precinct [pi'destriən 'pri:siŋkt] *n. Brit.* □ **calçadão**

peel¹ [pi:l] *n.* □ **casca**
orange peel. ◆ apple peel.
■ Compare **skin, shell, rind**:
skin of apples, bananas.
shell of nuts, eggs.
rind of oranges, yellow cheese.

peel² v. (peels, peeling, peeled)
1 descascar
to peel the potatoes.
2 descascar
The paint is peeling (off the ceiling).

peep¹ [pi:p] *n.* □ **espiada**
to take a peep (= to peep)

peep² v. (peeps, peeping, peeped)
1 espiar
to peep through the keyhole.
2 surgir
The sun peeped out from behind the clouds.

peg [peg] *n.*
1 cabide
I hung my coat on the peg.
2 (= clothes-peg; clothes-pin) **prendedor de roupa**
Take these pegs and hang the washing on the line.
3 (= tent-peg) **cavilha**
I used six pegs to hold the tent in place.

pen [pen] *n.*
1 caneta
to write in pen. ◆ a ballpoint pen.
2 cercado
a sheep pen.

pen friend, pen pal *n.* □ **amigo por correspondência**
I wrote a letter to my pen pal in Canada. ◆ I received a letter from my pen pal in Japan.

penalty ['penlti] *n.* (*pl.* **penalties**)
1 pena
a penalty of 5 years in prison. ◆ the death penalty.
2 (= fine) **multa**
The penalty for illegal parking is $100.

penalty kick ['penlti kik] *n.* □ **pênalti**

pence [pens] *n.* (*pl. of* **penny**) □ **centavos de libra esterlina**
It costs 60 pence. (= 60 p.)

pencil ['pensl] *n.* □ **lápis**
to write in pencil. ◆ to sharpen the pencil.

pencil box, pencil case ['pensl boks, 'pensl keis] *n.* □ **porta-lápis, estojo de lápis**

pencil sharpener ['pensl ʃa:pənə] *n*. □ **apontador de lápis**
penetrate ['penitreit] *v*. (**penetrates, penetrating, penetrated**) □ **penetrar**
The bullet did not penetrate the heart. ◆ The robbers penetrated the bank through a hole in the wall.
penetration [ˌpeni'treiʃən] *n*. □ **penetração**
penguin ['peŋgwin] *n*. □ **pinguim**
penknife ['penaif] *n*. (*pl*. **penknives**) □ **canivete**
penny ['peni] *n*. (*pl*. **pence or pennies**)
1 (= British money) **centavo de libra esterlina**
The price is 80 pence (= 80 p).
■ The plural **pence** (or **p**) is used for prices (*not* **pennies**).
2 (= 1 cent) *Amer*. **um centavo de dólar**
pension ['penʃən] *n*. □ **pensão, aposentadoria**
When he retires (= leaves work) at the age of 65, he will get a pension.
pensioner ['penʃənə] *n*. □ **pensionista, aposentado**
An old-age pensioner is also called a 'retiree' or a 'senior citizen'.
people ['pi:pl] *n*.
1 **pessoas**
How many people did you invite? ◆ Five people died in the fire.
■ The singular of **people** is **person** or **man / woman**.
2 (*pl*. **peoples**) **povo**
a brave people. ◆ the peoples of the world.
of all people □ **entre todas as pessoas**
You, of all people, should help them. ◆ Why me, of all people?
pepper ['pepə] *n*.
1 **pimenta**
salt and pepper.
2 **pimentão**
a green pepper.
peppermint ['pepəmint] *n*. □ **menta, hortelã**
per [pə:] *prep*. □ **por**
80 km per hour. ◆ It costs six dollars per kilo.
■ **a** or **an** are also possible: 80 km **an** hour six euros **a** kilo
percent [pə'sent] (also **per** cent) *adj*., *adv*., *n*. □ **por cento**
a 5 percent (= 5%) increase in sales. ◆ Ten percent of them voted for me. ◆ Unemployment dropped by 2 percent.
percentage [pə'sentidʒ] *n*. □ **porcentagem**
What percentage of the population have jobs? – About 88 percent.
perfect[1] ['pə:tikt] *adj*. □ **perfeito**
Your English is nearly perfect. ◆ She did a perfect job.
perfect[2] [pə'fekt] *v*. (**perfects, perfecting, perfected**) □ **aperfeiçoar**
to perfect the technique.
perfect[3] *n*. □ **perfeito (aspecto verbal)**
'I have gone' is in the present perfect, 'I had gone' is in the past perfect.
perfection [pə'fekʃən] *n*. □ **perfeição**
They planned everything to perfection.
perfectly ['pəfiktli] *adv*.
1 **perfeitamente**
They planned everything perfectly.
2 **perfeitamente**
It's perfectly legal. ◆ I'm perfectly all right.
perfectly well □ **perfeitamente bem**
You know perfectly well what I mean.
perform [pə'fo:m] *v*. (**performs, performing, performed**)

1 (= do; carry out) **executar**
This computer can perform many tasks. ◆ The doctor will perform the operation tomorrow.
2 **desempenhar**
The car performed well on the test.
3 **apresentar**
to perform a piece of music. ◆ The dance group is performing tonight.
performance [pə'fo:məns] *n*.
1 **performance, desempenho**
The team's performance is disappointing. ◆ to improve the car's performance.
2 **atuação, performance**
a live performance by the rock group.
performer [pə'fo:mə] *n*. □ **ator, músico, artista**
perfume ['pə:fju:m] *n*.
1 (= scent) **perfume**
to put on perfume. ◆ What perfume do you wear?
2 (= fragrance) **perfume, fragrância**
the perfume of roses.
perfumed [pə'fju:md] *adj*. □ **perfumado**
a perfumed letter.
perhaps [pə'haps] *adv*. (= maybe) □ **talvez**
Perhaps he will telephone. ◆ She is, perhaps, the best teacher in our school.
peril ['peril] *n*. □ **perigo**
They are in great peril.
■ **danger** is the usual word.
perilous ['periləs] *adj*. (= dangerous) □ **perigoso**
period ['piəriəd] *n*.
1 **período**
a period of 3 months. ◆ a long period of time.
2 **época, tempo**
in the period of Jesus Christ.
3 (= lesson) **aula**
We have six periods of English a week.
4 *Amer*. **ponto final**
End your sentences with a period!
■ *Brit*. **full stop**
perish ['periʃ] *v*. (**perishes, perishing, perished**) □ **perecer**
Hundreds perished in the earthquake.
permanent ['pə:mənənt] *n*. □ **permanente, fixo**
a permanent job.
■ antônimo: **temporary**
permanently ['pə:mənəntli] *adv*. □ **permanentemente**
permission [pə'miʃən] *n*. □ **permissão**
He took it without permission. ◆ They gave me permission to stay.
■ They gave me permission (*not* 'a permission').
with your permission □ **com a sua permissão**
permit[1] [pə'mit] *v*. (**permits, permitting, permitted** (= allow) □ **permitir, autorizar**
The doctors did not permit me to see him.
permit[2] *n*. □ **licença, autorização**
a work permit.
■ Ver **licence; license**.
persecute ['pə:sikju:t] *v*. (**persecutes, persecuting, persecuted**) □ **perseguir**
They were persecuted for their religious beliefs.
persecution [ˌpə:si'kju:ʃn] *n*. □ **perseguição**
perseverance [ˌpə:si'viərəns] *n*. □ **perseverança**

persevere [ˌpɔːsiˈviə] *v.* (**perseveres, persevering, persevered**) □ **perseverar**
She persevered in her efforts to break the world record.
persist [pəˈsist] *v.* (**persists, persisting, persisted**)
1 persistir
He persisted until he got an answer. ♦ She persists in her belief that it was my fault.
2 persisitir, continuar
If the pain persists, call the nurse.
persistence [pəˈsistəns] *n.* □ **persistência**
persistent [pəˈsistənt] *adj.*
1 persistente
his persistent attempts.
2 persistente
a persistent cold in the nose. ♦ a persistent smell.
persistently [pəˈsistəntli] *adv.* □ **persistentemente**
person [ˈpɔːsn] *n.* (*pl.* **people**) □ **pessoa**
We need one more person. ♦ She is the right person for the job.
in person □ **em pessoa, pessoalmente**
The President was here in person. ♦ I want to give it to her in person.
personal [ˈpɔːsnl] *adj.* □ **pessoal**
your personal problems. ♦ The letter is personal.
personal computer *n.* (Ver **PC**).
personal stereo *n.* □ **Walkman**
personality [ˌpɔːsəˈnaləti] *n.* (*pl.* **personalities**)
1 personalidade
She has a strong personality.
2 personalidade
a TV personality.
personally [ˈpɔːsnəli] *adv.* □ **pessoalmente**
Personally, I think it's a good plan. ♦ I'm personally responsible for them. ♦ I checked it personally.
perspire [pəˈspaiə] *v.* (**perspires, perspiring, perspired**) □ **transpirar**
He began to perspire.
■ The usual word is **sweat**.
persuade [pəˈsweid] *v.* (**persuades, persuading, persuaded**) (= **convince**) □ **persuadir**
Try to persuade her to stay. ♦ He persuaded me that he was innocent.
persuasion [pəˈsweiʒən] *n.* □ **persuasão**
After a lot of persuasion he agreed to help.
persuasive [pəˈsweisiv] *adj.* (= convincing) □ **persuasivo**
a persuasive speech / speaker.
pessimism [ˈpesimizəm] *n.* □ **pessimismo**
■ antônimo: **optimism**
pessimist [ˈpesimist] *n.* □ **pessimista**
■ antônimo: **optimist**
pessimistic [ˌpesiˈmistik] *adj.* □ **pessimista**
They are pessimistic about the future of the company.
■ antônimo: **optimistic**
pest [pest] *n.*
1 praga
Rats, cockroaches, etc. are pests.
2 peste
He is such a pest!
pester [ˈpestə] *v.* (**pesters, pestering, pestered**) (= nag) □ **perturbar, incomodar**
Stop pestering him with your questions!
pet [ˈpet] *n.*
1 animal de estimação
I have two pets – a dog and a rabbit.
2 queridinho
She's the teacher's pet.
petal [ˈpetl] *n.* □ **pétala**
petition [pəˈtiʃən] *n.* □ **petição**
They signed a petition against the project.
petrol [ˈpetrəl] *n. Brit.* □ **gasolina**
I'm running out of petrol. (= The petrol tank is almost empty.)
■ *Amer.* **gas; gasoline**
petrol station [ˈpetrəl ˈsteiʃən] *n. Brit.* □ **posto de combustível**
to fill up with petrol at the (petrol) station.
■ *Amer.* **gas station**
petrol tank [ˈpetrəl tank] *n. Brit.* (= fuel tank) □ **tanque de combustível**
to fill up the petrol tank.
■ *Amer.* **gas tank**
phantom [ˈfantəm] *n.* (= ghost) □ **fantasma**
pharmacist [ˈfɑːməsist] *n.* □ **farmacêutico**
■ *Amer.* also **druggist**
■ *Brit.* also **chemist**
pharmacy [ˈfɑːməsi] *n.* (*pl.* **pharmacies**) □ **farmácia**
phase [feiz] *n.* □ **fase**
a new phase in the relations between the two countries.
phenomenon [fəˈnomənən] *n.* (*pl.* **phenomena**) □ **fenômeno**
a natural phenomenon.
philosopher [fiˈlosəfə] *n.* □ **filósofo**
philosophical [filoˈsofikəl] *adj.* □ **filosófico**
philosophy [fiˈlosəfi] *n.*
1 filosofia
to study philosophy.
2 (*pl.* **philosophies**) **filosofia**
What's your philosophy of life?
phone[1] [foun] *n.* (= telephone) □ **telefone**
She is on the phone. (= She is speaking on the phone.) ♦ Answer the phone, please. ♦ What's your phone number?
phone[2] *v.* (**phones, phoning, phoned**) (= telephone; call) □ **telefonar, ligar**
She phoned me an hour ago. ♦ Did you phone the police?
phone book [ˈfoun buk] *n.* □ **lista telefônica**
to look up a number in the phone book.
phone booth [ˈfoun buːθ] *n.* □ **cabine telefônica, orelhão**
phone box [ˈfoun boks] *n. Brit.* □ **cabine telefônica, orelhão**
phonecard [ˈfounkɑːd] *n.* □ **cartão telefônico**
phone call [ˈfoun kɔːl] *n.* (= **call**) □ **ligação, telefonema**
I need to make a phone call. ♦ You had a (phone) call from Ron.
phoney [ˈfouni] *adj.* (mesmo que **phony**) □ **falso**
a phoney address.
■ Ver **false; forged; fake**[1].
photo [ˈfoutou] *n.* (= photograph) □ **foto**
She showed me her wedding photos. ♦ I took some photos of him.
photocopier [ˈfoutəkɔpiə] *n.* □ **fotocopiadora**
photocopy[1] [ˈfoutəkɔpi] *n.* (*pl.* **photocopies**) □ **fotocópia**
to make a photocopy of the letter.
photocopy[2] *v.* (**photocopies, photocopying, photocopied**) □ **fotocopiar**
He photocopied two pages from the book.

photograph¹ ['foutəgra:f] *n.* (Ver **photo**).

photograph² *v.* (**photographs, photographing, photographed**) □ **fotografar**
I usually photograph animals and flowers.

photographer [fə'tɔgrəfə] *n.* □ **fotógrafo**
A press photographer works for a newspaper.

photography [fə'tɔgrəfi] *n.* □ **fotografia**

phrasal verb ['freizl və:b] *n.* □ **verbo frásico**
■ A phrasal verb is a two-word verb (verb+preposition or verb+adverb), e.g.: find out; get up; go on; take off.

phrase¹ [freiz] *n.* □ **sintagma**
Examples of phrases are: 'at last', 'a bottle of wine', 'in order to'.

phrase² *v.* (**phrases, phrasing, phrased**) □ **expressar**
She phrased the question carefully.

physical ['fizikəl] *adj.* □ **físico**
physical exercises. ◆ physical work.

physical education ['fizikəl ˌedju'kei∫ən] *n.* □ **educação física**

physically ['fizikəli] *adv.* □ **fisicamente**
He is physically fit.

physician [fi'zi∫ən] *n. Amer.* □ **médico**

physicist ['fizisist] *n.* □ **físico**

physics ['fiziks] *n.* □ **física**

pianist ['piənist] *n.* □ **pianista**

piano [pi'anou] *n.* □ **piano**
She plays the piano very well.

pick¹ [pik] *v.* (**picks, picking, picked**)
1 (= choose; select) **escolher**
Pick any card you like.
2 colher
to pick flowers. ◆ I picked an orange.
3 cutucar
Don't pick your nose!
4 palitar
He picked his teeth.
pick on □ **pegar no pé, aporrinhar**
The boss is always picking on me.
pick out □ **distinguir**
It was impossible to pick him out in the crowd.
pick up
1 recolher
She picked up the toys from the floor.
2 pegar
He picked up the phone immediately.
3 pegar
Pick me up at 7.
4 entender
I picked up a few words in Chinese.
pick someone's pocket □ **bater a carteira de alguém**
They caught the thief who picked my pocket.

pick² *n.*
take your pick □ **fazer sua escolha**
We have toys for all ages. Take your pick.

pick³ *n.* □ **picareta**

pickle ['pikl] *n.* □ **picles**
a jar of pickles.

pickled ['pikld] *adj.* □ **em conserva**
pickled cabbage.

pickpocket ['pikpɔkit] *n.* □ **batedor de carteira**

picnic¹ ['piknik] *n.* □ **piquenique**
to go for a picnic. ◆ We had a picnic (in a picnic area).

picnic² *v.* (**picnics, picnicking, picnicked**) □ **fazer piquenique**
We picnicked by the lake.

picture ['pikt∫ə] *n.*
1 desenho, pintura, foto
I drew a picture of the building. ◆ a picture (= painting) by Picasso ◆ She showed me pictures of her children.
■ Ver **drawing; painting; photograph**.
2 (= film) **filme**
It's a good picture.
■ Ver **movie**.
3 (= the pictures) *Brit.* **cinema**
Let's go to the pictures (= the cinema).
■ *Amer.* **the movies**
take a picture (= to photograph) □ **tirar uma foto**
Let's take a picture. ◆ I took a picture of him.

pie [pai] *n.* □ **torta**
an apple pie. ◆ an onion and cheese pie.

piece [pi:s] *n.*
1 pedaço, fragmento
a piece of cake. ◆ broken pieces of glass. ◆ a piece of paper (*not* 'a paper').
2 parte
piece of furniture (e.g. a chair, a bed).
3 peça
a piece of music.
a piece of advice □ **um conselho**
Let me give you a piece of advice.
a piece of cake □ **muito fácil**
The test was a piece of cake (= very easy).
a piece of news □ **uma notícia**
That's a sensational piece of news!
fall to pieces □ **ficar em pedaços**
The chair fell to pieces.
take something to pieces □ **desmontar**
He took the machine to pieces.
to pieces, into pieces □ **em pedaços**
She tore the letter to pieces. ◆ The vase smashed to pieces.

pier [piə] *n.* □ **pier**

pierce [piəs] *v.* (**pierces, piercing, pierced**) □ **furar**
The needle pierced my finger.

piercing ['piəsiŋ] *adj.* □ **penetrante**
piercing cold. ◆ a piercing scream.

pig [pig] *n.* □ **porco**

pigeon ['pidʒən] *n.* □ **pombo**
There were a lot of pigeons in the square.
■ Ver **dove**.

piglet ['piglit] *n.* □ **leitão**

pigsty ['pigstai] *n.* (*pl.* **pigsties**) □ **chiqueiro**

pile¹ [pail] *n.*
1 monte
a pile of sand.
2 pilha
There's a pile of books on the table.

pile² *v.* (**piles, piling, piled**) □ **empilhar**
He piled the books on the desk.
pile up □ **acumular**
Snow is piling up outside.

pile-up ['pailʌp] *n.* □ **engavetamento**

pilgrim ['pilgrim] *n.* □ **peregrino**

pilgrimage ['pilgrimidʒ] *n.* □ **peregrinação**

pill [pil] *n.* (= tablet) □ **pílula**
Take one pill twice a day.
pillar ['pilə] *n.* □ **pilar**
pillar-box ['piləboks] *n. Brit.* □ **caixa do correio**
■ Ver **mailbox; postbox**.
pillow ['pilou] *n.* □ **travesseiro**
■ Ver **cushion**.
pillowcase ['piloukeis] *n.* (mesmo que **pillowslip**) □ **fronha**
pilot ['pailət] *n.* □ **piloto**
a helicopter pilot. ♦ The pilot landed the plane safely.
pimple ['pimpl] *n.* □ **espinha**
pin¹ ['pin] *n.* □ **alfinete**
The tailor pricked his finger on a pin.
■ Ver **drawing pin; hairpin; safety pin**.
pins and needles □ **comichão, formigamento**
pin² *v.* (**pins, pinning, pinned**)
 1 alfinetar
 Pin the dress together before sewing it.
 2 prender com tachinha
 She pinned the notice (up) on the board.
 3 fixar, prender
 He pinned me to the floor, so I couldn't move.
 4 depositar
 People pinned their hopes on him.
pinch¹ [pintʃ] *n.*
 1 beliscão
 She gave me a pinch on the cheek.
 2 pitada
 Add a pinch of salt to the salad.
pinch² *v.* (**pinches, pinching, pinched**)
 1 beliscar
 He pinched my arm.
 2 prender
 I pinched my finger in the door.
pine (tree) ['pain (tri:)] *n.* □ **pinho**
a pine forest. ♦ pine furniture.
pineapple ['painapl] *n.* □ **abacaxi**
pineapple juice.
ping-pong ['piŋpoŋ] *n.* (= table tennis) □ **pingue-pongue**
pink [piŋk] *n., adj.* □ **cor-de-rosa, rosa, pink**
She was dressed in pink.
■ Ver **rosy**.
pint [paint] *n.* □ **quartilho**
a pint of milk / beer.
pioneer [paiə'niə] *n.* □ **pioneiro**
The pioneers built houses and worked the land. ♦ He is one of the pioneers of laser technology.
pip [pip] *n.* □ **semente**
Oranges, apples and grapes have pips.
pipe [paip] *n.*
 1 tubo
 a water / gas pipe. ♦ a sewer pipe.
 ■ Ver **drainpipe; hose; tube**.
 2 cachimbo
 to smoke a pipe.
 3 gaita de foles
 She can play the pipe and the flute.
pipeline ['paiplain] *n.* □ **tubulação**
pirate¹ ['paiərət] *n.* □ **pirata**
pirate² *v.* (**pirates, pirating, pirated**) □ **piratear**
He pirated the latest videos and CDs, until he was caught by the police.

pistol ['pistl] *n.* (= revolver) □ **pistola**
He aimed his pistol and fired.
pit [pit] *n.*
 1 buraco
 They threw the rubbish into the pit.
 2 (= coalmine) **mina de carvão**
 Miners work in a pit.
 3 *Amer.* **caroço**
 a peach pit.
 ■ Ver **stone**.
pitch¹ [pitʃ] *n.*
 1 campo
 a football pitch (= a football field).
 ■ **court** is used for tennis or basketball.
 2 tom
 a high pitch (of sound).
pitch² *v.* (**pitches, pitching, pitched**) □ **armar**
to pitch a tent.
pitcher ['pitʃə] *n.*
 1 *Brit.* **jarro, cântaro**
 The pirates hid the treasure in pitchers.
 2 (= jug, *Brit.*) *Amer.* **jarro**
 a pitcher of water.
pitiful ['pitiful] *adj.* □ **comovente**
The cries of the injured dog were pitiful.
pity¹ ['piti] *n.* □ **pena, dó**
I felt pity for the poor child.
■ Compare with **mercy**.
take pity on □ **ter pena de**
I took pity on them and gave them some food.
it's a pity / what a pity □ **é uma pena / que pena**
I won't be able to come. – What a pity! ♦ It's a pity (that) you can't come.
pity² *v.* (**pities, pitying, pitied**) □ **ter pena, compadecer-se**
I pity them.
pizza ['pi:tsə] *n.* □ **pizza**
pl *abbr.* (= plural) □ **pl**
placard ['plaka:d] *n.* □ **cartaz**
The crowd carried placards against the government.
place¹ [pleis] *n.*
 1 lugar
 Let's look for a quiet place where we can talk. ♦ Put the picture back in its place.
 2 lugar
 Who finished in third place?
 3 (= seat) **lugar**
 Excuse me, you're sitting in my place. ♦ I changed places with him. ♦ He saved me a place next to him.
 4 casa
 We'll meet at my place at 7.
in place □ **no lugar**
Everything in the room was in place. ♦ Stick the label in place.
in place of (= instead of) □ **em lugar de**
He is ill, so I came in his place.
in the first place
 1 em primeiro lugar
 In the first place she is not here, and in the second place she can't help you.
 2 para começar
 It was wrong to say that in the first place.
in your / her / his place □ **no seu lugar**
In your place, I would take the job.

take place
1 ocorrer, realizar-se
The wedding will take place here tomorrow.
2 (= happen) **acontecer**
She told us what took place in that room.
place² *v.* (**places, placing, placed**) ▫ **colocar**
He placed a jug of water on the table.
plague [pleig] *n.*
1 peste
The plague killed thousands of people.
2 praga
a plague of mosquitoes.
plain¹ [plein] *adj.*
1 simples
a plain black dress.
2 liso
a plain carpet (= a carpet without designs). • plain paper.
3 simples
plain food.
4 natural
plain yoghurt.
5 (= clear) **claro**
to speak in plain English.
6 (= obvious; clear) **claro**
It was plain that he was angry.
7 sem atrativos
He is a plain child.
in plain clothes *Brit.* ▫ **à paisana**
a detective in plain clothes.
plain chocolate *n.* ▫ **chocolate puro**
■ *Amer.* **dark chocolate**
plain² *n.* ▫ **planície**
plainly [ˈpleinli] *adv.* (= clearly) ▫ **claramente**
We could see him plainly.
plait¹ [plat] *n.* ▫ **trança**
She wears her hair in a plait.
■ *Amer.* **braid**
plait² *v. Brit.* (**plaits, plaiting, plaited**) ▫ **trançar, fazer trança**
She plaited her hair.
■ *Amer.* **braid**
plan¹ [plan] *n.*
1 plano
What are your plans for tomorrow? • to make plans for the future. • Everything went according to plan.
2 planta
a street plan (= map) of the city. • a plan for a new office building.
plan² *v.* (**plans, planning, planned**) ▫ **planejar**
He planned the military operation. • I'm planning to visit them in Paris.
planned *adj.* ▫ **planejado**
It wasn't planned.
planning *n.* ▫ **planejamento**
The planning took a month.
plane [plein] *n.* ▫ **avião**
What time does the plane land? • The plane will take off in 30 minutes. • It's time to board (= get on) the plane.
■ Ver **aeroplane; airplane; aircraft**.
plane crash [ˈplein kraʃ] *n.* ▫ **queda de avião**
Six people died in the plane crash.

planet [ˈplanit] *n.* ▫ **planeta**
the planet Earth.
plank [plaŋk] *n.* ▫ **tábua**
plant¹ [plɑːnt] *n.*
1 planta, pé
to water the plants. • tomato plants.
2 planta, fábrica
a chemical plant.
plant² *v.* (**plants, planting, planted**) ▫ **plantar**
to plant flowers / trees.
plantation [planˈteiʃən] *n.* ▫ **plantação**
a cotton / sugar plantation.
plaster [ˈplɑːstə] *n.*
1 gesso
to cover the walls with plaster. • His leg was in plaster (= in a cast, *Amer.*) for four weeks.
2 (= sticking-plaster) *Brit.* **curativo**
Put a plaster on the cut.
■ *Amer.* **Band-aid™**
plastic¹ [ˈplastik] *adj.* ▫ **plástico**
plastic cups.
plastic bag *n.* ▫ **sacola plástica**
plastic² *n.* ▫ **plástico**
The flowers are made of plastic.
plastic surgery [ˈplastik ˈsɔːdʒəri] *n.* ▫ **cirurgia plástica**
He had plastic surgery on his nose.
plate [pleit] *n.* ▫ **prato**
plastic plates.
■ Ver **bowl; dish**.
platform [ˈplatfɔːm] *n.*
1 plataforma
The train to Paris will leave from platform 7.
2 tribuna
She went up to the platform to make her speech.
play¹ [plei] *n.*
1 peça
We saw a play by Shakespeare (at the theatre) last night.
2 peça
a radio play.
3 jogada, lance
There was a lot of rough play in the game.
4 lazer
You have enough time for homework and for play.
play² *v.* (**plays, playing, played**)
1 jogar, brincar
to play chess / basketball. • They are playing in the garden. • He likes to play with toys. • We are playing against a strong team tomorrow.
2 fazer um papel
I'm going to play the hero (of the play).
3 representar
She played an important part in the talks.
4 tocar
Can you play the piano?
■ play **the** piano (*not* 'a piano').
5 tocar
to play a disc.
play for time ▫ **ganhar tempo**
Don't give them an answer yet. Try to play for time.
player [ˈpleiə] *n.*
1 jogador
a football player.

2 pessoa que toca
a piano player (= pianist). ♦ a violin player (= violinist).
playfully ['pleifuli] *adv*. □ **alegremente**
The little child teased the dog playfully.
playground ['pleigraund] *n*. □ **playground, parquinho**
The children were playing in the school playground.
playmate ['pleimeit] *n*. □ **colega**
He was my playmate when we were children.
plea [pli:] *n*. □ **apelo**
to make a plea for help (= to ask for help).
plead [pli:d] *v*. *Amer.* (**pleads, pleading, pleaded** or **pled**) □ **suplicar**
They pleaded with him to help them.
plead guilty □ **alegar culpa**
He pleaded guilty to robbery.
plead not guilty □ **alegar inocência**
Do you plead guilty or not guilty?
pleasant ['pleznt] *adj*. (= nice)
1 agradável
What a pleasant surprise! ♦ pleasant weather.
2 agradável
She has a pleasant voice.
3 agradável
We had a pleasant time during the trip.
4 agradável
He was pleasant to them. ♦ She is a pleasant person.
■ antônimo: **unpleasant**
pleasantly ['plezntli] *adv*. □ **agradavelmente**
She smiled pleasantly. ♦ We were pleasantly surprised.
please[1] [pli:z] *excl*. □ **por favor**
Sit down, please. ♦ Please don't go. ♦ Two coffees, please. ♦ Will you help me, please? ♦ Would you like a lift? – Yes, please.
please[2] *v*. (**pleases, pleasing, pleased**)
1 agradar
It will please my parents to hear that I won a medal.
■ antônimo: **displease**
2 (= wish) **desejar, quiser**
Do as you please. ♦ You can say whatever you please.
please yourself □ **você é quem sabe**
please God □ **se Deus quiser**
We'll be there tomorrow, please God.
pleased [pli:zd] *adj*. □ **satisfeito**
I'm very pleased to see you. ♦ I'm pleased with your work.
pleasure ['pleʒə] *n*. □ **prazer**
I swim for pleasure. ♦ I had the pleasure of working with him. ♦ It's a pleasure to do business with you. ♦ Are you here on business or for pleasure?
it's a pleasure □ **é um prazer**
Thank you for the lift. – It's a pleasure.
it was a pleasure to... □ **foi um prazer...**
It was a pleasure to meet you.
take pleasure in □ **ter prazer em**
He takes pleasure in annoying me.
with pleasure □ **com prazer**
Could you help me, please? – With pleasure.
pled [pled] *v*. (Ver **plead**).
plentiful ['plentiful] *adj*. □ **abundante**
plenty ['plenti] *pron*. (= a lot) □ **muito**
We have plenty of time. ♦ There's plenty of food for everybody. ♦ We don't need any more pencils. We have plenty.
pliers ['plaiəz] *n*. □ **alicate**
Pull out the nail with the pliers.
plod [plod] *v*. (**plods, plodding, plodded**) □ **caminhar com dificuldade**
They plodded through the mud.
plot[1] [plot] *n*.
1 conspiração, trama
There was a plot to kill the King.
2 enredo, trama
The plot of the book is very complicated.
3 lote
a building plot.
plot[2] *v*. (**plots, plotting, plotted**) □ **conspirar, tramar**
They plotted to kill the President.
plough[1] [plau] *n*. *Brit*. **plow** *Amer*. □ **arado**
plough[2] *v*. (**ploughs, ploughing, ploughed**), **plow** *Amer*. (**plows, plowing, plowed**) □ **arar**
The farmer finished ploughing the field.
plug[1] [plʌg] *n*.
1 plugue
to pull out the plug. ♦ to put the plug into the socket ♦ This plug connects the keyboard to the computer.
2 tampão
Before you fill the bath with water, put in the plug.
plug[2] *v*. (**plugs, plugging, plugged**) □ **tapar**
I plugged the hole in the boat with a piece of wood.
plug in □ **conectar (na tomada etc.), ligar (na tomada etc.)**
Plug the TV in and switch it on. The antenna plugs in at the back of the TV.
■ antônimo: **unplug**
plum [plʌm] *n*. □ **ameixa**
plumber ['plʌmə] *n*. □ **encanador**
plump [plʌmp] *adj*. □ **rechonchudo**
plump cheeks. ♦ a plump baby.
plunge [plʌndʒ] *v*. (**plunges, plunging, plunged**)
1 pular
She plunged into the pool.
2 enfiar
He plunged his knife into the melon.
plural ['pluərəl] *n*., *adj*. □ **plural**
The plural of 'tooth' is 'teeth'. ♦ a plural noun.
■ abreviação: **pl.**
■ Ver **singular**.
plus[1] [plʌs] *prep*. □ **mais**
Five plus two minus three is four (5+2-3=4).
plus[2] *n*. (= advantage) □ **vantagem**
That's one of the pluses of this computer.
the plus sign (+) □ **o sinal de mais**
pm [,pi:'em] *abbr*., **p.m.** □ **da tarde, da noite**
at 6 pm. ♦ the 2 pm train.
■ Ver **a.m.**
PM [,pi:'em] *abbr*. (= Prime Minister) □ **primeiro-ministro**
pneumonia [nju:'məuniə] *n*. □ **pneumonia**
poach [pəutʃ] *v*. (**poaches, poaching, poached**) □ **caçar sem permissão**
He caught them when they poached on his land.
poached egg ['pəutʃt eg] *n*. □ **ovo quente**
poacher ['pəutʃə] *n*. □ **caçador ilegal**
The police arrested some poachers for killing elephants.
PO Box ['pi:əu bɒks] *n*. □ **caixa postal**
The address is PO Box 1099, Rome.
pocket ['pɒkit] *n*. □ **bolso**

There's a hole in my pocket. ◆ He put the money in his pocket.

pocketbook ['pokitbuk] *n. Amer.* □ **carteira**
■ *Brit.* **handbag**

pocketknife ['pokitnaif] *n.* (*pl.* **pocketknives**) □ **canivete**

pocket money ['pokit ˌmʌni] *n. Brit.* □ **dinheiro para pequenas despesas**
How much pocket money do you get?
■ *Amer.* **allowance**

pod [pod] *n.* □ **vagem**

poem ['pouim] *n.* □ **poema**
This poem was written by Shakespeare.
■ Compare **song**:
song = a poem with music.

poet ['pouit] *n.* □ **poeta**
She was a famous American poet.

poetic [pou'etik] *adj.* □ **poético**
poetic language.

poetry ['pouitri] *n.* □ **poesia**
modern French poetry.

point¹ [point] *n.*
1 ponto
four point eight (= 4.8).
■ Compare with **full stop; period**.
2 ponto
He scored 10 points.
3 ponto, questão
That's not the point. ◆ Please get to the point! ◆ I wrote down the main points of the lecture.
4 ponto, altura, ocasião
At that point we didn't know it.
5 propósito, razão
What's the point of staying here? ◆ Is there any point in speaking to him?
6 ponta
the point of a needle / pencil.
be on the point of □ **estar no ponto de**
I was on the point of leaving when he came.
point of view □ **ponto de vista**
It is a description from a child's point of view.
there's no point in... □ **não há razão para**
There's no point in complaining now.
to the point □ **direto ao ponto**
The lecture was short and to the point.

point² *v.* (**points, pointing, pointed**)
1 apontar
She pointed at me.
2 apontar, direcionar, assestar
He pointed the gun at the prisoner.
3 apontar, indicar
All the evidence points to him as the murderer.
point out
1 ressaltar
He pointed out that the plan was not good enough.
2 ressaltar
I pointed out the place on the map.

pointed ['pointid] *adj.* □ **pontiagudo**
a pointed stick.

pointless ['pointlis] *adj.* □ **inútil**
It's pointless to continue this discussion.

poison¹ ['poizn] *n.* □ **veneno**
a deadly poison. ◆ rat poison.
■ Compare with **venom**.

poison² *v.* (**poisons, poisoning, poisoned**) □ **envenenar**
Who poisoned the king? ◆ The food was poisoned.

poisoned ['poiznd] *adj.* □ **envenenado**
a poisoned arrow.

poisoning ['poizniŋ] *n.* □ **envenenamento**
They died of poisoning.

poisonous ['poiznəs] *adj.* □ **venenoso**
poisonous mushrooms. ◆ poisonous snakes. ◆ poisonous chemicals.

poke [pouk] *v.* (**pokes, poking, poked**)
1 cutucar
He poked me in the eye with his finger.
2 enfiar
She poked her head out of the window.
poke fun at □ **ridicularizar**
They like to poke fun at him.

polar ['poulə] *adj.* □ **polar**

polar bear ['poulə ˌbeə] *n.* □ **urso polar**

pole [poul] *n.*
1 polo
the North Pole. ◆ the South Pole.
2 polo
electricity poles.
3 mastro
a tent pole. ◆ a flagpole.
the pole vault □ **salto com vara**
He broke the world record in the pole vault.

police [pə'liːs] *n.* □ **polícia**
Call the police! ◆ The police are investigating. ◆ The police arrested two suspects. ◆ a police car.
■ the police **are** (*not* 'is').

police constable [pə'liːs 'kʌnstəbl] *n. Brit.* □ **policial**
■ abreviação: **PC**

police force [pə'liːs fɔːs] *n.* □ **força policial**

policeman [pə'liːsmən] *n.* (*pl.* **policemen**) □ **policial**

police officer [pə'liːs 'ofisə] *n.* □ **policial**
■ When you speak to a policeman or policewoman you say: **Officer.**

police station [pə'liːs 'steiʃən] *n.* □ **delegacia de polícia**

policewoman [pə'liːswumən] *n.* (*pl.* **policewomen**) □ **policial feminina**

policy ['polisi] *n.* (*pl.* **policies**)
1 política
an economic policy. ◆ What's the minister's policy on education?
2 apólice
an insurance policy.

polish¹ ['poliʃ] *v.* (**polishes, polishing, polished**) □ **polir**
to polish the furniture. ◆ I need to polish my shoes. ◆ to polish diamonds.

polish² *n.* □ **graxa, cera**
shoe polish. ◆ furniture polish.
■ **Polish** (Ver '**Geographical Names**').

polite [pə'lait] *adj.* □ **educado**
He was very polite (to us). ◆ a polite answer.
■ antônimo: **impolite; rude**

politely [pə'laitli] *adv.* □ **educadamente**
He asked them politely to wait outside.

politeness [pə'laitnis] *n.* □ **educação, polidez**

political [pə'litikəl] *adj.* □ **político**
What are your political opinions? ◆ a political party.

politically [pəˈlitikəli] *adv.* □ **politicamente**
politician [ˌpoliˈtiʃən] *n.* □ **político**
politics [ˈpolitiks] *n.*
 1 política
 She is interested in politics.
 2 política
 I'm studying politics at university.
 ■ *Amer.* **Political Science**
poll [poul] *n.* (mesmo que **opinion poll**) □ **pesquisa**
 The poll shows that 45% watch the news every evening.
pollute [pəˈlu:t] *v.* (**pollutes, polluting, polluted**) □ **poluir**
 Chemicals and smoke from factories are polluting the environment.
pollution [pəˈlu:ʃən] *n.* □ **poluição**
 air pollution. ♦ noise pollution. ♦ We must put a stop to the pollution of our rivers.
pond [pond] *n.* □ **laguinho, tanque**
 a fish pond. ♦ a duck pond.
pony [ˈpouni] *n.* (*pl.* **ponies**) □ **pônei**
ponytail [ˈpouniteil] *n.* □ **rabo de cavalo**
pool [pu:l] *n.*
 1 poça
 There were pools of water on the road.
 2 (= **swimming** pool) **piscina**
 He dived into the pool.
 the pools *n.* (mesmo que **football pools**) □ **loteria esportiva**
 I won a lot of money on the pools.
poor [puə] *adj.*
 1 pobre
 Many people in the slums are very poor. ♦ one of the poorest countries in the world.
 ■ The noun is **poverty**.
 2 pobre, coitado
 Poor Tim! He failed his driving test again.
 3 inferior
 a product of poor quality. ♦ poor results.
 4 pobre
 She is in poor health.
 the poor □ **os pobres**
 The rich must pay more taxes than the poor.
poorly [ˈpuəli] *adv.* □ **mal**
 They were poorly dressed. ♦ He did poorly in the exam.
pop[1] [pop] *n.*
 1 pop
 pop music. ♦ a pop group.
 2 estalo, estouro
 The cork came out of the bottle with a loud pop.
pop[2] *v.* (**pops, popping, popped**)
 1 estourar
 The balloon popped.
 2 estourar
 He popped the balloon with a needle.
 3 pôr
 She popped a piece of chocolate into her mouth.
 pop in / over □ **dar uma passada**
 Why don't you pop in for a cup of coffee?
 pop out □ **saltar**
 His eyes almost popped out of his head.
 pop up □ **aparecer, pipocar**
 Such problems might pop up from time to time.
popcorn [ˈpopko:n] *n.* □ **pipoca**

pope [poup] *n.* □ **papa**
Popsicle™ [ˈpopsikl] *n. Amer.* □ **picolé**
 ■ *Brit.* **ice lolly**
popular [ˈpopjulə] *adj.* □ **popular**
 a popular game. ♦ This teacher is very popular with his students.
 ■ antônimo: **unpopular**
popularity [ˌpopjuˈlariti] *n.* □ **popularidade**
 the growing popularity of computer games
populate [ˈpopjuleit] *v.* (**populates, populating, populated**) □ **povoar**
 be populated □ **ser habitado, ser povoado**
 This part of town is populated by poor families.
population [ˌpopjuˈleiʃən] *n.* □ **população**
 What is the population of your country? ♦ Sixty percent of the population there have cars.
porch [po:tʃ] *n.*
 1 pórtico
 He waited on the porch.
 2 *Amer.* **varanda**
 ■ *Brit.* **veranda**
pork [po:k] *n.* □ **carne de porco**
porridge [ˈporidʒ] *n. Brit.* □ **mingau de aveia**
 ■ *Amer.* **oatmeal**
port [po:t] *n.* □ **porto**
 Which city is the biggest port in Egypt? ♦ The ship is coming into port.
portable [ˈpo:təbl] *adj.* □ **portátil**
 a portable computer / TV set.
porter [ˈpo:tə] *n.*
 1 carregador
 The porter carried my suitcases into the train.
 2 porteiro
 The hotel porter opened the door for us.
porthole [ˈpo:thoul] *n.* □ **portinhola**
portion [ˈpo:ʃən] *n.*
 1 parte, quinhão
 He got a large portion of the money.
 2 porção
 I ordered another portion of rice.
 ■ Ver **course; helping**.
portrait [ˈpo:trət] *n.* □ **retrato**
 a portrait of the Queen.
position [pəˈziʃən] *n.*
 1 posição
 Find the position of the ship on the map. ♦ I was in a good position to see everything. ♦ to sit / lie in the same position for a long time. ♦ Turn the switch to the 'off' position. ♦ You put me in a difficult position. ♦ What's your position on this issue?
 2 (= job; post) **cargo**
 a teaching position.
positive [ˈpozətiv] *adj.*
 1 positivo
 a positive answer. ♦ a positive attitude.
 ■ antônimo: **negative**
 2 (= certain[1]) **ter certeza, estar seguro**
 Are you sure you saw him? – I'm positive.
 3 positivo
 We have a positive identification of the robber.
positively [ˈpozətivli] *adv.* □ **positivamente**
 It's positively ugly.

possess [pəˈzes] *v.* (**possesses, possessing, possessed**)
1 (= own) **possuir, ter**
They took everything that he possessed.
2 possuir
He was guilty of possessing a gun.
what possessed you (to...)? □ **o que deu em você (para...)**
What possessed him to do that?
possession [pəˈzeʃən] *n.* □ **porte, posse**
They arrested him for possession of drugs.
come into your possession □ **cair nas suas mãos**
The plans came into the possession of the enemy.
have in your possession □ **ter em seu poder**
They had in their possession the key to the safe.
take possession of □ **tomar posse de**
Our forces took possession of the island.
possessions *n. pl.* □ **posses**
They lost all their possessions in the fire.
possibility [ˌpɒsəˈbɪlɪti] *n.* (*pl.* **possibilities**) □ **possibilidade**
Is there any possibility that she will change her decision? ◆ There is a possibility of rain.
possible [ˈpɒsəbl] *adj.* □ **possível**
There are two possible answers. ◆ Is it possible to climb there?
■ antônimo: **impossible**
it's possible that... □ **é possível que...**
It's possible that he may not come.
as... as possible □ **tanto... quanto possível**
I need as much time as possible. ◆ Bring as many chairs as possible.
as soon as possible □ **assim que possível, o mais rápido possível**
Send it as soon as possible.
make it possible (for) □ **tornar algo possível (para)**
He made it possible for us to finish the project.
possibly [ˈpɒsəbli] *adv.*
1 (= perhaps) **talvez, possivelmente**
Will you finish it today? – Possibly. ◆ It will happen soon, possibly tomorrow.
2 possível
I'll do it as fast as I possibly can.
can't possibly □ **é impossível**
I can't possibly come now.
post[1] [poust] *n.*
1 trave
The ball hit the goal post.
2 correio, correspondência
Send the parcel by post. ◆ Is there any post for me?
■ **mail** is more usual in American English.
3 (= job; position) **cargo**
He got the post of teacher.
post[2] *v.* (**posts, posting, posted**)
1 *Brit.* **enviar pelo correio**
Don't forget to post him the cheque.
■ *Amer.* **mail**
2 mandar
The company posted her abroad.
3 colocar
The police posted guards around the building.
keep someone posted □ **manter alguém informado**
Keep me posted. (= Let me know if there is anything new.)

postage [ˈpoustɪdʒ] *n.* □ **postagem**
Add $4 for postage and packing.
postage stamp [ˈpoustɪdʒ stæmp] *n.* (= **stamp**) □ **selo**
postbox [ˈpoustbɒks] *n. Brit.* □ **caixa de correio**
■ *Amer.* **mailbox**
postcard [ˈpoustkɑːd] *n.* □ **cartão postal**
I'll send you a postcard when I get to Spain.
postcode [ˈpoustkoud] *n. Brit.* □ **código postal**
The letter will get there more quickly if you put the postcode on the envelope.
■ *Amer.* **zip code**
poster [ˈpoustə] *n.* □ **pôster**
to put up a poster (on the wall).
postman [ˈpoustmən] *n. Brit.* (*pl.* **postmen**) □ **carteiro**
The postman usually delivers the post in the morning.
■ *Amer.* **mailman**
post office [ˈpoustˌɒfɪs] *n.* □ **agência do correio**
postpone [pəsˈpoun] *v.* (**postpones, postponing, postponed**) (= put off) □ **adiar**
We'll have to postpone the meeting. ◆ The trip was postponed until next month.
postponement [pəsˈpounmənt] *n.* □ **adiamento**
postwoman [ˈpouswumən] *n.* (*pl.* **postwomen**) □ **carteira**
pot [pɒt] *n.*
1 panela
a cooking pot.
2 bule
a teapot. ◆ a coffee pot.
3 vaso
a plant pot. ◆ a flowerpot.
4 (= jar) **pote, frasco, vidro**
a pot of honey / jam.
5 galão, lata
a pot of paint (= a can of paint).
potato [pəˈteɪtou] *n.* □ **batata**
Peel the potatoes and cook them. ◆ a baked potato.
■ Ver **chips; crisps; mashed potatoes**.
potter [ˈpɒtə] *n.* □ **ceramista**
pottery [ˈpɒtəri] *n.*
1 cerâmica
They found antique pottery in the cave.
2 cerâmica
My hobby is pottery.
poultry [ˈpoultri] *n.* □ **carne de ave doméstica**
I eat no meat or poultry, only fish, dairy products and vegetables.
pounce [pauns] *v.* (**pounces, pouncing, pounced**) □ **lançar-se, saltar, dar o bote**
The cat pounced on the bird.
pound [paund] *n.*
1 libra
It cost £30 (= 30 pounds). ◆ a five-pound note.
2 libra
two pounds of flour. ◆ It weighs 8 lb (= 8 pounds).
3 (= the # sign) *Amer.* **cerquilha**
Press the pound sign (on the telephone or computer keyboard).
■ *Amer.* **hash**
pour [pɔː] *v.* (**pours, pouring, poured**)
1 servir, despejar
Pour me a cup of tea, please. ◆ I poured the sand out of my shoes.

2 verter
Blood is pouring from the wound.
3 chover torrencialmente
It's pouring (down) outside.
poverty ['povəti] *n*. □ **pobreza**
They live in poverty.
■ The adjective is **poor**.
powder¹ ['paudə] *n*. □ **pó**
Grind the sugar into powder.
powder² *v.* (**powders, powdering, powdered**) □ **passar pó**
She powdered her face. ◆ to powder the baby's bottom.
powdered milk [,paudəd 'milk] *n*. □ **leite em pó**
power ['pauə] *n*.
1 poder
the power of the engine. ◆ the power of the storm.
2 poder
the power of speech / sight.
3 poder
This minister has a lot of power in the government. ◆ The President has the power to give prisoners freedom.
4 alcance
I'll do everything in my power to help him.
5 potência
a world power.
6 poder
Which political party is in power in your country?
7 energia
nuclear power. ◆ to cut off the power (= electricity).
power outage *n*. (mesmo que **power cut**; **power failure**) □ **falta de energia**
■ *Brit.* **electricity cut**
power point *n*. (= socket) □ **tomada**
power station, power plant □ **usina elétrica**
powerful ['pauəful] *adj*. □ **potente, poderoso**
a powerful engine. ◆ a powerful microscope. ◆ the most powerful people in the organization.
pp *abbr.* (= pages), **pp.** □ **págs.**
See pp. 689-710.
practical ['præktɪkəl] *adj.*
1 prático
practical ideas. ◆ It's not practical to build the factory here. ◆ Do you have any practical experience as a mechanic?
2 útil
a practical present.
practical joke ['præktɪkəl dʒouk] *n*. □ **pegadinha, brincadeira**
He hid one of my shoes as a practical joke.
practically ['præktɪkəli] *adv.* (= almost) □ **praticamente**
Practically all the questions were about you. ◆ I know practically nothing about computers.
practice¹ ['præktɪs] *n*.
1 treino
It takes lots of practice to become a good pianist. ◆ We usually have a practice game two days before a match.
2 prática
In theory it was a good idea, but in practice it was a failure.
3 hábito
I make a practice of walking 5 km every day.
4 exercício (de profissão)
a dental practice (= the business of a dentist). ◆ a legal practice.

out of practice □ **destreinado**
She is out of practice, but she can still beat you at tennis.
practice² *v. Amer.* (**practices, practicing, practiced**), **practise** *Brit.* (**practises, practising, practised**)
1 praticar, treinar, ensaiar
She practices (the guitar) 2 hours a day.
2 exercer
to practise medicine. ◆ He practises as a lawyer.
praise¹ [preɪz] *n*. □ **elogio**
His new film received a lot of praise.
praise² *v.* (**praises, praising, praised**) □ **elogiar**
She praised them. ◆ He was praised for his courage.
pram [præm] *n. Brit.* □ **carrinho de bebê**
■ *Amer.* **baby carriage**
prank [præŋk] *n*. □ **pegadinha, peça**
pray [preɪ] *v.* (**prays, praying, prayed**) □ **orar, rezar**
They prayed to God to stop the storm. ◆ I'll pray for their safety.
prayer ['preɪə] *n*. □ **oração**
to say a prayer (= to pray). ◆ morning prayers. ◆ Their prayers were answered.
preach [pri:tʃ] *v.* (**preaches, preaching, preached**)
1 pregar
A priest preaches in church.
2 dar sermão
Stop preaching at me!
preacher ['pri:tʃə] *n*. □ **pregador**
precaution [prɪˈkɔːʃən] *n*. □ **precaução**
They took precautions against theft. ◆ He wore gloves as a precaution.
precede [prɪˈsiːd] *v.* (**precedes, preceding, preceded**) □ **preceder**
Lightning precedes thunder.
preceding [prɪˈsiːdɪŋ] *adj.* □ **anterior**
the preceding day (= the day before).
precinct [ˈpriːsɪŋkt] *n*.
1 *Brit.* recinto, área
a shopping precinct. ◆ a pedestrian precinct.
■ Ver **mall, shopping mall**.
2 *Amer.* distrito
a police precinct.
precious [ˈpreʃəs] *adj.*
1 precioso
precious stones (= diamonds, pearls, etc.).
2 precioso, valioso
My children are very precious to me.
precipice [ˈpresɪpɪs] *n*. □ **precipício**
He stood at the edge of the precipice and looked down at the sea below.
precise [prɪˈsaɪs] *adj.* □ **preciso**
precise instructions. ◆ precise measurements. ◆ I can't be precise about the time.
■ antônimo: **impreciso**
■ Ver **exact; accurate**.
precisely [prɪˈsaɪsli] *adv.* (= exactly) □ **precisamente**
at six o'clock precisely. ◆ What, precisely, is the problem?
precisely because □ **precisamente porque**
I didn't buy it precisely because it was too cheap.
precision [prɪˈsɪʒən] *n*. □ **precisão**
to measure the time with great precision.
predict [prɪˈdɪkt] *v.* (**predicts, predicting, predicted** (= **foretell**) □ **prever**

to predict the future. ◆ It's impossible to predict what he will do.

predictable [priˈdiktəbl] *adj.* ◻ **previsível**
Her reaction was predictable.
■ antônimo: **unpredictable**

prediction [priˈdikʃən] *n.* ◻ **previsão**

preface [ˈprefəs] *n.* (= foreword) ◻ **prefácio**

prefer [priˈfɜː] *v.* (**prefers, preferring, preferred**) ◻ **preferir**
I prefer swimming to running. ◆ She prefers to go by train rather than (go) by bus. ◆ I preferred not to answer.
I would prefer ◻ **eu prefiro**
I'm tired. I would prefer to stay at home tonight.
■ Ver **rather**.

preferable [ˈprefərəbl] *adj.* ◻ **preferível**
Sleeping at night is preferable to sleeping during the day.

preferably [ˈprefərəbli] *adv.* ◻ **preferivelmente, de preferência**
Call me tomorrow, preferably in the morning.

preference [ˈprefərəns] *n.*
1 preferência
What are your preferences in TV shows?
2 preferência
We give preference to those who come first.

prefix [ˈpriːfiks] *n.* ◻ **prefixo**
The prefix dis- in 'disagree' means 'not' (disagree = not agree).

pregnancy [ˈpregnənsi] *n.* (*pl.* **pregnancies**) ◻ **gravidez**

pregnant [ˈpregnənt] *adj.* ◻ **grávida**
She is pregnant. ◆ She is six months pregnant.

prejudice [ˈpredʒədis] *n.* ◻ **preconceito**
He has a prejudice against women drivers. ◆ racial prejudice.

prejudiced [ˈpredʒədist] *adj.* ◻ **preconceituoso**
They are prejudiced against black people.

prep. *abbr.* (= **preposition**).

preparation [ˌprepəˈreiʃən] *n.* ◻ **preparação**
The preparation of this meal will take two hours. ◆ exam preparation.

preparations *n. pl.* ◻ **preparativos**
Let's make preparations for the trip now.

prepare [priˈpeə] *v.* (**prepares, preparing, prepared**)
1 (= get… ready) **preparar**
I prepared a good meal. ◆ to prepare pupils for an exam.
2 preparar-se
We don't have enough time to prepare for their visit. ◆ I prepared well for the exam.
be prepared for ◻ **estar preparado para**
He was not prepared for this surprise.
be prepared to ◻ **estar preparado para**
I'm not prepared to discuss this here.

preposition [ˌprepəˈziʃən] *n.* ◻ **preposição**
'At', 'in', 'on' and 'with' are examples of prepositions.
■ abreviação: **prep**

prescribe [priˈskraib] *v.* (**prescribes, prescribing, prescribed**) ◻ **prescrever**
The doctor prescribed vitamins for him.

prescription [priˈskripʃən] *n.* ◻ **prescrição, receita**
You can't get this medicine without a prescription.

presence [ˈprezns] *n.* ◻ **presença**
He said it in the presence of my friends. ◆ Your presence is not necessary at the meeting.
■ antônimo: **absence**

present¹ [ˈpreznt] *adj.*
1 presente
How many people were present at the wedding? ◆ All pupils are present.
■ antônimo: **absent**
2 atual
What is your present address?

present² *n.*
1 presente
She bought me a birthday present. ◆ It's a present from my brother.
■ Ver **gift**.
2 presente
Think of the future, not only of the present. ◆ a verb in the present (tense).
at present (= at the moment) ◻ **no momento**
She's busy at present.
for the present (= for the moment) ◻ **por ora**
That's all for the present.

present³ [priˈzent] *v.* (**presents, presenting, presented**)
1 presentear
The president presented the cup to the captain.
2 (= introduce) **apresentar**
I presented him to the guests.
3 (= show) **apresentar**
They presented their passports to the officer.

presently [ˈprezntli] *adv.*
1 (= soon) **em breve, logo mais**
They will be here presently.
2 (= at the moment) *Amer.* **no momento, atualmente**
She is presently working on a new project.

preservation [ˌprezəˈveiʃən] *n.* ◻ **preservação**
the preservation of the forests / elephants.

preservative [priˈzɜːvətiv] *n.* ◻ **preservativo**

preserve [priˈzɜːv] *v.* (**preserves, preserving, preserved**)
1 preservar
to preserve old buildings. ◆ to preserve old customs.
2 pôr em conserva
to preserve fruit / vegetables.

president [ˈprezidənt] *n.* ◻ **presidente**
the President of France. ◆ The president of the company resigned.
Mr President ◻ **Sr. Presidente**

presidential [ˌpreziˈdenʃəl] *adj.* ◻ **presidencial**
the presidential elections. ◆ the presidential palace.

press¹ [pres] *n.*
1 imprensa
The Prime Minister spoke to the press today. ◆ The accident was reported in the press.
2 aperto
With a press of a button you get the information you need.
3 passada com ferro de passar
Give the shirt a press.
4 prensa
a printing press.

press² *v.* (**presses, pressing, pressed**)
1 apertar, pressionar
To operate the machine, press the red button. ◆ Press this key to print the file.
2 (= to iron) **passar a ferro**
He pressed his trousers.

3 (= urge) **pressionar**
I pressed him to make another effort.
be pressed for ◻ **ter pouco**
We're pressed for time / money.
press conference [pres 'confərəns] *n.* ◻ **coletiva de imprensa**
press-ups ['presʌps] *n. Brit.* ◻ **flexão**
Do 30 press-ups.
■ *Amer.* **push-ups**
pressure¹ ['preʃə] *n.*
1 pressão
Check the (air) pressure in the tyres. ♦ She has high / low blood pressure.
2 pressão
the pressures of modern life.
put pressure on ◻ **pôr pressão em, pressionar**
They put pressure on me to tell them the secret.
pressure² *v.* (**pressures, pressuring, pressured**) ◻ **pressionar**
They pressured him to sign.
prestige [pre'sti:ʒ] *n.* ◻ **prestígio**
There's a lot of prestige in this job.
prestigious [pre'sti:ʒiəs] *adj.* ◻ **prestigioso**
a prestigious prize. ♦ a prestigious school.
presumably [prə'zju:məbli] *adv.* ◻ **supostamente**
Presumably you know where you're going?
presume [prə'zju:m] *v.* (**presumes, presuming, presumed**) (= suppose) ◻ **presumir**
You are from England, I presume?
pretence [pri'tens] *Brit.,* **pretense** *Amer.* ◻ **pretensão**
pretend [pri'tend] *v.* (**pretends, pretending, pretended**) ◻ **fingir**
She pretended not to hear the question. ♦ I pretended that I was asleep.
pretty¹ ['priti] *adj.* (**prettier, prettiest**) ◻ **bonita**
a pretty girl. ♦ You look prettier in the white dress.
■ Use **handsome** or **good-looking** for men (*not* pretty).
pretty² *adv.* (= quite) ◻ **bem, bastante**
The picture was pretty ugly.
prevent [pri'vent] *v.* (**prevents, preventing, prevented**) ◻ **evitar, prevenir**
I tried to prevent him from going. ♦ how to prevent accidents
■ Ver **stop someone (from) (doing)**.
prevention [pri'venʃn] *n.* ◻ **prevenção**
the prevention of crime, disease, etc.
previous ['pri:viəs] *adj.* ◻ **prévio**
the previous owner of the car. ♦ on the previous day.
previously ['pri:viəsli] *adv.* ◻ **previamente**
Previously, he was the manager of a small business.
prey¹ [prei] *n.* ◻ **presa**
Mice are prey for cats. ♦ The lion jumped on its prey.
bird of prey *n.* ◻ **ave de rapina**
Eagles are birds of prey.
prey² *v.* (**preys, preying, preyed**) ◻ **alimentar-se de**
Some birds prey on other birds.
price [prais] *n.* ◻ **preço**
What's the price of this car? ♦ high / low prices.
priceless ['praislis] *adj.* ◻ **inestimável**
a priceless jewel.
prick¹ [prik] *n.* ◻ **picada**
I felt the prick of a needle.

prick² *v.* (**pricks, pricking, pricked**) ◻ **furar**
to prick a balloon with a pin. ♦ I accidentally pricked my finger with a needle.
prickle ['prikl] *n.* ◻ **espinho**
Look out! This bush has prickles. ♦ This fruit has prickles on its skin.
■ Ver **thorn**.
prickly ['prikli] *adj.* ◻ **espinhento**
a prickly bush.
pride [praid] *n.*
1 orgulho
He showed us his medal with great pride.
2 orgulho
They have too much pride to ask for help.
■ The adjective is **proud**.
take pride in ◻ **ter orgulho de**
They take pride in their work. (= They are proud of their work.)
priest [pri:st] *n.* ◻ **sacerdote**
A priest married them in the village church. ♦ a Buddhist priest.
primarily ['praimərili] *adv.* (= mainly) ◻ **principalmente**
primary ['praiməri] *adj.* ◻ **primário**
Their primary aim is to help the poor. ♦ a matter of primary importance.
primary school ['praiməri sku:l] *n.* ◻ **escola primária**
■ Ver **elementary school; junior school**.
prime [praim] *adj.* ◻ **principal**
a matter of prime importance. ♦ My prime concern is to save the animals.
prime minister ['praim ministə] *n.* ◻ **primeiro ministro**
The prime minister is the head of the government.
■ abreviação: **PM**
prince [prins] *n.* ◻ **príncipe**
princess [prin'ses] *n.* ◻ **princesa**
principal¹ ['prinsəpəl] *n.* (= **headmaster; headmistress**, *Brit.*) ◻ **diretor**
The new principal of our school is Ms Brown.
■ Do not confuse with **principle**.
principal² *adj.* (= main) ◻ **principal**
Their principal export is coffee. ♦ She is the principal character in the story.
principle ['prinsəpəl] *n.* ◻ **princípio**
It's against my principles to gamble. ♦ This new engine works on a simple principle.
in principle ◻ **a princípio**
I like the idea in principle, but I want to hear all the details.
on principle ◻ **por princípio**
He doesn't watch TV on principle.
print¹ [print] *n.*
1 letra impressa
Read the small print before you sign. ♦ books in large print for children
2 impressão digital
fingerprints.
3 gravura
I bought a print of a painting by Picasso.
4 (= photograph¹) **cópia**
black-and-white prints.
print² *v.* (**prints, printing, printed**)
1 imprimir
The book was printed in Hong Kong. ♦ They print 50,000 copies of the newspaper every day.

- Compare **type²**.

2 (= publish) **publicar**

The editor decided not to print her article.

3 escrever com letra de fôrma

Please print your name and address.

print out □ **imprimir**

I printed out the first file.

printer ['prɪntə] *n*. □ **impressora**

This printer is the smallest and fastest in the world. ◆ a laser printer.

printing ['prɪntɪŋ] *n*. □ **impressão**

a new invention in printing.

printout ['prɪntaʊt] *n*. □ **cópia impressa**

priority [praɪ'ɒrɪtɪ] *n*. (*pl*. **priorities**)

1 prioridade

to give priority to this matter.

2 (= right of way) **prioridade**

Ambulances and fire-engines have priority.

prison ['prɪzn] *n*. (= jail) □ **prisão**

The judge sent him to prison for five years. ◆ She escaped from prison.

prisoner ['prɪznə] *n*.

1 preso

The prisoner spent two years in jail.

2 prisioneiro

prisoners of war.

privacy ['praɪvəsɪ] *n*. □ **privacidade**

They need some privacy.

private¹ ['praɪvət] *n*. □ **soldado raso**

private² *adj*.

1 pessoal

a private letter. ◆ They met for a private discussion.

2 privado

private property. ◆ I refuse to talk about my private life.

3 particular

a private hospital. ◆ a private school.

in private □ **em particular**

Can we talk in private?

private detective [praɪvət dɪ'tektɪv] *n*. □ **detetive particular**

They hired a private detective.

privately ['praɪvətlɪ] *adv*. □ **em particular**

Where can we talk privately?

privilege ['prɪvəlɪdʒ] *n*. □ **privilégio**

They enjoy special privileges.

privileged ['prɪvəlɪdʒɪd] *adj*. □ **privilegiado**

prize [praɪz] *n*. □ **prêmio**

Who won first prize in the competition? ◆ the first prize in the lottery.

probability [ˌprɒbə'bɪlɪtɪ] *n*. □ **probabilidade**

There is a high probability that the plan will succeed.

probable ['prɒbəbl] *adj*. □ **provável**

It's probable that they will refuse.

■ antônimo: **improbable**

■ Ver **likely**.

probably ['prɒbəblɪ] *adv*. □ **provavelmente**

He'll probably come alone. ◆ The letter will arrive this week, probably tomorrow.

problem ['prɒbləm] *n*. □ **problema**

They have a lot of problems. ◆ There is a problem with the plan. ◆ Can you solve this mathematical problem?

problem child *n*. □ **criança-problema**

problematic [ˌprɒblə'mætɪk] *adj*. □ **problemático**

Teaching them a new language is problematic.

proceed [prə'siːd] *v*. (**proceeds, proceeding, proceeded**) □ **prosseguir**

Proceed with your work.

■ **continue** and **go on** are the usual words.

process ['prəʊses] *n*. □ **processo**

modern manufacturing processes. ◆ Writing a dictionary is a slow process.

processed ['prəʊsest] *adj*. □ **processado**

processed food.

procession [prə'seʃən] *n*. □ **desfile**

a carnival procession. ◆ a procession of cars.

processor ['prəʊsesə] *n*. □ **processador**

food processor. ◆ word processor.

produce¹ [prə'djuːs] *v*. (**produces, producing, produced**)

1 produzir

Our company produces plastic bags. ◆ to produce oil. ◆ Cows produce milk.

■ Ver **make**; **manufacture²**.

2 produzir

The film was produced by...

3 produzir

Our method can produce better results.

4 retirar

He produced his passport from the bag.

produce² ['prɒdjuːs] *n*. □ **produção**

agricultural produce.

producer [prə'djuːsə] *n*.

1 fabricante, produtor

a chocolate producer. ◆ Which country is the biggest oil producer?

■ Ver **maker**; **manufacturer**.

2 produtor

a TV producer. ◆ a movie producer. ◆ a record producer.

product ['prɒdʌkt] *n*. □ **produto**

dairy products (milk, yoghurt, etc.). ◆ We make plastic products of high quality.

■ **products** = **goods**

production [prə'dʌkʃən] *n*.

1 produção

This new car will go into production next year.

■ Ver **manufacture¹**.

2 produção

Production increased by 5%.

3 produção

The production of this film cost a lot.

productive [prə'dʌktɪv] *adj*.

1 produtivo

Are Japanese workers more productive than Americans workers?

2 produtivo

a productive discussion.

profession [prə'feʃən] *n*. □ **profissão**

She is a lawyer by profession.

■ When asking people what their profession is, we usually say: What do you do? – I'm a dentist.

professional¹ [prə'feʃənl] *adj*.

1 profissional

They did a professional job. ◆ to get professional advice from a lawyer, etc.

professional / properly

2 profissional
professional basketball. ♦ a professional boxer.
professional² *n*. □ **profissional**
He plays football as a professional, not as an amateur.
■ antônimo: **amateur**
professionally [prəˈfeʃənli] *adv*. □ **profissionalmente**
professor [prəˈfesə] *n*. □ **professor universitário**
Prof. (= Professor) Jones.
■ Ver **teacher**.
proficiency [prəˈfiʃənsi] *n*. □ **proficiência**
proficiency in cooking. ♦ proficiency in a language.
proficient [prəˈfiʃənt] *adj*. □ **proficiente**
a proficient swimmer. ♦ He is proficient in English, but not in French.
profile [ˈproufail] *n*. □ **perfil**
profit¹ [ˈprofit] *n*. □ **lucro**
I made a profit of $500 on my car. ♦ I sold it at a profit.
profit² *v*. (**profits, profiting, profited**)
1 (= benefit from) **lucrar**
I profited a lot from her advice.
2 lucrar
She profited (= made a profit) from selling her house.
profitable [ˈprofitəbl] *adj*. □ **lucrativo**
a profitable business
program¹ [ˈprougram] *n*.
1 □ **programa**
a computer program.
2 (= **programme**¹) *Amer.* **programa**
program² *v*. (**programs, programming, programmed**), **programme** *v*. *Brit.* (**programmes, programming, programmed**) □ **programar**
I programmed the computer to arrange all the names in alphabetical order.
programer [ˈprougramə] *n*. *Amer.*, **programmer** *Brit.* □ **programador**
programme¹ [ˈprougram] *n*. *Brit.*, **program** *Amer.*
1 programa
a TV / radio program.
2 programa
What's your programme for tomorrow?
3 programa
a theatre programme.
progress¹ [ˈprougres] *n*.
1 progresso
We are making good progress with the project.
2 progresso
technological progress.
in progress □ **em progresso, em andamento**
The game is still in progress.
progress² [prəˈgres] *v*. (**progresses, progressing, progressed**)
1 progredir, andar
How is the work progressing?
2 avançar
As the film progressed she got more and more bored.
progressive¹ [prəˈgresiv] *n*. (=**continuous**) (grammar) □ **progressivo**
The present progressive, e.g. 'I am standing'.
progressive² *adj*. □ **progressivo**
I hold progressive ideas, but my father is conservative in his politics.
prohibit [prəˈhibit] *v*. (**prohibits, prohibiting, prohibited**) □ **proibir**

The law prohibits cigarette ads on TV. ♦ Smoking is prohibited (= forbidden) here.
prohibition [ˌproui'biʃən] *n*. □ **proibição**
project [ˈproudʒekt] *n*. □ **projeto**
The project to computerize schools will cost millions.
projector [prəˈdʒektə] *n*. □ **projetor**
a slide projector.
prominent [ˈprominənt] *adj*. □ **proeminente, notório**
a prominent writer.
promise¹ [ˈpromis] *n*. □ **promessa**
break a promise □ **quebrar uma promessa**
They broke their promise to take me with them.
keep a promise □ **cumprir uma promessa**
He kept his promise not to tell anybody about it.
make a promise (= to promise) □ **fazer uma promessa**
She made a promise to try harder.
promise² *v*. (**promises, promising, promised**) □ **prometer**
You promised to buy him a computer. ♦ Promise me (that) you'll help them.
promising [ˈpromisiŋ] *adj*. □ **promissor**
a promising tennis player
promote [prəˈmout] *v*. (**promotes, promoting, promoted**)
1 promover
They promoted him to sergeant. ♦ She was promoted to manager.
2 promover
to promote peace and friendship between our two nations.
promotion [prəˈmouʃən] *n*. □ **promoção**
prompt [prompt] *adj*. □ **pronto, imediato**
They sent us a prompt reply.
promptly [ˈpromptli] *adv*.
1 prontamente
They answered our letter promptly.
2 pontualmente
He arrived promptly at 2 o'clock.
pronoun [ˈprounaun] *n*. □ **pronome**
'I', 'she', 'me', 'us', 'their' and 'who' are all examples of pronouns.
■ abreviação: **pron.**
pronounce [prəˈnauns] *v*. (**pronounces, pronouncing, pronounced**) □ **pronunciar**
How do you pronounce this word?
■ The noun is **pronunciation**.
pronunciation [prəˌnʌnsiˈeiʃən] *n*. □ **pronúncia**
There are two different pronunciations of this word. ♦ You can improve your pronunciation with practice.
■ The verb is **pronounce**.
proof [pru:f] *n*. □ **prova**
Do you have any proof that she stole your jewels?
■ The verb is **prove**.
■ Ver **evidence**.
propeller [prəˈpelə] *n*. □ **hélice**
proper [ˈpropə] *adj*.
1 apropriada, adequada
That's not the proper (= right) way to do it. ♦ to wear proper (= suitable) clothes for the wedding.
2 (= real) **de verdade, genuíno**
to eat a proper meal.
properly [ˈpropəli] *adv*. □ **adequadamente, bem**
She did the job properly.

proper name ['propə 'neim] *n.* (grammar) □ **nome próprio**
Proper names in English, such as 'London' or 'Mary', begin with a capital letter.

property ['propəti] *n.*
1 propriedade
Those books are my personal property.
2 (*pl.* **properties**) **propriedade**
They own a property in this area.

prophecy ['profəsi] *n.* (*pl.* **prophecies**) □ **profecia**

prophesy ['profisai] *v.* (**prophesies, prophesying, prophesied**) □ **profetizar**
He prophesied the end of the war.

prophet ['profit] *n.* □ **profeta**

prophetic [prə'fetik] *adj.* □ **profético**

proportion [prə'pɔ:ʃən] *n.*
1 proporção
What is the proportion of girls to boys in this school?
2 parte
A large proportion of the population lives in the center of the country.

proportions *n. pl.* □ **proporções**
a palace of huge proportions.

proposal [prə'pouzəl] *n.*
1 proposta
a peace proposal. ◆ They accepted my proposal to build a bridge.
■ Compare:
the offer of help / a job / a suggestion what to do.
2 pedido
She accepted his proposal of marriage.

propose [prə'pouz] *v.* (**proposes, proposing, proposed**)
1 (= **suggest**) **propor**
I propose that we start tomorrow.
■ that we start (*not* 'that we will start').
2 (= **intend**) **propor**
How do you propose to do it?
3 pedir em casamento
He proposed to me last night.
■ Compare:
to offer someone a job / help / coffee.
to propose a plan / marriage.

prosper ['prospə] *v.* (**prospers, prospering, prospered**) □ **prosperar**
The business prospered when she was manager.

prosperity [pro'speriti] *n.* □ **prosperidade**

prosperous ['prospərəs] *adj.* □ **próspero**
a prosperous businessman. ◆ a prosperous country.

prostitute ['prostitju:t] *n.* □ **prostituta**

protect [prə'tekt] *v.* (**protects, protecting, protected**) □ **proteger**
This cream will protect your skin against the sun. ◆ to protect the animals from danger.

protection [prə'tekʃən] *n.* □ **proteção**
They had police protection. ◆ The shelter gave them protection from the storm.

protest¹ ['proutest] *n.* □ **protesto**
They did not come to the meeting as a protest. ◆ to make a protest (= to protest) against.

protest² [prə'test] *v.* (**protests, protesting, protested**) □ **protestar**
They protested against the new tax.

protruding [prə'tru:diŋ] *adj.* □ **protuberante**
protruding teeth.

proud [praud] *adj.* □ **orgulhoso**
They are very proud of their son. ◆ I feel very proud to work with her. ◆ She's too proud to ask for help.
■ The noun is **pride**.

proudly ['praudli] *adv.* □ **orgulhosamente**
They talked proudly of their daughter's achievements.

prove [pru:v] *v. Amer.* (**proves, proving, proved** or **proven**) □ **provar**
There is enough evidence to prove that he is guilty. ◆ She proved to me that she was not the murderer.
■ The noun is **proof**.

proved to be □ **provar ser**
She proved to be a loyal friend.

proverb ['provə:b] *n.* □ **provérbio**
'A bird in the hand is worth two in the bush' is a proverb.

provide [prə'vaid] *v.* (**provides, providing, provided**) □ **prover**
He provided the money for the project. ◆ They provided us with food and clothes.
■ Ver **supply**.

provided (that) [prə'vaidid (ðət)] *conj.* (= **on condition that**) □ **desde que**
I'll go provided that you come with me.

providing (that) [prə'vaidiŋ (ðət)] (= **provided [that]**)

province ['provins] *n.* □ **província**
Ontario is a province of Canada.

provincial [prə'vinʃəl] *adj.* □ **provincial**
the provincial government.

provision [prə'viʒən] *n.* □ **provisão, fornecimento**
the provision of services to the public.

provisions [prə'viʒənz] *n. pl.* □ **provisões**
They took provisions for ten days.

prune [pru:n] *n.* □ **ameixa seca**

PS [pi:'es] *abbr.*, **P.S.** (= post scriptum) □ **P.S.**
Dear John, ... Yours Truly, Miriam. PS My new phone number is 6543982.

psychiatric [,saiki'ætrik] *adj.* □ **psiquiátrico**
psychiatric treatment.

psychiatrist [sai'kaiətrist] *n.* □ **psiquiatra**

psychological [,saikə'lodʒikəl] *adj.* □ **psicológico**

psychologist [sai'kolədʒist] *n.* □ **psicólogo**

psychology [sai'kolədʒi] *n.* □ **psicologia**

PTO [,pi: ti: 'ou] *abbr.* (= please turn over) □ **v.v., vire**

pub [pʌb] *n.* □ **bar**

public¹ ['pʌblik] *adj.* □ **público**
a public library / telephone ◆ *Brit.* public places.

public convenience *n.* □ **sanitário público**
■ *Amer.* **washroom; rest-room**

public opinion *n.* □ **opinião pública**

public opinion poll *n.* □ **pesquisa de opinião pública**

public relations *n.* □ **relações públicas**

public transport, public transportation □ **transporte público**

public² *n.*
the public □ **o público**
The park is open to the public.
in public □ **em público**
They never talk about it in public.
■ antônimo: **in private**

publication [,pʌbli'keiʃən] *n.*
1 publicação
Her book will be ready for publication next month.

publicity / pure

2 publicação
All their publications are very interesting.
- The verb is **publish**.

publicity [pʌˈblisəti] *n.* □ **publicidade**
There was a lot of publicity for his new book.
- Compare with **advertising**.

publicize [ˈpʌblisaiz] *v.* (**publicizes, publicizing, publicized**) □ **tornar público, divulgar**

publicly [ˈpʌblikli] *adv.* □ **publicamente**
He didn't say it publicly, only privately.

publish [ˈpʌbliʃ] *v.* (**publishes, publishing, published**) □ **publicar**
Our company publishes dictionaries and textbooks. ◆ Her article was published in the newspaper.
- Ver **publication**.

publisher [ˈpʌbliʃə] *n.* □ **editor**

pudding [ˈpudiŋ] *n.*
1 pudim, doce
rice pudding.
2 (= dessert) *Brit.* sobremesa
What's for pudding?

puddle [ˈpʌdl] *n.* □ **poça**

puff¹ [pʌf] *n.*
1 lufada
a puff of smoke.
2 baforada
He took a puff on the cigarette.

puff² *v.* (**puffs, puffing, puffed**)
1 arquejar
She was puffing hard at the end of the race.
2 baforar
He was puffing (on) his pipe.
3 soprar
Don't puff smoke into my face!

pull¹ [pul] *n.* □ **puxão**
Give the rope a pull.

pull² *v.* (**pulls, pulling, pulled**)
1 puxar
Stop pulling my hair!
2 puxar
The old horse pulled the cart slowly.

pull down □ **pôr abaixo, demolir**
They pulled the building down to build a cinema.

pull in *Brit.* □ **parar, encostar**
I pulled in because I was too tired to drive.

pull out
1 tirar, arrancar
I pulled the plug out. ◆ The dentist pulled out two of my teeth.
2 retirar
The General is pulling out his troops.

pull over □ **encostar**
Pull over and let the ambulance pass.

pull someone's leg □ **pregar uma peça em alguém**
I don't believe it! You're pulling my leg!

pull up □ **parar**
The driver pulled up at the 'Stop' sign.

pullover [ˈpulouvə] *n.* □ **pulôver**
- Ver **sweater; jumper**.

pulse [pʌls] *n.* □ **pulso, pulsação**
The doctor took the patient's pulse.

pump¹ [pʌmp] *n.* □ **bomba**
a gas pump. *Amer.* ◆ a petrol pump. *Brit.* ◆ a bicycle pump.

pump² *v.* (**pumps, pumping, pumped**)
1 bombear
They pumped the water out of the boat.
2 bombear
to pump air into the ball. ◆ to pump fuel into the fuel tank.

pump something up □ **encher algo**
I pumped up my bicycle tyres.

pumpkin [ˈpʌmpkin] *n.* □ **abóbora**

punch¹ [pʌntʃ] *n.* □ **soco**
He gave me a punch on / in the chin.

punch² *v.* (**punches, punching, punched**)
1 dar um soco
She punched me on / in the nose.
2 fazer furos, furar
to punch holes in a piece of paper.

punctual [ˈpʌŋktʃuəl] *adj.* □ **pontual**
She is very punctual and is never late for class.

punctuality [ˌpʌŋktʃuˈaliti] *n.* □ **pontualidade**

punctually [ˈpʌŋktʃuəli] *adv.* □ **pontualmente**
He arrived punctually at 5 o'clock.
- Ver **on time**.

punctuate [ˈpʌŋktʃueit] *v.* (**punctuates, punctuating, punctuated**) □ **pontuar**
Learn to punctuate your essays.

punctuation [ˌpʌŋktʃuˈeiʃən] *n.* □ **pontuação**
You get 5 points for correct punctuation.

punctuation mark [ˌpʌŋktʃuˈeiʃən maːk] *n.* □ **sinal de pontuação**
Commas (,), full stops (= periods, *Amer.*) (.), and colons (:) are examples of punctuation marks.

puncture¹ [ˌpʌŋktʃə] *n.* □ **furo**
There is a puncture in my football. ◆ My bicycle has a puncture.

puncture² *v.* (**punctures, puncturing, punctured**) □ **furar**
A nail punctured the tire.

punish [ˈpʌniʃ] *v.* (**punishes, punishing, punished**) □ **punir, castigar**
The teacher punished him for cheating on the exam.

punishment [ˈpʌniʃmənt] *n.* □ **punição, castigo**
What is the punishment for coming late to class? ◆ His parents didn't let him go out as a punishment.

pupil [ˈpuːpl] *n.*
1 aluno
There are 25 pupils in my class.
- **student** is the usual word in American English.
2 pupila
The pupil (of the eye) becomes smaller in bright light.

puppet [ˈpʌpit] *n.* □ **marionete**
a puppet show / theatre.

puppy [ˈpʌpi] *n.* (*pl.* **puppies**) □ **cachorrinho, filhote de cachorro**

purchase¹ [ˈpəːtʃəs] *n.* □ **aquisição, compra**
The date of purchase is on the receipt. ◆ We made some purchases at the department store.

purchase² *v.* (**purchases, purchasing, purchased**) □ **adquirir, comprar**
The company purchased (= bought) modern equipment.
- **buy** is the usual word.

pure [pjuə] *adj.* □ **puro**
pure gold. ◆ pure air. ◆ pure olive oil. ◆ a pure cotton shirt (100% cotton).

pure and simple □ **pura e simplesmente**
You don't work hard enough, pure and simple.
purely ['pjuəli] *adv*. □ **puramente**
I found it purely by accident.
purity ['pjuəriti] *n*. □ **pureza**
purple ['pə:pl] *n*., *adj*. □ **roxo**
green and purple grapes.
■ Ver **violet**, **mauve**.
purpose ['pə:pəs] *n*.
1 propósito, objetivo
What is the purpose of their visit? ◆ They need the information for research purposes.
■ Ver **aim**; **goal**.
2 finalidade
This computer is used for many purposes.
on purpose □ **de propósito**
He didn't break it on purpose.
purr [pə:] *v*. (**purrs, purring, purred**) □ **ronronar**
The cat purred when I brought it some food.
purse [pə:s] *n*.
1 bolsa
She opened her purse, but there was no money in it.
2 (= pocketbook) *Amer*. **carteira**
■ *Brit*. **handbag**
pursue [pə'sju:] *v*. (**pursues, pursuing, pursued**) (= chase) □ **perseguir**
The police are pursuing the robbers. ◆ We pursued their car.
pursuit [pə'sju:t] *n*. □ **perseguição**
The thief ran away with a policeman in pursuit (after him).
push¹ [puʃ] *n*.
1 empurrão
He gave the door a push and it closed.
2 aperto, toque
You can get all the information you need at the push of a button.
push² *v*. (**pushes, pushing, pushed**)
1 (= shove) **empurrar**
Don't push! ◆ We pushed the boat into the water.
2 apertar
Push the red button to start recording.
3 abrir caminho empurrando
We pushed our way through the crowd.
push-button ['puʃˌbʌtn] *adj*. □ **de tecla**
a push-button telephone / radio.
pushchair ['puʃˌtʃeə] *n Brit*. □ **carrinho de bebê**
■ *Amer*. **stroller**
push-ups ['puʃʌps] *n*. *Amer*. □ **flexões**
Do 30 push-ups!
■ *Brit*. **press-ups**
put [put] *v*. (**puts, putting, put**)
1 pôr, colocar
He put the box on the floor. ◆ She put her hand on my head. ◆ Put some more salt in the soup.
2 pôr, colocar
Put a tick (✓) for every correct answer.
put aside
1 pôr de lado
She put the paper aside and fell asleep.
2 economizar
They put aside (= saved) some money.

put away □ **guardar**
He put his toys away in the box.
put back
1 pôr de volta
Put your books back on the shelf.
2 atrasar
The clock is fast. I'd better put it back ten minutes.
put the blame on (Ver **blame**).
put down
1 baixar
Put down your gun!
2 sufocar
to put down the rebellion.
put in (= install) □ **instalar**
The garage put in a new motor.
put someone off □ **desestimular, desanimar**
The smell of the food put me off (eating).
put something off □ **adiar**
They put off the meeting until next week.
put on
1 vestir, calçar
He put on his hat and coat and went out. ◆ Put your shoes on. ◆ to put on a tie.
■ Compare with **wear**:
  I always wear socks. (habit)
  I put on my socks and shoes. (activity)
2 pôr
She put on her glasses to read the letter.
3 pôr
She put on her earrings, necklace, etc.
4 passar
to put on lipstick, makeup, etc.
■ antônimo: **take off**
5 (= switch / turn on) **ligar**
Put the lights on. ◆ to put on the TV.
■ antônimo: **put out**; **switch off**; **turn off**
6 ganhar
He puts on weight when he starts eating sweets.
put someone on □ **tirar sarro de alguém**
I don't believe it. You're putting me on!
put out □ **apagar**
Put out your cigarette! ◆ They put the fire out very quickly. ◆ to put out the lights / a candle.
put pressure on (Ver **pressure**).
put a stop to (Ver **stop**).
put someone through □ **passar a ligação**
I'd like to talk to the manager. Could you put me through (to him)?
put up
1 colocar
to put up a poster. ◆ to put up a notice (on the noticeboard).
2 erguer, montar
to put up a fence / tent / building.
put someone up □ **acolher, hospedar**
It was very late so he put me up for the night. ◆ Can you put up a friend of mine for the weekend?
put up with (= bear) □ **aguentar, tolerar, suportar**
How can you put up with this noise? ◆ I can't put up with him any longer.
puzzle¹ ['pʌzl] *n*.
1 mistério

Why she sent me this letter is a puzzle to me.
2 (= crossword puzzle) **palavras cruzadas**
to do (= find the answers to) a crossword puzzle
3 charada
I know a puzzle that you can't solve.
4 (= jigsaw puzzle) **quebra-cabeça**
puzzle² *v.* (**puzzles, puzzling, puzzled**) ☐ **intrigar**
His disappearance puzzled them.

puzzled ['pʌzld] *adj.* ☐ **intrigado**
She looked puzzled when she read his message.
puzzling ['pʌzliŋ] *adj.* ☐ **intrigante**
His reasons for coming here are very puzzling.
pyjamas [pə'dʒɑ:məz] *n.* ☐ **pijama**
■ *Amer.* **pajamas**
pyramid ['pirəmid] *n.* ☐ **pirâmide**
the pyramids of Egypt.

Qq

quack¹ [kwak] *n.* ▫ grasnido
quack² *v.* (**quacks, quacking, quacked**) ▫ grasnir
The ducks started to quack when we came to the farm.
qualification [ˌkwolifiˈkeiʃən] *n.* ▫ qualificação
Does he have the necessary qualifications for this job? ◆ academic qualifications (a diploma, a degree, etc.).
qualified [ˈkwolifaid] *adj.* (= trained) ▫ qualificado
a qualified nurse / teacher. ◆ Is she qualified for this job?
qualify [ˈkwolifai] *v.* (**qualifies, qualifying, qualified**) ▫ qualificar
He qualified as a doctor last year.
quality [ˈkwoliti] *n.* (*pl.* **qualities**)
1 qualidade
We sell goods of high quality. ◆ You must improve the quality of your work.
2 qualidades
What are the qualities of a good leader?
quantity [ˈkwontəti] *n.* (*pl.* **quantities**)
1 quantidade
a small quantity of sugar. ◆ large quantities of food.
■ Ver **amount**.
2 quantidade
We buy goods in quantity.
quarrel¹ [ˈkworəl] *n.* (= **row²**) ▫ briga
a family quarrel. ◆ They had a quarrel last night.
■ Ver **argument**; **fight¹**.
quarrel² *v.* (*Amer.* **quarrels, quarreling, quarreled**; *Brit.* **quarrelling, quarrelled**) (= **row⁴**) ▫ brigar
They quarreled about money. ◆ Stop quarreling!
■ Ver **argue**; **fight²**.
quarry [ˈkwori] *n.* (*pl.* **quarries**) ▫ pedreira
a marble quarry.
quarter [ˈkwo:tə] *n.*
1 quarto
a quarter of an hour (= 15 minutes). ◆ She gave me one quarter (= 1/4) of the apple. ◆ three-quarters (3/4). ◆ the last quarter (= 25 years) of the century.
2 trimestre
I pay the rent every quarter. ◆ in the first quarter of the year.
3 bairro, sector
They live in the rich quarter of the city.
4 *Amer.* **moeda de 25 centavos de dólar**
There are 25 cents in a quarter.
a quarter after / past ▫ ...e quinze
It's a quarter past 5 (= 5:15).
a quarter of / to ▫ quinze para
It's a quarter to 8 (= 7:45).
quarter-final [ˌkwo:təˈfainl] *n.* ▫ quarta de final
We're playing against a strong team in the quarter-final.
quarters [ˈkwo:təz] *n.* ▫ alojamento, acomodação
quay [ki:] *n.* ▫ cais
queen [kwi:n] *n.* ▫ rainha
the Queen of England. ◆ a beauty queen.
queer [kwiə] *adj.* (= strange; odd) ▫ esquisito
queer clothes. ◆ a queer way of talking.
query [ˈkwiəri] *n.* (*pl.* **queries**) ▫ pergunta
If you have any queries, you can call us anytime.

■ **question** is also possible.
question¹ [ˈkwestʃən] *n.*
1 pergunta, questão
He asked me a difficult question. ◆ I can't answer your question. ◆ The first question on the exam was easy.
2 pergunta, questão
The question is, who will pay for it?
3 dúvida
There's no question (= doubt) about it.
in question ▫ em questão
Where is the place in question?
out of the question ▫ fora de questão
It's out of the question. I won't let you go alone.
question² *v.* (**questions, questioning, questioned**)
1 interrogar
The police questioned them about the robbery.
■ Ver **interrogate**; **grill²**.
2 questionar
I question his ability to do the job.
question mark [ˈkwestʃən ma:k] *n.* (?) ▫ ponto de interrogação
questionnaire [ˌkwestʃəˈneə] *n.* ▫ questionário
Fill in (= Complete) the questionnaire.
question tag [ˈkwestʃən tag] *n.* ▫ pergunta de confirmação
■ Examples of question tags are:
He saw you, didn't he?
She won't come, will she?
They don't know, do they?
We can stay, can't we?
queue¹ [kju:] *n.* ▫ fila
to stand in a queue at the bus stop ◆ There is a long queue for the show.
■ *Amer.* **line¹**
queue² *v.* (**queues, queuing, queued**) (also **queue up**) ▫ fazer fila, ficar na fila
We queued (up) for the bus.
■ *Amer.* **line²**
quick [kwik] *adj.* ▫ rápido
to have a quick bath. ◆ to walk with quick steps. ◆ a quick decision / answer. ◆ It's quicker to go by car.
■ Ver **fast¹**; **rapid**.
■ antónimo: **slow**
quick! ▫ rápido!
Quick, give me that rope!
quickly [ˈkwikli] *adv.* ▫ rapidamente
He finished the job quickly. ◆ Come as quickly as possible.
■ antónimo: **slowly**
■ Ver **fast²**.
quid [kwid] *n. Brit.* (*pl.* **quid**) ▫ libra
You owe me 5 quid (= 5 pounds).
quiet¹ [ˈkwaiət] *adj.*
1 baixo
to speak in a quiet voice.
■ antónimo: **loud**
2 silencioso
It's very quiet here. ◆ The children are very quiet today.
■ antónimo: **noisy**
3 calma
to live a quiet life, far from the city.
be quiet ▫ fique quieto
Be quiet – the baby is asleep!
keep someone quiet ▫ manter alguém calado

Keep the children quiet! I can't work in this noise.
keep quiet ◻ **ficar calado**
She decided to keep quiet about the accident.
quiet² *n.* ◻ **silêncio**
I need some quiet here! ◆ the quiet of the night.
quietly ['kwaiətli] *adv.* ◻ **silenciosamente**
He walked quietly into the room. ◆ She closed the door quietly.
quilt [kwilt] *n.* ◻ **acolchoado**
quit [kwit] *v.* (**quits, quitting, quit**)
1 (= leave) **largar**
I quit my job.
2 (= stop) **parar**
When did you quit smoking?
quite [kwait] *adv.*
1 (= rather) **bem**
It's quite cold there. ◆ The book is quite good.
2 (= completely) **totalmente**
Are you quite sure that this is the place? ◆ You're quite right!
quite a few ◻ **pouquíssimo**
We met quite a few people at the party.
quite a lot (of) ◻ **bastante, um número expressivo**
There were quite a lot of people at the party. ◆ We slept quite a lot.
quiz [kwiz] *n.*
1 concurso de conhecimentos
a quiz show (on TV). ◆ a sports quiz.
2 teste
The teacher gave us a quiz about verb tenses.
quotation [kwou'teiʃən] *n.* ◻ **citação**
a quotation from the Bible / Koran.
quotation marks [kwou'teiʃən ma:ks] *n. pl.* (= **inverted commas**) ◻ **aspas**
quote [kwout] *v.* (**quotes, quoting, quoted**) ◻ **citar**
She likes to quote from Shakespeare's plays.

Rr

rabbi ['rabai] *n.* □ **rabino**
rabbit ['rabit] *n.* □ **coelho**
I keep a rabbit as a pet.
■ Ver **hare**.
race[1] [reis] *n.*
1 corrida
Who won the 400 metres race? ♦ She came second in the race. ♦ to take part in a race. ♦ a horse race. ♦ a boat race.
2 raça, etnia
people of different races. ♦ the human race.
the races *n.* □ **corrida de cavalos**
Did you lose money at the races?
race[2] *v.* (**races, racing, raced**)
1 apostar corrida
I'll race you to that tree. ♦ He is going to race against the best drivers in the world.
2 correr
We raced to catch the train.
racecourse ['reiskɔːs] *n.* □ **hipódromo**
racetrack ['reistrak] *n.* □ **pista de corridas, autódromo**
racial ['reiʃəl] *adj.* □ **racial**
racial problems (between different races). ♦ racial discrimination.
racing ['reisiŋ] *n.* □ **corrida**
I watched car racing on TV.
racing car □ **carro de corrida**
racism ['reisizəm] *n.* □ **racismo**
racist ['reisist] *n.*, *adj.* □ **racista**
The immigrants were attacked by racists. ♦ She has racist opinions.
rack [rak] *n.*
1 bagageiro, prateleira
a luggage rack (on a bus, train, etc.). ♦ a clothes rack.
2 porta-toalha
Brit. a towel rack.
plate rack *n.*
■ *Amer.* **dish drainer**
roof-rack *n.* □ **bagageiro**
Put the suitcases on the roof-rack of the car.
racket ['rakit] *n.*, **racquet** □ **raquete**
a tennis racket.
radar ['reidaː] *n.* □ **radar**
to spot a plane on the radar screen.
radiation [,reidi'eiʃən] *n.* □ **radiação**
High levels of radiation cause serious diseases and even death.
radiator ['reidieitə] *n.*
1 radiador
The radiator cools the engine.
2 aquecedor
It's cold. Turn on the radiator.
radio ['reidiou] *n.*
1 rádio
I turned on the radio to listen to the news. ♦ Switch / Turn off the radio. ♦ I heard it on the radio. ♦ Turn down the radio. It's too loud.
2 rádio
to send / receive a message by radio.

radio station ['reidiou 'steiʃən] *n.* □ **emissora de rádio**
radish ['radiʃ] *n.* □ **rabanete**
radius ['reidiəs] *n.* (*pl.* **radii**) □ **raio**
The radius of the circle is 10 cm. ♦ This wheel has a radius of 50 cm.
■ Ver **diameter**.
raft [raːft] *n.* □ **jangada, balsa**
rag [rag] *n.* □ **farrapo, trapo**
to clean the car with a rag.
rags *n.* □ **farrapos**
He was dressed in rags.
rage [reidʒ] *n.* □ **raiva, fúria**
She shouted with rage. ♦ He flew into a rage.
raid[1] [reid] *n.* □ **batida, ataque**
The police made a raid on their hiding place. ♦ an air raid.
raid[2] *v.* (**raids, raiding, raided**) □ **atacar, invadir**
The soldiers raided the enemy camp. ♦ Police raided the night club.
rail [reil] *n.*
1 *Brit.* □ **viga, barra**
a towel rail. ♦ a clothes rail (in the wardrobe).
■ *Amer.* **rack**
2 amurada
He leaned over the ship's rails.
3 vara
a curtain rail.
■ *Amer.* **rod**
4 trilho
to travel by rail.
rails *n.* □ **trilhos**
railings ['reiliŋz] *n. pl.* □ **grade, gradil**
the railings around the park.
railroad ['reilroud] *Amer.*
1 estrada de ferro, ferrovia
They are building a new railroad. ♦ the railroad line between the two cities.
2 ferroviária, de trem
a railroad station.
■ *Brit.* **railway**
rain[1] [rein] *n.* □ **chuva**
Don't go out in the rain. ♦ There was heavy rain last night.
rain[2] *v.* (**rains, raining, rained**) □ **chover**
Take an umbrella. It's starting to rain. ♦ It's raining. ♦ It rained hard all morning.
rainbow ['reinbou] *n.* □ **arco-íris**
raincoat ['reinkout] *n.* □ **capa de chuva**
raindrop ['reindrop] *n.* □ **gota de chuva**
rainy ['reini] *adj* (**rainier, rainiest**) □ **chuvoso**
It was a rainy day.
raise[1] [reiz] *n. Amer.* □ **aumento**
to get a raise (in salary). ♦ to ask for a raise.
■ *Brit.* **rise**
raise[2] *v.* (**raises, raising, raised**)
1 levantar
Raise your hand if you know the answer.
■ Compare with **lift**:
lift usually things that require some effort.
raise your hand / head, a cup, etc.; without any effort.
2 (= increase) **aumentar**
to raise prices / taxes / the temperature.
3 aumentar
Raise your voice. I can't hear you.

■ antônimo: **lower**
4 levantar
They raised the money for the project.
5 levantar
The article raises some interesting questions.
6 criar
to raise sheep / chickens.
7 (= bring up) criar
They are raising five children on one small salary.
to raise one's hat □ **tirar o chapéu (a título de cumprimento)**
He raised his hat when he saw her.
raisin ['reizn] *n.* □ **passa**
rake¹ [reik] *n.* □ **ancinho**
rake² *v.* **(rakes, raking, raked)** □ **limpar com ancinho**
to rake (up) the dead leaves
rally ['rali] *n.* **(pl. rallies)** □ **comício**
There were 50,000 people at the peace rally.
RAM [ram] *abbr.* □ **RAM**
ramble ['rambl] *v.* **(rambles, rambling, rambled)** □ **fazer uma excursão a pé**
We went rambling in the mountains in the vacation.
■ The noun is **ramble**.
ramp [ramp] *n.* □ **rampa**
to push a wheelchair up a ramp.
ran [ran] *v.* (Ver **run²**).
ranch [ra:ntʃ] *n.* □ **rancho, sítio**
to work on a ranch.
random ['randəm] *n., adj.* □ **casual, aleatório**
at random □ **aleatoriamente, ao acaso**
Choose a card at random.
rang [raŋ] *v.* (Ver **ring²**).
range¹ [reindʒ] *n.*
1 variedade
We sell a wide range of magazines.
2 alcance
What's the range of this gun?
3 autonomia
The range of the plane is 1,000 kilometers.
4 cadeia
a mountain range.
range² *v.* **(ranges, ranging, ranged)** □ **variar**
The temperatures in November range between seven and fifteen degrees Celsius (7-15° C).
rank [raŋk] *n.* □ **patente**
What's his rank? Sergeant.
ransom ['ransəm] *n.* □ **resgate**
The kidnappers demanded a ransom of 100,000 dollars.
rap¹ [rap] *n.* □ **batida leve**
I heard several raps on the window.
rap² *v.* **(raps, rapping, rapped)** □ **bater de leve**
He rapped on the table and asked them to be quiet.
rape¹ [reip] *n.* □ **estupro**
rape² *v.* **(rapes, raping, raped)** □ **estuprar**
rapid ['rapid] *adj.* □ **rápido**
a rapid movement. ✦ rapid changes.
■ Ver **fast¹**; **quick**.
rapidly ['rapidli] *adv.* □ **rapidamente**
Prices increased rapidly last year.
rare [reə] *adj.*
1 raro
a rare bird / disease. ✦ It's very rare to have rain in the desert.

■ antônimo: **common**
2 malpassado
rare meat
rarely ['reəli] *adv.* □ **raramente**
I rarely visit them.
rash¹ [raʃ] *n.* □ **erupção cutânea**
rash² *adj.* □ **precipitado, impetuoso**
a rash decision. ✦ It was rash of you to leave your job.
rashly ['raʃli] *adv.* □ **precipitadamente, impetuosamente**
raspberry ['ra:zbəri] *n.* **(pl. raspberries)** □ **framboesa**
raspberry jam.
rat [rat] *n.* □ **ratazana**
Rats are bigger than mice.
rate [reit] *n.*
1 taxa
the crime rate. ✦ the rate of inflation. ✦ The birth rate may increase by 2% next year.
2 razão, velocidade
We sell cars at the rate of three a week. ✦ to work at a fast / slow rate.
3 taxa
The rate of pay for this job is 15 dollars an hour.
-rate □ **linha, classe, nível**
a first-rate teacher (= an excellent teacher). ✦ third-rate goods.
at any rate
1 pelo menos
It's possible. At any rate, that's what she thinks.
2 de qualquer modo
He's coming with some friends. He won't come alone at any rate.
at this rate □ **dessa maneira**
At this rate, you'll lose all your friends.
rather ['ra:ðə] *adv.* □ **um tanto, meio**
It's rather cold in here. ✦ They were rather happy. ✦ It's rather a small amount. (= It's a rather small amount.)
■ Ver **quite**; **fairly**; **pretty**.
rather than □ **em vez de**
I prefer to do it today rather than tomorrow. ✦ I like the white shirt rather than the blue one.
would rather (mesmo que **'d rather**) □ **preferir**
I'd rather stay home tonight. ✦ She'd rather not wait. ✦ I'd rather go by train than by car.
■ Ver **prefer**.
ration¹ ['raʃən] *n.* □ **porção**
food rations.
ration² *v.* **(rations, rationing, rationed)** □ **racionar**
We had to ration the water.
rattle¹ ['ratl] *n.*
1 chocalho
The baby is playing with the rattle.
2 barulho
the rattle of bottles / a chain / an old car.
rattle² *v.* **(rattles, rattling, rattled)**
1 mover-se ruidosamente
I shook the money-box and the coins rattled inside. ✦ An old car rattled along the road.
2 chacoalhar
He rattled the keys in his pocket.
raven ['reivən] *n.* □ **corvo**
raw [ro:] *adj.*
1 cru, crua
raw meat / vegetables.

■ antônimo: **cooked**
2 não processado
raw sugar / cotton.
raw materials [ˈrɔːmətiəriəlz] *n. pl.* ▫ **matéria-prima**
Coal, oil, iron, cotton, etc. are raw materials.
ray [rei] *n.* ▫ **raio**
the sun's rays (= the rays of the sun).
razor [ˈreizə] *n.* ▫ **lâmina**
to shave with a razor. ◆ an electric razor.
razor-blade [ˈreizəˌbleid] *n.* ▫ **lâmina de barbear**
rd *abbr.* (= third) º, ª
the 3rd of June ◆ 23rd (= twenty-third)
Rd *abbr.* (= road) ▫ **est. (estrada)**
re- *pref.* ▫ **re-**
rearrange (= arrange again in a different way). ◆ rebuild (= build again). ◆ rename (= give a new name to).
reach¹ [riːtʃ] *n.*
out of reach, beyond reach ▫ **fora/longe do alcance**
Keep this medicine out of reach of children. ◆ I can't get to the top shelf. It's out of my reach.
within (easy) reach ▫ **ao alcance**
The school is within easy reach of my house. ◆ He put the alarm clock within easy reach.
reach² *v.* (**reaches, reaching, reached**)
1 (= arrive at / in; get to) **chegar**
They reached Moscow at 5 o'clock. ◆ We are reaching the end of the show.
■ They reached Moscow (*not* 'reached to Moscow').
2 esticar a mão para pegar algo
Reach out your hand and pick that orange. ◆ He reached for the door and opened it for me.
3 alcançar
Can you reach the ceiling?
4 conseguir falar com
You can reach me at this number.
react [riˈakt] *v.* (**reacts, reacting, reacted**) ▫ **reagir**
How did she react when she heard about it? ◆ He reacted quickly / angrily.
■ Ver **respond**.
reaction [riˈakʃən] *n.* ▫ **reação**
What was his reaction (to what you said)?
■ Ver **response**.
read [riːd] *v.* (**reads, reading, read**)
1 ler
He can read and write (Spanish). ◆ I read it in the newspaper. ◆ I read up to page 120. ◆ She enjoys reading detective stories. ◆ Read the sentence aloud.
2 ler
I read them a story. ◆ Read it to me.
read out (= read aloud) **ler**
I read out the letter to them.
reader [ˈriːdə] *n.*
1 leitor
the readers of a newspaper.
2 manual de leitura
an English reader for elementary learners.
readily [ˈredili] *adv.* ▫ **prontamente**
He readily agreed to help.
readiness [ˈredinis] *n.* ▫ **prontidão**
her readiness to help.
reading [ˈriːdiŋ] *n.* ▫ **leitura**
I like reading and dancing most.

ready [ˈredi] *adj.*
1 pronto
Are you ready? ◆ I'll be ready in a minute. ◆ Dinner is not ready yet. ◆ Is everything ready for the trip?
2 pronto
She is ready to help you.
get ready ▫ **aprontar-se, preparar-se**
I'm getting ready to receive the guests.
get something ready ▫ **preparar, ter algo à mão**
Get your tickets ready.
ready-made [ˌrediˈmeid] *adj.* ▫ **pronto**
ready-made frozen pizza.
real [riəl] *adj.*
1 real
Such things can't happen in real life, only in films and books.
2 verdadeiro
His real name is Sylvester, not Rambo. ◆ Is that a real diamond? ◆ real leather. ◆ We have a real problem.
realise [ˈriəlaiz] *v. Brit.* (Ver **realize**).
realistic [riəˈlistik] *adj.*
1 realista
Your ideas are not realistic.
2 realista
a realistic painting.
reality [riˈaləti] *n.* ▫ **realidade**
Her dream became a reality.
in reality (= in fact) ▫ **na realidade**
He says he is a millionaire, but in reality he is not so rich.
realization [ˌriəlaiˈzeiʃən] *n. Brit.*, **realisation**
1 compreensão, noção
the realization that it may happen soon.
2 realização
the realization of your dreams.
realize [ˈriəlaiz] *v.* (**realizes, realizing, realized**)
1 ter noção de, perceber
Do you realize the seriousness of the situation? ◆ I realize that it's difficult, but I'll try anyway. ◆ I didn't realize he was so ill.
2 realizar
She finally realized her dream of becoming world champion.
really [ˈriəli] *adv.*
1 realmente
Do you really think so? ◆ I really don't know. ◆ She is not really sorry. ◆ Did you like the film? Not really.
2 Verdade?, Sério?
I passed my driving test. – Really?
reap [riːp] *v.* (**reaps, reaping, reaped**) ▫ **ceifar, colher**
to reap the wheat.
rear¹ [riə] *adj.* ▫ **traseiro**
the rear lights / window of the car.
rear² *n.* (= back) ▫ **fundos, parte de trás, traseira**
We sat in the rear (of the train).
reason¹ [ˈriːzn] *n.* ▫ **razão**
What is the reason for the failure? ◆ The reason I didn't call was because there was no phone. ◆ Is there any reason why you did not come?
reason² *v.* (**reasons, reasoning, reasoned**) ▫ **argumentar, persuadir**
You can't reason with him – he has made up his mind.

reasonable ['ri:znəbl] *adj.*
1 razoável
Be reasonable! We can't go out in this rain. ♦ He is a reasonable man. He'll understand your problem.
2 razoável
a reasonable price. ♦ a reasonable offer.
■ antônimo: **unreasonable**
reasonably ['ri:znəbli] *adv.*
1 sensatamente
Let's discuss this reasonably.
2 (= quite) **razoavelmente**
The plan is reasonably good.
reassurance [,riə'ʃuərəns] *n.* □ **garantia**
I need reassurance that this is the right thing to do. ♦ They are asking for reassurances that the police will not arrest them.
reassure [riə'ʃuə] *v.* (**reassures, reassuring, reassured**) □ **tranquilizar**
He reassured us that there was no danger.
rebel[1] ['rebl] *n., adj.* □ **rebeldes, rebelde**
There was fighting between the rebels and the army. ♦ rebel soldiers.
rebel[2] *v.* (**rebels, rebelling, rebelled**) (= revolt) □ **rebelar-se, revoltar-se**
They rebelled against the king. ♦ They rebelled against the old style of music.
rebellion [rə'beljən] *n.* (= uprising) □ **rebelião**
a rebellion against a dictator.
reboot [ri'bu:t] *v.* (**reboots, rebooting, rebooted**) □ **reiniciar**
To 'reboot' your computer means to turn it off and then turn it on again.
rebuke[1] [rə'bju:k] *v.* (**rebukes, rebuking, rebuked**) (= scold, tell off) □ **repreender**
The teacher rebuked her for not doing her homework.
rebuke[2] *n.* □ **repreensão**
recall [ri'kɔ:l] *v.* (**recalls, recalling, recalled**) □ **recordar, lembrar**
I can't recall (= remember) what happened that night. ♦ I don't recall seeing you at the party.
receipt [rə'si:t] *n.* □ **recibo**
I paid for the watch and he gave me a receipt. ♦ Can I have a receipt, please?
receive [rə'si:v] *v.* (**receives, receiving, received**) (= get) □ **receber**
I was glad to receive your letter of May 10. ♦ When did you receive the invitation?
■ Compare **receive**; **accept**:
receive the invitation.
accept the invitation.
receiver [rə'si:və] *n.* □ **receptor, receptador**
recent ['ri:snt] *adj.* □ **recente**
Do you have a recent picture of her? ♦ This is the most recent information about him.
recently ['ri:sntli] *adv.*
1 recentemente
I only heard about it recently.
2 (= lately) **recentemente**
I haven't seen her recently.
reception [rə'sepʃən] *n.*
1 (= reception desk) **recepção**
I left the key at reception and went out (of the hotel).
2 recepção
The champion had a great reception when he returned home.
wedding reception *n.* □ **recepção do casamento**
receptionist [rə'sepʃənist] *n.* □ **recepcionista**
recess [ri'ses] *n. Amer.* □ **recesso**
They usually play during recess.
■ *Brit.* **break**
recharge [ri'tʃa:dʒ] *v.* (**recharges, recharging, recharged**) □ **recarregar**
I have to recharge the battery in my mobile phone.
recipe ['resəpi] *n.* □ **receita**
a recipe for chocolate cake.
reckless ['reklis] *adj.* □ **imprudente**
He was guilty of reckless driving. ♦ a reckless driver.
recklessly ['reklisli] *adv.* □ **imprudentemente**
to drive recklessly.
reckon ['rekən] *v.* (**reckons, reckoning, reckoned**)
1 (= think; believe) **achar, acreditar**
Do you reckon he will come today?
2 (= suppose) *Amer.* **achar, supor**
I reckon she knows what she is doing.
3 (= calculate) **calcular, estimar**
to reckon the cost of the party.
4 (= consider) **considerar**
Many people reckon her to be a great writer.
recognise ['rekəgnaiz] *v. Brit.* (Ver **recognize**).
recognition [,rekəg'niʃən] *n.* □ **reconhecimento**
He looked at me, but he showed no sign of recognition.
in recognition of □ **em reconhecimento por**
They gave him a medal in recognition of his achievements.
recognize ['rekəgnaiz] *v.* (**recognizes, recognizing, recognized**)
1 reconhecer
I didn't recognize you without your glasses. ♦ I recognized her voice.
■ Ver **identify**.
2 reconhecer
We recognize that there are a lot of difficulties.
recommend [rekə'mend] *v.* (**recommends, recommending, recommended**)
1 recomendar
Can you recommend (me) a good book? ♦ I recommended her for the job.
■ recommend me (*not* 'recommend to me').
2 recomendar
I recommend that you stay in bed.
■ recommend that you stay (not 'that you will stay')
recommendation [,rekəmən'deiʃən] *n.* □ **recomendação**
We ordered mushroom soup on his recommendation (= because he recommended it). ♦ The report made a number of recommendations. ♦ a letter of recommendation
record[1] ['rekɔ:d] *n.*
1 registro
They keep a record of all the births, marriages and deaths.
2 disco
to play a record (on the record-player).
■ Ver **disc**; **CD**.
3 recorde
She holds the world record for the long jump. ♦ He broke the record for the 100 metres race.
4 ficha
She has a criminal record.

5 histórico
This school has a good record.
off the record □ **em off, secretamente**
The Prime Minister admitted it off the record.
record² [rə'kɔ:d] *v.* (**records, recording, recorded**)
1 gravar, registrar
He recorded everything they said at the meeting. ◆ She recorded life in the village with her camera.
2 gravar
to record a song / TV programme.
recorder [rə'kɔ:də] *n.* □ **flauta doce**
A recorder is a musical instrument like a flute.
■ Ver **tape recorder; video cassette recorder**.
recording [rə'kɔ:diŋ] *n.* □ **gravação**
record-player ['rekɔ:d,pleiə] *n.* □ **toca-discos**
■ Ver **CD**.
recover [rə'kʌvə] *v.* (**recovers, recovering, recovered**)
1 recuperar
The patient is recovering (from his illness). ◆ It took me a long time to recover from the shock.
■ Ver **get better; get well; get over**.
2 recuperar
The police recovered the stolen jewels.
recovery [rə'kʌvəri] *n.* □ **recuperação**
The patient made a quick recovery after the operation. ◆ I wish you a speedy recovery.
recreation [rekri'eiʃən] *n.* □ **recreação, passatempo, lazer**
His recreation is to go fishing. ◆ Tennis is my favourite recreation.
■ Ver **pastime; hobby**.
recruit¹ [rə'kru:t] *v.* (**recruits, recruiting, recruited**)
□ **recrutar**
The police are recruiting volunteers.
recruit² *n.* □ **recruta**
a new recruit.
recruitment [rə'kru:tmənt] *n.* □ **recrutamento**
the recruitment of workers
rectangle ['rektəŋgl] *n.* (= oblong) □ **retângulo**
rectangular [rek'tæŋgjulə] *adj.* (= oblong) □ **retangular**
recycle [ri:'saikl] *v.* (**recycles, recycling, recycled**)
□ **reciclar**
to recycle paper, glass, plastics, etc.
recycled [ri:'saikld] *adj.* **reciclado**
recycled paper.
red¹ [red] *adj.* (**redder, reddest**) □ **tinto, vermelho, ruivo**
red wine. ◆ The leaves turned red (= their color / colour changed to red). ◆ She has red hair
red² *n.* □ **vermelho**
She was dressed in red.
reddish ['rediʃ] *adj.* □ **avermelhado**
red-handed ['red'hændid] *adj.* □ **em flagrante**
The police caught the thief red-handed.
redhead ['redhed] *n.* □ **ruivo**
She is a redhead.
red-hot [,red'hɒt] *adj.* □ **candente, em brasa**
reduce [rə'dju:s] *v.* (**reduces, reducing, reduced**)
1 reduzir
to reduce speed. ◆ to reduce the risk. ◆ They reduced the number of workers from 125 to 80. ◆ We reduced prices by 12%.
■ antônimo: **increase**
■ Ver **cut¹; decrease; lower²**.

2 emagrecer
Eat less fat if you want to reduce (= lose weight).
reduction [rə'dʌkʃən] *n.*
1 redução
a reduction of the number of accidents.
2 redução
price reductions.
reed [ri:d] *n.* □ **junco**
reef [ri:f] *n.* □ **recife**
reel [ri:l] *n.* □ **rolo, carretel, (rolo de) filme**
a film reel. ◆ a cotton reel. ◆ I put a new reel in the camera.
refer [rə'fə:] *v.* (**refers, referring, referred**)
1 referir-se
Are you referring to me when you say 'some lazy people'? ◆ What does the word 'condition' refer to in this article?
2 recorrer
I referred to a dictionary to find the meaning of the word.
3 encaminhar
My doctor referred me to an eye doctor.
referee [refə'ri:] *n.* □ **árbitro, juiz**
The referee blew his whistle for half-time.
■ Compare with **umpire**.
reference ['refərəns] *n.*
1 referência
The book is full of references to his childhood. ◆ I didn't make any reference to the money.
2 referências
I got a good reference from the boss.
with / in reference to (= in / with regard to) □ **com referência a, referente a**
I am writing to you in reference to your advertisement.
reference book ['refərəns buk] *n.* □ **obra de referência**
Dictionaries and encyclopedias are reference books.
reflect [rə'flekt] *v.* (**reflects, reflecting, reflected**)
1 refletir
He saw his face reflected in the water. ◆ Her face always reflects her true feelings.
2 refletir
I won't give you my answer now. I want time to reflect.
reflection [rə'flekʃən] *n.* □ **reflexo**
His reflection in the mirror frightened me. ◆ the reflection of heat / light.
reform¹ [rə'fɔ:m] *n.* □ **reforma**
The government decided on a reform of the education system.
reform² *v.* (**reforms, reforming, reformed**)
1 reformar
to reform the economic system.
2 recuperar-se
a criminal who is trying to reform.
refrain [rə'frein] *v.* (**refrains, refraining, refrained**)
□ **abster-se**
Please refrain from smoking.
refresh [rə'freʃ] *v.* (**refreshes, refreshing, refreshed**)
□ **refrescar**
I had a cold drink to refresh myself.
refresh your memory □ **refrescar sua memória**
Maybe this picture will help you refresh your memory.
refreshing [rə'freʃiŋ] *adj.* □ **refrescante**
a refreshing shower / sleep / drink.

refreshments [rəˈfreʃmənts] *n. pl.* □ **bebidas não alcoólicas**
Light refreshments will be available. ◆ You can buy refreshments before the show begins.

refrigerate [rəˈfridʒəreit] *v.* (**refrigerates, refrigerating, refrigerated**) □ **refrigerar**
Refrigerate after opening (the carton of juice).

refrigerator [rəˈfridʒəreitə] *n. Brit.* (mesmo que **fridge**) □ **refrigerador, geladeira**
Put the milk back in the refrigerator.

refuge [ˈrefjuːdʒ] *n.* □ **refúgio**
The mouse found refuge inside a hole.
take refuge from □ **abrigar-se de**
We took refuge from the rain in a bus shelter.

refugee [ˌrefjuːˈdʒiː] *n.* □ **refugiado**
to send food and blankets for the refugees. ◆ a refugee camp.

refund¹ [ˈriːfʌnd] *n.* □ **reembolso**
Did you get a refund on your broken watch?

refund² [riˈfʌnd] *v.* (**refunds, refunding, refunded**) □ **reembolsar**
I cancelled the trip and they refunded me the money.

refusal [rəˈfjuːzəl] *n.* □ **recusa**
Her refusal to accept the prize surprised everyone.

refuse¹ [rəˈfjuːz] *v.* (**refuses, refusing, refused**)
1 recusar-se
I asked him to leave, but he refused. ◆ She refused to tell us the secret.
2 recusar
They refused the gift.
■ antônimo: **agree**

refuse² *n.* (= **litter; rubbish; garbage; trash**) □ **refugo, lixo**

regard¹ [rəˈgɑːd] *n.*
1 consideração
She has no regard for other people's feelings.
2 consideração, apreço
I have a high regard for her / work.
in regard to, with regard to (= in / with reference to) □ **em / com relação a**
I'm writing in regard to your advertisement. ◆ With regard to your question, the answer is 'No'.

regards *n.* □ **lembranças**
Please give my regards to your father.
■ Ver **remember me to someone**.

regard² *v.* (**regards, regarding, regarded**) □ **considerar**
We regard him as our leader.

regiment [ˈredʒimənt] *n.* □ **regimento**

region [ˈriːdʒən] *n.* □ **região**
There isn't much rain in this region. ◆ tropical regions.

regional [ˈriːdʒənl] *adj.* □ **regional**

register¹ [ˈredʒistə] *n.* □ **livro de chamada, registro**
The teacher called out the names from the (class) register. ◆ the register of voters.

register² *v.* (**registers, registering, registered**)
1 registrar
I registered the car / house in my name.
2 inscrever-se, registrar-se, matricular-se
to register for a cookery course. ◆ to register at a hotel. ◆ to register for school.

registered letter *n.* □ **carta registrada**

registration [ˌredʒisˈtreiʃən] *n.* □ **registro**
registration of students for a course.

registration number [ˌredʒisˈtreiʃən ˈnʌmbə] *n.* □ **número da placa**
■ *Amer.* **license plate number**

regret¹ [rəˈgret] *n.* □ **desgosto, pesar**
Much to my regret (= I'm very sorry that), I can't come ◆ I have no regrets about my decision to stay.

regret² *v.* (**regrets, regretting, regretted**) □ **lamentar arrepender-se**
I regret (= I'm sorry) that I will not be able to come with you. ◆ She regrets what she said to me. ◆ We regret selling (= that we sold) the house.

regular [ˈregjulə] *adj.*
1 regular
He makes regular visits to that place. ◆ a regular pulse heartbeat. ◆ to eat regular meals.
2 habitual, frequente
She is not one of my regular customers.
3 simétrico
The buildings were regular in shape.
■ antônimo: **irregular**
4 normal
Do you want a large size packet or regular?
5 normal, comum
A regular shampoo is good enough.
6 regular
regular and irregular verbs.
7 de linha
the regular army.

regularity [ˌregjuˈlariti] *n.* □ **regularidade**
The school demands regularity of attendance.

regularly [ˈregjuləli] *adv.* □ **regularmente**
She visits them regularly. ◆ I get up regularly at 7 o'clock every morning.

regulate [ˈregjuleit] *v.* (**regulates, regulating, regulated**) □ **regular**
The thermostat regulates the temperature in the oven.

regulation [ˌregjuˈleiʃən] *n.* □ **regra, regulamento**
safety regulations to prevent accidents at work. ◆ It against the regulations to ride a motorbike without a he met.

rehearsal [rəˈhɔːsəl] *n.* □ **ensaio**
Tonight is the last rehearsal of the play.

rehearse [rəˈhɔːs] *v.* (**rehearses, rehearsing, rehearsed**) □ **ensaio**
The orchestra rehearsed for the concert. ◆ She rehearse her part in the play.

reign¹ [rein] *n.* □ **reinado**
during the reign of Queen Victoria.

reign² *v.* (**reigns, reigning, reigned**) □ **reinar**
How long did King George III reign over England?

rein [rein] *n.* □ **rédea**
He pulled (on) the reins to stop the horse.

reindeer [ˈreindiə] *n.* (*pl.* **reindeer**) □ **rena**

reinforce [ˌriːinˈfɔːs] *v.* (**reinforces, reinforcing, reinforced**) □ **reforçar**
to reinforce a building. ◆ to reinforce the army.

reinforcement [ˌriːinˈfɔsmənt] *n.* □ **reforço**

reject [rəˈdʒekt] *v.* (**rejects, rejecting, rejected**) □ **rejeita**
They rejected my plan. ◆ Two universities rejected me.
■ Ver **turn down**.

rejection [rəˈdʒekʃən] *n.* □ **rejeição**
I got a rejection from the college.

rejoice [rəˈdʒois] v. (**rejoices, rejoicing, rejoiced**) □ **alegrar-se**
They all rejoiced at her success.

relate [rəˈleit] v. (**relates, relating, related**) □ **relacionar**
There is a lot of evidence to relate heart disease to smoking.
■ Ver **connect**.
be related (to)
1 estar relacionado (a, com)
The two subjects are not related.
2 ser parente (de)
We are related. She is my aunt.

relation [rəˈleiʃən] n.
1 relação
There is no relation between the size of the computer and its power.
2 (= relative) **parente**
All her friends and relations came to the wedding.

relations n. pl. □ **relações**
We have good relations with our neighbours. ◆ diplomatic relations (between countries).

relationship [rəˈleiʃənʃip] n.
1 relação, relacionamento
I have a good relationship with the other members of the group. ◆ to have a serious relationship with a girl / boy.
2 parentesco
What is your relationship to him? We are brothers.
3 (= relation) **relação**
Is there any relationship between physical fitness and health?

relative[1] [ˈrelətiv] n. (= relation) □ **parente**
relative[2] adj. □ **relativo**
relative poverty.

relatively [ˈrelətivli] adv. □ **relativamente**
The exam was relatively easy. ◆ It's a relatively small car.

relative pronoun [ˈrelətiv ˈprounaun] n. □ **pronome relativo**
'Who', 'whom' and 'whose' are examples of relative pronouns.

relax [rəˈlaks] v. (**relaxes, relaxing, relaxed**) □ **relaxar**
A hot bath will help you relax. ◆ Let's relax for an hour. We can finish this later. ◆ Relax! There's nothing to worry about. ◆ to relax the muscles. ◆ Let your body relax.
■ Ver **take it easy**.

relaxation [ˌriːlakˈseiʃən] n.
1 descanso
She doesn't have much time for relaxation.
2 relaxamento
Your body is now in a state of relaxation.

relaxed [rəˈlakst] adj. □ **relaxado**
I feel relaxed when I listen to classical music.

release[1] [rəˈliːs] n. □ **libertação**
They were glad to hear of his release from prison.

release[2] v. (**releases, releasing, released**) □ **libertar**
The kidnappers released him after 10 days. ◆ I released the bird from the cage.
■ Ver **free**[3].

relevance [ˈreləvəns] n. □ **relevância**
What is the relevance of your question to this discussion?

relevant [ˈreləvənt] adj. □ **relevante**
What you say is not relevant to our problem. ◆ We need all the relevant details by tomorrow.
■ antônimo: **irrelevant**

reliable [rəˈlaiəbl] adj. □ **confiável**
a very reliable journalist. ◆ Is your information reliable? ◆ This machine is not very reliable.
■ antônimo: **unreliable**

relied [rəˈlaid] v. (Ver **rely**).

relief [rəˈliːf] n.
1 alívio
It was a great relief to hear that she was well. ◆ What a relief! I thought I was late.
2 ajuda, socorro
to send relief for the refugees.

relies [rəˈlaiz] v. (Ver **rely**).

relieve [rəˈliːv] v. (**relieves, relieving, relieved**) □ **aliviar**
I need a massage to relieve the pain in my arm.
be relieved □ **estar aliviado**
I'm relieved to hear that you are all right.

religion [rəˈlidʒən] n. □ **religião**

religious [rəˈlidʒəs] adj. □ **religioso**
religious education. ◆ Are you religious?

reluctance [rəˈlʌktəns] n. □ **relutância**
He joined us with great reluctance.

reluctant [rəˈlʌktənt] adj. (= unwilling) □ **relutante**
She was reluctant to talk about it.

reluctantly [rəˈlʌktəntli] adv. (= unwillingly) □ **relutantemente**
He reluctantly agreed to sing to us.

rely [rəˈlai] v. (**relies, relying, relied**)
rely on
1 (= count on) **contar com**
You can rely on her. She can keep a secret. ◆ Don't rely on the trains here to come on time.
2 (= depend on) **depender de**
He relies on his parents for money.

remain [rəˈmein] v. (**remains, remaining, remained**)
1 permanecer
Nothing remained on his plate when he finished eating.
2 (= stay) **permanecer**
The doctor told me to remain in bed.
3 (= stay) **ficar**
They remained friends. ◆ The shop will remain closed till the summer.

remainder [rəˈmeində] n. □ **resto, restante**
They spent the remainder of the day in the shops.

remaining [rəˈmeiniŋ] adj. □ **restante**
Mix the chocolate with the remaining butter. ◆ She gave me two of the remaining pictures.

remains [rəˈmeinz] n. □ **ruínas, restos**
the remains of an old building ◆ the remains of a meal

remark[1] [rəˈmaːk] n. (= comment) □ **comentário**
He made a remark about the loud music.

remark[2] v. (**remarks, remarking, remarked**) (= comment) □ **comentar**
She remarked that the film was very interesting. ◆ `It's nice', he remarked

remarkable [riˈmaːkəbl] adj. □ **notável**
a remarkable achievement ◆ a remarkable person

remarkably [rəˈmaːkəbli] adv. □ **notavelmente**
The party was remarkably successful. ◆ He speaks English remarkably well.

remedy [ˈremədi] n. (pl. **remedies**) □ **remédio**
They say that chicken soup is a good remedy for a cold.

remember [rə'membə] v. (**remembers, remembering, remembered**) ☐ **lembrar-se**
She couldn't remember his name. ♦ I remember writing (= that I wrote) him a letter. ♦ I remembered (= did not forget) to write him a letter.
■ Ver **recall**.

remember me to (someone) (= give my regards to) ☐ **dar lembranças minhas a (alguém)**
Remember me to your parents.

remind [rə'maind] v. (**reminds, reminding, reminded**) ☐ **lembrar (alguém) de**
Please remind me to buy him a present. ♦ She reminds me of her father. ♦ This song reminds me of my childhood.

reminder [rə'maində] n. ☐ **lembrete, aviso**
They sent me a reminder from the library to return the book.

remote [rə'mout] adj. ☐ **remoto, afastado**
a remote village.
■ Ver **distant**.

remote control [rə'mout kən'troul] n. ☐ **controle remoto**
to change channels (on the TV) with a remote control ♦ to fly little airplanes by remote control.

removal [rə'mu:vəl] n.
1 remoção
The removal of the furniture to the new office cost us a lot.
2 remoção
the removal of an obstacle.

remove [rə'mu:v] v. (**removes, removing, removed**) ☐ **remover**
to remove stains from clothes. ♦ She removed the picture from the wall.

renew [rə'nju:] v. (**renews, renewing, renewed**) ☐ **renovar**
He renewed his passport.

rent¹ [rent] n. ☐ **aluguel**
You pay a high rent for such a small apartment. ♦ How much rent did you pay for the car?

rent² v. (**rents, renting, rented**)
1 alugar
She rented a house in the village. ♦ They rented a car for the weekend.
■ Ver **hire²; let¹**.
2 (= rent out) **alugar**
We rent out rooms for students. ♦ They rent cars and boats.

repair¹ [ri'peə] n. ☐ **restauração, reparo**
The road / restaurant is closed for repairs.

repair² v. (**repairs, repairing, repaired**) ☐ **consertar, restaurar, reparar**
They are repairing the road. ♦ to repair a roof / clock / shoe. ♦ to repair the damage.
■ Ver **fix; mend**.

repairman [ri'peəmən] n. (Ver **repairperson**).
repairperson [ri'peə,pɔ:sn] n. ☐ **técnico**
The repairperson fixed my TV.

repay [ri'pei] v. (**repays, repaying, repaid**)
1 saldar, quitar
to repay a debt / loan.
2 retribuir
How can I ever repay you for your kindness?

repayment [ri'peimənt] n. ☐ **reembolso, pagamento**

repeat¹ [rə'pi:t] n. ☐ **reprise**
I never watch the repeats (of old shows) on TV.

repeat² v. (**repeats, repeating, repeated**)
1 repetir
Could you repeat the question, please? ♦ They will never repeat that mistake. ♦ You are repeating yourself. ♦ Repeat after me: one, two, three...
2 contar
Promise me not to repeat my secret to anyone.

repeatedly [rə'pi:tidli] adv. ☐ **repetidamente**
I warned him repeatedly of the danger.

repetition [repə'tiʃən] n. ☐ **repetição**
There mustn't be any repetition of such mistakes. ♦ Your essay is full of repetitions.

replace [rə'pleis] v. (**replaces, replacing, replaced**)
1 substituir
New and better computers replaced the old ones. ♦ Who will replace her as manager?
2 substituir
He replaced them with younger players.
3 recolocar
Please replace the books on the shelf.

replacement [rə'pleismənt] n.
1 substituição
the replacement of typewriters by computers.
2 (= substitute) **substituto**
She is going on holiday and we must find a replacement for her.

replay¹ [ri:plei] n. ☐ **replay**
to watch an action replay on TV of the goals during the game.

replay² [ri:plei] v. (**replays, replaying, replayed**) ☐ **repetir, repassar**

reply¹ [rə'plai] n. (= answer) ☐ **resposta**
What was his reply to your question? ♦ We must send them a reply immediately.

reply² v. (**replies, replying, replied** (= **answer**) ☐ **responder**
I asked her that question, but she didn't reply. ♦ Did he reply to your letter?
■ Ver **respond**.

report¹ [rə'pɔ:t] n.
1 relatório
What are the conclusions of the report on education?
2 matéria, reportagem
a newspaper report of the Prince's marriage. ♦ radio reports about the accident.
3 boletim escolar
to get a good (school) report. ♦ *Amer.* a report card.

report² v. (**reports, reporting, reported**)
1 fazer uma reportagem
A lot of newspaper and TV reporters came to report on the earthquake
2 comunicar
We reported the theft to the police.

reported speech [rə'pɔ:tid 'spi:tʃ] n. (grammar) ☐ **discurso indireto**
An example of reported speech is 'I asked him what his name was'.

reporter [rə'pɔ:tə] n. ☐ **repórter**
a TV reporter. ♦ a newspaper reporter.

represent [,reprə'zent] v. (**represents, representing, represented**)
1 representar

The red lines on the map represent roads. ◆ The painting represents the creation of the world.
2 representar
I hired a lawyer to represent me in court. ◆ She represents our company abroad.
representation [ˌreprəzen'teiʃən] *n.* □ **representação**
representative [ˌreprə'zentətiv] *n.* □ **representante, deputado**
Representatives from all over the world came to the exhibition. ◆ The House of the Representatives is part of the American Congress.
reproduce [ˌri:prə'dju:s] *v.* (**reproduces, reproducing, reproduced**)
1 reproduzir, fazer cópia
Can you reproduce (= make a copy of) this photograph? ◆ to reproduce a cassette.
2 reproduzir-se, procriar
Rabbits reproduce very quickly.
reproduction [ˌri:prə'dʌkʃən] *n.*
1 reprodução, réplica, cópia
This is not the original painting – it's only a reproduction.
2 reprodução
to study the reproduction of animals / plants.
reptile ['reptail] *n.* □ **réptil**
A snake is a reptile.
republic [rə'pʌblik] *n.* □ **república**
the Republic of France.
reputation [repju'teiʃən] *n.* □ **reputação**
This school has a good reputation.
reputed [ri'pju:tid] *adj.* □ **considerado**
She is reputed to be a good teacher.
request¹ [ri'kwest] *n.* □ **pedido**
a request for help.
request² *v.* (**requests, requesting, requested**) □ **solicitar, pedir**
We requested that they wait one more day.
be requested to □ **ser solicitado a**
Passengers are requested not to smoke.
require [rə'kwaiə] *v.* (**requires, requiring, required**)
1 (= need) **necessitar, precisar de**
We require more money and volunteers.
2 (= demand) **requerer, exigir**
This job requires a lot of effort.
requirement [rə'kwaiəmənt] *n.* □ **requisito**
What are the requirements for the job?
rescue¹ ['reskju:] *n.* □ **resgate**
The police came to their rescue and saved their lives. ◆ a rescue operation.
rescue² *v.* (**rescues, rescuing, rescued**) □ **resgatar**
They rescued the children from the burning house.
research¹ [ri'sɜ:tʃ] *n.* □ **pesquisa**
scientific / medical research. ◆ to do research on a disease.
research² *v.* (**researches, researching, researched**) □ **pesquisar**
They are researching into the causes of the disease. ◆ to research the market.
resemblance [rə'zembləns] *n.* □ **semelhança**
There's no resemblance between the two sisters.
resemble [rə'zembl] *v.* (**resembles, resembling, resembled**) □ **parecer-se com**
She resembles (= looks like) her father.

resent [ri'zent] *v.* (**resents, resenting, resented**) □ **ressentir-se, indignar-se com**
I resent your remark about my job.
resentment [ri'zentmənt] *n.* □ **ressentimento, indignação**
reservation [ˌrezə'veiʃən] *n.* □ **reserva**
to make a reservation at a restaurant. ◆ We canceled our hotel reservations. ◆ We have reservations for two on the plane to India.
■ Ver **book²**.
reserve¹ [rə'zɜ:v] *v.* (**reserves, reserving, reserved**) □ **reservar**
I reserved a table for two (at the restaurant). ◆ I'd like to reserve a seat on the next plane to Greece.
■ Ver **book²**.
be reserved □ **estar reservado**
These seats are reserved.
reserve² *n.*
1 reserva
a reserve of food, water, fuel, etc. ◆ Keep some money in reserve.
2 reserva
He always plays as a reserve.
3 em reserva, reservista
a soldier in the reserves. ◆ a reserve soldier.
reservoir ['rezəvwa:] *n.* □ **reservatório**
residence ['rezidəns] *n.*
1 residência
the Prime Minister's (official) residence. ◆ a family residence.
2 residência
during their residence in the USA.
resident ['rezidənt] *n.*
1 residente, morador
local residents. ◆ a resident of Korea. ◆ a resident of Madrid.
2 hóspede
The hotel restaurant is open for residents only.
resign [rə'zain] *v.* (**resigns, resigning, resigned**) □ **demitir-se de**
She wants to resign (from the company). ◆ He resigned (his job) as manager.
resign yourself to □ **resignar-se com**
They resigned themselves to the loss of their jobs.
resignation [ˌrezig'neiʃən] *n.* □ **demissão**
a letter of resignation. ◆ They demanded his resignation.
hand in your resignation □ **entregar sua carta de demissão**
She handed in her resignation to the President.
resist [rə'zist] *v.*
1 opor-se, oferecer resistência
They resisted the new tax. ◆ They did not resist when the enemy attacked.
2 resistir
I can't resist ice cream. ◆ I couldn't resist telling her the secret. ◆ He resisted the temptation to have another drink.
resistance [rə'zistəns] *n.* □ **resistência**
The enemy force gave in without any resistance. ◆ There is strong resistance to these changes.
resistant [rə'zistənt] *adj.* □ **resistente**
These tomato plants are resistant to disease.
resolution [ˌrezə'lu:ʃən] *n.*
1 resolução, decisão
He made a resolution to go on a diet.

2 determinação, resolução
They passed a resolution to stop the hunting of elephants.
resort [rə'zo:t] *n.* resort
a holiday resort. *Brit.* ◆ a vacation resort. *Amer.* ◆ a ski resort.
last resort □ **último recurso**
We have to ask him for help. This is our last resort. ◆ As a last resort we sold our house.
resource [rə'zo:s] *n.* □ **habilidade**
They showed great resource in dealing with the crisis.
resourceful [rə'zo:sful] *adj.* □ **habilidoso**
a very resourceful worker / soldier.
resources [rə'zo:siz] *n. pl.* □ **recursos**
natural resources such as oil, coal and iron.
respect¹ [rə'spekt] *n.*
1 respeito
I have great respect for him / his work. ◆ to treat them with respect.
■ antônimo: **disrespect**
2 aspecto
This car is better in every respect. ◆ In some respects, the plans are similar.
respect² *v.* (**respects, respecting, respected**)
1 respeitar
She respects you very much. ◆ They do not respect the law.
2 respeitar
We will respect his wishes.
respectable [rə'spektəbl] *adj.* □ **respeitável**
They are a respectable family. ◆ to behave in a respectable way.
respectably [rə'spektəbli] *adv.* □ **respeitavelmente**
respectful [rə'spektful] *adj.* □ **respeitoso/sa**
They are very respectful to their parents. ◆ respectful pupils.
respond [rə'spond] *v.* (**responds, responding, responded**)
1 (= react) **reagir**
I smiled at her, but she did not respond.
2 (= reply) (= answer) **responder**
They responded to my letter only yesterday.
response [rə'spons] *n.*
1 resposta
I received many responses to my ad in the newspaper.
■ **answer** is more usual.
2 (= reaction) **resposta, reação**
an angry response.
■ **reply** and **answer** are the usual words.
responsibility [rə,sponsə'biliti] *n.*
1 responsabilidade
She showed great responsibility by staying with the children all the time.
2 responsabilidade
He accepted full responsibility for the accident.
3 (*pl.* **responsibilities**) **responsabilidade**
We have a responsibility to our workers.
4 (*pl.* **responsibilities**) **responsabilidade**
My responsibility is to keep the place clean. ◆ I have too many responsibilities at work.
responsible [rə'sponsəbl] *adj.*
1 responsável
She is very responsible. ◆ a very responsible worker.
■ antônimo: **irresponsible**
2 responsável
The captain is responsible for the safety of the passengers. ◆ Who is responsible for the children?

3 responsável
Who is responsible for this mistake?
4 de responsabilidade
This is a very responsible job.
responsibly [rə'sponsəbli] *adv.* □ **responsavelmente**
to behave responsibly.
rest¹ [rest] *n.* □ **descanso**
You need some rest. ◆ I'm tired. Let's stop for a rest.
the rest
1 resto
The rest of the guests will come later. ◆ Two of them were red, and the rest (= the others) were green.
2 resto
They spent the rest of the day shopping. ◆ What did you buy with the rest of the money?
rest³ *v.* (**rests, resting, rested**)
1 descansar
Let's rest for an hour or so.
2 descansar
She stopped reading for a minute to rest her eyes.
3 apoiar
The ladder was resting against the wall. ◆ She rested her head on my shoulder.
restaurant ['restront] *n.* □ **restaurante**
He works as a waiter in an Chinese restaurant.
restful ['restful] *adj.* □ **repousante**
a restful sleep.
restless ['restlis] *adj.* □ **inquieto**
They began to get restless because of the long wait.
restlessly ['restlisli] *adv.* □ **intranquilamente**
restoration [,restə'reiʃən] *n.* □ **restauração**
the restoration of the old opera house
restore [rə'sto:] *v.* (**restores, restoring, restored**)
1 restaurar
to restore an old building / car.
2 restaurar
to restore law and order.
3 restituir
The police restored the stolen car to its owner.
restrain [rə'strein] *v.* (**restrains, restraining, restrained**) □ **segurar, reprimir**
He couldn't restrain his anger / tears. ◆ The police used force to restrain the violent man.
restraint [rə'streint] *n.* □ **controle, comedimento**
She showed a lot of restraint and did not get angry with him.
restrict [rə'strikt] *v.* (**restricts, restricting, restricted**) □ **restringir**
They restricted their expenses to $50 a week. ◆ to restrict their freedom.
restriction [rə'strikʃən] *n.* □ **restrição**
There are restrictions on hunting.
rest room ['rest ,ru:m] *n. Amer.* □ **banheiro**
■ Ver **toilet; lavatory; public convenience**.
result¹ [rə'zʌlt] *n.*
1 resultado
Their success was the result of hard work.
2 resultado
What is the result of the game? ◆ She got good exam results.
3 resultado
the result of a mathematical problem.

as a result (of) □ **como resultado (de), como consequência (de)**
I didn't study for the exam, and I failed as a result (of that). ◆ He died as a result of the accident.
result[2] *v.* (**results, resulting, resulted**)
result in □ **resultar em**
The talks resulted in a peace treaty.
result from □ **resultar de**
The problem results from bad planning.
resume [rə'zju:m] *v.* (**resumes, resuming, resumed**) □ **recomeçar**
He resumed his studies after his army service.
résumé [,rezu'mei] *n.* □ **currículo**
When you apply for a job, sometimes you have to send your résumé.
retire [rə'taiə] *v.* (**retires, retiring, retired**)
1 aposentar-se
She retired at the age of 60. ◆ He decided to retire from professional basketball.
2 retirar-se
She retired from the race because of an injury to her knee.
retired [rə'taiəd] *adj.* □ **aposentado**
a retired judge / teacher.
retiree [rə'taiəri] *n.* □ **aposentado**
a club for retirees.
■ Ver **pensioner, senior citizen**.
retirement [rə'taiəmənt] *n.* □ **aposentadoria**
What is the age of retirement in your country? ◆ Her retirement from tennis came too early.
retreat[1] [rə'tri:t] *n.* □ **recuo**
The enemy forces are now in retreat.
■ Compare with **withdraw**:
retreat = in the middle of battle.
withdrawal = to avoid fighting, or after the fighting has stopped, or as a result of an agreement.
retreat[2] *v.* (**retreats, retreating, retreated**) □ **recuar**
The general gave the order to retreat. ◆ The army is retreating.
■ Compare with **withdraw**.
return[1] [rə'tən] *n.* □ **retorno, volta**
I'll visit them on my return (= when I come back). ◆ her return to work.
in return (for) (= in exchange for) □ **em troca (de)**
What did they give you in return for your help? ◆ He helped me a lot and asked for nothing in return.
return ticket *n.* (= return) □ **bilhete de ida e volta**
A return to Liverpool, please. ◆ The return ticket costs the same as the single ticket.
■ *Amer.* **roundtrip (ticket)**
■ Ver **single (ticket)**.
many happy returns □ **que esta data se repita por muitos e muitos anos**
return[2] *v.* (**returns, returning, returned**)
1 (= come back; go back) **retornar, voltar**
They returned from Spain yesterday. ◆ He usually returns from work at 6 o'clock. ◆ She is returning to work next week.
2 (= give back) **devolver**
I have to return this book to the library.
return a call (= call back) □ **retornar uma ligação, ligar de volta**
I left them a message and I'm waiting for them to return my call.

reunion [ri:'ju:njən] *n.* □ **reencontro**
We have a class reunion every ten years. ◆ a family reunion (where you see your relatives again after a long time).
reveal [rə'vi:l] *v.* (**reveals, revealing, revealed**) □ **revelar**
He refused to reveal any information about the plan. ◆ to reveal secrets to the enemy.
revenge[1] [rə'vendʒ] *n.* □ **vingança**
They burnt his house in revenge for his actions.
get / have / take your revenge on (= take vengeance on) □ **vingar-se de**
They took revenge on him for revealing their names to the police.
revenge[2] *v.* (**revenges, revenging, revenged**) □ **vingar-se**
Our team wants to revenge their defeat of last week.
revenge yourself on (= take vengeance on) □ **vingar-se**
She revenged herself on her son's murderer.
reverse[1] [rə'vəːs] *n.*
1 inverso
We expected him to stay, but he did the reverse.
2 (= reverse gear) **marcha a ré**
She put the car into reverse.
reverse[2] *v.* (**reverses, reversing, reversed**)
1 ir de ré
He reversed (the car) into the parking place.
2 inverter
If you reverse the order of the letters BUT you get TUB.
reverse the charges □ **ligar / chamar a cobrar**
I always reverse the charges when I call them.
■ *Amer.* **to call collect**
reverse charge call *Brit.* □ **ligação / chamada a cobrar**
to make a reverse charge call to Los Angeles
■ *Amer.* **collect call**
review[1] [rə'vju:] *n.*
1 crítica, resenha
The book and the film got good reviews.
2 retrospecto
a review of the most important events of the year.
review[2] *v.* (**reviews, reviewing, reviewed**)
1 criticar, fazer resenha
He reviews films on a special TV programme.
2 rever
They are reviewing the plan. ◆ to review the situation.
3 *Amer.* **recapitular**
We are reviewing for the history exam tomorrow.
■ *Brit.* **revise**
revise [rə'vaiz] *v.* (**revises, revising, revised**)
1 fazer revisão, recapitular
I'm revising for my exam.
■ *Amer.* **review**
2 revisar
The book was revised.
revised edition [rə'vaizd i'diʃn] *n.* □ **edição revisada**
revision [rə'viʒən] *n.*
1 revisão
Your speech will need a lot of revision.
2 *Brit.* **recapitulação**
She got a low mark, because she didn't do any revision for the exam.
revive [rə'vaiv] *v.* (**revives, reviving, revived**) □ **reviver**
He fainted, but the doctor revived him.
■ The noun is **revival**.
revolt[1] [rə'vəult] *n.* (= rebellion, uprising) □ **rebelião**
The people were in revolt against the king.

revolt² *v.* (**revolts, revolting, revolted**) (= rebel) □ **rebelar-se**
The army revolted against the dictator.

revolting [rə'voultiŋ] *adj.* (= disgusting) □ **repugnante**
a revolting smell / taste.

revolution [,revə'lu:ʃən] *n.* □ **revolução**
the French Revolution. ◆ the Industrial Revolution. ◆ a revolution in the field of medicine.

revolutionary [,revə'lu:ʃənri] *adj.*, *n.* □ **revolucionário**
revolutionary ideas / inventions. ◆ He was a famous revolutionary.

revolver [rə'vɔlvə] *n.* (= pistol) □ **revólver**

revolving door [rə'vɔlviŋ dɔ:] *n.* □ **porta giratória**

reward¹ [rə'wɔ:d] *n.* □ **recompensa**
They are offering a reward of $100 to the person who finds their dog. ◆ She gave me a present as a reward for my help.

reward² *v.* (**rewards, rewarding, rewarded**) □ **recompensar**
His parents bought him a present to reward him for passing the exam.

rewind [ri:'waind] *v.* (**rewinds, rewinding, rewound**) □ **rebobinar**
I rewound the tape to hear the song again.

rewrite [ri:'rait] *v.* (**rewrites, rewriting, rewrote, rewritten**) □ **reescrever**
Rewrite the sentence without changing its meaning.

rhino ['rainou] *n.* (Ver **rhinoceros**).

rhinoceros [rai'nɔsərəs] *n.* (*pl.* **rhinoceros** or **rhinoceroses**) □ **rinoceronte**

rhyme¹ [raim] *n.*
1 rima
She writes all her poems in rhyme.
2 rima
'Fall' is a possible rhyme for 'call'.
3 poesia
to learn a new rhyme.
■ Ver **nursery rhyme**.

rhyme² *v.* (**rhymes, rhyming, rhymed**) □ **rimar**
'Boys' rhymes with 'toys'.

rhythm ['riðəm] *n.* □ **ritmo**
They danced to the rhythm of the drums. ◆ the rhythm of your heartbeat.

rib [rib] *n.* □ **costela**

ribbon ['ribən] *n.* □ **fita**
She always wears a red ribbon in her hair. ◆ I tied up the present with a ribbon.

rice [rais] *n.* □ **arroz**

rich [ritʃ] *adj.*
1 rico
She is very rich. ◆ one of the richest countries in the world.
2 abundante, farto
This area is rich in oil. ◆ Carrots are rich in vitamin A.
■ antônimo: **poor**
3 calórico
a rich meal / cake.
get rich □ **ficar rico, enriquecer**
He got rich very quickly.
the rich □ **os ricos**
the rich and the poor.

riches ['ritʃiz] *n.* (= wealth) □ **riqueza**

rid [rid] *v.*

get rid of □ **livrar-se de**
I got rid of the old furniture. ◆ They were glad to get rid of their guests. ◆ I can't get rid of my headache.

riddle ['ridl] *n.* □ **charada**
to find the answer to the riddle.

ride¹ [raid] *n.*
1 passeio
I went for a (horse) ride in the woods.
2 passeio, viagem
Let's go for a bike ride. ◆ a short bus ride (= bus journey). ◆ Do you want to come for a ride on my motorbike?
3 *Amer.* **carona**
I'm going to the station. Do you want a ride? ◆ She gave me a ride to town.
■ Ver **lift¹**

ride² *v.* (**rides, riding, rode, ridden**)
1 montar
I'm learning to ride (a horse). ◆ They rode on their camels for three days.
2 andar de
Can you ride a bicycle? ◆ They are riding on their bicycles.
3 andar de, viajar
to ride on a bus / train ◆ John and I rode in the back of the car.
go riding □ **cavalgar, montar**
They go riding once a week.

rider ['raidə] *n.* □ **cavaleiro, ciclista, motociclista**
The rider got off the horse / bicycle. ◆ a motorcycle rider.

ridiculous [rə'dikjuləs] *adj.* □ **ridículo**
You look ridiculous in that disguise. ◆ That's a ridiculous idea! ◆ Don't be so ridiculous! (= Don't be stupid!)

ridiculously [rə'dikjuləsli] *adv.* □ **ridiculamente**
He sold his car at a ridiculously low price.

riding ['raidiŋ] *n.* □ **montaria**
She takes riding lessons.

rifle ['raifl] *n.* □ **rifle**
He aimed his rifle at the target and fired.

right¹ [rait] *adj.*
1 direito
Raise your right arm, please. ◆ It's on the right side of the door.
■ antônimo: **left**
2 certo
That's not the right (= correct) answer. ◆ You did the right thing.
3 correto
It's not right to punish the whole class because of him.
4 certo
You're right, it's not a good idea.
5 certo, adequado
She is the right person for the job.
■ antônimo: **wrong**
■ Ver **all right**.

right² *adv.*
1 à direita
Amer. Turn right at the next traffic lights. (= Make a right at the next traffic light.)
■ antônimo: **left**
2 (= correctly) **corretamente**
Did I do it right?
■ antônimo: **wrong**
3 bem
It happened right here. ◆ She was standing right beside me.

4 (= immediately) **imediatamente**
I'll see him right after breakfast.
5 até
We drove right to the end of the road.
6 Certo
I'll meet you there at 8. – Right.
right away (= immediately) □ **imediatamente, agora mesmo**
I'll do it right away.
right now
1 no momento, agora
Call me later. I can't talk right now.
2 (= right away) **já, imediatamente**
right³ *n.*
1 direita
The red car on the right is mine. ◆ Look to the right. ◆ Do you support the Right or the Left in politics?
■ antônimo: **left**
2 direito
I have a right to say what I think. ◆ You have no right to do that. ◆ They are fighting for their rights.
3 certo
He knows the difference between right and wrong. ◆ to do right, not wrong.
right of way □ **preferência**
I have the right of way, because the other driver has a STOP sign.
right angle ['rait ,aŋgl] *n.* □ **ângulo reto**
An angle of 90º (90 degrees) is a right angle.
right-hand ['rait hand] *adj.* □ **direito**
on the right-hand side of the road. ◆ the right-hand shelf.
■ antônimo: **left-hand**
right-handed ['raithandid] *adj.* □ **destro**
She is right-handed.
■ antônimo: **left-handed**
rightly ['raitli] *adv.*
1 (= correctly) **direito**
If I remember rightly, you were against the plan.
2 corretamente
They were rightly punished.
■ Ver **justly**.
rigid ['ridʒid] *adj.*
1 rígido
rigid rules
2 resistente
a rigid plastic bag.
rim [rim] *n.* □ **borda**
the rim of a cup / plate.
rind [raind] *n.* □ **casca**
lemon rind. ◆ watermelon rind.
■ Ver **peel; skin**.
ring¹ [riŋ] *n.*
1 anel
a wedding ring. ◆ a gold ring.
2 roda
They sat in a ring around the fire.
3 ringue, picadeiro
a boxing ring. ◆ a circus ring.
4 argola
There was a ring at the door.
give someone a ring □ **dar um telefonema para alguém**
I'll give you a ring when I get home.

ring² *v.* (**rings, ringing, rang, rung**)
1 tocar
The phone is ringing. ◆ The pupils waited for the bell to ring.
2 tocar
I rang the doorbell but nobody answered.
3 (= telephone²) **ligar, telefonar**
I'll ring you tomorrow.
■ Ver **call**.
ring off □ **desligar**
She said 'Goodbye' and rang off.
■ Ver **hang up**.
ring up □ **ligar, telefonar**
Your friend rang up a moment ago. ◆ I'll ring him up later.
rinse¹ [rins] *v.* (**rinses, rinsing, rinsed**) □ **enxaguar**
I rinsed the vegetables (with water). ◆ Rinse your hair thoroughly (= well).
rinse² *n.* □ **enxaguada**
Give your hair a good rinse.
riot¹ ['raiət] *n.* □ **tumulto**
The riots started after the government raised prices.
riot² *v.* (**riots, rioting, rioted**) □ **tumultuar**
The football fans rioted after the match.
rip [rip] *v.* (**rips, ripping, ripped**)
1 rasgar
He ripped the package open. ◆ My shirt ripped when I raised my arm.
■ Ver **tear³**.
2 rasgar
I ripped my trousers on a nail.
rip up □ **rasgar**
She ripped the letter up.
ripe [raip] *adj.* □ **maduro**
These bananas are not ripe yet.
ripen ['raipn] *v.* (**ripens, ripening, ripened**) □ **amadurecer**
Tomatoes ripen quickly in the sunshine. ◆ The sun ripened the wheat.
rise¹ [raiz] *n.*
1 aumento
a rise in the price of meat. ◆ a rise in the number of accidents.
2 *Brit.* **aumento**
They got a 10% rise. ◆ a pay rise.
■ *Amer.* **raise**
rise² *v.* (**rises, rising, rose, risen**)
1 (= increase) **subir**
The temperature is rising. ◆ His salary rose by 15% last year.
2 nascer
The sun rises early in the morning.
3 sair
Smoke was rising from the chimney.
4 (= stand up) **ficar em pé, levantar-se**
They rose when the president came in.
5 insurgir-se
The people rose (up) against the king.
risk¹ [risk] *n.* □ **risco**
There is a risk of another earthquake. ◆ There are no risks in this business.
■ Ver **hazard**.
at risk (= in danger) □ **em risco**

The project is at risk because there is no money. ◆ His life is at risk.
take a risk □ arriscar-se, correr risco
She took a risk when she bought the business. ◆ Be careful! Don't take any risks!
risk² *v.* (**risks, risking, risked**)
1 arriscar
He risked his life to save the child.
2 arriscar-se
If you drive too fast, you risk an accident. ◆ It's dangerous to go there, but I'll risk it.
risky ['riski] *adj.* (**riskier, riskiest**) □ arriscado
a risky business. ◆ It's risky to let him keep the money.
■ Ver **dangerous**.
rival ['raivəl] *n., adj.* □ rival
They are rivals in business. ◆ rival teams.
river ['rivə] *n.* □ rio
the river Nile (in Egypt). ◆ We crossed the river by boat.
roach [routʃ] *n. Amer.* (= cockroach) □ barata
road [roud] *n.* □ rua
Be careful when you cross the road. ◆ Is this the road to the airport?
■ In addresses we use the short form **Rd.**
road accident ['roud aksidənt] *n.* □ acidente de trânsito
roadblock ['roudblok] *n.* □ barricada
The police put up roadblocks to catch the terrorist.
road safety ['roud 'seifti] *n.* □ segurança de trânsito
road sign ['roud sain] *n.* □ placa de sinalização
That road sign is a STOP sign.
roam [roum] *v.* (**roams, roaming, roamed**) □ vagar, perambular
He roams the streets every night.
roar¹ [ro:] *n.* □ rugido
The lion's roar frightened them. ◆ the roar of the engines.
roar² *v.* (**roars, roaring, roared**) □ rugir, dar gargalhadas
The lion roared angrily. ◆ They roared with laughter.
roast¹ [roust] *adj.* □ assado
roast beef.
■ Ver **roasted**.
roast² *v.* (**roasts, roasting, roasted**)
1 assar
Roast the meat for 30 minutes.
2 torrar
to roast peanuts, nuts, etc.
roast³ *n.* □ assado
We had roast for dinner.
roasted ['roustid] *adj.*
1 assado
roasted green peppers.
2 torrado
roasted peanuts.
rob [rob] *v.* (**robs, robbing, robbed**) □ roubar, assaltar
They robbed a bank. ◆ Two people robbed me.
robber ['robə] *n.* □ ladrão, assaltante
robbery ['robəri] *n.* (*pl.* **robberies**) □ roubo, assalto
The robbery took place in the middle of the day.
robin ['robin] *n.* □ melro, pintarroxo
robot ['roubot] *n.* □ robô
Robots are very useful in industry.
rock¹ [rɒk] *n.* □ pedra, rocha
The boat hit a big rock. ◆ Rocks fell from the hill down to the road. ◆ They threw rocks (= stones) into the river.

rock² *n.* (mesmo que **rock music**) □ rock
a rock concert. ◆ a rock star / singer.
rock³ *v.* (**rocks, rocking, rocked**) □ balançar, embalar, oscilar
The waves rocked the boat. ◆ I rocked the baby to stop her crying. ◆ The building rocked during the earthquake.
rocket ['rokit] *n.*
1 foguete
to launch a rocket into space.
2 míssil
The rockets destroyed the building. ◆ anti-tank rockets.
■ Ver **missile**.
rocky ['roki] *adj.* (**rockier, rockiest**) □ rochoso
a rocky hill.
rod [rod] *n.* □ barra
We use steel rods to make buildings stronger.
fishing rod *n.* □ vara de pescar
rode [roud] *v.* (Ver **ride**).
role [roul] *n.*
1 papel
She played the role (= part) of the queen.
2 parte, papel
He played an important (= part) role in this project.
role play ['roul plei] *n.* □ dramatização
We use role play in class to improve our English conversation.
roll¹ [roul] *n.*
1 rolo
a roll of film (for a camera). ◆ a roll of cloth. ◆ a toilet paper roll.
2 pãozinho
a roll and butter.
■ Ver **bun**.
roll² *v.* (**rolls, rolling, rolled**)
1 rolar
I dropped a coin and it rolled on the floor. ◆ He rolled the ball towards his child.
2 abrir com rolo
to roll pastry (to make a pie).
3 enrolar
to roll wool into a ball.
4 rodar, passar
The car rolled down the road.
roll over □ rolar
He rolled over onto his stomach.
roll up □ enrolar
to roll up a carpet. ◆ He rolled up his sleeves.
roller-coaster ['roulǝkoustǝ] *n.* □ montanha-russa
roller-skates ['roulǝskeits] *n. pl.* □ patins de rodas
roller-skating ['roulǝskeitiŋ] *n.* □ patinação
rolling pin ['rouliŋ 'pin] *n.* □ rolo de pastel
ROM [rom] *abbr.* □ ROM
romance [rǝ'mans] *n.*
1 romance
Their romance lasted six months.
2 romance
She loves to read romances.
romantic [rǝ'mantik] *adj.* □ romântico
a romantic story.
roof [ru:f] *n.* □ teto
the roof of the house / bus.
■ Ver **ceiling**.

roof-rack ['ru:fræk] *n*. □ **bagageiro**
Put the luggage on the roof-rack.

room¹ [rum] *n*.
1 quarto
The house has five rooms. ◆ I booked a room for a week (at the hotel).
■ Ver **bathroom; bedroom; dining-room; living-room; sitting-room**.
2 espaço
There's no room for more than five people in the car. ◆ Move the sofa to make room for the armchair.

room² *v*. (**rooms, rooming, roomed**) □ **dividir quarto / imóvel**
I roomed with him when I was at university.

room-mate ['rummeit] *n*. □ **colega de quarto**
She was my room-mate when we were at university.

room service ['rum 'sə:vis] *n*. □ **serviço de quarto**
At the hotel, I ordered breakfast from room service.

rooster ['ru:stə] *n*. *Amer*. □ **galo**
■ *Brit*. **cock**

root [ru:t] *n*. □ **raiz**
These plants have deep roots. ◆ to pull hair out by the roots.

rope [roup] *n*. □ **corda**
They tied him up with a rope.

rope ladder ['roup 'ladə] *n*. □ **escada de corda**

rose¹ [rouz] *v*. (Ver **rise**).

rose² *n*. □ **rosa**
I like the smell of roses. ◆ a rose garden.

rosy ['rouzi] *adj*. (**rosier, rosiest**) □ **rosado**
rosy cheeks.

rot [rot] *v*. (**rots, rotting, rotted**) □ **apodrecer**
The dead leaves rotted in the wet ground. ◆ One bad apple rotted all the apples in the basket.

rotate [rə'teit] *v*. (**rotates, rotating, rotated**) □ **girar**
The earth rotates (= turns) around the sun.

rotten ['rotn] *adj*.
1 podre
rotten apples / eggs.
2 péssimo, horrível
We had rotten weather yesterday.
3 horrível
That was a rotten thing to say!

rough [rʌf] *adj*.
1 áspero
He has rough hands. ◆ rough skin.
■ antônimo: **smooth**
2 acidentado
The motorcyclists had to drive over rough ground. ◆ a rough road (full of stones and holes).
3 violento
The game became rough and some players got injured.
4 bravo, agitado
The sea was rough.
■ antônimo: **smooth**
5 (= approximate) **aproximado**
I can give you a rough estimate of the cost.
6 áspero
a rough voice.

roughly ['rʌfli] *adv*.
1 bruscamente
They pushed him roughly into the car.
2 (= about) **cerca de**
It will cost us roughly $500.

round¹ [raund] *adj*. □ **redondo**
a round table. ◆ a round hole. ◆ a round stone. ◆ An orange is round.

round² *prep*.
1 ao redor
The earth moves round the sun. ◆ We sat round the fire. ◆ There's a fence round the garden.
2 por
We looked round the garden, but the cat wasn't there.
3 próximo, pertinho, virando a esquina
I live round the corner.
■ **around** is more usual in American English.

round³ *adv*.
1 à volta toda
The prison has a high wall all round.
2 por aqui
When can you come round to take the books?
■ **around** is more usual in American English.
■ Ver **go (a)round; look (a)round; pass (a)round; turn (a)round**.

round about □ **aproximadamente**
There were round about 100 people outside.

round and round □ **em círculo**
The wheel was going round and round.

round⁴ *n*.
1 ronda
The postman started his round late today.
2 round, rodada
The boxer won the match in the second round. ◆ Our team lost one game in the first round.

roundabout¹ ['raundəbaut] *n*.
1 *Brit*. **rotatória**
to go round a roundabout.
■ *Amer*. **traffic circle**
2 *Brit*. **carrossel**
At the fair the children had a ride on the roundabout.
■ *Amer*. **merry-go-round; carousel**

roundabout² *adj*. □ **indireto**
We went a roundabout way to avoid the traffic jam. ◆ She answered in a roundabout way.

round trip ['raund trip] *n*. □ **viagem de ida e volta**

round-trip ticket ['raundtrip 'tikit] *n*. *Amer*. □ **bilhete de ida e volta**
■ *Brit*. **return (ticket)**

route [ru:t] *n*. □ **rota**
We took the quickest route home. ◆ The birds always come from Europe by this route. ◆ a bus route. ◆ an escape route.

routine¹ [ru:'ti:n] *n*. □ **rotina**
What is your daily routine?

routine² *adj*. □ **rotineiro**
They do routine checks on the planes.

row¹ [rou] *n*.
1 fileira
They stood in a row in front of the flag. ◆ a row of books / houses.
2 fila
I never sit in the front row in the cinema.

row² *v*. (**rows, rowing, rowed**) □ **remar**
Take these oars and start rowing. ◆ to row a boat ◆ to row down the river.

row¹ [rau] *n.*
1 (= quarrel) **briga, discussão**
They had a row (about the money). ◆ She had a row with him.
2 balbúrdia
I can't study because of the terrible row that you are making.

row⁴ *v.* (**rows, rowing, rowed**) (= quarrel) □ **brigar, discutir**
They row all the time, but never hit each other.

rowing-boat ['rouiŋbout] *n. Amer.* (mesmo que **rowboat**) □ **barco a remo**

rowdy ['raudi] *adj.* (**rowdier, rowdiest**) □ **barulhento, agitado**
a rowdy party. ◆ rowdy behaviour.

royal ['roiəl] *adj.* □ **real**
the royal family.

royalty ['roiəlti] *n.* □ **realeza**

rub¹ [rʌb] *v.* (**rubs, rubbing, rubbed**)
1 esfregar
I rubbed my hands together to warm them. ◆ The cat rubbed itself against my leg.
2 passar
She rubbed the cream into her skin. *Brit.*

rub out □ **apagar**
I rubbed out the writing on the blackboard. ◆ Write the sentences in pencil, so you can rub the mistakes out.
■ *Amer.* **erase**

rub² *n.* □ **lustrada, massageada**
Give your shoes a rub. ◆ Give your hair a rub.

rubber ['rʌbə] *n.*
1 borracha
Car tyres are made of rubber. ◆ rubber gloves.
2 *Brit.* **borracha**
You can rub out pencil marks with a rubber.
■ *Amer.* **eraser**

rubber band ['rʌbə band] *n.* (also **elastic** band) □ **elástico**
I put a rubber band around the letters.

rubbish ['rʌbiʃ] *n.*
1 (= litter) *Brit.* **lixo**
Throw the rubbish in the bin. ◆ a rubbish bag.
■ Amer. **garbage; trash**
2 (= nonsense) **bobagem, besteira**
Don't talk rubbish!

rubbish bin ['rʌbiʃ bin] *n. Brit.* □ **cesto de lixo**
■ Compare **with dustbin**:
rubbish bin = inside the house.
dustbin = outside the house.

rubble ['rʌbl] *n.* □ **entulho, escombros**
They found two people alive under the rubble.

rucksack ['rʌksak] *n.* (also **backpack**) □ **mochila**
They climbed the hill with their rucksacks on their backs.

rudder ['rʌdə] *n.* □ **leme**

rude [ru:d] *adj.*
1 (= impolite) **descortês, grosso**
It's rude to talk with your mouth full. ◆ a rude man / remark. ◆ She was rude to me.
2 sujo, obsceno
a rude joke. ◆ a rude word.

rudely ['ru:dli] *adv.* □ **grosseiramente**
'Get out!', he said rudely.

rudeness ['ru:dnis] *n.* □ **rudeza, grossura**

rug [rʌg] *n.* □ **tapete**
There was a beautiful rug on the wall. ◆ He sat on the rug in front of the fire.
■ A **rug** is smaller than a **carpet**.

rugby ['rʌgbi] *n.* □ **rúgbi**

ruin¹ ['ru:in] *n.*
1 ruína
The war brought ruin to the country. ◆ Gambling was his ruin.
2 ruína
We visited the ruins of a Roman city. ◆ The building is now a ruin.
in ruins □ **em ruínas**
The town was in ruins after the bombing.

ruin² *v.* (**ruins, ruining, ruined**) □ **arruinar**
The rain ruined our trip. ◆ He spilled his drink on my dress and ruined it. ◆ Gambling ruined his career.

rule¹ [ru:l] *n.*
1 regra
to learn the rules of the game. ◆ It's against the rules to smoke in school. ◆ the rules of grammar.
2 domínio, governo
Under his rule the country became stronger. ◆ The country was under French rule for many years.
as a rule (= usually) □ **via de regra, geralmente**
As a rule, I eat breakfast, but today I got up late.

rule² *v.* (**rules, ruling, ruled**)
1 governar
The king ruled the country for 20 years.
2 decretar
The judge ruled that she was guilty.

ruler ['ru:lə] *n.*
1 soberano
The prince became the ruler after the queen died.
2 régua
to draw a straight line with a ruler.

rum [rʌm] *n.* □ **rum**

rumble¹ ['rʌmbl] *n.* □ **ribombar**
the rumble of guns / thunder.

rumble² *v.* (**rumbles, rumbling, rumbled**)
1 ribombar, ressoar
Thunder rumbled in the distance.
2 roncar
I want something to eat. My stomach is rumbling.

rumor ['ru:mə] *n. Amer.*, **rumour** *Brit.* □ **boato**
There's a rumour that he left the country last week.

run¹ [rʌn] *n.* □ **corrida**
We go for a run on the beach every morning.

run² *v.* (**runs, running, ran, run**)
1 correr
We ran as fast as possible to catch the train. ◆ I run 3 kilometers every day.
2 passar
The buses on this line run every five minutes.
3 funcionar
The engine is running.
4 gerenciar, dirigir
Who runs the business?
5 candidatar-se
He decided to run for president.
6 escorrer
You left the water / tap running.

7 seguir
The road runs up the hill.
8 passar
She ran her fingers through her hair.
9 ficar em cartaz
The play ran for nine months.
10 rodar
We are running the new program on the computer.
11 desbotar
When I washed the dress the colours ran.
run across (= meet by chance) □ **encontrar por acaso, topar com**
I ran across them yesterday.
run after □ **correr atrás**
I ran after the thief. ♦ He ran after the ball.
run away □ **fugir**
She ran away from home for two days. ♦ When he saw the police he ran away.
■ Ver **escape**.
run into someone (= run across) □ **dar com, topar com**
I ran into her in New York.
run into something □ **passar por algo / alguma coisa**
They ran into difficulties / trouble.
run on □ **ser movido a**
This car runs on electricity. ♦ This TV runs on batteries.
run out (of) □ **ficar sem**
Time is running out. ♦ We are running out of money.
run over
1 atropelar
A bus ran over our dog. ♦ She was almost run over by a car.
2 revisar
I had five minutes to run over my speech.
run through □ **recapitular**
He ran through the numbers in the report.
run-down ['rʌn 'daun] *adj*. (= in bad condition) □ **em péssimo estado**
The building is very run-down and needs immediate repair. ♦ a run-down old car.
rung[1] [rʌŋ] *v*. (Ver **ring**).
rung[2] *n*. □ **degrau**
I couldn't climb the ladder because three rungs were broken.
runner ['rʌnə] *n*. □ **corredores**
Six runners took part in the race.
runner-up [,rʌnə'rʌp] *n*. □ **segundo colocado**
The runner-up in the beauty contest was Miss Australia.
running[1] ['rʌniŋ] *n*. □ **corrida**
I like running and swimming. ♦ running shoes.

running[2] *adv*. □ **consecutivo**
Our team won the cup for four years running.
runway ['rʌnwei] *n*. □ **pista**
Planes take off and land on runways.
rural ['ruərəl] *adj*. □ **rural**
rural life.
■ Compare **urban**:
urban = of a city.
rush[1] [rʌʃ] *n*.
1 corrida
There was a rush for the door when the bell rang.
2 pressa
What's the rush?
be in a rush □ **estar com pressa**
I can't talk now – I'm in a rush.
there's no rush □ **não há pressa**
There's no rush! You can finish your breakfast.
the rush hour □ **hora do rush**
Traffic is heavy during the rush hour.
rush[2] *v*. (**rushes, rushing, rushed**)
1 apressar-se, correr
Don't rush – there's plenty of time. ♦ The children rushed into the classroom.
2 apressar
Don't rush me! I need time to think.
3 apressar
She was rushed to hospital (= to the hospital). *Amer*.
rust[1] [rʌst] *n*. □ **ferrugem**
There was rust all over the car.
rust[2] *v*. (**rusts, rusting, rusted**) □ **enferrujar**
Your bicycle will rust if you leave it out in the rain.
rustle[1] ['rʌsl] *n*. □ **farfalhada**
the rustle of leaves.
rustle[2] *v*. (**rustles, rustling, rustled**) □ **farfalhar**
Her dress rustled when she walked. ♦ It annoys me when he rustles his newspaper.
rusty ['rʌsti] *adj*. (**rustier, rustiest**) □ **enferrujado**
a rusty knife.
ruthless ['ru:θlis] *adj*. □ **impiedoso**
a ruthless ruler.
ruthlessly ['ru:θlisli] *adv*. □ **impiedosamente**
The army put down the revolt ruthlessly.
ruthlessness ['ru:θlisnis] *n*. □ **crueldade, desumanidade**
rye [rai] *n*. □ **centeio**
rye bread.

Ss

S *abbr.*
1 (= South) **S**
2 (= small size clothes) **P**

's *abbr.*
1 indica posse
John's car. ♦ the horse's mouth. ♦ men's clothes.
2 (= is; has)
It's here. (= It is here.) ♦ He's gone. (= He has gone.)

sabbath ['sabəθ] *n.* □ **sábado**
the Sabbath □ **o Sabá**
Friday is the Sabbath (day) for Moslems, Saturday for Jews, and Sunday for Christians.

sack¹ [sak] *n.* □ **saco**
a sack of potatoes.

sack² *v.* (**sacks, sacking, sacked**) (= fire, dismiss) □ **despedir, demitir**
The boss sacked the secretary.

sack³ *n.*
get the sack □ **ser demitido**
She got the sack for stealing.
give someone the sack □ **demitir alguém**
He was given the sack. ♦ His boss gave him the sack.

sacred ['seikrid] *adj.* □ **sagrado**
to visit the sacred places in Jerusalem. ♦ sacred writings (e.g. the Bible, the Koran).
■ Ver **holy**.

sacrifice¹ ['sakrifais] *n.*
1 sacrifício
They killed a lamb as a sacrifice.
2 sacrifício
His parents made big sacrifices to give him a university education.

sacrifice² *v.* (**sacrifices, sacrificing, sacrificed**)
1 sacrificar
They sacrificed animals to their gods.
2 sacrificar
They sacrificed their lives to defend their country.

sad [sad] *adj.* (**sadder, saddest**)
1 (= unhappy) **triste**
He is sad because his cat died.
2 triste
a sad story / film. ♦ It's sad to see so many poor people.

saddle¹ ['sadl] *n.* □ **sela, selim**
to put the saddle on the horse. ♦ a bicycle saddle.

saddle² *v.* (**saddles, saddling, saddled**) □ **selar**
to saddle (up) the horse.

sadly ['sadli] *adv.* □ **tristemente**
'We never saw him again', she said sadly.

sadness ['sadnis] *n.* (= unhappiness) □ **tristeza**

safe¹ [seif] *adj.*
1 seguro
Don't worry about them. They are in a safe place. ♦ I feel safe in this town. ♦ They are safe from danger.
2 seguro
Keep a safe distance from the car in front of you. ♦ This toy is safe for little children.
3 seguro
a safe journey.
4 cauteloso, cuidadoso
a safe driver.
safe and sound □ **são e salvo**
They were found safe and sound.

safe² *n.* □ **cofre**
They keep the jewels in a safe.

safely ['seifli] *adv.* □ **com segurança, a salvo**
The plane landed safely.

safety ['seifti] *n.* □ **segurança**
We are worried about the safety of the passengers. ♦ road safety.
■ Compare **security**:
security = for defence / defense, protection.

safety belt ['seiftibelt] *n.* (= **seat-belt**) □ **cinto de segurança**
Put on your safety belt before you start driving.

safety measures ['seifti 'meʒəz] *n. pl.* □ **medidas de segurança**
They took safety measures to prevent another accident.

safety pin ['seifti pin] *n.* □ **alfinete de segurança**

safety precautions ['seifti priˈkoːʃənz] *n. pl.* □ **precauções de segurança**
We took safety precautions to prevent a fire.

sag [sag] *v.* (**sags, sagging, sagged**) □ **ceder, vergar**
I put so many books on the shelf that it sagged.

said [sed] *v.* (Ver **say**).

sail¹ [seil] *n.*
1 vela
The sails help to increase the boat's speed when there is a wind.
2 passeio em barco à vela
to go for a sail.

sail² *v.* (**sails, sailing, sailed**)
1 navegar, velejar
The boat sailed down the river. ♦ We sailed around the world on a big ship.
2 (= **set sail**) **zarpar, içar velas**
The ship will sail at 2 o'clock. ♦ We sail for Cyprus tomorrow morning.
3 velejar
He learnt to sail (a sailing boat). ♦ I sailed the boat along the river.
go sailing □ **ir velejar**
We went sailing on the lake.

sailboard ['seilbo:d] *n.* □ **prancha de windsurfe**

sailboat ['seilbout] *n.* Amer., **sailing boat** Brit. □ **veleiro**

sailing ['seiliŋ] *n.*
1 nevegação à vela
a sailing club. ♦ I love sailing.
2 ato de zarpar
The time of sailing is 3 o'clock.

sailor ['seilə] *n.*
1 marinheiro, marujo
He is a sailor in the navy. ♦ The sailors on the ship were pirates.
2 velejador
The Australian sailor won the gold medal.

saint [seint] *n.* □ **são, santo**
Saint Peter (= St. Peter). ♦ St. Paul's Cathedral.
■ The short form **St.** is usually used with names.

sake [seik] *n.*
for the sake of □ **em consideração a**

Stay out of trouble for the sake of your parents. ♦ Don't do it for my sake.
for God's sake, for Heaven's sake ▫ **pelo amor de Deus**
For God's sake, stop that noise!
salad ['saləd] *n.* ▫ **salada**
to make a mixed salad (with all kinds of vegetables). ♦ chicken salad (= chicken with salad).
salary ['saləri] *n.* (*pl.* **salaries**) ▫ **salário**
He has a salary of $2,000 a month. ♦ a high salary.
■ Compare with **wages and pay**:
wages = weekly.
salary = monthly.
The general word is pay: What's the pay for the job?
sale [seil] *n.*
1 venda
Sales of computers will go up next year. ♦ The sale of guns to the public is legal in some countries.
2 liquidação
an end-of-season sale. ♦ I bought this dress in a sale (= on sale, *Amer.*).
for sale ▫ **à venda**
This car is not for sale.
on sale
1 *Amer.* **em promoção, em liquidação**
These shirts are on sale. I bought two for $15. ♦ I got it on sale for only $10.
2 à venda
The book is on sale now. (= It is in the shops now.)
sales assistant ['seilz ə'sistənt] *n. Brit.* (**mesmo que sales clerk**, *Amer.*) ▫ **vendedor, balconista**
'Can I help you?', asked the sales clerk. ♦ She works as a sales assistant in a department store.
■ *Brit.* also **shop assistant**
salesman ['seilzmən] *n.* (*pl.* **salesmen**) ▫ **vendedor**
salesperson ['seilz,pə:sən] *n.* (= **salesman; saleswoman**) ▫ **vendedor**
a computer salesperson.
saleswoman ['seilz,wumən] *n.* (*pl.* **saleswomen**) ▫ **vendedora**
salmon ['samən] *n.* ▫ **salmão**
salt [so:lt] *n.* ▫ **sal**
Pass the salt, please. ♦ The soup needs a little more salt.
salted ['so:ltid] *adj.* ▫ **salgado**
salted peanuts. ♦ salted butter.
salty ['so:lti] *adj.* (**saltier, saltiest**) ▫ **salgado**
The soup is too salty for me.
salute[1] [sə'lu:t] *n.* ▫ **continência**
The soldier raised the flag and gave a salute.
salute[2] *v.* (**salutes, saluting, saluted**) ▫ **bater continência**
The soldiers saluted their officer.
same [seim] *adj., pron.*
the same ▫ **o mesmo**
She has the same eyes as mine. ♦ They work in the same place. ♦ We feel the same. ♦ These pens are all the same.
all the same, just the same (= nevertheless) ▫ **mesmo assim, apesar de tudo**
I knew I couldn't win. All the same, I decided to try.
at the same time
1 ao mesmo tempo
Don't all speak at the same time. ♦ She can work and listen at the same time.

2 ao mesmo tempo
Our teacher is firm with us, but at the same time he is very patient.
the same to you ▫ **o mesmo para você, igualmente**
Have a nice Day! – The same to you! ♦ You're an idiot! – The same to you.
sample ['sa:mpl] *n.*
1 amostra
a free sample of shampoo.
2 amostra
a blood sample.
3 amostra
He is a good photographer. I saw samples of his work.
4 amostragem
a sample of the voters.
sand [sand] *n.* ▫ **areia**
a heap of sand. ♦ They are playing in the sand.
sandal ['sandl] *n.* ▫ **sandália**
He usually wears sandals in the summer.
sandpaper ['sandpeipə] *n.* ▫ **lixa**
sandwich ['sanwitʒ] *n.* ▫ **sanduíche**
a cheese sandwich.
sandy ['sandi] *adj.* (**sandier, sandiest**) ▫ **arenoso**
a sandy beach. ♦ sandy soil.
sane [sein] *adj.* ▫ **são**
The doctor said that the murderer was not sane.
■ antônimo: **insane**
sang [saŋ] *v.* (Ver **sing**).
sank [saŋk] *v.* (Ver **sink**).
Santa Claus ['santə 'klo:z] *n.* (= Father Christmas) ▫ **Papai Noel**
sarcastic [sa:'kastik] *adj.* ▫ **sarcástico**
a sarcastic remark.
sarcastically [sa:'kastikəli] *adv.* ▫ **sarcasticamente**
sardine [sa:'di:n] *n.* ▫ **sardinha**
a tin of sardines.
sat [sat] *v.* (Ver **sit**).
satchel ['satʃəl] *n.* ▫ **sacola**
They carry their satchels on their backs when they go to school.
satellite ['satəlait] *n.* ▫ **satélite**
They sent a spy satellite into space. ♦ a communications satellite. ♦ a satellite dish to receive satellite TV.
satin ['satin] *n.* ▫ **cetim**
satisfaction [,satis'fakʃən] *n.* ▫ **satisfação**
The agreement was to everyone's satisfaction. ♦ The success of my book gives me great satisfaction.
■ antônimo: **dissatisfaction**
satisfactory [,satis'faktəri] *adj.* ▫ **satisfatório**
Your progress in school is very satisfactory. ♦ We found a satisfactory solution to the problem.
■ antônimo: **unsatisfactory**
satisfied ['satisfaid] *adj.* ▫ **satisfeito**
satisfied customers
■ antônimo: **dissatisfied**
be satisfied (with) (= **estar satisfeito (com)**
I'm not satisfied with the results.
satisfy ['satisfai] *v.* (**satisfies, satisfying, satisfied**) ▫ **satisfazer**
Her answers to my questions satisfied me.
satisfying ['satisfaiiŋ] *adj.* ▫ **satisfatório**
a satisfying result.

Saturday ['satədei] *n.* □ **sábado**
I'll visit them on Saturday. ◆ She is coming next Saturday.
sauce [so:s] *n.* □ **molho**
tomato sauce.
saucepan ['so:spən] *n.* □ **caçarola**
Boil the rice in a saucepan for 15 minutes.
saucer ['so:sə] *n.* □ **pires**
a cup and saucer.
sausage ['sosidʒ] *n.* □ **salsicha**
I like hot sausages with mustard.
■ Ver **hot dog**.
savage ['savidʒ] *adj.*, *n.* □ **feroz, selvagem**
a savage dog. ◆ a savage attack by a wolf. ◆ He is a savage – he behaves very cruelly.
savagely ['savidʒli] *adv.* □ **ferozmente, selvagemente**
The wild animal fell savagely on its prey.
save [seiv] *v.* (**saves, saving, saved**)
1 salvar
They saved him from drowning. ◆ He saved my life.
■ Ver **rescue**.
2 guardar, economizar
to save money in the bank. ◆ I'm saving (up) for a new car.
3 poupar
This refrigerator saves electricity. ◆ Thanks for your help – you saved me a lot of trouble.
4 guardar
I saved all your pictures in my album.
5 evitar
The goalkeeper saved a goal.
savings ['seiviŋz] *n.* □ **economias**
I spent all my savings on the bicycle.
savings account ['seiviŋz ə'kaunt] *n.* □ **conta poupança**
I have $500 in my savings account.
saw[1] [so:] *v.* (Ver **see**).
saw[2] *n.* □ **serra**
a hand saw.
saw[3] *v.* (**saws, sawing, sawed** or **sawn**) □ **serrar**
I sawed the wood to make shelves.
sawdust ['so:dʌst] *n.* □ **serragem, pó de serra**
saxophone ['saksəfoun] *n.* □ **saxofone**
He plays the saxophone.
say[1] [sei] *n.*
have a say □ **dar uma opinião**
We all have a say in the planning of the trip.
have your say □ **ter a sua vez, dar a sua opinião**
Let him have his say.
say[2] *v.* (**says, saying, said**)
1 dizer, falar
'It's nice', she said. ◆ He said (that) we could wait here. ◆ She listened without saying anything.
■ Compare with **tell**:
"tell" is not followed by to: What did you say to him? What did you tell him?
"tell" must always be followed by 'me', 'her', 'him', 'them', etc.
"say" cannot be used when giving orders or advice: He told me to go. Tell her to come.
2 dizer
The notice says 'No Parking'. ◆ The clock says it's 5 o'clock.
3 (= let's say) **digamos**
We will finish the job in, (let's) say, two weeks.

that is to say □ **ou seja**
Come and see me on May 4, that is to say next Tuesday.
saying ['seiiŋ] *n.* □ **ditado**
scaffolding ['skafəldiŋ] *n.* □ **andaime**
scald[1] [sko:ld] *v.* (**scalds, scalding, scalded**) □ **escaldar**
He scalded his hand with boiling water.
scald[2] *n.* □ **escaldadura**
scale [skeil] *n.*
1 escala
The scale on this ruler is in centimeters.
2 balança
a kitchen scale.
■ Ver **scales**.
3 escala
On a scale of 1 to 10, I give the film an 8.
4 escala
What scale is this map? – 1:20,000 (one centimeter to twenty thousand).
5 escama
to scrape the scales from the fish. ◆ the scales of a snake.
on a large scale, large-scale □ **em larga escala, em grande escala**
They make this product on a large scale. ◆ a large-scale research.
on a small scale, small-scale □ **em pequena escala, em menor escala**
a small-scale experiment.
scales [skeilz] *n. Brit.,* **scale** *Amer.* □ **balança**
kitchen scale(s). ◆ bathroom scale(s).
scalp [skalp] *n.* □ **escalpo**
scan [skan] *v.* (**scans, scanning, scanned**)
1 esquadrinhar
The sailors scanned the horizon for any sign of land.
2 escanear
Scan the article and mark the key words.
3 escanear
to scan the body (with a scanner). ◆ He scanned the document and sent it by email.
scandal ['skandl] *n.* □ **escândalo**
There was a big scandal when they arrested the diplomat.
scanner ['skanə] *n.* □ **scanner**
a laser scanner. ◆ to scan the brain with a scanner. ◆ You can send data by email by means of a scanner.
scar[1] [ska:] *n.* □ **cicatriz**
He has a scar on his face.
scar[2] *v.* (**scars, scarring, scarred**) □ **marcar com cicatriz**
The cut may scar your chin.
scarce [skeəs] *adj.* □ **escasso**
Food was scarce during the war. ◆ Jobs are scarce in this town.
scarcely ['skeəsli] *adv.* (= hardly) □ **mal**
I could scarcely hear anything with all that noise.
scarcity ['skeəsiti] *n.* □ **falta, escassez, carência**
a scarcity of jobs / food.
scare[1] [skeə] *n.* □ **susto**
give someone a scare □ **dar um susto em alguém**
You gave me a scare! Why didn't you knock?
scare[2] *v.* (**scares, scaring, scared**)
1 (= frighten) **assustar, amedrontar**
The thunder scared them.
2 assustar-se, amedrontar-se
He doesn't scare easily.

scared *adj.* □ **amedrontado**
The first time I tried to ski I was really scared. ◆ I'm not scared (= afraid) of the dark.

scarecrow ['skeəkrou] *n.* □ **espantalho**

scarf [ska:f] *n.* (*pl.* **scarves**)
1 cachecol
Wrap a scarf around your neck. It's cold outside.
2 cachecol, lenço
a headscarf. ◆ She tied a silk scarf around her neck.

scarlet ['ska:lit] *adj.*, *n.* □ **escarlate**

scatter ['skatə] *v.* (**scatters, scattering, scattered**)
1 dispersar
They scattered in all directions when the police came.
■ Ver **disperse**.
2 espalhar
The wind scattered pieces of paper everywhere.
■ Ver **spread**.

scene [si:n] *n.*
1 local
the scene of the crime / accident.
2 cena
There was a scene when they asked him to leave.
3 cena
They get married in the last scene of the film. ◆ It happens in Act III, Scene 2 of the play.
4 cena
There were scenes of great joy in the streets.
5 cena
He painted scenes from village life.

scenery ['si:nəri] *n.*
1 cenário
the beautiful mountain scenery of Scotland.
■ Ver **landscape; view**.
2 cenário
They changed the scenery in each scene of the play.

scent [sent] *n.*
1 aroma
I like the scent of roses.
2 (= perfume) **perfume**
a bottle of scent.
3 odor, rastro
The dogs followed the scent of the foxes.

scented [centeds *adj.* □ **perfumado, aromatizado**
scented soap.

schedule¹ ['ʃedju:l] *n.*
1 agenda
The manager can't see you today, because he has a busy schedule.
2 *Amer.* **horário**
a train schedule. ◆ an airline schedule.
■ *Brit.* **timetable**
behind schedule □ **atrasado**
We are behind schedule with the project.
on schedule □ **dentro do prazo**
We can finish the work on schedule.

schedule² *v.* (**schedules, scheduling, scheduled**) □ **agendar, marcar**
to schedule the meeting for tomorrow.

scheme¹ [ski:m] *n.* (= plan) □ **trama, esquema**

scheme² *v.* (**schemes, scheming, schemed**) □ **tramar, maquinar**
They schemed against him.

scholar ['skolə] *n.* □ **erudito**
a history scholar.

scholarship ['skoləʃip] *n.* □ **bolsa de estudo**
She won a scholarship to the university.

school [sku:l] *n.*
1 escola
I usually go to school by bus. ◆ a driving school.
2 aula
What time do you start school? ◆ There's no school tomorrow.
3 (= college, university) *Amer.* □ **faculdade, universidade**
Where did you go to school? – New York State University.
■ Ver **elementary school; primary school; high school; secondary school**.

schoolbag ['sku:lbag] *n.* □ **mochila escolar**

schoolboy ['sku:lboi] *n.* □ **aluno**

schoolchildren ['sku:l,tʃildrən] *n.* □ **alunos**

schooldays ['sku:ldeiz] *n.* □ **tempo de escola**
They have happy memories of their schooldays.

schoolgirl ['sku:lgə:l] *n.* □ **aluna**

schooling ['sku:liŋ] *n.* (= years in school) □ **instrução, ensino**
He had ten years schooling.

schoolmaster ['sku:l,ma:stə] *n.* □ **diretor de escola**

schoolmistress ['sku:l,mistris] *n.* □ **diretora de escola**

schoolteacher ['sku:l,ti:tʃə] *n.* □ **professor**

school uniform ['sku:l 'ju:nifo:m] *n.* □ **uniforme escolar**
In this school pupils wear school uniform.

science ['saiəns] *n.* □ **ciência**
The government must invest more money in science and technology. ◆ Biology, chemistry and physics are all sciences. ◆ a science teacher. ◆ a science lab.

science fiction ['saiəns 'fikʃən] *n.*, *adj.* □ **ficção científica**
I read mainly science-fiction. ◆ a science-fiction film.
■ abreviação: **sci-fi**

scientific [,saiən'tifik] *adj.* □ **científico**
a scientific experiment. ◆ scientific research.

scientifically [,saiən'tifikli] *adv.* □ **cientificamente**
to prove the theory scientifically.

scientist ['saiəntist] *n.* □ **cientista**

sci-fi ['sai fai] *n.* (= **science fiction**).

scissors ['sizəz] *n.* □ **tesoura**
Cut it with your scissors. ◆ a pair of scissors. ◆ These scissors are very sharp.

scold [skould] *v.* (**scolds, scolding, scolded**) (= tell off) □ **repreender, dar bronca**
The teacher scolded us for coming late.

scoop¹ [sku:p] *n.*
1 concha de medida
He used a scoop to take rice out of the sack.
2 bola
three scoops of ice-cream.
3 furo
How did the newspaper get the scoop?

scoop² *v.* (**scoops, scooping, scooped**) □ **tirar com concha de medida**
I scooped out some ice-cream.

scooter ['sku:tə] *n.*
1 lambreta
You must wear a crash-helmet when you ride a scooter.
2 patinete
Children were riding their scooters in the playground.

score¹ [skoː] *n.*
1 placar
The score was 1-1 at half time.
2 nota
The average score in the test was 70%.
scores of □ **muitos, grande número de**
scores of people. ◆ scores of times.
score² *v.* (**scores, scoring, scored**)
1 pontuar, marcar (pontos, gols etc.)
He scored two goals. ◆ She scored 24 points.
2 pontuar, tirar
I scored the highest mark in the exam.
scorn¹ [skoːn] *n.* (= contempt) □ **escárnio**
She looked at him with scorn in her eyes.
scorn² *v.* (**scorns, scorning, scorned**) □ **desdenhar, desprezar**
They scorned him / his ideas.
scornful ['skoːnful] *adj.* □ **desdenhoso**
a scornful smile.
scorpion ['skoːpiən] *n.* □ **escorpião**
Scotch tape™ ['skotʃteip] *n. Amer.* □ **fita adesiva**
Put some Scotch tape across the torn page.
■ *Brit.* **Sellotape™**
Scout [skaut] *n.* (= **Boy Scout**) □ **escoteiro**
scramble ['skrambl] *v.* (**scrambles, scrambling, scrambled**) □ **escalar com dificuldade**
He scrambled over the wall.
scrambled egg(s) ['skrambld eg(z)] *n.* □ **ovo(s) mexido(s)**
scrap [skrap] *n.*
1 pedaço
a scrap of paper / cloth.
2 sucata
to sell a car for scrap.
scraps *n. pl.* □ **restos**
I gave the scraps to the dog.
scrape [skreip] *v.* (**scrapes, scraping, scraped**)
1 raspar
to scrape the paint off the wall. ◆ Scrape the mud off your shoes!
2 ralar
He fell and scraped his knee.
scratch¹ [skratʃ] *v.* (**scratches, scratching, scratched**)
1 coçar
The monkey scratched its head.
2 arranhar
Be careful! The cat may scratch you.
scratch² *n.* □ **arranhão**
There's a scratch on my car. ◆ His skin was covered with scratches from the bushes.
start from scratch □ **começar do zero**
She threw the letter in the basket and started from scratch. ◆ He started the business from scratch.
scream¹ [skriːm] *n.* □ **grito**
a scream of pain.
scream² *v.* (**screams, screaming, screamed**) □ **gritar**
He screamed with pain. ◆ They screamed for help. ◆ Stop screaming! It's only a spider.
screech¹ [skriːtʃ] *v.* (**screeches, screeching, screeched**) □ **ranger, guinchar**
The brakes screeched as the bus stopped.
■ Ver **creak**; **squeak**.
screech² *n.* □ **rangido, guincho**

The car stopped with a screech of the brakes. ◆ a screech of tyres.
screen¹ [skriːn] *n.*
1 tela
a television screen. ◆ a computer screen. ◆ a 21-inch screen.
2 telão
The screen in our classroom is used for showing slides.
3 biombo
The nurse put a screen around the patient's bed.
screen² *v.* (**screens, screening, screened**) □ **exibir**
They will screen the programme tonight (on television).
screw¹ [skruː] *n.* □ **parafuso**
to tighten a screw (with a screwdriver). ◆ to loosen a screw.
screw² *v.* (**screws, screwing, screwed**)
1 parafusar
I screwed the shelf to the wall.
2 rosquear
to screw the lid on the jar ◆ to screw a light-bulb in.
screwdriver ['skruːdraivə] *n.* □ **chave de fenda**
Use this screwdriver to loosen the screws.
scribble¹ ['skribl] *n.* □ **garrancho**
His signature is just a scribble. I can't read it.
scribble² *v.* (**scribbles, scribbling, scribbled**)
1 rabiscar
The doctor scribbled something on the prescription. ◆ to scribble a note.
2 rabiscar
My little brother scribbled all over the book.
script [skript] *n.* □ **script, roteiro**
the script of a play, film, etc.
scripture ['skriptʃə] *n.* (mesmo que **the scriptures**) □ **escritura**
scroll¹ [skroul] *n.* □ **pergaminho**
scrolls from ancient times
scroll² *v.* (**scrolls, scrolling, scrolled**) □ **rolar texto na tela do computador**
to scroll up / down the page ◆ to scroll to the left
scrub [skrʌb] *v.* (**scrubs, scrubbing, scrubbed**) □ **esfregar**
to scrub the floor
sculptor ['skʌlptə] *n.* □ **escultor**
sculpture ['skʌlptʃə] *n.* □ **escultura**
Sculpture is the art of making figures and shapes out of stone, wood, metal, etc. ◆ You can see her sculptures at the museum. ◆ a bronze sculpture.
■ A **statue** is a figure of a person or animal.
sea [siː] *n.* □ **mar**
to go for a swim in the sea. ◆ We live by the sea. ◆ the Mediterranean Sea.
at sea □ **em alto-mar**
They were three days at sea without food.
by sea □ **por mar**
We went there by sea.
seafood ['siːfuːd] *n.* □ **frutos do mar**
seagull ['siːgʌl] *n.* □ **gaivota**
seal¹ [siːl] *n.* □ **foca**
They want to stop the hunting of seals.
seal² *n.* □ **selo, lacre**
seal³ *v.* (**seals, sealing, sealed**)
1 selar

He sealed the envelope.
2 vedar
to seal a window, a container, etc.

seam [si:m] *n.* □ **bainha**

search[1] [sə:tʃ] *n.* □ **busca**
After a long search, they found the stolen car.
in search of □ **à procura de**
They went in search of the missing child.

search[2] *v.* (**searches, searching, searched**) □ **vasculhar, revistar**
The police searched his house. ◆ They searched him to see if he had drugs on him.
search for (= look for) □ **procurar**
They are searching for the missing child.

sea shell ['si: ʃel] *n.* □ **concha**

seashore ['si:ʃo:] *n.* □ **praia, litoral**
The children found some sea shells on the seashore.
■ Ver **beach**; **coast**.

seasick ['si:sik] *n.* □ **mareado**

seaside ['si:said] *n., adj.* □ **litoral**
We spent a week by the seaside. ◆ a seaside town.

season ['si:zn] *n.* □ **estação, temporada**
The four seasons of the year are spring, summer, autumn (or fall) and winter. ◆ the fishing season. ◆ the holiday season.

season ticket ['si:zn 'tikit] *n.* □ **bilhetes para a temporada**
a monthly season ticket for all bus lines. ◆ a season ticket for the Opera.

seat[1] [si:t] *n.* □ **assento, lugar**
We sat in the back seat (of the car). ◆ There are 1,000 seats in this theatre.
take a seat □ **sentar-se**
Please take a seat. (= Please sit down.)

seat[2] *v.* (**seats, seating, seated**)
1 acomodar
The hall seats 800 people.
2 reservar assento
He seated me next to his sister.
please be seated □ **por favor, sente-se**

seat-belt ['si:tbelt] *n.* (= **safety belt**) □ **cinto de segurança**
Please fasten your seat-belts. We are landing. ◆ Both drivers and passengers must wear seat-belts.

seaweed ['si:wi:d] *n.* □ **alga marinha**

second[1] ['sekənd] *adj., adv., pron.* □ **segundo**
February is the second month of the year. ◆ I finished second (= in second place) in the race. ◆ You are second on the list.
the second □ **o segundo, o segundo dia**
I'm the second of four children. ◆ the second of June (= 2nd June) ◆ She was the second to arrive.

second[2] *adv.* (Ver **secondly**).

second[3] *n.*
1 segundo
There are sixty seconds in a minute. ◆ She ran 100 meters in 11 seconds.
2 um segundo
Wait a second!
3 de segunda mão, usado
The clothes are cheap because they are seconds.

secondary ['sekəndəri] *adj.*
1 secundário
a matter of secondary importance
2 de segundo grau
secondary education

secondary school ['sekəndəri sku:l] *n. Brit.* □ **ensino médio**
■ *Amer.* **high school**

second-best [,sekənd'best] *adj.* □ **o segundo melhor**
the second-best result.

second class [sekənd kla:s] *n., adv.* □ **segunda classe, de segunda classe**
I usually travel (in) second class.

second-class [,sekənd'kla:s] *adj.*
1 de segunda classe
a second-class ticket.
2 de segunda classe
They feel like second-class citizens. ◆ second-class hotels.

second floor ['sekənd flo:] *n.*
1 *Brit.* primeiro andar
I live on the second floor.
2 *Amer.* segundo andar

second-hand [,sekənd'hand] *adj., adv. Brit.* □ **de segunda mão, usado**
a second-hand car. ◆ I bought the books second-hand.
■ *Amer.* **used**

secondly ['sekəndli] *adv.* (= **second**) □ **em segundo lugar**
Firstly, it's expensive, and secondly, we have two cameras already.

second person [,sekənd 'pə:sn] *n.*
the second person (grammar) □ **a segunda pessoa**
'You' is the second person pronoun.

second-rate [,sekənd'reit] *adj.* □ **de segunda (classe), inferior**
a second-rate player / film.

secrecy ['si:krəsi] *n.* □ **sigilo, reserva, segredo**

secret[1] ['si:krit] *adj.* □ **secreto**
They had secret talks / meetings. ◆ I hid it in a secret place.
keep something secret □ **manter algo em segredo**
They kept their plan secret.
secret agent *n.* □ **agente secreto**
the Secret Service *n.* □ **o Serviço Secreto**

secret[2] *n.* □ **segredo**
I can't tell you where – it's a secret. ◆ You can tell me. I can keep a secret. ◆ We have no secrets from each other.
in secret □ **em segredo, secretamente**
They meet in secret.

secretly *adv.* □ **secretamente**
The two leaders met secretly last week.

secretarial [,sekrə'teəriəl] *adj.* □ **secretariado**
secretarial work ◆ a secretarial college

secretary ['sekrətəri] *n.* (*pl.* **secretaries**)
1 secretário
A secretary types letters, answers the phone, arranges meetings, etc. ◆ a personal secretary.
2 *Amer.* secretário, ministro
the Secretary of Education.
■ *Brit.* **minister**
Secretary of State *n.*
1 *Brit.* Secretário de Estado
the Secretary of State for Education.
2 *Amer.* Secretário de Estado
The Secretary of State will meet today with the British Prime Minister.

secretive ['si:kritiv] *adj.* □ **reservado**
He is a very secretive person. ◆ She is secretive about her plans.
secretly ['si:kritli] *adv.* □ **secretamente**
They listened secretly to his telephone calls.
section ['sekʃən] *n.*
1 seção
the sports section (of the newspaper).
2 parte
This section of the road is very dangerous. ◆ The book is divided into three sections.
3 parte
to put together the sections of a model airplane.
4 setor
There is a special section for smokers in this restaurant.
sector ['sektə] *n.* □ **setor**
the public sector.
secular ['sekjulə] *adj.* □ **secular**
secure[1] [si'kjuə] *adj.*
1 seguro
They feel secure about the future of the company.
■ antônimo: **insecure**
2 seguro
Are the banks secure against robbery?
3 seguro
Be careful! This ladder is not very secure (= safe).
4 seguro
a secure job. ◆ a secure investment.
5 protegido
Make sure that the doors are secure.
secure[2] *v.* (**secures, securing, secured**) □ **guardar, proteger**
A large number of guards secured the building well.
security [si'kjuəriti] *n.*
1 segurança
We must improve security at the airport. ◆ the security forces (= the police, the army, etc).
■ Ver **safety; defence**.
2 segurança
Loving parents give their children a feeling of security.
■ antônimo: **insecurity**
■ Compare with **safety**:
safety = against danger from accidents, etc.
security = for protection, defence / defense.
security guard [si'kjuəriti ga:d] *n.* □ **guarda de segurança**
see [si:] *v.* (**sees, seeing, saw, seen**)
1 ver
I can't see clearly without my glasses. ◆ Look over there! Can you see that car? ◆ I saw what happened. ◆ Let me see the letter.
■ *No* [be + -ing]. Do *not* say 'I am / was seeing', etc.
2 ver
I saw (= watched) the concert on television last night. ◆ I've already seen that film.
■ *No* [be + -ing]. Do *not* say 'I am / was seeing', etc.
3 (= meet) **ver**
I'm seeing him tomorrow. ◆ I'll see you after school.
4 ver
You should see a doctor about your headaches. ◆ I went to see (= visit) her in hospital.
5 atender
The manager can't see you now.
6 (= understand) **entender, compreender**
I see what you mean. ◆ Open it like this. – I see.
7 ver
I'll see what I can do for you.
8 ver
Please see that everything is ready.
9 levar, acompanhar
My son will see you home.
I'll see, We'll see □ **vou ver, vamos ver**
Can I take the car tomorrow, Mum? – I'll see.
see about □ **ver**
When will you send it? – I'll see about it tomorrow.
see for yourself □ **ver você mesmo**
If you don't believe me, go and see for yourself.
see someone off □ **ver alguém partir**
They went to the airport to see their son off.
see through □ **perceber**
He didn't deceive me. I saw through him immediately.
see to □ **cuidar, tomar conta**
You see to the baby and I'll see to the dinner.
see you (later) (mesmo que **cheerio, see you soon, be seeing you**) □ **até mais tarde!, até mais!, até logo!**
seed [si:d] *n.* □ **semente**
to sow seeds. ◆ sunflower seeds.
seeing ['si:iŋ] *conj.* (mesmo que **seeing that; seeing as**) □ **visto que, considerando que**
Seeing that he is late, we'll start without him.
seek [si:k] *v.* (**seeks, seeking, sought**) (= look for) □ **buscar, procurar**
to seek a solution to a problem. ◆ to seek help.
seem [si:m] *v.* (**seems, seeming, seemed**) □ **parecer**
He seems like a very intelligent boy. ◆ She seems to like you. ◆ It seems to me that you need help.
seen [si:n] *v.* (Ver **see**).
seep [si:p] *v.* (**seeps, seeping, seeped**) □ **verter**
Water started seeping from the ground.
see-saw ['si:so:] *n.* □ **gangorra**
seize [si:z] *v.* (**seizes, seizing, seized**) □ **agarrar, pegar com força**
He seized me by the arm.
seizure ['si:ʒə] *n.* □ **apreensão**
the seizure of 50 kilos of drugs by the police.
seldom ['seldəm] *adv.* □ **raramente**
I seldom go there nowadays. ◆ She is seldom at home.
■ antônimo: **often**
■ Ver **rarely**.
select [sə'lekt] *v.* (**selects, selecting, selected**) (= choose carefully) □ **selecionar**
The coach selected the best players among the students.
selection [sə'lekʃən] *n.*
1 seleção
the selection of players for the team.
2 seleção
This shop has a good selection of gifts.
self- [self-] *pref.* **auto-**
self-control. ◆ self-educated.
self-confidence [,self'kɒnfidəns] *n.* □ **autoconfiança**
He doesn't have the self-confidence to tell them what he thinks.
self-confident [,self'kɒnfidənt] *adj.* □ **autoconfiante**
a self-confident person. ◆ She looks very self-confident.
self-confidently [,self'kɒnfidəntli] *adv.* □ **com autoconfiança**

self-conscious [self'kɔnʃəs] *adj.* □ **acanhado, tímido**
He feels very self-conscious about his appearance.

self-control [selfkən'troul] *n.* □ **autocontrole**
She lost her self-control and shouted angrily at them.

self-defence [selfdi'fens] *Brit.*, **self-defense** *Amer.* □ **auto-defesa, defesa própria**
He killed a man in self-defence.

self-employed [selfim'plɔid] *adj.* □ **autônomo**
Last year he was a worker in a factory, but now he is self-employed.

selfish ['selfiʃ] *adj.* □ **egoísta**
Don't be so selfish! ◆ selfish habits.
■ antônimo: **unselfish**

selfishly ['selfiʃli] *adv.* □ **egoisticamente**
to behave selfishly.
■ antônimo: **unselfishly**

selfishness ['selfiʃnis] *n.* □ **egoísmo**

self-respect [selfri'spekt] *n.* □ **amor-próprio**
Don't you have any self-respect?

self-service [self'sə:vis] *adj.* □ **self-service, autosserviço, autoatendimento**
a self-service restaurant.

sell [sel] *v.* (**sells, selling, sold**)
1 vender
They sold their house. ◆ They sold it to me. ◆ Don't sell him the car. ◆ I sold my camera for $20. ◆ That shop sells toys and games.
2 vender
Her discs sell very well.

be sold out □ **esgotado**
The concert was sold out a week ago. ◆ All the copies of that book were sold out within a week.

seller ['selə] *n.* □ **vendedor, artigo de muita saída**

Sellotape™ ['seləteip] *n. Brit.* □ **fita adesiva**
Put some Sellotape across the torn page.
■ *Amer.* **Scotch tape™**

semester [si'mestə] *n.* □ **semestre**
the Spring / Fall (Autumn) semester.

semi- [semi-] *pref.* □ **semi-**
a semi-circle. ◆ semi-automatic.

semicolon [semi'koulən] *n.* □ **ponto e vírgula**
A semicolon is a punctuation mark (;).

semifinal [semi'fainl] *n.* □ **semifinal**

senate ['senət] *n.* □ **senado**
the Senate □ **o Senado**

senator ['senətə] *n.* □ **senador**

send [send] *v.* (**sends, sending, sent**) □ **enviar, mandar**
She sent me a letter / postcard. ◆ Send them a fax / an e-mail. ◆ The judge sent her to prison. ◆ They sent him on a mission.

send for □ **mandar buscar**
to send for a doctor / taxi.

send off □ **enviar, remeter**
I'll send the letter off tomorrow.

senior ['si:njə] *adj.*
1 sênior, pessoa superior em cargo ou tempo de serviço
a senior officer in the army. ◆ a senior government minister.
2 mais velho
She is two years senior to me (= older than me).
3 mais antigo
He is senior to me, because he started to work here three years before me.
4 pai
Sammy Davis Sr. (= Senior)
■ antônimo: **junior**

senior citizen ['si:njə 'sitizn] *n.* (= old-age pensioner) □ **aposentado, reformado**

sensation [sen'seiʃən] *n.*
1 sensibilidade
After the accident she lost all sensation in her legs.
2 sensação
a wonderful sensation. ◆ a strange sensation.
3 sensação
Her new film caused a sensation all over Europe.

sensational [sen'seiʃənl] *adj.* □ **sensacional**
sensational news. ◆ a sensational victory.

sense¹ [sens] *n.*
1 sentido
I lost my sense of smell. ◆ the sense of taste / sight / hearing / touch.
2 senso
She has a good musical sense. ◆ your sense of duty.
3 (= meaning) **sentido**
Most words have more than one sense.
4 juízo, sentido
He has enough sense not to get into trouble. ◆ There's a lot of sense in what she is saying.
■ Ver **common sense**.
5 sentido
There's no sense in waiting. Let's start without him.

make sense □ **fazer sentido**
This sentence doesn't make sense.

make sense of □ **entender, compreender**
I can't make sense of his letter.

sense of humor / humour □ **senso de humor**
She has a good sense of humour.

sense² *v.* (**senses, sensing, sensed**) □ **sentir**
I sensed that something was wrong.

senseless ['senslis] *adj.* □ **sem sentido, absurdo**
senseless violence.

sensible ['sensibl] *adj.* □ **sensato**
a sensible person. ◆ a sensible decision.

sensitive ['sensitiv] *adj.*
1 sensível
sensitive skin. ◆ My teeth are very sensitive to cold.
2 sensível
Don't be so sensitive! We are only joking. ◆ Don't say anything about his hair. He is very sensitive about it.
3 sensível
She is sensitive to their feelings and needs.
■ antônimo: **insensitive**
4 sensível, delicado
a sensitive issue.

sent [sent] *v.* (Ver **send**).

sentence¹ ['sentəns] *n.*
1 sentença
Begin each sentence with a capital letter. ◆ Can you translate this sentence into Spanish?
2 sentença, pena
She got a sentence of five years in prison. ◆ a death sentence.

sentence² *v.* (**sentences, sentencing, sentenced**) □ **sentenciar**
The judge sentenced him to six years in prison.

sentimental [ˌsentiˈmentl] *adj.* ◻ **sentimental**
sentimental music.
sentry [ˈsentri] *n.* (*pl.* **sentries**) ◻ **sentinela**
separate¹ [ˈsepərət] *adj.* ◻ **separado**
Cut the pizza into four separate parts. ◆ Keep the vegetables separate from the fruit. ◆ They sleep in separate rooms. ◆ These are two separate problems.
separate² [ˈsepəreit] *v.* (**separates, separating, separated**)
1 separar
Separate the bad apples from the good ones. ◆ They started fighting, but I quickly separated them.
2 separar
The river separates the two countries.
3 separar-se
They separated at the airport.
4 separar
My parents separated when I was 5 years old.
5 separar-se
Let's separate. You go to the left, we'll go to the right.
separately [ˈsepərətli] *adv.* ◻ **separadamente**
They tested each of the students separately.
separation [ˌsepəˈreiʃən] *n.* ◻ **separação**
He saw his brother again after a separation of 20 years.
September [səpˈtembə] *n.* ◻ **setembro**
in September, 2002
■ For more example sentences see **April**.
sergeant [ˈsaːdʒənt] *n.* ◻ **sargento**
He is a sergeant in the air force.
serial [ˈsiəriəl] *n.* ◻ **seriado, série**
a television serial in six parts.
serial number [ˈsiəriəl ˈnʌmbə] *n.* ◻ **número de série**
Each soldier has a serial number. ◆ the serial number on a membership card.
series [ˈsiəriːz] *n.*
1 série
a series of events. ◆ a series of stamps.
2 série, seriado
a television series. ◆ a comedy series.
serious [ˈsiəriəs] *adj.*
1 sério
Be serious! This is not the time for jokes. ◆ a serious person. ◆ a serious discussion. ◆ Are you serious about leaving your job?
2 grave
a serious illness. ◆ a serious accident.
seriously [ˈsiəriəsli] *adv.*
1 seriamente
He is seriously ill. ◆ They were seriously injured in the accident.
2 seriamente, a sério
Let's talk about it seriously. ◆ Don't take him seriously. He is only joking.
seriousness [ˈsiəriəsnis] *n.* ◻ **seriedade**
Do you realize the seriousness of the situation?
sermon [ˈsəːmən] *n.* ◻ **sermão**
servant [ˈsəːvənt] *n.* ◻ **servo**
serve [səːv] *v.* (**serves, serving, served**)
1 servir
He served in the army for three years.
2 atender, servir
A young salesclerk served me at the department store. The waiter served us coffee and cake.

it serves you right ◻ **bem-feito para você**
I'm cold. – It serves you right. Why didn't you take your coat?
service [ˈsəːvis] *n.*
1 atendimento
The service in this restaurant is terrible.
2 serviço
military service. ◆ She retired after 20 years of service in the hospital.
3 assistência
You'll need the services of a lawyer.
4 serviço
There is a good bus service in this city.
5 revisão, manutenção
I take my car for service (= servicing, *Amer.*) every six months.
6 culto, cerimônia religiosa
They went to the morning service (at the church). ◆ a funeral service. ◆ a memorial service. ◆ a marriage service.
service station [ˈsəːvis ˈsteiʃən] *n.* ◻ **posto de combustível**
serviette [ˌsəːviˈet] *n. Brit.* (= napkin) ◻ **guardanapo**
set¹ [set] *n.*
1 kit, conjunto
a set of tools.
2 aparelho
a television set.
set² *v.* (**sets, setting, set**)
1 colocar, pôr
He set the plates on the table.
2 pôr a mesa
to set the table (= lay the table).
3 acertar, ajustar
I set the alarm clock for 5 o'clock. ◆ to set the video to record a programme.
4 marcar
to set a date for the exam.
5 pôr-se
The sun sets in the west.
■ antônimo: **rise**
6 endurecer
Leave the jelly (jello) in the refrigerator to set.
7 pôr no lugar
The doctor set my broken arm.
set a good example ◻ **dar um bom exemplo**
He sets a good example to his son.
set someone free (= release) ◻ **libertar**
He set the prisoners free. ◆ I set the animals free.
set something on fire, set fire to ◻ **pôr fogo em**
They set two cars on fire. ◆ Someone set fire to the building.
set off, set out ◻ **partir, sair**
We set off early in the morning.
set sail (= sail) ◻ **zarpar, içar vela**
The ship will set sail tomorrow.
set up ◻ **montar**
She set up the business ten years ago.
setback [ˈsetbak] *n.* ◻ **contratempo, revés**
Her exam failure was a serious setback to her hopes.
settee [seˈtiː] *n.* (= sofa) ◻ **sofá pequeno**
settle [ˈsetl] *v.* (**settles, settling, settled**)
1 estabelecer-se
They decided to leave the country and settle in Australia.

2 acertar, resolver
They settled their problems with the neighbours.
3 acertar, pagar
He settled his debts.
4 acomodar-se
After work she likes to settle in front of the television.
5 instalar-se
The bird settled on the top of a tree.
be settled □ **estar decido**
They want to get married, but nothing is settled yet. ◆ Everything is settled. You all know what to do.
settle down
1 acomodar-se
I settled down in the armchair to read the newspaper.
2 acalmar-se
Settle down, everyone!
3 estabelecer-se
It's time to get married and settle down.
settle for □ **partir para**
She couldn't afford a new car, so she had to settle for a used car.
settlement ['setlmənt] *n.*
1 acordo
They reached a settlement about the workers' demands.
2 assentamento
They built a new settlement near the border.
settler ['setlə] *n.* □ **colonizador**
seven ['sevn] *n., adj.* □ **sete**
It's seven o'clock. ◆ She is seven years old.
seventeen ['sevn'ti:n] *n., adj.* □ **dezessete**
I'm seventeen years old. ◆ Ten and seven are seventeen. ◆ It's seventeen minutes past six.
seventeenth[1] ['sevn'ti:nθ] *adj., adv., pron.* □ **décimo sétimo, dezesseté**
the seventeenth floor. ◆ the seventeenth century. ◆ June the seventeenth (= 17th June).
seventeenth[2] *n.* (= 1/17) □ **um dezessete avos**
seventh[1] ['sevnθ] *adj., adv., pron.* □ **sétimo, sete**
the seventh floor. ◆ He came seventh in the race. ◆ March the seventh (= 7th March).
seventh[2] *n.* (= 1/7) □ **um sétimo**
seventieth ['sevntiiθ] *adj., adv., pron.* □ **septuagésimo**
We are in the seventieth place on the list. ◆ It's his seventieth birthday.
seventy ['sevnti] *n., adj.* □ **setenta**
They came here seventy years ago. ◆ Seven times ten is seventy.
the seventies □ **os anos setenta, década de 1970**
Do you like the music of the seventies?
several ['sevrəl] (= a few) *adj., pron.* □ **vários**
The telephone rang several times before she picked it up. ◆ Several of them are my friends.
severe [sə'viə] *adj.*
1 severo
a severe punishment. ◆ severe criticism.
2 severo
a severe pain / illness. ◆ a severe winter.
3 severo
They are too severe with their children.
severely [sə'viəli] *adv.* □ **gravemente, severamente**
The building was severely damaged by fire.
severity [sə'veriti] *n.* □ **gravidade**
They did not realize the severity of the situation.

sew [sou] *v.* (**sews, sewing, sewed, sewn** or **sewed**) □ **costurar**
I need a needle and thread to sew a button on my shirt.
sewage ['sjuidʒ] *n.* □ **esgoto**
sewer ['sjuə] *n.* □ **esgoto**
a sewer pipe.
sewing ['souiŋ] *n.* □ **costura**
I like sewing and knitting. ◆ I have to do a lot of sewing today.
sewing machine ['souiŋ mə'ʃi:n] *n.* □ **máquina de costura**
sex [seks] *n.*
1 sexo
What sex is this bird? (= Is it male or female?)
■ **gender** is often used instead of **sex** for this meaning
2 sexo
She had sex with him. ◆ There's too much sex on TV.
sexual ['sekʃuəl] *adj.* □ **sexual**
sexual activity. ◆ the sexual organs.
sexual abuse *n.* □ **abuso sexual**
He was accused of sexual abuse.
sexual harassment *n.* □ **assédio sexual**
She accused her boss of sexual harassment.
sexy ['seksi] *adj.* □ **sexy, sensual**
a sexy dress.
sh! [ʃ] □ **psiu!**
Sh! The baby is sleeping.
shabby ['ʃabi] *adj.* (**shabbier, shabbiest**) □ **surrado**
a shabby old coat.
shade[1] [ʃeid] *n.*
1 sombra
to sit in the shade of a tree.
2 cúpula
to put a new shade over the lamp.
■ Ver **lampshade; sunshade**.
3 *Amer.* □ **persiana**
to pull down the shades
■ *Brit.* **blind**
4 tom, matiz
a shade of green.
shade[2] *v.* (**shades, shading, shaded**) □ **proteger da luz**
He shaded his eyes with his hand.
shadow ['ʃadou] *n.* □ **sombra**
The child enjoyed playing with his shadow.
■ Ver **shado**.
shady ['ʃeidi] *adj.* (**shadier, shadiest**) □ **à sombra, sombreado**
Here is a nice shady spot for the picnic.
shake [ʃeik] *v.* (**shakes, shaking, shook, shaken**)
1 tremer
I'm shaking with cold. ◆ They were shaking with fear.
2 tremer
The whole building shook when the bomb exploded.
3 sacudir, chacoalhar
They shook the tree and some apples fell down. ◆ Shake the bottle well before use. ◆ to shake a blanket (to remove the dust).
shake hands (with) □ **cumprimentar-se**
They shook hands and said 'Goodbye'.
■ The noun is **handshake**.
shake someone's hand □ **apertar a mão de alguém**
He shook my hand warmly.

shake your head □ **acenar negativamente com a cabeça**
She shook her head when I asked if I could take the car.

shaky ['ʃeiki] *adj.* (**shakier, shakiest**) □ **trêmulo**
shaky hands. ✦ a shaky voice. ✦ The baby camel tried to stand on its shaky legs.

shall [ʃəl, ʃal] *v.*
1 (= I / we will) *Brit.* □ **indica tempo futuro**
I shall try. ✦ I shan't (= shall not) be able to come. ✦ We shall be back soon.
2 dever
Where shall I put it? (= Where do you want me to put it?). ✦ Shall I close the window? (= Do you want me to close the window?)
shall we...? □ **vamos...?**
Shall we try again?

shallow ['ʃalou] *adj.* □ **raso**
The river is shallow here. ✦ shallow water. ✦ Cook it in a shallow dish.
■ antônimo: **deep**

shame [ʃeim] *n.*
1 vergonha
She was full of shame (= She was ashamed) because of her lies.
2 (= disgrace) □ **vergonha**
She brought shame on her family.
Shame on you! □ **Que vergonha!**
it's a shame, what a shame □ **é uma pena, que pena**
It's a shame you can't stay. ✦ Oh, what a shame!

shameful ['ʃeimful] *adj.* □ **vergonhoso, indecente**
Their attitude to us was shameful.

shampoo¹ [ʃam'pu:] *n.*
1 xampu
a shampoo for oily / dry hair.
2 lavagem de cabelo
to have a shampoo at the hairdresser's.

shampoo² *v.* (**shampoos, shampooing, shampooed**) □ **passar xampu**
The hairdresser shampooed my hair.

shan't [ʃa:nt] (= **shall not**).

shape¹ [ʃeip] *n.*
1 forma, formato
What shape is the table – round or square? ✦ He has a ring in the shape of a snake.
2 forma, condição
His heart is in good shape. ✦ The players are in good shape and ready for the match. ✦ The business is in bad shape.

shape² *v.* (**shapes, shaping, shaped**) □ **moldar, dar forma**
The children shaped the sand into a castle.

-shaped [ʃeipt] *adj.* □ **no formato de**
a star-shaped cookie (= a cookie in the shape of a star).

share¹ [ʃeə] *n.* □ **parte**
They all got their share of the money. ✦ He did his share of the work.

share² *v.* (**shares, sharing, shared**)
1 compartilhar, dividir
I share a room with another student.
2 partilhar
Share this chocolate with your brother.
3 (= share out) □ **repartir**
We shared the cake between the six of us.

shark [ʃa:k] *n.* □ **tubarão**

sharp¹ [ʃa:p] *adj.*
1 afiado
a sharp knife. ✦ Is the pencil sharp?
■ antônimo: **blunt**
2 agudo, cortante
I felt a sharp pain in my back.
■ antônimo: **dull**
3 fechado, acentuado
a sharp bend in the road.
4 duro, mordaz
sharp words. ✦ sharp criticism.
5 aguçado
Eagles have sharp eyes. ✦ sharp ears.
6 azedo, picante
Vinegar and lemons have a sharp taste. ✦ This cheese tastes sharp.
■ Compare with **hot**:
Food tastes hot when you add pepper to it.
7 perspicaz, esperto
She has a very sharp mind. ✦ That student is very sharp. ✦ He always asks sharp questions.
8 distinto, nítido
a sharp rise / fall in the number of accidents.

sharp² *adv.* (= exactly) □ **em ponto, pontualmente**
The meeting will start at 10 o'clock sharp.

sharpen ['ʃa:pən] *v.* (**sharpens, sharpening, sharpened**) □ **afiar, apontar**
to sharpen a knife / pencil.

sharpener ['ʃa:pənə] *n.* □ **apontador**
a pencil sharpener.

sharply ['ʃa:pli] *adv.*
1 duramente, rispidamente
He spoke sharply to them.
2 acentuadamente
Prices fell sharply last week.
3 abruptamente
The road turns sharply to the left.

shatter ['ʃatə] *v.* (**shatters, shattering, shattered**) □ **despedaçar, estilhaçar**
He dropped the vase and it shattered into pieces. ✦ The explosion shattered all the windows of the building.

shave¹ [ʃeiv] *n.* □ **ato de fazer a barba**
He has a shave every day.

shave² *v.* (**shaves, shaving, shaved**) □ **barbear-se**
He shaves every day. ✦ I'm going to shave my beard.

shaver ['ʃeivə] *n.* (= electric razor) □ **barbeador**

shawl [ʃɔ:l] *n.* □ **xale**
She wore a shawl over her shoulders.

she [ʃi:] *pron.* □ **ela**
She visits them once a week. ✦ Does she know you? ✦ She is a lawyer. ✦ She gave me a copy of her book.

shed¹ [ʃed] *n.* □ **barracão, galpão, abrigo**
We keep our tools in the garden shed. ✦ a bicycle shed.

shed² *v.* (**sheds, shedding, shed**)
1 perder
Trees shed their leaves in autumn. ✦ The snake shed its skin.
2 derramar
to shed tears (= cry).
3 derramar
to shed blood.

she'd [ʃi:d] (mesmo que **she had**; **she would**)

sheep [ʃi:p] *n.* (*pl.* **sheep**) □ ovelha
sheer [ʃiə] *adj.* □ puro
Your idea is sheer nonsense. ◆ It was sheer luck that I found it. ◆ a sheer waste of time.
sheet [ʃi:t] *n.*
1 lençol
to change the sheets.
2 folha
a sheet of paper.
3 chapa
plastic sheets.
shelf [ʃelf] *n.* (*pl.* **shelves**) □ estante, prateleira
Put the books back on the shelf. ◆ The shelves in the supermarket were full.
shell¹ [ʃel] *n.*
1 casca
to crack the shell of eggs, nuts, etc.
2 casco, concha
the shell of a snail / tortoise. ◆ sea-shells.
shell² *v.* (**shells, shelling, shelled**)
1 descascar
to shell peas, nuts, peanuts, etc.
■ Compare **peel**:
to peel fruit / potatoes.
2 bombardear
They shelled the enemy forces.
she'll [ʃi:l] (mesmo que **she will**).
shellfish [ˈʃelfɪʃ] *n.* □ marisco, molusco
shelter¹ [ˈʃeltə] *n.*
1 abrigo
The tree gave them some shelter from the rain. ◆ They ran for shelter when the shooting started.
2 abrigo
The shelter protected them from the bombs.
bus shelter *n.* □ abrigo de ponto de ônibus
shelter² *v.* (**shelters, sheltering, sheltered**)
1 abrigar
They shelter (= give shelter to) cats and dogs. ◆ The wall shelters the place from the wind.
2 abrigar-se
to shelter (= find shelter) from the rain.
shelves [ʃelvz] *n. pl.* (Ver **shelf**).
shepherd [ˈʃepəd] *n.* □ pastor
shepherdess [ˈʃepədɪs] *n.* □ pastora
sheriff [ˈʃerɪf] *n.* □ xerife
she's [ʃi:z] (mesmo que **she is**).
shield¹ [ʃi:ld] *n.* □ escudo
The policemen carried shields to protect themselves. ◆ Each warrior had a shield, bow and arrows.
shield² *v.* (**shields, shielding, shielded**) □ proteger
She shielded her eyes from the sun with her hand.
shift¹ [ʃɪft] *n.* □ turno
They work in shifts. ◆ He works the night shift.
shift² *v.* (**shifts, shifting, shifted**)
1 mover
Help me shift the sofa against the wall.
2 trocar
to shift (= change) gears.
shine¹ [ʃaɪn] *n.* □ brilho
the shine in his eyes. ◆ Her hair has a lovely shine. ◆ Give your shoes a shine.
shine² *v.* (**shines, shining, shone**)

1 brilhar
The sun is shining. ◆ I polished the table until it shone. ◆ Their eyes shone with joy. ◆ He shone a torch on the darkness.
2 (*past tense* **shined**) lustrar
I shined your shoes.
shiny [ˈʃaɪni] *adj.* (**shinier, shiniest**) □ brilhante
shiny hair. ◆ a shiny car.
ship¹ [ʃɪp] *n.* □ navio
The ship sailed an hour ago. ◆ All the passengers boarded the ship. ◆ The ship sank.
by ship □ navio
We went to Greece by ship.
ship² *v.* (**ships, shipping, shipped**) (= send by boat, air, train, truck / lorry) □ **enviar por navio, avião, trem, caminhão**
We ship oranges to Europe.
shipment [ˈʃɪpmənt] *n.* □ carregamento, expedição
a shipment of cars from Korea. ◆ The oil is ready for shipment.
shipwreck [ˈʃɪprek] *n.* □ naufrágio
A lighthouse warns against the danger of shipwreck. ◆ They died in a shipwreck.
be shipwrecked □ **sofrer um naufrágio**
They were shipwrecked off the coast.
shirt [ʃɜ:t] *n.* □ camisa
He put on his shirt and left. ◆ She was wearing a white shirt.
shiver [ˈʃɪvə] *v.* (**shivers, shivering, shivered**) □ tremer
I was shivering with cold.
shock¹ [ʃɒk] *n.*
1 choque
His death came as a shock to all of us.
2 choque
The sand reduced the shock of the fall.
3 (= electric shock) **choque elétrico**
He got a shock when he touched the wire.
shock² *v.* (**shocks, shocking, shocked**) □ chocar
The news of the accident shocked all of us.
shocking [ˈʃɒkɪŋ] *adj.* □ chocante
shocking news. ◆ shocking pictures.
shoe [ʃu:] *n.* □ sapato
What size shoes do you wear? ◆ I tried on the shoes, but they were too tight. ◆ a pair of tennis shoes. ◆ a shoe shop.
shoelace [ˈʃu:leɪs] *n.* Brit. (**mesmo que shoestring,** Amer.) □ **cadarço**
Can you tie your shoelaces by yourself? ◆ to untie the shoelaces.
shone [ʃɒn] *v.* (Ver **shine**).
shook [ʃʊk] *v.* (Ver **shake**).
shoot [ʃu:t] *v.* (**shoots, shooting, shot**)
1 atirar
Don't shoot! ◆ He pulled out his gun and shot (= fired) two bullets. ◆ She shot an arrow at the target.
2 atirar
He shot a rabbit. ◆ The police shot the robber in the leg. ◆ The Prime Minister was shot.
3 lançar
to shoot at the basket.
4 atirar
He shot three times (at the goal), but didn't score.
5 atravessar rapidamente

A falling star shot across the sky. ♦ He shot out of the door.
6 subir rapidamente
The pain shot up my arm.
7 rodar
to shoot a film.
shoot down □ **abater com um tiro**
They shot down the plane.
shop¹ [ʃɒp] *n.*
1 loja
a shoe shop. ♦ a clothes shop. ♦ a bookshop.
■ **store** is the usual word in American English.
2 oficina
I took the car to the shop for repair. ♦ a paint shop (for painting cars).
shop² *v.* (**shops, shopping, shopped**) □ **fazer compras**
I usually shop on Tuesdays.
go shopping □ **ir às compras**
We went shopping together.
shop assistant [ˈʃɒp əˈsɪstənt] *n.* □ **vendedor, balconista**
■ *Amer.* (**sales**) **clerk; salesperson**
shopkeeper [ˈʃɒpˌkiːpə] *n.* □ **lojista**
■ *Amer.* **storekeeper**
shoplifter [ˈʃɒplɪftə] *n.* □ **ladrão de loja**
shoplifting [ˈʃɒplɪftɪŋ] *n.* □ **roubo de artigos de lojas**
The police arrested them for shoplifting.
shopper [ˈʃɒpə] *n.* □ **comprador, carrinho de compras**
The shops, department stores and supermarkets were full of shoppers.
shopping [ˈʃɒpɪŋ] *n.*
1 ato de fazer compras
I do the shopping for them. ♦ I'm going shopping.
2 compra
to carry the shopping in shopping bags.
shopping centre [ˈʃɒpɪŋ ˌsentə] *n. Brit.* □ **centro comercial**
shopping mall [ˈʃɒpɪŋ mɔːl] *n. Amer.* (= **mall**) □ **centro comercial**
shopping precinct [ˈʃɒpɪŋ ˈpriːsɪŋkt] *n. Brit.* □ **calçadão**
shop-window [ˈʃɒpˈwɪndəʊ] *n.* □ **vitrine**
shore [ʃɔː] *n.* □ **praia, margem**
They swam to the shore.
■ Ver **coast**.
short [ʃɔːt] *adj.*
1 curto
She has short hair. ♦ a short skirt. ♦ a short line. ♦ This is the shortest way to town. ♦ a short letter / film. ♦ The days become shorter in winter. ♦ a short time ago.
■ antônimo: **long**
2 baixo
a short person. ♦ I'm too short to play basketball.
■ antônimo: **tall**
be short of □ **estar em falta de, estar para acabar**
They are short of money at the moment. ♦ We are a bit short of sugar, so don't forget to buy some.
for short □ **abreviando**
His name is Joseph, or Joe for short.
short for □ **abreviação de**
Joe is short for Joseph.
in short □ **em suma, para encurtar**
We buy them clothes, food, books; in short, we buy them everything they need.
shortage [ˈʃɔːtɪdʒ] *n.* □ **escassez**
There is a shortage of good engineers. ♦ a shortage of water (a water shortage).

short cut [ˈʃɔːt kʌt] *n.* □ **atalho**
We took a short cut to town.
shorten [ˈʃɔːtn] *v.* (**shortens, shortening, shortened**)
1 encurtar
Can you shorten my trousers? ♦ They shortened my story.
2 encurtar-se
The days are beginning to shorten.
■ antônimo: **lengthen**
shorthand [ˈʃɔːthænd] *n.* □ **taquigrafia**
shortly [ˈʃɔːtli] *adv.* (= **soon**) □ **logo**
They will be here shortly.
shortly after / before □ **pouco depois / antes**
He arrived shortly after ten o'clock.
shorts [ʃɔːts] *n. pl.*
1 shorts, calção
When the weather is hot I wear shorts. ♦ tennis shorts.
2 *Amer.* **cueca boxer**
Shorts are men's underpants.
■ a pair of shorts (*not* 'a shorts').
short-sighted [ˈʃɔːtˈsaɪtɪd] *adj.* □ **míope**
Short-sighted people should wear glasses or contact lenses.
■ *Amer.* **near-sighted**
shot¹ [ʃɒt] *v.* (Ver **shoot**).
shot² *n.*
1 tiro
He fired two shots.
2 jogada
With that great shot he scored his second goal.
3 foto
I took good shots of them.
4 (= injection) **injeção**
a flu shot.
should [ʃʊd] *v.* (= ought)
1 devia, deveria
He should see a doctor. ♦ Should I tell her the truth? ♦ You shouldn't work so hard.
2 deve
The train should arrive any moment now. ♦ There shouldn't be any problems.
should have (done) □ **devia / deveria ter**
You should have come earlier. It's too late now. ♦ She should have listened to me (but she didn't).
How should I know? □ **Como eu saberia?**
Who broke the window? – How should I know?
shoulder [ˈʃəʊldə] *n.* □ **ombro**
She carried a bag over her shoulder. ♦ He carried the child on his shoulders. ♦ He put his arm around my shoulder.
shouldn't [ˈʃʊdnt] (mesmo que **should not**).
shout¹ [ʃaʊt] *n.* □ **grito**
We could hear the shouts outside.
shout² *v.* (**shouts, shouting, shouted**) □ **gritar**
There's no need to shout – I'm not deaf. ♦ He shouted at them. ♦ Stop shouting!
shove [ʃʌv] *v.* (**shoves, shoving, shoved**) (= push) □ **empurrar**
They shoved him into the car. ♦ She shoved the box under the bed.
shovel¹ [ˈʃʌvl] *n.* □ **pá**
They used shovels to fill the hole with sand.
■ Compare with **spade**:
spade = square blade.

shovel² *v.* (**shovels, shoveling, shoveled, shovelling, shovelled**) □ **remover com pá**
I shovelled the snow from the path. ◆ We shovelled sand into buckets.

show¹ [ʃou] *n.*
1 programa
We have tickets for tonight's show. ◆ There is a good show on TV tonight. ◆ a TV show.
2 desfile, exposição
a fashion show. ◆ a flower show.
on show □ **em exposição**
His paintings are now on show at the museum.

show² *v.* (**shows, showing, showed**)
1 mostrar
Show me your hands! ◆ He showed us his watch. ◆ He showed it to us.
2 mostrar
She showed me how to use the computer.
3 acompanhar
Come, I'll show you to your room.
4 provar
This letter shows that he is guilty.
5 estar evidente
The disappointment showed on her face.
show off □ **exibir-se**
Stop showing off!
■ A show-off is a person who shows off.
show someone around □ **mostrar um local a alguém**
Come, I'll show you around. ◆ They showed him around the factory.
show up □ **aparecer**
She didn't show up (for the meeting).

shower¹ [ˈʃauə] *n.*
1 chuveiro
He is in the shower.
2 chuva leve e rápida
showers of rain.
have / take a shower □ **tomar uma ducha**
I took a shower and went to bed.

shower² *v.* (**showers, showering, showered**) □ **tomar banho de chuveiro, tomar uma ducha**
She showered and dressed.

shown [ʃoun] *v.* (Ver **show**).
shrank [ʃrank] *v.* (Ver **shrink**).
shred [ʃred] *n.* □ **tira**
Cut the vegetables into shreds.
tear something to shreds □ **picar algo em tiras**
I tore the letters to shreds.

shriek¹ [ʃriːk] *n.* □ **grito agudo**
He gave a shriek of pain. ◆ shrieks of delight.
shriek² *v.* (**shrieks, shrieking, shrieked**) □ **gritar, guinchar**
They shrieked with laughter. ◆ to shriek in fear.
shrill [ʃril] *adj.* □ **agudo, penetrante**
a shrill whistle.
shrimp [ʃrimp] *n.* □ **camarão**
shrine [ʃrain] *n.* □ **santuário, lugar sagrado ou histórico**
shrink [ʃriŋk] *v.* (**shrinks, shrinking, shrank, shrunk**) □ **encolher**
Don't wash your sweater in hot water. It will shrink.
shrivel [ˈʃrivl] *v.* (**shrivels, shriveling, shriveled, shrivelling, shrivelled**) □ **murchar**
The leaves are beginning to shrivel. ◆ The flowers shrivelled in the hot weather.

shrub [ʃrʌb] *n.* □ **arbusto**
shrug¹ [ʃrʌg] *n.* □ **meneio de ombros**
'Who cares?' he said with a shrug of his shoulders.
shrug² *v.* (**shrugs, shrugging, shrugged**) □ **dar de ombros**
'I don't know and I don't care', she said, and shrugged her shoulders.
shrunk [ʃrʌŋk] *v.* (Ver **shrink**).
shudder¹ [ˈʃʌdə] *n.* □ **tremor, estremecimento**
shudder² *v.* (**shudders, shuddering, shuddered**) □ **tremer, estremecer**
He shuddered when he drank the bitter medicine.
shuffle [ˈʃʌfl] *v.* (**shuffles, shuffling, shuffled**)
1 arrastar, arrastar-se
Stop shuffling your feet! ◆ The old man shuffled into his room.
2 embaralhar
to shuffle the cards.
shut¹ [ʃʌt] *adj.* (= closed) □ **fechado**
The windows and the curtains were shut.
shut² *v.* (**shuts, shutting, shut**)
1 (= close) **fechar**
Please shut the door behind you. ◆ Shut your books, please.
■ Ver **close³**.
2 (= close) **fechar**
The door shut behind her.
3 (= close) **fechar**
The shops shut early today.
4 fechar
They shut the dog inside the house.
shut down (= close down) □ **fechar**
They had to shut down the factory.
shut yourself in □ **fechar-se em**
He shut himself in his room for hours.
shut up □ **calar-se, calar a boca**
Shut up and pay attention! ◆ Tell him to shut up.
shut someone up
1 calar alguém, fazer alguém calar a boca
How can we shut him up?
2 trancafiar
They shut her up in prison for 5 years.
shutter [ˈʃʌtə] *n.* □ **veneziana**
shy [ʃai] *adj.* □ **tímido**
He is too shy to read out his homework in class. ◆ a shy smile.
shyness [ˈʃainis] *n.* □ **timidez**
sick [sik] *adj.* (= ill; not well) □ **doente**
a sick child. ◆ You look sick. ◆ She is sick in bed. ◆ The dog is very sick.
■ After 'be' or 'look' **sick** is the usual word in American English, **ill** in British English.
■ antônimo: **well, healthy**
be sick (= throw up) □ **ficar doente**
I'm going to be sick.
be sick of □ **estar farto de, cansado**
I'm sick of your complaints! ◆ I'm sick of doing everything for you!
feel sick □ **sentir-se mal**
I felt sick after eating that fish.
get sick (= become ill) □ **ficar doente**
I got sick, so I didn't go.

make someone sick □ **irritar / aborrecer alguém**
His insults made me sick!
the sick □ **os doentes**
The nurses looked after the sick.
sickly ['sikli] *adj.* (mesmo que **often ill**) □ **suscetível à doença**
a sickly child.
sickness ['siknis] *n.* (= illness) □ **doença, enfermidade**
There was a lot of sickness in the village.
▪ Ver **disease**.
side [said] *n.*
1 lado
on the left side of the road. ✦ There is a small garden at the side of the house.
2 lado
on the other side of the page / coin.
3 face
A box has a top, bottom and four sides.
4 lado
The French side won.
5 lado
A square has four sides.
be on someone's side □ **estar do lado de alguém**
My father blamed me, but my mother was on my side.
side by side □ **lado a lado**
They walked side by side.
take sides (with) □ **tomar partido (de)**
They had an argument, and I took sides with John (= I took John's side).
sideboard ['saidbo:d] *n.* □ **aparador**
sidewalk ['saidwo:k] *n. Amer.* □ **calçada**
▪ *Brit.* **pavement**
sideways ['saidweiz] *adj.*, *adv.*
1 lateralmente
This toy moves forwards, backwards and sideways.
2 de lado
We got the sofa in sideways.
siege [si:dʒ] *n.* □ **cerco**
The city was under siege for six months.
sieve [siv] *n.* □ **peneira**
I used a sieve to sift the flour.
sift [sift] *v.* (**sifts, sifting, sifted**) □ **peneirar**
to sift flour.
sigh¹ [sai] *n.* □ **suspiro**
'It's sad', she said with a sigh. ✦ 'Thank God', he said with a sigh of relief.
sigh² *v.* (**sighs, sighing, sighed**) □ **suspirar**
She sighed with sadness / disappointment.
sight [sait] *n.*
1 visão
He lost his sight (= became blind) when he was five. ✦ She wears glasses because she has poor sight.
2 vista
Their first sight of land made the sailors happy. ✦ We waited until the ship was out of sight, and left.
3 espetáculo, vista
The lake below was a beautiful sight.
the sights □ **pontos turísticos**
to see the sights. ✦ When you come to Rome I'll show you the sights.
at the sight of □ **diante de**
He cried at the sight of the big dog.

at first sight □ **à primeira vista**
It was love at first sight.
catch sight of □ **avistar**
I caught sight of him, but he disappeared in the crowd.
come into sight □ **ficar visível**
After two kilometers the farm came into sight.
lose sight of □ **perder de vista, perder contato**
We waited until we lost sight of the train.
sight-seeing ['saitsi:iŋ] *n.* □ **visita aos pontos turísticos**
We went sightseeing in Rome.
sightseer ['saitsiə] *n.* □ **pessoa que visita os pontos turísticos de um local**
sign¹ [sain] *n.*
1 sinal
The sign & means 'and'. ✦ The sign + means 'plus'.
2 sinal
I'll give you a sign when to start. ✦ He made a sign to us to stop.
3 sinal
The door is open, but there are no signs of breaking into the house. ✦ to show signs of boredom.
4 placa
a shop sign. ✦ The sign says No parking.
5 placa
road signs. ✦ traffic signs. ✦ The sign says it's 4 km to the airport.
sign² *v.* (**signs, signing, signed**) □ **assinar**
Sign here, please. ✦ Read the contract carefully before you sign. ✦ to sign a cheque.
▪ The noun is **signature**.
signal¹ ['signəl] *n.*
1 sinal
We waited for the signal to start the race. ✦ The signal was three knocks on the door.
2 sinal
radio / TV signals. *Amer.*
turn-signal *n.* □ **seta**
The turn-signal shows which way the car is turning.
▪ *Brit.* **indicator**
signal² *v.* (**signals, signaling, signaled, signalling, signalled**) □ **fazer sinal**
The policeman signalled to us to stop. ✦ She signalled with her flashlight.
signature ['signətʃə] *n.* □ **assinatura**
That's not my signature on the cheque.
▪ The verb is **sign**.
significance [sig'nifikəns] *n.* □ **significado**
a statement of great significance ✦ This ring has a special significance for him.
significant [sig'nifikənt] *adj.*
1 significativo
This fact is very significant (= important).
2 significativo
a significant improvement in his condition.
▪ antônimo: **insignificant**
significantly [sig'nifikəntli] *adv.* □ **significativamente**
The situation may change significantly next year.
signify ['signifai] *v.* (**signifies, signifying, signified**) □ **significar**
A red light signifies a warning.
signpost ['sainpoust] *n.* □ **placa de sinalização**
A signpost shows the direction and distance to towns, etc.

silence ['sailəns] *n.* □ **silêncio**
There was complete silence in the room. ◆ After a moment's silence he answered the question
in silence □ **em silêncio**
They looked at each other in silence.
Silence! □ **Silêncio!**

silent ['sailənt] *adj.*
1 silencioso
The place was dark and silent.
2 calado
She was silent for a moment before she answered.

silently ['sailəntli] *adv.* □ **silenciosamente**
He walked silently out of the room.

silk [silk] *n.*, *adj.* □ **seda**
a silk shirt. ◆ The shirt is made of silk.

sill [sil] *n.* (Ver **window-sill**).

silly ['sili] *adj.* (**sillier, silliest**) (= foolish) □ **bobo, tolo**
Don't be silly! ◆ a silly mistake. ◆ It was silly of you to go out in this weather.

silver ['silvə] *n.*
1 prata
The cup is made of silver. ◆ the silver medal.
2 prata
The thief stole all their silver.

silver wedding ['silvə 'wediŋ] *n.* □ **bodas de prata**

similar ['similə] *adj.* □ **similar, parecido, semelhante**
I have a similar dress, but it's a different size. ◆ Their problems are similar to ours.

similarity [,simi'lariti] *n.* (*pl.* **similarities**) □ **similaridade, semelhança**
There are some similarities between the two plans. ◆ I can't see any similarity between the two sisters.
■ antônimo: **difference**

simple ['simpl] *adj.*
1 simples
a simple solution. ◆ The instructions are written in simple English. ◆ I'll show you how to use it – it's very simple.
■ antônimo: **difficult**
2 (= plain) **simples**
a simple dress. ◆ a simple meal.
3 (grammar) **simples**
'It write letters' is in the present simple tense, and 'I wrote' is in the past simple tense.

simplicity [sim'plisəti] *n.* □ **simplicidade**
the simplicity of the plan. ◆ the simplicity of the writer's style.

simplified ['simplifaid] *adj.* □ **simplificado**
simplified English.

simplify ['simplifai] *v.* (**simplifies, simplifying, simplified**) □ **simplificar**
to simplify a sentence.

simply ['simpli] *adv.* □ **simplesmente**
I'll explain it more simply. ◆ I simply want to know the truth. ◆ The meal was simply delicious.

simultaneous [,siməl'teiniəs] *adj.* □ **simultâneo**

simultaneously [,siməl'teiniəsli] *adv.* □ **simultaneamente**
My friends arrived simultaneously at 8 o'clock exactly.

sin¹ [sin] *n.* □ **pecado**
He believes that God is punishing him for his sins.

sin² *v.* (**sins, sinning, sinned**) □ **pecar**
You sinned, but you can still repent.

since¹ [sins] *prep.* □ **desde**
I haven't seen him since 1980. ◆ She has worked here since June.

since² *conj.*
1 desde
I've known him since I was a child. ◆ We haven't met since we left the army.
2 (= because) **como, já que**
Since we don't know all the facts, we can't do anything.

since³ *adv.* □ **desde então**
She left three months ago and she hasn't written since.
ever since □ **desde que**
Ever since I was a child, I've wanted to be a doctor.
Since when...? □ **Desde quando...?**
Since when have you known him?

sincere [sin'siə] *adj.* □ **sincero**
I think he was sincere when he said 'sorry'. ◆ a sincere apology.
■ antônimo: **insincere**

sincerely [sin'siəli] *adv.* □ **sinceramente**
I sincerely hope that he will get the job.
Yours sincerely □ **Atenciosamente**
■ We use **Yours sincerely** in letters that begin with **Dear Mr. / Mrs.**
■ In American English **Sincerely yours** is more usual.

sincerity [sin'seriti] *n.* □ **sinceridade**
I believe in his sincerity.

sing [siŋ] *v.* (**sings, singing, sang, sung**) □ **cantar**
She sings beautifully. ◆ He sang a love song.

singer ['siŋə] *n.* □ **cantor**

singing ['siŋiŋ] *adj.*, *n.* □ **que canta, de canto, cantante, canto, cantoria, ato de cantar**
singing lessons ◆ His hobby is singing in a choir.

single¹ ['siŋgl] *adj.*
1 (= only one) **um só**
Give me a single reason why I should believe you. ◆ a single-parent family (only a father or a mother, not both).
2 (= even one) **um único**
There wasn't a single person in the street.
3 de solteiro
a single bed. ◆ Would you like a single or a double room?
4 (= unmarried) **solteiro**
Are you married or single? ◆ a single man. ◆ a single woman.
5 para uma pessoa só, individual
How much is a single ticket to Madrid, please?
■ *Amer.* **one way (ticket)**
■ Ver **return**.

single² *n.*
1 *Brit.* □ **só de ida**
One single to London, please, not a return.
■ *Amer.* **one-way ticket**
2 single, compacto simples
His new single will be a hit.

singles *n. pl.* □ **solteiros**
a singles bar.

singular ['siŋgjulə] (grammar) *adj.*, *n.* □ **singular**
a singular noun. ◆ a verb in the singular. ◆ The singular of 'teeth' is 'tooth'.
■ Ver **plural**.

sink¹ [siŋk] *n.* □ **pia**
The sink was full of dirty dishes.
■ Ver **washbasin**.

sink² v. (**sinks, sinking, sank, sunk**)
1 afundar
Water got into the boat and it began to sink. ♦ The empty box floated on the water, but the heavy box sank. ♦ They sank two enemy ships.
2 afundar
Their feet sank into the mud.
sip¹ [sip] n. □ **golinho**
He took a sip of coffee.
sip² v. (**sips, sipping, sipped**) □ **bebericar**
She sipped her tea slowly.
sir [sɔː] n. □ **senhor**
Can I help you, sir? ♦ Sorry, sir. I couldn't study for the exam. ♦ That's an order! – Yes, sir.
Sir □ **Sir**
Sir Winston (Churchill)
Dear Sir □ **Prezado senhor**
■ A formal letter to a man begins with **Dear Sir**; to a woman, **Dear Madam**.
siren ['saiərən] n. □ **sirene**
Police cars and ambulances have sirens.
sister ['sistə] n. □ **irmã**
She is my sister. ♦ We are sisters. ♦ I have one sister and one brother.
sister-in-law ['sistərinlɔː] n. (pl. **sisters-in-law**) □ **cunhada**
sit [sit] v. (**sits, sitting, sat**)
1 sentar-se
Don't sit on the floor. ♦ They sat in the back seat (of the car). ♦ to sit on a chair. ♦ to sit in an armchair.
2 sentar-se
They sat in the sun all morning.
3 sentar
He sat the child on a chair.
sit at □ **sentar-se a**
They sat at the table to eat dinner. ♦ to sit at a desk.
sit down □ **sentar-se**
Sit down, please. ♦ She sat (down) next to me.
sit up □ **sentar direito**
Sit up straight!
sitcom ['sitkom] n. □ **sitcom, seriado cômico de televisão, comédia de costumes**
I watch that sitcom on TV every evening and have a good laugh.
■ Compare **soap opera**.
site [sait] n.
1 local
a building site. ♦ a suitable site for the new factory.
2 site
web site (on the Internet).
sitting-room ['sitiŋrum] n. Brit. (= living room) □ **sala de estar**
They watched TV in the sitting-room.
situated ['sitjueitid] adj. (= located) □ **situado**
The theatre is situated in the city centre.
situation [,sitju'eiʃən] n. □ **situação**
the economic / political situation. ♦ They are in a difficult situation.
six [siks] adj., n. □ **seis**
It costs six dollars. ♦ It's six o'clock. ♦ He is six (years old).
sixteen [siks'tiːn] adj., n. □ **dezesseis**
sixteen pounds. ♦ Ten and six are sixteen. ♦ She is sixteen (years old).

sixteenth¹ [siks'tiːnθ] adj., adv., pron. □ **décimo sexto, dezesseis**
the sixteenth floor. ♦ the sixteenth century. ♦ August the sixteenth (= 16th August). Brit. ♦ August sixteenth (= August 16). Amer.
sixteenth² n. (= 1/16) □ **dezesseis avos**
sixth¹ [siksθ] adj., adv., pron. □ **sexto, seis**
the sixth name on the list ♦ I came sixth in the race. ♦ April sixth (= April 6). Amer. ♦ April the sixth (= 6th April). Brit.
sixth² n. (= 1/6) □ **um sexto**
Each of them ate a sixth of the cake.
sixtieth ['sikstiiθ] adj., adv., pron. □ **sexagésimo**
It's her sixtieth birthday. ♦ That tennis player is sixtieth in the world.
sixty ['siksti] adj., n. □ **sessenta**
There are sixty minutes in an hour. ♦ She is sixty (years old). ♦ The exercise is on page sixty.
the sixties □ **os anos sessenta, a década de 1960**
I like the music of the sixties.
in your sixties □ **nos seus sessenta e poucos anos**
He is in his sixties.
size [saiz] n.
1 tamanho
Our cars are the same size. ♦ How big is the computer? – It's the size of a notebook. ♦ an area the size of a football field.
2 tamanho, número
What size shoes do you wear? – Size 7. ♦ I want this dress in a bigger size.
skate¹ [skeit] n.
1 (= ice-skate) **patim de lâmina**
a pair of skates.
2 (= roller-skate) **patim com rodas**
skate² v. (**skates, skating, skated**)
1 (= ice-skate) **patinar**
They skated to the music (on the skating-rink).
2 patinar, andar de skate
Children were skating on the sidewalk.
skateboard ['skeitbɔːd] n. □ **skate**
skating rink ['skeitiŋriŋk] n. □ **ringue de patinação**
skeleton ['skelitn] n. □ **esqueleto**
a human skeleton.
sketch [sketʃ] n. □ **esboço**
to draw a sketch of a person, house, etc.
ski¹ [skiː] n. □ **esqui**
a pair of skis.
ski² v. (**skis, skiing, skied**) □ **esquiar**
I'm learning to ski. ♦ I can't ski.
go skiing □ **ir esquiar**
We went skiing last weekend.
skid [skid] v. (**skids, skidding, skidded**) □ **derrapar, deslizar**
There was some oil on the road and several cars skidded and hit each other.
skier ['skiːə] n. □ **esquiador**
I'm not a good skier.
skiing [kiin:iŋ] n. □ **esqui, ato de esquiar**
I like skiing. ♦ Let's go skiing.
skilful ['skilful] adj. Brit., **skillful** Amer. □ **hábil**
a skilful driver / dancer. ♦ She is very skillful at tennis.
skilfully ['skilfuli] adv. Brit., **skillfully** Amer. □ **habilmente**
She parked her car skilfully between two other cars.

skill [skil] *n.*
1 habilidade
He plays the guitar with great skill.
2 habilidade
He doesn't have the skills that we need for this job. ◆ the skills of reading and writing.

skilled [skild] *adj.* □ **habilidoso**
skilled workers.
■ antônimo: **unskilled**

skin[1] [skin] *n.*
1 pele
fair / dark skin. ◆ oily / dry skin. ◆ soft / rough skin.
2 casca, pele
a banana skin / tomato / potato skins.
■ Ver **peel**.

skin[2] *v.* (**skins, skinning, skinned**) □ **tirar a pele**
to skin a sheep.

skinhead ['skinhed] *n.* □ **skinhead**
violent attacks on foreigners by skinheads.
■ Ver **hooligan; thug**.

skinny ['skini] *adv.* (**skinnier, skinniest**) □ **muito magro, magricelo**
After his illness he was very skinny. ◆ skinny legs.

skip[1] [skip] *n.* □ **pulo, salto**

skip[2] *v.* (**skips, skipping, skipped**)
1 pular
They skipped around the playground. ◆ Take this skipping rope and skip for 15 minutes.
2 pular
I never skip breakfast. ◆ Skip pages 60-75.

skipping rope ['skipiŋroup] *n. Brit.* □ **corda de pular**
to play with a skipping rope.
■ *Amer.* **jump rope; skip rope**

skirt [skə:t] *n.* □ **saia**
She wears short skirts. ◆ She put on her skirt. ◆ She took off her skirt.

skull [skʌl] *n.* □ **crânio**

sky [skai] *n.* (*pl.* **skies**) □ **céu**
The sky is clear. (= There are no clouds in the sky.) ◆ a dark sky. ◆ blue skies.

skyscraper ['skai,skreipə] *n.* □ **arranha-céu**

slab [slab] *n.* □ **naco, pedaço grande**
slabs of marble beside the kitchen sink. ◆ a slab of cheese.

slack [slak] *adj.*
1 (= loose) **frouxo**
Leave the rope slack.
2 negligente, relapso
slack workers / students.

slam[1] [slam] *n.* □ **batida forte e barulhenta**
The door closed with a slam.

slam[2] *v.* (**slams, slamming, slammed**) □ **bater com força**
He slammed the door. ◆ She slammed the book on the table.

slang [slaŋ] *n., adj.* □ **gíria, de gíria**
slang words. ◆ 'Buck' is slang for 'dollar'

slant [sla:nt] *v.* (**slants, slanting, slanted**) □ **inclinar, inclinar-se**
In this sentence the letters slant to the right.

slap[1] [slæp] *n.* □ **tapa, bofetada**
She gave him a slap across the face.

slap[2] *v.* (**slaps, slapping, slapped**) □ **estapear, esbofetear**
I slapped her across the face. ◆ She slapped him / his face.

slash[1] [slaʃ] *v.* (**slashes, slashing**) □ **dar um talho, talhar**
Someone slashed my car tyres.

slash[2] *n.* □ **barra diagonal**
In this dictionary the slash (/) is used to show an alternative or another example (e.g. 'She slapped him / his face').

slaughter[1] ['slo:tə] *n.*
1 (= massacre) **massacre**
the slaughter of innocent people.
2 matança
the slaughter of animals for meat.

slaughter[2] *v.* (**slaughters, slaughtering, slaughtered**)
1 (= massacre) **matar, massacrar**
They slaughtered men, women and children.
2 abater
They slaughter animals for food.

slave [sleiv] *n.* □ **escravo**
The boss treats me like a slave.

slavery ['sleivəri] *n.* □ **escravidão**

sledge [sledʒ] *n. Amer.* (mesmo que **sled**) □ **trenó**
People use sledges to travel on snow.

sleep[1] [sli:p] *n.* □ **sono, soneca**
I'm tired – I must get some sleep. ◆ I had six hours' sleep last night.
go to sleep (= fall asleep) □ **dormir**
She sang to him until he went to sleep.

sleep[2] *v.* (**sleeps, sleeping, slept**) □ **dormir**
I didn't sleep well last night. ◆ I couldn't sleep because of the noise. ◆ The cat sleeps on the sofa. ◆ The baby is sleeping (= is asleep).
■ Ver **asleep**.

sleep late □ **dormir até tarde**
I slept late on Saturday.
■ Compare:
I went to sleep late last night.

sleeping bag ['sli:piŋbag] *n.* □ **saco de dormir**

sleepless ['sli:pləs] *adj.* □ **em claro, sem sono**
We had a sleepless night.

sleepy ['sli:pi] *adj.* (**sleepier, sleepiest**)
1 sonolento
to feel sleepy.
2 calmo, sossegado
a sleepy town.

sleet [sli:t] *n.* □ **granizo**

sleeve [sli:v] *n.* □ **manga**
a shirt / dress with short sleeves. ◆ Roll up your sleeves.

sleigh [slei] *n.* □ **trenó**

slender ['slendə] *adj.* (= slim) □ **esguio**
He has long, slender fingers. ◆ a slender girl.

slept [slept] *v.* (Ver **sleep**).

slice[1] [slais] *n.* □ **fatia**
a slice of bread. ◆ a slice of lemon. ◆ Cut the cheese into slices.

slice[2] *v.* (**slices, slicing, sliced**) □ **fatiar, cortar em fatias**
I sliced the tomatoes and the cheese.

slick [slik] *n.* (= oil slick) □ **mancha de óleo na superfície da água**

slide[1] [slaid] *n.*
1 slide
He showed us some slides of wild animals.
2 escorregador
Children were playing on the slide (in the playground).

slide² v. (**slides, sliding, slid**) ▫ **deslizar, introduzir discretamente**
I warned them not to slide on the ice. ♦ The drawer slid out easily. ♦ I slid (= slipped) a letter under his door.

slight [slait] adj. ▫ **leve**
We have a slight problem. ♦ There will be slight changes in the plan. ♦ a slight headache.

slightly ['slaitli] adv. (= a little) ▫ **levemente**
She is slightly taller than me.

slim¹ [slim] adj. (**slimmer, slimmest**) (= slender) ▫ **esguio**
a tall, slim girl. ♦ She has a slim figure.
- Compare **thin, skinny, slim**:
thin = not fat.
skinny = too thin.
slim = with a nice figure.

slim² v. (**slims, slimming, slimmed**) ▫ **emagrecer**
I'm on a diet – I'm trying to slim.

sling¹ [sliŋ] n. ▫ **tipoia**
He has his arm in a sling.

sling² v. (**slings, slinging, slung**) ▫ **atirar, arremessar**
He slung the newspaper angrily at me.

slingshot ['sliŋʃot] n. Amer. ▫ **estilingue**
He is shooting small stones with a slingshot.
- Brit. **catapult**

slip¹ [slip] n.
1 pedaço pequeno
He wrote my phone number on a slip of paper.
2 cometer um deslize
to make a slip.

slip² v. (**slips, slipping, slipped**)
1 escorregar
I slipped on a banana skin. ♦ The wheels slipped on the wet road. ♦ The cup slipped out of my hand.
2 escapar, escapulir
She slipped out of the room.
3 (= slide) **introduzir discretamente**
He slipped the letter into his pocket.

slipper ['slipə] n. ▫ **chinelo**
a pair of slippers.

slippery ['slipəri] adj. ▫ **escorregadio**
Drive carefully. The roads are slippery.

slit¹ [slit] n. ▫ **fenda**
The sunlight came in through a slit in the curtains. ♦ My skirt has a slit in front.

slit² v. (**slits, slitting, slit**) ▫ **abrir cortando em linha reta**
Use this knife to slit open the envelope. ♦ The murderer slit his victim's throat.

slither ['sliðə] v. (**slithers, slithering, slithered**) ▫ **serpentear**
The snake slithered down the tree.

slogan ['slougən] n. ▫ **slogan**
'Give peace a chance' is a political slogan.

slope¹ [sloup] n. ▫ **declive, rampa**
the slope of a hill. ♦ a ski slope.

slope² v. (**slopes, sloping, sloped**) ▫ **fazer declive**
The road slopes up to the entrance of the city.

sloping ['sloupiŋ] adj. ▫ **inclinado**
a sloping roof.

sloppy ['slopi] adj. (**sloppier, sloppiest**) ▫ **desleixado**
sloppy work. ♦ a sloppy worker.

slot [slot] n. ▫ **fenda, abertura para inserir moedas**
I put a coin in the slot and pressed the button for coffee.

slot machine ['slotməʃi:n] n.
1 máquina caça-níqueis
He lost a lot of money on the slot machines.
2 (= vending machine) **máquina**
You can buy a drink or a snack from a slot machine.

slow¹ [slou] adj.
1 lento
a slow train / runner. ♦ to drive at a slow speed.
- antônimo: **quick; fast**
2 atrasado
My watch is five minutes slow.
- antônimo: **fast**

slow² v. (**slows, slowing, slowed**)
slow (down) ▫ **diminuir a velocidade, desacelerar**
The car slowed until it stopped at the traffic-lights. ♦ Slow down – there is a narrow bridge ahead. ♦ The heavy rain slowed the work down.
- antônimo: **speed up**

slowly ['slouli] adv. ▫ **devagar, vagarosamente, lentamente**
Drive more slowly. ♦ He spoke very slowly.

slug [slʌg] n. ▫ **lesma, bala**

slum [slʌm] n. (also **the slum**) ▫ **favela**

slung [slʌŋ] v. (Ver **sling²**).

sly [slai] adj. (= cunning) ▫ **dissimulado, astuto**
a sly smile. ♦ a sly child.

smack¹ [smak] n. ▫ **palmada**
She gave the child a smack on the bottom.

smack² v. (**smacks, smacking, smacked**) ▫ **dar palmada**
They never smack their child.

small [smo:l] adj.
1 pequeno
a small house, table, bottle, etc. ♦ a small family. ♦ My car is smaller than yours. ♦ the smallest tree in the world.
- antônimo: **big; large**
- Use **little** instead of **small** when you want to express an emotional idea with the size:
a beautiful little garden; a sweet little girl.
2 pequeno
a small number of people. ♦ a small amount of money.
- antônimo: **large**
3 pequeno
That shirt is too small for you.
- antônimo: **large**
4 (= little) **pequeno**
a small problem / mistake.
- antônimo: **big**
5 (= young; little) **pequeno**
They have two small children.

get smaller ▫ **ficar menor, diminuir de tamanho**
Computers get smaller and smaller every year.

smart [sma:t] adj.
1 elegante
You look smart in that suit. ♦ smart clothes.
- Used especially in British English.
2 (= clever) **inteligente**
She is a smart girl. ♦ He is one of the smartest students in school.
- Used especially in American English.

smart bomb ['sma:t bom] n. ▫ **bomba teleguiada**

smart card ['sma:t ka:d] n. ▫ **smart card, cartão inteligente**

smash¹ [smaʃ] n. ▫ **choque violento e barulhento**
We heard the smash of breaking glass.

smash² v. (**smashes, smashing, smashed**) ☐ **despedaçar**
The glass hit the floor and smashed to pieces. ◆ The thief smashed the window to get into the house.

smear¹ [smiə] n. ☐ **mancha, nódoa**
a smear of paint, jam, lipstick, etc.

smear² v. (**smears, smearing, smeared**) ☐ **lambuzar, espalhar**
They smeared mud on the floor. ◆ The child smeared jam over his clothes.

smell¹ [smel] n.
1 olfato, faro
Dogs have a very good sense of smell.
2 cheiro
There's a strong smell of gas here. ◆ We complained about the smells from the factory. ◆ a pleasant smell ◆ A stink is an unpleasant smell.

smell² v. (**smells, smelling, smelt or, smelled**)
1 sentir cheiro
I smell something burning in the kitchen. ◆ Can you smell it? (= Do you smell it?)
2 cheirar
The egg smells bad – in fact, it stinks. ◆ This perfume smells good.
3 ter cheiro
Your feet smell.

smelly ['smeli] adj. (**smellier, smelliest**) ☐ **fedido**
smelly feet / socks

smile¹ [smail] n. ☐ **sorriso**
He welcomed me with a big smile.

smile² v. (**smiles, smiling, smiled**) ☐ **sorrir**
She smiled at me. ◆ Smile at the camera.

smock [smok] n. Amer. ☐ **jaleco, guarda-pó**
■ Brit. **overall**

smog [smog] n. ☐ **combinação de nevoeiro e fumaça**
Smog is a serious problem in this city.

smoke¹ [smouk] n. ☐ **fumaça**
The room was full of cigarette smoke.

smoke² v. (**smokes, smoking, smoked**) ☐ **fumar**
I don't smoke. ◆ to smoke a cigarette / pipe. ◆ I quit (= stopped) smoking.

smoked [smoukt] adj. ☐ **defumado**
smoked sausage / cheese.

smoker ['smoukə] n. ☐ **fumante**
If you smoke 15 cigarettes a day, you are a heavy smoker.
■ antônimo: **non-smoker**

smoking ['smoukiŋ] n. ☐ **ato de fumar**
The doctor told him to give up smoking (= to stop smoking). No smoking, please.

smoky ['smouki] adj. (**smokier, smokiest**) ☐ **enfumaçado**
smoky room (full of cigarette smoke). ◆ a smoky chimney.

smooth [smu:ð] adj.
1 liso
smooth skin / paper.
2 suave
The ride in this car is very smooth.
3 calmo
smooth sea.
■ antônimo: **rough**

smoothly ['smu:ðli] adv. ☐ **tranquilamente, uniformemente**
Everything went smoothly according to plan. ◆ The machine is working smoothly.

smother ['smʌðə] v. (**smothers, smothering, smothered**)
1 asfixiar
The murderer smothered her with a pillow.
2 abafar
He smothered the fire with sand.
3 cobrir totalmente
She smothered the burger with ketchup.

smuggle ['smʌgl] v. (**smuggles, smuggling, smuggled**) ☐ **contrabandear**
They smuggled diamonds out of the country. ◆ She tried to smuggle drugs into prison. ◆ to smuggle people across the border.

smuggler ['smʌglə] n. ☐ **contrabandista**
drug smugglers.

smuggling ['smʌgliŋ] n. ☐ **contrabando**

snack [snak] n. ☐ **lanchinho**
I had a snack (= a sandwich, a chocolate bar, etc.) on the train.

snack bar ['snak ba:] n. ☐ **lanchonete**
I had tea and a cheese sandwich at the snack bar.

snag [snag] n. ☐ **porém, empecilho**
There's one snag in the plan – it's too risky.

snail [sneil] n. ☐ **caracol, lesma**

snail mail ['sneil meil] n. ☐ **correio normal**
I sent the invitation by snail mail (= by post, not electronically).
■ Ver **email**.

snake [sneik] n. ☐ **cobra**
a poisonous snake. ◆ A snake bit him.

snap¹ [snap] v. (**snaps, snapping, snapped**)
1 romper-se com estalo
The branch snapped. ◆ The rope snapped. ◆ He snapped a piece of chalk in two.
2 falar brusca e asperamente
'Do it now!' he snapped.
3 tentar morder
The dog snapped at my hand.

snap your fingers ☐ **estalar os dedos**
My dog comes immediately when I snap my fingers.

snap² n. (mesmo que **snapshot**) ☐ **foto instantânea**
They showed us some snaps from their holiday in Turkey.

snarl¹ [sna:l] n. ☐ **rosnado**
The dog gave a snarl.

snarl² v. (**snarls, snarling, snarled**) ☐ **rosnar**
The dog snarled at me.

snatch [snatʃ] v. (**snatches, snatching, snatched**) (= grab) ☐ **arrancar**
A thief snatched my bag and ran away.

sneak [sni:k] v. (**sneaks, sneaking, sneaked**) ☐ **mover-se furtivamente**
I sneaked out of the room. ◆ She sneaked into the house.

sneaker ['sni:kə] n. Amer. ☐ **tênis**
a pair of sneakers.

sneer¹ [sniə] n. ☐ **sorriso desdenhoso**
'Is that all?' she said with a sneer.

sneer² v. (**sneers, sneering, sneered**) ☐ **sorrir com desdém**
He always sneers at my ideas.

sneeze¹ [sni:z] n. ☐ **espirro**

sneeze² v. (**sneezes, sneezing, sneezed**) ☐ **espirrar**
The smell made me sneeze.

sniff¹ [snif] *n.* □ fungada
sniff² *v.* (**sniffs, sniffing, sniffed**) (mesmo que **sniffle**)
1 fungar
I can't stop sniffing – I have a cold. ◆ She always sniffs when she cries.
2 cheirar, farejar
The dogs sniffed each other.
snore [sno:] *v.* (**snores, snoring, snored**) □ roncar
I can't sleep when you snore so loudly.
snort [sno:t] *v.* (**snorts, snorting, snorted**) □ resfolegar
He snorts when he laughs. ◆ The horse snorted.
snow¹ [snou] *n.* □ neve
to play in the snow. ◆ Heavy snow fell during the night.
snow² *v.* (**snows, snowing, snowed**) □ nevar
Look, it's snowing! ◆ It snowed all night.
snowball ['snoubo:l] *n.* □ bola de neve
We threw snowballs at each other.
snowflakes ['snoufleiks] *n. pl.* □ flocos de neve
snowplough ['snouplau] *n. Brit.*, **snowplow** *Amer.* □ removedor de neve
snowy ['snoui] *adj.* (**snowier, snowiest**) □ nevado, cheio de neve
snowy mountains. ◆ a snowy winter.
so¹ [sou] *adv.*
1 tão
Why is the bag so heavy? ◆ You're so lazy!
2 tão
The coffee is so hot (that) I can't drink it. (= The coffee is too hot to drink.)
■ The following sentences mean the same: The book was **so good** that I read it twice. It was **such a good book** that I read it twice
3 sim
Is it true? – I think so. ◆ I don't think so. (= I think not.) ◆ I hope so. (antônimo: I hope not.)
4 também
She can drive and so can I. ◆ I like ice-cream. – So do I.
and so on □ e assim por diante
They sell washing-machines, refrigerators, TVs and so on.
not so... as (mesmo que **not as... as**) □ não tão / tanto... quanto
This car is not so expensive as that one.
or so □ cerca de, aproximadamente
I learnt 200 or so words in Spanish.
so as to (= in order to) □ a fim de
I got up early so as not to miss the train.
so far (= until now) □ até agora
We haven't seen anything so far.
so far as (Ver **as far as**).
so long as (Ver **as long as**).
so many
1 tantos
I receive so many letters that I can't answer all of them.
■ Used with countable nouns.
2 muitos
You have to answer so many questions in an hour.
so much
1 tanto
I can't pay so much (money).
■ Used with uncountable nouns.
2 muito
You have to do so much work a day.

so-so □ mais ou menos
How are you today? – So-so.
so² *conj.*
1 por isso, portanto
I'm very busy so I can't do it today. ◆ He wanted to com so I invited him.
2 (= so that) **para que**
Raise your hand so (that) I can see you.
So what? □ E daí?
He is the manager's son. – So what?
soak [souk] *v.* (**soaks, soaking, soaked**)
1 deixar de molho
Leave the clothes to soak for five minutes. ◆ I soaked t dishes in hot water before washing them.
2 encharcar
My glass of water fell over and soaked the tablecloth. ◆ soak a sponge in water.
get soaked □ ficar encharcado
I went out in the rain and got soaked.
soak up □ absorver, enxugar
I soaked the water up with a cloth.
soaking ['soukiŋ] *adj.* (mesmo que **soaking we** □ encharcado
My clothes are soaking wet.
soap [soup] *n.* □ sabão, sabonete
Wash your hands with soap.
a bar of soap □ sabão, sabonete
I bought two bars of soap.
soap opera ['soup 'opərə] *n.* □ novela
I don't like to watch soap operas. They make me cry.
■ Ver **sitcom**.
soap powder ['soup'audə] *n.* □ sabão em pó
soapy ['soupi] *adj.* □ com sabão
Soak the dishes in soapy water.
soar [so:] *v.* (**soars, soaring, soared**)
1 planar
The plane soared into the clouds.
2 elevar-se
Prices are soaring. ◆ Temperatures soared to 40° C.
sob¹ [sob] *n.* □ soluço
sob² *v.* (**sobs, sobbing, sobbed**) □ soluçar
The child was sobbing, because he couldn't find his moth
sober ['soubə] *adj.* □ sóbrio
Dan is sober (= not drunk), so he will drive.
so-called [sou'ko:ld] *adj.* □ pretenso, suposto
Your so-called friends only want to use you.
soccer ['sokə] *n. Brit.* □ futebol
■ Ver **football**.
sociable ['souʃəbl] *adj.* □ sociável
He is a very sociable man.
social ['souʃəl] *adj.* □ social
social problems. ◆ their social and economic backgrou
social life ['souʃəl laif] *n.* □ vida social
social services ['souʃəl 'sə:visiz] *n.* □ serviços sociais
social worker ['souʃəl 'wə:kə] *n.* □ assistente social
society [sə'saiəti] *n.*
1 sociedade
Crime is a danger to society.
■ Do *not* say **the society** in this meaning.
2 (*pl.* **societies**) **sociedade**
a civilized society.
3 (*pl.* **societies**) **sociedade, companhia**

sock [sok] *n.* □ **meia**
Put on your shoes and socks.

socket ['sokit] *n.* □ **tomada, soquete**
Plug the TV into the socket. ◆ a socket for the (computer) keyboard.

soda ['soudə] *n.*
1 (= **soda water**) **água com gás**
I like my lemonade with soda.
2 (= soda pop) *Amer.* **refrigerante**
a glass of raspberry soda.
■ *Brit.* a fizzy drink

sofa ['soufə] *n.* (= settee) □ **sofá**
to sit on the sofa.

soft [soft] *adj.*
1 macio
a soft pillow.
■ antônimo: **hard**
2 macio
soft skin. ◆ soft hair.
■ antônimo: **rough**
3 suave
She has a soft voice. ◆ soft music.
4 suave
a soft blue.
■ antônimo: **bright**
5 suave
the soft light from the lamp.
6 mole
Their teacher is too soft with them.
■ antônimo: **strict**

soft-boiled egg [soft'boild eg] *n.* □ **ovo quente**
This isn't a soft-boiled egg – it's hard-boiled!

soft drink ['soft driŋk] *n.* □ **drinque sem álcool**
There isn't any alcohol in soft drinks.

soften ['sofn] *v.* (**softens, softening, softened**) □ **amaciar, amolecer**
This cream softens the skin. ◆ Leave the butter to soften.

softly ['softli] *adv.* □ **suavemente**
to speak softly.

softness ['softnis] *n.* □ **maciez, suavidade**

software ['softweə] *n.* □ **software**
Computers are useless without software.
■ Ver **hardware**.

soggy ['sogi] *adj.* □ **encharcado, empapado**
soggy ground.

soil [soil] *n.* □ **solo**
This soil is good for growing oranges.
■ Ver **earth; ground**.

solar ['soulə] *adj.* □ **solar**
solar energy.

the solar system *n.* □ **o sistema solar**

sold [sould] *v.* (Ver **sell**).

sold out □ **esgotado**
The book is sold out. ◆ The concert was sold out a week ago.

soldier ['souldʒə] *n.* □ **soldado**
He was a soldier in the German army. ◆ The soldiers fought bravely.

sole¹ [soul] *adj.* (= only) □ **único**
My sole purpose is to find out the truth. ◆ She is the sole owner of the shop.

sole² *n.*
1 sola, solado
Tennis shoes have rubber soles.
2 sola, planta
the sole of the foot.

solemn ['soləm] *adj.*
1 sério
a solemn face.
2 solene
solemn music.

solemnly ['soləmli] *adv.* □ **solenemente, com seriedade**
They listened to the news solemnly.

solicitor [so'lisitə] *n. Brit.* □ **advogado**
■ Ver **lawyer**.

solid¹ ['solid] *adj.*
1 sólido
The patient can't eat solid food.
2 maciço
solid gold. **solid²** *n.*
1 sólido
Water is a liquid and ice is a solid.
2 corpo sólido
A pyramid is a solid.

solitary ['solitəri] *adj.* □ **solitário**
to go for a solitary walk (= to go for a walk alone).

solo¹ ['soulou] *adj., adv.* □ **solo**
That's his first solo flight (as a pilot).

solo² *n.* □ **solo**
to play a piano solo.

solution [sə'lu:ʃən] *n.* □ **solução**
There is more than one solution to this problem.

solve [solv] *v.* (**solves, solving, solved**) □ **resolver, solucionar**
They are trying to solve the problem of violence in schools. ◆ The police solved the crime. ◆ The scientists cannot solve the mystery.

some [sʌm] *adj., pron.*
1 certa quantidade
I bought some eggs and some meat.
■ In questions and negative sentences **any** is used instead of **some**, except for questions when you expect the answer 'yes':
Would you like some tea / cake?
Can I have some (coffee)?
2 alguns
Some students think that it's a good idea. ◆ Some of them came late.
3 algum
There's some man waiting outside. ◆ There must be some way to tell him.

some more □ **um pouco mais de**
We don't have enough money. We need some more. ◆ Can I have some more biscuits / coffee?

some time □ **algum tempo**
I waited for some time and left. ◆ We saw them some time ago.

somebody ['sʌmbodi] *pron.* (= **someone**) □ **alguém, uma pessoa**
Someone asked about you. ◆ There's somebody waiting for you.

■ In questions and negative sentences **anybody** or **anyone** are used instead of **somebody** or **someone**.

somebody else, someone else □ **uma outra pessoa**
I need him here. Take someone else.
somehow ['sʌmhau] *adv.* □ **de alguma forma, de algum modo**
We must get there somehow.
someone ['sʌmwʌn] *pron.* (Ver **somebody**).
someplace ['sʌmpleis] *adv. Amer.* (= somewhere) □ **em algum lugar**
They live someplace in the north.
somersault ['sʌməso:lt] *n.* □ **salto-mortal, cambalhota**
to do a somersault.
something ['sʌmθiŋ] *n.* □ **algo, alguma coisa**
I saw something moving. ◆ Something is bothering me.
■ In questions and negative sentences **anything** is usually used instead of **something**, except in questions when you expect the answer 'yes':
Can I tell you something?
Do you want something to drink?
something else □ **algo mais, mais alguma coisa**
I expected to hear something else. ◆ I'll give you something else to eat.
■ Compare with **anything else**.
sometime ['sʌmtaim] *adv.* □ **qualquer hora**
I'll visit them sometime next month.
sometimes ['sʌmtaimz] *adv.* □ **às vezes**
She sometimes comes for a visit. ◆ Sometimes I think about them.
somewhere ['sʌmweə] *adv.* □ **algum lugar**
They went somewhere. ◆ He lives somewhere in the north.
■ In questions and negative sentences **anywhere** is usually used instead of **somewhere**, except in questions when you expect the answer 'yes':
Do you want to go somewhere?
somewhere else □ **outro lugar**
Let's go somewhere else.
son [sʌn] *n.* □ **filho**
They have a son and two daughters.
song [soŋ] *n.*
1 canção
a pop song. ◆ He sang a love song.
2 canto, ato de cantar
to burst into song (= to start singing).
son-in-law ['sʌninlo:] *n.* (*pl.* **sons-in-law**) □ **genro**
My daughter and my son-in-law have a happy marriage.
soon [su:n] *adv.*
1 (= shortly) **logo, em breve, daqui a pouco**
You will soon hear from him. ◆ The film will start soon.
2 cedo
Why are you leaving so soon?
as soon as □ **assim que**
I'll do it as soon as I get home.
■ **as soon as I get...** (*not* 'as soon as I will get...').
as soon as possible, as soon as you can □ **assim que possível, o mais rápido possível**
Please answer as soon as possible. ◆ Come here as soon as you can.
soon after □ **logo depois, pouco depois**
He phoned soon after six o'clock.
sooner or later □ **mais cedo ou mais tarde**
Sooner or later you'll have to tell them the truth.
too soon □ **antes da hora, cedo demais**
I can't tell you all about it – it's too soon. ◆ You answered too soon.

soot [sut] *n.* □ **fuligem**
soothe [su:ð] *v.* (**soothes, soothing, soothed**) □ **acalmar, sossegar**
She knows how to soothe a crying baby.
soothing ['su:ðiŋ] *adj.* □ **calmante, relaxante**
soothing music. ◆ a soothing bath.
sophisticated [sə'fistikeitid] *adj.* □ **sofisticado**
sophisticated equipment.
sophistication [sə,fisti'keiʃən] *n.* □ **sofisticação**
sore [so:] *adj.* □ **dolorido, irritado**
My feet are sore after standing for so long. ◆ sore eyes.
sore throat □ **garganta inflamada**
I have a sore throat.
sorrow ['sorou] *n.* □ **tristeza**
They felt deep sorrow at the death of their mother.
sorry[1] ['sori] *adj.*
1 pesaroso
I'm sorry I didn't write to you sooner.
2 triste
We are sorry you can't stay.
3 contrito
I'm sorry, but the answer is 'no'.
feel sorry for □ **ter pena de**
I felt sorry for the hungry child and gave him my sandwich.
sorry[2]
1 (= excuse me) **sinto muito, perdão, desculpe**
Sorry, I didn't mean to hurt you.
2 (= Pardon?) **como?, como disse?**
Sorry? Did you say tea or coffee?
sort[1] [so:t] *n.* (= kind; type) □ **tipo**
What sort of movies do you like? ◆ They sell all sorts (= many types) of pens.
sort of (= kind of) □ **um tanto, um pouco, meio**
It's sort of round, something like an egg. ◆ Are you ready? – Sort of.
sort[2] *v.* (**sorts, sorting, sorted**) □ **separar**
A machine sorts the letters according to the postcode.
sort out □ **resolver**
Take some money until you sort out your problems.
SOS [esou'es] *n.* □ **SOS, pedido de socorro**
The ship sent out an SOS.
sought [so:t] *v.* (Ver **seek**).
soul [soul] *n.*
1 alma
He is dead, but his soul is in Heaven.
2 soul
soul music.
not a soul □ **nem uma alma viva**
I was alone there. There wasn't a soul around.
sound[1] [saund] *n.* □ **som**
I heard the sound of something breaking. ◆ The sound of this TV is very clear. ◆ vowel sounds.
not make a sound □ **não dar um pio**
He hid under the bed and didn't make a sound.
sound[2] *v.* (**sounds, sounding, sounded**)
1 soar, parecer
The song sounds nice. ◆ Your idea sounds interesting.
2 tocar
to sound the horn (of the car). ◆ He sounded the alarm when he saw the fire.
sound[3] *adj.*

1 (= healthy) □ **saudável**
a sound body. ♦ sound teeth.
2 sensato
sound advice.
safe and sound □ **são e salvo**
They returned home safe and sound.
sound⁴ *adv.*
sound asleep □ **em sono profundo**
The baby is sound asleep.
soup [su:p] *n.* □ **sopa**
I had some chicken soup for lunch. ♦ a bowl of soup.
sour ['sauə] *adj.* □ **azeda**
The lemonade is too sour – add sugar to make it sweet.
go sour □ **ficar azedo, azedar**
Put the milk back in the fridge or it will go sour.
source [so:s] *n.*
1 fonte
That journalist has good sources in the government.
2 fonte
The sun is a good source of energy.
3 nascente
the source of the river Nile.
south¹ [sauθ] *n.* □ **sul**
They live somewhere in the south (of the country). ♦ north, south, east and west.
south² *adj.* □ **do sul, meridional**
a south wind. ♦ the south coast. ♦ South America. ♦ South Africa.
south³ *adv.* □ **ao sul**
to travel south.
south of □ **ao sul de**
sixty kilometers south of Paris.
southern ['sʌðən] *adj.* □ **do sul**
a village in southern France.
souvenir [su:və'niə] *n.* □ **suvenir**
I bought some souvenirs in India.
sow [sou] *v.* (**sows, sowing, sowed, sown** or **sowed**) □ **semear**
to sow seeds. ♦ The farmer sowed the field with wheat.
space [speis] *n.*
1 (= room) **espaço**
There isn't enough space for another bed in the room. ♦ I need more space in my office. ♦ The chairs take up too much space here.
2 espaço
Can you park in the space between these two cars? ♦ Leave more space between the words.
■ Ver **parking space**.
3 (= outer space) **espaço, espaço sideral**
to send a satellite into space. ♦ creatures from outer space.
spacecraft ['speiskra:ft] *n.* (*pl.* **spacecraft**) □ **espaçonave**
spaceman ['speismən] *n.* (*pl.* **spacemen**) (= astronaut) □ **astronauta (homem)**
spaceship ['speiʃip] *n.* □ **espaçonave, nave espacial**
space shuttle ['speis 'ʃʌtl] *n.* □ **ônibus espacial**
The space shuttle carried a big telescope into space.
space station ['speis 'steiʃən] *n.* □ **estação espacial**
spacesuit ['speisu:t] *n.* □ **traje espacial**
Astronauts wear spacesuits.
spacewoman ['speiswumən] *n.* (*pl.* **spacewomen**) (= astronaut) □ **astronauta (mulher)**
spacious ['speiʃəs] *adj.* □ **espaçoso**

a spacious room ♦ a spacious park.
spade [speid] *n.* □ **pá**
Take this spade and dig a hole here.
■ Compare **shovel, spade**:
  shovel = round blade.
  spade = square blade.
spades *n. pl.* □ **espadas**
the queen of spades.
spaghetti [spə'geti] *n.* □ **espaguete**
spanner ['spanə] *n. Brit.* □ **chave inglesa**
to tighten a bolt with a spanner.
■ *Amer.* **wrench**
spare¹ [speə] *adj.*
1 sobressalente
a spare key. ♦ a spare wheel.
2 extra
Do you have a spare pencil?
3 livre
What do you do in your spare time?
spare part *n.* □ **peça sobressalente**
spare tyre *n. Brit.*, **spare tire** *Amer.* □ **pneu sobressalente**
spare² *v.* (**spares, sparing, spared**)
1 dispor
Can you spare me five minutes of your time? ♦ How much can you give me? – I can spare $20.
2 poupar
The king spared their lives.
spark [spa:k] *n.* □ **fagulha, faísca**
A spark started the fire in the building.
sparkle¹ ['spa:kl] *n.* □ **brilho, cintilação**
the sparkle of jewels.
sparkle² *v.* (**sparkles, sparkling, sparkled**) □ **brilhar, cintilar**
The sea sparkled in the sunlight.
sparkling ['spa:kliŋ] *adj.*
1 cintilante
sparkling diamonds.
2 (= fizzy) **frisante, com gás**
sparkling wine. ♦ sparkling mineral water.
sparrow ['sparou] *n.* □ **pardal**
spat [spat] *v.* (Ver **spit**).
speak [spi:k] *v.* (**speaks, speaking, spoke, spoken**)
1 falar
Can I speak to the manager, please? ♦ Can I speak with...? *Amer.* ♦ Try to speak more slowly.
■ **talk** is also possible.
2 falar
Do you speak English? ♦ I can speak three languages.
■ **talk** is not possible here.
3 falar
Who spoke at the meeting? ♦ She spoke about the economic problems.
■ **talk** is also possible.
speak up □ **falar alto**
Speak up! I can't hear you.
speaker ['spi:kə] *n.*
1 palestrante
Our speaker tonight is a famous scientist.
2 falante
an English speaker. ♦ a Chinese speaker.
3 (= loudspeaker) **alto-falante**
spear [spiə] *n.* □ **lança, arpão**

special ['speʃəl] *adj.* □ especial
This is a special day for all of us. ◆ The pop star got special treatment at the hotel. ◆ a special computer program for blind people. ◆ Are you doing anything special tonight?
special² *n. Amer.* □ promoção
This week's special: perfumes at half price.
on special □ na promoção
We have frozen vegetables on special.
special offer *n.* □ promoção especial
It's a special offer. You get two for the price of one.
specialise ['speʃəlaiz] *v. Brit.* (= **specialize**).
specialist ['speʃəlist] *n.*
1 (= expert) **especialista**
She is a specialist in Greek philosophy. ◆ a computer specialist.
2 especialista
an eye specialist. ◆ a heart specialist.
speciality [speʃi'aləti] *n. Brit.* (= **specialty**, *Amer.*) □ especialidade
His speciality is English grammar.
specialization [,speʃəlai'zeiʃən] *n.*, **specialisation** *Brit.* □ especialização
specialize ['speʃəlaiz] *v.* (**specializes, specializing, specialized**)
This school specializes in art and music.
specialize in □ especializar-se em
She specialized in skin diseases.
specially ['speʃəli] *adv.* (also **especially**) □ especialmente
I prepared this meal specially for you.
specialty ['speʃəlti] *n. Amer.* (= **speciality**, *Brit.*) □ especialidade
His speciality is English grammar.
species ['spi:ʃi:z] *n.* □ espécie
Elephants are an endangered species. (= Their existence is in danger.)
specific [spə'sifik] *adj.* □ específico
I asked you a specific question, but you gave me a general answer. ◆ He gave us specific instructions on how to do it.
specifically [spə'sifikli] *adv.*
1 especificamente
I specifically told you to wait for us.
2 especificamente
TV programmes specifically for little children.
specify ['spesifai] *v.* (**specifies, specifying, specified**) □ especificar
He did not specify who will be in the team.
speck [spek] *n.* □ partícula, pontinha
a speck of dust.
spectacle ['spektəkl] *n.* □ espetáculo
The carnival was a great spectacle.
spectacles ['spektəklz] *n. pl.* □ óculos
spectacular [spek'tækjulə] *adj.* □ espetacular
The view from the top of the hill was spectacular.
spectator [spek'teitə] *n.* □ espectador
There were 30,000 spectators in the stadium.
■ Compare with **viewer**.
sped [sped] *v.* (Ver **speed**).
speech [spi:tʃ] *n.*
1 discurso
The President's speech was very good. ◆ She writes the Prime Minister's speeches.
2 fala
Only humans have the power of speech.
make a speech, give a speech □ fazer um discurso
He made a speech about the economic situation.
freedom of speech □ liberdade de expressão
speed¹ [spi:d] *n.* □ velocidade
I drove at a speed of 80 kph (kilometers per hour). ◆ The boat travelled at high speed. ◆ to lower the speed. ◆ to increase the speed. ◆ What's the speed limit here?
speed² *v.* (**speeds, speeding, sped or speeded**)
1 acelerar
When the pop star got into the car, the driver sped away.
2 ir em alta velocidade
The police stopped him because he was speeding.
■ The form **sped** is used only in meaning 1
speed up □ acelerar
They speeded up the building of the road.
speeding ['spi:diŋ] *n.* □ excesso de velocidade
She had to pay a fine for speeding.
■ Ver **ticket**.
speed limit ['spi:d 'limit] *n.* □ limite de velocidade
The speed limit on this road is 50 kph (kilometers per hour).
speedy recovery ['spi:di rə'kʌvəri] *n.* □ recuperação rápida
I wish you a speedy recovery!
spell¹ [spel] *n.* □ feitiço
put a spell on □ enfeitiçar
The witch put a spell on the princess.
spell² *v.* (**spells, spelling, spelled or spelt**) □ soletrar
How do you spell your name? – 'E-D-D-Y'. ◆ He spelled the name wrong.
spell check ['speltʃek] *n.* □ corretor ortográfico
Your email was full of spelling mistakes – why dont you use a spell check?
spelling ['speliŋ] *n.* □ ortografia
What's the American spelling for 'plough'?
spelling mistake ['speliŋ mis'teik] *n.* □ erro de ortografia
You make too many spelling mistakes! ◆ Please correct your spelling mistakes.
spelt [spelt] *v.* (Ver **spell²**).
spend [spend] *v.* (**spends, spending, spent**)
1 gastar
He spends a lot of money on computer games. ◆ I went shopping and spent $100.
2 passar
I spend one hour every day on my homework. ◆ She spent six months in prison. ◆ He spent a year abroad.
spice¹ [spais] *n.* □ condimento, especiarias
Pepper, cinnamon and paprika are spices.
spice² *v.* (**spices, spicing, spiced**) □ temperar, condimentar
I spiced the soup with black pepper.
spicy ['spaisi] *adj.* (**spicier, spiciest**) □ condimentado
I like spicy food.
spider ['spaidə] *n.* □ aranha
spiderweb ['spaidəweb] *n. Amer.* (= **cobweb**, *Brit.*) □ teia de aranha
Spiders make spiderwebs to catch insects.
spied [spaid] *v.* (Ver **spy²**).
spies [spaiz] *n.*, *v.* (Ver **spy¹**; **spy²**).
spike [spaik] *n.* □ ponta
a fence with spikes on top.

spill [spil] *v.* (**spills, spilling, spilled** or, **spilt**) □ derramar
Be careful not to spill your coffee on the sofa. ◆ I poured sugar into a jar, but some of it spilled on the floor.
spin [spin] *v.* (**spins, spinning, spun**)
1 rodar
to spin a top. ◆ The dancer spun round and round.
2 girar, rodar
My head is spinning.
3 fiar
He spun threads of wool.
4 tecer
Spiders spin webs.
spinach ['spinidʒ] *n.* □ espinafre
spine [spain] *n.* □ espinha
spinster ['spinstə] *n.* □ solteirona, solteira
spiral[1] ['spaiərəl] *adj.* □ espiral
a spiral staircase.
spiral[2] *n.* □ espiral
spirit ['spirit] *n.*
1 espírito
the spirits of the dead.
2 espírito
All those failures broke his spirit. ◆ He is 90 years old, but he is young in spirit.
spirits *n. pl.*
1 astral, humor
She is in high spirits (= in a happy mood) today.
2 bebida alcoólica
Whisky and vodka are spirits.
spiritual ['spiritʃuəl] *adj.* □ espiritual
spiritual guidance / needs.
spit[1] [spit] *v. Amer.* (**spits, spitting, spat** or, **spit**) □ cuspir
He spits when he talks. ◆ She spat at him.
spit[2] *n.* □ cuspe
spite [spait] *n.*
out of spite □ por despeito
He tore up her letters out of spite.
in spite of □ apesar de
We went out in spite of the rain.
■ Other ways of saying this:
We went out despite the rain.
We went out although it was raining.
splash [splæʃ] *v.* (**splashes, splashing, splashed**)
1 salpicar
A car splashed me with mud.
2 respingar
Some paint splashed on the window.
3 chapinhar
The children were splashing in the pool.
splendid ['splendid] *adj.*
1 esplêndido
a splendid view of the valley. ◆ a splendid palace.
2 esplêndido
What a splendid idea!
splinter ['splintə] *n.* □ farpa
I have a splinter (of wood, glass or metal) in my finger.
split[1] [split] *n.*
1 abertura, fenda
You have a split down your shirt. ◆ a split in the skirt.
2 racha
a split in the (political) party.
do the splits □ abrir espacate
split[2] *v.* (**splits, splitting, split**)
1 partir
I split the melon in half.
2 abrir-se
His jeans split at the sides.
3 dividir
They split the money between them.
split up
1 (= break up) **terminar**
She split up with her boyfriend.
2 dividir-se
The class split up to work in groups (divided up).
split second ['split 'sekənd] *n.* □ fração de segundo
It happened in a split second.
spoil [spoil] *v.* (**spoils, spoiling, spoiled** or **spoilt**)
1 (= ruin) **estragar**
He spoiled all the fun with his bad jokes. ◆ The cold weather spoilt our holiday. ◆ Don't add any more salt – you'll spoil the meal.
2 (= indulge) **mimar**
They spoil their son.
spoilt [spoilt] *adj.* □ mimado
a spoilt child.
spoke[1] [spouk] *n.* □ raio de roda
spoke[2] *v.* (Ver **speak**).
spoken ['spoukən] *v.* (Ver **speak**).
spokesman ['spouksmən] *n.* (*pl.* **spokesmen**) □ porta-voz
the government spokesman.
spokesperson ['spoukspə:sən] *n.* □ porta-voz
spokeswoman ['spoukswumən] *n.* (*pl.* **spokeswomen**) □ porta-voz
sponge [spʌndʒ] *n.* □ esponja
He soaked up the water with a sponge.
sponge cake [pɒnʌndʒ keik] *n.* □ pão-de-ló
sponsor[1] ['spɒnsə] *n.* □ patrocinador
Each team in the football league has a sponsor.
sponsor[2] *v.* (**sponsors, sponsoring, sponsored**) □ patrocinar
A big computer company will sponsor the broadcast of the game on TV.
spontaneous [spɒn'teiniəs] *adj.* □ espontâneo
a spontaneous reaction.
spool [spu:l] *n.* (= reel) **carretel**
to rewind the spool (of a fishing-line).
spoon [spu:n] *n.*
1 colher
a soup spoon. ◆ a wooden spoon.
■ Ver **teaspoon**; **tablespoon**.
2 (= spoonful) **colherada**
sport [spɔ:t] *n.*
1 esporte
They do a lot of sport at school.
2 (= game) **esporte**
I like team sports, especially football and basketball.
sports [spɔ:ts] *adj.* □ esportes
sports equipment. ◆ a sports club. *Amer.*
sports car *n. Amer.* (mesmo que **sport car**) □ carro esportivo

sports jacket *n.* (mesmo que **sport coat**) ◻ jaqueta esportiva, paletó esportivo
the sports page *n.* (mesmo que **the sports section**) ◻ página de esportes
I always read the sports page.
sportsman ['spɔːtsmən] *n.* (*pl.* **sportsmen**) ◻ esportista
sportsmanship ['spɔːtsmənʃip] *n.* ◻ esportividade
sportswoman ['spɔːtswumən] *n.* (*pl.* **sportswomen**) ◻ esportista
spot¹ [spɔt] *n.*
 1 bolinha, ponto
 The dress was red with black spots. ◆ There were spots of paint on the floor.
 2 ponto, local
 We found a good spot for a picnic. ◆ This is the exact spot where it happened.
 on the spot
 1 na hora
 When they met, they recognized each other on the spot.
 2 no local
 The ambulance was on the spot very quickly.
spot² *v.* (**spots, spotting, spotted**) ◻ localizar
 The police spotted him in the crowd. ◆ He spotted the problem in my TV and fixed it.
spotlight ['spɔtlait] *n.* ◻ holofote, refletor
spout [spaut] *n.* ◻ bico
 Kettles and teapots have spouts.
sprain [sprein] *v.* (**sprains, spraining, sprained**) ◻ torcer, distender
 I sprained my ankle when I jumped down.
sprang [spraŋ] *v.* (Ver **spring**).
spray¹ [sprei] *n.*
 1 aerossol
 (a can of) hair spray. ◆ insect spray (for killing flies, mosquitoes, etc.).
 2 líquido espalhado pelo uso de pulverizador
 Chemical sprays are used in agriculture.
 3 jato, borrifo
 a quick spray of perfume.
spray² *v.* (**sprays, spraying, sprayed**) ◻ borrifar
 He sprayed black paint on my door. ◆ She sprayed herself with perfume.
spray can ['sprei 'kan] *n.* ◻ lata de spray
 He painted a picture on the wall with spray cans.
spread¹ [spred] *n.*
 1 difusão, propagação
 to stop the spread of a disease.
 2 pasta
 anchovy spread.
spread² *v.* (**spreads, spreading, spread**)
 1 abrir, desdobrar
 I spread a tablecloth over the table. ◆ The officer spread out a map on the table. ◆ The bird spread its wings.
 2 passar
 I spread butter on a slice of bread.
 3 espalhar
 Fire spread quickly to the top floor. ◆ The news spread very quickly.
 4 espalhar
 Rats spread disease. ◆ Nobody knows who spread the lies about her.
 5 estender-se
 The desert spreads for hundreds of kilometers.

spread out
 1 espalhar-se
 The police spread out in search of the missing child.
 2 abrir
 He spread out his sleeping-bag on the ground.
spring¹ [spriŋ] *n.*
 1 mola
 The springs in my mattress make too much noise.
 2 primavera
 Many trees blossom in spring. ◆ The four seasons are spring, summer, autumn (= fall) and winter.
 3 fonte
 They drank water from the spring. ◆ spring water.
spring² *v.* (**springs, springing, sprang, sprung**) ◻ pular
 I sprang out of bed to answer the telephone.
springboard ['spriŋbɔːd] *n.* ◻ trampolim
sprinkle ['spriŋkl] *v.* (**sprinkles, sprinkling, sprinkled**) ◻ borrifar, salpicar
 Sprinkle some oil and vinegar on the salad. ◆ Sprinkle the cookies with sugar before baking.
sprinkler ['spriŋklə] *n.* ◻ aspersor
sprint¹ [sprint] *n.* ◻ corrida de velocidade de pequeno percurso
 a 100 meter / metre sprint.
sprint² *v.* (**sprints, sprinting, sprinted**) ◻ correr a toda velocidade
 He sprinted to catch the train.
sprout [spraut] *v.* (**sprouts, sprouting, sprouted**) ◻ brotar
 The seeds are beginning to sprout.
sprung [sprʌŋ] *v.* (Ver **spring**).
spun [spʌn] *v.* (Ver **spin**).
spur [spɔː] *n.* ◻ espora
 The rider had spurs on his boots.
spy¹ [spai] *n.* (*pl.* **spies**) ◻ espião
 The spy passed on secret information to the enemy.
spy² *v.* (**spies, spying, spied**) ◻ espionar
 She spied for the enemy.
spy on ◻ espionar
 How do you know I was there? Are you spying on me?
spy³ *adj.* ◻ de espião
 spy stories.
spy satellite ['spai 'satəlait] *n.* ◻ satélite espião
Sq. *abbr.*, **Sq** (= **Square**) Pç.
 8 Victory Sq.
sq (or **Sq.**) *abbr.* (= square) ◻ quadrado (unidade de medida)
 10 sq km (= 10 square kilometers / kilometres).
squad [skwɔd] *n.*
 1 esquadrão
 the police drugs squad.
 2 seleção, equipe
 the Brazilian athletics squad.
squad car ['skwɔd 'kaː] *n.* ◻ viatura
square¹ [skweə] *n.*
 1 quadrado
 Draw a square, a rectangle and a triangle.
 2 (= Sq.) **praça**
 There is an exhibition in the town square.
square² *adj.*
 1 quadrado
 a square window.

2 quadrado
an area of 1,000 square meters / metres ◆ The room is 16 metres square.
- abreviação: **sq.**

square³ [squares, squaring, squared] □ **endireitar, acertar, ajustar**

squash¹ [skwoʃ] *n.*
1 *Brit.* **suco**
orange squash.
2 *Amer.* **abóbora**
- *Brit.* **marrow**
- Ver **courgette; zucchini.**

squash² *v.* (**squashes, squashing, squashed**)
1 amassar
He sat on the box and squashed it. ◆ The bananas got squashed.
2 espremer-se, espremer
Twenty people squashed into my room. ◆ I squashed the clothes into the suitcase.

squat [skwɒt] *v.* (**squats, squatting, squatted**) □ **agachar-se**
They all squatted around the fire.

squeak¹ [skwi:k] *n.* □ **guincho**
the squeak of a mouse.

squeak² *v.* (**squeaks, squeaking, squeaked**) □ **guinchar, ranger**
I heard the mice squeaking. ◆ His shoes squeaked when he walked. ◆ The door squeaked when I opened it.

squeaky ['skwi:ki] *adj.*
1 estridente
She has a squeaky voice.
2 rangente
a squeaky door. ◆ a squeaky chair.

squeal¹ [skwi:l] *n.* □ **guincho**
the squeals of pigs. ◆ a squeal of brakes.

squeal² *v.* (**squeals, squealing, squealed**) □ **dar gritos agudos, guinchar**
The children squealed with joy. ◆ The tires squealed when she stopped the car.

squeeze¹ [skwi:z] *n.* □ **aperto**
He gave my hand a squeeze.

squeeze² *v.* (**squeezes, squeezing, squeezed**)
1 apertar
He squeezed my arm to show his sympathy. ◆ to squeeze the toothpaste tube.
2 espremer
I squeezed two oranges.
3 espremer-se
We squeezed into the back of the car.
4 forçar
We can squeeze another person in the car.

squeeze something out of □ **arrancar algo de**
Try to squeeze more information out of him.

squirrel ['skwɪrəl] *n.* □ **esquilo**
Squirrels live in trees and eat nuts.

st *abbr.* **º**
1st July (= the first of July) ◆ Today is my 21st birthday.
- Ver **first.**

St *abbr.*, **St.**
1 (= street) **R.**
I live at 10 Flower St., Chicago.

2 (= Saint) **S., Sto.**
St Peter. ◆ St. Paul's Cathedral.

stab [stab] *v.* (**stabs, stabbing, stabbed**) □ **esfaquear**
The murderer stabbed him twice in the stomach. ◆ She was stabbed to death.

stability [stə'bɪlɪti] *n.* □ **estabilidade**
economic and political stability.
- antônimo: **instability**

stable¹ ['steɪbl] *adj.* □ **firme, estável**
Be careful! The ladder isn't very stable. ◆ The patient's condition is stable. ◆ a stable country. ◆ a stable marriage.
- antônimo: **unstable**

stable² *n.* □ **estábulo**
He is feeding the horses in the stable.

stack¹ [stak] *n.* □ **pilha**
a stack of books. ◆ a stack of papers.
- Ver **heap; pile.**

stack² *v.* (**stacks, stacking, stacked**) □ **empilhar**
I helped him stack the chairs after the party.

be stacked (with) □ **estar lotado (de)**
The refrigerator was stacked with food.

stadium ['steɪdɪəm] *n.* □ **estádio**
There are 50,000 seats in the stadium. ◆ a football stadium.

staff [sta:f] *n.*
1 pessoal, equipe
We need more staff in the office. ◆ the hotel staff.
2 corpo docente
The school has a staff of 45 teachers.

staff room ['sta:f,rum] *n.* □ **sala dos professores, sala dos funcionários**

stage [steɪdʒ] *n.*
1 palco
All the actors went on stage at the end of the play.
2 estágio
They will finish the first stage of the project in May. ◆ At this stage, it's too early to know what happened.

stagger ['stagə] *v.* (**staggers, staggering, staggered**) □ **cambalear**
A drunk staggered down the street.

stain¹ [steɪn] *n.* □ **mancha**
There are coffee stains on the sofa. ◆ an oil stain. ◆ to remove a stain.
- Ver **mark; spot.**

stain² *v.* (**stains, staining, stained**) □ **manchar**
The blood stained his shirt.

stainless steel ['steɪnlɪs sti:l] *n.* □ **aço inoxidável**
stainless steel knives and forks.

staircase ['steəkeɪs] *n.* (mesmo que **stairway**) □ **escada**

stairs [steəz] *n. pl.* □ **escada**
She climbed up the stairs to the second floor. ◆ He went down the stairs to the kitchen. ◆ wooden stairs.
- Ver **downstairs; upstairs.**
- Compare **with steps:**
  stairs = inside a building.
  steps = outside a building.

stale [steɪl] *adj.*
1 amanhecido, passado
stale bread / biscuits.
2 de mofo, mofado
There was a stale smell in the kitchen. ◆ The air was stale because the windows were closed.

stalk [stɔ:k] *n.* □ **talo, haste**

stall / start

the stalk of a flower.
■ Ver **stem**.
stall [sto:l] *n.* □ **banca**
a market stall. ◆ a fruit stall.
stammer ['stamə] *v.* (**stammers, stammering, stammered**) (= stutter) □ **gaguejar**
He stammered when he spoke.
stamp¹ [stamp] *n.*
1 selo
She stuck a stamp on the envelope. ◆ I collect stamps as a hobby.
2 carimbo
a date stamp (= stamping dates).
3 carimbo
The stamps in my passport show that I was in Spain, France and Italy last year.
stamp² *v.* (**stamps, stamping, stamped**)
1 bater com o pé sobre algo
He stamped on the cockroach and killed it. ◆ She stamped her foot in anger.
2 carimbar
She stamped the date on the check. ◆ to stamp a passport.
stand¹ [stand] *n.*
1 barraca, quiosque, estande
a hot-dog stand (where you can buy hot dogs). ◆ Our company has a stand at the electronics exhibition.
2 suporte
a hat-stand (where you can hang your hat). ◆ a music stand.
3 arquibancada
The fans in the stands cheered when the game started.
stand² *v.* (**stands, standing, stood**)
1 estar, encontrar-se
She stood by the window and looked outside. ◆ Don't just stand there – come and help me!
2 (= stand up) **levantar-se**
He stood up and gave his seat to an old man.
3 ficar
Can you stand on your head?
4 encontrar-se
The bookcase stands in the corner.
5 aguentar, suportar
The building won't stand another storm.
6 pôr, colocar
Stand the ladder against that tree.
7 estar de pé
My offer still stands – 15,000 for your car.
can't / couldn't stand (= can't / couldn't bear) □ **não poder aguentar**
I can't stand that man. ◆ She couldn't stand the heat and went out.
stand aside □ **afastar-se**
They stood aside to let the ambulance pass.
stand back □ **recuar**
The policemen asked the crowd to stand back.
stand by
1 assistir, ficar olhando
How can you stand by and let them cheat your friend?
2 ficar a postos
Stand by! We are landing.
3 ficar do lado de, apoiar
He needs our support and we'll stand by him.

stand for □ **significar**
'PM' stands for 'Prime Minister'. *Amer.*
stand in line □ **ficar na fila**
We stood in line for hours to buy a ticket.
■ *Brit.* **stand in a queue**
stand out □ **destacar-se**
You'll stand out in the crowd in that dress.
stand still □ **ficar imóvel**
Stand still while I brush your hair.
stand up for □ **defender**
My father blamed me, but my mother stood up for me.
stand up for your rights □ **defender seus direitos**
We must stand up for our rights.
stand up to □ **enfrentar**
It was brave of her to stand up to the boss.
standard¹ ['standəd] *adj.* □ **padrão**
This is the standard size of compact discs. ◆ They speak standard English.
standard² *n.*
1 padrão
We have very high safety standards in our factory.
2 média, nível
His work is above standard. ◆ Your work is of a very high standard.
standard of living ['standəd ov 'livin] *n.* (mesmo que **living standard**) □ **padrão de vida**
The standard of living may rise by 3% next year. ◆ a high standard of living.
stand-by ['standbai] *n.*
on stand-by
1 de prontidão
Five ambulances were on standby.
2 na lista de espera
They put me on standby (because there are no seats on the plane at the moment).
standpoint ['standpoint] *n.* (= point of view) □ **ponto de vista**
Let's try to look at the problem from their standpoint.
stank [staŋk] *v.* (Ver **stink**).
staple¹ ['steipl] *n.* □ **grampo**
staple² *v.* (**staples, stapling, stapled**) □ **grampear**
Staple the copies of this letter together.
stapler ['steiplə] *n.* □ **grampeador**
star¹ [sta:] *n.*
1 estrela
The stars were shining brightly that night.
2 estrela
I made cookies / biscuits in the shape of a star.
3 astro, estrela
She is a big rock star in Russia. ◆ a film / movie star.
star² *v.* (**stars, starring, starred**) □ **estrelar**
He usually stars in cowboy films.
starch ['sta:tʃ] *n.* □ **amido**
Rice, bread and potatoes contain a lot of starch.
stare¹ [steə] *v.* (**stares, staring, stared**) □ **olhar fixamente**
She is staring at you. ◆ He stared at the picture in amazement.
stare² *n.* □ **olhar fixo**
start¹ [sta:t] *n.* (= beginning) □ **início, começo**
He thanked us at the start of the meeting. ◆ at the start of the month.
from the start □ **desde o início**

We knew it wasn't a good plan from the start.
for a start □ **para começar**
We can't go there now. It's late, for a start.

start² *v.* (**starts, starting, started**)
1 (= begin) **começar**
I start work at eight o'clock. ◆ She started laughing. (= She started to laugh.) ◆ It's starting to snow.
2 (= begin) **começar**
The concert starts at nine o'clock.
3 (= begin) **começar**
She started the lecture with a joke.
4 provocar
Nobody knows who started the fire.
5 ligar
I can't start the car.
6 montar
They started a business.
7 constituir, formar
to start a family.
8 (= start off) **iniciar, começar**
We started early in order to get there before noon.

start out as □ **começar**
She started out as a secretary and now she is the head of the company.

start over (= begin again) □ **começar de novo**
He began to write a letter, then he tore it up and started over.

starter ['staːtə] *n.* □ **entrada**
A starter is the first course in a meal. ◆ What would you like for starters?

startle ['staːtl] *v.* (**startles, startling, startled**) □ **assustar**
You startled me! Why didn't you knock?

start-up ['staːtʌp] *adj.* □ **iniciante, novo**
a start-up company in hi-tech.

starvation [staːˈveiʃən] *n.* □ **inanição, fome**
Some of them died of starvation.

starve [staːv] *v.* (**starves, starving, starved**) □ **morrer de inanição**
Many people are starving there, so we must send them food immediately.

I'm starving! □ **Estou morrendo de fome!**
Let's eat first. I'm starving!

state¹ [steit] *n.*
1 estado
The house was in a terrible state (= condition). ◆ The state of the economy is quite good this year.
2 Estado
member states of the United Nations ◆ The state provides education for every citizen.
■ Ver **country**.
3 estado
the State of Arizona.

state² *v.* (**states, stating, stated**) □ **declarar**
In his letter, he stated his demands. ◆ Please state your name and address.

statement ['steitmənt] *n.* □ **declaração**
make a statement □ **dar uma declaração**
The Prime Minister will make a statement about the peace talks.

statesman ['steitsmən] *n.* (*pl.* **statesmen**) □ **estadista**
station ['steiʃən] *n.*
1 estação
the railway station. ◆ the train station. *Amer.* ◆ the bus station.
2 delegacia, posto
a police station. ◆ a fire station. ◆ a gas / petrol station.
3 emissora
a radio station. ◆ a TV station.

stationary ['steiʃənəri] *adj.* □ **estacionário, parado**
He crashed into a stationary car.

stationery ['steiʃənəri] *n.* □ **artigos de papelaria e escritório**
stationery (= paper, envelopes, pens and pencils) and office equipment (= staplers, paper clips, etc.).

statistics [stəˈtistiks] *n. pl.* □ **estatística**
Statistics show that the number of smokers is going down.

statue ['statjuː] *n.* □ **estátua**
The statue of the first president is in the capital city.
■ Ver **sculpture**.

stay¹ [stei] *n.* □ **estada, estadia**
I hope you will enjoy your stay in our city.

stay² *v.* (**stays, staying, stayed**)
1 (= remain) **ficar**
Stay here until I call you! ◆ She has to stay in bed. ◆ I can't stay (for) long.
2 (= remain) **ficar**
I stayed awake all night.
3 ficar
We stayed at the hotel for a week. ◆ My uncle is staying with us for the weekend.

stay behind □ **ficar por um tempo**
The teacher asked me to stay behind after class.

stay in □ **ficar em casa**
I'm staying in tonight. I have an exam tomorrow.

stay up □ **ficar acordado**
We stayed up all night.

steadily ['stedili] *adv.* □ **constantemente**
The temperatures are rising steadily.

steady ['stedi] *adj.* (**steadier, steadiest**)
1 firme
I'll hold the ladder steady while you climb.
■ antônimo: **unsteady**
2 fixo
a steady job. ◆ a steady income.
3 constante
I drove at a steady speed.

steak [steik] *n.* □ **filé**
We had steak and chips for dinner.

steal [stiːl] *v.* (**steals, stealing, stole, stolen**) □ **roubar, furtar**
The thief stole my watch and wallet. ◆ His car was stolen yesterday.
■ Compare:
He stole my money.
He robbed me.
He robbed a bank.

steam¹ [stiːm] *n.*
1 vapor
When the water boiled, steam came out of the kettle. ◆ Steam covered the windows.
2 máquina a vapor
a steam engine.

steam² *v.* (**steams, steaming, steamed**) □ **cozinhar no vapor**
I don't cook my vegetables; I steam them.

steamed [sti:md] *adj.* □ **cozido no vapor**
steamed vegetables.
steaming ['sti:miŋ] *adj.* □ **muito quente, pelando**
a steaming cup of coffee.
steamroller ['sti:m,roulə] *n.* □ **rolo compressor**
steamship ['sti:mʃip] *n.* □ **navio a vapor**
steel *n.* □ **aço**
The gate is made of steel.
steep [sti:p] *adj.* □ **íngreme**
a steep hill.
steer [stiə] *v.* (**steers, steering, steered**) □ **guiar, conduzir**
He steered the boat carefully between the rocks.
steering wheel ['stiəriŋwi:l] *n.* □ **volante**
stem [stem] *n.* □ **haste**
the stem of a mushroom.
step¹ [step] *n.*
1 passo
He took a step forward (towards me). ◆ I heard steps on the floor above.
2 passo
What's the next step? ◆ a big step forward in the talks.
3 escadaria
I'll meet you on the steps of the cinema.
■ Compare with **stairs**:
stairs = inside a building.
steps = outside a building.
take steps □ **tomar providências**
The government is taking steps to reduce unemployment.
step by step □ **passo a passo**
She showed me how to use the computer, step by step.
watch your step □ **olhar por onde pisa, tomar cuidado**
Watch your step! There's no light here.
■ *Brit.* also **mind your step**
step² *v.* (**steps, stepping, stepped**)
1 recuar
He stepped backwards slowly when he saw the snake. ◆ Step aside (= Move aside), please.
2 pisar
You stepped on my foot!
step- [step] *pref.* □ **indica parentesco por casamento**
stepbrother ['stepbrʌðə] *n.* □ **meio-irmão**
stepdaughter ['stepdɔ:tə] *n.* □ **enteada**
stepfather ['stepfa:ðə] *n.* □ **padrasto**
stepmother ['stepmʌðə] *n.* □ **madrasta**
stepsister ['stepsistə] *n.* □ **meia-irmã**
stepson ['stepsʌn] *n.* □ **enteado**
stepladder ['steplædə] *n.* □ **escada portátil**
He climbed up the stepladder.
stereo¹ ['steriou] *n.*
1 estéreo
You can hear the programme in stereo.
2 (= stereo system) **aparelho de som**
■ A **personal stereo** means the same as a **walkman**.
stereo² *adj.* □ **estereofônico**
a stereo broadcast (of a concert, etc.).
stern [stɔ:n] *adj.* □ **severo, austero**
a stern teacher. ◆ a stern warning. ◆ She had a stern look on her face.
stew¹ [stju:] *n.* □ **cozido**
beef stew.

stew² *v.* (**stews, stewing, stewed**) □ **cozinhar**
Stew the meat for an hour.
stewed *adj.* □ **cozido**
stewed apples.
steward ['stjuəd] *n.* □ **comissário de bordo, organizador de eventos**
Stewards serve food and drinks to passengers on a plane, ship or train. ◆ Stewards and stewardesses guided the visitors at the exhibition.
■ A steward or stewardess on a plane is usually called a **flight attendant in** American English.
stewardess ['stjuədis] *n.* □ **comissária de bordo, organizador de eventos**
■ Ver **steward**.
stick¹ [stik] *n.*
1 graveto
They threw dry sticks into the fire.
2 vara
He hit me with a stick.
3 *Brit.* (= cane) **bengala**
He leans on a stick when he walks.
4 bastão
a stick of chalk.
5 talo
a stick of celery.
stick² *v.* (**sticks, sticking, stuck**)
1 espetar
He stuck a fork into the potato to see if it was cooked. ◆ Something stuck in my finger.
■ The adjective is **stuck**.
2 colar
Don't forget to stick a stamp on the envelope. ◆ Use glue to stick the pieces together. ◆ Chocolate sticks to your teeth.
3 (=get stuck) **encalhar**
The car stuck in the mud.
stick out □ **projetar-se**
One of his teeth sticks out.
stick something out □ **pôr algo para fora**
Don't stick your head out of the window!
stick to / by □ **manter, sustentar**
I made a decision, and I'm going to stick to it.
stick to the point / subject □ **ater-se ao ponto/assunto**
Stick to the subject. We don't have the time to listen to your stories.
stick together □ **ficar junto**
Everything will be all right if we stick together.
sticker ['stikə] *n.* □ **adesivo**
The sticker on the back of my car says 'keep a safe distance'.
sticking-plaster ['stikiŋ 'pla:stə] *n.* *Brit.* □ **curativo adesivo, band-aid**
Put a sticking-plaster over the cut in your finger.
■ *Amer.* Band-Aid™
stick-up ['stikʌp] *n.* (= robbery) □ **roubo, assalto**
sticky ['stiki] *adj.* (**stickier, stickiest**) □ **grudento, melado**
Wash your hands! They are sticky with chocolate. ◆ sticky sweets.
stiff [stif] *adj.*
1 duro
The box is made of stiff cardboard. ◆ a stiff brush.

2 rígido
My muscles were stiff after the exercise.
still¹ ['stil] *adv.*
1 ainda
She still lives there. ◆ They're still waiting. ◆ Do you still love her?
■ antônimo: **not anymore**; **no longer**
■ Compare with **not yet**:
  She doesn't live here yet. (= She still lives somewhere else.)
2 ainda assim, mesmo assim
It was a nice day, but I still took an umbrella. ◆ There was no chance. Still, we decided to try once more.
3 ainda
It will be still colder tomorrow.
4 (= don't move) **sem se mexer**
Stand still while I brush your hair.
still² *adj.*
1 (= not moving) **parado, imóvel**
still water.
2 (= not fizzy) **sem gás**
still mineral water.
stillness ['stilnis] *n.* □ **quietude, imobilidade**
the stillness of the night.
sting¹ [stiŋ] *n.*
1 ferrão
Bees and wasps have a sting in their tails.
■ *Amer.* **stinger**
2 picada
The sting of a jellyfish is very painful.
sting² *v.* (**stings, stinging, stung**)
1 picar
A bee stung me on the arm. ◆ Bees, scorpions and jellyfish sting, but mosquitoes and snakes bite. ◆ Careful! That plant stings.
2 queimar, arder
The smoke is stinging my eyes.
stink¹ [stiŋk] *n.* (= a bad smell) □ **fedor**
The stink was unbearable.
stink² *v.* (**stinks, stinking, stunk**) (= smell bad) □ **cheirar mal, feder**
This place stinks. ◆ Wash your hair! It stinks of smoke.
stir [stɜː] *v.* (**stirs, stirring, stirred**)
1 mexer
He put sugar in his tea and stirred it. ◆ Stir the paint with this stick.
2 remexer, mover-se
A light wind stirred the leaves. ◆ He stirred in his sleep.
stir up □ **agitar, tumultuar**
The new pupil stirred up trouble among the other pupils.
stitch¹ [stitʃ] *n.*
1 ponto
The cut in his hand needed eight stitches.
2 ponto
There are different kinds of stitches in knitting.
stitch² *v.* (**stitches, stitching, stitched**) □ **pregar**
I stitched a button onto my shirt.
stitch up □ **dar ponto**
The doctor stitched up my wound.
stock¹ [stok] *n.* □ **estoque**
We have a large stock of refrigerators.
out of stock □ **esgotado**
That disc is out of stock at the moment.

stock² *v.* (**stocks, stocking, stocked**) □ **estocar**
We stock all kinds of bread.
well stocked □ **abastecer**
The supermarkets here are well stocked. ◆ a well-stocked library.
stock exchange ['stok iks,tʃeindʒ] *n.* □ **Bolsa de Valores**
stocking ['stokiŋ] *n.* □ **meia**
a pair of stockings.
stole [stoul] *v.* (Ver **steal**).
stolen ['stoulən] *v.* (Ver **steal**).
stomach ['stʌmək] *n.*
1 estômago
How long does food stay in the stomach?
2 barriga
He was lying on his stomach.
stomach-ache ['stʌməkeik] *n.* □ **dor de estômago**
I have a terrible stomach-ache.
stone¹ [stoun] *n.*
1 pedra
They built houses of stone. ◆ a stone wall.
2 pedra
They threw stones at the soldiers.
■ *Amer.* also **rock**
3 *Brit.* **caroço**
Peaches, plums, olives and cherries have a stone inside them.
■ *Amer.* **pit**
4 (= precious stone) **pedra preciosa**
stone² *v.* (**stones, stoning, stoned**) □ **apedrejar**
They stoned him to death. ◆ They stoned the police.
stony ['stouni] *adj.* (**stonier, stoniest**) □ **pedregoso**
stony ground.
stood [stud] *v.* (Ver **stand**).
stool [stuːl] *n.* □ **banco, tamborete**
a bar stool.
stoop [stuːp] *v.* (**stoops, stooping, stooped**) □ **curvar-se**
He is so tall that he has to stoop when he comes into the room. ◆ She stooped (down) to pick up her bag.
stop¹ [stop] *n.*
1 parada
I get off at the next stop. ◆ a bus stop.
2 parada, escala
We will make one stop on our journey. ◆ A non-stop bus or train has no stops on the way.
come to a stop □ **parar, terminar**
The train came to a stop. ◆ The work came to a stop.
put a stop to □ **pôr um ponto final em, acabar com**
How can we put a stop to air pollution?
stop² *v.* (**stops, stopping, stopped**)
1 parar
The bus stopped and I got off. ◆ He started to run, but he stopped when he saw me. ◆ If your watch stops, change the battery. ◆ Stop the car, please.
2 parar
She stopped the lecture in the middle.
3 parar
When did the rain stop?
stop (doing) □ **parar de (fazer)**
Stop laughing at him! ◆ She stopped smoking a month ago.
stop to (do) □ **parar para (fazer)**
He stopped to buy something to eat.

stop behind (= stay behind)
stop someone (from) (doing) (= prevent) ▫ **impedir alguém de (fazer)**
He tried to stop me (from) going there.
stop it! ▫ **pare!**
Stop it! You're hurting me!
stop over ▫ **fazer escala**
The plane stops over in Athens on the way to New York.
storage ['stɔ:ridʒ] *n.* ▫ **depósito**
We can use this room for storage.
■ The verb is **store²**.
store¹ [stɔ:] *n.*
1 *Amer.* **loja**
a shoe store. ◆ a furniture store. ◆ a clothing store. ◆ a grocery store.
■ *Brit.* **shop**
2 loja
a department store.
3 estoque
Ants always have a store of food for the winter.
store² *v.* (**stores, storing, stored**)
1 guardar
The farmer stored the wheat in the barn. ◆ to store information on a computer.
■ The noun is **storage**.
2 (= store up) **estocar**
Ants store up food for the winter.
storekeeper ['stɔ:ˌki:pə] *n. Amer.* ▫ **lojista**
■ *Brit.* **shopkeeper**
storeroom ['stɔ:rum] *n.* ▫ **depósito**
We use this spare room as a storeroom.
storey ['stɔ:ri] *n. Brit.* (*pl.* **storeys**), **story** *Amer.* (*pl.* **stories**) ▫ **andar**
a seven-storey / story building (= seven-storeyed / storied).
■ Ver **floor**.
stork [stɔ:k] *n.* ▫ **cegonha**
storm¹ [stɔ:m] *n.* ▫ **tempestade**
There was a heavy storm last night. ◆ a rainstorm. ◆ a sandstorm.
storm² *v.* (**storms, storming, stormed**)
1 mover-se demonstrando raiva
He stormed out of the room.
2 atacar violentamente
The soldiers stormed the building.
stormy ['stɔ:mi] *adj.* (**stormier, stormiest**) ▫ **tempestuoso**
a stormy night. ◆ stormy weather.
story¹ ['stɔ:ri] *n.* (Ver **storey**).
story² *n.* (*pl.* **stories**)
1 história
Our teacher tells us beautiful stories. ◆ a love story. ◆ a detective story. ◆ It's a true story.
2 matéria
The main story in the newspaper today is (about) the President's visit to China.
stove [stouv] *n.*
1 fogão
He put a kettle of water on the stove.
2 estufa, fornalha
A stove is a heater or a cooker.
■ Ver **oven**.
camp stove *n.* ▫ **fogareiro, fogão portátil**

stowaway ['stouəwei] *n.* ▫ **passageiro clandestino**
There was a stowaway on the ship.
straight¹ [streit] *adj.*
1 reto, liso
a straight line. ◆ She has straight hair.
2 reto
The picture isn't straight. ◆ Your tie isn't straight.
3 (= honest) **sincero, franco**
Give me a straight answer. ◆ Be straight with me.
let's get it / this straight ▫ **vamos esclarecer**
Let's get this straight. You sold our car without asking me?
straight² *adv.*
1 diretamente
Look straight at the camera.
2 direto
After the game, we went straight home.
go straight on, keep straight on ▫ **ir sempre reto, continuar em linha reta**
Go straight on and turn right at the next traffic light.
straight away (= immediately) ▫ **já, imediatamente**
Do it straight away!
straight out ▫ **francamente**
I'll tell him straight out what I think of him.
straighten ['streitn] *v.* (**straightens, straightening, straightened**)
1 endireitar
Let me straighten your tie.
2 endireitar, ficar reto
The road straightens out after five kilometers.
straighten up ▫ **endireitar-se**
Bend over and then straighten up again.
straightforward [streit'fɔ:wəd] *adj.*
1 simples
a straightforward grammar exercise. ◆ The instructions are straightforward.
2 direto
a straightforward person.
strain¹ [strein] *n.*
1 pressão
She is under a lot of strain at work.
2 pressão
The rope broke under the strain. ◆ Working too hard puts a strain on the heart.
strain² *v.* (**strains, straining, strained**)
1 forçar, distender
Don't read in the dark! You'll strain your eyes. ◆ He strained a muscle.
2 esforçar-se
She had to strain to hear what he said.
3 coar, escorrer
to strain vegetables. ◆ to strain the tea.
strainer ['streinə] *n.* ▫ **coador**
a tea strainer.
stranded ['strandid] *adj.* (= stuck) ▫ **preso**
Someone stole my bag and I was stranded there with no passport and no money.
strange [streindʒ] *adj.*
1 (= odd) **estranho, esquisito**
We heard a strange noise. ◆ It's strange that she didn't say anything about it.
2 estranho

I woke up and found myself in a strange room.
- Compare **foreign**:
foreign = from / of another country.

strangely ['streindʒli] *adv.* □ **estranhamente**
The dog is behaving strangely. ◆ The house was strangely quiet.

stranger ['streindʒə] *n.* □ **estranho**
Don't talk to strangers!
- Compare **foreigner**:
foreigner = someone from another country.

strangle ['straŋgl] *v.* (**strangles, strangling, strangled**) □ **estrangular**
The murderer strangled her with his hands.
- Ver **choke; suffocate**.

strap¹ [strap] *n.* □ **correia, alça**
a leather watch-strap. ◆ My suitcase has straps round it.
shoulder strap *n.* □ **tiracolo**
strap² *v.* (**straps, strapping, strapped**) □ **prender com correia, tira**
I strapped the suitcases to the car roof.
be strapped in □ **estar com cinto de segurança**
All the passengers were strapped in.

straw [strɔ:] *n.*
1 palha
a straw hat.
2 canudinho
She drank her apple juice through a straw.

strawberry ['strɔ:bəri] *n.* (*pl.* **strawberries**) □ **morango**
She picked some strawberries from her garden. ◆ strawberry jam.

stray [strei] *adj.* □ **cachorro de rua**
a stray dog.

streak [stri:k] *n.* □ **mecha**
She has grey streaks in her hair.

stream¹ [stri:m] *n.*
1 ribeirão
A stream is a small river.
2 filete
A stream of blood came out of the wound.
3 corrente
a stream of cold air.

stream² *v.* (**streams, streaming, streamed**)
1 (= flow) **correr, verter**
Tears were streaming down his cheeks.
2 afluir
The crowd streamed out of the stadium.

street [stri:t] *n.* □ **rua**
Look left and right before you cross the street. ◆ to walk down the street (= along the street). ◆ I live in Flower Street. *Brit.* ◆ I live on Flower Street. *Amer.*
- abreviação: **St.**

streetcar ['stri:tka:] *n. Amer.* □ **bonde**
- *Brit.* **tram**

strength [streŋθ] *n.*
1 força
The patient didn't have the strength to get up. ◆ I pushed it with all my strength.
- Ver **force; power**.
2 força, resistência
materials of great strength.
- The adjective is **strong**.
- antônimo: **weakness**

strengthen ['streŋθən] *v.* (**strengthens, strengthening, strengthened**) □ **fortalecer, reforçar**
I walk a lot to strengthen my leg muscles. ◆ to strengthen a building.
- antônimo: **weaken**

stress¹ [stres] *n.*
1 estresse
She is under a lot of stress, because of pressure of work.
2 acento, tonicidade
In the word 'enter', the stress is on the first part of the word.

stress² *v.* (**stresses, stressing, stressed**)
1 (= emphasize) **enfatizar**
He stressed the importance of working together.
2 acentuar
The first part of the word 'comedy' is stressed.

stretch¹ [stretʃ] *n.*
1 espreguiçada
He got out of bed and had a good stretch.
2 faixa
Traffic is slow along a ten-kilometer stretch of the road. ◆ a wide stretch of stony land.

stretch² *v.* (**stretches, stretching, stretched**)
1 esticar
He stretched the elastic band until it broke. ◆ This material can stretch like rubber.
2 espreguiçar-se
The cat got up and stretched. ◆ He stretched his arms.
3 esticar
The dress stretched when I washed it.
4 estender-se
The river stretches for miles through the jungle.
stretch out
1 espreguiçar-se
He stretched out on the grass.
2 esticar
She stretched out her hand to take a book from the shelf.

stretcher ['stretʃə] *n.* □ **maca**
They carried the injured person on a stretcher.

strict [strikt] *adj.* □ **rigoroso**
They are very strict with their children. ◆ a strict teacher. ◆ strict rules.

strictly ['striktli] *adv.* □ **rigorosamente, terminantemente**
This message is strictly confidential. ◆ Smoking is strictly forbidden.

stride¹ [straid] *n.* □ **passo largo**
stride² *v.* (**strides, striding, strode, stridden**) □ **andar a passos largos**
He strode up to the door to open it for her.

strike¹ [straik] *n.*
1 greve
The nurses are on strike. ◆ a hunger strike.
2 ataque
an air strike against enemy bases.
go on strike □ **fazer greve**
They went on strike for higher pay.

strike² *v.* (**strikes, striking, struck**)
1 (= hit) **acertar**
The ball struck him on the face. ◆ She struck him with her bag.
2 atingir
Their car was struck by lightning.

3 (= hit) **bater**
The boat struck a rock.
4 atacar
The bandits may strike again.
5 bater
The clock struck eight.
6 fazer greve
They are striking for better pay.
7 ocorrer
It suddenly struck me that they needed help. ◆ A thought struck me.
8 afetar, tocar
How does the place strike you?
9 riscar
We had to strike him from the list.
strike a match □ **riscar um fósforo**
He struck a match and lit a candle.
strike out (= cross out) □ **tirar fora**
Strike his name out from the list. ◆ The editor struck out the last paragraph.
striker ['straikə] *n.*
1 grevista
The strikers want better working conditions.
2 atacante
The young striker scored 28 goals last season.
string [striŋ] *n.*
1 barbante
She tied up the package with string.
■ **a piece of string** (*not* 'a string').
■ Ver **rope; thread**.
2 cordão
a string of pearls.
3 corda
A violin has four strings. ◆ guitar strings.
strip[1] [strip] *n.* □ **tira, faixa**
a strip of paper. ◆ a strip of land. ◆ Cut the vegetables into strips.
strip[2] *v.* (**strips, stripping, stripped**)
1 descascar
He stripped the paper off the present. ◆ to strip the paint off the wall.
2 (= undress completely) **tirar a roupa, despir**
She stripped (off) and went into the bathroom. ◆ They stripped the prisoner.
stripe [straip] *n.* □ **listra**
A zebra has black and white stripes.
striped [straipt] *adj.* □ **listrado**
a striped shirt.
strode [stroud] *v.* (Ver **stride**).
stroke[1] [strouk] *n.*
1 derrame cerebral
She had a stroke and died.
2 golpe
He cut the rope with one stroke of his sword.
3 batidas
His punishment was ten strokes of the whip.
4 traço, pincelada
a brush stroke. ◆ a stroke of a pen.
5 afago
She gave the dog a stroke.
6 braçada
He swam with quick strokes.

■ Ver **backstroke; breaststroke**.
7 som da batida do relógio
She arrived at the stroke of midnight.
stroke[2] *v.* (**strokes, stroking, stroked**) □ **acariciar, afagar**
She stroked the cat. ◆ He stroked his beard.
■ Ver **pat**.
stroll[1] [stroul] *n.* □ **passeio, caminhada**
They went for a stroll in the park.
stroll[2] *v.* (**strolls, strolling, strolled**) □ **caminhar**
We strolled by the sea.
stroller ['stroulə] *n. Amer.* □ **carrinho de bebê**
■ *Brit.* **pushchair**
strong [stroŋ] *adj.*
1 forte
He has strong arms / muscles. ◆ He is a very strong man.
2 forte, resistente
Steel is a stronger material than iron. ◆ a strong rope. ◆ a strong door.
3 forte, intenso
strong winds. ◆ strong light.
4 forte
There was a strong smell of gas in the kitchen. ◆ She likes strong coffee.
5 grande, forte
She has a strong influence on them.
6 forte
a strong country. ◆ a strong team.
7 forte, bom
She is strong in math but weak in English.
■ antônimo: **weak**
■ The noun is **strength**.
make something stronger □ **tornar algo mais forte, fortalecer**
They made the wall stronger.
strongly ['stroŋli] *adv.* □ **firmemente, profundamente**
I strongly believe that we made the right decision.
struck [strʌk] *v.* (Ver **strike**).
structure ['strʌktʃə] *n.*
1 estrutura
the structure of the brain. ◆ the structure of the story.
2 construção, estrutura
The Eiffel Tower is a structure made of steel.
struggle[1] ['strʌgl] *n.* □ **luta**
The police will continue the struggle against drug dealers. ◆ At last they won their struggle for independence.
struggle[2] *v.* (**struggles, struggling, struggled**)
1 batalhar
They struggled for freedom.
2 lutar
He struggled with his attacker.
struggle to do something □ **esforçar-se para fazer algo**
She struggled to open the box.
stubborn ['stʌbən] *adj.* (= obstinate) □ **teimoso**
Take his advice. Don't be so stubborn.
stubbornly ['stʌbənli] *adv.* □ **teimosamente**
stuck[1] [stʌk] *v.* (Ver **stick**).
stuck[2] *adj.* □ **emperrado**
The window is stuck.
be stuck in... □ **ficar preso em...**
The car is stuck in the mud. ◆ I was stuck (= stranded) in a strange town with no money.

get stuck □ **ficar preso**
I got stuck in traffic for an hour.
student ['stju:dənt] *n.* □ **aluno, estudante**
She was a student at Harvard University. ◆ a biology student. ◆ high school students.
■ *Brit.* **pupil** (in primary and secondary schools)
student council ['stju:dənt 'kaunsəl] *n. Amer.* (mesmo que **student government**) □ **conselho de alunos**
The student council discussed the subject of a school uniform.
studio ['stju:diou] *n.*
1 ateliê, estúdio
an artist's studio. ◆ a photographer's studio.
2 estúdio
a TV studio. ◆ a recording studio.
studious ['stju:diəs] *adj.* □ **estudioso**
She is a studious girl. (= She likes to study.)
study[1] ['stʌdi] *n.* (*pl.* **studies**)
1 estudo
They are doing a study of old customs. ◆ Studies show that smoking is harmful.
2 estúdio, escritório
He is in his study, writing letters.
studies ['stʌdiz] *n. pl.*
1 estudos
She will continue her studies at college next year.
2 estudos
business studies. ◆ media studies.
study[2] *v.* (**studies, studying, studied**)
1 estudar
She studied law at university. ◆ I'm studying for the exam.
■ Ver **learn**.
2 estudar
We will study your ideas carefully.
3 estudar
The scientist studied how bees behave.
stuff[1] [stʌf] *n.*
1 (= substance) **coisa**
What's that stuff in the soup? ◆ There was some sticky stuff on the floor.
2 coisas, pertences
Put your stuff in these boxes.
stuff[2] *v.* (**stuffs, stuffing, stuffed**)
1 rechear
I stuffed the peppers with rice.
2 socar
He stuffed everything into the drawers.
stuffed [stʌft] *adj.* □ **recheado**
stuffed vegetables.
stuffy ['stʌfi] *adj.* (**stuffier, stuffiest**) □ **abafado**
Open the window – it's hot and stuffy in here.
stumble ['stʌmbl] *v.* (**stumbles, stumbling, stumbled**) □ **tropeçar**
He stumbled, but didn't fall. ◆ She stumbled over the step.
stump [stʌmp] *n.* □ **toco**
a tree stump.
stun [stʌn] *v.* (**stuns, stunning, stunned**)
1 atordoar
They stunned the guard and tied him up.
2 assombrar
His sudden death stunned all of us.
stung [stʌŋ] *v.* (Ver **sting**).

stunk [stʌŋk] *v.* (Ver **stink**).
stunning ['stʌniŋ] *adj.* □ **estonteante, atordoante**
a stunning dress. ◆ a stunning view. ◆ stunning news.
stunt [stʌnt] *n.* □ **dublê**
Some actors do the stunts themselves.
stuntman ['stʌntmən] *n.* □ **dublê**
stuntwoman ['stʌnt,wumən] *n.* □ **dublê**
stupid ['stju:pid] *adj.* (= foolish) □ **idiota, burro**
He is not so stupid as you think. ◆ You made a stupid mistake. ◆ It was stupid of her to go there.
stupidity [stju:'piditi] *n.* □ **idiotice, burrice**
stupidly ['stju:pidli] *adv.* □ **estupidamente, tolamente**
stutter[1] ['stʌtə] *v.* (**stutters, stuttering, stuttered**) (= stammer) □ **gaguejar**
She stutters a little.
stutter[2] *n.* □ **gagueira**
style [stail] *n.*
1 estilo
His style of writing is very original.
2 estilo
a style of architecture from Roman times.
3 estilo
They sell swimsuits in different styles. ◆ a new style of car.
■ Ver **hairstyle**.
4 (= fashion) **moda**
the latest style.
subject ['sʌbdʒikt] *n.*
1 (= topic) **assunto**
What was the subject of the discussion? ◆ She wrote several books on the subject. ◆ Don't change the subject.
■ Ver **topic**.
2 matéria, disciplina
He teaches two subjects – history and geography.
3 (grammar) **sujeito**
In the sentence 'The dog is sleeping', 'the dog' is the subject.
4 súditos
The king was good to his subjects. ◆ British subjects.
subjective [səb'dʒektiv] *adj.* □ **subjetivo**
a subjective impression, not an objective analysis.
submarine [sʌbmə'ri:n] *n.* □ **submarino**
The submarine began to dive.
submission [səb'miʃən] *n.* □ **submissão, apresentação**
submit [səb'mit] *v.* (**submits, submitting, submitted**)
1 (= surrender) **submeter-se**
He will not submit to their threats.
2 (= present) **apresentar**
You must submit your application before May 6.
subscribe [səb'skraib] *v.* (**subscribes, subscribing, subscribed**) □ **assinar**
He subscribes to a computer magazine.
subscriber [səb'skraibə] *n.* □ **assinante**
a newspaper with a lot of subscribers. ◆ telephone subscribers.
subscription [səb'skripʃən] *n.* □ **assinatura**
I have a subscription to a fashion magazine.
substance ['sʌbstəns] *n.* □ **substância**
Rubber is an elastic substance. ◆ Cigarette smoke contains harmful substances.
■ Ver **material; matter; stuff**.
substantial [səb'stanʃəl] *adj.* □ **substancial**

The fire caused substantial damage. ◆ a substantial amount of money.

substitute¹ ['sʌbstitjuːt] *n.* □ **substituto**
His substitute (= replacement) is also a good player. ◆ a sugar substitute.

substitute² *v.* (**substitutes, substituting, substituted**)
1 substituir
You can substitute honey for sugar.
2 substituir
He substituted for me in the second half.

subtitle ['sʌbtaitl] *n. pl.* □ **legenda**
a Chinese film with English subtitles.

subtract [səb'trakt] *v.* (**subtracts, subtracting, subtracted**) □ **subtrair**
If you subtract four from ten, you get six (10-4=6).
■ antônimo: **add**

subtraction [səb'trakʃən] *n.* □ **subtração**
She can do addition and subtraction.

suburb ['sʌbəːb] *n.* □ **subúrbio, periferia**
They live in the suburbs.

suburban [sʌ'bəːbən] *adj.* □ **suburbano**
a suburban villa.

subway ['sʌbwei] *n.*
1 *Amer.* **metrô**
I took the subway to the city center.
■ *Brit.* **underground; tube**
2 *Brit.* **passagem subterrânea**
A subway is a passage under a busy road.
■ *Amer.* **underpass**

succeed [sək'siːd] *v.* (**succeeds, succeeding, succeeded**)
1 ser bem-sucedido, ter êxito, dar-se bem
She succeeded in finding a job. ◆ He will succeed in life. ◆ The plan succeeded.
■ **succeed in doing something** (*not* 'succeed to do something').
■ The noun is **success**.
■ antônimo: **fail**
2 suceder
Who succeeded President Kennedy?
■ The noun is **succession**.

success [sək'ses] *n.*
1 sucesso
Her success in business is amazing. ◆ I wish you success in your new job. ◆ The success of the plan depends on all of you.
2 sucesso
The book was a great success. ◆ He was a success as a teacher.
■ antônimo: **failure**

successful [sək'sesful] *adj.* □ **bem-sucedido, de sucesso**
The meeting was very successful. ◆ a successful writer. ◆ a successful career.
■ antônimo: **unsuccessful**
be successful in (doing) □ **conseguir (fazer), ter êxito (em)**
He was successful in finding a job.

successfully [sək'sesfuli] *adv.* □ **com sucesso, com êxito**
They did their job successfully.

successive [sək'sesiv] *adj.* □ **consecutivo**
We won six successive games.

such [sʌtʃ] *adj.*
1 tanto
It was such a good story that I saw it twice. ◆ She is such a lovely baby!
■ You can also say: The story was so good that I read it twice.
2 tal
I don't go to such places. ◆ What can you do in such a situation?
3 semelhante
Mr. Jones? There's no such person here.
such as (= for example) □ **tal como**
Some animals, such as cows and sheep, give milk.

suck [sʌk] *v.* (**sucks, sucking, sucked**)
1 sugar
The baby is sucking milk from a bottle.
2 sorver, chupar
to suck chocolate. ◆ Don't suck your thumb!

sudden ['sʌdn] *adj.* □ **repentino**
His sudden death shocked all of us. ◆ a sudden decision.
all of a sudden (= suddenly) □ **de repente, do nada**
All of a sudden it started to rain.

suddenly ['sʌdnli] *adv.* □ **repentinamente, subitamente**
Everything happened so suddenly! ◆ Suddenly, the car stopped and a woman got out.

suddenness ['sʌdnis] *n.* □ **subitaneidade**

sue [suː] *v.* (**sues, suing, sued**) **processar**
He sued the newspaper (for $20,000).

suffer ['sʌfə] *v.* (**suffers, suffering, suffered**) □ **sofrer**
The patient is suffering. ◆ She suffers from backaches.

suffering ['sʌfəriŋ] *n.* □ **sofrimento**
The war caused great suffering to many people.

sufficient [sə'fiʃənt] *adj.* (= enough) □ **suficiente**
There is sufficient food for five people. ◆ There was sufficient air to last five hours. ◆ Fifty dollars will be sufficient.
■ antônimo: **insufficient**

sufficiently [sə'fiʃəntli] *adv.* □ **suficientemente**
The water was sufficiently warm. (= The water was warm enough.)

suffix ['sʌfiks] *n.* □ **sufixo**
Examples of suffixes:
-ment (e.g. develop – development).
-ly (quick – quickly).
-ness (dark – darkness).
-ful (hope – hopeful).
■ Ver **prefix**.

suffocate ['sʌfəkeit] *v.* (**suffocates, suffocating, suffocated**) □ **sufocar-se**
Two people suffocated from poisonous gases.
■ Ver **choke; strangle**.

suffocation ['sʌfəkeiʃən] *n.* □ **sufocamento**
They died of suffocation when there was no air left.

sugar ['ʃugə] *n.*
1 açúcar
Do you take sugar in your coffee? ◆ There's too much sugar in the lemonade. (= It's too sweet.)
2 torrão de açúcar, colher de açúcar
Two sugars, please.

suggest [sə'dʒest] *v.* (**suggests, suggesting, suggested**)
1 (= propose) **sugerir, propor**
I suggest that we talk to him first. ◆ What do you suggest? ◆ He suggested going for a swim. ◆ Who suggested this place (for the picnic)?

suggestion / superior

- suggest **that we talk** (*not* that we will talk).
- Compare **offer, propose**:
  to offer someone a job / help / coffee.
  to propose a plan / marriage.

2 sugerir

His questions suggest (that) he doesn't trust me. ◆ Are you suggesting (that) I'm lying?

suggestion [sə'dʒestʃən] *n*. □ **sugestão**

I don't know where to start. Do you have any suggestions?

- Compare **offer, proposal**:
  an offer of a job.
  a proposal of marriage.

make a suggestion □ **dar uma sugestão**

Can I make a suggestion? ◆ He made an excellent suggestion.

suicide ['su:isaid] *n*. □ **suicídio**

The number of suicides was very high last year.

commit suicide □ **cometer suicídio**

She commited suicide by jumping from the bridge.

suit¹ [su:t] *n*. □ **terno, conjunto, tailleur**

She was wearing a grey suit.

- Ver **spacesuit; swimsuit; track suit**.

suit² *v*. (**suits, suited**)

1 ficar bem

I like your new haircut – it really suits you. ◆ I prefer skirts – trousers / pants don't suit me.

2 convir

We can meet at ten o'clock – does that suit you?

- *No* [be + -ing]. Do *not* say 'It is not suiting you'.

suitable ['su:təbl] *adj*. □ **adequado**

I must find a suitable time to talk to her. ◆ This place is not suitable for a picnic. ◆ He is not suitable for the job.

- antônimo: **unsuitable**

suitably ['su:təbli] *adv*. □ **adequadamente**

You are not suitably dressed for a party.

suitcase ['su:tkeis] *n*. □ **mala**

Let's pack the suitcases.

suite [swi:t] *n*. □ **suíte**

We met him at his hotel suite.

sulk [sʌlk] *v*. (**sulks, sulking, sulked**) □ **ficar emburrado**

He is sulking because I told him to stay here.

sum¹ [sʌm] *n*.

1 soma

a large sum (of money).

2 soma

The sum of two and eight is ten.

do sums □ **calcular o dinheiro necessário para fazer alguma coisa**

My parents sometimes help me to do sums.

sum² *v*. (**sums, summing, summed**)

sum up (= summarize) □ **resumir**

Sum up the story in ten lines.

summarize ['sʌməraiz] *v*. (**summarizes, summarizing, summarized**), **summarise** *Brit*. (= **sum up**) □ **resumir**

I summarized the main points of the article.

summary ['sʌməri] *n*. (*pl*. **summaries**) □ **resumo**

The speaker gave us a summary of the report. ◆ Write a summary of the book.

summer ['sʌmə] *n*. □ **verão**

Summer is the warmest season of the year. ◆ In (the) summer I usually get up early.

summer camp ['sʌmə kʌmp] *n*. □ **acampamento de verão**

summer holidays ['sʌmə 'hɔlədiz] *n*. *Brit*. (**mesmo que summer vacation**, *Amer*.) □ **férias de verão**

Where are you going for the summer holidays / vacation?

summit ['sʌmit] *n*. □ **cume**

The climbers finally reached the summit (of the mountain).

sun [sʌn] *n*. □ **sol**

The sun rises in the east and sets in the west. ◆ The sun is shining. ◆ My dog likes to sit in the sun.

sunbathe ['sʌnbeið] *v*. (**sunbathes, sunbathing, sunbathed**) □ **tomar banho de sol**

They went to the beach to swim and sunbathe.

sunburn ['sʌnbə:n] *n*. □ **queimadura de sol**

You'll get sunburn if you sit too long in the sun.

sunburned ['sʌnbə:nd] *adj*. (mesmo que **sunburnt**) □ **queimado de sol**

a sunburnt face.

Sunday ['sʌndi] *n*. □ **domingo**

I'll see you on Sunday. ◆ My birthday is next Sunday. ◆ She visited them last Sunday.

sunflower ['sʌn,flauə] *n*. □ **girassol**

sung [sʌŋ] *v*. (Ver **sing**).

sunglasses ['sʌngla:siz] *n*. □ **óculos de sol, óculos escuros**

He usually wears sunglasses in the summer.

sunk [sʌŋk] *v*. (Ver **sink²**).

sunlight ['sʌnlait] *n*. □ **luz do sol**

There's not enough sunlight in my room.

sunlit ['sʌnlit] *adj*. □ **iluminado, claro**

a sunlit room.

sunny ['sʌni] *adj*. (**sunnier, sunniest**) □ **ensolarado**

a sunny day. ◆ a sunny room.

sunrise ['sʌnraiz] *n*. □ **nascer do sol**

My father always gets up at sunrise.

sunset ['sʌnset] *n*. □ **pôr do sol**

We returned home at sunset.

sunshade ['sʌnʃeid] *n*. □ **para-sol, guarda-sol**

sunshine ['sʌnʃain] *n*. □ **luz do sol**

These plants need a lot of sunshine. ◆ to sit in the sunshine.

sunstroke ['sʌnstrouk] *n*. □ **insolação**

suntan ['sʌntan] *n*. (= **tan**) □ **bronzeado, bronzeamento**

get a suntan □ **ficar bronzeado**

You got a good suntan on your holiday.

suntanned ['sʌntand] *adj*. (= **tanned**) □ **bronzeado**

He is suntanned. ◆ suntanned legs.

super ['su:pə] *adj*. (= **great**) □ **super**

That was a super game. ◆ What a super idea!

superb [su:'pəb] *adj*. □ **excelente**

The meal was superb. ◆ a superb player.

supercomputer ['su:pəkəm,pju:tə] *n*. □ **supercomputador**

superficial [su:pə'fiʃəl] *adj*.

1 superficial

The discussion was very superficial.

2 superficial

There were superficial wounds on his body.

superior [su'piəriə] *adj*.

1 superior

Fresh vegetables are superior to frozen vegetables. ◆ He is superior to the other players.

- antônimo: **inferior**

2 superior

superior wine.

■ antônimo: **inferior**
3 **superior**
a superior officer.
superiority [su,piəri'oriti] *n.* □ **superioridade**
superlative [su'pə:lətiv] *adj.*, *n.* □ **superlativo**
'Best' is the superlative form of 'good'. ◆ The superlative of 'expensive' is 'most expensive'.
■ The **comparative** form is 'better', 'more expensive', etc.
supermarket ['su:pəma:kit] *n.* □ **supermercado**
I buy my food at the supermarket.
supernatural [su:pə'nat∫ərəl] *adj.* □ **sobrenatural**
People believe that he has supernatural powers.
supersonic [su:pə'sɔnik] *adj.* □ **supersônico**
a supersonic airplane.
superstar ['su:pəsta:] *n.* □ **superastro, superestrela**
She is a superstar in America.
superstition [su:pə'sti∫ən] *n.* □ **superstição**
Some people think that a black cat brings bad luck, but that is just a superstition.
superstitious [,su:pə'sti∫əs] *adj.* □ **supersticioso**
I'm not superstitious.
supervise ['su:pəvaiz] *v.* (**supervises, supervising, supervised**) □ **supervisionar**
Her job is to supervise the project. ◆ He supervises a team of workers.
supervision [,su:pə'viʒən] *n.* □ **supervisão**
The patient is still under supervision.
supervisor ['su:pəvaizə] *n.* □ **supervisor**
■ Ver **school supervisor**.
supper ['sʌpə] *n.* □ **jantar, ceia**
We usually have supper at 7 pm.
■ **dinner** can also be the evening meal, if it is the big meal of the day.
supply[1] [sə'plai] *n.* □ **suprimento, fornecimento**
We get a supply of food once a week. ◆ They cut off the water supply to the city.
be in short supply □ **estar em falta**
Food and water are in short supply because of the fighting.
supplies *n. pl.* □ **provisões**
An airplane brought them food and medical supplies.
supply[2] *v.* (**supplies, supplying, supplied**) (= provide) □ **suprir, fornecer**
We supplied them with food and fuel. ◆ The heart supplies blood to the whole body.
support[1] [sə'pɔ:t] *n.* □ **apoio**
I need the support of all of you.
■ antônimo: **opposition**
support[2] *v.* (**supports, supporting, supported**)
1 **apoiar**
He supported me when everybody else was against me. ◆ We all supported his decision.
■ antônimo: **oppose**
2 (= keep) **sustentar**
I have four children to support.
3 **torcer**
Which team do you support?
4 **amparar, suportar**
The injured player was supported by two people. ◆ That chair will not support his weight.
supporter [sə'pɔ:tə] *n.*
1 (= fan) **torcedor**
football supporters.

2 **apoiador**
She is a strong supporter of the President. ◆ the supporters of the plan.
■ antônimo: **opponent**
suppose[1] [sə'pouz] *v.* (**supposes, supposing, supposed**)
1 (= guess) **supor**
I suppose you know what happened.
2 (= think) **achar**
What do you suppose will happen now?
I suppose so
1 **Acho que sim.**
Does she know I'm here? – I suppose so.
2 **Acho que sim.**
Can I use the phone? – Yes, I suppose so.
suppose[2] *conj.* (= supposing) □ **supondo que, caso**
Suppose he asks, what will you tell him?
supposed [sə'pouzd] *adj.*
be supposed to □ **dever fazer algo**
I can't go. I'm supposed to wait for them. ◆ The plane was supposed to (= due to) land an hour ago. ◆ They are supposed to (= due to) arrive tomorrow.
be not supposed to
1 (= can't) **não poder**
It's a secret. I'm not supposed to tell you.
2 (= not due to) **não dever**
They are not supposed to come before Tuesday.
supposing [sə'pouziŋ] *conj.* (Ver **suppose**[2]).
supreme [su'pri:m] *adj.* □ **supremo**
the Supreme Court □ **o Supremo Tribunal, a Suprema Corte**
sure[1] [∫uə] *adj.* (= certain) □ **certo**
I'm sure I can do it. ◆ I think it was here, but I'm not sure. ◆ If you're not sure what to do, you can ask John.
■ antônimo: **unsure**
be sure to... □ **certificar-se de...**
Be sure to lock the door when you leave.
make sure □ **assegurar-se de**
I think the exam is next Thursday, but I'll ask again to make sure. ◆ Make sure you lock the door when you leave.
sure[2] *adv. Amer.* (= of course) □ **claro**
Can I use the phone? – Sure.
for sure □ **ao certo, com certeza**
We don't know for sure who did it.
sure enough □ **com certeza**
I expected him to be there, and sure enough he was there.
that's for sure □ **é certo, certamente**
He won't help us, that's for sure.
surely ['∫uəli] *adv.*
1 **com certeza, certamente**
Surely you know where she is!
2 **certamente**
Surely we can't leave him here alone!
3 **certamente**
If they don't study, they will surely fail.
surf[1] [sə:f] *n.* □ **surfe**
surf[2] *v.* (**surfs, surfing, surfed**)
1 **surfar, navegar**
Can you teach me how to surf?
2 **surfar, navegar**
to surf the Internet.
go surfing □ **ir surfar**
They went surfing almost every day.

surface ['sə:fis] *n.*
1 superfície
A mirror has a smooth surface. ◆ the Earth's surface
2 superfície
He dived below the surface and then rose to the surface again.
surfboard ['sə:fbo:d] *n.* □ **prancha de surfe**
surfer ['sə:fə] *n.* □ **surfista**
surfing ['sə:fiŋ] *n.* □ **surfe**
Surfing is my favorite sport.
surgeon ['sə:dʒən] *n.* □ **cirurgião**
The surgeon operated on the patient for five hours. ◆ a brain surgeon. ◆ a heart surgeon.
surgery ['sə:dʒəri] *n.* □ **cirurgia**
She had surgery on her eye. ◆ open-heart surgery.
■ Ver **operation**.
surname ['sə:neim] *n.* (= family name; last name) □ **sobrenome**
His first name is Kevin and his surname is Brown.
surprise¹ [sə'praiz] *n.* □ **surpresa**
His visit was a pleasant surprise. ◆ It's a surprise party, so don't tell her about it.
in / with surprise □ **com surpresa**
They looked at me in surprise when I told them about my marriage.
take someone by surprise □ **pegar alguém de surpresa**
The rain took us by surprise, in the middle of our trip.
to my surprise □ **para a minha surpresa**
To my surprise, he agreed with me.
surprise² *v.* (surprises, surprising, surprised) □ **surpreender**
Don't tell him about my visit – I want to surprise him. ◆ The news surprised everyone.
surprised [sə'praizd] *adj.* □ **surpreso**
I'm surprised (that) he didn't say anything. ◆ She was surprised to see me.
surprising [sə'praiziŋ] *adj.* □ **surpreendente**
It's surprising that they agreed to come. ◆ His answer was surprising.
surprisingly [sə'praiziŋli] *adv.* □ **surpreendentemente**
The lecture was surprisingly interesting. ◆ Surprisingly, she was not angry with them.
surrender¹ [sə'rendə] *n.* □ **rendição**
surrender² *v.* (surrenders, surrendering, surrendered) (= yield) □ **render-se**
They surrendered to the enemy.
surround [sə'raund] *v.* (surrounds, surrounding, surrounded) □ **cercar**
The police surrounded the house.
be surrounded (by) □ **estar cercado (por)**
The place is surrounded – you have two minutes to surrender! ◆ The house is surrounded by a wall.
surroundings [sə'raundiŋz] *n.* □ **arredores, cercanias**
They live in very beautiful surroundings.
survey ['sə:vei] *n.* □ **pesquisa**
They are doing a survey of people's eating habits. ◆ Surveys show that young people watch TV more than in the past.
survival [sə'vaivəl] *n.* □ **sobrevivência**
They have no chance of survival after so many days in that jungle.
survive [sə'vaiv] *v.* (survives, surviving, survived) □ **sobreviver**

How long can they survive without food and water? ◆ Not many people survived the earthquake.
survivor [sə'vaivə] *n.* □ **sobrevivente**
They rescued the survivors of the accident.
suspect¹ ['sʌspekt] *n.* □ **suspeito**
The police arrested two suspects in connection with the murder.
suspect² [sə'spekt] *v.* (suspects, suspecting, suspected)
1 suspeitar
The police suspect that he is the robber. ◆ They suspected her of kidnapping the child.
2 desconfiar
I suspect it won't be easy.
suspicion [sə'spiʃən] *n.* □ **suspeita, desconfiança**
I'm arresting you on suspicion of murder. ◆ His movements aroused our suspicions.
suspicious [sə'spiʃəs] *adj.*
1 suspeito
Her sudden disappearance was very suspicious. ◆ The driver found a suspicious package on the bus.
2 desconfiado
He is a very suspicious man. ◆ She is suspicious of strangers.
get suspicious □ **ficar desconfiado**
I started to be suspicious when he talked about the money.
make someone suspicious □ **deixar alguém desconfiado**
His questions made me suspicious.
suspiciously [sə'spiʃəsli] *adv.*
1 suspeitosamente
They behaved suspiciously.
2 com desconfiança
She looked at them suspiciously.
swallow ['swolou] *v.* (swallows, swallowing, swallowed) □ **engolir**
Chew your food well before swallowing it. ◆ Don't swallow your chewing-gum.
swam [swam] *v.* (Ver **swim**).
swamp [swomp] *n.* □ **pântano, brejo**
swan [swon] *n.* □ **cisne**
swap [swop] *v.* (swaps, swapping, swapped) □ **trocar**
I like to sit by the window – can we swap places? ◆ I swapped jackets with him.
swarm¹ [swo:m] *n.* □ **enxame**
a swarm of bees. ◆ a swarm of flies.
swarm² *v.* (swarms, swarming, swarmed) □ **aglomerar-se**
The crowd swarmed into the stadium.
be swarming with □ **estar lotado de**
The place was swarming with tourists.
sway [swei] *v.* (sways, swaying, swayed) □ **oscilar**
The trees were swaying in the wind.
swear [sweə] *v.* (swears, swearing, swore, sworn)
1 (= curse) □ **dizer palavrão, praguejar**
He swore when he lost the game. ◆ She never swears at her workers.
2 jurar
I swear I didn't take the money!
swear word ['sweə wə:d] *n.* □ **palavrão**
The only swear words in this dictionary are 'damn' and 'bloody'.
sweat¹ [swet] *n.* □ **suor**

sweat / syllabus

He wiped the sweat from his forehead.
sweat[2] *v.* (**sweats, sweating, sweated**) □ suar
I sweated with fear. ♦ She felt hot and started to sweat.
sweater ['swetə] *n.* □ **suéter**
Put on your sweater – it's cold outside.
■ *Brit.* also **jumper; pullover**
sweatshirt ['swetʃəːt] *n.* □ **blusa de moletom**
I usually wear a sweatshirt when I go jogging.
sweaty ['sweti] *adj.* (**sweatier, sweatiest**) □ **suado**
I was sweaty after the long run. ♦ sweaty clothes.
sweep[1] [swiːp] *n.* □ **varrida**
Give the floor a sweep.
sweep[2] *v.* (**sweeps, sweeping, swept**)
1 varrer
I swept the floor.
2 varrer
A big wave swept her towards the shore.
sweep up □ **varrer**
She gave me a broom to sweep up the dead leaves.
sweet[1] [swiːt] *adj.*
1 doce
The coffee is too sweet. I put too much sugar in. ♦ a sweet apple.
2 doce
She is a sweet little girl.
3 doce
The sweet smell of roses filled the air.
4 gentil
It was sweet of you to buy her a present.
sweet[2] *n.* □ **doce, guloseima**
Eating sweets is bad for your teeth. ♦ a bag of sweets.
■ The usual word in American English is **candy**.
sweeten ['swiːtn] *v.* (**sweetens, sweetening, sweetened**) □ **adoçar**
Add a little honey to sweeten the tea.
sweetly ['swiːtli] *adv.* □ **docemente, com doçura**
She smiled sweetly at them.
sweetness ['swiːtnəs] *n.* □ **doçura**
swell [swel] *v.* (**swells, swelling, swelled, swelled or swollen**)
swell (up) □ **inchar**
My ankle started to swell immediately after I fell.
swelling ['sweliŋ] *n.* □ **inchaço**
I have a swelling on my arm where the bee stung me.
swept [swept] *v.* (Ver **sweep**).
swerve [sweːv] *v.* (**swerves, swerving, swerved**) □ **desviar**
The driver swerved to avoid the cat. ♦ The car suddenly swerved and crashed into a tree.
swift [swift] *adj.* □ **veloz, rápido**
a swift runner (= a fast runner). ♦ a swift reply (= a quick reply).
swiftly ['swiftli] *adv.* □ **velozmente, rapidamente**
The bird flew swiftly out of the cage.
swim[1] [swim] *n.* □ **nadar**
We had a swim in the lake. ♦ Let's go for a swim.
swim[2] *v.* (**swims, swimming, swam, swum**) □ **nadar**
Can you swim? (= Do you know how to swim?). ♦ They swam back to the shore.
go swimming □ **ir nadar, fazer natação**
We go swimming once a week.
swimmer ['swimə] *n.* □ **nadador**
I'm not a very good swimmer.

swimming ['swimiŋ] *n.* □ **natação**
Swimming is good for your health.
swimming costume ['swimiŋ 'kɒstjuːm] *n.* □ **traje para natação**
swimming pool ['swimiŋ puːl] *n.* (= **pool**) □ **piscina**
swimming trunks ['swimiŋ trʌŋks] *n.* (= **trunks**) □ **calção de banho**
swimsuit ['swimsuːt] *n.* □ **maiô**
a one-piece swimsuit. ♦ a two-piece swimsuit.
swindle ['swindl] *v.* (**swindles, swindling, swindled**) □ **trapacear**
He swindled several businessmen.
swindler ['swindlə] *n.* □ **vigarista**
swing[1] [swiŋ] *n.* □ **balanço**
The children like to play on the swings.
swing[2] *v.* (**swings, swinging, swung**)
1 balançar
The monkey swung from one tree to another. ♦ A rope was swinging from a tree.
2 balançar
He swung the sack onto his shoulder. ♦ The soldier swung his arms as he walked.
3 oscilar
The door swung open.
switch[1] [switʃ] *n.* □ **interruptor**
a light switch. ♦ the on / off switch.
switch[2] *v.* (**switches, switching, switched**)
1 trocar, mudar
She said something in Spanish and then switched to English. ♦ They switched the meeting from Tuesday to Thursday.
2 trocar, mudar
He switches jobs very often.
switch off (= turn off) □ **desligar**
He switched the lights off and went to bed. ♦ Don't forget to switch off the oven.
switch on (= turn on) □ **ligar**
Switch the TV on.
switchboard ['switʃbɔːd] *n.* □ **mesa telefônica**
I rang the hotel switchboard and they connected me to room nº 310.
swollen[1] ['swəulən] *v.* (Ver **swell**).
swollen[2] *adj.* □ **inchado**
Her ankle is swollen.
swoop [swuːp] *v.* (**swoops, swooping, swooped**) □ **precipitar-se**
The eagle swooped down on the mouse.
swop [swɒp] *v.* (= **swap**).
sword [sɔːd] *n.* □ **espada**
They drew their swords and started to fight.
swore [swɔː] *v.* (Ver **swear**).
sworn [swɔːn] *v.* (Ver **swear**).
swot [swɒt] *v. Brit.* (**swots, swotting, swotted**) (= **cram**) □ **estudar muito**
He is swotting for his biology exam.
swum [swʌm] *v.* (Ver **swim**).
swung [swʌŋ] *v.* (Ver **swing**).
syllable ['siləbl] *n.* □ **sílaba**
The word 'expensive' has three syllables (ex-pen-sive).
syllabus ['siləbəs] *n.* □ **plano de estudos**
the English syllabus.
■ Compare **curriculum**:
curriculum = all the subjects studied.

symbol ['simbəl] *n.* □ **símbolo**
The dove is a symbol of peace. ◆ The symbol $ means 'dollar(s)'. ◆ % is a symbol for percent.
symmetrical [si'metrikəl] *adj.* □ **simétrico**
sympathetic [,simpə'θetik] *adj.* □ **simpático**
The boss was very sympathetic about my problems.
■ antônimo: **unsympathetic**
■ Be careful. Don't use the word 'sympathetic' when you want to say that a person is nice or likeable.
sympathetically [,simpə'θetikli] *adv.* □ **compreensivamente, solidariamente**
She listened to my story sympathetically.
sympathize ['simpəθaiz] *v. Brit.* (**sympathizes, sympathizing, sympathized**), **sympathise**
sympathize with □ **ser solidário, solidarizar-se**
I sympathize with her, but there's nothing I can do.
sympathy ['simpəθi] *n.* □ **simpatia**
She received many letters of sympathy when her husband died. ◆ I have a lot of sympathy for him. He is in big trouble.
symphony ['simfəni] *n.* (*pl.* **symphonies**) □ **sinfonia**
symptom ['simptəm] *n.* □ **sintoma**
What are the symptoms of the disease?

synagogue ['sinəgog] *n.* □ **sinagoga**
Jews pray in synagogues.
synonym ['sinənim] *n.* □ **sinônimo**
The words 'buy' and 'purchase' are synonyms.
synthetic [sin'θetik] *adj.* □ **sintético**
Plastic is a synthetic material.
syringe [si'rindʒ] *n.* □ **seringa**
syrup ['sirəp] *n.* □ **calda**
pineapple slices in syrup.
system ['sistəm] *n.*
1 sistema
an alarm system. ◆ a central-heating system. ◆ the nervous system. ◆ a computer system.
2 sistema
the metric system. ◆ the decimal system.
3 sistema
There is a system for arranging books in a library.
systematic [,sistə'matik] *adj.* □ **sistemático**
a systematic analysis of the information.
systematically [,sistə'mætikli] *adv.* □ **sistematicamente**

Tt

table ['teibl] *n.*
1 mesa
The teapot is on the table. ◆ a kitchen table.
2 tabela
The table shows the number of students in the last five years.
■ Ver **timetable**.
set the table (mesmo que **lay the table**) □ **arrumar a mesa, pôr a mesa**
Help me set the table for dinner.
sit at the table □ **sentar-se à mesa**
The whole family sat at the table.
table of contents *n.* □ **sumário**
tablecloth ['teiblkloθ] *n.* □ **toalha de mesa**
tablespoon ['teiblspu:n] *n.* □ **colher de sopa**
a silver tablespoon. ◆ two tablespoons of sugar.
tablet ['tablit] *n.* (= pill) □ **comprimido**
Take one tablet three times a day.
table tennis ['teibl 'tenis] *n.* (= ping pong) □ **tênis de mesa**
tackle[1] ['takl] *n.*
1 equipamento, apetrechos
fishing tackle.
2 entrada
a good tackle by the defender (in football).
tackle[2] *v.* (**tackles, tackling, tackled**)
1 (= deal with) **lidar com, atacar, abordar**
There is a way to tackle this problem.
2 derrubar
I tackled him before he shot at the goal.
3 atacar
Someone tackled the thief.
tact [takt] *n.* □ **tato**
Show some tact when you talk to him and don't mention his failure.
tactful ['taktful] *adj.* □ **diplomático**
He gave her a tactful answer.
tactfully ['taktfuli] *adv.* □ **diplomaticamente**
tactics ['taktiks] *n. pl.* □ **tática**
We must use different tactics in our fight against drug dealers.
tactless ['tAktlis] *adj.* □ **sem diplomacia**
It was tactless of you to tell him the joke about a fat man.
tag [tag] *n.*
1 etiqueta
There isn't a price tag on this hat. How much is it? ◆ All those at the meeting had a name tag on their jackets.
2 pega-pega
The children are playing tag outside.
tag question *n.* (Ver **question tag**).
tail [teil] *n.*
1 rabo
The dog wagged its tail. ◆ Cut off the fish's tail.
2 cauda
the tail of an airplane.
■ Ver **heads or tails**.
tailor ['teilə] *n.* □ **alfaiate**
A tailor makes or alters clothes, especially suits.
take [teik] *v.* (**takes, taking, took, taken**)

1 pegar
She took the baby in her arms. ◆ Take my hand.
2 levar
Don't forget to take your umbrella. ◆ She took the dog for a walk.
3 levar
This bus will take you to the station. ◆ He took me to school in his car.
4 pegar, tomar
I took a taxi to the airport.
5 aceitar
Take my advice and wait here. ◆ Sorry, we don't take cheques.
6 levar
The journey by bus takes 2 hours. ◆ It didn't take me long to find it.
7 tomar
Take the medicine once a day. ◆ Do you take milk in your coffee?
8 levar
I didn't take it seriously. I thought it was a joke.
9 pegar, levar
Someone took my umbrella last night.
10 tomar
I'll take a bath and go to bed.
11 tirar
She took a photograph of me and the children.
12 tomar
Enemy forces took the town.
■ Ver **take action; take into account; take care; take notes; take part; take place; take pleasure; take pride; take a risk; take the trouble; take a walk**
it takes □ **é preciso**
It takes a lot of courage to do what she did.
take after □ **puxar a, sair à**
He takes after his mother.
take something apart □ **desmontar algo**
He took the machine apart.
take away □ **levar embora**
I took the knife away from him. ◆ I don't want to see it – take it away!
take back □ **devolver**
If you don't like the dress, I can take it back.
take down
1 anotar
She took down my name and address.
2 abaixar
He took down his trousers. ◆ Take that suitcase down.
take in
1 aceitar
We have no money, so we have to take in tenants.
2 receber
She took them in with her elegant clothes.
take off □ **decolar**
The plane is taking off now.
take something off
1 tirar algo
Take your coat off. ◆ He took off his glasses. ◆ Don't take your shoes off.
■ antônimo: **put on**
2 tirar
Take a few days off until you feel better.

take out □ tirar
She took out a driving licence.
take something out of □ tirar algo de dentro de
He took his wallet out of his pocket.
take over □ assumir
She took over (the company) when her father died.
take up
1 ocupar
The furniture takes up too much space.
2 ocupar
His hobby takes up all his time.
3 começar a estudar / treinar
I'm not good at skiing. I only took it up last week.
take-away ['teikəwei] *n. Brit.* (**mesmo que take-out**)
1 refeição para viagem
Let's get something to eat at a Chinese take-away.
2 comida pronta
Let's have a take-away supper tonight.
take-off ['teiko:f] *n.* □ **decolagem**
The pilot had to land five minutes after take-off.
take-out ['teikaut] *n. Amer.* (Ver **take-away**).
talcum powder ['talkəm 'paudə] *n.* (mesmo que **talc**) □ **talco**
tale [teil] *n.* □ **conto**
He told us a tale about a magic lamp.
talent ['talənt] *n.* (= gift²) □ **talento**
She has a talent for singing. ◆ His musical talent is amazing.
talented ['taləntid] *adj.* (= gifted) □ **talentoso**
a talented actor. ◆ a talented tennis player.
talk¹ [to:k] *n.*
1 conversa
I'll have a talk with her (= I'll talk to her) tonight. ◆ The peace talks will take place in Switzerland.
2 (= lecture) palestra
She gave an interesting talk about dolphins.
3 conversa, papo
I don't believe he can do anything. It's just talk!
talk² *v.* (**talks, talking, talked**) □ **conversar, falar**
What did you talk about? ◆ We talked about the party. ◆ Can I talk to you?
■ Ver **speak**.
talk about □ falar sobre
She talked about the history of the city. ◆ He didn't want to talk about his problems.
talkative ['to:kətiv] *adj.* □ **falante**
She is a very talkative person.
tall [to:l] *adj.*
1 alto
You are taller than me. ◆ a tall tree.
■ antônimo: **short**.
■ Ver **high**.
2 de altura
She is 1.68 metres tall.
How tall...? □ **O quanto mede...?**
How tall are you? ◆ How tall is she?
tame¹ [teim] *adj.* □ **domesticado, domado**
a tame lion.
tame² *v.* (**tames, taming, tamed**) □ **domesticar, domar**
He tames wild animals.
tan [tan] *n.* (= suntan) □ **bronzeado**
I got a nice tan after a week by the sea.

■ The adjective is **tanned**.
tangerine [tandʒə'ri:n] *n.* □ **tangerina**
tangle¹ ['tangl] *n.* □ **emaranhado**
The wool is in a tangle.
tangle² *v.* (**tangles, tangling, tangled**) □ **emaranhar**
Try not to tangle the wires.
tangled ['tangld] *adj.* □ **emaranhado**
tangled string. ◆ The dog's hair is tangled.
tank [tank] *n.*
1 tanque
to fill up the petrol tank. *Brit.* ◆ gas tank. *Amer.* ◆ My fuel tank holds 40 liters.
2 tanque
The air force destroyed many enemy tanks.
tanker ['tankə] *n.* □ **petroleiro, carro-tanque**
An oil tanker is a ship that carries oil. ◆ Tanker trucks can carry gas, water, oil, etc.
tanned [tand] *adj.* (= **suntanned**) □ **bronzeado**
She is very tanned. ◆ tanned legs.
■ The noun is **tan**.
tap¹ [tap] *n.*
1 torneira
Turn off the tap. ◆ I turned on the hot water tap.
■ *Amer.* **faucet**
2 batidinha, tapinha
I heard a tap on the door. ◆ a tap on the shoulder.
tap² *v.* (**taps, tapping, tapped**) □ **bater levemente**
He tapped me on the shoulder. ◆ She tapped her fingers on the table.
tape¹ [teip] *n.*
1 fita
I have the film on tape. ◆ We listened to her voice on tape.
2 (= cassette) fita cassete
Use this blank tape to record the songs. ◆ Rewind the tape and play it again. ◆ a video tape.
3 fita adesiva
I stuck the pieces of paper together with some tape.
tape² *v.* (**tapes, taping, taped**)
1 (= record) gravar em fita
I taped the concert (from TV or the radio).
2 colar com fita adesiva
He taped some magazine pictures on the wall.
tape deck ['teip ,dek] *n.* □ **gravador de mesa**
tape measure ['teip ,meʒə] *n.* □ **fita métrica**
tape recorder ['teip rə'ko:də] *n.* □ **gravador, toca-fitas**
tapestry ['tapəstri] *n.* (*pl.* **tapestries**) □ **tapeçaria**
tar [ta:] *n.* □ **piche**
Tar is used for making roads.
target ['ta:git] *n.* □ **alvo**
The missile hit the target. ◆ to miss the target. ◆ a military target.
tarmac ['ta:mak] *n.* (= runway) □ **pista, asfalto**
Planes wait on the tarmac when passengers go on board.
tart [ta:t] *n.* □ **torta**
apple tart. ◆ strawberry tart.
tartan ['ta:tən] *n.* □ **xadrez escocês**
a tartan skirt.
task [ta:sk] *n.* □ **tarefa**
Your task is to organize the party.
taste¹ [teist] *n.*
1 gosto
Sugar has a sweet taste. ◆ I hate the taste of cigarettes.

taste / telephone

■ Ver **flavor**.
2 sabor
Have a taste of the soup to see if there is enough salt.
3 gosto
He and I have the same taste in music. ◆ She has bad taste in clothes.
sense of taste □ **sentido do paladar**
an animal with a sharp sense of taste.
taste² *v.* (**tastes, tasting, tasted**)
1 ter gosto
The soup tastes good. ◆ This jam tastes of strawberries.
2 provar
The cook tasted the soup, then added some more salt. ◆ Come on, just taste it!
3 sentir o gosto
I can't taste any garlic in the soup.
tasteful ['teistful] *adj.* □ **de bom gosto**
tasteful furniture.
tasteless ['teistlis] *adj.*
1 sem gosto, insípido
The soup was tasteless.
2 sem graça
tasteless jokes.
3 sem graça, de mau gosto
tasteless furniture.
tasty ['teisti] *adj.* (**tastier, tastiest**) □ **saboroso**
The meal was very tasty.
■ **delicious** means 'very tasty'.
tatters ['tatəz] *n.*
in tatters □ **em farrapos**
His clothes were in tatters.
tattoo [tə'tu:] *n.* □ **tatuagem**
He had a tattoo of a dragon on his arm.
taught [to:t] *v.* (Ver **teach**).
tax¹ [taks] *n.* □ **imposto**
There's a 10% tax on cigarettes in this country. ◆ to lower the taxes. ◆ to increase the taxes. ◆ income tax.
tax² *v.* (**taxes, taxing, taxed**) □ **tributar**
be taxed □ **ser tributado**
Very low incomes are not taxed (= are free of tax).
tax-free ['taks,fri:] *adj., adv.* □ **isento de imposto**
tax-free incomes. ◆ to buy goods tax-free.
taxi ['taksi] *n.* (= cab) □ **táxi**
I took a taxi to the station. ◆ to go by taxi. ◆ to call a taxi (= to telephone for a taxi).
taxi driver ['taksi 'draivə] *n.* □ **taxista**
tea [ti:] *n.* □ **chá**
Would you like a cup of tea? ◆ I'll make some tea. ◆ a packet of tea. ◆ Two teas, please. ◆ They usually have tea at four o'clock.
tea bag [ti: bag] *n.* □ **saquinho de chá**
teach [ti:tʃ] *v.* (**teaches, teaching, taught**) □ **ensinar, dar aula de, lecionar**
She taught me (how) to swim. ◆ He teaches French.
teacher ['ti:tʃə] *n.* □ **professor**
He is my history teacher. ◆ She is a teacher at a high school.
teaching ['ti:tʃiŋ] *n.* □ **ensino**
new teaching methods.
team [ti:m] *n.*
1 time, seleção
Which team do you support? ◆ He plays for the national team.

2 equipe
a team of scientists.
teamwork ['ti:mwɜ:k] *n.* □ **trabalho em equipe**
Teamwork is very important in this project.
teapot ['ti:pot] *n.* □ **bule de chá**
tear¹ [tiə] *n.* □ **lágrima**
There were tears in her eyes.
in tears □ **aos prantos**
He was in tears. (= He was crying.)
burst into tears □ **cair no choro, irromper em lágrimas**
He burst into tears when he heard the sad news.
tear² [teə] *n.* □ **rasgo**
You have a tear in your shirt.
tear³ [teə] *v.* (**tears, tearing, tore, torn**)
1 rasgar
He tore the newspaper to pieces.
2 rasgar
I tore my skirt on a nail.
3 arrancar rasgando
She tore a page from her notebook.
4 rasgar
Paper tears easily.
tear down
1 demolir
They tore down the old buildings.
2 arrancar
He tore the note down from the notice-board.
tear up □ **rasgar**
She tore up his letter in anger.
tease [ti:z] *v.* (**teases, teasing, teased**) □ **atazanar**
Stop teasing her! ◆ They teased me about my red hair.
teaspoon ['ti:spu:n] *n.* □ **colher de chá**
He stirred his tea with a silver teaspoon.
technical ['teknikəl] *adj.* □ **técnico**
technical knowledge. ◆ technical problems.
technician [tek'niʃən] *n.* □ **técnico**
a laboratory technician. ◆ an aircraft technician.
technique [tek'ni:k] *n.* □ **técnica**
Her driving technique is perfect. ◆ a new technique for improving your memory.
technological [,teknə'lodʒikəl] *adj.* □ **tecnológico**
a technological breakthrough in photography.
technology [tek'nolədʒi] *n.* □ **tecnologia**
High technology (= hi-tech) is used a lot in industry today. ◆ computer technology.
teddy ['tedi] *n. Brit.* (*pl.* **teddies**) (= **teddy bear**)
teddy bear ['tedi beə] *n.* □ **ursinho de pelúcia**
tedious ['ti:diəs] *adj.* (= boring and tiring) □ **entediante, chato**
a tedious lecture. ◆ a tedious job.
teenage ['ti:neidʒ] *adj.* □ **adolescente**
teenage children. ◆ teenage problems.
teenager ['ti:neidʒə] *n.* (= adolescent) □ **adolescente**
a club for teenagers.
teens [ti:nz] *n.* □ **adolescência**
He is in his teens.
teeth [ti:θ] *n.* (*plural of* **tooth**) □ **dentes**
tel. *abbr.* (mesmo que **telephone number**) □ **tel.**
telegram ['teligram] *n.* □ **telegrama**
Send him a telegram.
■ *Amer.* also **wire**
telephone¹ ['telifoun] *n.* (= **phone**) □ **telefone**

May I use your telephone? ◆ Can I make a telephone call? ◆ What's your telephone number? ◆ You can order pizza by telephone.
on the (tele)phone ☐ **ao telefone**
I spoke to her on the phone yesterday. ◆ Just a minute! I'm on the telephone.
telephone² *v.* (**telephones, telephoning, telephoned**) ☐ **telefonar, ligar**
I'll telephone her to invite her for dinner. ◆ I telephoned him, but someone answered "wrong number".
■ **phone** and **call** are the more usual words.
telephone booth ['telifoun buːθ] *n.* *Amer.* (**mesmo que telephone box**, *Brit.*) ☐ **cabine telefônica, orelhão, telefone público**
telephone call ['telifoun koːl] *n.* (= **phone** call) ☐ **ligação (telefônica)**
I had a telephone call from Sarah yesterday.
telephone directory ['telifoun diˈrektəri] *n.* (= **phone book**) ☐ **lista telefônica**
I looked up his number in the telephone directory.
telephone number ['telifoun ˈnʌmbə] *n.* ☐ **número de telefone**
What's your telephone number?
■ abreviação: **tel.**
■ Examples of how you say your telephone number: nine, two, four, seven, two, three, six (9247236).
■ Zero is sometimes said as the letter "o": six o two, seven, five, double o (6027500).
telescope ['teliskoup] *n.* ☐ **telescópio**
to look through the telescope.
television ['teliviʒən] *n.* (= **TV**)
1 (= television set) **aparelho de tevê, televisor, televisão**
I bought a new television. ◆ Turn on the television. ◆ Turn off the television.
2 televisão
I don't watch television every day. ◆ There's an interesting programme on television tonight. ◆ a television show. ◆ a television interview. ◆ cable / satellite television.
tell [tel] *v.* (**tells, telling, told**)
1 dizer
She'll tell you what to do. ◆ I told him to wait for me. ◆ Can you tell me how to get to the station?
■ Compare **say**:
 She'll say what to do.
 I said: 'Wait for me!'
2 dizer, contar
Tell me the truth! ◆ Tell them what happened. ◆ She told them a beautiful story.
3 indicar
That traffic sign tells you that you can't stop here.
can tell
1 distinguir
It's going to snow. – How can you tell?
2 distinguir
I can't tell the difference between David and his twin brother.
tell someone off (= scold) ☐ **repreender alguém, dar bronca em alguém**
He told me off because I came late.
tell the time ☐ **dizer as horas**
Can you tell me the time please? – It's five o'clock.
■ Ver **time¹**.

teller ['telə] *n.* ☐ **caixa**
a bank teller.
telly ['teli] *n.* *Brit.* (*pl.* **tellies**) (= television) ☐ **televisão**
What's on telly tonight?
temper ['tempə] *n.* ☐ **temperamento**
She has a bad temper. (= She gets angry easily.)
in a temper ☐ **de mau humor**
He is in a temper, because he didn't sleep well last night.
lose your temper ☐ **perder a paciência**
She lost her temper and slapped me on the face.
temperature ['temprətʃə] *n.* ☐ **temperatura**
Water boils at a temperature of 100° C (= 100 degrees Celsius) ◆ Temperatures may rise / fall. ◆ a high / low temperature.
have a temperature (= have a fever) ☐ **ter febre**
She must stay in bed – she has a temperature.
take someone's temperature ☐ **tirar a temperatura de alguém**
The nurse took my temperature.
temple ['templ] *n.* ☐ **templo**
a Buddhist temple. ◆ an ancient Greek temple.
temporarily ['tempərərili] *adv.* ☐ **temporariamente**
The office is temporarily closed.
temporary ['tempərəri] *adj.* ☐ **temporário**
a temporary job. ◆ a temporary secretary.
■ antônimo: **permanent**
tempt [tempt] *v.* (**tempts, tempting, tempted**) ☐ **tentar, seduzir**
They lowered the prices to tempt people to buy more.
be tempted to ☐ **estar tentado a**
I'm tempted to buy the house.
be tempted into ☐ **ser induzido a**
I was tempted into buying the house.
temptation [tempˈteiʃən] *n.*
1 tentação
They offered me a very high salary as a temptation.
2 tentação
I felt a temptation to tell her the secret.
resist the temptation ☐ **resistir à tentação**
He couldn't resist the temptation to eat all the chocolate.
tempting ['temptiŋ] *adj.* ☐ **tentador**
a tempting offer.
ten [ten] *adj., n.* ☐ **dez**
It costs ten dollars. ◆ We need ten people. ◆ It's ten o'clock. ◆ She is ten years old.
a ten ☐ **um dez**
I got a ten in (= on) the exam.
■ Ver **tenth**.
tenant ['tenənt] *n.* ☐ **inquilino, arrendatário**
Tenants pay rent to a landlord.
tend [tend] *v.* (**tends, tending, tended**) ☐ **tender**
Young children tend to watch TV more than read books.
tendency ['tendənsi] *n.* (*pl.* **tendencies**) ☐ **tendência**
He has a tendency to complain about everything.
tender ['tendə] *adj.*
1 tenro
tender meat. ◆ Cook the vegetables until they are tender.
■ antônimo: **tough**
2 terno
a tender look. ◆ tender words.
3 sensível, dolorido
My ankle is still tender.

tenderly ['tendəli] *adv.* □ **ternamente, com ternura**
He put his arm around her tenderly.
tenderness ['tendənis] *n.* □ **ternura**
the tenderness in his look.
tennis ['tenis] *n.* □ **tênis**
We play tennis once a week.
tennis court ['tenis kɔ:t] *n.* □ **quadra de tênis**
tennis racket ['tenis 'rakit] *n.* □ **raquete de tênis**
tennis shoe ['tenis ʃu:] *n.* □ **tênis**
tense[1] [tens] *n.* (grammar) □ **tempo**
The past tense of 'break' is 'broke'.
tense[2] *adj.*
1 tenso
They were tense because they are waiting.
2 tenso
The situation is very tense.
3 tenso
tense muscles.
tension ['tenʃən] *n.*
1 tensão
I felt a lot of tension before the test.
2 tensão
There's some tension between the two countries.
tent [tent] *n.* □ **barraca, tenda**
We put up a tent very quickly. ◆ They sleep in tents when they go camping.
tenth[1] [tenθ] *adj., pron., adv.* □ **décimo, dez**
The office is on the tenth floor. ◆ July the tenth (= 10th July). *Brit.* ◆ July tenth (= July 10). *Amer.* ◆ He came tenth in the race.
tenth[2] *n.* (= 1/10) □ **um décimo**
He got a tenth of the profits.
term [tə:m] *n.*
1 termo
technical terms. ◆ medical terms.
2 mandato
The President's second term in office was from 1984 to 1988.
3 *Brit.* **trimestre**
The summer term in British schools is from April to July.
■ Compare **semester**:
   semester = half the school / university year.
terms *n. pl.* □ **termos**
the terms of the contract.
terminal ['tə:minəl] *n.*
1 terminal
They are building a new air terminal (at the airport). ◆ a rail terminal. ◆ a bus terminal.
2 terminal
Every desk in the room / office has a terminal connected to the central computer.
terminus ['tə:minəs] *n.* □ **término, terminal**
terrace ['terəs] *n.* □ **terraço**
We had lunch on the terrace (of the house, of the hotel, etc.).
terrible ['terəbl] *adj.*
1 terrível
a terrible accident.
2 (= awful) **horrível**
The food was terrible.
3 (= awful) **horrível**
I feel terrible. I'm going to lie down.

terribly ['terəbli] *adv.*
1 (= very) *Brit.* **terrivelmente**
I'm terribly sorry!
2 (= very badly) **terrivelmente**
They suffered terribly.
3 (= very badly) **pessimamente**
They played terribly.
terrific [tə'rifik] *adj.*
1 (= excellent) **excelente**
That was a terrific show!
2 (= very great) **tremendo**
It moved at a terrific speed. ◆ a terrific storm.
terrified ['terifaid] *adj.* (= very scared) □ **apavorado**
I'm terrified of snakes. ◆ She looked terrified.
terrify ['terifai] *v.* (**terrifies, terrifying, terrified**) □ **aterrorizar**
The storm terrified them.
terrifying ['terifaiŋ] *adj.* □ **aterrorizante**
a terrifying experience.
territorial [teri'tɔ:riəl] *adj.* □ **territorial**
territory ['teritəri] *n.* (*pl.* **territories**) □ **território**
They crossed the border into enemy territory.
terror ['terə] *n.* (= great fear) □ **terror**
They ran away in terror.
terrorism ['terərizəm] *n.* □ **terrorismo**
an act of terrorism.
terrorist ['terərist] *n.* □ **terrorista**
Five terrorists hijacked a plane.
terrorist attack *n.* □ **ataque terrorista**
Five people were killed in a terrorist attack.
test[1] [test] *n.*
1 avaliação, prova
She passed her driving test. ◆ I failed my grammar test.
2 exame
a blood test. ◆ a hearing test.
3 teste
Tests show that this car is the safest.
test[2] *v.* (**tests, testing, tested**)
1 examinar
The doctor tested her eyes / hearing.
2 testar
The new drug was tested on animals.
3 avaliar
The teacher tests us in grammar once a week.
testify ['testifai] *v.* (**testifies, testifying, testified**) □ **testemunhar**
The witness testified in court.
testimony ['testiməni] *n.* (*pl.* **testimonies**) □ **testemunho**
test tube ['test tju:b] *n.* □ **tubo de ensaio**
Test tubes are used in scientific experiments in the lab.
text [tekst] *n.*
1 texto
Each page of the book has both text and pictures.
2 texto
The newspaper printed the text of his speech.
textbook ['tekstbuk] *n.* □ **livro didático**
a history textbook.
than [ðən, ðan] *conj., prep.* □ **(do) que**
He is taller than me. ◆ I cook better than she does. ◆ It costs less than 50 dollars.
thank [θaŋk] *v.* (**thanks, thanking, thanked**) □ **agradecer**
I thanked them for their help.

thank you, thanks □ obrigado
Thank you (for your help). ♦ Would you like some more tea? – No, thanks. ♦ How are you? – Fine, thank you.
thank you very much □ muito obrigado
Thank you very much. – You're welcome.
thanks *n.* □ agradecimento
I wrote them a letter of thanks.
thanks to □ graças a
Thanks to you we finished the job on time.
thankful ['θaŋkful] *adj.* □ grato
They were thankful that the war was over.
thankfully ['θaŋkfuli] *adv.* □ felizmente
Thankfully, nobody got hurt.
Thanksgiving ['θaŋksgiviŋ] *n.* □ Ação de Graças
that[1] [ðat] *conj.* □ que
He said (that) he was tired. ♦ I'm sure (that) she will succeed.
that[2] *pron.*
1 (= who, whom) **que**
The girl that we saw is my cousin. ♦ The boy that is riding the bicycle is my best friend.
2 (= which) **que**
the best book that I've ever read. ♦ This is the only copy that we have. ♦ The tree that fell down was old.
3 aquele, aquilo
Did you see that? ♦ What was that? ♦ That's my sister. ♦ That's what I said. ♦ That's my house over there. ♦ That is more expensive than this one. ♦ Who's that on the phone?
■ Say **this** for something or someone near you, **that** for something or someone not near.
after that □ depois disso, em seguida
We had dinner and after that we went out.
at that time □ naquela época
At that time, he was a student.
that's why □ é por isso
He was busy. That's why he couldn't come.
that[3] *adj.* (*pl.* **those**) □ aquele, aquilo
That car is bigger than this one. ♦ Who is that man over there? ♦ Did you see that bird?
■ Ver **those**.
that[4] *adv.* (= so) □ tão
I can't swim that far. ♦ The situation isn't that bad.
thaw [θɔː] *v.* (**thaws, thawing, thawed**) □ derreter-se, degelar-se
The snow is thawing. ♦ Thaw frozen meat before cooking it.
■ You **thaw** something frozen, you **melt** something solid.
the [ðə, ði] □ o, a
The man who bought your car is my uncle. ♦ The weather will be clear tomorrow. ♦ the sun. ♦ the sky. ♦ the government. ♦ the third of June. ♦ Can you play the guitar? ♦ the poor. ♦ the rich. ♦ the blind.
in the, at the □ no, na
Put the eggs in the refrigerator. ♦ They are in the garden. ♦ at the office. ♦ at the end of the road.
the... the □ quanto (mais)... (mais)
The more I think about it, the more I'm certain that the decision was right. ♦ The less we talk about it, the better.
■ We use **the** before names of rivers, seas, deserts, regions, etc.:
the Nile, the Volga, the Baltic, the Arctic, the Mediterranean, the Sahara, the Middle / Far East

■ We don't use **the** before the names of most countries (see appendix of geographical names).
theater ['θɪətə] *n. Amer.*, **theatre** *Brit.*
1 teatro
We're going to the theatre tonight.
2 *Amer.* **cinema**
a movie theater.
■ *Brit.* **cinema**
theft [θeft] *n.* □ roubo, furto
There are too many car thefts in this neighbourhood. ♦ She is guilty of theft.
■ A **thief** is someone who commits a **theft**; he steals things.
their [ðeə] *adj.* □ seu, deles, seus, deles
Their house is large. ♦ They got into their cars. ♦ Every student took their (her or his) exam paper.
theirs [ðeəz] *pron.* □ o deles, a delas
Our plan is better than theirs.
them [ðəm, ðem] *pron.*
1 os, as, lhes, a eles, a elas
I know them. ♦ She bought them presents. ♦ I'll talk to them. ♦ Dr. Brown treated them.
2 (= him / her) **lhe, a ele, a ela**
If anyone asks, tell them you don't know.
theme [θiːm] *n.*
1 (= subject) **tema**
The theme of the book is 'traffic in the year 2025'.
2 *Amer.* (= paper) **texto**
My homework is to write a one-page theme on peace.
themselves [ðem'selvz] *pron.*
1 se, a si mesmos
They built themselves a small house. ♦ They are proud of themselves.
2 eles mesmos, elas mesmas
They made it themselves. ♦ David and Jane themselves told me.
by themselves
1 (= alone) **sozinhos**
They live by themselves.
2 por si mesmos
They solved the problem by themselves.
then [ðen] *adv.*
1 então, na época
I was a student then (= at that time). ♦ I can't come next Tuesday, I'll be in Paris then.
2 depois, em seguida
Finish your homework and then you can watch TV. ♦ I'll talk to her and then I'll decide.
3 então
Then you agree with me. ♦ It's a nice house. – Why don't you buy it then?
theoretical [ˌθɪəˈretɪkəl] *adj.* (mesmo que **theoretic**) □ teórico
theory ['θɪəri] *n.* (*pl.* **theories**) □ teoria
There are different theories about how people learn a language.
in theory □ na teoria
Your idea is good in theory, but I'm not sure it will work in practice.
therapy ['θerəpi] *n.* □ terapia
speech therapy (for people who stutter). ♦ a therapy for breast cancer.

there¹ [ðeə, ðə] *adv.* □ **aí, lá**
Don't come here – I'll meet you there. ◆ I'm going there tomorrow. ◆ The noise came from there.

there² *pron.* □ **usado para formar os verbos "haver" e "ter" no presente e no passado**
There's someone at the door. ◆ Is there anything I can do? ◆ There weren't many people outside. ◆ There aren't any eggs in the refrigerator.

there... no □ **indica ausência total**
There's no milk in the bottle. ◆ There was no hope. ◆ There were no trees there.

there... nothing □ **indica ausência total**
There's nothing you can do. ◆ There was nothing in the box.

there you are □ **tome**
He broke off a piece of chocolate and said to me 'There you are'. ◆ He showed me how to do it and said 'There you are'.

therefore ['ðeəfo:] *adv.* □ **portanto**
I got up late, and therefore decided to take a taxi. ◆ The number of pupils is growing every day. Therefore, the government must build more schools.

thermometer [θə'momitə] *n.* □ **termômetro**

thermostat ['θe:məstat] *n.* □ **termostato**

these [ði:z] *adj., pron.* (*plural of* **this**) □ **estes, estas**
Who put these boxes here? ◆ These chairs are stronger than those. ◆ What are these?

they [ðei] *pron.* □ **eles, elas**
They know what happened. ◆ Where are the letters? – They're on your desk.

they say □ **dizem que**
They say it's going to rain tomorrow.

they'd [ðeid] **they had; they would**)
they'll [ðeil] (mesmo que **they will; they shall**)
they're [ðeə] (mesmo que **they are; they were**)
they've [ðeiv] (mesmo que **they have**)

thick [θik] *adj.*
1 grosso, espesso
a thick book. ◆ a thick coat. ◆ thick walls. ◆ a thick rope.
■ antônimo: **thin**
2 de espessura
The wall is 50 centimeters thick.
3 grosso, denso
He has thick hair. ◆ a thick forest.
■ antônimo: **thin**
4 grosso
The soup was thick.
■ antônimo: **thin**
5 denso
thick smoke. ◆ thick fog.

How thick...? □ **O quão grosso?**
How thick is the rope? ◆ How thick are the walls?

thicken ['θikən] *v.* (**thickens, thickening, thickened**) □ **engrossar**
Thicken the sauce with two spoons of flour. ◆ The fog is beginning to thicken.

thickness ['θiknis] *n.* □ **espessura, grossura**
The glass is three centimeters in thickness.

thief [θi:v] *n.* (*pl.* **thieves**) □ **ladrão, ladra**
The thief stole my wallet and my car. ◆ a car thief.
■ Ver **theft**.

thigh [θai] *n.* □ **coxa**

thin [θin] *n.* (**thinner, thinnest**)
1 fino
a thin book. ◆ a thin cable. ◆ a thin slice of bread. ◆ thin walls.
■ antônimo: **thick**
2 magro
She doesn't eat enough. She is too thin.
■ antônimo: **fat**
■ Compare with **slim**.
3 fino, ralo
The paint is very thin.
■ antônimo: **thick**
4 fino
thin hair.
■ antônimo: **thick**

thing [θiŋ] *n.* □ **coisa**
What's that thing on the table? ◆ We don't talk about these things. ◆ There's another thing I want to know. ◆ Strange things are happening there. ◆ That was a stupid thing to do.

things *n. pl.* □ **coisas**
Pack your things and go!

first thing □ **prioridade, primeira coisa**
I'll send it first thing in the morning.

think [θiŋk] *v.* (**thinks, thinking, thought**)
1 pensar
Be quiet! I'm trying to think. ◆ She thought for a moment and then answered.
2 achar
I think (that) she is right. ◆ Do you think (that) it is possible?

I think so □ **Acho que sim**
Is he here? – Yes, I think so.

I don't think so □ **Acho que não**
Do you think he can do it? – No, I don't think so.

think about
1 pensar sobre
Think about it and give me your answer tomorrow. ◆ She thinks about him every day.
2 pensar em
I'm thinking about visiting them.
3 achar
What do you think about the plan?

think of
1 pensar em
I can't think of any other way. ◆ I can't think of her name.
2 achar
What do you think of his idea?
3 pensar sobre
We're thinking of buying the house.

think something over □ **refletir sobre algo**
I'll think it over before I decide.

third¹ [θə:d] *adj., pron., adv.* □ **terceiro, três**
We live on the third floor. ◆ May the third (= 3rd May). *Brit.* ◆ May third (= May 3). *Amer.* ◆ She came third in the race.

third² *n.* (= 1/3) □ **um terço**
He got a third of the money.

third person ['θə:d 'pə:sn] *n.* (grammar) □ **terceira pessoa**
'he / she / it / they' and 'him / her / them' are third person pronouns. ◆ The third person singular of the verb ends with 's' in the present simple tense, such as 'takes'.

thirst [θə:st] *n.* □ **sede**
The animal died of thirst.

thirsty [ˈθɔːsti] *adj.* (**thirstier, thirstiest**) □ com sede, sedento
I'm thirsty. ♦ The long walk made me thirsty.
thirteen [θɔːˈtiːn] *adj., pron., n.* □ treze
It costs thirteen dollars. ♦ thirteen people. ♦ She is thirteen years old.
thirteenth [θɔːˈtiːnθ] *adj., pron., adv.* □ décimo terceiro, treze
the thirteenth name on the list. ♦ June the thirteenth (= 13th June). *Brit.* ♦ June thirteenth (= June 13). *Amer.* ♦ He came thirteenth in the race.
thirtieth [ˈθɔːtiiθ] *adj., pron., adv.* □ trigésimo, treze
It's her thirtieth birthday. ♦ What date is it today? – The thirtieth.
thirty [ˈθɔːti] *adj., pron., n.* □ trinta
There are thirty people here. ♦ page thirty. ♦ I'm thirty years old.
the thirties □ os anos trinta, década de 1930
This song was very popular in the thirties.
in your thirties □ nos seus trinta e poucos anos
She is in her thirties.
this[1] [ðis] *adj., pron.* (*pl.* **these**) □ este, isto
Sarah gave me this pen. ♦ This is my friend James. ♦ What is this? ♦ This (car) is better than that.
■ Ver **these**.
this week / month □ esta semana / mês
I'll telephone this week.
like this
1 como este
Can you find me another box like this?
2 deste jeito, assim
Is she always like this?
3 desta maneira, assim
Try to do it like this.
this[2] *adv.* □ deste
The chair is about this high. ♦ The table is about this long.
thorn [θɔːn] *n.* □ espinho
Rose bushes have thorns.
thorough [ˈθʌrə] *adj.* □ minucioso
They made a thorough search of the place.
thoroughly [ˈθʌrəli] *adv.*
1 minuciosamente
The doctor examined me thoroughly.
2 profundamente
I felt thoroughly bored.
thoroughness [ˈθʌrənis] *n.* □ meticulosidade, minuciosidade
those[1] [ðəʊz] *adj.* □ aqueles, aquelas
Bring those chairs here. ♦ Those girls are in my class. ♦ These pens are better than those pens.
■ Ver **that**.
those[2] *pron.* (*plural of* **that**) □ aqueles, aquelas
Those are our suitcases over there.
though[1] [ðəʊ] *conj.*
1 (= although) **embora**
I enjoyed the film, though it was very long. ♦ Though I tried, I couldn't do it.
2 (= but) **porém**
He can drive, though not very well.
as though □ como se
It looks as though it's broken.
even though (= although) □ ainda que, mesmo que
I think I'll buy it, even though it's expensive.

though[2] *adv.* □ mesmo assim
We can try. It won't be easy, though.
thought[1] [θɔːt] *v.* (Ver **think**).
thought[2] *n.*
1 consideração, reflexão
Give it some thought (= Think about it) before you decide.
2 ideia, opinião
We would like to hear your thoughts on the subject.
thoughtful [ˈθɔːtful] *adj.*
1 pensativo
She had a thoughtful look on her face.
2 atencioso
It was very thoughtful of you to invite them.
thoughtfulness [ˈθɔːtfulnis] *n.* □ atenção, consideração
thousand [ˈθaʊzənd] *adj., pron.* □ mil, milhar
a thousand dollars. ♦ three thousand and six (= 3.006). ♦ Thousands of people came to the concert.
thousandth[1] [ˈθaʊzəndθ] *adj., pron., adv.* □ milésimo
the thousandth time. ♦ the thousandth anniversary.
thousandth[2] *n.* □ milésimo
a thousandth of a second.
thrash [θraʃ] *v.* (**thrashes, thrashing, thrashed**) □ surrar, bater
He thrashed the horse with the whip.
thread[1] [θred] *n.* □ linha
a needle and thread.
thread[2] *v.* (**threads, threading, threaded**)
1 passar linha
to thread a needle.
2 passar por
She threaded the beads on a string.
threat [θret] *n.*
1 ameaça
I'm not afraid of his threats. ♦ Is that a threat?
2 ameaça
Drugs are a threat to society.
threaten [ˈθretən] *v.* (**threatens, threatening, threatened**) □ ameaçar
He threatened to kill me. ♦ Don't threaten me!
threatening [ˈθretənɪŋ] *adj.* □ ameaçador
a threatening voice. ♦ a threatening letter.
threateningly [ˈθretənɪŋli] *adv.* □ ameaçadoramente
She looked threateningly at him.
three [θriː] *adj., pron.* □ três
It costs three dollars. ♦ We need three people. ♦ It's three o'clock. ♦ He is three years old.
■ Compare **third**:
third child.
a third of the price.
threw [θruː] *v.* (Ver **throw**).
thrill[1] [θril] *n.* □ emoção
He climbs mountains because it gives him a thrill.
thrill[2] *v.* (**thrills, thrilling, thrilled**) □ emocionar
It thrilled her to see the view from the top of the mountain.
thrilled [θrild] *adj.* □ emocionado
They were thrilled to meet the pop star.
thriller [ˈθrilə] *n.* □ obra de suspense
Thrillers are my favourite TV films. ♦ I like to read thrillers.
thrilling [ˈθrilɪŋ] *adj.* □ emocionante, empolgante
a thrilling experience. ♦ a thrilling adventure story.

throat [θrout] *n.*
1 garganta
He grabbed me by the throat.
2 garganta
Something got stuck in my throat.
throb [θrob] *v.* (**throbs, throbbing, throbbed**) □ **soluçar**
Her heart was throbbing with excitement.
throne [θroun] *n.* □ **trono**
through[1] [θru:] *prep.*
1 por, através de
We walked through the fields. ◆ The train goes through a tunnel. ◆ He looked through the window. ◆ to look through a telescope.
2 durante
Bears sleep through the winter.
3 *Amer.* **até**
We are open Monday through Thursday.
4 por meio de, por causa de
They lost money through bad management. ◆ He got the job through his father.
through[2] *adv.*
1 através
They cut the fence and went through.
2 completamente
I read the article through.
■ Ver **get through; put someone through**.
throughout [θru:'aut] *prep.*
1 em todo
Millions of people throughout the world watched the programme.
2 durante todo
throughout the year.
throw [θrou] *v.* (**throws, throwing, threw, thrown**)
1 jogar, atirar
Throw me those keys. ◆ Throw the ball to Karen. ◆ They threw tomatoes at the speaker.
2 jogar
He threw me to the floor. ◆ She threw her bag down.
3 jogar
The horse threw its rider up into the air.
throw something away / out □ **jogar algo fora**
I need these magazines. Don't throw them away. ◆ to throw away old clothes.
throw up (= be sick) □ **vomitar**
The bad smell made me throw up.
thrust [θrʌst] *v.* (**thrusts, thrusting, thrust**) □ **enfiar**
She thrust some money into my hand.
thud [θʌd] *n.* □ **baque**
The bag hit the floor with a thud.
thug [θʌg] *n.* (= hooligan) □ **bandido**
Some thugs wrecked his car.
■ Ver **skinhead**.
thumb [θʌm] *n.* □ **polegar**
thumbtack [θʌmtak] *n. Amer.* □ **tachinha**
I need some thumbtacks to put up this poster.
■ *Brit.* **drawing-pin**
thump [θʌmp] *v.* (**thumps, thumping, thumped**)
1 esmurrar
He thumped on the door, but there was no answer.
2 bater forte
His heart was thumping with fear.
thunder[1] ['θʌndə] *n.* □ **trovão**
Thunder comes after lightning.
thunder[2] *v.* (**thunders, thundering, thundered**) □ **trovejar**
It rained and thundered last night.
thunderstorm ['θʌndəstɔ:m] *n.* □ **tempestade**
Thursday ['θə:zdi] *n.* □ **quinta-feira**
They arrived on Thursday. ◆ We meet every Thursday. ◆ What day is it today? – It's Thursday. ◆ I saw her last Thursday. ◆ I'll see her again next Thursday.
thus [ðʌs] *adv.*
1 assim, desse modo
Open it with your thumb, thus.
2 consequentemente
They decided to buy a small house and thus save some money.
tick[1] [tik] *n.*
1 tique-taque
We could hear the ticks of the clock.
2 *Brit.* **marca**
Put a tick by every correct answer.
■ *Amer.* **check**
tick[2] *v.* (**ticks, ticking, ticked**)
1 fazer tique-taque
The clock is ticking.
2 *Brit.* **ticar, fazer uma marca**
Tick the names (on the list) of those who are here.
■ *Amer.* **check**
ticket ['tikit] *n.*
1 tíquete, entrada, passagem, bilhete
I bought two tickets for the basketball game. ◆ a cinema ticket. ◆ a bus ticket. ◆ a train ticket. ◆ a plane ticket ◆ a return ticket ◆ a single ticket.
2 multa
He got a ticket for speeding. ◆ a parking ticket.
ticket office ['tikit 'ofis] *n.* □ **bilheteria**
tickle ['tikl] *v.* (**tickles, tickling, tickled**)
1 fazer cócegas
She laughed when I tickled her feet.
2 coçar, pinicar
My nose is tickling. ◆ This blanket tickles.
tide [taid] *n.* □ **maré**
The tide is coming in (= at high tide). ◆ The tide is going out (= at low tide).
tidily ['taidili] *adv.* □ **ordenadamente**
Put the books tidily on the shelf.
tidiness ['taidinis] *n.* □ **ordem**
tidy[1] ['taidi] *adj.* (**tidier, tidiest**)
1 arrumado
She always keeps her room neat and tidy.
2 ordeiro
He is a very tidy worker.
tidy[2] *v.* (**tidies, tidying, tidied**) □ **arrumar**
Tidy (up) your room before you go. ◆ She tidied her desk.
tie[1] [tai] *n.*
1 gravata
He wore a blue suit and red tie.
2 (= draw) **empate**
The game ended in a tie.
ties *n. pl.* □ **laços**
We have strong ties with that country.
tie[2] *v.* (**ties, tying, tied**)
1 amarrar
I tied a rope round the tree. ◆ He tied his horse to a tree. ◆ Tie the parcel with a piece of string.

tiger / times

2 empatar
They tied in the third game (of chess).
tie someone up □ **amarrar alguém**
The robbers tied up the guard.
tie something up □ **amarrar algo**
Tie up the package with string.

tiger ['taigə] *n.* □ **tigre**
A tiger has yellow fur with black stripes.
■ Compare **leopard**:
A leopard has black spots.

tight¹ [tait] *adj.*
1 apertado
a tight knot. ◆ The screw is tight enough. ◆ Can you open this jar? The lid is too tight.
2 apertado, justo
These shoes are too tight. I need a bigger size. ◆ He wore tight jeans. ◆ This shirt is too tight.
3 esticado
The cable between the two poles is tight enough.
■ antônimo: **loose**

tight² *adv.* □ **com firmeza**
Hold tight! There's a hole in the road!
■ Ver **tightly**.

tighten ['taitn] *v.* (**tightens, tightening, tightened**) □ **apertar**
He tightened the screws. ◆ She tightened her belt. ◆ The rope tightened around his neck.
■ antônimo: **loosen**

tightly ['taitli] *adv.* □ **firmemente**
Close the lid tightly. ◆ I tied the rope tightly around the tree.

tightrope ['taitroup] *n.* □ **corda bamba**
Acrobats walk the tightrope in a circus.

tights [taits] *n. pl.*
1 *Brit.* **meia-calça**
a pair of tights.
■ *Amer.* **pantyhose**
2 collant
Dancers wear tights.

tile [tail] *n.* □ **telha, ladrilho**
(red) roof tiles. ◆ a floor tile. ◆ bathroom tiles.

till¹ [til] *conj.* (= until) □ **até que**
We waited till he arrived. ◆ Go straight on till you get to a traffic light, then turn right.

till² *prep.* (= until) □ **até**
I'll wait for you till tomorrow. ◆ She worked there till 1990. ◆ The office is open from nine till six.

till now □ **até agora**
I never thought that he could do it till now.

till³ *n. Brit.* □ **caixa de guardar dinheiro**
She put the money in the till.
■ *Amer.* **register**

tilt [tilt] *v.* (**tilts, tilting, tilted**) □ **inclinar**
He tilts his shoulders to one side when he sings. ◆ The seats tilt forward a little.

timber ['timbə] *n.* □ **madeira**
Timber is used especially for building.

time¹ [taim] *n.*
1 hora
What time is it? (= What's the time?) ◆ Could you tell me the time please?
2 tempo
How do you pass the time in the evenings? ◆ Time passed quickly. ◆ It took me a long time to find it. ◆ I haven't got much time. ◆ Don't waste my time! ◆ What do you do in your free time?
3 vez
Every time I see that picture, I laugh. ◆ Next time don't forget to take it. ◆ The last time I saw him was yesterday. ◆ We meet three times a week.

times *n. pl.*
1 horários
Can you tell me the times of the trains to London, please?
2 vezes
Knock three times on the door.
3 tempos
There were no cars in ancient times. ◆ in Roman times.
4 vezes
This box is four times heavier than that one.

times *prep.* □ **vezes**
Five times six is thirty (5x6=30).

at a time □ **por vez**
I can carry two boxes at a time.

at that time □ **naquela época**
At that time, she was ten years old.

at the time □ **na época**
My parents married in 1980. They were students at the time.

at times (= sometimes) □ **às vezes**
She annoys me at times.

by the time □ **na hora em que, quando**
By the time you get home everything will be ready.
■ you get (*not* 'you will get').

for the time being □ **por enquanto**
You can use my car for the time being.

from time to time □ **de vez em quando**
I visit them from time to time.

have a good / great time □ **divertir-se muito**
We had a great time at the party.

in good time □ **na hora certa**
I want everything to be ready in good time.

in time
1 com o tempo
You'll get used to your new school in time.
2 a tempo
We'll arrive home in time (for dinner). ◆ I finished the exam in time to check the answers.

on time □ **na hora, pontualmente**
The train arrived on time. ◆ The concert started right on time.

it's about time □ **já não era sem tempo, até que enfim**
It's about time (that) you found a job.
■ it's about time (that) you **found** (*not* 'that you will find').

it's time to □ **é hora, está na hora**
It's time to make some changes. ◆ Is it time to go home?

save time □ **economizar tempo**
You can save a lot of time if you go by train.

spend time □ **passar um tempo**
I spent some time in the market. ◆ She spends a lot of time watching TV.

take time □ **levar tempo**
It took me a long time to prepare the meal.

take your time □ **não tenha pressa**

time / to

There's no hurry – take your time.
tell the time, tell time □ **dizer as horas, ver as horas**
He can't tell the time yet – he's only four years old.
time after time, time and time again □ **várias vezes, várias e várias vezes**
I've warned them time after time not to go there.
time² *v.* (**times, timing, timed**)
1 programar
They timed the robbery perfectly. ♦ The bomb was timed to explode in the rush-hour.
2 marcar o tempo
There is a special watch to time the runners in a race.
times [taimz] *n., prep.* (Ver **time¹**).
timetable ['taimteibl] *n.*
1 *Brit.* **horário**
a train timetable. ♦ a school timetable. ♦ What's the first lesson on your timetable today?
■ The usual word in American English is **schedule**.
2 (= schedule) **programação**
There's no timetable yet for the peace talks.
timid ['timid] *adj.* □ **tímido**
He is so timid that he never raises his hand in class.
timidly ['timidli] *adv.* □ **timidamente**
She spoke timidly to her teacher.
timing ['taimiŋ] *n.* □ **timing**
Your timing is perfect – everything is ready.
tin [tin] *n.*
1 latão
a tin box. ♦ a tin roof.
2 *Brit.* **lata**
a tin of sardines.
■ *Amer.* **can**
3 lata
a biscuit tin. ♦ a cake tin.
4 *Brit.* **lata**
a bread tin. ♦ a cake tin.
■ *Amer.* **pan**
tinned [tind] *adj. Brit.* □ **enlatado**
tinned pineapple. ♦ tinned tomatoes.
■ *Amer.* **canned**
tin-opener ['tin ,oupənə] *n.* □ **abridor de lata**
■ *Amer.* **can-opener**
tiny [taini] *adj.* (**tinier, tiniest**) (= minute¹) □ **pequenino**
the baby's tiny feet. ♦ a tiny insect.
tip¹ [tip] *n.*
1 gorjeta
He gave the waiter a good tip.
2 dica
She gave me some useful tips on how to make a good pizza.
3 ponta
She touched the tip of her nose with the tip of her finger. ♦ the tip of an arrow.
tip² *v.* (**tips, tipping, tipped**)
1 dar gorjeta
Did you tip the taxi driver?
2 inclinar
Don't tip your chair back, or you'll fall! ♦ The boat tipped to one side.
3 *Brit.* **esvaziar**
She opened her bag and tipped everything out onto the table.

tip over □ **emborcar**
He tipped a chair over when he ran out. ♦ The boat tipped over.
tiptoe¹ ['tiptou] *n.*
on tiptoe(s) □ **na ponta dos pés**
He walked on tiptoe into the bedroom.
tiptoe² *v.* (**tiptoes, tiptoeing, tiptoed**) □ **andar na ponta dos pés**
She tiptoed quietly out of the room.
tire¹ ['taiə] *n. Amer.* (= tyre, *Brit.*) □ **pneu**
to change a tire.
tire² *v.* (**tires, tiring, tired**) □ **cansar, cansar-se**
The hard work tired them. ♦ The runners are beginning to tire.
tired ['taiəd] *adj.* □ **cansado**
You need some rest – you look tired. ♦ I was tired after the long walk.
be tired of (= be worn-out) □ **estar cansado de**
I'm tired of waiting for him – let's go!
be tired out □ **estar exausto**
I was tired out after playing football.
get tired □ **ficar cansado**
He is ill and gets tired very easily. ♦ She got tired and sat down to rest.
tiring ['taiəriŋ] *adj.* □ **cansativo**
I had a tiring day at work.
tissue ['tiʃu:] *n.*
1 (= a paper hankerchief) **lenço de papel**
a box of tissues.
2 (= tissue paper) **papel de seda**
Tissue paper is used for wrapping and packing.
3 tecido
brain tissue.
title ['taitl] *n.*
1 título
What was the title of her first book?
2 título
'Professor', 'Dr.', 'Mr.', 'Mrs.' and 'Sir' are examples of titles.
3 título
He lost his title to the Italian boxer.
to¹ [tə, tu] *prep.*
1 a, para
We're going to the market. ♦ This is the road to Paris. ♦ She pointed to the ceiling.
2 a, para
Give it to him. ♦ Listen to her. ♦ I sent a letter to Edna.
3 a, até
We are open from 8 am to 7 pm. ♦ Can you count from one to ten? ♦ from beginning to end.
4 para
It's ten minutes to four.
5 a
The journey will take two to three hours.
6 a
He tied his horse to a tree.
7 para
The colour changed from green to blue.
8 para
I came to see the children. ♦ She is too young to understand this. ♦ He is tall enough to reach that shelf.
9 a
I prefer walking to running.

10 de
Is this the key to the door?
11 para
There's no solution to this problem. ◆ a danger to your health.
12 com
My car does ten kilometers to the liter.
13 usado para expressar o infinitivo do verbo
We want to help. ◆ Show me how to do it. ◆ I don't want to go, but I have to (= to go).
to and fro (Ver **fro**).

toad [toud] *n.* □ **sapo**

toast¹ [toust] *n.*
1 torrada
I had toast and marmalade for breakfast.
2 brinde
We drank a toast to the bride and groom.

toast² *v.* (**toasts, toasting, toasted**)
1 tostar
Don't toast the bread too much.
2 brindar
We toasted the bride and groom.

toasted ['toustid] *adj.* □ **tostado**
a toasted sandwich.

toaster ['toustə] *n.* □ **tostador, torradeira**

toaster oven ['toustər ʌvn] *n.* □ **forno tostador**
We use the toaster oven for grilling fish and baking pies.

tobacco [tə'bækou] *n.* □ **tabaco, fumo**
a packet of pipe tobacco.

today [tə'dei] *n., adv.*
1 hoje
Today is Tuesday. ◆ I can't come today.
2 hoje
Children today watch too much TV.

today's [tə'deiz] □ **de hoje**
Is this today's paper? ◆ today's parents.

toe [tou] *n.* □ **dedo do pé**
She tickled the baby's toes.

toenail ['touneil] *n.* □ **unha do dedo do pé**
Cut your toenails.

toffee ['tɔfi] *n.* □ **caramelo**
a bag of toffees.

together [tə'geðə] *adv.*
1 junto
We go everywhere together. ◆ Together we can do it.
2 junto
Stick the two pieces together. ◆ Mix the flour, butter and eggs together.

toilet ['tɔilit] *n.* (= lavatory) □ **toalete, banheiro**
I need to go to the toilet.
■ The usual words are **bathroom and washroom**.

toilet paper ['tɔilit 'peipə] *n.* □ **papel higiênico**
toilet roll ['tɔilit roul] *n.* □ **rolo de papel higiênico**

token ['toukən] *n.*
1 sinal, prova
Please accept this gift as a token of our friendship.
2 *Brit.* **vale**
a gift token. ◆ a book token.
■ *Amer.* **gift certificate**
3 ficha
You don't need tokens for this machine – you can use money.

told [tould] *v.* (Ver **tell**).

tolerable ['tɔlərəbl] *adj.* □ **tolerável**
The pain in my leg is tolerable.
■ antônimo: **intolerable**

tolerance ['tɔlərəns] *n.* (= toleration) □ **tolerância**
religious tolerance. ◆ tolerance towards other opinions.
■ antônimo: **intolerance**

tolerant ['tɔlərənt] *adj.* □ **tolerante**
a tolerant person. ◆ He is very tolerant towards other religions.
■ antônimo: **intolerant**

tolerate ['tɔləreit] *v.* (**tolerates, tolerating, tolerated**)
1 tolerar
I won't tolerate any disturbance in my class.
2 tolerar, suportar
We couldn't tolerate the heat.

toleration [ˌtɔlə'reiʃən] *n.* (= tolerance) □ **tolerância**
religious toleration.

tomato [tə'ma:tou] *n.* □ **tomate**
Cut the tomatoes and the lettuce to make a salad. ◆ tomato juice.

tomb [tu:m] *n.* □ **tumba**
A tomb is a grave, especially of an important person.

tombstone ['tu:mstoun] *n.* □ **lápide**

tomorrow [tə'mɔrou] *n., adv.* □ **amanhã**
I'll call you tomorrow morning. ◆ She is coming tomorrow.
the day after tomorrow □ **depois de amanhã**
We are going away the day after tomorrow.

ton [tʌn] *n.* □ **tonelada**
In Britain, a ton equals 1,016 kilograms, and in the USA 907 kilograms.
■ Compare **tonne**:
tonne = 1000 kilos

tons of (= a lot of) □ **um monte de**
They bought tons of food for the party.

tone [toun] *n.*
1 tom
'Not now!' he said in an angry tone (of voice).
2 sinal
a dialing / dialling tone. ◆ Please leave a message after the tone.

tongue [tʌŋ] *n.*
1 língua
Stick your tongue out.
2 língua, idioma
Your mother tongue is the first language you learnt as a child.

tonight [tə'nait] *adv., n.* □ **hoje à noite, esta noite**
We are going out tonight. ◆ What's on TV tonight? ◆ Tonight at 7 o'clock.

tonne [tʌn] *n.* (mesmo que **metric ton**) □ **tonelada**
There are 1,000 kilos in a tonne.
■ Compare **ton**:
ton = 1,016 kilos.

too [tu:] *adv.*
1 também
She saw it too. (= She also saw it.) ◆ I agree. – Me too.
■ Ver **also**.
2 demais
The box is too heavy. ◆ It's too cold outside. ◆ too many books; too much milk.

took / touching

not too (= not so) □ **não tão**
The meal is not too bad.
too... to □ **demais... para**
The tea is too hot (for me) to drink. ◆ I'm too short to reach the top shelf.

took [tuk] *v.* (Ver **take**).

tool [tu:l] *n.* □ **ferramenta**
I keep my tools (= a hammer, a saw, a screwdriver, a drill, pliers, etc.) in that box. ◆ garden tools.
■ Compare with **instrument**:
instrument is used for technical or delicate work (optical instruments, medical instruments, surgical instruments, etc.).

tooth [tu:θ] *n.* (*pl.* **teeth**)
1 dente
The dentist took out my crooked tooth. ◆ to fill a tooth.
2 dente
the teeth of a comb, saw, etc.

toothache ['tu:θeik] *n.* □ **dor de dente**
I have a terrible toothache.

toothbrush ['tu:θbrʌʃ] *n.* □ **escova de dente**

toothpaste ['tu:θpeist] *n.* □ **pasta de dente**
a tube of toothpaste.

top¹ [top] *adj.*
1 mais alto, máximo
The book is on the top shelf. ◆ at top speed.
2 principal, mais importante
She is one of the world's top scientists.

top² *n.*
1 topo
After a week they reached the top of the mountain. ◆ on top of the hill.
■ antônimo: **foot**
2 topo
He stood at the top of the stairs. ◆ The restaurant is at the top of the building.
3 topo
Write your name at the top of the page.
■ antônimo: **bottom**
4 topo
Our team is at the top of the league. ◆ Mary is at the top of the class in mathematics.
■ antônimo: **bottom**
5 superfície
the top of the table.
6 tampa
a bottle top. ◆ the top (= cap) of a pen. ◆ Put the top (= cap) back on the toothpaste.
■ Ver **cap**.
7 pião
to spin a top.

on top □ **por cima**
The ice cream had a cherry on top.
on top of □ **sobre, em cima de**
There is a TV antenna on top of the roof. ◆ He put the books one on top of the other.
top secret, top-secret □ **altamente confidencial**
These documents are top secret. ◆ a top-secret project.

topic ['topik] *n.* (= subject) □ **tópico**
What was the topic of the discussion?

topical ['topikəl] *adj.* □ **principal**
topical issues of today.

torch [to:tʃ] *n.*
1 *Brit.* **lanterna**
He shone the torch on me.
■ *Amer.* **flashlight**
2 tocha
Which athlete will carry the Olympic torch?

tore [to:] *v.* (Ver **tear³**).

torn [to:n] *v.* (Ver **tear³**).

tornado [to:'neidou] *n.* □ **tornado**

torpedo [to:'pi:dou] *n.* □ **torpedo**
A torpedo hit the ship and it sank.

tortoise ['to:təs] *n.* □ **tartaruga**
A tortoise moves very slowly and has a shell to protect it.
■ Ver **turtle**.

torture¹ ['to:tʃə] *n.* □ **tortura**
The prisoner died of torture.

torture² *v.* (**tortures, torturing, tortured**) □ **torturar**
They tortured the prisoner until he confessed.

toss [tos] *v.* (**tosses, tossing, tossed**)
1 arremessar, atirar
She tossed the newspaper to him. ◆ I tossed the empty can into the bin.
2 sacudir-se
The boat tossed up and down.
3 jogar
Let's toss a coin to decide who will start.

total¹ ['toutəl] *adj.*
1 total
The total number of pupils in our school is 600.
2 (= complete) **total**
It was a total failure. ◆ There was total silence in the room.

total² *n.* □ **total**
We paid a total of $200. ◆ There were 150 people there in total.

totally ['toutəli] *adv.* □ **totalmente**
I totally agree with you.

touch¹ [tʌtʃ] *v.* (**touches, touching, touched**)
1 tocar, pôr a mão
She touched me on the arm. ◆ Be careful not to touch the paint – it's still wet. ◆ He touched the water to see if it was hot.
2 encostar
Her dress was so long that it touched the ground.

touch² *n.*
1 toque
I felt the touch of his hand on my shoulder.
2 tato
the sense of touch.
3 toque
Wool is soft to the touch.

be / keep in touch (with) □ **estar / manter contato (com)**
We kept in touch with them until they left the country.
◆ Keep in touch! ◆ We are not in touch any more.
get in touch with □ **entrar em contato com**
I got in touch with her by telephone.
lose touch (with) □ **perder contato (com)**
I lost touch with him when we left school.

touchdown ['tʌtʃdaun] *n.* □ **aterrissagem**
Touchdown is the moment of landing (of an airplane or spacecraft).

touching ['tʌtʃiŋ] *adj.* □ **tocante, emocionante**
The ending of the film was very touching.

touchy ['tʌtʃi] *adj.* □ **sensível**
Don't be so touchy – I'm only joking.

tough [tʌf] *adj.*
1 (= difficult) **duro, difícil**
a tough job. ◆ a tough problem. ◆ It's a tough competition.
2 duro
tough plastic. ◆ a tough material.
3 durão
He is a tough guy. ◆ You need to be tough to succeed in business.
4 duro, violento
The police are taking tough measures against drug dealers.
5 duro
tough meat.
■ antônimo: **tender**
get tough with □ **ser duro com**
It's necessary to get tough with such criminals.

tour¹ [tuə] *n.*
1 visita, excursão
He gave us a tour of the factory. ◆ We went on a guided tour around the museum.
2 viagem
a 6-day tour of Italy.
3 turnê
The tour of the rock band will start in Greece.

tour² *v.* (**tours, touring, toured**) □ **excursionar por**
We toured North Africa for a month.

tour guide ['tuə gaid] *n.* □ **guia turístico**
The tour guide gave us a tour of the museum.

tourism ['tuərizm] *n.* □ **turismo**
Tourism is a big industry in this country.

tourist ['tuərist] *n.* □ **turismo**
The tourists went sightseeing around the city.

tournament ['tuənəmənt] *n.* □ **torneio**
a tennis tournament. ◆ a chess tournament.

tow [tou] *v.* (**tows, towing, towed**) □ **guinchar**
My car broke down and was towed to a garage.

toward(s) [tə'wɔ:d(z)] *prep.*
1 em direção a
He walked towards the door. ◆ She ran towards me.
2 para com
They were friendly towards us. ◆ What is your attitude towards violence on TV?
3 rumo a
This is the first step towards peace.
4 em direção a
We will finish the project towards the end of the year.

towel ['tauəl] *n.* □ **toalha**
He dried himself with the bath towel. ◆ paper towels.

tower ['tauə] *n.* □ **torre**
The tower is 300 metres high. ◆ the Eiffel Tower.

town [taun] *n.* □ **cidade**
A town is smaller than a city. ◆ a fishing town.

town hall ['taunhɔ:l] *n.* □ **prefeitura**
■ **city hall** for a city.

toxic ['toksik] *adj.* (= poisonous) □ **tóxico**
toxic chemicals / gases.

toy [toi] *n., adj.* □ **brinquedo, de brinquedo**
Pick up the toys from the floor. ◆ a toy car. ◆ toy soldiers.

trace¹ [treis] *n.*
1 vestígio, sinal
There is no trace of the missing child. ◆ The animal disappeared without trace.
2 vestígio
The police found traces of poison in the cup.

trace² *v.* (**traces, tracing, traced**)
1 rastrear
The police are trying to trace the robbers. ◆ They traced the stolen car. ◆ to trace a telephone call.
2 esboçar, traçar
I traced the map.

track¹ [trak] *n.*
1 (= path) **trilha**
This track leads to the village.
2 pista
The runners are waiting on the track.
3 trilhos
Snow blocked the track and the train was six hours late.
4 *Amer.* **plataforma**
Our train is on Track 12.
■ *Brit.* **platform**
5 faixa
The best song is on the second track of the disc.

tracks *n. pl.* □ **pegadas**
They found the tracks of the bear in the snow. ◆ We followed the tracks. ◆ dirt tracks.

track² *v.* (**tracks, tracking, tracked**) □ **rastrear**
The radar tracks the rocket in the air.

track down □ **seguir a pista de**
The police tracked down the robbers.

tracksuit [traksu:t] *n.* (mesmo que **jogging suit**) □ **moletom, roupa para correr**

tractor ['traktə] *n.* □ **trator**

trade¹ [treid] *n.*
1 comércio
Our trade with Japan will double next year. ◆ a trade agreement.
2 (= job) **profissão**
to learn a trade.
by trade □ **de profissão**
He is a carpenter by trade.

trade² *v.* (**trades, trading, traded**) □ **negociar, comerciar**
We trade with many countries in Europe.

trade something for □ **trocar algo por**
I traded my car for his van.

trademark [treidma:k] *n.* □ **marca registrada**

trader [treidə] *n.* □ **comerciante**
■ Ver **merchant**.

tradesman ['treidzmən] *n.* (*pl.* **tradesmen**) □ **lojista**

trade union ['treid 'ju:njən] *n. Brit.* □ **sindicato**
■ *Amer.* **labor union**

tradition [trə'diʃən] *n.* □ **tradição**
In many countries it's a tradition for the bride to wear a white dress.

traditional [trə'diʃənl] *adj.* □ **tradicional**
traditional customs. ◆ traditional music. ◆ a traditional ceremony.

traditionally [trə'diʃənli] *adv.* □ **tradicionalmente**
Traditionally, English people eat turkey on Christmas Day.

traffic ['trafik] *n.* □ **tráfego**
There was a lot of traffic on the road to the airport. ◆ air traffic.

traffic circle ['trafik 'sɜ:kl] *n. Amer.* □ **rotatória**
Go around the traffic circle.
■ *Brit.* **roundabout**

traffic jam ['trafik dʒam] *n.* □ **congestionamento de trânsito**
I was stuck in a traffic jam.
traffic lights ['trafik laits] *n. pl.* (mesmo que **traffic light**, *Amer.*) □ **semáforo**
Turn right at the next traffic lights.
traffic sign ['trafik sain] *n.* □ **placa de trânsito**
A Stop sign on the road is a traffic sign.
traffic warden ['trafik 'wo:dn] *n. Brit.* □ **guarda de trânsito**
tragedy ['tradʒədi] *n.* (*pl.* **tragedies**)
1 tragédia
The Prime Minister's death was a great tragedy for all of us.
2 tragédia
Shakespeare wrote tragedies as well as comedies.
tragic ['tradʒik] *adj.* □ **trágico**
a tragic accident.
tragically ['tradʒikəli] *adv.* □ **tragicamente**
They died tragically in a road accident.
trail¹ [treil] *n.*
1 rastro
The wounded robber left a trail of blood behind him.
2 (= path) **trilha**
We went up the trail to the top of the hill.
be on someone's trail □ **estar no rastro de alguém**
The prisoner escaped, but the police are on his trail.
trail² *v.* (**trails, trailing, trailed**)
1 arrastar-se
Her dress trailed along the floor.
2 perder
Our team is trailing by one goal to two (1-2).
trail along behind □ **ir atrás**
The children trailed along behind their teacher.
trailer ['treilə] *n.*
1 *Amer.* **trailer**
They are touring the country in a trailer.
■ *Brit.* **caravan**
2 trailer
The car pulled a trailer with a small boat on it.
train¹ [trein] *n.* □ **trem**
I like to travel by train. ◆ Does this train go to London? ◆ I got on the train at 7 and got off at 7:30.
catch the train □ **pegar o trem**
I caught the 8 o'clock train.
miss the train □ **perder o trem**
Hurry up or you'll miss the train.
train² *v.* (**trains, training, trained**)
1 treinar
He is training them for the swimming competition. ◆ She trains horses for races. ◆ The athletes trained hard for the Olympic Games.
2 instruir
A teachers' college trains new teachers. ◆ She is training to be a tourist guide.
trained [treind] *adj.*
1 (= qualified) **qualificado**
She is a trained nurse. ◆ trained teachers.
2 treinado
a trained guide dog (for the blind)
trainee [trei'ni:] *n.* □ **pessoa em treinamento**
a trainee teacher / technician.
trainer ['treinə] *n.*
1 (= coach) **treinador**
The trainer taught the players to play as a team.

2 treinador
a guide-dog trainer.
3 *Brit.* **tênis**
a pair of trainers.
■ *Amer.* **running shoe; sneaker**
training ['treiniŋ] *n.*
1 treinamento
military training. ◆ The runners are in training for the race.
2 treinamento
The new workers will need some training. ◆ a training course.
traitor ['treitə] *n.* □ **traidor**
A traitor is a person who commits treason. ◆ He is a traitor. He betrayed his country and friends.
■ Ver **unfaithful**.
tram [tram] *n.* □ **bonde**
■ *Amer.* **streetcar**
tramp [tramp] *n.* □ **andarilho**
A tramp has no home or job and moves from place to place.
trample ['trampl] *v.* (**tramples, trampling, trampled**) □ **pisotear**
The dog trampled (on) the flowers.
transfer¹ ['transfə:] *n.* □ **transferência**
He asked for a transfer to another class.
transfer² *v.* (**transfers, transferring, transferred**) □ **transferir**
They transferred her to another hospital. ◆ The money was transferred to my account.
transform [trans'fo:m] *v.* (**transforms, transforming, transformed**) (= change completely) □ **transformar**
Computers may transform people's lives in the next few years.
transformation [ˌtransfɔ:'meiʃən] *n.* □ **transformação**
transistor [tran'sistə] *n.* (mesmo que **transistor radio**) □ **transistor**
translate [trans'leit] *v.* (**translates, translating, translated**) □ **traduzir**
Can you translate this sentence into Chinese? ◆ She translates books from Polish into English.
■ Compare **interpret**:
interpret = to translate speech as it is being spoken.
translation [trans'leiʃən] *n.* □ **tradução**
a translation exercise. ◆ This is a good translation of the poem. ◆ What is the translation of 'lion' in French?
translator [trans'leitə] *n.* □ **tradutor**
■ Ver **interpreter**.
transparent [trans'parənt] *adj.* □ **transparente**
a transparent glass box. ◆ a transparent shirt.
transplant¹ [trans'pla:nt] *n.* □ **transplante**
a heart transplant. ◆ a transplant operation.
transplant² *v.* (**transplants, transplanting, transplanted**) □ **transplantar**
The doctors transplanted a heart and lungs into him.
transport¹ ['transpo:t] *n. Brit.*
1 transporte
the Ministry of Transport. ◆ public transport (= buses, trains, etc.).
2 transporte
the transport of goods by trains. ◆ a transport plane. *Brit.*
means of transport □ **meio de transporte**

My bicycle is my only means of transport.
- *Amer.* **transportation**

transport² *v.* (**transports, transporting, transported**) □ **transportar**
It takes over two hours to transport the goods by plane.

transportation [ˌtrænspɔːˈteɪʃən] *n. Amer.*
1 transporte
public transportation (= buses, trains, etc.).
2 transporte
the transportation of gas by road. *Amer.*
means of transportation □ **meios de transporte**
- *Brit.* **transport**

trap¹ [træp] *n.* □ **armadilha**
The animal was caught in a trap. ◆ to set a trap (= to prepare it). ◆ Don't go in there – it's a trap! ◆ He is very clever – he won't fall into the trap.

trap² *v.* (**traps, trapping, trapped**)
1 pegar com armadilha
to trap an animal.
2 capturar
The police used clever tricks to trap her.
be trapped □ **ficar preso**
Five people were trapped in the burning building.

trash [træʃ] *n. Amer.* (= garbage) □ **lixo**
- *Brit.* **rubbish**

trash can [træʃ kæn] *n. Amer.* (= garbage can) □ **lata de lixo**
- *Brit.* **dustbin**

travel¹ [ˈtrævl] *v.* (**travels, travelling, travelled**; *Amer.* **traveling, traveled**)
1 viajar
I travel to work by bus. (= I go to work by bus.) ◆ to travel by sea. ◆ to travel by air.
- Compare **drive**:
  I drive to work (in my car).
- *Ver* **ride**².
2 viajar
to travel around the world.
3 viajar
We travelled at 90 kilometres per hour. ◆ They traveled 100 kilometers every day.

travel² *n.* **viagem**
air travel (= by plane). ◆ a travel book.
- *Ver* **journey**.

travels *n. pl.* □ **viagens**
She wrote a book about her travels in Africa.
- Compare **journey**:
  journey – going from one place to another.

travel agency [ˈtrævl ˈeɪdʒənsi] *n.* (*pl.* **travel agencies**) □ **agência de viagem**

travel agent [ˈtrævl ˈeɪdʒənt] *n.* □ **agente de viagem**

traveler's check [ˈtrævələz tʃek] *n. Amer.* (Ver **traveller's cheque**.)

traveller [ˈtrævələ] *n. Amer.*, **traveler** □ **viajante**
Marco Polo was a famous traveller.
- Compare **passenger**:
  50 passengers on a bus.

traveller's cheque [ˈtrævələz tʃek] *n. Brit.* □ **cheque de viagem**
I paid by traveller's cheque.
- *Amer.* **traveler's check**

travelling [ˈtrævəlɪŋ] *n. Amer.* (also **traveling**) □ **viagem**
I do a lot of travelling in this job. *Amer.*

travelling bag *n.* (mesmo que **travel bag**) □ **mala de mão**
When you go on a plane you can take your travelling bag with you. *Amer.*

travelling expenses *n.* (mesmo que **travel expenses**) □ **despesas de viagem**

tray [treɪ] *n.* □ **bandeja**

treacherous [ˈtretʃərəs] *adj.* □ **traiçoeiro**
His treacherous friend told them his secret.

treachery [ˈtretʃəri] *n.* □ **traição**
- Compare **treason**:
  treason = against your country.

tread [tred] *v.* (**treads, treading, trod, trodden**) □ **pisar**
He trod on my foot.

treason [ˈtriːzn] *n.* □ **traição**
The spy got 20 years in prison for treason.
- *Ver* **betrayal; treachery**.

treasure [ˈtreʒə] *n.* □ **tesouro**
The pirates buried the treasure in the sand.

treasurer [ˈtreʒərə] *n.* □ **tesoureiro**

treasury [ˈtreʒəri] *n.* □ **tesouro**
the Treasury □ **o Tesouro Nacional**

treat¹ [triːt] *v.* (**treats, treating, treated**)
1 tratar
They treat the prisoners well / badly. ◆ We treated them with respect. ◆ Don't treat her like a child!
2 tratar
They treated my suggestion seriously. ◆ She treated it as a joke.
3 tratar
In this hospital they treat cancer patients with a new drug.
4 tratar
Treat the camera with care!
treat someone to... □ **convidar alguém para...**
She took us to a restaurant and treated us to a meal.

treat² *n.* □ **regalo, presente**
As a special treat he took us for a sail in his boat.

treatment [ˈtriːtmənt] *n.*
1 tratamento
His treatment of his workers is fair. ◆ Important guests get special treatment at the hotel.
2 tratamento
medical treatment. ◆ a new treatment for cancer.

treaty [ˈtriːti] *n.* (*pl.* **treaties**) □ **tratado**
The two countries signed a peace treaty.

tree [triː] *n.* □ **árvore**
She climbed (up / down) the tree. ◆ We planted an apple tree in our garden. ◆ a tall tree.

tremble [ˈtrembl] *v.* (**trembles, trembling, trembled**) □ **tremer**
He trembled with fear.
- *Ver* **shake, shiver**.

tremendous [trəˈmendəs] *adj.*
1 (= enormous) □ **tremendo**
The rocket travels at a tremendous speed. ◆ a tremendous amount of work
2 (= great) □ **extraordinário**
The show was tremendous. ◆ a tremendous player.

tremendously [trəˈmendəsli] *adv.* (very much) □ **tremendamente, extremamente**
The book is tremendously funny. ◆ I enjoyed the film tremendously.

trench [trentʃ] *n.* □ **trincheira**
The soldiers took shelter in the trenches.

trend [trend] *n*. □ **tendência**
The trend today is towards eating natural food. ♦ the latest trend in music, fashion, etc.
trespass ['trespəs] *v*. (**trespasses, trespassing, trespassed**) □ **invadir**
to trespass on private land.
trespasser ['trespəsə] *n*. □ **invasor**
trial [traiəl] *n*.
1 julgamento
The court was full during the murder trial.
■ The verb is **try²**.
2 teste
trials to test the safety of a car, drug, etc.
on trial
1 experiência
I got the machine on trial for three weeks.
2 julgamento
She is on trial for robbery.
trial period *n*. □ **período de experiência**
You will work here for a trial period (of three months).
triangle ['traiæŋgl] *n*. □ **triângulo**
to draw a triangle.
triangular [trai'æŋgjulə] *adj*. □ **triangular**
tribal ['traibəl] *adj*. □ **tribal**
tribal dances.
tribe [traib] *n*. □ **tribo**
a tribe of Indians. ♦ African tribes.
tribute ['tribju:t] *n*. □ **tributo**
When he retired from basketball, they played a game as a tribute to him.
pay tribute to □ **fazer um tributo a, fazer uma homenagem a**
trick¹ [trik] *n*.
1 truque
He uses clever tricks to cheat people.
2 brincadeira
Is that one of your silly tricks again?
3 truque
card tricks. ♦ The magician's tricks were funny.
play a trick on □ **pregar uma peça em**
The children played a trick on their grandfather.
trick² *v*. (**tricks, tricking, tricked**) □ **enganar**
The police tricked him and he had to admit his guilt.
trickery ['trikəri] *n*. □ **logro, trapaça**
trickle¹ ['trikl] *n*. □ **pingo, filete**
a trickle of blood.
trickle² *v*. (**trickles, trickling, trickled**) □ **pingar, gotejar**
Tears trickled down his cheeks.
tricky ['triki] *adj*. (**trickier, trickiest**) □ **capcioso**
a tricky situation. ♦ It was very tricky to translate the book from Chinese into English.
tricycle ['traisikl] *n*. □ **triciclo**
tried [traid] *v*. (Ver **try²**).
tries [traiz] *v*., *n*. (Ver **try¹, try²**).
trigger ['trigə] *n*. □ **gatilho**
He aimed the gun at the target and pulled the trigger.
trim¹ [trim] *v*. (**trims, trimming, trimmed**) □ **aparar, podar**
The barber trimmed his beard. ♦ I trimmed the rose bush.
trim² *n*. □ **aparada**
My beard needs a trim.

trip¹ [trip] *n*. □ **viagem**
We went on a trip around the world. ♦ a day trip to the mountains. ♦ a business trip. ♦ a boat trip. ♦ a school trip.
■ An **excursion** or **outing** is a short trip for pleasure.
trip² *v*. (**trips, tripping, tripped**) □ **tropeçar**
He tripped over the step. ♦ She tripped and fell.
trip someone up □ **passar rasteira em alguém**
He stretched out his leg and tried to trip me up.
triple ['tripl] *v*. (**triples, tripling, tripled**) □ **triplicar**
Sales may triple next year.
triple jump ['tripl dʒʌmp] *n*. □ **salto triplo**
She won the gold medal in the triple jump.
triplet ['triplit] *n*. □ **trigêmeos**
She gave birth to triplets.
triumph ['traiʌmf] *n*. (= victory) □ **triunfo**
The landing on the moon was a triumph for man. ♦ shouts of triumph.
triumphant [trai'ʌmfənt] *adj*. □ **triunfante**
The triumphant soldiers returned home.
triumphantly [trai'ʌmfəntli] *adv*. □ **triunfantemente**
trivial ['triviəl] *adj*. □ **trivial**
It's not a trivial matter – we can't just ignore it.
triviality [,trivi'aliti] *n*. (*pl*. **trivialities**) □ **trivialidade**
Don't bother the boss with such trivialities.
trod, trodden [trod, 'trodn] *v*. (Ver **tread**).
trolley ['troli] *n*. *Brit*. □ **carrinho**
luggage trolley (= baggage cart, *Amer*.). ♦ supermarket trolley (= shopping cart, *Amer*.). ♦ tea trolley (= tea wagon, *Amer*.).
trolley-bus ['trolibʌs] *n*. □ **ônibus elétrico**
trombone [trom'boun] *n*. □ **trombone**
troops [tru:ps] *n*. *pl*. □ **tropas**
trophy ['troufi] *n*. (*pl*. **trophies**) □ **troféu**
The tennis champion got a prize of $150,000 and a trophy.
tropic ['tropik] *n*.
the tropics *pl*. □ **os trópicos**
The tropics are the hottest place of the world.
tropical ['tropikəl] *adj*. □ **tropical**
tropical fruit (= banana, mango, coconut, pineapple, etc.).
trot¹ [trot] *v*. (**trots, trotting, trotted**) □ **trotar**
The horse trotted along the path. ♦ The child trotted beside his mother.
trot² *n*. □ **trote**
trouble¹ ['trʌbl] *n*.
1 problema
She told me all about her troubles.
2 (= difficulty; problem) **problema**
I had a lot of trouble finding the place. ♦ The trouble is I don't know his address. ♦ What's the trouble? (= What's wrong?)
3 (= bother²) **incômodo**
I can come again tomorrow – it's no trouble.
4 problema
He has heart trouble. ♦ She has trouble with her hearing.
5 encrenca, problema
I don't want any trouble with the police.
6 problema
The trouble started when they got drunk.
be in trouble □ **estar encrencado**
You'll be in trouble if you don't finish the job in time. ♦ She is in trouble with the police.
get into trouble □ **ficar encrencado**
He got into trouble with the police.

get someone into trouble ◻ meter alguém em apuros
Don't say anything or you'll get us into trouble.
go to a lot of trouble ◻ ter muito trabalho para fazer algo
take the trouble ◻ dar-se ao trabalho
He didn't take the trouble to read the instructions.

trouble² *v.* (**troubles, troubling, troubled**) (= **bother¹**)
1 incomodar
I don't know what's troubling him.
2 incomodar
I'm sorry to trouble you, but I have to ask you some questions.
3 incomodar
Please don't trouble – I'll call a taxi.

trough [trof] *n.* ◻ cocho, gamela

trousers ['trauzəz] *n. pl.* ◻ calça(s)
I bought a new pair of trousers. ◆ Take off your trousers and put these on. ◆ She never wears trousers.
■ The usual word in American English is **pants**.

trout [traut] *n.* ◻ truta

truant ['truənt] *n.* ◻ gazeteiro
play truant ◻ matar aula
■ *Amer.* **play hooky**

truce [tru:s] *n.* ◻ trégua

truck [trʌk] *n.* ◻ caminhão
They carry the goods in big trucks. ◆ a truck driver. ◆ a delivery truck.
■ The usual word in British English is **lorry**.

true [tru:] *adj.* ◻ verdadeiro
Is it true (that) she got married? ◆ That's not true! ◆ A dolphin is a fish: true or false? ◆ It's a true story. ◆ a true friend.
come true ◻ virar realidade
My dream came true.
■ The noun is **truth**.
■ antônimo: **false; untrue**

truly ['tru:li] *adv.* ◻ verdadeiramente
I'm truly sorry about yesterday. ◆ He truly wants to help.
Yours truly ◻ atenciosamente
■ We use **Yours truly** to end formal letters that begin with **Dear Sir** or **Dear Madam**.
■ Ver **Yours sincerely; Yours faithfully**.

trumpet ['trʌmpit] *n.* ◻ trompete
Can you play the trumpet?

trunk [trʌŋk] *n.*
1 tronco
Oak trees have thick trunks.
2 baú
All his clothes are in that trunk.
3 *Amer.* porta-malas
Put the bags in the trunk (of my car).
■ *Brit.* **boot**
4 tromba
The elephant lifted the man with its trunk.

trunks [trʌŋks] *n.* (= **swimming** trunks) ◻ calção de banho

trust¹ [trʌst] *n.* ◻ confiança
Put your trust in God. ◆ I have absolute trust in him.

trust² *v.* (**trusts, trusting, trusted**)
1 confiar
He trusts me and I'll never betray him. ◆ I don't trust her.
2 confiar
You can trust her to do the job well.
trust in ◻ confiar
We trust in God.

trustworthy ['trʌst,wɜ:ði] *adj.* ◻ confiável
He is honest and trustworthy. ◆ trustworthy information.

truth [tru:θ] *n.* ◻ verdade
It's the truth – she is not lying. ◆ There's no truth in what he says – it's all lies. ◆ They will find out the truth soon.
■ The adjective is **true**.
tell the truth ◻ dizer a verdade
Tell me the truth – did you take it? ◆ She told (us) the whole truth.
to tell you the truth ◻ para falar a verdade
To tell you the truth, I don't trust him.

truthful ['tru:θful] *adj.*
1 sincero
She is a truthful child. ◆ Be truthful. (= Tell me the truth.)
2 sincero, honesto
He gave us truthful answers.

truthfully ['tru:θfuli] *adv.* ◻ verdadeiramente, sinceramente

try¹ [trai] *n.* (*pl.* **tries**) ◻ tentativa
Let me have a try. (= Let me try.) ◆ You may fail again, but it's worth a try. ◆ I'm not sure I can do it, but I'll give it a try.

try² *v.* (**tries, trying, tried**)
1 tentar
He tried to open the door, but it was locked. ◆ I'm trying to help you. ◆ Try this chair – it's more comfortable.
2 tentar
Try to come early.
3 provar
I tried the new ice cream – it was delicious.
4 julgar
They tried him for murder.
try and... (mesmo que **try to**) ◻ tentar...
Try and come tonight.
try hard ◻ esforçar-se muito
He tried hard not to get angry.
try harder ◻ esforçar-se mais
You must try harder if you want to succeed.
try something on ◻ experimentar
Try this shirt on. ◆ I tried on the dress, but it was too small.
try out ◻ experimentar
He tried out the car before he paid for it.

T-shirt ['ti:ʃɜ:t] *n.* ◻ camiseta

tub [tʌb] *n.*
1 tubo
a tub of margarine. ◆ a tub of ice cream.
2 tina
a tub for washing clothes.
3 *Amer.* (= bathtub) banheira

tube [tju:b] *n.*
1 tubo, cano
There's a rubber tube behind the gas cooker. ◆ a glass tube.
■ Ver **pipe**.
2 tubo
a tube of toothpaste. ◆ a tube of glue.
3 câmara
the inner tube of a tyre.

tuck / turn

4 (= underground) *Brit.* **metrô**
I go to work by tube.
■ *Amer.* **subway**
tuck [tʌk] *v.* (**tucks, tucking, tucked**) □ **enfiar, pôr para dentro**
Tuck your shirt into your trousers.
tuck someone in / up □ **pôr / colocar na cama**
She tucked him in and said 'Good night'.
Tuesday ['tju:zdi] *n.* □ **terça-feira**
They will come on Tuesday. ◆ I saw her last Tuesday. ◆ My birthday is next Tuesday.
tuft [tʌft] *n.* □ **tufo**
a tuft of hair. ◆ a tuft of grass.
tug[1] [tʌg] *v.* (**tugs, tugging, tugged**) (= pull) □ **puxar**
The child tugged (at) my sleeve.
tug[2] *n.*
1 puxão
He gave the rope a tug.
2 (= tugboat) **rebocador**
tug-of-war [tʌgəv'wɔ:] *n.* □ **cabo de guerra, disputa**
tuition [tju'iʃən] *n.*
1 aula
I had private tuition (= lessons) in mathematics.
2 *Amer.* **taxa escolar, anuidade**
Tuition is higher this year (at college).
■ *Brit.* **tuition fees**
tulip ['tju:lip] *n.* □ **tulipa**
tumble ['tʌmbl] *v.* (**tumbles, tumbling, tumbled**) □ **cair**
He slipped and tumbled down the stairs.
tumble down □ **ruir**
The old building is tumbling down.
tumbler ['tʌmblə] *n.* □ **copo**
a tumbler (= a glass) of milk.
tummy ['tʌmi] *n.* (*pl.* **tummies**) □ **barriga**
Children often say 'tummy' instead of stomach.
tumor ['tju:mə] *n. Amer.*, **tumour** *Brit.* □ **tumor**
a brain tumour.
tuna ['tju:nə] *n.* □ **atum**
tune[1] [tju:n] *n.* □ **canção**
He whistled a tune. ◆ to sing a tune.
tune[2] *v.* (**tunes, tuning, tuned**) □ **afinar**
to tune a piano. ◆ to tune an engine.
tune in (to) □ **sintonizar**
to tune in to a station.
tunnel ['tʌnl] *n.* □ **túnel**
A tunnel connects Britain and France. ◆ to dig a tunnel.
turban ['tɜ:bən] *n.* □ **turbante**
turkey ['tɜ:ki] *n.* □ **peru**
Turkey (Ver '**Geographical Names**').
turn[1] [tɜ:n] *n.*
1 curva
Make a left turn after the traffic lights. (= Turn left after the traffic lights.) ◆ a sharp turn to the right.
■ Ver **U-turn**.
2 volta
Give the handle another turn. (= Turn the handle one more time.)
3 vez
Wait patiently for your turn! ◆ It's your turn to take the dog out.
in turn □ **um após outro**
He interviewed each of us in turn.

take turns □ **revezar**
We take turns to do the housework.
turn[2] *v.* (**turns, turning, turned**)
1 virar
Turn the handle clockwise. ◆ to turn the key. ◆ The wheel turned slowly.
2 virar
Turn right at the second traffic lights. ◆ She turned towards me. ◆ The road turns north there.
3 virar
I smiled at him, but he turned his back on me. ◆ She turned her eyes towards him.
4 (= become) **tornar-se**
His hair turned white. ◆ Water turns into ice at zero degrees Celsius (0° C.)
5 transformar
The witch turned the prince into a frog.
6 ir para
Turn to page 66.
■ Do not confuse with:
turn a / the page.
7 recorrer
We turned to her for help.
turn against □ **virar-se contra**
They all turned against him.
turn someone against □ **colocar alguém contra**
He turned all my friends against me.
turn (a)round □ **virar-se**
She turned around to look at the woman behind her.
turn back □ **voltar**
We had to turn back because of the bad weather.
turn someone down □ **recusar alguém**
I applied for the job, but they turned me down.
turn something down
1 (= reject) **rejeitar algo**
He turned down our offer. ◆ I can't turn down their invitation.
2 baixar
Turn the radio down – it's too loud. ◆ to turn down the gas, the heat, etc.
turn off (= switch off) □ **desligar, fechar**
I turned the light off. ◆ Don't forget to turn off the gas. ◆ Turn off the tap / faucet. ◆ Turn off the water. ◆ to turn off the switch.
■ Compare with **put out**:
put out the fire.
turn on (= switch on) □ **ligar, abrir**
She turned the TV on. ◆ Turn on the oven. ◆ to turn on the switch, the tap, etc.
turn out □ **acontecer que**
It turns out (that) she didn't know anything about it.
turn something out
1 (= turn off) **desligar**
She turned out the lights. ◆ He turned the gas fire out.
2 esvaziar
Turn out your pockets. ◆ to turn out the cupboard.
turn over □ **capotar, revirar, virar para outro lado**
The car turned over. (= The car overturned.) ◆ Turn over on your stomach. ◆ The doctor turned the patient over.
turn someone over to □ **entregar alguém para**
They turned him over to the police.
turn to

1 recorrer a
They turned to us for help.
2 (= turn into) **virar**
The water turned to ice.
turn up
1 (= arrive) **aparecer, chegar**
Did they turn up late or on time?
2 aumentar
Turn up the TV – I can't hear anything.
turning ['tɜːnɪŋ] *n*. □ **entrada, curva**
Take the first turning on the left.
turnip ['tɜːnɪp] *n*. □ **nabo**
turn signal [tɜːn 'sɪgnə] *n*. *Amer*. □ **seta**
■ *Brit*. **indicator**
turnstile ['tɜːnstaɪl] *n*. □ **roleta, catraca**
turquoise ['tɜːkwɔɪz] *adj*., *n*. □ **turquesa**
turtle ['tɜːtl] *n*.
1 (= tortoise) *Amer*. □ **tartaruga**
I keep a turtle as a pet. ◆ A turtle has a hard shell on its back.
2 (= sea turtle) **tartaruga**
Turtles are very heavy and live in the sea.
tusk [tʌsk] *n*. □ **presa**
Elephants have tusks.
tutor ['tjuːtə] *n*. (= private teacher) □ **tutor**
TV ['tiːˈviː] *abbr*. (= television) □ **TV**
What's on TV tonight? ◆ Turn on the TV. ◆ a 21-inch TV.
tweezers ['twiːzəz] *n*. □ **pinça**
twelfth[1] [twelfθ] *adj*., *adv*., *pron*. □ **décimo segundo, doze**
We went up to the twelfth floor. ◆ The twelfth of May (= 12th May). ◆ I came twelfth in the race.
twelfth[2] *n*. (= 1/12) □ **um doze avos**
twelve [twelv] *adj*., *n*. □ **doze**
It's twelve o'clock. ◆ She is twelve years old. ◆ twelve eggs (= a dozen eggs).
twentieth ['twentiiθ] *adj*., *adv*., *pron*. □ **vigésimo, vinte**
the twentieth century. ◆ the twentieth of June (= 20th June). ◆ I came twentieth in the competition.
twenty ['twenti] *adj*., *n*. □ **vinte**
She is twenty years old. ◆ You owe me twenty dollars.
the twenties □ **os anos vinte, a década de 1920**
That song was popular in the twenties.
in your twenties □ **nos seus vinte e poucos anos**
She is in her twenties.
twice [twaɪs] *adv*. □ **duas vezes**
We go there twice a week. ◆ She is twice your age.
twice as... □ **duas vezes mais...**
Your camera is twice as big as mine. ◆ She got twice as much money.
twig [twɪg] *n*. □ **graveto**
We collected dry twigs for the fire.
twilight ['twaɪlaɪt] *n*. (= dusk) □ **crepúsculo, meia-luz**
I can't see well in the twilight. ◆ at twilight time.
twin [twɪn] *n*. □ **gêmeo**
They are twins, but they don't look alike. ◆ My twin sister is getting married.
twinkle ['twɪŋkl] *v*. (**twinkles, twinkling, twinkled**) □ **cintilar**
The stars twinkled in the sky.
twist[1] [twɪst] *v*. (**twists, twisting, twisted**)
1 virar
He twisted his head around to look at the man behind him.

2 retorcer
I twisted the pieces of string into a rope.
3 serpentear
The road twists through the hills.
4 torcer
I twisted my ankle in a tennis match.
5 entortar
The plastic cups twisted in the heat.
6 distorcer
That's not what I said – you're twisting my words!
twist something off □ **tirar retorcendo**
Can you twist the lid of this jar off?
twist something (a)round □ **enrolar, entrelaçar**
I twisted the rope round the tree.
twist[2] *n*.
1 torção
Straighten out the telephone wire – it has a lot of twists in it. ◆ Give the lid another twist to close it tight.
2 curva
There are many twists in the road.
twitter ['twɪtə] *v*. (**twitters, twittering, twittered**) □ **chilrear**
Birds twittered in a tree outside my window.
two [tuː] *adj*., *n*. □ **dois**
Two people came to visit you. ◆ It's two o'clock. ◆ She is two years old.
in two □ **em dois**
I cut the apple in two. ◆ The vase broke in two.
two by two □ **de dois em dois**
They came out two by two.
type[1] [taɪp] *n*.
1 (= sort, kind) **tipo**
What type of music do you like? ◆ This cream is good for your type of skin.
2 tipos
What type of man is he? ◆ She is not my type.
3 tipo
What's your blood type? – Type A.
4 fonte
Children's books are printed in large type.
type[2] *v*. (**types, typing, typed**) □ **datilografar, digitar**
Can you type? ◆ The secretary types my letters (on a typewriter). ◆ Today most people use personal computers for typing.
■ You can also say **key in** for typing on a computer keyboard.
typewriter ['taɪpraɪtə] *n*. □ **máquina de escrever**
typical ['tɪpɪkəl] *adj*. □ **típico**
a typical Spanish house. ◆ It's typical of him to be late.
typically ['tɪpɪkəli] *adv*. □ **tipicamente**
This ancient building is not typically Greek.
typing ['taɪpɪŋ] *n*. □ **datilografia, digitação**
typist ['taɪpɪst] *n*. □ **datilógrafo, digitador**
tyrannical [tɪ'rænɪkəl] *adj*. **tirânico**
a tyrannical ruler.
tyrant ['taɪrənt] *n*. □ **tirano**
a tyrant is a cruel dictator.
tyre [taɪə] *n*. *Brit*. □ **pneu**
a spare tyre. ◆ to change the tyre.
■ *Amer*. **tire**
flat tyre *n*. (= a flat) □ **pneu murcho**
I had a puncture on the way here, so now I have a flat tyre / tire.

Uu

UFO [ˌjuːˈefou] *abbr.* (= unidentified flying object) □ **óvni**
I don't believe that UFOs exist.
ugliness [ˈʌglinis] *n.* □ **feiura**
ugly [ˈʌgli] *adj.* (**uglier, ugliest**) □ **feio**
She is not so ugly. ◆ his ugly face. ◆ an ugly building.
umbrella [ʌmˈbrelə] *n.* □ **guarda-chuva**
You put up your umbrella when it starts raining and take it down when it stops raining.
umpire [ˈʌmpaiə] *n.* □ **árbitro, juiz**
■ Compare **referee**:
referee = for football, basketball, etc.
un- [ʌn-] *pref.*
1 des-, in-
uncomfortable (= not comfortable). ◆ unusual (= not usual).
2 des-
uncover (= opposite of cover). ◆ unlock (= opposite of lock).
UN [ˈjuːˈen] *abbr.* (mesmo que **the United Nations**) □ **ONU**
unable [ʌnˈeibl] *adj.* □ **ser incapaz de, não poder fazer algo**
She was unable to come. (= She couldn't come.) ◆ He is unable to stay. (= He can't stay.) ◆ I'm unable to move my leg. (= I can't move my leg.)
■ The noun is **inability**.
unacceptable [ˈʌnəkˈseptəbl] *adj.* □ **inaceitável**
The plan is totally unacceptable.
unaccustomed [ˈʌnəˈkʌstəmd] *adj.* □ **desacostumado**
She is unaccustomed to the heat.
unanimous [juˈnanıməs] *adj.* □ **unânime**
a unanimous decision.
unanimously [juˈnanıməsli] *adv.* □ **unanimamente**
They decided unanimously to sell the company.
unarmed [ʌnˈɑːmd] *adj.* □ **desarmado**
Don't shoot! I'm unarmed!
unavailable [ˌʌnəˈveiləbl] *adj.* □ **indisponível, inacessível**
The manager is unavailable – call him later.
unavoidable [ˌʌnəˈvoidəbl] *adj.* □ **inevitável**
The delay was unavoidable, because of the bad weather.
unaware [ˌʌnəˈweə] *adj.* □ **despercebido, inconsciente, alheio**
She is unaware of the risks. ◆ He was unaware that it was a trap.
unbearable [ʌnˈbeərəbl] *adj.* □ **intolerável**
The heat was unbearable. ◆ unbearable pain.
unbearably [ʌnˈbeərəbli] *adv.* □ **intoleravelmente**
The weather is unbearably hot.
unbelievable [ˌʌnbiˈliːvəbl] *adj.* (= incredible) □ **inacreditável**
It's unbelievable how he jumped so high!
unbelievably [ˌʌnbiˈliːvəbli] *adv.* (= incredibly) □ **inacreditavelmente**
It's unbelievably cheap.
unborn [ʌnˈbɔːn] *adj.*, *adj.* □ **em gestação, futuro**
an unborn child.
uncertain [ʌnˈsɜːtn] *adj.*, *adj.*
1 incerto, vago
It's uncertain when they will come. ◆ Their future is uncertain.

2 em dúvida
I'm uncertain what to do.
uncertainty [ʌnˈsɜːtnti] *adj.*, *n.* (*pl.* **uncertainties**) □ **incerteza**
There is some uncertainty about when they will meet.
uncle [ˈʌŋkl] *adj.*, *n.* □ **tio**
My aunt and uncle are coming today.
uncomfortable [ʌnˈkʌmfətəbl] *adj.*, *adj.*
1 desconfortável
an uncomfortable chair. ◆ uncomfortable shoes. ◆ It's uncomfortable to sit on that chair.
■ Compare **inconvenient**:
inconvenient = for time, meeting place, etc.
2 desconfortável
She feels uncomfortable when she sees us.
uncomfortably [ʌnˈkʌmfətəbli] *adv.*
1 desconfortavelmente
Her skirt was uncomfortably tight.
2 desconfortavelmente
He moved uncomfortably in his chair when I asked him about the money.
uncommon [ʌnˈkomən] *adj.* □ **incomum**
an uncommon name.
■ Ver **rare**.
unconscious [ʌnˈkonʃəs] *adj.*
1 inconsciente
The patient was unconscious for ten hours.
2 inconsciente
She was unconscious of the mistake she made during her speech.
unconsciously [ʌnˈkonʃəsli] *adv.* □ **inconscientemente**
unconsciousness [ʌnˈkonʃəsnis] *n.* □ **inconsciência**
uncountable noun [ʌnˈkauntəbl naun] *n.* (grammar) □ **substantivo incontável**
'Milk', 'information' and 'money' are examples of uncountable nouns.
uncover [ʌnˈkʌvə] *v.* (**uncovers, uncovering, uncovered**)
1 descobrir
She uncovered her face and we saw tears in her eyes.
2 descobrir
The journalist uncovered the truth about the minister.
under[1] [ˈʌndə] *prep.*
1 sob, embaixo de
The box is under the bed. ◆ He felt warm under the blanket. ◆ The boat sailed under the bridge. ◆ under the water ◆ He held the bag under his arm.
■ Ver **below**[2].
■ antônimo: **over**
2 sob, embaixo de
I hid the letter under my shirt.
3 menor de
You can't vote if you are under 18.
■ antônimo: **above; over**
4 sob o comando de
The team of scientists is working under Professor Jones. ◆ The restaurant is under new management.
5 sob
The matter is under investigation. ◆ Your suggestions are under discussion.
6 sob
The town was under attack / fire.

■ Ver **under the circumstances**; **be under control**.

under[2] *adv.* □ **inferior**

children aged seven and under.

go under □ **afundar**

The boat went under.

undercover agent [ˌʌndəˈkʌvə ˈeidʒənt] *n.* □ **agente secreto, infiltrado**

undercover detective [ˌʌndəˈkʌvə diˈtektiv] *n.* □ **detetive secreto, disfarçado**

underestimate [ˌʌndərˈestimeit] *v.* (**underestimates, underestimating, underestimated**) □ **subestimar**

Don't underestimate him – he's very clever.

undergo [ˌʌndəˈgou] *v.* (**undergoes, undergoing, underwent, undergone**) □ **sofrer, passar por**

She's undergoing an operation on her leg. ◆ The organization underwent a lot of changes.

undergraduate [ˌʌndəˈgradjuət] *n.* □ **universitário**

underground[1] [ˈʌndəgraund] *n.*

the underground

1 (= tube) *Brit.* **metrô**

I travel to work by underground.

■ *Amer.* **subway**

2 organização clandestina, grupo subversivo

The underground fought against the enemy during the war.

underground[2] [ˌʌndəˈgraund] *adj.*

1 subterrâneo

an underground tunnel.

2 subversivo, clandestino

an underground newspaper.

undergrowth [ˈʌndəgrouθ] *n.* □ **pequenos arbustos**

underline [ˌʌndəˈlain] *v.* (**underlines, underlining, underlined**) □ **sublinhar**

Underline all the new words in the article.

be underlined □ **estar sublinhado**

All the mistakes are underlined in red.

underneath[1] [ˌʌndəˈniːθ] *prep.* (= under) □ **sob, embaixo de**

underneath the bed. ◆ underneath the blanket.

underneath[2] *adv.*

1 por baixo

He wore a jacket with a T-shirt underneath.

2 (= below) **abaixo, inferior**

Take the books from the top shelf and put them on the shelf underneath.

underpants [ˈʌndəpants] *n. pl.* □ **cueca**

He put on a clean pair of underpants.

■ *Brit.* also **pants**

■ In American English **underpants** are also for women.

underpass [ˈʌndəpaːs] *n. Amer.* □ **passagem**

An underpass is a passage under a busy road.

■ *Brit.* **subway**

underprivileged [ˌʌndəˈprivəlidʒid] *adj.* □ **menos favorecido**

underprivileged children in the slums.

undershirt [ˈʌndəʃəːt] *n. Amer.* □ **camiseta**

Are you wearing an undershirt?

■ *Brit.* **vest**

understand [ˌʌndəˈstand] *v.* (**understands, understood**)

1 entender, compreender

He understood exactly what I meant. ◆ Do you understand (me)? ◆ I don't understand Japanese.

2 entender

He doesn't understand why we want to sell it. ◆ Do you understand how it works?

3 entender, compreender

I understand how you feel. ◆ Tell her the truth – I'm sure she'll understand.

4 entender, compreender

I understand that you want to leave us.

■ *No* [be + -ing]: do *not* say 'am understanding', etc.

understandable [ˌʌndəˈstandəbl] *adj.* □ **compreensível**

He doesn't speak English well, but that's understandable because he only started to learn a month ago.

understanding[1] [ˌʌndəˈstandiŋ] *adj.* □ **compreensivo**

The teacher was very understanding and forgave him.

understanding[2] *n.*

1 entendimento, compreensão

She has a good understanding of the subject.

2 entendimento, acordo

We came to an understanding. ◆ We have an understanding.

understood [ˌʌndəˈstud] *v.* (Ver **understand**).

undertake [ˌʌndəˈteik] *v.* (**undertakes, undertaking, undertook, undertaken**)

1 empreender

A large company undertook the project.

2 encarregar-se de

They undertook to send the money by Tuesday.

undertaker [ˈʌndəteikə] *n.* □ **agente funerário**

■ also **funeral director,** especially in American English.

underwear [ˈʌndəweə] *n.* □ **roupa íntima, roupa de baixo**

Underpants, undershirts and bras are underwear.

underwent [ˌʌndəˈwent] *v.* (Ver **undergo**).

underworld [ˈʌndəwəːld] *n., adj.* □ **submundo**

an underworld gang leader.

undo [ʌnˈduː] *v.* (**undoes, undoing, undid, undone**) □ **desfazer, desatar, tirar**

She undid the parcel. ◆ Help him to undo his coat / belt. ◆ to undo the buttons / string.

■ You can also say **unfasten** (a belt, buttons) and **untie** (a knot, a parcel / package).

undone [ʌnˈdʌn] *adj.* □ **desatado, desfeito**

Your shoelace is undone.

come undone □ **desfazer-se**

The knot came undone.

undoubtedly [ʌnˈdautidli] *adv.* (= without doubt) □ **indubitavelmente, sem dúvida**

This is undoubtedly his best book.

undress [ʌnˈdres] *v.* (**undresses, undressing, undressed**) □ **despir, despir-se, tirar a roupa**

He undressed and put on his pyjamas. ◆ I undressed him and sent him to bed.

get undressed □ **despir-se, tirar a roupa**

She got undressed and took a bath.

■ antônimo: **get dressed**

uneasily [ʌnˈiːzili] *adv.* □ **ansiosamente, apreensivamente**

She looked at her watch uneasily.

uneasy [ʌnˈiːzi] *adj.* □ **ansioso, apreensivo**

It made her feel a little uneasy to ask him to do it. ◆ Their son was four hours late and they were beginning to feel uneasy (= worried).

unemployed [ˌʌnimˈploid] *adj.* □ **desempregado**

He was unemployed for six months before he got this job.

the unemployed *n.* □ **os desempregados**

unemployment [ˌʌnimˈplɔimənt] *n.* □ **desemprego**
Unemployment may rise by 2%. ◆ The level of unemployment is very high in our town. ◆ to reduce unemployment.
unemployment benefit [ˌʌnimˈplɔimənt ˈbenəfit] *n.* Brit. □ **seguro-desemprego**
■ *Amer.* **unemployment**; **unemployment compensation**
uneven [ʌnˈiːvn] *adj.*
1 irregular
an uneven handwriting. ◆ The floor is uneven in places.
2 desequilibrado
an uneven contest / match.
unexpected [ˌʌniksˈpektid] *adj.* □ **inesperado**
an unexpected visit / visitor. ◆ The results were unexpected.
unexpectedly [ˌʌniksˈpektidli] *adv.* □ **inesperadamente**
She returned unexpectedly.
unfair [ʌnˈfeə] *adj.* □ **injusto**
This decision is unfair (to them). ◆ It was unfair to let him do all the work.
unfairly [ʌnˈfeəli] *adv.* □ **injustamente**
The boss treats him unfairly. ◆ He was unfairly blamed for the failure.
unfairness [ʌnˈfeənis] *n.* □ **injustiça**
unfaithful [ʌnˈfeiθful] *adj.* □ **infiel**
He is unfaithful to his wife. ◆ an unfaithful wife / husband.
unfamiliar [ˌʌnfəˈmiljə] *adj.* □ **desconhecido**
unfamiliar faces. ◆ an unfamiliar place.
be unfamiliar with □ **não ter familiaridade com, não estar familiarizado com**
I'm unfamiliar with this place / subject.
unfashionable [ʌnˈfaʃənəbl] *adj.* □ **fora de moda, antiquado**
unfashionable clothes. ◆ unfashionable ideas.
unfasten [ʌnˈfɑːsn] *v.* (**unfastens, unfastening, unfastened**) (= undo) □ **desatar, soltar**
He unfastened his belt / seat-belt. ◆ to unfasten a button.
■ Compare **untie**:
a parcel / package, a knot.
unfavourable [ʌnˈfeivərəbl] *adj. Amer.*, **unfavourable** *Brit.*
1 desfavorável
He made an unfavourable impression on us.
2 desfavorável
unfavorable weather.
unfinished [ʌnˈfiniʃt] *adj.* □ **inacabado**
an unfinished job.
unfit [ʌnˈfit] *adj.*
1 impróprio
The water is unfit for drinking.
2 fora de forma
You're unfit because you don't do any exercise.
unfold [ʌnˈfould] *v.* (**unfolds, unfolding, unfolded**)
1 abrir, desdobrar
He unfolded the map and spread it on the floor.
2 desdobrar-se
The armchair unfolds into a bed.
unforgettable [ˌʌnfəˈgetəbl] *adj.* □ **inesquecível**
The trip was an unforgettable experience.
unforgivable [ˌʌnfəˈgivəbl] *adj.* □ **imperdoável**
an unforgivable mistake.
unfortunate [ʌnˈfɔːtʃənət] *adj.* (= unlucky) □ **desafortunado**
We have to help these unfortunate people. ◆ It's unfortunate that you lost at the last minute.

unfortunately [ʌnˈfɔːtʃənətli] *adv.* (= unluckily) □ **infelizmente**
Unfortunately, there's nothing we can do to help. ◆ She almost won the race, but unfortunately she fell and broke her leg.
unfriendly [ʌnˈfrendli] *adj.* □ **não amistoso, hostil, antipático**
They were unfriendly to him. ◆ an unfriendly look.
ungrateful [ʌnˈgreitful] *adj.* □ **ingrato**
He's so ungrateful – he didn't even say thank you.
unhappily [ʌnˈhapili] *adv.* □ **com tristeza**
She looked at his picture unhappily.
unhappiness [ʌnˈhapinis] *n.* (= sadness) □ **infelicidade, tristeza**
unhappy [ʌnˈhapi] *adj.* (= sad) □ **triste, infeliz**
He was very unhappy when his dog died. ◆ She had an unhappy childhood.
unhealthy [ʌnˈhelθi] *adj.* (**unhealthier, unhealthiest**)
1 (= ill, sick) □ **doente, sem saúde**
an unhealthy child. ◆ an unhealthy look on his face.
2 insalubre
unhealthy climate. ◆ an unhealthy habit.
unidentified [ˌʌnaiˈdentifaid] *adj.* □ **não identificado**
an unidentified person. ◆ an unidentified body.
unidentified flying object *n.* (Ver **UFO**).
uniform [ˈjuːnifɔːm] *n.* □ **uniforme**
We have to wear uniform in our school. ◆ The nurse was not wearing a uniform. ◆ military uniforms. ◆ a police uniform. ◆ a school uniform.
in uniform □ **fardado**
a soldier in uniform. ◆ soldiers in uniform
uninhabited [ˌʌninˈhabitid] *adj.* □ **desabitado, deserto**
an uninhabited island.
uninterested [ʌnˈintristid] *adj.* □ **indiferente, desinteressado**
I am uninterested in this matter. (= I don't care. It is not interesting.)
union [ˈjuːnjən] *n.*
1 união, sindicato
The National Union of Students. ◆ the engineers' union. ◆ a trade union. *Brit.* ◆ a labor union. *Amer.*
2 união
The union between the two countries ended in 1992.
unique [juːˈniːk] *adj.* □ **único, singular, sem igual**
The building is unique in its style. ◆ The ability to speak is unique to humans.
unit [ˈjuːnit] *n.*
1 célula
The family is the basic social unit.
2 unidade
The book has ten units.
3 unidade
an army unit.
4 unidade
The kilogram(me) is a unit of weight and the meter is a unit of length.
unite [juːˈnait] *v.* (**unites, uniting, united**) □ **unir-se**
The two countries united to fight their enemy. ◆ The new leader united the different groups.
united [juːˈnaitəd] *adj.* □ **unido**
The workers are united against the management.
unity [ˈjuːnəti] *n.* □ **unidade**
There's a need for national unity.

universal [ˌjuːniˈvɜːsəl] *adj.* ▫ **universal**
Pollution is a universal problem.
universe [ˈjuːnivɜːs] *n.* ▫ **universo**
The universe consists of the earth and all the stars and planets.
university [juːniˈvɜːsəti] *n.* (*pl.* **universities**) ▫ **universidade**
She is studying law at university. ◆ He has a degree in mathematics from Harvard University.
go to university ▫ **fazer faculdade**
When she finished high school she went to university.
unjust [ʌnˈdʒʌst] *adj.* ▫ **injusto**
The new tax is unjust. ◆ unjust accusations.
unkind [ʌnˈkaind] *adj.* ▫ **indelicado, duro**
It was unkind of you to say that. ◆ an unkind remark.
unkindly [ʌnˈkaindli] *adv.* ▫ **indelicadamente, duramente**
unknown [ʌnˈnoun] *adj.*
1 desconhecido
an unknown star. ◆ The exact amount is unknown.
2 desconhecido
an unknown writer.
▪ antônimo: **well-known**
unless [ʌnˈles] *conj.* (mesmo que **if... not**) ▫ **a menos que**
I'll come tomorrow unless it rains. ◆ Don't come back unless you change your mind. ◆ Unless you apologize, she won't forgive you.
unlike [ʌnˈlaik] *prep.*
1 ao contrário de, diferente de
He likes to read, unlike his brother.
2 diferente
Their house is unlike any of the houses here.
unlikely [ʌnˈlaikli] *adj.* (= improbable) ▫ **improvável**
It is unlikely that he will win the race. ◆ He is unlikely to win the race.
unload [ʌnˈloud] *v.* (**unloads, unloading, unloaded**) ▫ **descarregar**
They unloaded the goods from the truck. ◆ to unload a ship.
unlock [ʌnˈlok] *v.* (**unlocks, unlocking, unlocked**) ▫ **destravar, destrancar**
I unlocked the door.
unlocked [ʌnˈlokt] *adj.* ▫ **destravado, destrancado**
Don't leave your car unlocked. ◆ The safe was unlocked.
unluckily [ʌnˈlʌkili] *adv.* (= unfortunately) ▫ **infelizmente**
Unluckily, there was no one there to help.
unlucky [ʌnˈlʌki] *adj.* (**unluckier, unluckiest**)
1 (= unfortunate) **desafortunado**
We played well but we were unlucky.
2 azarado
an unlucky number.
unmarried [ʌnˈmarid] *adj.* (= single) ▫ **descasado**
He / She is still unmarried.
unnatural [ʌnˈnatʃərəl] *adj.*
1 forçado, não natural
an unnatural smile.
2 (= not normal) **anormal**
unnatural behavior.
unnecessarily [ʌnˈnesəsərili] *adv.* ▫ **desnecessariamente**
I don't want to worry him unnecessarily, so I won't tell him.
unnecessary [ʌnˈnesəsəri] *adj.* ▫ **desnecessário**

It was unnecessary to call the police. ◆ unnecessary information / details.
unpack [ʌnˈpak] *v.* (**unpacks, unpacking, unpacked**) ▫ **desfazer, desfazer a mala**
Unpack the suitcases. ◆ It didn't take me long to unpack (my clothes).
unpaid [ʌnˈpeid] *adj.* ▫ **não pago**
an unpaid bill. ◆ an unpaid debt.
unpleasant [ʌnˈpleznt] *adj.* ▫ **desagradável**
an unpleasant smell. ◆ an unpleasant surprise.
unpleasantly [ʌnˈplezntli] *adv.*
1 desagradavelmente
The cake was unpleasantly sweet.
2 mal
He spoke unpleasantly to us.
unplug [ʌnˈplʌg] *v.* (**unplugs, unplugging, unplugged**) ▫ **desplugar, desligar**
Unplug the oven before cleaning it.
▪ antônimo: **plug in**
unpopular [ʌnˈpopjulə] *adj.* ▫ **impopular**
unpopular opinions.
unreal [ʌnˈriəl] *adj.* ▫ **irreal**
an unreal world.
unreasonable [ʌnˈriːzənəbl] *adj.* ▫ **absurdo, insensato**
The workers' demands are unreasonable.
unreliable [ʌnriˈlaiəbl] *adj.* ▫ **não confiável**
an unreliable machine. ◆ an unreliable person.
unsafe [ʌnˈseif] *adj.* ▫ **inseguro, perigoso**
It's unsafe to go there alone at night.
unsatisfactory [ʌnˌsatisˈfaktəri] *adj.* ▫ **insatisfatório**
Your work is unsatisfactory – you must try harder.
unscrew [ʌnˈskruː] *v.* (**unscrews, unscrewing, unscrewed**) ▫ **abrir, desatarraxar**
Unscrew the top of the bottle. ◆ to unscrew the jar, the toothpaste tube, etc. ◆ to unscrew a light bulb.
unskilled [ʌnˈskild] *adj.* ▫ **não especializado**
unskilled workers.
unstable [ʌnˈsteibl] *adj.* ▫ **instável**
That chair is unstable. ◆ an unstable government.
unsuccessful [ʌnsəkˈsesful] *adj.* ▫ **malsucedido**
His attempt to climb the tree was unsuccessful. ◆ unsuccessful results. ◆ an unsuccessful writer.
to be unsuccesful ▫ **ser malsucedido**
I tried to make a cake but I was unsuccessful.
unsuccessfully [ʌnsəkˈsesfuli] *adv.* ▫ **sem sucesso**
She tried again and again unsuccessfully.
unsuitable [ʌnˈsuːtəbl] *adj.* ▫ **inadequado**
He is unsuitable for the job. ◆ These books are unsuitable for children.
unsure [ʌnˈʃuə] *adj.*
1 inseguro
She is unsure of herself.
2 (= uncertain) **inseguro**
I'm unsure of the facts. ◆ She was unsure what to say.
untidiness [ʌnˈtaidinis] *n.* ▫ **desarrumação, bagunça**
untidy [ʌnˈtaidi] *adj.* (**untidier, untidiest**) ▫ **desarrumado, bagunçado**
His desk is always untidy. ◆ an untidy room.
untie [ʌnˈtai] *v.* (**unties, untying, untied**)
1 (= undo) **desfazer, desatar**
to untie a knot, a rope, etc.
2 desamarrar, soltar

He untied the prisoner.
3 (= undo) **desfazer**
Untie the parcel.
until¹ [ən'til] *conj.* (= **till**) □ **até (que)**
I waited until they were ready. ✦ Call him every day until he agrees to come.
■ **until he agrees** (*not* 'until he will agree').
until² *prep.* (also **till**) □ **até**
We waited until midnight. ✦ The bank is open until 6:30 pm.
■ Compare:
until tomorrow / 8 o'clock / Monday.
as far as page 60 / the post office / London.
up to ten / page 50 / 35 kilos.
■ **until** is written with one **l**, **till** is written with two.
untrue [ʌn'truː] *adj.* (= false) □ **falso**
Everything they said was untrue. ✦ an untrue story.
unusual [ʌn'juːʒuəl] *adj.* □ **incomum**
It's unusual to see children behave like that. ✦ Her clothes are very unusual.
unusually [ʌn'juːʒuəli] *adv.* □ **extraordinariamente**
an unusually big diamond. ✦ It's unusually hot today. ✦ The place was unusually quiet.
unwanted [ʌn'wontid] *adj.* □ **indesejado, indesejável**
unwelcome [ʌn'welkəm] *adj.* □ **inoportuno, desagradável**
an unwelcome visitor. ✦ an unwelcome surprise.
unwell [ʌn'wel] *adj.* (= ill, sick) □ **indisposto**
Stay in bed if you are feeling unwell.
unwilling [ʌn'wiliŋ] *adj.* (= reluctant) □ **relutante**
She was unwilling to help.
unwillingly [ʌn'wiliŋli] *adv.* (= reluctantly) □ **relutantemente**
He agreed unwillingly to give us the money.
unwrap [ʌn'ræp] *v.* (**unwraps, unwrapping, unwrapped**) □ **desembrulhar**
Unwrap the present.
unzip [ʌn'zip] *v.* (**unzips, unzipping, unzipped**) □ **abrir o zíper de**
He unzipped the suitcase. ✦ She unzipped her dress.
up¹ [ʌp] *adv.*
1 para cima
Put your hands up. ✦ The little child looked up at me. ✦ Is the elevator going up or down?
2 para cima
Put in the cassette this side up.
3 até o fim, totalmente
Drink up your milk. ✦ Eat up your dinner.
■ Ver **break up; bring up; call up; catch up; come up; end up; get up; give up; go up; grow up; hold up; hurry up; lock up; make up; pick up; pull up; put up; set up; sit up; show up; shut up; speak up; stand up; stay up; sum up; take up; tear up; throw up; tie up; turn up; use up; wake up**.
it's up to you □ **você é quem sabe**
He can stay or go – it's up to him.
up to
1 até
Up to five people can get into the car. ✦ He counted up to ten.
2 (= as far as) **até**
Read up to page 65.
up to now (mesmo que **up till now**) □ **até agora**

Up to now, there haven't been any problems.
up until □ **até**
Up until yesterday, we didn't hear from him.
What is he / she up to? □ **O que ele / ela está aprontando?**
What are you up to? Are you trying to trick me?
up² *prep.*
1 subir
They walked up the hill. ✦ He climbed up the tree. ✦ She went up the stairs.
2 (= along) **ao longo de**
to drive up the road.
up³ *adj.*
1 de pé, acordado
Is she still up? ✦ Are the children up yet?
2 aumentar
Sales are up by 10%.
up⁴ *n.*
ups and downs □ **altos e baixos**
There are ups and downs in our business.
update [ʌp'deit] *v.* (**updates, updating, updated**) □ **atualizar**
to update a dictionary, a map, etc. ✦ He updated me on the situation.
■ Ver **up-to-date**.
updated [ʌp'deitid] *adj.* □ **atualizado**
an updated dictionary.
upgrade [ʌp'greid] *v.* (**upgrades, upgrading, upgraded**) □ **melhorar**
How much will it cost to upgrade my computer?
uphill [ʌp'hil] *adv.* □ **morro acima**
to drive uphill.
uphold [ʌp'hould] *v.* (**upholds, upholding, upheld**) □ **defender, preservar**
We want to uphold our traditions and beliefs.
upkeep ['ʌpkiːp] *n.* (= maintenence) □ **manutenção**
I pay for the upkeep of the house. ✦ He is responsible for the upkeep of the park.
upon [ə'pɒn] *prep.* □ **sobre**
■ **on** is the usual word we use.
upper ['ʌpə] *adj.* □ **superior**
the upper lip and the lower lip.
■ Compare **top**:
the top shelf and the bottom shelf.
upper class ['ʌpə klaːs] *adj.* □ **de classe alta**
They speak English with an upper-class accent.
■ with a hyphen when before a noun.
■ Compare **middle class; working class**.
upright ['ʌprait] *adj., adv.* □ **vertical, verticalmente**
Stand upright!
uprising ['ʌpraiziŋ] *n.* (= rebellion) □ **levante, rebelião**
upset¹ [ʌp'set] *n., adj.* □ **bravo, abalado**
He is upset because I didn't let him take the car. ✦ She is still upset about the accident.
upset² *v.* (**upsets, upsetting, upset**)
1 perturbar, abalar, deixar bravo
I'm sorry. I didn't mean to upset you. ✦ It upsets her when you talk about the accident.
2 atrapalhar
The rain upset their plans (for a picnic).
3 virar
He upset a cup of coffee all over the table. ✦ The wave upset the boat.

upset³ [ˈʌpset] *n., adj.* □ **desarranjo, indisposição, desarranjado, indisposto**
I have a stomach upset. (= My stomach is upset.)

upside down [ˈʌpsaidˈdaun] *adv., adj.* □ **de ponta-cabeça, de pernas para o ar, de cabeça para baixo**
The pupils put their chairs upside down on the desks.
• That picture is upside down.
■ Compare with **inside out**.

upstairs [ʌpˈsteəz] *adv., adj.* □ **para cima, no andar de cima**
He went upstairs. • She lives upstairs. • an upstairs window / room.
■ antônimo: **downstairs**

up-to-date [ˌʌp tə ˈdeit] *adj.*
1 atualizado
an up-to-date dictionary. • an up-to-date map. • up-to-date news.
2 atual
up-to-date clothes (= the clothes are up to date). • up-to-date methods (= the methods are up to date).
■ No hyphen when **up to date** comes after the verb
■ antônimo: **out-of-date; out of date; outdated**
bring... up to date (= update) □ **atualizar, modernizar**
We need to bring the system up to date.

upward(s) [ˈʌpwɔːd(z)] *adv.* □ **para cima**
The bird flew upwards. • He pointed his finger upwards.
■ antônimo: **downwards**

urban [ˈɜːbən] *adj.* □ **urbano**
urban areas.
■ Compare **rural**:
rural (= of the countryside / villages.

urge¹ [ɜːdʒ] *n.* □ **ímpeto, vontade**
I had an urge to hit him.

urge² *v.* (**urges, urging, urged**) □ **incitar, instigar, encorajar**
He urged her to stop smoking. • I urge you not to sell it.

urgency [ˈɜːdʒənsi] *n.* □ **urgência**
a matter of great urgency.

urgent [ˈɜːdʒənt] *adj.* □ **urgente**
an urgent telephone call. • an urgent message. • It's not urgent – we can do it later.

urgently [ˈɜːdʒəntli] *adv.* □ **urgentemente**
We must meet urgently.

us [ʌs] *pron.* □ **nos, nós, conosco**
He didn't see us. • They gave us some food. • He looked at us. • She stayed with us.

use¹ [juːz] *v.* (**uses, using, used**)
1 usar
Can I use your phone? • I never use that word. • They used my room as an office.
2 usar
Don't trust him. He is just using you. • She used her influence to get him a job.
3 usar
He uses too much sugar.

use up □ **esgotar**
Don't use up all the butter. We need it for the other cake.

use² *n.*
1 uso
a school library for the use of the pupils. • The use of computers in industry is increasing.
2 usos
the use of energy from the sun for heating water.

3 (*pl.* **uses**) **usos**
This tool has many uses.
4 movimento
After the accident he lost the use of his legs.

it's no use (doing) □ **não adianta (fazer)**
It's no use complaining – there's nothing they can do.

make use of □ **fazer uso de**
She makes good use of her time. • They made use of energy from the sun.

what's the use of (doing)? □ **De que adianta (fazer)?**
What's the use of crying?

be of use to □ **ser útil a**
Take this rope – it will be of use to you. • Can I be of any use to you?

used¹ [juːzd] *adj. Amer.* □ **usado**
used cars. • used clothes.
■ *Brit.* **second-hand**

used² [juːst] *adj.*
be used to (= be accustomed to) □ **ser/estar acostumado a**
I'm used to the noise here. • She's not used to getting up early.
get used to (= get accustomed to) □ **acostumar-se a**
I'm getting used to the changes. • They got used to living in the village.

used³ [juːst] *v.*
used to □ **ter o costume de, estar acostumado a**
I used to visit them every day. • She used to like him, but now she hates him. • I didn't use to eat breakfast, but now I do.
■ Compare:
I am used to eating a big breakfast every day.

useful [ˈjuːsful] *adj.* □ **útil**
Dictionaries are very useful for learning a language.

usefully [ˈjuːsfuli] *adv.* □ **utilmente**

usefulness [ˈjuːsfulnis] *n.* □ **utilidade**

useless [ˈjuːslis] *adj.* □ **inútil**
A computer is useless without a program.
it's useless to □ **é inútil**
It's useless to shout – nobody will hear you.

user [ˈjuːzə] *n.* □ **usuário**
telephone users.

user-friendly [ˈjuːzəˌfrendli] *adj.* □ **simples para o usuário**
a user-friendly computer program

usual [ˈjuːʒuəl] *adj.* □ **comum, de sempre**
It's warmer than usual today • It's usual for him to work ten hours a day. • The key is in its usual place.

as usual □ **como sempre**
She is late, as usual. • As usual, he didn't say much.

usually [ˈjuːʒuəli] *adv.* (= as a rule) □ **normalmente**
I usually get up at 7 am. • Usually he goes to work by bus.
• What do you usually do in the evenings?

utensil [juːˈtensl] *n.* □ **utensílio**
kitchen utensils (e.g. pots and pans).

utter¹ [ˈʌtə] *v.* (**utters, uttering, uttered**) □ **proferir, emitir, pronunciar**
He uttered a cry of pain. • She uttered some words in Russian.

utter² *adj.* (= total) □ **total, completo**
It's utter madness to go there at night. • an utter failure.

utterly [ˈʌtəli] *adv.* □ **profundamente**
The room was utterly dark.

U-turn [ˈjuː tɜːn] *n.* □ **retorno, mudança de direção**

Vv

V (= 5) V
VI (= 6) ♦ IV (= 4)
v. *abbr.* (Ver **versus**).
vacancy ['veikənsi] *n.* (*pl.* **vacancies**)
1 vaga
We have a vacancy for a technician.
2 vaga
There are no vacancies in this hotel.
vacant ['veikənt] *adj.* □ **vago**
a vacant room / seat.
vacation[1] [və'keiʃən] *n.*
1 *Amer.* **férias**
We went to Turkey on vacation. ♦ He is on vacation. ♦ to take a vacation. ♦ a week's vacation.
■ Brit. **holiday**
2 *Amer.* **férias**
They are going to summer camp on their summer vacation.
■ *Brit.* **holiday**
3 feriados
the Christmas vacation (at a university).
vacation[2] *v. Amer.* (**vacations, vacationing, vacationed**)
□ **passar férias**
They are vacationing in Brazil.
vacuum ['vakjum] *n.* □ **vácuo**
vacuum cleaner ['vakjum 'kli:nə] *n.* □ **aspirador de pó**
vague [veig] *adj.* □ **vago**
vague memories. ♦ vague instructions.
vaguely ['veigli] *adv.* □ **vagamente**
I vaguely remember his face.
vagueness ['veignis] *n.* □ **incerteza, imprecisão**
vain [vein] *adj.*
1 vaidoso
He is so vain – he thinks I wrote this song about him.
■ The noun is **vanity**.
2 vão
She made a vain attempt to reach the shelf.
in vain □ **em vão**
All her efforts were in vain. ♦ I tried in vain to lift the box.
valid ['valid] *adj.* □ **válido**
The tickets are valid for the next show. ♦ My passport is valid for five years.
validity [və'liditi] *n.* □ **validade**
the validity of a passport / a contract / an argument.
valley ['vali] *n.* □ **vale**
valuable ['valjuəbl] *adj.*
1 valioso
valuable jewels.
2 valioso
She gave us valuable information. ♦ Let's not waste valuable time.
■ antônimo: **worthless; unimportant**
valuables ['valjuəblz] *n. pl.* □ **valores**
I keep the jewels and other valuables in the safe.
value[1] ['valju:] *n.*
1 valor
Do you know the value of this diamond?
2 valor
This information is of little value. ♦ The discovery was of great value.
values *n. pl.* □ **valores**
the values of a democratic society.
value[2] *v.* (**values, valuing, valued**)
1 valorizar
I value his advice greatly.
2 avaliar
He valued the house at $120,000.
vampire ['vampaiə] *n.* □ **vampiro**
van [van] *n.* □ **van**
a delivery van. ♦ a furniture van. ♦ a police van.
vandal ['vandəl] *n.* □ **vândalo**
vandalism ['vandəlizəm] *n.* □ **vandalismo**
vanilla [və'nilə] *n.* □ **baunilha**
vanish ['vaniʃ] *v.* (**vanishes, vanishing, vanished**) (= disappear) □ **desaparecer**
The sun vanished behind the clouds.
vanity ['vanəti] *n.* □ **vaidade**
■ The adjective is **vain**.
variation [,veəri'eiʃən] *n.* □ **variação**
There are great variations in prices from shop to shop.
varied ['veərid] *adj.* □ **variado**
She had an interesting and varied career.
variety [və'raiəti] *n.*
1 variedade
There's a lot of variety in this job.
2 variedade
They sell a wide variety of goods.
3 (*pl.* **varieties**) **variedades**
We have many varieties of oranges.
various ['veəriəs] *adj.* □ **vários**
At the zoo, we saw birds of various sizes. ♦ He did it for various reasons.
varnish ['va:niʃ] *n.* □ **verniz**
wood varnish.
vary ['veəri] *v.* (**varies, varying, varied**)
1 variar
The buildings vary in style. ♦ Prices vary from 20 to 50 dollars.
2 variar
Try to vary your diet.
vase [va:z] *n.* □ **vaso**
vast [va:st] *adj.* (= enormous) □ **vasto**
The Sahara is a vast desert. ♦ a vast amount of money.
VCR [,vi: si: 'a:(r)] *n., abbr.* (= video cassette recorder) □ **aparelho de videocassete**
veal [vi:l] *n.* □ **carne de vitela**
vegetable ['vedʒtəbl] *n.* □ **vegetal, legume**
Potatoes and peppers are vegetables. ♦ green vegetables (e.g. lettuce, spinach, cucumbers).
vegetable oil ['vedʒtəbl oil] *n.* □ **óleo vegetal**
vegetable soup ['vedʒtəbl su:p] *n.* □ **sopa de legumes**
vegetarian [,vedʒi'təriən] *n.* □ **vegetariano**
I don't eat meat – I'm a vegetarian.
vehicle ['viəkl] *n.* □ **veículo**
Cars, buses, trucks and bikes are vehicles.
veil [veil] *n.* □ **véu**
a bride's veil. ♦ Some Muslim women wear veils.
vein [vein] *n.* □ **veias**
arteries and veins.
velvet ['velvit] *n.* □ **veludo**
a blue velvet jacket.

vending machine ['vendiŋ mə‚ʃi:n] *n.* □ **máquina**
You can buy coffee, sandwiches, etc. from a vending machine.
vendor ['vendə] *n.* □ **máquina de...**
the ice-cream vendor. ◆ the hot dog vendor.
vengeance ['vendʒəns] *n.* □ **vingança**
take vengeance on (= take revenge on) □ **vingar-se de**
They took vengeance on the killer.
venom ['venəm] *n.* □ **veneno**
veranda(h) [və'rændə] *n.* □ **varanda**
We sat on the veranda.
■ *Amer.* also **porch**
■ Compare **balcony**.
verb [və:b] *n.* □ **verbo**
'Went' is the past tense of the verb 'go'. ◆ irregular verbs (e.g. eat, cut).
verdict ['və:dikt] *n.* □ **veredicto**
The jury's verdict was 'not guilty'.
verify ['verifai] *v.* (**verifies, verifying, verified**) □ **verificar**
to verify the facts.
verse [və:s] *n.*
1 verso
The story is written in verse.
2 verso
the first verse of the song / poem.
3 versículo
a verse from the Bible.
version ['və:ʃən] *n.*
1 versão
a new version of the song. ◆ the first version of the film.
2 versão
Give me your version of what happened.
versus ['və:səs] *prep.* (= against) □ **versus, contra**
The first match will be Italy versus Poland.
■ abreviação: **v.**; **vs**
vertical ['və:tikəl] *adj.* □ **vertical**
The letter L has a vertical line and a horizontal line.
very[1] ['veri] *adv.* □ **muito**
a very high mountain. ◆ He did it very quickly.
not very □ **não muito**
I'm not very interested in football.
very much
1 muito
I like him very much.
2 muito, muita coisa
She didn't say very much.
3 muito, muitíssimo
It's very much the same.
very well
1 muito bem
I know her very well.
2 muito bem, está bem
Call me tomorrow. – Very well.
■ Do not confuse with 'I am very well' (= very healthy, not sick).
very[2] *adj.* □ **exato, exatamente**
At that very moment she came in. ◆ He is the very man we need. ◆ It happened in this very room.
vessel ['vesl] *n.* □ **embarcação**
A ship or large boat is a vessel.
blood vessel *n.* □ **vaso sanguíneo**
Arteries and veins are blood vessels.

vest [vest] *n.*
1 *Amer.* **colete**
She wore a gray vest over her shirt.
■ *Brit.* **waistcoat**
2 *Brit.* **camiseta**
I wear only white cotton vests.
■ *Amer.* **undershirt**
bullet-proof vest *n.* □ **colete à prova de balas**
Policemen sometimes wear bullet-proof vests.
vet [vet] *n.* (= **veterinarian**) □ **veterinário**
I took my dog to the vet.
veterinarian [‚vetəri'neəriən] *n.* (**mesmo que veterinary surgeon,** *Amer.*) □ **veterinário**
veteran ['vetərən] *n.*
1 (= ex-soldier) **veterano**
veterans of the Second World War.
2 veterano
a veteran politician / teacher.
veto[1] ['vi:tou] *n.* □ **veto**
veto[2] *v.* (**vetoes, vetoing, vetoed**) □ **vetar**
The chairman vetoed the project.
via ['vaiə] *prep.*
1 via
We flew to Scotland via Newcastle.
2 via
We received these pictures via satellite.
vibrate [vai'breit] *v.* (**vibrates, vibrating, vibrated**) □ **vibrar**
The walls vibrated with the loud music.
vice- [vais-] *pref.* (= deputy) □ **vice**
the Vice-President of the USA.
vice[1] [vais] *n.* □ **vício, imoralidade**
vice and corruption.
vice squad *n.* □ **esquadrão da delegacia de costumes**
vice[2] *n.*, **vise** *Amer.* □ **torno**
vicious ['viʃəs] *adj.*
1 cruel, feroz
a vicious attack. ◆ a vicious criminal.
2 maldoso, malicioso
vicious lies. ◆ a vicious rumour.
victim ['viktim] *n.* □ **vítima**
the murderer's victims. ◆ a rape victim. ◆ the victims of the earthquake.
victorious [vik'to:riəs] *adj.* □ **vitorioso**
The victorious team received a warm welcome.
■ Ver **triumphant**.
victory ['viktəri] *n.* (*pl.* **victories**) □ **vitória**
to win a victory in war, a game, the elections, etc.
■ Ver **triumph**.
video ['vidiou] *n.*
1 vídeo
We watched the video of the wedding. ◆ to rent a video from a video shop / store.
2 vídeo
We will record everything on video.
3 (= videotape) **fita de vídeo**
4 (= video cassette recorder) **aparelho de videocassete**
video camera ['vidiou 'kamərə] *n.* □ **câmera de vídeo**
video cassette ['vidiou kə'set] *n.* □ **fita de vídeo**
video cassette recorder ['vidiou kə'set rə'ko:də] *n.* (= VCR; video) □ **aparelho de videocassete**

videotape ['vidiouteip] *n*. □ **fita de vídeo**
view [vju:] *n*.
1 vista
There's a beautiful view from our hotel room.
2 vista
The bus blocked my view of the road.
3 visão
What are your views on education?
come into view □ **aparecer, ficar à mostra**
After two days at sea the island came into view.
in view of □ **em vista de**
In view of the situation, we decided to stay.
on view □ **à mostra**
The artist's works are on view at the museum.
point of view (Ver **point**).
viewer ['vju:ə] *n*. □ **telespectador**
Millions of viewers will watch the broadcast on TV.
viewpoint ['vju:point] *n*. (= **point of view**)
vigor ['vigə] *n*. *Amer*., **vigour** *Brit*. □ **vigor**
They started to work again with greater vigor.
vigorous ['vigərəs] *adj*. □ **vigoroso**
to do vigorous physical exercise. ♦ vigorous efforts.
vigorously ['vigərəsli] *adv*.
1 (= energetically) **com vigor, com vida**
Don't dance too vigorously.
2 vigorosamente
He denied the accusations vigorously.
villa ['vilə] *n*. □ **mansão, casa de campo**
village ['vilidʒ] *n*. □ **vilarejo**
They live in a small village.
villager ['vilidʒə] *n*. □ **aldeão**
villain ['vilən] *n*. □ **vilão**
The villain dies at the end of the play.
■ antônimo: **hero**
vine [vain] *n*. □ **vinha, videira, parreira**
vinegar ['vinigə] *n*. □ **vinagre**
Put some oil and vinegar on the salad.
vineyard ['vinja:d] *n*. □ **vinha, vinhedo, parreiral**
viola [vi'oulə] *n*. □ **viola de arco**
He plays the viola.
violate ['vaiəleit] *v*. (**violates, violating, violated**)
1 (= break) **violar**
to violate an agreement / the rules.
2 violar
They violated our rights.
violation [,vaiə'leiʃən] *n*. □ **violação**
a violation of human rights. ♦ traffic violations (e.g. speeding).
violence ['vaiələns] *n*. □ **violência**
There's too much violence on TV.
violent ['vaiələnt] *adj*. □ **violento**
a violent man. ♦ a violent crime. ♦ a violent film. ♦ She became violent.
violently ['vaiələntli] *adv*. □ **violentamente**
They beat him violently.
violet[1] ['vaiəlit] *n*. □ **violeta**
Violets have purple or white flowers.
violet[2] *n*., *adj*. □ **violeta**
■ Ver **mauve**; **purple**.
violin [,vaiə'lin] *n*. □ **violino**
She plays the violin.
violinist ['vaiəlinist] *n*. □ **violinista**

VIP ['vi:'ai'pi:] *abbr*. (mesmo que **very important person**) □ **VIP**
virtually ['və:tʃuəli] *adv*. □ **virtualmente**
The room was virtually empty. ♦ Virtually all of them were women.
virtual reality ['və:tʃuəl ri'aləti] *n*. □ **realidade virtual**
virtual reality video games on computer.
virtue ['və:tʃu:] *n*. □ **virtude**
Patience is only one of her many virtues.
virus ['vaiərəs] *n*. □ **vírus**
a flu virus. ♦ The virus can destroy all your computer files.
visa ['vi:zə] *n*. □ **visto**
You need a visa to get into America.
vise [vais] *n*. *Amer*., **vice** *Brit*. □ **torno**
visibility [,vizə'biliti] *n*. □ **visibilidade**
Visibility was bad because of the fog.
visible ['vizəbl] *adj*. □ **visível**
The tracks were clearly visible in the snow.
■ antônimo: **invisible**
vision ['viʒən] *n*.
1 visão
I don't need glasses – I have perfect vision.
2 visão
a leader of great vision.
visit[1] ['vizit] *n*. □ **visita**
This is my first visit to Jordan. ♦ It was a short visit.
pay a visit to, pay someone a visit □ **fazer uma visita a, fazer uma visita a alguém**
Let's pay a visit to his parents. ♦ We paid him a visit.
visit[2] *v*. (**visits, visiting, visited**)
1 visitar
I visit them once a week. ♦ We visited him in hospital.
2 visitar
Many tourists are visiting Paris now. ♦ to visit the zoo.
3 ir
I must visit the dentist.
visitor ['vizitə] *n*. □ **visita, visitante**
We had a visitor today. ♦ Many visitors are coming to the museum.
visual ['viʒuəl] *adj*. □ **visual**
visual aids *n*. *pl*. □ **artifícios visuais**
Some teachers use visual aids (e.g. films, pictures) in class.
vital ['vaitl] *adj*. □ **vital**
It's vital that we (should) finish the job quickly. ♦ vital information.
vitamin ['vitəmin] *n*. □ **vitamina**
Oranges are rich in vitamin C.
vivid ['vivid] *adj*.
1 vivo
vivid colours.
2 vívido
I have a vivid memory of my visit there.
vivid imagination *n*. □ **imaginação viva**
vividly ['vividli] *adv*. □ **vividamente, claramente**
I vividly remember the first time I met him.
vocabulary [və'kabjuləri] *n*. (*pl*. **vocabularies**)
1 vocabulário
These exercises will help you increase your English vocabulary. ♦ He has a rich vocabulary.
2 vocabulário
At the end of the book there is a vocabulary of 2,000 words.

vocation [vəˈkeiʃən] *n.* □ **vocação**
Teaching is a vocation, not just a job.
vocational guidance [vəˈkeiʃənl ˈgaidəns] *n.* □ **orientação vocacional**
Students can get vocational guidance before they finish school.
vocational school [vəˈkeiʃənl sku:l] *n.* □ **escola vocacional**
vocational training [vəˈkeiʃənl ˈtreiniŋ] *n.* □ **treinamento vocacional**
voice [vois] *n.* □ **voz**
Lower your voice! (= Speak more quietly!). ◆ a beautiful voice. ◆ an angry voice. ◆ She spoke in a loud voice. ◆ I can hear voices outside.
at the top of your voice □ **o mais alto que pôde**
She shouted at the top of her voice.
raise your voice □ **erguer a voz**
There's no need to raise your voice – I can hear you.
voicemail [ˈvoismeil] *n.* □ **correio de voz**
No one answered the phone, so I left a message on the voicemail.
volcano [volˈkeinou] *n.* □ **vulcão**
volcanic [volˈkanik] *adj.* □ **vulcânico**
volcanic rocks.
volleyball [ˈvolibo:l] *n.* □ **voleibol**
volume [ˈvoljum] *n.*
1 volume
Turn down the volume – it's too loud.
2 volume
What is the volume of this bottle?
3 volume
a dictionary in two volumes ◆ This library has 20,000 volumes (= books).
voluntarily [ˈvoləntərəli] *adv.* □ **espontaneamente**
They returned the money voluntarily.
voluntary [ˈvoləntəri] *adj.*
1 voluntário
voluntary work. ◆ a voluntary organization.
2 espontâneo
Nobody forced him to say anything – it was voluntary.
volunteer¹ [ˌvolənˈtiə] *n.* □ **voluntário**
I need ten volunteers for this dangerous job.

volunteer² *v.* (**volunteers, volunteering, volunteered**)
1 oferecer-se como voluntário
Everybody volunteered to help. ◆ He volunteered for the army.
2 oferecer
We didn't force her to tell us – she volunteered the information.
vomit¹ [ˈvomit] *v.* (**vomits, vomiting, vomited**) (= throw up) □ **vomitar**
He felt sick and vomited.
vomit² *n.* □ **vômito**
vote¹ [vout] *n.*
1 voto
They are counting the votes. ◆ There were 6 votes for me and 12 for the other candidate.
2 voto
We decided the matter by a vote.
have a vote, take a vote □ **fazer uma votação**
We can't agree on this, so let's take a vote.
vote² *v.* (**votes, voting, voted**) □ **votar**
I voted for the plan and she voted against it. ◆ Who are you going to vote for in the election? ◆ I don't have the right to vote yet.
voter [ˈvoutə] *n.* □ **eleitores**
Five million voters voted in the elections.
vow¹ [vau] *v.* (**vows, vowing, vowed**) □ **jurar**
He vowed to take revenge.
vow² *n.* □ **voto, jura**
vowel [ˈvauəl] *n.* □ **vogal**
The vowels are a, e, i, o, u.
■ Compare **consonant**:
consonant = b, c, d, etc.
voyage [ˈvoiidʒ] *n.* □ **viagem**
We went on a voyage around the world (by ship). ◆ a voyage to the moon.
vs *abbr.* (Ver **versus**).
vulgar [ˈvʌlgə] *adj.* (= rude) □ **vulgar**
a vulgar joke. ◆ vulgar manners.
vulnerable [ˈvʌlnərəbl] *adj.* □ **vulnerável**
He is lonely and vulnerable.
vulture [ˈvʌltʃə] *n.* □ **abutre, urubu**

Ww

W *abbr.* (= West) ▫ **O, oeste**

wade [weid] *v.* (**wades, wading, waded**) ▫ **atravessar com dificuldade**
We can wade across the river here.

wafer ['weifə] *n.* ▫ **wafer, biscoito, bolacha**
chocolate wafers.

waffle ['wofl] *n.* ▫ **waffle**
I had a waffle for breakfast.

wag [wag] *v.* (**wags, wagging, wagged**) ▫ **abanar**
The dog wags its tail when it sees me. ◆ The dog's tail wagged.

wage [weidʒ] *n.* ▫ **salário**
1 salário
How many people earn only the minimum wage? ◆ She earns a weekly wage of $200. ◆ a wage increase of 4%.
2 (= **wages**) *pl.* **salário**
Her wages are $200 a week.
■ Compare **wages**:
  wages = weekly
  salary = monthly
  pay is the general word (e.g. What's your pay?)

wagon ['wagən] *n.* (mesmo que **freight car**), *Brit.* **waggon**
1 carroça
A wagon is pulled by horses.
2 vagão
goods waggons.

wail [weil] *v.* (**wails, wailing, wailed**) ▫ **lamentar, tocar**
'I broke my leg', he wailed. ◆ An ambulance siren wailed outside.

waist [weist] *n.* ▫ **cintura**
He put his hands around her waist.
■ Ver **hip**.

waistcoat ['weistkout] *n. Brit.* ▫ **colete**
■ *Amer.* **vest**

wait¹ [weit] *n.* ▫ **espera**
After a long wait she finally arrived.

wait² *v.* (**waits, waiting, waited**) ▫ **esperar**
Don't wait for me. ◆ He waited outside. ◆ I'm waiting for the bus.
I can't wait ▫ **mal posso esperar, não vejo a hora**
I can't wait to hear your new song.
keep someone waiting ▫ **deixar alguém esperando, fazer alguém esperar**
She kept me waiting for twenty minutes.

wait at tables, wait tables ▫ **servir mesas, trabalhar como garçom**
I'm waiting tables to pay for my university studies.

wait on ▫ **servir**
Five people waited on the guests.

wait up
1 esperar acordado
Don't wait up for me – I'll be home late tonight.
2 (= **Wait up!**) *Amer.* **Espere!**
Wait up! I can't walk so fast.

waiter ['weitə] *n.* ▫ **garçom**
The waiter gave us the menu and waited to take our order.
■ Ver **waitress**.

waiting room ['weitiŋ rum] *n.* ▫ **sala de espera**
The waiting room at the railway station was full. ◆ the dentist's waiting room.

waitress ['weitris] *n.* ▫ **garçonete**
It's a small restaurant with one waiter and two waitresses.

wake [weik] *v.* (**wakes, waking, woke, woken**)

wake (up)
1 acordar
I woke (up) in the middle of the night. ◆ Wake up! You'll be late for school!
2 acordar
Speak quietly – you'll wake the baby! ◆ The noise woke me up. ◆ Wake me (up) at six.

walk¹ [wo:k] *v.* (**walks, walking, walked**) ▫ **andar, caminhar**
I usually walk to school. ◆ Babies can learn to walk without help. ◆ to walk in the park.

walk² *n.*
1 caminhada
It's a five minutes' walk to the station.
2 passeio, caminhada
I took the dog for a walk.
go for a walk ▫ **sair para caminhar**
We went for a walk in the park.

walkie-talkie [,wo:ki'to:ki] *n.* ▫ **rádio comunicador**
The police carry walkie-talkies to talk to each other.

walking stick ['wo:kiŋ stik] *n.* ▫ **bengala**

Walkman™ ['wo:kmən] *n.* (= personal stereo) ▫ **walkman**

wall [wo:l] *n.* ▫ **parede, muro**
There were no pictures on the walls. ◆ He climbed over the wall. ◆ There is a high wall around the building.

wallet ['wolit] *n.* ▫ **carteira**
He took his wallet out of his pocket.

wallpaper ['wo:lpeipə] *n.* ▫ **papel de parede**

walnut ['wo:lnʌt] *n.* ▫ **noz, nogueira, imbuia**

wander ['wondə] *v.* (**wanders, wandering, wandered**) ▫ **perambular**
They wandered around town.

want [wont] *v.* (**wants, wanted**)
1 querer
I don't want to go. ◆ She wants more money. ◆ That's not what I wanted.
■ **Would you like...?** is more polite than **Do you want...?**
Would you like some tea?
■ *No* [be + -ing]: *do not* say 'am wanting' etc.
■ In short answers we say **want to**:
Why didn't you come? – I didn't want to.
2 (= **need**) **precisar, pedir**
The walls want painting.

want ad ['wont 'ad] *n.* ▫ **classificados**

war [wo:] *n.* ▫ **guerra**
Millions died in the Second World War. ◆ They won / lost the war. ◆ A war broke out between the two countries.
at war ▫ **em guerra**
Great Britain was at war with Germany from 1939 to 1945.
declare war on ▫ **declarar guerra a**
They declared war on their enemy.

ward [wo:d] *n.* ▫ **ala**
the children's ward (of a hospital).

warden ['wo:dn] *n.*
1 diretor
She is the warden of a youth hostel.

2 *Amer.* **diretor**
a prison warden.
3 (= **traffic warden**) **guarda**
warder ['wɔ:də] *n*. □ **carcereiro**
a prison warder.
wardrobe ['wɔ:droub] *n*. □ **guarda-roupa**
Hang the jacket in the wardrobe.
warehouse ['weəhaus] *n*. □ **depósito**
A warehouse is a big building for storing goods.
warfare ['wɔ:feə] *n*. □ **guerra**
psychological warfare.
warm¹ [wɔ:m] *adj*.
1 quente
The water is not warm enough. • warm weather.
■ antônimo: **cool**
2 quente
His hand was warm.
■ antônimo: **cold**
3 de inverno
warm clothes. • a warm coat.
4 acolhedor
a warm person. • a warm welcome.
■ antônimo: **cold**
get warm □ **aquecer-se**
Come and get warm by the fire.
keep something warm □ **manter algo aquecido**
I covered my feet to keep them warm. • Put the food in the oven to keep it warm.
warm² *v*. (**warms, warming, warmed**)
warm up □ **aquecer, esquentar**
I'll warm up the baby's food. • The weather is still cold, but it's warming (up).
warmly ['wɔ:mli] *adv*.
1 calorosamente
He shook my hand warmly. • She smiled warmly.
2 com roupa de inverno
She is warmly dressed.
warmth [wɔ:mθ] *n*.
1 calor
the warmth of your bed, the sun, your body, etc.
2 calor
the warmth of his smile.
warn [wɔ:n] *v*. (**warns, warning, warned**) □ **avisar, alertar**
I warned him not to go there. • I'm warning you!
warning ['wɔ:niŋ] *n*. □ **aviso, alerta**
I'm giving you a last warning. • There is a warning on the cigarette packet about the dangers of smoking.
warrant ['wɔrənt] *n*. □ **mandado**
I have a warrant for your arrest.
warranty ['wɔrənti] *n*. (= guarantee) □ **garantia**
You have a one-year warranty on this watch.
warrior ['wɔriə] *n*. □ **guerreiro**
warship ['wɔ:ʃip] *n*. □ **navio de guerra**
wartime ['wɔ:taim] *n*. □ **tempo de guerra**
was [wɔz, wəz] *v*. (Ver **be**).
wash¹ [wɔʃ] *n*.
1 lavagem, lavada
The car needs a wash. • Give it a wash. (= Wash it.)
2 *Amer.* **roupa lavada, roupa suja**
to hang out the wash (to dry) • to do the wash (= to wash dirty clothes).
■ *Brit.* **washing**

have a wash □ **lavar-se**
He is having a wash.
wash² *v*. (**washes, washing, washed**)
1 lavar, lavar-se
Go and wash your hands. • It's your turn to wash the dishes. • She washed and went to bed.
2 lavar
to wash the dirty clothes
wash away □ **tirar lavando, arrastar**
The rain washed the dust away. • Many houses were washed away by the floods.
wash up
1 *Brit.* **lavar a louça**
It's your turn to wash up (the dishes).
2 *Amer.* **lavar-se**
Go and wash up (your hands and face).
washbasin ['wɔʃ,beisn] *n. Brit*. □ **pia**
A wash-basin is a sink in a bathroom.
■ *Amer.* **sink**
washing ['wɔʃiŋ] *n. Brit*. □ **roupa suja, roupa lavada**
to do the washing (= to wash dirty clothes). • Hang the washing on the line to dry.
■ *Amer.* **wash**
washing machine ['wɔʃiŋ məˈʃi:n] *n*. □ **máquina de lavar roupa, lavadora de roupa**
washing powder ['wɔʃiŋ 'paudə] *n*. □ **sabão em pó**
washing-up [,wɔʃiŋˈʌp] *n. Brit*. □ **lavar a louça**
It's your turn to do the washing-up.
■ *Amer.* **dishes**
washing-up liquid [,wɔʃiŋˈʌp 'likwid] *n*. □ **sabão líquido**
washroom ['wɔʃrum] *n. Amer*. (= toilet) □ **banheiro**
■ Ver **bathroom; lavatory; WC**.
wasn't ['wɔznt] (mesmo que **was not**).
wasp [wɔsp] *n*. □ **vespa**
A wasp stung him in the arm.
waste¹ [weist] *n*.
1 desperdício
It's a waste of time and money.
2 lixo
industrial waste. • nuclear waste. • to recycle waste materials.
waste² *v*. (**wastes, wasting, wasted**) □ **desperdiçar**
Don't waste my time! • to waste food. • to waste energy.
waste-basket ['weist,ba:skit] *n. Amer*. (= waste-paper basket) □ **cesto de lixo**
wasteful ['weistful] *adj*. □ **desperdiçador**
wasteful use of water.
waste-paper basket ['weistpeipə 'ba:skit] *n. Brit*. (= waste-basket) □ **cesto de lixo**
watch¹ [wɔtʃ] *n*. □ **relógio de pulso**
It's five o'clock by my watch. • My watch is five minutes fast, according to the clock on the wall. • Your watch is slow.
watch² *n*. □ **vigia, guarda**
keep watch □ **ficar de guarda**
My dog keeps watch over our house.
watch³ *v*. (**watches, watching, watched**)
1 assistir a, ver
I watch television four hours a day. • We watched the game on TV. • Watch how I do it.
2 (= look after) **olhar**
Watch the baby – I'm going out for a minute.

watchdog / weakness

3 ver, olhar
Watch where you're going!
Watch it! ☐ **Cuidado!**
Watch it! You almost cut my face!
watch out ☐ **Cuidado!**
Watch out! There's a red light!
watch out for ☐ **ter cuidado com**
Watch out for the dog – it bites.
Watch your language! ☐ **Olha a boca!**
watch your step (Ver **step**).
watchdog ['wotʃdog] *n.* ☐ cão de guarda
watchmaker ['wotʃmeikə] *n.* ☐ relojoeiro
watchman ['wotʃmən] *n.* (*pl.* **watchmen**) ☐ **vigia, guarda**
water¹ ['wo:tə] *n.* ☐ água
a glass of water. ♦ The water is not hot enough for a bath.
♦ The water is very deep here.
water² *v.* (**waters, watering, watered**)
1 aguar, molhar
to water the garden / plants.
2 lacrimejar
His eyes watered when he cut the onion.
watercolor ['wo:tə,kʌlə] *n. Amer.*, **watercolour** *Brit.*
☐ aquarela
to paint in watercolors.
waterfall ['wo:təfo:l] *n.* ☐ cascata, cachoeira
■ Ver **falls**.
watering can ['wo:təriŋ kan] *n.* ☐ regador
She watered the plants with a watering can.
watermelon ['wo:tə,melən] *n.* ☐ melancia
I cut a slice of watermelon.
waterproof ['wo:təpru:f] *adj.* ☐ à prova d'água, impermeável
a waterproof coat.
water resistant ['wo:tə rə'zistənt] *adj.* ☐ à prova d'água
This watch is water resistant.
water-skiing ['wo:tə ski:iŋ] *n.* ☐ esqui aquático
to go water-skiing.
wave¹ [weiv] *n.*
1 onda
high waves.
2 aceno
He asked me to come in with a wave of his hand.
3 ondas
radio waves. ♦ light waves.
wave² *v.* (**waves, waving, waved**)
1 acenar
I waved to him and he waved back. ♦ She waved goodbye to us.
2 acenar com
He waved a white handkerchief. ♦ to wave a flag.
3 tremular
The flags were waving in the wind.
wavy ['weivi] *adj.* ☐ ondulado
She has wavy hair. ♦ a wavy line.
wax [waks] *n.* ☐ **cera, parafina**
Wax is used for making candles.
way [wei] *n.*
1 caminho
Can you tell me the way to the airport? ♦ They lost their way in the forest. ♦ A bus blocked our way.
2 lado, direção
Go that way. ♦ They went the wrong way. ♦ She looked the other way.

3 modo, maneira
Is there a way to do it more quickly? ♦ You can solve the problem in different ways.
4 modo
They behaved in a very strange way.
5 percurso
It's a long way from home to the station. ♦ She ran all the way from school.
by the way ☐ **a propósito**
By the way, I saw David today.
feel your way (Ver **feel**).
give way
1 *Brit.* dar passagem
Give way to traffic coming from the right.
■ *Amer.* yield
2 ceder
They gave way to the workers' demands.
3 (= collapse) desmoronar
The bridge gave way.
in the way ☐ **no caminho**
We can't cross the bridge. There's a big truck in the way.
get in the way of ☐ **atrapalhar**
Don't let your hobbies get in the way of your studies.
make way for ☐ **dar passagem para**
Make way for the ambulance!
No way! ☐ **Nada disso!, De jeito nenhum!**
I need more money. – No way!
on the way, on your way (to) ☐ **a caminho**
They met him on the way to the station. ♦ Buy some bread on your way home.
one way or another ☐ **de uma forma ou de outra**
We'll get the money, one way or another.
the other way (a)round ☐ **ao contrário**
He always wears his hats the other way around.
way out
1 (= exit) saída
Where's the way out (of the building)?
2 saída
We must find a way out of this difficult situation.
way of life ☐ **modo de vida**
She likes the Spanish way of life.
WC [dʌblju:'si:] *n.* (= toilet) ☐ **toalete, banheiro**
we [wi:] *pron.* ☐ nós
We sold our house. ♦ We saw him, but he didn't see us.
♦ We don't need it.
weak [wi:k] *adj.*
1 fraco
The patient is too weak to get up. ♦ to feel weak. ♦ She has a weak heart.
2 fraco
a weak leader. ♦ a weak government.
3 fraco
weak pupils ♦ They are weak in mathematics.
4 fraco
weak tea / coffee.
■ antônimo: **strong**
weaken ['wi:kən] *v.* (**weakens, weakening, weakened**)
☐ enfraquecer
The heat weakened them. ♦ This patient is weakening, but that patient is getting stronger.
■ antônimo: **strengthen**
weakness ['wi:knis] *n.*

1 fraqueza
The enemy is showing signs of weakness.
- antônimo: **strength**

2 fraqueza
The plan has many weaknesses.

3 fraco
I have a weakness for sweets.

wealth [welθ] *n.* (= riches) □ **posses**
a family of great wealth (= a very rich family).

wealthy [ˈwelθi] *adj.* (= rich) □ **rico**
He is a very wealthy man. ◆ a wealthy country.

weapon [ˈwepən] *n.* (= arms) □ **arma**
Guns and swords are weapons.

wear[1] [weə] *v.* (**wears, wearing, wore, worn**)

1 usar
She was wearing a black dress. ◆ I never wear a hat / tie. ◆ I always wear socks / shoes.
- Ver **put on**.

2 usar
Do you wear glasses?

3 usar
He wears a gold ring. ◆ She was wearing earrings and a diamond necklace.

4 usar
to wear lipstick, makeup, perfume, etc.

wear off □ **passar**
The pain is wearing off. ◆ The effect of the injection wore off quickly.

wear out □ **desgastar-se, desgastar**
These shoes will wear out quickly. ◆ Don't use the mixer too long – you'll wear the motor out.

wear someone out □ **desgastar alguém**
You're wearing yourself out with hard work.

wear[2] *n.*

1 uso
clothes for everyday wear.

2 vestuário, roupa, traje
men's wear. ◆ women's wear. ◆ children's wear.

weary [ˈwiəri] *adj.* (= tired) □ **fatigado**
They were weary after the long walk.

weather [ˈweðə] *n.* □ **tempo**
We have fine weather here in spring. ◆ bad weather. ◆ cold / hot weather.

weather forecast *n.* □ **previsão do tempo**
What's the weather forecast for tomorrow?

weather forecaster *n.* □ **meteorologista**
According to the weather forecaster, it will snow tomorrow.

weatherman [ˈweðəmən] *n.* □ **meteorologista**
A weatherman studies and forecasts the weather.

weave [ˈwiːv] *v.* (**weaves, weaving, wove, woven**)

1 tecer
He weaves carpets. ◆ to weave cloth.

2 tecer
She wove a beautiful basket.

weaver [ˈwiːvə] *n.* □ **tecelão**

web [web] *n.*

1 (= cobweb) **teia**
Spiders use their web to catch insects.

2 (= **the Web**) **internet**
to surf the Web (= Internet sites).
- Ver **www**.

website [ˈwebsait] *n.* □ **website, site**
I surfed the Internet to find the website about the famous scientist.

we'd [wiːd] (mesmo que **we had; we would**)

wedding [ˈwediŋ] *n.* □ **casamento**
They invited me to their wedding.

wedding anniversary *n.* □ **aniversário de casamento**

wedding dress *n.* □ **vestido de noiva**

wedding ring *n.* □ **aliança**
- Ver **golden wedding; silver wedding**.

Wednesday [ˈwenzdi] *n.* □ **quarta-feira**
They arrived on Wednesday. ◆ They will come next Wednesday. ◆ last Wednesday. ◆ every Wednesday.

weed[1] [wiːd] *n.* □ **erva daninha**
The garden is full of weeds.

weed[2] *v.* (**weeds, weeding, weeded**) □ **capinar**
They are weeding the garden.

week [wiːk] *n.*

1 semana
I go to the beach once a week. ◆ We'll finish it next week. ◆ He bought it two weeks ago.

2 (= working week) **semana de trabalho**
We work a five-day week.

weekday [ˈwiːkdei] *n.* □ **dia de semana**
Most people work on weekdays.

weekend [ˌwiːkˈend] *n.* □ **fim de semana**
Brit. at the weekend. ◆ *Amer.* on the weekend. ◆ He stayed with us over the weekend.

weekly[1] [ˈwiːkli] *adj., adv.* □ **semanal, semanalmente**
This magazine is a weekly, not a monthly. ◆ a weekly visit. ◆ We visit her weekly.

weekly[2] *n.* (*pl.* **weeklies**) □ **semanário**

weep [wiːp] *v.* (**weeps, weeping, wept**) (= cry) □ **chorar**
The child wept when he lost his mother.

weigh [wei] *v.* (**weighs, weighing, weighed**)

1 pesar
He weighed (out) a kilo of rice (on the scales). ◆ They weigh your luggage (= baggage) at the airport.

2 pesar
How much do you weigh? – I weigh 52 kilos. ◆ The baby weighs 3 kilos.

weight [weit] *n.*

1 peso
What is the weight of this truck? ◆ His weight is 65 kg.

2 peso
a 250 gram weight.

lift weights □ **levantar peso**
He lifts weights to strengthen his muscles.

lose weight □ **perder peso**
She lost weight during her illness.

put on weight □ **ganhar peso**
You need to put on some weight – you're too thin.

weightlifting [ˈweitliftiŋ] *n.* □ **levantamento de peso**

weird [wiəd] *adj.* (= very strange) □ **estranho, esquisito**
a weird feeling. ◆ He's really weird. ◆ weird clothes.

welcome[1] [ˈwelkəm] *adj.* □ **bem-vindo**
a welcome visitor. ◆ a welcome change in the weather. ◆ She didn't feel welcome.

be welcome to □ **ficar à vontade para**
You're welcome to join us.

make someone welcome □ **fazer alguém se sentir à vontade**
They are important guests, so try to make them welcome.

welcome / what

Welcome (to) □ **Bem-vindo (a)**
Welcome home! ◆ Welcome to Japan.
You're welcome □ **De nada**
Thank you for the ride. – You're welcome.
welcome² *v.* (**welcomes, welcoming, welcomed**)
1 receber
She welcomed us with a smile.
2 acolher
He always welcomes new ideas.
welcome³ *n.* □ **acolhida**
They gave us a warm welcome.
welfare ['welfeə] *n.* □ **bem-estar, assistência social**
We must think of the child's welfare. ◆ the welfare services.
well¹ [wel] *adj.* (**better, best**) □ **bem**
How are you? – I'm very well, thank you. ◆ He looks well (= in good health). ◆ a well-child clinic.
■ antônimo: **ill, sick**
get well (= recover) □ **de recuperação, de melhoras**
You'll stay in hospital until you get well. ◆ I am sending a get-well card to my friend in the hospital.
well² *adv.* (**better, best**)
1 bem
He behaved well. ◆ She plays the piano very well.
■ antônimo: **badly**
2 bem
Shake the bottle well before use. ◆ I remember it very well.
3 bem
I went to bed well before midnight. ◆ He is well over fifty.
as well □ **também**
I read that book as well.
as well as (= and also) □ **bem como, e também**
He plays tennis as well as football.
■ Compare:
He plays tennis as well as he plays football.
as well as I can □ **o melhor que eu posso**
I'm doing as well as I can. (= I'm doing my best.)
do well □ **ir bem**
She is doing well at / in school. ◆ He did well in / on the exam.
may / might as well □ **é / seria uma boa ideia**
We have nothing else to do. We might as well finish what we started.
Well done! □ **Muito bem!**
I passed the test! – Well done!
well³ *excl.*
1 bem, bom
Well, they did it!
■ used to show surprise.
2 bem, bom
Well, what did I tell you?
■ used when expecting some comment.
3 bem, bom
What do you think? – Well, I'm not really sure.
■ used to express doubt, uncertainty, etc.
4 então
Well, the next day he came again.
■ used when continuing a story.
5 bem, bom
Well, I must go now.
■ used when ending a conversation

well⁴ *n.* □ **poço**
They get the water from wells. ◆ an oil well. ◆ to dig a well.
we'll [wi:l] (mesmo que **we will**)
well-known [,wel'noun] *adj.* (= famous) □ **conhecido**
a well-known architect.
■ antônimo: **unknown**
well known (= familiar) □ **conhecido, familiar**
Her opinions are well known.
well-off [,wel'of] *adj.* (= rich) □ **bem de vida**
His family is very well-off.
well-to-do [,weltə'du:] *adj.* (= rich) □ **bem de vida**
They used to be poor, but now they are well-to-do.
went [went] *v.* (Ver **go**).
wept [wept] *v.* (Ver **weep**).
were [wɔː, wə] *v.* (Ver **be**).
we're [wiə] (mesmo que **we are**).
weren't ['wɔːnt] (mesmo que **were not**).
west¹ [west] *adj.* □ **do oeste, ocidental, zona oeste**
a west wind. ◆ the west bank of the river. ◆ West London.
west² *adv.* □ **para o oeste**
to travel / sail west.
west of □ **a oeste de**
six km west of the city.
west³ *n.* □ **oeste**
from the west. ◆ in the west of the country.
the West □ **o Ocidente**
The West includes North America and many European countries.
western¹ ['westən] *adj.* □ **ocidental**
western Europe / Argentina. ◆ western parts of the country.
western² *n.* □ **faroeste, bangue-bangue**
A western is a film about cowboys and Indians in the USA.
wet¹ [wet] *adj.* (**wetter, wettest**)
1 molhado
Be careful! The floor is wet. ◆ wet hands. ◆ My shirt is wet.
2 fresco
The paint is still wet.
3 (= rainy) **úmido**
a wet day. ◆ wet weather.
■ antônimo: **dry**
get wet □ **molhar-se**
Take an umbrella if you don't want to get wet.
wet² *v.* (**wets, wetting, wetted** or **wet**)
1 molhar
He wet his hair and combed it.
2 molhar
He still wets (the bed).
we've [wi:v] (mesmo que **have**).
whale [weil] *n.* □ **baleia**
what¹ [wot] *pron., adj.*
1 o que, qual
What do you want? ◆ What's your name? ◆ What happened?
2 que, qual
What size is it? ◆ What kind of books do you like?
■ Ver **which**.
3 o que
He didn't know what to do. ◆ I don't know what happened.
4 que
What a big egg! ◆ What a lovely evening!

What time...?
1 Que horas...?
What time is it? – It's 5 o'clock.
2 A que horas...?
What time did you arrive?
What about...? (= How about...?) □ **Que tal...?**
What about going for a swim? ◆ What about a cold drink?
What... for?
1 Por que...?
What did you do that for? (= Why did you do that?)
2 Para que...?
What do you need it for?
3 Para que...?
What's this tool for?
What is... like? □ **Como... é?**
What is she like? – Well, she is tall, beautiful and very intelligent.
What's the matter? □ **O que foi?, Qual o problema?**
What's the matter? Don't you feel well? ◆ What's the matter with the TV? *Amer.*
What's up? □ **E aí?**
What's up, guys?
What² *excl.*
1 (= Pardon?, Sorry?) □ **Quê?, O quê?**
What? I can't hear you!
2 Quê?, O quê?
Hey, Johnny! – What?
3 Quê?, O quê?
They got married. – What?! When?
whatever¹ [wot'evə] *adj.* □ **qualquer**
He will buy whatever goods you want to sell.
whatever² *pron., adv.*
1 tudo, qualquer coisa
They ate whatever they found there. ◆ I'll do whatever you tell me to do.
2 seja qual for, seja o que for
She will buy it, whatever the price. ◆ Whatever happens, don't tell her.
3 o que
Whatever do you mean by that remark?
4 em absoluto
Do you have questions? – None whatever.
what's [wots] (mesmo que **what is; what has**)
wheat [wi:t] *n.* □ **trigo**
to grow wheat. ◆ to grind wheat into flour.
wheel [wi:l] *n.*
1 roda
Cars, bicycles and planes have wheels.
2 (= **steering-wheel**) □ **volante**
Don't take your hands off the wheel!
at the wheel; behind the wheel □ **no volante**
I feel safe when she is behind the wheel (= when she is driving).
wheelbarrow ['wi:lbarou] *n.* □ **carrinho de mão**
wheelchair ['wi:ltʃeə] *n.* □ **cadeira de rodas**
when¹ [wen] *adv.*
1 quando
When did you see her? ◆ When will she come? ◆ I don't know when it happened.
2 quando
It happened last month, when we were on holiday. ◆ Tuesday is the day when I go shopping.

when² *conj.* □ **quando**
I saw him when he arrived. ◆ Tell him to call me when you see him.
■ **when you see him** (*not* 'when you will see him').
whenever [wen'evə] *conj.*
1 sempre que, quando
Come whenever you want.
2 sempre que, quando
Whenever I think about it, I get angry.
where¹ [weə] *adv.*
1 onde, por onde
Where is she? ◆ Where do you live? ◆ I don't know where to start.
2 onde, aonde
Where are you going?
3 onde
This is the place where we met.
where² *conj.*
1 onde
You'll find the keys where you put them.
2 (= wherever) **onde**
Put it where you like.
whereas [weər'az] *conj.* □ **ao passo que**
She likes dogs, whereas I like cats.
wherever [weər'evə] *adv., conj.* □ **onde (quer que)**
Put it wherever you like. ◆ He follows me wherever I go.
whether ['weðə] *conj.* (= if) **se**
I don't know whether it's possible. ◆ She can't decide whether to stay or to go.
whether... or not □ **quer... quer não, se... ou não**
You must do it whether you like it or not. ◆ I can't decide whether to go or not. (= I can't decide whether or not to go.)
which [witʃ] *adv., pron.*
1 qual, quais
Which is your book – this one or that one? ◆ Which of the books is yours? ◆ Which way did he go?
■ Compare:
  What color / colour is the door?
  Which color / colour do you prefer – red or green?
2 qual
Which of you knows the answer?
■ Compare:
  Who knows the answer?
3 (= that) **que**
Here is the book (which) you gave me. ◆ Can you see the cat which is lying there?
4 qual
This is the box in which he hid the key ◆ The house about which we talked costs a lot.
5 que, o qual
The leaves, which were green, became brown.
■ **that** cannot be used instead of **which** in meanings 4 and 5 (i.e. **that** cannot be used after a preposition or a comma).
whichever [witʃ'evə] *adj., pron.* □ **qual**
Take whichever pen you want. ◆ Take whichever is less expensive.
while¹ [wail] *conj.*
1 (= during the time that) **enquanto**
It happened while we were out.
2 (= although) **embora**
While we understand your difficulties, we can't help you.

3 (= whereas) **ao passo que**
She likes dogs, while I like cats.
while² *n.* □ **tempo, momento**
Let's rest here for a while. ◆ The show will start in a short while.
■ Ver **worthwhile**.
■ Compare:
It's not worth my while. It's not worthwhile for me.
whine [wain] *v.* (**whines, whining, whined**)
1 choramingar
The dog is whining outside the door.
2 resmungar, choramingar
Stop whining – you'll get your present!
whip¹ [wip] *n.* □ **chicote**
whip² *v.* (**whips, whipping, whipped**)
1 chicotear
He whipped the horse.
2 bater
to whip egg whites.
whipped cream ['wipt kri:m] *n.* □ **creme batido**
whirl [wə:l] *v.* (**whirls, whirling, whirled**) □ **rodopiar**
The kite whirled round and round in the wind.
whirlpool ['wə:lpu:l] *n.* □ **redemoinho**
whisk¹ [wisk] *v.* (**whisks, whisking, whisked**) □ **bater**
to whisk egg whites.
whisk² *n.* □ **batedeira, batedor**
an electric whisk.
whisker ['wiskə] *n.* □ **bigode**
Cats and rats have whiskers.
whisper¹ ['wispə] *n.* □ **sussurro**
I can hear whispers behind the door. ◆ He said it in a whisper.
whisper² *v.* (**whispers, whispering, whispered**) □ **sussurrar**
Why are you whispering? No one can hear us.
whistle¹ ['wisl] *n.*
1 apito
The referee blew his whistle.
2 assovio, assobio
He gave a whistle when he saw the beautiful view.
whistle² *v.* (**whistles, whistling, whistled**) □ **assoviar, assobiar**
Can you whistle? ◆ The kettle is whistling.
white¹ [wait] *adj.*
1 branco
a white horse. ◆ white walls. ◆ white hair. ◆ They painted the walls white.
2 branco
black people and white people.
3 branco
white coffee (= coffee with milk).
4 branco, refinado
white bread. ◆ white sugar. ◆ white rice.
white² *n.*
1 branco
The bride was dressed in white.
2 (*pl.* **whites**) **brancos**
equal rights for blacks and whites.
3 (*pl.* **whites**) **clara**
the white of an egg.
whiz [wiz] *v.* (mesmo que **whizz**) □ **passar em alta velocidade**
A bullet whizzed by his head.

who [hu:] *pron.*
1 quem
Who are you? ◆ Who knows the answer? ◆ Tell me who did it.
2 quem
Who did you give it to? ◆ Who are you talking about?
■ Ver **whom**.
3 (= that) **que**
That is the man who sold me the car.
4 que
Our neighbour, who is a very nice woman, is a teacher.
who'd [hu:d] (mesmo que **who had / would**).
whoever [hu:'evə] *pron.*
1 quem (quer que)
Whoever finds the key must bring it here immediately.
2 quem
Whoever is that man?
whole¹ [houl] *adj.* □ **todo, inteiro**
I read the whole book in two hours. ◆ a whole apple. ◆ We stayed there for a whole week.
whole² *n.*
1 o tempo todo
I spent the whole of the morning in the kitchen.
2 todo
Two halves make a whole.
on the whole □ **como um todo, no conjunto**
The plan is good, on the whole.
who'll [hu:l] (mesmo que **who will**).
whom [hu:m] *pron.*
1 quem
Whom are you meeting today? ◆ To whom did you send it?
■ It is more usual to say:
Who are you meeting today?
Who did you send it to?
2 que
He is the man (whom) you wanted to see. ◆ They are the people with whom we spent the weekend. ◆ My cousin, whom you saw yesterday, is a banker.
■ **whom** may be left out except after a preposition or a comma.
who're [hu:ə] (mesmo que **who are; who were**).
who's [hu:z] (mesmo que **who is; who has**).
whose [hu:z] *adj., pron.*
1 de quem
Whose bag is this? (or: Whose is this bag?). ◆ In whose room did you find it?
2 cujo, cujos
That's the girl whose father is a writer. ◆ a village whose name is very funny.
who've [hu:v] (mesmo que **who have**).
why [wai] *adv.* □ **Por que...?, Por quê?**
Why did he take it? ◆ Why didn't you tell me? ◆ Why are you sitting in the dark? ◆ I want to wait here. – Why? ◆ Everyone knows why she left.
that's why □ **é por isso (que)**
She wasn't happy here. That's why she left.
why not
1 Por que não...?
Why not tell her the truth?
2 Por que não?
Would you like to go for a swim? – Yes, why not?

wicked ['wikid] *adj.* □ **malvado, perverso**
a wicked witch.

wickedly ['wikidli] *adv.* □ **malvadamente, perversamente**

wickedness ['wikidnis] *n.* □ **maldade, perversidade**

wide¹ [waid] *adj.*
1 largo
a wide river. ◆ wide streets.
■ antônimo: **narrow**
2 de largura
The road is ten metres wide.
3 vasto
She has a wide knowledge of computers.
■ Ver **wide range**.
How wide...? □ **O quão largo...?**
How wide is the door?

wide² *adv.* □ **muito, bem**
Open your eyes wide.

wide apart □ **bem aberto**
He stood with his legs wide apart.

wide awake □ **totalmente acordado**
He is wide awake.

wide open □ **escancarado**
The door was wide open.

widen ['waidn] *v.* (**widens, widening, widened**) □ **alargar-se, alargar**
The road widens here. ◆ We must widen the road (= make it wider).

widespread ['waidspred] *adj.*
1 disseminado
Crime is widespread in this city.
2 espalhado
The fire caused widespread damage.

widow ['widou] *n.* □ **viúva**

widower ['widouə] *n.* □ **viúvo**

width [widθ] *n.* □ **largura**
The room is six metres in width. ◆ Measure the length and width of the floor. ◆ What is the width? (= How wide is it?)

wife [waif] *n.* (*pl.* **wives**) □ **esposa**
My wife says that I'm a good husband.

wig [wig] *n.* □ **peruca**

wild [waild] *adj.*
1 silvestre, selvagem
wild flowers. ◆ wild animals. ◆ a wild cat.
2 furioso, louco
The crowd was wild with excitement. ◆ She was wild with anger.
3 tempestuoso
a wild night (= a stormy night).
4 louco, extravagante
a wild guess. ◆ a wild idea.

wildlife ['waildlaif] *n.* □ **vida selvagem**
to protect the wildlife in the jungles.

wildlife park *n.* □ **reserva natural**

will¹ [wil] *v.*
1 usado para formar o futuro do presente dos verbos
I'll (= I will) send it tomorrow. ◆ It'll be ready next week. ◆ Will you need me tomorrow?
■ *Brit.* also 'I / we **shall**'
2 usado para formar o futuro do presente dos verbos
She will help you for free. ◆ I won't (= will not) do it!
3 usado para fazer um pedido educadamente
Will you help me, please? ◆ Close the door, will you?

will have to □ **terei / terá / teremos / terão de**
You'll have to wait for him.

will² *n.*
1 força de vontade
She has a strong will.
2 vontade
I went with them against my will. (= They forced me to go with them.)
3 testamento
He made his won a month before he died. ◆ She left us the house in her will.
of your own free will □ **por livre e espontânea vontade**
He came of his own free will.

willing ['wiliŋ] *adj.* □ **disposto**
She is willing to help.

willingly ['wiliŋli] *adv.* □ **de boa vontade, de bom grado**
He willingly agreed to come with us.

willingness ['wiliŋnis] *n.* □ **disposição, boa vontade**

win¹ [win] *n.* □ **vitória**
The team had two wins and two defeats last month.

win² *v.* (**wins, winning, won**)
1 vencer, ganhar
They won the war. ◆ I'm sure she will win the race. ◆ Who won the elections?
■ Compare:
France won the game against Brazil.
France beat Brazil.
2 ganhar
He won a gold medal in the high jump. ◆ Who won the (first) prize?

wind¹ [wind] *n.* □ **vento**
There's a cold wind blowing outside.

wind² *v.* (**winds, winding, wound**)
1 serpentear
The river winds through the jungle.
2 colocar, envolver
I wound a bandage around her finger.
3 dar corda (em)
Don't forget to wind (up) the alarm clock.
wind down / up (a car window) □ **baixar / erguer, abrir / fechar**
The driver wound the window down.
■ *Amer.* **roll down / up**

winding ['waindiŋ] *adj.* □ **sinuoso**
a long and winding road.

windmill ['winmil] *n.* □ **moinho de vento**

window ['windou] *n.* □ **janela**
Open the window, please. ◆ Will you close the window, please? ◆ to look through the window.
■ Ver **shop-window**.

windowpane ['windoupein] *n.* □ **vidraça**

windowsill ['windousil] *n.* □ **parapeito, peitoril**

window-shopping ['windou'ʃɔpiŋ] *n.* □ **ver vitrines**
I'm not going to buy anything, I just want to go window-shopping.

windscreen ['windouskri:n] *n.* *Brit.* □ **para-brisa**

windscreen wiper *n.* □ **limpador de para-brisa**

windshield ['windʃi:ld] *n.* *Amer.* □ **para-brisa**

windshield wiper *n.* □ **limpador de para-brisa**

windsurfer ['windsə:fə] *n.*
1 windsurfista
He is a good windsurfer.

2 (= sailboard) **prancha de windsurfe**
windsurfing ['winds:fiŋ] *n.* □ **windsurfe**
windy ['windi] *adj.* (**windier, windiest**) □ **ventoso**
 windy weather. ◆ a windy day.
wine [wain] *n.* □ **vinho**
 a glass of red wine. ◆ a wine glass.
wing [wiŋ] *n.* □ **asa**
 Birds, butterflies and flies have wings. ◆ the plane's wings.
wink¹ [wiŋk] *n.* □ **piscada, piscadela**
 He gave me a wink.
wink² *v.* (**winks, winking, winked**) □ **piscar**
 He winked at me to show that he was joking.
winner ['winə] *n.* □ **vencedor**
 The winner will get a prize of $25,000. ◆ the winner of the match.

 ■ antônimo: **loser**

winning ['winiŋ] *adj.* □ **vencedor**
 the winning team. ◆ the winning ticket.
winter ['wintə] *n.* □ **inverno**
 It rains a lot here in (the) winter. ◆ It was very cold last winter. ◆ a typical winter's day.

 ■ The adjective is **wintry**.

wintry ['wintri] *adj.* □ **frio, de inverno**
 wintry weather.
wipe¹ [waip] *n.* □ **passada de pano**
 Give the table a quick wipe.
wipe² *v.* (**wipes, wiping, wiped**)
 1 passar um pano, enxugar
 Wipe the table with this cloth. ◆ to wipe the floor. ◆ He wiped his hands on a towel.
 2 enxugar
 She wiped the tears from her eyes.
wipe off □ **apagar**
 Wipe that writing off the blackboard.
wipe out □ **devastar**
 The bombing wiped out the whole village.
wipe up □ **enxugar**
 I wiped up the water on the floor.
wire ['waiə] *n.*
 1 fio, arame
 an electric wire. ◆ a wire fence.
 2 (= telegram) *Amer.* **telegrama**
 Send them a wire before you come.
barbed wire *n.* □ **arame farpado**
wireless ['waiəlis] *n.*
 1 rádio
 The old word for 'radio' is 'wireless'.
 2 sem fio
 Mobile phones work by wireless.
wisdom ['wizdəm] *n.* □ **sabedoria**
 a man of great wisdom.
wise [waiz] *adj.* □ **sábio**
 a wise old man. ◆ She is a very wise woman. ◆ It was a wise decision.
wisely ['waizli] *adv.* □ **sabiamente**
 She wisely refused to answer.
wish¹ [wiʃ] *v.* (**wishes, wishing, wished**)
 1 querer, desejar
 Where is she? – I wish I knew. ◆ I wish I could come, but I'm very busy. ◆ I wish I was rich.

 ■ Use with a verb in the past: I wish I knew the answer (*not* 'I know').

 2 desejar
 Wish me luck. ◆ I wish you a Happy New Year.
 3 querer
 I wish to speak to the manager. ◆ I'll go with you if you wish.
wish for □ **desejar**
 All I wish for is good health.
wish² *n.*
 1 desejo, pedido
 All his wishes came true.
 2 desejo
 I have no wish to see him.
best wishes □ **melhores votos**
 Please send him my best wishes. ◆ She ended her letter with 'Best wishes'.
make a wish □ **fazer um pedido**
 He closed his eyes and made a wish.
wit [wit] *n.* □ **sagacidade, presença de espírito**
 His books are full of amusing stories and wit.
witch [witʃ] *n.* □ **bruxa**
 The witch put a magic spell on the prince.
witchcraft ['witʃkra:ft] *n.* □ **bruxaria**
witch doctor ['witʃ ,doktə] *n.* □ **feiticeiro, pajé**
with [wið] *prep.*
 1 com
 He came with his son. ◆ Mix it with the flour. ◆ I agree with you.
 2 com
 a woman with white hair. ◆ a wall with a window.
 3 com
 Break it with a hammer. ◆ The mountain was covered with snow.
 4 com
 He argued with his sister. ◆ They are competing with us. ◆ France is playing with (= against) Spain.
 5 com
 The teacher is pleased with them. ◆ She is angry with me.
 6 de
 He was shaking with fear.
with no (= without any) □ **sem**
 a small room, with no windows.

 ■ Ver **with pleasure; with your permission**.

withdraw [wið'drɔ:] *v.* (**withdraws, withdrawing, withdrew, withdrawn**)
 1 retirar
 I withdrew all the money from my bank account.
 2 bater em retirada
 The army withdrew when the enemy approached.

 ■ Compare **retreat**:
  retreat = after a battle.

 3 retirar-se
 She wants to withdraw from the race.

 ■ The noun is **withdrawal**.

wither ['wiðə] *v.* (**withers, withering, withered**) □ **murchar**
 The flowers withered in the heat.
within [wi'ðin] *prep.*
 1 dentro de
 They can finish the job within two days. ◆ I'll be back within an hour.
 2 a
 The school is within two kilometers / kilometres of home.

3 (= inside) **dentro**
within the building. • from within the house.
within reach (Ver **reach**).
without [wi'ðaut] *prep.*
1 sem
One coffee, without milk.
2 sem
She left without saying goodbye.
3 sem
Don't go without me.
do without □ **passar sem, ficar sem**
I can't do without a car.
witness[1] ['witnis] *n.*
1 testemunha
The witness testified (in court).
2 testemunha
There were no witnesses to the accident.
witness[2] *v.* (**witnesses, witnessing, witnessed**) □ **testemunhar**
They witnessed the tragic accident.
witty ['witi] *adj.* (**wittier, wittiest**) □ **sagaz, espirituoso**
a witty (= amusing) remark. • a witty person.
wives [waivz] *n.* (*plural of* **wife**).
wizard ['wizəd] *n.* □ **mago**
■ Compare **magician; witch**.
wobble ['wobl] *v.* (**wobbles, wobbling, wobbled**) □ **bambear, balançar**
It wobbled like jelly. • Stop wobbling the table!
wobbly ['wobli] *adj.* □ **bambo**
a wobbly table.
woke [wouk] *v.* (Ver **wake**).
woken ['woukən] *v.* (Ver **wake**).
wolf [wulf] *n.* (*pl.* **wolves**) □ **lobo**
woman ['wumən] *n.* (*pl.* **women**)
1 mulher
men, women and children. • a young woman. • women's clothes.
2 mulher
a woman driver. • a woman soldier. • a woman doctor.
■ Ver **businesswoman; chairwoman; policewoman**.
womanhood ['wumənhud] *n.* □ **maturidade feminina**
to reach womanhood.
■ Ver **manhood; childhood**.
won [wʌn] *v.* (Ver **win**).
wonder[1] ['wʌndə] *v.* (**wonders, wondering, wondered**) □ **conjeturar, imaginar**
He began to wonder what was happening there.
I wonder where / how... □ **Pergunto a mim mesmo onde / como...**
I wonder what he wants. • I wonder where she is.
I wonder if □ **Será que...?**
I wonder if you could help me.
wonder[2] ['wʌndə] *n.*
1 maravilhado
We looked in wonder at the pyramids.
2 milagre, maravilha
It's a wonder that no one was killed. • the wonders of modern technology
no wonder □ **não é à toa que, não é de admirar que**
It's a lovely dog. No wonder they want to keep it.
wonderful ['wʌndəful] *adj.* □ **maravilhoso**
What a wonderful feeling! • We had a wonderful time. • He is wonderful.

wonderfully ['wʌndəfuli] *adv.* □ **maravilhosamente**
won't [wount] (mesmo que **will not**).
wood [wud] *n.*
1 madeira
The table is made of wood.
2 lenha
We need more wood for the fire.
wood(s) *n.* □ **bosque**
They went for a walk in the woods.
wooden ['wudn] *adj.* □ **de pau, de madeira**
a wooden spoon. • wooden furniture.
wool [wul] *n.* □ **lã**
lamb's wool. • a ball of wool (for knitting). • This sweater is made of wool.
woolen ['wulin] *adj. Amer.,* **woollen** *Brit.* □ **de lã**
woolen socks. • woolen gloves.
woolly ['wuli] *adj. Amer.,* **wooly** □ **de lã**
a woolly hat.
word [wɜːd] *n.*
1 palavra
Learn the new words. • What's the meaning of this word? • Write a composition of 250 words.
2 (= promise) **palavra**
I give you my word that I won't tell anyone.
have a word with □ **dar uma palavrinha com**
Can I have a word with you?
in other words □ **em outras palavras**
The film is too long. – In other words you didn't like it.
keep your word □ **manter sua palavra**
She kept her word and came to see me.
not say a word □ **não dizer uma palavra**
He was angry, but he didn't say a word.
take someone's word for it □ **acreditar no que alguém diz**
It's hard to believe that they will come, but I'll take your word for it.
word for word □ **palavra por palavra**
It's not a good idea to translate idioms word for word. • Tell me what she said word for word.
word processor ['wɜːd 'prousəsə] *n.* □ **processador de texto**
Word processors are used today instead of typewriters.
wore [wɔː] *v.* (Ver **wear**).
work[1] [wɜːk] *n.*
1 trabalho
We have a lot of work to do. • hard work. • physical work.
2 trabalho
What time do you finish work? • He is looking for work (= a job). • We can meet after work.
3 trabalho
She is not here – she is at work. • I usually go to work by bus.
4 trabalho
Your work is not good enough – you must try harder.
5 obra
a work of art. • the works of Shakespeare.
works *n.*
1 sistema
iron works. • gas works.
2 obras
public works (= building roads, etc.).
at work
1 no trabalho
Please phone me at work.

2 ocupado
He is at work on a new project.
get to work □ trabalhar
Come on! Let's get to work – we don't have much time.
out of work □ sem trabalho, desempregado
She is looking for a job now that she is out of work.
work² v. (works, working, worked)
1 trabalhar
She works five days a week. ◆ He works for / at a computer company. ◆ I worked hard on this plan.
2 funcionar, operar
How does this machine work? ◆ The phone doesn't work (= isn't working). ◆ He showed me how to work (= operate) the dishwasher.
3 funcionar, dar certo
Do you think the plan will work?
work out
1 dar certo
I hope everything will work out in the end. ◆ Our plan didn't work out.
2 malhar
I work out in the gym twice a week.
work something out
1 bolar
to work out a plan. ◆ to work out a solution. ◆ to work out the details of the plan.
2 (= solve) **resolver**
to work out a problem.
3 calcular
I worked out the cost of the trip.
workbook ['wɔːkbuk] *n.* □ **livro de exercícios**
worker ['wɔːkə] *n.* □ **trabalhador, funcionário**
factory workers. ◆ office workers. ◆ a skilled worker.
working ['wɔːkiŋ] *adj.*
1 de trabalho, horário de expediente
The working conditions are not good enough. ◆ working hours. ◆ working clothes.
2 que trabalha
a working mother.
working class ['wɔːkiŋ klɑːs] *n., adj.* □ **classe operária**
a working-class district. ◆ This politician comes from the working class.
■ **working-class** (with a hyphen) before a noun.
■ Compare **upper class, middle class**.
workman ['wɔːkmən] *n.* (*pl.* **workmen**) (= worker) □ **operário**
We need more workmen to finish the building quickly.
workout ['wɔːkaut] *n.* □ **ginástica, malhação**
workshop ['wɔːkʃop] *n.*
1 oficina
He built this machine in his workshop.
2 oficina
a workshop on reading skills.
world [wɔːld] *n.*
1 mundo
the highest mountain in the world. ◆ people from all over the world. ◆ We went on a trip around the world.
2 mundo
the world of fashion. ◆ the scientific world. ◆ the animal world. ◆ the plant world.
think the world of □ **achar alguém o máximo**
He thinks the world of you.

world champion *n.* □ **campeão mundial**
the world chess champion.
World Cup *n.* □ **Copa do Mundo**
world power *n.* □ **potência mundial**
world record *n.* □ **recorde mundial**
She broke the world record in the long jump.
world war *n.* □ **guerra mundial**
The Second World War ended in 1945.
world-famous ['wɔːldfeiməs] *adj.* □ **mundialmente famoso**
a world-famous actor.
worldwide ['wɔːldwaid] *adj., adv.* □ **mundial, mundialmente**
a worldwide problem. ◆ Their cars are sold worldwide. ◆ the worldwide web (= www).
worm [wɔːm] *n.* □ **verme**
There is a worm in the apple.
worn [wɔːn] *v.* (Ver **wear**).
worn-out ['wɔːn'aut] *adj.*
1 gasto
worn-out shoes.
2 (= exhausted) **exausto**
He is wornout after 18 hours of work.
worried ['wʌrid] *adj.* □ **preocupado**
He is worried about your health. ◆ I'm not worried – she'll be all right.
get worried □ **ficar preocupado**
I got worried when you didn't call.
worry¹ ['wʌri] *v.* (**worries, worrying, worried**)
1 preocupar-se
Don't worry! I know what to do. ◆ There is nothing to worry about. ◆ She worries when I get home late.
2 preocupar
What's worrying you? ◆ It worries me when you come home late.
worry² *n.*
1 preocupação
You could see the worry on their faces.
2 (*pl.* **worries**) **preocupação**
I have a lot of worries. ◆ That's not my biggest worry.
worrying ['wʌriiŋ] *adj.* □ **preocupante**
This new situation is worrying. ◆ a worrying problem.
worse¹ [wɔːs] *adj.* (**bad, worse, worst**)
1 pior
Is the situation now better or worse? ◆ His plan is bad, but yours is even worse. ◆ Your grammar is worse than mine.
2 pior
I feel worse today. ◆ The patient is worse today.
get worse □ **ficar pior, piorar**
The problem is getting worse. ◆ The patient's condition got worse.
worse² *adv.* (**badly, worse, worst**) □ **pior**
She sings worse than I do.
worship¹ ['wɔːʃip] *n.* □ **culto, adoração**
a place of worship (= church, mosque, synagogue, temple, etc.).
worship² *v.* (**worships, worshiping, worshiped, worshipping, worshipped**)
1 adorar
to worship God. ◆ Muslims worship in a mosque.
2 adorar
She worships her father / pop singers.

worshiper [ˈwɔːʃipə] *n. Amer.*, **worshipper** *Brit.* □ **adorador**
The worshippers filled the church.

worst¹ [wɔːst] *adj.* (**bad, worse, worst**) □ **pior**
He is the worst player in the team.

worst² *adv.* (**badly, worse, worst**) □ **pior**
I sang badly, but he sang worst of all.

worst³ *n.*
the worst □ **o pior, os piores**
We all played badly, but you were the worst. ◆ A pessimist always expects the worst.
at worst □ **na pior das hipóteses**
At worst you'll have to do it again.
if (the) worst comes to (the) worst □ **se acontecer o pior**
If the worst comes to the worst, we can always sell the house.

worth¹ [wɔːθ] *adj.*
1 valer
This watch is worth $1,000.
2 ser digno de, valer a pena
The book is worth reading. ◆ It's not worth the trouble (to fix that radio).
it's worth a try □ **vale a pena tentar**
The chance of winning isn't good, but it's worth a try.
it's worth it □ **vale a pena**
I studied hard for the exam, but it was worth it.

worth² *n.*
1 valor
The jewels are of great worth.
2 em
They sold $20,000 worth of jewels.
■ Ver **worthwhile**.

worthless [ˈwɔːθlis] *adj.* □ **inútil**
This painting is worthless. ◆ a worthless exercise.

worthwhile [wɔːθˈwail] *adj.* □ **louvável, que vale a pena**
The effort was worthwhile, because I got the job.
■ Compare:
It's not worthwhile.
It's not worth our while.

worthy [ˈwɔːði] *adj.* □ **merecedor**
She is worthy of the prize.

would [wud] *v.*
1 usado para formar o futuro do pretérito dos verbos
I knew that she would come.
■ Compare:
He said, 'I will stay another day'.
He said that he would stay another day.
2 usado em orações condicionais
What would you do if you won a million dollars? ◆ If I were you, I wouldn't (= would not) go.
3 querer
I warned him, but he wouldn't listen.
4 (= used to) ter o costume de
When we were young, we would play for hours on the beach.
would like; 'd like □ **gostaria/gostaríamos/gostariam de**
I'd like to speak to the manager. ◆ Would you like a cold drink?
Would you...? □ **usado para fazer um pedido educadamente**
Would you close the door, please? ◆ Would you mind waiting outside?

wouldn't [ˈwudənt] (mesmo que **would not**)
would've [ˈwudəv] (mesmo que **would have**)
wound¹ [waund] *v.* (Ver **wind²**).
wound² [wuːnd] *n.* □ **ferimento**
a knife wound. ◆ a bullet wound. ◆ The nurse bandaged his wound.
wound³ [wuːnd] *v.* (**wounds, wounding, wounded**) □ **ferir**
The bullet wounded her in the arm. ◆ The robber wounded the guard.
be wounded □ **ser ferido**
He was seriously wounded in the war.
■ Compare:
be wounded (by a knife, gun, etc.).
be injured (in an accident, a game, etc.).

wounded [ˈwuːndid] *adj.* □ **ferido**
a wounded soldier.
the wounded □ **os feridos**
The wounded were taken to hospital.

wove [wouv] *v.* (Ver **weave**).
woven [ˈwouvən] *v.* (Ver **weave**).
wow [wau] *excl.* □ **uau!**
Wow! Look at his muscles!

wrap [rap] *v.* (**wraps, wrapping, wrapped**) □ **embrulhar, enrolar-se**
She wrapped the parcel in brown paper. ◆ He wrapped himself in a blanket.
wrap something round / around □ **colocar algo em volta de**
Wrap the scarf around your neck.
wrap something up □ **embrulhar**
She wrapped up the presents.

wrapper [ˈrapə] *n.* □ **invólucro**
a candy wrapper. ◆ a brown paper wrapper.

wrapping [ˈrapiŋ] *n.* (= **wrapper**) □ **invólucro**
He took the present out of its wrapping. ◆ The new chairs were still in plastic wrappings.

wrapping paper [ˈrapiŋ ˈpeipə] *n.* □ **papel de embrulho**

wreath [riːθ] *n.* □ **guirlanda**
I put the wreath on the grave.

wreck¹ [rek] *n.* □ **ruínas, destroços, escombros**
Divers found a treasure in the wreck. ◆ a car wreck. ◆ the wreck of the plane.
■ Ver **shipwreck**.

wreck² *v.* (**wrecks, wrecking, wrecked**) □ **destroçar, destruir**
The thieves wrecked my car.
be wrecked □ **ser destroçado**
The ship was wrecked on rocks.

wreckage [ˈrekidʒ] *n.* □ **destroços**
They are looking for survivors in the wreckage of the plane.

wrench [rentʃ] *n. Amer.* □ **chave-inglesa**
to tighten a bolt with a wrench.
■ *Brit.* **spanner**.

wrestle [ˈresl] *v.* (**wrestles, wrestling, wrestled**) □ **lutar**
You'll see him wrestling with the champion on TV tonight.

wrestler [ˈreslə] *n.* □ **lutador**
wrestling [ˈresliŋ] *n.* □ **luta**
wretched [ˈretʃid] *adj.* (= **miserable**) □ **arrasado, infeliz**
He feels wretched because he is very lonely.
wriggle [ˈrigl] *v.* (**wriggles, wriggling, wriggled**) □ **remexer-se, contorcer-se**

Stop wriggling and sit still! ◆ The dancer wriggled like a snake.

wring [riŋ] *v.* (**wrings, wringing, wrung**)
wring something out □ **torcer**
He wrung (out) the wet towel. ◆ She wrung the water (out) from the shirt.

wrinkle ['riŋkl] *n.*
1 ruga
the wrinkles on her face.
2 prega
The shirt is full of wrinkles.

wrinkled ['riŋkld] *adj.* □ **enrugado, amarrotado**
his wrinkled face. ◆ a wrinkled skirt.

wrist [rist] *n.* □ **pulso**

wristwatch [ristwat:tʃ] *n.* □ **relógio de pulso**

write [rait] *v.* (**writes, writing, wrote, written**)
1 escrever
He is learning to read and write. ◆ Write the answer on the blackboard.
2 escrever
She writes (to) us every month. ◆ I wrote him a letter / postcard.
3 escrever, compor
He wrote a book about animals. ◆ to write a song.

write down □ **escrever**
Write down your name and address.

write out □ **copiar, escrever**
Write out the answers in full. ◆ He wrote out a cheque for $200.

writer ['raitə] *n.* □ **escritor, autor**
She is a famous writer. ◆ the writer of the article.

writing ['raitiŋ] *n.*
1 escrita
First they learn reading and then writing.
2 (= handwriting) **letra, caligrafia**
I can't read your writing.
3 dizeres
Can you read the writing on that wall?

in writing □ **por escrito**
I want your answer in writing.

writings *n. pl.* □ **escritos**
the writings of the Greek philosophers.

writing materials *n. pl.* □ **material para escrever**
We need writing materials (= pens, pencils, paper, ink, etc.).

writing pad *n.* □ **bloco de anotações**

writing paper *n.* □ **papel para escrever**

written[1] ['ritn] *v.* (Ver **write**).

written[2] *adj.* □ **escrito, por escrito**
a written examination. ◆ a written agreement.

wrong[1] [roŋ] *adj.*
1 errado
The answer is wrong. ◆ They went in the wrong direction.
2 errado
He is the wrong man for the job.
3 errado
My watch is wrong.
4 errado, enganado
I think you're wrong. ◆ I thought she was happy, but I was wrong.
5 errado
It's wrong to steal.
■ antônimo: **right**

there's nothing wrong (with) □ **não há nada (de) errado (com)**
There's nothing wrong with your heart – you just need a rest.

there's something wrong (with) □ **há algo errado (com)**
There's something wrong with the TV – it's not working.

What's wrong (with)...? □ **O que foi?, O que há de errado (com)...?**
What's wrong? Don't you like it? ◆ What's wrong with him? – He's a little tired.

wrong number □ **número errado, ligação errada**
I'm sorry, you have the wrong number.

wrong[2] *adv.* □ **errado**
You did it all wrong. You must do it again.

go wrong
1 dar errado
What went wrong? – The computer stopped working.
2 (= make a mistake) **errar, cometer um erro**
Where did we go wrong?

wrong[3] *n.*
1 errado
Does he know the difference between right and wrong?
2 injustiça
You do him a great wrong. He's not lying to you.

wrongly ['roŋli] *adv.*
1 erroneamente
The letter was wrongly addressed. (= It had a wrong address.)
2 erroneamente
She was wrongly accused.

wrote [rout] *v.* (Ver **write**).

wrung [rʌŋ] *v.* (Ver **wring**).

www [ˌdʌblju: dʌblju: 'dʌblju:] *abbr.* □ **www, rede mundial de computadores**
The address of their website is www.iht.com/.

Xx

X
1 (= 10) **X**
King Louis X.
2 (= times) **vezes**
5 X 2 = 10.

Xerox™ ['ziəroks] *n.* (= photocopy) □ **cópia xerox**
Make a Xerox of the letter.

xerox ['ziəroks] *v.* (**xeroxes, xeroxing, xeroxed**) □ **xerografar**
to xerox a document, letter, etc. ◆ To xerox is to photocopy.

Xerox machine™ ['ziəroks məˈʃiːn] *n.* □ **fotocopiadora**
A Xerox machine is a photocopier.

Xmas ['krisməs] *abbr.* (= Christmas) □ **Natal**
■ **Xmas** is used as a short form, especially on signs and cards.

X-ray[1] [eks'rei] *n.* □ **raio-X**
The X-ray shows that your arm is broken.

X-ray[2] *v.* (**X-rays, X-raying, X-rayed**) □ **radiografar**
My leg was X-rayed.

XS *abbr.* (= extra small [size]) □ **PP**

xylophone ['zailəfoun] *n.* □ **xilofone**

Yy

yacht [jɒt] *n*. □ **iate**
a yacht race. ◆ The rich buy yachts for pleasure trips.
yard [jɑːd] *n*.
1 jarda
The fence is ten yards long.
■ abreviação: **yd**
2 pátio
the school yard. ◆ the prison yard.
3 (= garden) **jardim, quintal**
They were sitting on the grass in the yard.
yawn[1] [jɔːn] *n*. □ **bocejar**
People yawn when they are tired or bored.
yawn[2] *n*. □ **bocejo**
yd *abbr*. (Ver **yard**).
yeah [jeə] *n., excl.* □ **sim**
year [jiə] *n*.
1 ano
It happened in the year 1965. ◆ this year. ◆ last year. ◆ next year.
2 ano
I came here two years ago.
He is ten (years old). ◆ We'll see you in a year's time (= in a year from now).
-year-old □ **anos (de idade)**
a six-year-old girl.
all year round □ **o ano todo**
The sun shines there all year round.
for years □ **há anos**
I haven't seen him for years (= in years).
year after year □ **ano após ano**
They meet at the same place, year after year.
school year *n*. □ **ano escolar**
yearly ['jiəli] *adj., adv.* □ **anual, anualmente, por ano**
a yearly visit. ◆ It happens twice yearly.
yeast [jiːst] *n*. □ **fermento**
yell[1] [jel] *n*. □ **gritos**
The neighbor's yells frightened the children.
yell[2] *v*. (**yells, yelling, yelled**) □ **gritar**
'Stop it!' he yelled ◆ Stop yelling at them! ◆ to yell out in fear.
yellow ['jeləu] *adj., n*. □ **amarelo**
a yellow blouse. ◆ They painted the car yellow. ◆ a shade of yellow.
yes [jes] *excl.* □ **sim**
Are you sure? – Yes, I am. ◆ Do you speak English? – Yes, I do. ◆ Would you like a lift? – Yes, thank you.
yesterday ['jestədi] *adv., n*. □ **ontem**
I saw her yesterday. ◆ Where did you go yesterday? ◆ She left yesterday morning. ◆ yesterday afternoon / evening.
■ **last night** (*not* 'yesterday night').
the day before yesterday □ **antes de ontem, anteontem**
They came the day before yesterday.
yesterday's paper □ **jornal de ontem**
I read it in yesterday's paper.
yet[1] [jet] *adv*.
1 ainda
I haven't seen him yet. ◆ I'm not ready yet.
■ Compare with **still**:
He's still here – he hasn't gone yet.

2 já
Have you eaten yet?
■ In American English **yet** is often used with the *past tense*: Did you eat yet?
● Ver **already**.
yet[2] *conj*. □ **mesmo assim**
It's an interesting story, and yet I don't think it's true.
yield [jiːld] *v*. (**yields, yielding, yielded**)
1 produzir
Trees yield fruit. ◆ The investment did not yield any profits.
2 (= surrender) **render-se**
They yielded to the workers' demands.
3 *Amer*. **dar passagem**
Drivers must usually yield to traffic from the right.
■ *Brit*. **give way**
yoghurt ['jɒgət] *n*. (mesmo que **yogurt**) □ **iogurte**
yolk [jəuk] *n*. □ **gema**
you [juː] *pron*.
1 você, vocês
You are a big girl now. ◆ You are a good father. ◆ You all know the answer.
2 você, vocês
I saw you walking together. ◆ She bought you a present. ◆ Did he phone you?
3 você, vocês
You can't always get what you want.
you'd [juːd] (mesmo que **you had; you would**)
you'll [juːl] (mesmo que **you will; you shall**)
young[1] [jʌŋ] *adj*. □ **jovem, novo**
a young teacher. ◆ young babies. ◆ a young tree / animal. ◆ She is younger than me. ◆ He is my youngest son.
young[2] *n*. □ **filhote**
The cat will attack you if you try to touch her young.
the young □ **jovem**
books for the young.
youngster ['jʌŋstə] *n*. □ **jovem, moço**
your [jɔː] *adj*. □ **seu, sua, seus, suas**
Bring your children with you. ◆ Is that your car? ◆ Your husband was there.
you're [juə] (mesmo que **you are; you were**).
yours [jɔːz] *pron*. □ **teu, tua, teus, tuas, seu, sua, seus, suas**
That's my car. Which is yours? ◆ A friend of yours called today.
● Ver **Yours faithfully; Yours sincerely; Yours truly**.
yourself [jɔːˈself] *pron*. (*pl*. **yourselves**)
1 se, você mesmo
Look at yourself in the mirror. ◆ Buy yourself a nice dress. ◆ Are you proud of yourselves?
■ Ver **enjoy yourself; help yourself**.
2 você mesmo
You yourself told me. ◆ Did you do it yourself?
(all) by yourself
1 (= alone) **sozinho**
Why are you sitting all by yourself?
2 por conta própria
You can do it by yourself.
youth [juːθ] *n*.
1 juventude, mocidade
I was a good swimmer in my youth.
2 juventude
She has youth and ambition. (= She is young and ambitious.)

3 (*pl.* **youths**) **jovens**
a group of youths.

4 (**the youth**) **a juventude, os jovens**
The youth of today like this kind of music. ◆ The youth of this country are wonderful.

ˈyouth club [ˈjuːθ klʌb] *n.* □ **clube de jovens**

ˈyouth hostel [juːθ ˈhostəl] *n.* □ **albergue da juventude**

you've [juːv] (mesmo que **you had**).

yummy [ˈjʌmi] *adj.* □ **saboroso**
a yummy cake.

yuppie [ˈjʌpi] (mesmo que **yuppy**) *n.*, *adj.* □ **yuppie**
'Yuppies' are rich, young and fashionable people in a city. ◆ a yuppie district. ◆ Yuppies like to eat at that restaurant.

Zz

zap [zap] *v.* (**zaps, zapping, zapped**) ▫ **zapear**
to zap between channels (with a remote control).

zebra ['ziːbrə] *n.* ▫ **zebra**
A zebra has black and white stripes.

zebra crossing ['ziːbrə 'krosiŋ] *n. Brit.* ▫ **faixa de pedestre**
Vehicles must stop at a zebra crossing to let pedestrians cross the road.
- *Amer.* **crosswalk**

zero ['ziərou] *n.* ▫ **zero**
My ID number is nine zero six two five (90625). ✦ The temperature is five degrees below zero (-5° C).
- When speaking numbers such as telephone or room numbers, we usually say **o** instead of **zero**:
room number 307 (three o seven).
- In giving the results of games such as soccer, we usually say **nil**:
Manchester United won 2-0 (two nil).
- In American English the usual word is **nothing**:
They won 6-0 (six nothing).
- In British English **nought** means 'zero' when speaking of numbers: There are three noughts in 1000.

zigzag[1] ['zigzag] *n., adj.* ▫ **zigue-zague**
a zigzag road

zigzag[2] *v.* (**zigzags, zigzagging, zigzagged**) ▫ **zigue-zaguear**
The motorcycle zigzagged across the field.

zip[1] [zip] *n. Brit.* ▫ **zíper**
Do up your zip. ✦ Undo your zip.
- *Amer.* **zipper**

zip[2] *v.* (**zips, zipping, zipped**)
zip up ▫ **fechar o zíper**
He zipped up his trousers. ✦ Zip your jacket up.
- antônimo: **unzip**

zip code ['zip 'koud] *n. Amer.* ▫ **código postal**
- *Brit.* **postcode**

zipper ['zipə] *n. Amer.* ▫ **zíper**
Do up your zipper. ✦ He undid his zipper.
- *Brit.* **zip**

zone [zoun] *n.* ▫ **zona**
a war zone. ✦ a danger zone.

zoo [zuː] *n.* ▫ **zoológico**
In some zoos they keep the animals in cages.

zoom [zuːm] *v.* (**zooms, zooming, zoomed**) ▫ **passar zunindo**
He zoomed past on his motorbike.

zucchini [zuˈkiːni] *n.* (*pl.* **zucchini** or **zucchinis**) *Amer.*
▫ **abobrinha**
- *Brit.* **courgette**
- Ver **marrow**.

GLOSSÁRIO PORTUGUÊS/INGLÊS

Aa

a *art.* the
a bordo aboard, on board
à cabeceira da mesa at the head of the table
a cada every
a caminho en route, on the way, on your way to
a cavalo on horseback
a cobrar collect
a despeito de despite
a família de alguém one's folks
a favor for, in favor
a fim de in order to, so as to
a fio on end
à frente ahead
a leste de east of
a maioria de most
a mais additional, extra, further
a mais velha the eldest
à mão at hand, by hand, handy
a meio caminho midway
a menos que unless
à mercê de be at the mercy of
à mostra on view
a não ser but, except
a oeste de west of
a olho nu with the naked eye
a paisana in plain clothes
a pé on foot
a pior *adj.* the worst
à primeira vista at first sight
a princípio at first, initially
à procura de in search of
a propósito by the way, incidentally
à prova d'água water resistant, waterproof
à prova de fogo fireproof
a saber namely
a salvo safely
a sério seriously
a tempo in good time, in time
à toa idle
a trabalho on business
a última vez the last time
à venda for sale
à vista cash
à vontade comfortable
a.C. *abr.* B.C.
aba *s.* flap
abacaxi *s.* pineapple
abadia *s.* abbey
abafado *adj.* stuffy
abafar *v.* smother
abaixar *v.* duck, lower
abaixo *adv.* below, beneath, down, underneath
abaixo do preço at a loss
abajur *s.* lamp, lampshade
abalado *adj.* upset
abalar *v.* jolt, upset
abanar *v.* wag
abanar a cabeça negativamente shake your head
abandonado *adj.* abandoned
abandonar *v.* abandon, desert
abandono *s.* abandonment, neglect
abarrotar *v.* cram
abastecer *v.* fuel, well stocked
abater *v.* slaughter
abatido *adj.* dismal
abduzir *v.* abduct
abelha *s.* bee
abençoar *v.* bless
abertamente *adv.* openly
aberto *adj.* open
abertura *s.* break, opening
abeto *s.* fir
abóbora *s.* marrow, pumpkin, squash
abobrinha *s.* courgette, zucchini
abolição *s.* abolition
abolir *v.* abolish, do away with
abominável *adj.* infamous
abordagem *s.* approach
abordar *v.* deal with, tackle
aborrecer *v.* bore
aborto *s.* abortion
abotoar *v.* do up
abraçar *v.* cuddle, embrace, hug
abraço *s.* cuddle, embrace, hug
abrandar *v.* die down
abrangente *adj.* comprehensive, extensive
abreviação *s.* abbreviation
abridor *s.* opener
abridor de garrafa *s.* bottle opener
abridor de lata *s.* tin-opener
abrigar *v.* house, shelter
abrigar-se de take refuge from
abrigo *s.* cover, shed, shelter
abril *s.* April
abrir *v.* open, spread, untold
abruptamente *adv.* sharply
absolutamente *adv.* absolutely, by no means, not at all
absoluto *adj.* absolute
absolver *v.* acquit
absorção *s.* absorption
absorver *v.* absorb, soak up
abster-se *v.* refrain
abstrato *adj.* abstract
absurdo *s.* absurdity
absurdo *adj.* absurd, outrageous, senseless, unreasonable
abundante *adj.* plentiful
abusar *v.* abuse
abuso *s.* abuse
abuso de drogas *s.* drug abuse
abuso sexual *s.* sexual abuse
abutre *s.* vulture
acabado *adj.* finished, over
acabar *v.* end (up), finish, put a stop to
acabar de just
academia *s.* gym
acadêmico *adj.* academic
acalmar-se *v.* calm down, settle down
acampamento *s.* camp
acampamento de verão *s.* summer camp
acampar *v.* camp
acanhado *adj.* self-conscious
ação *s.* action
Ação de Graças *s.* Thanksgiving
acariciar *v.* stroke
acasalamento *s.* breeding
acasalar-se *v.* mate
acaso *s.* random
aceitação *s.* acceptance
aceitar *v.* accept, take, take in
aceitável *adj.* acceptable
acelerador *s.* accelerator
acelerar *v.* accelerate, hasten, speed (up)
acenar *v.* wave
acenar com a cabeça *v.* nod
acender *v.* come on, light
aceno *s.* wave
acento *s.* stress
acentuadamente *adv.* sharply
acentuado *adj.* sharp
acentuar *v.* stress
acertar *v.* hit, settle, square, strike
acessar *v.* access
acesso *s.* access
achados e perdidos lost property
achar *v.* believe, figure out, find, guess, make of, reckon, suppose, think
achar alguém o máximo think the world of
achar de think about, think of
achar defeito em find fault with
achatar *v.* flatten
acho que não I don't think so
acho que sim I suppose so, I think so
acidentado *adj.* bumpy, rough
acidental *adj.* accidental
acidentalmente *adv.* accidentally
acidente *s.* accident
acidente de trânsito *s.* road accident
ácido *s.* acid
acima *adv.* above, overhead
acima de tudo above all
acirrado *adj.* close
aço *s.* steel
aço inoxidável *s.* stainless steel

acolchoado *s.* quilt
acolhedor *adj.* warm
acolher *v.* put up, welcome
acolhida *s.* welcome
acomodação *s.* accommodation, quarters
acomodar *v.* accommodate
acomodar-se *v.* settle (down)
acompanhamento *s.* accompaniment
acompanhar *v.* accompany, escort, follow, keep up with, see
acompanhar o passo de keep pace with
aconchegante *adj.* cosy, cozy
acondicionamento *s.* packaging
aconselhamento *s.* counselling
aconselhar *v.* advise
acontecer *v.* come about, go on, happen, take place
acontecimento *s.* event, happening
acordado *adj.* awake, up
acordar *v.* wake, wake up
acordeão *s.* accordion
acordo *s.* accord, agreement, arrangement, compromise, deal, settlement, understanding
acorrentar *v.* chain
acostumado *adj.* accustomed
acostumar-se *v.* become accustomed to, get accustomed to, get used to
açougue *s.* butchery
açougueiro *s.* butcher
acre *s.* acre
acreditar *v.* believe, reckon, think
acreditar no que alguém diz take someone's word for it
acrescentar *v.* add
acrobata *s.* acrobat
acrobático *adj.* acrobatic
açúcar *s.* sugar
açúcar refinado *s.* white sugar
acumular *v.* accumulate, hoard, pile up
acúmulo *s.* accumulation
acusação *s.* accusation, charge
acusado *s.* defendant, the accused
acusar *v.* accuse, charge
adaga *s.* dagger
adaptação *s.* adaptation, adjustment
adaptar *v.* adapt
adaptar-se *v.* adjust, get used to
adega *s.* cellar
adequadamente *adv.* accordingly, appropriately, properly, suitably
adequado *adj.* adequate, appropriate, fit, proper, suitable
adesivo *s.* sticker
adeus *s.* goodbye

adiamento *s.* postponement
adiantado *adj.* early, in advance
adiar *v.* delay, postpone, put off
adição *s.* addition
adicional *adj.* additional, extra, further
adicionar *v.* add
adivinhar *v.* guess
adjetivo *s.* adjective
administração *s.* administration
administração pública *s.* civil service
administrar *v.* administer
admiração *s.* admiration
admirar *v.* admire
admirável *adj.* admirable
admissão *s.* admission, confession, entrance
admitir *v.* admit, own up
adoção *s.* adoption
adoçar *v.* sweeten
adolescência *s.* adolescence, teens
adolescente *adj.* adolescent, teenage
adolescente *s.* adolescent, teenager
adoração *s.* worship
adorador *s.* worshiper
adorar *v.* adore, love, worship
adorável *adj.* adorable, lovable, lovely
adormecido *adj.* asleep
adotado *adj.* adopted
adotar *v.* adopt
adquirir *v.* acquire, buy, purchase
adulto *adj.* adult, grown(-up)
advérbio *s.* adverb
adversário *s.* opponent
advogado *s.* attorney, lawyer, solicitor
aeróbica *s.* aerobics
aerodeslizador *s.* hovercraft
aeromoça *s.* (air) hostess, flight attendant, stewardess
aeronave *s.* aircraft
aeroporto *s.* airport
aerosol *s.* aerosol
afabilidade *s.* friendliness
afagar *v.* stroke
afago *s.* stroke
afastado *adj.* remote
afastar-se *v.* back away, move over, stand aside
afeição *s.* affection
afetar *v.* affect, strike
afeto *s.* affection
afetuosamente *adv.* affectionately
afetuoso *adj.* affectionate
afiado *adj.* sharp
afiar *v.* sharpen
afinar *v.* tune
afirmação *s.* claim

afluente *adj.* affluent
afluir *v.* stream out
afogar-se *v.* drown
afortunado *adj.* fortunate, lucky
afro-americano *adj., s.* African American
afrouxar *v.* loosen
afundar *v.* go under, sink
agachar-se *v.* crouch, squat
agarrar(-se) *v.* cling, clutch, clutch at, get hold of, grasp, grip, seize
agência *s.* agency
agência de empregos *s.* employment agency
agência de viagem *s.* travel agency
agência do correio *s.* post office
agenda *s.* calendar, diary, schedule
agendar *v.* schedule
agente *s.* agent
agente de viagem *s.* travel agent
agente duplo *s.* double agent
agente funerário *s.* undertaker
agente infiltrado *s.* undercover agent
agente secreto *s.* secret agent, undercover agent
agir *v.* act, behave, take action
agitadamente *adv.* feverishly
agitado *adj.* hectic, rough, rowdy
agitar *v.* stir up
aglomerar-se *v.* swarm
agonia *s.* agony
agonizar *v.* agonize
agora *adv.* now, right now
agora mesmo immediately, just now, right away
agosto *s.* August
agradar *v.* please
agradável *adj.* agreeable, delightful, enjoyable, fair, nice, pleasant
agradavelmente *adv.* pleasantly
agradecer *v.* thank
agradecimento *s.* thanks
agredir *v.* assault
agressão *s.* aggression, assault
agressivamente *adv.* aggressively
agressivo *adj.* aggressive
agressor *s.* attacker
agrícola *adj.* agricultural
agricultor *s.* farmer
agricultura *s.* agriculture, farming
água *s.* water
água com gás *s.* soda, soda water
água mineral *s.* mineral water
aguar *v.* water
aguardado *adj.* due
aguardar ansiosamente look forward to

água-viva s. jellyfish
aguçado adj. sharp
agudo adj. sharp, shrill
aguentar v. bear, carry, cope, endure, put up with, stand
águia s. eagle
agulha s. needle
agulha de tricô s. knitting-needle
aí adv. here, there
aids s. AIDS
ainda adv. still, yet
ainda assim still
ainda que conj. although, even though
aipo s. celery
airbag s. airbag
ajoelhar-se v. kneel
ajuda s. a helping hand, aid, hand, help, relief
ajudante s. aide
ajudar v. aid, help
ajustar v. adjust, alter
ajustar as contas com get even with
ajuste s. adjustment, alteration
ala s. ward
alargar v. broaden, widen
alargar-se v. widen
alarido s. din
alarmar v. alarm
alarme s. alarm
alarme contra ladrão s. burglar alarm
alarme de incêndio s. fire-alarm
alarme falso s. false alarm
alastramento s. spread
alavanca s. lever
albergue s. hostel
albergue da juventude s. youth hostel
álbum s. album
alça s. strap
alcançar v. achieve, catch up with, get up to, reach
alcance s. power, range
álcool s. alcohol
alcoólico adj. alcoholic
Alcorão s. Koran
aldeão s. villager
aleatoriamente s. at random
aleatório adj. random
alegação s. claim
alegar v. allege, claim
alegar ausência de culpa plead not guilty
alegar culpa plead guilty
alegrar(-se) v. brighten, cheer up, rejoice
alegre adj. cheerful, gay, jolly, joyful, lively
alegremente adv. cheerfully, joyfully, playfully

aleijado v. cripple
além da conta over-
além de apart from, besides, beyond, in addition to, other than, past
além de todas as expectativas beyond all expectations
além disso also, besides, furthermore, moreover
além do mais morcover
além do período estabelecido overtime
alerta s. alert, warning
alertar v. alert, caution, warn
alfabético adj. alphabetical
alfabeto s. ABC, alphabet
alface s. lettuce
alfândega s. customs
alfinetar v. pin
alfinete s. pin
alfinete de segurança s. safety pin
alga marinha s. seaweed
algemas s. handcuffs
algo pron. anything, something
algo mais anything else, something else
algodão s. cotton, cotton wool
alguém pron. anybody, somebody
alguém mais anybody else, anyone else
algum dia some day
algum lugar anywhere, somewhere
algum modo any way, some way
algum tempo some time
algum pron. any, some
alguma coisa anything, something
alguma vez ever
algumas pron. a couple, a few, several, some
alguns pron. a couple, a few, several, some
alheio adj. unaware
alho s. garlic
alho-poró s. leek
aliado s. ally
aliança s. alliance, wedding ring
aliás adv. incidentally
álibi s. alibi
alicate s. pliers
alicerces s. foundations
alienígena s. alien
aligátor s. alligator
alimentar(-se) v. feed, feed on, prey
alimento s. food
alinhar v. be lined with
alistar-se v. join up
aliviar v. relieve
alívio s. comfort, relief

alma s. soul
almirante s. admiral
almoçar v. lunch
almoço s. lunch
almofada s. cushion
alô int. hello
alojamento s. quarters
alongar v. lengthen
alpinismo s. climbing, mountaineering
alpinista s. climber, mountaineer
alta s. discharge
alta-classe adj. high-class
altamente adv. highly
altamente confidencial top-secret
altamente tecnológico hi-tech
alterar v. alter, change
alternado adj. alternate
alternativa s. alternative, choice
alternativo adj. alternative
alteza s. highness
altitude s. height
alto adv. high, loudly
alto adj. high, loud, tall
alto-falante s. loudspeaker, speaker
altos e baixos ups and downs
altura s. height
alturas s. heights
alugar v. hire (out), let, rent (out)
aluguel s. hire, rent
alumínio s. aluminium / aluminum
aluna s. pupil, schoolgirl, student
aluno s. pupil, schoolboy, student
alvo s. aim, target
alvoroçar-se v. fuss
amaciar v. soften
amador adj. amateurish
amador s. amateur
amadurecer v. mature, ripen
amaldiçoado adj. cursed
amaldiçoar v. curse
amanhã s. tomorrow
amanhecer s. dawn
amanhecido adj. stale
amante s. lover
amar v. love
amarelo adj. yellow
amargamente adv. bitterly
amargo adj. bitter
amargor s. bitterness
amargura s. bitterness
amarrar v. bind, do up, knot, tie
amarrar algo tie something up
amarrar alguém tie someone up
amarrotado adj. wrinkled
amarrotar v. crease
amassado s. dent
amassar v. crease, crumple, dent, knead, mash, squash
ambição s. ambition

ambicioso *adj.* ambitious
ambiental *adj.* environmental
ambiente *s.* atmosphere, environment
ambos *n.* both
ambulância *s.* ambulance
ameaça *s.* menace, threat
ameaçador *adj.* threatening
ameaçadoramente *adv.* threateningly
ameaçar *v.* threaten
amedrontado *adj.* frightened, scared
amedrontar *v.* frighten, scare
ameixa *s.* plum
ameixa seca *s.* prune
amêndoa *s.* almond
amendoim *s.* peanut
ameno *adj.* mild
americano *s.* American
amido *s.* starch
amigo por correspondência *s.* pen friend, pen pal
amigo *s.* friend, mate, pal
amistoso *adj.* friendly, neighborly
amizade *s.* friendliness, friendship
amolar *v.* nag
amolecer *v.* soften
amontoar *v.* heap
amor *s.* love
amora silvestre *s.* blackberry
amordaçar *v.* gag
amoroso *adj.* loving
amor-próprio *s.* self-respect
amostra *s.* sample
amostragem *s.* sample
amotinar(-se) *v.* mutiny
amparar *v.* support
ampliação *s.* enlargement
ampliar *v.* enlarge, extend, magnify, stretch
amuleto *s.* charm
amurada *s.* rail
anã *s.* dwarf, midget
analfabeto *adj.* illiterate
analisar *v.* analyse, analyze
análise *s.* analysis
anão *s.* dwarf, midget
ancestral *s.* ancestor
anchova *s.* anchovy
ancinho *s.* rake
âncora *s.* anchor, newscaster
anda logo! hurry up!
andaime *s.* scaffolding
andar *s.* floor, storey
andar *v.* progress, walk
andar a passos largos stride
andar de *v.* ride
andar de bicicleta cycle
andar de cima *s.* top deck, upstairs
andar de skate skate

andar logo get a move on, hurry
andar na ponta dos pés tiptoe
andar térreo *s.* first floor
andarilho *s.* tramp
anel *s.* ring
anestesia *s.* anaesthetic
anestésico *s.* anaesthetic
anexar *v.* attach, enclose
anexo *s.* attachment, extension
anfitriã *s.* hostess
anfitrião *s.* host
ângulo *s.* angle
ângulo reto *s.* right angle
angústia *s.* distress
animado *adj.* cheerful, lively
animal *s.* animal
animal de estimação *s.* pet
animar *v.* brighten
animar-se *v.* cheer up, come to life
aninhar-se *v.* nest
aniversário *s.* anniversary, birthday
aniversário de casamento *s.* wedding anniversary
anjo *s.* angel
ano *s.* year
ano após ano year after year
ano bissexto *s.* leap year
ano escolar *s.* school year
anoitecer *s.* dusk
anônimo *adj.* anonymous
anormal *adj.* not normal, unnatural
anotações *s.* notes
anotar *v.* jot down, make note of, note down, take down, write down
anseio *s.* longing
ansiar *v.* long
ansiedade *s.* anxiety
ansiosamente *adv.* anxiously
ansioso *adj.* anxious, eager
antena *s.* aerial, antenna
anteontem *adv.* the day before yesterday
antepassado *s.* ancestor
anterior *adj.* former, last, preceding
anteriormente *adv.* before, formerly
antes *adv.* before
antes da hora too soon
antigamente *adv.* long ago
antigo *adj.* ancient, old-fashioned
antiguidade *s.* antique
anti-horário *adj.* anticlockwise
antipático *adj.* unfriendly
antiquado *v.* out of date, outdated
antiquado *adj.* unfashionable
antissemita *adj.* anti-Semitic
antissemitismo *s.* anti-Semitism
anual *adj.* annual, yearly

anualmente *adv.* annually, yearly
anuidade *s.* tuition
anulação *s.* deletion
anunciador *s.* announcer
anunciar *v.* advertise, announce
anúncio *s.* ad, advertisement, announcement, notice
anzol *s.* hook
ao acaso at random
ao alcance within easy reach
ao ar livre in the open air, open-air, out of doors, outdoors
ao certo for sure
ao contrário the other way around
ao contrário de as opposed to, unlike
ao dia a day
ao invés de instead of
ao lado beside, next door, next to
ao longe in the distance
ao longo de along, down, up
ao mar overboard
ao mesmo tempo at once, at the same time
ao norte de north of
ao redor round
ao sul de south of
ao telefone on the telephone
ao todo in all
ao vivo live
aonde *adv.* where
aos prantos in tears
apagado *adj.* out
apagador *s.* eraser
apagamento *s.* deletion
apagar *v.* erase, put out, rub out, wipe off
apagar com o sopro blow out
apagar o fogo put out the fire
apagar-se *v.* die down, go out
apaixonadamente *adv.* passionately
apaixonado *adj.* in love, passionate
apaixonar-se *v.* fall in love
apaixonar-se por fall in love with
aparada *s.* trim
aparador *s.* sideboard
aparar *v.* clip, cut, mow, trim
aparato *s.* apparatus
aparecer *v.* appear, arrive, come by/out, come into view, pop up, show up, turn up
aparelhagem *s.* apparatus
aparelhar *v.* equip
aparelhar-se *v.* equip oneself
aparelho *s.* aid, appliance, instrument, set
aparelho de CD *s.* compact disc player
aparelho de som *s.* stereo, stereo system

aparelho de tevê *s.* television, television set
aparelho de videocassete *s.* VCR, videocassette recorder
aparelhos *s.* goods
aparência *s.* appearance, look, looks
aparentar *v.* look
aparente *adj.* apparent
aparentemente *adv.* apparently
aparição *s.* appearance
apartamento *s.* apartment, flat
apavorado *adj.* terrified
apedrejar *v.* stone
apelar *v.* appeal
apelidar *v.* nickname
apelido *s.* alias, nickname
apelo *s.* appeal, plea
apenas *adv.* barely, nothing but, only
apêndice *s.* appendix, intestine tube
aperfeiçoar *v.* perfect
apertado *adj.* fast, tight
apertar *v.* clasp, fasten, press, push, squeeze, tighten
apertar a mão de alguém shake someone's hand
aperto *s.* push, squeeze
aperto de mão *s.* handshake
apesar de despite, in spite of
apesar de tudo all the same, just the same, nevertheless
apesar disso nevertheless
apetecer *v.* appeal
apetite *s.* appetite
apetitoso *adj.* appetizing
apetrechos *s.* tackle
apimentado *adj.* hot
apinhar-se *v.* crowd into
apito *s.* whistle
aplainar *v.* flatten
aplaudir *v.* applaud, cheer, clap
aplauso *s.* applause, clap, hand
aplicação *s.* application
aplicar *v.* apply, enforce
aplicar-se *v.* apply
apodrecer *v.* decay, rot
apoiar *v.* back, back up, favor, lean, stand by, support
apoiar-se *v.* lean
apoio *s.* support
apólice *s.* policy
apontador *s.* sharpener
apontador de lápis *s.* pencil sharpener
apontar *v.* appoint, point, sharpen
aporrinhar *v.* pick on
após *prep.* after
aposentado *s.* pensioner, retiree
aposentado *adj.* retired
aposentadoria *s.* pension, retirement

aposentadoria por velhice *s.* old-age pension
aposentar-se *v.* retire
aposta *s.* bet
apostar *v.* bet
apostar corrida *v.* race
aprazível *adj.* delightful
apreço *s.* regard
apreensão *s.* alarm, seizure
apreensivamente *adv.* uneasily
apreensivo *adj.* uneasy
aprender *v.* learn
aprender a lição learn your lesson
aprendiz *s.* apprentice, learner
aprendizado *s.* learning
apresentação *s.* introduction, submission
apresentar *v.* introduce, model, perform, present, show, submit
apressadamente *adv.* hastily, hurriedly
apressado *adj.* hasty
apressar *v.* hurry, rush
apressar-se *v.* get a move on, hurry, rush
aprofundar *v.* deepen
aprontar *v.* get up to
aprontar-se *v.* get ready
apropriado *adj.* proper
aprovação *s.* approval, pass
aprovar *v.* approve
aproveitar *v.* make the most of
aproveitar a oportunidade take the opportunity
aproveitar-se de take advantage of
aproximação *s.* approach
aproximadamente *adv.* approximately, or so, round about
aproximado *adj.* approximate, rough
aproximar-se *v.* approach, draw, gain on, get nearer/closer
aptidão *s.* aptitude, fitness
aquarela *s.* watercolor
aquecedor *s.* fire, heater, heating
aquecer *v.* heat, warm up
aquecer-se *v.* get warm
aquecimento central *s.* central heating
aqueles *pron.* those
aquele *pron.* former, that
aqui *adv.* here
aqui está here, over here
aquilo *pron.* that
árabe *adj.* Arabic
árabe *s.* Arab
arame *s.* wire
arame farpado *s.* barbed wire
aranha *s.* spider
arar *v.* plough, plow

árbitro *s.* referee, umpire
arbusto *s.* bush, shrub
arcar com *v.* bush, shrub
arcebispo *s.* archbishop
arco *s.* arch, bow
arco-íris *s.* rainbow
ar-condicionado *s.* air-conditioning
arder *v.* blaze, sting
árduo *adj.* hard
área *s.* area, field
área rural *s.* countryside
areia *s.* sand
arejar *v.* air
arena *s.* arena
arenoso *adj.* sandy
arfada *s.* gap
argila *s.* clay
argola *s.* ring
argumentação *s.* argument, dispute
argumentar *v.* argue, reason
argumento *s.* argument
aridez *s.* dryness
aritmética *s.* arithmetic
arma *s.* gun, weapon
armação *s.* frame
armadilha *s.* trap
armado *adj.* armed
armadura *s.* armor
armamento *s.* gun
armário *s.* cabinet, closet, cupboard, locker
armas *s.* arms
aroma *s.* aroma, scent
aromatizado *s.* scented
arpão *adj.* spear
arquear *v.* arch
arquejar *v.* puff
arqueologia *s.* archaelogy
arqueológico *adj.* archaeological
arqueólogo *s.* archaeologist
arquibancada *s.* grandstand, stand
arquiteto *s.* architect
arquitetura *s.* architecture
arquivar *v.* file
arquivo *s.* file
arrancar *v.* grab, pull out, snatch, tear down
arranha-céu *s.* skyscraper
arranhão *s.* scratch
arranhar *v.* graze, scratch
arranjar-se *v.* manage
arranjo *s.* arrangement
arrasado *adj.* wretched
arrasador *adj.* overwhelming
arrastar *v.* drag, shuffle, wash away
arrastar-se *v.* crawl, drag, shuffle, trail
arrebentar *v.* break

arredores s. surroundings
arreios s. harness
arremessar v. sling, toss
arrepender-se v. regret, repent
arriscado adj. risky
arriscar v. risk
arriscar-se v. risk, take a chance, take a risk
arrogância s. arrogance, haughtiness
arrogante adj. arrogant, haughty
arrogantemente adv. arrogantly
arrombar v. break in
arroz s. rice
arruinar v. ruin
arrumado adj. tidy
arrumar v. arrange, get, lay, tidy
arrumar a cama make the bed
arrumar a mesa lay the table, set the table
arrumar-se v. dress up
arte s. art
arteiro adj. mischievous
artéria s. artery
artesã s. craftswoman
artesanal adj. handmade
artesanato s. craft
artesão s. craftsman
articulação s. joint
articulação dos dedos s. knuckle
artificial adj. artificial, man-made
artifício s. device
artifícios visuais s. visual aids
artigo s. article, grammar, paper
artigo definido s. definite article
artigo indefinido s. indefinite article
artilharia s. artillery
artista s. artist, performer
artístico adj. artistic
árvore s. tree
árvore genealógica s. family tree
às avessas inside out
às custas de alguém at someone's expense
as duas s. both
as quais pron. which
às vezes adv. at times, sometimes
asa s. handle, wing
asa-delta s. hang-glider
asfalto s. tarmac
asfixiar v. smother
asilo s. asylum, home
asno s. ass
aspas s. inverted commas, quotation marks
aspecto s. aspect, respect
asperamente adv. harshly
áspero adj. coarse, harsh, rough
aspersor s. sprinkler
aspirador de pó s. vacuum cleaner
assado s. roast
assado adj. baked, roasted
assaltante s. mugger, robber
assaltar v. burgle, hold up, mug, rob
assalto s. hold-up, robbery, stick-up
assar v. bake, roast
assassinato s. assassination, killing, murder
assassina s. murderess
assassinar v. assassinate, murder
assassino s. killer, murderer
assassino adj. murderous
asseado adj. neat
assédio sexual s. sexual harassment
assegurar v. assure, ensure, insure
assegurar-se v. make sure
assembleia s. assembly
assentamento s. settlement
assentar v. fit
assento s. seat
assim adv. like this, thus
assim que as soon as, just as, once
assim que possível as soon as possible, as soon as you can
assinante s. subscriber
assinar v. sign, subscribe
assinatura s. signature, subscription
assistência s. assistance, service
assistência social s. welfare
assistente s. aide, assistant
assistente social s. social worker
assistir v. assist, stand by
assistir a v. watch
assoar o nariz blow your nose
assobiar v. whistle
assobio s. whistle
associação s. association
associar v. associate
associar-se v. associate, join
assombrado adj. haunted
assombrar v. astonish, haunt, stun
assombro s. astonishment
assombroso adj. astonishing
assoviar v. whistle
assovio s. whistle
assumir v. take over
assunto s. affair, matter, subject, topic
assustado adj. afraid
assustador adj. frightening
assustar v. alarm, frighten, scare, startle
assustar-se v. scare
astral s. spirits
astro s. star
astro de cinema s. film star
astronauta s. astronaut, spaceman, spacewoman
astúcia s. cunning
astuto adj. cunning, sly
atacante s. attacker, striker
atacar v. attack, charge, raid, strike, tackle
atacar em bando gang together; gang up
atadura s. bandage
atalho s. footpath, short cut
ataque s. attack, raid, strike
ataque aéreo s. air raid
ataque cardíaco s. heart attack
ataque terrorista s. terrorist attack
atarefado adj. busy
atazanar v. nag, tease
até adv. as far as, even, no later than, up to, up until
até prep. through, till, to, until
até agora so far, until now, up to/till now
até certo ponto to a certain extent, to some extent
até então so far
até logo! see you later!
até mesmo even
até onde...? how far...?
até que till, until
até que enfim at last, it's about time
até que ponto...? how far...?
até segunda ordem until further notice
até tarde until late
ateliê s. studio
atenção s. attention, thoughtfulness
atenciosamente adv. (Yours) faithfully, (Yours) sincerely, Yours truly
atencioso adj. considerate, thoughtful
atendente s. attendant
atender v. meet, see, serve
atender à demanda go around, go round
atender a porta answer the door
atender ao telefone answer the telephone
atentado s. attempt
atento adj. alert
aterrissagem s. landing, touchdown
aterrissar v. land
aterrorizante adj. terrifying
aterrorizar v. terrify
ater-se ao ponto stick to the point/subject
atestado s. certificate
atestar v. certify
atingir v. strike
atiradeira s. catapult

atirar *v.* fire, shoot, sling, throw, toss
atitude *s.* attitude
ativamente *adv.* busily
atividade *s.* activity
ativo *adj.* active
atlas *s.* atlas
atleta *s.* athlete
atlético *adj.* athletic
atletismo *s.* athletics
atmosfera *s.* atmosphere
ato *s.* act, action, law
ato de cantar *s.* singing
ato de dirigir *s.* driving
ato de esquiar *s.* skiing
ato de fazer a barba *s.* shave
ato de fazer compras *s.* shopping
ato de fritar *s.* frying
ato de fumar *s.* smoking
ato de pescar *s.* fishing
ato de voar de asa-delta *s.* hang-gliding
ato de zarpar *s.* sailing
atômico *adj.* atomic
átomo *s.* atom
ator *s.* actor, performer
atordoado *s.* in a daze
atordoamento *s.* daze
atordoante *adj.* stunning
atordoar *v.* daze, stun
atração *s.* appeal, attraction
atraente *adj.* appealing, attractive
atrair *v.* attract, draw
atrapalhar *v.* get in the way of, mess up, obstruct, upset
atrás *prep.* after, ago, behind
atrasado *adj.* backward, behind schedule, late, overdue
atrasar *v.* delay, put back
atrasar-se *v.* fall behind
atraso *s.* delay, hold-up
através *adv.* through
atravessar *v.* cross, get/go/pass through
atravessar com dificuldade wade
atrever-se *v.* dare
atrevido *adj.* cheeky, daring
atrevimento *s.* cheek, daring

atriz *s.* actress
atropelar *v.* hit, run over
atuação *s.* performance
atual *adj.* current, present, up-to-date
atualizado *adj.* updated, up-to-date
atualizar *v.* bring... up to date, update
atualmente *adv.* at the moment, currently, nowadays, presently
atuante *adj.* active
atuar *v.* act as
atum *s.* tuna
ATV *s.* all-terrain vehicle, ATV
au pair *s.* au pair
audição *s.* hearing
audiência *s.* audience
áudio *adj.* audio / audio-
auge *s.* height, peak
aula *s.* class, lecture, lesson, period, school, tuition
aumentar *v.* enlarge, go up, grow, increase, magnify, turn up
aumento *s.* enlargement, increase, raise, rise
aurora *s.* dawn
ausência *s.* absence
ausente *adj.* absent, missing
austero *adj.* stern
autêntico *adj.* authentic
auto *s.* self-
autobiografia *s.* autobiography
autobiográfico *adj.* autobiographical
autoconfiança *s.* self-confidence
autoconfiante *adj.* self-confident
autocontrole *s.* self-control
autódromo *s.* racetrack
autoestrada *s.* freeway
autoestrada *s.* motorway
autógrafo *s.* autograph
automaticamente *adv.* automatically
automático *adj.* automatic
automobilismo *s.* motor racing
automóvel *s.* automobile
autonomia *s.* range

autônomo *adj.* self-employed
autor *s.* author, writer
autoridade *s.* authority, official
autorização *s.* permit
autorizado *adj.* licensed
autorizar *v.* authorize, license, okay
auxiliar *v.* help
auxílio *s.* help, unemployment benefit
avaliar *v.* estimate, value
avançado *adj.* advanced
avançar *v.* advance, fast forward, make headway, progress
avanço *s.* advance
avarento *adj.* miserly
ave *s.* bird
ave de rapina *s.* bird of prey
aveia *s.* oats
avelã *s.* hazelnut
avenida *s.* avenue
avental *s.* apron, overall
aventura *s.* adventure
aventureiro *adj.* adventurous
avermelhado *adj.* reddish
aversão *s.* dislike
avestruz *s.* ostrich
aviador *s.* flyer
avião *s.* airplane, plane
avião jumbo *s.* jumbo jet
avidamente *adv.* eagerly, greedily
avidez *s.* eagerness
ávido *adj.* eager, keen
avisar *v.* let know, warn
aviso *s.* notice, warning
avistar *s.* catch sight of
avó *s.* grandmother
avô *s.* grandfather
avós *s.* grandparents
avulso *adj.* odd
azar *s.* misfortune
azarado *adj.* unlucky
azedar *v.* go sour
azedo *adj.* sour
azeite *s.* olive oil
azeitona *s.* olive
azul *adj., s.* blue

Bb

babá s. babysitter, nanny
bacalhau s. cod
bacana adj. attractive, cool, fashionable, great
bacon s. bacon
bactérias s. bacteria
baforada s. puff
baforar v. puff
baga s. berry
bagageiro s. rack, roof-rack
bagagem s. baggage, luggage
bagagem de mão s. hand luggage
bagunça s. mess, muddle, untidiness
bagunçado adj. messy, untidy
bagunçar v. mess up, muddle something up
baía s. bay, harbor
bailarina s. ballerina
baile s. ball, dance
bainha s. hem, seam
bairro s. neighborhood, quarter
baixa s. casualty, loss
baixar v. come down, dip, download, go down, lower, put down, turn something down
baixar a cabeça hang your head
baixo adv. low
baixo adj. low, quiet, short
bajulação s. flattery
bajular v. flatter
bala s. bullet, slug
bala de hortelã s. mint
balança s. balance, scale, scales
balançar v. rock, swing, wobble
balanceado adj. balanced
balanço s. swing
balão s. balloon, hot-air balloon
balbúrdia s. row
balcão s. counter, desk
balconista s. clerk
balde s. bucket, pail
balé s. ballet
baleia s. whale
balsa s. ferry, raft
bambear v. wobble
bambo adj. wobbly
bambu s. bamboo
banana s. banana
banca s. stall
banca de jornal s. newsstand
bancada s. bench
banco s. bank, bench, stool
banco da frente s. front seat
banco de trás s. back seat
banda s. band, group
bandagem s. dressing
band-aid s. Band-Aid, sticking plaster
bandas s. part
bandeira s. flag
bandeja s. tray
bandido s. bandit, thug
bando s. bunch, flock, pack
bangalô s. bungalow
bangue-bangue s. western
banhar-se v. bathe
banheira s. bathtub, tub
banheiro s. bathroom, lavatory, loo, rest room, toilet, washroom, WC
banheiro feminino s. Ladies
banheiro masculino s. Gents
banhista s. bather
banho s. bath, bathing
banner s. banner
banqueiro s. banker
banquete s. banquet, feast
baque s. blow, thud
bar s. bar, pub
baralho s. pack
barão s. baron
barata s. cockroach, roach
barato adv. cheaply
barato adj. cheap, inexpensive
barba s. beard
barbado adj. bearded
barbante s. string
bárbaro adj. excellent, terrific
barbatana s. fin
barbeador s. shaver
barbearia s. barber
barbear-se v. shave
barbeiro s. barber
barbudo adj. bearded
barcaça s. barge
barco s. boat
barco a motor s. motorboat
barco a remo s. rowing-boat
barganha s. bargain
barman s. barman, bartender
barômetro s. barometer
baronesa s. baroness
barra s. bar, rod
barra diagonal s. slash
barraca s. stand, tent
barragem s. dam
barreira s. barrier
barreira contra acidentes s. crash barrier
barrento adj. muddy
barricada s. barricade, roadblock
barriga s. belly, stomach, tummy
barril s. barrel
barro s. mud
barulhentamente adv. noisily
barulhento adj. noisy, rowdy
barulhinho s. murmur
barulho s. clatter, crash, noise, rattle
base s. base, basis
basicamente adv. basically
básico adj. basic, elementary
basquetebol s. basketball
basta! int. enough!
bastante adj. a good/great deal of, ample, quite a lot of
bastão s. club, stick
bastardo s. bastard
batalha s. battle
batalhar v. battle, struggle
batata s. potato
batata frita s. chips, French fries
batedeira s. mixer, whisk
batedor s. whisk
batedor de carteira s. pickpocket
batente s. frame
bate-papo s. chat
bater v. beat, bounce, bump, crash, flap, hit, knock, strike, thrash, whip, whisk
bater a cabeça em bang your head on
bater a carteira de alguém pick someone's pocket
bater com força bang, bash, slam
bater com o pé sobre algo stamp
bater continência salute
bater de leve rap
bater em retirada withdraw
bater forte thump
bater levemente tap
bater palmas clap
bater papo chat
bateria s. battery, drum
baterista s. drummer
batida s. beat, bump, knock, raid
batida forte e barulhenta s. slam
batida leve s. rap
batidinha s. tap
batimento s. beat
batimento cardíaco s. heartbeat
batismo s. baptism, christening
batizar v. baptize, christen
batom s. lipstick
baú s. chest, trunk
baunilha s. vanilla
bazar s. bazaar
bêbado adj. drunk
bebê s. baby
bebedeira s. drunkenness
beber v. drink
bebericar v. sip
bebida s. drink
bebida alcoólica s. spirits
bebidas não alcoólicas s. refreshments
beco s. alley
beco sem saída s. dead end
beijar v. kiss
beijo s. kiss
beirada s. edge
beisebol s. baseball

beleza *s.* beauty
beliche *s.* bunk
beliscão *s.* pinch
beliscar *v.* pinch
belo *adj.* fine
bem *adj.* fine, good, well
bem *adv.* all right, nicely, pretty, properly, quite, well
bem *s.* good
bem como also, as well as
bem cozido hard-boiled
bem de vida well-off, well-to-do
bem-sucedido successful
bem-estar *s.* welfare
bem-feito pra você it serves you right
bem-vindo welcome
bênção *s.* blessing
beneficiar(-se) *v.* benefit
benefício *s.* advantage, benefit
bengala *s.* cane, stick, walking stick
bens *s.* goods
berço *s.* cot, cradle, crib
beringela *s.* aubergine, eggplant
besouro *s.* beetle
besta *s.* beast
besteira *s.* nonsense, rubbish
best-seller *s.* bestseller
beterraba *s.* beetroot
bezerro *s.* calf
Bíblia *s.* Bible
biblioteca *s.* library
bibliotecário *s.* librarian
bicar *v.* peck
bicicleta *s.* bicycle, bike, cycle
bico *s.* beak, spout
bifurcação *s.* fork
bifurcar-se *v.* branch
bigode *s.* moustache, mustache, whisker
bike *s.* bicycle, bike
bilhão *adj.* billion
bilhete *s.* note, ticket
bilhete de ida e volta *s.* return ticket, round-trip ticket
bilheteria *s.* booking office, box office, ticket office
bilhetes para a temporada *s.* season tickets
binóculo *s.* binoculars
biografia *s.* biography
biologia *s.* biology
biológico *adj.* biological
biólogo *s.* biologist
biombo *s.* screen
bisavó *s.* great-grandmother
bisavô *s.* great-grandfather
biscoito *s.* biscuit, cookie, cracker, wafer
bispo *s.* bishop
blazer *s.* blazer

blefar *v.* bluff
blefe *s.* bluff
blockbuster *s.* blockbuster
bloco *s.* block, pad
bloco de anotações *s.* notepad, writing pad
bloqueado *adj.* blocked
bloquear *v.* bar, barricade, block, jam
bloqueio *s.* block, blockade
blusa *s.* blouse
blusa de moletom *s.* sweatshirt
boa *adj.* good, nice, pleasant
boa forma *s.* fitness
boa sorte *s.* luck
boa tarde *s.* good afternoon
boa vontade *s.* willingness
boate *s.* nightclub
boato *s.* rumor
bobagem *s.* nonsense, rubbish
bobo *adj.* foolish
boca *s.* mouth
bocado *s.* nibble
bocejar *v.* yawn
bocejo *s.* yawn
bochecha *s.* cheek
bodas de ouro *s.* golden wedding
bodas de prata *s.* silver wedding
bofetada *s.* slap
boi *s.* ox
boia *s.* buoy
boia de salvamento *s.* lifebuoy
boiar *v.* float
boicotar *v.* boycott
boicote *s.* boycott
boina *s.* beret
bola *s.* ball, scoop
bola de futebol *s.* ball, football
bola de neve *s.* snowball
bolacha *s.* wafer
bolachinha *s.* cookie
bolar *v.* make up, work out
boleia *s.* cab
boletim escolar *s.* card, school report
bolha *s.* blister, bubble
boliche *s.* bowling
bolinha *s.* dot, spot
bolinha de gude *s.* marble
bolo *s.* cake
bolor *s.* mold, mould
bolorento *adj.* moldy, mouldy
bolsa *s.* handbag, purse
bolsa de estudo *s.* grant, scholarship
bolsa de valores *s.* stock exchange
bolso *s.* pocket
bom *adj.* fine, good, nice, okay, pleasant
bom senso *s.* common sense
bom trabalho good job
bomba *s.* bomb, pump

bomba teleguiada *s.* smart bomb
bombardear *v.* bomb, shell
bombardeio *s.* air raid
bombardeiro *s.* bomber
bombear *v.* pump
bombeiro *s.* firefighter, fireman
bombinha *s.* cracker, firecracker
bondade *s.* goodness
bonde *s.* cable-car, streetcar, tram
boné *s.* cap
boneca *s.* doll
bonito *adj.* beautiful, good-looking, handsome, pretty
bônus *s.* bonus
borboleta *s.* butterfly
borbulhar *v.* bubble
borda *s.* border, brim, edge, rim
bordado *s.* embroidery
bordado *adj.* embroidered
bordar *v.* embroider
borracha *s.* eraser, rubber
borrifar *v.* spray, sprinkle
borrifo *s.* spray
bosque *s.* wood, woods
bota *s.* boot
botânica *s.* botany
botânico *adj.* botanic
botão *s.* bud, button, knob
botar *v.* lay
bote *s.* dinghy
bote salva-vidas *s.* lifeboat
boxe *s.* boxing
boxeador *s.* boxer
braçada *s.* stroke
bracelete *s.* bracelet
braço *s.* arm
branco *s.* white
branco *adj.* white
brasa *s.* coal
bravamente *adv.* bravely
bravo *adj.* angry, brave, cross, fierce, mad, rough
bravura *s.* bravery, courage
break *s.* break
brecha *s.* gap
brejo *s.* swamp
breque *s.* brake
bretão *s.* Britisher
breve *adj.* brief
briga *s.* fight, fighting, quarrel, row
brigada *s.* brigade
brigada de incêndio *s.* fire brigade
brigar *v.* fall out with, fight, quarrel, row
brilhante *adj.* bright, brilliant, clever, glaring, shiny
brilhantemente *adv.* brightly, brilliantly
brilhar *v.* flash, glare, gleam, shine, sparkle
brilho *s.* brightness, brilliance, gleam, shine, sparkle

brincadeira *s.* hoax, practical joke, trick
brincar *v.* fiddle, fool about/around, joke, kid, mess about/around, play
brinco *s.* earring
brindar *v.* toast
brinde *s.* toast
brinquedo *s.* toy
brisa *s.* breeze
britânico *adj.* British
britânico *s.* Britisher
broca *s.* drill
brocar *v.* drill
brocha *s.* brush
broche *s.* brooch
brochura *s.* paperback
bronze *s.* bronze
bronzeado *s.* suntan, tan
bronzeado *adj.* suntanned, tanned
brotar *v.* sprout
browser *s.* browser
bruscamente *adv.* roughly
brutal *adj.* brutal
brutalmente *adv.* brutally
bruxa *s.* witch
bruxaria *s.* witchcraft
budista *adj.* Buddhist
bueiro *s.* drain, gutter
bugigangas *s.* odds and ends
bulbo *s.* bulb
bule *s.* pot
bule de chá *s.* teapot
buquê *s.* bouquet
buraco *s.* hole, pit
burrice *s.* stupidity
burro *s.* donkey
burro *adj.* stupid
busca *s.* search
buscar *v.* search, seek
bússola *s.* compass
buzina *s.* horn
buzinar *v.* honk, hoot
byte *s.* byte

Cc

cabana *s.* cabin, hut
cabeça *s.* brain, brains, head, mind
cabecear *v.* head
cabeleireiro *s.* hairdresser
cabelo *s.* hair
cabelo longo *s.* long hair
cabeludo *adj.* hairy
caber *v.* fit
cabide *s.* coat-hanger, hanger, peg
cabina *s.* booth, box, cabin, cockpit, compartment
cabine telefônica *s.* call-box, phone booth/box, telephone booth/kiosk
cabo *s.* cable, corporal, handle
cabo de guerra *s.* tug-of-war
cabra *s.* goat
cabrito *s.* kid
caça *s.* fighter, hunt, hunting
caçada *s.* hunt
caçador *s.* hunter
caçador ilegal *s.* poacher
caçar *v.* hunt
caçar sem permissão poach
caçarola *s.* saucepan
cacau *s.* cocoa
cacheado *adj.* curly
cachear *v.* curl
cachecol *s.* scarf
cachimbo *s.* pipe
cacho *s.* bunch, curl
cachoeira *s.* waterfall
cachorrinho *s.* puppy
cachorro de rua *s.* stray
cachorro *s.* dog
cachorro-quente *s.* hot dog
cacto *s.* cactus
cada *pron.* each, every
cada vez menos less and less
cadarço *s.* lace, shoelace
cadáver *s.* corpse
cadeado *s.* padlock
cadeia *s.* jail, range
cadeira *s.* chair
cadeira de lona *s.* deck-chair
cadeira de rodas *s.* wheelchair
cadela *s.* bitch
caderno *s.* book, exercise book, notebook
café *s.* bar, cafe, coffee, coffee shop
café com leite *s.* coffee with milk, white coffee
café da manhã *s.* breakfast
cai fora! clear off!, get lost!, go away!, leave me alone!
cair *v.* decline, decrease, drop, fall (down), tumble
cair doente fall ill
cair nas suas mãos come into your possession
cair no choro burst into tears, burst out crying
cair no sono fall asleep
cais *s.* dock, quay
caixa *s.* box, carton, case, cash desk, cashier, checkout, chest, clerk, crate, teller
caixa alta *s.* capital, capital letter
caixa de correio *s.* postbox
caixa de correspondência *s.* letter-box, mailbox
caixa de fósforos *s.* matchbox
caixa de guardar dinheiro *s.* till
caixa do correio *s.* mailbox, pillar-box, postbox
caixa eletrônico *s.* ATM, cash machine
caixa postal *s.* PO Box
caixão *s.* coffin
calabouço *s.* dungeon
calado *adj.* quiet, silent
calar a boca shut up
calar alguém shut someone up
calar-se *v.* shut up
calça *s.* pants, trousers
calçada *s.* pavement, sidewalk
calçadão *s.* pedestrian mall, pedestrian precinct, shopping precinct
calção *s.* shorts
calção de banho *s.* (swimming) trunks
calçar *v.* put on
calcinha *s.* knickers, panties
calculado *adj.* calculated
calculadora *s.* calculator
calcular *v.* calculate, estimate, reckon
cálculo *s.* calculation
calda *s.* syrup
caldeira *s.* boiler
calendário *s.* calendar
caligrafia *s.* handwriting, writing
calmamente *adv.* calmly
calmante *adj.* soothing
calmo *adj.* calm, sleepy, smooth
calombo *s.* bump, lump
calor *s.* heat, warmth
caloria *s.* calorie
calórico *adj.* rich
calorosamente *adv.* warmly
calouro *s.* freshman
cama *s.* bed
cama de lona *s.* camp bed, cot
cama-beliche *s.* bunk bed
camada *s.* coat, covering, layer
camaleão *s.* chameleon
câmara *s.* council, hall, tube
camarada *s.* pal
camarão *s.* shrimp
camarim *s.* dressing room
camarote *s.* cabin
cambalear *v.* stagger
cambalhota *s.* somersault
câmbio! *int.* over!
camelo *s.* camel
câmera *s.* camera
câmera de vídeo *s.* video camera
caminhada *s.* hike, stroll, walk
caminhante *s.* hiker
caminhão *s.* lorry, truck
caminhar *v.* hike, stroll, walk
caminhar com dificuldade plod
caminho *s.* lane, path, way
camisa *s.* shirt
camisa de malha *s.* jersey
camiseta *s.* T-shirt, undershirt, vest
camisola *s.* nightdress
campainha *s.* bell, doorbell
campanha *s.* campaign
campanha publicitária *s.* advertising campaign
campeão *s.* champion
campeão de bilheteria *s.* blockbuster
campeão de vendas *s.* best-selling
campeão mundial *s.* world champion
campeonato *s.* championship, contest
campina *s.* meadow
camping *s.* camping
campismo *s.* camping
campista *s.* camper
campo *s.* countryside, course, field, ground, pitch
campo de batalha *s.* battlefield
campo de futebol *s.* football pitch
campo de golfe *s.* golf course
campo de petróleo *s.* oilfield
campo minado *s.* minefield
camponês *s.* peasant
camuflagem *s.* camouflage
camuflar *v.* camouflage
cana *s.* cane
canal *s.* canal, channel
caneleta *s.* groove
canário *s.* canary
canção *s.* song, tune
cancelado *adj.* off
cancelamento *s.* cancellation
cancelar *v.* call off, cancel
câncer *s.* cancer
candelabro *s.* candlestick
candente *adj.* red-hot
candidatar-se *v.* apply, run
candidato *s.* applicant, candidate, examinee
candidatura *s.* candidacy
caneca *s.* mug
canela *s.* cinnamon
caneta *s.* pen
caneta esferográfica *s.* ball-point

caneta hidrográfica *s.* felt-pen
caneta-tinteiro *s.* fountain-pen
canguru *s.* kangaroo
canhão *s.* cannon
canhoto *adj.* left-handed
canibal *s.* cannibal
canil *s.* kennel
canivete *s.* penknife, pocketknife
cano *s.* barrel, drain, tube
cano de esgoto *s.* drainpipe
canoa *s.* canoe
cansado *adj.* sick of, tired
cansar(-se) *v.* tire
cansativo *adj.* tiring
cantante *adj.* singing
cantar *v.* sing
cântaro *s.* pitcher
cantarolar *v.* hum
canteiro *s.* bed, flowerbed
cantiga de ninar *s.* lullaby, nursery rhyme
cantil *s.* canteen
cantina *s.* cafeteria, canteen, coffee shop
canto *s.* corner, singing, song
cantor *s.* singer
cantoria *s.* singing
canudinho *s.* straw
cão *s.* dog
cão de guarda *s.* watchdog
capa *s.* cloak, cover
capa de chuva *s.* raincoat
capa dura *s.* hardback
capacete *s.* crash-helmet, helmet
capacho *s.* mat
capacidade *s.* capability, capacity
capataz *s.* foreman
capaz *adj.* able, capable
capcioso *adj.* tricky
capela *s.* chapel
capim *s.* grass
capinar *v.* weed
capital *s.* capital
capitão *s.* captain
capítulo *s.* chapter, installment, part
capô *s.* bonnet, hood
capotar *v.* overturn, turn over
caprichado *adj.* neat
captura *s.* capture
capturar *v.* capture, trap
capuz *s.* hood
cáqui *adj.* khaki
cara *s.* fellow, guy, lad
cara a cara face to face
cara ou coroa heads or tails
caracol *s.* snail
característica *s.* characteristic, feature
característico *adj.* characteristic
caramelo *s.* toffee

caranguejo *s.* crab
caratê *s.* karate
caráter *s.* character
caravana *s.* caravan
carcereiro *s.* warder
cardápio *s.* menu
cardeal *s.* cardinal
cardigã *s.* cardigan
cardinal *s.* cardinal
careca *adj., s.* bald
carecer *v.* lack
carência *s.* scarcity
carestia *s.* famine
carga *s.* cargo, freight, load
cargo *s.* job, office, position, post
cariar *v.* decay
caridade *s.* charity
cárie *s.* decay, filling
carimbar *v.* stamp
carimbo *s.* stamp
carinhosamente *adv.* lovingly
carmesim *s.* crimson
carnaval *s.* carnival
carne *s.* flesh, meat
carne de ave doméstica *s.* poultry
carne de caça *s.* game
carne de carneiro *s.* mutton
carne de porco *s.* pork
carne bovina *s.* beef
carne de vitela *s.* veal
carneiro *s.* lamb
caro *adv.* dearly
caro senhor dear sir
caro *adj.* costly, dear, expensive
caroço *s.* pit, stone
carona *s.* lift, ride
caronista *s.* hitchhiker
carpete *s.* carpet
carpintaria *s.* carpentry
carpinteiro *s.* carpenter
carranca *s.* frown
carrasco *s.* hangman
carregado *adj.* deep, loaded
carregador *s.* porter
carregamento *s.* cargo, shipment
carregar *v.* carry, load
carreira *s.* career
carretel *s.* reel, spool
carrinho *s.* barrow, cart, trolley
carrinho de bebê *s.* baby carriage, pram, pushchair, stroller
carrinho de compras *s.* shopper
carrinho de mão *s.* wheelbarrow
carro *s.* automobile, car, motor car
carro de bombeiro *s.* fire-engine
carro de corrida *s.* racing car
carro esportivo *s.* sport car, sports car
carroça *s.* cart, wagon
carrossel *s.* carousel, merry-go-round, roundabout
carro-tanque *s.* tanker

carruagem *s.* carriage, coach
carta *s.* card, letter
carta de navegação *s.* chart
carta registrada *s.* registered letter
cartão *s.* card
cartão de crédito *s.* credit card
cartão de embarque *s.* boarding card
cartão de índice *s.* card index
cartão de saque *s.* cash card
cartão inteligente *s.* smart card
cartão postal *s.* postcard
cartão telefônico *s.* phonecard
cartaz *s.* notice, placard
carteira *s.* pocketbook, postwoman, purse, wallet
carteira de habilitação *s.* driving licence
carteira de identidade *s.* ID, identity card
carteira de motorista *s.* driver's license, licence
carteiro *s.* mailman, postman
cartomante *s.* fortune teller
cartum *s.* cartoon
carvalho *s.* oak
carvão *s.* coal
casa *s.* home, house
casa de cachorro *s.* kennel
casa de campo *s.* villa
casa de repouso *s.* nursing home
casa e comida *s.* board
casaco *s.* coat
casado *adj.* married
casal *s.* couple
casamenteiro *s.* matchmaker
casamento *s.* marriage, wedding
casar-se *v.* get married, marry
casca *s.* bark, peel, rind, shell, skin
cascalho *s.* gravel
cascata *s.* waterfall
casco *s.* hoof, shell
caseiro *adj.* homemade
caso *conj.* suppose
caso *s.* affair, case
casquinha *s.* cone
cassetete *s.* club
cassis *s.* blackcurrant
castanha *s.* chestnut, nut
castanho *adj.* brown
castelo *s.* castle
castiçal *s.* candlestick
castigar *v.* punish
castigo *s.* punishment
casual *adj.* casual
casualmente *adv.* casually
catálogo *s.* catalog
catálogo telefônico *s.* directory, telephone directory
catapulta *s.* catapult
catarata *s.* falls

catedral *s.* cathedral
categórico *adj.* definite
cativeiro *s.* captivity
cativo *s.* captive
católico *adj.* Catholic
catorze *s.* fourteen
catraca *s.* turnstile
caubói *s.* cowboy
cauda *s.* tail
causa *s.* cause
causar *v.* cause
cautela *s.* caution
cautelosamente *adv.* cautiously
cauteloso *adj.* cautious, safe
cavalariço *s.* groom
cavaleiro *s.* knight, rider
cavalgar *v.* go riding
cavalheiro *s.* gentleman
cavalo *s.* horse
cavar *v.* dig
caverna *s.* cave
cavilha *s.* peg
cavoucar *v.* dig
caxumba *s.* mumps
CD *s.* CD, compact disc
CD player *s.* compact disc player
CD-ROM *s.* CD-ROM
cebola *s.* onion
ceder *s.* give way
ceder *v.* give in, sag
cedo *adj.* early
cedo *adv.* at an early hour, soon
cedo demais too soon
cédula *s.* ballot
cegar *v.* blind
cego *adj.* blind, blunt
cegonha *s.* stork
cegueira *s.* blindness
ceia *s.* supper
ceifar *v.* reap
cela *s.* cell
celebração *s.* celebration
celebrar *v.* celebrate
celeiro *s.* barn
Celsius *s.* Celsius
célula *s.* cell, unit
cem *s., num.* one hundred
cemitério *s.* cemetery, graveyard
cena *s.* scene
cenário *s.* scenery
cenho *s.* frown
cenoura *s.* carrot
centavo *s.* cent, pence, penny
centeio *s.* rye
centelha *s.* gleam
centena *s.* hundred
centenas *s.* hundreds
centésimo *s.* hundredth
centígrados *s.* Celsius
centilitro *s.* centiliter
centímetro *s.* centimeter
central *adj.* central

centro *s.* center, centre, heart
centro comunitário *s.* community center
centro da cidade *s.* downtown
centro de compras *s.* shopping centre/mall
cera *s.* polish, wax
cerâmica *s.* pottery
ceramista *s.* potter
cerca *s.* fence
cerca de *adv.* about, roughly
cerca viva *s.* hedge
cercado *s.* farmyard, pen
cercanias *s.* surroundings
cercar *v.* enclose, surround
cerco *s.* siege
cerda *s.* bristle
cereal *s.* cereal
cérebro *s.* brain
cereja *s.* cherry
cerimônia *s.* ceremony
cerimônia religiosa *s.* religious ceremony
cerimonial *adj.* ceremonial
cerquilha *s.* hash
cerração *s.* haze
certamente *adv.* certainly, surely
certeza *s.* certainty
certidão *s.* certificate
certificar *v.* certify
certificar-se *v.* be sure to, make certain
certo *s.* right
certo *adj.* certain, correct, definite, okay, right, sure
cerveja *s.* beer
cervo *s.* deer
cessar *v.* cease
cessar-fogo *s.* cease-fire
cesta *s.* basket
cesto *s.* bin
cesto de lixo *s.* rubbish bin, waste(-paper) basket
cetim *s.* satin
céu *s.* heaven, sky
cevada *s.* barley
chá *s.* tea
chacal *s.* jackal
chacoalhar *v.* rattle, shake
chacota *s.* jeer
chalé *s.* cottage
chaleira *s.* kettle
chama *s.* flame
chamada *s.* call
chamada a cobrar *s.* reverse charge call
chamado *s.* call
chamar *v.* call
chamar a atenção de alguém catch someone's eye, draw someone's attention to

chamar a cobrar *v.* reverse the charges
chamar-se *v.* be called
chamejar *v.* flare
chaminé *s.* chimney, funnel
champanhe *s.* champagne
chance *s.* chance
chances *s.* odds
chantagear *v.* blackmail
chantagem *s.* blackmail
chão *s.* earth, floor, ground, land
chapa *s.* sheet
chapéu *s.* hat
chapinhar *v.* splash
charada *s.* puzzle, riddle
charme *s.* charm
charmoso *adj.* charming
charuto *s.* cigar
chassis *s.* framework
chato *adj.* boring, dull, tedious
chave *s.* key
chave de fenda *s.* screwdriver
chave inglesa *s.* spanner, wrench
checar *v.* check, check out, check up
check-in *s.* check-in
check-up *s.* check-up
chef *s.* chef
chefe *s.* boss, chief, head
chefe de polícia *s.* police constable
chega! *v.* enough!
chegada *s.* approach, arrival
chegado *adj.* close
chegar *v.* arrive, arrive at/in, come (by), get, get to, make it, reach, turn up
chegar a um acordo compromise
chegar ao fim come to an end, get through
chegar ao fundo de get to the bottom of
chegar até come up to, get up to, reach
chegar mais perto de get/come closer
chegar perto come near/nearer, gain on
cheio *adj.* busy, full of/up, loaded
cheio de altos e baixos bumpy
cheio de neve snowy
cheirar *v.* smell, sniff
cheirar mal stink
cheiro *s.* smell
cheque *s.* check, cheque
cheque de viagem *s.* traveller's cheque
chiado *s.* hiss
chiclete *s.* (chewing) gum
chicote *s.* whip
chicotear *v.* whip
chifre *s.* horn

chimpanzé s. chimpanzee
chinelo s. slipper
chip s. chip, microchip
chiqueiro s. pigsty
chocalho s. rattle
chocante adj. appalling, shocking
chocar v. hatch, shock
chocolate s. chocolate, cocoa
chocolate ao leite s. milk chocolate
chocolate puro s. plain chocolate
chofer s. chauffeur
choque s. shock
choque elétrico s. electric shock, shock
choramingar v. whine
chorar v. cry, weep
chorar a morte de v. mourn
chover v. rain
chover granizo hail
chover torrencialmente pour
chumbo s. lead
chupar v. suck
churrasco s. barbecue
chutar v. kick
chute s. kick
chute de pênalti s. penalty kick
chuva s. rain
chuva fina s. drizzle
chuva leve e rápida s. shower
chuveiro s. shower
chuviscar v. drizzle
chuvisco s. drizzle
chuvoso adj. rainy
cibercafé s. cybercafe
ciberespaço s. cyberspace
cicatriz s. scar
cicatrizar v. heal
ciclismo s. cycling
ciclista s. cyclist, rider
cidadania s. citizenship
cidadão s. citizen, national
cidade s. city, town
ciência s. science
ciente adj. aware, conscious
cientificamente adv. scientifically
científico adj. scientific
cientista s. scientist
cigano s. gypsy
cigarro s. cigarette
cilíndrico adj. cylindrical
cilindro s. cylinder
cílios s. eyelashes
cimento s. cement
cinco s., num. five
cinegrafista s. cameraman / camerawoman
cinema s. cinema, movie theater, theater
cinquenta s., num. fifty
cintilação s. sparkle
cintilante adj. sparkling

cintilar v. gleam, glimmer, glisten, sparkle, twinkle
cinto s. belt
cinto de segurança s. safety/seat belt
cinto salva-vidas s. life preserver, lifebelt
cintura s. waist
cinza adj. gray, grey
cinza s. ash
cinzeiro s. ashtray
circo s. circus
circuito s. circuit
circulação s. circulation
circular adj. circular
circular s. circular
circular v. circulate
círculo s. circle
circundar v. encircle
circunferência s. circumference
circunstância s. circumstance
cirurgia s. surgery
cirurgia plástica s. plastic surgery
cirurgião s. surgeon
cisne s. swan
citação s. quotation
citar v. name, quote
ciumento adj. jealous
ciúmes s. jealousy
civil adj. civil, civilian
civil s. civilian
civilização s. civilization
civilizado adj. civil, civilized, polite
clamor s. outcry
clandestino adj. underground
clara s. white, whites
claramente adv. clearly, obviously, plainly, vividly
clarão s. flash
clarear v. brighten
claro int. certainly, of course, sure
claro que não certainly not
claro adj. bright, clear, definite, light, obvious, plain, sunlit
classe s. class, classroom, rate
classe alta s. upper class
classe média s. middle class
classe operária s. working class
clássico adj. classical
classificação s. classification
classificados s. want ad
classificar v. classify, grade
cliente s. client, customer
clima s. climate
clínico s. clinic
clipe s. clip
clipe de papel s. paper-clip
clique s. click
clonar v. clone
closet s. closet
clube s. club

clube de jovens s. youth club
clube noturno s. nightclub
coador s. strainer
coar v. strain
coaxar v. croak
coaxo s. croak
cobaia s. guinea pig
cobertor s. blanket
cobertura s. covering, icing
cobra s. snake
cobrador s. conductor
cobrança s. charge
cobrar v. charge, collect
cobrar a mais v. overcharge
cobre s. copper
cobrir v. coat, cover
coçar v. itch, scratch, tickle
coceira s. itch
cochilar v. doze, nap
cochilo s. doze, nap
cocho s. trough
cockpit s. cockpit
coco s. coconut
cocoricar v. crow
código s. code
código de área s. area code, code, dialling code
código postal s. postcode, zip code
coelhinho s. bunny
coelho s. rabbit
coffee break s. coffee break
cofre s. safe
cogumelo s. mushroom
coincidência s. coincidence
coincidir v. clash, overlap
coisa s. stuff, substance, thing
coisas velhas s. junk
cola s. glue, gum, paste
colante s. tights
colapso s. breakdown, collapse
colar s. necklace
colar v. cheat, copy, glue, paste, stick
colar com fita adesiva v. tape
colarinho s. collar
colchão s. mattress
colchetes s. brackets
coleção s. collection
colecionador s. collector
colecionar v. collect
colega s. buddy, colleague, mate, playmate
colega de classe s. classmate
colega de quarto s. room-mate
colégio s. high school
coleira s. collar, lead, leash
coleta s. collection
colete s. vest, waistcoat
colete à prova de balas s. bullet-proof vest
colete salva-vidas s. life jacket
coletiva de imprensa s. news conference, press conference

coletivo *adj.* collective
colheita *s.* harvest
colher *s.* spoon
colher *v.* harvest, pick, reap
colher de chá *s.* teaspoon
colher de sopa *s.* tablespoon
colherada *s.* spoon, spoonful
colidir *v.* collide
colina *s.* hill
colisão *s.* collision
colmeia *s.* beehive, hive
colo *s.* lap
colocar *v.* lay, load, place, put, put up, set
colocar algo em volta de wrap something round/around
colocar alguém contra turn someone against
colocar na cama *v.* tuck someone in/up
cólon *s.* colon
colônia *s.* colony
colonizador *s.* settler
colorido *adj.* colored, colorful
colorir *v.* color
coluna *s.* column, file
coluna vertebral *s.* backbone
com *prep.* along, with
com a condição de que on condition that
com a exceção de with the exception of
com a idade aged, with age
com a sua permissão with your permission
com amor love
com ânimo cheerfully
com ar-condicionado air-conditioned
com autoconfiança self-confidently
com calma calmly, in your own time
com calor hot
com certeza certainly, definitely, for certain/sure, indeed, of course, sure enough, surely
com ciúmes jealous, jealously
com clareza clearly
com confiança confidently
com cuidado carefully
com defeito faulty, out of order
com desconfiança suspiciously
com doçura sweetly
com entusiasmo enthusiastically
com exceção de aside/apart from
com êxito successfully
com extravagância extravagantly
com facilidade easily, with ease
com felicidade happily
com firmeza firmly, tight
com fome hungry

com força hard
com franqueza bluntly
com gás fizzy, sparkling
com gratidão gratefully
com inteligência cleverly
com inveja enviously
com justiça fairly, justly
com leite milky
com licença excuse me
com medo afraid, frightened
com meus próprios olhos with my own eyes
com modos nicely
com muito prazer gladly
com névoa foggy
com o tempo in time
com paciência patiently
com prazer with pleasure
com precisão accurately
com pressa hastily, in a hurry
com que frequência...? how often...?
com referência a in/with regard to, with/in reference to
com relação a in connection with, in/with reference to, in/with regard to
com sabor de -flavored, -flavoured
com saudades de casa homesick
com sede thirsty
com segurança safely
com seriedade solemnly
com sucesso successfully
com surpresa in/with surprise
com ternura tenderly
com tristeza gloomily, unhappily
com vertigem giddy
com vigor energetically, vigorously
comandante *s.* commander
comandar *v.* direct
comando *s.* command
comarca *s.* county
combate *s.* combat
combatente *s.* fighter
combinação *s.* combination, match
combinado *adj.* combined
combinar *v.* arrange, blend, combine, fix, match
comboio *s.* convoy
combustível *s.* fuel
começar *v.* begin, break out, get down to, to open, start, start off, start out as
começar de novo begin again, start over
começar do zero start from scratch
começo *s.* beginning, start

começo ao fim *s.* from beginning to end
comédia *s.* comedy
comédia de costumes *s.* sitcom
comediante *s.* comedian
comedimento *s.* restraint
comemoração *s.* celebration
comemorar *v.* celebrate
comentar *v.* comment, remark
comentário *s.* comment, commentary, remark
comentarista *s.* commentator
comer *v.* eat
comercial *adj., s.* commercial
comercializar *v.* deal in, market
comerciante *s.* dealer, merchant, trader
comerciar *v.* trade
comércio *s.* business, commerce, trade
comércio eletrônico *s.* e-commerce
cometer *v.* commit, make
cometer suicídio commit suicide
cometer um deslize slip
cometer um erro make a mistake
comichão *s.* pins and needles
comichoso *adj.* itchy
comício *s.* rally
cômico *adj.* comical
cômico *s.* comic
comida *s.* food
comida pronta *s.* takeaway
comissária de bordo *s.* air-hostess, flight attendant, hostess, stewardess
comissário de bordo *s.* flight attendant, steward
comitê *s.* committee
como *adv.* how, however
como *conj.* as, because, like, since
como... é? what is... like?
como consequência de as a result of
como disse? pardon?, sorry
como é que eu vou saber? How should I know?
como é que? how come?
como eu ia saber? how should I know?
como num passe de mágica as if by magic, like magic
como resultado de as a result of
como se as though/if
como sempre as usual
como um todo on the whole
como vai? how do you do?
como você está? how are you doing?
como você ousa...? how dare you...?
como? I beg your pardon?, pardon?, sorry?

cômoda s. chest of drawers
comodidades s. comforts
comovente adj. emotional, pitiful
comovido adj. emotional
compadecer-se v. pity
companheiro s. companion
companhia s. company, societies, society
companhia aérea s. airline
comparação s. comparison
comparado adj. compared
comparar v. compare, contrast
comparativo s. comparative
comparecer v. attend
comparecimento s. attendance
compartilhar v. share
compartimento s. compartment
compasso s. compass, compasses
compensação s. compensation
compensar v. compensate, make it up to, make up for, pay
competência s. expertise
competente adj. able, efficient
competição s. competition
competidor s. competitor
competir v. compete
competitivo adj. competitive
complementar adj. complimentary
complementar v. complement
completamente adv. completely, through
completar v. complete
completo adj. closed, complete, full
complexo s. complex
complexo adj. complex
complicação s. complication
complicado adj. complex, complicated
complicar v. complicate
complô s. plot
componente s. component
compor v. compose, write
compor-se de v. consist of
comportamento s. behavior
comportamento indevido s. misbehavior
comportar v. hold
comportar-se v. behave (yourself)
comportar-se mal v. misbehave
composição s. composition
compositor s. composer
compra s. purchase, shopping
comprador s. shopper
comprar v. buy, purchase
compreender v. make sense of, see, understand
compreensão s. comprehension, realization, understanding
compreensivamente adv. sympathetically
compreensível adj. understandable
compreensivo adj. understanding
comprido adj. lengthy, long
comprimento s. length
comprimido s. tablet
comprometido adj. engaged
compromisso s. appointment
compulsão s. compulsion
compulsório adj. compulsory
computador s. computer
computador de mesa s. desktop computer
computador pessoal s. personal computer
comum adj. (out of the) ordinary, common, general, unusual, usual
comunicação s. communication
comunicações s. communications
comunicado s. announcement
comunicar v. announce, report
comunicar-se v. communicate, contact
comunidade s. community
conceder v. award, grant
concentração s. concentration
concentrar v. concentrate
concerto s. concert
concha s. sea shell, shell
concha de medida s. scoop
conciso adj. concise
concluir v. accomplish, conclude
conclusão s. conclusion
concordar v. agree
concorrente s. contestant
concreto s. concrete
concreto adj. concrete
concurso s. contest
condado s. county
conde s. count, earl
condecoração s. decoration
condecorar v. decorate
condenação s. condemnation, conviction
condenado s. convict
condenar v. condemn, convict
condessa s. countess
condição s. condition
condicionador de ar s. air--conditioner
condicional adj. conditional
condicionar v. condition
condições s. conditions
condimentado adj. spicy
condimentar v. spice
condimento s. spice
condizer v. fit
condolências s. condolences
conduta s. conduct
conduzir v. conduct, lead, steer
cone s. cone
conectar v. connect
conexão s. connection
conferência s. conference, lecture
conferencista s. lecturer
conferir v. check (out/up)
confessar v. admit, confess, own up
confiança s. confidence, trust
confiante adj. confident
confiantemente adv. confidently
confiar v. depend, trust, trust in
confiável adj. reliable, trustworthy
confidencial adj. confidential
confirmação s. confirmation
confirmar v. confirm
confissão s. confession
conflitar v. conflict
conflito s. conflict
conflito de gerações s. generation gap
conforme conj. according to
confortar v. comfort
confortável adj. comfortable
confortavelmente adv. comfortably
conforto s. comfort
confundir v. confuse, mistake, mix-up, muddle up
confusão s. confusion, mix-up, muddle
confuso adj. confused, confusing, fuzzy
congelado adj. frozen
congelador s. freezer
congelar v. freeze
congestionamento de trânsito s. traffic jam
congresso s. congress
conhecer v. get to know someone, know, meet
conhecido adj. familiar, well-known
conhecido s. acquaintance
conhecimento s. acquaintance, knowledge
conhecimentos gerais s. general knowledge
conjeturar v. wonder
conjunção s. conjunction
conjuntamente adv. jointly
conjunto s. mass, set, suit
conjunto de escritórios s. office block
conjunto habitacional s. estate, housing development, housing estate
conjunto adj. joint
conosco pron. us
conquista s. conquest
conquistar v. conquer
consciência s. awareness, conscience, consciousness
consciencioso adj. conscientious
consciente adj. conscious
conscrito s. conscript
consecutivo adj. running, successive

conseguir *v.* be able to, can, come by, could, gain, get, manage
conseguir controlar algo bring something under control
conseguir fazer be successful in [doing]
conseguir fugir make your escape
conselheiro *s.* counsellor
conselho *s.* advice, board, council
conselho de alunos *s.* student council
consentimento *s.* consent
consequência *s.* consequence
consequentemente *adv.* consequently, thus
consertar *v.* fix, mend, repair
conservação *s.* conservation
conservador *adj.* conservative
consideração *s.* consideration, regard, thought, thoughtfulness
considerado *adj.* reputed
considerando que considering
considerar *v.* consider, reckon, regard, take something into account
considerável *adj.* considerable
consideravelmente *adv.* considerably
consistente *adj.* consistent
consistir de *v.* consist
consoante *s.* consonant
consolação *s.* consolation
consolar *v.* comfort, console
consolo de lareira *s.* mantelpiece
conspícuo *adj.* conspicuous
conspiração *s.* conspiracy
conspirador *s.* conspirator
conspirar *v.* gang together/up, plot
constante *adj.* constant, steady
constantemente *adv.* constantly, steadily
consternação *s.* dismay
constituição *s.* constitution
constituir *v.* start
constrangedor *adj.* embarrassing
constranger *v.* embarrass
constrangido *adj.* embarrassed
constrangimento *s.* embarrassment
construção *s.* construction, structure
construir *v.* build, construct
construtivo *adj.* constructive
construtor *s.* builder
cônsul *s.* consul
consulta *s.* consultation
consultar *v.* consult
consultor *s.* adviser, consultant
consumidor *s.* consumer, customer
consumir *v.* consume

consumo *s.* consumption
conta *s.* account, bead, bill, check, concern, count
conta poupança *s.* savings account
contabilidade *s.* accountancy, accounts, book-keeping
contador *s.* accountant
contagioso *adj.* contagious
contaminar *v.* infect
contar *v.* count on, give away, rely on, repeat, tell
contar mentirinhas fib
contato *s.* contact
contável *adj.* countable
contêiner *s.* container
contenda *s.* dispute
contentar-se *v.* make do with
contente *adj.* content
conter *v.* contain
conteúdo *s.* content, contents
contexto *s.* context
continência *s.* salute
continente *s.* continent
continuação *s.* continuation, follow-up
continuamente *adv.* continually, continuously
continuar *v.* carry on, continue, get on with, go on, keep on, keep on [doing], persist
continuar em linha reta go straight on, keep straight on
contínuo *adj.* continual, continuous
conto *s.* tale
conto de fadas *s.* fairy tale
contorcer-se *v.* wriggle
contorno *s.* outline
contra *prep.* against, versus
contrabaixo *s.* bass
contrabandear *v.* smuggle
contrabandista *s.* smuggler
contrabando *s.* smuggling
contradição *s.* contradiction
contraditório *adj.* contradictory
contradizer *v.* contradict
contrair dívidas *s.* get into debt
contrário *adj.* contrary, opposite
contrário *adj.* contrary
contrastar *v.* contrast
contraste *s.* contrast
contratar *v.* contract, hire
contratempo *s.* setback
contrato *s.* contract
contribuição *s.* contribution
contribuir *v.* contribute
contrito *adj.* sorry
controlar *v.* control
controle *s.* control, grasp, restraint
controle remoto *s.* remote control
controles *s.* controls

controvérsia *s.* controversy
controverso *adj.* controversial
contudo *adv.* however, nevertheless, nonetheless
convencer *v.* convince
convencido *adj.* conceited, convinced
convenhamos *v.* let's face it
conveniência *s.* convenience
conveniente *adj.* convenient
convento *s.* convent
conversa *s.* chat, conversation, talk
conversar *v.* chat, converse, talk
converter *v.* convert
convicção *s.* conviction
convicto *adj.* convinced
convidado *s.* guest
convidar *v.* ask, invite
convidar alguém para treat someone to...
convincente *adj.* convincing
convir *v.* suit
convite *s.* invitation
convocar *v.* call someone up, draft
cookie *s.* cookie
cooperação *s.* cooperation
cooperar *v.* cooperate
cooperativo *adj.* cooperative
copa *s.* cup
Copa do Mundo *s.* World Cup
copas *s.* hearts
cópia *s.* copy, photograph, print, reproduction
cópia impressa *s.* printout
cópia xerox *s.* Xerox
copiar *v.* copy
copo *s.* glass, tumbler
coquetel *s.* cocktail
cor *s.* color
coração *s.* heart
coragem *s.* bravery, courage, guts, nerve
corajosamente *adv.* bravely, courageously
corajoso *adj.* brave, courageous
coral *s.* chorus
corante *s.* dye
corar *v.* blush, flush
corcova *s.* hump
corda *s.* rope, string
corda bamba *s.* tightrope
corda de pular *s.* jump rope, skipping rope
cordão *s.* cord, string
cor-de-rosa *adj., s.* pink
coro *s.* choir, chorus
coroa *s.* crown
coroar *v.* crown
coronel *s.* colonel
corpo *s.* body
corpo de bombeiros *s.* fire brigade

corpo de jurados *s.* jury
corpo docente *s.* staff
corporação *s.* corporation
correção *s.* correction
corredor *s.* aisle, corridor, passage
correia *s.* strap
correio *s.* mail, post
correio aéreo *s.* airmail
correio de voz *s.* voicemail
correio eletrônico *s.* electronic mail
corrente *s.* chain, current, stream
corrente de ar *s.* draft, draught
correr *v.* dash, flow, hurry, jog, race, run, rush, sprint, stream
correr atrás *v.* run after
correr risco *s.* take a chance, take a risk
correspondência *s.* correspondence, mail, post
corresponder(-se) *v.* correspond
corretamente *adv.* correctly, rightly
correto *adj.* correct
corretor ortográfico *s.* spell check
corretor *s.* real estate agent
corrida *s.* jog, jogging, race, racing, run, running, rush
corrida curta e rápida *s.* dash, sprint
corrida de carro *s.* motor racing
corridinha *s.* dash
corrigir *v.* correct, grade, mark
corrimão *s.* banister
corromper *v.* corrupt
corrupção *s.* corruption
corrupto *adj.* corrupt
cortador de grama *s.* lawnmower, mower
cortante *adj.* sharp
cortar *v.* axe, be cut off, break off, chop, clip, cut (back/out of/off/up)
cortar em fatias *v.* slice
cortar fora *v.* cut something off
corte *s.* court, cut
corte de cabelo *s.* haircut, hairstyle
cortês *adj.* courteous
cortina *s.* curtain
cortinas *s.* drapes
coruja *s.* owl
corvo *s.* crow, raven
cosmético *s.* cosmetic
cosmonauta *s.* spaceman, spacewoman
costa *s.* coast
costela *s.* rib
costeleta *s.* chop
costeletas *s.* bristle

costume *s.* custom
costumeiro *adj.* customary
costura *s.* sewing
costurar *v.* sew
costureira *s.* dressmaker
cotovelada *s.* nudge
cotovelo *s.* elbow
coturno *s.* combat boots
couro *s.* leather
couve-flor *s.* cauliflower
covarde *s.* coward
covinha *s.* dimple
coxa *s.* thigh
coxeadura *s.* limp
cozido *s.* stew
cozido *adj.* cooked, stewed
cozido no vapor *adj.* steamed
cozinha *s.* kitchen
cozinhar *v.* boil, cook, stew
cozinhar no vapor *v.* steam
cozinheiro *s.* cook
crânio *s.* skull
creche *s.* nursery, nursery school
credenciado *adj.* licensed
credencial *s.* pass
crédito *s.* credit
creme *s.* cream, custard
creme batido *s.* whipped cream
cremoso *adj.* creamy
crença *s.* faith, religion, belief
crepitar *v.* crackle
crepúsculo *s.* dusk, twilight
crer *v.* believe
crescente *adj.* growing
crescer *v.* grow (up)
crescido *adj.* grown
crescimento *s.* growth
crespo *adj.* curly
cretino *adj.*, *s.* jerk
cria *s.* calf, foal
criação *s.* creation
criador *s.* creator
criança *s.* child, infant, kid
criar *v.* breed, bring up, create, keep
criatividade *s.* creativity
criativo *adj.* creative
criatura *s.* creature
crime *s.* crime, murder
criminal *adj.* criminal
criminoso *adj.*, *s.* criminal
crina *s.* mane
críquete *s.* cricket
crise *s.* crisis
cristal *s.* crystal
cristandade *s.* Christianity
cristão *adj.* Christian
crítica *s.* criticism, review
criticar *v.* criticise, criticize, fault, review
crítico *adj.* critical
crítico *s.* critic

crocante *adj.* crisp
crocodilo *s.* crocodile
cru *adj.* raw
crucial *adj.* crucial
cruel *adj.* cruel, vicious
crueldade *s.* cruelty, ruthlessness
cruelmente *adv.* cruelly
cruz *s.* cross
cruzada *s.* crusade
cruzamento *s.* junction
cruzar *v.* cross
cruzeiro *s.* cruise
cúbico *adj.* cubic
cubo *s.* cube
cubo de gelo *s.* ice cube
cuco *s.* cuckoo
cueca *s.* pants, underpants
cueca boxer *s.* shorts
cuidado *s.* care, caution
cuidado com *v.* beware of
cuidado! *int.* be careful!, look out!, watch it/out!
cuidador *s.* caregiver, carer, nurse, nursemaid
cuidadosamente *adv.* carefully
cuidadoso *adj.* careful, safe
cuidar *v.* care for, look after, mind, nurse, see to, take care of
cuja(s) *pron.* whose
cujo(s) *pron.* whose
culinária *s.* cookery, cooking
culpa *s.* blame, fault, guilt
culpado *adj.* guilty
culpar *v.* blame
cultivar *v.* cultivate, grow
cultivo *s.* cultivation
culto *s.* cult, worship
culto *adj.* learned
cultura *s.* crops, culture
cultural *adj.* cultural
cume *s.* summit
cumprimentar *v.* greet, shake hands with
cumprimento *s.* greeting
cumprir *v.* fulfil, observe
cumprir uma promessa keep a promise
cunhada *s.* sister-in-law
cunhado *s.* brother-in-law
cupom *s.* coupon
cúpula *s.* dome, shade
cura *s.* cure
curar *v.* cure
curativo *s.* dressing
curiosamente *adv.* curiously
curiosidade *s.* curiosity
curioso *s.* bystander
curioso *adj.* curious, inquisitive, nosy, strange
curral *s.* farmyard
currículo *s.* curriculum, resumé
curso *s.* course

curso noturno *s.* night school
cursor *s.* cursor
curto *adj.* short
curva *s.* bend, curve, turn, turning, twist
curvar *v.* bend, bow, stoop
cuspe *s.* spit
cuspir *v.* spit
custar *v.* cost
custe o que custar at all costs
custo *s.* cost
custoso *adj.* costly
cutelaria *s.* cutlery
cutucada *s.* nudge
cutucar *v.* nudge, pick, poke

Dd

d.C. *abr.* AD
da mesma forma likewise
da moda fashionable
dado *s.* dice, input
dados *s.* data
daltônico *adj.* color-blind
dama de honra *s.* bridesmaid
damasco *s.* apricot
danado *adj.* mischievous
dança *s.* dance, dancing
dança do ventre *s.* belly-dance
dança folclórica *s.* folk dance
dançar *v.* dance
dançarino *s.* dancer
danificar *v.* damage
dano *s.* damage
daqui a pouco shortly, soon
dar *v.* attach, deal, equal, give, hand, make
dar a entender hint
dar à luz give birth to
dar a sua opinião have your say
dar alta discharge
dar aulas coach, lecture, teach
dar baforadas puff
dar bronca scold, tell off
dar certo work (out)
dar conta cope
dar corda em wind
dar de ombros shrug
dar descarga flush
dar errado go wrong
dar forma shape
dar gargalhadas roar
dar gorjeta tip
dar lembranças a give my regards to
dar licença a license
dar nó knot
dar no mesmo make no difference
dar nos nervos get on your nerves
dar nota grade, mark
dar o troco get your own back
dar ordem a alguém dictate
dar palmadas smack
dar passagem give way, make way for, yield
dar ponto stitch up
dar por certo take something for granted
dar ré back
dar risadinhas bobas giggle
dar sermão preach
dar tapinhas em pat
dar testemunho give evidence
dar um bom exemplo set a good example
dar um fim em put an end to
dar um soco punch
dar um susto em alguém give someone a scare
dar um tempo hang on, linger
dar um tranco jerk
dar uma declaração make a statement
dar uma olhada browse, have/take a look, look over
dar uma opinião have a say
dar uma palavrinha com have a word with
dar uma passada drop by/in, pop in/over
dar uma sugestão make a suggestion
dardo *s.* dart
dardo de arremesso *s.* javelin
dar-se o trabalho *s.* bother, take the trouble
dar-se bem *v.* get away with, succeed
dar-se com *v.* get along (with), get on (with)
data *s.* date
datar *v.* date
datilografar *v.* type
datilografia *s.* typing
datilógrafo *s.* typist
de *pron.* by, from, in, of, out of, to, with
de acordo com in accordance/agreement with
de agora em diante from now on
de algum modo somehow
de alguma forma somehow
de antemão beforehand
de avião by air, flying
de boa aparência good-looking
de boa qualidade fine
de boa vontade willingly
de bom coração kind-hearted
de bom gênio good-tempered
de bom gosto nice, tasteful
de bom grado willingly
de braços abertos with open arms
de braços dados arm in arm
de brincadeira for fun
de cabeça head first
de cabeça para baixo upside down
de canto singing
de casal double
de cima above
de cinema movie
de classe alta upper-class
de classe média middle-class
de comprimento long
de cor by heart
de costas back
de cristal crystal
de desconto off
de distância apart, away, off
de dois em dois two by two
de duas em duas two by two
de escritório clerical
de espessura thick
de espião spy
de ficção fictional
de folga off, off duty
de forma nenhuma not at all
de frente head-on
de gênio bom good-natured
de graça for nothing, free, free of charge
de guarda on guard
de hoje today's
de hora em hora hourly
de idade aged
de inverno warm, wintry
de jeito nenhum by no means, no way, not at all, on no account
de lã woolen, woolly
de lado sideways
de lado aside
de largura broad, wide
de lazer leisure
de linha regular
de longe by far
de lua moody
de madeira wooden
de mal a pior go from bad to worse
de maneira nenhuma not at all, not in the least
de mão única one-way
de mãos dadas hand in hand
de massa mass
de mau gosto tasteless
de mau humor in a temper
de medicina medical
de melhoras get well, recover
de mentira fake
de modo indolor painlessly
de nada don't mention it, not at all, you're welcome
de noite overnight
de novo again, once more
de ouro golden
de ouro gold
de pau wooden
de pé up
de perto closely
de plantão on duty
de ponta-cabeça upside down
de pouca importância minor
de prestígio prestigious
de primeira first-rate
de primeira classe first class
de prisão imprisonment
de profissão by trade
de profundidade deep
de prontidão on standby

de propósito deliberately, on purpose
de qualquer forma anyway, in any case
de qualquer modo anyway
de quatro on all fours
de quatro patas four-legged
de quem whose
de repente all at once, all of a sudden, suddenly
de segunda classe second-class, second-rate
de segunda mão second-hand
de segundo grau secondary
de sempre usual
de serviço on duty
de solteiro bachelor, single
de sorte lucky
de sucesso successful
de tempo integral full-time
de tempos em tempos every so often, from time to time
de terra dirt
de todo dia everyday
de trabalho working
de trás para frente backward
de trem railroad, railway
de última hora red-hot
de uma forma ou de outra one way or another
de uma vez por todas once and for all
de uma vez só at one go
de verdade proper, real, true
de vez em quando every now and again, every now and then, from time to time, occasionally, once in a while
de volta back
debate *s.* debate
debater *v.* confer, debate
débil *adj.* feeble
debilitado *adj.* frail
débito *s.* debt
debruçar-se *v.* lean
década *s.* decade
decência *s.* decency
decente *adj.* decent
decepção *s.* disappointment
decepcionado *adj.* disappointed
decepcionante *adj.* disappointing
decepcionar *v.* disappoint, let someone down
decidido *adj.* decisive
decidir *v.* be settled, decide
decifrar *v.* make out
decimal *s.* decimal
décimo *s.* tenth
décimo nono *s., num.* nineteenth
décimo oitavo *s., num.* eighteenth
décimo primeiro *s., num.* eleventh

décimo quinto *s., num.* fifteenth
décimo segundo *s., num.* twelfth
décimo sétimo *s., num.* seventeenth
décimo terceiro *s., num.* thirteenth
decisão *s.* decision, resolution
decisivo *adj.* decisive
declaração *s.* declaration, statement
declarar *v.* declare, state
declarar guerra a *s.* declare war on
declinar *v.* decline
declive *s.* slope
decolagem *s.* take-off
decolar *v.* take off
decoração *s.* decoration
decorar *v.* decorate, learn
decorrer *s.* course
decretar *v.* rule
dedicação *s.* dedication
dedicado *adj.* devoted
dedicar *v.* dedicate, devote
dedo *s.* finger
dedo do pé *s.* toe
default *s.* default
defeito *s.* fault
defeituoso *adj.* faulty
defender *v.* champion, defend, stand up for, uphold
defender seus direitos stand up for your rights
defensivo *adj.* defensive
defesa *s.* defence, defense
defesa própria *s.* self-defence
deficiência *s.* handicap
deficiente *adj.* deficient, disabled, handicapped
definição *s.* definition
definir *v.* define
deflagração *s.* outbreak
defraudar *v.* swindle
defumado *adj.* smoked
degelar(-se) *v.* thaw
degenerado *s.* degenerate
degenerar *v.* degenerate
degrau *s.* rung
deitar-se *v.* lie, lie down
deixa pra lá never mind
deixar *v.* drop, keep, leave, let, quit
deixar... em algum lugar leave... behind
deixar alguém desconfiado make someone suspicious
deixar alguém em paz leave someone alone
deixar alguém entrar let someone in
deixar alguém esperando keep someone waiting

deixar alguém louco drive someone crazy/mad
deixar alguém sair let someone out
deixar alguém zangado make someone angry
deixar bravo upset
deixar cair drop
deixar crescer grow
deixar de fazer algo fail to do something
deixar de fora leave out
deixar de frequentar drop out
deixar de molho soak
deixar passar miss, overlook
deixe que eu... deixe-me... let me...
dela *pron.* her, its
delas *pron.* their
delatar *v.* inform on
dele *pron.* his, its
delegação *s.* deputation
delegacia *s.* station
delegacia de polícia *s.* police station
deleitar *v.* delight
deles *pron.* their
deletar *v.* delete
deliberadamente *adv.* deliberately
deliberado *adj.* deliberate
delicadamente *adv.* gently, graciously
delicado *adj.* dainty, delicate, gentle, sensitive
delicatéssen *s.* delicatessen
deliciar-se *v.* indulge
delicioso *adj.* delicious
delinquente *s.* offender
delinquente juvenil *s.* juvenile delinquent
delito *s.* offence, offense
delivery *s.* delivery
demais *adj.* over-, too, too many, too much
demanda *s.* demand
demão *s.* coat, layer
demente *adj.* mad, mentally ill
demissão *s.* dismissal, resignation
demitir *v.* dismiss, fire, sack
demitir-se *v.* resign
democracia *s.* democracy
democrata *s.* democrat
democrático *adj.* democratic
demolir *v.* demolish, knock down, pull down, tear down
demônio *s.* devil
demonstração *s.* demonstration
demonstrar *v.* demonstrate
demora *s.* delay, hold-up
demorar-se *v.* linger
denim *s.* denims
densamente *adv.* densely

densidade *s.* density
denso *adj.* dense, thick
dental *adj.* dental
dentário *adj.* dental
dente *s.* tooth
dentista *s.* dentist
dentre *prep.* out of
dentro *prep.* inside, within
departamento *s.* department
depende (de) it depends (on)
dependência *s.* dependence
dependente *adj.* dependent
depender *v.* rely/depend on
depois *adv.* after, afterward, later, next, then
depois de amanhã *adv.* the day after tomorrow
depositar *v.* deposit
depósito *s.* deposit, dump, storage, storeroom, warehouse
depósito de bagagem *s.* left luggage office
depravado *adj.* vicious
depressa! *int.* hurry up!
depressão *s.* depression
deprimente *adj.* depressing
deprimido *adj.* depressed
deprimir *v.* depress
deputado *s.* representative
deque *s.* deck
derivado *s.* derivative
derramar *v.* shed, spill
derrame cerebral *s.* stroke
derrapar *v.* skid
derreter *v.* melt
derrota *s.* defeat
derrotar *v.* beat, defeat
derrubar *v.* break/cut down, drop, knock down/over, tackle
desabar *v.* collapse, come down
desacelerar *v.* slow down
desacordo *s.* disagreement
desacostumado *adj.* unaccustomed
desafiador *adj.* defiant
desafiadoramente *adv.* defiantly
desafiar *v.* challenge, defy
desafio *s.* challenge
desafortunado *adj.* unfortunate, unlucky
desagradável *adj.* unpleasant, unwelcome
desagradavelmente *adv.* unpleasantly
desagrado *s.* dislike
desajeitadamente *adv.* clumsily
desajeitado *adj.* clumsy
desamarrar *v.* untie
desamparado *adj.* helpless
desamparo *s.* helplessness
desanimar *v.* lose heart

desaparecer *v.* disappear, vanish
desaparecido *adj.* missing
desaparecimento *s.* disappearance
desapontado *adj.* disappointed
desapontamento *s.* disappointment
desapontar *v.* disappoint
desaprovação *s.* disapproval
desaprovar *v.* disapprove
desarmado *adj.* unarmed
desarrumação *s.* untidiness
desarrumado *adj.* untidy
desastre *s.* crash, disaster
desastroso *adj.* disastrous
desatado *adj.* undone
desatar *v.* undo, unfasten, untie
desatar a *v.* break into, burst into
desatar a chorar *v.* break down
desatarraxar *v.* unscrew
desatencioso *adj.* inconsiderate
desatualizado *adj.* out of date, outdated
desavença *s.* argument, disagreement
desbotar *v.* fade
descalço *adv.* barefoot
descansar *v.* rest
descanso *s.* relaxation, rest
descarga *s.* discharge
descarregar *v.* dump, unload
descartar *v.* dispose of
descartável *adj.* disposable
descarte *s.* disposal
descasado *adj.* unmarried
descascar *v.* flake, peel, shell, strip
descendente *s.* descendant
descer *v.* climb/come down, descend, dismount, get down/off/out of, go down
descida *s.* descent
desclassificar *v.* disqualify
descoberta *s.* discovery, finding
descobrir *v.* discover, figure out, find out, uncover
desconectar *v.* disconnect
desconfiado *adj.* suspicious
desconfiança *s.* suspicion
desconfiar *v.* distrust, suspect
desconfortável *adj.* uncomfortable
desconfortavelmente *adv.* uncomfortably
desconhecido *adj.* unfamiliar, unknown
desconsiderar *v.* disregard
descontar *v.* cash
descontente *adj.* discontented, displeased
desconto *s.* discount
descortês *adj.* impolite, rude
descrever *v.* describe
descrição *s.* description
descuidadamente *adv.* carelessly

descuidado *adj.* careless
descuido *s.* carelessness
desculpa *s.* apology, excuse
desculpar *v.* excuse, forgive
desculpar-se *v.* apologize
desculpe! excuse me, sorry
desde *prep.* since
desde então ever since, since
desde quando...? since when...?
desde que as long as, ever since
desdenhar *v.* scorn
desdenhoso *adj.* scornful
desdobrar *v.* spread, unfold
desejar *v.* desire, may, please, wish (for)
desejável *adj.* desirable
desejo *s.* desire, longing, wish
desembrulhar *v.* unwrap
desempenhar *v.* perform
desempenho *s.* performance
desempregado *adj.* out of work, unemployed
desemprego *s.* unemployment
desencorajar *v.* discourage
desengonçado *adj.* awkward, clumsy
desenhar *v.* design, draw
desenho *s.* drawing, picture
desenho animado *s.* cartoon
desenterrar *v.* dig up
desenvolver *v.* develop, grow
desenvolvido *adj.* developed
desenvolvimento *s.* development
desequilibrado *adj.* uneven
desertar *v.* desert
deserto *s.* desert
deserto *adj.* deserted, uninhabited
desesperadamente *adv.* badly, desperately, hopelessly
desesperado *adj.* desperate
desesperador *adj.* desperate
desespero *s.* despair, desperation
desestimular *v.* put someone off
desfavorável *adj.* unfavorable
desfazer *v.* undo, unpack, untie
desfazer-se *adj.* come undone
desfeito *adj.* undone
desfiladeiro *s.* pass
desfilar *v.* parade
desfile *s.* parade, procession, show
desfile de moda *s.* fashion show
desgastar(-se) *v.* wear out
desgosto *s.* grief, regret
desgostosamente *adv.* disgustedly
desgraça *s.* disgrace
desgraçado *s.* bastard
desgraçar *v.* disgrace
design *s.* design
designar *v.* assign
designer *s.* designer
designer de moda *s.* fashion designer

desincentivar *v.* discourage
desinfetante *s.* disinfectant
desinteressado *adj.* disinterested, uninterested
desistente *s.* drop-out
desistir *v.* give up
desjejum *s.* breakfast
desleixado *adj.* sloppy
desligado *adv.* off, out
desligar *v.* disconnect, hang up, ring/switch off, turn off/out, unplug
deslizar *v.* glide, skid, slide
desmaiar *v.* faint, pass out
desmanchar *v.* come/fall to bits
desmontar *v.* come apart, fall apart
desmoronar *v.* collapse, crumble, give way
desnecessariamente *adv.* needlessly, unnecessarily
desnecessário *adj.* needless, unnecessary
desobedecer *v.* disobey
desobediência *s.* disobedience
desobediente *adj.* disobedient
desodorante *s.* deodorant
desodorizador de ambiente *s.* air freshener
desolador *adj.* dismal
desonesto *adj.* crooked, dishonest
desordeiro *s.* hooligan
desordem *s.* disorder, disturbance
desorganizar *v.* disrupt
despedaçar *v.* shatter, smash
despedida *s.* farewell
despedir *v.* fire, sack
despejar *v.* pour
despercebido *adj.* unaware
desperdiçador *adj.* wasteful
desperdiçar *v.* waste
desperdício *s.* waste
despertador *s.* alarm, alarm clock
despesa *s.* expense
despesas de viagem *s.* travel expenses, travelling expenses
despir(-se) *v.* get undressed, strip, undress
desplugar *v.* unplug
desprazer *s.* displeasure
desprender *v.* detach
despreocupadamente *adv.* leisurely
desprezar *v.* despise, look down on, scorn
desprezo *s.* contempt
desrespeito *s.* disrespect
desse modo *conj.* thus
destacar(-se) *v.* detach, stand out
destemidamente *adv.* fearlessly
destemido *adj.* fearless
destinar-se a be bound for
destino *s.* destination, destiny, fate

destrancado *adj.* unlocked
destrancar *v.* unlock
destravado *adj.* unlocked
destravar *v.* unlock
destreinado *adj.* out of practice
destro *adj.* right-handed
destroçar *v.* wreck
destroços *s.* wreck, wreckage
destróier *s.* destroyer
destruição *s.* destruction
destruir *v.* destroy, wreck
desumanidade *s.* ruthlessness
desvantagem *s.* disadvantage, handicap
desviar *v.* divert, swerve
desvio *s.* detour
detalhado *adj.* detailed
detalhe *s.* detail
detecção *s.* detection
detectar *v.* detect
detergente *s.* detergent
deteriorado *adj.* dilapidated
deteriorar *v.* deteriorate
determinação *s.* determination, resolution
determinado *adj.* determined
determinar *v.* determine
detestar *v.* detest, hate
detetive *s.* detective
detetive particular *s.* private detective
detetive secreto *s.* undercover detective
deus *s.* god
deusa *s.* goddess
devagar *adv.* slowly
devanear *v.* day-dream
devaneio *s.* day-dream
devastar *v.* wipe out
dever *s.* duty
dever *v.* must, ought to, owe, shall
dever de casa *s.* homework
deveria *v.* ought to, should
devido a *prep.* because of
devido a *adj.* due to, owing to
devoção *s.* devotion
devolver *v.* bring/give/take back, return
devorar *v.* devour
devotado *adj.* devoted
devotar *v.* devote
dez *s., num.* ten
dezembro *s.* December
dezenove *s., num.* nineteen, nineteenth
dezesseis *s., num.* sixteen
dezessete *s., num.* seventeen
dezoito *s., num.* eighteen
dia *s.* day
dia a dia *s.* day by day
dia das bruxas *s.* Halloween

dia de semana *s.* weekday
dia sim, dia não *s.* day in, day out
diabetes *s.* diabetes
diagnosticar *v.* diagnose
diagnóstico *s.* diagnosis
diagonal *s.* diagonal
diagrama *s.* diagram
dial *s.* dial
dialeto *s.* dialect
diálogo *s.* dialog
diamante *s.* diamond
diâmetro *s.* diameter
diante de *adv.* before, in front of
dianteira *s.* lead
dianteiro *adj.* front
diariamente *adv.* daily
diário *s.* diary, journal
diário *adj.* daily, everyday
dica *s.* hint, tip
dicionário *s.* dictionary
dieta *s.* diet
dietético *adj.* diet
diferença *s.* difference
diferenciação *s.* differentiation
diferenciar(-se) *v.* differ, differentiate
diferente *adj.* different, unlike
diferentemente *adv.* differently
diferir *v.* differ
difícil *adj.* difficult, hard, tough
dificuldade *s.* difficulty
digerir *v.* digest
digestão *s.* digestion
digitação *s.* typing
digitador *s.* typist
digital *adj.* digital
digitar *v.* type
dígito *s.* figure
dignidade *s.* dignity
digno *adj.* dignified
diligente *adj.* diligent, industrious
diluir *v.* dilute
diminuição *s.* decrease
diminuir *v.* decline, decrease, die down, diminish, lessen, lower
dinâmico *adj.* dynamic
dinamitar *v.* blast
dinamite *s.* dynamite
dinheiro *s.* money
dinheiro para pequenas despesas *s.* pocket money
dinheiro trocado *s.* change
dinossauro *s.* dinosaur
diploma *s.* degree, diploma
diplomata *s.* diplomat
diplomaticamente *adv.* tactfully
diplomático *adj.* diplomatic, tactful
direção *s.* direction, driving, way
direcionar *v.* direct
direita *s.* right

direito *adv.* correctly, nicely, rightly
direito *s.* law, right
direito *adj.* right, right-hand
direitos humanos *s.* human rights
diretamente *adv.* directly, straight
direto *adj.* non-stop
direto *adv.* direct, straight
direto ao ponto *s.* to the point
direto *adj.* direct, straightforward
diretor *s.* chairman, director, governor, head, managing director, principal
diretor de escola *s.* schoolmaster/schoolmistress
dirigir *v.* direct, drive, run
discador *s.* dial
discar *v.* dial
discernimento *s.* judgement
disciplina *s.* discipline, subject
disciplinar *v.* discipline
discípulo *s.* disciple
disc-jóquei *s.* disc-jockey
disco *s.* disc, disco, disk, record
disco rígido *s.* hard disk
disco voador *s.* flying saucer
discordância *s.* disagreement
discordar *v.* disagree
discoteca *s.* disco
discriminação *s.* discrimination
discriminar *v.* discriminate
discurso *s.* speech
discurso direto *s.* direct speech grammar
discurso indireto *s.* indirect/reported speech
discussão *s.* argument, discussion, quarrel, row
discutir *v.* argue, confer, discuss, row
disfarçar(-se) *v.* disguise
disfarce *s.* disguise
disparar *v.* bang, bolt, dart, explode, fire, go off
dispensa *s.* dismissal
dispensar *v.* dismiss, excuse
dispersar *v.* break up, disperse, scatter
displicência *s.* carelessness
displicente *adj.* careless
displicentemente *adv.* carelessly
disponível *adj.* available
dispor *v.* spare
disposição *s.* willingness
dispositivo *s.* device
disposto *adj.* willing
disputa *s.* feud, tug-of-war
disquete *s.* diskette, floppy disk
disseminado *adj.* widespread
dissertação *s.* paper
dissimulado *adj.* deceitful, sly

dissolver *v.* dissolve
distância *s.* distance
distante *adj.* distant
distender *v.* sprain, strain
distinção *s.* distinction
distinguir *v.* differentiate, distinguish, pick out, tell the difference
distintamente *adv.* distinctly
distintivo *s.* badge
distinto *adj.* distinct, distinguished, sharp
distorcer *v.* twist
distração *s.* distraction
distrair *v.* distract
distribuição *s.* distribution
distribuir *v.* distribute, give/hand out, issue
distrito *s.* district, precinct
distrito policial *s.* police station
distúrbio *s.* disorder
ditado *s.* dictation, saying
ditador *s.* dictator
ditar *v.* dictate
divergir *v.* conflict
diversão *s.* amusement, amusements, entertainment, fun
divertido *adj.* amusing, entertaining
divertimento *s.* fun
divertir-se *v.* enjoy oneself, have a good time
dividir *v.* divide, share, split
dividir ao meio *v.* halve
divino *adj.* divine
divisa *s.* boundary
divisão *s.* division
divorciado *adj.* divorced
divorciar-se *v.* divorce
divórcio *s.* divorce
divulgar *v.* publicize
dizer *v.* say, tell
dizer respeito a concern
dizeres *s.* writing
dó *s.* pity
do leste east, eastern
do nada all of a sudden, suddenly
do norte north, northern
do oeste west, western
do outro lado across
do que *conj.* than
do sul south, southern
doação *s.* donation
doar *v.* donate, give away
dobra *s.* crease, fold
dobradiça *s.* hinge
dobrado *adj.* folded
dobrar *v.* bend, double, fold
dobrável *adj.* folding
dobro *s.* double
doca *s.* dock
doce *adj.* sweet

doce *s.* candy, pudding, sweet
docemente *adv.* sweetly
doces de confeitaria *s.* pastries, pastry
documentário *s.* documentary
documento *s.* document
doçura *s.* sweetness
doença *s.* disease, illness, sickness
doente *adj.* ill, sick, unhealthy
doer *v.* ache, hurt
doida *s.* madwoman
doido *s.* madman
doido *adj.* crazy
doido por *adj.* crazy about
dois *s., num.* two
dólar *s.* buck, dollar
dolorido *adj.* painful, sore, tender
dolorosamente *adv.* painfully
doloroso *adj.* painful
domado *adj.* tame
domar *v.* tame
domesticado *adj.* tame
domesticar *v.* domesticate, tame
doméstico *adj.* domestic, internal
dominante *adj.* dominant
dominar *v.* dominate, master
domingo *s.* Sunday
domínio *s.* grasp, rule
dona de casa *s.* housewife
dono *s.* owner
donut *s.* doughnut
dor *s.* ache, grief, pain
dor de cabeça *s.* headache
dor de dente *s.* toothache
dor de estômago *s.* stomachache
dor de ouvido *s.* earache
dor nas costas *s.* backache
dormente *adj.* numb
dormir *v.* fall asleep, go to sleep, sleep
dormir além da conta oversleep
dormir até tarde sleep late
dormitório *s.* dormitory
dose *s.* dose
dourado *adj.* golden
doutor *s.* doctor
doze *s.* twelve
dragão *s.* dragon
drama *s.* drama, play
dramaticamente *adv.* dramatically
dramático *adj.* dramatic
dramatização *s.* role play
drástico *adj.* drastic
drenar *v.* drain
drinque *s.* drink
drive *s.* (disk) drive
droga *s.* drug
droga! *int.* damn!
drogadição *s.* drug addiction

drogadito *s.* drug addict
drogado *s.* drug addict
drogar *v.* drug
drogaria *s.* drugstore
duas vezes twice
duelo *s.* duel
duna *s.* dune
duplo *adj.* double

duque *s.* duke
duquesa *s.* duchess
duramente *adv.* sharply, unkindly
durante *prep.* during, through
durante a noite overnight
durante o dia daytime
durão *adj.* tough
durar *v.* last

duro *adj.* difficult, hard, harsh, sharp, stiff, tough, unkind
durão *adj.* tough
dúvida *s.* doubt, question
duvidar *v.* doubt
duvidoso *adj.* doubtful
dúzia *s.* dozen
DVD *s.* DVD

Ee

e *conj.* and
e assim por diante and so forth, and so on
é claro of course
e daí? so what?
é hora de it's time to
é melhor que 'd better, had better
é por isso que that's why
é possível que... it's possible that...
é proibido no
é um prazer it's a pleasure
é uma pena it's a pity/shame, what a pity/shame
eclipse *s.* eclipse
eco *s.* echo
ecoar *v.* echo
ecologia *s.* ecology
ecológico *adj.* eco-friendly, ecological
e-commerce *s.* e-commerce
economia *s.* economics, economy
economias *s.* savings
econômico *adj.* economic, economical
economista *s.* economist
economizar *v.* economize, put aside, save
economizar tempo save time
edição *s.* edition, issue
edifício *s.* building
editar *v.* edit
editor *s.* editor, publisher
educação *s.* education, politeness
educação física *s.* physical education
educacional *adj.* educational
educadamente *adv.* courteously, politely
educado *adj.* courteous, polite
educar *v.* bring someone up, educate
educativo *adj.* educational
efeito *s.* effect
efetivo *adj.* effective
efetuar *v.* effect
eficaz *adj.* effective
eficazmente *adv.* efficiently
eficiência *s.* efficiency
eficiente *adj.* efficient
eficientemente *adv.* efficiently
egoísmo *s.* selfishness
egoísta *adj.* selfish
egoisticamente *adv.* selfishly
ela *pron.* it, she
ela mesma *pron.* herself
elas *pron.* they
elas mesmas *pron.* themselves
elástico *s.* elastic, elastic band, rubber band
elástico *adj.* elastic
ele *pron.* he, it
ele mesmo himself, itself
elefante *s.* elephant
elegante *adj.* elegant, neat, smart
elegantemente *adv.* elegantly
eleger *v.* elect
eleição *s.* election, general election
eleitores *s.* voter
elemento *s.* element
eles *pron.* they
eles mesmos themselves
eletricidade *s.* electricity
eletricista *s.* electrician
elétrico *adj.* electric, electrical
eletrônica *s.* electronics
eletrônico *adj.* electronic
elevador *s.* elevator, lift
elevar-se *v.* soar
elo *s.* link
elogiar *v.* compliment, praise
elogio *s.* compliment, praise
eloquência *s.* eloquence
eloquente *adj.* eloquent
em *prep.* at, in, into, onto
em andamento in progress
em boas mãos in good hands
em branco blank
em breve before long, presently, shortly, soon
em casa at home
em caso de in case of
em chamas alight, burning, on fire
em cima da hora at short notice
em cima de on top of
em círculo round and round
em comum mutual
em confidência in confidence
em conjunto combined
em conserva pickled
em consideração a for the sake of
em detalhes in detail
em diante onward
em dias alternados on alternate days
em dinheiro cash
em direção a towards
em dúvida in doubt, uncertain
em espécie cash
em exposição on show
em farrapos in tatters
em flagrante red-handed
em forma fit
em frente *adv.* in front (of), opposite
em frente onward
em geral in general
em grande escala large-scale, on a large scale
em guerra at war
em hipótese alguma under no circumstances
em homenagem a in honor/honour of
em intervalos at intervals
em larga escala large-scale, on a large scale
em liquidação on sale
em lugar de in place of, instead of
em lugar nenhum nowhere
em más condições dilapidated
em meados de mid, mid-
em média on the average
em melhor situação better off
em memória de in memory of
em menor escala on a small scale, small-scale
em nome de on behalf of
em ordem in order, neat
em ordem alfabética alphabetically
em outras palavras in other words
em parte in part
em particular in particular/private, privately
em pedaços into pieces, to pieces
em pequena escala on a small scale, small-scale
em perigo in distress
em péssimo estado run-down
em pessoa in person
em ponto on the dot, sharp
em poucas palavras briefly
em primeira classe first class
em primeiro lugar first of all, firstly
em primeiro lugar in the first place
em princípio in principle
em progresso in progress
em promoção on sale
em público in public
em qualquer lugar anywhere
em resumo in brief
em risco at risk, in danger
em ruínas in ruins
em segredo in secret
em seguida after (that), next, then
em seu horário livre in/on your own time
em seu lugar in your/her/his place
em silêncio in silence
em sono profundo sound asleep
em suma in short
em tempo integral full-time
em termos gerais generally speaking
em terra ashore
em todo caso anyway, in any case
em todo lugar all over, everywhere

em troca de in exchange/return for
em vão in vain
em vez de instead (of), rather than
em volta de around, round
em voz alta aloud, out loud
emagrecer v. reduce, slim
e-mail s. e-mail / email
emaranhado s. tangle
emaranhado adj. tangled
emaranhar v. tangle
embaçado adj. blurred
embaixada s. embassy
embaixador s. ambassador
embaixo de adv. beneath, under, underneath
embalagem s. carton, packet, packing
embalar v. rock
embaralhar v. shuffle
embarcação s. vessel
embarcar v. board
emblema s. badge
embolorado adj. mouldy
embora adv. (even) though, although, while
emborcar v. capsize, tip over
emboscada s. ambush
emboscar v. ambush
embriaguez s. drunkenness
embrulhar v. wrap, wrap something up
emendar v. mend
emergência s. casualty department, emergence, emergency
emergir v. emerge
emigrar v. emigrate
emigração s. emigration
eminente adj. distinguished
emissão s. issue
emissora s. station
emissora de rádio s. radio station
emitir v. issue, utter
emoção s. emotion, thrill
emocionado adj. emotional, thrilled
emocional adj. emotional
emocionante adj. thrilling, touching
emocionar v. move, thrill
emoldurar v. frame
empacotamento s. packing
empacotar v. pack
empapado adj. soggy
empatar v. draw, equal, tie
empate s. draw, tie
empecilho s. snag
emperrado adj. jammed, stuck
emperrar v. jam
empilhar v. pile, stack
empinar v. fly

empoeirado adj. dusty
empolgação s. excitement
empolgado adj. excited
empolgante adj. exciting, thrilling
empolgar v. excite
emporcalhar v. foul
empreender v. undertake
empreendimento s. enterprise
empregada doméstica s. housekeeper, maid
empregado s. employee
empregador s. employer
empregar v. employ
emprego s. employment, job
empresa s. business, company, firm
empresária s. businesswoman
empresário s. businessman
emprestado s. on loan
emprestar v. lend, loan
empréstimo s. loan
empurrão s. push
empurrar v. jog, push, shove
encabeçar v. head
encaixar(-se) v. fit (in)
encaixe s. joint
encalhar v. stick
encaminhar v. direct, forward, refer
encanador s. plumber
encantado adj. bewildered, enchanted
encantador adj. charming
encantar v. charm, delight
encarar v. face
encarcerar v. imprison
encardido adj. grubby
encarregar-se v. undertake
encerrado adj. closed
encerrar atividade close/shut down
encharcado adj. drenched, soaking, soggy
encharcar v. soak
enchente s. flood
encher v. cram, fill (up), flood, heap, inflate
enchimento s. pad, patch
enciclopédia s. encyclopedia
encolher v. shrink
encompridar v. lengthen
encontrar v. come across, encounter, find, meet
encontrar por acaso meet by chance, run across
encontro s. date, encounter, meeting
encorajado adj. encouraged
encorajador adj. encouraging
encorajamento s. encouragement
encorajar v. encourage, urge
encostar v. pull in/over, touch

encrespar v. curl
encruzilhada s. crossroads
encurtar v. shorten
endereçar v. address
endereço s. address
endireitar v. square, straighten
endireitar(-se) v. straighten up
endividar-se v. get into debt
endurecer v. harden
energia s. energy, power
enevoado adj. hazy
enfaixar v. bandage
ênfase s. emphasis
enfatizar v. emphasize, stress
enfeite s. ornament
enfeitiçar v. bewitch, put a spell on
enfermagem s. nursing
enfermeira s. nurse, nursemaid
enfermidade s. sickness
enferrujado adj. rusty
enferrujar v. rust
enfiar v. plunge, poke, thrust, tuck
enfileirar-se v. line
enforcar v. hang
enforcar aula v. play hooky
enfraquecer v. weaken
enfrentar v. experience, face, stand up to
enfumaçado adj. smoky
engajar-se v. engage
enganado adj. mistaken, wrong
enganador adj. deceitful
enganar v. deceive, fool, mislead, trick
engano s. deceit, misunderstanding
enganoso adj. misleading
engasgar v. choke
engatinhar v. crawl
engavetamento s. pile-up
engenharia s. engineering
engenheiro s. engineer
engenhoca s. gadget
engolir v. swallow
engolir apressadamente gulp
engordar v. gain weight, get fat
engraçado adj. comical, funny, humorous
engrossar v. thicken
enguia s. eel
enguiço s. breakdown
enlameado adj. muddy
enlatado adj. canned, tinned
enluarado adj. moonlit
enojar v. disgust
enojar alguém make someone sick
enorme adj. enormous, huge, massive
enormemente adv. enormously
enquanto conj. as, during the time that, when, whereas, while

enquanto isso meanwhile
enredo s. plot
enriquecer adj. get rich
enrolar v. coil, roll (up), twist around
enrolar-se v. wrap
enrubescer v. blush, flush
enrugado adj. wrinkled
ensaiar v. practice, rehearse
ensaio s. essay, rehearsal
ensanguentado adj. bloody
ensinar v. direct, teach
ensino s. schooling, teaching
ensino a distância s. distance learning, e-learning
ensino básico s. elementary school
ensino médio s. high/secondary school
ensino superior s. higher education
ensolarado adj. sunny
ensurdecedor adj. deafening
ensurdecer v. deafen
entalhar v. carve
então adv. then
enteada s. stepdaughter
enteado s. stepson
entediado adj. bored
entediante adj. boring, dull, tedious
entediar v. bore
entender v. catch, figure out, follow, gather, get, grasp, make out, make sense of, pick up, see, understand
entender mal misunderstand
entendimento s. understanding
enterrar v. bury
enterro s. burial
entonação s. intonation
entorpecido adj. numb
entortar v. bend, twist
entrada s. admission, doorway, entrance, entry, starter, tackle, ticket, turning
entrada para carro s. drive, driveway
entrar v. climb, come/get in, draw, enter, get in/into/on, go into
entrar em conflito clash
entrar em contato com contact, get in touch with
entrar em erupção erupt
entrar em pânico panic
entrar para o exército join the army
entre prep. among, amongst, between
entre outras coisas among other things
entre uma coisa e outra in between

entre você e eu between you and me
entrega s. delivery
entregador s. delivery boy
entregar v. deliver, hand in/over, inform on
entregar alguém para turn someone over to
entregar sua carta de demissão hand in your resignation
entregar-se v. give oneself up
entrelaçar v. twist something a round
entretanto conj. nonetheless
entretenimento s. amusements, entertainment
entreter v. entertain
entrevista s. interview
entrevistador s. interviewer
entrevistar v. interview
entroncamento s. junction
entulho s. rubble
entusiasmado adj. enthusiastic
entusiasmo s. enthusiasm
entusiasta s. enthusiast
enumerar v. name, number
envelhecer v. get old
envelope s. envelope
envenenado adj. poisoned
envenenamento s. poisoning
envenenar v. poison
envergonhado adj. ashamed
enviar v. send (off)
enviar pelo correio mail, post
enviar por fax v. fax
enviar por navio v. ship
envolver v. concern, involve
envolver-se v. engage
envolvimento s. involvement
enxada s. hoe
enxaguada s. rinse
enxaguar v. rinse
enxame s. hive, swarm
enxugar v. dry, soak up, wipe (up)
enxurrada s. flood
epidemia s. epidemic
episódico adj. incidental
episódio s. episode
época s. day, period
equação s. equation
Equador s. Equator
equilibrado adj. balanced, even
equilibrar(-se) v. balance
equilíbrio s. balance
equipamento s. equipment, gear, tackle
equipar v. equip
equipar-se v. equip oneself
equipe s. crew, squad, team
equivocado adj. mistaken
era s. age, ivy
era uma vez once upon a time
ereto adj. erect

erguer v. erect, lift, put up, wind up [a car window]
erguer a voz v. raise your voice
erigir v. erect
errado s. wrong
errado adj. mistaken, wrong
errar v. make a mistake, miss
erro s. error, mistake
erro de ortografia s. spelling mistake
erroneamente adv. wrongly
erudição s. learning
erudito s. scholar
erupção s. eruption
erupção cutânea s. rash
erva s. herb
erva daninha s. weed
ervilha s. pea
ervoso adj. grassy
esbanjador/ra adj. wasteful
esboçar v. sketch, trace
esboço s. drawing, outline, sketch
esbofetear v. slap
escada s. ladder, staircase, stairs
escada de corda s. rope ladder
escada de incêndio s. fire-escape
escada portátil s. stepladder
escada rolante s. escalator
escadaria s. step
escala s. scale, stop
escalada s. climb
escalar v. climb, scramble
escaldadura s. scald
escaldar v. scald
escalpo s. scalp
escama s. scale
escamar v. flake
escancarado adj. wide open
escândalo s. scandal
escandaloso adj. outrageous
escanear v. scan
escapamento s. exhaust
escapar v. break out, escape, slip
escapulir v. slip
escarlate adj. scarlet
escárnio s. scorn
escassez s. lack, scarcity, shortage
escasso adj. scarce
escavação s. excavation
escavadora s. bulldozer
escavar v. dig
esclarecer v. clarify, enlighten
esclarecido adj. enlightened
escoar v. drain
escola s. school
escola de ensino fundamental s. junior high/school
escola de ensino médio s. high/secondary school
escola inclusiva s. comprehensive school
escola maternal s. nursery school

escola noturna s. night school
escola primária s. primary school
escola secundária s. grammar school
escola vocacional s. vocational school
escolha s. choice
escolher v. choose, pick, select
escoltar v. escort
escombros s. debris, rubble, wreck
esconde-esconde s. hide-and-seek
esconder v. conceal, hide, hold back, keep something from someone
esconderijo s. hide-out, hiding
escondido adj. hidden
escorpião s. scorpion
escorredor de prato s. plate rack
escorregadio adj. slippery
escorregador s. slide
escorregar v. slip
escorrer v. drain, run
escoteira s. girl guide
escoteiro s. boy scout
escoteiro s. scout
escova s. brush
escova de cabelo s. hairbrush
escova de dente s. toothbrush
escovar v. brush
escravidão s. slavery
escravo s. slave
escrever v. drop a line, write (down), write out
escrever com letra de forma print
escrita s. writing
escrito adj. written
escritor s. writer
escritório s. office, study
escritório de advocacia s. firm
escritos s. writings
escritura s. scripture
escudo s. shield
esculpir v. carve
escultor s. sculptor
escultura s. sculpture
escurecer v. darken
escuridão s. darkness
escuro s. dark
escuro adj. dark
escutar v. hear, listen
esfaquear v. stab
esfarelar v. crumble
esfera s. field
esfolar v. graze
esforçado adj. industrious
esforçar-se v. strain
esforçar-se mais try harder
esforçar-se muito try hard
esforçar-se para fazer algo struggle to do something
esforço s. effort
esfregão s. mop

esfregar v. mop, rub, scrub
esfriar v. cool (down)
esfriar a cabeça cool down
esgotado adj. out of stock, sold out
esgotamento s. breakdown
esgotar v. exhaust, use up
esgoto s. gutter, sewage, sewer
esguichar v. gush
esguio adj. lean, slender, slim
esmagar v. crush
esmerado adj. painstaking
esmeralda s. emerald
esmurrar v. thump
espaço s. box, room, space
espaço em branco s. blank
espaço sideral s. outer space, space
espaçonave s. spacecraft, spaceship
espaçoso adj. spacious
espada s. sword
espadas s. spades
espaguete s. spaghetti
espalhado adj. widespread
espalhar v. scatter, smear, spread
espalhar-se v. get around, spread out
espanador s. duster
espanar v. dust
espantalho s. scarecrow
espantar v. amaze, astonish, chase away
espanto s. astonishment
espantoso adj. astonishing
esparadrapo s. adhesive plaster, sticking plaster
espatifar-se v. crash
especial adj. particular, special
especialidade s. speciality
especialista s. expert, specialist
especialização s. specialization
especializar-se v. specialize
especialmente adv. especially, specially
especiarias s. spice
espécie s. species
especificamente adv. specifically
especificar v. specify
específico adj. particular, specific
espectador s. bystander, spectator
espelho s. mirror
espera s. wait
esperado adj. due
esperança s. hope
esperançosamente adv. hopefully
esperançoso adj. hopeful
esperar v. anticipate, expect, hang/hold on, hope, wait
esperar acordado wait up
esperto adj. sharp
espesso adj. thick

espessura s. thickness
espetacular adj. spectacular
espetáculo s. sight, spectacle
espetar v. stick
espiada s. peep
espião s. spy
espiar v. peep
espiga de milho s. corn on the cob
espinafre s. spinach
espinha s. pimple, spine
espinhento adj. prickly
espinho s. prickle, thorn
espionar v. spy (on)
espiral adj. spiral
espiral s. spiral
espírito s. spirit
espiritual adj. spiritual
espirituoso adj. witty
espirrar v. sneeze
espirro s. sneeze
esplêndido adj. splendid
esplendor s. glitter
esponja s. sponge
espontaneamente adv. voluntarily
espontâneo adj. spontaneous, voluntary
espora s. spur
esporadicamente adv. infrequently
esporádico adj. infrequent
esporte s. game, sport
esportes s. sports
esportista s. sportsman, sportswoman
esportividade s. sportsmanship
esposa s. wife
espreguiçada s. stretch
espreguiçadeira s. deck-chair
espreguiçar-se v. stretch, stretch out
espremer(-se) v. squeeze
espuma s. foam, froth
esquadra s. fleet
esquadrão s. squad
esquadrinhar v. scan
esquecer v. forget, leave ...behind
esquecido adj. forgetful
esqueleto s. skeleton
esquema s. scheme
esquentar v. heat, warm up
esquerda s. left
esquerdo adj. left, left-hand
esqui s. ski, skiing
esqui aquático s. water-skiing
esquiador s. skier
esquiar v. ski
esquilo s. squirrel
esquina s. corner
esquisito adj. awkward, funny, odd, queer, strange, weird
esquivar-se v. dodge
essência s. essence

essencial *adj.* essential
esta *pron.* this
estabelecer(-se) *v.* establish, settle (down)
estabelecimento *s.* establishment
estabilidade *s.* stability
Establishment *s.* Establishment
estábulo *s.* stable
estação *s.* season, station
estação espacial *s.* space station
estação rodoviária *s.* bus station
estacionado *adj.* stationary
estacionamento *s.* car park, parking (garage), parking lot
estacionar *v.* park
estada *s.* stay
estadia *s.* stay
estádio *s.* stadium
estadista *s.* statesman
estado *s.* condition, state
estado de espírito *s.* morale
estagiário *s.* trainee
estágio *s.* stage
estalar *v.* click
estalar os dedos snap your fingers
estalo *s.* crack, pop
estampa *s.* pattern
estande *s.* booth, stand
estante *s.* bookcase, bookshelf
estapear *v.* slap
estar a fim de fancy, feel like
estar acostumado be accustomed/used to
estar alerta be on the alert
estar aliviado be relieved
estar apaixonado be in love
estar arrasado be overwhelmed
estar cansado be tired of, be worn-out
estar cercado be surrounded by
estar cheio be fed up with
estar coberto be covered with
estar com cinto de segurança be strapped in
estar com pressa be in a rush/hurry
estar com sorte be in luck
estar de acordo com see eye to eye with
estar de dieta be on a diet
estar de pé stand
estar de volta be back
estar destinado be intended for
estar diante de be faced with
estar dormindo pesado be fast asleep
estar em falta be in short supply
estar em falta de be short of
estar em maus lençóis to be in a mess
estar empregado be employed
estar encrencado be in trouble

estar envolvido be involved in
estar espantado be amazed
estar exausto be tired out
estar fadado a be bound to
estar familiarizado be familiar with
estar farto be fed up with, be sick of, have had enough of
estar ferido be injured
estar garantido be guaranteed
estar grávida be pregnant
estar impressionado be impressed by
estar incluído be included
estar influenciado be influenced
estar interessado be interested in
estar localizado be located, be situated
estar lotado be stacked/swarming with
estar louco be dying
estar na liderança be in the lead
estar no aguardo de to look forward to
estar no comando de be in charge of
estar no meio de be in the middle of
estar no ponto de be on the point of
estar no rastro de alguém be on someone's trail
estar obcecado com be obsessed with
estar para acabar be short of
estar perdido be lost
estar precisando de be in need of
estar preparado be prepared for, be prepared to
estar prestes a be about to
estar proibido de must not
estar relacionado be related to
estar reservado be reserved
estar satisfeito be satisfied with, have had enough of
estar situado be located, be situated
estar sob controle be under control
estar sobrando be left over
estar sublinhado be underlined
estar sujeito a be liable to
estar tentado be tempted to
estar trancado be locked
estar travado be locked
estar vestido de be dressed in
estardalhaço *s.* fuss
estatística *s.* statistics
estátua *s.* statue
estável *adj.* stable
este *pron.* this
estender *v.* extend

estender-se *v.* spread, stretch
estepe *s.* spare tyre/tire
estéreo *s.* stereo
estereofônico *adj.* stereo
estes *adj.* these
estiagem *s.* drought
esticado *adj.* tight
esticar *v.* hold out, stretch (out)
estilhaçar *v.* shatter
estilíngue *s.* catapult, slingshot
estilo *s.* style
estilo de cabelo *s.* hairstyle
estilo de vida *s.* lifestyle
estimar *v.* calculate, estimate, make, reckon
estimativa *s.* estimate
estimulado *adj.* encouraged
estimulante *adj.* encouraging
estímulo *s.* encouragement
estocar *v.* hoard, stock, store (up)
estojo *s.* box, case
estojo de lápis *s.* pencil box, pencil case
estômago *s.* stomach
estonteante *adj.* stunning
estoque *s.* hoard, stock, store
estourar *v.* blow up, burst, pop
estouro *s.* pop
estrada *s.* lane
estrada de ferro *s.* railroad, railway
estrada principal *s.* main road
estragar *v.* go off/bad, ruin, spoil
estrangeiro *s.* alien, foreigner
estrangeiro *adj.* foreign, overseas
estrangular *v.* strangle
estranhamente *adv.* oddly, strangely
estranho *s.* stranger
estranho *adj.* awkward, funny, odd, strange, weird
estreitar *v.* narrow
estreito *adj.* narrow
estrela *s.* star
estrelar *v.* star
estremecer *v.* shudder
estremecimento *s.* shudder
estresse *s.* stress
estribilho *s.* chorus
estridente *adj.* squeaky
estrondo *s.* bang
estrutura *s.* structure
estudante *s.* student
estudar *v.* study
estúdio *s.* studio, study
estudioso *adj.* studious
estudo *s.* study
estudos *s.* studies
estufa *s.* greenhouse, stove
estupidamente *adv.* stupidly
estuprar *v.* rape
estupro *s.* rape

esvaziar v. clear, empty, turn out
esvoaçar v. flap
eternamente adv. eternally
eterno adj. eternal
etiqueta s. label, tag
etiquetar v. label
étnico adj. ethnic
eu pron. I, me
eu acho difícil... I find it difficult/hard to...
eu desafio você a... I dare you
eu duvido que você... I dare you
eu juro! I cross my heart!
eu mesmo myself
eu não faço ideia I haven't got a clue
eucalipto s. eucalyptus
euforia s. excitement
euro s. euro
evacuação s. evacuation
evacuar v. evacuate
evento s. event, happening
eventual adj. incidental
evidente adj. conspicuous, evident
evitamento s. avoidance
evitar v. avoid, prevent, save
ex- prefix ex-, former
exagerar v. exaggerate
exagero s. exaggeration
exalar v. give off
exame s. exam, examination, paper, test
exame de direção s. driving test
exame de sangue s. blood test
exame médico s. medical
exames finais s. finals
examinar v. examine, go over/through, inspect, look into, test
exatamente adv. exactly, just, just as
exatidão s. accuracy
exato adj. accurate, exact
exaustão s. exhaustion
exausto adj. exhausted, exhausting, worn-out
exaustor s. exhaust
exceçao s. exception
exceder v. exceed
excelente adj. excellent, superb, terrific
excepcional adj. exceptional, extraordinary
excepcionalmente adv. exceptionally

excessivamente adv. heavily
excesso de velocidade s. speeding
exceto prep. apart from, except (for)
excitação s. excitement
excitado adj. excited
excitante adj. exciting
excitar v. excite
exclamação s. exclamation
exclamar v. exclaim
excluído s. outsider
excluir v. exclude, leave out
exclusão s. exclusion
exclusivo adj. exclusive
excursão s. excursion, outing
excursionar v. tour
execução s. execution
executar v. carry out, do, execute, perform
executivo adj. executive
executor s. executioner
exemplar s. copy, issue, model
exemplo s. example
exercer v. practice
exercício s. exercise
exercitar v. exercise
exército s. army
exibir v. display, exhibit, model, screen
exibir-se v. show off
exigência s. demand
exigente adj. fussy, particular
exigir v. demand, involve, require
exilar v. exile
exílio s. exile
existência s. existence
existir v. exist
expandir v. expand
expansão s. expansion
expectativa s. expectation
expedição s. expedition, shipment
experiência s. experience
experiente adj. experienced
experimental adj. experimental
experimentar v. try out, try something on
experimento s. experiment
expert s. expert
expertise s. expertise
expirar v. breathe out
explicação s. explanation
explicar v. account, explain
explodir v. blow up, explode, go off

exploração s. exploitation, exploration
explorador s. explorer
explorar v. exploit, explore
explosão s. bang, blast, burst, explosion, outburst
explosivo s. explosive
explosivo adj. explosive
expor v. display, exhibit, expose
exportação s. exports
exportador s. exporter
exportar v. export
exposição s. display, exhibit, exhibition, show
expositor s. display
expressão s. expression
expressão idiomática s. idiom, phrasal verb
expressar-se v. express oneself
expresso s. express
expresso adj. express
expulsão s. expulsion
expulsar v. banish, expel, kick out
extensão s. extent, length
exterior s. exterior, outside
exterminar v. exterminate
externo adj. exterior, outer, outside
extinção s. extinction
extinguir v. extinguish
extinto adj. extinct
extintor s. extinguisher
extintor de incêndio s. fire extinguisher
extra adj. extra, spare
extrair v. draw, mine
extraordinariamente adv. extraordinarily, unusually
extraordinário adj. extraordinary, out of the ordinary, unusual
extraterrestre adj. extraterrestrial
extravagância s. extravagance
extravagante adj. extravagant, fancy, wild
extravagantemente adv. extravagantly
extremamente adv. extremely, jolly
extremidade s. end
extremismo s. extremism
extremista s. extremist
Extremo Oriente s. Far East
extremo adj. extreme

Ff

fã s. fan
fábrica s. factory, mill, plant
fabricação s. manufacture
fabricado adj. man-made
fabricante s. maker, manufacturer, producer
fabricar v. manufacture
fábula s. fable
faca s. knife
façanha s. deed
fácil adj. easy
facilidade s. ease
facilmente adv. easily
faculdade s. college, school, university
fada s. fairy
fagulha s. spark
Fahrenheit s. Fahrenheit
faísca s. spark
faiscar v. glisten
faixa s. band, banner, crossing, patch, stretch, strip, track
faixa de pedestres s. crosswalk, pedestrian/zebra crossing
fala s. speech
falante adj. talkative
falante nativo s. native speaker
falar v. say, speak, talk
falar a verdade tell the truth
falar alto speak up
falar brusca e asperamente snap
falar ofegantemente gasp
falcão s. hawk
falecer v. die, pass away
falecido adj. late
falência s. bankruptcy
falha s. fault
falhar v. fail, fall through
falido adj. bankrupt
falsificação s. fake, forgery
falsificado adj. forged
falsificador s. forger
falsificar v. fake, forge
falso adj. bogus, fake, false, forged, phoney, untrue
falta s. foul, lack, scarcity
falta de energia s. power outage
falta de jeito s. awkwardness, clumsiness
fama s. fame, name
família s. family
familiar adj. familiar, well known
faminto adj. hungry
famoso adj. famous
fanático s. bigot
fanatismo s. bigotry
fanfarronice s. boast
fantasia s. fancy dress, fantasy
fantasiar-se v. dress up
fantasma s. ghost, phantom
fantasmagórico adj. ghostly
fantástico adj. fantastic
fardado s. in uniform
fardo s. burden, pack
farejar v. sniff
farelo s. crumb
farfalhada s. rustle
farfalhar v. rustle
farinha de trigo s. flour
farmacêutico s. druggist, pharmacist
farmácia s. chemist, drugstore, pharmacy
faro s. smell
faroeste s. western
farol s. headlight, lamp, lighthouse
farpa s. splinter
farrapo s. rag
fascinação s. fascination
fascinante adj. fascinating
fascinar v. fascinate
fase s. phase
fast-food s. fast food
fatal adj. fatal
fatalmente adv. fatally
fatia s. slice
fatiar v. slice
fatídico adj. fateful
fatigado adj. weary
fato s. fact
fator s. factor
fatura s. invoice
favela s. slum
favor s. favor
favorável adj. favorable
favorecer v. favor, flatter
favoritismo s. favoritism
favorito adj. favorite
fax s. fax
fazenda s. farm, finance
fazendeiro s. farmer
fazer v. do, make
fazer algo desaparecer make something disappear
fazer alguém calar a boca shut someone up
fazer alguém de bobo make a fool of
fazer alguém esperar keep someone waiting
fazer alguém rir make someone laugh
fazer alguém se sentir à vontade make someone welcome
fazer alguma diferença make any difference
fazer amizade make friends with
fazer as malas pack
fazer as pazes com make up
fazer barricada barricade
fazer campanha campaign
fazer cócegas tickle
fazer companhia a alguém keep someone company
fazer compras shop
fazer contato get through
fazer cópia reproduce
fazer cumprir enforce
fazer curva curve
fazer declive slope
fazer dieta diet
fazer economias economize
fazer escala stop over
fazer escândalo get into a fuss
fazer experiências experiment
fazer faculdade go to university
fazer fila line up, queue
fazer furos punch
fazer greve go on strike
fazer lavagem cerebral brainwash
fazer ligação a cobrar reverse the charges
fazer mal harm
fazer malabarismo juggle
fazer mímica mime
fazer natação go swimming
fazer nenhuma diferença make any difference
fazer ninho nest
fazer o check-in check in
fazer o check-out check out
fazer o favor de kindly
fazer o melhor possível do/try your best
fazer o papel de act, play
fazer parte de participate, take part in
fazer piquenique picnic
fazer ponte aérea airlift
fazer sentido make sense
fazer sinal signal
fazer sua escolha take your pick
fazer um cruzeiro cruise
fazer um discurso give a speech, make a speech
fazer um elogio a alguém pay someone a compliment
fazer um escândalo get into a fuss
fazer um favor a oblige
fazer um pedido make a wish
fazer um tributo a pay tribute to
fazer uma homenagem a pay tribute to
fazer uma promessa make a promise, promise
fazer uma visita a alguém pay someone a visit
fazer uso de make use of
faz-tudo s. handyman
fé s. faith, religion

febre *s.* fever
febril *adj.* feverish
febrilmente *adv.* feverishly
fechado *adj.* closed, dense, sharp, shut
fechadura *s.* keyhole, lock
fechar *v.* close (down), draw, fasten, shut, shut down, turn/switch off, wind/zip up
fecho *s.* clasp
feder *v.* stink
fedido *adj.* smelly
fedor *s.* stink
feedback *s.* feedback
feição *s.* feature
feijão *s.* bean
feio *adj.* ghastly, ugly
feira *s.* fair
feiticeiro *s.* witch doctor
feitiço *s.* spell
feito *s.* accomplishment, deed, feat
feito mágica as if by magic, like magic
feito à mão handmade
feiura *s.* ugliness
felicidade *s.* gladness, happiness, joy
feliz *adj.* content, glad, happy, merry
felizmente *adv.* fortunately, happily, luckily, thankfully
fêmea *s.* female
feminino *adj.* feminine
fenda *s.* gap, slit, slot, split
feno *s.* hay
fenômeno *s.* phenomenon
feriado *s.* holiday
feriado bancário *s.* bank holiday
feriados *s.* vacation
férias *s.* holiday, vacation
férias de verão *s.* summer holidays
ferido *adj.* injured, wounded
ferimento *s.* injury, wound
ferino *adj.* vicious
ferir *v.* hurt, injure, wound
ferir-se *v.* get hurt
fermento *s.* yeast
feroz *adj.* ferocious, fierce, savage
ferozmente *adv.* savagely
ferradura *s.* horseshoe
ferragens *s.* hardware
ferramenta *s.* tool
ferrão *s.* sting
ferreiro *s.* blacksmith
ferro *s.* iron
ferro de passar *s.* iron
ferrolho *s.* bolt
ferrovia *s.* railroad, railway
ferroviária *adj.* railroad, railway
ferrugem *s.* rust
fértil *adj.* fertile

fertilizante *s.* fertilizer
fervente *adj.* boiling
ferver *v.* boil, bubble
fervido *adj.* boiled
fervilhar *v.* crawl
festa *s.* festival, fête, party
festim *s.* feast
festival *s.* festival
festividades *s.* festivities
fétido *adj.* foul
fevereiro *s.* February
fiar *v.* spin
fibra *s.* fiber
ficar *v.* keep, lie, remain, stand, stay
ficar à mostra come into view
ficar a postos stand by
ficar à vontade help yourself
ficar à vontade para be welcome to
ficar acordado stay up
ficar ao lado de alguém be on someone's side
ficar bêbado get drunk
ficar boquiaberto gape
ficar bronzeado get a suntan
ficar calado keep quiet
ficar cansado get tired
ficar careca go bald
ficar cego go blind
ficar com nojo be disgusted
ficar com raiva get angry
ficar confuso get confused, get mixed up
ficar consternado be dismayed
ficar de guarda keep watch
ficar de olho em keep an eye on
ficar desanimado be discouraged
ficar desconfiado get suspicious
ficar detido be held up
ficar do lado de stand by
ficar doente be taken ill, become ill, get sick
ficar em cartaz run
ficar em casa stay in
ficar em pé rise, stand up
ficar emburrado sulk
ficar encantado be enchanted by
ficar encharcado get soaked
ficar encrencado get into trouble
ficar entediado get bored with
ficar feliz em be happy to
ficar imóvel stand still
ficar isolado be isolated
ficar junto stick together
ficar louco go crazy
ficar melhor get better, improve
ficar na fila queue, stand in line
ficar nervoso get nervous
ficar ofendido feel insulted, take offence
ficar para trás lag behind

ficar perdido get lost, lose your way
ficar pior get worse
ficar preocupado get worried
ficar preso be stuck, be trapped
ficar rico get rich
ficar sem do without, run out of
ficar sério keep a straight face
ficar torcendo keep your fingers crossed
ficar trancado be locked in
ficar velho get old
ficar visível come into sight
ficar zangado get angry
ficção *s.* fiction
ficção científica *s.* science fiction
ficha *s.* application form, file, record, token
ficha criminal *s.* criminal record
fictício *adj.* fictional, fictitious
fiel *adj.* faithful
fièlmente *adv.* faithfully
fígado *s.* liver
figo *s.* fig
figura *s.* figure
figura de linguagem *s.* figure of speech
fila *s.* file, line, queue, row
filão *s.* loaf
filé *s.* steak
fileira *s.* line, row
filete *s.* band, stream, trickle
filha *s.* daughter, girl
filha única an only child
filho *s.* son
filho único an only child
filho *s.* child
filho único *s.* an only child
filhote *s.* offspring, young
filhote de animal selvagem *s.* cub
filial *s.* branch, chapter
filmar *v.* film
filme *s.* feature, film, movie, picture
filosofia *s.* philosophy
filosófico *adj.* philosophical
filósofo *s.* philosopher
filtrar *v.* filter
filtro *s.* filter
fim *s.* end, finish
fim de semana *s.* weekend
final *adj.* final, last
finalidade *s.* purpose
finalizar *v.* finalize
finalmente *adv.* at last, eventually, finally, in the end, lastly
finanças *s.* finances
financeiro *adj.* financial
financiamento *s.* finance
financiar *v.* finance
fingir *v.* make believe, pretend
fino *adj.* fine, thin

fio *s.* flex, glimmer, wire
firma *s.* firm
firme *adj.* decisive, fine, firm, stable, steady
firmemente *adv.* firmly, strongly, tightly
física *s.* physics
fisicamente *adv.* physically
físico *adj.* physical
físico *s.* physicist
fita *s.* band, ribbon, tape
fita adesiva *s.* (adhesive) tape, Scotch tape, Sellotape
fita cassete *s.* cassette, tape
fita de vídeo *s.* video (cassette), videotape
fita métrica *s.* tape measure
fivela *s.* buckle
fixar *v.* fasten, fix, pin
fixo *adj.* fixed, permanent, steady
flagrar *v.* catch
flash *s.* flash
flat *s.* flat
flauta *s.* flute
flecha *s.* arrow
flertar *v.* flirt
flexão *s.* press-ups
flexível *adj.* flexible
flexões *s.* push-ups
floco *s.* flakes
flocos de milho *s.* cornflakes
flocos de neve *s.* snowflakes
flor *s.* flower
floração *s.* blossom
florescer *v.* bloom, flourish
floresta *s.* forest
florido *adj.* flowery
florir *v.* blossom
florista *s.* florist
fluência *s.* fluency
fluente *adj.* fluent
fluentemente *adv.* fluently
fluido *adj.* fluid
fluir *v.* flow, stream
flutuar *v.* float
fluxo *s.* flow
flyer *s.* flyer
foca *s.* seal
focar *v.* focus
focinheira *s.* muzzle
foco *s.* focus
fofinho *adj.* plump
fofoca *s.* gossip
fofocar *v.* gossip
fofoqueiro *s.* gossip
fogão *s.* cooker, stove
fogareiro *s.* camp stove
fogo *s.* fire, light
fogos de artifício *s.* fireworks
fogueira *s.* bonfire, campfire
foguete *s.* rocket
folder *s.* folder

fôlego *s.* breath
folgado *adj.* loose
folha *s.* leaf, page, sheet
folhas *s.* greens, leaves, lettuce
folheto *s.* brochure, flyer, leaflet
follow-up *s.* follow-up
fome *s.* famine, hunger, starvation
fones de ouvido *s.* earphones, headphones
fonte *s.* fountain, source, spring
fora *adv.* out
fora de alcance beyond reach, out of reach
fora de forma unfit
fora de moda old-fashioned, unfashionable
fora de ordem out of order
fora de perigo out of danger
fora do alcance out of reach
fora do normal out of the ordinary, unusual
fora dos limites out of bounds
forca *s.* gallows
força *s.* force, strength
força aérea *s.* air force
força de vontade *s.* will
força policial *s.* police force
forçado *adj.* unnatural
forçar *v.* force, squeeze, strain
forças armadas *s.* the armed forces
forjado *adj.* forged
forjar *v.* forge
forma *s.* form, grammar, mould, pan, shape
formação *s.* background
formado *s.* graduate
formal *adj.* formal
formalmente *adv.* formally
formar(-se) *v.* form, graduate, start
formato *s.* shape
formatura *s.* graduation
formidável *adj.* grand
formiga *s.* ant
formigamento *s.* pins and needles
fórmula *s.* formula
formulário *s.* application form, form
fornada *s.* batch
fornalha *s.* furnace, stove
fornecer *v.* provide, supply
fornecimento *s.* provision, supply
forno *s.* oven
forno de micro-ondas *s.* microwave
forno tostador *s.* toaster oven
forquilha *s.* fork
forro *s.* lining
fortalecer *v.* strengthen
fortaleza *s.* fortress
forte *adj.* fierce, heavy, strong

forte *s.* fort
fortuna *s.* fortune
fórum *s.* forum
fósforo *s.* match
fóssil *s.* fossil
fosso *s.* ditch
foto *s.* photo, picture, shot
foto instantânea *s.* snap
fotocópia *s.* photocopy
fotocopiadora *s.* photocopier, Xerox machine
fotocopiar *v.* photocopy
fotografar *v.* photograph
fotografia *s.* photography
fotógrafo *s.* photographer
fração *s.* fraction
fração de segundo *s.* split second
fracassado *s.* loser
fracasso *s.* failure
fraco *adj.* dim, faint, feeble, frail, weak
frágil *adj.* brittle, fragile
fragmento *s.* fragment
fragrância *s.* fragrance, perfume
fralda *s.* diaper, nappy
framboesa *s.* raspberry
francamente *adv.* frankly, straight out
franco *adj.* frank, honest, straight
frango *s.* chicken
franja *s.* fringe
franzir as sobrancelhas frown
fraqueza *s.* weakness
frasco *s.* jar, pot
frase *s.* phrase
fratura *s.* fracture
fraturar *v.* fracture
fraude *s.* fraud
frear *v.* brake
freezer *s.* freezer
freguês *s.* customer
freio *s.* brake
freira *s.* nun
frente *s.* front
frequência *s.* attendance, frequency
frequentar *v.* attend
frequente *adj.* frequent, regular
frequentemente *adv.* frequently, often
fresco *adj.* cool, fresh, wet
friamente *adv.* coldly
fricção *s.* friction
frieza *s.* coldness
frigideira *s.* frying-pan
frio *s.* cold
frio *adj.* cold, wintry
frisante *adj.* fizzy, sparkling
fritar *v.* fry
fritas *s.* chips
frito *adj.* fried
fritura *s.* frying

fronha *s.* pillowcase
fronte *s.* brow, forehead, front
fronteira *s.* border, frontier
frouxamente *adv.* loosely
frouxo *adj.* loose, slack
frustração *s.* frustration
frustrado *adj.* frustrated
frustrante *adj.* frustrating
fruta *s.* fruit
frutinha vermelha *s.* berry
frutos do mar *s.* seafood
fuga *s.* escape
fugir *v.* break out, escape, flee, get/run away
fulgir *v.* glow
fulgor *s.* glow
fuligem *s.* soot
fumaça *s.* smoke
fumante *s.* smoker
fumar *v.* smoke
fumo *s.* tobacco
função *s.* function
funcionar *v.* function, run, work
funcionário *s.* employee, worker
fundação *s.* establishment, foundation
fundador *s.* founder
fundamental *adj.* fundamental
fundar *v.* establish, found
fundir(-se) *v.* merge
fundo *s.* bottom, fund
fundo *adj.* deep
fundos *s.* funds, rear
funeral *s.* funeral
fungada *s.* sniff
fungar *v.* sniff
funil *s.* funnel
furacão *s.* hurricane
furar *v.* pierce, prick, punch, puncture
fúria *s.* fury, rage
furiosamente *adv.* furiously
furioso *adj.* furious, wild
furo *s.* hole, puncture, scoop
furtar *v.* steal
furto *s.* theft
fusível *s.* fuse
futebol *s.* football, soccer
futebol americano *s.* (American) football
futuro *s.* future
futuro *adj.* future, unborn
fuzuê *s.* fuss

Gg

gabar-se *v.* boast
gado *s.* cattle
gafanhoto *s.* grasshopper, locust
gagueira *s.* stutter
gaguejar *v.* stammer, stutter
gaiola *s.* cage
gaita de foles *s.* bagpipes
gaivota *s.* seagull
galão *s.* gallon, pot
galáxia *s.* galaxy
galera *s.* gang
galeria *s.* gallery
galho *s.* branch
galinha *s.* chicken, hen
galo *s.* bump, cock, lump, rooster
galopar *v.* gallop
galope *s.* gallop
galpão *s.* shed
gamela *s.* trough
ganância *s.* greed
gananciosamente *adv.* greedily
ganancioso *adj.* greedy
gancho *s.* hook
gangorra *s.* see-saw
gângster *s.* gangster
gangue *s.* gang
ganhar *v.* earn, gain, get, make, put on, win
ganhar a vida make a living
ganhar peso put on weight
ganhar tempo play for time
ganhar vida come to life
ganso *s.* goose
gansos *s.* geese
garagem *s.* garage
garantia *s.* assurance, guarantee, reassurance, warranty
garantir *v.* ensure, guarantee
garçom *s.* waiter
garçonete *s.* barmaid, waitress
garfo *s.* fork
garganta *s.* throat
garganta inflamada *s.* sore throat
gargantilha *s.* necklace
garoa *s.* mist
garota *s.* girl
garoto *s.* boy
garoto de recados *s.* errand boy
garra *s.* claw
garrafa *s.* bottle
garrancho *s.* scribble
gás *s.* gas
gasolina *s.* gas, gasoline, petrol
gasoso *adj.* fizzy
gastar *v.* spend
gasto *adj.* worn-out
gatilho *s.* trigger
gatinho *s.* kitten
gato *s.* cat

gaveta *s.* drawer
gay *adj., s.* gay, homosexual
gazetear *s.* play hooky
gazeteiro *s.* truant
geada *s.* frost
geladeira *s.* fridge, refrigerator
gelado *adj.* chilly, frosty, icy
gelar *v.* freeze
gelatina *s.* jelly
geleia *s.* jam, jelly
geleia de fruta cítrica *s.* marmalade
gélido *adj.* icy
gelo *s.* ice
gema *s.* gem, yolk
gêmeo *s.* twin
gemer *v.* groan, moan
gemido *s.* groan, moan
general *s.* general
generalizar *v.* generalize
gênero *s.* gender, grammar, sex
gêneros alimentícios *s.* groceries
generosamente *adv.* generously
generosidade *s.* generosity
generoso *adj.* generous, kind-hearted
gengibre *s.* ginger
gengivas *s.* gums
gênio *s.* genius
genitor *s.* parent
genro *s.* son-in-law
gentil *adj.* gentle, kind, kindly, sweet
gentileza *s.* kindness
gentilmente *adv.* kindly
genuinamente *adv.* genuinely
genuíno *adj.* genuine, proper, real
geografia *s.* geography
geográfico *adj.* geographic
geometria *s.* geometry
geométrico *adj.* geometric
geração *s.* generation
gerador *s.* generator
geral *adj.* general
geralmente *adv.* generally, ordinarily, usually
gerar *v.* generate
gerência *s.* management
gerenciamento *s.* management
gerenciar *v.* manage, run
gerente *s.* manager, manageress
gerente administrativo *s.* managing director
germe *s.* germ
gesso *s.* cast, plaster
gesto *s.* gesture
gibi *s.* comic, comic book, comics
gigante *s.* giant
gigantesco *adj.* gigantic
ginásio *s.* gym, gymnasium
ginástica *s.* gym, gymnastics, workout

girafa *s.* giraffe
girar *v.* go around/round, rotate, spin
girassol *s.* sunflower
gíria *s.* slang
giz *s.* chalk
glacê *s.* icing
glitter *s.* glitter
global *adj.* global
globo *s.* globe
glória *s.* glory
glorioso *adj.* glorious
gol *s.* goal
gola *s.* collar, neck
gole *s.* gulp
goleiro *s.* goalkeeper, keeper
golfe *s.* golf
golfinho *s.* dolphin
golfo *s.* gulf
golinho *s.* sip
golpe *s.* blow, hit, kick, knock, stroke
golpear com soco bash
golpear insistentemente hammer
goma *s.* gum
goma de mascar *s.* chewing-gum
gordinho *adj.* plump
gordo *adj.* fat
gordura *s.* fat, grease
gorduroso *adj.* greasy
gorila *s.* gorilla
gorjear *v.* twitter
gorjeta *s.* tip
gorro *s.* cap
gostar *v.* enjoy, like
gosto *s.* taste
gota *s.* drop, raindrop
gotejar *v.* trickle
governador *s.* governor
governadora *s.* governess
governanta *s.* housekeeper
governar *v.* govern, rule
governo *s.* government, rule
graça *s.* grace
graças a *s.* owing to, thanks to
graças a Deus! *int.* thank goodness!
graciosamente *adv.* gracefully
gracioso *adj.* cute, graceful
gradativamente *adv.* gradually
gradativo *adj.* gradual
grade *s.* bar, railings
gradil *s.* railings
graduado *adj.* graded
gradual *adj.* gradual
gradualmente *adv.* gradually
gráfico *s.* chart, graph
grafite *s.* lead
grama *s.* gram, grass, lawn
gramado *s.* lawn
gramática *s.* grammar
gramatical *adj.* grammatical

gramaticalmente *adv.* grammatically
gramínio *adj.* grassy
grampeador *s.* stapler
grampear *v.* staple
grampo *s.* clip, hairpin, staple
granada *s.* grenade
granada de mão *s.* hand grenade
grande *adj.* big, great, large, strong
grandemente *adv.* greatly, largely
grandeza *s.* greatness
grandioso *adj.* grand, huge
granizo *s.* hail, hailstone, sleet
grão *s.* bean, corn, grain
grapefruit *s.* grapefruit
grasnido *s.* quack
grasnir *v.* quack
gratidão *s.* gratitude
grátis *adj.* free (of charge)
grato *adj.* grateful, thankful
gratuito *adj.* complimentary, free
grau *s.* degree
gravação *s.* recording
gravador *s.* cassette/tape recorder
gravador de mesa *s.* tape deck
gravar *v.* record, tape
gravata *s.* tie
gravata-borboleta *s.* bow tie
grave *adj.* bad, bass, critical, grave, serious
gravemente *adv.* badly, critically, gravely, severely
graveto *s.* stick, twig
grávida *adj.* pregnant

gravidade *s.* gravity, severity
gravidez *s.* pregnancy
gravura *s.* print
graxa *s.* grease, polish
grelha *s.* grill
grelhar *v.* broil, grill
greve *s.* strike
grevista *s.* striker
grill *s.* grill
grilo *s.* cricket
gripe *s.* flu
grisalho *adj.* grey
gritar *v.* call, cry, scream, shout, shriek, yell
gritaria *s.* cry
grito *s.* cry, scream, shout, yell
groselha *s.* currant, gooseberry
groselha preta *s.* blackcurrant
grosseiramente *adv.* harshly, rudely
grosseiro *adj.* nasty
grosso *adj.* impolite, rude, thick
grossura *s.* rudeness, thickness
grudento *adj.* sticky
grupo *s.* group, party
gruta *s.* cave
guarda *s.* constable, guard, keeper, warden, watch, watchman
guarda costeira *s.* coastguard
guarda de segurança *s.* security guard
guarda de trânsito *s.* traffic warden
guarda-chuva *s.* umbrella

guarda-costas *s.* bodyguard
guardanapo *s.* napkin, serviette
guarda-pó *s.* smock
guardar *v.* guard, keep, put away, save, secure, store
guardar em lugar não lembrado mislay
guardar rancor de *s.* have a grudge against
guarda-roupa *s.* wardrobe
guarda-sol *s.* sunshade
guarda-vidas *s.* lifeguard
guardião *s.* guardian, keeper
guerra *s.* war, warfare
guerra civil *s.* civil war
guerra mundial *s.* world war
guerreiro *s.* fighter, warrior
guerrilha *s.* guerrilla
guia *s.* guide, guidebook, kerb
guia turístico *s.* tour guide
guiar *v.* guide, steer
guidão *s.* handlebars
guinchar *v.* screech, shriek, squeak, squeal, tow
guincho *s.* screech, squeak, squeal
guindaste *s.* crane
guirlanda *s.* wreath
guitarra *s.* guitar
guitarrista *s.* guitarist
gula *s.* greed
guloseima *s.* candy, sweet
guloso *adj.* greedy
gusano *s.* maggot

Hh

há anos for years
há muito tempo long ago
hábil *adj.* clever, skilful
habilidade *s.* ability, resource, skill
habilidoso *adj.* resourceful, skillful
habilmente *adv.* skilfully
habitação *s.* dwelling, housing
habitado *adj.* inhabited
habitante *s.* inhabitant
hábito *s.* habit, practice
habitual *adj.* habitual, regular
hacker *s.* hacker
hall *s.* hall
halloween *s.* Halloween
hambúrguer *s.* burger, hamburger
hamster *s.* hamster
hardware *s.* hardware
harmonia *s.* harmony
harpa *s.* harp
hashtag *s.* pound, the # sign
haste *s.* stalk, stem
hastear *v.* hoist
HD *abr.* hard disk
hectare *s.* hectare
hediondo *adj.* hideous
hélice *s.* propeller
helicóptero *s.* helicopter
hematoma *s.* bruise
hemisfério *s.* hemisphere
herança *s.* inheritance
herdar *v.* inherit
herdeira *s.* heiress
herdeiro *s.* heir
herói *s.* hero
heroico *adj.* heroic
heroína *s.* hero, heroin, heroine
heroísmo *s.* heroism
hesitação *s.* hesitation
hesitante *adj.* hesitant
hesitar *v.* hesitate

hidrogênio *s.* hydrogen
hífen *s.* dash, hyphen
higiene *s.* hygiene
higiênico *adj.* hygienic
hino *s.* anthem, hymn
hino nacional *s.* national anthem
hipermercado *s.* hypermarket
hipocrisia *s.* hypocrisy
hipócrita *adj.* hypocritical
hipócrita *s.* hypocrite
hipódromo *s.* racecourse
hipopótamo *s.* hippopotamus
hipoteca *s.* mortgage
hipotecar *v.* mortgage
hippie *s.* hippie
história *s.* history, story
historiador *s.* historian
histórico *s.* record
histórico *adj.* historic, historical
hi-tech *s.* hi-tech
hobby *s.* hobby
hoje *adv.* today
hoje à noite tonight
hoje em dia nowadays, these days
Holocausto *s.* Holocaust
holofote *s.* spotlight
homem *s.* man
homem armado *s.* gunman
homem de negócios *s.* businessman
homens *s.* men
homossexual *adj., s.* homosexual
honestamente *adv.* honestly
honestidade *s.* honesty
honesto *adj.* honest, truthful
honorários *s.* fee
honra *s.* honor
honrado *adj.* honorable
honrar *v.* honor
hooligan *s.* hooligan
hóquei *s.* hockey
hóquei no gelo *s.* ice hockey
hora *s.* appointment, hour, o'clock, time

hora do almoço *s.* lunch-time
hora do rush *s.* the rush hour
hora extra *s.* overtime
horário *s.* hours, schedule, timetable
horário de expediente *s.* working/office hours
horizontal *adj.* horizontal
horizonte *s.* horizon
horrível *adj.* awful, dreadful, foul, frightful, horrible, miserable, rotten, terrible
horrivelmente *adv.* awfully
horror *s.* horror
horrorizado *adj.* horrified
horrorizar *v.* horrify
horroroso *adj.* hideous, horrid
hortelã *s.* mint, peppermint
hospedar *v.* put someone up
hospedaria *s.* inn
hospedar-se *v.* lodge
hóspede *s.* boarder, guest, lodger, resident
hospital *s.* hospital
hospitaleiro *adj.* hospitable
hospitalidade *s.* hospitality
hostil *adj.* hostile, unfriendly
hostilidade *s.* hostility
hotel *s.* hotel
humanidade *s.* humanity, mankind
humanitário *adj.* humane
humano *s.* (human) being
humano *adj.* human, humane
humilde *adj.* humble
humildemente *adv.* humbly
humilhação *s.* humiliation
humilhado *adj.* humiliated
humilhante *adj.* humiliating
humilhar *v.* humiliate
humor *s.* humor, humour, mood, spirits
humorista *s.* comic

Ii

iate *s.* yacht
içar vela (set) sail
iceberg *s.* iceberg
idade *s.* age
Idade Média *s.* Middle Ages
ideal *adj.* ideal
ideia *s.* idea, notion, thought
idêntico *adj.* identical
identidade *s.* identity
identificação *s.* ID, identification
identificar *v.* identify
idioma *s.* language
idiota *adj.* dumb, idiotic, stupid
idiota *s.* idiot
idiotice *s.* dumbness, stupidity
ídolo *s.* idol
idoso *adj., s.* senior citizen
idoso *adj.* aged, elderly, old
aposentado *s.* senior citizen
ignorância *s.* ignorance
ignorante *adj.* ignorant
ignorar *v.* ignore, overlook
igreja *s.* church
igual *adj.* equal
igualar *v.* equal
igualdade *s.* equality
igualmente *adv.* alike, equally
ilegal *adj.* illegal
ilegalmente *adv.* illegally
ilegível *adj.* illegible
ilha *s.* island
ilha deserta *s.* desert island
iluminação *s.* lighting
iluminado *adj.* sunlit
iluminar *v.* illuminate
Iluminismo *s.* Enlightenment
ilustração *s.* illustration
ilustrar *v.* illustrate
ímã *s.* magnet
imagem *s.* image
imaginação *s.* imagination
imaginação viva *s.* vivid imagination
imaginar *v.* figure, guess, imagine, suppose, wonder
imaginário *adj.* imaginary
imaginar-se *v.* fancy
imaginativo *adj.* imaginative
imagine...! *v.* fancy...!
imbuia *s.* walnut
imediatamente *adv.* at once, immediately, instantly, right away/ now, straight away
imediato *adj.* immediate, prompt
imensamente *adv.* immensely
imenso *adj.* immense
imigração *s.* immigration
imigrante *s.* immigrant
imigrar *v.* immigrate

imitação *s.* imitation
imitar *v.* copy, imitate, mime, mimic
imobilidade *s.* stillness
imoral *adj.* immoral
imoralidade *s.* vice
imortal *adj.* immortal
imóvel *adj.* not moving, still
impaciência *s.* eagerness, impatience
impaciente *adj.* impatient
impacientemente *adv.* impatiently
ímpar *adj.* odd
imparcial *adj.* impartial
impecável *adj.* faultless
impedimento *s.* deterrent
impedir *v.* deter, keep from, prevent
imperador *s.* emperor
imperativo *s.* imperative
imperatriz *s.* empress
imperdoável *adj.* unforgivable
império *s.* empire
impermeável *adj.* waterproof
impertinente *adj.* impertinent
ímpeto *s.* urge
impetuosamente *adv.* rashly
impetuoso *adj.* rash
impiedosamente *adv.* heartlessly, mercilessly, ruthlessly
impiedoso *adj.* heartless, merciless, ruthless
implicação *s.* implication
implicar *v.* imply, involve
implorar *v.* beg, implore
impopular *adj.* unpopular
impor *v.* impose
importação *s.* import
importado *adj.* imported
importador *s.* importer
importância *s.* importance
importante *adj.* important, major, meaningful
importar *v.* import, matter
importar-se *v.* care, care about, mind
impossível *adj.* impossible
imposto *s.* customs, duty, tax
imposto de renda *s.* income tax
impostor *s.* fraud
impotência *s.* helplessness
impotentemente *adv.* helplessly
imprecisamente *adv.* inaccurately
imprecisão *s.* vagueness
impreciso *adj.* inaccurate
imprensa *s.* press
impressão *s.* impression, printing
impressão digital *s.* fingerprint, print
impressionado *adj.* impressed
impressionante *adj.* impressive
impressionar *v.* impress

impressora *s.* printer
imprimir *v.* print, print out
impróprio *adj.* unfit
improvável *adj.* improbable, unlikely
imprudente *adj.* reckless
imprudentemente *adv.* recklessly
impulsivo *adj.* impulsive
impulso *s.* impulse
imundície *s.* filth
imundo *adj.* filthy
imune *adj.* immune
imunizar *v.* immunize
inacabado *adj.* unfinished
inaceitável *adj.* unacceptable
inacessível *adj.* unavailable
inacreditável *adj.* unbelievable
inacreditavelmente *adv.* unbelievably
inadequado *adj.* inadequate, unsuitable
inanição *s.* hunger, starvation
inaptidão *s.* disability
incandescência *s.* glow
incapacidade *s.* disability, inability
incapaz *adj.* helpless, incapable
incendiar *v.* burn down
incêndio *s.* blaze, fire
incentivado *adj.* encouraged
incentivador *adj.* encouraging
incentivar *v.* encourage
incentivo *s.* encouragement
incerteza *s.* uncertainty, vagueness
incerto *adj.* insecure, uncertain
incessantemente *adv.* endlessly
inchaço *s.* swelling
inchado *adj.* swollen
inchar *v.* swell up
incidente *s.* incident
incitar *v.* urge
inclinação *s.* addiction
inclinado *adj.* sloping
inclinar *v.* slant, tilt, tip
inclinar-se *v.* slant
incluir *v.* include
inclusão *s.* inclusion
inclusive *adv.* including, inclusive
incomodado *adj.* bothered
incomodar *v.* bother, pester, trouble
incômodo *s.* bother, nuisance, trouble
incompleto *adj.* incomplete
incomum *adj.* uncommon, unusual
inconsciência *s.* unconsciousness
inconsciente *adj.* unaware, unconscious
inconscientemente *adv.* unconsciously

inconsistente *adj.* inconsistent
incontável *adj.* countless
inconveniência *s.* awkwardness, inconvenience
inconveniente *adj.* inconvenient
incorretamente *adv.* inaccurately, incorrectly
incorreto *adj.* incorrect
incrível *adj.* awesome, extraordinary, incredible
incrivelmente *adv.* incredibly
incumbência *s.* assignment
incumbir *v.* assign
incurável *adj.* incurable
indagação *s.* inquiry
indagar *v.* enquire
indecente *adj.* shameful
indeciso *adj.* hesitant
indefinidamente *adv.* indefinitely
indelicadamente *adv.* impolitely, unkindly
indelicado *adj.* impolite, unkind
independência *s.* independence
independente *adj.* independent
indesejado *adj.* unwanted
indesejável *adj.* unwanted
indiano *s.* Indian
indicação *s.* appointment, indication
indicador *s.* dial
indicar *v.* appoint, indicate, tell
índice *s.* index
indiferente *adj.* indifferent, uninterested
indígena americano *s.* American Indian, Native American
indignação *s.* indignation, resentment
indignadamente *adv.* indignantly
indignado *adj.* indignant
indignar-se *v.* resent
índio *s.* Indian
indiretamente *adv.* indirectly
indireto *adj.* indirect, roundabout
indisponível *adj.* unavailable
indisposição *s.* upset
indisposto *s.* unwell, upset
individual *adj.* individual, single
individualmente *adv.* individually
indivíduo *s.* individual
indolor *adj.* painless
indubitavelmente *adv.* doubtless, undoubtedly
indultar *v.* pardon
indústria *s.* industry
industrial *adj.* industrial
induzir a erro *v.* mislead
ineficiente *adj.* inefficient
ineficientemente *adv.* inefficiently
inesperadamente *adv.* unexpectedly
inesperado *adj.* unexpected
inesquecível *adj.* unforgettable
inestimável *adj.* invaluable, priceless
inevitável *adj.* inevitable, unavoidable
inevitavelmente *adv.* inevitably
inexato *adj.* inaccurate
inexperiente *adj.* inexperienced
inexpressivo *adj.* meaningless
infame *adj.* infamous
infância *s.* childhood, infancy
infantaria *s.* infantry
infantil *adj.* childish
infecção *s.* infection
infeccionado *adj.* infected
infeccioso *adj.* infectious
infectado *adj.* infected
infectar *v.* infect
infelicidade *s.* unhappiness
infeliz *adj.* unhappy, wretched
infelizmente *adv.* unfortunately, unluckily
inferior *adj.* inferior, lower, poor, second-rate
inferno *s.* hell
infiel *adj.* unfaithful
infinitamente *adv.* endlessly, infinitely
infinitivo *s.* infinitive
infinito *adj.* infinite
inflação *s.* inflation
inflar *v.* inflate
inflável *adj.* inflatable
influência *s.* influence
influenciar *v.* influence
influente *adj.* influential
informação *s.* information, input
informado *adj.* enlightened
informal *adj.* informal
informalmente *adv.* informally
informar *v.* brief, enlighten, inform, instruct
informatizado *adj.* computerized
informatizar *v.* computerize
infringir *v.* break
infringir a lei break the law
ingênuo *adj.* naive
ingrato *adj.* ungrateful
ingrediente *s.* ingredient
íngreme *adj.* steep
iniciais *s.* initials
inicial *adj.* initial
inicialmente *adv.* initially
iniciante *adj.* start-up
iniciante *s.* beginner, learner
iniciar *v.* initiate, start (off)
início *s.* beginning, outset, start
inimigo *adj.* hostile
inimigo *s.* enemy
injeção *s.* injection, shot
injetar *v.* inject

injustamente *adv.* unfairly
injustiça *s.* injustice, unfairness, wrong
injusto *adj.* unfair, unjust
inocência *s.* innocence
inocentar *v.* acquit
inocente *adj.* innocent
inocentemente *adv.* innocently
inofensivo *adj.* harmless
inoportuno *adj.* unwelcome
inquérito *s.* inquiry
inquietamente *adv.* restlessly
inquieto *adj.* restless
inquilino *s.* lodger, tenant
insalubre *adj.* unhealthy
insano *adj.* insane
insatisfação *s.* displeasure
insatisfatório *adj.* unsatisfactory
insatisfeito *adj.* displeased, dissatisfied
inconsciente *adj.* unconscious
inscrever(-se) *v.* apply, enrol, register
inscrição *s.* application, enrolment
insegurança *s.* insecurity
inseguro *adj.* insecure, uncertain, unsafe, unsure
insensatamente *adv.* foolishly
insensatez *s.* foolishness
insensato *adj.* foolish, unreasonable
inserir *v.* insert
inseto *s.* bug, insect
inseto nocivo *s.* pest
insignificante *adj.* insignificant
insinuar *v.* hint
insípido *adj.* tasteless
insistência *s.* insistence
insistente *adj.* insistent
insistir *v.* insist
insolação *s.* sunstroke
insolência *s.* insolence
insolente *adj.* defiant, impudent, insolent
inspeção *s.* check, inspection
inspecionar *v.* inspect
inspetor *s.* inspector, officer
inspiração *s.* inspiration
inspirar *v.* breathe in / out, inspire
instalação *s.* installation
instalações *s.* facilities
instalar *v.* install, put in
instalar-se *v.* settle
instância *s.* instance
instantâneo *adj.* instant
instante *s.* instant
instável *adj.* fluid, unstable
instigar *v.* urge
instintivamente *adv.* instinctively
instintivo *adj.* instinctive
instinto *s.* instinct
instituição *s.* institution

instituição de caridade *s.* charities, charity
instituto *s.* institute
instrução *s.* education, instruction, schooling
instruções *s.* directions, instruction
instruído *adj.* educated
instruir *v.* educate, instruct
instrumento *s.* instrument, musical instrument
instrutivo *adj.* instructional
instrutor *s.* coach, instructor
insuficiente *adj.* inadequate, insufficient
insultado *adj.* insulted
insultante *adj.* insulting
insultar *v.* insult
insulto *s.* insult
insultos *s.* abuse
inteiramente *adv.* entirely
inteiro *adj.* entire, whole
intelecto *s.* intellect
inteligência *s.* cleverness, intelligence
inteligência artificial *s.* artificial intelligence
inteligente *adj.* clever, intelligent, smart
inteligentemente *adv.* intelligently
intenção *s.* intention
intencional *adj.* deliberate, intentional
intencionalmente *adv.* intentionally
intencionar *v.* intend
intensamente *adv.* intensely
intenso *adj.* intense
interativo *adj.* interactive
intercâmbio *s.* exchange
interessado *s.* applicant
interessante *adj.* interesting
interessar *v.* interest
interesse *s.* interest
interferência *s.* disturbance, interference
interferir *v.* interfere
interfone *s.* intercom
interino *adj.* acting
interior *adj.* inner
interior *s.* countryside, inside, interior
interjeição *s.* interjection
intermediário *s.* middleman
intermediário *adj.* intermediate
intermitentemente *adv.* off and on, on and off
internacional *adj.* international
internato *s.* boarding school

internet *s.* internet, the net
interno *adj.* indoor, inside, internal
interpretação *s.* acting, interpretation
interpretar *v.* interpret
intérprete *s.* interpreter
interrogação *s.* interrogation
interrogar *v.* grill, interrogate, question
interrogativo *adj.* interrogative
interromper *v.* disrupt, interrupt
interrupção *s.* interruption
interruptor *s.* switch
interurbano *adj.* long-distance
intervalo *s.* (coffee) break, gap, intermission, interval
intestinal *adj.* bowel
intestino *s.* bowel
intimidar *v.* bully, deter
intimo *s.* interior
íntimo *adj.* close, inner
intitulado *adj.* entitled
intolerância *s.* bigotry
intolerante *s.* bigot
intolerável *adj.* unbearable
intoleravelmente *adv.* unbearably
intrigado *adj.* puzzled
intrigante *adj.* puzzling
intrigar *v.* baffle, puzzle
introdução *s.* introduction
introduzir *v.* introduce
intrometer-se *v.* meddle
intrometido *adj.* nosy
inúmeros *adj.* numerous
inundar *v.* flood
inútil *adj.* pointless, useless, worthless
invadir *v.* invade, raid, trespass
inválido *s.* invalid
invasão *s.* invasion
invasor *s.* invader, trespasser
inveja *s.* envy
invejar *v.* envy, grudge
invejoso *adj.* envious
invenção *s.* invention
inventar *v.* invent, make up
inventor *s.* inventor
inverno *s.* winter
inverso *s.* reverse
inverter *v.* reverse
investidor *s.* investor
investigação *s.* inquiry, investigation
investigar *v.* inquire/look into, investigate
investimento *s.* investment
investir *v.* invest
inveterado *adj.* habitual

invisível *adj.* invisible
invólucro *s.* wrapper, wrapping
iogurte *s.* yoghurt
ir *v.* do, go
ir à deriva drift
ir à falência go bankrupt
ir acampar go camping
ir às compras go shopping
ir atrás chase/go after, trail along/behind
ir bem do well
ir buscar call for
ir caminhar go for a walk
ir de avião fly
ir de ré reverse
ir depressa dash
ir dormir go to bed
ir em alta velocidade speed
ir em direção a head for
ir em frente go ahead
ir embora go, go away
ir esquiar go skiing
ir nadar go swimming
ir por água abaixo go down the drain
ir sempre reto go/keep straight on
ir surfar go surfing
ir vagarosamente lag
ir velejar go sailing
ir... de... go... by...
irmã *s.* sister
irmão *s.* brother
irreal *adj.* unreal
irregular *adj.* irregular, uneven
irrelevante *adj.* irrelevant
irremediável *adj.* hopeless
irrequietamente *adv.* restlessly
irrequieto/ta *adj.* restless
irresponsabilidade *s.* irresponsibility
irresponsável *adj.* irresponsible
irritação *s.* annoyance, irritation
irritadiço *adj.* irritable
irritado *adj.* annoyed, sore
irritante *adj.* annoying, irritating
irritar *v.* annoy, get on someone's nerves, irritate
irromper *v.* burst into
irromper em lágrimas burst into tears
isca *s.* bait
Islã *s.* Islam
islâmico *adj.* Islamic
isolado *adj.* isolated, lonely
isolamento *s.* isolation
isolar *v.* be cut off, isolate
isqueiro *s.* lighter
isto *pron.* this
isto é namely

Jj

já already, at once, before, ever, immediately, right now/away, straight away, yet
já chega! enough
já já in a moment
já não era sem tempo it's about time
já que because, for, since
jaguar *s.* jaguar
jaleco *s.* overall, smock
jamais *adv.* never
janeiro *s.* January
janela *s.* window
jangada *s.* raft
jantar *s.* dinner, supper
jantar *v.* dine
jaqueta *s.* jacket
jaqueta esportiva *s.* sport coat, sports jacket
jarda *s.* yard
jardim *s.* garden, yard
jardim de infância *s.* kindergarten
jardinagem *s.* gardening
jardineiro *s.* gardener
jardins *s.* gardens
jarra *s.* jug
jarro *s.* jug, pitcher
jato *s.* jet, spray
jaula *s.* cage
javali *s.* boar
jazz *s.* jazz
jeans *s.* denims, jeans
jeito *s.* manner
jejuar *v.* fast
jejum *s.* fast
jérsei *s.* jersey
Jesus *s.* Jesus
jipe *s.* jeep
joalheiro *s.* jeweler
jocosamente *adv.* humorously
joelheira *s.* pad
joelho *s.* knee
jogada *s.* move, play
jogador de futebol *s.* footballer
jogador *s.* gambler, player
jogar *v.* bet, dump, fling, gamble, play, throw, toss
jogar algo fora throw something away/out
jogar lixo litter
jogatina *s.* gambling
jogo *s.* gambling, match
jogo da velha *s.* hashtag, pound
jogo de damas *s.* checkers, draughts
jogos *s.* games
joia *s.* jewel
joias *s.* jewellery
jóquei *s.* jockey
jornada *s.* journey
jornal *s.* newspaper, paper
jornal de ontem *s.* yesterday's paper
jornaleiro *s.* newsagent
jornalismo *s.* journalism
jornalista *s.* journalist
jovem *adj.* young
jovem *s.* the young, youngster
jovens *s.* youth, youths
joystick *s.* joystick
juba *s.* mane
jubileu *s.* jubilee
judaico *adj.* Jewish
judaísmo *s.* Judaism
judeu *adj.* Jewish
judeu *s.* Jew
judia *adj.* Jewish
judia *s.* Jew
judô *s.* judo
juiz *s.* judge, justice, referee
juiz *s.* umpire
juíza *s.* justice, referee
juízo *s.* sense
julgamento *s.* judgement, trial
julgar *v.* judge, try
julho *s.* July
jumbo jet *s.* jumbo jet
jumento *s.* donkey
junco *s.* reed
junho *s.* June
júnior *adj.* junior
junk food *s.* junk food
junta *s.* joint, knuckle
juntamente *adv.* jointly
juntar *v.* collect, gather
juntar-se *v.* band together, join
junto *adv.* together
jura *s.* vow
jurados *s.* judge
juramento *s.* oath
jurar *v.* swear, vow
júri *s.* jury
jurídico *adj.* legal
juros *s.* interest
justamente *adv.* justly
justiça *s.* justice
justificado *adj.* justified
justificar *v.* account for, justify
justificar-se *v.* justify yourself
justificativa *s.* justification
justo *adj.* fair, just, tight
juventude *s.* youth

Kk

ketchup *s.* ketchup
kit *s.* kit, set
know-how *s.* know-how
kosher *adj.* kosher

Ll

lá *adv.* over there, there
lã *s.* wool
lá fora *adv.* outside
lábio *s.* lip
laboratório *s.* lab, laboratory
laço *s.* bow, loop
laços *s.* ties
lacrimejar *v.* water
lacuna *s.* gap
ladear *v.* line
ladeira *s.* hill
ladino *adj.* cunning
lado *s.* side, way
lado a lado side by side
lado de fora outside
ladra *s.* burglar, robber, thief
ladrão *s.* burglar, robber, thief
ladrão de estrada *s.* highwayman
ladrão de loja *s.* shoplifter
ladrilho *s.* tile
lagarta *s.* caterpillar
lagarto *s.* lizard
lago *s.* lake
lagosta *s.* lobster
lágrima *s.* tear
laguinho *s.* pond
lama *s.* mud
lamber *v.* lick
lambida *s.* lick
lambreta *s.* scooter
lambuzar *v.* smear
lamentador *s.* mourner
lamentar *v.* grieve, mourn, regret, wail
lamento que... I'm afraid...
lâmina *s.* blade, razor
lâmina de barbear *s.* razor-blade
lâmpada *s.* bulb, lamp, light-bulb
lança *s.* spear
lançar *v.* fling, hurl, launch, shoot
lançar-se *v.* pounce
lance *s.* flight
lanchinho *s.* snack
lanchonete *s.* (snack) bar, coffee shop
lanterna *s.* flashlight, torch
lápide *s.* gravestone, tombstone

lápis *s.* pencil
lápis de cera *s.* crayon
laptop *s.* laptop
lar *s.* home
laranja *adj., s.* orange
laranja *s.* orange
lareira *s.* fireplace, hearth
largar *v.* desert, drop (out), give up, leave, quit
largar de *v.* let go of
largar do pé de alguém get off someone's back
largo *adj.* broad, loose, wide
largura *s.* breadth, width
larva *s.* grub
larva de inseto *s.* maggot
lasca *s.* chip
laser *s.* laser
lata *s.* bin, can, pot, tin
lata de lixo *s.* (litter) bin, dustbin, garbage/trash can
lata de spray *s.* spray can
latão *s.* brass, tin
lateralmente *adv.* sideways
laticínios *s.* dairy
latido *s.* bark
latir *v.* bark
lava *s.* lava
lavadora de roupa *s.* washing machine
lavagem *s.* wash
lavagem de cabelo *s.* shampoo
lavanderia *s.* laundry
lavanderia automática *s.* launderette, laundromat
lavanderia que lava a seco *s.* dry-cleaner's
lavar a louça wash up
lavar a seco dry-clean
lavar roupa do the laundry
lavar(-se) *v.* bathe, wash, wash up
lavoura *s.* farming, field
lavrador *s.* farmer
lazer *s.* leisure, recreation
leal *adj.* loyal
lealdade *s.* loyalty
leão *s.* lion
lebre *s.* hare
lecionar *v.* teach
legal *adj.* attractive, cool, great, lawful, legal, nice
legalmente *adv.* legally
legenda *s.* key, subtitles
legítima defesa *s.* self-defence
legítimo *adj.* legitimate
legível *adj.* legible
legume *s.* vegetable
lei *s.* law
leilão *s.* auction
leitãozinho *s.* piglet
leite *s.* milk
leite em pó *s.* powdered milk

leiteiro *s.* milkman
leiteria *s.* dairy
leito *s.* bed
leitor *s.* reader
leitoso *adj.* milky
leitura *s.* reading
lema *s.* slogan
lembrança *s.* memory
lembranças *s.* regards
lembrar alguém de remind
lembrar-se *v.* recall, remember
lembrete *s.* reminder
leme *s.* rudder
lenço *s.* handkerchief, hanky, scarf
lenço de papel *s.* paper handkerchief, tissue
lençol *s.* sheet
lenda *s.* legend
lendário *adj.* legendary
lenha *s.* log, wood
lentamente *adv.* slowly
lente *s.* lens
lente de aumento *s.* magnifying glass
lente de contato *s.* contact lens
lentilha *s.* lentil
lento *adj.* slow
leoa *s.* lioness
leopardo *s.* leopard
leque *s.* fan
ler *v.* read, read aloud, read out
lesma *s.* slug, snail
leste *adj., s.* east
letra *s.* handwriting, letter, lyrics, writing
letra impressa *s.* print
letra maiúscula *s.* capital, capital letter
levado *adj.* naughty
levantamento de peso *s.* weightlifting
levantar *v.* arouse, erect, lift, raise
levantar os olhos look up
levantar peso lift weights
levantar-se *v.* get up, rise, stand (up)
levante *s.* uprising
levar *v.* lead, see, take
levar a culpa por get/take the blame for
levar a sério take something to heart
levar às pressas rush
levar de carro drive
levar em consideração take into consideration
levar embora take away
levar tempo take time
levar uma boa surra get a good hiding
levar uma vida lead a life

leve *adj.* faint, gentle, light, mild, slight
levemente *adv.* lightly, slightly
lhe *pron.* her, him, it
lhes *pron.* them
liberal *adj.* liberal
liberar *v.* discharge
liberar alguém *v.* let someone off
liberdade *s.* freedom, liberty
liberdade de expressão *s.* freedom of speech
libertação *s.* liberation, release
libertar *v.* free, liberate, release, set free
libra *s.* pound, quid
lição *s.* lesson
licença *s.* furlough, leave, licence, permit
lícito *adj.* lawful, legal
lidar com *v.* deal with, handle, tackle
lider *adj.* leading
líder *s.* leader
líder de torcida *s.* cheerleader
liderança *s.* leadership
liderar *v.* lead
liga *s.* league
ligação *s.* call, connection, phone call
ligação a cobrar *s.* reverse charge call
ligação telefônica *s.* telephone call
ligado *adv.* on
ligar *v.* call, care for, connect, link, phone, plug in, put on, ring (up), start, switch/ turn on, telephone
ligar a cobrar call collect
ligar de volta call back, return a call
lima *s.* lime
limão *s.* lemon, lime
limitado *adj.* limited
limitar *v.* limit
limite *s.* limit
limite de velocidade *s.* speed limit
limo *s.* moss
limonada *s.* lemonade
limpada *s.* clean
limpador de para-brisa *s.* windscreen/windshield wiper
limpar *v.* bathe, clean, mop up
limpo *adj.* clean, fresh
lindamente *adv.* beautifully
lindo *adj.* beautiful, gorgeous, lovely
língua *s.* language, tongue
língua materna *s.* mother tongue
linguagem chula *s.* bad language
linha *s.* line, -rate, thread

linhagem *s.* ancestry
linhas gerais *s.* outline
liquidação *s.* sale
liquidificador *s.* blender
líquido *s.* fluid, liquid
líquido *adj.* liquid
lírio *s.* lily
liso *adj.* even, plain, smooth, straight
lista *s.* list
lista telefônica *s.* (phone) book, (telephone) directory, catalog
listar *v.* list
listra *s.* stripe
listrado *adj.* striped
literalmente *adv.* pure and simple
literário *adj.* literary
literatura *s.* literature
litoral *s.* coast, seashore, seaside
litro *s.* liter, litre
livraria *s.* bookshop, bookstore
livrar-se de *v.* get rid of
livre *adj.* clear, free, spare
livre-arbítrio *s.* free will
livre de free from/of
livre de impostos *adj.* duty-free
livremente *adv.* freely
livreto *s.* booklet
livrinho *s.* booklet
livro *s.* book
livro de chamada *s.* register
livro de referência *s.* reference book
livro de exercícios *s.* workbook
livro didático *s.* textbook
lixa *s.* file, sandpaper
lixão *s.* dump
lixar *v.* file
lixeira *s.* dustbin
lixeiro *s.* dustman
lixo *s.* garbage, litter, refuse, rubbish, trash, waste
lobby *s.* lobby
lobo *s.* wolf
local *adj.* local
local *s.* scene, site, spot
local de nascimento *s.* birthplace
local para estacionar *s.* parking space
localidade *s.* locality
localização *s.* location
localizar *v.* locate, spot
loção *s.* lotion
locomotiva *s.* engine, locomotive
locutor *s.* announcer
logo *adv.* shortly, soon
logo depois soon after
logo mais presently, soon
logo que as soon as
logro *s.* trickery
loira *adj.* blonde

loiro *adj.* blond
loja *s.* shop, store
loja de departamento *s.* department store
lojista *s.* shopkeeper, storekeeper, tradesman
lombada *s.* bump
lona *s.* canvas
longe *adj., adv.* away, far
longe de far from
longe do alcance beyond reach, out of reach
longo *adj.* lengthy, long
lorde *s.* lord
lorota *s.* fib
loroteiro *s.* fibber
lotado *adj.* crowded, full up, fully booked, overcrowded
lotar *v.* crowd
lote *s.* plot
loteria *s.* lottery
loteria esportiva *s.* football pools, pools
louca *s.* madwoman
louça *s.* china, crockery, dish
loucamente *adv.* crazily, madly
louco *s.* madman
louco *adj.* crazy, insane, mad, wild
louco por crazy/mad about
loucura *s.* madness
lounge *s.* lounge
lousa *s.* blackboard
louvável *adj.* worthwhile
lua *s.* moon
lua de mel *s.* honeymoon
luar *s.* moonlight
lubrificar *v.* oil
lucrar *v.* benefit, profit
lucrativo *adj.* profitable
lucro *s.* profit
lufada *s.* blast, puff
lugar *s.* place, seat
lugar algum *adv.* anywhere
lugar sagrado *s.* shrine
luminosidade *s.* glare
lustrada *s.* rub
lustrar *v.* shine
lustroso *adj.* glossy
luta *s.* struggle, wrestling
lutador *s.* boxer, fighter, wrestler
lutar *v.* fight, struggle, wrestle
luto *s.* mourning
luva *s.* glove
luxo *s.* luxury
luxuoso *adj.* fancy, luxurious
luz *s.* light, lights
luz do dia *s.* daylight
luz do sol *s.* sunlight
luz trêmula *s.* glimmer
luzes *s.* light, lights

Mm

má *adj.* bad, nasty
maca *s.* stretcher
maçã *s.* apple
macacão *s.* dungarees, overalls
macaco *s.* jack, monkey
maçaneta *s.* handle, knob
macarrão *s.* noodle
machadinha *s.* hatchet
machado *s.* axe
macho *adj., s.* male
machucar *v.* hurt
machucar-se *v.* get hurt
maciço *adj.* solid
maciez *s.* softness
macio *adj.* not rough, soft
maço *s.* bunch, bundle, pack
madame *s.* madam
madeira *s.* timber, wood
madrasta *s.* stepmother
madrinha *s.* godmother
maduro *adj.* mature, ripe
mãe *s.* ma, mom, mother, mum
maestro *s.* conductor
mãezinha *s.* mommy, mummy
magazine *s.* department store
magia *s.* magic
mágica *s.* magic
magicamente *adv.* magically
mágico *adj.* magic, magical
mágico *s.* conjurer, magician
magistrado *s.* magistrate
magnético *adj.* magnetic
magnífico *adj.* magnificent
mago *s.* magician, wizard
magoado *adj.* hurt
magoar *v.* hurt
magoar alguém hurt someone's feelings
magricelo *adv.* skinny
magro *adj.* lean, thin
maio *s.* May
maiô *s.* swimsuit
maior parte de *adj.* most
maioria *s.* majority
maioridade *s.* adulthood
mais *adv.* any more, best, else, more, most
mais *conj.* and
mais *prep.* plus
mais adiante beyond
mais além farther, further
mais algum lugar anywhere else
mais alguma coisa anything else, something else
mais cedo ou mais tarde sooner or later
mais de over
mais distante farther
mais jovem junior
mais longe farther, furthest
mais novo junior
mais ou menos kind/sort of, more or less, so-so
mais perto nearer
mais recente latest
mais seco drier
mais tarde later, later on
mais tempo any longer
mais um another
mais uma vez once again, once more
mais velho big, elder, older, senior
majestade *s.* Majesty
major *s.* major
mal *adv.* badly, barely, hardly, poorly, scarcely, unpleasantly
mal *s.* evil, harm
mala *s.* case, suitcase
mala de mão *s.* travelling/travel bag
mala escolar *s.* schoolbag
malabarista *s.* juggler
malcriado *adj.* impudent
maldade *s.* meanness, wickedness
maldição *s.* curse
maldoso *adj.* vicious
mal-educado *adj.* impolite
mal-entendido *s.* misunderstanding
males *s.* evil
malhação *s.* workout
malhar *v.* work out
mal-humorado *adj.* bad-tempered
malpassado *adj.* rare
malsucedido *adj.* unsuccessful
malicioso *adj.* vicious
maltratar *v.* abuse, ill-treat
maluco *adj.* crazy, nuts
malva *s.* mauve
malvadamente *adv.* wickedly
malvado *adj.* wicked
mamãe *s.* mom, momma
mamãezinha *s.* mommy, mummy
mamífero *s.* mammal
mamilo *s.* nipple
manada *s.* herd
mancar *v.* limp
mancha *s.* smear, stain
mancha de óleo/petróleo *s.* oil slick
manchar *v.* stain
manchete *s.* headline
manco *adj.* lame
mandado *s.* warrant
mandão *adj.* bossy
mandar *v.* command, fax, order, post, send
mandar buscar *v.* send for
mandar em boss around/about
mandar e-mail e-mail/email
mandar lembranças a alguém give/send regards to
mandíbula *s.* jaw, jaws
mandona *adj.* bossy
maneira *s.* way
maneiras *s.* manners
manga *s.* mango, sleeve
mangueira *s.* hose
manhã *s.* morning
manifestação *s.* demonstration
manifestante *s.* demonstrator
manifestar-se *v.* demonstrate
manobra *s.* maneuver
manqueira *s.* limp
mansão *s.* mansion, villa
manteiga *s.* butter
mantenedor *s.* keeper
manter *v.* keep, maintain, stick to
manter algo aquecido keep something warm
manter algo em segredo keep something secret
manter alguém informado keep someone posted
manter alguém quieto keep someone quiet
manter contato com be/keep in touch with
manter distância keep out
manter sua palavra keep your word
manter-se longe de keep ...out
mantimentos *s.* groceries
manual *adj.* manual
manual *s.* guide, guidebook, handbook, manual
manualmente *adv.* manually
manufaturar *v.* manufacture
manusear *v.* handle
manutenção *s.* maintenance, upkeep
mão *s.* hand
mão de obra *s.* labor, manpower
mãos ao alto hands up
mapa *s.* map
maquiagem *s.* make-up
maquiar-se *v.* make up
máquina *s.* (vending) machine machinery
máquina a vapor *s.* steam engine
máquina caça-níqueis *s.* slot machine
máquina de costura *s.* sewing machine
máquina de escrever *s.* typewriter
máquina de lavar louça *s.* dishwasher
máquina de lavar roupa *s.* washing machine
maquinar *v.* scheme
maquinário *s.* machinery

maquinista *s.* engine-driver, engineer
mar *s.* sea
maratona *s.* marathon
maravilha *s.* marvel, wonder
maravilhado *s.* wonder
maravilhar-se *v.* marvel
maravilhosamente *adv.* wonderfully
maravilhoso *adj.* marvellous, wonderful
marca *s.* brand, check, make, mark, tick
marca registrada *s.* trademark
marcar *v.* mark, schedule, score
marcha *s.* gear, march
marcha à ré *s.* reverse, reverse gear
marchar *v.* march
março *s.* March
maré *s.* tide
mareado *adj.* seasick
marfim *s.* ivory
margarida *s.* daisy
margarina *s.* margarine
margem *s.* bank, fringe, margin, shore
marido *s.* husband
marinha *s.* navy
marinheiro *s.* sailor, tailor
marionete *s.* puppet
mariposa *s.* moth
marisco *s.* shellfish
marketing *s.* marketing
mármore *s.* marble
marrom *adj., s.* brown
martelar *v.* hammer
martelo *s.* hammer
marujo *s.* sailor, tailor
mas *conj.* but, only
máscara *s.* mask
mascarado *adj.* masked
masculino *adj.* male, masculine
massa *s.* dough, mass, pastry
massacrar *v.* massacre, slaughter
massacre *s.* massacre, slaughter
massageada *s.* rub
massagear *v.* massage
massagem *s.* massage
mastigar *v.* chew, crunch
mastro *s.* mast, pole
mastro de bandeira *s.* flagpole
matador *s.* killer
matança *s.* slaughter
matar *v.* kill, massacre, slaughter
matar aula *v.* play truant
matar-se *v.* kill yourself
matemática *s.* math, mathematics
matematicamente *adv.* mathematically
matemático *adj.* mathematical
matemático *s.* mathematician

matéria *s.* material, report, story, subject
material *adj.* material
material *s.* material, matter
matéria-prima *s.* raw materials
matiz *s.* shade
matrícula *s.* enrolment
matricular(-se) *v.* enrol, register
matriz *s.* head
maturidade *s.* adulthood, maturity
maturidade feminina *s.* womanhood
maturidade masculina *s.* manhood
mau *adj.* bad, evil, nasty
mau trato *s.* ill-treatment
máximo *adj.* maximum, top
me *pron.* me, myself
mecânica *s.* mechanics
mecânico *adj.* mechanical
mecânico *s.* mechanic
mecanismo *s.* mechanism
mecha *s.* streak
medalha *s.* medal
média *s.* average
mediar *v.* moderate
medicamento *s.* drug, medicine
medicina *s.* medicine
médico *s.* doctor, physician
médico *adj.* medical
medida *s.* measure, measurement
medidas *s.* measures
medidas de segurança *s.* safety measures
medidor *s.* gauge, meter
medieval *adj.* medieval
médio *adj.* medium
medíocre *adj.* mediocre
medir *v.* gauge, measure
Mediterrâneo *s.* Mediterranean
medo *s.* fear
medonho *adj.* ghastly
meia *s.* sock, stocking
meia-calça *s.* pantyhose, tights
meia-idade *adj.* middle-aged
meia-irmã *s.* stepsister
meia-lua *s.* crescent
meia-luz *s.* twilight
meia-noite *s.* midnight
meio *adv.* a little, half, kind/sort of, rather
meio *s.* center, centre, half, heart, middle
meio ambiente *s.* environment
meio caminho halfway
meio da semana *s.* midweek
meio de intimidação *s.* deterrent
meio de transporte *s.* means of transport
meio expediente *adj.* part-time
meio período part-time

meio *adj.* half
meio-dia *s.* midday, noon
meio-fio *s.* curb, kerb
meio-irmão *s.* stepbrother
meios *s.* form, means
meio-termo *s.* compromise
mel *s.* honey
melado *adj.* sticky
melancia *s.* watermelon
melancolicamente *adv.* gloomily
melancólico *adj.* moody
melão *s.* melon
melhor *adj., adv.* best, better
melhora *s.* improvement
melhorar *v.* get better, improve, recover, upgrade
melhores votos best wishes
melodia *s.* melody
melro *s.* blackbird, robin
membro *s.* limb, member
memorando *s.* memo
memorável *adj.* memorable
memória *s.* memory
memorial *s.* memorial
memorizar *v.* memorize
menção *s.* mention
menção honrosa *s.* distinction
mendigar *v.* beg
mendigo *s.* beggar
menina *s.* daughter, girl
menino *s.* boy
menor *adj., s.* minor
menos *adj.* fewer, less
menos *adv.* least, less
menos *prep.* apart from, except (for)
menos favorecido disadvantaged, underprivileged
mensageiro *s.* errand boy
mensageiro *s.* messenger
mensagem *s.* message
mensal *adj.* monthly
mensalmente *adv.* monthly
mensário *s.* monthly
menta *s.* mint, peppermint
mental *adj.* mental
mentalidade *s.* mentality
mentalmente *adv.* mentally
mente *s.* mind
mentir *v.* lie
mentira *s.* lie
mentirinha *s.* fib
mentiroso *s.* fibber, liar
menu *s.* menu
meramente *adv.* merely
mercadinho *s.* greengrocery, grocer, grocery
mercado *s.* market
mercadoria *s.* merchandise
mercearia *s.* delicatessen
merecedor *adj.* worthy
merecer *v.* deserve, merit

merecido *adj.* due
mergulhador *s.* diver
mergulhar *v.* dip, dive
mergulho *s.* diving
meridional *adj.* south
Meritíssimo *s.* Your Honor/Honour
mérito *s.* merit
mero *adj.* mere
mês *s.* month
mesa *s.* desk, table
mesada *s.* allowance
mescla *s.* mixture
mesmo *adj., s.* the same
mesmo assim *adv.* anyway, even so, still, though
mesmo que *adv.* although, even if, even though
mesmo se even if
mesquinhez *s.* meanness
mesquinho *adj.* cheap, mean, miserly
mesquita *s.* mosque
mestre *s.* master
metade *s.* half
metade do caminho halfway
metades *s.* halves
metal *s.* metal
metálico *adj.* metallic
meteorologista *s.* weather forecaster, weatherman
meter-se *v.* meddle
meticuloso *adj.* fussy, painstaking
método *s.* method
metralhadora *s.* machine-gun
métrico *adj.* metric
metro *s.* meter, metre
metrô *s.* subway, tube, underground
meu *pron.* mine, my
mexer *v.* move, stir
mexer-se *v.* move
miar *v.* miaow
miau *s.* miaow
micróbio *s.* bug, microbe
microfone *s.* microphone, mike
microscópico *adj.* microscopic
microscópio *s.* microscope
mídia *s.* media
migalha *s.* crumb
migrante *s.* migrant
migrar *v.* migrate
mil *s., num.* thousand
milagre *s.* miracle, wonder
milagrosamente *adv.* miraculously
milagroso *adj.* miraculous
milênio *s.* millennium
milésimo *adj.* thousandth
milha *s.* mile
milhão *s., num.* million
milhar *s., num.* thousand

milho *s.* corn, maize
milho cozido *s.* corn on the cob
miligrama *s.* milligram
milímetro *s.* millimeter
milionário *s.* millionaire
milionésimo *adj.* millionth
militar *adj.* military
mim mesmo *pron.* myself
mimado *adj.* spoilt
mimar *v.* indulge, spoil
mímica *s.* mime, pantomime
mímico *s.* mimic
mina *s.* mine
mina de carvão *s.* coalmine, pit
mina de ouro *s.* goldmine
mineirador *s.* miner
mineiro *s.* miner
mineral *s.* mineral
mingau de aveia *s.* porridge
minha *pron.* mine, my
minha casa *s.* my place
miniatura *adj.* miniature
mínimo *s.* minimum
mínimo *adj.* minimal, minimum
ministério *s.* department, ministry, office
ministro *s.* minister
minoria *s.* minority
minuciosamente *adv.* closely, thoroughly
minuciosidade *s.* thoroughness
minucioso *adj.* thorough
minúsculo *adj.* minute
minuto *s.* minute, moment
miolo *s.* core
míope *adj.* near-/short-sighted
mirante *s.* lookout, look-out point
mirar *s.* aim, take aim at
miscelânia *s.* jumble
miserável *adj.* miserable
miséria *s.* misery
misericórdia *s.* mercy
misericordioso *adj.* merciful
missa *s.* Mass
missão *s.* mission
míssil *s.* missile
missionário/a *s.* missionary
mistério *s.* mystery, puzzle
misteriosamente *adv.* mysteriously
misterioso *adj.* mysterious
misto *adj.* mixed
mistura *s.* blend, mixture
misturar(-se) *v.* blend, mix
mitene *s.* mitten
mito *s.* myth
mobília *s.* furniture
mobiliado *adj.* furnished
mobiliar *v.* furnish
mobiliário *s.* furniture
moça *s.* miss, youngster
mochila *s.* backpack, pack, rucksack

mocidade *s.* girlhood, youth
moço *s.* youngster
moda *s.* fashion, style
modal *s.* modal
modelagem *s.* modelling
modelar *v.* form, model
modelo *s.* model
modem *s.* modem
moderadamente *adv.* moderately
moderado *adj.* moderate
moderar *v.* moderate
modernizar *v.* bring... up to date, update
moderno *adj.* modern
modestamente *adv.* modestly
modéstia *s.* modesty
modesto *adj.* modest
modismo *s.* buzzword
modo *s.* way
modo de vida *s.* way of life
modos *s.* manners
moeda *s.* coin, currency
moeda de 25 centavos de dólar *s.* quarter
moeda de dez centavos de dólar *s.* dime
moedas *s.* change
moedor *s.* grinder, mill
moer *v.* grind, mince
mofado *adj.* moldy, stale
mofo *s.* mold
moído *adj.* ground, minced
moinho *s.* mill
moinho de vento *s.* windmill
moita *s.* bush
mola *s.* spring
moldar *v.* mold, mould, shape
molde *s.* mold
moldura *s.* frame
mole *adj.* soft
moleiro *s.* miller
moleque *s.* errand boy
moletom *s.* tracksuit
molhado *adj.* wet
molhar *v.* water, wet
molhar-se *v.* get wet
molho *s.* bunch, sauce
molusco *s.* shellfish
momento *s.* moment
monarca *s.* monarch
monarquia *s.* monarchy
monge *s.* monk
monótono *adj.* dreary, monotonous
monstro *s.* monster
monstruoso *adj.* monstrous
montanha *s.* batch, mountain
montanha-russa *s.* roller-coaster
montanhista *s.* mountaineer
montanhoso *adj.* hilly, mountainous
montar *v.* form, go riding, mount, put/set up, start

montaria *s.* riding
monte *s.* batch, heap, mount, pack, pile
monumento *s.* monument
moradia *s.* dwelling
morador *s.* resident
moral *adj., s.* moral
moralidade *s.* morality
moralmente *adv.* morally
morango *s.* strawberry
morar *v.* live, room
morcego *s.* bat
mordaz *adj.* sharp
morder *v.* bite
mordida *s.* bite
mordiscar *v.* nibble
morno *adj.* lukewarm
morrendo *v.* dying
morrer *v.* die
morrer congelado freeze to death
morrer de chorar cry your eyes out
morrer de inanição starve
morro *s.* hill
morro acima uphill
mortal *adj.* deadly
morte *s.* death
morto *adj.* dead
mosca *s.* fly
mostarda *s.* mustard
mosteiro *v.* abbey, monastery
mostra *s.* display, exhibit, exhibition
mostrador *s.* dial
mostrar *v.* show
mostrar o caminho direct
mostrar um local a alguém show someone around
motel *s.* motel
motim *s.* mutiny
motivo *s.* motive
moto *s.* bike, motorbike, motorcycle
motocicleta *s.* cycle, motorbike, motorcycle
motociclista *s.* motorcyclist, rider
motoneta *s.* moped
motor *s.* engine, motor
motorista *s.* chauffeur, driver, motorist
motorzinho *s.* drill
mouse *s.* mouse
móvel *adj.* mobile
móvel *s.* piece
mover *v.* budge, shift
mover-se *v.* move, stir
mover-se demonstrando raiva storm
mover-se furtivamente sneak
mover-se lentamente creep
mover-se ruidosamente rattle
movimento *s.* motion, move, movement, use
muçulmano *s.* Muslim
mudança *s.* change, move
mudança de direção *s.* U-turn
mudar *v.* change, move, switch
mudar de ideia *v.* change your mind
mudar-se *v.* move, move in
mudo *adj.* dead, dumb
mugido *s.* moo
mugir *v.* moo
muitíssimo *adv.* very/too much
muito *adv.* a lot, awfully, bloody, so/very much, very
muito *pron.* plenty
muito *s.* lot, many, much
muito bem highly, very well
muito longe far away
muito magro skinny
muito obrigado thank you very much
muito quente boiling, steaming
muito tempo a long time
muito tempo atrás long ago, long before
muito tempo depois long after
muito triste miserable
muito *adj.* a good/great deal of, a lot of, too much
muitos *adj.* (a great) many, lots of, scores of
mula *s.* mule
muleta *s.* crutch
mulher *s.* woman
mulher de negócios *s.* businesswoman
multa *s.* fine, penalty, ticket
multa por estacionamento proibido *s.* parking ticket
multar *v.* fine
multicolorido *adj.* multicolored
multidão *s.* crowd, mob
multiplicação *s.* multiplication
multiplicar(-se) *v.* multiply
mundial *adj.* worldwide
mundialmente *adv.* worldwide
mundialmente famoso world-famous
mundo *s.* globe, world
munição *s.* ammunition
murchar *v.* shrivel, wither
murcho *adj.* flat
murmurar *v.* murmur
murmúrio *s.* murmur
muro *s.* wall
muscular *adj.* muscular
músculo *s.* muscle
musculoso *adj.* muscular
museu *s.* museum
musgo *s.* moss
música *s.* music
música folclórica *s.* folk song
musical *adj.* musical
musical *s.* musical
musicista *s.* musician
músico *s.* musician, performer
mútuo *adj.* mutual

Nn

na época *adv.* at the time, then
na esperança de in the hope of
na frente de in front of
na hora on time
na hora em que by the time
na íntegra in full
na lista de espera on standby
na metade do caminho midway
na moda fashionably
na parte externa outside
na pior das hipóteses at worst
na ponta dos pés on tiptoes
na realidade in fact, in reality
na retaguarda behind
na verdade actually, as a matter of fact, in fact
nabo *s.* turnip
nação *s.* nation
nacional *adj.* national
nacionalidade *s.* nationality
naco *pron.* slab
nada *pron.* anything, none, nothing
nada além de *pron.* nothing but
nada disso! no way!
nadadeira *s.* fin
nadador *s.* swimmer
nadar *v.* swim
nado crawl *s.* crawl
nado de costas *s.* backstroke
nado de peito *s.* breast-stroke
náilon *s.* nylon
namorada *s.* girlfriend
namorado *s.* boyfriend
não *adv.* no, not
não adianta it's no good, it's no use
não adianta [fazer] it's no use [doing]
não aguentar can't bear, can't stand
não conseguir fail (to do something)
não dar em nada come to nothing
não dar um pio not make a sound
não dever be not due/supposed to
não dizer uma palavra not say a word
não é da sua conta! it's none of your business!
não é de admirar que no wonder
não entender can't make head or tail of
não estar familiarizado com be unfamiliar with
não estar no seu juízo perfeito be out of your mind
não fazer diferença make no difference

não gostar de dislike
não gosto da aparência I don't like the look of
não há pressa there's no rush
não há razão para there's no point in
não haver mal em there's no harm in...
não importa o que no matter what
não invejar not grudge
não mais no longer, not any longer/more
não me importo I don't mind
não mexer em algo leave something alone
não muito not very much
não nítido fuzzy, unclear
não passar de nothing but
não poder be not supposed to, can't
não poder deixar de can't help
não por isso don't mention it, not at all, you're welcome
não querer saber will/would not hear of
não se afobar take it/things easy
não se atrever don't you dare
não se ofender no offence
não servir be no good, not be any good
não só... como também not only... but also
não suportar can't bear/stand
não tão not as... as, not so, not so... as, not too
não tenha pressa take your time
não ter condição de can't afford
não ter coragem de not have the heart to
não ter nada a ver com have/has nothing to do with
não ter permissão be not allowed to
não tirar os olhos de not take your eyes off
não vejo a hora I can't wait
não confiável *adj.* unreliable
não especializado *adj.* unskilled
não ficção *adj.* non-fiction
não fumante *adj.* non-smoker
não habitado *adj.* uninhabited
não identificado *adj.* unidentified
não natural *adj.* unnatural
não pago *adj.* unpaid
naquela época at that time
narciso *s.* daffodil
narina *s.* nostril
nariz *s.* nose
nascente *s.* source
nascer *v.* be born, rise
nascer do sol *s.* sunrise

nascimento *s.* birth
natação *s.* swimming
Natal *s.* Christmas, Xmas
nativo *s.* native
nativo americano *s.* Native American
nativo *adj.* native
natural *adj.* natural, plain
natural *s.* native
naturalmente *adv.* naturally
natureza *s.* nature
naufrágio *s.* shipwreck
naval *adj.* naval
nave espacial *s.* spaceship
navegação *s.* navigation, surfing
navegação a vela *s.* sailing
navegador *s.* browser, navigator
navegar *v.* browse, navigate, sail, surf
navio *s.* liner, ship
navio a vapor *s.* steamship
navio de guerra *s.* warship
neblina *s.* fog, haze, mist
necessariamente *adv.* necessarily
necessário *adj.* necessary
necessidade *s.* necessity, need
necessitar *v.* need, require
negar *v.* deny
negativa *s.* denial
negativo *s.* negative
negativo *adj.* negative
negligência *s.* neglect, negligence
negligenciado *adj.* neglected
negligenciar *v.* neglect
negligente *adj.* negligent, slack
negociação *s.* negotiation
negociar *v.* bargain, deal with, negotiate, trade
negócio *s.* business
negro *s.* black
nem *conj.* neither, nor
nem de longe not at all, not in the least
nem perto not nearly, nowhere near
nem... nem neither... nor
nenhum *pron.* neither, none
néon *s.* neon
nerd *s.* nerd
nervo *s.* nerve
nervosamente *adv.* nervously
nervosismo *s.* nervousness
nervoso *adj.* nervous
nessas circunstâncias in/under the circumstances
nesse caso in that case
nesse meio-tempo in the meantime
nesse passo at this rate
net *s.* internet, the net
neta *s.* granddaughter
neto *s.* grandson

neto *s.* grandchild
network *s.* network
neutro *adj.* neutral
nevado *adj.* snowy
nevar *v.* snow
nevasca *s.* blizzard
neve *s.* snow
nevoento *adj.* foggy
ninguém *pron.* anybody, nobody
ninhada *s.* litter
ninho *s.* nest
nítido *adj.* clear, sharp
nitrogênio *s.* nitrogen
nível *s.* count, level, standard
nivelar *v.* flatten
nó *s.* knot
no andar de baixo downstairs
no caminho in the way
no conjunto on the whole
no entanto however
no exterior overseas
no final at last, finally, in the end
no formato de -shaped
no início at first
no lugar de in your/her/his place
no mais tardar at the latest
no máximo at the most
no meio de mid, mid-
no mínimo at least
no momento at the moment, just/right now, presently
no que me diz respeito as far as I'm concerned
no total altogether
no trabalho at work
no volante at/behind the wheel
nobre *adj.* noble
noção *s.* awareness, notion, realization
nocautear *v.* knock down/out
nódoa *s.* smear
nogueira *s.* walnut
noite *s.* evening, night, night-time

noiva *s.* bride, fiancée
noivado *s.* engagement
noivo *s.* bridegroom, fiancé, groom
noivo *adj.* engaged
nojento *adj.* disgusting, gross, nasty
nome *s.* name
nome de batismo *s.* Christian/first name
nome de família *s.* family name
nome próprio *s.* proper name
nonagésimo *s., num.* ninetieth
nono *s., num.* ninth
nora *s.* daughter-in-law
normal *adj.* normal, regular
normalmente *adv.* normally, usually
norte *adj., s.* north
nós *pron.* us, we
nos anos cinquenta in the fifties
nos anos oitenta in the eighties
nos anos quarenta in the forties
nós mesmos ourselves
nos seus cinquenta anos in your fifties
nos seus quarenta anos in your forties
nos seus sessenta e poucos anos in your sixties
nos seus trinta e poucos anos in your thirties
nos seus vinte e poucos anos in your twenties
nos tempos antigos in former times
nosso *pron.* our, ours
nota *s.* banknote, bill, grade, mark, note, score
nota fiscal *s.* invoice
notar *v.* note, notice
notável *adj.* distinguished, noticeable, outstanding, remarkable

notavelmente *adv.* remarkably
notícia *s.* news
notícia de última hora *s.* newsflash
noticiário *s.* news
notificar *v.* notify
notório *adj.* glaring, notorious, prominent
noturno *adj.* nightly, overnight
novamente *adv.* again
nove *s., num.* nine, ninth
novela *s.* novel, soap opera
novela de mistério *s.* mystery novel
novelista *s.* novelist
novelo *s.* ball
novembro *s.* November
noventa *s., num.* ninety
novinho *adj.* brand-new
novo *adj.* fresh, further, new, start-up, young
novo em folha brand-new
noz *s.* nut, walnut
nu *adj.* bare, naked
nublado *adj.* cloudy, dull, misty
nuclear *adj.* nuclear
num instante *s.* in a flash
num minuto *s.* in a minute, in a moment
numerado *adj.* numbered
número *s.* act, issue, number, size
número da placa *s.* registration number
número de série *s.* serial number
número de telefone *s.* telephone number
números *s.* figures
nunca *adv.* never
nutricional *adj.* nutritional
nutritivo *adj.* nourishing, nutritious
nuvem *s.* cloud

Oo

o ano todo s. all year round
o dia seguinte s. the next day
o fato é que the fact is
o mais adv. the most
o mais cedo possível as soon as possible
o mais distante the farthest, the furthest
o mais longe the farthest
o mais rápido possível as soon as possible, as soon as you can
o mais velho the eldest
o pior adj. the worst
o quanto antes as soon as possible
o que what, whatever
o que foi? what's the matter?
o que há de errado com...? what's wrong with...?
o que você faz? what do you do?
o quê? pardon?, sorry?, what?
o tempo todo s. all along
o art. the
oásis s. oasis
obedecer v. go by, obey, observe
obediência s. obedience
obediente adj. obedient
obedientemente adv. obediently
objeção s. objection
objetivamente adv. objectively
objetivo s. aim, goal, object, objective, purpose
objetivo adj. objective
objeto s. missile, object
objeto direto s. direct object [grammar]
objeto exposto s. exhibit
objeto indireto s. indirect object [grammar]
obra s. work
obra de referência s. reference book
obra de suspense s. thriller
obra exposta s. exhibit
obra-prima s. masterpiece
obras s. works
obrigação s. obligation
obrigado adj. thank you, thanks
obrigar v. compel, force, oblige
obrigatório adj. compulsory
obscuro adj. obscure
observação s. observation
observador adj. observant
observância s. observance
observar v. observe, remark
observatório s. observatory
obsessão s. obsession
obstáculo s. obstacle

obstinação s. obstinacy
obstinadamente adv. obstinately
obstinado adj. obstinate
obstrução s. blockage, obstruction
obstruir v. obstruct
obter v. obtain
obturar v. fill
obviamente adv. clearly, obviously
óbvio adj. apparent, obvious
ocasião s. instance, occasion, point
ocasional adj. occasional
ocasionalmente adv. occasionally
oceano s. ocean
ocidental adj. west, western
Ocidente s. West
ociosidade s. idleness
oco adj. hollow
ocorrência s. occurrence
ocorrer v. come (about), happen, occur, strike, take place
octogésimo s., num. eightieth
oculista s. optician
óculos s. glasses, spectacles
óculos de proteção s. goggles
óculos de sol s. sunglasses
óculos escuros s. sunglasses
ocultar v. conceal
ocupação s. occupation
ocupado adj. busy, engaged, occupied, taken
ocupar v. occupy, take up
odiado adj. hated
odiar v. hate
ódio s. hate, hatred
odioso adj. hateful
odor s. odor, scent
oeste s. west
ofegar v. gasp, pant
ofender v. offend
oferecer v. offer
oferecer-se como voluntário volunteer
oferta s. offer
oficial adj. official
oficial s. officer
oficialmente adv. officially
oficina s. garage, shop, workshop
ofuscante adj. blinding
ofuscar v. dazzle
oi int. hi
oitavo s., num. eighth
oitenta s., num. eighty
oito s., num. eight
OK int. fine, OK, okay
olá int. hallo, hello
óleo s. oil
óleo vegetal s. vegetable oil
oleoso adj. oily
olfato s. smell
olhada s. look
olhar s. glance, look

olhar v. examine, look (at), look after, mind, take care of, watch
olhar ao redor look around/round
olhar através look through
olhar de relance glance
olhar em volta look around/round
olhar fixamente gaze, stare
olhar fixo gaze, stare
olhar furiosamente glare
olhar furioso glare
olhar por onde pisa watch your step
olho s. eye
Olimpíadas s. the Olympic Games
olímpico adj. Olympic
oliva s. olive
ombro s. shoulder
omelete s. omelette
omissão s. omission
omitir v. leave out
onça s. ounce
onda s. wave
onde adv. where
onde quer que adv. wherever
ondulado adj. wavy
ônibus s. bus
ônibus de dois andares s. double-decker
ônibus elétrico s. trolleybus
ônibus espacial s. space shuttle
ônibus-leito s. bus, coach
ontem adv. yesterday
ontem à noite last night
ONU abr. UN
onze s., num. eleven
opaco adj. dull, not bright
opção s. alternative, choice, option
opcional adj. optional
ópera s. opera
operação s. operation
operador s. operator
operar v. operate, work
operário s. laborer, workman
operário da construção s. construction worker
opinião s. notion, opinion, thought
opinião pública s. public opinion
oponente s. opponent
opor-se v. contradict, object, oppose, resist
oportunidade s. opportunity
oposição s. opposition
opositor s. opponent
oposto s. opposite
oposto adj. opposite
optar v. choose
oração s. clause, prayer

oração condicional *s.* conditional clause
oração principal *s.* main clause grammar
oração subordinada *s.* dependent clause, subordinate clause
oral *adj.* oral
orar *v.* pray
órbita *s.* orbit
orbitar *v.* orbit
orçamento *s.* budget
ordeiro *adj.* tidy
ordem *s.* command, order, tidiness
ordenadamente *adv.* tidily
ordenar *v.* command, direct, order
ordenhar *v.* milk
orelhão *s.* call-box, pay phone, phone booth/box, telephone booth/kiosk
orelha *s.* ear
orfanato *s.* orphanage
órfão *s.* orphan
orgânico *adj.* organic
organização *s.* organization
Organização das Nações Unidas *s.* the United Nations
organizado *adj.* organized
organizador *s.* organizer
organizar *v.* arrange, organize
organizar-se *v.* get organized
órgão *s.* organ
orgulho *s.* pride
orgulhosamente *adv.* proudly
orgulhoso *adj.* proud
orientação *s.* guidance
orientação vocacional *s.* vocational guidance
oriental *adj.* east, eastern, oriental
orientar *v.* guide

oriente *s.* east
Oriente Médio *s.* Middle East
origem *s.* origin
original *adj., s.* original
originalmente *adv.* originally
ornamental *adj.* ornamental
ornamento *s.* ornament
ornar *v.* blend, match
orquestra *s.* orchestra
orquídea *s.* orchid
ortografia *s.* spelling
orvalho *s.* dew
os anos noventa *s.* the nineties
os anos sessenta *s.* the sixties
os anos setenta *s.* the seventies
os anos trinta *s.* the thirties
os anos vinte *s.* the twenties
os antigos *s.* the ancients
os cegos *s.* the blind
os clássicos *s.* the ancients
os deficientes *s.* the disabled
os desempregados *s.* the unemployed
os doentes *s.* the sick
os dois *s.* both
os feridos *s.* the injured, the wounded
os idosos *s.* the aged, the elders, the old
os Jogos Olímpicos *s.* the Olympic Games
os jovens *s.* the youth
os militares *s.* the military
os mortos *s.* the dead
os outros *s.* the others
os pobres *s.* the poor
os ricos *s.* the rich
os surdos *s.* the deaf
os trópicos *s.* the tropics

oscilar *v.* rock, sway, swing
osso *s.* bone
ostra *s.* oyster
ótico *adj.* optical
otimismo *s.* optimism
otimista *adj.* optimistic
otimista *s.* optimist
ótimo *adj.* gorgeous, great, lovely
ou *conj.* or
ou... ou either... or
ou seja that is to say
ouriço *s.* hedgehog
ourives *s.* goldsmith
ouro *s.* gold
ousadamente *adv.* boldly
ousadia *s.* boldness, daring
ousado *adj.* bold, daring
outdoor *s.* billboard
outono *s.* autumn, fall
outro dia *s.* the other day
outro lugar *s.* elsewhere, somewhere else
outro *pron.* another, other
outros *pron.* others
outubro *s.* October
ouvido *s.* ear
ouvinte *s.* listener
ouvir *v.* hear, listen
ouvir falar de hear of
ouvir por acaso overhear
oval *adj.* oval
ovelha *s.* sheep
óvni *s.* UFO
ovo *s.* egg
ovo quente *s.* soft-boiled egg
ovo poché *s.* poached egg
ovos mexidos *s.* scrambled egg
oxigênio *s.* oxygen
ozônio *s.* ozone

Pp

pá *s.* shovel, spade
pá de lixo *s.* dustpan
paciência *s.* patience
paciente *adj.* patient
paciente *s.* patient
pacientemente *adv.* patiently
pacificamente *adv.* peacefully
pacífico *adj.* peaceful
pacote *s.* pack, package, packaging, packet, parcel
pacote turístico *s.* package tour
pacto *s.* pact
padaria *s.* baker, bakery
padeiro *s.* baker
padrão *adj.* default, standard
padrão de vida *s.* standard of living
padrasto *s.* stepfather
padrinho *s.* best man, godfather
pagamento *s.* pay, payment
pagar *v.* give, pay, settle
pagável *adj.* due
página *s.* page
pai *s.* father
painel *s.* panel
pairar *v.* hover
pais *s.* parents
país *s.* country
país de origem *s.* native country
país em desenvolvimento *s.* developing country
paisagem *s.* landscape
paixão *s.* passion
pajé *s.* witch doctor
pala *s.* peak
palácio *s.* palace
palavra *s.* promise, word
palavra da moda *s.* buzzword
palavra por palavra *s.* word for word
palavrão *s.* bad language, curse, oath, swear word
palavras cruzadas *s.* (crossword) puzzle
palco *s.* stage
palestra *s.* conference, lecture, talk
palestrante *s.* lecturer, speaker
paletó *s.* jacket
paletó esportivo *s.* sport coat, sports jacket
palha *s.* straw
palhaço *s.* clown
pálido *adj.* pale
palitar *v.* pick
palma *s.* palm
palmada *s.* smack
palmadinha *s.* pat
palmas *s.* clap
palmeira *s.* palm
palmtop *s.* palmtop
pálpebra *s.* eyelid, lid
palpite *s.* guess
pancada *s.* bang
pane *s.* breakdown
panela *s.* pan, pot, saucepan
pânico *s.* panic
pano *s.* cloth
panqueca *s.* pancake
pântano *s.* marsh, swamp
pantera *s.* panther
pantomima *s.* pantomime
pão *s.* bread
pão de hambúrguer *s.* bun
pão doce *s.* bun
pão de ló *s.* sponge cake
pão-duro *adj.* mean
pão-duro *s.* miser
pãozinho *s.* roll
papa *s.* pope
papagaio *s.* parrot
papai *s.* dad
Papai Noel *s.* Father Christmas, Santa Claus
papaizinho *s.* daddy
paparicar *v.* fuss over
papel *s.* paper, part, role
papel de embrulho *s.* wrapping paper
papel de parede *s.* wallpaper
papel de seda *s.* tissue, tissue paper
papel higiênico *s.* toilet paper
papel para anotações *s.* notepaper
papel para escrever *s.* writing paper
papelada *s.* papers
papelão *s.* cardboard
papo *s.* talk
páprica *s.* paprika
par *adj.* even
par *s.* pair
para a frente forward
para baixo down, downward
para casa home
para cima up, upward
para começar for a start, to begin with
para dentro inside, inward
para falar a verdade to tell you the truth
para fora outward
para frente forward, forwards
para frente e para trás backwards and forwards
para lá e para cá to and fro
para nada for nothing
para o leste east, eastwards
para o norte northerly
para o oeste west
para o outro lado across
para o seu próprio bem for your own good
para o sul south
para que so, so that
para que...? what...for?
para sempre for ever, forever
para sempre for good, forever
para trás behind
para trás back, backward
parabenizar *v.* congratulate
parabéns *s.* congratulations
para-brisa *s.* windscreen, windshield
para-choque *s.* bumper
parada *s.* halt, parade, stop
parada de ônibus *s.* bus stop
parado *adj.* not moving, still
parafina *s.* paraffin, wax
parafusar *v.* screw
parafuso *s.* screw
parágrafo *s.* paragraph
paraíso *s.* paradise
para-lama *s.* fender
paralelo *adj.* parallel
paralisado *adj.* paralysed
paralisar *v.* paralyse
paralisia *s.* paralysis
paralítico *v.* cripple
parapeito *s.* windowsill
paraquedas *s.* parachute
parar *v.* (come to a) stop, abandon, draw up, drop, halt, quit
parar de funcionar break down
para-sol *s.* sunshade
parceiro *s.* buddy, mate, partner
parcela *s.* installment
parceria *s.* partnership
parcial *adj.* partial
parcialmente *adv.* partly
pardal *s.* sparrow
pare! *v.* hold it!
parece que it looks as if
parecer *s.* opinion
parecer *v.* appear, look, seem, sound
parecer-se com *v.* look like, resemble
parecido *adj.* alike, similar
parede *s.* wall
parente *s.* relation, relative
parentesco *s.* relationship
parênteses *s.* parentheses
páreo *s.* match
parir *v.* give birth to
parlamento *s.* parliament
parque *s.* park
parque de diversões *s.* amusement park, carnival, fair

parquímetro s. parking meter
parquinho s. playground
parreira s. vine
parreiral s. vineyard
parte s. installment, part, party, portion, proportion, role, section, share
parte de trás s. back, rear
parte dianteira s. nose
parte do discurso s. part of speech
parte externa s. outside
parteira s. midwife
participação s. participation
participação como sócio ou membro s. membership
participante s. contestant, participant
participar v. join in, participate
particípio s. participle
partícula s. speck
particular adj. individual, private
particularmente adv. particularly
partida s. departure, game, match
partido s. party
partilhar v. share
partir v. depart, leave, set off/out, split
partir o coração de alguém break someone's heart
Páscoa s. Easter
pasmar v. amaze
pasmo s. gaze
passa s. raisin
passado s. past
passado adj. last, late, past, stale
passageiro s. passenger
passageiro clandestino s. stowaway
passagem s. gateway, passage, ticket, underpass
passagem de nível s. grade crossing, level crossing
passagem subterrânea s. subway
passaporte s. passport
passar v. blow over, get through, go by, hand (down), pass (by), run, spend, wear off
passar a ferro iron, press
passar a ligação connect, put someone through
passar a roupa iron
passar algo para as pessoas pass something around/round
passar férias vacation
passar fome starve
passar mal fall ill
passar manteiga butter
passar o ferrolho bolt
passar o tempo hang about/around
passar para move on, pass on to

passar pela sua cabeça cross your mind
passar por experience, get/go/live through, thread, undergo
passar rasteira em alguém trip someone up
passar sem do without
passar um pano wipe
passar um tempo spend time
passar xampu shampoo
passar zunindo zoom
pássaro s. bird
passatempo s. pastime, recreation
passe s. pass
passeata s. demonstration, march
passeio s. outing, ride, stroll, walk
passinho s. patter
passivo s. passive
passo s. move, pace, step
passo a passo step by step
passo largo s. stride
passos s. footsteps
pasta s. briefcase, file, folder, paste, spread
pasta de dente s. toothpaste
pastar v. graze
pastor s. shepherd
pastora s. shepherdess
pata s. paw
patamar s. landing
patê s. paste
patente s. rank
patim com rodinha s. roller-skate, skate
patim de lâmina s. ice-skate, skate
patinação no gelo s. ice skating
patinar s. roller-skating
patinar v. ice-skate, skate
patinete s. scooter
patinho s. duckling
patins de rodas s. roller-skates
pátio s. courtyard, yard
pato s. duck
patrão s. boss
pátria s. native country
patroa s. boss
patrocinador s. sponsor
patrocinar v. sponsor
patrulha s. patrol
patrulhar v. patrol
paus s. clubs
pausa s. pause
pausar v. pause
pavão s. peacock
paz s. peace
paz de espírito s. peace of mind
PC s. PC, personal computer
pé s. bottom, foot, plant
peão s. top
peça s. item, part, piece, play
peça sobressalente s. spare part

pecado s. sin
pecar v. sin
pechincha s. bargaining
pechinchar v. bargain
peculiar adj. peculiar
peculiaridade s. peculiarity
pedacinho s. bit
pedaço s. nibble, piece, scrap
pedaço grande s. slab
pedaço pequeno s. slip
pedal s. pedal
pedalar v. pedal
pedestre s. passer-by, pedestrian
pedido s. order, proposal, request, wish
pedido de socorro s. SOS
pedinte s. beggar
pedir v. ask (for someone/something for), need, order, request, want
pedir demissão give/hand in your notice
pedir desculpas apologize
pedir em casamento propose
pedir esmola beg
pedir informações inquire
pedra s. rock, stone
pedra grande e redonda s. boulder
pedra preciosa s. precious stone, stone
pedregoso adj. stony
pedregulho s. pebble
pedreira s. quarry
pegada s. footprint, grasp, grip, hold
pegadas s. tracks
pegadinha s. practical joke, prank
pega-pega s. tag
pegar v. catch, collect, get, pick up, take
pegar alguém de surpresa take someone by surprise
pegar carona hitch
pegar com armadilha trap
pegar com força seize
pegar fogo catch fire
pegar no pé pick on
pegar um resfriado catch a cold
peito s. breast, chest
peitoril s. ledge, windowsill
peixe s. fish
peixinho dourado s. goldfish
pela força by force
pela metade half
pela primeira vez for the first time
pelagem s. coat
pelando adj. steaming
pelas costas de alguém behind someone's back
pele s. skin

pelo s. fur
pelo contrário on the contrary
pelo menos at least
pelo menos uma vez for once
pelo que eu sei as far as
pelota s. lump
peludo adj. furry, hairy
pena s. feather, penalty, pity, sentence
penal adj. criminal
pender v. hang
pendurar v. hang
peneira s. sieve
peneirar v. sift
penetração s. penetration
penetrante adj. keen, piercing, shrill
penetrar v. penetrate
penhasco s. cliff, crag
pensão s. boarding house, pension
pensão completa s. board, full board
pensar v. think about/of
pensativo adj. thoughtful
pensionista s. pensioner
pente s. comb
penteadeira s. dressing table
penteado s. hairstyle
pentear v. comb
pepino s. cucumber
pequena quantidade s. dash, handful
pequenino adj. little, tiny
pequenino s. midget
pequeno bosque s. grove
pequeno adj. little, minor, small, young
pequenos arbustos s. undergrowth
pera s. pear
perambular v. roam, wander
perceber v. see through
percentagem s. percentage
perceptível adj. noticeable
percurso s. way
percurso de carro s. drive
perda s. loss
perdão s. forgiveness, pardon
perdão! int. pardon me, sorry
perdão? int. pardon?
perdedor s. loser
perder v. lose, mislay, miss
perder a conta de lose count of
perder a esperança give up hope
perder a paciência lose your temper
perder contato lose sight of
perder contato com lose touch with
perder de vista lose sight of
perder o controle de lose control of

perder o trem miss the train
perder peso lose weight
perder-se v. get lost, lose your way
perdido adj. lost
perdoar v. excuse, forgive, pardon
perdulário adj. wasteful
perecer v. perish
peregrinação s. pilgrimage
peregrino s. pilgrim
perfeição s. perfection, thoroughness
perfeitamente adv. perfectly
perfeito s. perfect
perfeito adj. perfect
perfil s. profile
performance s. performance
perfumado adj. perfumed, scented
perfume s. fragrance, perfume, scent
perfurar v. drill
pergaminho s. scroll
pergunta s. enquiry, inquiry, query, question
perguntar v. ask, enquire, inquire
perguntar por alguém ask after someone
periferia s. outskirts, suburb
perigo s. danger, hazard, peril
perigosamente adv. dangerously
perigoso adj. dangerous, hazardous, perilous, unsafe
perímetro s. area
periódico s. journal
período s. length, period, term
período de experiência s. trial period
periquito s. budgie
perito s. expert
permanecer v. remain, stay
permanente adj. permanent
permanentemente adv. permanently
permissão s. permission
permitir v. allow, let, permit
perna s. leg
pernilongo s. mosquito
pérola s. pearl
perseguição s. chase, persecution, pursuit
perseguir v. chase (after), go after, persecute
perseverança s. perseverance
perseverar v. persevere
persiana s. blind, shade
persistência s. persistence
persistente adj. persistent
persistentemente adv. persistently
persistir v. persist
personagem s. character
personalidade s. personality

personalizado adj. one-on-one, one-to-one
perspectiva s. outlook
perspicaz adj. sharp
persuadir v. persuade, reason
persuasão s. persuasion
persuasivo adj. persuasive
pertencer a v. belong, belong to
pertences s. belongings, stuff
perto adv. close, near
perturbar v. disturb, pester, upset
peru s. turkey
peruca s. wig
perversamente adv. wickedly
perversidade s. wickedness
perverso adj. wicked
pesadamente adv. heavily
pesadelo s. nightmare
pesado adj. hard, heavy
pêsames s. condolences
pesar s. distress, grief, regret
pesar v. weigh
pesaroso adj. sorry
pescador s. fisherman
pescar v. fish
pescaria s. fishing
pescoço s. neck
peso s. heaviness, weight
pesquisa s. poll, research, survey
pesquisa de opinião pública s. public opinion poll
pesquisar v. research
pêssego s. peach
pessimamente adv. terribly, very badly
pessimismo s. pessimism
pessimista adj. pessimistic
pessimista s. pessimist
péssimo adj. hopeless
pessoa s. person
pessoa de idade s. elder
pessoal adj. personal, private
pessoal s. staff
pessoalmente adv. in person, personally
pessoas s. people
peste s. pest, plague
pétala s. petal
petição s. petition
petroleiro s. oil tanker
petróleo s. oil
pia s. basin, sink, washbasin
piada s. joke
pianista s. pianist
piano s. piano
piar v. chirp
picada s. bite, prick, sting
picadeiro s. ring
picante adj. hot, sharp
picar v. bite, chop, cut up, sting
picar algo em tiras tear something to shreds

picareta s. pick
piche s. tar
picles s. pickle
pico s. peak
picolé s. ice lolly, lolly, Popsicle
píer s. pier
pifar v. crash
pijama s. pajamas, pyjamas
pilar s. pillar
pilha s. heap, pile, stack
pilotar v. fly, navigate
piloto s. pilot
pílula s. pill
pimenta s. pepper
pimentão s. pepper
pinça s. tweezers
pinças s. claws
pincel s. brush, paintbrush
pincelada s. stroke
pingar v. drip, trickle
pingente de gelo s. icicle
pingo s. dot, trickle
pingo de chuva s. raindrop
pingue-pongue s. ping-pong
pinha s. cone
pinho s. pine
pinicar v. tickle
pink s. pink
pintar v. paint
pintarroxo s. robin
pintinho s. chick
pintor s. painter
pintura s. oil painting, painting, picture
pio s. chirp, hoot
pioneiro s. pioneer
pior adj., adv. worse, worst
piorar v. get worse
pipa s. kite
pipoca s. popcorn
piquenique s. picnic
pirâmide s. pyramid
pirata s. pirate
piratear v. pirate
pires s. saucer
pirulito s. lollipop, lolly
pisar v. step, tread
piscada s. wink
piscadela s. wink
piscar v. blink, flash, wink
piscina s. pool, swimming pool
pisotear v. trample
pista s. clue, course, lane, lead, runway, tarmac, track
pista de corridas s. racetrack
pista de patinação no gelo s. ice rink
pistola s. pistol
pitada s. pinch
pizza s. pizza
placa s. number plate, sign
placa de identificação do veículo s. license plate
placa de sinalização s. road sign, signpost
placa de trânsito s. traffic sign
placar s. score
planador s. glider, gliding
planar v. soar
planejado adj. planned
planejamento s. planning
planejar v. plan
planeta s. planet
planície s. plain
plano s. level, plan
plano de estudos s. syllabus
plano de fundo s. background
plano adj. even, flat
planta s. plan, plant, sole
plantação s. plantation
plantar v. plant
plástico s. plastic
plástico adj. plastic
plataforma s. platform, track
plataforma de petróleo s. oil rig
plateia s. audience
playground s. ground, playground
plugar v. plug in
plugue s. plug
plural s. plural
pneu s. tire, tyre
pneu furado s. a flat, flat tyre
pneumonia s. pneumonia
pó s. dust, powder
pó de serra s. sawdust
pobre adj. deficient, poor
pobreza s. poverty
poça s. pool, puddle
poço s. well
poço de petróleo s. oil well
podar v. trim
pode ser maybe
poder s. power
poder v. can, may
poderia v. could, may, might
poderoso adj. mighty, powerful
podre adj. bad, rotten
poeira s. dust
poema s. poem
poesia s. poetry, rhyme
poeta s. poet
poético adj. poetic
poetisa s. poet
pois conj. for
polar adj. polar
polegada s. inch
polegar s. thumb
polêmico adj. controversial
polícia s. police
policial s. constable, cop, police officer, policeman
policial feminina s. policewoman
polidez s. politeness
polir v. polish
política s. policy, politics
politicamente adv. politically
político adj. political
político s. politician
polo s. pole
poltrona s. armchair, easy chair
poluição s. pollution
poluição do ar s. air pollution
poluir v. pollute
polvo s. octopus
pólvora s. gunpowder
pomar s. grove, orchard
pombo s. dove, pigeon
ponderação s. consideration
pônei s. pony
ponta s. end, lead, point, spike, tip
pontapé inicial s. kick-off
ponte s. bridge
ponteiro s. hand, needle
pontiagudo adj. pointed
pontinha s. speck
ponto s. bus stop, point, spot, stitch
ponto alto s. highlight
ponto de eletricidade s. power point, socket
ponto de exclamação s. exclamation mark
ponto de interrogação s. question mark
ponto de vista s. outlook, point of view, standpoint
ponto e vírgula s. semicolon
ponto final s. full stop, period
ponto fraco s. weakness
pontocom s. dot-com
pontos turísticos s. the sights
pontuação s. punctuation
pontual adj. punctual
pontualidade s. punctuality
pontualmente adv. on time, promptly, punctually, sharp
pontuar v. punctuate
pontudo adj. jagged
pop s. pop
população s. population
popular adj. popular
popularidade s. popularity
por prep. by, for, per, through
pôr v. lay, pop, put (on), set, stand, tuck someone in/up
pôr a culpa em put/lay the blame on
pôr a mão touch
pôr a mesa lay/set the table
pôr abaixo pull down
por acaso by chance
por acidente by accident
pôr algo para fora stick something out
por ano yearly
por aqui round
pôr as mãos em lay your hands on

por baixo underneath
por causa de because of, on account of
por cento percent
por cima de above
por coincidência by coincidence
pôr de lado put aside
pôr de volta put back
por despeito out of spite
por Deus! for goodness' sake
por dia a day
pôr do sol *s.* sunset
pôr em conserva preserve
pôr em ordem do up
por engano by mistake
por enquanto for now, for the time being
por escrito in writing, written
por exemplo for example, for instance
por extenso in full
por favor please
por fim eventually, finally
pôr fim a do away with
pôr fogo em set fire to, set something on fire
por gentileza kindly
por iniciativa própria of your own accord
por isso so
pôr linha na agulha thread
por livre e espontânea vontade of your own free will
por mais... que however
por meio de by means of, through
por mês a month
por mim mesmo by myself, on your own
por nada don't mention it
pôr no correio mail
por outro lado by/in contrast
pôr para dentro tuck
por perto around, by
por pessoa a head, per head
por pouco narrowly
pôr pressão em put pressure on
por princípio on principle
Por que...? Por quê? why?
Por que não...? why not?
por quê? how come?
por séculos for ages
por si mesmo by oneself
por si mesmos by themselves
por si só by itself
por sua própria iniciativa of your own accord
por toda parte all over
por último lastly
por último, mas não menos importante last but not least

por um lado... por outro lado on the one hand... on the other hand
pôr um ponto final em put a stop to
por um triz a narrow escape
por vez at a time
por volta de about, around
porão *s.* basement
porca *s.* nut
porção *s.* helping, portion, ration
porcentagem *s.* percentage
porco *s.* pig
porco *adj.* messy
porém *conj.* but, though
porém *s.* snag
porque *conj.* because, for
porquinho-da-índia *s.* guinea pig
porta *s.* door
porta giratória *s.* revolving door
porta-aviões *s.* aircraft-carrier
porta-lápis *s.* pencil box / pencil case
porta-malas *s.* boot, trunk
portanto *conj.* so, therefore
portão *s.* gate, gateway
portátil *adj.* portable
porta-toalha *s.* rack
porta-voz *s.* spokesman, spokesperson, spokeswoman
porte *s.* possession
porteiro *s.* porter
pórtico *s.* porch
portinhola *s.* porthole
porto *s.* harbor, port
pós-escrito *s.* postscript
posição *s.* position
posicionamento *s.* attitude
positivamente *adv.* positively
positivo *adj.* certain, positive
posse *s.* possession
posses *s.* possessions, wealth
possibilidade *s.* possibility
possibilitar *v.* enable
possível *adj.* possible
possivelmente *adv.* possibly
posso tomar emprestado? can I borrow?
possuir *v.* have, own, possess
postagem *s.* postage
poste de luz *s.* lamppost
pôster *s.* poster
posteriormente *adv.* later
posto *s.* station
posto de combustível *s.* garage, gas/petrol/service station
pote *s.* jar, pot
potência *s.* power
potência mundial *s.* world power
potente *adj.* powerful
potro *s.* foal
pouco *adv.* little

pouco a pouco bit by bit, little by little
pouco depois *adv.* shortly after, soon after
poucos *adj.* few
poupar *v.* save, spare
pouquinho *adv.* a bit, a little
pouquíssimo *adj.* quite a few
pousada *s.* bed and breakfast, boarding house, inn
pousar *v.* land
pouso *s.* landing
povo *s.* people, peoples
povoar *v.* populate
pra variar for a change
praça *s.* square
prado *s.* meadow
praga *s.* curse, plague
praguejar *v.* curse, swear
praia *s.* beach, seashore, shore
prancha de embarque *s.* gangway
prancha de surfe *s.* surfboard
prancha de windsurfe *s.* sailboard, windsurfer
prata *s.* silver
prateleira *s.* rack, shelf
prática *s.* practice
praticamente *adv.* as good as, practically
praticante *adj.* observant
praticar *v.* practice
prático *adj.* practical
prato *s.* course, dish, meal, plate
prato principal *s.* main course
pratos *s.* cymbals
prazer *s.* delight, enjoyment, pleasure
prazer em conhecê-lo nice to meet you, pleased to meet you
prazer em vê-lo nice to see you
prazeroso *adj.* enjoyable
prazo final *s.* deadline
precaução *s.* precaution
precauções de segurança *s.* safety precautions
preceder *v.* precede
precioso *adj.* precious
precipício *s.* precipice
precipitadamente *adv.* rashly
precipitado *adj.* hasty, rash
precipitar-se *v.* swoop
precisamente *adv.* precisely
precisão *s.* accuracy, precision
precisar *v.* need, require, want
precisar partir must be off
preciso *adj.* accurate, precise
preço *s.* price
preconcebido *adj.* biased
preconceito *s.* bias, prejudice
preconceituoso *adj.* prejudiced
prédio *s.* building

prédio comercial *s.* office block
predizer *v.* foretell
preencher *v.* fill in
prefácio *s.* foreword, preface
prefeita *s.* mayoress
prefeito *s.* mayor
prefeitura *s.* hall, town hall
preferência *s.* preference, right of way
preferido *adj.* favorite
preferir *v.* prefer, would rather
preferível *adj.* preferable
preferivelmente *adv.* preferably
prefixo *s.* prefix
prega *s.* wrinkle
pregado *adj.* exhausted, worn-out
pregador *s.* preacher
pregar *v.* nail, preach, stitch
pregar uma peça em play a joke/trick on
prego *s.* nail
preguiça *s.* laziness
preguiçosamente *adv.* lazily
preguiçoso *adj.* idle, lazy
prejudicar *v.* damage, endanger, harm
prejudicial *adj.* bad, harmful
prejuízo *s.* damage, loss
prêmio *s.* award, prize
prendedor de cabelo *s.* hairpin
prendedor de roupa *s.* clothespeg, clothespin, peg
prender *v.* arrest, attach, bind, catch, imprison, jail, pin, pinch, tie
prender a respiração hold your breath
prender com clipe clip
prender com correia strap
prender com tachinha pin
prensa *s.* press
preocupação *s.* concern, worries, worry
preocupado *adj.* anxious, concerned, very worried, worried
preocupante *adj.* worrying
preocupar(-se) *v.* concern, worry
preparação *s.* preparation
preparar *v.* get... ready, make, prepare
preparar-se *v.* get ready
preparativos *s.* preparations
preposição *s.* preposition
presa *s.* prey, tusk
presciência *s.* foresight
prescrever *v.* prescribe
prescrição *s.* prescription
presença *s.* presence
presença de espírito *s.* wit
presente *adj.* present
presente *s.* gift, present, treat
presentear *v.* present

preservação *s.* preservation
preservar *v.* preserve, uphold
preservativo *s.* preservative
presidencial *adj.* presidential
presidente *s.* president
presidiário *s.* convict
presidir *v.* chair
preso *adj.* stranded, under arrest
pressa *s.* haste, hurry, rush
pressão *s.* pressure, strain
pressão sanguínea *s.* blood pressure
pressionar *v.* press, pressure, urge
prestar atenção a *v.* pay attention to
prestar para nada *v.* be no good, not be any good
prestativo *adj.* helpful, neighborly
prestígio *s.* prestige
presumir *v.* presume
presunto *s.* ham
pretender *v.* aim, intend
pretensão *s.* pretence
pretenso *adj.* so-called
pretérito passado *s.* past tense [grammar]
preto *s.* black
preto *adj.* black
prevenção *s.* prevention
prevenir *v.* prevent
prever *v.* forecast, foresee, predict
previamente *adv.* previously
prévio *adj.* previous
previsão *s.* forecast, outlook, prediction
previsão do tempo *s.* weather forecast
previsível *adj.* predictable
Prezada senhora Dear Madam
Prezado senhor Dear Sir
prezado *adj.* dear
primário *adj.* primary
primavera *s.* spring
primeira classe *s.* first class
primeira coisa *s.* first thing
primeiramente *adv.* first, firstly
primeiro andar *s.* first floor
primeiro-ministro *s.* prime minister
primeiro nome *s.* first name
primeiro *adj.* first, leading
primeiros-socorros *s.* first aid
primo *s.* cousin
primorosamente *adv.* nicely
primoroso *adj.* exquisite
princesa *s.* princess
principal *adj.* chief, leading, main, major, prime, principal, top
principalmente *adv.* chiefly, mainly, mostly, primarily
príncipe *s.* prince
princípio *s.* outset, principle

prioridade *s.* first thing, priority, right of way
prisão *s.* arrest, prison
prisão perpétua *s.* life sentence
prisioneiro *s.* prisoner
privacidade *s.* privacy
privilegiado *adj.* privileged
privilégio *s.* privilege
probabilidade *s.* probability
problema *s.* difficulty, problem, trouble
problemático *adj.* problematic
processado *adj.* processed
processador *s.* processor
processador de alimentos *s.* food processor
processador de texto *s.* word processor
processar *v.* sue
processo *s.* process
procriar *v.* breed
procurar *v.* look for, look up, search for, seek
produção *s.* output, produce, production
produtivo *adj.* productive
produto *s.* product
produto químico *s.* chemical
produtor *s.* producer
produtos *s.* goods
produzir *v.* produce, yield
proeminente *adj.* prominent
profecia *s.* prophecy
proferir *v.* utter
professor *s.* lecturer, professor, schoolteacher, teacher
profeta *s.* prophet
profético *adj.* prophetic
profetizar *v.* prophesy
proficiência *s.* proficiency
proficiente *adj.* proficient
profissão *s.* job, occupation, profession, trade
profissional *adj., s.* professional
profissionalmente *adv.* professionally
profundamente *adv.* deeply, thoroughly, utterly
profundidade *s.* depth
profundo *adj.* deep
programa *s.* program, programme, show
programa de entrevista *s.* chat show
programação *s.* schedule, timetable
programador *s.* programer
programar *v.* program, programme, time
progredir *v.* get on/along, make headway, progress
progressivo *adj.* progressive

progresso *s.* progress
proibição *s.* ban, prohibition
proibir *v.* ban, forbid, prohibit
projetar *v.* design
projetar-se *v.* stick out
projétil *s.* bullet
projeto *s.* project
projetor *s.* projector
prole *s.* offspring
promessa *s.* promise
prometer *v.* promise
promissor *adj.* promising
promoção *s.* promotion, special
promoção especial *s.* special offer
promover *v.* promote
pronome *s.* pronoun
pronome relativo *s.* relative pronoun
prontamente *adv.* promptly, readily
prontidão *s.* readiness, standby
pronto *adj.* prompt, ready, ready-made
pronto-socorro *s.* accident and emergency, casualty department, emergency room
pronúncia *s.* pronunciation
pronunciar *v.* pronounce, utter
pronunciar incorretamente *v.* mispronounce, misspell
propaganda *s.* advertising
propenso *adj.* likely
propor *v.* intend, propose, suggest
proporção *s.* proportion
proporções *s.* proportions
propósito *s.* point, purpose
proposta *s.* offer, proposal

propriedade *s.* estate, ownership, properties, property
proprietária *s.* landlady
proprietário *s.* landlord
proprietário *s.* owner
próprio *adj.* of your own, own
prosperar *v.* flourish, prosper
prosperidade *s.* prosperity
próspero *adj.* prosperous
prosseguir *v.* go ahead, proceed
prostituta *s.* prostitute
proteção *s.* protection
proteger *v.* protect, secure, shield
proteger da luz *v.* shade
protestar *v.* object, protest
protesto *s.* outcry, protest
protetor *adj.* defensive
protuberante *adj.* protruding
prova *s.* evidence, paper, proof, token, trial
provação *s.* ordeal
provar *v.* prove, show, taste, try
provável *adj.* likely, probable
provavelmente *adv.* probably
provérbio *s.* proverb
providências *s.* arrangements
província *s.* province
provincial *adj.* provincial
provisão *s.* provision
provisões *s.* provisions, supplies
provocador *adj.* defiant
provocadoramente *adv.* defiantly
provocar *v.* start
próxima vez next time
próximo a *adv.* close, near, next to
próximo *adj.* close, nearby, next
pseudônimo *s.* alias

psicologia *s.* psychology
psicológico *adj.* psychological
psicólogo *s.* psychologist
psiquiatra *s.* psychiatrist
psiquiátrico *adj.* psychiatric
psiu! *int.* hush!, sh!
publicação *s.* publication
publicamente *adv.* publicly
publicar *v.* print, publish
publicidade *s.* publicity
público *adj.* public
pudim *s.* pudding
pugilismo *s.* boxing
pugilista *s.* boxer
pular *v.* bounce, hop, jump, plunge, skip, spring
pulga *s.* flea
pulmão *s.* lung
pulo *s.* hop, jump, skip
pulôver *s.* pullover
pulsação *s.* pulse
pulseira *s.* bracelet
pulso *s.* pulse, wrist
punhado *s.* handful
punhal *s.* dagger
punho *s.* fist
punição *s.* punishment
punir *v.* punish
pupila *s.* pupil
puramente *adv.* purely
purê de batata *s.* mashed potatoes
pureza *s.* purity
puro *adj.* clear, pure, sheer
puxão *s.* pull, tug
puxar *v.* draw, haul, pull
puxar a *v.* take after
puxar ferro lift weights

Qq

quadra *s.* block, court, gym, gymnasium
quadra de tênis *s.* tennis court
quadrado *s.* square
quadrado *adj.* square
quadriciclo *s.* all-terrain vehicle, ATV
quadril *s.* hip
quadro *s.* board, painting
quadro a óleo *s.* oil painting
quadro de avisos *s.* bulletin-board, noticeboard
quadro-negro *s.* blackboard
quais *pron.* what, which
qual *pron.* what, which
qual a altitude...? how high...?
qual a distância...? how far...?
qual a duração...? how long...?
qual a idade...? how old...?
qual a largura...? how wide...?
qual a profundidade...? how deep...?
qual o comprimento...? how long...?
qual o problema? what's the matter?
qual altura...? how tall...?
qual espessura...? how thick...?
qualidade *s.* grade, quality
qualificação *s.* qualification
qualificado *adj.* qualified, trained
qualificar *v.* qualify
qualquer *pron.* any, whatever
qualquer coisa anything, whatever
qualquer hora sometime
qualquer pessoa anybody
qualquer um anybody
qualquer um dos dois either
quando *adv.* just as, when
quando *conj.* as, by the time, once, when, whenever, while
quantidade *s.* amount, quantity

quanto...? *pron.* how much...?
quanto custa...? how much...?
quanto é? how much?
quanto mais... mais the more... the more..., the... the...
quanto tempo...? how long...?
quantos...? *pron.* how many...?
quantos anos...? how old...?
quantos...? how many...?
quão pesado...? how heavy...?
quarta de final *s.* quarter-final
quarta-feira *s.* Wednesday
quarteirão *s.* block
quartel *s.* barracks
quartel-general *s.* headquarters
quartilho *s.* pint
quarto *s.* bedroom, joint, quarter, room
quarto de brinquedo *s.* nursery
quarto *num., s.* fourth
quase *adv.* almost, narrowly, nearly
quase nada hardly anything, next to nothing
quase nunca hardly
quatro *num., s.* four
que *pron.* that, which
que bom! good for you!
que está por vir ...to come
que horas são? what time is it?
que horas...? what time...?
que idade...? how old...?
que não faz parte the odd man out, the odd one out
que pena! it's/what a pity, it's/what a shame, too bad
que tal...? how about...?, what about...?
que vale a pena worthwhile
que vergonha! shame on you!
quê? *int.* pardon?, sorry?, what?
quebra-cabeça *s.* jigsaw puzzle, puzzle
quebrado *adj.* bankrupt, broken, out of order
quebra-luz *s.* lampshade
quebrar *v.* break, break down

quebrar uma promessa break a promise
queda *s.* drop, fall
queda d'água *s.* falls
queda de avião *s.* plane crash
queijo *s.* cheese
queimado de sol *adj.* sunburned
queimadura *s.* burn
queimadura de sol *s.* sunburn
queimar *v.* burn, fire
queixa *s.* grievance
queixar-se *v.* complain, moan
queixo *s.* chin
quem *pron.* who, whoever, whom
quem quer que whoever
quente *adj.* hot, warm
quer dizer que it means that
quer... quer não whether... or not
querer *v.* fancy, like, want, wish
querer dizer *v.* mean
queridinho *s.* darling
querido *adj.* darling, dear
querosene *s.* kerosene
questão *s.* affair, issue, question
questionar *v.* question
questionário *s.* questionnaire
quietude *s.* stillness
quilo *s.* kilo
quilômetro *s.* kilometer
quilowat *s.* kilowatt
química *s.* chemistry
químico *s.* chemist
químico *adj.* chemical
quinhão *s.* portion
quinquagésimo *s., num.* fiftieth
quinta-feira *s.* Thursday
quintal *s.* garden, yard
quinto *s., num.* fifth
quinze *s., num.* fifteen
quinze para a quarter of/to
quiosque *s.* kiosk, parlor, stand
quitanda *s.* greengrocery, grocery
quitar *v.* repay
quite *adj.* even

Rr

rabanete *s.* radish
rabino *s.* rabbi
rabiscar *v.* scribble
rabo *s.* tail
rabo de cavalo *s.* ponytail
rabugento *adj.* grumpy
raça *s.* breed, race
raça humana *s.* human race
racha *s.* split
rachar *v.* crack
rachar de estudar cram, swot
racial *adj.* racial
racionar *v.* ration
racismo *s.* racism
racista *s.* racist
radar *s.* radar
radiação *s.* radiation
radiador *s.* radiator
rádio *s.* radio
rádio comunicador *s.* intercom, walkie-talkie
radiografar *v.* X-ray
raia *s.* lane
rainha *s.* queen
raio *s.* beam, lightning, radius, ray
raio de roda *s.* spoke
raio-X *s.* X-ray
raiva *s.* anger, rage
raivosamente *adv.* angrily
raiz *s.* root
rajada *s.* gust
ralado *adj.* grated
ralador *s.* grater
ralar *v.* grate, scrape
ralo *adj.* thin
ramal *s.* extension
rampa *s.* ramp, slope
rancho *s.* ranch
rancor *s.* grudge
rangente *adj.* squeaky
ranger *v.* creak, screech, squeak
rangido *s.* creak, screech
rango *s.* food, grub
ranhura *s.* groove
rapidamente *adv.* quickly, rapidly, swiftly
rápido *adj.* brief, hasty, quick, rapid, swift
raposa *s.* fox
raquete *s.* bat, racket
raquete de tênis *s.* tennis racket
raramente *adv.* infrequently, rarely, seldom
raro *adj.* infrequent, rare
rascunho *s.* draft
rasgar *v.* rip (up), tear (up)
rasgo *s.* tear
raso *adj.* level, shallow
raspar *v.* scrape
rastejar *v.* creep
rastrear *v.* trace, track
rastro *s.* scent, trail
ratazana *s.* rat
rato *s.* mouse
ratos *s.* mice
razão *s.* rate, reason
razoável *adj.* fair, reasonable
razoavelmente *adv.* quite, reasonably
ré *s.* defendant
reação *s.* reaction, response
reagir *v.* react, respond
real *adj.* actual, real, royal
realeza *s.* royalty
realidade *s.* reality
realidade virtual *s.* virtual reality
realista *adj.* realistic
realização *s.* accomplishment, achievement, fulfilment, realization
realizar *v.* accomplish, carry out, conduct, effect, fulfil, hold, realize
realizar-se *v.* come true, take place
realmente *adv.* actually, indeed, really
rebanho *s.* flock, herd, livestock
rebelar-se *v.* rebel
rebelde *s.* rebel
rebelião *s.* rebellion, revolt, uprising
rebobinar *v.* rewind
rebocador *s.* tug, tugboat
reboque *s.* camper
recado *s.* message
recapitular *v.* review, revise, run through
recarregar *v.* recharge
receber *v.* entertain, receive, take in, welcome
receio que... I'm afraid...
receita *s.* pattern, recipe
receita médica *s.* prescription
recém *adv.* newly
recém-chegado *s.* newcomer
recente *adj.* recent
recentemente *adv.* lately, recently
recepção *s.* reception, reception desk
recepção do casamento *s.* wedding reception
recepcionar *v.* entertain
recepcionista *s.* receptionist
receptador *s.* receiver
receptor *s.* receiver
recesso *s.* recess
recesso escolar no meio do ano *s.* half-term, midterm
recheado *adj.* stuffed
rechear *v.* stuff
recheio *s.* filling
recibo *s.* receipt
reciclado *adj.* recycled
reciclar *v.* recycle
recife *s.* reef
recipiente *s.* container
reclamação *s.* complaint
reclamar *v.* claim, complain
recolher *v.* pick up
recolocar *v.* replace
recomeçar *v.* resume
recomendação *s.* recommendation
recomendar *v.* recommend
recompensa *s.* reward
recompensar *v.* reward
reconciliar-se *v.* make up
reconhecer *v.* acknowledge, appreciate, recognize
reconhecidamente *adv.* gratefully
reconhecimento *s.* appreciation, recognition
recordar *v.* recall
recorde *s.* record
recorde mundial *s.* world record
recorrer *v.* appeal, refer, turn to
recreação *s.* recreation
recruta *s.* recruit
recrutado *s.* conscript
recrutamento *s.* conscription, recrutamento
recrutar *v.* conscript, recruit
recuar *v.* retreat, stand back, step back
recuo *s.* retreat
recuperação *s.* recovery
recuperação rápida *s.* speedy recovery
recuperar *v.* recover, reform
recurso *s.* resource
recusa *s.* refusal
recusar alguém turn someone down
recusar(-se) *v.* refuse
rede *s.* hammock, net, network
rédea *s.* rein
redemoinho *s.* whirlpool
redigir *v.* draw up
redondo *adj.* round
redução *s.* reduction
reduzir *v.* cut back/down on, reduce
reduzir à metade *v.* halve
reembolsar *v.* refund
reembolso *s.* refund, repayment
reencontro *s.* reunion
reescrever *v.* rewrite
refeição *s.* meal
refeição para viagem *s.* takeaway
refém *s.* hostage
referência *s.* reference

referente a concerning, in/with regard to, with/in reference to
referir-se *v.* refer
refletir *v.* reflect
refletir sobre algo think something over
refletor *s.* spotlight
reflexão *s.* reflection, thought
reflexo *s.* reflection
reforçar *v.* reinforce, strengthen
reforço *s.* reinforcement
reforma *s.* reform
reformar *v.* reform
refrão *s.* chorus
refrescante *adj.* refreshing
refrescar *v.* cool, refresh
refrescar sua memória refresh your memory
refrigerador *s.* fridge, refrigerator
refrigerante *s.* soda, soda pop
refrigerar *v.* refrigerate
refugiado *s.* evacuee, refugee
refúgio *s.* refuge
refugo *s.* refuse
regador *s.* watering can
regalo *s.* treat
reger *v.* conduct
região *s.* area, district, region
regime *v.* diet
regimento *s.* regiment
regional *adj.* regional
registrar(-se) *v.* record, register
registro *s.* record, register, registration
regra *s.* regulation, rule
régua *s.* ruler
regulamento *s.* regulation
regular *adj.* average, regular
regular *v.* regulate
regularidade *s.* regularity
regularmente *adv.* regularly
rei *s.* king
reinado *s.* reign
reinar *v.* reign
reiniciar *v.* reboot
reino *s.* kingdom
reivindicação *s.* claim
reivindicar *v.* claim
rejeição *s.* rejection
rejeitar *v.* reject, turn down
relação *s.* relation, relationship
relacionamento *s.* relationship
relacionar *v.* relate
relações *s.* connections, relations
relações públicas *s.* public relations
relâmpago *s.* lightning
relance *s.* glimpse
relapso *adj.* slack
relativamente *adv.* relatively
relativo *adj.* relative
relato *s.* account
relatório *s.* report
relaxado *adj.* relaxed
relaxamento *s.* relaxation
relaxante *adj.* soothing
relaxar *v.* relax
relevância *s.* relevance
relevante *adj.* relevant
religião *s.* religion
religioso *adj.* religious
relinchar *v.* neigh
relincho *s.* neigh
relógio cuco *s.* cuckoo clock
relógio de parede *s.* clock
relógio de pulso *s.* watch, wristwatch
relojoeiro *s.* watchmaker
relutância *s.* reluctance
relutante *adj.* reluctant, unwilling
relutantemente *adv.* reluctantly, unwillingly
reluzir *v.* glow
remar *v.* paddle, row
remédio *s.* drug, medicine, remedy
remeter *v.* send off
remexer *v.* stir
remexer-se *v.* wriggle
remo *s.* oar, paddle
remoção *s.* removal
remontar *v.* go back
remoto *adj.* isolated, remote
removedor de neve *s.* snowplough
remover *v.* remove
rena *s.* reindeer
renda *s.* earnings, income, lace
render-se *v.* surrender, yield
rendição *s.* surrender
rendimento *s.* income
renovar *v.* renew
reparar *v.* repair
reparo *s.* repair
repartir *v.* share, share out
repassar *v.* replay
repentinamente *adv.* suddenly
repentino *adj.* overnight, sudden
repetição *s.* repetition
repetidamente *adv.* over and over again, repeatedly
repetidas vezes again and again
repetir *v.* repeat, replay
replay *s.* replay
réplica *s.* reproduction
repolho *s.* cabbage
reportagem *s.* report
repórter *s.* reporter
repousante *adj.* restful
repreender *v.* rebuke, scold, tell off
repreensão *s.* rebuke
represa *s.* dam
representação *s.* representation
representante *s.* representative
representar *v.* play, represent
repressão *s.* crackdown
reprimir *v.* restrain
reprise *s.* repeat
reprodução *s.* breeding, reproduction
reproduzir *v.* reproduce
reproduzir-se *v.* breed
reprovar *v.* fail
réptil *s.* reptile
república *s.* republic
repugnância *s.* disgust
repugnante *adj.* disgusting, revolting
repugnar *v.* disgust
repulsivamente *adv.* disgustedly
reputação *s.* reputation
requerer *v.* demand, require
requintado *adj.* exquisite
requisito *s.* requirement
reserva *s.* booking, reservation, reserve
reserva natural *s.* wildlife park
reservado *adj.* secretive
reservar *v.* book, reserve
reservatório *s.* reservoir
resfolegar *v.* snort
resfriado *s.* cold
resfriar *v.* cool
resgatar *v.* rescue
resgate *s.* ransom, rescue
residência *s.* residence
residencial *adj.* home
residente *s.* resident
resignar-se com resign yourself to
resistência *s.* endurance, resistance, strength
resistente *adj.* resistant, rigid, strong
resistir *v.* endure, resist
resistir à tentação resist the temptation
resmungar *v.* grumble, mumble, mutter, nag, whine
resolução *s.* resolution
resolver *v.* settle, solve, sort/work out
resort *s.* resort
respeitar *v.* respect
respeitável *adj.* respectable
respeitavelmente *adv.* respectably
respeito *s.* respect
respeitoso *adj.* respectful
respingar *v.* splash
respiração *s.* breath, breathing
respirar *v.* breathe
resplandecer *v.* glitter
responder *v.* answer, reply, respond
responder por account for
responsabilidade *s.* responsibility
responsável *adj.* responsible

responsavelmente *adv.* responsibly
resposta *s.* answer, reaction, reply, response
ressaltar *v.* point out
ressentimento *s.* grudge, hard feelings, resentment
ressentir(-se) *v.* resent
ressoar *v.* rumble
restante *adj.* remaining
restante *s.* remainder
restauração *s.* repair, restoration
restaurante *s.* restaurant
restaurar *v.* repair, restore
restituir *v.* restore
resto *s.* remainder, rest
restos *s.* remains, scraps
restrição *s.* restriction
restringir *v.* restrict
resultado *s.* outcome, result
resultar de result from
resultar em result in
resumir *v.* sum up, summarize
resumo *s.* abstract, summary
retangular *adj.* oblong, rectangular
retângulo *s.* oblong, rectangle
retardatário *s.* latecomer
reter *v.* hold back
retirar *v.* draw, pull out, withdraw
retirar-se *v.* retire, withdraw
reto *adj.* straight
retorcer *v.* twist
retornar *v.* come/get/go back, return
retornar uma ligação call back, return a call
retorno *s.* return, U-turn
retrato *s.* portrait
retribuir *v.* repay
retrospecto *s.* review
réu *s.* defendant
reunião *s.* assembly, gathering, meeting
reunir *v.* gather
reunir-se *v.* assemble, gather, get together
revelar *v.* develop, give away, reveal, turn out
rever *v.* review
reverência *s.* bow
revés *s.* setback
revezar *s.* take turns
revigorante *adj.* brisk
revirar *v.* turn over
revisão *s.* overhaul, revision
revisar *v.* revise, run over
revista *s.* magazine
revista em quadrinhos *s.* comic, comic book, comics
revistar *v.* go through, search
reviver *v.* revive

revoltar-se *v.* revolt
revolução *s.* revolution
revolucionário *adj.* revolutionary
revólver *s.* revolver
rezar *v.* pray
RG *s.* ID
ribeirão *s.* stream
ribombar *v.* rumble
rico *adj.* rich, wealthy
ridiculamente *adv.* ridiculously
ridicularizar *v.* poke fun at
ridículo *adj.* absurd, ridiculous
rifle *s.* rifle
rígido *adj.* rigid, stiff, strict
rigorosamente *adv.* strictly
rim *s.* kidney
rima *s.* rhyme
rimar *v.* rhyme
ringue *s.* ring
ringue de patinação *s.* skating rink
rinite *s.* hay fever
rinoceronte *s.* rhinoceros
rio *s.* river
riqueza *s.* affluence, riches
rir *v.* laugh
rir com discrição *v.* chuckle
risada *s.* laugh, laughter
risadinha *s.* chuckle, giggle
riscar *v.* cross out, strike
riscar um fósforo *v.* strike a match
risco *s.* gamble, risk
rispidamente *adv.* sharply
ritmo *s.* pace, rhythm
rival *s.* rival
rixa *s.* feud
robô *s.* robot
rocha *s.* rock
rochedo *s.* crag
rochoso *adj.* rocky
rock *s.* rock
roda *s.* ring, wheel
rodada *s.* round
rodar *v.* roll, run, shoot, spin
rodear *v.* circle, encircle
rodopiar *v.* whirl
rodovia *s.* highway
roer *v.* bite, gnaw
rolar *v.* roll, roll over
rolar texto na tela do computador *v.* scroll
roleta *s.* turnstile
rolha *s.* cork
rolo *s.* coil, reel, roll
rolo compressor *s.* steamroller
rolo de filme *s.* reel
rolo de papel higiênico *s.* toilet roll
rolo de pastel *s.* rolling pin
ROM *s.* ROM
romance *s.* mystery novel, romance

romântico *adj.* romantic
romper *v.* break/split up with
romper-se *v.* snap
roncar *v.* rumble, snore
ronda *s.* round
ronronar *v.* purr
rosa *s.* pink, rose
rosado *adj.* rosy
rosnado *s.* growl, snarl
rosnar *v.* growl, snarl
rosquear *v.* screw
rosto *s.* face
rota *s.* route
rotatória *s.* roundabout, traffic circle
roteiro *s.* script
rotina *s.* routine
rotineiro *adj.* routine
rotular *v.* label
rótulo *s.* label
roubar *v.* cheat, hold up, rob, steal
roubo *s.* burglary, robbery, stick-up, theft
roubo de artigos de lojas *s.* shoplifting
roucamente *adv.* hoarsly
rouco *adj.* hoarse
round *s.* round
roupa *s.* clothing, outfit, wear
roupa de baixo *s.* underwear
roupa de cama e mesa *s.* linen
roupa íntima *s.* underwear
roupa lavada *s.* wash, washing
roupa para correr *s.* tracksuit
roupa para passar *s.* ironing
roupa suja *s.* wash, washing
roupão *s.* dressing gown
roupão de banho *s.* bathrobe
roupas *s.* clothes
roupas de cama *s.* bedclothes
rouxinol *s.* nightingale
roxo *adj.* purple
roxo *s.* purple
rua *s.* road, street
rudeza *s.* rudeness
ruga *s.* crease, line, wrinkle
rúgbi *s.* rugby
rugido *s.* roar
rugir *v.* roar
ruído *s.* noise
ruidosamente *adv.* noisily
ruim *adj.* bad, foul
ruína *s.* ruin
ruínas *s.* remains
ruir *v.* tumble down
ruivo *adj.* red
ruivo *s.* redhead
rum *s.* rum
rumo a towards
ruptura *s.* breakthrough, burst
rural *adj.* rural

Ss

sã *adj.* sane
Sabá *s.* Sabbath
sábado *s.* sabbath, Saturday
sabão *s.* a bar of soap, soap
sabão em pó *s.* soap powder, washing powder
sabão líquido *s.* washing-up liquid
sabedoria *s.* wisdom
saber *s.* learning
saber como fazer algo know how to do something
saber sobre hear about
sabiamente *adv.* wisely
sábio *adj.* wise
sabonete *s.* a bar of soap, soap
sabor *s.* flavor, taste
saboroso *adj.* tasty, yummy
sacada *s.* balcony
sacanear alguém pull someone's leg
sacar *v.* draw money out, figure out, grasp, see through, understand
saca-rolhas *s.* corkscrew
sacerdote *s.* priest
saco *s.* bag, carrier bag, sack
saco de dormir *s.* sleeping bag
sacola *s.* bag, carrier bag, satchel
sacola plástica *s.* plastic bag
sacolão *s.* greengrocery, grocer, grocery
sacolejar *v.* jolt
sacrificar *v.* sacrifice
sacrifício *s.* sacrifice
sacudida *s.* jolt
sacudir *v.* shake
safar-se *v.* get away with
safra *s.* crop
sagacidade *s.* wit
sagaz *adj.* witty
sagrado *adj.* holy, sacred
saguão *s.* hall, lobby, lounge
saia *s.* skirt
saia escocesa *s.* kilt
saída *s.* exit, fire-escape, way out
sair *v.* come out, get away/off/out of, go away/out, leave, rise, set off/out
sair com go out with
sair da casca hatch
sair de come/get out of
sair de moda go out of fashion
sair do controle to get out of hand
sair para caminhar go for a walk
sal *s.* salt
sala *s.* hall, office
sala de aula *s.* classroom
sala de espera *s.* waiting room
sala de estar *s.* living room, sitting-room
sala de jantar *s.* dining room
sala de primeiros-socorros *s.* emergency room
sala dos funcionários *s.* staff room
salada *s.* salad
salão *s.* parlor
salão de baile *s.* ballroom
salário *s.* salary, wage
saldar *v.* repay
saldo *s.* balance
salgadinho *s.* chips, crisps
salgado *adj.* salted, salty
saliência *s.* bulge
salmão *s.* salmon
salpicar *v.* splash, sprinkle
salsão *s.* celery
salsicha *s.* sausage
salsinha *s.* parsley
saltar *v.* hop, leap, pop out
saltar de paraquedas parachute
salteador *s.* highwayman
salto *s.* heel, hop, jump, leap, skip
salto com vara *s.* pole vault
salto em altura *s.* high jump
salto em distância *s.* long jump
salto triplo *s.* triple jump
salto-mortal *s.* somersault
salvar *v.* save
salva-vidas *s.* lifeguard
samba-canção *s.* boxer shorts
sandália *s.* sandal
sanduíche *s.* sandwich
sangrar *v.* bleed
sangrento *adj.* bloody
sangue *s.* blood
sanitário público *s.* public convenience
santo *s.* saint
Santo Deus! *int.* Good God!
santuário *s.* shrine
são *s.* saint
são e salvo safe and sound
são *adj.* sane
sapato *s.* shoe
sapo *s.* frog, toad
saquinho *s.* bag
saquinho de chá *s.* tea bag
sarampo *s.* measles
sarar *v.* heal
sarcasticamente *adv.* sarcastically
sarcástico *adj.* sarcastic
sardas *s.* freckles
sardinha *s.* sardine
sargento *s.* sergeant
sarjeta *s.* kerb
satélite *s.* satellite
satélite espião *s.* spy satellite
satisfação *s.* fulfilment, satisfaction
satisfatório/a *adj.* satisfactory, satisfying
satisfazer *v.* indulge, satisfy
satisfeito *adj.* contented, full up, pleased, satisfied
saudável *adj.* healthful, healthy, sound
saúde *s.* health
saúde! *int.* bless you!, cheers!
saxofone *s.* saxophone
scanner *s.* scanner
scooter *s.* scooter
script *s.* script
se *conj.* if, whether
se *pron.* herself, himself, itself, oneself, themselves, yourself
se acontecer o pior if the worst comes to the worst
se alguma vez if ever
se ao menos if only
se eu fosse você if I were you
se necessário if necessary
se por acaso just in case
se... ou não whether... or not
seca *s.* drought
secador *s.* drier, hair-drier
secador de cabelo *s.* hair-drier
secadora *s.* drier
seção *s.* section
secar *v.* dry
secar totalmente dry up
seco *adj.* blunt, dried, dry
secretamente *adv.* in secret, secretly
secretariado *adj.* secretarial
secretária eletrônica *s.* answering machine
Secretário de Estado *s.* Secretary of State
secretário/a *s.* secretary
secreto *adj.* secret
secular *adj.* secular
século *s.* century
secundário/a *adj.* secondary
secura *s.* dryness
seda *s.* silk
sede *s.* headquarters, thirst
sede regional *s.* branch, chapter
sedento *adj.* thirsty
seduzir *v.* tempt
segredo *s.* combination, secrecy, secret
seguinte *adj.* following, next
seguir *v.* follow, go by
seguir a pista de track down
segunda classe *s.* second class
segunda-feira *s.* Monday
segundo *s.* runner-up, second
segundo *prep.* according to
segundo andar *s.* second floor
segundo *adj.* latter, second
segundo colocado runner-up

segundo melhor second-best
segurança s. safety, security
segurança de trânsito s. road safety
segurar s. get hold of
segurar v. hold (back/up), insure, restrain
segurar-se v. hang on to
seguro s. insurance
seguro-desemprego s. unemployment benefit
seguro adj. safe, secure
seio s. breast
seis num., s. six
seja o que for whatever
seja qual for whatever
sela s. saddle
selar v. saddle, seal
seleção s. selection, squad, team
selecionar v. select
self-service adj. self-service
selim s. saddle
selo s. postage stamp, stamp
selva s. jungle
selvagem adj. savage, wild
selvagemente adv. savagely
sem prep. no, with no, without
sem comentário! no comment!
sem contar not counting
sem coração heartless
sem demora without delay
sem dó mercilessly
sem dúvida definitely, doubtless, undoubtedly
sem emprego out of a job, unemployed
sem escala non-stop
sem exceção without exception
sem expressão blank
sem falar not to mention
sem falta without fail
sem fim endless
sem fio wireless
sem fôlego breathless
sem gás not fizzy, still
sem gosto tasteless
sem graça tasteless
sem igual unique
sem imposto tax-free
sem instrução illiterate
sem parar around the clock, non-stop, on and on
sem ponta blunt
sem pressa leisurely
sem qualquer dúvida without a doubt
sem razão for nothing
sem remédio helpless
sem ressentimentos no hard feelings
sem saída dead end
sem saúde ill, sick, unhealthy
sem se mexer still
sem sentido meaningless, senseless
sem sono sleepless
sem sucesso unsuccessfully
sem trabalho out of work
semáforo s. traffic lights
semana s. week
semana de trabalho s. working week
semanada s. weekly allowance
semanal adj. weekly
semanalmente adv. weekly
semanário s. weekly
semear v. sow
semelhança s. likeness, resemblance, similarity
semelhante adj. alike, similar, such
semente s. pip, seed
semestre s. semester
semifinal s. semifinal
sempre adv. always, forever
sempre que every time, whenever
sem-teto adj., s. homeless
senado s. senate
senador s. senator
senão conj. or, or else, otherwise
sendo v. being
senha s. password
Senhor s. God, Lord
senhor s. gentleman, mister, sir
senhora s. lady, madam
senhoras e senhores! ladies and gentlemen!
senhoria s. landlady
senhorio s. landlord
senhorita s. Miss
sênior adj. senior
sensação s. feeling, sensation
sensacional adj. sensational
sensatamente adv. reasonably
sensato adj. sensible, sound
sensibilidade s. feeling, sensation
sensível adj. irritable, sensitive, tender, touchy
senso s. sense
senso de humor s. sense of humor
sensual adj. sexy
sentar direito sit up
sentar-se v. sit, sit down, take a seat
sentar-se à mesa sit at the table
sentença s. sentence
sentença de morte s. death sentence
sentenciar v. sentence
sentido s. meaning, sense
sentido anti-horário s. counterclockwise
sentido horário s. clockwise
sentido norte s. north

sentimental adj. sentimental
sentimento s. feeling
sentinela s. sentry
sentir v. feel, sense
sentir falta de miss
sentir muita vontade de be keen on
sentir o cheiro de smell
sentir o gosto taste
sentir prazer be delighted
sentir tonteira faint
sentir(-se) v. feel
sentir-se lisonjeado feel/be flattered
sentir-se mal feel sick
separação s. separation
separadamente adv. apart, individually, separately
separado adj. separate
separar v. separate, sort
separar-se v. break up, part, separate
septuagésimo s., num. seventieth
sequestrador s. hijacker, kidnapper
sequestrar v. abduct, hijack, kidnap
sequestro s. abduction, hijacking, kidnapping
ser abençoado com/por be blessed with
ser acompanhado de be accompanied by
ser apelidado be nicknamed
ser baseado em be based on
ser bem-sucedido v. succeed
ser bem-intencionado mean well
ser capaz de be able to, can
ser composto de be composed of
ser constituído de be made up of
ser cuidadoso be careful
ser demitido get the sack
ser destroçado be wrecked
ser digno de be worth of
ser doido be crazy, be nuts
ser dono own
ser duro com get tough with
ser feito de be made of, become of
ser ferido be wounded
ser habitado be populated
ser igual a equal to
ser incapaz de unable to
ser induzido a be tempted into
ser levado blow, drift
ser ligado a be attached to
ser louco por be mad about
ser malsucedido be unsuccessful
ser motivo de honra para be an honor/honour to
ser movido a run on
ser o lugar de belong to

ser obrigado a be obliged to
ser parente de be related to
ser preso be jailed
ser publicado come out
ser ruim em be bad at
ser solidário com sympathize with
ser tributado be taxed
ser útil come in handy
ser útil a be of use to
será que...? I wonder if...
sereia *s.* mermaid
seriado *s.* serial, series
seriado cômico na tevê *s.* sitcom
seriamente *adv.* seriously
série *s.* form, grade, serial, series
seriedade *s.* seriousness
seringa *s.* syringe
sério *adj.* serious, solemn
sério? *int.* really?
sermão *s.* sermon
serpentear *v.* slither, twist, wind
serra *s.* saw
serragem *s.* sawdust
serrar *v.* saw
serviço *s.* service
serviço de quarto *s.* room service
serviço doméstico *s.* housework
Serviço Secreto *s.* Secret Service
serviços sociais *s.* social services
servir *v.* do, fit, pour, serve, wait on
servir de intérprete interpret
servir mesas wait at tables, wait tables
servir-se *v.* help yourself
servo *s.* servant
sessenta *s., num.* sixty
seta *s.* indicator, turn signal, turn-signal
sete *s., num.* seven
setembro *s.* September
setenta *s., num.* seventy
setentrional *adj.* northern
sétimo *s., num.* seventh
setor *s.* division, quarter, section, sector
seu *pron.* her, his, its, your
seus *pron.* her, his, its, your
severamente *adv.* severely
severo *adj.* harsh, severe, stern
sexagésimo *s., num.* sixtieth
sexo *s.* sex
sexta-feira *s.* Friday
sexto *adj.* sixth
sexual *adj.* sexual
sexy *adj.* sexy
shopping center *s.* (shopping) mall
shorts *s.* shorts
show *s.* concert
si mesma herself
si mesmo himself, itself, oneself

si própria herself
si próprio himself, itself, oneself
sibilar *v.* hiss
sigilo *s.* secrecy
significa que it means that
significado *s.* meaning, significance
significar *v.* mean, signify, stand for
significar muito para mean a lot to
significativamente *adv.* significantly
significativo *adj.* meaningful, significant
sílaba *s.* syllable
silêncio *s.* quiet, silence
silêncio! *int.* hush!, silence!
silenciosamente *adv.* quietly, silently
silencioso *adj.* quiet, silent
silvestre *adj.* wild
sim *adv.* yeah, yes
símbolo *s.* symbol
simétrico *adj.* regular, symmetrical
similar *adj.* similar
similaridade *s.* similarity
símio *s.* ape
simpático *adj.* friendly
simples *adj.* plain, simple, straightforward
simples para o usuário user-friendly
simplesmente *adv.* just, simply
simplicidade *s.* simplicity
simplificado *adj.* simplified
simplificar *v.* simplify
simultaneamente *adv.* simultaneously
simultâneo *adj.* simultaneous
sinagoga *s.* synagogue
sinal *s.* deposit, light, mark, sign, signal, token, tone, trace
sinal afirmativo com a cabeça *s.* nod
sinal de pontuação *s.* punctuation mark
sinal verde *s.* go-ahead
sinalizar *v.* indicate, signal
sinceramente *adv.* honestly, sincerely, truthfully
sinceridade *s.* sincerity
sincero *adj.* honest, sincere, straight, truthful
sindicato *s.* trade union, union
sinfonia *s.* symphony
single *s.* single
singular *adj.* singular, unique
sino *s.* bell
sinônimo *s.* synonym
sinta-se em casa! make yourself at home!

sintético *adj.* synthetic
sinto muito! excuse me, I beg your pardon, sorry!
sintoma *s.* symptom
sintonizar *v.* tune in
sinuoso *adj.* winding
sirene *s.* siren
siri *s.* crab
sistema *s.* system, works
sistema solar *s.* solar system
sistematicamente *adv.* systematically
sistemático *adj.* systematic
sitcom *s.* sitcom
site *s.* site, website
sítio *s.* ranch
situação *s.* situation
situado *adj.* situated
skate *s.* skateboard
skinhead *s.* skinhead
slide *s.* slide
slogan *s.* slogan
smart card *s.* smart card
só *adv.* all, just, only
só de ida one-way
só um minuto just a minute/moment
soar *v.* chime, sound
sob *prep.* beneath, under, underneath
sob observação under observation
soberano *s.* ruler
soberba *s.* haughtiness
sobrancelha *s.* brow, eyebrow
sobre *prep.* on, on top of, onto, over, upon
sobremesa *s.* dessert
sobrenatural *adj.* supernatural
sobrenome *s.* family/last name, surname
sobrepor-se *v.* overlap
sobressalente *adj.* spare
sobretudo *s.* overcoat
sobretudo *adv.* above all
sobrevivência *s.* survival
sobrevivente *s.* survivor
sobreviver *v.* get by, manage, survive
sobrinha *s.* niece
sobrinho *s.* nephew
sóbrio *adj.* sober
socar *v.* squash, stuff
social *adj.* social
sociável *adj.* sociable
sociedade *s.* partnership, societies, society
sócio *s.* partner
soco *s.* blow, punch
socorrer *v.* help
socorro *s.* aid, help, relief
socorro! *int.* help!
sofá *s.* couch, settee, sofa

sofisticação s. sophistication
sofisticado adj. sophisticated
sofrer v. grieve, have, suffer, undergo
sofrer um naufrágio be shipwrecked
sofrimento s. suffering
software s. software
sogra s. mother-in-law
sogro s. father-in-law
sol s. sun, sunshine
sola s. sole
solado s. sole
solar adj. solar
solavanco s. jerk
soldado raso s. private
soldado s. soldier
solene adj. solemn
solenemente adv. solemnly
soletrar v. spell
solicitação s. application
solicitar v. request
solidão s. loneliness
solidariamente adv. sympathetically
solidariedade s. sympathy
solidário adj. sympathetic
solidarizar-se v. sympathize with
sólido s. solid
sólido adj. solid
solitário adj. lonely, lonesome, solitary
solo adj. solo
solo s. soil
soltar v. spin, unfasten, untie
soltar alguém let someone go
soltar-se v. come off, get loose
solteira s. spinster
solteiro s. bachelor
solteiro adj. single, unmarried
solteirona s. spinster
solto adj. loose
solução s. answer, solution
soluçar v. sob, throb
solucionar v. solve
soluço s. hiccup, sob
som s. chime, sound
som da batida do relógio s. stroke
soma s. addition, amount, figure, sum
somar v. add
sombra s. shade, shadow
sombreado adj. shady
sombrio adj. dreary, gloomy
somente adv. only
soneca s. nap, sleep
sonhar v. dream
sonhar acordado day-dream
sonho s. dream
sono s. sleep
sono leve s. doze

sonolento adj. sleepy
sopa s. soup
sopa de legumes s. vegetable soup
sopé s. foot
soprar v. blow
sopro s. blow
soquete s. socket
sorrir v. smile
sorrir com desdém sneer
sorriso s. smile
sorriso desdenhoso s. sneer
sorriso largo s. grin
sorte s. fortune, luck
sorte grande s. jackpot
sortear v. draw
sorteio s. draw
sortudo adj. lucky
sorver v. suck
sorvete s. ice-cream
SOS abr. SOS
sossegado adj. peaceful, sleepy
sossegar v. settle down, soothe
sossego s. peacefulness
sótão s. attic
sotaque s. accent
soul s. soul
sovina s. miser
sozinha pron. alone, by herself, by myself, by yourself, on her own
sozinho pron. alone, by himself, by myself, by oneself, by yourself, on his own
sozinhos pron. alone, by ourselves, by themselves, by yourselves
spray s. spray
Sr. abr. Mr.
Sra. abr. Mrs., Ms.
Srta. abr. Miss
Sto. abr. Saint, St
sua pron. her, his, its, your
suado adj. sweaty
suar v. sweat
suas pron. her, his, its, your
suave adj. mild, smooth, soft
suavemente adv. softly
suavidade s. softness
subdesenvolvido adj. backward
subestimar v. underestimate
subir v. climb, climb/go up, get on, increase, rise
subir à sua cabeça go to your head
subir muito soar
subir rapidamente shoot
subitamente adv. suddenly
subitaneidade s. suddenness
subjetivo adj. subjective
sublinhar v. underline
submarino s. submarine
submergir v. dive
submeter-se v. submit, surrender

submissão s. submission
submundo s. underworld
subornar v. bribe
suborno s. bribe
subproduto s. by-product
subsistência s. livelihood
subsolo s. basement
substância s. substance
substância química s. chemical
substancial adj. substantial
substantivo s. noun
substantivo composto s. compound noun
substantivo incontável s. uncountable noun
substituição s. replacement
substituir v. replace, substitute
substituto s. deputy
substituto adj. deputy, replacement, substitute
subterrâneo adj. underground
subtração s. subtraction
subtrair v. subtract
suburbano adj. suburban
subúrbio s. suburb
subversivo adj. underground
sucata s. scrap
suceder v. succeed
sucesso s. hit, success
sucesso de vendas s. best-selling
suco s. juice, squash
suculento adj. juicy
súdito s. subject
suéter s. jumper, sweater
suficiente adj. enough, sufficient
suficientemente adv. enough, sufficiently
sufixo s. suffix
sufocamento s. suffocation
sufocar(-se) v. choke, put down, suffocate
sugar v. suck
sugerir v. propose, suggest
sugestão s. suggestion
suicídio s. suicide
suíte s. suite
sujar v. dirty, litter, mess
sujeira s. dirt, filth
sujeito s. fellow, subject
sujo adj. dirty, rude
sul s. south
sulco s. groove
sumário s. (table of) contents
sumiço s. disappearance
sumir v. disappear, go away
suor s. sweat
super prefix super
superar v. get over, overcome
superastro s. superstar
supercomputador s. supercomputer
superestimar v. overestimate

superestrela *s.* superstar
superficial *adj.* superficial
superfície *s.* surface, top
superior *adj.* superior, upper
superioridade *s.* superiority
superlativo *adj.* superlative
supermercado *s.* supermarket
superpovoado *adj.* overcrowded
supersônico *adj.* supersonic
superstição *s.* superstition
supersticioso *adj.* superstitious
supervisão *s.* supervision
supervisionar *v.* oversee, supervise
supervisor *s.* supervisor
suplicar *v.* plead
suplício *s.* ordeal
supondo que suppose
supor *v.* assume, expect, guess, reckon, suppose
suportar *v.* bear, put up with, stand, support, tolerate

suposição *s.* assumption
supostamente *adv.* presumably
suposto *adj.* so-called
Suprema Corte *s.* Supreme Court
Supremo Tribunal *s.* Supreme Court
supremo *adj.* supreme
suprimento *s.* supply
suprir *v.* supply
surdez *s.* deafness
surdo *adj.* deaf
surfar *v.* surf
surfe *s.* surf, surfing
surfista *s.* surfer
surgir *v.* appear, come up, peep
surpreendente *adj.* amazing, surprising
surpreendentemente *adv.* amazingly, surprisingly
surpreender *v.* surprise
surpresa *s.* amazement, surprise

surpreso *adj.* surprised
surra *s.* beating
surrado *adj.* shabby
surrar *v.* thrash
suscetível a doença sickly
suspeita *s.* suspicion
suspeitar *v.* suspect
suspeito *adj.* suspicious
suspeito *s.* suspect
suspeitosamente *adv.* suspiciously
suspender *v.* call off
suspenso *adj.* overhead
suspirar *v.* sigh
suspiro *s.* sigh
sussurrar *v.* whisper
sussurro *s.* whisper
sustentar *v.* keep, support
susto *s.* fright, scare
sutiã *s.* bra
suvenir *s.* souvenir

Tt

tabaco *s.* tobacco
tabela *s.* table
tábua *s.* board, plank
tábua de passar *s.* ironing board
tabuada *s.* multiplication table
taça *s.* cup, glass
tachinha *s.* drawing-pin, thumbtack
taco *s.* club
tagarelar *v.* chatter
tagarelice *s.* chatter
tailleur *s.* suit
tais como for example, such as
tal *pron.* such
tal como for example, such as
talão *s.* book
talão de cheques *s.* cheque-book
talco *s.* talcum powder
talento *s.* ability, gift, talent
talentoso *adj.* gifted, talented
talhar *v.* slash
talheres *s.* cutlery
talo *s.* stalk, stick
talvez *adv.* maybe, perhaps, possibly
tamanho *s.* size
tâmara *s.* date
também *adv.* also, as well, either, so, too
também não either, neither
tambor *s.* drum
tamborete *s.* stool
tamborilada *s.* patter
tamborilar *v.* patter
tampa *s.* cap, cover, lid, top
tampão *s.* patch
tampouco *adv.* either, neither
tangerina *s.* tangerine
tanque *s.* cylinder, pond, tank
tanque de combustível *s.* fuel tank
tanque de gasolina *s.* petrol tank
tanto *adv.* so much
tanto... quanto both... and
tanto... quanto possível as... as possible
tanto *pron.* so much, such
tantos *pron.* so many
tantos quantos as many as
tão *adv.* so, such
tão bem quanto as well as
tão... quanto as... as
tão... quanto possível as... as possible
tapa *s.* slap
tapar *v.* plug
tapeçaria *s.* tapestry
tapete *s.* carpet, rug
tapetinho *s.* mat
tapinha *s.* pat, tap
taquigrafia *s.* shorthand
tarde *adv.* late
tarde *s.* afternoon
tarefa *s.* assignment, homework, job, task
tarefa de rotina *s.* chore
tarefas esporádicas *s.* odd jobs
tarifa *s.* fare
tartaruga *s.* tortoise, turtle
tatame *s.* mat
tatear *v.* feel, grope
tática *s.* tactics
tato *s.* tact, touch
tatuagem *s.* tattoo
taxa *s.* charge, fee, rate
taxa de adesão *s.* membership, membership fee
taxa de câmbio *s.* exchange rate
taxa escolar *s.* tuition
táxi *s.* cab, taxi
taxista *s.* taxi driver
tchau *int.* bye, bye-bye, cheerio, goodbye
teatro *s.* acting, drama, theater
tecedor *s.* weaver
tecelão *s.* weaver
tecer *v.* spin, weave
tecido *s.* cloth, material, tissue
tecla *s.* key
teclado *s.* keyboard
teclar *v.* key in
técnica *s.* technique
técnico *s.* repairperson
técnico *adj.* technical
técnico *s.* technician
tecnologia *s.* technology
tecnologia da informação *s.* information technology
tecnológico *adj.* technological
tédio *s.* boredom
teia *s.* cobweb, web
teia de aranha *s.* cobweb, spiderweb
teimosamente *adv.* stubbornly
teimoso *adj.* stubborn
tel. *abr.* tel.
tela *s.* canvas, screen
telão *s.* screen
teleférico *s.* cable-car
telefonar *v.* call (up), phone, ring (up), telephone
telefone *s.* phone, telephone
telefone celular *s.* cellular phone
telefone público *s.* pay phone, telephone booth
telefonema *s.* call, phone call
telefonista *s.* operator
telegrama *s.* cable, telegram, wire
telescópio *s.* telescope
telespectador *s.* viewer
televisão *s.* television, television set
televisão a cabo *s.* cable television
televisor *s.* television, television set
telha *s.* tile
tema *s.* subject, theme
temer *v.* fear
temperamento *s.* temper
temperar *v.* flavor, spice
temperatura *s.* temperature
tempero *s.* dressing
tempestade *s.* rainstorm, storm
tempestade de areia *s.* sandstorm
tempestade de neve *s.* snowstorm
tempestuoso *adj.* stormy, wild
templo *s.* temple
tempo *s.* half, tense, time, weather, while
tempo de escola *s.* schooldays
tempo de guerra *s.* wartime
temporada *s.* season
temporal *s.* thunderstorm
temporariamente *adv.* temporarily
temporário *adj.* temporary
tenda *s.* tent
tendência *s.* tendency, trend
tender *v.* tend
tenente *s.* lieutenant
tenha modos! mind your manners!
tênis *s.* sneaker, tennis (shoe), trainer
tênis de mesa *s.* table tennis
tenro *adj.* tender
tensão *s.* tension
tenso *adj.* tense
tentação *s.* temptation
tentador *adj.* tempting
tentar *v.* attempt, have a go at, tempt, try
tentativa *s.* attempt, try
teor *s.* content
teoria *s.* theory
teórico *adj.* theoretical
ter a consciência pesada have a guilty conscience
ter a consciência tranquila have a clear conscience
ter a intenção de mean
ter a obrigação de to be under an obligation to
ter a sua vez have your say
ter a ver com have to do with
ter algo à mão get something ready
ter algo em comum have something in common
ter algo feito por alguém have something [done]

ter algo na cabeça have something on your mind
ter aversão a dislike
ter boa vontade mean well
ter calma take it easy/things easy
ter capacidade para hold
ter carinho por be fond of
ter cheiro smell
ter conhecimento de be acquainted with
ter cuidado be careful
ter cuidado com mind, watch out for
ter de have (got) to
ter direito a be entitled to
ter em mente bear/keep in mind
ter em seu poder have in your possession
ter esperança hope
ter êxito be successful, succeed
ter febre have a fever, have a temperature
ter garantia be guaranteed
ter gosto taste
ter interesse em take an interest in
ter licença be licensed
ter medo de fear of
ter muito trabalho para fazer algo go to a lot of trouble
ter noção de realize
ter notícias de hear from
ter o costume de used to, would
ter orgulho de take pride in
ter pena (de) pity, take pity on
ter pena de feel sorry for
ter permissão de can, may
ter prazer em enjoy, take delight/pleasure in
ter ressentimento contra have a grudge against
ter saudade de miss
ter senso de humor have a sense of humor
ter seu cabelo cortado have/get your hair cut
ter um papel em play a part in
ter vergonha de be ashamed of/to
ter vista para overlook
terapia *s.* therapy
terça-feira *s.* Tuesday
terceira idade *s.* old age
terceiro *adj.* third
terminação *s.* ending
terminado *adj.* complete, finished, over
terminal *s.* terminal, terminus
terminantemente *adv.* strictly
terminar *v.* break/split up with complete, conclude, end, finish, get through
término *s.* terminus

termo *s.* term
termômetro *s.* thermometer
termos *s.* terms
termostato *s.* thermostat
ternamente *adv.* dearly, tenderly
terno *s.* suit
terno *adj.* tender
ternura *s.* tenderness
terra *s.* country, earth, ground, land, soil
terra natal *s.* homeland
terraço *s.* terrace
terremoto *s.* earthquake
terreno *s.* grounds
térreo *s.* ground floor
territorial *adj.* territorial
território *s.* territory
terrível *adj.* frightful, terrible
terrivelmente *adv.* terribly, very, very badly
terror *s.* horror film, terror
terrorismo *s.* terrorism
terrorista *s.* terrorist
tesoura *s.* scissors
tesoureiro *s.* treasurer
tesouro *s.* treasure, treasury
Tesouro Nacional *s.* Treasury
testa *s.* brow, forehead
testamento *s.* will
testar *v.* test
teste *s.* quiz, test, trial
teste de múltipla-escolha *s.* multiple-choice test
testemunha *s.* witness
testemunha ocular *s.* eye-witness
testemunhar *v.* testify, witness
testemunho *s.* testimony
teto *s.* ceiling, roof
teu *pron.* your
teus *pron.* your
tevê *s.* telly, TV
texto *s.* paper, text, theme
tia *s.* aunt
ticar *v.* tick
tigela *s.* basin, bowl
tigre *s.* tiger
tijolo *s.* brick
tilintar *v.* jingle
time *s.* team
timidamente *adv.* timidly
timidez *s.* shyness
tímido *adj.* self-conscious, shy, timid
timing *s.* timing
tina *s.* tub
tingir *v.* dye
tinta *s.* ink, paint
tinto *adj.* red
tintura *s.* dye
tio *adj.* uncle
tipicamente *adv.* typically
típico *adj.* typical

tipo *s.* grade, kind, sort, type
tipoia *s.* sling
tíquete *s.* ticket
tira *s.* cop, shred, strap, strip
tiracolo *s.* shoulder strap
tirânico *adj.* tyrannical
tirano *s.* tyrant
tirar *v.* clear, draw, get, pull out, score, take out/off
tirar a febre de alguém take someone's temperature
tirar a pele kin
tirar a roupa get undressed, strip, undress
tirar a sorte draw lots
tirar algo take something off
tirar algo de dentro de take something out of
tirar conclusões pressipitadas jump to conclusions
tirar fora cross out, strike out
tirar o chapéu raise one's hat
tirar o pó dust
tirar proveito de take advantage of
tirar sarro de to make fun of
tirar uma foto photograph, take a picture
tirinha *s.* cartoon
tiro *s.* shot
título *s.* heading, title
toalete *s.* lavatory, toilet, WC
toalha *s.* towel
toalha de mesa *s.* cloth, tablecloth
toca *s.* burrow, den
toca-discos *s.* record-player
toca-fitas *s.* cassette player, tape recorder
tocante *adj.* touching
tocar *v.* go off, move, play, ring, sound, strike, touch
tocar novamente replay
tocha *s.* torch
toco *s.* stump
toda vez every time
todas as coisas everything
todavia *conj.* nevertheless, nonetheless
todo mundo everybody
todo *adj.* all, every, whole
todos *pron.* everybody
todos a bordo! all aboard!
todos *adj.* all, every
toga *s.* gown
tolamente *adv.* foolishly, stupidly
tolerância *s.* tolerance, toleration
tolerante *adj.* tolerant
tolerar *v.* bear, put up with, tolerate
tolerável *adj.* tolerable
tolice *s.* foolishness
tolo *s.* fool

tolo *adj.* foolish
tom *s.* pitch, shade, tone
tomada *s.* socket
tomar *v.* capture, catch, have, make, take
tomar banho de chuveiro have/take a shower, shower
tomar banho de sol sunbathe
tomar conhecimento de become acquainted with
tomar conta look after, see to
tomar conta de criança babysit
tomar cuidado watch your step
tomar cuidado take care
tomar emprestado borrow
tomar nota make a note, note/write down, take notes
tomar o rumo de head for
tomar o trem catch the train
tomar parte em participate, take part in
tomar partido de take sides with
tomar posse de take possession of
tomar providência take action, take steps
tomar uma coisa por outra mistake
tomar uma decisão decide, make up your mind
tomar uma ducha have/take a shower
tomara que hopefully
tomate *s.* tomato
tombo *s.* fall
tonelada *s.* ton, tonne
tonto *adj.* dizzy
tontura *s.* dizziness
topar com *v.* bump/run into, meet by chance, run across
tópico *s.* topic
topo *s.* top
toque *s.* push, touch
tora *s.* log
toranja *s.* grapefruit
torção *s.* twist
torcedor *s.* fan, supporter
torcer *v.* sprain, support, twist, wring out
tormenta *s.* rainstorm
tornado *s.* tornado
tornar *v.* make
tornar algo mais forte make something stronger
tornar algo possível para make it possible for
tornar público publicize
tornar-se *v.* be going to, become, turn
torneio *s.* tournament
torneira *s.* faucet, tap
tornozelo *s.* ankle
torpedo *s.* torpedo

torrada *s.* toast
torradeira *s.* toaster
torrado *adj.* roasted
torrão *s.* lump
torrar *v.* roast
torre *s.* tower
torre de controle *s.* control tower
torta *s.* pie, tart
torto *adj.* crooked
tortura *s.* torture
torturar *v.* torture
tosse *s.* cough
tossir *v.* cough
tostado *adj.* toasted
tostador *s.* toaster
tostar *v.* toast
total *adj.* absolute, complete, full, overall, total, utter
totalidade *s.* entirety
totalizar *v.* amount to, number
totalmente *adv.* altogether, completely, fully, totally
totalmente acordado wide awake
touca *s.* bonnet, cap
toucinho *s.* bacon
toupeira *s.* mole
touro *s.* bull
tóxico *adj.* toxic
toxicomania *s.* drug addiction
trabalhador *s.* laborer, worker
trabalhar *v.* work
trabalho *s.* job, paper, work
trabalho em equipe *s.* teamwork
trabalho manual *s.* labor
traça *s.* moth
traçar *v.* chart, trace
traço *s.* stroke
tradição *s.* tradition
tradicional *adj.* traditional
tradicionalmente *adv.* traditionally
tradução *s.* translation
tradutor *s.* translator
traduzir *v.* translate
tráfego *s.* traffic
traficante *s.* dealer, drug dealer
tragédia *s.* tragedy
tragicamente *adv.* tragically
trágico *adj.* tragic
traição *s.* betrayal, treachery, treason
traiçoeiro *adj.* treacherous
traidor *s.* traitor
trailer *s.* camper, caravan, trailer
trair *v.* betray
traje *s.* costume, dress, outfit, wear
traje de mergulho *s.* diving suit
traje espacial *s.* spacesuit
traje para natação *s.* swimming costume
trama *s.* scheme

tramar *v.* plot, scheme
trampolim *s.* diving board, springboard
trança *s.* braid, plait
trancafiar *v.* shut up
trancar *v.* lock
trançar *v.* plait
trancar algo em algum lugar lock something away
trancar alguém do lado de fora lock someone out
trancar tudo lock up
tranco *s.* jerk, jolt
tranquilamente *adv.* smoothly
tranquilidade *s.* peacefulness
tranquilizar *v.* reassure
tranquilo *adj.* peaceful
transbordar *v.* overflow
transeunte *s.* passer-by
transferência *s.* transfer
transferir *v.* transfer
transformação *s.* transformation
transformar *v.* transform, turn
transformar algo em make something into
transistor *s.* transistor
transmissão *s.* broadcast
transmissor *s.* broadcaster
transmitir *v.* broadcast
transparente *adj.* clear, transparent
transpirar *v.* perspire
transplantar *v.* transplant
transplante *s.* transplant
transpor *s.* bridge
transportar *v.* airlift, carry, transport
transporte *s.* transport, transportation
transporte público *s.* public transport/transportation
trapaça *s.* trickery
trapacear *v.* cheat
trapaceiro *s.* cheat
trapo *s.* rag
traquina *adj.* naughty
traquinagem *s.* naughtiness
traseira *s.* rear
traseiro *adj.* back, rear
tratado *s.* treaty
tratamento *s.* treatment
tratar *v.* treat
tratar com deal with
trato *s.* bargain, deal
trator *s.* tractor
travar *v.* lock
trave *s.* post
travessão *s.* dash
travesseiro *s.* pillow
travessia *s.* crossing
travessura *s.* mischief, naughtiness
trazer *v.* bring (about)

trazer à baila bring something up, raise
trazer algo para mais perto bring something nearer/closer
trazer de volta bring back
trazer para baixo take down
trecho *s.* passage
trégua *s.* truce
treinado *adj.* trained
treinador *s.* coach, trainer
treinamento *s.* training
treinamento vocacional *s.* vocational training
treinar *v.* coach, drill, practice, take up, train
treino *s.* practice
trem *s.* rail, train
tremendamente *adv.* tremendously
tremendo *adj.* enormous, great, terrific, tremendous, very great
tremer *v.* shake, shiver, shudder, tremble
tremor *s.* shudder
tremular *v.* flicker, wave
trêmulo *adj.* shaky
trenó *s.* sledge, sleigh
três *s., num.* three
três vivas para three cheers for
treze *s., num.* thirteen
triangular *adj.* triangular
triângulo *s.* triangle
tribal *adj.* tribal
tribo *s.* tribe
tribuna *s.* platform
tribuna de honra *s.* grandstand
tribunal *s.* court (of law), lawcourt
tributar *v.* tax
tributo *s.* tribute

triciclo *s.* tricycle
tricô *s.* knitting
tricotar *v.* knit
trigêmeos *s.* triplet
trigésimo *s., num.* thirtieth
trigo *s.* wheat
trilha *s.* footpath, path, track, trail
trilhos *s.* rails, track
trimestre *s.* quarter
trinca *s.* crack
trincar *v.* crack
trinchar *v.* carve
trincheira *s.* trench
trinco *s.* bolt
trinta *s., num.* thirty
triplicar *v.* triple
tripulação *s.* crew
tripular *v.* man
triste *adj.* bleak, gloomy, sad, sorry, unhappy
tristemente *adv.* sadly
tristeza *s.* dismay, sadness, sorrow, unhappiness
triunfante *adj.* triumphant
triunfantemente *adv.* triumphantly
triunfo *s.* triumph
trivial *adj.* trivial
trivialidade *s.* triviality
troca *s.* exchange
trocar *v.* change, exchange, shift, swap, switch
trocar algo por trade something for
trocar de roupa change
troco *s.* change
troféu *s.* trophy
tromba *s.* trunk
trombone *s.* trombone
trompa *s.* horn
trompete *s.* trumpet

tronco *s.* log, trunk
trono *s.* throne
tropas *s.* troops
tropeçar *v.* stumble, trip
tropical *adj.* tropical
trotar *v.* trot
trote *s.* hoax, trot
trouxa *s.* bundle
trovão *s.* thunder
trovejar *v.* thunder
truque *s.* trick
truta *s.* trout
tubarão *s.* shark
tubo *s.* pipe, tub, tube
tubo de ensaio *s.* test tube
tubulação *s.* pipeline
tudo *pron.* all, everything, whatever
tudo a seu tempo all in good time
tudo bem all right, fine, OK
tudo de bom all the best, best wishes
tudo de novo all over again
tudo outra vez all over again
tufo *s.* bush, tuft
tulipa *s.* tulip
tumba *s.* tomb
tumor *s.* tumor
túmulo *s.* grave
tumulto *s.* disturbance, riot
tumultuar *v.* riot, stir up
túnel *s.* tunnel
turbante *s.* turban
turismo *s.* tourism, tourist
turma *s.* class, gang, guys
turnê *s.* tour
turno *s.* shift
turno da noite *s.* night shift
turquesa *adj.* turquoise
tutor *s.* tutor
TV *s.* TV

Uu

uau! *int.* wow!
UE *abr.* EU
uivar *v.* howl
uivo *s.* howl
ultimamente *adv.* lately
último recurso *s.* last resort
último *adj.* final, last, latest, past
ultrapassado *adj.* outdated
ultrapassar *v.* overtake
um a um one by one
um ao outro each other, one another
um grande número quite a few
um grande número de a large number of
um monte de a lot of, tons of
um número expressivo quite a lot of
um pequeno número de a few, a small number of
um por um one by one
um pouco a little, kind/sort of
um pouco mais de some more
um quarto para a quarter of/to
um tanto rather
um tipo de a kind of
um *art.* a/an, one
um ou outro either
uma espécie de a kind of
uma folha de papel a piece/sheet of paper
uma ligação a cobrar a reverse charge call
uma notícia a piece of news
uma outra pessoa somebody else, someone else
uma outra vez some other time
uma pena too bad
uma vez once
uma vez mais once again, once more
uma vez ou outra once or twice
uma vez por ano annually, once a year
umedecer *v.* dampen, moisten
umidade *s.* dampness, moisture
úmido *adj.* damp, moist, rainy, wet
unanimemente *adv.* unanimously
unânime *adj.* unanimous
unha *s.* fingernail, nail
unha do dedo do pé *s.* toenail
união *s.* union
União Europeia *s.* European Union
único *adj.* only, sole, unique
unidade *s.* unit, unity
unidade de disco *s.* disk drive, drive
unido *adj.* united
uniforme *adj.* level
uniforme *s.* uniform
uniforme escolar *s.* school uniform
uniformemente *adv.* smoothly
unir(-se) *v.* combine, join, unite
universal *adj.* universal
universidade *s.* college, school, university
universitário *s.* undergraduate
universo *s.* universe
untar *v.* grease
untar com manteiga *v.* butter
urbano *adj.* urban
urgência *s.* urgency
urgente *adj.* urgent
urgentemente *adv.* urgently
ursinho de pelúcia *s.* teddy bear
urso *s.* bear
urso polar *s.* polar bear
urubu *s.* vulture
usado *adj.* second-hand, used
usar *v.* use, wear
usina *s.* mill
usina elétrica *s.* power plant, power station
uso *s.* use, wear
usuário *s.* user
utensílio *s.* utensil
útil *adj.* handy, helpful, practical, useful
utilidade *s.* usefulness
utilmente *adv.* usefully
uva *s.* grape

Vv

vá em frente! go ahead!
vaca *s.* cow
vacina *s.* injection
vacinar *v.* inject
vácuo *s.* emptiness, vacuum
vadiagem *s.* loitering
vadiar *v.* loiter
vaga *s.* opening, parking space, vacancy
vagamente *adv.* vaguely
vagão *s.* carriage, freight car, wagon
vagar *v.* roam
vagarosamente *adv.* lazily, slowly
vagem *s.* pod
vago *adj.* general, uncertain, vacant, vague
vai que just in case
vaiar *v.* hiss
vaidade *s.* vanity
vaidoso *adj.* conceited, vain
vale *s.* token, valley
vale a pena it's worth it
vale a pena tentar it's worth a try
valentão *s.* bully
valer *v.* be worth
valer a pena be worth
valete *s.* jack
valeu! *slang* cheers!
validade *s.* validity
válido *adj.* good, valid
valioso *adj.* valuable
valor *s.* value, worth
valores *s.* valuables, values
valorizar *v.* value
vamos *v.* let's..., shall we...?
vamos esclarecer isso let's get it/this straight
vampiro *s.* vampire
van *s.* van
vandalismo *s.* vandalism
vândalo *s.* hooligan
vândalo *s.* vandal
vangloriar-se *v.* flatter yourself, gloat
vantagem *s.* advantage, lead, plus
vão *adj.* vain
vapor *s.* steam
vaporizador *s.* spray
vara *s.* cane, stick
vara de pescar *s.* fishing rod
varal *s.* line
varanda *s.* porch, veranda
varão *s.* rail
variação *s.* variation
variado *adj.* varied
variar *v.* range, vary
várias vezes time after time, time and time again
variedade *s.* choice, range, variety
varinha mágica *s.* magic wand
vários *adj.* quite a few, several, various
varrer *v.* blow, sweep, sweep up
varrida *s.* sweep
vasculhar *v.* search
vaso *s.* flowerpot, pot, vase
vaso sanguíneo *s.* blood vessel
vassoura *s.* broom
vasto *adj.* vast, wide
vazamento *s.* leak
vazar *v.* escape, leak
vazio *s.* emptiness
vazio *adj.* bare, empty, hollow
veado *s.* deer
vedar *v.* seal
vegetal *s.* vegetable
vegetariano *s.* vegetarian
veia *s.* vein
veículo *s.* vehicle
vela *s.* candle, sail
veleiro *s.* sailboat
velejar *v.* sail
velhice *s.* old age
velho *adj.* old

velocidade s. pace, rate, speed
veloz adj. swift
velozmente adv. swiftly
veludo s. velvet
vencedor adj. winning
vencedor s. winner
vencer v. overcome, win
venda s. blindfold, sale
vendar v. blindfold
vendaval s. gale
vendedor s. salesman, seller
vendedor s. clerk, sales/shop assistant, salesperson
vendedora s. saleswoman
vender v. sell
veneno s. poison, venom
venenoso adj. poisonous
veneziana s. shutter
ventilador s. fan
vento s. wind
ventoso adj. windy
ver v. see, watch
ver alguém partir see someone off
ver de relance (catch a) glimpse
ver vitrine window-shop
ver você mesmo see for yourself
veranista s. holidaymaker
verão s. summer
verba s. finance, fund
verbas s. funds
verbo s. verb
verdade s. truth
verdade? really?
verdadeiramente adv. truly, truthfully
verdadeiro adj. actual, real, true
verde adj., s. green
verde-esmeralda adj., s. emerald
verdureiro s. greengrocer
veredicto s. verdict
vergar v. sag
vergonha s. disgrace, shame
vergonhoso adj. shameful
verificar v. check (out/up), verify
verme s. worm
vermelho adj., s. crimson, red
verniz s. varnish
verruga s. mole
versão s. version
versículo s. verse
verso s. back, rear, verse
verter v. flow, pour, seep, stream
vertical adj. upright, vertical
verticalmente adj. upright
vespa s. wasp
véspera s. eve
véspera de ano-novo s. New Year's Eve
vestiário s. cloakroom
vestido s. dress, frock
vestido de noiva s. gown, wedding dress

vestígio s. trace
vestir v. clothe, dress, put on
vestir-se v. dress, get dressed
vestir-se elegantemente dress up
vestuário s. clothing, wear
vetar v. veto
veterano s. ex-soldier, veteran
veterinário s. vet
veto s. veto
véu s. veil
vez s. go, time, turn
vezes s. times
via prep. via
via de regra as a rule
via expressa s. expressway, motorway
viagem s. journey, ride, travel, travelling, trip, voyage
viagem de ida e volta s. round trip
viajante s. traveller
viajar v. go away, ride, travel
viajar de carona hitch, hitchhike
viajar diariamente para trabalhar commute
viatura s. squad car
vibrar v. vibrate
vice s. vice, vise
viciado adj. addicted
viciado s. addict
viciado em drogas s. drug addict
viciante adj. addictive
vício s. addiction, vice
vida s. life, lifetime, livelihood, lives
vida selvagem s. wildlife
vida social s. social life
videira s. vine
vídeo s. video
videogame s. videogame
vidraça s. pane, windowpane
vidro s. glass, jar, pot
viela s. alley
viga s. beam
vigarista s. crook, swindler
vigia s. lookout, watch, watchman
vigiar v. guard
vigor s. vigor
vigorosamente adv. vigorously
vigoroso adj. energetic, vigorous
vilão s. villain
vilarejo s. village
vinagre s. vinegar
vindouro adj. ...to come
vingança s. revenge, vengeance
vingar-se (de) v. revenge (on), take vengeance (on)
vinha s. vine, vineyard
vinhedo s. vineyard
vinho s. wine
vinte s., num. twenty
violação s. violation
viola de arco s. viola

violão s. guitar
violar v. break, violate
violência s. violence
violentamente adv. violently
violento adj. rough, violent
violeta s. violet
violinista s. violinist
violino s. fiddle, violin
violoncelo s. cello
violonista s. guitarist
VIP s. VIP
vir v. come (on/along)
vir a calhar come in handy
vir à mente come to mind
vir a ser moda come into fashion
vir à tona come out
vir de come from
vir depois de follow
vir junto come along
virar v. capsize, turn (to/into)
virar para outro lado turn over
virar realidade come true
virar-se v. get by, make do with, manage, turn around
virar-se contra turn against
vírgula s. comma
virtualmente adv. virtually
virtude s. goodness, virtue
vírus s. bug, virus
visão s. eyesight, sight, view, vision
visibilidade s. visibility
visita s. call, visit, visitor
visitante s. caller, visitor
visitar v. call on, go round, visit
visitar casualmente drop by/in/around
visitar pontos turísticos go sightseeing
visível adj. conspicuous, visible
vista s. eyesight, sight, view
visto s. visa
visto que seeing that
visual adj. visual
visual s. look, looks
vital adj. vital
vitamina s. vitamin
vítima s. casualty, victim
vitória s. victory, win
vitorioso adj. victorious
vitrina s. shop-window
viúva s. widow
viúvo s. widower
viva! int. cheers!, hip, Hip, hurray!
viveiro s. nursery
vivenciar v. experience
viver s. living
viver v. live
viver de live on
viver dentro do orçamento make ends meet

vividamente *adv.* vividly
vívido *adj.* vivid
vivo *adj.* alive, live, living, vivid
vizinhança *s.* neighborhood
vizinho *s.* neighbor
vó *s.* grandma, granny
vô *s.* grandad, grandpa
voador *adj.* flying
voar *v.* fly
vocabulário *s.* vocabulary
vocação *s.* vocation
você *pron.* you
você é quem sabe it's up to you, please yourself
você gostaria de...? would you care for...?
você mesmo yourself
você poderia...? would you mind ...?
você se importa de/se...? do you mind...?
vocês mesmos yourself
vogal *s.* vowel
volante *s.* steering wheel, wheel
voleibol *s.* volleyball
volta *s.* lap, return, turn
voltar *v.* come/get/go back, return, turn back
volume *s.* volume
volumoso *adj.* bulky
voluntário *adj.* voluntary
voluntário *s.* volunteer
vomitar *v.* be sick, throw up, vomit
vômito *s.* vomit

vontade *s.* urge, will
voo *s.* flight
votar *v.* vote
voto *s.* vote, vow
vovó *s.* grandma, granny
vovô *s.* grandad, grandpa
voz *s.* voice
voz ativa *s.* active voice
vulcânico *adj.* volcanic
vulcão *s.* volcano
vulgar *adj.* common, vulgar
vulnerável *adj.* vulnerable
vulto *s.* figure
vultuoso *adj.* massive

Ww

wafer *s.* wafer
waffle *s.* waffle
walkman *s.* personal stereo, walkman
website *s.* website
windsurfe *s.* windsurfing
windsurfista *s.* windsurfer
workshop *s.* workshop

Xx

xadrez *adj.* checked
xadrez *s.* chess
xadrez escocês *adj.* tartan
xale *s.* shawl

xampu *s.* shampoo
xeque *s.* check
xerife *s.* sheriff
xerocar *v.* xerox
xícara *s.* cup
xilofone *s.* xylophone
xingamento *s.* curse
xingar *v.* curse

Yy

yuppie *s.* yuppie

Zz

zangado *adj.* angry, cross
zapear *v.* zap
zarpar *v.* sail, set sail
zebra *s.* zebra
zelador *s.* caretaker, janitor
zero *s.* love, nil, nought, zero
zigue-zague *s.* zigzag
zigue-zaguear *v.* zigzag
ziper *s.* zip, zipper
zombar *v.* jeer, mock
zombaria *s.* jeer
zona *s.* zone
zona comercial *s.* shopping precinct
zoológico *s.* zoo
zumbido *s.* buzz
zumbir *v.* buzz, hum